to Karen,
with Love,
Tony
Christmas 85'

# 200 Years of Great
# American Short Stories

# 200 Years of Great American Short Stories

EDITED BY

*Martha Foley*

Galahad Books • *New York*

*Published by*
*Galahad Books*
*166 Fifth Avenue*
*New York, NY 10016*

*Published by arrangement with Houghton Mifflin Company*

*Manufactured in the United States of America*

*10 9 8 7 6 5 4 3 2*

*Library of Congress Catalog Card Number 82-82360*

*ISBN 0-88365-665-5*

For permission to reprint stories still protected by copyright, grateful acknowledgement is made to the authors, proprietors, and publishers named below:

Conrad Aiken, "Silent Snow, Secret Snow." Copyright, 1932, by Conrad Aiken. Copyright renewed 1960 by Conrad Aiken.

Sherwood Anderson, "The Strength of God" and "The Teacher." Copyright 1919 by B. W. Huebsch, Inc., Copyright 1947 by Eleanor Copenhager Anderson. Reprinted by permission of The Viking Press, Inc.

James Baldwin, "Tell Me How Long the Train's Been Gone." Adapted from *Tell Me How Long the Train's Been Gone* by James Baldwin. Copyright © 1968 by James Baldwin. This version originally published in *McCall's Magazine*. Reprinted by arrangement with The Dial Press.

Stephen Vincent Benét, "A Tooth for Paul Revere." From *The Selected Works of Stephen Vincent Benét*, Holt, Rinehart and Winston, Inc. Copyright, 1937 by Stephen Vincent Benét. Copyright renewed © 1965 by Thomas C. Benét, Stephanie B. Mahin, Benét Lewis.

Kay Boyle, "Seven Say You Can Hear Corn Grow." Copyright, 1966, by Kay Boyle.

Ray Bradbury, "February 1999: Ylla." Copyright, 1950, by Ray Bradbury.

Erskine Caldwell, "Masses of Men." Copyright 1933, copyright © 1961 by Erskine Caldwell. Reprinted from *The Complete Stories of Erskine Caldwell*, by permission of the publishers, Little, Brown and Company.

Willa Cather, "Double Birthday." Copyright © 1929 by Willa Cather and the Forum Publishing Co.

John Cheever, "The Country Husband." Copyright, © 1954, by The New Yorker Magazine, Inc.

James T. Farrel, "Spring Evening." Reprinted from *The Short Stories of James T. Farrell* by permission of the publisher, Vanguard Press, Inc. Copyright 1932, 1933, 1934

*To Those
Wonderful Guardians
of Our
Literary Treasure
the Librarians of America*

# Contents

*Table of Contents*

# 200 Years of Great American Short Stories

# Introduction

The American short story is, like the United States of America, two hundred years old. The first one, "A Pretty Story," by Francis Hopkinson, was published coincidental with the founding of the First Continental Congress in 1774 and was a rallying cry to the colonists to revolt against the British. Since then more short stories have been published in the United States than in any other nation. The authoritative *Short Story Index*, published by H. W. Wilson and Company, lists 96,336 short stories that were published in books in the United States up to 1968. Excluded from this total are folk tales, humorous sketches, character sketches, and stories for children under twelve. Nor does it include the uncounted thousands of short stories that have been published only in magazines. The astounding number shows the short story is America's most characteristic literary form and its most popular. European literature reflects its influence, especially the English and French. Kipling and Conrad, Baudelaire and de Maupassant are examples.

This anthology is a literary bicentennial celebration in recognition of a great American achievement. No single volume could possibly encompass the enormous range of that achievement and it is sad that the number of superb stories omitted has to exceed by far the number that can be included. Thus this is not a collection of "best" stories. Nor is it a presentation of only patriotic writing. Important writers are seldom national chauvinists. For that reason many of the finest authors in every country and in every time have been misunderstood and unappreciated during their lives. Only too true is the old verse: "Seven cities warr'd for Homer being dead/"Who living had no roofe to shroude his head."

When Francis Hopkinson wrote the first short story to be published in the United States it heralded the start of all American fiction. Not that the colonists before the Revolution had been idle in the realm of letters: poems, plays, essays, journals, histories, biographies, military accounts, and travel books abounded. To say nothing of such hair-raising depictions of the Salem witchcraft trials as Cotton Mather's *The Wonders of the Invisible World*. And, with no telephone or telegraph, there was endless written correspondence. Among the most delightful of these epistles are the letters of Abigail Adams whose husband, John, was to succeed George Washington as president. If Abigail had had her way the Declaration of Independence today would read "We hold these Truths to be self-evident, that all Men and Women are created equal": so she wrote to her husband. Shocked, he wrote back "What next?"

During the actual fighting of the Revolutionary War, from the battles of Lexington and Concord in 1775 to the signing of the Treaty of Paris in 1783, practically nothing of consequence was published. Two exceptions were books by Thomas Paine, *Common Sense* and *The American Crisis*. Muskets were heard instead of the printing press. In 1789, when peace had been established and there had been a few quiet years in which to sharpen the quill pens, the first novel appeared, fifteen years after the first short story. It was based on a notorious family scandal and was called *The Power of Sympathy* by William Hill Brown. It was a "romance" of seduction, incest, and suicide, its advertised purpose "To Expose the dangerous Consequences of Seduction" and "the Advantages of Female Education."

In 1820, Sydney Smith, a famous English literary critic, demanded, "In the four quarters of the globe, who reads an American book? or goes to an American play? or looks at an American picture or statue? What does the world yet owe to American physicians and surgeons? What new substances have their chemists discovered? Or what old ones have they analyzed? What new constellations have been discovered by the telescopes of Americans? What have they done in mathematics? Who drinks out of American glasses? Or wears American coats or gowns? Or sleeps in American blankets?"

Smith's harangue had an immediate answer. An American book of short stories, *The Sketch Book* by Washington Irving, was sweeping not only the United States but Smith's own native British Isles. In it were such immortal tales as "Rip Van Winkle" and "The Legend of Sleepy Hollow." English society clasped Irving to its bosom and he was equally lionized by the French. Renowned writers such as Sir Walter Scott, Lord Byron, and Thomas Moore became his friends. If Hopkinson was the first American story writer recognized nationally, Irving was the first recognized internationally.

In 1923, Edward J. O'Brien, in his *The Advance of the American Short Story*, lamented that two of our finest story writers were ignored and forgotten. One was Herman Melville, who certainly has not been ignored in recent years. The other was William Austin, whose work has long been out of print and is unknown to contemporary readers. But, in addition to being as fine a writer as O'Brien claimed, Austin had a profound influence on many writers who came after him, poets as well as story authors. Even Edward Everett Hale, while writing army recruiting propaganda, got the idea for his well-known "Man Without a Country" from Austin. Peter Rugg was the original man in American literature who couldn't go home again.

What is a short story? In her foreword to *Best American Short Stories 1974*, this editor wrote, "The businesslike *Short Story Index* defines it as 'a story of more than two average-sized pages and not more than one hundred and fifty average-sized pages.' The more literary *American Heritage Dictionary* states it is 'a short prose fiction aiming at unity of characterization, theme, and effect.' Robert Penn Warren says 'It is a story that is not too long.' Then a novel might be defined as a story that is not too short? Henry James said a story could be an anecdote or a picture and 'I prefer the picture.' Edward J. O'Brien thought the modern short story grew out of the essay. Others think its genesis was in tales told by prehistoric people around cave fires. A Supreme Court Justice, struggling with a pornography case decision, exclaimed, 'I can't define obscenity but I know it when I see it!' So it is, I believe, with a short story. You know a short story when you read it!"

America has always been a country in a hurry. The pioneer had too much work to do in exploring and developing new frontiers to afford the time for either writing long works or reading them. The frontier is gone, yet Americans are still impatient and restless, still mobile, as proved by the traffic on any interstate highway. Short stories are ideal for such a culture.

Hopkinson, Austin, and Irving, our first important short-story writers, were all born in the eighteenth century. Although there were only three of them, differences in their work early emphasized the distinction between two kinds of fiction, the realistic or naturalistic and the romantic. It was a distinction that was to prevail in the following two centuries with American literature seesawing between the two. All fiction must have a springboard of reality. Story authors write out of their own knowing and feeling. The difference between the realistic writer and the romantic is that the first tries for strict objectivity and the second adds imaginative wish-fulfillment to his impression of the objective. One tries to keep his feet on the ground, the other flies off into the wild blue yonder.

No writer could be more realistic than Hopkinson. He may have given people, places, and things disguised names but he recorded with meticulous accuracy the actual events that he saw leading up to the

Revolution. No writer could be more happily romantic than Irving in his tale of Rip Van Winkle's escape from domestication, the intermittent wish of so many husbands. And no writer could be more gloomily and romantically Gothic than Austin describing Peter Rugg's accursed ride.

The United States may be known as a land of pragmatism, with the majority of its citizens proud to be called practical people, but romanticism has dominated much of its literature. Hopkinson was the last realist for a long time. Sociologists trace the cause to the rise of the American middle class. Literary genealogists point to Rousseau and his belief that man is good and that only institutions are evil. Philosophers cite the idealism of the eighteenth century's most discussed philosopher, Immanuel Kant. Economists fight over Adam Smith and Karl Marx. And the writers? They just go on writing.

Nathaniel Hawthorne was the first memorable writer born in the nineteenth century and the most memorable chronicler of the Puritans. Like Hopkinson he based much of his writing on actual historic events but in style he was another William Austin, only far more productive. He was a pioneer in the development of the American short story as a literary form in its own right, distinct and separate from the European. So aware were European writers of what the Americans were doing that a verbal duel was fought between Hawthorne and Alexandre Dumas, each accusing the other of plagiarism, but publication dates proved Hawthorne innocent.

Hawthorne lived in Gothic gloom as well as wrote about it. At one time in his life he did not leave his home for twelve years until after dark. In a preface to *The Marble Faun*, he decried the lack of material for romantic writing in the United States "where there is no shadow, no antiquity, no mystery, no picturesque and gloomy wrong, nor anything but a commonplace prosperity, as is happily the case with my dear native land."

The two greatest romantic short-story writers of the nineteenth century and two of the greatest American writers of any type or period are Edgar Allan Poe and Herman Melville. Both had to endure Homer's fate, Poe even more than Melville.

However he may have been regarded in his own country, Poe was idolized in France. Charles Baudelaire translated his short stories, entitling them "extraordinary." Remy de Gourmont said of Poe, "No poet since the Greeks has had such an understanding of the liability to disaster, of the tragic necessity . . . Poe is an American much more representative of America than Emerson or Walt Whitman." The Goncourt brothers in their *Journals* in 1856 declared: "Poe's is a literature of the coming Twentieth Century, of the scientifically miraculous ordained to chronicle what happens in the brain of humanity rather than what happens in its heart." How Poe would have hated that last statement! He himself said, "I write for the feeling." English writers who admired and were influenced by him are Swinburne, Dowson, and Robert Louis Stevenson. A fellow American, Vernon Parrington, said it best. "He was the first of our artists and the first of our critics . . . He went his own way, a rebel in the cause of beauty."

If only one story had ever been written in the United States and that story Herman Melville's "Bartleby the Scrivener," this country could rise up and call itself blessed. What happened to the story when it was published in a collection of magnificent stories by Melville, *The Piazza Tales*, is one more comment on what can befall a writer at the hands of the Philistines. Melville's first five books were based on his South Sea adventures and were a terrific commercial success. He bought a Massachusetts farm, became a close friend of Nathaniel Hawthorne's, and prospered until he wrote *Moby Dick*. That masterpiece was dismissed as too highbrow by readers who wanted more superficial adventure stories. His next book, *Pierre*, again failed his public and *The Piazza Tales* was coolly received and soon out of print. Poor and forgotten, he begged for jobs and finally got one as a minor customs clerk at which he worked for thirteen obscure years until his death, which went unnoticed.

Edward J. O'Brien, who with Raymond Weaver was responsible for rediscovering Melville, said that in "Bartleby the Scrivener" the author had written his own epitaph:

> The round face of the grub-man peered upon me now. "His dinner is ready. Won't he dine to-day, either? Or does he live without dining?"
> "Lives without dining," said I, and closed the eyes.
> "Eh! — He's asleep, ain't he?"
> "With kings and counselors," murmured I.

The American frontier came into its own in the writing of the nineteenth century. The miners, trappers, and cattlemen reveled in yarn-swapping, and the taller the tale the better. Of that species Thorpe's "The Big Bear of Arkansas" is a classic. Those rugged tobacco-chewing, usually unshorn pioneers were a sentimental lot and Bret Harte was one of the most sentimental of them all. Harte's crony, Samuel L. Clemens, or Mark Twain, was not. He was a realist who tempered his realism with humorous exaggeration. The West did leave a permanent impression on Clemens and he retained something of its spirit all his life.

"The Unwritten War" is what a modern historian, Daniel Aaron, calls the Civil War, next to the Revolution the most momentous war in our history. All our other wars, the Indian, the War of 1812, the Mexican

War, the Spanish-American, the two World Wars, and now the war in Vietnam have resulted in far more writing, both fiction and nonfiction, than the one that during four terrible years tore our country apart. But a civil war is the saddest of all wars and like many a fight in a family leaves lasting bitterness too deep for words.

Only three important authors came close enough to write at first hand about the war. One was Ambrose Bierce, who fought for the North and two of whose short-story collections are based on his experiences; another was Charles Egbert Craddock (Mary Noailles Murfree), who as a child saw some of the war's bloodiest fighting in her native Tennessee; and Walt Whitman, whose role was the noblest of all, for he nursed both Northern and Southern soldiers in army hospitals. Samuel Clemens served for two weeks with the Confederate Army and deserted. Years later, of course, Stephen Crane and William Faulkner were to write of it. It would be interesting to know what Whitman would think of their books for he declared: "The actual soldier of 1862–65, North and South, with all his ways, his incredible dauntlessness, habits, practices, tastes, language, his fierce friendship, his appetite, rankness, his superb strength and animality, lawless gait and a hundred unnamed lights and shades of camp, I say, will never be written — perhaps must not and should not be."

Until done to death by its constant repetition in the stories of O. Henry, the "surprise ending" was a popular device that began in the nineteenth century and endured until well into the twentieth. Unless deftly handled it is also annoying since it often fools the unsuspecting reader into believing a lie implicit in the story. Besides, a surprise is a surprise only once. Of its many devotees two of the best writers were Frank Stockton with his "The Lady or the Tiger?" and William Bailey Aldrich with "Marjorie Daw."

Expatriation was common among American authors long before the celebrated "Lost Generation" of the twenties in Paris. There have been many reasons for this emigration, cheaper living and lower taxes, the perspective that distance can give a writer on his native material, the stimulation of foreign peoples and sights, but the prime one is the very reason that makes the short story popular in the United States. The great speed and high pressure of life here drive writers to seek the more contemplative, less mechanized ways of living in the security of an older, more settled civilization. Irving, Hawthorne, Crane, B. Traven, Pound, Eliot, Stein, O'Brien, Hemingway, Wright, and many, many more make the list of our literary expatriates a long one. Of them all, Henry James is the most extraordinary.

His long love-hate relationship with the United States dominated the life and writing of Henry James. A national dichotomy developed in him early when at the impressionable age of twelve he was taken to live for several years in Europe. He returned to study at Harvard but from the age of twenty-three, when he went again to Europe, he never was really happy on either side of the Atlantic. When he was in the United States he felt its atmosphere was unfriendly to artists and left for Europe. In Europe he yearned for America. Commenting on one of his return trips to America in 1870, he wrote: "The nostalgic poison had been distilled for him, the future presented to him as a single intense question: was he to spend it in brooding exile, or might he somehow come into his 'own'?" In 1875 he finally decided to make Europe his permanent home and, except for an intermission of two years, spent his last forty years there. Even then he gave his home address as Cambridge, Massachusetts. In 1915, a year before his death, James put a period to his long Europe-versus-America debate. To show his sympathy for the Allied cause in the First World War he became a British citizen.

James was a realist but not in the usual meaning of the term as applied to a writer dedicated to factual representation. He was a "psychological realist." His chosen territory is the one of mind and emotion and he was a brave man to venture as a fiction writer into such elusive places. He hated facts and he hated plots and there is little action in his stories. Instead there is tremendous tension in the psychological give-and-take of his characters and great suspense. His stories and novels are among the most subtle ever written. Someone has compared them to "a waking dream."

Our most mysterious expatriate is Ambrose Bierce. He was one of the few well-known American writers to serve on either side in the Civil War and his short stories, *Tales of Soldiers and Civilians,* are some of the finest ever to have been written about the conflict. His brilliance as a writer and editor made him the most influential and popular literary figure on the West Coast. But in 1913, when he was seventy-one years old, he said he was tired of American civilization and went to Mexico where war was raging to seek what he called "the good, kind darkness." He was never heard from again. Some reports said he had been captured and executed by one of the warring Mexican generals, others said he had been killed by bandits or that he was living in the same kind of deep Mexican seclusion as that of the Chicago-born author, B. Traven, who became such a remote expatriate people forgot he was an American. Nobody knows.

Although the United States was to be incredibly tardy in granting equal rights, American women almost from the beginning succeeded in literature. Her name is not familiar now but Sara Josepha Hale (1788–1879) was an important person to short-story writers. As editor, first of the Boston *Ladies' Magazine* (1828 to 1837), and for forty years after of *Godey's Lady's Book*, she published a great number of them. Her contributors included Hawthorne, Poe, and Stowe. Hale also wrote stories but none ever achieved the permanent recognition of her children's verse, "Mary Had A Little Lamb"!

Harriet Beecher Stowe (1811–1896) was the first major American woman short-story writer in the nineteenth century. Because of the antislavery impact of her novel *Uncle Tom's Cabin*, which was the first American novel to sell more than a million copies, it is usually forgotten that she wrote other fiction, including several volumes of short stories. Set either in her native New England or in Florida, they were strongly regional in scene and character types. In fact, nearly all the early women writers were to lean heavily toward the regional. Sarah Orne Jewett, with her New England scenes and people, and Kate Chopin, with her Creole stories, are famous examples. An exception was Rebecca Harding Davis, who wrote beautifully and poignantly of the plight of women mill workers.

Although all the women writers mentioned were active in feminist causes, particularly suffrage and higher education for women, feminism in their fiction writing emerged rather late. Mary Wilkins Freeman stressed it in "The Revolt of Mother," in which a wife successfully opposes a husband's plans to build a second new barn instead of a badly needed family home. Susan Glaspell also wrote a feminist short story in "A Jury of Her Peers," in which women who have discovered that a neighbor has committed a murder they consider justified band together to conceal her guilt.

Willa Cather, one of our all-time major writers of either sex, started out by writing beautiful local color stories of her Nebraska farm neighbors. She was to roam far from them in stories about people from other regions such as New York and New Mexico. The majority of her many novels and short stories is devoted to penetrating studies of a woman's character done with great beauty and sensitivity. The women range from the sturdy young farm women to frustrated women artists hungry for a career to the gracefully poised and sophisticated mature woman in the novel, *A Lost Lady*.

Edith Wharton, another outstanding woman writer who was born and matured in the nineteenth century, also was one who, like Cather, could write of greatly varying types of women. Although she is generally thought of as devoted to "high society" types, such as the dowager in "After Holbein," she wrote magnificently of poor seamstresses struggling to survive in "The Bunner Sisters" and the simple farm wife in her novella *Ethan Frome*.

One American woman writer who used a masculine alias was Mary

Noailles Murfree. Her disguise was not discovered until long after she had become famous as the "Charles Craddock" author of vivid accounts of bloody Civil War battles. Then the editor of the *Atlantic Monthly* and her admiring public were stunned to find "he" was a sickly, crippled woman. Beside her many novels she wrote eleven volumes of short stories. As a child she had witnessed some of the bloodiest Civil War fighting in her native Tennessee and used this experience together with love for the beauty of the Cumberland mountains and the simple folk who lived there as basis for her fiction. She was considered a pioneer in the use of American dialect.

At the beginning of this introduction, romanticism and realism were mentioned as the dominant influences in American fiction. There is a third term, used by some literary scholars, "naturalism." It is so close to realism it hardly seems worth the bother. If the term were to be "determinism" it might be more understandable. It comes to the fore in the late nineteenth century and is attributed to the influence of Darwin's theory of biological determinism and Karl Marx's theory of economic determinism. It was first used in France to explain the writing of Zola with his emphasis on the physical heritage of his characters as opposed to Flaubert's concern with their social environment. An interesting example of how impossible it is to pin down an exact definition of literary technique is Hamlin Garland. He has been called all three, realistic because of his accurately factual descriptions, naturalistic because of the determinism enforced by the poverty that victimizes his characters, and romantic because of their "ethical idealism."

All hair-splitting aside, Hamlin Garland is a significant writer who heralds the coming of a long line of socially conscious writers whose sympathies were with the poor and who stressed the harshness of the life they endured. Short-story writers in this group include Stephen Crane, Jack London, Theodore Dreiser, James Farrell, and the entire group of proletarian writers who were to emerge in the thirties. Garland's toil-worn farmers struggling to survive on bleak midwestern prairies and his war-scarred soldiers in their weary resignation are described with such warmth that, saddened though a reader may be, he is glad to know them. Like the thirties' writers who became active in radical movements, Garland was active in politics and campaigned for the Populist Party, a combination of farmer and labor reform groups.

Two years after Hamlin Garland's *Main-Travelled Roads* was published, Stephen Crane's first book, *Maggie: A Girl of the Streets*, appeared, privately printed at the author's expense because publishers turned it down as too grim. The first was a collection of short stories, the second a novel; one depicted the cruel life on midwestern wheat farms, the other the cruel life in New York City slums. It is problematical as to how much influence writers have upon one another. Some cases are indisputable, especially when an author is honest enough to acknowledge a debt as Willa Cather did to Sarah Orne Jewett; Sherwood Anderson to Gertrude Stein; William Faulkner to Sherwood Anderson: unlike Hemingway who, far more than Faulkner, was indebted to Anderson. Often, though, literary likeness may be attributed to *Zeitgeist*, the spirit of the times.

By the eighteen-nineties, when Garland and Crane emerged, the Industrial Revolution had long since taken hold. An increasing number of unions had been organized by farm laborers and factory workers, emphatic in their protests against injustice, to which the sensitive ears of writers were not deaf. Few writers become rich and of those who do even fewer seem to produce work of lasting merit or even lasting popular appeal, as a glance at any best-seller list of ten years or so back will show. Most writers also know long periods of financial uncertainty. It is natural they should feel empathy for others who do. The terrified rookie soldier in *The Red Badge of Courage* is the best known of Crane's characters but in his short stories he also had a miraculous way of creating empathy for ordinary workaday people.

A literary phenomenon of this period was the writing of Jack London. It is as amazingly ambivalent as London himself. Like Garland and Crane, he identified with the oppressed but took more direct action and became a Socialist, active in the Socialist Party and an ardent admirer of Karl Marx. He also worshipped Neitzsche with his myth of the Superman and gloried in writing about elemental man in violent conflict with raw nature. It is hard to believe that any author could, at one and the same time, write with equal power of the triumph of a lone individual and of workers massed together in collective action. London did. His first writing, magazine stories of rugged life in the Klondike, were collected in his first book, *Son of the Wolf*, and were followed almost immediately by *People of the Abyss*, a study of London slum life, and soon after *The Iron Heel*, a widely read and influential Socialist novel.

The end of the nineteenth century marked a swift and dramatic change in the national status of the United States, altering its character forever and consequently the character of its literature. Within three months in 1898, the brief time it took this country to conquer Spain in the Spanish-American War, the United States became a world power. With the acquisition in the Atlantic of Puerto Rico and Cuba, the latter nominally independent but with part of its territory, Guantanamo, retained as an American naval base, and with the acquisition of Hawaii, the Philippines, and Guam far out in the Pacific, we were no longer one nation among many nations but a burgeoning empire.

Many authors fought in the war. Among the short-story writers participating were Sherwood Anderson and Stephen Crane. *Wounds in the Rain*, Crane's short-story collection, was based on his experiences in it as was one of his most admired stories, "The Open Boat." A long list of novels and nonfiction works also grew out of it. As did Elbert Hubbard's notoriously sentimental *Message to Garcia*, which by 1940 had sold more than forty million copies, many of them bought by industrialists to promote efficiency among their employees.

When the nation's borders expanded after the war so did all aspects of its life. In 1900 the population of the United States was 75,944,575. In 1972 it was 208,232,000. Back in 1774 when Hopkinson wrote the first American short story the population was approximately 2,450,000. Like the people, American short stories rapidly increased. Beginning singly in the eighteenth century, they multiplied arithmetically in the nineteenth and geometrically in the twentieth until in 1968 *The Short Story Index* could tabulate the 96,336 entries already noted at the beginning of this introduction.

Any survey of the short story in the United States must recognize the role of periodicals. American magazines have been and still are very important to the success of the American short story. They are every bit as important to it as book publishers are to the promulgation of longer literary works. The overwhelming majority of our writers were first printed in magazines. Without such publication many would never become known. Magazines were preceded in colonial times by "gift books." These were miscellanies published annually or on special occasions and usually lavishly illustrated and bound.

Benjamin Franklin conceived the first magazine to be published in the colonies. He and the editor he engaged for it had an angry disagreement and the editor brought out his own magazine, *The American Magazine*, in 1741, just three days before Franklin's, which was called *The General Magazine*. Thus *The American Magazine* was acclaimed as the first and Franklin's only second and an imitation. Both magazines were short-lived. Franklin was so hurt he never mentioned either periodical in his autobiography. Most readers associate Franklin with *The Saturday Evening Post*, which for many years carried his picture and his name as founder on the cover. This was a publicity gimmick. Franklin died in 1790 and the *Post* was founded in 1821.

The oldest of American literary magazines is *The North American Review*, founded in Boston in 1815. It was suspended in 1939, revived in 1963, and is now published at Cornell College in Iowa. The stature of its early editors and contributors was remarkable. The former included R. H. Dana and Henry Adams. The latter included, in addition to a brilliant array of poets, essayists, and novelists, such short-story writers as Irving, Twain, Tolstoy, and James. Another equally influential early magazine was, as already mentioned, *Godey's Lady's Book*, founded in 1830, and edited by Sarah Hale, a feminist, for forty years from 1837 to 1877. In the same period belongs *The Southern Literary Messenger*, 1834 to 1864, which was edited for two years, from 1835 to 1837, by Edgar Allan Poe. That "impractical" poet increased its circulation from 500 to 3500 subscribers, a huge figure for those days.

*The Atlantic Monthly* (now *The Atlantic*) and *Harper's Magazine* were started in the middle of the nineteenth century and their titles have been almost omnipresent in literary bibliography ever since. This is also true of *Scribner's Magazine* and *Lippincott's*, magazines that came some years later but are no longer published. In the earlier part of the twentieth century notable literary magazines were *The Smart Set*, *The Dial*, *Double-Dealer*, *Hound and Horn*, *The Little Review*, *American Caravan*, and *transition*. What a good magazine can accomplish is proved by the tremendous achievement of *The Little Review* in serializing Joyce's *Ulysses* when no other publisher would touch that masterpiece. And *The New Yorker*, by printing one or more distinguished short stories weekly, has been indispensable to hundreds of leading authors, both American and foreign.

Less fortunately, as magazines increased in number so did an inferior sort, the so-called "slicks" and "pulps" and "women's magazines," many of which attained enormous circulations. While an occasional worthwhile story appeared in them, they were ruled by advertisers whose unabashedly admitted credo was that the average American reader has the mentality of a twelve-year-old. This led to a plethora of shoddy adventure and crime stories in the pulps; the boy-meets-girl-boy-loses-girl-boy-gets-girl-back-and-job-in-the-bank formula in the slicks; and the Patient-Griselda type in the women's magazines who discovers that happiness is to be found in a domestic purdah. It was his disgust with this type of writing that led a young New England poet, Edward J. O'Brien, a couple of years out of Harvard, to found in 1915 his annual collection, *The Best American Short Stories*, in order to rescue from the welter of print those stories that are of permanent value. It was so successful a second similar anthology was started in 1919, the *O. Henry Memorial Award* series.

The twentieth century that was to be even more productive of American fiction than its predecessors had an interesting start. Two important story collections were published in 1900: *Whilomville Stories*, by Stephen Crane, and *Son of the Wolf*, by Jack London. It was also the year that another of our literary giants, Theodore Dreiser, better known for his novels than his short stories, finished his first book, *Sister Carrie*, which was accepted, printed, bound, made ready for book store distribution, and at the last minute withheld from circulation by the publisher.

The publisher's wife had read a copy, was shocked by what she considered its immorality, and persuaded her husband to keep the book hidden from the light of day in his vaults for twelve years. They were long hard years for the shaken author, who had to toil at hack jobs. Not until after Dreiser's second book, *Jennie Gerhard*, was published and enthusiastically received, did the publisher free *Sister Carrie* from captivity. It, too, was applauded and Dreiser was recognized for the genius he was.

Queen Victoria died in 1901 and the pall cast by her ultra-respectable, matronly presence on the use of the English language on both sides of the Atlantic began to lift. Piano legs — er — er — limbs no longer wore petticoats and people no longer had to say they were retiring when they meant going to bed. Still, along with all literary expression, short stories continued to be severely circumscribed. Organizations such as the Watch and Ward Society and the Society for the Suppression of Vice maintained strict censorship over subject matter and vocabulary.

In 1920 Margaret Anderson and Jane Heap, the two editors of *The Little Review*, were hauled into court on charges of obscenity by the Society for the Suppression of Vice. Since 1914, when the magazine was founded in Chicago, the young women had struggled against terrific odds to keep *The Little Review* going. Nearly always financially straitened, sometimes close to starving, doing most of the manual labor themselves, as described by Margaret Anderson in *My Thirty Years' War* (1930), they were to sustain the magazine for twenty-five years. During that time they printed such notable writers as T. S. Eliot, William Carlos Williams, W. B. Yeats, Malcolm Cowley, Ford Madox Ford, Amy Lowell, and Sherwood Anderson. Ezra Pound became the European editor in 1917 and it was he who recommended *Ulysses* to them with the warning that it might be censorable. As quoted by Janet Flanner in *The New Yorker*, Margaret Anderson exclaimed, "This is the most beautiful thing we'll ever have! We'll print it if it is the last effort of our lives." Their serialized publication of *Ulysses* caused an uproar. Four times issues of the magazine were burned by the United States Post Office. When, finally, the editors were tried in court before three judges they were found guilty of obscenity, fingerprinted, and fined one hundred dollars.

H. L. Mencken caused another uproar when he printed "Hatrack," a short story by Herbert Asbury, in *The American Mercury*. It had only the mildest of any sex relevance but the literary vigilantes tried to prosecute the magazine. Mencken went to Boston to protest and he was arrested on the Common for possession of obscene literature. At the station house it was discovered he had put the jacket from a suppressed book around a copy of the Bible. In the nineteen-thirties, after the court dismissed obscenity charges against Erskine Caldwell's *God's Little Acre*, and James Joyce's *Ulysses*, copies of which U. S. Customs inspectors had been confiscating at the docks along with forbidden liquor, the priggishness abated. Today writers can use the English language as freely as did William Shakespeare.

The early years of this century were to be the source of much nostalgic writing. They were years of peace before the Great War: an extraordinary number of gifted writers in all fields of literature were born around the turn of the century and much of their work grew out of childhood impressions, which are the most acute. Among the many short-story writers whose names were to become familiar to present-day readers are Dorothy Parker, Vardis Fisher, Edmund Wilson, F. Scott Fitzgerald, William Faulkner, Stephen Vincent Benét, Ernest Hemingway, E. B. White, Thomas Wolfe, John Steinbeck, Kay Boyle, Erskine Caldwell, James T. Farrell, Jesse Stuart, Robert Penn Warren, William Saroyan, Richard Wright, James Agee, and Eudora Welty.

Another portent of things to come in those halcyon years was the first work by three new writers. One was *Three Lives*, in 1909, by Gertrude Stein. It was a story collection and quite conventionally written compared to her later work. The stories were considered radical by reviewers because they had no conventional plots. Another first book was Ring Lardner's baseball stories entitled *You Know Me Al*, in 1916 and a progenitor of a long line of baseball tales by many writers. The book received only casual attention and it was not until several books later that Lardner was seen as an important writer.

Of the greatest significance at this period, however, was the appearance of Sherwood Anderson, who was to have a profound effect on American short-story writing. His first book was a novel, *Windy McPherson's Son*, in 1916, followed by another novel and a book of poems. Not until 1919 did a book of his short stories appear, *Winesburg, Ohio*. No American book in this century engendered such excitement among writers, particularly the young. It was like a great current of fresh air sweeping across what had threatened to become a parched desert of contrived, dishonest writing. Writers felt freed by it, including Faulkner and Hemingway, whose name was given to what should be called "the Anderson influence." The New York *World Telegram* reviewed an early book by Hemingway in three parallel columns of similar passages from the writings of Gertrude Stein, Sherwood Anderson, and Ernest Hemingway, and headlined the review like a racing chart: "Hemingway out of Stein by Anderson."

In 1917, an American Expeditionary Force was dispatched to Europe and the United States joined the First World War on the side of the Allies. A number of American writers had previously volunteered as ambulance drivers, including e. e. cummings and Ernest Hemingway. William Faulkner tried to enlist but was turned down as too frail by the United States Army and joined the British Royal Air Force in Canada. The war ended before his training did and he saw no action. Hemingway, of course, saw plenty of action on the Italian front, was wounded, and wrote of it in *A Farewell to Arms*.

Also in the army was a young man from Princeton who, sergeants or no sergeants, achieved the unmilitary feat of writing the first draft of his first novel while training in boot camp. He was F. Scott Fitzgerald and the novel was *This Side of Paradise*, published in 1920 along with his first book of short stories, *Flappers and Philosophers*. In 1922 a second book of his short stories, *Tales of the Jazz Age*, was published. The twenties had got their most popular label, "The Jazz Age."

The designation, with its connotation of giddiness, is misleading. The literary life was not all jumping into fountains or running with the bulls at Pamplona. The twenties was the richest decade thus far in the number of important literary works produced. The list is too long to print here. A wonderfully concise tabulation can be found in the Chronological Index to the *Oxford Companion to American Literature*. A historic short-story first was Ernest Hemingway's "My Old Man," published by O'Brien in *The Best American Short Stories 1923*, the only short story in the series not previously printed in a magazine.

Writers were affected by the Sacco-Vanzetti case, which became the American version of the Dreyfus controversy. The two men, political radicals, were accused of murdering a Massachusetts paymaster and guard. After the alleged evidence against them was proved false and they were still condemned to die, there were widespread demonstrations. Many of our most famous authors participated, picketing the courthouse and prison. The case inspired 144 poems, six plays, eight novels, and uncounted short stories, all by well-known hands and all in sympathy with the condemned men.

"Wall Street Lays An Egg!" *Variety*, Broadway's theatrical journal, proclaimed in November, 1929. The twenties ended with a bang. Their real epitaph was a short story. It was by the same author whose stories had ushered in the boom years, F. Scott Fitzgerald. His "Babylon Revisited" is the penetrating story of a man who lost in the boom everything he had ever wanted.

Suddenly the Depression was upon us. Banks closing and businesses failing, yesterday's tycoons selling apples on street corners or killing themselves, millions of unemployed, and endless breadlines — the long, horrid litany can still make an American shudder. It shocked the nation into a kind of class consciousness it had never known. There was a widespread feeling of imminent revolution. A publisher needing capital was told by a financier he approached, "I might as well let you have the money. It will all be taken away from me tomorrow anyhow." "Why?" the publisher asked. "There's going to be a revolution." A prize for the best novel by a Communist was offered by a large publishing house. The main entrance of the newly built Rockefeller Center on Fifth Avenue featured an enormous mural by the Mexican artist, Diego Rivera, since erased. It portrayed the heroic figure of a triumphantly smiling laborer bearing a huge red flag and leading forward masses of people. To one side was a caricature of John D. Rockefeller, his face wizened like a monkey's. Evidently the mural was meant as a kind of protective coloring.

From Europe during those years came thousands of refugees, many outstanding intellectuals, scientists, and artists, fleeing the devastation being wrought by Hitler and Mussolini. Among the English writers were Aldous Huxley, Christopher Isherwood, and W. H. Auden; among the Continental were Thomas Mann and Berthold Brecht. They added a valuable new dimension to the American literary scene with Huxley and Mann being the most admired short-story writers.

"I'll Take My Stand," in 1930, was the first of a series of symposia by important Southern writers calling themselves Agrarians who earlier had published *The Fugitive*, a little magazine in Nashville, Tennessee. Most of the Agrarians were poets and critics, such as John Crowe Ransom and Donald Davidson, but also included Robert Penn Warren and Allen Tate, who wrote fiction. The Agrarians were opposed to realism in literature and, to quote the words of Allan Tate, "Only a return to the provinces, to the small self-contained centres of life, will put the all destroying abstraction America to rest." Out of the Agrarian movement grew another one, the New Criticism. This was a form of analysis that isolated a piece of writing from all externals, such as the author's life, the period, and other environmental circumstances to concentrate solely on the style and content of the actual words on the printed page. The theory spread north and led to much heated argument among writers throughout the country.

It is fortunate that the South has stayed in the United States. Otherwise this nation would be without some of its most glorious literature, for Dixie abounds in literary talent. William Faulkner stands the tallest. No American author, north, south, east, or west surpasses the writing in his many stories and novels. "Yoknapatawpha County," the scene of most of his writing, has become as real to readers as has his native Mississippi. The South is proud of Faulkner now, although for a number of years his books were out of print and he had to resort to hack writing in Hollywood to earn money for his family. But Georgia has not yet forgiven Erskine Caldwell for his descriptions of the sharecropper's merciless life in *Tobacco Road* and *God's Little Acre.* Their power lies in the dead seriousness with which Caldwell wrote them, pulling no punches. The South will forgive Caldwell as it has Thomas Wolfe, whose native Asheville, which reviled him during his lifetime, has restored his mother's old boarding house as a memorial to him.

There have been and are so many brilliant Southern authors who emerged in the Depression years it is impossible to give each his due share. But in a book of short stories four must be mentioned. They are Katherine Anne Porter, Carson McCullers, Eudora Welty, and Flannery O'Connor. Their state's long border with Mexico has affected the work of the many good writers in Texas and Katherine Anne Porter is an excellent example. She has located her stories in both the United States and Mexico. It doesn't matter where they take place. Her stories are to be cherished for their sheer beauty. Both Carson McCullers and Eudora Welty use grotesque characters and write with extreme sensitivity. McCullers is the more realistic while Welty prefers fantasy. Flannery O'Connor's people and the events befalling them are both extraordinary.

In 1930, a mimeographed publication entitled *Story* was produced by two young American foreign correspondents, Whit Burnett and Martha Foley, stationed in Vienna, Austria. It opened with a statement that it would "present short narratives of significance by no matter whom and coming from no matter where" and that if it used any nonfiction articles they "will be as rare as short stories of creative importance are today in the article-ridden magazines of America." It further stated that it was a sort of "proof-book of hitherto unpublished manuscripts" the rights to which would remain with the authors because they might appear later in more permanent pages. In other words, the editors originally planned a crusade to impress public and publishers with the importance of stories. Almost overnight it was flooded with hundreds of manuscripts of remarkably high quality and by the time of its third bi-monthly issue became a magazine, the only one devoted to the literary short story. Demand for copies grew rapidly and *Story* was moved from Europe to America where it became the focus for a whole generation of thirties writers. Splendid little magazines had been coming and going since the founding of the Republic. The 1929 crash had a devastating effect on those of the twenties. Only a few survived. They were *transition, Sewanee Review, Prairie Schooner, Hound and Horn,* and *This Quarter.* Quality magazines such as the *Atlantic, Harper's,* and *Scribner's* cut down sharply the amount of fiction they published following the lead of Mencken and Nathan, who had abandoned the old *Smart Set* with its plentiful fiction for the *American Mercury* with its emphasis on factual writing. *Story* was a success because it filled a publishing vacuum.

*Story* had the golden opportunity to be the first to publish John Cheever, Carson McCullers, William Saroyan, Norman Mailer, James Farrell, Tennessee Williams, J. D. Salinger, Jesse Stuart, Nelson Algren, Jerome Weidman, James Laughlin, Emily Hahn, Peter de Vries, and Elizabeth Janeway, plus many more. Already well-established authors became contributors, among them William Faulkner, William March, Katherine Anne Porter, Manuel Komroff, Dorothy Canfield Fisher, and Kay Boyle. Among foreign authors were Robert Musil, Malcolm Lowry, Ivan Bunin, H. E. Bates, and Graham Greene. Now it reads like a literary hall of fame but many of these writers had been rejected elsewhere because they wrote short stories. Today more than a hundred magazines are printing short stories of literary merit.

Proletarian literature, the story of laboring humanity's struggle to overcome inimical social and economic circumstances, has existed from the earliest times. The classics and the Bible are studded with it. In the United States Emerson, Thoreau, and Whitman have been considered its progenitors, along with William Dean Howells, Edwin Markham, Hamlin Garland, Jack London, Frank Norris, and Upton Sinclair. Theodore Dreiser, B. Traven, Sinclair Lewis, and Sherwood Anderson came later. American proletarian writing came of age in the thirties. There were more writers disturbed by social problems than ever before. Some of the best were James Farrell, Howard Fast, Albert Maltz, Richard Wright, Jack Conroy, Nelson Algren, Pietro di Donato, Irwin Shaw, Josephine Johnson, Waldo Frank, Josephine Herbst, Michael Gold, and Albert Halper.

A matter of life and death for writers in the thirties was the Federal Writers' Project. It literally saved many of them from starvation and homelessness. Organized in 1935 in the most desperate part of the Depression for the relief of writers, editors, and researchers, it employed at one time more than 6,600 literary people. Project alumni include renowned authors, among them Conrad Aiken and Richard Wright, whose stories are classics.

History sometimes seems like blowing up and popping a paper bag. Boom! Bust! Bang! In the twenties we had the Boom, in the thirties the Bust, and in the forties we got the Bang — the Second World War. The First World War was horrible enough, God knows, but the Second was even worse. It gave us the Holocaust. And Hiroshima.

Because military action has never really stopped for Americans even though peace was signed in 1945 and thirty years have passed, it is not yet possible to assess the full impact on our literature of the Second World War. Almost immediately we were embroiled in the Korean War. When fighting there was more or less finished, along came Vietnam and the longest war in United States history. Although it now presumably has ended, we still seem to be deeply involved in Southeast Asia. Words-worth's adage for writing still holds — "emotion recollected in tran-quility." If tranquillity can be equated with peace American writers since the nineteen-forties have had little of it.

Powerful writing did come out of the Second World War, however. Some of the best is in *The Gallery*, by John Horne Burns, whose early death robbed the country of an incipient great writer. Other distin-guished World War II fiction was Saul Bellow's *Dangling Man*, Norman Mailer's *The Naked and the Dead*, Irwin Shaw's *The Young Lions*, Herman Wouk's *The Caine Mutiny*, James Michener's *Tales of the South Pacific*, and *Guard of Honor* by James Gould Cozzens. With the excep-tion of the last-named they are all collections of short stories. The Michener book announces that fact in its title. The others were published and reviewed as "novels."

These books emphasize a trend in American fiction that has become pronounced in this century. In the eighteenth and nineteenth centuries when the novel first developed importance, it generally took two forms. One is as seen in Fielding, Smollett, and Dickens, and usually concerned three couples, upper class, lower class, and comic. Their interwoven adventures made the plot. Or, as in the case of Jane Austen, George Eliot, and Henry James, the novel is a long, tightly knit story, parts of which could not be separated without bringing the whole structure toppling down.

Nowadays many so-called novels, even though they concern the same group of characters from cover to cover, can easily be divided into their component parts. These parts then turn out to be short stories and can be published separately in magazines to the financial benefit of the author and the promotional advantage of the book publisher. *Life with Father* and *My Sister Eileen*, printed in *The New Yorker* in the twenties and thirties as short stories first and then as highly successful books, are well-known examples. The short-story form seems destined to pre-dominate in American literature.

The United States has not been the melting pot it so frequently is called in its fiction, although it is certainly rich in ethnic writing. Instead it is more like a pot-au-feu, that flavorsome stew that simmers constantly on peasant stoves. To it are added continually whatever ingredients become available with each maintaining its own distinct taste while contributing to the savoriness of the whole. Many and varied cultures have contributed to our writing. The European cultures are the most recognized and taken for granted. But those cultures are, after all, derivative.

America has two kinds of ethnic literature that it has not always appreciated. One is that of our black authors. In colonial times two of the most gifted poets were black slaves, Jupiter Hammon (1720–1800) and Phillis Wheatley (1753–1784). In the nineteenth century Charles Waddell Chesnutt (1858–1932) was a black who wrote a number of novels and a well-known collection of black dialect stories, *The Conjure Woman*. William Stanley Braithwaite (1878–1962), black poet and short-story writer, founded and edited for many years the highly regarded *Annual Anthology of Magazine Verse and Year Book of American Poetry*. There are, of course, many other black men and women who have written splendidly. Some of the more contemporary black short-story authors are Zora Neale Hurston, Langston Hughes, Richard Wright, James Baldwin, Ralph Ellison, Eldridge Cleaver, Alice Walker, Ernest Gaines, and Ishmael Reed.

The most neglected American literature and the only indigenous one is that of the American Indian. We have had intriguing samples of it brilliantly relayed by Oliver LaFarge and Mary Austin. But the American Indian storyteller himself? Hounded from state to state, forcibly deported on the infamous Cherokee "Trail of Tears," segregated on reservations, harassed by innumerable cruel bureaucratic restrictions, betrayed by false treaties — what opportunity did the Indian have to write? So his literature has been kept oral and we have been deprived of his age-old tales, rich in poetic imagery and religious symbolism. Out of that forced obscurity impressive Indian writers are now finally emerging. One is Vine Deloria who wrote the moving best seller, *Custer Died for Your Sins*. *Rabbit Boss* is a novel of permanent literary value by Thomas Sanchez, while another fine Indian writer, N. Scott Momaday, won the Pulitzer Prize for his novel, *House Made of Dawn*. Two other important native American writers are James Welch, author of *Winter in the Blood*, and Leslie Silko with her many fine short stories and poems. Other Indian short stories are also finding their way into print. A recent fascinating collection of them is *The Man to Send Rain Clouds* (1974), edited by Kenneth Rosen.

Just as the twenties were known as the Jazz Age, the fifties were to be known as the age of the Beat movement. The term "Beat," as defined by the *Oxford Companion to American Literature*, "expressed both exhaustion and beatification in that the writers, tired of conventional society, and disgusted by it, believed that thoroughgoing disaffiliation from all aspects of the manners and mores of what they saw as a corrupt, crass, commercial world would bring its own kind of blissful illumination, aided by drink and drugs." And, it could be added, Zen Buddhism. Allen Ginsberg was their poet laureate, Jack Kerouac their historian. The Beats recognized themselves in Ginsberg's famous poem, "Howl": "I saw the best minds of my generation destroyed by madness, starving hysterical naked." They relived their experiences in the stories about them in Kerouac's books, particularly *On the Road* (1957), *The Dharma Bums* (1958), and *The Subterraneans* (1959). Among the leading literary figures of the Beat movement are Ken Kesey, author of *One Flew Over the Cuckoo's Nest*, William Gaddis, author of *The Recognitions*, and Terry Southern and Mason Hoffenberg, who collaborated on *Candy*. Older writers associated with the Beats included Henry Miller, Paul Bowles, Kenneth Rexroth, William Burroughs, and Norman Mailer.

The century grew older and a kind of restlessness overtook many writers in the sixties. They wanted something different but they didn't seem to know what. Some, like John Barth in his *The Sotweed Factor* and Donald Barthelme in *Snow White*, took to parodying ancient works. Others, viewing the French vogue for the *nouvel roman*, tried minimizing the role of characters in their stories. Still others, perhaps influenced by Marshall McLuhan and his linear theory of the "medium is the message," try combining graphics with writing. Or, to cite an extreme example of experimentation, an able writer like Ronald Sukenik throws away the words he can write so well to confront the reader with long stretches of blank paper. This trend has continued into the seventies and is given the awkward name of "innovative writing." Poets, when they rebel against restrictions of rhyme and meter, call their writing "free verse." What these new experimental story writers are doing might be termed "free fiction."

One of the most important, perhaps the most important, of this present group of writers is Thomas Pynchon. His latest novel, *Gravity's Rainbow*, won the National Book Award for 1973. Both in content and style it is considered the most daringly original work of fiction since James Joyce's *Ulysses*. Even more, in some ways, than *Ulysses*, it takes a reader beyond the words on the page into what critics, when they have the rare experience of encountering it, call a literary fourth dimension.

Today's fermentation among writers is of a kind that usually foretells a new kind of burgeoning and it augurs well for a third American literary century. Providing, of course, the world is spared the Bomb. Our present scene is fantastically rich in a host of splendid story writers, both the many well-loved ones already here, the less known, and those newly approaching over the horizon.

When this survey was begun, it sounded like a breeze. Choices seemed so obvious. Irving, Hawthorne, Poe, Melville, Twain, James, Crane, Cather, down to Hemingway and Faulkner in the twentieth century — they were all there just waiting to be picked. Then one encountered the frightening statistic of 96,336 short stories published in books in the United States from 1774 to 1968, plus the innumerable thousands that appeared only in magazines. And one discovered that Irving had not been the first American story writer as taught in literature classes and generally assumed, but that an author named Francis Hopkinson, who wrote stories, plays, and poems and also designed the American flag, had written a short story with a powerful catalytic effect on the starting of the American Revolution. It took many hours of research extending for more than a year and the help of a number of patient librarians to track down the original version, which had been out of print for more than a century. That was only the beginning. Even with the well-known authors there was such a plethora of choices. Irving, for example. How to choose between such equally good tales as "Rip Van Winkle" and "The Legend of Sleepy Hollow"? Hawthorne presented a dozen immortal stories. And Poe? One might as well pick a number out of a hat.

All through the nineteenth century reading there was the consolation of thinking how much easier it would be when the twentieth century was reached where the literary territory was familiar. It was a vain hope. There is a multitude of good writers and one admires so many of them that preferences are impossible. This writer will be haunted for the rest of her days by the choices she did not make. She has been like that legendary child with a penny in a candy store. There is only one defense. Readers are invited to make out their own list of favorite American short stories. They may be amazed and delighted and also overwhelmed to find out how very many of them there are.

As was said at the beginning of this introduction, *200 Years of Great American Short Stories* is no flag-in-the-lapel collection of chauvinistic writings. But it is a sampling of literary masterpieces of which any nation could be proud. To quote a recent critic, "The short story, though not a domestic invention, has been perfected in America." The United States, founded in 1776, can now in 1976 look back with unequivocal and patriotic pride on two hundred years of literary genius and its very own unique contribution to world literature, the American short story.

# *Acknowledgments*

I owe a debt of gratitude to so many writers, scholars, editors, and friends for help and guidance in preparing this anthology that it is impossible to list them all. First, it is no exaggeration to say that the collection certainly could not have been compiled without the skilled research of many patient librarians. Those I was able to consult personally and thus can name are Margaret A. Kately and Lia Smits of the New Canaan, Connecticut, Public Library, and Eleanor Shea, Rowena Lebow, and Lee Snook of the Forbes Library in Northampton, Massachusetts. There are also the hundreds of librarians I never met but who helped me greatly through their cooperation in the Inter Library system, which gave me access to more than a million books in public and college libraries. A very special example of the important help I received is in connection with the tracking down of one of the four surviving copies of the original edition of Hopkinson's "A Pretty Story." Through Inter Library, the American Antiquarian Society, and the librarian in charge of the rare books division of the Boston Public Library, a copy was located in the rare book collection of the University of Pennsylvania Library. Its curator, Neda Westlake, provided much needed information about the author and the history of the publication of his story. Through her it was learned that the G. K. Hall Co. of Boston had only lately reproduced it for a gift book and Elizabeth Kubik there was kind enough to provide a facsimile of the gift book's one remaining copy.

Invaluable source books have been the *Short Story Index* published by H. W. Wilson Co., the *American Fiction Series* issued by the Garrett Press, the *Cambridge History of American Literature,* and the *Oxford Companion to American Literature.* James D. Hart, the editor, is to be congratulated on his brilliant organization of the *Oxford Companion*'s "Chronological Index of Literary and Social History" which I consulted innumerable times. Another very helpful survey of our literary history was Vernon Parrington's *Main Currents in American Thought* which links economic and social events with the country's literary development. Two other surveys that also helped were *American Short Stories* (1904) edited by Charles Baldwin Sears with abundant comments, and *The Advance of the American Short Story* (1923) by Edward J. O'Brien, who had such an important influence on the course of the modern story.

Credit also should go to David Harris, the managing editor of Houghton Mifflin Company, who suggested this book; Jane Wilson, my agent, who held my hand whenever I was overcome by the magnitude of the task; Dr. Abraham Rothberg, who was generous with excellent suggestions; Judith Stark, who deciphered in her typing my messy, written-over copy; and Phillip Schmidt, who stood on his feet for hours making Xerox copies for twice as many stories as finally could be used for reprinting.

MARTHA FOLEY

# Francis Hopkinson (1737–1791)

THE FIRST American short story, "A Pretty Story," was published in 1774, the year the Continental Congress was founded. Its author, Francis Hopkinson, born in Philadelphia in 1737, was a member of the Second Continental Congress, a signer of the Declaration of Independence, and the designer of the American flag. Extraordinarily versatile, he was our first native music composer, a prolific writer of verses, plays, and essays, and for many years a judge in the Admiralty. Copies of the first edition of "A Pretty Story," are very rare, only four being known to exist, and only nine of a second edition, also printed in 1774. The story was widely popular with the colonists, arousing in them the same furious indignation *Uncle Tom's Cabin* was to excite in their descendants before the Civil War. It was published for a second time in 1857 and now, with minor modernization of the antiquated spelling and typography, it is being published here for the third time to celebrate the Bicentennial of the revolution it helped start.

The story is a capsule account in fiction form of the events that led to the American Revolution. The identity of the characters was easily recognized by the angry colonists who were the "children." The old Farm is England and the new Farm, America. The Nobleman is King George III, the Nobleman's "wife" and the children's "mother" the British Parliament, which was elected every seven years; the Great Paper, Magna Charta; the Steward, Lord North, the Prime Minister; the Gruel Merchants, the East India Tea Company; the Overseer, General Gage; Jack is Massachusetts and the padlock on his gate the Fort Bill blockading Boston Harbor. The various abuses inflicted on the children are metaphors for such harsh laws as the Stamp Act, the Mutiny Act, and the tax that instigated the Boston Tea Party. The dramatic ending is the most original way of ending a story ever encountered by this reader.

# A Pretty Story

## Written in the Year of Our Lord 1774
## by Peter Grievous, Esq. A. B. C. D. E.

### *Veluti in Speculo*

ONCE UPON A TIME, a great while ago, there lived a certain Nobleman, who had long possessed a very valuable Farm, and had a great number of children and grandchildren. Besides the annual profits of his land, which were very considerable, he kept a large shop of goods; and being very forceful in trade, he became in time, exceeding rich and powerful; insomuch that all his neighbors feared and respected him. With respect to the management of his family, it was thought he had adopted the most perfect mode that could be devised, for he had been at pains to examine the economy of all his neighbors, and had selected from their plans all that appeared to be equitable and beneficial, and omitted those which from experience were found to be inconvenient. Or rather, by blending their several constitutions together, he had so ingeniously counterbalanced the evils of one mode of government with the benefits of another that the advantages were richly enjoyed, and the inconveniences scarcely felt. In short, his family was thought to be the best ordered of any in his neighborhood.

He never exercised any undue authority over his children or servants; neither indeed could he oppress them if he was so disposed; for it was particularly convenanted in his marriage articles that he should not at any time impose any tasks or hardships whatever upon his children without the free consent of his wife.

Now the custom in his family was this, that at the end of every seven years his marriage became null and void; at which time his children and grandchildren met together and chose another wife for him, whom the old gentleman was obliged to marry under the same articles and restrictions as before. If his late wife had conducted herself during her seven years' marriage, with mildness, discretion and integrity, she was re-elected; if otherwise, deposed: by which means the children always had a great interest in their elected mother; and, through her, a reasonable check upon their father's temper. For besides that he could do nothing material respecting his children without her approbation; she was sole mistress of the purse strings; and gave him, from time to time, such sums of money as she thought necessary for the expenses of the family.

Being one day in a very extraordinary good humor, he gave his children a writing under his hand and seal, by which he released them from many badges of dependence, and confirmed for them several very important privileges. The chief were the two following, viz. that none of his children should be punished for any offense, or supposed offense, until his brethren had first declared him worthy of such punishment; and secondly, he gave fresh assurances that he would impose no hardships upon them without the consent of their elected mother.

This writing, on account of its singular importance, was called THE GREAT PAPER. After it was executed with the utmost solemnity, he caused his chaplain to publish a dire *anathema* against all who should attempt to violate the articles of the Great Paper, in the words following.

*"In the Name of the Father, Son and Holy Ghost, Amen! Whereas our Lord and Master, to the honor of God and for the common profit of this Farm hath granted for him and his heirs forever, these articles above written: I, his Chaplain and spiritual pastor of all this Farm, do admonish the people of the Farm Once, Twice and Thrice: Because that shortness will not suffer so much delay as to give knowledge to the people of these presents in writing; I therefore enjoin all persons, of what estate

soever they be, that they and every of them, as much as in them is, shall uphold and maintain these articles, granted by our Lord and Master in all points. And all those that in any point do resist, or break, or in any manner hereafter procure, counsel or any ways assent to, resist or break these ordinances, or go about it by word or deed, openly or privately, by any manner of pretence or color: I the aforesaid Chaplain, by my authority do *excommunicate* and *accurse*, and from the Body of our Lord Jesus Christ, and from all the Company of Heaven, and from all the sacraments of the holy Church do *sequester* and *exclude*."

"*This is a true and genuine denunciation copied from the Archives of the family."

## II

Now it came to pass that this Nobleman had, by some means or other, obtained the right to an immense tract of wild uncultivated country at a vast distance from his mansion house. But he set little store by this acquisition, as it yielded him no profit; nor was it likely to do so, being not only difficult of access on account of the distance, but was also overrun with innumerable wild beasts very fierce and savage; so that it would be extremely dangerous to attempt taking possession of it.

In process of time, however, some of his children, more stout and enterprising than the rest, requested leave of their father to go and settle on this distant tract of land. Leave was readily obtained; but before they set out certain agreements were stipulated between them — the principal were — the old gentleman, on his part, engaged to protect and defend the adventurers in their new settlements; to assist them in chasing away the wild beasts, and to extend to them all the benefits of the government under which they were born: assuring them that although they should be removed so far from his preference they should nevertheless be considered as the children of his family, and treated accordingly. At the same time he gave each of them a bond for the faithful performances; in which among other things, it was covenanted that they should, each of them in their several families, have a liberty of making such rules and regulations for their own good government as they should find convenient; provided these rules and regulations should not contradict or be in conflict with the general standing orders established on his Farm.

In return for these favors he insisted that they, on their parts, should at all times acknowledge him to be their father; that they should not deal with their neighbors without his leave, but send to his shop only for such merchandise as they should want. But in order to enable them to pay for such goods as they should purchase, they were permitted to sell the produce of their lands to certain of his neighbors.

These preliminaries being duly adjusted, our adventurers bid adieu to the comforts and conveniences of their father's house, and set off on their journey — Many and great were the difficulties they encountered on their way: but many more and much greater had they to combat on their arrival in the new country. Here they found nothing but wild nature. Mountains, over-grown with inaccessible foliage, and plains steeped in stagnant waters. Their ears are no longer attentive to the repeated strokes of industrious labor and the busy hum of men, instead of these, the roaring tempest and incessant howlings of beasts of prey fill their minds with horror and dismay. The needful comforts of life are no longer in their power — no friendly roof to shelter them from inclement skies; no fortress to protect them from surrounding dangers. Unaccustomed as they were to hardships like these, some were cut off by sickness and disease, and others snatched away by the hands of barbarity. They began, however, with great perseverance to clear the land of encumbering rubbish, and the woods resound with the strokes of labor; they drain the waters from the sedged morass; and pour the sun beams on the reeking soil; they are forced to exercise all the powers of industry and economy for bare subsistence, and like their first parent when driven from Paradise, to earn their bread with the sweat of their brows. In this work they were frequently interrupted by the incursions of the wild beasts, against whom they defended themselves with heroic prowess and magnanimity.

After some time, however, by dint of indefatigable perseverance, they found themselves comfortably settled on this new Farm; and had the delightful prospect of vast tracts of land waving with luxuriant harvests, and perfuming the air with delicious fruits, which before had been a dreary wilderness, unfit for the habitation of men.

In the meantime they kept up a constant correspondence with their father's family, and at a great expense provided wagons, horses and drivers to bring from his shop such goods and merchandise as they wanted for which they paid out of the produce of their lands.

### III

Now the new settlers had adopted a mode of government in their several families similar to that their Father had established on the old Farm; in taking a new wife at the end of certain periods of time; which wife was chosen for them by their children, and without whose consent they could do nothing material in the conduct of their affairs. Under these circumstances they thrived exceedingly, and became very numerous; living in great harmony among themselves, and in constitutional obedience to their father and his wife.

Notwithstanding their successful progress, however, they were frequently annoyed by the wild beasts, which were not yet expelled from the country; and were moreover troubled by some of their neighbors who wanted to drive them off the land and take possession of it themselves.

To assist them in their difficulties, and protect them from danger, the old Nobleman sent over several of his servants, who with the help of the new settlers drove away their enemies. But then he required that they should reimburse him for the trouble and expense he was at in their behalf; this they did with great cheerfulness, by applying from time to time to their respective wives, who always commanded their cash.

Thus did matters go for a considerable time, to their mutual happiness and benefit. But now the Nobleman's wife began to cast an avaricious eye upon the new settlers; saying to herself, if, by the natural consequence of their intercourse with us my wealth and power are much increased, how much more would they accumulate if I can persuade them that all they have belong to us, and therefore I may at any time demand from them such part of their earnings as I please. At the same time she was fully sensible of the promises and agreements her husband had made when they left the old Farm, and of the tenor and purport of the Great Paper. She therefore thought it necessary to proceed with great caution and art, and endeavored to gain her point by imperceptible steps.

In order to do this, she first issued an edict setting forth, that whereas the tailors of her family were greatly injured by the people of the new Farm, insomuch as they presumed to make their own clothes whereby the said tailors were deprived of the benefit of their custom; it was therefore ordained that for the future the new settlers should not be permitted to have amongst them any shears or scissors larger than a certain fixed size. In consequence of this, our adventurers were compelled to have their clothes made by their father's tailors: but out of regard to the old gentleman, they patiently submitted to this grievance.

Encouraged by this success, she proceeded in her plan. Observing that the new settlers were very fond of a particular kind of cider which they purchased of a neighbor, who was friendly with their father (the apples proper for making this cider not growing on their own farm) she published another edict obliging them to pay her for every barrel of cider used in their families! To this likewise they submitted: not yet seeing the scope of her designs against them.

After this manner she proceeded, imposing taxes upon them on various pretenses, and receiving the fruits of their industry with both hands. Moreover she persuaded her husband to send amongst them from time to time a number of the most lazy and useless of his servants under the specious pretext of defending them in their settlements, and of assisting to destroy the wild beasts; but in fact to rid his own house of their company, not having employment for them; and at the same time to be a watch and a check upon the people of the new Farm.

It was likewise ordered that these Protectors, as they were called, should be supplied with bread and butter cut in a particular form: but the head of one of the families refused to comply with this order. He engaged to give the guests, thus forced upon him, bread and butter sufficient; but insisted that his wife should have the liberty of cutting it in what shape she pleased.

This put the old Nobleman into a violent passion, so that he had his son's wife put into jail for presuming to cut her loaf otherwise than as had been directed.

IV

As the old gentleman advanced in years he began to neglect the affairs of his family, leaving them chiefly to the management of his steward. Now the steward had debauched the wife, and by that means gained an entire ascendancy over her. She no longer deliberated as to what would most benefit either the old Farm or the new; but said and did whatever the steward pleased. Nay, so much was she influenced by him that she could neither utter *Ay* or *No* but as he directed. For he had cunningly persuaded her that it was very fashionable for women to wear padlocks on their lips, and that he was sure they would become her exceedingly. He therefore fashioned a padlock to each corner of her mouth; when the one was opened she could only say *Ay*; and when the other was loosed, could only cry *No*. He took care to keep the keys of these locks himself; so that her will became entirely subject to his power.

Now the old lady and the steward had set themselves against the people of the new Farm; and began to devise ways and means to impoverish and distress them. They prevailed upon the Nobleman to sign an edict against the new settlers, in which it was declared that it was their duty as children to pay something towards the supplying of their father's table with provisions and to supporting the dignity of his family; for that purpose it was ordained that all their spoons, knives and forks, plates and porringers, should be marked with a certain mark by officers appointed for that end; for which marking they were to pay a certain stipend; and that they should not, under severe penalties, presume to make use of any spoon, knife or fork, plate or porringer, before it had been marked, and the said stipend paid to the officer.

The inhabitants of the new Farm began to see that their father's affections were alienated from them; and that their elected mother was a base mother, debauched by their enemy the steward. They were thrown into great confusion and distress. They wrote the most supplicating letters to the old gentleman, in which they acknowledged him to be their father in terms of the greatest respect and affection — they recounted to him the hardships and difficulties they had suffered in settling his new Farm; and pointed out the great addition of wealth and power his family had acquired by the improvement of that wilderness; and showed him that all the fruits of their labor must in the natural course of things unite, in the long run, in his money box. They also, in humble terms, reminded him of his promises and engagements on their leaving home, and of the bonds he had given them; of the solemnity and importance of the Great Paper with the curse annexed. They acknowledged that he ought to be reimbursed the expense he was at on their account, and that it was their duty to assist in supporting the dignity of his family. All this they declared they were willing and ready to do; but requested that they might do it agreeable to the purport of the Great Paper; by applying to their several wives for the keys of their money boxes and furnishing him from thence; and not be subject to the tyranny and caprice of an avaricious mother whom, being far away, they had never chosen and of a steward who was their enemy.

Some of these letters were intercepted by the steward; others were delivered to the old gentleman, who was at the same time persuaded to take no notice of them; but, on the contrary, to insist more strenuously on the right his wife claimed of marking their spoons, knives and forks, plates and porringers.

The new settlers observing how matters were conducted in their father's family became exceedingly distressed and mortified. They met together and agreed one and all that they would no longer submit to the arbitrary impositions of the mother, and their enemy the steward. They determined to pay no manner of regard to the new decree, considering it a violation of the Great Paper. But to go on and eat their broth and pudding as usual. The cooks also and butlers served their spoons, knives and forks, plates and porringers without having them marked by the new officers.

The Nobleman at length thought fit to reverse the order which had been made respecting the spoons, knives and forks, plates and porringers of the new settlers. But he did this with a very ill grace: for he, at the same time avowed and declared that he and his wife had the right to mark all their furniture, if they pleased, from the silver tankard down to the very chamber pots: that as he was their father he had an absolute control over them and that their liberties, lives and properties were at the disposal of him and his wife: that it was not fit that he who was allowed to be omnipresent, immortal and incapable of error, should be confined by the shackles of the Great Paper; or obliged to fulfill the bonds he had given them; which he averred he had a right to cancel whenever he pleased.

His wife became intoxicated with vanity. The steward had told her she was an omnipotent goddess and ought to be worshipped as such:

that it was the height of impudence and disobedience in the new settlers to dispute her authority, which, with respect to them, was unlimited: that as they had removed from their father's family, they had forfeited all pretensions to be considered as his children, and lost the privileges of the Great Paper: that therefore she might look on them only as tenants at will on her husband's Farm, and extract from them what rent she pleased.

All this was perfectly agreeable to madam, who admitted this new doctrine in its full sense.

The people of the new Farm, however, took little notice of these pompous declarations. They were glad the marking degree was reversed, and were in hopes that things would gradually settle into their former channel.

## V

In the meantime the new settlers increased exceedingly, and as they increased, their dealings at their father's shop were proportionably enlarged.

It is true that they suffered some inconveniences from the protectors that had been sent amongst them, who became very troublesome in their houses: they seduced their daughters; introduced riot and intemperance into their families, and derided and insulted the orders and regulations they had made for their own good government. Moreover the old Nobleman had sent amongst them a great number of thieves, ravishers and murderers, who did a great deal of mischief by practicing those crimes for which they had been banished from the old Farm. But they bore their grievances with as much patience as could be expected; not choosing to trouble their aged father with complaints, unless in case of important necessity.

Now the steward continued to hate the new settlers with exceeding great hatred and determined to renew his attack upon their peace and happiness. He artfully insinuated to the old gentleman and his foolish wife, that it was very mean and unbecoming of them to receive the contributions of the people of the new Farm, towards supporting the dignity of his family, through the hands of their respective wives: that upon this footing it would be in their power to refuse his requisitions whenever they should be thought to be unreasonable, of which they would pretend to be judges themselves; and that it was high time they should be compelled to acknowledge his arbitrary power and his wife's omnipotence.

For this purpose another decree was prepared and published, ordering that the new settlers should pay a certain stipend upon particular goods, which they were not allowed to purchase anywhere but at their father's shop; and that this stipend should not be deemed an advance upon the original price of the goods, but be paid on their arrival at the new Farm, for the express purpose of supporting the dignity of the old gentleman's family, and of defraying the expenses he affected to afford them.

This new decree gave our adventurers the utmost uneasiness. They saw that the steward and the mother were determined to oppress and enslave them. They again met together and wrote to their father, as before, the most humble and persuasive letters; but to little purpose: a deaf ear was turned to all their remonstrances; and their dutiful requests treated with contempt.

Finding this moderate and decent conduct brought them no relief, they had recourse to another expedient. They bound themselves in a solemn engagement not to deal any more at their father's shop until this unconstitutional decree should be reversed; which they declared to be a violation of the Great Paper.

This agreement was so strictly adhered to, that in a few months the clerks and apprentices in the old gentleman's shop began to make a sad outcry. They declared that their master's trade was declining exceedingly, and that his wife and steward would, by their mischievous machinations, ruin the whole farm: they forthwith sharpened their pens and attacked the steward and even the old lady herself with great severity. Insomuch it was thought proper to withdraw this attempt likewise upon the rights and liberties of the new settlers. One part only of the decree remained unreversed — viz. the tax upon water gruel.

Now there were certain men on the old Farm, who had obtained from the old gentleman an exclusive right of selling water gruel. Vast quantities of this gruel were vended among the new settlers; for it became very fashionable for them to use it in their families in great abundance. They did not however trouble themselves much about the tax on water gruel: they were well pleased with the reversal of the other parts of the decree, and considering gruel as not absolutely necessary to the comfort of life, they were determined to endeavor to do without it, and by that means avoid the remaining effects of the new decree.

The steward found his designs once more frustrated; but was not discouraged by this disappointment. He formed another scheme so artfully contrived that he thought himself sure of success. He sent for the persons who had the sole right of vending water gruel, and after reminding them of the obligations they were under to the Nobleman and his wife for their exclusive privilege, he desired they would send sundry wagon loads of gruel to the new Farm, promising that the accustomed duty which they paid for their exclusive right should be taken off from all the gruel they sent amongst the new settlers: and that in case their cargoes should come to any damage, he would take care that the loss should be repaired out of the old gentleman's coffers.

The gruel merchants readily consented to this proposal, knowing that if their cargoes were sold, they would reap considerable profits; and if they failed, the steward was to make good the damage. On the other hand the steward concluded that the new settlers could not resist purchasing the gruel to which they had been so long accustomed; and if they did purchase it when subject to the tax aforesaid, this would be an avowed acknowledgment on their part that their father and his wife had a right to break through the tenor of the Great Paper, and to lay on them what impositions they pleased without the consent of their respective wives.

But the new settlers were well aware of this decoy. They saw clearly that the gruel was not sent to accommodate but to enslave them; and that if they suffered any part to be sold amongst them, it would be deemed a submission to the assumed omnipotence of the great madam.

## VI

On the arrival of the water gruel, the people of the new Farm were again thrown into great alarms and confusions. Some of them would not suffer the wagons to be unloaded at all, but sent them immediately back to the gruel merchants; others permitted the wagons to unload but would not touch the hateful commodity so that it lay about their roads and highways until it grew sour and spoiled. But one of the new settlers, whose name was Jack, either from a keener sense of the injuries attempted against him, or from the necessity of his situation, which was such that he could not send back the gruel because of a number of mercenaries whom his father had stationed before his house to watch and be a check upon his conduct: he, I say, being almost driven to despair, fell to work, and with great zeal stove to pieces the casks of gruel, which had been sent him, and utterly demolished the whole cargo.

These proceedings were soon known at the old Farm. Great and terrible was the uproar there. The old gentleman fell into great wrath, declaring that his absent children meant to throw off all dependence upon him, and to become altogether disobedient. His wife also tore the padlocks from her lips, and raved and stormed like a billingsgate. The steward lost all patience and moderation, swearing most profanely that he would leave no stone unturned until he had humbled the new settlers at his feet, and caused their father to trample on their necks. Moreover the gruel merchants roared and bellowed for the loss of their gruel; and the clerks and apprentices were in the utmost consternation lest the people of the new Farm should again agree to have no dealings at their father's shop. Vengeance was immediately set on foot, particularly against Jack. With him they determined to begin; hoping that by making an example of him they should so terrify the other families of the new settlers, that they would all submit to the designs of the steward and the omnipotence of the old lady.

A very large padlock was, accordingly, prepared to be fastened upon Jack's great gate; the key of which was to be given to the old gentleman; who was not to open it again until he paid for the gruel he had spilled, and resigned all claim to the privileges of the Great Paper: nor then either unless he saw fit. Secondly, a decree was made to new model the regulations and economy of Jack's family in such a manner that they might for the future be more subject to the will of the steward: and, thirdly, a large gallows was erected before the mansion house in the old Farm, and an order given that if any of Jack's children or servants should be suspected of misbehavior, they should not be convicted or acquitted by the consent of their brethren, agreeable to the purpose of the Great Paper but be tied neck and heels and dragged to the gallows at the mansion house and there be hanged without mercy.

No sooner did tidings of this undue severity reach the new Farm, but the people were almost ready to despair. They were altogether at a loss how to act, or by what means they should avert the vengeance to which they were doomed: but the old lady and the steward soon determined the matter; for the padlock was sent over and without ceremony fastened upon Jack's great gate. They did not wait to know whether he would pay for the gruel or not, or make the required acknowledgments; nor give him the least opportunity to make his defense — the great gate was locked, and the key given to the old Nobleman, as had been determined.

Poor Jack found himself in a deplorable condition. The great inlet to his Farm was entirely blocked up, so that he could neither carry out the produce of his land for sale, nor receive from abroad the necessities for his family.

But this was not all — his father, along with the padlock aforesaid, had sent an overseer to hector and domineer over him and his family; and to endeavor to break his spirit by exercising every possible severity: for which purpose he was attended by a great number of mercenaries, and armed with more than common authority.

On this first arrival in Jack's family he was received with considerable respect, because he was the delegate of their aged father: for, notwithstanding all that had passed, the people of the new settlements loved and revered the old gentleman with a truly filial attachment; attributing his unkindness entirely to the intrigues of their enemy, the steward. But this fair weather did not last long. The new overseer took the first opportunity of showing he had no intentions of living in harmony and friendship with the family. Some of Jack's domestics had put on their Sunday clothes, and attended the overseer in the great parlor, in order to pay him their compliments on his arrival, and to request his assistance in reconciling them to their father; but he rudely stopped them short in the midst of their speech; called them a parcel of disobedient scoundrels, and bid them go about their business. So saying, he turned upon his heel, and with great contempt left the room.

## VII

Now Jack and his family finding themselves oppressed, insulted and tyrannized over in the most cruel and arbitrary manner, advised with their brethren what measures should be adopted to relieve them from their intolerable grievances. Their brethren, one and all, united in sympathizing with their afflictions; they advised them to bear their sufferings with fortitude for a time, assuring them they looked upon the punishments and insults laid upon them with the same indignation as if they had been inflicted upon themselves, and that they would stand by and support them to the last. But, above all, earnestly recommended it to them to be firm and steady in the cause of liberty and justice, and never acknowledge the omnipotence of the mother; nor yield to the machinations of their enemy the steward.

In the meantime, lest Jack's family suffer for the want of necessities, their great gate being fast locked, liberal and very generous contributions were raised among the several families of the new settlements for their present relief. This seasonable bounty was handed to Jack over the garden wall — all access to the front of his house being shut.

Now the overseer observed that the children and domestics of Jack's family had frequent meetings and consultations together: sometimes in the garret, and sometimes in the stable: understanding, likewise, that an agreement not to deal at their father's shop, until their grievances should be redressed, was much talked of amongst them, he wrote a thundering prohibition, much like a Pope's Bull, which he caused to be pasted up in every room in the house; in which he declared and protested that these meetings were treasonable, traitorous and rebellious; contrary to the dignity of their father, and inconsistent with the omnipotence of their mother: denouncing terrible punishments against any two of the family who from thenceforth should be seen whispering together, and strictly forbidding the domestics to hold any more meetings in the garret or stable.

These harsh and unconstitutional proceedings irritated Jack and the other inhabitants of the new Farm to such a degree that

★  ★  ★  ★  ★  ★  ★  ★  ★  ★  ★  ★  ★

# Washington Irving (1783–1859)

TWO YEARS after the end of the American Revolution in which his father, a wealthy merchant, had been active, Washington Irving was born in 1783 in New York City. He studied law but abandoned it to write, finding a rich source of inspiration in the Dutch settlers who had preceded the English as the first colonists of his native state. Suffering from melancholia after the woman to whom he was engaged died, he gave up writing to go into business but, still depressed, sought surcease by traveling in Europe. There he became a close friend of Sir Walter Scott, who persuaded him to resume writing. Scott was responsible for the publication in 1820 of *The Sketch Book*, in which "Rip Van Winkle" appeared, to be followed by many other stories and writings. With the publication of "Rip Van Winkle" American literature really got under way and Irving became the first internationally famous American writer.

If, like this editor, you have not read "Rip Van Winkle" since childhood, you may be pleasantly surprised by the freshness and mature charm of the writing in this tale of lovable, lazy old Rip. Irving knew how to round out his characters so you not only understand Rip but sympathize with his wife in the frenzy to which his happy-go-lucky ways drove her. The description of the beauty and atmosphere of the Hudson River Valley, Irving's "Sleepy Hollow" country, is enchanting. The story's dramatic power is attested to by the theatrical productions of it that have toured the country for years with great popular success. In 1859 Joseph Jefferson achieved lasting fame for his acting in the title role.

# Rip Van Winkle

WHOEVER has made a voyage up the Hudson must remember the Kaatskill mountains. They are a dismembered branch of the great Appalachian family, and are seen away to the west of the river, swelling up to a noble height, and lording it over the surrounding country. Every change of season, every change of weather, indeed, every hour of the day, produces some change in the magical hues and shapes of these mountains, and they are regarded by all the good wives, far and near, as perfect barometers. When the weather is fair and settled, they are clothed in blue and purple, and print their bold outlines on the clear evening sky; but sometimes, when the rest of the landscape is cloudless, they will gather a hood of gray vapors about their summits, which, in the last rays of the setting sun, will glow and light up like a crown of glory.

At the foot of these fairy mountains, the voyager may have descried the light smoke curling up from a village, whose shingle-roofs gleam among the trees, just where the blue tints of the upland melt away into the fresh green of the nearer landscape. It is a little village, of great antiquity, having been founded by some of the Dutch colonists in the early times of the province, just about the beginning of the government of the good Peter Stuyvesant, (may he rest in peace!) and there were some of the houses of the original settlers standing within a few years, built of small yellow bricks brought from Holland, having latticed windows and gable fronts, surmounted with weathercocks.

In that same village, and in one of these very houses (which, to tell the precise truth, was sadly time-worn and weather-beaten), there lived, many years since, while the country was yet a province of Great Britain, a simple, good-natured fellow, of the name of Rip Van Winkle. He was a descendant of the Van Winkles who figured so gallantly in the chivalrous days of Peter Stuyvesant, and accompanied him to the siege of Fort Christina. He inherited, however, but little of the martial character of his ancestors. I have observed that he was a simple, good-natured man; he was, moreover, a kind neighbor, and an obedient, hen-pecked husband. Indeed, to the latter circumstance might be owing that meekness of spirit which gained him such universal popularity; for those men are most apt to be obsequious and conciliating abroad, who are under the discipline of shrews at home. Their tempers, doubtless, are rendered pliant and malleable in the fiery furnace of domestic tribulation; and a curtain-lecture is worth all the sermons in the world for teaching the virtues of patience and long-suffering. A termagant wife may, therefore, in some respects, be considered a tolerable blessing; and if so, Rip Van Winkle was thrice blessed.

Certain it is, that he was a great favorite among all the good wives of the village, who, as usual with the amiable sex, took his part in all family squabbles; and never failed, whenever they talked those matters over in their evening gossipings, to lay all the blame on Dame Van Winkle. The children of the village, too, would shout with joy whenever he approached. He assisted at their sports, made their playthings, taught them to fly kites and shoot marbles, and told them long stories of ghosts, witches, and Indians. Whenever he went dodging about the village, he was surrounded by a troop of them, hanging on his skirts, clambering on his back, and playing a thousand tricks on him with impunity; and not a dog would bark at him throughout the neighborhood.

The great error in Rip's composition was an insuperable aversion to all kinds of profitable labor. It could not be from the want of assiduity or perseverance; for he would sit on a wet rock, with a rod as long and heavy as a Tartar's lance, and fish all day without a murmur, even though he should not be encouraged by a single nibble. He would carry a fowling-piece on his shoulder for hours together, trudging through woods and swamps, and up hill and down dale, to shoot a few squirrels or wild pigeons. He would never refuse to assist a neighbor even in the roughest toil, and was a foremost man at all country frolics for husking Indian corn, or building stone fences; the women of the village, too, used to employ him to run their errands, and to do such little odd jobs as their less obliging husbands would not do for them. In a word, Rip was ready to attend to anybody's business but his own; but as to doing family duty, and keeping his farm in order, he found it impossible.

In fact, he declared it was of no use to work on his farm; it was the most pestilent little piece of ground in the whole country; everything about it went wrong, and would go wrong in spite of him. His fences were continually falling to pieces; his cow would either go astray, or get among the cabbages; weeds were sure to grow quicker in his fields than anywhere else; the rain always made a point of setting in just as he had some out-door work to do; so that though his patrimonial estate had dwindled away under his management, acre by acre, until there was little more left than a mere patch of Indian corn and potatoes, yet it was the worst conditioned farm in the neighborhood.

His children, too, were as ragged and wild as if they belonged to nobody. His son Rip, an urchin begotten in his own likeness, promised to inherit the habits, with the old clothes of his father. He was generally seen trooping like a colt at his mother's heels, equipped in a pair of his father's cast-off galligaskins, which he had much ado to hold up with one hand, as a fine lady does her train in bad weather.

Rip Van Winkle, however, was one of those happy mortals, of foolish, well-oiled dispositions, who take the world easy, eat white bread or brown, whichever can be got with least thought or trouble, and would rather starve on a penny then work for a pound. If left to himself, he would have whistled life away, in perfect contentment; but his wife kept continually dinning in his ears about his idleness, his carelessness, and the ruin he was bringing on his family. Morning, noon, and night, her tongue was incessantly going, and everything he said or did was sure to produce a torrent of household eloquence. Rip had but one way of replying to all lectures of the kind, and that, by frequent use, had grown into a habit. He shrugged his shoulders, shook his head, cast up his eyes, but said nothing. This, however, always provoked a fresh volley from his wife; so that he was fain to draw off his forces, and take to the outside of the house — the only side which, in truth, belongs to a hen-pecked husband.

Rip's sole domestic adherent was his dog Wolf, who was as much hen-pecked as his master; for Dame Van Winkle regarded them as companions in idleness, and even looked upon Wolf with an evil eye, as the cause of his master's going so often astray. True it is, in all points of spirit befitting an honorable dog, he was as courageous an animal as ever scoured the woods; but what courage can withstand the enduring and all-besetting terrors of a woman's tongue? The moment Wolf entered the house his crest fell, his tail drooped to the ground, or curled between his legs, he sneaked about with a gallows air, casting many a sidelong glance at Dame Van Winkle, and at the least flourish of a broomstick or ladle he would fly to the door with yelping precipitation.

Times grew worse and worse with Rip Van Winkle as years of matrimony rolled on; a tart temper never mellows with age, and a sharp tongue is the only edged tool that grows keener with constant use. For a long while he used to console himself, when driven from home, by frequenting a kind of perpetual club of the sages, philosophers, and other idle personages of the village, which held its sessions on a bench before a small inn, designated by a rubicund portrait of His Majesty George the Third. Here they used to sit in the shade through a long, lazy summer's day, talking listlessly over village gossip, or telling endless sleepy stories about nothing. But it would have been worth any states-man's money to have heard the profound discussions that sometimes took place, when by chance an old newspaper fell into their hands from some passing traveller. How solemnly they would listen to the contents, as drawled out by Derrick Van Bummel, the schoolmaster, a dapper learned little man, who was not to be daunted by the most gigantic word in the dictionary; and how sagely they would deliberate upon public events some months after they had taken place.

The opinions of this junto were completely controlled by Nicholas Vedder, a patriarch of the village, and landlord of the inn, at the door of which he took his seat from morning till night, just moving sufficiently to avoid the sun and keep in the shade of a large tree; so that the neighbors could tell the hour by his movements as accurately as by a sun-dial. It is true he was rarely heard to speak, but smoked his pipe incessantly. His adherents, however (for every great man has his adherents), perfectly understood him, and knew how to gather his opinions. When any-thing that was read or related displeased him, he was observed to smoke his pipe vehemently, and to send forth short, frequent, and angry puffs; but when pleased, he would inhale the smoke slowly and tranquilly, and emit it in light and placid clouds; and sometimes, taking the pipe from his mouth, and letting the fragrant vapor curl about his nose, would gravely nod his head in token of perfect approbation.

From even this stronghold the unlucky Rip was at length routed by his termagant wife, who would suddenly break in upon the tranquillity of the assemblage and call the members all to naught; nor was that august personage, Nicholas Vedder himself, sacred from the daring tongue of this terrible virago, who charged him outright with encouraging her husband in habits of idleness.

Poor Rip was at last reduced almost to despair; and his only alternative, to escape from the labor of the farm and clamor of his wife, was to take gun in hand and stroll away into the woods. Here he would sometimes seat himself at the foot of a tree, and share the contents of his wallet with Wolf, with whom he sympathized as a fellow-sufferer in persecution. "Poor Wolf," he would say, "thy mistress leads thee a dog's life of it; but never mind, my lad, whilst I live thou shalt never want a friend to stand by thee!" Wolf would wag his tail, look wistfully in his master's face; and if dogs can feel pity, I verily believe he reciprocated the sentiment with all his heart.

In a long ramble of the kind on a fine autumnal day, Rip had unconsciously scrambled to one of the highest parts of the Kaatskill mountains. He was after his favorite sport of squirrel-shooting, and the still solitudes had echoed and re-echoed with the reports of his gun. Panting and fatigued, he threw himself, late in the afternoon, on a green knoll, covered with mountain herbage, that crowned the brow of a precipice. From an opening between the trees he could overlook all the lower country for many a mile of rich woodland. He saw at a distance the lordly Hudson, far, far below him, moving on its silent but majestic course, with the reflection of a purple cloud, or the sail of a lagging bark, here and there sleeping on its glassy bosom, and at last losing itself in the blue highlands.

On the other side he looked down into a deep mountain glen, wild, lonely, and shagged, the bottom filled with fragments from the impending cliffs, and scarcely lighted by the reflected rays of the setting sun. For some time Rip lay musing on this scene; evening was gradually advancing; the mountains began to throw their long blue shadows over the valleys; he saw that it would be dark long before he could reach the village, and he heaved a heavy sigh when he thought of encountering the terrors of Dame Van Winkle.

As he was about to descend, he heard a voice from a distance, hallooing, "Rip Van Winkle! Rip Van Winkle!" He looked round, but could see nothing but a crow winging its solitary flight across the mountain. He thought his fancy must have deceived him, and turned again to descend, when he heard the same cry ring through the still evening air: "Rip Van Winkle! Rip Van Winkle!" — at the same time Wolf bristled up his back, and giving a low growl, skulked to his master's side, looking fearfully down into the glen. Rip now felt a vague apprehension stealing over him; he looked anxiously in the same direction, and perceived a strange figure slowly toiling up the rocks, and bending under the weight of something he carried on his back. He was surprised to see any human being in this lonely and unfrequented place; but supposing it to be some one of the neighborhood in need of his assistance, he hastened down to yield it.

On nearer approach he was still more surprised at the singularity of the stranger's appearance. He was a short, square-built old fellow, with thick bushy hair, and a grizzled beard. His dress was of the antique Dutch fashion, — a cloth jerkin strapped round the waist — several pair of breeches, the outer one of ample volume, decorated with rows of buttons down the sides, and bunches at the knees. He bore on his shoulder a stout keg, that seemed full of liquor, and made signs for Rip to approach and assist him with the load. Though rather shy and distrustful of this new acquaintance, Rip complied with his usual alacrity; and mutually relieving one another, they clambered up a narrow gully, apparently the dry bed of a mountain torrent. As they ascended, Rip every now and then heard long rolling peals, like distant thunder, that seemed to issue out of a deep ravine, or rather cleft, between lofty rocks, toward which their rugged path conducted. He paused for an instant, but supposing it to be the muttering of one of those transient thunder-showers which often take place in mountain heights, he proceeded. Passing through the ravine, they came to a hollow, like a small amphitheatre, surrounded by perpendicular precipices, over the brinks of which, impending trees shot their branches, so that you only caught glimpses of the azure sky and the bright evening cloud. During the whole time, Rip and his companion had labored on in silence; for though the former marvelled greatly what could be the object of carrying a keg of liquor up this wild mountain, yet there was something strange and incomprehensible about the unknown, that inspired awe, and checked familiarity.

On entering the amphitheatre, new objects of wonder presented themselves. On a level spot in the centre was a company of odd-looking personages playing at ninepins. They were dressed in a quaint outlandish fashion: some wore short doublets, other jerkins, with long knives in their belts, and most of them had enormous breeches, of similar style with that of the guide's. Their visages, too, were peculiar: one had a large head, broad face, and small piggish eyes; the face of another seemed to consist entirely of nose, and was surmounted by a white sugar-loaf hat, set off with a little red cock's tail. They all had beards of various shapes and colors. There was one who seemed to be the commander. He was a stout old gentleman, with a weather-beaten countenance; he wore a laced doublet, broad belt and hanger, high-crowned hat and feather, red stockings, and high-heeled shoes, with roses in them. The whole group reminded Rip of the figures in an old Flemish painting, in the parlor of Domine Van Schaick, the village parson, and which had been brought over from Holland at the time of the settlement.

What seemed particularly odd to Rip was, that though these folks were evidently amusing themselves, yet they maintained the gravest faces, the most mysterious silence, and were, withal, the most melancholy party of pleasure he had ever witnessed. Nothing interrupted the stillness of the scene but the noise of the balls, which, whenever they were rolled, echoed along the mountains like rumbling peals of thunder.

As Rip and his companion approached them, they suddenly desisted from their play, and stared at him with such a fixed statue-like gaze, and such strange, uncouth, lack-lustre countenances, that his heart turned within him, and his knees smote together. His companion now emptied the contents of the keg into large flagons, and made signs to him to wait upon the company. He obeyed with fear and trembling; they quaffed the liquor in profound silence, and then returned to their game.

By degrees, Rip's awe and apprehension subsided. He even ventured, when no eye was fixed upon him, to taste the beverage, which he found had much of the flavor of excellent Hollands. He was naturally a thirsty soul, and was soon tempted to repeat the draught. One taste provoked another, and he reiterated his visits to the flagon so often, that at length his senses were overpowered, his eyes swam in his head, his head gradually declined, and he fell into a deep sleep.

On waking, he found himself on the green knoll from whence he had first seen the old man of the glen. He rubbed his eyes — it was a bright sunny morning. The birds were hopping and twittering among the bushes, and the eagle was wheeling aloft, and breasting the pure mountain breeze. "Surely," thought Rip, "I have not slept here all night." He recalled the occurrences before he fell asleep. The strange man with the keg of liquor — the mountain ravine — the wild retreat among the rocks — the woe-begone party at ninepins — the flagon — "Oh! that flagon! that wicked flagon!" thought Rip, — "what excuse shall I make to Dame Van Winkle?"

He looked round for his gun, but in place of the clean, well-oiled fowling-piece, he found an old fire-lock lying by him, the barrel incrusted with rust, the lock falling off, and the stock worm-eaten. He now suspected that the grave roisters of the mountain had put a trick upon him, and having dosed him with liquor, had robbed him of his gun. Wolf, too, had disappeared but he might have strayed away after a squirrel or partridge. He whistled after him, and shouted his name, but all in vain; the echoes repeated his whistle and shout, but no dog was to be seen.

He determined to revisit the scene of the last evening's gambol, and if he met with any of the party, to demand his dog and gun. As he rose to walk, he found himself stiff in the joints and wanting in his usual activity. "These mountain beds do not agree with me," thought Rip, "and if this frolic should lay me up with a fit of the rheumatism, I shall have a blessed time with Dame Van Winkle." With some difficulty he got down into the glen: he found the gully up which he and his companion had ascended the preceding evening; but to his astonishment a mountain stream was now foaming down it, leaping from rock to rock, and filling the glen with babbling murmurs. He, however, made shift to scramble up its sides, working his toilsome way through thickets of birch, sassafras, and witch-hazel, and sometimes tripped up or entangled by the wild grape-vines that twisted their coils or tendrils from tree to tree, and spread a kind of network in his path.

At length he reached to where the ravine had opened through the clifts to the amphitheatre; but no traces of such opening remained. The rocks presented a high, impenetrable wall, over which the torrent came tumbling in a sheet of feathery foam and fell into a broad deep basin, black from the shadows of the surrounding forest. Here, then, poor Rip was brought to a stand. He again called and whistled after his dog; he was only answered by the cawing of a flock of idle crows, sporting high in the air about a dry tree that overhung a sunny precipice; and who, secure in their elevation, seemed to look down and scoff at the poor man's perplexities. What was to be done? the morning was passing away, and Rip felt famished for want of his breakfast. He grieved to give up his dog and gun; he dreaded to meet his wife; but it would not do to starve among the mountains. He shook his head, shouldered the rusty fire-lock, and, with a heart full of trouble and anxiety, turned his steps homeward.

As he approached the village he met a number of people, but none whom he knew, which somewhat surprised him, for he had thought himself acquainted with every one in the country round. Their dress, too, was of a different fashion from that to which he was accustomed. They all stared at him with equal marks of surprise, and whenever they cast their eyes upon him, invariably stroked their chins. The constant recurrence of this gesture induced Rip, involuntarily, to do the same, when, to his astonishment, he found his beard had grown a foot long!

He had now entered the skirts of the village. A troop of strange children ran at his heels, hooting after him, and pointing at his gray beard. The dogs, too, not one of which he recognized for an old acquaintance, barked at him as he passed. The very village was altered; it was larger and more populous. There were rows of houses which he had never seen before, and those which had been his familiar haunts had disappeared. Strange names were over the doors — strange faces at the windows — everything was strange. His mind now misgave him; he began to doubt whether both he and the world around him were not bewitched. Surely this was his native village, which he had left but the day before. There stood the Kaatskill mountains — there ran the silver Hudson at a distance — there was every hill and dale precisely as it had always been. Rip was sorely perplexed. "That flagon last night," thought he, "has addled my poor head sadly!"

It was with some difficulty that he found the way to his own house, which he approached with silent awe, expecting every moment to hear the shrill voice of Dame Van Winkle. He found the house gone to decay — the roof fallen in, the windows shattered, and the doors off the hinges. A half-starved dog that looked like Wolf was skulking about it. Rip called him by name, but the cur snarled, showed his teeth, and passed on. This was an unkind cut indeed. "My very dog," sighed poor Rip, "has forgotten me!"

He entered the house, which, to tell the truth, Dame Van Winkle had always kept in neat order. It was empty, forlorn, and apparently abandoned. This desolateness overcame all his connubial fears — he called loudly for his wife and children — the lonely chambers rang for a moment with his voice, and then all again was silence.

He now hurried forth, and hastened to his old resort, the village inn — but it too was gone. A large rickety wooden building stood in its place, with great gaping windows, some of them broken and mended with old hats and petticoats, and over the door was painted, "The Union Hotel, by Jonathan Doolittle." Instead of the great tree that used to shelter the quiet little Dutch inn of yore, there now was reared a tall naked pole, with something on the top that looked like a red nightcap, and from it was fluttering a flag, on which was a singular assemblage of stars and stripes; — all this was strange and incomprehensible. He recognized on the sign, however, the ruby face of King George, under which he had smoked so many a peaceful pipe: but even this was singularly metamorphosed. The red coat was changed for one of blue and buff, a sword was held in the hand instead of a sceptre, the head was decorated with a cocked hat, and underneath was painted in large characters, GENERAL WASHINGTON.

There was, as usual, a crowd of folk about the door, but none that Rip recollected. The very character of the people seemed changed. There was a busy, bustling, disputatious tone about it, instead of the accustomed phlegm and drowsy tranquillity. He looked in vain for the sage Nicholas Vedder, with his broad face, double chin, and fair long pipe, uttering clouds of tobacco-smoke instead of idle speeches; or Van Bummel, the schoolmaster, doling forth the contents of an ancient newspaper. In place of these, a lean, bilious-looking fellow, with his pockets full of hand-bills, was haranguing vehemently about rights of citizens — elections — members of Congress — liberty — Bunker's Hill — heroes of seventy-six — and other words, which were a perfect Babylonish jargon to the bewildered Van Winkle.

The appearance of Rip, with his long, grizzled beard, his rusty fowling-piece, his uncouth dress, and an army of women and children at his heels, soon attracted the attention of the tavern-politicians. They crowded round him, eying him from head to foot with great curiosity. The orator bustled up to him, and, drawing him partly aside, inquired, "On which side he voted?" Rip stared in vacant stupidity. Another short but busy little fellow pulled him by the arm, and, rising on tiptoe, inquired in his ear, "Whether he was Federal or Democrat?" Rip was equally at a loss to comprehend the question; when a knowing, self-important old gentleman, in a sharp cocked hat, made his way through the crowd, putting them to the right and left with his elbows as he passed, and planting himself before Van Winkle, with one arm akimbo, the other resting on his cane, his keen eyes and sharp hat penetrating, as it were, into his very soul, demanded in an austere tone, "What brought him to the election with a gun on his shoulder, and a mob at his heels; and whether he meant to breed a riot in the village?" — "Alas! gentlemen," cried Rip, somewhat dismayed, "I am a poor quiet man, a native of the place, and a loyal subject of the King, God bless him!"

Here a general shout burst from the by-standers — "A tory! a tory! a spy! a refugee! hustle him! away with him!" It was with great difficulty that the self-important man in the cocked hat restored order; and, having assumed a tenfold austerity of brow, demanded again of the unknown culprit, what he came there for, and whom he was seeking? The poor man humbly assured him that he meant no harm, but merely came there in search of some of his neighbors, who used to keep about the tavern.

"Well — who are they? — name them."

Rip bethought himself a moment, and inquired, "Where's Nicholas Vedder?"

There was a silence for a little while, when an old man replied, in a thin piping voice, "Nicholas Vedder! why, he is dead and gone these eighteen years! There was a wooden tombstone in the churchyard that used to tell all about him, but that's rotten and gone too."

"Where's Brom Dutcher?"

"Oh, he went off to the army in the beginning of the war; some say he was killed at the storming of Stony Point — others say he was drowned in a squall at the foot of Antony's Nose. I don't know — he never came back again."

"Where's Van Bummel, the schoolmaster?"

"He went off to the wars too, was a great militia general, and is now in Congress."

Rip's heart died away at hearing of these sad changes in his home and friends, and finding himself thus alone in the world. Every answer puzzled him too, by treating of such enormous lapses of time, and of matters which he could not understand: war — Congress — Stony Point — he had no courage to ask after any more friends, but cried out in despair, "Does nobody here know Rip Van Winkle?"

"Oh, Rip Van Winkle!" exclaimed two or three, "Oh, to be sure! that's Rip Van Winkle yonder, leaning against the tree."

Rip looked, and beheld a precise counterpart of himself, as he went up the mountain; apparently as lazy, and certainly as ragged. The poor fellow was now completely confounded. He doubted his own identity, and whether he was himself or another man. In the midst of his bewilderment, the man in the cocked hat demanded who he was, and what was his name.

"God knows," exclaimed he, at his wit's end; "I'm not myself — I'm sombody else — that's me yonder — no — that's somebody else got into my shoes — I was myself last night, but I fell asleep on the mountain, and they've changed my gun, and everything's changed, and I'm changed, and I can't tell what's my name, or who I am!"

The by-standers began now to look at each other, nod, wink significantly, and tap their fingers against their foreheads. There was a whisper, also, about securing the gun, and keeping the old fellow from doing mischief, at the very suggestion of which the self-important man in the cocked hat retired with some precipitation. At this critical moment a fresh, comely woman pressed through the throng to get a peep at the gray-bearded man. She had a chubby child in her arms, which, frightened at his looks, began to cry. "Hush, Rip," cried she. "Hush you little fool; the old man won't hurt you." The name of the child, the air of the mother, the tone of her voice, all awakened a train of recollections in his mind. "What is your name, my good woman?" asked he.

"Judith Gardenier."

"And your father's name?"

"Ah, poor man, Rip Van Winkle was his name, but it's twenty years since he went away from home with his gun, and never has been heard of since, — his dog came home without him; but whether he shot himself, or was carried away by the Indians, nobody can tell. I was then but a little girl."

Rip had but one question more to ask; but he put it with a faltering voice:

"Where's your mother?"

"Oh, she too had died but a short time since; she broke a blood-vessel in a fit of passion at a New-England pedler."

There was a drop of comfort, at least, in this intelligence. The honest man could contain himself no longer. He caught his daughter and her child in his arms. "I am your father!" cried he — "Young Rip Van Winkle once — old Rip Van Winkle now! — Does nobody know poor Rip Van Winkle?"

All stood amazed, until an old woman, tottering out from among the crowd, put her hand to her brow, and peering under it in his face for a moment, exclaimed, "Sure enough! it is Rip Van Winkle — it is himself! Welcome home again, old neighbor. Why, where have you been these twenty long years?"

Rip's story was soon told, for the whole twenty years had been to him but as one night. The neighbors stared when they heard it; some were seen to wink at each other, and put their tongues in their cheeks: and the self-important man in the cocked hat, who, when the alarm was over, had returned to the field, screwed down the corners of his mouth, and shook his head — upon which there was a general shaking of the head throughout the assemblage.

It was determined, however, to take the opinion of old Peter Vander-donk, who was seen slowly advancing up the road. He was a descendant of the historian of that name, who wrote one of the earliest accounts of the province. Peter was the most ancient inhabitant of the village, and well versed in all the wonderful events and traditions of the neighborhood. He recollected Rip at once, and corroborated his story in the most satisfactory manner. He assured the company that it was a fact, handed down from his ancestor the historian, that the Kaatskill mountains had always been haunted by strange beings. That it was affirmed that the great Hendrick Hudson, the first discoverer of the river and country, kept a kind of vigil there every twenty years, with his crew of the Half-moon; being permitted in this way to revisit the scenes of his enterprise, and keep a guardian eye upon the river and the great city called by his name. That his father had once seen them in their old Dutch dresses playing at ninepins in a hollow of the mountain; and that he himself had heard, one summer afternoon, the sound of their balls, like distant peals of thunder.

To make a long story short, the company broke up and returned to the more important concerns of the election. Rip's daughter took him home to live with her; she had a snug, well-furnished house, and a stout, cheery farmer for a husband, whom Rip recollected for one of the urchins that used to climb upon his back. As to Rip's son and heir, who was the ditto of himself, seen leaning against the tree, he was employed to work on the farm; but evinced an hereditary disposition to attend to anything else but his business.

Rip now resumed his old walks and habits; he soon found many of his former cronies, though all rather the worse for the wear and tear of time; and preferred making friends among the rising generation, with whom he soon grew into great favor.

Having nothing to do at home, and being arrived at that happy age when a man can be idle with impunity, he took his place once more on the bench at the inn-door, and was reverenced as one of the patriarchs of the village, and a chronicle of the old times "before the war." It was some time before he could get into the regular track of gossip, or could be made to comprehend the strange events that had taken place during his torpor. How that there had been a revolutionary war, — that the country had thrown off the yoke of old England, — and that, instead of being a subject of his Majesty George the Third, he was now a free citizen of the United States. Rip, in fact, was no politician; the changes of states and empires made but little impression on him; but there was one species of despotism under which he had long groaned, and that was — petticoat government. Happily that was at an end; he had got his neck out of the yoke of matrimony, and could go in and out whenever he pleased, without dreading the tyranny of Dame Van Winkle. Whenever her name was mentioned, however, he shook his head, shrugged his shoulders, and cast up his eyes; which might pass either for an expression of resignation to his fate, or joy at his deliverance.

He used to tell his story to every stranger that arrived at Mr. Doolittle's hotel. He was observed, at first, to vary on some points every time he told it, which was, doubtless, owing to his having so recently awaked. It at last settled down precisely to the tale I have related, and not a man, woman, or child in the neighborhood but knew it by heart. Some always pretended to doubt the reality of it, and insisted that Rip had been out of his head, and that this was one point on which he always remained flighty. The old Dutch inhabitants, however, almost universally gave it full credit. Even to this day they never hear a thunderstorm of a summer afternoon about the Kaatskill, but they say Hendrick Hudson and his crew are at their game of ninepins; and it is a common wish of all hen-pecked husbands in the neighborhood, when life hangs heavy on their hands, that they might have a quieting draught out of Rip Van Winkle's flagon.

# William Austin (1778-1841)

LIKE HERMAN MELVILLE, who was forgotten for so many years, William Austin has been consigned to undeserved oblivion. He was born in Lunenburg, Massachusetts, graduated from Harvard University in 1798, and thereupon wrote a censorious "Strictures on Harvard University," which would endear him to our present-day progressive educators. He studied for the law in England whence he wrote *Letters from London* (1804) exposing British lawyers and politicians from the viewpoint of a New England Yankee. Austin was chaplain on several cruises aboard the *Constitution,* the famous United States frigate saved from being scrapped when popular indignation was aroused by Holmes's poem "Old Ironsides" (1830). The reason Austin is not better remembered is that he was not a prolific writer. His short stories, however, now out of print, have influenced American literature. Far back in 1923, Edward J. O'Brien said a collected edition of Austin's stories was highly to be desired but they remain out of print to this day. "Peter Rugg, the Missing Man," was one of the most widely read stories in the early part of the nineteenth century. The character of Peter Rugg figured in Hawthorne's writing and Edward Everett Hale transmuted him into his mundane but popular "The Man without a Country." Amy Lowell and Louise Imogen Guiney used Austin's story in their poetry.

*"Let the storm increase,"* said Rugg, with a fearful oath, *"I will see home to-night in spite of the last tempest, or may I never see home!"* And he set off in the teeth of a furious gale in an open carriage with his little daughter for the Boston that he was not to see for many years. In 1824, when this story was written, curses were not spelled out as in 1974. It was enough to refer throughout the story to Rugg's defiant use of profanity to explain why heavenly wrath descended on him. Quite apart from the moral, the tale's gloomy ambience has power to haunt a reader much as poor Rugg was haunted by that storm. It is easy to understand why other authors should have drawn on this story for use in their own writings.

# Peter Rugg, the Missing Man

### From Jonathan Dunwell of New York to Mr. Herman Krauff

SIR, — Agreeably to my promise, I now relate to you all the particulars of the lost man and child which I have been able to collect. It is entirely owing to the humane interest you seemed to take in the report, that I have pursued the inquiry to the following result.

You may remember that business called me to Boston in the summer of 1820. I sailed in the packet to Providence, and when I arrived there I learned that every seat in the stage was engaged. I was thus obliged either to wait a few hours or accept a seat with the driver, who civilly offered me that accommodation. Accordingly, I took my seat by his side, and soon found him intelligent and communicative. When we had travelled about ten miles, the horses suddenly threw their ears on their neck, as flat as a hare's. Said the driver, "Have you a surtout with you?"

"No," said I; "why do you ask?"

"You will want one soon," said he. "Do you observe the ears of all the horses?"

"Yes; and was just about to ask the reason."

"They see the storm-breeder, and we shall see him soon."

At this moment there was not a cloud visible in the firmament. Soon after, a small speck appeared in the road.

"There," said my companion, "comes the storm-breeder. He always leaves a Scotch mist behind him. By many a wet jacket do I remember him. I suppose the poor fellow suffers much himself, — much more than is known to the world."

Presently a man with a child beside him, with a large black horse, and a weather-beaten chair, once built for a chaise-body, passed in great haste, apparently at the rate of twelve miles an hour. He seemed to grasp the reins of his horse with firmness, and appeared to anticipate his speed. He seemed dejected, and looked anxiously at the passengers, particularly at the stage-driver and myself. In a moment after he passed us, the horse's ears were up, and bent themselves forward so that they nearly met.

"Who is that man?" said I; "he seems in great trouble."

"Nobody knows who he is, but his person and the child are familiar to me. I have met him more than a hundred times, and have been so often asked the way to Boston by that man, even when he was travelling directly from that town, that of late I have refused any communication with him; and that is the reason he gave me such a fixed look."

"But does he never stop anywhere?"

"I have never known him to stop anywhere longer than to inquire the way to Boston; and let him be where he may, he will tell you he cannot stay a moment, for he must reach Boston that night."

We were now ascending a high hill in Walpole; and as we had a fair view of the heavens, I was rather disposed to jeer the driver for thinking of his surtout, as not a cloud as big as a marble could be discerned.

"Do you look," said he, "in the direction whence the man came; that is the place to look. The storm never meets him; it follows him."

We presently approached another hill; and when at the height, the driver pointed out in an eastern direction a little black speck about as big as a hat. "There," said he, "is the seed-storm. We may possibly reach Polley's before it reaches us, but the wanderer and his child will go to Providence through rain, thunder, and lightning."

And now the horses, as though taught by instinct, hastened with increased speed. The little black cloud came on rolling over the turnpike, and doubled and trebled itself in all directions. The appearance of this cloud attracted the notice of all the passengers, for after it had spread itself to a great bulk it suddenly became more limited in circumference, grew more compact, dark, and consolidated. And now the successive flashes of chain lightning caused the whole cloud to appear like a sort of irregular net-work, and displayed a thousand fantastic images. The driver bespoke my attention to a remarkable configuration in the cloud. He said every flash of lightning near its centre discovered to him, distinctly, the form of a man sitting in an open carriage drawn by a black horse. But in truth I saw no such thing; the man's fancy was doubtless at fault. It is a very common thing for the imagination to paint for the senses, both in the visible and invisible world.

In the mean time the distant thunder gave notice of a shower at hand; and just as we reached Polley's tavern the rain poured down in torrents. It was soon over, the cloud passing in the direction of the turnpike toward Providence. In a few moments after, a respectable-looking man in a chaise stopped at the door. The man and child in the chair having excited some little sympathy among the passengers, the gentleman was asked if he had observed them. He said he had met them; that the man seemed bewildered, and inquired the way to Boston; that he was driving at great speed, as though he expected to outstrip the tempest; that the moment he had passed him, a thunder-clap broke directly over the man's head, and seemed to envelop both man and child, horse and carriage. "I stopped," said the gentleman, "supposing the lightning had struck him, but the horse only seemed to loom up and increase his speed; and as well as I could judge, he travelled just as fast as the thunder-cloud."

While this man was speaking, a pedler with a cart of tin merchandise came up, all dripping; and on being questioned, he said he had met that man and carriage, within a fortnight, in four different States; that at each time he had inquired the way to Boston; and that a thunder-shower like the present had each time deluged his wagon and his wares, setting his tin pots, etc. afloat, so that he had determined to get a marine insurance for the future. But that which excited his surprise most was the strange conduct of his horse, for long before he could distinguish the man in the chair, his own horse stood still in the road, and flung back his ears. In short," said the pedler, "I wish never to see that man and horse again; they do not look to me as though they belonged to this world."

This was all I could learn at that time; and the occurrence soon after would have become with me, "like one of those things which had never happened," had I not, as I stood recently on the door-step of Bennett's hotel in Hartford, heard a man say, "There goes Peter Rugg and his child! he looks wet and weary, and farther from Boston than ever." I was satisfied it was the same man I had seen more than three years before; for whoever has once seen Peter Rugg can never after be deceived as to his identity.

"Peter Rugg!" said I; "and who is Peter Rugg?"

"That," said the stranger, "is more than any one can tell exactly. He is a famous traveller, held in light esteem by all innholders, for he never stops to eat, drink, or sleep. I wonder why the government does not employ him to carry the mail."

"Ay," said a by-stander, "that is a thought bright only on one side; how long would it take in that case to send a letter to Boston, for Peter has already, to my knowledge, been more than twenty years travelling to that place."

"But," said I, "does the man never stop anywhere; does he never converse with any one? I saw the same man more than three years since, near Providence, and I heard a strange story about him. Pray, sir, give me some account of this man."

"Sir," said the stranger, "those who know the most respecting that man, say the least. I have heard it asserted that Heaven sometimes sets a mark on a man, either for judgment or a trial. Under which Peter Rugg now labors, I cannot say; therefore I am rather inclined to pity than to judge."

"You speak like a humane man," said I; "and if you have known him so long, I pray you will give me some account of him. Has his appearance much altered in that time?".

"Why, yes. He looks as though he never ate, drank, or slept; and his child looks older than himself, and he looks like time broken off from eternity, and anxious to gain a resting-place."

"And how does his horse look?" said I.

"As for his horse, he looks fatter and gayer, and shows more animation and courage than he did twenty years ago. The last time Rugg spoke to me he inquired how far it was to Boston. I told him just one hundred miles."

" 'Why,' said he, 'how can you deceive me so? It is cruel to mislead a traveller. I have lost my way; pray direct me the nearest way to Boston.'

"I repeated, it was one hundred miles.

" 'How can you say so?' said he; 'I was told last evening it was but fifty, and I have travelled all night.'

" 'But,' said I, 'you are now travelling from Boston. You must turn back.'

" 'Alas,' said he, 'it is all turn back! Boston shifts with the wind, and plays all around the compass. One man tells me it is to the east, another to the west; and the guide-posts too, they all point the wrong way.'

" 'But will you not stop and rest?' said I; 'you seem wet and weary.'

" 'Yes,' said he, ' it has been foul weather since I left home.'

" 'Stop, then, and refresh yourself.'

" 'I must not stop; I must reach home to-night, if possible: though I think you must be mistaken in the distance to Boston.'

"He then gave the reins to his horse, which he restrained with difficulty, and disappeared in a moment. A few days afterward I met the man a little this side of Claremont,[1] winding around the hills in Unity, at the rate, I believe, of twelve miles an hour."

"Is Peter Rugg his real name, or has he accidentally gained that name?"

"I know not, but presume he will not deny his name; you can ask him, — for see, he has turned his horse, and is passing this way."

In a moment a dark-colored, high-spirited horse approached, and would have passed without stopping, but I had resolved to speak to Peter Rugg, or whoever the man might be. Accordingly I stepped into the street; and as the horse approached, I made a feint of stopping him. The man immediately reined in his horse. "Sir," said I, "may I be so bold as to inquire if you are not Mr. Rugg? for I think I have seen you before."

"My name is Peter Rugg," said he. "I have unfortunately lost my way; I am wet and weary, and will take it kindly of you to direct me to Boston."

"You live in Boston, do you; and in what street?"

"In Middle Street."

"When did you leave Boston?"

"I cannot tell precisely; it seems a considerable time."

"But how did you and your child become so wet? It has not rained here to-day."

"It has just rained a heavy shower up the river. But I shall not reach Boston to-night if I tarry. Would you advise me to take the old road or the turnpike?"

"Why, the old road is one hundred and seventeen miles, and the turnpike is ninety-seven."

"How can you say so? You impose on me; it is wrong to trifle with a traveller; you know it is but forty miles from Newburyport to Boston."

"But this is not Newburyport; this is Hartford."

"Do not deceive me, sir. Is not this town Newburyport, and the river that I have been following the Merrimack?"

"No, sir; this is Hartford, and the river the Connecticut."

He wrung his hands and looked incredulous. "Have the rivers, too, changed their courses, as the cities have changed places? But see! the clouds are gathering in the south, and we shall have a rainy night. Ah, that fatal oath!"

---

[1] In New Hampshire.

He would tarry no longer; his impatient horse leaped off, his hind flanks rising like wings: he seemed to devour all before him, and to scorn all behind.

I had now, as I thought, discovered a clew to the history of Peter Rugg; and I determined, the next time my business called me to Boston, to make a further inquiry. Soon after, I was enabled to collect the following particulars from Mrs. Croft, an aged lady in Middle Street, who has resided in Boston during the last twenty years. Her narration is this:

Just at twilight last summer a person stopped at the door of the late Mrs. Rugg. Mrs. Croft on coming to the door perceived a stranger, with a child by his side, in an old weather-beaten carriage, with a black horse. The stranger asked for Mrs. Rugg, and was informed that Mrs. Rugg had died at a good old age, more than twenty years before that time.

The stranger replied, "How can you deceive me so? Do ask Mrs. Rugg to step to the door."

"Sir, I assure you Mrs. Rugg has not lived here these twenty years; no one lives here but myself, and my name is Betsy Croft."

The stranger paused, looked up and down the street, and said, "Though the paint is rather faded, this looks like my house."

"Yes," said the child, "that is the stone before the door that I used to sit on to eat my bread and milk."

"But," said the stranger, "it seems to be on the wrong side of the street. Indeed, everything here seems to be misplaced. The streets are all changed, the people are all changed, the town seems changed, and what is strangest of all, Catherine Rugg has deserted her husband and child. Pray," continued the stranger, "has John Foy come home from sea? He went a long voyage; he is my kinsman. If I could see him, he could give me some account of Mrs. Rugg."

"Sir," said Mrs. Croft, "I never heard of John Foy. Where did he live?"

"Just above here, in Orange-tree Lane."

"There is no such place in this neighborhood."

"What do you tell me! Are the streets gone? Orange-tree Lane is at the head of Hanover Street, near Pemberton's Hill."

"There is no such lane now."

"Madam, you cannot be serious! But you doubtless know my brother, William Rugg. He lives in Royal Exchange Lane, near King Street."

"I know of no such lane; and I am sure there is no such street as King Street in this town."

"No such street as King Street! Why, woman, you mock me! You may as well tell me there is no King George. However, madam, you see I am wet and weary, I must find a resting-place. I will go to Hart's tavern, near the market."

"Which market, sir? for you seem perplexed; we have several markets."

"You know there is but one market near the town dock."

"Oh, the old market; but no such person has kept there these twenty years."

Here the stranger seemed disconcerted, and uttered to himself quite audibly: "Strange mistake; how much this looks like the town of Boston! It certainly has a great resemblance to it; but I perceive my mistake now. Some other Mrs. Rugg, some other Middle Street. — Then," said he, "madam, can you direct me to Boston?"

"Why, this is Boston, the city of Boston; I know of no other Boston."

"City of Boston it may be; but it is not the Boston where I live. I recollect now, I came over a bridge instead of a ferry. Pray, what bridge is that I just came over?"

"It is Charles River bridge."

"I perceive my mistake: there is a ferry between Boston and Charlestown; there is no bridge. Ah, I perceive my mistake. If I were in Boston my horse would carry me directly to my own door. But my horse shows by his impatience that he is in a strange place. Absurd, that I should have mistaken this place for the old town of Boston! It is a much finer city than the town of Boston. It has been built long since Boston. I fancy Boston must lie at a distance from this city, as the good woman seems ignorant of it."

At these words his horse began to chafe, and strike the pavement with his forefeet. The stranger seemed a little bewildered, and said, "No home to-night;" and giving the reins to his horse, passed up the street, and I saw no more of him.

It was evident that the generation to which Peter Rugg belonged has passed away.

This was all the account of Peter Rugg I could obtain from Mrs. Croft; but she directed me to an elderly man, Mr. James Felt, who lived near her, and who had kept a record of the principal occurrences for the last fifty years. At my request she sent for him; and after I had related to him the object of my inquiry, Mr. Felt told me he had known Rugg in his youth, and that his disappearance had caused some surprise; but as it sometimes happens that men run away, — sometimes to be rid of others, and sometimes to be rid of themselves, — and Rugg took his child with him, and his own horse and chair, and as it did not appear that any creditors made a stir, the occurrence soon mingled itself in the stream of oblivion; and Rugg and his child, horse, and chair were soon forgotten.

"It is true," said Mr. Felt, "sundry stories grew out of Rugg's affair, whether true or false I cannot tell; but stranger things have happened in my day, without even a newspaper notice."

"Sir," said I, "Peter Rugg is now living. I have lately seen Peter Rugg and his child, horse, and chair; therefore I pray you to relate to me all you know or ever heard of him."

"Why, my friend," said James Felt, "that Peter Rugg is now a living man, I will not deny; but that you have seen Peter Rugg and his child, is impossible, if you mean a small child; for Jenny Rugg, if living, must be at least — let me see — Boston massacre, 1770 — Jenny Rugg was about ten years old. Why, sir, Jenny Rugg, if living, must be more than sixty years of age. That Peter Rugg is living, is highly probable, as he was only ten years older than myself, and I was only eighty last March; and I am as likely to live twenty years longer as any man."

Here I perceived that Mr. Felt was in his dotage, and I despaired of gaining any intelligence from him on which I could depend.

I took my leave of Mrs. Croft, and proceeded to my lodgings at the Marlborough Hotel.

"If Peter Rugg," thought I, "has been travelling since the Boston massacre, there is no reason why he should not travel to the end of time. If the present generation know little of him, the next will know less, and Peter and his child will have no hold on this world."

In the course of the evening, I related my adventure in Middle Street.

"Ha!" said one of the company, smiling, "do you really think you have seen Peter Rugg? I have heard my grandfather speak of him, as though he seriously believed his own story."

"Sir," said I, "pray let us compare your grandfather's story of Mr. Rugg with my own."

"Peter Rugg, sir, — if my granfather was worthy of credit, — once lived in Middle Street, in this city. He was a man in comfortable circumstances, had a wife and one daughter, and was generally esteemed for his sober life and manners. But unhappily, his temper, at times, was altogether ungovernable, and then his language was terrible. In these fits of passion, if a door stood in his way, he would never do less than kick a panel through. He would sometimes throw his heels over his head, and come down on his feet, uttering oaths in a circle; and thus in a rage, he was the first who performed a somerset, and did what others have since learned to do for merriment and money. Once Rugg was seen to bite a tenpenny nail in halves. In those days everybody, both men and boys, wore wigs; and Peter, at these moments of violent passion, would become so profane that his wig would rise up from his head. Some said it was on account of his terrible language; others accounted for it in a more philosophical way, and said it was caused by the expansion of his scalp, as violent passion, we know, will swell the veins and expand the head. While these fits were on him, Rugg had no respect for heaven or earth. Except this infirmity, all agreed that Rugg was a good sort of man; for when his fits were over, nobody was so ready to commend a placid temper as Peter.

"One morning, late in autumn, Rugg, in his own chair, with a fine large bay horse, took his daughter and proceeded to Concord. On his return a violent storm overtook him. At dark he stopped in Menotomy, now West Cambridge, at the door of a Mr. Cutter, a friend of his, who urged him to tarry the night. On Rugg's declining to stop, Mr. Cutter urged him vehemently. 'Why, Mr. Rugg,' said Cutter, 'the storm is overwhelming you. The night is exceedingly dark. Your little daughter will perish. You are in an open chair, and the tempest is increasing.' *'Let the storm increase,'* said Rugg, with a fearful oath, *'I will see home to-night, in spite of the last tempest, or may I never see home!'* At these words he gave his whip to his high-spirited horse and disappeared in a moment. But Peter Rugg did not reach home that night, nor the next; nor, when he became a missing man, could he ever be traced beyond Mr. Cutter's, in Menotomy.

"For a long time after, on every dark and stormy night the wife of Peter Rugg would fancy she heard the crack of a whip, and the fleet tread of a horse, and the rattling of a carriage passing her door. The neighbors, too, heard the same noises, and some said they knew it was Rugg's horse; the tread on the pavement was perfectly familiar to them. This occurred so repeatedly that at length the neighbors watched with lanterns, and saw the real Peter Rugg, with his own horse and chair and the child sitting beside him, pass directly before his own door, his head turned toward his house, and himself making every effort to stop his horse, but in vain.

"The next day the friends of Mrs. Rugg exerted themselves to find her husband and child. They inquired at every public house and stable in town; but it did not appear that Rugg made any stay in Boston. No one, after Rugg had passed his own door, could give any account of him, though it was asserted by some that the clatter of Rugg's horse and carriage over the pavements shook the houses on both sides of the streets. And this is credible, if indeed Rugg's horse and carriage did pass on that night; for at this day, in many of the streets, a loaded truck or team in passing will shake the houses like an earthquake. However, Rugg's neighbors never afterward watched. Some of them treated it all as a delusion, and thought no more of it. Others of a different opinion shook their heads and said nothing.

"Thus Rugg and his child, horse, and chair were soon forgotten;

and probably many in the neighborhood never heard a word on the subject.

"There was indeed a rumor that Rugg was seen afterward in Connecticut, between Suffield and Hartford, passing through the country at headlong speed. This gave occasion to Rugg's friends to make further inquiry; but the more they inquired, the more they were baffled. If they heard of Rugg one day in Connecticut, the next they heard of him winding round the hills in New Hampshire; and soon after a man in a chair, with a small child, exactly answering the description of Peter Rugg, would be seen in Rhode Island inquiring the way to Boston.

"But that which chiefly gave a color of mystery to the story of Peter Rugg was the affair at Charleston bridge. The toll-gatherer asserted that sometimes, on the darkest and most stormy nights, when no object could be discerned, about the time Rugg was missing, a horse and wheel-carriage, with a noise equal to a troop, would at midnight, in utter contempt of the rates of toll, pass over the bridge. This occurred so frequently that the toll-gatherer resolved to attempt a discovery. Soon after, at the usual time, apparently the same horse and carriage approached the bridge from Charlestown square. The toll-gatherer, prepared, took his stand as near the middle of the bridge as he dared, with a large three-legged stool in his hand; as the appearance passed, he threw the stool at the horse, but heard nothing except the noise of the stool skipping across the bridge. The toll-gatherer on the next day asserted that the stool went directly through the body of the horse, and he persisted in that belief ever after. Whether Rugg, or whoever the person was, ever passed the bridge again, the toll-gatherer would never tell; and when questioned, seemed anxious to waive the subject. And thus Peter Rugg and his child, horse, and carriage, remain a mystery to this day."

This, sir is all that I could learn of Peter Rugg in Boston.

# Further Account of Peter Rugg
## By Jonathan Dunwell

IN THE AUTUMN of 1825 I attended the races at Richmond in Virginia. As two new horses of great promise were run, the race-ground was never better attended, nor was expectation ever more deeply excited. The partisans of Dart and Lightning, the two race-horses, were equally anxious and equally dubious of the result. To an indifferent spectator, it was impossible to perceive any difference. They were equally beautiful to behold, alike in color and height, and as they stood side by side they measured from heel to forefeet within half an inch of each other. The eyes of each were full, prominent, and resolute; and when at times they regarded each other, they assumed a lofty demeanor, seemed to shorten their necks, project their eyes, and rest their bodies equally on their four hoofs. They certainly showed signs of intelligence, and displayed a courtesy to each other unusual even with statesmen.

It was now nearly twelve o'clock, the hour of expectation, doubt, and anxiety. The riders mounted their horses; and so trim, light, and airy they sat on the animals as to seem a part of them. The spectators, many deep in a solid column, had taken their places, and as many thousand breathing statues were there as spectators. All eyes were turned to Dart and Lightning and their two fairy riders. There was nothing to disturb this calm except a busy woodpecker on a neighboring tree. The signal was given, and Dart and Lightning answered it with ready intelligence. At first they proceed at a slow trot, then they quicken to a canter, and then a gallop; presently they sweep the plain. Both horses lay themselves flat on the ground, their riders bending forward and resting their chins between their horses' ears. Had not the ground been perfectly level, had there been any undulation, the least rise and fall, the spectator would now and then have lost sight of both horses and riders.

While these horses, side by side, thus appeared, flying without wings, flat as a hare, and neither gaining on the other, all eyes were diverted to a new spectacle. Directly in the rear of Dart and Lightning, a majestic black horse of unusual size, drawing an old weather-beaten chair, strode over the plain; and although he appeared to make no effort, for he maintained a steady trot, before Dart and Lightning approached the goal the black horse and chair had overtaken the racers, who, on perceiving this new competitor pass them, threw back their ears, and suddenly stopped in their course. Thus neither Dart nor Lightning carried away the purse.

The spectators now were exceedingly curious to learn whence came the black horse and chair. With many it was the opinion that nobody was in the vehicle. Indeed, this began to be the prevalent opinion; for those at a short distance, so fleet was the black horse, could not easily discern who, if anybody, was in the carriage. But both the riders, very near to whom the black horse passed, agreed in this particular, — that a sad-looking man and a little girl were in the chair. When they stated this I was satisfied that the man was Peter Rugg. But what caused no little surprise, John Spring, one of the riders (he who rode Lightning) asserted that no earthly horse without breaking his trot could, in a carriage, outstrip his race-horse; and he persisted, with some passion, that it was not a horse, — or, he was sure it was not a horse, but a large black ox. "What a great black ox can do," said John, "I cannot pretend to say; but no race-horse, not even flying Childers, could out-trot Lightning in a fair race."

This opinion of John Spring excited no little merriment, for it was obvious to every one that it was a powerful black horse that interrupted the race; but John Spring, jealous of Lightning's reputation as a horse, would rather have it thought that any other beast, even an ox, had been the victor. However, the "horse-laugh" at John Spring's expense was soon suppressed; for as soon as Dart and Lightning began to breathe more freely, it was observed that both of them walked deliberately to the track of the race-ground, and putting their heads to the earth, suddenly raised them again and began to snort. They repeated this till John Spring said, — "These horses have discovered something strange; they suspect foul play. Let me go and talk with Lightning."

He went up to Lightning and took hold of his mane; and Lightning put his nose toward the ground and smelt of the earth without touching it, then reared his head very high, and snorted so loudly that the sound echoed from the next hill. Dart did the same. John Spring stooped down to examine the spot where Lightning had smelled. In a moment he raised himself up, and the countenance of the man was changed. His strength failed him, and he sidled against Lightning.

At length John Spring recovered from his stupor and exclaimed, "It was an ox! I told you it was an ox. No real horse ever yet beat Lightning."

And now, on a close inspection of the black horse's tracks in the path, it was evident to every one that the forefeet of the black horse were cloven. Notwithstanding these appearances, to me it was evident that the strange horse was in reality a horse. Yet when the people left the race-ground, I presume one half of all those present would have testified that a large black ox had distanced two of the fleetest coursers that ever trod the Virginia turf. So uncertain are all things called historical facts.

While I was proceeding to my lodgings, pondering on the events of the day, a stranger rode up to me, and accosted me thus, — "I think your name is Dunwell, sir."

"Yes, sir," I replied.

"Did I not see you a year or two since in Boston, at the Marlborough Hotel?"

"Very likely, sir, for I was there."

"And you heard a story about one Peter Rugg."

"I recollect it all," said I.

"The account you heard in Boston must be true, for here he was to-day. The man has found his way to Virginia, and for aught that appears, has been to Cape Horn. I have seen him before to-day, but never saw him travel with such fearful velocity. Pray, sir, where does Peter Rugg spend his winters, for I have seen him only in summer, and always in foul weather, except this time?"

I replied, "No one knows where Peter Rugg spends his winters; where or when he eats, drinks, sleeps, or lodges. He seems to have an indistinct idea of day and night, time and space, storm and sunshine. His only object is Boston. It appears to me that Rugg's horse has some control of the chair; and that Rugg himself is, in some sort, under the control of his horse."

I then inquired of the stranger where he first saw the man and horse.

"Why, sir," said he, "in the summer of 1824, I travelled to the North for my health; and soon after I saw you at the Marlborough Hotel I returned homeward to Virginia, and, if my memory's correct, I saw this man and horse in every State between here and Massachusetts. Sometimes he would meet me, but oftener overtake me. He never spoke but once, and that once was in Delaware. On his approach he checked his horse with some difficulty . A more beautiful horse I never saw; his hide was as fair and rotund and glossy as the skin of a Congo beauty. When Rugg's horse approached mine he reined in his neck, bent his ears forward until they met, and looked my horse full in the face. My horse immediately withered into half a horse, his hide curling up like a piece of burnt leather; spell-bound, he was fixed to the earth as though a nail had been driven through each hoof.

" 'Sir,' said Rugg, 'perhaps you are travelling to Boston; and if so, I should be happy to accompany you, for I have lost my way, and I must reach home to-night. See how sleepy this little girl looks; poor thing, she is a picture of patience.'

" 'Sir,' said I, 'it is impossible for you to reach home to-night, for you are in Concord, in the county of Sussex, in the State of Delaware.'

" 'What do you mean,' said he, 'by State of Delaware? If I were in Concord, that is only twenty miles from Boston, and my horse Lightfoot could carry me to Charlestown ferry in less than two hours. You mistake, sir; you are a stranger here; this town is nothing like Concord. I am well acquainted with Concord. I went to Concord when I left Boston.'

" 'But,' said I, 'you are in Concord, in the State of Delaware.'

" 'What do you mean by State?' said Rugg.

" 'Why, one of the United States.'

" 'States!' said he, in a low voice; 'the man is a wag, and would persuade me I am in Holland.' Then, raising his voice, he said, 'You seem, sir, to be a gentleman, and I entreat you to mislead me not: tell me, quickly, for pity's sake, the right road to Boston, for you see my horse will swallow his bits, he has eaten nothing since I left Concord.'

" 'Sir, said I, 'this town is Concord, — Concord in Delaware, not Concord in Massachusetts; and you are now five hundred miles from Boston.'

"Rugg looked at me for a moment, more in sorrow than resentment, and then repeated, 'Five hundred miles! Unhappy man, who would have thought him deranged; but nothing in this world is so deceitful as appearances. Five hundred miles! This beats Connecticut River.'

"What he meant by Connecticut River, I know not; his horse broke away, and Rugg disappeared in a moment."

I explained to the stranger the meaning of Rugg's expression, "Connecticut River," and the incident respecting him that occurred at Hartford, as I stood on the door-stone of Mr. Bennett's excellent hotel. We both agreed that the man we had seen that day was the true Peter Rugg.

Soon after, I saw Rugg again, at the toll-gate on the turnpike between Alexandria and Middleburgh. While I was paying the toll, I observed to the toll-gatherer that the drought was more severe in his vicinity than farther south.

"Yes," said he, "the drought is excessive; but if I had not heard yesterday, by a traveller, that the man with the black horse was seen in Kentucky a day or two since, I should be sure of a shower in a few minutes."

I looked all around the horizon, and could not discern a cloud that could hold a pint of water.

"Look, sir," said the toll-gatherer, "you perceive to the eastward, just above that hill, a small black cloud not bigger than a blackberry, and while I am speaking it is doubling and trebling itself, and rolling up the turnpike steadily, as if its sole design was to deluge some object."

"True," said I, "I do perceive it; but what connection is there between a thunder-cloud and a man and horse?"

"More than you imagine, or I can tell you; but stop a moment, sir, I may need your assistance. I know that cloud; I have seen it several times before, and can testify to its identity. You will soon see a man and black horse under it."

While he was speaking, true enough, we began to hear the distant thunder, and soon the chain-lightning performed all the figures of a country-dance. About a mile distant we saw the man and black horse under the cloud; but before he arrived at the toll-gate, the thunder-cloud had spent itself, and not even a sprinkle fell near us.

As the man, whom I instantly knew to be Rugg, attempted to pass, the toll-gatherer swung the gate across the road, seized Rugg's horse by the reins, and demanded two dollars.

Feeling some little regard for Rugg, I interfered, and began to question the toll-gatherer, and requested him not to be wroth with the man. The toll-gatherer replied that he had just cause, for the man had run his toll ten times, and moreover that the horse had discharged a cannon-ball at him, to the great danger of his life; that the man had always before approached so rapidly that he was too quick for the rusty hinges of the toll-gate; "but now I will have full satisfaction."

Rugg looked wistfully at me, and said, "I entreat you, sir, to delay me not; I have found at length the direct road to Boston, and shall not reach home before night if you detain me. You see I am dripping wet, and ought to change my clothes."

The toll-gatherer then demanded why he had run his toll so many times.

"Toll! Why," said Rugg, "do you demand toll? There is no toll to pay on the king's highway."

"King's highway! Do you not perceive this is a turnpike?"

"Turnpike! there are no turnpikes in Massachusetts."

"That may be, but we have several in Virginia."

"Virginia! Do you pretend I am in Virginia?"

Rugg, then, appealing to me, asked how far it was to Boston.

Said I, "Mr. Rugg, I perceive you are bewildered, and am sorry to see you so far from home; you are, indeed, in Virginia."

"You know me, then, sir, it seems; and you say I am in Virginia. Give me leave to tell you, sir, you are the most impudent man alive; for I was never forty miles from Boston, and I never saw a Virginian in my life. This beats Delaware!"

"Your toll, sir, your toll!"

"I will not pay you a penny," said Rugg; "you are both of you highway robbers. There are no turnpikes in this country. Take toll on the king's highway! Robbers take toll on the king's highway!" Then in a low tone, he said, "Here is evidently a conspiracy against me; alas, I shall never see Boston! The highways refuse me a passage, the rivers change their courses, and there is no faith in the compass."

But Rugg's horse had no idea of stopping more than one minute; for in the midst of this altercation, the horse, whose nose was resting on the upper bar of the turnpike-gate, seized it between his teeth, lifted it gently off its staples, and trotted off with it. The toll-gatherer, confounded, strained his eyes after his gate.

"Let him go," said I, "the horse will soon drop your gate, and you will get it again."

I then questioned the toll-gatherer respecting his knowledge of this man; and he related the following particulars: —

"The first time," said he, "that man ever passed this toll-gate was in the year 1806, at the moment of the great eclipse. I thought the horse was frightened at the sudden darkness, and concluded he had run away with the man. But within a few days after, the same man and horse repassed with equal speed, without the least respect to the toll-gate or to me, except by a vacant stare. Some few years afterward, during the late war, I saw the same man approaching again, and I resolved to check his career. Accordingly I stepped into the middle of the road, and stretched wide both my arms, and cried, 'Stop, sir, on your peril!' At this the man said, 'Now, Lightfoot, confound the robber!' at the same time he gave the whip liberally to the flank of his horse, which bounded off with such force that it appeared to me two such horses, give them a place to stand, would overcome any check man could devise. An ammunition wagon which had just passed on to Baltimore had dropped an eighteen pounder in the road; this unlucky ball lay in the way of the horse's heels, and the beast, with the sagacity of a demon, clinched it with one of his heels and hurled it behind him. I feel dizzy in relating the fact, but so nearly did the ball pass my head, that the wind thereof blew off my hat; and the ball embedded itself in that gate-post, as you may see if you will cast your eye on the post. I have permitted it to remain there in memory of the occurrence, — as the people of Boston, I am told, preserve the eighteen-pounder which is now to be seen half imbedded in Brattle Street church."

I then took leave of the toll-gatherer, and promised him if I saw or heard of his gate I would send him notice.

A strong inclination had possessed me to arrest Rugg and search his pockets, thinking great discoveries might be made in the examination; but what I saw and heard that day convinced me that no human force could detain Peter Rugg against his consent. I therefore determined if I ever saw Rugg again to treat him in the gentlest manner.

In pursuing my way to New York, I entered on the turnpike in Trenton; and when I arrived at New Brunswick, I perceived the road was newly macadamized. The small stones had just been laid thereon. As I passed this piece of road, I observed that, at regular distances of about eight feet, the stones were entirely displaced from spots as large as the circumference of a half-bushel measure. This singular appearance induced me to inquire the cause of it at the turnpike-gate.

"Sir," said the toll-gatherer, "I wonder not at the question, but I am unable to give you a satisfactory answer. Indeed, sir, I believe I am bewitched, and that the turnpike is under a spell of enchantment; for what appeared to me last night cannot be a real transaction, otherwise a turnpike-gate is a useless thing."

"I do not believe in witchcraft or enchantment," said I; "and if you will relate circumstantially what happened last night, I will endeavor to account for it by natural means."

"You may recollect the night was uncommonly dark. Well, sir, just after I had closed the gate for the night, down the turnpike, as far as my eye could reach, I beheld what at first appeared to be two armies engaged. The report of the musketry, and the flashes of their firelocks, were incessant and continuous. As this strange spectacle approached me with the fury of a tornado, the noise increased; and the appearance rolled on in one compact body over the surface of the ground. The most splendid fireworks arose out of the earth and encircled this moving spectacle. The divers tints of the rainbow, the most brilliant dyes that the sun lays in the lap of spring, added to the whole family of gems, could not display a more beautiful, radiant, and dazzling spectacle than accompanied the black horse. You would have thought all the stars of heaven had met in merriment on the turnpike. In the midst of this luminous configuration sat a man, distinctly to be seen, in a miserable-looking chair, drawn by a black horse. The turnpike-gate ought, by the laws of Nature and the laws of the State, to have made a wreck of the whole, and have dissolved the enchantment; but no, the horse without an effort passed over the gate, and drew the man and chair horizontally after him without touching the bar. This was what I call enchantment. What think you, sir?"

"My friend," said I, "you have grossly magnified a natural occurrence. The man was Peter Rugg, on his way to Boston. It is true, his horse travelled with unequalled speed, but as he reared high his forefeet, he could not help displacing the thousand small stones on which he trod, which flying in all directions struck one another, and resounded and scintillated. The top bar of your gate is not more than two feet from the ground, and Rugg's horse at every vault could easily lift the carriage over that gate."

This satisfied Mr. McDoubt, and I was pleased at that occurrence; for otherwise Mr. McDoubt, who is a worthy man, late from the Highlands, might have added to his calendar of superstitions. Having thus disenchanted the macadamized road and the turnpike-gate, and also Mr. McDoubt, I pursued my journey homeward to New York.

Little did I expect to see or hear anything further of Mr. Rugg, for he was now more than twelve hours in advance of me. I could hear nothing of him on my way to Elizabethtown, and therefore concluded that during the past night he had turned off from the turnpike and pursued a westerly direction; but just before I arrived at Powles's Hook, I observed a considerable collection of passengers in the ferry-boat, all standing motionless, and steadily looking at the same object. One of the ferry-men, Mr. Hardy, who knew me well, observing my approach delayed a minute, in order to afford me a passage, and coming up, said, "Mr. Dunwell, we have a curiosity on board that would puzzle Dr. Mitchell."

"Some strange fish, I suppose, has found its way into the Hudson."

"No," said he, "it is a man who looks as if he had lain hidden in the ark, and had just now ventured out. He has a little girl with him, the counterpart of himself, and the finest horse you ever saw, harnessed to the queerest-looking carriage that ever was made."

"Ah, Mr. Hardy," said I, "you have, indeed, hooked a prize; no one before you could ever detain Peter Rugg long enough to examine him."

"Do you know the man?" said Mr. Hardy.

"No, nobody knows him, but everybody has seen him. Detain him as long as possible; delay the boat under any pretence, cut the gear of the horse, do anything to detain him."

As I entered the ferry-boat, I was struck at the spectacle before me. There, indeed, sat Peter Rugg and Jenny Rugg in the chair, and there stood the black horse, all as quiet as lambs, surrounded by more than fifty men and women, who seemed to have lost all their senses but one. Not a motion, not a breath, not a rustle. They were all eye. Rugg appeared to them to be a man not of this world; and they appeared to Rugg a strange generation of men. Rugg spoke not, and they spoke not; nor was I disposed to disturb the calm, satisfied to reconnoitre Rugg in a state of rest. Presently, Rugg observed in a low voice, addressed to nobody, "A new contrivance, horses instead of oars; Boston folks are full of notions."

It was plain that Rugg was of Dutch extraction. He had on three pairs of small clothes, called in former days of simplicity breeches, not much the worse for wear; but time had proved the fabric, and shrunk one more than another, so that they showed at the knees their different qualities and colors. His several waistcoats, the flaps of which rested on his knees, made him appear rather corpulent. His capacious drab coat would supply the stuff for half a dozen modern ones; the sleeves were like meal bags, in the cuffs of which you might nurse a child to sleep. His hat, probably once black, now of a tan color, was neither round nor crooked, but in shape much like the one President Monroe wore on his late tour. This dress gave the rotund face of Rugg an antiquated dignity. The man, though deeply sunburned, did not appear to be more than thirty years of age. He had lost his sad and anxious look, was quite composed, and seemed happy. The chair in which Rugg sat was very capacious, evidently made for service, and calculated to last for ages; the timber would supply material for three modern carriages. This chair, like a Nantucket coach, would answer for everything that ever went on wheels. The horse, too, was an object of curiosity; his majestic height, his natural mane and tail, gave him a commanding appearance, and his large open nostrils indicated inexhaustible wind. It was apparent that the hoofs of his forefeet had been split, probably on some newly macadamized road, and were now growing together again; so that John Spring was not altogether in the wrong.

How long this dumb scene would otherwise have continued I cannot tell. Rugg discovered no sign of impatience. But Rugg's horse having been quiet more than five minutes, had no idea of standing idle; he began to whinny, and in a moment after, with his right forefoot he started a plank. Said Rugg, "My horse is impatient, he sees the North End. You must be quick, or he will be ungovernable."

At these words, the horse raised his left forefoot; and when he laid it down every inch of the ferry-boat trembled. Two men immediately seized Rugg's horse by the nostrils. The horse nodded, and both of them were in the Hudson. While we were fishing up the men, the horse was perfectly quiet.

"Fret not the horse," said Rugg, "and he will do no harm. He is only anxious, like myself, to arrive at yonder beautiful shore; he sees the North Church, and smells his own stable."

"Sir," said I to Rugg, practising a little deception, "pray tell me, for I am a stranger here, what river is this, and what city is that opposite, for you seem to be an inhabitant of it?"

"This river, sir, is called Mystic River, and this is Winnisimmet ferry, — we have retained the Indian names, — and that town is Boston. You must, indeed, be a stranger in these parts, not to know that yonder is Boston, the capital of the New England provinces."

"Pray, sir, how long have you been absent from Boston?"

"Why, that I cannot exactly tell. I lately went with this little girl of mine to Concord, to see my friends; and I am ashamed to tell you, in returning lost the way, and have been travelling ever since. No one would direct me right. It is cruel to mislead a traveller. My horse, Lightfoot, has boxed the compass; and it seems to me he has boxed it back again. But, sir, you perceive my horse is uneasy; Lightfoot, as yet, has only given a hint and a nod. I cannot be answerable for his heels."

At these words Lightfoot reared his long tail, and snapped it as you would a whiplash. The Hudson reverberated with the sound. Instantly the six horses began to move the boat. The Hudson was a sea of glass, smooth as oil, not a ripple. The horses, from a smart trot, soon pressed into a gallop; water now ran over the gunwale; the ferry-boat was soon buried in an ocean of foam, and the noise of the spray was like the roaring of many waters. When we arrived at New York, you might see the beautiful white wake of the ferry-boat across the Hudson.

Though Rugg refused to pay toll at turnpikes, when Mr. Hardy reached his hand for the ferriage, Rugg readily put his hand into one of his many pockets, took out a piece of silver, and handed it to Mr. Hardy.

"What is this?" said Mr. Hardy.

"It is thirty shillings," said Rugg.

"It might once have been thirty shillings, old tenor," said Mr. Hardy, "but it is not at present."

"The money is good English coin," said Rugg; "my grandfather brought a bag of them from England, and had them hot from the mint."

Hearing this, I approached near to Rugg, and asked permission to see the coin. It was a half-crown, coined by the English Parliament, dated in the year 1649. On one side, "The Commonwealth of England," and St. George's cross encircled with a wreath of laurel. On the other, "God with us," and a harp and St. George's cross united. I winked at Mr. Hardy, and pronounced it good current money; and said loudly, "I will not permit the gentleman to be imposed on, for I will exchange the money myself."

On this, Rugg spoke, — "Please to give me your name, sir."

"My name is Dunwell, sir," I replied.

"Mr. Dunwell," said Rugg, "you are the only honest man I have seen since I left Boston. As you are a stranger here, my house is your home; Dame Rugg will be happy to see her husband's friend. Step into my chair, sir, there is room enough; move a little, Jenny, for the gentleman, and we will be in Middle Street in a minute."

Accordingly I took a seat by Peter Rugg.

"Were you never in Boston before?" said Rugg.

"No," said I.

"Well, you will now see the queen of New England, a town second only to Philadephia, in all North America.

"You forget New York," said I.

"Poh, New York is nothing; though I never was there. I am told you might put all New York in our mill-pond. No, sir, New York, I assure you, is but a sorry affair; no more to be compared with Boston than a wigwam with a palace."

As Rugg's horse turned into Pearl Street, I looked Rugg as fully in the face as good manners would allow, and said, "Sir, if this is Boston, I acknowledge New York is not worthy to be one of its suburbs."

Before we had proceeded far in Pearl Street, Rugg's countenance changed: his nerves began to twitch; his eyes trembled in their sockets;

he was evidently bewildered. "What is the matter, Mr. Rugg; you seem disturbed."

"This surpasses all human comprehension; if you know, sir, where we are, I beseech you to tell me."

"If this place," I replied, "is not Boston, it must be New York."

"No, sir, it is not Boston; nor can it be New York. How could I be in New York, which is nearly two hundred miles from Boston?"

By this time we had passed into Broadway, and then Rugg, in truth, discovered a chaotic mind. "There is no such place as this in North America. This is all the effect of enchantment; this is a grand delusion, nothing real. Here is seemingly a great city, magnificent houses, shops and goods, men and women innumerable, and as busy as in real life, all sprung up in one night from the wilderness; or what is more probable, some tremendous convulsion of Nature has thrown London or Amsterdam on the shores of New England. Or, possibly, I may be dreaming, though the night seems rather long; but before now I have sailed in one night to Amsterdam, bought goods of Vandogger, and returned to Boston before morning."

At this moment a hue-and-cry was heard, "Stop the madmen, they will endanger the lives of thousands!" In vain hundreds attempted to stop Rugg's horse. Lightfoot interfered with nothing; his course was straight as a shooting-star. But on my part, fearful that before night I should find myself behind the Alleghanies, I addressed Mr. Rugg in a tone of entreaty, and requested him to restrain the horse and permit me to alight.

"My friend," said he, "we shall be in Boston before dark, and Dame Rugg will be most exceeding glad to see us."

"Mr. Rugg," said I, "you must excuse me. Pray look to the west; see that thunder-cloud swelling with rage, as if in pursuit of us."

"Ah!" said Rugg, "it is in vain to attempt to escape. I know that cloud; it is collecting new wrath to spend on my head." Then checking his horse, he permitted me to descend, saying, "Farewell, Mr. Dunwell, I shall be happy to see you in Boston; I live in Middle Street."

It is uncertain in what direction Mr. Rugg pursued his course, after he disappeared in Broadway; but one thing is sufficiently known to everybody, — that in the course of two months after he was seen in New York, he found his way most opportunely to Boston.

It seems the estate of Peter Rugg had recently fallen to the Commonwealth of Massachusetts for want of heirs; and the Legislature had ordered the solicitor-general to advertise and sell it at public auction. Happening to be in Boston at the time, and observing his advertisement, which described a considerable extent of land, I felt a kindly curiosity to see the spot where Rugg once lived. Taking the advertisement in my hand, I wandered a little way down Middle Street, and without asking a question of any one, when I came to a certain spot I said to myself, "This is Rugg's estate; I will proceed no farther. This must be the spot; it is a counterpart of Peter Rugg." The premises, indeed, looked as if they had fulfilled a sad prophecy. Fronting on Middle Street, they extended in the rear to Ann Street, and embraced about half an acre of land. It was not uncommon in former times to have half an acre for a house-lot; for an acre of land then, in many parts of Boston, was not more valuable than a foot in some places at present. The old mansion-house had become a powder-post, and been blown away. One other building, uninhabited, stood ominous, courting dilapidation. The street had been so much raised that the bed-chamber had descended to the kitchen and was level with the street. The house seemed conscious of its fate; and as though tired of standing there, the front was fast retreating from the rear, and waiting the next south wind to project itself into the street. If the most wary animals had sought a place of refuge, here they would have rendezvoused. Here, under the ridge-pole, the crow would have perched in security; and in the recesses below, you might have caught the fox and the weasel asleep. "The hand of destiny," said I, "has pressed heavy on this spot; still heavier on the former owners. Strange that so large a lot of land as this should want an heir! Yet Peter Rugg, at this day, might pass by his own door-stone, and ask, 'Who once lived here?' "

The auctioneer, appointed by the solicitor to sell this estate, was a man of eloquence, as many of the auctioneers of Boston are. The occasion seemed to warrant, and his duty urged, him to make a display. He addressed his audience as follows, —

"The estate, gentlemen, which we offer you this day, was once the property of a family now extinct. For that reason it has escheated to the Commonwealth. Lest any one of you should be deterred from bidding on so large an estate as this for fear of a disputed title, I am authorized by the solicitor-general to proclaim that the purchaser shall have the best of all titles, — a warranty-deed from the Commonwealth. I state this, gentlemen, because I know there is an idle rumor in this vicinity, that one Peter Rugg, the original owner of this estate, is still living. This rumor, gentlemen, has no foundation, and can have no foundation in the nature of things. It originated about two years since, from the incredible story of one Jonathan Dunwell, of New York. Mrs. Croft, indeed, whose husband I see present, and whose mouth waters for this estate, has countenanced this fiction. But, gentlemen, was it ever known that any estate, especially an estate of this value, lay unclaimed for nearly half a century, if any heir, ever so remote, were existing? For, gentlemen, all agree that old Peter Rugg, if living, would be at least one hundred years of age. It is said that he and his daughter, with a horse and chaise, were missed more than half a century ago; and because they never returned home, forsooth, they must be now living, and will some day come and claim this great estate. Such logic, gentlemen, never led to a good investment. Let not this idle story cross the noble purpose of consigning these ruins to the genius of architecture. If such a contingency could check the spirit of enterprise, farewell to all mercantile excitement. Your surplus money, instead of refreshing your sleep with the golden dreams of new sources of speculation, would turn to the nightmare. A man's money, if not employed, serves only to disturb his rest. Look, then, to the prospect before you. Here is half an acre of land, — more than twenty thousand square feet, — a corner lot, with wonderful capabilities; none of your contracted lots of forty feet by fifty, where in dog-days, you can breathe only through your scuttles. On the contrary, an architect cannot contemplate this lot of land without rapture, for here is room enough for his genius to shame the temple of Solomon. Then the prospect — how commanding! To the east, so near to the Atlantic that Neptune, freighted with the select treasures of the whole earth, can knock at your door with his trident. From the west, the produce of the river of Paradise — the Connecticut — will soon, by the blessings of steam, railways, and canals pass under your windows; and thus, on this spot, Neptune shall marry Ceres, and Pomona from Roxbury, and Flora from Cambridge, shall dance at the wedding.

"Gentlemen of science, men of taste, ye of the literary emporium, — for I perceive many of you present — to you this holy ground. If the spot on which in times past a hero left only the print of a footstep is now sacred, of what price is the birthplace of one who all the world knows was born in Middle Street, directly opposite to this lot; and who, if his birthplace were not well known, would now be claimed by more than seven cities. To you, then, the value of these premises must be inestimable. For ere long there will arise in full view of the edifice to be erected here, a monument, the wonder and veneration of the world. A column shall spring to the clouds; and on that column will be engraven one word which will convey all that is wise in intellect, useful in science, good in morals, prudent in counsel, and benevolent in principle, — a name of one who, when living, was the patron of the poor, the delight of the cottage, and the admiration of kings; now dead, worth the whole seven wise men of Greece. Need I tell you his name? He fixed the thunder and guided the lightning.

"Men of the North End! Need I appeal to your patriotism, in order to enhance the value of this lot? The earth affords no such scenery as this; there, around that corner, lived James Otis; here, Samuel Adams; there, Joseph Warren; and around that other corner, Josiah Quincy.

Here was the birthplace of Freedom; here Liberty was born, and nursed, and grew to manhood. Here man was newly created. Here is the nursery of American Independence — I am too modest — here began the emancipation of the world; a thousand generations hence millions of men will cross the Atlantic just to look at the north end of Boston. Your fathers — what do I say — yourselves, — yes, this moment, I behold several attending this auction who lent a hand to rock the cradle of Independence.

"Men of speculation, — ye who are deaf to everything except the sound of money, — you, I know, will give me both of your ears when I tell you the city of Boston must have a piece of this estate in order to widen Ann Street. Do you hear me, — do you all hear me? I say the city must have a large piece of this land in order to widen Ann Street. What a chance! The city scorns to take a man's land for nothing. If it seizes your property, it is generous beyond the dreams of avarice. The only oppression is, you are in danger of being smothered under a load of wealth. Witness the old lady who lately died of a broken heart when the mayor paid her for a piece of her kitchen-garden. All the faculty agreed that the sight of the treasure, which the mayor incautiously paid her in dazzling dollars, warm from the mint, sped joyfully all the blood of her body into her heart, and rent it with raptures. Therefore, let him who purchases this estate fear his good fortune, and not Peter Rugg. Bid, then, liberally, and do not let the name of Rugg damp your ardor. How much will you give per foot for this estate?"

Thus spoke the auctioneer, and gracefully waved his ivory hammer. From fifty to seventy-five cents per foot were offered in a few moments. The bidding labored from seventy-five to ninety. At length one dollar was offered . The auctioneer seemed satisfied; and looking at his watch, said he would knock off the estate in five minutes, if no one offered more.

There was a deep silence during this short period. While the hammer was suspended, a strange rumbling noise was heard, which arrested the attention of every one. Presently, it was like the sound of many shipwrights driving home the bolts of a seventy-four. As the sound approached nearer, some exclaimed, "The buildings in the new market are falling in promiscuous ruins." Others said, "No, it is an earthquake; we perceive the earth tremble." Others said, "Not so; the sound proceeds from Hanover Street, and approaches nearer;" and this proved true, for presently Peter Rugg was in the midst of us.

"Alas, Jenny," said Peter, "I am ruined; our house has been burned, and here are all our neighbors around the ruins. Heaven grant your mother, Dame Rugg, is safe."

"They don't look like our neighbors," said Jenny; "but sure enough our house is burned, and nothing left but the door-stone and an old cedar post. Do ask where mother is."

In the mean time more than a thousand men had surrounded Rugg and his horse and chair. Yet neither Rugg personally, nor his horse and carriage, attracted more attention than the auctioneer. The confident look and searching eyes of Rugg carried more conviction to every one present that the estate was his, than could any parchment or paper with signature and seal. The impression which the auctioneer had just made on the company was effaced in a moment; and although the latter words of the auctioneer were, "Fear not Peter Rugg," the moment the auctioneer met the eye of Rugg his occupation was gone; his arm fell down to his hips, his late lively hammer hung heavy in his hand, and the auction was forgotten. The black horse, too, gave his evidence. He knew his journey was ended; for he stretched himself into a horse and a half, rested his head over the cedar post, and whinnied thrice, causing his harness to tremble from headstall to crupper.

Rugg then stood upright in his chair, and asked with some authority, "Who has demolished my house in my absence, for I see no signs of conflagration? I demand by what accident this has happened, and wherefore this collection of strange people has assembled before my doorstep. I thought I knew every man in Boston, but you appear to me a new generation of men. Yet I am familiar with many of the countenances here present, and I can call some of you by name; but in truth I do not recollect that before this moment I ever saw any one of you. There, I am certain, is a Winslow, and here a Sargent; there stands a Sewall, and next to him a Dudley. Will none of you speak to me, — or is this all a delusion? I see, indeed, many forms of men, and no want of eyes, but of motion, speech, and hearing, you seem to be destitute. Strange! Will no one inform me who has demolished my house?"

Then spake a voice from the crowd, but whence it came I could not discern: "There is nothing strange here but yourself, Mr. Rugg. Time, which destroys and renews all things, has dilapidated your house, and placed us here. You have suffered many years under an illusion. The tempest which you profanely defied at Menotomy has at length subsided; but you will never see home, for your house and wife and neighbors have all disappeared. Your estate, indeed, remains, but no home. You were cut off from the last age, and you can never be fitted to the present. Your home is gone, and you can never have another home in this world."

# Nathaniel Hawthorne (1804–1864)

THE GREAT-GRANDSON of a judge who condemned men and women to death in the Salem witchcraft trials, Nathaniel Hawthorne led a life that seems like one long atonement for his ancestor's sins. The son of a sea captain, he was born in Salem, Massachusetts. His father died of yellow fever in Dutch Guiana four years later and Nathaniel's mother withdrew into such lifelong, melancholy seclusion she did not even share mealtimes with her children. Nathaniel remained extremely devoted to her. His first book, *Fanshawe* (1828), an amateurish novel, was published at his own expense while he was a student at Bowdoin College in Maine. Not until his short stories were published in an annual miscellany and reprinted in 1837 in *Twice-Told Tales* did his writing attract attention. They were followed by a tremendous outpouring of literary masterpieces, both short stories and novels, all reflecting his fascination with the effects of Puritanism on America, and all with an emphasis on morality. "Irving had dealt with manners and Poe was to deal with passions. Hawthorne was solely preoccupied with the drama of conscience" was the succinct way O'Brien summed up the three writers in his *The Advance of the American Short Story*. Apart from his short stories, Hawthorne's best known writings are *The Scarlet Letter* and *The House of the Seven Gables*. He worked at various times as a magazine and book editor and as a customs collector. He was one of our first literary expatriates, living abroad for seven years. Returning to his native Massachusetts he spent the last four years of his life in Concord.

For a writer as dedicated as he was to the historic events in colonial New England, "The Grey Champion" was a made-to-order story for Hawthorne. There was the regicide, William Goffe, who signed the order for the beheading of King Charles I, a fugitive from the Restoration hiding out in Hadley, Massachusetts. There was the hated Sir Edmund Andros, tyrannical governor of the Dominion of New England and the appointed representative of British royalty. And there was Cotton Mather, witch-hunter, religious zealot, and ardent spokesman for seventeenth-century New Englanders. Andros and Mather were equally violent, headstrong men. Their clash was inevitable and climaxed in the Boston uprising described by Hawthorne in "The Grey Champion," which ended the governorship of Andros. And Goffe, the regicide? He was the Grey Champion. It is not known whether he was present at this particular Boston event but he did participate in a battle with the Indians during King Philip's War. Goffe also became a favorite character in the writings of James Fenimore Cooper, James Paulding, and Sir Walter Scott. But none used him more awesomely than did Hawthorne in this story.

# The Grey Champion

THERE was once a time when New England groaned under the actual pressure of heavier wrongs than those threatened ones which brought on the Revolution. James II, the bigoted successor of Charles the Voluptuous, had annulled the charters of all the colonies, and sent a harsh and unprincipled soldier to take away our liberties and endanger our religion. The administration of Sir Edmund Andros lacked scarcely a single characteristic of tyranny: a Governor and Council, holding office from the King, and wholly independent of the country; laws made and taxes levied without concurrence of the people immediate or by their representatives; the rights of private citizens violated, and the titles of all landed property declared void; the voice of complaint stifled by restrictions on the press; and, finally, disaffection overawed by the first band of mercenary troops that ever marched on our free soil. For two years our ancestors were kept in sullen submission by that filial love which had invariably secured their allegiance to the mother country, whether its head chanced to be a Parliament, Protector, or Popish Monarch. Till these evil times, however, such allegiance had been merely nominal, and the colonists had ruled themselves, enjoying far more freedom than is even yet the privilege of the native subjects of Great Britain.

At length a rumor reached our shores that the Prince of Orange had ventured on an enterprise, the success of which would be the triumph of civil and religious rights and the salvation of New England. It was but a doubtful whisper; it might be false, or the attempt might fail; and, in either case, the man that stirred against King James would lose his head. Still the intelligence produced a marked effect. The people smiled mysteriously in the streets, and threw bold glances at their oppressors; while far and wide there was a subdued and silent agitation, as if the slightest signal would rouse the whole land from its sluggish despondency. Aware of their danger, the rulers resolved to avert it by an imposing display of strength, and perhaps to confirm their despotism by yet harsher measures. One afternoon in April, 1689, Sir Edmund Andros and his favorite councillors, being warm with wine, assembled the redcoats of the Governor's Guard, and made their appearance in the streets of Boston. The sun was near setting when the march commenced.

The roll of the drum at that unquiet crisis seemed to go through the streets, less as the martial music of the soldiers, than as a muster-call to the inhabitants themselves. A multitude, by various avenues, assembled in King Street, which was destined to be the scene, nearly a century afterwards, of another encounter between the troops of Britain, and a people struggling against her tyranny. Though more than sixty years had elapsed since the pilgrims came, this crowd of their descendants still showed the strong and sombre features of their character perhaps more strikingly in such a stern emergency than on happier occasions. There were the sober garb, the general severity of mien, the gloomy but undismayed expression, the scriptural forms of speech, and the confidence in Heaven's blessing on a righteous cause, which would have marked a band of the original Puritans, when threatened by some peril of the wilderness. Indeed, it was not yet time for the old spirit to be extinct; since there were men in the street that day who had worshipped there beneath the trees, before a house was reared to the God for whom they had become exiles. Old soldiers of the Parliament were here, too, smiling grimly at the thought that their aged arms might strike another blow against the house of Stuart. Here, also, were the veterans of King Philip's war, who had burned villages and slaughtered young and old, with pious fierceness, while the godly souls throughout the land were helping them with prayer. Several ministers were scattered among the crowd, which, unlike all other mobs, regarded them with such reverence, as if there were sanctity in their very garments. These holy men exerted their influence to quiet the people, but not to disperse them. Meantime, the purpose of the Governor, in disturbing the peace of the town at a period when the slightest commotion might throw the country into a ferment, was almost the universal subject of inquiry, and variously explained.

"Satan will strike his master-stroke presently," cried some, "because he knoweth that his time is short. All our godly pastors are to be dragged to prison! We shall see them at a Smithfield fire in King Street!"

Hereupon the people of each parish gathered closer round their minister, who looked calmly upwards and assumed a more apostolic dignity, as well befitted a candidate for the highest honor of his pro-fession, the crown of martyrdom. It was actually fancied, at that period, that New England might have a John Rogers of her own to take the place of that worthy in the Primer.

"The Pope of Rome has given orders for a new St. Bartholomew!" cried others. "We are to be massacred, man and male child!"

Neither was this rumor wholly discredited, although the wiser class believed the Governor's object somewhat less atrocious. His predecessor under the old charter, Bradstreet, a venerable companion of the first settlers, was known to be in town. There were grounds for conjecturing, that Sir Edmund Andros intended at once to strike terror by a parade of military force, and to confound the opposite faction by possessing himself of their chief.

"Stand firm for the old charter Governor!" shouted the crowd, seizing upon the idea. "The good old Governor Bradstreet!"

While this cry was at the loudest, the people were surprised by the well-known figure of Governor Bradstreet himself, a patriarch of nearly ninety, who appeared on the elevated steps of a door, and, with character-istic mildness, besought them to submit to the constituted authorities.

"My children," concluded this venerable person, "do nothing rashly. Cry not aloud, but pray for the welfare of New England, and expect patiently what the Lord will do in this matter!"

The event was soon to be decided. All this time, the roll of the drum had been approaching through Cornhill, louder and deeper, till with reverberations from house to house, and the regular tramp of martial footsteps, it burst into the street. A double rank of soldiers made their appearance, occupying the whole breadth of the passage, with shouldered matchlocks, and matches burning, so as to present a row of fires in the dusk. Their steady march was like the progress of a machine, that would roll irresistibly over everything in its way. Next, moving slowly, with a confused clatter of hoofs on the pavement, rode a party of mounted gentlemen, the central figure being Sir Edmund Andros, elderly, but erect and soldier-like. Those around him were his favorite councillors, and the bitterest foes of New England. At his right hand rode Edward Randolph, our arch-enemy, that "blasted wretch," as Cotton Mather calls him, who achieved the downfall of our ancient government, and was followed with a sensible curse, through life and to his grave. On the other side was Bullivant, scattering jests and mockery as he rode along. Dudley came behind, with a downcast look, dreading, as well he might, to meet the indignant gaze of the people, who beheld him, their only countryman by birth, among the oppressors of his native land. The captain of a frigate in the harbor, and two or three civil officers under the Crown, were also there. But the figure which most attracted the public eye, and stirred up the deepest feeling, was the Episcopal clergyman of King's Chapel, riding haughtily among the magistrates in his priestly vestments, the fitting representative of prelacy and persecution, the union of church and state, and all those abominations which had driven the Puritans to the wilderness. Another guard of soldiers, in double rank, brought up the rear.

The whole scene was a picture of the condition of New England, and its moral, the deformity of any government that does not grow out of the nature of things and the character of the people. On one side the religious multitude, with their sad visages and dark attire, and on the other, the group of despotic rulers, with the high churchman in the midst, and here and there a crucifix at their bosoms, all magnificently clad, flushed with wine, proud of unjust authority, and scoffing at the universal groan. And the mercenary soldiers, waiting but the word to deluge the street with blood, showed the only means by which obedience could be secured.

"O Lord of Hosts," cried a voice among the crowd, "provide a Champion for thy people!"

This ejaculation was loudly uttered, and served as a herald's cry, to introduce a remarkable personage. The crowd had rolled back, and were now huddled together nearly at the extremity of the street, while the soldiers had advanced no more than a third of its length. The intervening space was empty — a paved solitude, between lofty edifices, which threw almost a twilight shadow over it. Suddenly, there was seen the figure of an ancient man, who seemed to have emerged from among the people, and was walking by himself along the centre of the street, to confront the armed band. He wore the old Puritan dress, a dark cloak and a steeple-crowned hat, in the fashion of at least fifty years before, with a heavy sword upon his thigh, but a staff in his hand to assist the tremulous gait of age.

When at some distance from the multitude, the old man turned slowly round, displaying a face of antique majesty, rendered doubly venerable by the hoary beard that descended on his breast. He made a gesture at once of encouragement and warning, then turned again, and resumed his way.

"Who is this grey patriarch?" asked the young men of their sires.

"Who is this venerable brother?" asked the old men among themselves.

But none could make reply. The fathers of the people, those of fourscore years and upwards, were disturbed, deeming it strange that they should forget one of such evident authority, whom they must have known in their early days, the associate of Winthrop, and all the old councillors, giving laws, and making prayers, and leading them against the savage. The elderly men ought to have remembered him, too, with locks as grey in their youth, as their own were now. And the young! How could he have passed so utterly from their memories — that hoary sire, the relic of long-departed times, whose awful benediction had surely been bestowed on their uncovered heads, in childhood?

"Whence did he come? What is his purpose? Who can this old man be?" whispered the wondering crowd.

Meanwhile, the venerable stranger, staff in hand, was pursuing his solitary walk along the centre of the street. As he drew near the advancing soldiers, and as the roll of their drum came full upon his ear, the old man raised himself to a loftier mien, while the decrepitude of age seemed to fall from his shoulders, leaving him in grey but unbroken dignity. Now, he marched onward with a warrior's step, keeping time to the military music. Thus the aged form advanced on one side, and the whole parade of soldiers and magistrates on the other, till, when scarcely twenty yards remained between, the old man grasped his staff by the middle, and held it before him like a leader's truncheon.

"Stand!" cried he.

The eye, the face, and attitude of command; the solemn, yet warlike peal of that voice, fit either to rule a host in the battle-field or be raised to God in prayer, were irresistible. At the old man's word and outstretched arm, the roll of the drum was hushed at once, and the advancing line stood still. A tremulous enthusiasm seized upon the multitude. That stately form, combining the leader and the saint, so grey, so dimly seen, in such an ancient garb, could only belong to some old champion of the righteous cause, whom the oppressor's drum had summoned from his grave. They raised a shout of awe and exultation, and looked for the deliverance of New England.

The Governor, and the gentlemen of his party, perceiving themselves brought to an unexpected stand, rode hastily forward, as if they would have pressed their snorting and affrighted horses right against the hoary apparition. He, however, blenched not a step, but glancing his severe eye round the group, which half encompassed him, at last bent it sternly on Sir Edmund Andros. One would have thought that the dark old man was chief ruler there, and that the Governor and Council, with soldiers at their back, representing the whole power and authority of the Crown, had no alternative but obedience.

"What does this old fellow here?" cried Edward Randolph, fiercely. "On, Sir Edmund! Bid the soldiers forward, and give the dotard the same choice that you give all his countrymen — to stand aside or be trampled on!"

"Nay, nay, let us show respect to the good grandsire," said Bullivant, laughing. "See you not, he is some old round-headed dignitary, who hath lain asleep these thirty years, and knows nothing of the change of times? Doubtless, he thinks to put us down with a proclamation in Old Noll's name!"

"Are you mad, old man?" demanded Sir Edmund Andros, in loud and harsh tones. "How dare you stay the march of King James's Governor?"

"I have stayed the march of a King himself, ere now," replied the grey figure, with stern composure. "I am here, Sir Governor, because the cry of an oppressed people hath disturbed me in my secret place; and beseeching this favor earnestly of the Lord, it was vouchsafed me to appear once again on earth, in the good old cause of his saints. And what speak ye of James? There is no longer a Popish tyrant on the throne of England, and by to-morrow noon, his name shall be a byword in this very street, where ye would make it a word of terror. Back, thou that wast a Governor, back! With this night thy power is ended — to-morrow, the prison! — back, lest I foretell the scaffold!"

The people had been drawing nearer and nearer, and drinking in the words of their champion, who spoke in accents long disused, like one unaccustomed to converse, except with the dead of many years ago. But his voice stirred their souls. They confronted the soldiers, not wholly without arms, and ready to convert the very stones of the street into deadly weapons. Sir Edmund Andros looked at the old man; then he cast his hard and cruel eye over the multitude, and beheld them burning with that lurid wrath, so difficult to kindle or to quench; and again he fixed his gaze on the aged form, which stood obscurely in an open space, where neither friend nor foe had thrust himself. What were his thoughts, he uttered no word which might discover. But whether the oppressor were overawed by the Grey Champion's look, or perceived his peril in the threatening attitude of the people, it is certain that he gave back, and ordered his soldiers to commence a slow and guarded retreat. Before another sunset, the Governor, and all that rode so proudly with him, were prisoners, and long ere it was known that James had abdicated, King William was proclaimed throughout New England.

But where was the Grey Champion? Some reported that, when the troops had gone from King Street, and the people were thronging tumultuously in their rear, Bradstreet, the aged Governor, was seen to embrace a form more aged than his own. Others soberly affirmed, that while they marvelled at the venerable grandeur of his aspect, the old man had faded from their eyes, melting slowly into the hues of twilight, till, where he stood, there was an empty space. But all agreed that the hoary shape was gone. The men of that generation watched for his reappearance, in sunshine and in twilight, but never saw him more, nor knew when his funeral passed, nor where his gravestone was.

And who was the Grey Champion? Perhaps his name might be found in the records of that stern Court of Justice, which passed a sentence, too mighty for the age, but glorious in all after-times, for its humbling lesson to the monarch and its high example to the subject. I have heard, that whenever the descendants of the Puritans are to show the spirit of their sires, the old man appears again. When eighty years had passed, he walked once more in King Street. Five years later, in the twilight of an April morning, he stood on the green, beside the meeting-house, at Lexington, where now the obelisk of granite, with a slab of slate inlaid, commemorates the first fallen of the Revolution. And when our fathers were toiling at the breastwork on Bunker's Hill, all through that night the old warrior walked his rounds. Long, long may it be, ere he comes again! His hour is one of darkness, and adversity, and peril. But should domestic tyranny oppress us, or the invader's step pollute our soil, still may the Grey Champion come, for he is the type of New England's hereditary spirit; and his shadowy march, on the eve of danger, must ever be the pledge, that New England's sons will vindicate their ancestry.

# T. B. Thorpe (1815–1878)

AROUND campfires in the Old Southwest and in frontier saloons throughout the still really Wild West, jovial yarns were swapped among the explorers and early settlers. In time the less earthy were printed and became a popular part of early American literature. One of the best known of their writers was T. B. Thorpe. He was born in 1815 in Massachusetts and went to Louisiana where he lived for twenty years. His life as a frontiersman was interrupted by service in the Mexican War, started by the annexation of Texas and resulting in the acquisition of all the territory between Louisiana and the Pacific Ocean. One authority in 1919 declared twelve hundred books and pamphlets had been written about the war. Thorpe wrote several of them. He is most remembered for such tales as "The Big Bear of Arkansas."

In "The Big Bear of Arkansas," this most famous of American Tall Tales, a chauvinist from Arkansas, the "state without a fault," where beets are mistaken for cedar stumps and potato hills are big as Indian burial mounds, out-prevaricates that most renowned of classical European literary liars, Baron Munchausen. This reader detests hunting but she found herself laughing all the way from the story's opening amid the wonderful mixture of early-American types aboard the old-time Mississippi "high-pressure-and-beat-every-thing" steamboat to the ending when the liar invites all present to "liquor" before going to bed. As if they needed to get drunk after listening to him! The dialect, which the author uses with a sparing hand, is delightful as when the braggart refers delicately to his underdrawers as "inexpressibles." Read and enjoy!

# *The Big Bear of Arkansas*

A STEAMBOAT on the Mississippi frequently, in making her regular trips, carries between places varying from one to two thousand miles apart; and as these boats advertise to land passengers and freight at "all intermediate landings," the heterogeneous character of the passengers of one of these up-country boats can scarcely be imagined by one who has never seen it with his own eyes. Starting from New Orleans in one of these boats, you will find yourself associated with men from every state in the Union, and from every portion of the globe; and a man of observation need not lack for amusement or instruction in such a crowd, if he will take the trouble to read the great book of character so favourably opened before him. Here may be seen jostling together the wealthy Southern planter, and the pedlar of tin-ware from New England — the Northern merchant, and the Southern jockey — a venerable bishop, and a desperate gambler — the land speculator, and the honest farmer — professional men of all creeds and characters — Wolvereens, Suckers, Hoosiers, Buckeyes, and Corn-crackers, beside a "plentiful sprinkling" of the half-horse and half-alligator species of men, who are peculiar to "old Mississippi," and who appear to gain a livelihood simply by going up and down the river. In the pursuit of pleasure or business, I have frequently found myself in such a crowd.

On one occasion, when in New Orleans, I had occasion to take a trip of a few miles up the Mississippi, and I hurried on board the well-known "high-pressure-and-beat-every-thing" steamboat *Invincible*, just as the last note of the last bell was sounding; and when the confusion and bustle that is natural to a boat's getting under way had subsided, I discovered that I was associated in as heterogeneous a crowd as was ever got together. As my trip was to be of a few hours' duration only, I made no endeavours to become acquainted with my fellow passengers, most of whom would be together many days. Instead of this, I took out of my pocket the "latest paper," and more critically than usual examined its contents; my fellow passengers at the same time disposed themselves in little groups. While I was thus busily employed in reading, and my companions were more busily employed in discussing such subjects as suited their humours best, we were startled most unexpectedly by a loud Indian whoop, uttered in the "social hall," that part of the cabin fitted off for a bar; then was to be heard a loud crowing, which would not have continued to have interested us — such sounds being quite common in that place of spirits — had not the hero of these windy accomplishments stuck his head into the cabin and hallooed out, "Hurra for the Big Bar of Arkansaw!" and then might be heard a confused hum of voices, unintelligible, save in such broken sentences as "horse," "screamer," "lightning is slow," &c. As might have been expected, this continued interruption attracted the attention of every one in the cabin; all conversation dropped, and in the midst of this surprise the "Big Bar" walked into the cabin, took a chair, put his feet on the stove, and looking back over his shoulder, passed the general and familiar salute of "Strangers, how are you?" He then expressed himself as much at home as if he had been at "the Forks of Cypress," and "perhaps a little more so." Some of the company at this familiarity looked a little angry, and some astonished; but in a moment every face was wreathed in a smile. There was something about the intruder that won the heart on sight. He appeared to be a man enjoying perfect health and content-ment: His eyes were as sparkling as diamonds, and good-natured to simplicity. Then his perfect confidence in himself was irresistibly droll. "Perhaps," said he, "gentlemen," running on without a person speaking, "perhaps you have been to New Orleans often; I never made *the first visit before*, and I don't intend to make another in a crow's life. I am thrown away in that ar place, and useless, that ar a fact. Some of the gentlemen thar called me *green* — well, perhaps I am, said I, *but I arn't so at home*; and if I ain't off my trail much, the heads of them perlite chaps themselves wern't much the hardest; for according to my notion, they were real *know-nothings*, green as a pumpkin-vine — couldn't, in farming, I'll bet, raise a crop of turnips: and as for shooting, they'd miss a barn if the door was swinging, and that, too, with the best rifle in the country. And then they talked to me 'bout hunting, and laughed at my calling the principal game in Arkansaw poker, and high-low-jack. 'Perhaps,' said I, 'you prefer chickens and rolette'; at this they laughed harder than ever, and asked me if I lived in the woods, and didn't know what *game* was? At this I rather think I laughed. 'Yes,' I roared, and says, 'Strangers, if you'd asked me *how we got our meat* in Arkansaw, I'd a told you at once, and given you a list of varmints that would make a caravan, beginning with the bar, and ending off with the cat; that's *meat* though, not game.' Game, indeed, that's what city folks call it; and with them it means chippen-birds and shite-pokes; maybe such trash live in my diggens, but I arn't noticed them yet: a bird any way is too trifling. I never did shoot at but one, and I'd never forgiven myself for that, had it weighed less than forty pounds. I wouldn't draw a rifle on any thing less than that; and when I meet with another wild turkey of the same weight I will drap him."

"A wild turkey weighing forty pounds!" exclaimed twenty voices in the cabin at once.

"Yes, strangers, and wasn't it a whopper? You see, the thing was so fat that it couldn't fly far; and when he fell out of the tree, after I shot him, on striking the ground he bust open behind, and the way the pound gobs of tallow rolled out of the opening was perfectly beautiful."

"Where did all that happen?" asked a cynical-looking Hoosier.

"Happen! happened in Arkansaw: where else could it have happened, but in the creation state, the finishing-up country — a state where the *sile* runs down to the centre of the 'arth, and government gives you a title to every inch of it? Then its airs — just breathe them, and they will make you snort like a horse. It's a state without a fault, it is."

"Excepting mosquitoes," cried the Hoosier.

"Well, stranger, except them; for it ar a fact that they ar rather *enormous*, and do push themselves in somewhat troublesome. But, stranger, they never stick twice in the same place; and give them a fair chance for a few months, and you will get as much above noticing them as an alligator. They can't hurt my feelings, for they lay under the skin; and I never knew but one case of injury resulting from them, and that was to a Yankee: and they take worse to foreigners, any how, than they do to natives. But the way they used that fellow up! first they punched him until he swelled up and busted; then he su-per-a-ted, as the doctor called it, until he was as raw as beef; then he took the ager, owing to the warm

weather, and finally he took a steamboat and left the country. He was
the only man that ever took mosquitoes to heart that I know of. But
mosquitoes is natur, and I never find fault with her. If they ar large,
Arkansaw is large, her varmints ar large, her trees ar large, her rivers
ar large, and a small mosquito would be of no more use in Arkansaw
than preaching in a cane-brake.''

This knock-down argument in favour of big mosquitoes used the
Hoosier up, and the logician started on a new track, to explain how
numerous bear were in his "diggins," where he represented them to be
"about as plenty as blackberries, and a little plentifuler.''

Upon the utterance of this assertion, a timid little man near me
inquired if the bear in Arkansaw ever attacked the settlers in numbers.

"No," said our hero, warming with the subject, "no, stranger, for
you see it ain't the natur of bar to go in droves; but the way they squander
about in pairs and single ones is edifying. And then the way I hunt
them the old black rascals know the crack of my gun as well as they know
a pig's squealing. They grow thin in our parts, it frightens them so, and
they do take the noise dreadfully, poor things. That gun of mine is
perfect *epidemic among bar*; if not watched closely, it will go off as
quick on a warm scent as my dog Bowie-knife will; and then that dog —
whew! why the fellow thinks that the world is full of bar, he finds them
so easy. It's lucky he don't talk as well as think; for with his natural
modesty, if he should suddenly learn how much he is acknowledged to
be ahead of all other dogs in the universe, he would be astonished to
death in two minutes. Strangers, the dog knows a bar's way as well as
a horse-jockey knows a woman's: he always barks at the right time, bites
at the exact place, and whips without getting a scratch. I never could
tell whether he was made expressly to hunt bar, or whether bar was
made expressly for him to hunt: any way, I believe they were ordained
to go together as naturally as Squire Jones says a man and woman is,
when he moralizes in marrying a couple. In fact, Jones once said,
said he, 'Marriage according to law is a civil contract of divine origin;
it's common to all countries as well as Arkansaw, and people take to it
as naturally as Jim Dogget's Bowie-knife takes to bar.' ''

"What season of the year do your hunts take place?" inquired a
gentlemanly foreigner, who, from some peculiarities of his baggage, I
suspected to be an Englishman, on some hunting expedition, probably
at the foot of the Rocky Mountains.

"The season for bar hunting, stranger," said the man of Arkansaw,
"is generally all the year round, and the hunts take place about as regular.
I read in history that varmints have their fat season, and their lean season.
That is not the case in Arkansaw, feeding as they do upon the *sponte-
nacious* productions of the sile, they have one continued fat season the

year round: though in winter things in this way is rather more greasy than in summer, I must admit. For that reason bar with us run in warm weather, but in winter, they only waddle. Fat, fat! it's an enemy to speed; it tames everything that has plenty of it. I have seen wild turkeys, from its influence, as gentle as chickens. Run a bar in this fat condition, and the way it improves the critter for eating is amazing; it sort of mixes the ile up with meat, until you can't tell t'other from which. I've done this often. I recollect one perty morning in particular, of putting an old fellow on the stretch, and considering the weight he carried, he run well. But the dogs soon tired him down, and when I came up with him wasn't he in a beautiful sweat — I might say fever; and then to see his tongue sticking out of his mouth a feet, and his sides sinking and opening like a bellows, and his cheeks so fat he couldn't look cross. In this fix I blazed at him, and pitch me naked into a briar patch if the steam didn't come out of the bullet-hole ten foot in a straight line. The fellow, I reckon, was made on the high-pressure system, and the lead sort of bust his biler."

"That column of steam was rather curious, or else the bear must have been *warm*," observed the foreigner, with a laugh.

"Stranger, as you observe, that bar was WARM, and the blowing off of the steam show'd it, and also how hard the varmint had been run. I have no doubt if he had kept on two miles farther his insides would have been stewed; and I expect to meet with a varmint yet of extra bottom, who will run himself into a skinfull of bar's grease: it is possible, much on-likelier things have happened."

"Whereabouts are these bears so abundant?" inquired the foreigner, with increasing interest.

"Why, stranger, they inhabit the neighbourhood of my settlement, one of the prettiest places on old Mississippi — a perfect location, and no mistake; a place that had some defects until the river made the 'cut-off' at 'Shirt-tail bend,' and that remedied the evil, as it brought my cabin on the edge of the river — a great advantage in wet weather, I assure you, as you can now roll a barrel of whiskey into my yard in high water from a boat, as easy as falling off a log. It's a great improvement, as toting it by land in a jug, as I used to do, *evaporated* it too fast, and it became expensive. Just stop with me, stranger, a month or two, or a year if you like, and you will appreciate my place. I can give you plenty to eat; for beside hog and hominy, you can have bar-ham, and bar-sausages, and a mattress of bar-skins to sleep on, and a wildcat-skin, pulled off hull, stuffed with corn-shucks, for a pillow. That bed would put you to sleep if you had the rheumatics in every joint in your body. I call that ar bed a *quietus*. Then look at my land — the government ain' got another such a piece to dispose of. Such timber, and such bottom land, why you can't preserve any thing natural you plant in it unless you pick it young, things thar will grow out of shape so quick. I once planted in those diggins a few potatoes and beets: they took a fine start, and after that an ox team couldn't have kept them from growing. About that time I went off to old Kentuck on bisiness, and did not hear from them things in three months, when I accidentally stumbled on a fellow who had stopped at my place, with an idea of buying me out. 'How did you like things?' said I. 'Pretty well,' said he; 'the cabin is convenient, and the timber land is good; but that bottom land ain't worth the first red cent.' 'Why?' said I. ' 'Cause,' said he. ' 'Cause what?' said I. ' 'Cause it's full of cedar stumps and Indian mounds,' said he, *'and it can't be cleared.'* 'Lord,' said I, 'them ar "cedar stumps" is beets, and them ar "Indian mounds" ar tater hills.' As I expected, the crop was overgrown and useless: the sile is too rich, *and planting in Arkansaw is dangerous.* I had a good-sized sow killed in that same bottom land. The old thief stole an ear of corn, and took it down where she slept at night to eat. Well, she left a grain or two on the ground, and lay down on them: before morning the corn shot up, and the percussion killed her dead. I don't plant any more: natur intended Arkansaw for a hunting ground, and I go according to natur."

The questioner who thus elicited the description of our hero's settlement, seemed to be perfectly satisfied, and said no more; but the "Big Bar of Arkansaw" rambled on from one thing to another with a volubility perfectly astonishing, occasionally disputing with those around him, particularly with a "live Sucker" from Illinois, who had the daring to say that our Arkansaw friend's stories "smelt rather tall."

In this manner the evening was spent; but conscious that my own association with so singular a personage would probably end before morning, I asked him if he would not give me a description of some particular bear hunt; adding that I took great interest in such things, though I was no sportsman. The desire seemed to please him, and he squared himself round towards me, saying, that he could give me an idea of a bar hunt that was never beat in this world, or in any other. His manner was so singular, that half of his story consisted in his excellent way of telling it, the great peculiarity of which was, the happy manner he had of emphasizing the prominent parts of his conversation. As near as I can recollect, I have italicized them, and given the story in his own words.

"Stranger," said he, "in bar hunts *I am numerous*, and which particular one, as you say, I shall tell, puzzles me. There was the old she devil I shot at the Hurricane last fall — then there was the old hog thief I popped over at the Bloody Crossing, and then — Yes, I have it! I will give you an idea of a hunt, in which the greatest bar was killed that ever lived, *none excepted*; about an old fellow that I hunted, more or less, for two or three years; and if that ain't a particular bar hunt, I ain't got any to tell. But in the first place, stranger, let me say, I am pleased with you because you ain't ashamed to gain information by asking, and listening and that's what I say to Countess's pups every day when I'm home; and I have got great hopes of them ar pups, because they are continually *nosing* about; and though they stick it sometimes in the wrong place, they gain experience any how, and may learn something useful to boot. Well, as I was saying about this big bar, you see when I and some more first settled in our region, we were drivin to hunting naturally; we soon liked it, and after that we found it an easy matter to make the thing our business. One old chap who had pioneered 'afore us, gave us to understand that we had settled in the right place. He dwelt upon its merits until it was affecting, and showed us, to prove his assertions, more marks on the sassafras trees than I ever saw on a tavern door 'lection time. 'Who keeps that ar reckoning?' said I. 'The bar,' said he. 'What for?' said I. 'Can't tell,' said he; 'but so it is: the bar bite the bark and wood too, at the highest point from the ground they can reach, and you can tell, by the marks,' said he, 'the length of the bar to an inch.' 'Enough,' said I. 'I've learned something here a'ready, and I'll put it in practice.'

"Well, stranger, just one month from that time I killed a bar, and told its exact length before I measured it, by those very marks; and when I did that, I swelled up considerable — I've been a prouder man ever since. So I went on, larning something every day, until I was reckoned a buster and allowed to be decidedly the best bar hunter in my district; and that is a reputation as much harder to earn than to be reckoned first man in Congress, as an iron ramrod is harder than a toadstool. Did the varmint grow over-cunning by being fooled with by green-horn hunters, and by this means get troublesome, they send for me as a matter of course; and thus I do my own hunting, and most of my neighbours'. I walk into the varmints though, and it has become about as much the same to me as drinking. It is told in two sentences — a bar is started, and he is killed. The thing is somewhat monotonous now — I know just how much they will run, where they will tire, how much they will growl, and what a thundering time I will have in getting them home. I could give you the history of the chase with all particulars at the commencement, I know the signs so well — *Stranger, I'm certain.* Once I met with a match though, and I will tell you about it; for a common hunt would not be worth relating.

"On a fine fall day, long time ago, I was trailing about for bar, and what should I see but fresh marks on the sassafras trees, about eight inches above any in the forests that I knew of. Says I, 'them marks is a hoax, or it indicates the d——t bar that was ever grown.' In fact, stranger, I couldn't believe it was real, and I went on. Again I saw the same marks, at the same height, and *I knew the thing lived.* That conviction came home to my soul like an earthquake. Says I, 'here is something a-purpose for me: that bar is mine, or I give up the hunting business.' The very next morning what should I see but a number of buzzards hovering over my cornfield. 'The rascal has been there,' said I, 'for that sign is certain:' and, sure enough, on examining, I found the bones of what had been as beautiful a hog the day before, as was ever raised by a Buckeye. Then I tracked the critter out of the field to the woods, and all the marks he left behind, showed me that he was *the bar*.

"Well, stranger, the first fair chase I ever had with that big critter, I saw him no less than three distinct times at a distance: the dogs run him over eighteen miles and broke down, my horse gave out, and I was as nearly used up as a man can be, made on *my* principle, *which is patent*. Before this adventure, such things were unknown to me as possible; but, strange as it was, that bar got me used to it before I was done with him; for he got so at last, that he would leave me on a long chase *quite easy*. How he did it, I never could understand. That a bar runs at all, is puzzling; but how this one could tire down and bust up a pack of hounds and a horse, that were used to overhauling everything they started after in no time, was past my understanding. Well, stranger, that bar finally go so sassy, that he used to help himself to a hog off my premises whenever he wanted one; the buzzards followed after what he left, and so between *bar and buzzard*, I rather think I was *out of pork*.

"Well, missing that bar so often took hold of my vitals, and I wasted away. The thing had been carried to far, and it reduced me in flesh faster than an ager. I would see that bar in every thing I did: *he hunted me*, and that, too, like a devil, which I began to think he was. While in this fix, I made preparations to give him a last brush, and be done with it. Having completed every thing to my satisfaction, I started at sunrise, and to my great joy, I discovered from the way the dogs run, that they were near him; finding his trail was nothing, for that had become as plain to the pack as a turnpike road. On we went, and coming to an open country, what should I see but the bar very leisurely ascending a hill, and the dogs close at his heels, either a match for him in speed, or else he did not care to get out of their way — I don't know which. But wasn't he a beauty, though? I loved him like a brother.

"On he went, until he came to a tree, the limbs of which formed a crotch about six feet from the ground. Into this crotch he got and seated himself, the dogs yelling all around it; and there he sat eyeing them as quiet as a pond in low water. A green-horn friend of mine, in company, reached shooting distance before me, and blazed away, hitting the critter in the centre of his forehead. The bar shook his head as the ball struck it, and then walked down from that tree as gently as a lady would from a carriage. 'Twas a beautiful sight to see him do that — he was in such a rage that he seemed to be as little afraid of the dogs as if they had been sucking pigs; and the dogs warn't slow in making a ring around him at a respectful distance, I tell you; even Bowie-knife, himself, stood off. Then the way his eyes flashed — why the fire of them would have singed a cat's hair; in fact that bar was in a *wrath all over*. Only one pup came near him, and he was brushed out so totally with the bar's left paw, that he entirely disappeared; and that made the old dogs more cautious still. In the mean time, I came up, and taking deliberate aim as a man should do, at his side, just back of his foreleg, *if my gun did not snap*, call me a coward, and I won't take it personal. Yes, stranger, *it snapped*, and I could not find a cap about my person. While in this predicament, I turned round to my fool friend — says I, 'Bill,' says I, 'you're an ass — you're a fool — you might as well have tried to kill that bar by barking the tree under his belly, as to have done it by hitting him in the head. Your shot has made a tiger of him, and blast me, if a dog gets killed or wounded when they come to blows, I will stick my knife into your liver, I will — ' my wrath was up. I had lost my caps, my gun had snapped, the fellow with me had fired at the bar's head, and I expected every moment to see him close in with the dogs, and kill a dozen of them at least. In this thing I was mistaken, for the bar leaped over the ring formed by the dogs, and giving a fierce growl, was off — the pack, of course, in full cry after him. The run this time was short, for coming to the edge of a lake the varmint jumped in, and swam to a little island in the lake, which it reached just a moment before the dogs. 'I'll have him now,' said I, for I had found my caps in the *lining of my coat* — so, rolling a log into the lake, I paddled myself across to the island, just as the dogs had cornered the bar in a thicket. I rushed up and fired — at the same time the critter leaped over the dogs and came within three feet of me, running like mad; he jumped into the lake, and tried to mount the log I had just deserted, but every time he got half his body on it, it would roll over and send him under; the dogs, too, got around him, and pulled him about, and finally Bowie-knife clenched with him, and they sunk into the lake together. Stranger, about this time, I was excited, and I stripped off my coat, drew my knife, and intended to have taken a part with Bowie-knife myself, when the bar rose to the surface. But the varmint staid under — Bowie-knife came up alone, more dead than alive, and with the pack came ashore. 'Thank God,' said I, 'the old villain has got his deserts at last.' Determined to have the body, I cut a grape-vine for a rope, and dove down where I could see the bar in the water, fastened my queer rope to his leg, and fished him, with great difficulty, ashore. Stranger, may I be chawed to death by young alligators, if the thing I looked at wasn't a *she bar, and not the old critter after all*. The way matters got mixed on that island was onaccountably curious, and thinking of it made me more than ever convinced that I was hunting the devil himself. I went home that night and took to my bed — the thing was killing me. The entire team of Arkansaw in bar-hunting, acknowledged himself used up, and the fact sunk into my feelings like a snagged boat will in the Mississippi. I grew as cross as a bar with two cubs and a sore tail. The thing got out 'mong my neighbours, and I was asked how come on that individu-al that never lost a bar when once started? and if that same individu-al didn't wear telescopes when he turned a she bar, of ordinary size, into an old he one, a little larger than a horse? 'Perhaps,' said I, 'friends' — getting wrathy — 'perhaps you want to call somebody a liar,' 'Oh, no,' said they, 'we only heard such things as being *rather common* of late, but we don't believe one word of it; oh, no,' — and then they would ride off and laugh like so many hyenas over a dead nigger. It was too much, and I determined to catch that bar, go to Texas, or die, — and I made my preparations accordin'. I had the pack shut up and rested. I took my rifle to pieces and iled it. I put caps in every pocket about my person, *for fear of the lining.* I then told my neighbours, that on Monday morning — naming the day — I would start THAT BAR, and bring him home with me, or they might divide my settlement among them, the owner having disappeared. Well, stranger, on the morning previous to the great day of my hunting expedition, I went into the woods near my house, taking my gun and Bowie-knife along, just *from habit,* and there sitting down also from habit, what should I see, getting over my fence, but *the bar!* Yes, the old varmint was within a hundred yards of me, and the way he walked *over that fence* — stranger, he loomed up like a *black mist,* he seemed so large, and he walked right towards me. I raised myself, took deliberate aim, and fired. Instantly the varmint wheeled, gave a yell, and *walked through the fence* like a falling tree would through a cobweb. I started after, but was tripped up by my inexpressibles, which either from habit, or the excitement of the moment, were about my heels, and before I had really gathered myself up, I heard the old varmint groaning in a thicket near by, like a thousand sinners, and by the time I reached him he was a corpse. Stranger, it took five niggers and myself to put the carcase on a mule's back, and old long-ears waddled under the load, as if he was foundered in every leg of his body, and with a common whopper of a bar, he would have trotted off, and enjoyed himself. 'Twould astonish you to know how big he was: I made a *bed-spread of his skin,* and the way it used to cover my bar mattress, and leave several feet on each side to tuck up, would have delighted you. It was in fact a creation bar, and if it had lived in Samson's time, and had met him, in a fair fight, it would have licked him in the twinkling of a dice-box. But, strangers, I never like the way I hunted, and *missed him*. There is something curious about it, I could never understand, — and I never was satisfied at his giving in so easy at last. Prehaps, he had heard of my preparations to hunt him the next day, so he jist come in, like Capt. Scott's coon, to save his wind to grunt with in dying; but that ain't likely. My private opinion is, that that bar was an *unhuntable bar, and died when his time come.*"

When the story was ended, our hero sat some minutes with his auditors in a grave silence; I saw there was a mystery to him connected with the bear whose death he had just related, that had evidently made a strong impression on his mind. It was also evident that there was some superstitious awe connected with the affair, — a feeling common with all "children of the wood," when they meet with any thing out of their everyday experience. He was the first one, however, to break the silence, and jumping up, he asked all present to "liquor" before going to bed, — a thing which he did, with a number of companions, evidently to his heart's content.

Long before day, I was put ashore at my place of destination, and I can only follow with the reader, in imagination, our Arkansas friend, in his adventures at the "Forks of Cypress" on the Mississippi.

# Edgar Allan Poe (1809–1849)

ONE DOES NOT know whether to weep in anguish or explode in rage when one considers the life of Poe. Left an orphan at three by the death of parents who were traveling actors; adopted and then rejected as a boy by a rich and close-fisted foster father; poor all his life; frail in health; widowed when the young wife he adored died; scorned as a ne'er-do-well when no man worked harder as an editor and a writer of poetry, short stories, and criticism; dead at forty and viciously lied about by his literary executor, a man ambitious to make a name for himself; yet Poe was one of America's and the world's greatest literary geniuses. He was born in Boston and reared in Richmond. He attended the University of Virginia and later West Point where he neglected military duty for his writing and was dismissed. He was only eighteen when his first book of poems, *Tamerlane*, was published. A short story, "Ms. Found in a Bottle," published in 1833, also bestowed early fame on him. This was to be followed by many more short stories, all of them renowned today. Among them was the world's first detective story, "Murders in the Rue Morgue." In spite of the great popularity of his poem, "The Raven," Poe was no ornithologist. It would have been extremely difficult for a raven to perch above his chamber door. Ravens are as big as turkeys.

"The Cask of Amontillado" is a classic horror story. While Poe was in the army, he was stationed at Fort Independence on Castle Island in Boston Harbor. There he learned of a murder that had taken place in the fort ten years earlier. A young lieutenant, Robert F. Massie, was accused of cheating at cards by an older officer and was killed in the sword duel that followed at dawn on Christmas Day in 1817. Massie's killer was detested by his fellow officers. Soon after the duel he mysteriously disappeared. Poe discovered that, to avenge Massie, his friends had gotten the killer drunk, taken him to the deepest dungeon in the fort, chained him to the floor of a niche there, walled it up, and left him to die. With the background changed to Italy, "The Cask of Amontillado" was published in *Godey's Lady's Book* in 1846. Fifty-nine years later, in 1905, workmen renovating the fort knocked down a wall and discovered a skeleton's bones in the tattered remnants of an 1812 army uniform. "For the half of a century no mortal has disturbed them," Poe wrote at the end of his story. Poe's "fiction" proved to be historical fact.

# The Cask of Amontillado

THE THOUSAND injuries of Fortunato I had borne as I best could; but when he ventured upon insult, I vowed revenge. You, who so well know the nature of my soul, will not suppose, however, that I gave utterance to a threat. *At length* I would be avenged; this was a point definitively settled — but the very definitiveness with which it was resolved, precluded the idea of risk. I must not only punish, but punish with impunity. A wrong is unredressed when retribution overtakes its redresser. It is equally unredressed when the avenger fails to make himself felt as such to him who has done the wrong.

It must be understood, that neither by word nor deed had I given Fortunato cause to doubt my good-will. I continued, as was my wont, to smile in his face, and he did not perceive that my smile *now* was at the thought of his immolation.

He had a weak point — this Fortunato — although in other regards he was a man to be respected and even feared. He prided himself on his connoisseurship in wine. Few Italians have the true virtuoso spirit. For the most part their enthusiasm is adopted to suit the time and opportunity — to practise imposture upon the British and Austrian *millionnaires*. In painting and gemmary Fortunato, like his countrymen, was a quack — but in the matter of old wines he was sincere. In this respect I did not differ from him materially: I was skilful in the Italian vintages myself, and bought largely whenever I could.

It was about dusk, one evening during the supreme madness of the carnival season, that I encountered my friend. He accosted me with excessive warmth, for he had been drinking much. The man wore motley. He had on a tight-fitting parti-striped dress, and his head was surmounted by the conical cap and bells. I was so pleased to see him, that I thought I should never have done wringing his hand.

I said to him: "My dear Fortunato, you are luckily met. How remarkably well you are looking to-day! But I have received a pipe of what passes for Amontillado, and I have my doubts."

"How?" said he. "Amontillado? A pipe? Impossible! And in the middle of the carnival!"

"I have my doubts," I replied; "and I was silly enough to pay the full Amontillado price without consulting you in the matter. You were not to be found, and I was fearful of losing a bargain."

"Amontillado!"

"I have my doubts."

"Amontillado!"

"And I must satisfy them."

"Amontillado!"

"As you are engaged, I am on my way to Luchesi. If any one has a critical turn, it is he. He will tell me — "

"Luchesi cannot tell Amontillado from Sherry."

"And yet some fools will have it that his taste is a match for your own."

"Come, let us go."

"Whither?"

"To your vaults."

"My friend, no; I will not impose upon your good nature. I perceive you have an engagment. Luchesi — "

"I have no engagement; — come."

"My friend, no. It is not the engagement, but the severe cold with which I perceive you are afflicted. The vaults are insufferably damp. They are encrusted with nitre."

"Let us go, nevertheless. The cold is merely nothing. Amontillado! You have been imposed upon. And as for Luchesi, he cannot distinguish Sherry from Amontillado."

Thus speaking, Fortunato possessed himself of my arm. Putting on a mask of black silk, and drawing a *roquelaire* closely about my person, I suffered him to hurry me to my palazzo.

There were no attendants at home; they had absconded to make merry in honor of the time. I had told them that I should not return until the morning, and had given them explicit orders not to stir from the house. These orders were sufficient, I well knew, to insure their immediate disappearance, one and all, as soon as my back was turned.

I took from their sconces two flambeaux, and giving one to Fortunato, bowed him through several suites of rooms to the archway that led into the vaults. I passed down a long and winding staircase, requesting him to be cautious as he followed. We came at length to the foot of the descent, and stood together on the damp ground of the catacombs of the Montresors.

The gait of my friend was unsteady, and the bells upon his cap jingled as he strode.

"The pipe?" said he.

"It is farther on," said I; "but observe the white web-work which gleams from these cavern walls."

He turned toward me, and looked into my eyes with two filmy orbs that distilled the rheum of intoxication.

"Nitre?" he asked, at length.

"Nitre," I replied. "How long have you had that cough?"

"Ugh! ugh! ugh! — ugh! ugh! ugh! — ugh! ugh! ugh! — ugh! ugh! ugh! — ugh! ugh! ugh!"

My poor friend found it impossible to reply for many minutes.

"It is nothing," he said, at last.

"Come," I said, with decision, "we will go back; your health is precious. You are rich, respected, admired, beloved; you are happy, as once I was. You are a man to be missed. For me it is no matter. We will go back; you will be ill, and I cannot be responsible. Besides, there is Luchesi — "

"Enough," he said; "the cough is a mere nothing; it will not kill me. I shall not die of a cough."

"True — true," I replied; "and, indeed, I had no intention of alarming you unnecessarily; but you should use all proper caution. A draught of this Medoc will defend us from the damps."

Here I knocked off the neck a bottle which I drew from a long row of its fellows that lay upon the mould.

"Drink," I said, presenting him the wine.

He raised it to his lips with a leer. He paused and nodded to me familiarly, while his bells jingled.

"I drink," he said, "to the buried that repose around us."

"And I to your long life."

He again took my arm, and we proceeded.

"These vaults," he said, "are extensive."

"The Montresors," I replied, "were a great and numerous family."

"I forget your arms."

"A huge human foot d'or, in a field azure; the foot crushes a serpent rampant whose fangs are imbedded in the heel."

"And the motto?"

"*Nemo me impune lacessit.*"

"Good!" he said.

The wine sparkled in his eyes and the bells jingled. My own fancy grew warm with the Medoc. We had passed through walls of piled bones, with casks and puncheons intermingling, into the inmost recesses of the catacombs. I paused again, and this time I made bold to seize Fortunato by an arm above the elbow.

"The nitre!" I said; "see, it increases. It hangs like moss upon the vaults. We are below the river's bed. The drops of moisture trickle among the bones. Come, we will go back ere it is too late. Your cough — "

"It is nothing," he said; "let us go on. But first, another draught of the Medoc."

I broke and reached him a flagon of De Grâve. He emptied it at a breath. His eyes flashed with a fierce light. He laughed and threw the bottle upward with a gesticulation I did not understand.

I looked at him in surprise. He repeated the movement — a grotesque one.

"You do not comprehend?" he said.

"Not I," I replied.

"Then you are not of the brotherhood."

"How?"

"You are not of the masons."

"Yes, yes," I said; "yes, yes."

"You? Impossible! A mason?"

"A mason," I replied.

"A sign," he said.

"It is this," I answered, producing a trowel from beneath the folds of my *roquelaire*.

"You jest," he exclaimed, recoiling a few paces. "But let us proceed to the Amontillado."

"Be it so," I said, replacing the tool beneath the cloak, and again offering him my arm. He leaned upon it heavily. We continued our route in search of the Amontillado. We passed through a range of low arches, descended, passed on, and descending again, arrived at a deep crypt, in which the foulness of the air caused our flambeaux rather to glow than flame.

At the most remote end of the crypt there appeared another less spacious. Its walls had been lined with human remains, piled to the vault overhead, in the fashion of the great catacombs of Paris. Three sides of this interior crypt were still ornamented in this manner. From the fourth the bones had been thrown down, and lay promiscuously upon the earth, forming at one point a mound of some size. Within the wall thus exposed by the displacing of the bones, we perceived a still interior recess, in depth about four feet, in width three, in height six or seven. It seemed to have been constructed for no especial use within itself, but formed merely the interval between two of the colossal supports of the roof of the catacombs, and was backed by one of their circumscribing walls of solid granite.

It was in vain the Fortunato, uplifting his dull torch, endeavored to pry into the depth of the recess. Its termination the feeble light did not enable us to see.

"Proceed," I said; "herein is the Amontillado. As for Luchesi — "

"He is an ignoramus," interrupted my friend, as he stepped unsteadily forward, while I followed immediately at his heels. In an instant he had reached the extremity of the niche, and finding his progress arrested by the rock, stood stupidly bewildered. A moment more and I had fettered him to the granite. In its surface were two iron staples, distant from each other about two feet, horizontally. From one of these depended a short chain, from the other a padlock. Throwing the links about his waist, it was but the work of a few seconds to secure it. He was too much astounded to resist. Withdrawing the key I stepped back from the recess.

"Pass your hand," I said, "over the wall; you cannot help feeling the nitre. Indeed it is *very* damp. Once more let me *implore* you to return. No? Then I must positively leave you. But I must first render you all the little attentions in my power."

"The Amontillado!" ejaculated my friend, not yet recovered from his astonishment.

"True," I replied; "the Amontillado."

As I said these words I busied myself among the piles of bones of which I have before spoken. Throwing them aside, I soon uncovered a quantity of building stone and mortar. With these materials and with the aid of my trowel, I began vigorously to wall up the entrance of the niche.

I hard scarcely laid the first tier of the masonry when I discovered that the intoxication of Fortunato had in a great measure worn off. The earliest indication I had of this was a low moaning cry from the depth of the recess. It was *not* the cry of a drunken man. There was then a long and obstinate silence. I laid the second tier, and the third, and the fourth; and then I heard the furious vibrations of the chain. The noise lasted for several minutes during which, that I might hearken to it with the more satisfaction, I ceased my labors and sat down upon the bones. When at last the clanking subsided, I resumed the trowel, and finished without interruption the fifth, the sixth, and the seventh tier. The wall was now nearly upon a level with my breast. I again paused, and holding the flambeaux over the mason-work, threw a few feeble rays upon the figure within.

A succession of loud and shrill screams, bursting suddenly from the throat of the chained form, seemed to thrust me violently back. For a brief moment I hesitated — I trembled. Unsheathing my rapier, I began to grope with it about the recess; but the thought of an instant reassured me. I placed my hand upon the solid fabric of the catacombs, and felt satisfied. I reapproached the wall. I replied to the yells of him who clamored. I re-echoed — I aided — I surpassed them in volume and in strength. I did this, and the clamorer grew still.

It was now midnight, and my task was drawing to a close. I had completed the eighth, the ninth, and the tenth tier. I had finished a portion of the last and the eleventh; there remained but a single stone to be fitted and plastered in. I struggled with its weight; I placed it partially in its destined position. But now there came from out the niche a low laugh that erected the hairs upon my head. It was succeeded by a sad voice, which I had difficulty in recognizing as that of the noble Fortunato. The voice said —

"Ha! ha! ha! — he! he! — a very good joke indeed — an excellent jest. We will have many a rich laugh about it at the palazzo — he! he! he! — over our wine — he! he! he!"

"The Amontillado!" I said.

"He! he! he! — he! he! he! — yes, the Amontillado. But is it not getting late? Will not they be awaiting us at the palazzo, the Lady Fortunato and the rest? Let us be gone."

"Yes," I said, "let us be gone."

*"For the love of God, Montresor!"*

"Yes," I said, "for the love of God!"

But to these words I hearkened in vain for a reply. I grew impatient. I called aloud:

"Fortunato!"

No answer. I called again:

"Fortunato!"

No answer still. I thrust a torch through the remaining aperture and let it fall within. There came forth in return only a jingling of the bells. My heart grew sick — on account of the dampness of the catacombs. I hastened to make an end of my labor. I forced the last stone into its position; I plastered it up. Against the new masonry I re-erected the old rampart of bones. For the half of a century no mortal has disturbed them. *In pace requiescat!*

# Herman Melville (1818–1891)

OF ALL American writers Melville had the most adventurous life. He was born in New York City in 1819 of English and Dutch colonial ancestry. When he was twelve years old, his father, a bankrupt, died and left Melville's mother destitute with eight children to support. Herman worked at odd jobs and at fifteen shipped as a cabin boy to Liverpool. Two years later he sailed on a whaler for the South Seas, an eighteen-month voyage that was to be the basis for *Moby Dick*. He jumped ship at the Marquesas, was captured and held prisoner by savages. He escaped on an Australian trader from which he deserted and became a field laborer in Tahiti, left there on another whaler, left it and in Honolulu enlisted as an ordinary seaman aboard a U. S. frigate which a year later brought him home to America, where he started writing. His first five books of his experiences made him a literary idol. He bought a Massachusetts farm, became close friends with Nathaniel Hawthorne, a neighbor, and in 1851 wrote *Moby Dick*. Today it seems incredible that *Moby Dick*, so universally judged a masterpiece, cost Melville his popularity. The books that followed were ignored by a public which preferred his more exotic romances. In 1856 a collection of his magnificent short stories, *The Piazza Tales*, was published and was soon out of print. One more poorly received novel followed and he wrote no more prose, save for the novella, *Billy Budd*, and turned to verse. Poor and forgotten, he begged for jobs and finally landed one as a minor customs inspector. He worked at this for thirteen years until his death in 1891. Melville remained forgotten until the 1920s when readers were startled to discover what a great American literary treasure had been buried for so long.

"Bartleby the Scrivener," this tale of the clerk from the Dead Letter Office, has been applauded countless times as "America's greatest short story." The words are too mundane to convey the awe a reader can feel. If ever a story was "fourth dimensional" it is "Bartleby the Scrivener." Many readers have been startled after finishing it to find themselves back in the everyday world. Yet there is a terrible reality to the story. It was published in 1853 in *Putnam's Magazine*, the editor of which rejected a later story for fear of "offending the religious sensibilities of the public and the congregation of Grace Church."

# Bartleby the Scrivener

I AM A rather elderly man. The nature of my avocations, for the last thirty years, has brought me into more than ordinary contact with what would seem an interesting and somewhat singular set of men, of whom, as yet, nothing, that I know of, has ever been written — I mean, the law-copyists, or scriveners. I have known very many of them, professionally and privately, and, if I pleased, could relate divers histories, at which good-natured gentlemen might smile, and sentimental souls might weep. But I waive the biographies of all other scriveners, for a few passages in the life of Bartleby, who was a scrivener, the strangest I ever saw, or heard of. While, of other law-copyists, I might write the complete life, of Bartleby nothing of that sort can be done. I believe that no materials exist, for a full and satisfactory biography of this man. It is an irreparable loss to literature. Bartleby was one of those beings of whom nothing is ascertainable, except from the original sources, and, in his case, those are very small. What my own astonished eyes saw of Bartleby, *that* is all I know of him, except, indeed, one vague report, which will appear in the sequel.

Ere introducing the scrivener, as he first appeared to me, it is fit I make some mention of myself, my *employés*, my business, my chambers, and general surroundings; because some such description is indispensable to an adequate understanding of the chief character about to be presented. Imprimis: I am a man who, from his youth upwards, has been filled with a profound conviction that the easiest way of life is the best. Hence, though I belong to a profession proverbially energetic and nervous, even to turbulence, at times, yet nothing of that sort have I ever suffered to invade my peace. I am one of those unambitious lawyers who never address a jury, or in any way draw down public applause; but, in the cool tranquillity of a snug retreat, do a snug business among rich men's bonds, and mortgages, and title-deeds. All who know me, consider me an eminently *safe* man. The late John Jacob Astor, a personage little given to poetic enthusiasm, had no hesitation in pronouncing my first grand point to be prudence; my next, method. I do not speak it in vanity, but simply record the fact, that I was not unemployed in my profession by the late John Jacob Astor; a name which, I admit, I love to repeat; for it hath a rounded and orbicular sound to it, and rings like unto bullion. I will freely add, that I was not insensible to the late John Jacob Astor's good opinion.

Some time prior to the period at which this little history begins, my avocations had been largely increased. The good old office, now extinct in the State of New York, of a Master in Chancery, had been conferred upon me. It was not a very arduous office, but very pleasantly remunerative. I seldom lose my temper; much more seldom indulge in dangerous indignation at wrongs and outrages; but I must be permitted to be rash here and declare, that I consider the sudden and violent abrogation of the office of Master in Chancery, by the new Constitution, as a — premature act; inasmuch as I had counted upon a life-lease of the profits, whereas I only received those of a few short years. But this is by the way.

My chambers were upstairs, at No. — Wall Street. At one end, they looked upon the white wall of the interior of a spacious sky-light shaft, penetrating the building from top to bottom.

This view might have been considered rather tame than otherwise,

deficient in what landscape painters call "life." But, if so, the view from
the other end of my chambers offered, at least, a contrast, if nothing
more. In that direction, my windows commanded an unobstructed
view of a lofty brick wall, black by age and everlasting shade; which wall
required no spy-glass to bring out its lurking beauties, but, for the benefit
of all near-sighted spectators, was pushed up to within ten feet of my
windowpanes. Owing to the great height of the surrounding buildings,
and my chambers being on the second floor, the interval between this
wall and mine not a little resembled a huge square cistern.

At the period just preceding the advent of Bartleby, I had two
persons as copyists in my employment, and a promising lad as an office-
boy. First, Turkey; second, Nippers; third, Ginger Nut. These may
seem names, the like of which are not usually found in the Directory.
In truth, they were nicknames, mutually conferred upon each other
by my three clerks, and were deemed expressive of their respective persons
or characters. Turkey was a short, pursy Englishman, of about my own
age — that is, somewhere not far from sixty. In the morning, one
might say, his face was of a fine florid hue, but after twelve o'clock,
meridian — his dinner hour — it blazed like a grate full of Christmas
coals; and continued blazing — but, as it were, with a gradual wane
— till six o'clock, P.M., or thereabouts; after which, I saw no more
of the proprietor of the face, which, gaining its meridian with the sun,
seemed to set with it, to rise, culminate, and decline the following day,
with the like regularity and undiminished glory. There are many
singular coincidences I have known in the course of my life, not the least
among which was the fact, that, exactly when Turkey displayed his
fullest beams from his red and radiant countenance, just then, too, at
that critical moment, began the daily period when I considered his
business capacities as seriously disturbed for the remainder of the
twenty-four hours. Not that he was absolutely idle, or averse to business
then; far from it. The difficulty was, he was apt to be altogether too
energetic. There was a strange, inflamed, flurried, flighty recklessness
of activity about him. He would be incautious in dipping his pen into
his inkstand. All his blots upon my documents were dropped there after
twelve o'clock, meridian. Indeed, not only would he be reckless, and
sadly given to making blots in the afternoon, but, some days, he went
further, and was rather noisy. At such times, too, his face flamed with
augmented blazonry, as if cannel coal had been heaped on anthracite.
He made an unpleasant racket with his chair; spilled his sand-box; in
mending his pens, impatiently split them all to pieces, and threw them
on the floor in a sudden passion; stood up, and leaned over his table,
boxing his papers about in a most indecorous manner, very sad to
behold in an elderly man like him. Nevertheless, as he was in many

ways a most valuable person to me, and all the time before twelve o'clock, meridian, was the quickest, steadiest creature, too, accomplishing a great deal of work in a style not easily to be matched — for these reasons, I was willing to overlook his eccentricities, though, indeed, occasionally, I remonstrated with him. I did this very gently, however, because, though the civilest, nay, the blandest and most reverential of men in the morning, yet, in the afternoon, he was disposed, upon provocation, to be slightly rash with his tongue — in fact, insolent. Now, valuing his morning services as I did, and resolved not to lose them — yet, at the same time, made uncomfortable by his inflamed ways afer twelve o'clock — and being a man of peace, unwilling by my admonitions to call forth unseemly retorts from him, I took upon me, one Saturday noon (he was always worse on Saturdays) to hint to him, very kindly, that, perhaps, now that he was growing old, it might be well to abridge his labors; in short, he need not come to my chambers after twelve o'clock, but, dinner over, had best go home to his lodgings, and rest himself till tea-time. But no; he insisted upon his afternoon devotions. His countenance became intolerably fervid, as he oratorically assured me — gesticulating with a long ruler at the other end of the room — that if his services in the morning were useful, how indispensable, then, in the afternoon?

"With submission, sir," said Turkey, on this occasion, "I consider myself your right-hand man. In the morning I but marshall and deploy my columns; but in the afternoon I put myself at their head, and gallantly charge the foe, thus" — and he made a violent thrust with the ruler.

"But the blots, Turkey," intimated I.

"True; but, with submission, sir, behold these hairs! I am getting old. Surely, sir, a blot or two of a warm afternoon is not to be severely urged against gray hairs. Old age — even if it blot the page — is honorable. With submission, sir, we *both* are getting old."

This appeal to my fellow-feeling was hardly to be resisted. At all events, I saw that go he would not. So, I made up my mind to let him stay, resolving, nevertheless, to see to it that, during the afternoon, he had to do with my less important papers.

Nippers, the second on my list, was a whiskered, sallow, and, upon the whole, rather piratical-looking young man, of about five-and-twenty. I always deemed him the victim of two evil powers — ambition and indigestion. The ambition was evinced by a certain impatience of the duties of a mere copyist, an unwarrantable usurpation of strictly professional affairs, such as the original drawing up of legal documents. The indigestion seemed betokened in an occasional nervous testiness and grinning irritability, causing the teeth to audibly grind together over mistakes committed in copying; unnecessary maledictions, hissed, rather than spoken, in the heat of business; and especially by a continual discontent with the height of the table where he worked. Though of a very ingenious mechanical turn, Nippers could never get this table to suit him. He put chips under it, blocks of various sorts, bits of pasteboard, and at last went so far as to attempt an exquisite adjustment, by final pieces of folded blotting-paper. But no invention would answer. If, for the sake of easing his back, he brought the table-lid at a sharp angle well up towards his chin, and wrote there like a man using the steep roof of a Dutch house for his desk, then he declared that it stopped the circulation in his arms. If now he lowered the table to his waistbands, and stooped over it in writing, then there was a sore aching in his back. In short, the truth of the matter was, Nippers knew not what he wanted. Or, if he wanted anything, it was to be rid of a scrivener's table altogether. Among the manifestations of his diseased ambition was a fondness he had for receiving visits from certain ambiguous-looking fellows in seedy coats, whom he called his clients. Indeed, I was aware that not only was he, at times, considerable of a ward-politician, but he occasionally did a little business at the Justices' courts, and was not unknown on the steps of the Tombs. I have good reason to believe, however, that one individual who called upon him at my chambers, and who, with a grand air, he insisted was his client, was no other than a dun, and the alleged title-deed, a bill. But, with all his failings, and the annoyances he caused me, Nippers, like his compatriot Turkey, was a very useful man to me; wrote a neat, swift hand; and, when he chose, was not deficient in a gentlemanly sort of deportment. Added to this, he always dressed in a gentlemanly sort of way; and so, incidentally, reflected credit upon my chambers. Whereas, with respect to Turkey, I had much ado to keep him from being a reproach to me. His clothes were apt to look oily, and smell of eating-houses. He wore his pantaloons very loose and baggy in summer. His coats were execrable; his hat not to be handled. But while the hat was a thing of indifference to me, inasmuch as his natural civility and deference, as a dependent Englishman, always led him to doff it the moment he entered the room, yet his coat was another matter. Concerning his coats, I reasoned with him; but with no effect. The truth was, I suppose, that a man with so small an income could not afford to sport such a lustrous face and a lustrous coat at one and the same time. As Nippers once observed, Turkey's money went chiefly for red ink. One winter day, I presented Turkey with a highly respectable-looking coat of my own — a padded gray coat, of a most comfortable warmth, and which buttoned straight up from the knee to the neck. I thought Turkey would appreciate the favor, and abate his rashness and obstreperousness of afternoons. But no; I verily believe that buttoning himself up in so downy and blanket-like a coat had a pernicious effect upon him — upon the same principle that too much oats are bad for horses. In fact, precisely as a rash, restive horse is said to feel his oats, so Turkey felt his coat. It made him insolent. He was a man whom prosperity harmed.

Though, concerning the self-indulgent habits of Turkey, I had my own private surmises, yet, touching Nippers, I was well persuaded that, whatever might be his faults in other respects, he was, at least, a temperate young man. But, indeed, nature herself seemed to have been his vintner, and, at his birth, charged him so thoroughly with an irritable, brandy-like disposition, that all subsequent potations were needless. When I consider how, amid the stillness of my chambers, Nippers would sometimes impatiently rise from his seat, and stooping over his table, spread his arms wide apart, seize the whole desk, and move it, and jerk it, with a grim, grinding motion on the floor, as if the table were a perverse voluntary agent, intent on thwarting and vexing him, I plainly perceive that, for Nippers, brandy-and-water were altogether superfluous.

It was fortunate for me that, owing to its peculiar cause — indigestion — the irritability and consequent nervousness of Nippers were mainly observable in the morning, while in the afternoon he was comparatively mild. So that, Turkey's paroxysms only coming on about twelve o'clock, I never had to do with their eccentricities at one time. Their fits relieved each other, like guards. When Nipper's was on, Turkey's was off; and *vice versa*. This was a good natural arrangement, under the circumstances.

Ginger Nut, the third on my list, was a lad, some twelve years old. His father was a carman, ambitious of seeing his son on the bench instead of a cart, before he died. So he sent him to my office, as student at law, errand-boy, cleaner and sweeper, at the rate of one dollar a week. He had a little desk to himself, but he did not use it much. Upon inspection, the drawer exhibited a great array of the shells of various sorts of nuts. Indeed, to this quick-witted youth, the whole noble science of the law was contained in a nutshell. Not the least among the employments of Ginger Nut, as well as one which he discharged with the most alacrity, was his duty as cake and apple purveyor for Turkey and Nippers. Copying law-papers being proverbially a dry, husky sort of business, my two scriveners were fain to moisten their mouths very often with Spitzenbergs, to be had at the numerous stalls nigh the Custom House and Post Office. Also, they sent Ginger Nut very frequently for that peculiar cake — small, flat, round, and very spicy — after which he had been named by them. Of a cold morning, when business was but dull, Turkey would gobble up scores of these cakes, as if they were mere wafers — indeed, they sell them at the rate of six or eight for a penny — the scrape of his pen blending with the crunching of the crisp particles in his mouth. Of all the fiery afternoon blunders and flurried rashnesses of Turkey, was his once moistening a ginger-cake between his lips, and clapping it on to a mortgage, for a seal. I came within an ace of dismissing him then. But he mollified me by making an oriental bow, and saying —

"With submission, sir, it was generous of me to find you in stationery on my own account."

Now my original business — that of a conveyancer and title hunter, and drawer-up of recondite documents of all sorts — was considerably increased by receiving the Master's office. There was now great work for scriveners. Not only must I push the clerks already with me, but I must have additional help.

In answer to my advertisement, a motionless young man one morning stood upon my office threshold, the door being open, for it was summer. I can see that figure now — pallidly neat, pitiably respectable, incurably forlorn! It was Bartleby.

After a few words touching his qualifications, I engaged him, glad to have among my corps of copyists a man of so singularly sedate an aspect, which I thought might operate beneficially upon the flighty temper of Turkey, and the fiery one of Nippers.

I should have stated before that ground-glass folding-doors divided my premises into two parts, one of which was occupied by my scriveners, the other by myself. According to my humor, I threw open these doors, or closed them. I resolved to assign Bartleby a corner by the folding-doors, but on my side of them, so as to have this quiet man within easy call, in case any trifling thing was to be done. I placed his desk close up to a small side-window in that part of the room, a window which originally had afforded a lateral view of certain grimy backyards and bricks, but which, owing to subsequent erections, commanded at present no view at all, though it gave some light. Within three feet of the panes was a wall, and the light came down from far above, between two lofty buildings, as from a very small opening in a dome. Still further to a satisfactory arrangement, I procured a high green folding screen, which might entirely isolate Bartleby from my sight, though not remove him from my voice. And thus, in a manner, privacy and society were conjoined.

At first, Bartleby did an extraordinary quantity of writing. As if long famishing for something to copy, he seemed to gorge himself on my documents. There was no pause for digestion. He ran a day and night line, copying by sunlight and by candlelight. I should have been quite delighted with his application, had he been cheerfully industrious. But he wrote on silently, palely, mechanically.

It is, of course, an indispensable part of a scrivener's business to verify the accuracy of his copy, word by word. Where there are two or more scriveners in an office, they assist each other in this examination, one reading from the copy, the other holding the original. It is a very dull, wearisome, and lethargic affair. I can readily imagine that, to some sanguine temperaments, it would be altogether intolerable. For example, I cannot credit that the mettlesome poet, Byron, would have contentedly sat down with Bartleby to examine a law document of, say five hundred pages, closely written in a crimpy hand.

Now and then, in the haste of business, it had been my habit to assist in comparing some brief document myself, calling Turkey or Nippers for this purpose. One object I had, in placing Bartleby so handy to me behind the screen, was, to avail myself of his services on such trivial occasions. It was on the third day, I think, of his being with me, and before any necessity had arisen for having his own writing examined, that, being much hurried to complete a small affair I had in hand, I abruptly called to Bartleby. In my haste and natural expectancy of instant compliance, I sat with my head bent over the original on my desk, and my right hand sideways, and somewhat nervously extended with the copy, so that, immediately upon emerging from his retreat, Bartleby might snatch it and proceed to business without the least delay.

In this very attitude did I sit when I called to him, rapidly stating what it was I wanted him to do — namely, to examine a small paper with me. Imagine my surprise, nay, my consternation, when, without moving from his privacy, Bartleby, in a singularly mild, firm voice, replied, "I would prefer not to."

I sat awhile in perfect silence, rallying my stunned faculties. Immediately it occurred to me that my ears had deceived me, or Bartleby had entirely misunderstood my meaning. I repeated my request in the clearest tone I could assume; but in quite as clear a one came the previous reply, "I would prefer not to."

"Prefer not to," echoed I, rising in high excitement, and crossing the room with a stride. "What do you mean? Are you moon-struck? I want you to help me compare this sheet here — take it," and I thrust it towards him.

"I would prefer not to," said he.

I looked at him steadfastly. His face was leanly composed; his gray eye dimly calm. Not a wrinkle of agitation rippled him. Had there been the least uneasiness, anger, impatience or impertinence in his manner; in other words, had there been anything ordinarily human about him, doubtless I should have violently dismissed him from the premises. But as it was, I should have as soon thought of turning my pale plaster-of-paris bust of Cicero out of doors. I stood gazing at him awhile, as he went on with his own writing, and then reseated myself at my desk. This is very strange, thought I. What had one best do? But my business hurried me. I concluded to forget the matter for the present, reserving it for my future leisure. So, calling Nippers from the other room, the paper was speedily examined.

A few days after this, Bartleby concluded four lengthy documents, being quadruplicates of a week's testimony taken before me in my High Court of Chancery. It became necessary to examine them. It was an important suit, and great accuracy was imperative. Having all things arranged, I called Turkey, Nippers, and Ginger Nut from the next room, meaning to place the four copies in the hands of my four clerks, while I should read from the original. Accordingly, Turkey, Nippers, and Ginger Nut had taken their seats in a row, each with his document in his hand, when I called to Bartleby to join this interesting group.

"Bartleby! quick, I am waiting."

I heard a slow scrape of his chair legs on the uncarpeted floor, and soon he appeared standing at the entrance of his hermitage.

"What is wanted?" said he, mildly.

"The copies, the copies," said I, hurriedly. "We are going to examine them. There" — and I held towards him the fourth quadruplicate.

"I would prefer not to," he said, and gently disappeared behind the screen.

For a few moments I was turned into a pillar of salt, standing at the head of my seated column of clerks. Recovering myself, I advanced towards the screen, and demanded the reason for such extraordinary conduct.

"*Why* do you refuse?"

"I would prefer not to."

With any other man I should have flown outright into a dreadful passion, scorned all further words, and thrust him ignominiously from my presence. But there was something about Bartleby that not only strangely disarmed me, but, in a wonderful manner, touched and disconcerted me. I began to reason with him.

"These are your own copies we are about to examine. It is labor saving to you, because one examination will answer for your four papers. It is common usage. Every copyist is bound to help examine his copy. Is it not so? Will you not speak? Answer!"

"I prefer not to," he replied in a flute-like tone. It seemed to me that, while I had been addressing him, he carefully revolved every statement that I made; fully comprehended the meaning; could not gainsay the irresistible conclusion; but, at the same time, some paramount consideration prevailed with him to reply as he did.

"You are decided, then, not to comply with my request — a request made according to common usage and common sense?"

He briefly gave me to understand, that on that point my judgment was sound. Yes: his decision was irreversible.

It is not seldom the case that, when a man is browbeaten in some unprecedented and violently unreasonable way, he beings to stagger in his own plainest faith. He begins, as it were, vaguely to surmise that, wonderful as it may be, all the justice and all the reason is on the other side. Accordingly, if any disinterested persons are present, he turns to them for some reinforcement for his own faltering mind.

"Turkey," said I, "what do you think of this? Am I not right?"

"With submission, sir," said Turkey, in his blandest tone, "I think that you are."

"Nippers," said I, "what do *you* think of it?"

"I think I should kick him out of the office."

(The reader of nice perceptions will here perceive that, it being morning, Turkey's answer is couched in polite and tranquil terms, but Nippers replies in ill-tempered ones. Or, to repeat a previous sentence, Nippers's ugly mood was on duty, and Turkey's off.)

"Ginger Nut," said I, willing to enlist the smallest suffrage in my behalf, "what do *you* think of it?"

"I think, sir, he's a little *luny*," replied Ginger Nut, with a grin.

"You hear what they say," said I, turning towards the screen, "come forth and do your duty."

But he vouchsafed no reply. I pondered a moment in sore perplexity. But once more business hurried me. I determined again to postpone the consideration of this dilemma to my future leisure. With a little trouble we made out to examine the papers without Bartleby, though at every page or two Turkey deferentially dropped his opinion, that this proceeding was quite out of the common; while Nippers, twitching in his chair with a dyspeptic nervousness, ground out, between his set teeth, occasional hissing maledictions against the stubborn oaf behind the screen. And for his (Nippers's) part, this was the first and the last time he would do another man's business without pay.

Meanwhile Bartleby sat in his hermitage, oblivious to everything but his own peculiar business there.

Some days passed, the scrivener being employed upon another lengthy work. His late remarkable conduct led me to regard his ways narrowly. I observed that he never went to dinner; indeed, that he never went anywhere. As yet I had never, of my personal knowledge, known him to be outside of my office. He was a perpetual sentry in the corner. At about eleven o'clock though, in the morning, I noticed that Ginger Nut would advance toward the opening in Bartleby's screen, as if silently beckoned thither by a gesture invisible to me where I sat. The boy would then leave the office, jingling a few pence, and reappear with a handful of ginger-nuts, which he delivered in the hermitage, receiving two of the cakes for his trouble.

He lives, then, on ginger-nuts, thought I; never eats a dinner, properly speaking; he must be a vegetarian, then, but no; he never eats even vegetables, he eats nothing but ginger-nuts. My mind then ran on in reveries concerning the probable effects upon the human constitution of living entirely on ginger-nuts. Ginger-nuts are so called, because they contain ginger as one of their peculiar constituents, and the final flavoring one. Now, what was ginger? A hot, spicy thing. Was Bartleby hot and spicy? Not at all. Ginger, then, had no effect upon Bartleby. Probably he preferred it should have none.

Nothing so aggravates an earnest person as a passive resistance. If the individual so resisted be of a not inhumane temper, and the resisting one perfectly harmless in his passivity, then, in the better moods of the former, he will endeavor charitably to construe to his imagination what proves impossible to be solved by his judgment. Even so, for the most part, I regarded Bartleby and his ways. Poor fellow! thought I, he means no mischief; it is plain he intends no insolence; his aspect sufficiently evinces that his eccentricities are involuntary. He is useful to me. I can get along with him. If I turn him away, the chances are he will fall in with some less indulgent employer, and then he will be rudely treated, and perhaps driven forth miserably to starve. Yes. Here I can cheaply purchase a delicious self-approval. To befriend Bartleby; to humor him in his strange wilfulness, will cost me little or nothing, while I lay up in my soul what will eventually prove a sweet morsel for my conscience. But this mood was not invariable with me. The passiveness of Bartleby sometimes irritated me. I felt strangely goaded on to encounter him in new opposition — to elicit some angry spark from him answerable to my own. But, indeed, I might as well have essayed to strike fire with my knuckles against a bit of Windsor soap. But one afternoon the evil impulse in me mastered me, and the following little scene ensued:

"Bartleby," said I, "when those papers are all copied, I will compare them with you."

"I would prefer not to."

"How? Surely you do not mean to persist in that mulish vagary?" No answer.

I threw open the folding-doors near by, and turning upon Turkey and Nippers, exclaimed:

"Bartleby a second time says, he won't examine his papers. What do you think of it, Turkey?"

It was afternoon, be it remembered. Turkey sat glowing like a brass boiler; his bald head steaming; his hands reeling among his blotted papers.

"Think of it?" roared Turkey. "I think I'll just step behind his screen, and black his eyes for him!"

So saying, Turkey rose to his feet and threw his arms into a pugilistic position. He was hurrying away to make good his promise, when I detained him, alarmed at the effect of incautiously rousing Turkey's combativeness after dinner.

"Sit down, Turkey," said I, "and hear what Nippers has to say. What do you think of it, Nippers? Would I not be justified in immediately dismissing Bartleby?"

"Excuse me, that is for you to decide, sir. I think his conduct quite unusual, and, indeed, unjust, as regards Turkey and myself. But it may only be a passing whim."

"Ah," exclaimed I, "you have strangely changed your mind, then — you speak very gently of him now."

"All beer," cried Turkey; "gentleness is effects of beer — Nippers and I dined together to-day. You see how gentle *I* am, sir. Shall I go and black his eyes?"

"You refer to Bartleby, I suppose. No, not to-day, Turkey," I replied; "pray, put up your fists."

I closed the doors, and again advanced towards Bartleby. I felt additional incentives tempting me to my fate. I burned to be rebelled against again. I remembered that Bartleby never left the office.

"Bartleby," said I, "Ginger Nut is away; just step around to the post-office, won't you?" (it was but a three minutes' walk) "and see if there is anything for me."

"I would prefer not to."

"You *will* not?"

"I *prefer* not."

I staggered to my desk, and sat there in a deep study. My blind inveteracy returned. Was there any other thing in which I could procure myself to be ignominiously repulsed by this lean, penniless wight? — my hired clerk? What added thing is there, perfectly reasonable, that he will be sure to refuse to do?

"Bartleby!"

No answer.

"Bartleby," in a louder tone.

No answer.

"Bartleby," I roared.

Like a very ghost, agreeably to the laws of magical invocation, at the third summons, he appeared at the entrance of his hermitage.

"Go to the next room, and tell Nippers to come to me."

"I prefer not to," he respectfully and slowly said, and mildly disappeared.

"Very good, Bartleby," said I, in a quiet sort of serenely-severe self-possessed tone, intimating the unalterable purpose of some terrible retribution very close at hand. At the moment I half intended something of the kind. But upon the whole, as it was drawing towards my dinner-hour, I thought it best to put on my hat and walk home for the day, suffering much from perplexity and distress of mind.

Shall I acknowledge it? The conclusion of this whole business was, that it soon became a fixed fact of my chambers, that a pale young scrivener, by the name of Bartleby, had a desk there; that he copied for me at the usual rate of four cents a folio (one hundred words); but he was permanently exempt from examining the work done by him, that duty being transferred to Turkey and Nippers, out of compliment, doubtless, to their superior acuteness; moreover, said Bartleby was never, on any account, to be dispatched on the most trivial errand of any sort; and that even if entreated to take upon him such a matter, it was generally understood that he would "prefer not to" —in other words, that he would refuse point-blank.

As days passed on, I became considerably reconciled to Bartleby. His steadiness, his freedom from all dissipation, his incessant industry (except when he chose to throw himself into a standing revery behind his screen), his great stillness, his unalterableness of demeanor under all circumstances, made him a valuable acquisition. One prime thing was this — *he was always there* — first in the morning, continually through the day, and the last at night. I had a singular confidence in his honesty. I felt my most precious papers perfectly safe in his hands. Sometimes, to be sure, I could not, for the very soul of me, avoid falling into sudden spasmodic passions with him. For it was exceeding difficult to bear in mind all the time those strange peculiarities, privileges, and unheard-of exemptions, forming the tacit stipulations on Bartleby's part under which he remained in my office. Now and then, in the eagerness of dispatching pressing business, I would inadvertently summon Bartleby, in a short, rapid tone, to put his finger, say, on the incipient tie of a bit of red tape with which I was about compressing some papers. Of course, from behind the screen the usual answer, "I prefer not to," was sure to come; and then, how could a human creature, with the common infirmities of our nature, refrain from bitterly exclaiming upon such perverseness — such unreasonableness? However, every added repulse of this sort which I received only tended to lessen the probability of my repeating the inadvertence.

Here it must be said, that, according to the custom of most legal gentlemen occupying chambers in densely-populated law buildings, there were several keys to my door. One was kept by a woman residing in the attic, which person weekly scrubbed and daily swept and dusted my apartments. Another was kept by Turkey for convenience sake. The third I sometimes carried in my own pocket. The fourth I knew not who had.

Now, one Sunday morning I happened to go to Trinity Church, to hear a celebrated preacher, and finding myself rather early on the ground I thought I would walk round to my chambers for a while. Luckily I had my key with me; but upon applying it to the lock, I found it resisted by something inserted from the inside. Quite surprised, I called out; when to my consternation a key was turned from within; and thrusting his lean visage at me, and holding the door ajar, the apparition of Bartleby appeared, in his shirt-sleeves, and otherwise in a strangely tattered deshabille, saying quietly that he was sorry, but he was deeply engaged just then, and — preferred not admitting me at present. In a brief word or two, he moreover added, that perhaps I had better walk round the block two or three times, and by that time he would probably have concluded his affairs.

Now, the utterly unsurmised appearance of Bartleby, tenanting my law-chambers of a Sunday morning, with his cadaverously gentlemanly *nonchalance*, yet withal firm and self-possessed, had such a strange effect upon me, that incontinently I slunk away from my own door, and did as desired. But not without sundry twinges of impotent rebellion against the mild effrontery of this unaccountable scrivener. Indeed, it was his wonderful mildness chiefly, which not only disarmed me, but unmanned me, as it were. For I consider that one, for the time, is a sort of unmanned when he tranquilly permits his hired clerk to dictate to him, and order him away from his own premises. Furthermore, I was full of uneasiness as to what Bartleby could possibly be doing in my office in his shirt-sleeves, and in an otherwise dismantled condition of a Sunday morning. Was anything amiss going on? Nay, that was out of the question. It was not to be thought of for a moment that Bartleby was an immoral person. But what could he be doing there? — copying? Nay again, whatever might be his eccentricities, Bartleby was an eminently decorous person. He would be the last man to sit down to his desk in any state approaching to nudity. Besides, it was Sunday; and there was something about Bartleby that forbade the supposition that he would by any secular occupation violate the proprieties of the day.

Nevertheless, my mind was not pacified; and full of a restless curiosity, at last I returned to the door. Without hindrance I inserted my key, opened it and entered. Bartleby was not to be seen. I looked round anxiously, peeped behind his screen; but it was very plain that he was gone. Upon more closely examining the place, I surmised that for an indefinite period Bartleby must have ate, dressed, and slept in my office, and that too without plate, mirror, or bed. The cushioned seat of a rickety old sofa in one corner bore the faint impress of a lean, reclining form. Rolled away under his desk, I found a blanket; under the empty grate, a blacking box and brush; on a chair, a tin basin, with soap and a ragged towel; in a newspaper a few crumbs of ginger-nuts and a morsel of cheese. Yes, thought I, it is evident enough that Bartleby has been making his home here, keeping bachelor's hall all by himself. Immediately then the thought came sweeping across me, what miserable friendlessness and loneliness are here revealed! His poverty is great; but his solitude, how horrible! Think of it. Of a Sunday, Wall Street is deserted as Petra; and every night of every day it is an emptiness. This building, too, which of week-days hums with industry and life, at nightfall echoes with sheer vacancy, and all through Sunday is forlorn. And here Bartleby makes his home; sole spectator of a solitude which he has seen all populous — a sort of innocent and transformed Marius brooding among the ruins of Carthage!

For the first time in my life a feeling of overpowering stinging melancholy seized me. Before, I had never experienced aught but a not unpleasing sadness. The bond of a common humanity now drew me irresistibly to gloom. A fraternal melancholy! For both I and Bartleby were sons of Adam. I remembered the bright silks and sparkling faces I had seen that day, in gala trim, swan-like sailing down the Mississippi of Broadway; and I contrasted them with the pallid copyist, and thought to myself, Ah, happiness courts the light, so we deem the world is gay; but misery hides aloof, so we deem that misery there is none. These sad fancyings — chimeras, doubtless, of a sick and silly brain — led on to other and more special thoughts, concerning the eccentricities of Bartleby. Presentiments of strange discoveries hovered round me. The scrivener's pale form appeared to me laid out, among uncaring strangers, in its shivering winding-sheet.

Suddenly I was attracted by Bartleby's closed desk, the key in open sight left in the lock.

I mean no mischief, seek the gratification of no heartless curiosity, thought I; besides, the desk is mine, and its contents, too, so I will make bold to look within. Everything was methodically arranged, the papers smoothly placed. The pigeon-holes were deep, and removing the files of documents, I groped into their recesses. Presently I felt something there, and dragged it out. It was an old bandanna handkerchief, heavy and knotted. I opened it, and saw it was a saving's bank.

I now recalled all the quiet mysteries which I had noted in the man. I remembered that he never spoke but to answer; that, though at intervals he had considerable time to himself, yet I have never seen him reading — no, not even a newspaper; that for long periods he would stand looking out, at his pale window behind the screen, upon the dead brick wall; I was quite sure he never visited any refectory or eating-house; while his pale face clearly indicated that he never drank beer like Turkey, or tea and coffee even, like other men; that he never went anywhere in particular that I could learn; never went out for a walk, unless, indeed, that was the case at present; that he had declined telling who he was, or whence he came, or whether he had any relatives in the world; that though so thin and pale, he never complained of ill-health. And more than all, I remembered a certain unconscious air of pallid — how shall I call it? — of pallid haughtiness, say, or rather an austere reserve about him, which had positively awed me into my tame compliance with his eccentricities, when I had feared to ask him to do the slightest incidental thing for me, even though I might know, from his long-continued motionlessness, that behind his screen he must be standing in one of those dead-wall reveries of his.

Revolving all these things, and coupling them with the recently discovered fact, that he made my office his constant abiding place and home, and not forgetful of his morbid moodiness; revolving all these things, a prudential feeling began to steal over me. My first emotions had been those of pure melancholy and sincerest pity; but just in proportion as the forlornness of Bartleby grew and grew to my imagination, did that same melancholy merge into fear, that pity into repulsion. So true it is, and so terrible, too, that up to a certain point the thought or sight of misery enlists our best affections; but in certain special cases, beyond that point it does not. They err who would assert that invariably this is owing to the inherent selfishness of the human heart. It rather proceeds from a certain hopelessness of remedying excessive and organic ill. To a sensitive being, pity is not seldom pain. And when at last it is perceived that such pity cannot lead to effectual succor, common sense bids the soul be rid of it. What I saw that morning persuaded me that the scrivener was the victim of innate and incurable disorder. I might give alms to his body; but his body did not pain him; it was his soul that suffered, and his soul I could not reach.

I did not accomplish the purpose of going to Trinity Church that morning. Somehow, the things I had seen disqualified me for the time from church-going. I walked homeward, thinking what I would do with Bartleby. Finally, I resolved upon this — I would put certain calm questions to him the next morning, touching his history, etc., and if he declined to answer them openly and unreservedly (and I supposed he would prefer not), then to give him a twenty dollar bill over and above whatever I might owe him, and tell him his services were no longer required; but that if in any other way I could assist him, I would be happy to do so, especially if he desired to return to his native place, wherever that might be, I would willingly help to defray the expenses. Moreover, if, after reaching home, he found himself at any time in want of aid, a letter from him would be sure of a reply.

The next morning came.

"Bartleby," said I, gently calling to him behind his screen.

No reply.

"Bartleby," said I, in a still gentler tone, "come here; I am not going to ask you to do anything you would prefer not to do — I simply wish to speak to you."

Upon this he noiselessly slid into view.

"Will you tell me, Bartleby, where you were born?"

"I would prefer not to."

"Will you tell me *anything* about yourself?"

"I would prefer not to."

"But what reasonable objection can you have to speak to me? I feel friendly towards you."

He did not look at me while I spoke, but kept his glance fixed upon my bust of Cicero, which, as I then sat, was directly behind me, some six inches above my head.

"What is your answer, Bartleby?" said I, after waiting a considerable time for a reply, during which his countenance remained immovable, only there was the faintest conceivable tremor of the white attenuated mouth.

"At present I prefer to give no answer," he said, and retired into his hermitage.

It was rather weak in me I confess, but his manner, on this occasion, nettled me. Not only did there seem to lurk in it a certain calm disdain, but his perverseness seemed ungrateful, considering the undeniable good usage and indulgence he had received from me.

Again I sat ruminating what I should do. Mortified as I was at his behavior, and resolved as I had been to dismiss him when I entered my office, nevertheless I strangely felt something superstitious knocking at my heart, and forbidding me to carry out my purpose, and denouncing me for a villain if I dared to breathe one bitter word against this forlornest of mankind. At last, familiarly drawing my chair behind his screen, I sat down and said: "Bartleby, never mind, then, about revealing your history; but let me entreat you, as a friend, to comply as far as may be with the usages of this office. Say now, you will help to examine papers to-morrow or next day: in short, say now, that in a day or two you will begin to be a little reasonable: — say so, Bartleby."

"At present I would prefer not to be a little reasonable," was his mildly cadaverous reply.

Just then the folding-doors opened, and Nippers approached. He seemed suffering from an unusually bad night's rest, induced by severer indigestion than common. He overheard those final words of Bartleby.

"*Prefer not*, eh?" gritted Nippers — "I'd *prefer* him, if I were you, sir," addressing me — "I'd *prefer* him; I'd give him preferences, the stubborn mule! What is it, sir, pray, that he *prefers* not to do now?"

Bartleby moved not a limb.

"Mr. Nippers," said I, "I'd prefer that you would withdraw for the present."

Somehow, of late, I had got into the way of involuntarily using this word "prefer" upon all sorts of not exactly suitable occasions. And I trembled to think that my contact with the scrivener had already and seriously affected me in a mental way. And what further and deeper aberration might it not yet produce? This apprehension had not been without efficacy in determining me to summary measures.

As Nippers, looking very sour and sulky, was departing, Turkey blandly and deferentially approached.

"With submission, sir," said he, "yesterday I was thinking about Bartleby here, and I think that if he would but prefer to take a quart of good ale every day, it would do much towards mending him, and enabling him to assist in examining his papers."

"So you have got the word, too," said I, slightly excited.

"With submission, what word, sir?" asked Turkey, respectfully crowding himself into the contracted space behind the screen, and by so doing, making me jostle the scrivener. "What word, sir?"

"I would prefer to be left alone here," said Bartleby, as if offended at being mobbed in his privacy.

"*That's* the word, Turkey," said I — "*that's* it."

"Oh, *prefer*? oh yes — queer word. I never use it myself. But, sir, as I was saying, if he would but prefer — "

"Turkey," interrupted I, "you will please withdraw."

"Oh certainly, sir, if you prefer that I should."

As he opened the folding-door to retire, Nippers at his desk caught a glimpse of me, and asked whether I would prefer to have a certain paper copied on blue paper or white. He did not in the least roguishly accent the word "prefer." It was plain that it involuntarily rolled from his tongue. I thought to myself, surely I must get rid of a demented man, who already has in some degree turned the tongues, if not the heads of myself and clerks. But I thought it prudent not to break the dismission at once.

The next day I noticed that Bartleby did nothing but stand at his window in his dead-wall revery. Upon asking him why he did not write, he said that he had decided upon doing no more writing.

"Why, how now? what next?" exclaimed I, "do no more writing?"

"No more."

"And what is the reason?"

"Do you not see the reason for yourself?" he indifferently replied.

I look steadfastly at him, and perceived that his eyes looked dull and glazed. Instantly it occurred to me, that his unexampled diligence in copying by his dim window for the first few weeks of his stay with me might have temporarily impaired his vision.

I was touched. I said something in condolence with him. I hinted that of course he did wisely in abstaining from writing for a while; and urged him to embrace that opportunity of taking wholesome exercise in the open air. This, however, he did not do. A few days after this, my other clerks being absent, and being in a great hurry to dispatch certain letters by the mail, I thought that, having nothing else earthly to do, Bartleby would surely be less inflexible than usual, and carry these letters to the post-office. But he blankly declined. So, much to my inconvenience, I went myself.

Still added days went by. Whether Bartleby's eyes improved or not, I could not say. To all appearance, I thought they did. But when I asked him if they did, he vouchsafed no answer. At all events, he would do no copying. At last, in reply to my urgings, he informed me that he had permanently given up copying.

"What!" exclaimed I; "suppose your eyes should get entirely well — better than ever before — would you not copy then?"

"I have given up copying," he answered, and slid aside.

He remained as ever, a fixture in my chamber. Nay — if that were possible — he became still more a fixture than before. What was to be done? He would do nothing in the office; why should he stay there? In plain fact, he had now become a millstone to me, not only useless as a necklace, but afflictive to bear. Yet I was sorry for him. I speak less than truth when I say that, on his own account, he occasioned me uneasiness. If he would but have named a single relative or friend, I would instantly have written, and urged their taking the poor fellow away to some convenient retreat. But he seemed alone, absolutely alone in the universe. A bit of wreck in the mid-Atlantic. At length, necessities connected with my business tyrannized over all other considerations. Decently as I could, I told Bartleby that in six days' time he must unconditionally leave the office. I warned him to take measures, in the interval, for procuring some other abode. I offered to assist him in this endeavor, if he himself would but take the first step towards a removal.

"And when you finally quit me, Bartleby," added I, "I shall see that you go not away entirely unprovided. Six days from this hour, remember."

At the expiration of that period, I peeped behind the screen, and lo! Bartleby was there.

I buttoned up my coat, balanced myself; advanced slowly towards him, touched his shoulder, and said, "The time has come; you must quit this place; I am sorry for you; here is money; but you must go."

"I would prefer not," he replied, with his back still towards me.

"You *must*."

He remained silent.

Now I had an unbounded confidence in this man's common honesty. He had frequently restored to me sixpences and shillings carelessly dropped upon the floor, for I am apt to be very reckless in such shirt-button affairs. The proceeding, then, which followed will not be deemed extraordinary.

"Bartleby," said I, "I owe you twelve dollars on account; here are thirty-two; the odd twenty are yours — Will you take it?" and I handed the bills towards him.

But he made no motion.

"I will leave them here, then," putting them under a weight on the table. Then taking my hat and cane and going to the door, I tranquilly turned and added — "After you have removed your things from these offices, Bartleby, you will of course lock the door — since every one is now gone for the day but you — and if you please, slip your key underneath the mat, so that I may have it in the morning. I shall not see you again; so good-bye to you. If, hereafter, in your new place of abode, I can be of any service to you, do not fail to advise me by letter. Good-bye, Bartleby, and fare you well."

But he answered not a word; like the last column of some ruined temple, he remained standing mute and solitary in the middle of the otherwise deserted room.

As I walked home in a pensive mood, my vanity got the better of my pity. I could not but highly plume myself on my masterly management in getting rid of Bartleby. Masterly I call it, and such it must appear to any dispassionate thinker. The beauty of my procedure seemed to consist in its perfect quietness. There was no vulgar bullying, no bravado of any sort, no choleric hectoring, and striding to and fro across the apartment, jerking out vehement commands for Bartleby to bundle himself off with his beggarly traps. Nothing of the kind. Without loudly bidding Bartleby depart — as an inferior genius might have done — I *assumed* the ground that depart he must; and upon that assumption built all I had to say. The more I thought over my procedure, the more I was charmed with it. Nevertheless, next morning, upon awakening,

I had my doubts — I had somehow slept off the fumes of vanity. One of the coolest and wisest hours a man has, is just after he awakes in the morning. My procedure seemed as sagacious as ever — but only in theory. How it would prove in practice — there was the rub. It was truly a beautiful thought to have assumed Bartleby's departure; but, after all, that assumption was simply my own, and none of Bartleby's. The great point was, not whether I had assumed that he would quit me, but whether he would prefer so to do. He was more a man of preferences than assumptions.

After breakfast, I walked down town, arguing the probabilities *pro* and *con*. One moment I thought it would prove a miserable failure, and Bartleby would be found all alive at my office as usual; the next moment it seemed certain that I should find his chair empty. And so I kept veering about. At the corner of Broadway and Canal Street, I saw quite an excited group of people standing in earnest conversation.

"I'll take odds he doesn't," said a voice as I passed.

"Doesn't go? — done!" said I, "put up your money."

I was instinctively putting my hand in my pocket to produce my own, when I remembered that this was an election day. The words I had overheard bore no reference to Bartleby, but to the success or non-success of some candidate for the mayoralty. In my intent frame of mind, I had, as it were, imagined that all Broadway shared in my excitement, and were debating the same question with me. I passed on, very thankful that the uproar of the street screened my momentary absent-mindedness.

As I had intended, I was earlier than usual at my office door. I stood listening for a moment. All was still. He must be gone. I tried the knob. The door was locked. Yes, my procedure had worked to a charm; he indeed must be vanished. Yet a certain melancholy mixed with this: I was almost sorry for my brilliant success. I was fumbling under the door mat for the key, which Bartleby was to have left there for me, when accidentally my knee knocked against a panel, producing a summoning sound, and in response a voice came to me from within — "Not yet; I am occupied."

It was Bartleby.

I was thunderstruck. For an instant I stood like the man who, pipe in mouth, was killed one cloudless afternoon long ago in Virginia, by summer lightning; at his own warm open window he was killed, and remained leaning out there upon the dreamy afternoon, till some one touched him, when he fell.

"Not gone!" I murmured at last. But again obeying that wondrous ascendancy which the inscrutable scrivener had over me, and from which ascendancy, for all my chafing, I could not completely escape, I slowly

went down stairs and out into the street and while walking round the
block, considered what I should next do in this unheard-of perplexity.
Turn the man out by an actual thrusting I could not; to drive him away
by calling him hard names would not do; calling in the police was an
unpleasant idea; and yet, permit him to enjoy his cadaverous triumph
over me — this, too, I could not think of. What was to be done? or, if
nothing could be done, was there anything further that I could *assume* in
the matter? Yes, as before I had prospectively assumed that Bartleby
would depart, so now I might retrospectively assume that departed he
was. In the legitimate carrying out of this assumption, I might enter my
office in a great hurry, and pretending not to see Bartleby at all, walk
straight against him as if he were air. Such a proceeding would in a
singular degree have the appearance of a home-thrust. It was hardly
possible that Bartleby could withstand such an application of the doctrine of assumptions. But upon second thoughts the success of the plan
seemed rather dubious. I resolved to argue the matter over with him
again.

"Bartleby," said I, entering the office, with a quietly severe expression, "I am seriously displeased. I am pained, Bartleby. I had thought
better of you. I had imagined you of such a gentlemanly organization,
that in any delicate dilemma a slight hint would suffice — in short, an
assumption. But it appears I am deceived. Why," I added, unaffectedly
starting, "you have not even touched that money yet," pointing to it, just
where I had left it the evening previous.

He answered nothing.

"Will you, or will you not, quit me?" I now demanded in a sudden
passion, advancing close to him.

"I would prefer *not* to quit you," he replied, gently emphasizing the
*not*.

"What earthly right have you to stay here? Do you pay any rent?
Do you pay my taxes? Or is this property yours?"

He answered nothing.

"Are you ready to go on and write now? Are your eyes recovered?
Could you copy a small paper for me this morning? or help examine a
few lines? or step round to the post-office? In a word, will you do
anything at all, to give a coloring to your refusal to depart the premises?"

He silently retired into his hermitage.

I was now in such a state of nervous resentment that I thought it
but prudent to check myself at present from further demonstrations.
Bartleby and I were alone. I remembered the tragedy of the unfortunate
Adams and the still more unfortunate Colt in the solitary office of the
latter; and how poor Colt, being dreadfully incensed by Adams, and
imprudently permitting himself to get wildly excited, was at unawares

hurried into his fatal act — an act which certainly no man could possibly deplore more than the actor himself. Often it had occurred to me in my ponderings upon the subject that had that altercation taken place in the public street, or at a private residence, it would not have terminated as it did. It was the circumstance of being alone in a solitary office, up stairs, of a building entirely unhallowed by humanizing domestic associations — an uncarpeted office, doubtless, of a dusty, haggard sort of appearance — this it must have been, which greatly helped to enhance the irritable desperation of the hapless Colt.

But when this old Adam of resentment rose in me and tempted me concerning Bartleby, I grappled him and threw him. How? Why, simply by recalling the divine injunction: "A new commandment give I unto you, that ye love one another." Yes, this it was that saved me. Aside from higher considerations, charity often operates as a vastly wise and prudent principle — a great safeguard to its possessor. Men have committed murder for jealousy's sake, and anger's sake, and hatred's sake, and selfishness' sake, and spiritual pride's sake; but no man, that ever I heard of, ever committed a diabolical murder for sweet charity's sake. Mere self-interest, then, if no better motive can be enlisted, should, especially with high-tempered men, prompt all beings to charity and philanthrophy. At any rate, upon the occasion in question, I strove to drown my exasperated feelings towards the scrivener by benevolently construing his conduct. Poor fellow, poor fellow! thought, I, he don't mean anything; and besides, he has seen hard times, and ought to be indulged.

I endeavored, also, immediately to occupy myself, and at the same time to comfort my despondency. I tried to fancy, that in the course of the morning, at such time as might prove agreeable to him, Bartleby, of his own free accord, would emerge from his hermitage and take up some decided line of march in the direction of the door. But no. Half-past twelve o'clock came; Turkey began to glow in the face, overturn his inkstand, and become generally obstreperous; Nippers abated down into quietude and courtesy; Ginger Nut munched his noon apple; and Bartleby remained standing at his window in one of his profoundest dead-wall reveries. Will it be credited? Ought I to acknowledge it? That afternoon I left the office without saying one further word to him.

Some days now passed, during which, at leisure intervals I looked a little into "Edwards on the Will," and "Priestley on Necessity." Under the circumstances, those books induced a salutary feeling. Gradually I slid into the persuasion that these troubles of mine, touching the scrivener, had been all predestinated from eternity, and Bartleby was billeted upon me for some mysterious purpose of an all-wise Providence, which it was not for a mere mortal like me to fathom. Yes, Bartleby, stay there behind your screen, thought I; I shall persecute you no more; you are harmless and noiseless as any of these old chairs; in short, I never feel so private as when I know you are here. At last I see it; I penetrate to the predestinated purpose of my life. I am content. Others may have loftier parts to enact; but my mission in this world, Bartleby, is to furnish you with office-room for such period as you may see fit to remain.

I believe that this wise and blessed frame of mind would have continued with me, had it not been for the unsolicited and uncharitable remarks obtruded upon me by my professional friends who visited the rooms. But thus it often is, that the constant friction of illiberal minds wears out at last the best resolves of the more generous. Though to be sure, when I reflected upon it, it was not strange that people entering my office should be struck by the peculiar aspect of the unaccountable Bartleby, and so be tempted to throw out some sinister observations concerning him. Sometimes an attorney, having business with me, and calling at my office, and finding no one but the scrivener there, would undertake to obtain some sort of precise information from him touching my whereabouts; but without heeding his idle talk, Bartleby would remain standing immovable in the middle of the room. So after contemplating him in that position for a time, the attorney would depart, no wiser than he came.

Also, when a reference was going on, and the room full of lawyers and witnesses, and business driving fast, some deeply-occupied legal gentleman present, seeing Bartleby wholly unemployed, would request him to run round to his (the legal gentleman's) office and fetch some papers for him. Thereupon, Bartleby would tranquilly decline, and yet remain idle as before. Then the lawyer would give a great stare, and turn to me. And what could I say? At last I was made aware that all through the circle of my professional acquaintance, a whisper of wonder was running round, having reference to the strange creature I kept at my office. This worried me very much. And as the idea came upon me of his possibly turning out a long-lived man, and keep occupying my chambers, and denying my authority; and perplexing my visitors; and scandalizing my professional reputation; and casting a general gloom over the premises; keeping soul and body together to the last upon his savings (for doubtless he spent but half a dime a day), and in the end perhaps outlive me, and claim possession of my office by right of his perpetual occupancy: as all these dark anticipations crowded upon me more and more, and my friends continually intruded their relentless remarks upon the apparition in my room; a great change was wrought in me. I resolved to gather all my faculties together, and forever rid me of this intolerable incubus.

Ere revolving any complicated project, however, adapted to this end,

I first simply suggested to Bartleby the propriety of his permanent departure. In a calm and serious tone, I commended the idea to his careful and mature consideration. But, having taken three days to meditate upon it, he apprised me, that his original determination remained the same; in short, that he still preferred to abide with me.

What shall I do? I now said to myself, buttoning up my coat to the last button. What shall I do? what ought I to do? what does conscience say I *should* do with this man, or, rather, ghost. Rid myself of him, I must; go, he shall. But how? You will not thrust him, the poor, pale, passive mortal — you will not thrust such a helpless creature out of your door? you will not dishonor yourself by such cruelty? No, I will not, I cannot do that. Rather would I let him live and die here, and then mason up his remains in the wall. What, then, will you do? For all your coaxing, he will not budge. Bribes he leaves under your own paperweight on your table; in short, it is quite plain that he prefers to cling to you.

Then something severe, something unusual must be done. What! surely you will not have him collared by a constable, and commit his innocent pallor to the common jail? And upon what ground could you procure such a thing to be done? — a vagrant, is he? What! he a vagrant, a wanderer, who refuses to budge? It is because he will *not* be a vagrant, then, that you seek to count him *as* a vagrant. That is too absurd. No visible means of support: there I have him. Wrong again: for indubitably he *does* support himself, and that is the only unanswerable proof that any man can show of his possessing the means so to do. No more, then. Since he will not quit me, I must quit him. I will change my offices; I will move elsewhere, and give him fair notice, that if I find him on my new premises I will then proceed against him as a common trespasser.

Acting accordingly, next day I thus addressed him: "I find these chambers too far from the City Hall; the air is unwholesome. In a word, I propose to remove my offices next week, and shall no longer require your services. I tell you this now, in order that you may seek another place."

He made no reply, and nothing more was said.

On the appointed day I engaged carts and men, proceeded to my chambers, and, having but little furniture, everything was removed in a few hours. Throughout, the scrivener remained standing behind the screen, which I directed to be removed the last thing. It was withdrawn; and, being folded up like a huge folio, left him the motionless occupant of a naked room. I stood in the entry watching him a moment, while something from within me upbraided me.

I re-entered, with my hand in my pocket — and — and my heart in my mouth.

"Good-bye, Bartleby; I am going — good-bye, and God some way bless you; and take that," slipping something in his hand. But it dropped upon the floor, and then — strange to say — I tore myself from him whom I had so longed to be rid of.

Established in my new quarters, for a day or two I kept the door locked, and started at every footfall in the passages. When I returned to my rooms, after any little absence, I would pause at the threshold for an instant, and attentively listen, ere applying my key. But these fears were needless. Bartleby never came nigh me.

I thought all was going well, when a perturbed-looking stranger visited me, inquiring whether I was the person who had recently occupied rooms at No. — Wall Street.

Full of forebodings, I replied that I was.

"Then, sir," said the stranger, who proved a lawyer, "you are responsible for the man you left there. He refuses to do any copying; he refuses to do anything; he says he prefers not to; and he refuses to quit the premises."

"I am very sorry, sir," said I, with assumed tranquillity, but an inward tremor, "but, really, the man you allude to is nothing to me — he is no relation or apprentice of mine, that you should hold me responsible for him."

"In mercy's name, who is he?"

"I certainly cannot inform you. I know nothing about him. Formerly I employed him as a copyist; but he has done nothing for me now for some time past."

"I shall settle him, then — good morning, sir."

Several days passed, and I heard nothing more; and, though I often felt a charitable prompting to call at the place and see poor Bartleby, yet a certain squeamishness, of I know not what, withheld me.

All is over with him, by this time, thought I, at last, when, through another week, no further intelligence reached me. But, coming to my room the day after, I found several persons waiting at my door in a high state of nervous excitement.

"That's the man — here he comes," cried the foremost one, whom I recognized as the lawyer who had previously called upon me alone.

"You must take him away, sir, at once," cried a portly person among them, advancing upon me, and whom I knew to be the landlord of No. — Wall Street. "These gentlemen, my tenants, cannot stand it any longer; Mr. B — — ," pointing to the lawyer, "has turned him out of his room, and he now persists in haunting the building generally, sitting upon the banisters of the stairs by day, and sleeping in the entry by night. Everybody is concerned; clients are leaving the offices; some fears are entertained of a mob; something you must do, and that without delay."

Aghast at this torrent, I fell back before it, and would fain have locked myself in my new quarters. In vain I persisted that Bartleby was nothing to me — no more than to any one else. In vain — I was the last person known to have anything to do with him, and they held me to the terrible account. Fearful, then, of being exposed in the papers (as one person present obscurely threatened), I considered the matter, and, at length, said, that if the lawyer would give me a confidential interview with the scrivener, in his (the lawyer's) own room, I would, that afternoon, strive my best to rid them of the nuisance they complained of.

Going up stairs to my old haunt, there was Bartleby silently sitting upon the banister at the landing.

"What are you doing here, Bartleby?" said I.

"Sitting upon the banister," he mildly replied.

I motioned him into the lawyer's room, who then left us.

"Bartleby," said I, "are you aware that you are the cause of great tribulation to me, by persisting in occupying the entry after being dismissed from the office?"

No answer.

"Now one of two things must take place. Either you must do something, or something must be done to you. Now what sort of business would you like to engage in? Would you like to re-engage in copying for some one?"

"No; I would prefer not to make any change."

"Would you like a clerkship in a dry-goods store?"

"There is too much confinement about that. No, I would not like a clerkship; but I am not particular."

"Too much confinement," I cried, "why, you keep yourself confined all the time!"

"I would prefer not to take a clerkship," he rejoined, as if to settle that little item at once.

"How would a bar-tender's business suit you? There is no trying of the eye-sight in that."

"I would not like it at all; though, as I said before, I am not particular."

His unwonted wordiness inspirited me. I returned to the charge.

"Well, then, would you like to travel through the country collecting bills for the merchants? That would improve your health."

"No, I would prefer to be doing something else."

"How, then, would going as a companion to Europe, to entertain some young gentleman with your conversation — how would that suit you?"

"Not at all. It does not strike me that there is anything definite about that. I like to be stationary. But I am not particular."

"Stationary you shall be, then," I cried, now losing all patience, and, for the first time in all my exasperating connection with him, fairly flying into a passion. "If you do not go away from these premises before night, I shall feel bound — indeed, I *am* bound — to — to — to quit the premises myself!" I rather absurdly concluded, knowing not with what possible threat to try to frighten his immobility into compliance. Despairing of all further efforts, I was precipitately leaving him, when a final thought occurred to me — one which had not been wholly un-indulged before.

"Bartleby," said I, in the kindest tone I could assume under such exciting circumstances, "will you go home with me now — not to my office, but my dwelling — and remain there till we can conclude upon some convenient arrangement for you at our leisure? Come, let us start now, right away."

"No: at present I would prefer not to make any change at all."

I answered nothing; but, effectually dodging every one by the suddenness and rapidity of my flight, rushed from the building, ran up Wall Street towards Broadway, and, jumping into the first omnibus, was soon removed from pursuit. As soon as tranquillity returned, I distinctly perceived that I had now done all that I possibly could, both in respect to the demands of the landlord and his tenants, and with re-gard to my own desire and sense of duty, to benefit Bartleby, and shield him from rude persecution. I now strove to be entirely care-free and quiescent; and my conscience justified me in the attempt; though, indeed, it was not so successful as I could have wished. So fearful was I of being again hunted out by the incensed landlord and his exasperated tenants, that, surrendering my business to Nippers, for a few days, I drove about the upper part of the town and through the suburbs, in my rockaway; crossed over to Jersey City and Hoboken, and paid fugitive visits to Manhattanville and Astoria. In fact, I almost lived in my rockaway for the time.

When again I entered my office, lo, a note from the landlord lay upon the desk. I opened it with trembling hands. It informed me that the writer had sent to the police, and had Bartleby removed to the Tombs as a vagrant. Moreover, since I knew more about him than any one else, he wished me to appear at that place, and make a suitable statement of the facts. These tidings had a conflicting effect upon me. At first I was indignant; but, at last, almost approved. The landlord's energetic, sum-mary disposition, had led him to adopt a procedure which I do not think

I would have decided upon myself; and yet, as a last resort, under such peculiar circumstances, it seemed the only plan.

As I afterwards learned, the poor scrivener, when told that he must be conducted to the Tombs, offered not the slightest obstacle, but, in his pale, unmoving way, silently acquiesced.

Some of the compassionate and curious by-standers joined the party; and headed by one of the constables arm-in-arm with Bartleby, the silent procession filed its way through all the noise, and heat, and joy of the roaring thoroughfares at noon.

The same day I received the note, I went to the Tombs, or, to speak more properly, the Halls of Justice. Seeking the right officer, I stated the purpose of my call, and was informed that the individual I described was, indeed, within. I then assured the functionary that Bartleby was a perfectly honest man, and greatly to be compassionated, however unaccountably eccentric. I narrated all I knew, and closed by suggesting the idea of letting him remain in as indulgent confinement as possible, till something less harsh might be done — though, indeed, I hardly knew what. At all events, if nothing else could be decided upon, the alms-house must receive him. I then begged to have an interview.

Being under no disgraceful charge, and quite serene and harmless in all his ways, they had permitted him freely to wander about the prison, and, especially, in the inclosed grass-plated yards thereof. And so I found him there, standing all alone in the quietest of the yards, his face towards a high wall, while all around, from the narrow slits of the jail windows, I thought I saw peering out upon him the eyes of murderers and thieves.

"Bartleby!"

"I know you," he said, without looking around — "and I want nothing to say to you."

"It was not I that brought you here, Bartleby," said I, keenly pained at his implied suspicion. "And to you, this should not be so vile a place. Nothing reproachful attaches to you by being here. And see, it is not so sad a place as one might think. Look, there is the sky, and here is the grass."

"I know where I am," he replied, but would say nothing more, and so I left him.

As I entered the corridor again, a broad meat-like man, in an apron, accosted me, and, jerking his thumb over his shoulder, said — "Is that your friend?"

"Yes."

"Does he want to starve? If he does, let him live on the prison fare, that's all."

"Who are you?" asked I, not knowing what to make of such an unofficially speaking person in such a place.

"I am the grub-man. Such gentlemen as have friends here, hire me to provide them with something good to eat."

"Is this so?" said I, turning to the turnkey.

He said it was.

"Well, then," said I, slipping some silver into the grub-man's hands (for so they called him), "I want you to give particular attention to my friend there; let him have the best dinner you can get. And you must be as polite to him as possible."

"Introduce me, will you?" said the grub-man, looking at me with an expression which seemed to say he was all impatience for an opportunity to give a specimen of his breeding.

Thinking it would prove of benefit to the scrivener, I acquiesced; and, asking the grub-man his name, went up with him to Bartleby.

"Bartleby, this is a friend; you will find him very useful to you."

"Your sarvant, sir, your sarvant," said the grub-man, making a low salutation behind his apron. "Hope you find it pleasant here, sir; nice grounds — cool apartments — hope you'll stay with us some time — try to make it agreeable. What will you have for dinner to-day?"

"I prefer not to dine to-day," said Bartleby, turning away. "It would disagree with me; I am unused to dinners." So saying, he slowly moved to the other side of the inclosure, and took up a position fronting the dead-wall.

"How's this?" said the grub-man, addressing me with a stare of astonishment. "He's odd, ain't he?"

"I think he is a little deranged," said I, sadly.

"Deranged? deranged is it? Well, now, upon my word, I thought that friend of yourn was a gentleman forger; they are always pale and genteel-like, them forgers. I can't help pity 'em — can't help it, sir. Did you know Monroe Edwards?" he added, touchingly, and paused. Then, laying his hand piteously on my shoulder, sighed, "He died of consumption at Sing-Sing. So you weren't acquainted with Monroe?"

"No, I was never socially acquainted with any forgers. But I cannot stop longer. Look to my friend yonder. You will not lose by it. I will see you again."

Some few days after this, I again obtained admission to the Tombs, and went through the corridors in quest of Bartleby; but without finding him.

"I saw him coming from his cell not long ago," said a turnkey, "may be he's gone to loiter in the yards."

So I went in that direction.

"Are you looking for the silent man?" said another turnkey, passing me. "Yonder he lies — sleeping in the yard there. 'Tis not twenty minutes since I saw him lie down."

The yard was entirely quiet. It was not accessible to the common prisoners. The surrounding walls, of amazing thickness, kept off all sounds behind them. The Egyptian character of the masonry weighed upon me with its gloom. But a soft imprisoned turf grew under foot. The heart of the eternal pyramids, it seemed, wherein, by some strange magic, through the clefts, grass-seed, dropped by birds, had sprung.

Strangely huddled at the base of the wall, his knees drawn up, and lying on his side, his head touching the cold stones, I saw the wasted Bartleby. But nothing stirred. I paused; then went close up to him; stooped over, and saw that his dim eyes were open; otherwise he seemed profoundly sleeping. Something prompted me to touch him. I felt his hand, when a tingling shiver ran up my arm and down my spine to my feet.

The round face of the grub-man peered upon me now. "His dinner is ready. Won't he dine to-day, either? Or does he live without dining?"

"Lives without dining," said I, and closed the eyes.

"Eh! — He's asleep, ain't he?"

"With kings and counselors," murmured I.

There would seem little need for proceeding further in this history. Imagination will readily supply the meagre recital of poor Bartleby's interment. But, ere parting with the reader, let me say, that if this little narrative has sufficiently interested him, to awaken curiosity as to who Bartleby was, and what manner of life he led prior to the present narrator's making his acquaintance, I can only reply, that in such curiosity I fully share, but am wholly unable to gratify it. Yet here I hardly know whether I should divulge one little item of rumor, which came to my ear a few months after the scrivener's decease. Upon what basis it rested, I could never ascertain; and hence, how true it is I cannot now tell. But, inasmuch as this vague report has not been without a certain suggestive interest to me, however sad, it may prove the same with some others; and so I will briefly mention it. The report was this: that Bartleby had been a subordinate clerk in the Dead Letter Office at Washington, from which he had been suddenly removed by a change in the administration. When I think over this rumor, hardly can I express the emotions which seize me. Dead letters! does it not sound like dead men? Conceive a man by nature and misfortune prone to a pallid hopelessness, can any business seem more fitted to heighten it than that of continually handling these dead letters, and assorting them for the flames? For by the cart-load they are annually burned. Sometimes from out the folded paper the pale clerk takes a ring — the finger it was meant for, perhaps, moulders in the grave; a bank-note sent in swiftest charity — he whom it would relieve, nor eats nor hungers any more; pardon for those who died despairing; hope for those who died unhoping; good tidings for those who died stifled by unrelieved calamities. On errands of life, these letters speed to death.

Ah, Bartleby! Ah, humanity!

# Bret Harte (1836–1902)

FRANCIS BRETT HARTE, who abbreviated his name for his writing, was born in Albany, New York. In 1854, a little too late to be a Forty-niner, he went to California while the impact of the frenzied Gold Rush was still being felt there. He mined in the fabulous Mother Lode, the richest gold source in America, but found no fortune. He went to San Francisco to work as printer and journalist. There he did find riches — in tales of his fellow miners. A collection, *The Luck of Roaring Camp and Other Sketches*, was published in 1870. This book and his comic ballad, "Plain Language from Truthful James," retitled "The Heathen Chinee," about two card sharps outwitted by Ah Sin, a Chinese gambler with "ways that are dark," swept Harte into tumultuous nationwide popularity. The *Atlantic Monthly* paid him ten thousand dollars for twelve short stories and publishing offers flooded him. But the writing in the novels, short stories, and plays, even one on which Samuel Clemens collaborated, became mediocre. He was a U.S. consul in Europe for a few years, then retired to London where he spent the last eleven years of his life as a hack writer.

"Tennessee's Partner" is a sentimental story, but one that, between laughter and tears, is a vivid evocation of the life in those long ago western mining camps. Especially is it the story of a friendship between two men, one a gambler and thief, the other a simple, steadfast man with a "serious, simple face." Nothing can destroy the friendship, not even when a faithless wife runs off with one. A wonderful court scene is highlighted by terrific irony when the "Partner" offers his entire life's savings and a gold watch to save Tennessee from hanging. Harte shows the rough-and-ready, fast-shooting, hard-drinking miners as really a warmhearted lot.

# *Tennessee's Partner*

I DO not think that we ever knew his real name. Our ignorance of it certainly never gave us any social inconvenience, for at Sandy Bar in 1854 most men were christened anew. Sometimes these appellatives were derived from some distinctiveness of dress, as in the case of "Dungaree Jack"; or from some peculiarity of habit, as shown in "Saleratus Bill," so called from an undue proportion of that chemical in his daily bread; or from some unlucky slip, as exhibited in "The Iron Pirate," a mild, inoffensive man, who earned that baleful title by his unfortunate mispronunciation of the term "iron pyrites." Perhaps this may have been the beginning of a rude heraldry; but I am constrained to think that it was because a man's real name in that day rested solely upon his own unsupported statement. "Call yourself Clifford, do you?" said Boston, addressing a timid new-comer with infinite scorn; "hell is full of such Cliffords!" He then introduced the unfortunate man, whose name happened to be really Clifford, as "Jay-bird Charley," — an unhallowed inspiration of the moment, that clung to him ever after.

But to return to Tennessee's Partner, whom we never knew by any other than this relative title; that he had ever existed as a separate and distinct individuality we only learned later. It seems that in 1853 he left Poker Flat to go to San Francisco, ostensibly to procure a wife. He never got any farther than Stockton. At that place he was attracted by a young person who waited upon the table at the hotel where he took his meals. One morning he said something to her which caused her to smile not unkindly, to somewhat coquettishly break a plate of toast over his upturned, serious, simple face, and to retreat to the kitchen. He followed her, and emerged a few moments later, covered with more toast and victory. That day week they were married by a Justice of the Peace, and returned to Poker Flat. I am aware that something more might be made of this episode, but I prefer to tell it as it was current at Sandy Bar, — in the gulches and bar-rooms, — where all sentiment was modified by a strong sense of humor.

Of their married felicity but little is known, perhaps for the reason that Tennessee, then living with his partner, one day took occasion to say something to the bride on his account, at which, it is said, she smiled not unkindly and chastely retreated, — this time as far as Marysville, where Tennessee followed her, and where they went to housekeeping without the aid of a Justice of the Peace. Tennessee's Partner took the loss of his wife simply and seriously, as was his fashion. But to everybody's surprise, when Tennessee one day returned from Marysville, without his partner's wife, — she having smiled and retreated with somebody else, — Tennessee's Partner was the first man to shake his hand and greet him with affection. The boys who had gathered in the cañon to see the shooting were naturally indignant. Their indignation might have found vent in sarcasm but for a certain look in Tennessee's Partner's eye that indicated a lack of humorous appreciation. In fact, he was a grave man, with a steady application to practical detail which was unpleasant in a difficulty.

Meanwhile a popular feeling against Tennessee had grown up on the Bar. He was known to be a gambler; he was suspected to be a thief. In these suspicions Tennessee's Partner was equally compromised; his continued intimacy with Tennessee after the affair above quoted could only be accounted for on the hypothesis of a copartnership of crime. At last Tennessee's guilt became flagrant. One day he overtook a stranger on his way to Red Dog. The stranger afterward related that Tennessee beguiled the time with interesting anecdote and reminiscence, but illogically concluded the interview in the following words: "And now, young man, I'll trouble you for your knife, your pistols, and your money. You see your weppings might get you into trouble at Red Dog, and your money's a temptation to the evilly disposed. I think you said your address was San Francisco. I shall endeavor to call." It may be stated here that Tennessee had a fine flow of humor, which no business preoccupation could wholly subdue.

This exploit was his last. Red Dog and Sandy Bar made common cause against the highwayman. Tennessee was hunted in very much the same fashion as his prototype, the grizzly. As the toils closed around him, he made a desperate dash through the Bar, emptying his revolver at the crowd before the Arcade Saloon, and so on up Grizzly Cañon; but at its farther extremity he was stopped by a small man on a gray horse. The men looked at each other a moment in silence. Both were fearless, both self-possessed and independent; and both types of a civilization that in the seventeenth century would have been called heroic, but, in the nineteenth, simply "reckless." "What have you got there? — I call," said Tennessee, quietly. "Two bowers and an ace," said the stranger, as quietly, showing two revolvers and a bowie-knife. "That takes me," returned Tennessee; and with this gamblers' epigram, he threw away his useless pistol, and rode back with his captor.

It was a warm night. The cool breeze which usually sprang up with the going down of the sun behind the *chaparral*-crested mountain was that evening withheld from Sandy Bar. The little cañon was stifling with heated resinous odors, and the decaying drift-wood on the Bar sent forth faint, sickening exhalations. The feverishness of day, and its fierce passions, still filled the camp. Lights moved restlessly along the bank of the river, striking no answering reflection from its tawny current. Against the blackness of the pines the windows of the old loft above the express-office stood out staringly bright; and through their curtainless panes the loungers below could see the forms of those who were even then deciding the fate of Tennessee. And above all this, etched on the dark firmament, rose the Sierra, remote and passionless, crowned with remoter passionless stars.

The trial of Tennessee was conducted as fairly as was consistent with a judge and jury who felt themselves to some extent obliged to justify, in their verdict, the previous irregularities of arrest and indictment. The law of Sandy Bar was implacable, but not vengeful. The excitement and personal feeling of the chase were over; with Tennesse safe in their hands they were ready to listen patiently to any defence, which they were already satisfied was insufficient. There being no doubt in their own minds, they were willing to give the prisoner the benefit of any that might exist. Secure in the hypothesis that he ought to be hanged, on general principles, they indulged him with more latitude of defence than his reckless hardihood seemed to ask. The Judge appeared to be more anxious than the prisoner, who, otherwise unconcerned, evidently took a grim pleasure in the responsibility he had created. "I don't take any hand in this yer game," had been his invariable, but good-humored reply to all questions. The Judge — who was also his captor — for a moment vaguely regretted that he had not shot him "on sight," that morning, but presently dismissed this human weakness as unworthy of the judicial mind. Nevertheless, when there was a tap at the door, and it was said that Tennessee's Partner was there on behalf of the prisoner, he was admitted at once without question. Perhaps the younger members of the jury, to whom the proceedings were becoming irksomely thoughtful, hailed him as a relief.

For he was not, certainly, an imposing figure. Short and stout, with a square face, sunburned into a preternatural redness, clad in a loose duck "jumper," and trousers streaked and splashed with red soil, his aspect under any circumstances would have been quaint, and was now even ridiculous. As he stooped to deposit at his feet a heavy carpet-bag he was carrying, it became obvious, from partially developed legends and inscriptions, that the material with which his trousers had been patched had been originally intended for a less ambitious covering. Yet he advanced with great gravity, and after having shaken the hand of each person in the room with labored cordiality, he wiped his serious, perplexed face on a red bandanna handkerchief, a shade lighter than his complexion, laid his powerful hand upon the table to steady himself, and thus addressed the Judge: —

"I was passin' by," he began, by way of apology, "and I thought I'd just step in and see how things was gittin' on with Tennessee thar, — my partner. It's a hot night. I disremember any sich weather before on the Bar."

He paused a moment, but nobody volunteering any other meteorological recollection, he again had recourse to his pocket-handkerchief, and for some moments mopped his face diligently.

"Have you anything to say in behalf of the prisoner?" said the Judge, finally.

"Thet's it," said Tennessee's Partner, in a tone of relief. "I come yar as Tennessee's pardner, — knowing him nigh on four year, off and on, wet and dry, in luck and out o' luck. His ways ain't allers my ways, but thar ain't any p'ints in that young man, thar ain't any liveliness as he's been up to, as I don't know. And you sez to me, sez you, — confidential-like, and between man and man, — sez you, 'Do you know anything in his behalf?' and I sez to you, sez I, — confidential-like, as between man and man, — 'What should a man know of his pardner?' "

"Is this all you have to say?" asked the Judge, impatiently, feeling, perhaps, that a dangerous sympathy of humor was beginning to humanize the Court.

"Thet's so," continued Tennessee's Partner. "It ain't for me to say anything agin' him. And now, what's the case? Here's Tennessee wants money, wants it bad, and doesn't like to ask it of his old pardner. Well, what does Tennessee do? He lays for a stranger, and he fetches that stranger. And you lays for *him*, and you fetches *him*; and the honors is easy. And I put it to you, bein' a far-minded man, and to you, gentlemen, all, as far-minded men, ef this is n't so."

"Prisoner," said the Judge, interrupting, "have you any questions to ask this man?"

"No! no!" continued Tennessee's Partner, hastily. "I play this yer hand alone. To come down to the bed-rock, it's just this: Tennessee, thar, has played it pretty rough and expensive-like on a stranger, and on this yer camp. And now, what's the fair thing? Some would say more; some would say less. Here's seventeen hundred dollars in coarse gold and a watch, — it's about all my pile, — and call it square!" And before a hand could be raised to prevent him, he had emptied the contents of the carpet-bag upon the table.

For a moment his life was in jeopardy. One or two men sprang to their feet, several hands groped for hidden weapons, and a suggestion to "throw him from the window" was only overridden by a gesture from the Judge. Tennessee laughed. And apparently oblivious of the excitement, Tennessee's Partner improved the opportunity to mop his face again with his handkerchief.

When order was restored, and the man was made to understand, by the use of forcible figures and rhetoric, that Tennessee's offence could not be condoned by money, his face took a more serious and sanguinary hue, and those who were nearest to him noticed that his rough hand trembled slightly on the table. He hesitated a moment as he slowly returned the gold to the carpet-bag, as if he had not yet entirely caught the elevated sense of justice which swayed the tribunal, and was perplexed with the belief that he had not offered enough. Then he turned to the Judge, and saying, "This yer is a lone hand, played alone, and without my pardner," he bowed to the jury and was about to withdraw, when the Judge called him back. "If you have anything to say to Tennessee, you had better say it now." For the first time that evening the eyes of the prisoner and his strange advocate met. Tennessee smiled, showed his white teeth, and, saying, "Euchred, old man!" held out his hand. Tennessee's Partner took it in his own, and saying, "I just dropped in as I was passin' to see how things was gettin' on," let the hand passively fall, and adding that "it was a warm night," again mopped his face with his handkerchief, and without another word withdrew.

The two men never again met each other alive. For the unparalleled insult of a bribe offered to Judge Lynch — who, whether bigoted, weak, or narrow, was at least incorruptible — firmly fixed in the mind of that mythical personage any wavering determination of Tennessee's fate; and at the break of day he was marched, closely guarded, to meet it at the top of Marley's Hill.

How he met it, how cool he was, how he refused to say anything, how perfect were the arrangements of the committee, were all duly reported, with the addition of a warning moral and example to all future evil-doers, in the Red Dog Clarion, by its editor, who was present, and to whose vigorous English I cheerfully refer the reader. But the beauty of that midsummer morning, the blessed amity of earth and air and sky, the awakened life of the free woods and hills, the joyous renewal and promise of Nature, and above all, the infinite Serenity that thrilled through each, was not reported, as not being a part of the social lesson. And yet, when the weak and foolish deed was done, and a life, with its possibilities and responsibilities, had passed out of the misshapen thing that dangled between earth and sky, the birds sang, the flowers bloomed, the sun shone, as cheerily as before; and possibly the Red Dog Clarion was right.

Tennessee's Partner was not in the group that surrounded the ominous tree. But as they turned to disperse attention was drawn to the singular appearance of a motionless donkey-cart halted at the side of the road. As they approached, they at once recognized the venerable "Jenny" and the two-wheeled cart as the property of Tennessee's Partner, — used by him in carrying dirt from his claim; and a few paces distant the owner of the equipage himself, sitting under a buckeye-tree, wiping the perspiration from his glowing face. In answer to an inquiry, he said he had come for the body of the "diseased," "if it was all the same to the committee." He didn't wish to "hurry anything"; he could "wait." He was not working that day; and when the gentlemen were done with the "diseased," he would take him. "Ef thar is any present," he added, in his simple, serious way, "as would care to jine in the fun'l, they kin come." Perhaps it was from a sense of humor, which I have already intimated was a feature of Sandy Bar, — perhaps it was from something even better than that; but two thirds of the loungers accepted the invitation at once.

It was noon when the body of Tennessee was delivered into the hands of his partner. As the cart drew up to the fatal tree, we noticed that it contained a rough, oblong box, — apparently made from a section of sluicing, — and half filled with bark and the tassels of pine. The cart was further decorated with slips of willow, and made fragrant with buckeye-blossoms. When the body was deposited in the box, Tennessee's Partner drew over it a piece of tarred canvas, and gravely mounting the narrow seat in front, with his feet upon the shafts, urged the little donkey forward. The equipage moved slowly on, at that decorous pace which was habitual with "Jenny" even under less solemn circumstances. The men — half curiously, half jestingly, but all good-humoredly — strolled along beside the cart; some in advance, some a little in the rear of the homely catafalque. But, whether from the narrowing of the road or some present sense of decorum, as the cart passed on, the company fell to the rear in couples, keeping step, and otherwise assuming the external show of a formal procession. Jack Folinsbee, who had at the outset played a funeral march in dumb show upon an imaginary trombone, desisted, from a lack of sympathy and appreciation, — not having, perhaps, your true humorist's capacity to be content with the enjoyment of his own fun.

The way led through Grizzly Cañon, — by this time clothed in funereal drapery and shadows. The redwoods, burying their moccasined feet in the red soil, stood in Indian-file along the track, trailing an uncouth benediction from their bending boughs upon the passing bier. A hare, surprised into helpless inactivity, sat upright and pulsating in the ferns by the roadside, as the *cortège* went by. Squirrels hastened to gain a secure outlook from higher boughs; and the blue-jays, spreading their wings, fluttered before them like outriders, until the outskirts of Sandy Bar were reached, and the solitary cabin of Tennessee's Partner.

Viewed under more favorable circumstances, it would not have been a cheerful place. The unpicturesque site, the rude and unlovely outlines, the unsavory details, which distinguish the nestbuilding of the California miner, were all here, with the dreariness of decay superadded. A few paces from the cabin there was a rough enclosure, which, in the brief days of Tennessee's Partner's matrimonial felicity, had been used as a garden, but was now overgrown with fern. As we approached it we were surprised to find that what we had taken for a recent attempt at cultivation was the broken soil about an open grave.

The cart was halted before the enclosure; and rejecting the offers of assistance with the same air of simple self-reliance he had displayed throughout, Tennessee's Partner lifted the rough coffin on his back, and deposited it, unaided, within the shallow grave. He then nailed down the board which served as a lid; and mounting the little mound of earth beside it, took off his hat, and slowly mopped his face with his handkerchief. This the crowd felt was a preliminary to speech; and they disposed themselves variously on stumps and boulders, and sat expectant.

"When a man," began Tennessee's Partner, slowly, "has been running free all day, what's the natural thing for him to do? Why, to come home. And if he ain't in a condition to go home, what can his best friend do? Why, bring him home! And here's Tennessee has been running free, and we brings him home from his wandering." He paused, and picked up a fragment of quartz, rubbed it thoughtfully on his sleeve, and went on: "It ain't the first time that I've packed him on my back, as you see'd me now. It ain't the first time that I brought him to this yer cabin when he could n't help himself; it ain't the first time that I and 'Jinny' have waited for him on yon hill, and picked him up and so fetched him home, when he could n't speak, and did n't know me. And now that it's the last time, why — " he paused, and rubbed the quartz gently on his sleeve — "you see it's sort of rough on his pardner. And now, gentlemen," he added, abruptly, picking up his long-handled shovel, "the fun'l's over; and my thanks, and Tennessee's thanks, to you for your trouble."

Resisting any proffers of assistance, he began to fill in the grave, turning his back upon the crowd, that after a few moments' hesitation gradually withdrew. As they crossed the little ridge that hid Sandy Bar from view, some, looking back, thought they could see Tennessee's Partner, his work done, sitting upon the grave, his shovel between his knees, and his face buried in his red bandanna handkerchief. But it was argued by others that you could n't tell his face from his handkerchief at that distance; and this point remained undecided.

In the reaction that followed the feverish excitement of that day, Tennessee's Partner was not forgotten. A secret investigation had cleared him of any complicity in Tennessee's guilt, and left only a suspicion of his general sanity. Sandy Bar made a point of calling on him, and proffering various uncouth, but well-meant kindnesses. But from that day his rude health and great strength seemed visibly to decline; and when the rainy reason fairly set in, and the tiny grass-blades were beginning to peep from the rocky mound above Tennessee's grave, he took to his bed.

One night, when the pines beside the cabin were swaying in the storm and trailing their slender fingers over the roof, and the roar and rush of the swollen river were heard below, Tennessee's Partner lifted his head from the pillow, saying, "It is time to go for Tennessee; I must put 'Jinny' in the cart"; and would have risen from his bed but for the restraint of his attendant. Struggling, he still pursued his singular fancy: "There, now, steady, 'Jinny,' — steady, old girl. How dark it is! Look out for the ruts, — and look out for him, too, old gal. Sometimes, you know, when he's blind drunk, he drops down right in the trail. Keep on straight up to the pine on the top of the hill. Thar — I told you so! — thar he is, — coming this way, too, — all by himself, sober, and his face a-shining. Tennessee! Pardner!"

And so they met.

# Harriet Beecher Stowe (1811–1896)

HARRIET BEECHER STOWE is the first important American woman fiction writer. Her father, brother, and husband were all famous theologians and she grew up in Connecticut in a severe Calvinist atmosphere. While stressing morality, her writing was compassionate. *Uncle Tom's Cabin* was based on the slave life she witnessed first hand in the South and in Maine where her home was a station for slaves escaping on the underground railroad to Canada. Called the most popular American book ever published, *Uncle Tom's Cabin* was followed by many other novels and short stories and a book defending women's rights called *My Wife and I*. Stowe was almost as popular in England as in the United States, becoming a friend of Queen Victoria, until she wrote *Lady Byron Vindicated* (1870), charging the poet with incestuous relations with his sister, which bitterly antagonized much of the British public. Her later writing set in America regained her some of her lost appeal for English readers. During the Civil War she met Lincoln who demanded "Is this the little lady who started such a big war?" Her last years she spent writing about Florida, where she had settled.

Buried treasure! Especially Captain Kidd's. The belief that fabulous riches await the lucky one to discover them fascinates Americans. It is a legend occurring in much of their fiction and Harriet Beecher Stowe has fun with it in this story in the collection, *Sam Lawson's Oldtown Fireside Stories*. It is definitely a period piece, but despite the "quaintness," Sam Lawson's natural astuteness is plain; his humor penetrating. As is his depiction of his greedy neighbors. And, for its time, the story has an unconventional ending with no heavy-handed preaching.

# Captain Kidd's Money

ONE of our most favorite legendary resorts was the old barn.

Sam Lawson preferred it on many accounts. It was quiet and retired, that is to say, at such distance from his own house, that he could not hear if Hepsy called ever so loudly, and farther off than it would be convenient for that industrious and painstaking woman to follow him. Then there was the soft fragrant cushion of hay, on which his length of limb could be easily bestowed.

Our barn had an upper loft with a swinging outer door that commanded a view of the old mill, the waterfall, and the distant windings of the river, with its grassy green banks, its graceful elm draperies, and its white flocks of water-lilies; and then on this Saturday afternoon we had Sam all to ourselves. It was a drowsy, dreamy October day, when the hens were lazily "craw, crawing," in a soft, conversational undertone with each other, as they scratched and picked the hay-seed under the barn windows. Below in the barn black Caesar sat quietly hatchelling flax, sometimes gurgling and giggling to himself with an overflow of that interior jollity with which he seemed to be always full. The African in

New England was a curious contrast to everybody around him in the joy and satisfaction that he seemed to feel in the mere fact of being alive. Every white person was glad or sorry for some appreciable cause in the past, present, or future, which was capable of being definitely stated: but black Caesar was in an eternal giggle and frizzle and simmer of enjoyment for which he could give no earthly reason: he was an "embodied joy," like Shelley's skylark.

"Jest hear him," said Sam Lawson, looking pensively over the haymow, and strewing hayseed down on his wool. "How that 'are critter seems to tickle and laugh all the while 'bout nothin'. Lordy massy he don't seem never to consider that 'this life's a dream, an empty show.'"

"Look here, Sam," we broke in, anxious to cut short a threatened stream of morality, "you promised to tell us about Capt. Kidd, and how you dug for his money."

"Did I, now? Wal, boys, that 'are history o' Kidd's is a warnin' to fellers. Why, Kidd had pious parents and Bible and sanctuary privileges when he was a boy, and yet come to be hanged. It's all in this 'ere song I'm going' to sing ye. Lordy massy! I wish I had my bass-viol now. — Caesar," he said, calling down from his perch, "can't you strike the pitch o' 'Cap'n Kidd,' on your fiddle?"

Caesar's fiddle was never far from him. It was, in fact, tucked away in a nice little nook just over the manger; and he often caught an interval from his work to scrape a dancing-tune on it, keeping time with his heels, to our great delight.

A most wailing minor-keyed tune was doled forth, which seemed quite refreshing to Sam's pathetic vein, as he sang in his most lugubrious tones, —

> " 'My name was Robert Kidd
>   As I sailed, as I sailed,
> My name was Robert Kidd;
> God's laws I did forbid,
> And so wickedly I did,
>   As I sailed, as I sailed.'

"Now ye see, boys, he's a goin' to tell how he abused his religious privileges; just hear now: —

> " 'My father taught me well,
>   As I sailed, as I sailed;
> My father taught me well
> To shun the gates of hell,
> But yet I did rebel,
>   As I sailed, as I sailed.

> " 'He put a Bible in my hand,
>     As I sailed, as I sailed;
> He put a Bible in my hand,
> And I sunk it in the sand
> Before I left the strand,
>     As I sailed, as I sailed.'

"Did ye ever hear o' such a hardened, contrary critter, boys? It's awful to think on. Wal, ye see that 'are's the way fellers allers begin the ways of sin, by turnin' their backs on the Bible and the advice o' pious parents. Now hear what he come to:—

> " 'Then I murdered William More,
>     As I sailed, as I sailed;
> I murdered William More,
> And left him in his gore,
> Not many leagues from shore,
>     As I sailed, as I sailed.

> " 'To execution dock
>     I must go, I must go.
> To execution dock,
> While thousands round me flock,
> To see me on the block,
>     I must go, I must go'.

"There was a good deal more on't," said Sam, pausing, "but I don't seem to remember it; but it's real solemn and affectin'."

"Who was Capt. Kidd, Sam?" said I.

"Wal, he was an officer in the British navy, and he got to bein' a pirate: used to take ships and sink 'em, and murder the folks; and so they say he got no end o' money, — gold and silver and precious stones, as many as the wise men in the East. But ye see, what good did it all do him? He couldn't use it, and dar'sn't keep it; so he used to bury it in spots round here and there in the awfullest heathen way ye ever heard of. Why, they say he allers used to kill one or two men or women or children of his prisoners, and bury with it, so that their sperits might keep watch on it ef anybody was to dig arter it. That 'are thing has been tried and tried and tried, but no man nor mother's son on 'em ever got a cent that dug. 'Twas tried here'n Oldtown; and they come pretty nigh gettin' on't, but it gin 'em the slip. Ye see, boys, *it's the Devil's money*, and he holds a pretty tight grip on't."

"Well, how was it about digging for it? Tell us, did *you* do it?

Were *you* there? Did you see it? And why couldn't they get it?" we both asked eagerly and in one breath.

"Why, Lordy massy! boys, your questions tumbles over each other thick as martins out o' a martin-box. Now, you jest be moderate and let alone, and I'll tell you all about it from the beginnin' to the end. I didn't railly have no hand in't, though I was knowin' to 't, as I be to most things that goes on round here; but my conscience wouldn't railly a let me start on no sich undertakin'.

"Wal, the one that fust sot the thing a goin' was old Mother Hokum, that used to live up in that little tumble-down shed by the cranberry-pond up beyond the spring pastur'. They had a putty bad name, them Hokums. How they got a livin' nobody knew; for they didn't seem to pay no attention to raisin' nothin' but childun, but the duce knows, there was plenty o' them. Their old hut was like a rabbit-pen: there was a tow-head to very crack and cranny. 'Member what old Caesar said once when the word come to the store that old Hokum had got twins. 'S'pose de Lord knows best,' says Caesar, 'but *I* thought dere was Hokums enough afore.' Wal, even poor workin' industrious folks like me finds it's hard gettin' along when there's so many mouths to feed. Lordy massy! there don't never seem to be no end on't, and so it ain't wonderful, come to think on't, ef folks like them Hokums gets tempted to help along in ways that ain't quite right. Anyhow, folks did use to think that old Hokum was too sort o' familiar with their wood-piles 'long in the night, though they couldn't never prove it on him; and when Mother Hokum come to houses round to wash, folks use sometimes to miss pieces, here and there, though they never could find 'em on her; then they was allers a gettin' in debt here and a gettin' in debt there. Why, they got to owin' two dollars to Joe Gidger for butcher's meat. Joe was sort o' good-natured and let 'em have meat, 'cause Hokum he promised so fair to pay; but he couldn't never get it out o' him. 'Member once Joe walked clear up to the cranberry-pond arter that 'are two dollars; but Mother Hokum she see him a comin' jest as he come past the juniper-bush on the corner. She says to Hokum, 'Get into bed, old man, quick, and let me tell the story,' says she. So she covered him up; and when Gidger come in she come up to him, and says she, 'Why, Mr. Gidger, I'm jest ashamed to see ye: why, Mr. Hokum was jest a comin' down to pay ye that 'are money last week, but ye see he was took down with the small-pox' — Joe didn't hear no more: he just turned round, and he streaked it out that 'are door with his coat-tails flyin' out straight ahind him; and old Mother Hokum she jest stood at the window holdin' her sides and laughin' fit to split, to see him run. That 'are's jest a sample of the ways them Hokums cut up.

"Wal, you see, boys, there'a a queer kind o' rock down on the bank

o' the river, that looks sort o' like a grave-stone. The biggest part on't
is sunk down under ground, and it's pretty well growed over with black-
berry-vines; but, when you scratch the bushes away, they used to make
out some queer marks on that 'are rock. They was sort o' lines and
crosses; and folks would have it that them was Kidd's private marks, and
that there was one o' the places where he hid his money.

"Wal, there's no sayin' fairly how it come to be thought so; but
fellers used to say so, and they used sometimes to talk it over to the
tahvern; and kind o' wonder whether or no, if they should dig, they
wouldn't come to suthin'.

"Wal, old Mother Hokum she heard on't, and she was a sort o' en-
terprisin' old crittur: fact was, she had to be, 'cause the young Hokums
was jest like bag-worms, the more they growed the more they eat, and I
expect she found it pretty hard to fill their mouths; and so she said ef
there *was* any thing under that 'are rock, they'd as good's have it as the
Devil; and so she didn't give old Hokum no peace o' his life, but he must
see what there was there.

"Wal, I was with 'em the night they was a talkin' on't up. Ye see,
Hokum he got thirty-seven cents' worth o' lemons and sperit. I see him
goin' by as I was out a splittin' kindlin's; and says he, 'Sam, you jest
go 'long up to our house to-night,' says he: 'Toddy Whitney and Harry
Wiggin's comin' up, and we're goin' to have a little suthin' hot,' says he;
and he kind o' showed me the lemons and sperit. And I told him I
guessed I would go 'long. Wal, I kind o' wanted to see what they'd be
up to, ye know.

"Wal, come to find out, they was a talkin' about Cap'n Kidd's treasures, and layin' out how they should get it, and a settin' one another on
with gret stories about it.

"'I've heard that there was whole chists full o' gold guineas,' says
one.

"'And I've heard o' gold bracelets and ear-rings and finger-rings
all sparklin' with diamonds,' says another.

"'Maybe it's old silver plate from some o' them old West Indian
grandees,'' says another.

"'Wal, whatever it is,' says Mother Hokum, 'I want to be into it,'
says she.

"'Wal, Sam, won't you jine?' says they.

"'Wal, boys,' says I, 'I kind o' don't feel jest like j'inin'. I sort o'
ain't clear about the rights on't: seems to me it's mighty nigh like goin'
to the Devil for money.'

"'Wal,' says Mother Hokum, 'what if 'tis? Money's money, get
it how ye will; and the Devil's money 'll buy as much meat as any. I'd
go to the Devil, if he gave good money.'

" 'Wal, I guess I wouldn't,' says I. 'Don't you 'member the sermon Parson Lothrop preached about hastin' to be rich, last sabba' day?'

" 'Parson Lothrop be hanged!' says she. 'Wal, now,' says she, 'I like to see a parson with his silk stockin's and great gold-headed cane, a lollopin' on his carriage behind his fat, prancin' hosses, comin' to meetin' to preach to us poor folks not to want to be rich! How'd he like to have forty-'leven children, and nothin' to put onto 'em or into 'em, I wonder? Guess if Lady Lothrop had to rub and scrub, and wear her fingers to the bone as I do, she'd want to be rich; and I guess the parson, if he couldn't get a bellyful for a week, would be for diggin' up Kidd's money, or doing 'most any thing else to make the pot bile.'

" 'Wal,' says I, 'I'll kind o' go with ye, boys, and sort o' see how things turn out; but I guess I won't take no shere in't,' says I.

"Wal, they got it all planned out. They was to wait till the full moon, and then they was to get Primus King to go with 'em and help do the diggin'. Ye see, Hokum and Toddy Whitney and Wiggin are all putty softly fellers, and hate dreffully to work; and I tell you the Kidd money ain't to be got without a pretty tough piece o' diggin'. Why, it's jest like diggin' a well to get at it. Now, Primus King was the master hand for diggin' wells, and so they said they'd get him by givin' on him a shere.

"Harry Wiggin he didn't want no nigger a sherin' in it, he said; but Toddy and Hokum they said that when there was such stiff diggin' to be done, they didn't care if they did go in with a nigger.

"Wal, Wiggin he said he hadn't no objection to havin' the nigger do the diggin',' it was *sherin' the profits* he objected to.

" 'Wal,' says Hokum, 'you can't get him without,' says he. 'Primus knows too much,' says he: 'you can't fool him.' Finally they 'greed that they was to give Primus twenty dollars, and shere the treasure 'mong themselves.

" 'Come to talk with Primus, he wouldn't stick in a spade, unless they'd pay him aforehand. Ye see, Primus was up to 'em; he knowed about Gidger and there wa'n't none on 'em that was particular good pay; and so they all jest hed to rake and scrape, and pay him down the twenty dollars among 'em; and they 'greed for the fust full moon, at twelve o'clock at night, the 9th of October.

"Wal, ye see I had to tell Hepsy I was goin' out to watch. Wal, so I was; but not jest in the way she took it: but, Lordy massy! a feller has to tell his wife suthin' to keep her quiet, ye know, 'specially Hepsy.

"Wal, wal, of all the moonlight nights that ever I did see, I never did see one equal to that. Why, you could see the color o' every thing. I 'member I could see how the huckleberry-bushes on the rock was red as blood when the moonlight shone through 'em; 'cause the leaves, you see, had begun to turn.

"Goin' on our way we got to talkin' about the sperits.

" 'I ain't afraid on 'em,' says Hokum. 'What harm can a sperit do me?' says he. 'I don't care ef there's a dozen on 'em;' and he took a swig at his bottle.

" 'Oh! there ain't no sperits,' says Harry Wiggin. 'That 'are talk's all nonsense;' and he took a swig at *his* bottle.

" 'Wal,' says Toddy, 'I don't know 'bout that 'are. Me and Ike Sanders has seen the sperits in the Cap'n Brown house. We thought we'd jest have a peek into the window one night; and there was a whole flock o' black colts without no heads on come rushin' on us and knocked us flat.'

" 'I expect you'd been at the tahvern,' said Hokum.

" 'Wal, yes, we had; but them was sperits: we wa'n't drunk, now; we was jest as sober as ever we was.'

" 'Wal, they won't get away my money,' says Primus, 'for I put it safe away in Dinah's teapot afore I come out;' and then he showed all his ivories from ear to ear. 'I think all this 'are's sort o' foolishness,' says Primus.

" 'Wal,' says I, 'boys, I ain't a goin' to have no part or lot in this 'ere matter, but I'll jest lay it off to you how it's to be done. Ef Kidd's money is under this rock, there's *sperits* that watch it, and you mustn't give 'em no advantage. There mustn't be a word spoke from the time ye get sight o' the treasure till ye get it safe up on to firm ground,' says I. 'Ef ye do, it'll vanish right out o' sight. I've talked with them that has dug down to it and seen it; but they allers lost it, 'cause they'd call out and say suthin'; and the minute they spoke, away it went.'

"Wal, so they marked off the ground; and Primus he begun to dig, and the rest kind o' sot round. It was so still it was kind o' solemn. Ye see, it was past twelve o'clock, and every critter in Oldtown was asleep; and there was two whippoorwills on the great Cap'n Brown elm-trees, that kep' a answerin' each other back and forward sort o' solitary like; and then every once in a while there'd come a sort o' strange whisper up among the elm-tree leaves, jest as if there was talkin' goin' on; and every time Primus struck his spade into the ground it sounded sort o' holler, jest as if he'd been a diggin' a grave. 'It's kind o' melancholy,' says I, 'to think o' them poor critters that had to be killed and buried jest to keep this 'ere treasure. What awful things 'll be brought to light in the judgment day! Them poor critters they loved to live and hated to die as much as any on us; but no, they had to die jest to satisfy that critter's wicked will. I've heard them as thought they could tell the Cap'n

Kidd places by layin' their ear to the ground at midnight, and they'd hear groans and wailin's.' "

"Why, Sam! were there really people who could tell where Kidd's money was?" I here interposed.

"Oh, sartin! why, yis. There was Shebna Bascom, he was one. Shebna could always tell what was under the earth. He'd cut a hazel-stick and hold it in his hand when folks was wantin' to know where to dig wells; and that 'are stick would jest turn in his hand, and p'int down till it would fairly grind the bark off; and ef you dug in that place you was sure to find a spring. Oh, yis! Shebna he's told many where the Kidd money was, and been with 'em when they dug for it; but the pester on't was they allers lost it, 'cause they would some on 'em speak afore they thought."

"But, Sam, what about this digging? Let's know what come of it," said we, as Sam appeared to lose his way in his story.

"Wal, ye see, they dug down about five feet, when Primus he struck his spade smack on something that chincked like iron.

"Wal, then Hokum and Toddy Whitney was into the hole in a minute: they made Primus get out, and they took the spade, 'cause they wanted to be sure to come on it themselves.

"Wal, they begun, and they dug and he scraped, and sure enough they come to a gret iron pot as big as your granny's dinner-pot, with an iron bale to it.

"Wal, then they put down a rope, and he put the rope through the handle; then Hokum and Toddy they clambered upon the bank, and all on 'em began to draw up jest as still and silent as could be. They drawed and they drawed, till they jest got it even with the ground, when Toddy spoke out all in a tremble, 'There,' says he, *'we've got it!'* And the minit he spoke they was both struck by *suthin'* that knocked 'em clean over; and the rope give a crack like a pistol-shot, and broke short off; and the pot went down, down, down, and they heard it goin', jink, jink, jink; and it went way down into the earth, and the ground closed over it; and then they heard the screechin'est laugh ye ever did hear."

"I want to know, Sam, did you see that pot?" I exclaimed at this part of the story.

"Wal, no, I didn't. Ye see, I jest happened to drop asleep while they was diggin', I was so kind o' tired, and I didn't wake up till it was all over.

"I was waked up, 'cause there was consid'able of a scuffle; for Hokum was so mad at Toddy for speakin', that he was a fistin' on him; and old Primus he jest haw-hawed and laughed. 'Wal, I got *my* money safe, anyhow,' says he.

" 'Wal, come to,' says I. ' 'Tain't no use cryin' for spilt milk:

you've jest got to turn in now and fill up this 'ere hole, else the selectmen 'll be down on ye.'

" 'Wal,' says Primus, 'I didn't engage to fill up no holes;' and he put his spade on his shoulder and trudged off.

"Wal, it was putty hard work, fillin' in that hole; but Hokum and Toddy and Wiggin had to do it, 'cause they didn't want to have everybody a laughin' at 'em; and I kind o' tried to set it home to 'em, showin' on 'em that 'twas all for the best.

" 'Ef you'd a been left to get that 'are money, there'd a come a cuss with it,' says I. 'It shows the vanity o' hastin' to be rich.'

" 'Oh, you shet up!' says Hokum, says he. 'You never hasted to any thing,' says he. Ye see, he was riled, that's why he spoke so."

"Sam," said we, after maturely reflecting over the story, "what do you suppose was in that pot?"

"Lordy massy! boys: ye never will be done askin questions. Why, how should I know?"

# Thomas Bailey Aldrich (1836–1907)

LIKE SO MANY American fiction writers, Aldrich, who was born in Portsmouth, New Hampshire, started out by writing verse. His plans for a Harvard education were shattered by his father's death and he took a routine clerical job. After the first collection of his verses, *The Bells,* appeared, he got newspaper work and was a Civil War correspondent for the New York *Tribune.* He went on to magazine editing, finally becoming editor of the *Atlantic Monthly,* and settled in Boston, then known as "the Athens of America." In 1870 his popular *Story of a Bad Boy* was published and still lures young readers with its title. Other novels and verse collections were to follow but his many short stories were his most effective form of writing.

The meretricious "surprise ending" that features so many of O. Henry's stories and those of other imitators of H. C. Bunner and Thomas Bailey Aldrich is absent in the unexpected ending to this delightful story. It is so uncontrived the reader has no feeling of having been duped by the story's earlier part. Written in letter form, the surprise at the end grows naturally out of the characters of the two young men and their situation. Talk about a young Lochinvar riding to the rescue! Don't — just read the story and laugh.

# *Marjorie Daw*

*Dr. Dillon to Edward Delaney, Esq., at The Pines, Near Rye, N. H.*

August 8, 187 — .

MY DEAR SIR: I am happy to assure you that your anxiety is without reason. Flemming will be confined to the sofa for three or four weeks, and will have to be careful at first how he uses his leg. A fracture of this kind is always a tedious affair. Fortunately, the bone was very skillfully set by the surgeon who chanced to be in the drug-store where Flemming was brought after his fall, and I apprehend no permanent inconvenience from the accident. *Flemming is doing perfectly well physically;* but I must confess that the irritable and morbid state of mind into which he has fallen causes me a great deal of uneasiness. He is the last man in the world who ought to break his leg. You know how impetuous our friend is ordinarily, what a soul of restlessness and energy, never content unless he is rushing at some object, like a sportive bull at a red shawl; but amiable withal. He is no longer amiable. His temper has become something frightful. Miss Fanny Flemming came up from Newport, where the family are staying for the summer, to nurse him; but he packed her off the next morning in tears. He has a complete set of Balzac's works, twenty-seven volumes piled up near his sofa, to throw at Watkins whenever that

exemplary serving-man appears with his meals. Yesterday I very innocently brought Flemming a small basket of lemons. You know it was
a strip of lemon-peel on the curbstone that caused our friend's mischance. Well, he no sooner set his eyes upon these lemons than he fell
into such a rage as I cannot adequately describe. This is only one of his
moods, and the least distressing. At other times he sits with bowed head
regarding his splintered limb, silent, sullen, despairing. When this fit
is on him — and it sometimes lasts all day — nothing can distract his
melancholy. He refuses to eat, does not even read the newspapers; books,
except as projectiles for Watkins, have no charms for him. His state is
truly pitiable.

Now, if he were a poor man, with a family depending on his daily
labor, this irritability and despondency would be natural enough. But in
a young fellow of twenty-four, with plenty of money and seemingly not a
care in the world, the thing is monstrous. If he continues to give way to
his vagaries in this manner, he will end by bringing on an inflammation
of the fibula. It was the fibula he broke. I am at my wits' end to know
what to prescribe for him. I have anaesthetics and lotions, to make
people sleep and to soothe pain; but I've no medicine that will make a man
have a little common-sense. That is beyond my skill, but maybe it is not
beyond yours. You are Flemming's intimate friend, his *fidus Achates*.
Write to him, write to him frequently, distract his mind, cheer him up,
and prevent him from becoming a confirmed case of melancholia. Perhaps he has some important plans disarranged by his present confinement. If he has you will know, and will know how to advise him judiciously. I trust your father finds the change beneficial? I am, my
dear sir, with great respect, etc.


II

*Edward Delaney to John Flemming, West 38th Street, New York*

August 9, — .

MY DEAR JACK: I had a line from Dillon this morning, and was rejoiced
to learn that your hurt is not so bad as reported. Like a certain personage, you are not so black and blue as you are painted. Dillon will
put you on your pins again in two or three weeks, if you will only have
patience and follow his counsels. Did you get my note of last Wednesday?
I was greatly troubled when I heard of the accident.

I can imagine how tranquil and saintly you are with your leg in
a trough! It is deuced awkward, to be sure, just as we had promised ourselves a glorious month together at the seaside; but we must make the
best of it. It is unfortunate, too, that my father's health renders it impossible for me to leave him. I think he has much improved; the sea air is

his native element; but he still needs my arm to lean upon in his walks, and requires some one more careful that a servant to look after him. I cannot come to you, dear Jack, but I have hours of unemployed time on hand, and I will write you a whole post-office full of letters if that will divert you. Heaven knows, I haven't anything to write about. It isn't as if we were living at one of the beach houses; then I could do you some character studies, and fill your imagination with groups of sea-goddesses, with their (or somebody else's) raven and blond manes hanging down their shoulders. You should have Aphrodite in morning wrapper, in evening costume, and in her prettiest bathing suit. But we are far from all that here. We have rooms in a farm-house, on a cross-road, two miles from the hotels, and lead the quietest of lives.

I wish I were a novelist. This old house, with its sanded floors and high wainscots, and its narrow windows looking out upon a cluster of pines that turn themselves into aeolian-harps every time the wind blows, would be the place in which to write a summer romance. It should be a story with the odors of the forest and the breath of the sea in it. It should be a novel like one of that Russian fellow's, — what's his name? — Tourguénieff, Turgenef, Turgenif, Toorguniff, Turgénjew, — nobody knows how to spell him. Yet I wonder if even a Liza or an Alexandra Paulovna could stir the heart of a man who has constant twinges in his leg. I wonder if one of our own Yankee girls of the best type, haughty and *spirituelle*, would be of any comfort to you in your present deplorable condition. If I thought so, I would hasten down to the Surf House and catch one for you; or, better still, I would find you one over the way.

Picture to yourself a large white house just across the road, nearly opposite our cottage. It is not a house, but a mansion, built, perhaps, in the colonial period, with rambling extensions, and gambrel roof, and a wide piazza on three sides — a self-possessed, high-bred piece of architecture, with its nose in the air. It stands back from the road, and has an obsequious retinue of fringed elms and oaks and weeping willows. Sometimes in the morning, and oftener in the afternoon, when the sun has withdrawn from that part of the mansion, a young woman appears on the piazza with some mysterious Penelope web of embroidery in her hand, or a book. There is a hammock over there, — of pineapple fibre, it looks from here. A hammock is very becoming when one is eighteen, and has golden hair, and dark eyes, and an emerald-colored illusion dress looped up after the fashion of a Dresden china shepherdess, and is *chaussée* like a belle of the time of Louis Quatorze. All this splendor goes into that hammock, and sways there like a pond-lily in the golden afternoon. The window of my bedroom looks down on that piazza, — and so do I.

But enough of this nonsense, which ill becomes a sedate young attorney taking his vacation with an invalid father.  Drop me a line, dear Jack, and tell me how you really are. State your case. Write me a long, quiet letter. If you are violent or abusive, I'll take the law to you.

## III

### *John Flemming to Edward Delaney*

August 11, — .

YOUR LETTER, dear Ned, was a godsend. Fancy what a fix I am in, — I, who never had a day's sickness since I was born. My left leg weighs three tons. It is embalmed in spices and smothered in layers of fine linen, like a mummy. I can't move. I haven't moved for five thousand years. I'm of the time of Pharaoh.

I lie from morning till night on a lounge, staring into the hot street. Everybody is out of town enjoying himself. The brown-stone-front houses across the street resemble a row of particularly ugly coffins set up on end. A green mould is settling on the names of the deceased, carved on the silver door-plates. Sardonic spiders have sewed up the key-holes. All is silence and dust and desolation.  — I interrupt this a moment, to take a shy at Watkins with the second volume of César Birotteau. Missed him! I think I could bring him down with a copy of Sainte-Beuve or the Dictionnaire Universel, if I had it. These small Balzac books somehow don't quite fit my hand; but I shall fetch him yet. I've an idea Watkins is tapping the old gentleman's Château Yquem. Duplicate key of the wine-cellar. Hibernian swarries in the front basement. Young Cheops up stairs, snug in his cerements. Watkins glides into my chamber, with that colorless, hypocritical face of his drawn out long like an accordion; but I know he grins all the way down stairs, and is glad I have broken my leg. Was not my evil star in the very zenith when I ran up to town to attend that dinner at Delmonico's? I didn't come up altogether for that. It was partly to buy Frank Livingstone's roan mare Margot. And now I shall not be able to sit in the saddle these two months. I'll send the mare down to you at The Pines, — is that the name of the place?

Old Dillon fancies that I have something on my mind. He drives me wild with lemons. Lemons for a mind diseased! Nonsense. I am only as restless as the devil under this confinement, — a thing I'm not used to. Take a man who has never had so much as a headache or a tooth-ache in his life, strap one of his legs in a section of water-spout, keep him in a room in the city for weeks, with the hot weather turned on, and then expect him to smile and purr and be happy! It is preposterous. I can't be cheerful or calm.

Your letter is the first consoling thing I have had since my disaster, ten days ago. It really cheered me up for half an hour. Send me a screed, Ned, as often as you can, if you love me. Anything will do. Write me more about that little girl in the hammock. That was very pretty, all that about the Dresden china shepherdess and the pond-lily; the imagery a little mixed, perhaps, but very pretty. I didn't suppose you had so much sentimental furniture in your upper story. It shows how one may be familiar for years with the reception-room of his neighbor, and never suspect what is directly under his mansard. I supposed your loft stuffed with dry legal parchments, mortgages and affidavits; you take down a package of manuscript, and lo! there are lyrics and sonnets and canzonettas. You really have a graphic descriptive touch, Edward Delaney, and I suspect you of anonymous love-tales in the mgazines.

I shall be a bear until I hear from you again. Tell me all about your pretty *inconnue* across the road. What is her name? Who is she? Who's her father? Where's her mother? Who's her lover? You cannot imagine how this will occupy me. The more trifling the better. My imprisonment has weakened me intellectually to such a degree that I find your epistolary gifts quite considerable. I am passing into my second childhood. In a week or two I shall take to India-rubber rings and prongs of coral. A silver cup, with an appropriate inscription, would be a delicate attention on your part. In the meantime, write!

## IV

*Edward Delaney to John Flemming*

August 12, — .

THE SICK pasha shall be amused. *Bismillah!* he wills it so. If the story-teller becomes prolix and tedious, — the bow-string and the sack, and two Nubians to drop him into the Piscataqua! But, truly, Jack, I have a hard task. There is literally nothing here, — except the little girl over the way. She is swinging in the hammock at this moment. It is to me compensation for many of the ills of life to see her now and then put out a small kid boot, which fits like a glove, and set herself going. Who is she, and what is her name? Her name is Daw. Only daughter of Mr. Richard W. Daw, ex-colonel and banker. Mother dead. One brother at Harvard, elder brother killed at the battle of Fair Oaks, nine years ago. Old, rich family, the Daws. This is the homestead, where father and daughter pass eight months of the twelve; the rest of the year in Baltimore and Washington. The New England winter too many for the old gentleman. The daughter is called Marjorie, — Marjorie Daw. Sounds odd at first, doesn't it? But after you say it over to yourself half a dozen times, you like it. There's a pleasing quaintness to it, something prim and violet-like. Must be a nice sort of girl to be called Marjorie Daw.

I had mine host of The Pines in the witness-box last night, and drew the foregoing testimony from him. He has charge of Mr. Daw's vegetable-garden, and has known the family these thirty years. Of course I shall make the acquaintance of my neighbors before many days. It will be next to impossible for me not to meet Mr. Daw or Miss Daw in some of my walks. The young lady has a favorite path to the sea-beach. I shall intercept her some morning, and touch my hat to her. Then the princess will bend her fair head to me with courteous surprise not unmixed with haughtiness. Will snub me, in fact. All this for thy sake, O Pasha of the Snapt Axle-tree! . . . How oddly things fall out! Ten minutes ago I was called down to the parlor, — you know the kind of parlors in farmhouses on the coast, a sort of amphibious parlor, with sea-shells on the mantle-piece and spruce branches in the chimney-place, — where I found my father and Mr. Daw doing the antique polite to each other. He had come to pay his respects to his new neighbors. Mr. Daw is a tall, slim gentleman of about fifty-five, with a florid face and snow-white mustache and side-whiskers. Looks like Mr. Dombey, or as Mr. Dombey would have looked if he had served a few years in the British Army. Mr. Daw was a colonel in the late war, commanding the regiment in which his son was a lieutenant. Plucky old boy, backbone of New Hampshire granite. Before taking his leave, the colonel delivered himself of an invitation as if he were issuing a general order. Miss Daw has a few friends coming, at 4 P.M., to play croquet on the lawn (parade-ground) and have tea (cold rations) on the piazza. Will we honor them with our company? (or be sent to the guard-house.) My father declines on the plea of ill-health. My father's son bows with as much suavity as he knows, and accepts.

In my next I shall have something to tell you. I shall have seen the little beauty face to face. I have a presentiment, Jack, that this Daw is a *rara avis*! Keep up your spirits, my boy, until I write you another letter, — and send me along word how's your leg.


V

*Edward Delaney to John Flemming*

August 13, — .

THE PARTY, my dear Jack, was as dreary as possible. A lieutenant of the navy, the rector of the Episcopal church at Stillwater, and a society swell from Nahant. The lieutenant looked as if he had swallowed a couple of his buttons, and found the bullion rather indigestible; the rector was a pensive youth, of the daffydowndilly sort; and the swell from Nahant was a very weak tidal wave indeed. The women were much better, as they always are; the two Miss Kingsburys of Philadelphia, staying at the Sea-shell House, two bright and engaging girls. But Marjorie Daw!

The company broke up soon after tea, and I remained to smoke a cigar with the colonel on the piazza. It was like seeing a picture to see Miss Marjorie hovering around the old soldier, and doing a hundred gracious little things for him. She brought the cigars and lighted the tapers with her own delicate fingers, in the most enchanting fashion. As we sat there, she came and went in the summer twilight, and seemed, with her white dress and pale gold hair, like some lovely phantom that had sprung into existence out of the smoke-wreaths. If she had melted into air, like the statue of Galatea in the play, I should have been more sorry than surprised.

It was easy to perceive that the old colonel worshipped her, and she him. I think the relation between an elderly father and a daughter just blooming into womanhood the most beautiful possible. There is in it a subtle sentiment that cannot exist in the case of mother and daughter, or that of son and mother. But this is getting into deep water.

I sat with the Daws until half past ten, and saw the moon rise on the sea. The ocean, that had stretched motionless and black against the horizon, was changed by magic into a broken field of glittering ice, inter-spersed with marvellous silvery fjords. In the far distance the Isles of Shoals loomed up like a group of huge bergs drifting down on us. The Polar Regions in a June thaw! It was exceedingly fine. What did we talk about? We talked about the weather — and *you!* The weather has been disagreeable for several days past, — and so have you. I glided from one topic to the other very naturally. I told my friends of your accident; how it had frustrated all our summer plans, and what our plans were. I played quite a spirited solo on the fibula. Then I described you; or, rather, I didn't. I spoke of your amiability, of your patience under this severe affliction; of your touching gratitude when Dillon brings you little presents of fruit; of your tenderness to your sister Fanny, whom you would not allow to stay in town to nurse you, and how you heroically sent her back to Newport, preferring to remain alone with Mary, the cook, and your man Watkins, to whom, by the way, you were devotedly attached. If you had been there, Jack, you wouldn't have known yourself. I should have excelled as a criminal lawyer, if I had not turned my attention to a different branch of jurisprudence.

Miss Marjorie asked all manner of leading questions concerning you. It did not occur to me then, but it struck me forcibly afterwards, that she evinced a singular interest in the conversation. When I got back to my room, I recalled how eagerly she leaned forward, with her full, snowy throat in strong moonlight, listening to what I said. Posi-tively, I think I made her like you!

Miss Daw is a girl whom you would like immensely, I can tell you that. A beauty without affectation, a high and tender nature, — if one can read the soul in the face. And the old colonel is a noble character, too.

I am glad the Daws are such pleasant people. The Pines is an isolated spot, and my resources are few. I fear I should have found life here somewhat monotonous before long, with no other society than that of my excellent sire. It is true, I might have made a target of the defenceless invalid; but I haven't a taste for artillery, *moi*.

## VI

### *John Flemming to Edward Delaney*

August 17, —

FOR A MAN who hasn't a taste for artillery, it occurs to me, my friend, you are keeping up a pretty lively fire on my inner works. But go on. Cynicism is a small brass field-piece that eventually bursts and kills the artilleryman.

You may abuse me as much as you like, and I'll not complain; for I don't know what I should do without your letters. They are curing me. I haven't hurled anything at Watkins since last Sunday, partly because I have grown more amiable under your teaching, and partly because Watkins captured my ammunition one night, and carried it off to the library. He is rapidly losing the habit he had acquired of dodging whenever I rub my ear, or make any slight motion with my right arm. He is still suggestive of the wine-cellar, however. You may break, you may shatter Watkins, if you will, but the scent of the Roederer will hang round him still.

Ned, that Miss Daw must be a charming person. I should certainly like her. I like her already. When you spoke in your first letter of seeing a young girl swinging in a hammock under your chamber window, I was somehow strangely drawn to her. I cannot account for it in the least. What you have subsequently written of Miss Daw has strengthened the impression. You seem to be describing a woman I have known in some previous state of existence, or dreamed of in this. Upon my word, if you were to send me her photograph, I believe I should recognize her at a glance. Her manner, that listening attitude, her traits of character, as you indicate them, the light hair and the dark eyes, — they are all familiar things to me. Asked a lot of questions, did she? Curious about me? That is strange.

You would laugh in your sleeve, you wretched old cynic, if you knew how I lie awake nights, with my gas turned down to a star, thinking of The Pines and the house across the road. How cool it must be down there! I long for the salt smell in the air. I picture the colonel smoking his cheroot on the piazza. I send you and Miss Daw off on afternoon rambles along the beach. Sometimes I let you stroll with her under the elms in the moonlight, for you are great friends by this time, I take it, and see each other every day. I know your ways and your manners! Then I fall into a truculent mood, and would like to destroy somebody. Have you noticed anything in the shape of a lover hanging around the colonial Lares and Penates? Does that lieutenant of the horse-marines or that young Stillwater parson visit the house much? Not that I am pining for news of them, but any gossip of the kind would be in order. I wonder, Ned, you don't fall in love with Miss Daw. I am ripe to do it myself. Speaking of photographs, couldn't you manage to slip one of her *cartes-de-visite* from her album, — she must have an album, you know, — and send it to me? I will return it before it could be missed. That's a good fellow! Did the mare arrive safe and sound? It will be a capital animal this autumn for Central Park.

O — my leg? I forgot about my leg. It's better.

## VII

### *Edward Delaney to John Flemming*

August 20, —

YOU are correct in your surmises. I am on the most friendly terms with our neighbors. The colonel and my father smoke their afternoon cigar together in our sitting-room or on the piazza opposite, and I pass an hour or two of the day or the evening with the daughter. I am more and more struck by the beauty, modesty, and intelligence of Miss Daw.

You ask me why I do not fall in love with her. I will be frank, Jack: I have thought of that. She is young, rich, accomplished, uniting in herself more attractions, mental and personal, than I can recall in any girl of my acquaintance; but she lacks the something that would be necessary in inspire in me that kind of interest. Possessing this unknown quality, a woman neither beautiful nor wealthy nor very young could bring me to her feet. But not Miss Daw. If we were shipwrecked together on an uninhabited island, — let me suggest a tropical island, for it costs no more to be picturesque, — I would build her a bamboo hut, I would fetch her bread-fruit and cocoanuts, I would fry yams for her, I would lure the ingenuous turtle and make her nourishing soups, but I wouldn't make love to her, — not under eighteen months. I would like to have her for a sister, that I might shield her and counsel her, and spend half my income on thread-laces and camel's-hair shawls. (We are off the island now.) If such were not my feeling, there would still be an obstacle to my loving Miss Daw. A greater misfortune could scarcely befall me than to love her. Flemming, I am about to make a revelation that will astonish you. I may be all wrong in my premises and consequently in my conclusions; but you shall judge.

That night when I returned to my room after the croquet party at the Daws', and was thinking over the trivial events of the evening, I was suddenly impressed by the air of eager attention with which Miss Daw had followed my account of your accident. I think I mentioned this to you. Well, the next morning, as I went to mail my letter, I overtook Miss Daw on the road to Rye, where the post-office is, and accompanied her thither and back, an hour's walk. The conversation again turned on you, and again I remarked that inexplicable look of interest which had lighted up her face the previous evening. Since then, I have seen Miss Daw perhaps ten times, perhaps oftener, and on each occasion I found that when I was not speaking of you, or your sister, or some person or place associated with you, I was not holding her attention. She would be absent-minded, her eyes would wander away from me to the sea, or to some distant object in the landscape; her fingers would play with the leaves of a book in a way that convinced me she was not listening. At these moments if I abruptly changed the theme, — I did it several times as an experiment, — and dropped some remark about my friend Flemming, then the sombre blue eyes would come back to me instantly.

Now, is this not the oddest thing in the world? No, not the oddest. The effect which you tell me was produced on you by my casual mention of an unknown girl swinging in a hammock is certainly as strange. You can conjecture how that passage in your letter of Friday startled me. Is it possible, then, that two people who have never met, and who are hundreds of miles apart, can exert a magnetic influence on each other? I have read of such psychological phenomena, but never credited them. I leave the solution of the problem to you. As for myself, all other things being favorable, it would be impossible for me to fall in love with a woman who listens to me only when I am talking of my friend!

I am not aware that any one is paying marked attention to my fair neighbor. The lieutenant of the navy — he is stationed at Rivermouth — sometimes drops in of an evening, and sometimes the rector from Stillwater; the lieutenant the oftener. He was there last night. I would not be surprised if he had an eye to the heiress; but he is not formidable. Mistress Daw carries a neat little spear of irony, and the honest lieutenant seems to have a particular facility for impaling himself on the point of it. He is not dangerous, I should say; though I have known a woman to satirize a man for years, and marry him after all. Decidedly, the lowly rector is not dangerous; yet, again, who has not seen Cloth of Frieze victorious in the lists where Cloth of Gold went down?

As to the photograph. There is an exquisite ivorytype of Marjorie, in passe-partout, on the drawing-room mantel-piece. It would be missed at once, if taken. I would do anything reasonable for you, Jack, but I've no burning desire to be hauled up before the local justice of the peace, on a charge of petty larceny.

P. S. — Enclosed is a spray of mignonette, which I advise you to treat tenderly. Yes, we talked of you again last night, as usual. It is becoming a little dreary for me.


## VIII

### *Edward Delaney to John Flemming*

August 22, — .

YOUR letter in reply to my last has occupied my thoughts all the morning. I do not know what to think. Do you mean to say that you are seriously half in love with a woman whom you have never seen, — with a shadow, a chimera? for what else can Miss Daw be to you? I do not understand it at all. I understand neither you nor her. You are a couple of ethereal beings moving in finer air that I can breathe with my commonplace lungs. Such delicacy of sentiment is something I admire without comprehending. I am bewildered. I am of the earth earthy, and I find myself in the incongruous position of having to do with mere souls, with natures so finely tempered that I run some risk of shattering them in my awkwardness. I am as Caliban among the spirits!

Reflecting on your letter, I am not sure it is wise in me to continue this correspondence. But no, Jack; I do wrong to doubt the good sense that forms the basis of your character. You are deeply interested in Miss Daw; you feel that she is a person whom you may perhaps greatly admire when you know her: at the same time you bear in mind that the chances are ten to five that, when you do come to know her, she will fall far short of your ideal, and you will not care for her in the least. Look at it in this sensible light, and I will hold back nothing from you.

Yesterday afternoon my father and myself rode over to Rivermouth with the Daws. A heavy rain in the morning had cooled the atmosphere and laid the dust. To Rivermouth is a drive of eight miles, along a winding road lined all the way with wild barberry-bushes. I never saw anything more brilliant than these bushes, the green of the foliage and the pink of the coral berries intensified by the rain. The colonel drove, with my father in front, Miss Daw and I on the back seat. I resolved that for the first five miles your name should not pass my lips. I was amused by the artful attempts she made, at the start, to break through my reticence. Then a silence fell upon her; and then she became suddenly gay.

That keenness which I enjoyed so much when it was exercised on the lieutenant was not so satisfactory directed against myself. Miss Daw has great sweetness of disposition, but she can be disagreeable. She is like the young lady in the rhyme, with the curl on her forehead,

> "When she is good,
> She is very, very good,
> And when she is bad, she is horrid!"

I kept to my resolution, however; but on the return home I relented, and talked of your mare! Miss Daw is going to try a side-saddle on Margot some morning. The animal is a trifle too light for my weight. By the by, I nearly forgot to say Miss Daw sat for a picture yesterday to a River-mouth artist. If the negative turns out well, I am to have a copy. So our ends will be accomplished without crime. I wish, though, I could send you the ivorytype in the drawing-room; it is cleverly colored, and would give you an idea of her hair and eyes, which of course the other will not.

No, Jack, the spray of mignonette did not come from me. A man of twenty-eight doesn't enclose flowers in his letters — to another man. But don't attach too much significance to the circumstance. She gives sprays of mignonette to the rector, sprays to the lieutenant. She has even given a rose from her bosom to your slave. It is her jocund nature to scatter flowers, like Spring.

If my letters sometimes read disjointedly, you must understand that I never finish one at a sitting, but write at intervals, when the mood is on me.

The mood is not on me now.


## IX

### *Edward Delaney to John Flemming*

August 23, — .

I HAVE just returned from the strangest interview with Marjorie. She has all but confessed to me her interest in you. But with what modesty and dignity! Her words elude my pen as I attempt to put them on paper; and, indeed, it was not so much what she said as her manner; and that I cannot reproduce. Perhaps it was of a piece with the strangeness of this whole business, that she should tacitly acknowledge to a third party the love she feels for a man she has never beheld! But I have lost, through your aid, the faculty of being surprised. I accept things as people do in dreams. Now that I am again in my room, it all appears like an illusion, — the black masses of Rembrandtish shadow under the trees, the fireflies whirling in Pyrrhic dances among the shrubbery, the sea over there, Marjorie sitting on the hammock!

It is past midnight, and I am too sleepy to write more.

Thursday Morning.

My father has suddenly taken it into his head to spend a few days at the Shoals. In the meanwhile you will not hear from me. I see Marjorie walking in the garden with the colonel. I wish I could speak to her alone, but shall probably not have an opportunity before we leave.

## X

*Edward Delaney to John Flemming.*

August 28, — .

YOU WERE passing into your second childhood, were you? Your intellect was so reduced that my epistolary gifts seemed quite considerable to you, did they? I rise superior to the sarcasm in your favor of the 11th instant, when I notice that five days' silence on my part is sufficient to throw you into the depths of despondency.

We returned only this morning from Appledore, that enchanted island, — at four dollars per day. I find on my desk three letters from you! Evidently there is no lingering doubt in *your* mind as to the pleasure I derive from your correspondence. These letters are undated, but in what I take to be the latest are two passages that require my consideration. You will pardon my candor, dear Flemming, but the conviction forces itself upon me that as your leg grows stronger your head becomes weaker. You ask my advice on a certain point. I will give it. In my opinion you could do nothing more unwise than to address a note to Miss Daw, thanking her for the flower. It would, I am sure, offend her delicacy beyond pardon. She knows you only through me; you are to her an abstraction, a figure in a dream, — a dream from which the faintest shock would awaken her. Of course, if you enclose a note to me and insist on its delivery, I shall deliver it; but I advise you not to do so.

You say you are able, with the aid of a cane, to walk about your chamber, and that you purpose to come to The Pines the instant Dillon thinks you strong enough to stand the journey. Again I advise you not to. Do you not see that every hour you remain away, Marjorie's glamour deepens, and your influence over her increases? You will ruin everything by precipitancy. Wait until you are entirely recovered; in any case, do not come without giving me warning. I fear the effect of your abrupt advent here — under the circumstances.

Miss Daw was evidently glad to see us back again, and gave me both hands in the frankest way. She stopped at the door a moment, this afternoon, in the carriage; she had been over to Rivermouth for her pictures. Unluckily the photographer had spilt some acid on the plate, and she was obliged to give him another sitting. I have an intuition that something is troubling Marjorie. She had an abstracted air not usual with her. However, it may be only my fancy . . . I end this, leaving several things unsaid, to accompany my father on one of those long rides which are now his chief medicine, — and mine!

## XI

### *Edward Delaney to John Flemming*

August 29, — .

I WRITE in great haste to tell you what has taken place here since my letter of last night. I am in the utmost perplexity. Only one thing is plain, — *you* must not dream of coming to The Pines. Marjorie has told her father everything! I saw her for a few minutes, an hour ago, in the garden; and, as near as I could gather from her confused statement, the facts are these: Lieutenant Bradly — that's the naval officer stationed at Rivermouth — has been paying court to Miss Daw for some time past, but not so much to her liking as to that of the colonel, who it seems is an old friend of the young gentleman's father. Yesterday (I knew she was in some trouble when she drove up to our gate) the colonel spoke to Marjorie of Bradly, — urged his suit, I infer. Marjorie expressed her dislike for the lieutenant with characteristic frankness, and finally confessed to her father — well, I really do not know what she confessed. It must have been the vaguest of confessions, and must have sufficiently puzzled the colonel. At any rate, it exasperated him. I suppose I am implicated in the matter, and that the colonel feels bitterly towards me. I do not see why: I have carried no messages between you and Miss Daw; I have behaved with the greatest discretion. I can find no flaw anywhere in my proceeding. I do not see that anybody has done anything, — except the colonel himself.

It is probable, nevertheless, that the friendly relations between the two houses will be broken off. "A plague o' both your houses," say you. I will keep you informed, as well as I can, of what occurs over the way. We shall remain here until the second week in September. Stay where you are, or, at all events, do not dream of joining me . . . Colonel Daw is sitting on the piazza looking rather wicked. I have not seen Marjorie since I parted with her in the garden.

## XII

### *Edward Delaney to Thomas Dillon,*
### *M. D., Madison Square, New York*

August 30, — .

MY DEAR DOCTOR: If you have any influence over Flemming, I beg of you to exert it to prevent his coming to this place at present. There are circumstances, which I will explain to you before long, that make it of the first importance that he should not come into this neighborhood. His appearance here, I speak advisedly, would be disastrous to him. In urging him to remain in New York, or to go to some inland resort, you will be doing him and me a real service. Of course you will not mention my name in this connection. You know me well enough, my dear doctor, to be assured that, in begging your secret co-operation, I have reasons that will meet your entire approval when they are made plain to you. We shall return to town on the 15th of next month, and my first duty will be to present myself at your hospitable door and satisfy your curiosity, if I have excited it. My father, I am glad to state, has so greatly improved that he can no longer be regarded as an invalid. With great esteem, I am, etc., etc.

## XIII

### *Edward Delaney to John Flemming*

August 31, — .

YOUR letter, announcing your mad determination to come here, has just reached me. I beseech you to reflect a moment. The step would be fatal to your interests and hers. You would furnish just cause for irritation to R. W. D.; and, though he loves Marjorie tenderly, he is capable of going to any lengths if opposed. You would not like, I am convinced, to be the means of causing him to treat *her* with severity. That would be the result of your presence at The Pines at this juncture. I am annoyed to be obliged to point out these things to you. We are on very delicate ground, Jack; the situation is critical, and the slightest mistake in a move would cost us the game. If you consider it worth the winning, be patient. Trust a little to my sagacity. Wait and see what happens. Moreover, I understand from Dillon that you are in no condition to take so long a journey. He thinks the air of the coast would be the worst thing possible for you; that you ought to go inland, if anywhere. Be advised by me. Be advised by Dillon.

## XIV

*Telegrams*

September 1, — .

### 1. — To EDWARD DELANEY

Letter received. Dillon be hanged. I think I ought to be on the ground.

J. F.

### 2. — To JOHN FLEMMING

Stay where you are. You would only complicate matters. Do not move until you hear from me.

E. D.

### 3. — To EDWARD DELANEY

My being at The Pines could be kept secret. I must see her.

J. F.

### 4. — To JOHN FLEMMING

Do not think of it. It would be useless. R. W. D. has locked M. in her room. You would not be able to effect an interview.

E. D.

### 5. — To EDWARD DELANEY

Locked her in her room. Good God. That settles the question. I shall leave by the twelve-fifteen express.

J. F.

## XV

*The Arrival*

ON the second of September, 187 — , as the down express due at 3:40 left the station at Hampton, a young man, leaning on the shoulder of a servant, whom he addressed as Watkins, stepped from the platform into a hack, and requested to be driven to "The Pines." On arriving at the gate of a modest farm-house, a few miles from the station, the young man descended with difficulty from the carriage, and, casting a hasty glance across the road, seemed much impressed by some peculiarity in the landscape. Again leaning on the shoulder of the person Watkins, he walked to the door of the farm-house and inquired for Mr. Edward Delaney. He was informed by the aged man who answered his knock, that Mr. Edward Delaney had gone to Boston the day before, but that Mr. Jonas Delaney was within. This information did not appear satisfactory to the stranger, who inquired if Mr. Edward Delaney had left any message for Mr. John Flemming. There *was* a letter for Mr. Flemming, if he were that person. After a brief absence the aged man reappeared with a letter.

## XVI

### *Edward Delaney to John Flemming*

September 1, — .

I AM horror-stricken at what I have done! When I began this correspondence I had no other purpose than to relieve the tedium of your sick-chamber. Dillon told me to cheer you up. I tried to. I thought you entered into the spirit of the thing. I had no idea, until within a few days, that you were taking matters *au sérieux.*

What can I say? I am in sackcloth and ashes. I am a pariah, a dog of an outcast. I tried to make a little romance to interest you, something soothing and idyllic, and, by Jove! I have done it only too well! My father doesn't know a word of this, so don't jar the old gentleman any more than you can help. I fly from the wrath to come — when you arrive! For O, dear Jack, there isn't any colonial mansion on the other side of the road, there isn't any piazza, there isn't any hammock, — there isn't any Marjorie Daw! !

# Frank Stockton (1834–1902)

A NATIVE Philadelphian, Stockton began his literary career as a writer of children's stories, many of which appeared in *St. Nicholas Magazine*, of which he was the editor. He was to become much better known as the author of a "whimsically fantastic novel," *Rudder Grange* (1879). In it a young couple trying to economize by living aboard a canal boat have their lives complicated by a maid who tries to pattern her life according to the Gothic romances that are her favorite reading. A Stockton book that this reader adored as a child was *The Casting Away of Mrs. Lecks and Mrs. Aleshine* (1886), about two middle-aged housewives cast adrift by a shipwreck in the middle of the Pacific Ocean with a string of frankfurters floating along beside them. Stockton was a prolific writer, his novels and short stories totaling twenty-three volumes. None, however, equalled the sensation caused by his "The Lady or the Tiger?" published in *The Century Magazine* in 1882.

This story led to lively debates between the male chauvinists of the eighteen-eighties and the followers of Susan B. Anthony, whose classic four-volume *History of Woman Suffrage* was appearing during the same years. Masculine opponents of equal rights who were then very much in the majority asserted women were such jealous creatures that the girl in the story would rather sacrifice the life of a lover than surrender him to another member of her sex. More than one woman retorted that the king who devised such a fiendish ordeal was male. And that only a man writer could dream up a tale like this. Either way, "The Lady or the Tiger?" is a literary riddle and still continues to tease thousands of readers today.

# The Lady or the Tiger?

IN THE very olden time, there lived a semi-barbaric king, whose ideas, though somewhat polished and sharpened by the progressiveness of distant Latin neighbors, were still large, florid, and untrammelled, as became the half of him which was barbaric. He was a man of exuberant fancy, and, withal, of an authority so irresistible that, at his will, he turned his varied fancies into facts. He was greatly given to self-communing, and when he and himself agreed upon anything, the thing was done. When every member of his domestic and political systems moved smoothly in its appointed course, his nature was bland and genial; but whenever there was a little hitch, and some of his orbs got out of their orbits, he was blander and more genial still, for nothing pleased him so much as to make the crooked straight, and crush down uneven places.

Among the borrowed notions by which his barbarism had become semified was that of the public arena, in which, by exhibitions of manly and beastly valor; the minds of his subjects were refined and cultured.

But even here the exuberant and barbaric fancy asserted itself. The arena of the king was built, not to give the people an opportunity of hearing the rhapsodies of dying gladiators, nor to enable them to view the inevitable conclusion of a conflict between religious opinions and hungry jaws, but for purposes far better adapted to widen and develop the mental energies of the people. This vast amphitheatre, with its encircling galleries, its mysterious vaults, and its unseen passages, was an agent of poetic justice, in which crime was punished, or virtue rewarded, by the decrees of an impartial and incorruptible chance.

When a subject was accused of a crime of sufficient importance to interest the king, public notice was given that on an appointed day the fate of the accused person would be decided in the king's arena — a structure which well deserved its name; for, although its form and plan were borrowed from afar, its purpose emanated solely from the brain of this man, who, every barleycorn a king, knew no tradition to which he owed more allegiance than pleased his fancy, and who ingrafted on every adopted form of human thought and action the rich growth of his barbaric idealism.

When all the people had assembled in the galleries, and the king, surrounded by his court, sat high up on his throne of royal state on one side of the arena, he gave a signal, a door beneath him opened, and the accused subject stepped out into the amphitheatre. Directly opposite him, on the other side of the enclosed space, were two doors, exactly alike and side by side. It was the duty and the privilege of the person on trial to walk directly to these doors and open one of them. He could open either door he pleased. He was subject to no guidance or influence but that of the aforementioned impartial and incorruptible chance. If he opened the one, there came out of it a hungry tiger, the fiercest and most cruel that could be procured, which immediately sprang upon him, and tore him to pieces, as a punishment for his guilt. The moment that the case of the criminal was thus decided, doleful iron bells were clanged, great wails went up from the hired mourners posted on the outer rim of the arena, and the vast audience, with bowed heads and downcast hearts, wended slowly their homeward way, mourning greatly that one so young and fair, or so old and respected, should have merited so dire a fate.

But if the accused person opened the other door, there came forth from it a lady, the most suitable to his years and station that his Majesty could select among his fair subjects; and to this lady he was immediately married, as a reward of his innocence. It mattered not that he might already possess a wife and family, or that his affections might be engaged upon an object of his own selection. The king allowed no such subordinate arrangements to interfere with his great scheme of retribution and reward. The exercises, as in the other instance, took place immediately, and in the arena. Another door opened beneath the king, and a priest, followed by a band of choristers, and dancing maidens blowing joyous airs on golden horns and treading an epithalamic measure, advanced to where the pair stood side by side, and the wedding was promptly and cheerily solemnized. Then the gay brass bells rang forth their merry peals, the people shouted glad hurrahs, and the innocent man, preceded by children strewing flowers on his path, led his bride to his home.

This was the king's semi-barbaric method of administering justice. Its perfect fairness is obvious. The criminal could not know out of which door would come the lady. He opened either he pleased, without having the slightest idea whether, in the next instant, he was to be devoured or married. On some occasions the tiger came out of one door, and on some out of the other. The decisions of this tribunal were not only fair — they were positively determinate. The accused person was instantly punished if he found himself guilty, and if innocent he was rewarded on the spot, whether he liked it or not. There was no escape from the judgments of the king's arena.

The institution was a very popular one. When the people gathered together on one of the great trial days, they never knew whether they were to witness a bloody slaughter or a hilarious wedding. This element of uncertainty lent an interest to the occasion which it could not otherwise have attained. Thus the masses were entertained and pleased, and the thinking part of the community could bring no charge of unfairness against this plan; for did not the accused person have the whole matter in his own hands?

This semi-barbaric king had a daughter as blooming as his most florid fancies, and with a soul as fervent and imperious as his own. As is usual in such cases, she was the apple of his eye, and was loved by him above all humanity. Among his courtiers was a young man of that fineness of blood and lowness of station common to the conventional heroes of romance who love royal maidens. This royal maiden was well satisfied with her lover, for he was handsome and brave to a degree unsurpassed in all this kingdom, and she loved him with an ardor that had enough of barbarism in it to make it exceedingly warm and strong. This love affair moved on happily for many months, until, one day, the king happened to discover its existence. He did not hesitate nor waver in regard to his duty in the premises. The youth was immediately cast into prison, and a day was appointed for his trial in the king's arena. This, of course, was an especially important occasion, and his Majesty, as well as all the people, was greatly interested in the workings and development of this trial. Never before had such a case occurred — never before had a subject dared to love the daughter of a king. In after years such things became commonplace enough, but then they were, in no slight degree, novel and startling.

The tiger cages of the kingdom were searched for the most savage and relentless beasts, from which the fiercest monster might be selected for the arena, and the ranks of maiden youth and beauty throughout the land were carefully surveyed by competent judges, in order that the young man might have a fitting bride in case fate did not determine for him a different destiny. Of course, everybody knew that the deed with which the accused was charged had been done. He had loved the princess, and neither he, she, nor any one else thought of denying the fact. But the king would not think of allowing any fact of this kind to interfere with the workings of the tribunal, in which he took such great delight and satisfaction. No matter how the affair turned out, the youth would be disposed of, and the king would take an aesthetic pleasure in watching the course of events which would determine whether or not the young man had done wrong in allowing himself to love the princess.

The appointed day arrived. From far and near the people gathered, and thronged the great galleries of the arena, while crowds, unable to gain admittance, massed themselves against its outside walls. The king and his court were in their places, opposite the twin doors — those fateful portals, so terrible in their similarity!

All was ready. The signal was given. A door beneath the royal party opened, and the lover of the princess walked into the arena. Tall, beautiful, fair, his appearance was greeted with a low hum of admiration and anxiety. Half the audience had not known so grand a youth had lived among them. No wonder the princess loved him! What a terrible thing for him to be there!

As the youth advanced into the arena, he turned, as the custom was, to bow to the king. But he did not think at all of that royal personage; his eyes were fixed upon the princess, who sat to the right of her father. Had it not been for the moiety of barbarism in her nature, it is probable that lady would not have been there. But her intense and fervid soul would not allow her to be absent on an occasion in which she was so terribly interested. From the moment that the decree had gone forth that her lover should decide his fate in the king's arena, she had thought of nothing, night or day, but this great event and the various subjects connected with it. Possessed of more power, influence, and force of character than any one who had ever before been interested in such a case, she had done what no other person had done — she had possessed herself of the secret of the doors. She knew in which of the two rooms behind those doors stood the cage of the tiger, with its open front, and in which waited the lady. Through these thick doors, heavily curtained with skins on the inside, it was impossible that any noise or suggestion should come from within to the person who should approach to raise the latch of one of them. But gold, and the power of a woman's will, had brought the secret to the princess.

Not only did she know in which room stood the lady, ready to emerge, all blushing and radiant, should her door be opened, but she knew who the lady was. It was one of the fairest and loveliest of the damsels of the court who had been selected as the reward of the accused youth, should he be proved innocent of the crime of aspiring to one so far above him; and the princess hated her. Often had she seen, or imagined that she had seen, this fair creature throwing glances of admiration upon the person of her lover, and sometimes she thought these glances were perceived and even returned. Now and then she had seen them talking together. It was but for a moment or two, but much can be said in a brief space. It may have been on most unimportant topics, but how could she know that? The girl was lovely, but she had dared to raise her eyes to the loved one of the princess, and, with all the intensity of the savage blood transmitted to her through long lines of wholly barbaric ancestors, she hated the woman who blushed and trembled behind that silent door.

When her lover turned and looked at her, and his eye met hers as she sat there paler and whiter than any one in the vast ocean of anxious faces about her, he saw, by the power of quick perception which is given to those whose souls are one, that she knew behind which door crouched the tiger, and behind which stood the lady. He had expected her to know it. He understood her nature, and his soul was assured that she would never rest until she had made plain to herself this thing, hidden to all other lookers-on, even to the king. The only hope for the youth in which there was any element of certainty was based upon the success of the princess in discovering this mystery, and the moment he looked upon her, he saw she had succeeded.

Then it was that his quick and anxious glance asked the question, "Which?" It was as plain to her as if he shouted it from where he stood. There was not an instant to be lost. The question was asked in a flash; it must be answered in another.

Her right arm lay on the cushioned parapet before her. She raised her hand, and made a slight, quick movement toward the right. No one but her lover saw her. Every eye but his was fixed on the man in the arena.

He turned, and with a firm and rapid step he walked across the empty space. Every heart stopped beating, every breath was held, every eye was fixed immovably upon that man. Without the slightest hesitation, he went to the door on the right, and opened it.

Now, the point of the story is this: Did the tiger come out of that door, or did the lady?

The more we reflect upon this question, the harder it is to answer. It involves a study of the human heart which leads us through devious mazes of passion, out of which it is difficult to find our way. Think of it, fair reader, not as if the decision of the question depended upon yourself, but upon that hot-blooded, semi-barbaric princess, her soul at a white heat beneath the combined fires of despair and jealousy. She had lost him, but who should have him?

How often, in her waking hours and in her dreams, had she started in wild horror and covered her face with her hands as she thought of her lover opening the door on the other side of which waited the cruel fangs of the tiger!

But how much oftener had she seen him at the other door! How in her grievous reveries had she gnashed her teeth and torn her hair when she saw his start of rapturous delight as he opened the door of the lady! How her soul had burned in agony when she had seen him rush to meet that woman, with her flushing cheek and sparkling eye of triumph; when she had seen him lead her forth, his whole frame kindled with the joy of recovered life; when she had heard the glad shouts from the multitude, and the wild ringing of the happy bells; when she had seen the priest, with his joyous followers, advance to the couple, and make them man and wife before her very eyes; and when she had seen them walk away together upon their path of flowers, followed by the tremendous shouts of the hilarious multitude, in which her one despairing shriek was lost and drowned!

Would it not be better for him to die at once, and go to wait for her in the blessed regions of semi-barbaric futurity?

And yet, that awful tiger, those shrieks, that blood!

Her decision had been indicated in an instant, but it had been made after days and nights of anguished deliberation. She had known she would be asked, she had decided what she would answer, and, without the slightest hesitation, she had moved her hand to the right.

The question of her decision is one not to be lightly considered, and it is not for me to presume to set up myself as the person able to answer it. So I leave it with all of you: Which came out of the opened door — the lady or the tiger?

# Charles Egbert Craddock (1850–1922)

TO THE AMAZEMENT of "his" thousands of enthusiastic readers who had been following the Craddock short stories in leading magazines, and even of the editors themselves, the author turned out to be, in the words of *The Oxford Companion to American Literature*, a "frail, crippled spinster." She was Mary Noailles Murfree, born in Murfreesboro, Tennessee, in 1850, and she became her native state's foremost regional writer. She wrote eleven collections of short stories, as well as many novels, most of them historical. Called by Thomas Jefferson the "Volunteer State," because it was the first to volunteer in both the War of 1812 and the Mexican War, Tennessee, next to Virginia, endured the bloodiest fighting of the Civil War. As a child, Mary Murfree saw it personally and many of her novels were inspired by that conflict.

"Over on the T'Other Mounting" was included in the author's first book, *In the Tennessee Mountains*, published in 1884. To the modern reader it may seem overladen with dialect since the custom today is to suggest native speech more by inflection and rhythm than by such meticulously misspelled and overpunctuated language. But literary critics attribute much of its appeal to this very excess. Mary Noailles Murfree was a pioneer in the use of American dialect. Her use of it convinced her readers of the authenticity of her material and delighted them with its novelty. The writing has some of the loveliest nature description in American fiction. And her Cumberland Mountain people, in their little cabins with their simple ways and folk tales of the supernatural, live for us today as vividly as they did for the author so many years ago.

# Over on the T'other Mounting

STRETCHING out laterally from a long oblique line of the Southern Alleghanies are two parallel ranges, following the same course through several leagues, and separated by a narrow strip of valley hardly half a mile in width. As they fare along arm in arm, so to speak, sundry differences between the close companions are distinctly apparent. One is much the higher, and leads the way; it strikes out all the bold curves and angles of the course, meekly attended by the lesser ridge; its shadowy coves and sharp ravines are repeated in miniature as its comrade falls into the line of march; it seems to have its companion in charge, and to conduct it away from the majestic procession of mountains that traverses the State.

But, despite its more imposing appearance, all the tangible advantages are possessed by its humble neighbor. When Old Rocky-Top, as the lower range is called, is fresh and green with the tender verdure of spring, the snow still lies on the summit of the T'other Mounting, and drifts deep into treacherous rifts and chasms, and muffles the voice of the singing pines; and all the crags are hung with gigantic glittering icicles, and the woods are gloomy and bleak. When the sun shines bright on Old Rocky-Top, clouds often hover about the loftier mountain, and storms brew in that higher atmosphere; the all-pervading winter winds surge wildly among the groaning forests, and wrench the limbs from the trees, and dash huge fragments of cliffs down deep gorges, and spend their fury before they reach the sheltered lower spur. When the kindly shades of evening slip softly down on drowsy Rocky-Top, and the work is laid by in the rough little houses, and the simple home-folks draw around the hearth, day still lingers in a weird, paralytic life among the tree-tops of the T'other Mounting; and the only remnant of the world visible is that stark black line of its summit, stiff and hard against the faint green and saffron tints of the sky. Before the birds are well awake on Old Rocky-Top, and while the shadows are still thick, the T'other Mounting has been called up to a new day. Lonely dawns these: the pale gleam strikes along the October woods, bringing first into uncertain twilight the dead yellow and red of the foliage, presently heightened into royal gold and crimson by the first ray of sunshine; it rouses the timid wild-fowl; it drives home the plundering fox; it meets, perhaps, some lumbering bear or skulking mountain wolf; it flecks with light and shade the deer, all gray and antlered; it falls upon no human habitation, for the few settlers of the region have a persistent predilection for Old Rocky-Top. Somehow, the T'other Mounting is vaguely in ill repute among its neighbors, — it has a bad name.

"It's the onluckiest place ennywhar nigh about," said Nathan White, as he sat one afternoon upon the porch of his log-cabin, on the summit of Old Rocky-Top, and gazed up at the heights of the T'other Mounting across the narrow valley. "I hev hearn tell all my days ez how, ef ye go up thar on the T'other Mounting, suthin' will happen ter ye afore ye kin git away. An' I knows myself ez how — 't war ten year ago an' better — I went up thar, one Jan'ry day, a-lookin' fur my cow, ez hed strayed off through not hevin' enny calf ter our house; an' I fund the cow, but jes' tuk an' slipped on a icy rock, an' bruk my ankle-bone. 'Twar sech a job a-gittin' off 'n that thar T'other Mounting an' back over hyar, it hev l'arned me ter stay away from thar."

"Thar war a man," piped out a shrill, quavering voice from within the door, — the voice of Nathan White's father, the oldest inhabitant of Rocky-Top, — "thar war a man hyar, nigh on ter fifty year ago, — he war mightily gin ter thievin' horses; an' one time, while he war a-runnin' away with Pete Dilks's dapple-gray mare, — they called her Luce, five year old she war, — Pete, he war a-ridin' a-hint him on his old sorrel mare, — *her* name 't war Jane, an' — the Jeemes boys, they war a-ridin' arter the horse-thief too. Thar, now! I clar forgits what horses them

Jeemes boys war a-ridin' of." He paused for an instant in anxious reflection. "Waal, sir! it do beat all that I can't remember them Jeemes boys' horses! Anyways, they got ter that thar tricky ford through Wild-Duck River, thar on the side o' the T'other Mounting, an' the horse-thief war ahead, an' he hed ter take it fust. An' that thar river, — it rises yander in them pines, nigh about," pointing with a shaking fore-finger, — "an' that thar river jes' spun him out 'n the saddle like a top, an' he war n't seen no more till he hed floated nigh ter Colbury, ez dead ez a door-nail, nor Pete's dapple-gray mare nuther; she bruk her knees agin them high stone banks. But he war a good swimmer, an' he war drowned. He war witched with the place, ez sure ez ye air born."

A long silence ensued. Then Nathan White raised his pondering eyes with a look of slow curiosity. "What did Tony Britt say he war a-doin' of, when ye kem on him suddint in the woods on the T'other Mounting?" he asked, addressing his son, a stalwart youth, who was sitting upon the step, his hat on the back of his head, and his hands in the pockets of his jeans trousers.

"He said he war a-huntin', but he hed n't hed no sort 'n luck. It 'pears ter me ez all the game thar is witched somehow, an' ye can't git no good shot at nuthin'. Tony tole me to-day that he got up three deer, an' hed toler'ble aim; an' he missed two, an' the t'other jes' trotted off with a rifle-ball in his flank, ez onconsarned ez ef he hed hit him with an acorn."

"I hev always hearn ez everything that belongs on that thar T'other Mounting air witched, an 'ef ye brings away so much ez a leaf, or a stone, or a stick, ye fetches a curse with it," chimed in the old man, "'kase thar hev been sech a many folks killed on the T'other Mounting."

"I tole Tony Britt that thar word," said the young fellow, "an' 'lowed ter him ez how he hed tuk a mighty bad spot ter go a-huntin'."

"What did he say?" demanded Nathan White.

"He say he never knowed ez thar war murders commit on T'other Mounting, an' ef thar war he 'spects 't war nuthin' but Injuns, long time ago. But he 'lowed the place war powerful onlucky, an' he believed the mounting war witched."

"Ef Tony Britt's arter enny harm," said the octogenarian, "he'll never come off 'n that thar T'other Mounting. It's a mighty place fur bad folks ter make thar eend. Thar's that thar horse thief I war a-tellin' 'bout, an' that dapple-gray mare, — her name 't war Luce. An' folks ez is a-runnin' from the sheriff jes' takes ter the T'other Mounting ez nateral ez ef it war home; an' ef they don't git cotched, they is never hearn on no more." He paused impressively. "The rocks falls on 'em, an' kills 'em; an' I'll tell ye jes' how I knows," he resumed, oracularly. "'T war sixty year ago, nigh about, an' me an' them Jeemes boys war a-burnin' of lime tergether over on the T'other Mounting. We hed a lime-kiln over thar, jes' under Piney Notch, an' never hed no luck, but jes stuck ter it like fools, till Hiram Jeemes got one of his eyes put out. So we quit burnin' of lime on the T'other Mounting, 'count of the place bein' witched, an' kem over hyar ter Old Rocky-Top, an' got along toler'ble well, cornsiderin'. But one day, whilst we war a-workin' on the T'other Mounting, what d'ye think I fund in the rock? The print of a bare foot in the solid stone, ez plain an' ez nateral ez ef the track hed been lef' in the clay yestiddy. Waal, I knowed it war the track o' Jeremiah Stubbs, what shot his step-brother, an' gin the sheriff the slip, an' war las' seen on the T'other Mounting, 'kase his old shoe jes' fit the track, fur we tried it. An' a good while arterward I fund on that same T'other Mounting — in the solid stone, mind ye — a fish, what he had done br'iled fur supper, jes' turned ter a stone."

"So thar's the Bible made true," said an elderly woman, who had come to the door to hear this reminiscence, and stood mechanically stirring a hoe-cake batter in a shallow wooden bowl. "Ax fur a fish, an' ye'll git a stone."

The secret history of the hills among which they lived was indeed as a sealed book to these simple mountaineers.

"The las' time I war ter Colbury," said Nathan White, "I hearn the sheriff a-talkin' 'bout how them evil-doers an' sech runs fur the T'other Mounting fust thing; though he 'lowed ez it war powerful foxy in 'em ter try ter hide thar, kase he said, ef they wunst reaches it, he mought ez well look fur a needle in a hay-stack. He 'lowed ef he hed a posse a thousand men strong he could n't git 'em out."

"He can't find 'em, 'kase the rocks falls on 'em, or swallers 'em in," said the old man. "Ef Tony Britt is up ter mischief he'll never come back no more. He'll git into worser trouble than ever he see afore."

"He hev done seen a powerful lot of trouble, fust one way an' another, 'thout foolin' round the T'other Mounting," said Nathan White. "They tells me ez he got hisself indicted, I believes they calls it, or suthin', down yander ter the court at Colbury, — that war year afore las', — an' he hed ter pay twenty dollars fine; 'kase when he war overseer of the road he jes' war constant in lettin' his friends, an' folks ginerally, off 'thout hevin' 'em fined, when they didn't come an' work on the road, — though that air the way ez the overseers hev always done, without nobody a-tellin' on 'em an' sech. But them ez war n't Tony Britt's friends seen a mighty differ. He war dead sure ter fine Caleb Hoxie seventy-five cents, 'cordin' ter the law, fur every day that he war summonsed ter work an' never come; 'kase Tony an' Caleb hed some sort 'n grudge agin one another 'count of a spavined horse what Caleb sold ter Tony, makin' him out to be a sound critter, — though Caleb swears he never knowed the horse war spavined when he sold him ter Tony, no more 'n nuthin'. Caleb war mightily worked up 'bout his hyar finin' business, an' him an' Tony hed a tussle 'bout it every time they kem tergether. But Caleb war always sure ter git the worst of it, 'kase Tony, though he air toler'ble spindling sort o' build, he air somehow or other sorter stringy an' tough, an' makes a right smart show in a reg'lar knock-down an' drag-out fight. So Caleb he war beat every time, an' fined too. An' he tried wunst ter shoot Tony Britt, but he missed his aim. An' when he war a-layin' off how ter fix Tony, fur treatin' him that way, he war a-stoppin', one day, at Jacob Green's blacksmith's shop, yander, a mile down the valley, an' he war a-talkin' 'bout it ter a passel o' folks thar. An' Lawyer Rood from Colbury war thar, an' Jacob war a-shoein' of his mare; an' he hearn the tale, an' axed Caleb why n't he report Tony ter the court, an' git him fined fur neglect of his duty, bein' overseer of the road. An' Caleb never knowed before that it war the law that everybody what war summonsed an' didn't come must be fined, or the overseer must be fined hisself; but he knowed that Tony hed been a-lettin' of his friends off, an' folks ginerally, an' he jes' 'greed fur Lawyer Rood ter stir up trouble fur Tony. An' he done it. An' the court fined Tony twenty dollars fur them ways o' his'n. An' it kept him so busy a-scufflin' ter raise the twenty dollars that he never hed a chance ter give Caleb Hoxie more 'n one or two beatin's the whole time he war a-scrapin' up the money."

This story was by no means unknown to the little circle, nor did its narrator labor under the delusion that he was telling a new thing. It was merely a verbal act of recollection, and an attentive silence reigned as he related the familiar facts. To people who live in lonely regions this habit of retrospection (especially noticeable in them) and an enduring interest in the past may be something of a compensation for the scanty happenings of the present. When the recital was concluded, the hush for a time was unbroken, save by the rush of the winds, bringing upon their breath the fragrant woodland odors of balsams and pungent herbs, and a fresh and exhilarating suggestion of sweeping over a volume of falling water. They stirred the fringed shadow of a great pine that stood, like a sentinel, before Nathan White's door and threw its colorless simulacrum, a boastful lie twice its size, far down the sunset road. Now and then the faint clangor of a cow-bell came from out the tangled woods about the little hut, and the low of homeward-bound cattle sounded upon the air, mellowed and softened by the distance. The haze that rested above the long, narrow valley was hardly visible, save in the illusive beauty with which it invested the scene, — the tender azure of the far-away ranges; the exquisite tones of the gray and purple shadows that hovered about the darkening coves and along the deep lines marking the gorges; the burnished brilliance of the sunlight, which, despite its splendor, seemed lonely enough, lying motionless upon the lonely landscape and on the still figures clustered about the porch. Their eyes were turned toward the opposite steeps, gorgeous with scarlet oak and sumac, all in autumnal array, and their thoughts were busy with the hunter on the T'other Mounting and vague speculations concerning his evil intent.

"It 'pears ter me powerful strange ez Tony goes a-foolin' round that thar T'other Mounting, cornsiderin' what happened yander in its shadow," said the woman, coming again to the door, and leaning idly against the frame; the bread was baking over the coals. "That thar wife o' his'n, afore she died, war always frettin' 'kase way down thar on the backbone, whar her house war, the shadow o' the T'other Mounting laid on it fur an hour an' better every day of the worl'. She 'lowed ez it always put her in mind o' the shadow o' death. An' I thought 'bout that thar sayin' o' hern the day when I see her a-lyin' stiff an' cold on the bed, an' the shadow of the T'other Mounting drappin' in at the open door, an' a-creepin' an' a-creepin' over her face. An' I war plumb glad when they got that woman under ground, whar, ef the sunshine can't git ter her, neither kin the shadow. Ef ever thar war a murdered woman, she war one. Arter all that hed come an' gone with Caleb Hoxie, fur Tony Britt ter go arter him, 'kase he war a yerb-doctor, ter git him ter physic his wife, who war nigh about dead with the lung fever, an' gin up by old Dr. Marsh! — it looks ter me like he war plumb crazy, — though him an' Caleb hed sorter made friends 'bout the spavined horse an' sech afore then. Jes' ez soon ez she drunk the stuff that Caleb fixed fur her she laid her head back an' shet her eyes, an' never opened 'em no more in this worl'. She war a murdered woman, an' Caleb Hoxie done it through the yerbs he fixed fur her."

A subtile amethystine mist had gradually overlaid the slopes of the T'other Mounting, mellowing the brilliant tints of the variegated foliage to a delicious hazy sheen of mosaics; but about the base the air seemed dun-colored, though transparent; seen through it, even the red of the crowded trees was but a sombre sort of magnificence, and the great masses of gray rocks, jutting out among them here and there, wore a darkly frowning aspect. Along the summit there was a blaze of scarlet and gold in the full glory of the sunshine; the topmost cliffs caught its rays, and gave them back in unexpected gleams of green or grayish-yellow, as of mosses, or vines, or huckleberry bushes, nourished in the heart of the deep fissures.

"Waal," said Nathan White, "I never did believe ez Caleb gin her ennythink ter hurt, — though I knows thar is them ez does. Caleb is the bes' yerb-doctor I ever see. The rheumatiz would nigh on ter hev killed me, ef it warn't fur him, that spell I hed las' winter. An' Dr. Marsh, what they hed up afore the gran' jury, swore that the yerbs what Caleb gin her war nuthin' ter hurt; *he* said, though, they couldn't holp nor hender. An' but fur Dr. Marsh they would hev jailed Caleb ter stand his trial, like Tony wanted 'em ter do. But Dr. Marsh said she died with the consumption, jes' the same, an' Caleb's yerbs war wholesome, though they warn't no 'count at all."

"I knows I ain't a-goin' never ter tech nuthin' he fixes fur me no more," said his wife, "an' I'll be bound nobody else in these hyar mountings will, nuther."

"Waal," drawled her son, "I knows fur true ez he air tendin' now on old Gideon Croft, what lives over yander in the valley on the t'other side of the T'other Mounting, an' is down with the fever. He went over thar yestiddy evening, late; I met him when he war goin', an' he tole me."

"He hed better look out how he comes across Tony Britt," said Nathan White; "fur I hearn, the las' time I war ter the Settlemint, how Tony hev swore ter kill him the nex' time he see him, fur a-givin' of pizenous yerbs ter his wife. Tony air mightily outdone 'kase the gran' jury let him off. Caleb hed better be sorter keerful how he goes a-foolin' round these hyar dark woods."

The sun had sunk, and the night, long held in abeyance, was coming fast. The glooms gathered in the valley; a soft gray shadow hung over the landscape, making familiar things strange. The T'other Mounting was all a dusky, sad purple under the faintly pulsating stars, save that high along the horizontal line of its summit gleamed the strange red radiance of the dead and gone sunset. The outline of the foliage was clearly drawn against the pure lapis lazuli tint of the sky behind it; here and there the uncanny light streamed through the bare limbs of an early leafless tree, which looked in the distance like some bony hand beckoning, or warning, or raised in horror.

"*Anythink* mought happen thar!" said the woman, as she stood on night-wrapped Rocky-Top and gazed up at the alien light, so red in the midst of the dark landscape. When she turned back to the door of the little hut, the meagre comforts within seemed almost luxury, in their cordial contrast to the desolate, dreary mountain yonder and the thought of the forlorn, wandering hunter. A genial glow from the hearth diffused itself over the puncheon floor; the savory odor of broiling venison filled the room as a tall, slim girl knelt before the fire and placed the meat upon the gridiron, her pale cheeks flushing with the heat; there was a happy suggestion of peace and unity when the four generations trooped in to their supper, grandfather on his grandson's arm, and a sedate two-year-old bringing up the rear. Nathan White's wife paused behind the others to bar the door, and once more, as she looked up at the T'other Mounting, the thought of the lonely wanderer smote her heart. The red sunset light had died out at last, but a golden aureola heralded the moon-rise, and a gleaming thread edged the masses of foliage; there was no faint suggestion now of mist in the valley, and myriads of stars filled a cloudless sky. "He hev done gone home by this time," she said to her daughter-in-law, as she closed the door, "an' ef he ain't, he'll hev a moon ter light him."

"Air ye a-studyin' 'bout Tony Britt yit?" asked Nathan White. "He hev done gone home a good hour by sun, I'll be bound. Jes' ketch Tony Britt a-huntin' till sundown, will ye! He air a mighty pore hand ter work. 'Stonishes me ter hear he air even a-huntin' on the T'other Mounting."

"I don't believe he's up ter enny harm," said the woman; "he hev jes' tuk ter the woods with grief."

"'Pears ter me," said the daughter-in-law, rising from her kneeling posture before the fire, and glancing reproachfully at her husband, — "'pears ter me ez ye mought hev brought him hyar ter eat his supper along of we-uns, stiddier a-leavin' him a-grievin' over his dead wife in them witched woods on the T'other Mounting."

The young fellow looked a trifle abashed at this suggestion. "I never wunst thought of it," he said. "Tony never stopped ter talk more 'n a minit, nohow."

The evening wore away; the octogenarian and the sedate two-year-old fell asleep in their chairs shortly after supper; Nathan White and his son smoked their cob-pipes, and talked fitfully of the few incidents of the day; the women sat in the firelight with their knitting, silent and absorbed, except that now and then the elder, breaking from her reverie, declared, "I can't git Tony Britt out'n my head nohow in the worl'."

The moon had come grandly up over the T'other Mounting, casting long silver lights and deep black shadows through all the tangled recesses and yawning chasms of the woods and rocks. In the vast wilderness the bright rays met only one human creature, the belated hunter making his way homeward through the dense forest with an experienced woodman's craft. For no evil intent had brought Tony Britt to the T'other Mounting; he had spent the day in hunting, urged by that strong necessity without which the mountaineer seldom makes any exertion. Dr. Marsh's unavailing skill had cost him dear; his only cow was sold to make up the twenty dollars fine which his revenge on Caleb Hoxie had entailed upon him; without even so much as a spavined horse tillage was impossible, and the bounteous harvest left him empty-handed, for he had no crops to gather. The hardships of extreme poverty had reinforced the sorrows that came upon him in battalions, and had driven him far through long aisles of the woods, where the night fell upon him unaware. The foliage was all embossed with exquisite silver designs that seemed to stand out some little distance from the dark masses of leaves; now and then there came to his eyes that emerald gleam never seen upon vendure in the day-time, — only shown by some artificial light, or the moon's sweet uncertainty. The wind was strong and fresh, but not cold; here and there was a glimmer of dew. Once, and once only, he thought of the wild traditions which peopled the T'other Mounting with evil spirits. He paused with a sudden chill; he glanced nervously over his shoulder down the illimitable avenues of the lonely woods. The grape-vines, hanging in festoons from tree to tree, were slowly swinging back and forth, stirred by the wind. There was a dizzy dance of shadows whirling on every open space where the light lay on the ground. The roar and fret of Wild-Duck River, hidden there somewhere in the pines, came on the breeze like a strange, weird, fitful voice, crying out amid the haunted solitudes of the T'other Mounting. He turned abruptly, with his gun on his shoulder, and pursued his way through the trackless desert in the direction of his home. He had been absorbed in his quest and his gloomy thoughts, and did not realize the distance he had traversed until it lay before him to be retraced; but his superstitious terror urged him to renewed exertions. "Ef ever I gits off'n this hyar witched mounting," he said to himself, as he tore away the vines and brambles that beset his course, "I'll never come back agin while I lives." He grew calmer when he paused on a huge projecting crag, and looked across the narrow valley at the great black mass opposite, which he knew was Old Rocky-Top; its very presence gave him a sense of companionship and blunted his fear, and he sat down to rest for a few minutes, gazing at the outline of the range he knew so well, so unfamiliar from a new stand-point. How low it seemed from the heights of the T'other Mounting! Could that faint gleam be the light in Nathan White's house? Tony Britt glanced further down the indistinct slope, where he knew his own desolate, deserted hut was crouched. "Jes' whar the shadow o' the T'other Mounting can reach it," he thought, with a new infusion of bitterness. He averted his eyes; he would look no longer; he threw him-self at full length among the ragged clumps of grass and fragments of rock, and turned his face to the stars. It all came back to him then. Sometimes, in his sordid cares and struggles for his scanty existence, his past troubles were dwarfed by the present. But here on the lonely cliff, with the infinite spaces above him and the boundless forest below, he felt anew his isolation. No light on earth save the far gleam from another man's home, and in heaven only the drowning face of the moon, drifting slowly through the blue floods of the skies. He was only twenty-five; he had youth and health and strength, but he felt that he had lived his life; it seemed long, marked as it was by cares and privation and persis-tent failure. Little as he knew of life, he knew how hard his had been, even meted by those of the poverty-stricken wretches among whom his lot was cast. "An' sech luck!" he said, as his sad eyes followed the drifting dead face of the moon. "Along o' that thar step-mother o' mine till I war growed; an' then when I war married, an' we hed got the house put up, an' war beginnin' ter git along like other folks kin, an' Car'line's mother gin her that thar calf what growed ter a cow, an' through pinchin' an' savin' we made out ter buy that thar horse from Caleb Hoxie, jes' ez we war a-startin' ter work a crap he lays down an' dies; an' that cussed twenty dollars ez I hed ter pay ter the court; an' Car'line jes' a-gittin' sick, an' a-wastin' an' a-wastin' away, till I, like a fool, brung Caleb thar, an' he pizens her with his yerbs — God A'mighty! ef I could jes' lay my hands wunst on that scoundrel I wouldn't leave a mite of him, ef he war pertected by a hundred lyin', thievin' gran' juries! But he can't stay a-hidin' forevermo'. He's got ter 'count ter me, ef he ain't ter the law; an' he'll see a mighty differ atwixt us. I swear he'll never draw another breath!"

He rose with a set, stern face, and struck a huge bowlder beside him with his hard clenched hand as he spoke. He had not even an ignorant idea of an impressive dramatic pose; but if the great gaunt cliff had been the stage of a theatre his attitude and manner at that instant would have won him applause. He was all alone with his poverty and his anguished memories, as men with such burdens are apt to be.

The bowlder on which, in his rude fashion, he had registered his oath was harder than his hard hand, and the vehemence of the blow brought blood; but he had scarcely time to think of it. His absorbed reverie was broken by a rustling other than that of the eddying wind. He raised his head and looked about him, half expecting to see the antlers of a deer. Then there came to his ears the echo of the tread of man. His eyes mechanically followed the sound. Forty feet down the face of the crag a broad ledge jutted out, and upon it ran a narrow path, made by stray cattle, or the feet of their searching owners; it was visible from the summit for a distance of a hundred yards or so, and the white glamour of the moonbeams fell full upon it. Before a speculation had suggested itself, a man walked slowly into view along the path, and with starting eyes the hunter recognized his dearest foe. Britt's hand lay upon the bowlder; his oath was in his mind; his unconscious enemy had come within his power. Swifter than a flash the temptation was presented. He remembered the warnings of his lawyer at Colbury last week, when the grand jury had failed to find a true bill against Caleb Hoxie, — that he was an innocent man, and must go unscathed, that any revenge for fancied wrongs would be dearly rued; he remembered, too, the mountain traditions of the falling rocks burying evil-doers in the heart of the hills. Here was his opportunity. He would have a life for a life, and there would be one more legend of the very stones conspiring to punish malefactors escaped from men added to the terrible "sayin's" of the T'other Mounting. A strong belief in the supernatural influences of the place was rife within him; he knew nothing of Gideon Croft's fever and the errand that had brought the herb-doctor through the "witched mounting"; had he not been transported thither by some invisible agency, that the rocks might fall upon him and crush him?

The temptation and the resolve were simultaneous. With his hand upon the bowlder, his hot heart beating fast, his distended eyes burning upon the approaching figure, he waited for the moment to come. There lay the long, low, black mountain opposite, with only the moon beams upon it, for the lights in Nathan White's house were extinguished; there was the deep, dark gulf of the valley; there, forty feet below him, was the narrow, moon-flooded path on the ledge, and the man advancing carelessly. The bowlder fell with a frightful crash, the echoes rang with a scream of terror, and the two men — one fleeing from the dreadful danger he had barely escaped, the other from the hideous deed he thought he had done — ran wildly in opposite directions through the tangled autumnal woods.

Was every leaf of the forest endowed with a woful voice, that the echo of that shriek might never die from Tony Britt's ears? Did the storied, retributive rocks still vibrate with this new victim's frenzied cry? And what was this horror in his heart! Now, — so late, — was coming a terrible conviction of his enemy's innocence, and with it a fathomless remorse.

All through the interminable night he fled frantically along the mountain's summit, scarcely knowing whither, and caring for nothing except to multiply the miles between him and the frightful object that he believed lay under the bowlder which he had dashed down the precipice. The moon sank beneath the horizon; the fantastic shadows were merged in the darkest hour of the night; the winds died, and there was no voice in all the woods, save the wail of Wild-Duck River and the forever-resounding screams in the flying wretch's ears. Sometimes he answered them in a wild, hoarse, inarticulate cry; sometimes he flung his hands above his head and wrung them in his agony; never once did he pause in his flight. Panting, breathless, exhausted, he eagerly sped through the darkness; tearing his face upon the brambles; plunging now and then into gullies and unseen quagmires; sometimes falling heavily, but recovering himself in an instant, and once more struggling on; striving to elude the pursuing voices, and to distance forever his conscience and his memory.

And then came that terrible early daylight that was wont to dawn upon the T'other Mounting when all the world besides was lost in slumber; the wan, melancholy light showed dimly the solemn trees and dense undergrowth; the precarious pitfalls about his path; the long deep gorges; the great crags and chasms; the cascades, steely gray, and white; the huge mass, all hung about with shadows, which he knew was Old Rocky-Top, rising from the impenetrably dark valley below. It seemed wonderful to him, somehow, that a new day should break at all. If, in a revulsion of nature, that utter blackness had continued forever and ever it would not have been strange, after what had happened. He could have borne it better than the sight of the familiar world gradually growing into day, all unconscious of his secret. He had begun the descent of the T'other Mounting, and he seemed to carry that pale dawn with him; day was breaking when he reached the foot of Old Rocky-Top, and as he climbed up to his own deserted, empty little shanty, it too stood plainly defined in the morning light. He dragged himself to the door, and impelled by some morbid fascination he glanced over his shoulder at the T'other Mounting. There it was, unchanged, with the golden largess of a gracious season blazing upon every autumnal leaf. He shuddered, and went into the fireless, comfortless house. And then he made an appalling discovery. As he mechanically divested himself of his shot-pouch and powder-horn he was stricken by a sudden consciousness that he did not have his gun! One doubtful moment, and he remembered that he had laid it upon the crag when he had thrown himself down to rest. Beyond question, it was there yet. His conscience was still now, — his remorse had fled. It was only a matter of time when his crime would be known. He recollected his meeting with young White while he was hunting, and then Britt cursed the gun which he had left on the cliff. The discovery of the weapon there would be strong evidence against him, taken in connection with all the other circumstances. True, he could even yet go back and recover it, but he was mastered by the fear of meeting some one on the unfrequented road, or even in the loneliness of the T'other Mounting, and strengthening the chain of evidence against him by the fact of being once more seen in the fateful neighborhood. He resolved that he would wait until night-fall, and then he would retrace his way, secure his gun, and all might yet be well with him. As to the bowlder, — were men never before buried under the falling rocks of the T'other Mounting?

Without food, without rest, without sleep, his limbs rigid with the strong tension of his nerves, his eyes bloodshot, haggard, and eager, his brain on fire, he sat through the long morning hours absently gazing across the narrow valley at the solemn, majestic mountain opposite, and that sinister jutting crag with the indistinctly defined ledges of its rugged surface.

After a time, the scene began to grow dim; the sun was still shining, but through a haze becoming momently more dense. The brilliantly tinted foliage upon the T'other Mounting was fading; the cliffs showed strangely distorted faces through the semi-transparent blue vapor, and presently they seemed to recede altogether; the valley disappeared, and all the country was filled with the smoke of distant burning woods. He was gasping when he first became sensible of the smoke-laden haze, for he had seen nothing of the changing aspect of the landscape. Before his vision was the changeless picture of a night of mingled moonlight and shadow, the ill-defined black mass where Old Rocky-Top rose into the air, the impenetrable gloom of the valley, the ledge of the crag, and the unconscious figure slowly coming within the power of his murderous hand. His eyes would look on no other scene, no other face, so long as he should live.

He had a momentary sensation of stifling, and then a great weight was lifted. For he had begun to doubt whether the unlucky locality would account satisfactorily for the fall of that bowlder and the horrible object beneath it; a more reasonable conclusion might be deduced from the fact that he had been seen in the neighborhood, and the circumstance of the deadly feud. But what wonder would there be if the dry leaves on the T'other Mounting should be ignited and the woods burned! What explanations might not such a catastrophe suggest? — a frantic flight from the flames toward the cliff and an accidental fall. And so he waited throughout the long day, that was hardly day at all, but an opaque twilight, through which could be discerned only the stony path leading down the slope from his door, only the blurred outlines of the bushes close at hand, only the great gaunt limbs of a lightning-scathed tree, seeming entirely severed from the unseen trunk, and swinging in the air sixty feet above the earth.

Toward night-fall the wind rose and the smoke-curtain lifted, once more revealing to the settlers upon Old Rocky-Top the sombre T'other Mounting, with the belated evening light still lurid upon the trees, — only a strange, faint resemblance of the sunset radiance, rather the ghost of a dead day. And presently this apparition was gone, and the deep purple line of the witched mountain's summit grew darker against the opaline skies, till it was merged in a dusky black, and the shades of the night fell thick on the landscape.

The scenic effects of the drama, that serve to widen the mental vision and cultivate the imagination of even the poor in cities, were denied these primitive, simple people; but that magnificent pageant of the four seasons, wherein was forever presented the imposing splendor of the T'other Mounting in an ever-changing grandeur of aspect, was a gracious recompense for the spectacular privileges of civilization. And this evening the humble family party on Nathan White's porch beheld a scene of unique impressiveness.

The moon had not yet risen; the winds were awhirl; the darkness draped the earth as with a pall. Out from the impenetrable gloom of the woods on the T'other Mounting there started, suddenly, a scarlet globe of fire; one long moment it was motionless, but near it the spectral outline of a hand appeared beckoning, or warning, or raised in horror, — only a leafless tree, catching in the distance a semblance of humanity. Then from the still ball of fire there streamed upward a long, slender plume of golden light, waving back and forth against the pale horizon. Across the dark slope of the mountain below, flashes of lightning were shooting in zigzag lines, and wherever they gleamed were seen those frantic skeleton hands raised and wrung in anguish. It was cruel sport for the cruel winds; they maddened over gorge and cliff and along the wooded steeps, carrying far upon their wings the sparks of desolation. From the summit, myriads of jets of flame reached up to the placid stars; about the base of the mountain lurked a lake of liquid fire, with wreaths of blue smoke hovering over it; ever and anon, athwart the slope darted the sudden lightning, widening into sheets of flame as it conquered new ground.

The astonishment on the faces grouped about Nathan White's door was succeeded by a startled anxiety. After the first incoherent exclamations of surprise came the pertinent inquiry from his wife, "Ef Old Rocky-Top war ter ketch too, whar would we-uns run ter?"

Nathan White's countenance had in its expression more of astounded excitement than of bodily fear. "Why, bless my soul!" he said at length, "the woods away over yander, what hev been burnin' all day, ain't-nigh enough ter the T'other Mounting ter ketch it, — nuthin' like it."

"The T'other Mounting would burn, though, ef fire war put ter it," said his son. The two men exchanged a glance of deep significance.

"Do ye mean ter say," exclaimed Mrs. White, her fire-lit face agitated by a sudden superstitious terror, "that that thar T'other Mounting is fired by witches an' sech?"

"Don't talk so loud, Matildy," said her husband. "Them knows best ez done it."

"Thar's one thing sure," quavered the old man: "that thar fire will never tech a leaf on Old Rocky-Top. Thar's a church on this hyar mounting, — bless the Lord fur it! — an' we lives in the fear o' God."

There was a pause, all watching with distended eyes the progress of the flames.

"It looks like it mought hev been kindled in torment," said the young daughter-in-law.

"It looks down thar," said her husband, pointing to the lake of fire, "like the pit itself."

The apathetic inhabitants of Old Rocky-Top were stirred into an activity very incongruous with their habits and the hour. During the conflagration they traversed long distances to reach each other's houses and confer concerning the danger and the questions of supernatural agency provoked by the mysterious firing of the woods. Nathan White had few neighbors, but above the crackling of the timber and the roar of the flames there rose the quick beat of running footsteps; the undergrowth of the forest near at hand was in strange commotion; and at last, the figure of a man burst forth, the light of the fire showing the startling pallor of his face as he staggered to the little porch and sank, exhausted, into a chair.

"Waal, Caleb Hoxie!" exclaimed Nathan White, in good-natured raillery; "ye're skeered, fur true! What ails ye, ter think Old Rocky-Top air a-goin' ter ketch too? 'T ain't nigh dry enough, I'm a-thinkin'."

"Fire kindled that thar way can't tech a leaf on Old Rocky-Top," sleepily piped out the old man, nodding in his chair, the glare of the flames which rioted over the T'other Mounting gilding his long white hair and peaceful, slumberous face. "Thar's a church on Old Rocky-Top, — bless the" — The sentence drifted away with his dreams.

"Does ye believe — them — them" — Caleb Hoxie's trembling white lips could not frame the word — "them — done it?"

"Like ez not," said Nathan White. "But that ain't a-troublin' of ye an' me. I ain't never hearn o' them witches a-tormentin' of honest folks what ain't done nuthin' hurtful ter nobody," he added, in cordial reassurance.

His son was half hidden behind one of the rough cedar posts, that his mirth at the guest's display of cowardice might not be observed. But the women, always quick to suspect, glanced meaningly at each other with widening eyes, as they stood together in the door-way.

"I dunno, — I dunno," Caleb Hoxie declared huskily. "I ain't never done nuthin' ter nobody, an' what do ye s'pose them witches an' sech done ter me las' night, on that T'other Mounting? I war a-goin' over yander to Gideon Croft's fur ter physic him, ez he air mortal low with the fever; an' ez I war a-comin' alongside o' that thar high bluff" — it was very distinct, with the flames wreathing fantastically about its gray, rigid features — "they throwed a bowlder ez big ez this hyar porch down on ter me. It jes' grazed me, an' knocked me down, an' kivered me with dirt. An' I run home a-hollerin'; an' it seemed ter me ter-day ez I war a-goin' ter screech an' screech all my life, like some onsettled crazy critter. It 'peared like 't would take a bar'l o' hop tea ter git me quiet. An' now look yander!" and he pointed tremulously to the blazing mountain.

There was an expression of conviction on the women's faces. All their lives afterward it was there whenever Caleb Hoxie's name was mentioned; no more to be moved or changed than the stern, set faces of the crags among the fiery woods.

"Thar's a church on this hyar mounting," said the old man feebly, waking for a moment, and falling asleep the next.

Nathan White was perplexed and doubtful, and a superstitious awe had checked the laughing youngster behind the cedar post.

A great cloud of flame came rolling through the sky toward them, golden, pellucid, spangled through and through with fiery red stars; poising itself for one moment high above the valley, then breaking into myriads of sparks, and showering down upon the dark abysses below.

"Look-a-hyar!" said the elder woman in a frightened under-tone to her daughter-in-law; "this hyar wicked critter air too onlucky ter be a-sittin' 'longside of us; we'll all be burnt up afore he gits hisself away from hyar. An' who is that a-comin' yander?" For from the encompassing woods another dark figure had emerged, and was slowly approaching the porch. The wary eyes near Caleb Hoxie saw that he fell to trembling, and that he clutched at a post for support. But the hand pointing at him was shaken as with a palsy, and the voice hardly seemed Tony Britt's as it cried out, in an agony of terror, "What air ye a-doin' hyar, a-sittin' 'longside o' livin' folks? Yer bones air under a bowlder on the T'other Mounting an' ye air a dead man!"

They said ever afterward that Tony Britt had lost his mind "through goin' a-huntin' jes' one time on the T'other Mounting. His spirit air all broke, an' he's a mighty tame critter nowadays." Through his persistent endeavor he and Caleb Hoxie became quite friendly, and he was even reported to "'low that he war sati'fied that Caleb never gin his wife nuthin' ter hurt." "Though," said the gossips of Old Rocky-Top, "them women up ter White's will hev it no other way but that Caleb pizened her, an' they wouldn't take no yerbs from him no more 'n he war a rattlesnake. But Caleb always 'pears sorter skittish when he an' Tony air tergether, like he did n't know when Tony war a-goin' ter fotch him a lick. But law! Tony air that changed that ye can't make him mad 'thout ye mind him o' the time he called Caleb a ghost."

A dark, gloomy, deserted place was the charred T'other Mounting through all the long winter. And when spring came, and Old Rocky-Top was green with delicate fresh verdure, and melodious with singing birds and chorusing breezes, and bedecked as for some great festival with violets and azaleas and laurel-blooms, the T'other Mounting was stark and wintry and black with its desolate, leafless trees. But after a while the spring came for it, too: the buds swelled and burst; flowering vines festooned the grim gray crags; and the dainty freshness of the vernal season reigned upon its summit, while all the world below was growing into heat and dust. The circuit-rider said it reminded him of a tardy change in a sinner's heart: though it come at the eleventh hour, the glorious summer is before it, and a full fruition; though it work but an hour in the Lord's vineyard, it receives the same reward as those who labored through all the day.

"An' it always did 'pear ter me ez thar war mighty little jestice in that," was Mrs. White's comment.

But at the meeting when that sermon was preached Tony Britt told his "experience." It seemed a confession, for according to the gossips he "'lowed that he hed flung that bowlder down on Caleb Hoxie, — what the witches flung, ye know, — 'kase he believed then that Caleb hed killed his wife with pizenous yerbs; an' he went back the nex' night an' fired the woods, ter make folks think when they fund Caleb's bones that he war a-runnin' from the blaze an' fell off'n the bluff." And everybody on Old Rocky-Top said incredulously, "Pore Tony Britt! He hev los' his mind through goin' a-huntin' jes' one time on the T'other Mounting."

# Mary Wilkins Freeman (1852–1930)

WHEN HER now celebrated regional short stories were first published, Mary Wilkins Freeman, although her skill as a writer was acknowledged, was criticized as "too harshly realistic"! It was an unfortunate period in American literary history when women writers were expected to be sentimental and editors wanted only happy endings. Freeman was born and grew up in Randolph, Massachusetts, then farming country that had fallen on hard times. Her first two books of prose, *A Humble Romance* (1887) and *A New England Nun* (1891), were collections of her short stories. Although she wrote four novels and a play, none was a major work. Her final book, *Edgewater People* (1918), consisted of short stories and was hailed as having the merit of her early work.

It is almost impossible to believe that "Revolt of Mother" is one of the stories that, when they appeared in *A New England Nun*, were called "grim." To us today it is a warmhearted, humorous story of a wife and mother wanting a few comforts for her children. And all of us in traveling through New England have seen those huge old barns dwarfing tiny houses. But even though the author is fair in showing that the farmer is gentle and contrite when he understands he has been neglecting his family, Freeman evidently offended some male sensibilities. Such direct action by a woman should not be tolerated, they thought, nor should the joke be at the expense of a husband. Today, however, only the most recalcitrant sexist could fail to find some pleasure in reading it.

# *The Revolt of Mother*

"FATHER!"

"What is it?"

"What are them men diggin' over in the field for?"

There was a sudden dropping and enlarging of the lower part of the old man's face, as if some heavy weight had settled therein; he shut his mouth tight, and went on harnessing the great bay mare. He hustled the collar on to her neck with a jerk.

"Father!"

The old man slapped the saddle on the mare's back.

"Look here, Father, I want to know what them men are diggin' over in the field for, an' I'm going' to know."

"I wish you'd go into the house, Mother, an' tend to your own affairs," the old man said then. He ran his words together, and his speech was almost as inarticulate as a growl.

But the woman understood; it was her most native tongue. "I ain't goin' into the house till you tell me what them men are doin' over there in the field," said she.

Then she stood waiting. She was a small woman, short and straight-waisted like a child in her brown cotton gown. Her forehead was mild and benevolent between the smooth curves of gray hair; there were meek downward lines about her nose and mouth; but her eyes, fixed upon the old man, looked as if the meekness had been the result of her own will, never of the will of another.

They were in the barn, standing before the wide-open doors. The spring air, full of the smell of growing grass and unseen blossoms, came in their faces. The deep yard in front was littered with farm wagons and piles of wood; on the edges, close to the fence and the house, the grass was a vivid green, and there were some dandelions.

The old man glanced doggedly at his wife as he tightened the last buckles on the harness. She looked as immovable to him as one of the rocks in his pasture land, bound to the earth with generations of black-berry vines. He slapped the reins over the horse, and started forth from the barn.

"*Father!*" said she.

The old man pulled up. "What is it?"

"I want to know what them men are diggin' over there in that field for."

"They're diggin' a cellar, I s'pose, if you've got to know."

"A cellar for what?"

"A barn."

"A barn? You ain't goin' to build a barn over there where we was goin' to have a house, Father?"

The old man said not another word. He hurried the horse into the farm wagon and clattered out of the yard, jouncing as sturdily on his seat as a boy.

The woman stood a moment looking after him, then she went out of the barn across a corner of the yard to the house. The house, standing at right angles with the great barn and a long reach of sheds and out-buildings, was infinitesimal compared with them. It was scarcely as commodious for people as the little boxes under the barn eaves were for doves.

A pretty girl's face, pink and delicate as a flower, was looking out of one of the house windows. She was watching three men who were digging over in the field which bounded the yard near the road line. She turned quickly when the woman entered.

"What are they diggin' for, Mother?" said she. "Did he tell you?"

"They're diggin' for — a cellar for a new barn."

"Oh, Mother, he ain't going to build another barn?"

"That's what he says."

A boy stood before the kitchen glass combing his hair. He combed slowly and painstakingly, arranging his brown hair in a smooth hillock over his forehead. He did not seem to pay any attention to the conversation.

"Sammy, did you know Father was going to build a new barn?" asked the girl.

The boy combed assiduously.

"Sammy!"

He turned, and showed a face like his father's under his smooth crest of hair. "Yes, I s'pose I did," he said, reluctantly.

"How long have you known it?" asked his mother.

" 'Bout three months, I guess."

"Why didn't you tell of it?"

"Didn't think 'twould do no good."

"I don't see what Father wants another barn for," said the girl, in her sweet, slow voice. She turned again to the window and stared out at the digging men in the field. Her tender, sweet face was full of a gentle distress. Her forehead was as bald and innocent as a baby's, with the light hair strained from it in a row of curl papers. She was quite large, but her soft curves did not look as if they covered muscles.

Her mother looked sternly at the boy. "Is he goin' to buy more cows?" said she.

The boy did not reply; he was tying his shoes.

"Sammy, I want you to tell me if he's going' to buy more cows."

"I s'pose he is."

"How many?"

"Four, I guess."

His mother said nothing more. She went into the pantry, and there was a clatter of dishes. The boy got his cap from a nail behind the door, took an old arithmetic from the shelf, and started for school. He was lightly built, but clumsy. He went out of the yard with a curious spring in his hips that made his loose homemade jacket tilt up in the rear.

The girl went to the sink and began to wash the dishes that were piled up there. Her mother came promptly out of the pantry and shoved her aside. "You wipe 'em," said she. "I'll wash. There's a good many this mornin'."

The mother plunged her hands vigorously into the water, the girl wiped the plates slowly and dreamily. "Mother," said she, "don't you think it's too bad Father's going to build that new barn, much as we need a decent house to live in?"

Her mother scrubbed a dish fiercely. "You ain't found out yet, we're womenfolks, Nanny Penn," said she. "You ain't seen enough of menfolks yet to. One of these days you'll find it out, and then you'll know that we know only what menfolks think we do, so far as any use of it goes, an' how we'd ought to reckon menfolks in with Providence, an' not complain of what they do any more than we do of the weather."

"I don't care; I don't believe George is anything like that, anyhow," said Nanny. Her delicate face flushed pink; her lips pouted softly, as if she were going to cry.

"You wait an' see. I guess George Eastman ain't no better than other men. You hadn't ought to judge Father, though. He can't help it, 'cause he don't look at things jest the way we do. An' we've been pretty comfortable here, after all. The roof don't leak — ain't never but once — that's one thing. Father's kept it shingled right up."

"I do wish we had a parlor."

"I guess it won't hurt George Eastman any to come to see you in a nice clean kitchen. I guess a good many girls don't have as good a place as this. Nobody's ever heard me complain."

"I ain't complained either, Mother."

"Well, I don't think you'd better, a good father an' a good home as you've got. S'pose your father made you go out an' work for your livin'? Lots of girls have to that ain't no better able to than you be."

Sarah Penn washed the frying pan with a conclusive air. She scrubbed the outside of it as faithfully as the inside. She was a masterly keeper of her box of a house. Her one living room never seemed to have in it any of the dust which the friction of life with inanimate matter produces. She swept, and there seemed to be no dirt to go before the broom; she cleaned, and one could see no difference. She was like an artist so perfect that he has apparently no art. Today she got out a mixing bowl and a board, and rolled some pies, and there was no more flour upon her than upon her daughter who was doing finer work. Nanny was to be married in the fall, and she was sewing on some white cambric and embroidery. She sewed industriously while her mother cooked; her soft milk-white hands and wrists showed whiter than her delicate work.

"We must have the stove moved out in the shed before long," said Mrs. Penn. "Talk about not havin' things, it's been a real blessin' to be able to put a stove up in that shed in hot weather. Father did one good thing when he fixed that stove pipe out there."

Sarah Penn's face as she rolled her pies had that expression of meek vigor which might have characterized one of the New Testament saints. She was making mince pies. Her husband, Adoniram Penn, liked them better than any other kind. She baked twice a week. Adoniram often liked a piece of pie between meals. She hurried this morning. It had been later than usual when she began, and she wanted to have a pie baked for dinner. However deep a resentment she might be forced to hold against her husband, she would never fail in sedulous attention to his wants.

Nobility of character manifests itself at loopholes when it is not provided with large doors. Sarah Penn's showed itself today in flaky dishes of pastry. She made the pies faithfully, while across the table she could see, when she glanced up from work, the sight that rankled in her patient and steadfast soul — the digging of the cellar of the new barn in the place where Adoniram forty years ago had promised her their new house should stand.

The pies were done for dinner. Adoniram and Sammy were home a few minutes after twelve o'clock. The dinner was eaten with serious haste. There was never much conversation at the table in the Penn family. Adoniram asked a blessing, and they ate promptly, then rose up and went about their work.

Sammy went back to school, taking soft sly lopes out of the yard like a rabbit. He wanted a game of marbles before school, and feared his father would give him chores to do. Adoniram hastened to the door and called after him, but he was out of sight.

"I don't see what you let him go for, Mother," said he. "I wanted him to help me unload that wood."

Adoniram went to work out in the yard unloading wood from the wagon. Sarah put away the dinner dishes, while Nanny took down her curl papers and changed her dress. She was going down to the store to buy some more embroidery and thread.

When Nanny was gone, Mrs. Penn went to the door. "Father!" she called.

"Well, what is it!"

"I want to see you jest a minute, Father."

"I can't leave this wood nohow. I've got to git it unloaded and go for a load of gravel afore two o'clock. Sammy had ought to help me. You hadn't ought to let him go to school so early."

"I want to see you jest a minute."

"I tell ye I can't, nohow, Mother."

"Father, you come here." Sarah Penn stood in the door like a queen: she held her head as if it bore a crown; there was that patience which makes authority in her voice. Adoniram went.

Mrs. Penn led the way into the kitchen, and pointed to a chair. "Sit down, Father," said she; "I've got somethin' I want to say to you."

He sat down heavily; his face was quite stolid, but he looked at her with restive eyes. "Well, what is it, Mother?"

"I want to know what you're buildin' that new barn for, Father?"

"I ain't got nothin' to say about it."

"It can't be you think you need another barn?"

"I tell ye I ain't got nothin' to say about it, Mother; an' I ain't goin' to say nothin'."

"Be you goin' to buy more cows?"

Adoniram did not reply; he shut his mouth tight.

"I know you be, as well as I want to. Now, Father, look here" — Sarah Penn had not sat down; she stood before her husband in the humble fashion of a Scripture woman — "I'm goin' to talk real plain to you; I never have sence I married you, but I'm goin' to now. I ain't never complained, an' I ain't goin' to complain now, but I'm goin' to talk plain. You see this room here, Father; you look at it well. You see there ain't no carpet on the floor, an' you see the paper is all dirty and droppin' off the walls. We ain't had no new paper on it for ten year, an' then I put it on myself, an' it didn't cost but nine cents a roll. You see this room, Father; it's all the one I've had to work in an' eat in an' sit in sence we was married. There ain't another woman in the whole town whose husband ain't got half the means you have but what's got better. It's all the room Nanny's got to have her company in; an' there ain't one of her mates but what's got better, an' their fathers not so able as hers is. It's all the room she'll have to be married in. What would you have thought, Father, if we had had our weddin' in a room no better than this? I was married in my mother's parlor, with a carpet on the floor, an' stuffed furniture, an' a mahogany card table. An' this is all the room my daughter will have to be married in. Look here, Father!"

Sarah Penn went across the room as though it were a tragic stage. She flung open a door and disclosed a tiny bedroom only large enough for a bed and bureau, with a path between. "There, Father," said she, "there's all the room I've had to sleep in in forty year. All my children were born there — the two that died an' the two that's livin'. I was sick with a fever, there."

She stepped to another door and opened it. It led into the small ill-lighted pantry. "Here," said she, "is all the buttery I've got — every place I've got for my dishes, to set away my victuals in, an' to keep my milk pans in. Father, I've been takin' care of the milk of six cows in this place, an' now you're goin' to build a new barn, an' keep more cows, an' give me more to do in it."

She threw open another door. A narrow, crooked flight of stairs wound upward from it. "There, Father," said she, "I want you to look at the stairs that go up to them two unfinished chambers that are all the places our son and daughter have had to sleep in all their lives. There ain't a prettier girl in town nor a more ladylike one than Nanny, an' that's the place she has to sleep in. It ain't so good as your horse's stall; it ain't so warm an' tight."

Sarah Penn went back and stood before her husband. "Now, Father," said she, "I want to know if you think you're doin' right and accordin' to what you profess. Here, where we was married forty year ago, you promised me faithful that we should have a new house built in that lot over in the field before the year was out. You said you had money enough, an' you wouldn't ask me to live in no such place as this. It is forty year now, an' you've been makin' more money an' I've been savin' of it for you ever sence, an' you ain't built no house yet. You've built sheds an' cow houses an' one new barn, an' now you're goin' to build another. Father, I want to know if you think it's right. You're lodgin' your dumb beasts better than you are your own flesh and blood. I want to know if you think it's right."

"I ain't got nothin' to say."

"You can't say nothin' without ownin' it ain't right, Father. An' there's another thing — I ain't complained; I've got along forty year an' I s'pose I should forty more, if it wa'n't for that — if we don't have another house, Nanny, she can't live with us after she's married. She'll have to go somewhere else to live away from us, an' it don't seem as if I could have it so, noways, Father. She wa'n't ever strong. She's got considerable color, but there wa'n't never any backbone to her. I've always took the heft of everything off her, an' she ain't fit to keep house an' do everything herself. Think of her doin' all the washin' and ironin' and bakin' with them soft white hands and arms, an' sweepin'. I can't have it so, noways, Father."

Mrs. Penn's face was burning; her mild eyes gleamed. She had pleaded her little cause like a Webster; she had ranged from severity to pathos; but her opponent employed that obstinate silence which makes eloquence futile with mocking echoes. Adoniram arose clumsily.

"Father, ain't you got nothin' to say?" said Mrs. Penn.

"I've got to go off after that load of gravel. I can't stan' talkin' all day."

"Father, won't you think it over an' have a house built there instead of a barn?"

"I ain't got nothin' to say."

Adoniram shuffled out. Mrs. Penn went into her bedroom. When she came out, her eyes were red. She had a roll of unbleached cotton. She spread it out on the kitchen table, and began cutting out some shirts for her husband. The men over in the field had a team to help them this afternoon; she could hear their halloos. She had a scanty pattern for the shirts; she had to plan and piece the sleeves.

Nanny came home with her embroidery and sat down with her needlework. She had taken down her curl papers, and there was a soft roll of fair hair like an aureole over her forehead; her face was as delicately fine and clear as porcelain. Suddenly she looked up and the tender red flamed over her face and neck. "Mother," said she.

"What say?"

"I've been thinking — I don't see how we're goin' to have any wedding in this room. I'd be ashamed to have his folks come if we didn't have anybody else."

"Mebbe we can have some new paper before then; I can put it on. I guess you won't have no call to be ashamed of your belongin's."

"We might have the wedding in the new barn," said Nanny, with gentle pettishness. "Why, Mother, what makes you look so?"

Mrs. Penn had started and was staring at her with a curious expression. She turned again to her work, and spread out a pattern carefully on the cloth. "Nothin'," said she.

Presently Adoniram clattered out of the yard in his two-wheeled dump cart, standing as proudly upright as a Roman charioteer. Mrs. Penn opened the door and stood there a minute looking out; the halloos of the men sounded louder.

It seemed to her all through the spring months that she heard nothing but the halloos and the noises of saws and hammers. The new barn grew fast. It was a fine edifice for this little village. Men came on pleasant Sundays, in their meeting suits and clean shirt bosoms, and stood around it admiringly. Mrs. Penn did not speak of it and Adoniram did not mention it to her, although sometimes upon a return from inspecting it, he bore himself with injured dignity.

"It's a strange thing how your mother feels about the new barn," he said, confidentially, to Sammy one day.

Sammy only grunted after an odd fashion for a boy; he had learned it from his father.

The barn was all completed ready for use by the third week in July. Adoniram had planned to move his stock in on Wednesday; on Tuesday he received a letter which changed his plans. He came in with it early in the morning. "Sammy's been to the post office," said he, "an' I've got a letter from Hiram." Hiram was Mrs. Penn's brother who lived in Vermont.

"Well," said Mrs. Penn, "what does he say about the folks?"

"I guess they're all right. He says he thinks if I come up country right off ther's a chance to buy jest the kind of a horse I want." He stared reflectively out of the window at the new barn.

Mrs. Penn was making pies. She went on clapping the rolling pin into the crust, although she was very pale, and her heart beat loudly.

"I dun' know but what I'd better go," said Adoniram. "I hate to go off jest now, right in the midst of hayin', but the ten-acre lot's cut, an' I guess Rufus an' the others can git along without me three or four days. I can't get a horse round here to suit me, nohow, an' I've got to have another for all that wood haulin' in the fall. I told Hiram to watch out an' if he got wind of a good horse to let me know. I guess I'd better go."

"I'll get out your clean shirt an' collar," said Mrs. Penn calmly.

She laid out Adoniram's Sunday suit and his clean clothes on the bed in the little bedroom. She got his shaving water and razor ready. At last she buttoned on his collar and fastened his black cravat.

Adoniram never wore his collar and cravat except on extra occasions. He held his head high, with a rasped dignity. When he was all ready, with coat and hat brushed, and a lunch of pie and cheese in a paper bag, he hesitated on the threshold of the door. He looked at his wife and his manner was defiantly apologetic. "*If* them cows come today Sammy can drive them into the new barn," said he, "an' when they bring the hay up they can pitch it in there."

"Well," replied Mrs. Penn.

Adoniram set his shaven face ahead and started. When he had cleared the doorstep, he turned and looked back with a kind of nervous solemnity. "I shall be back by Saturday if nothin' happens," said he.

"Do be careful, Father," returned his wife.

She stood in the door with Nanny at her elbow and watched him out of sight. Her eyes had a strange, doubtful expression in them; her peaceful forehead was contracted. Nanny sat sewing. Her wedding day was drawing nearer and she was getting pale and thin with her steady sewing. Her mother kept glancing at her.

"Have you got that pain in your side this mornin'?" she asked.

"A little."

Mrs. Penn's face as she worked, changed; her perplexed forehead smoothed; her eyes were steady, her lips firmly set. She formed a maxim for herself, although incoherently with her unlettered thoughts. "Unsolicited opportunities are the guideposts of the Lord to the new roads of Life," she repeated in effect, and she made up her mind to her course of action.

"S'posin' I *had* wrote to Hiram," she muttered once, when she was in the pantry. "S'posin' I had wrote and asked him if he knew of any horse? But I didn't, an' Father's goin' wa'n't any of my doin'. It looks like a providence." Her mother's voice rang out quite loud at the last.

"What you talkin' about, Mother?" called Nanny.

"Nothin'."

Mrs. Penn hurried her baking; at eleven o'clock it was all done. The load of hay from the west field came slowly down the cart track and drew up at the new barn. Mrs. Penn ran out. "Stop!" she screamed. "Stop!"

The men stopped and looked; Sammy upreared from the top of the load and stared at his mother.

"Stop!" she cried out again. "Don't you put the hay in that barn; put it in the old one."

"Why, he said to put it in here," returned one of the haymakers, wonderingly. He was a young man, a neighbor's son, whom Adoniram hired by the year to work on the farm.

"Don't you put the hay in the new barn; there's room enough in the old one, ain't there?" said Mrs. Penn.

"Room enough," returned the hired man, in his thick, rustic tones. "Didn't need the new barn, nohow, as far as room's concerned. Well, I s'pose he changed his mind." He took hold of the horses' bridles.

Mrs. Penn went back to the house. Soon the kitchen windows were darkened and a fragrance like warm honey came into the room.

Nanny laid down her work. "I thought Father wanted them to put the hay into the new barn?" she said, wonderingly.

"It's all right," replied her mother.

Sammy slid down from the load of hay and came in to see if dinner was ready.

"I ain't goin' to get a regular dinner today, as long as Father's gone," said his mother. "I've let the fire go out. You can have some bread an' milk an' pie. I thought we could get along." She set out some bowls of milk, some bread and a pie on the kitchen table. "You'd better eat your dinner now," said she. "You might jest as well get through with it. I want you to help me afterward."

Nanny and Sammy stared at each other. There was something strange in their mother's manner. Mrs. Penn did not eat anything herself. She went into the pantry and they heard her moving dishes while they ate. Presently she came out with a pile of plates. She got the clothes basket out of the shed and packed them in it. Nanny and Sammy watched. She brought out cups and saucers and put them in with the plates.

"What you goin' to do, Mother?" inquired Nanny, in a timid voice. A sense of something unusual made her tremble, as if it were a ghost. Sammy rolled his eyes over his pie.

"You'll see what I'm goin' to do," replied Mrs. Penn. "If you're through, Nanny, I want you to go upstairs and pack your things; an' I want you, Sammy, to help me take down the bed in the bedroom."

"Oh, Mother, what for?" gasped Nanny.

"You'll see."

During the next few hours a feat was performed by this simple pious New England mother which was equal in its way to Wolfe's storming of the Heights of Abraham. It took no more genius and audacity of bravery for Wolfe to cheer his wondering soldiers up those steep precipices, under the sleeping eyes of the enemy, than for Sarah Penn, at the head of her children, to move all their little house-hold goods into the new barn while her husband was away.

Nanny and Sammy followed their mother's instructions without a murmur; indeed, they were overawed. There is a certain uncanny and super-human quality about all such purely original undertakings as their mother's was to them. Nanny went back and forth with her light loads and Sammy tugged with sober energy.

At five o'clock in the afternoon the little house in which the Penns had lived for forty years had emptied itself into the new barn.

Every builder builds somewhat for unknown purposes, and is in a measure a prophet. The architect of Adoniram Penn's barn, while he designed it for the comfort of four-footed animals, had planned better than he knew for the comfort of humans. Sarah Penn saw at a glance its possibilities. Those great box stalls, with quilts hung before them, would make better bedrooms than the one she had occupied for forty years, and there was a tight carriage room. The harness room, with its chimney and shelves, would make a kitchen of her dreams. The great middle space would make a parlor, by-and-by, fit for a palace. Upstairs there was as much room as down. With partitions and windows, what a house there would be! Sarah looked at the row of stanchions before the allotted space for cows, and reflected she would have a front entry there.

At six o'clock the stove was up in the harness room, the kettle was boiling, and the table set for tea. It looked almost as homelike as the abandoned house across the yard had ever done. The young hired man milked, and Sarah directed him calmly to bring the milk to the new barn. He came gasping, dropping little blots of foam from the brimming pails on the grass. Before the next morning he had spread the story of Adoniam Penn's wife moving into the new barn all over the little village. Men assembled in the store and talked it over; women with shawls over their heads scuttled into each other's houses before their work was done. Any deviation from the ordinary course of life in this quiet town was enough to stop all progress in it. Everybody paused to look at the staid, independent figure on the side track. There was a difference of opinion with regard to her. Some held her to be insane; some, of a lawless and rebellious spirit.

Friday the minister went to see her. It was in the forenoon, and she was at the barn door shelling peas for dinner. She looked up and returned his salutation with dignity; then she went on with her work. She did not invite him in. The saintly expression of her face remained fixed, but there was an angry flush over it.

The minister stood awkwardly before her, and talked. She handled the peas as if they were bullets. At last she looked up and her eyes showed a spirit that her meek front had covered for a lifetime.

"There ain't no use talkin', Mr. Hersey," said she. "I've thought it all over and over, an' I believe I'm doin' what's right. I've made it the subject of prayer, and it's betwixt me an' the Lord an' Adoniram. There ain't no call for nobody else to worry about it."

"Well, of course, if you have brought it to the Lord in prayer, and feel satisfied that you are doing right, Mrs. Penn," said the minister helplessly. His thin, gray-bearded face was pathetic. He was a sickly man; his youthful confidence had cooled; he had to scourge himself up to some of his pastoral duties, and then he was prostrated by the smart.

"I think it's right jest as much as I think it was right for our forefathers to come over from the old country 'cause they didn't have what belonged to 'em," said Mrs. Penn. She arose. The barn threshold might have been Plymouth Rock from her bearing. "I don't doubt you mean well, Mr. Hersey," said she, "but there are things people hadn't ought to interfere with. I've been a member of the church for over forty year. I've got my mind an' my own feet, an' I'm goin' to think my own thoughts an' go my own ways, an' nobody but the Lord is goin' to dictate to me unless I've a mind to have him. Won't you come in an' set down? How is Mis' Hersey?"

"She is well, I thank you," replied the minister. He added some more perplexed, apologetic remarks; then he retreated.

He could expound the intricacies of every character study in the Scriptures; he was competent to grasp the Pilgrim Fathers and all historical innovators; but Sarah Penn was beyond him. He could deal with primal cases, but parallel ones worsted him. But, after all, although it was aside from his province, he wondered more how Adoniram Penn would deal with his wife than how the Lord would. Everybody shared the wonder. When Adoniram's four new cows arrived, Sarah ordered three put in the old barn, the other in the house shed where the cooking stove had stood. That added to the excitement. It was whispered that all four cows were domiciled in the house.

Toward sunset on Saturday, when Adoniram was expected home, there was a knot of men in the road near the new barn. The hired man milked, but he still hung around the premises. There were brown bread and baked beans and a custard pie; it was the supper that Adoniram loved on a Saturday night. She had on a clean calico and she bore herself imperturbably. Nanny and Sammy kept close at her heels. Their eyes were large, and Nanny was full of nervous tremors. Still there was to them more pleasant excitement than anything else. An inborn confidence in their mother over their father asserted itself.

Sammy looked out of the harness-room window. "There he is," he announced, in an awed whisper. He and Nanny peeped around the casing. Mrs. Penn kept on about her work. The children watched Adoniram leave the new horse standing in the drive while he went to the house-door. It was fastened. Then he went around to the shed. That door was seldom locked, even when the family was away. The thought how her father would be confronted by the cow flashed upon Nanny. There was a hysterical sob in her throat. Adoniram emerged from the shed and stood looking about in a dazed fashion. His lips moved; he was saying something, but they could not hear what it was. The hired man was peeping around a corner of the old barn but nobody saw him.

Adoniram took the new horse by the bridle and led him across the yard to the new barn. Nanny and Sammy slunk close to their mother. The barn doors rolled back and there stood Adoniram, with the long mild face of the great Canadian farm horse looking over his shoulder.

Nanny kept behind her mother, but Sammy stepped suddenly forward and stood in front of her.

Adoniram stared at the group. "What on airth you all down here for?" said he. "What's the matter over to the house?"

"We've come here to live, Father," said Sammy. His shrill voice quavered out bravely.

"What — " Adoniram sniffed — "what is it smells like cookin?" said he. He stepped forward and looked in at the open door of the harness room. Then he turned to his wife. His old bristling face was pale and frightened. "What on airth does this mean, Mother?"

"You come in here, Father," said Sarah. She led the way into the harness room and shut the door. "Now, Father," said she, "you needn't be scared. I ain't crazy. There ain't nothin' to be upset over. But we've come here to live an' we're goin' to live here. We've got jest as good a right here as new horses and cows. The house wa'n't fit for us to live in any longer, an' I made up my mind I wa'n't goin' to stay there. I've done my duty by you forty year an' I'm goin' to do it now, but I'm goin' to live here. You've got to put in some windows an' partitions, an' you'll have to buy some furniture."

"Why, Mother!" the old man gasped.

"You'd better take your coat off an' get washed — there's the wash basin — an' then we'll have supper."

"Why, Mother!"

Sammy went past the window, leading the new horse to the old barn. The old man saw him and shook his head speechlessly. He tried to take off his coat, but his arms seemed to lack the power. His wife helped him. She poured some water into the tin basin and put in a piece of soap. She got the comb and brush and smoothed his thin gray hair after he had washed. Then she put the beans, hot bread and tea on the table. Sammy came in and the family drew up. Adoniram sat looking dazedly at his plate and they waited.

"Ain't you goin' to ask a blessin', Father?" said Sarah.

And the old man bent his head and mumbled.

All through the meal he stopped eating at intervals and stared furtively at his wife, but he ate well. The home food tasted good to him and his old frame was too sturdily healthy to be affected by his mind. But after supper he went out and sat down on the step of the smaller door at the right of the barn, through which he had meant his Jerseys to pass in stately file, but which Sarah designed for her front house-door, and he leaned his head on his hands.

After the supper dishes were cleared away and the milk pans washed, Sarah went out to him. The twilight was deepening. There was a clear green glow in the sky. Before them stretched the smooth level of field; in the distance was a cluster of haystacks like the huts of a village; the air was very calm and sweet. The landscape might have been an ideal one of peace.

Sarah bent over and touched her husband on one of his thin, sinewy shoulders. "Father!"

The old man's shoulders heaved; he was weeping.

"Why, don't do so, Father," said Sarah.

"I'll — put up the — partitions, an' — everything you — want, Mother."

Sarah put her apron up to her face; she was overcome by her own triumph.

Adoniram was like a fortress whose walls had no active resistance, and went down the instant the right besieging tools were used. "Why, Mother," he said hoarsely, "I hadn't no idee you was so set on't it as all this comes to."

# Ambrose Bierce (1842–1914?)

A QUESTION MARK must be put after that supposed date of Bierce's death, for although he was one of the most famous writers of his time, no one knows when, where, or how he died. He was born in Ohio, served in the Civil War, and became a journalist in San Francisco where he was noted for both brilliance and bitterness. His first three books were collections of witty but acrimonious sketches published under the pseudonym of Dod Grile. He first attained real literary stature with *Tales of Soldiers and Civilians* (1891), later retitled *In the Midst of Life*, which included powerful stories of the Civil War. His second most important book was *Can Such Things Be?* (1893) and contains more stories of the Civil War and of the California frontier. His *The Devil's Dictionary* (1911), first published in 1906 as *The Cynic's Word Book*, addressed to "enlightened souls who prefer dry wines to sweet, sense to sentiment, wit to humor and clean English to slang" was notorious for the cynicism of its definitions. In 1913, saying he was tired of American civilization, he left California for Mexico where a war was raging to "seek the good, kind darkness" and was never heard of again.

Because of the macabre quality of many of his stories, the best of which are based on his experiences as a soldier in the Civil War, Ambrose Bierce has frequently been likened to Poe. Once Poe is mentioned the resemblance can be seen in this account of the trapped soldier, but Bierce was his own man and an important artist in his own right. There is more of daylight in Bierce's writing and less of Poe's frequent suggestion of the supernatural. The Civil War was a domestic war and, as Bierce wrote elsewhere, the Mason-Dixon Line cut families in half, but the brothers in "One of the Missing" are both with the Northern Army. The irony in this tragic story indicts any and all war.

# *One of the Missing*

JEROME SEARING, a private soldier of General Sherman's army, then confronting the enemy at and about Kenesaw Mountain, Georgia, turned his back upon a small group of officers, with whom he had been talking in low tones, stepped across a light line of earthworks, and disappeared in a forest. None of the men in line behind the works had said a word to him, nor had he so much as nodded to them in passing, but all who saw understood that this brave man had been intrusted with some perilous duty. Jerome Searing, though a private, did not serve in the ranks; he was detailed for service at division headquarters, being borne upon the rolls as an orderly. "Orderly" is a word covering a multitude of duties. An orderly may be a messenger, a clerk, an officer's servant — anything. He may perform services for which no provision is made in orders and army regulations. Their nature may depend upon his aptitude, upon favour, upon accident. Private Searing, an incomparable marksman, young — it is surprising how young we all were in those days — hardy, intelligent, and insensible to fear, was a scout. The general commanding his division was not content to obey orders blindly without knowing what was in his front, even when his command was not on detached service, but formed a fraction of the line of the army; nor was he satisfied to receive his knowledge of his *vis-à-vis* through the customary channels; he wanted to know more than he was apprised of by the corps commander and the collisions of pickets and skirmishers. Hence Jerome Searing — with his extraordinary daring, his woodcraft, his sharp eyes and truthful tongue. On this occasion his instructions were simple: to get as near the enemy's lines as possible and learn all that he could.

In a few moments he had arrived at the picket line, the men on duty there lying in groups of from two to four behind little banks of earth scooped out of the slight depression in which they lay, their rifles protruding from the green boughs with which they had masked their small defences. The forest extended without a break toward the front, so solemn and silent that only by an effort of the imagination could it be conceived as populous with armed men, alert and vigilant — a forest formidable with possibilities of battle. Pausing a moment in one of the rifle pits to apprise the men of his intention, Searing crept stealthily forward on his hands and knees and was soon lost to view in a dense thicket of underbrush.

"That is the last of him," said one of the men; "I wish I had his rifle; those fellows will hurt some of us with it."

Searing crept on, taking advantage of every accident of ground and growth to give himself better cover. His eyes penetrated everywhere, his ears took note of every sound. He stilled his breathing, and at the cracking of a twig beneath his knee stopped his progress and hugged the earth. It was slow work, but not tedious; the danger made it exciting, but by no physical signs was the excitement manifest. His pulse was as regular, his nerves were as steady, as if he were trying to trap a sparrow.

"It seems a long time," he thought, "but I cannot have come very far; I am still alive."

He smiled at his own method of estimating distance, and crept forward. A moment later he suddenly flattened himself upon the earth and lay motionless, minute after minute. Through a narrow opening in the bushes he had caught sight of a small mound of yellow clay — one of the enemy's rifle pits. After some little time he cautiously raised his head, inch by inch, then his body upon his hands, spread out on each side of him, all the while intently regarding the hillock of clay. In another moment he was upon his feet, rifle in hand, striding rapidly forward with little attempt at concealment. He had rightly interpreted the signs, whatever they were; the enemy was gone.

To assure himself beyond a doubt before going back to report upon so important a matter, Searing pushed forward across the line of abandoned pits, running from cover to cover in the more open forest, his eyes vigilant to discover possible stragglers. He came to the edge of a plantation — one of those forlorn, deserted homesteads of the last years of the war, upgrown with brambles, ugly with broken fences, and desolate with vacant buildings having blank apertures in place of doors and windows. After a keen reconnoissance from the safe seclusion of a clump of young pines, Searing ran lightly across a field and through an orchard to a small structure which stood apart from the other farm buildings, on a slight elevation, which he thought would enable him to overlook a large scope of country in the direction that he supposed the enemy to have taken in withdrawing. This building, whch had originally consisted of a single room, elevated upon four posts about ten feet high, was now little more than a roof; the floor had fallen away, the joists and planks loosely piled on the ground below or resting on end at various angles, not wholly torn from their fastenings above. The supporting posts were themselves no longer vertical. It looked as if the whole edifice would go down at the touch of a finger. Concealing himself in the débris of joists and flooring, Searing looked across the open ground between his point of view and a spur of Kenesaw Mountain, a half mile away. A road leading up and across this spur was crowded with troops — the rear guard of the retiring enemy, their gun barrels gleaming in the morning sunlight.

Searing had now learned all that he could hope to know. It was his duty to return to his own command with all possible speed and report his discovery. But the grey column of infantry toiling up the mountain road was singularly tempting. His rifle — an ordinary "Springfield," but fitted with a globe sight and hair trigger — would easily send its ounce and a quarter of lead hissing into their midst. That would probably not affect the duration and result of the war, but it is the business of a soldier to kill. It is also his pleasure if he is a good soldier. Searing cocked his rifle and "set" the trigger.

But it was decreed from the beginning of time that Private Searing was not to murder anybody that bright summer morning, nor was the Confederate retreat to be announced by him. For countless ages events had been so matching themselves together in that wondrous mosaic to some parts of which, dimly discernible, we give the name of history, that the acts which he had in will would have marred the harmony of the pattern.

Some twenty-five years previously the Power charged with the execution of the work according to the design had provided against that mischance by causing the birth of a certain male child in a little village at the foot of the Carpathian Mountains, had carefully reared it, supervised its education, directed its desires into a military channel, and in due time made it an officer of artillery. By the concurrence of an infinite number of favouring influences and their preponderance over an infinite number of opposing ones, this officer of artillery had been made to commit a breach of discipline and fly from his native country to avoid punishment. He had been directed to New Orleans (instead of New York), where a recruiting officer awaited him on the wharf. He was enlisted and promoted, and things were so ordered that he now commanded a Confederate battery some three miles along the line from where Jerome Searing, the Federal scout, stood cocking his rifle. Nothing had been neglected — at every step in the progress of both these men's lives, and in the lives of their ancestors and contemporaries, and of the lives of the contemporaries of their ancestors — the right thing had been done to bring about the desired result. Had anything in all this vast concatenation been overlooked, Private Searing might have fired on the retreating Confederates that morning, and would perhaps have missed. As it fell out, a captain of artillery, having nothing better to do while awaiting his turn to pull out and be off, amused himself by sighting a field piece obliquely to his right at what he took to be some Federal officers on the crest of a hill, and discharged it. The shot flew high of its mark.

As Jerome Searing drew back the hammer of his rifle, and, with his eyes upon the distant Confederates, considered where he could plant his shot with the best hope of making a widow or an orphan or a childless mother — perhaps all three, for Private Searing, although he had repeatedly refused promotion, was not without a certain kind of ambition — he heard a rushing sound in the air, like that made by the wings of a great bird swooping down upon its prey. More quickly that he could apprehend the gradation, it increased to a hoarse and horrible roar, as the missile that made it sprang at him out of the sky, striking with a deafening impact one of the posts supporting the confusion of timbers above him, smashing it into matchwood, and bringing down the crazy edifice with a loud clatter, in clouds of blinding dust!

Lieutenant Adrian Searing, in command of the picket guard on that part of the line through which his brother Jerome had passed on his mission, sat with attentive ears in his breastwork behind the line. Not the faintest sound escaped him; the cry of a bird, the barking of a squirrel, the noise of the wind among the pines — all were anxiously noted by his overstrained sense. Suddenly, directly in front of his line, he heard a faint, confused rumble, like the clatter of a falling building translated by distance. At the same moment an officer approached him on foot from the rear and saluted.

"Lieutenant," said the aide, "the colonel directs you to move forward your line and feel the enemy if you find him. If not, continue the advance until directed to halt. There is reason to think that the enemy has retreated."

The lieutenant nodded and said nothing; the other officer retired. In a moment the men, apprised of their duty by the non-commissioned officers in low tones, had deployed from their rifle pits and were moving forward in skirmishing order, with set teeth and beating hearts. The lieutenant mechanically looked at his watch. Six o'clock and eighteen minutes.

When Jerome Searing recovered consciousness, he did not at once understand what had occurred. It was, indeed, some time before he opened his eyes. For a while he believed that he had died and been buried, and he tried to recall some portions of the burial service. He thought that his wife was kneeling upon his grave, adding her weight to that of the earth upon his breast. The two of them, widow and earth, had crushed his coffin. Unless the children should persuade her to go home, he would not much longer be able to breathe. He felt a sense of wrong. "I cannot speak to her," he thought; "the dead have no voice; and if I open my eyes I shall get them full of earth."

He opened his eyes — a great expanse of blue sky, rising from a fringe of the tops of trees. In the foreground, shutting out some of the trees, a high, dun mound, angular in outline and crossed by an intricate, patternless system of straight lines; in the centre a bright ring of metal — the whole an immeasurable distance away — a distance so inconceivably great that it fatigued him, and he closed his eyes. The moment that he did so he was conscious of an insufferable light. A sound was in his ears like the low, rhythmic thunder of a distant sea breaking in successive waves upon the beach, and out of this noise, seeming a part of it, or possibly coming from beyond it, and intermingled with its ceaseless undertone, came the articulate words: "Jerome Searing, you are caught like a rat in a trap — in a trap, trap, trap."

Suddenly there fell a great silence, a black darkness, an infinite tranquillity, and Jerome Searing, perfectly conscious of his rathood, and well assured of the trap that he was in, remembered all, and, nowise alarmed, again opened his eyes to reconnoitre, to note the strength of his enemy, to plan his defence.

He was caught in a reclining posture, his back firmly supported by a solid beam. Another lay across his breast, but he had been able to shrink a little way from it so that it no longer oppressed him though it was immovable. A brace joining it at an angle had wedged him against a pile of boards on his left, fastening the arm on that side. His legs, slightly parted and straight along the ground, were covered upward to the knees with a mass of débris which towered above his narrow horizon.

His head was as rigidly fixed as in a vice; he could move his eyes, his chin — no more. Only his right arm was partly free. "You must help us out of this," he said to it. But he could not get it from under the heavy timber athwart his chest, nor move it outward more than six inches at the elbow.

Searing was not seriously injured, nor did he suffer pain. A smart rap on the head from a flying fragment of the splintered post, incurred simultaneously with the frightfully sudden shock to the nervous system, had momentarily dazed him. His term of unconsciousness, including the period of recovery, during which he had had the strange fancies, had probably not exceeded a few seconds, for the dust of the wreck had not wholly cleared away as he began an intelligent survey of the situation.

With his partly free right hand he now tried to get hold of the beam which lay across, but not quite against, his breast. In no way could he do so. He was unable to depress the shoulder so as to push the elbow beyond that edge of the timber which was nearest his knees; failing in that, he could not raise the forearm and hand to grasp the beam. The brace that made an angle with it downward and backward prevented him from doing anything in that direction, and between it and his body the space was not half as wide as the length of his forearm. Obviously he could not get his hand under the beam nor over it; he could not, in fact, touch it at all. Having demonstrated his inability, he desisted, and began to think if he could reach any of the débris piled upon his legs.

In surveying the mass with a view to determining that point, his attention was arrested by what seemed to be a ring of shining metal immediately in front of his eyes. It appeared to him at first to surround some perfectly black substance, and it was somewhat more than a half inch in diameter. It suddenly occurred to his mind that the blackness was simply shadow, and that the ring was in fact the muzzle of his rifle protruding from the pile of débris. He was not long in satisfying himself that this was so — if it was a satisfaction. By closing either eye he could look a little way along the barrel — to the point where it was hidden by the rubbish that held it. He could see the one side, with the corresponding eye, at apparently the same angle as the other side with the other eye. Looking with the right eye, the weapon seemed to be directed at a point to the left of his head, and *vice versa*. He was unable to see the upper surface of the barrel, but could see the under surface of the stock at a slight angle. The piece was, in fact, aimed at the exact centre of his forehead.

In the perception of this circumstance, in the recollection that just previously to the mischance of which this uncomfortable situation was the result, he had cocked the gun and set the trigger so that a touch would discharge it, Private Searing was affected with a feeling of uneasiness.

But that was as far as possible from fear; he was a brave man, somewhat familiar with the aspect of rifles from that point of view, and of cannon, too; and now he recalled, with something like amusement, an incident of his experience at the storming of Missionary Ridge, where, walking up to one of the enemy's embrasures from which he had seen a heavy gun throw charge after charge of grape among the assailants, he thought for a moment that the piece had been withdrawn; he could see nothing in the opening but a brazen circle. What that was he had understood just in time to step aside as it pitched another peck of iron down that swarming slope. To face firearms is one of the commonest incidents in a soldier's life — firearms, too, with malevolent eyes blazing behind them. That is what a soldier is for. Still, Private Searing did not altogether relish the situation, and turned away his eyes.

After groping, aimless, with his right hand for a time, he made an ineffectual attempt to release his left. Then he tried to disengage his head, the fixity of which was the more annoying from his ignorance of what held it. Next he tried to free his feet, but while exerting the powerful muscles of his legs for that purpose it occurred to him that a disturbance of the rubbish which held them might discharge the rifle; how it could have endured what had already befallen it he could not understand, although memory assisted him with various instances in point. One in particular he recalled, in which, in a moment of mental abstraction, he had clubbed his rifle and beaten out another gentleman's brains, observing afterward that the weapon which he had been diligently swinging by the muzzle was loaded, capped, and at full cock — knowledge of which circumstance would doubtless have cheered his antagonist to longer endurance. He had always smiled in recalling that blunder of his "green and salad days" as a soldier, but now he did not smile. He turned his eyes again to the muzzle of the gun, and for a moment fancied that it had moved; it seemed somewhat nearer.

Again he looked away. The tops of the distant trees beyond the bounds of the plantation interested him; he had not before observed how light and feathery they seemed, nor how darkly blue the sky was, even among their branches, where they somewhat paled it with their green; above him it appeared almost black. "It will be uncomfortably hot here," he thought, "as the day advances. I wonder which way I am looking."

Judging by such shadows as he could see, he decided that his face was due north; he would at least not have the sun in his eyes, and north — well, that was toward his wife and children.

"Bah!" he exclaimed aloud, "what have they to do with it?"

He closed his eyes. "As I can't get out, I may as well go to sleep. The rebels are gone, and some of our fellows are sure to stray out here foraging. They'll find me."

But he did not sleep. Gradually he became sensible of a pain in his forehead — a dull ache, hardly perceptible at first, but growing more and more uncomfortable. He opened his eyes and it was gone — closed them and it returned. "The devil!" he said irrelevantly, and stared again at the sky. He heard the singing of birds, the strange metallic note of the meadow lark, suggesting the clash of vibrant blades. He fell into pleasant memories of his childhood, played again with his brother and sister, raced across the fields, shouting to alarm the sedentary larks, entered the sombre forest beyond, and with timid steps followed the faint path to Ghost Rock, standing at last with audible heart-throbs before the Dead Man's Cave and seeking to penetrate its awful mystery. For the first time he observed that the opening of the haunted cavern was encircled by a ring of metal. Then all else vanished, and left him gazing into the barrel of his rifle as before. But whereas before it had seemed nearer, it now seemed an inconceivable distance away, and all the more sinister for that. He cried out, and, startled by something in his own voice — the note of fear — lied to himself in denial: "If I don't sing out I may stay here till I die."

He now made no further attempt to evade the menacing stare of the gun barrel. If he turned away his eyes an instant it was to look for assistance (although he could not see the ground on either side the ruin), and he permitted them to return, obedient to the imperative fascination. If he closed them, it was from weariness, and instantly the poignant pain in his forehead — the prophecy and menace of the bullet — forced him to reopen them.

The tension of nerve and brain was too severe; nature came to his relief with intervals of unconsciousness. Reviving from one of these, he became sensible of a sharp, smarting pain in his right hand, and when he worked his fingers together, or rubbed his palm with them, he could feel that they were wet and slippery. He could not see the hand, but he knew the sensation; it was running blood. In his delirium he had beaten it against the jagged fragments of the wreck, had clutched it full of splinters. He resolved that he would meet his fate more manly. He was a plain, common soldier, had no religion and not much philosophy; he could not die like a hero, with great and wise last words, even if there were someone to hear them, but he could die "game," and he would. But if he could only know when to expect the shot!

Some rats which had probably inhabited the shed came sneaking and scampering about. One of them mounted the pile of débris that held the rifle; another followed, and another. Searing regarded them at first with indifference, then with friendly interest; then, as the thought flashed into his bewildered mind that they might touch the trigger of his rifle, he screamed at them to go away. "It is no business of yours," he cried.

The creatures left; they would return later, attack his face, gnaw his nose, cut his throat — he knew that, but he hoped by that time to be dead.

Nothing could now unfix his gaze from the little ring of metal with its black interior. The pain in his forehead was fierce and constant. He felt it gradually penetrating the brain more and more deeply, until at last its progress was arrested by the wood at the back of his head. It grew momentarily more insufferable; he began wantonly beating his lacerated hand against the splinters again to counteract that horrible ache. It seemed to throb with a slow, regular recurrence, each pulsation sharper than the preceding, and sometimes he cried out, thinking he felt the fatal bullet. No thoughts of home, of wife and children, of country, of glory. The whole record of memory was effaced. The world had passed away — not a vestige remained. Here, in this confusion of timbers and boards, is the sole universe. Here is immortality in time — each pain an everlasting life. The throbs tick off eternities.

Jerome Searing, the man of courage, the formidable enemy, the strong, resolute warrior, was as pale as a ghost. His jaw was fallen; his eyes protruded; he trembled in every fibre; a cold sweat bathed his entire body; he screamed with fear. He was not insane — he was terrified.

In groping about with his torn and bleeding hand he seized at last a strip of board, and, pulling, felt it give way. It lay parallel with his body, and by bending his elbow as much as the contracted space would permit, he could draw it a few inches at a time. Finally it was altogether loosened from the wreckage covering his legs; he could lift it clear of the ground its whole length. A great hope came into his mind: perhaps he could work it upward, that is to say backward, far enough to lift the end and push aside the rifle; or, if that were too tightly wedged, so hold the strip of board as to deflect the bullet. With this object he passed it backward inch by inch, hardly daring to breath, lest that act somehow defeat his intent, and more than ever unable to remove his eyes from the rifle, which might perhaps now hasten to improve its waning opportunity. Something at least had been gained; in the occupation of his mind in this attempt at self-defence he was less sensible of the pain in his head and had ceased to scream. But he was still dreadfully frightened, and his teeth rattled like castanets.

The strip of board ceased to move to the suasion of his hand. He tugged at it with all his strength, changed the direction of its length all he could, but it had met some extended obstruction behind him, and the end in front was still too far away to clear the pile of débris and reach the muzzle of the gun. It extended, indeed, nearly as far as the trigger-guard, which, uncovered by the rubbish, he could imperfectly see with his right eye. He tried to break the strip with his hand, but had no leverage. Perceiving his defeat, all his terror returned, augmented tenfold. The black aperture of the rifle appeared to threaten a sharper and more imminent death in punishment of his rebellion. The track of the bullet through his head ached with an intenser anguish. He began to tremble again.

Suddenly he became composed. His tremor subsided. He clinched his teeth and drew down his eyebrows. He had not exhausted his means of defence; a new design had shaped itself in his mind — another plan of battle. Raising the front end of the strip of board, he carefully pushed it forward through the wreckage at the side of the rifle until it pressed against the trigger guard. Then he moved the end slowly outward until he could feel that it had cleared it, then, closing his eyes, thrust it against the trigger with all his strength! There was no explosion; the rifle had been discharged as it dropped from his hand when the building fell. But Jerome Searing was dead.

A line of Federal skirmishers swept across the plantation toward the mountain. They passed on both sides of the wrecked building, observing nothing. At a short distance in their rear came their commander, Lieutenant Adrian Searing. He casts his eyes curiously upon the ruin and sees a dead body half buried in boards and timbers. It is so covered with dust that its clothing is Confederate grey. Its face is yellowish white; the cheeks are fallen in, the temples sunken, too, with sharp ridges about them, making the forehead forbiddingly narrow; the upper lip, slightly lifted, shows the white teeth, rigidly clinched. The hair is heavy with moisture, the face as wet as the dewy grass all about. From his point of view the officer does not observe the rifle; the man was apparently killed by the fall of the building.

'Dead a week,' said the officer curtly, moving on, mechanically pulling out his watch as if to verify his estimate of time. Six o'clock and forty minutes.

# Hamlin Garland (1860-1940)

A CLASS-CONSCIOUS agrarian proletarian, if such nomenclature is permissible, Hamlin Garland, born in Wisconsin in 1860, had his character and writing shaped by the hard, poorly paid labor he endured as a young man on Midwest wheat farms. He espoused the single tax and campaigned for the Populist Party, then almost as strong as the Republican and Democratic parties are now. He wrote several collections of short stories of which *Main-Travelled Roads*, published in 1891, is the best known. Of his novels, *Rose of Dutcher's Coolly* is the most popular. His two-part autobiography, *A Son of the Middle Border* and *A Daughter of the Middle Border*, won the Pulitzer Prize in 1921.

"The Return of a Private" is taken from *Main-Travelled Roads*, in which Garland defines a "Main-Travelled Road in the West" as one that "may lead past a bend in the river where the water laughs eternally over its shadows . . . Mainly it is long and weariful . . . Like the main-travelled road of life it is traversed by many classes of people, but the poor and the weary predominate." Back from three years of fighting with the Union Army in the Civil War, Private Smith — the commonplace name signifies his universality — is no triumphant conquering hero but a bone-tired man in shabby blue uniform returning to his poverty-stricken family and neglected farm. It is a simple tale simply told. Its bleakness is redeemed by the love of a family glad to be together once more.

# The Return of a Private

THE nearer the train drew toward La Crosse, the soberer the little group of "vets" became. On the long way from New Orleans they had beguiled tedium with jokes and friendly chaff; or with planning with elaborate detail what they were going to do now, after the war. A long journey, slowly, irregularly, yet persistently pushing northward. When they entered on Wisconsin territory they gave a cheer, and another when they reached Madison, but after that they sank into a dumb expectancy. Comrades dropped off at one or two points beyond, until there were only four or five left who were bound for La Crosse County.

Three of them were gaunt and brown, the fourth was gaunt and pale, with signs of fever and ague upon him. One had a great scar down his temple, one limped, and they all had unnaturally large, bright eyes, showing emaciation. There were no bands greeting them at the station, no banks of gayly dressed ladies waving handkerchiefs and shouting "Bravo!" as they came in on the caboose of a freight train into the towns that had cheered and blared at them on their way to war. As they looked out or stepped upon the platform for a moment, while the train stood at the station, the loafers looked at them indifferently. Their blue coats, dusty and grimy, were too familiar now to excite notice, much less a friendly word. They were the last of the army to return, and the loafers were surfeited with such sights.

The train jogged forward so slowly that it seemed likely to be midnight before they should reach La Crosse. The little squad grumbled and swore, but it was no use; the train would not hurry, and, as a matter of fact, it was nearly two o'clock when the engine whistled "down brakes."

All of the group were farmers, living in districts several miles out of the town, and all were poor.

"Now, boys," said Private Smith, he of the fever and ague, "we are landed in La Crosse in the night. We've got to stay somewhere till mornin'. Now I ain't got no two dollars to waste on a hotel. I've got a wife and children, so I'm goin' to roost on a bench and take the cost of a bed out of my hide."

"Same here," put in one of the other men. "Hide'll grow on again, dollars'll come hard. It's goin' to be mighty hot skirmishin' to find a dollar these days."

"Don't think they'll be a deputation of citizens waitin' to 'scort us to a hotel, eh?" said another. His sarcasm was too obvious to require an answer.

Smith went on, "Then at daybreak we'll start for home — at least, I will."

"Well, I'll be dummed if I'll take two dollars out of *my* hide," one of the younger men said. "I'm goin' to a hotel, ef I don't never lay up a cent."

"That'll do f'r you," said Smith; "but if you had a wife an' three younguns dependin' on yeh — "

"Which I ain't, thank the Lord! and don't intend havin' while the court knows itself."

The station was deserted, chill, and dark, as they came into it at exactly a quarter to two in the morning. Lit by the oil lamps that flared a dull red light over the dingy benches, the waiting room was not an inviting place. The younger man went off to look up a hotel, while the rest remained and prepared to camp down on the floor and benches. Smith was attended to tenderly by the other men, who spread their blankets on the bench for him, and, by robbing themselves, made quite a comfortable bed, though the narrowness of the bench made his sleeping precarious.

It was chill, though August, and the two men, sitting with bowed heads, grew stiff with cold and weariness, and were forced to rise now and again and walk about to warm their stiffened limbs. It did not occur to them, probably, to contrast their coming home with their going forth, or with the coming home of the generals, colonels, or even captains — but to Private Smith, at any rate, there came a sickness at heart almost deadly as he lay there on his hard bed and went over his situation.

In the deep of the night, lying on a board in the town where he had enlisted three years ago, all elation and enthusiasm gone out of him, he faced the fact that with the joy of home-coming was already mingled the bitter juice of care. He saw himself sick, worn out, taking up the work on his half-cleared farm, the inevitable mortgage standing ready with open jaw to swallow half his earnings. He had given three years of his life for a mere pittance of pay, and now! —

Morning dawned at last, slowly, with a pale yellow dome of light rising silently above the bluffs, which stand like some huge storm-devastated castle, just east of the city. Out to the left the great river swept on its massive yet silent way to the south. Bluejays called across the water from hillside to hillside through the clear, beautiful air, and hawks began to skim the tops of the hills. The older men were astir early, but Private Smith had fallen at last into a sleep, and they went out without waking him. He lay on his knapsack, his gaunt face turned toward the ceiling, his hands clasped on his breast, with a curious pathetic effect of weakness and appeal.

An engine switching near woke him at last, and he slowly sat up and stared about . He looked out of the window and saw that the sun was lightening the hills across the river. He rose and brushed his hair as well as he could, folded his blankets up, and went out to find his companions. They stood gazing silently at the river and at the hills.

"Looks natcher'l, don't it?" they said, as he came out.

"That's what it does," he replied. "An' it looks good. D' yeh see that peak?" He pointed at a beautiful symmetrical peak, rising like a slightly truncated cone, so high that it seemed the very highest of them all. It was touched by the morning sun and it glowed like a beacon, and a light scarf of gray morning fog was rolling up its shadowed side.

"My farm's just beyond that. Now, if I can only ketch a ride, we'll be home by dinner-time."

"I'm talkin' about breakfast," said one of the others.

"I guess it's one more meal o' hardtack f'r me," said Smith.

They foraged around, and finally found a restaurant with a sleepy old German behind the counter, and procured some coffee, which they drank to wash down their hardtack.

"Time'll come," said Smith, holding up a piece by the corner, "when this'll be a curiosity."

"I hope to God it will! I bet I've chawed hardtack enough to shingle every house in the coolly. I've chawed it when my lampers was down, and when they wasn't. I've took it dry, soaked, and mashed. I've had it wormy, musty, sour, and blue-mouldy. I've had it in little bits and big bits; 'fore coffee an' after coffee. I'm ready f'r a change. I'd like t' git holt jest about now o' some of the hot biscuits my wife c'n make when she lays herself out f'r company."

"Well, if you set there gabblin', you'll never *see* yer wife."

"Come on," said Private Smith. "Wait a moment, boys; less take suthin'. It's on me." He led them to the rusty tin dipper which hung on a nail beside the wooden water-pail, and they grinned and drank. Then shouldering their blankets and muskets, which they were "takin' home to the boys," they struck out on their last march.

"They called that coffee Jayvy," grumbled one of them, "but it never went by the road where government Jayvy resides. I reckon I know coffee from peas."

They kept together on the road along the turnpike, and up the winding road by the river, which they followed for some miles. The river was very lovely, curving down along its sandy beds, pausing now and then under broad basswood trees, or running in dark, swift, silent currents under tangles of wild grapevines, and drooping alders, and haw trees. At one of these lovely spots the three vets sat down on the thick green sward to rest, "on Smith's account." The leaves of the trees were as fresh and green as in June, the jays called cheery greetings to them, and kingfishers darted to and fro with swooping, noiseless flight.

"I tell yeh, boys, this knocks the swamps of Loueesiana into kingdom come."

"You bet. All they c'n raise down there is snakes, niggers, and p'rticler hell."

"An' fightin' men," put in the older man.

"An' fightin' men. If I had a good hook an' line I'd sneak a pick'rel out o' that pond. Say, remember that time I shot that alligator — "

"I guess we'd better be crawlin' along," interrupted Smith, rising and shouldering his knapsack, with considerable effort, which he tried to hide.

"Say, Smith, lemme give you a lift on that."

"I guess I c'n manage," said Smith, grimly.

"Course. But, yo' see, I may not have a chance right off to pay yeh back for the times you've carried my gun and hull caboodle. Say, now, gimme that gun, anyway."

"All right, if yeh feel like it, Jim," Smith replied, and they trudged along doggedly in the sun, which was getting higher and hotter each half-mile.

"Ain't it queer there ain't no teams comin' along," said Smith, after a long silence.

"Well, no, seein's it's Sunday."

"By jinks, that's a fact. It *is* Sunday. I'll git home in time f'r dinner, sure!" he exulted. "She don't hev dinner usially till about *one* on Sundays." And he fell into a muse, in which he smiled.

"Well, I'll git home jest about six o'clock, jest about when the boys are milkin' the cows," said old Jim Cranby. "I'll step into the barn, an' then I'll say: '*Heah*! why ain't this milkin' done before this time o' day?' An' then won't they yell!" he added, slapping his thigh in great glee.

Smith went on. "I'll jest go up the path. Old Rover'll come down the road to meet me. He won't bark; he'll know me, an' he'll come down waggin' his tail an' showin' his teeth. That's his way of laughin'. An' so I'll walk up to the kitchen door, an' I'll say, '*Dinner* f'r a hungry man!' An' then she'll jump up, an' — "

He couldn't go on. His voice choked at the thought of it. Saunders, the third man, hardly uttered a word, but walked silently behind the others. He had lost his wife the first year he was in the army. She died of pneumonia, caught in the autumn rains while working in the fields in his place.

They plodded along till at last they came to a parting of the ways. To the right the road continued up the main valley; to the left it went over the big ridge.

"Well, boys," began Smith, as they grounded their muskets and looked away up the valley, "here's where we shake hands. We've marched together a good many miles, an' now I s'pose we're done."

"Yes, I don't think we'll do any more of it f'r a while. I don't want to, I know."

"I hope I'll see yeh once in a while, boys, to talk over old times."

"Of course," said Saunders, whose voice trembled a little, too. "It ain't *exactly* like dyin'." They all found it hard to look at each other.

"But we'd ought'r go home with you," said Cranby. "You'll never climb that ridge with all them things on yer back."

"Oh, I'm all right! Don't worry about me. Every step takes me nearer home, yeh see. Well, good-by, boys."

They shook hands. "Good-by. Good luck!"

"Same to you. Lemme know how you find things at home."

"Good-by."

"Good-by."

He turned once before they passed out of sight, and waved his cap, and they did the same, and all yelled. Then all marched away with their long, steady, loping, veteran step. The solitary climber in blue walked on for a time, with his mind filled with the kindness of his comrades, and musing upon the many wonderful days they had had together in camp and field.

He thought of his chum, Billy Tripp. Poor Billy! A "minie" ball fell into his breast one day, fell wailing like a cat, and tore a great ragged hole in his heart. He looked forward to a sad scene with Billy's mother and sweetheart. They would want to know all about it. He tried to recall all that Billy had said, and the particulars of it, but there was little to remember, just that wild wailing sound high in the air, a dull slap, a short, quick, expulsive groan, and the boy lay with his face in the dirt in the ploughed field they were marching across.

That was all. But all the scenes he had since been through had not dimmed the horror, the terror of that moment, when his boy comrade fell, with only a breath between a laugh and a death-groan. Poor handsome Billy! Worth millions of dollars was his young life.

These sombre recollections gave way at length to more cheerful feelings as he began to approach his home coolly. The fields and houses grew familiar, and in one or two he was greeted by people seated in the doorways. But he was in no mood to talk, and pushed on steadily, though he stopped and accepted a drink of milk once at the well-side of a neighbor.

The sun was burning hot on that slope, and his step grew slower, in spite of his iron resolution. He sat down several times to rest. Slowly he crawled up the rough, reddish-brown road, which wound along the hillside, under great trees, through dense groves of jack oaks, with tree-tops far below him on his left hand, and the hills far above him on his right. He crawled along like some minute, wingless variety of fly.

He ate some hardtack, sauced with wild berries, when he reached the summit of the ridge, and sat there for some time, looking down into his home coolly.

Sombre, pathetic figure! His wide, round, gray eyes gazing down into the beautiful valley, seeing and not seeing, the splendid cloud-shadows sweeping over the western hills and across the green and yellow wheat far below. His head drooped forward on his palm, his shoulders took on a tired stoop, his cheek-bones showed painfully. An observer might have said, "He is looking down upon his own grave."

## II

Sunday comes in a Western wheat harvest with such sweet and sudden relaxation to man and beast that it would be holy for that reason, if for no other, and Sundays are usually fair in harvest-time. As one goes out into the field in the hot morning sunshine, with no sound abroad save the crickets and the indescribably pleasant silken rustling of the ripened grain, the reaper and the very sheaves in the stubble seem to be resting, dreaming.

Around the house, in the shade of the trees, the men sit, smoking, dozing, or reading the papers, while the women, never resting, move about at the housework. The men eat on Sundays about the same as on other days, and breakfast is no sooner over and out of the way than dinner begins.

But at the Smith farm there were no men dozing or reading. Mrs.

Smith was alone with her three children, Mary, nine, Tommy, six, and little Ted, just past four. Her farm, rented to a neighbor, lay at the head of a coolly or narrow gully, made at some far-off post-glacial period by the vast and angry floods of water which gullied these tremendous furrows in the level prairie — furrows so deep that undisturbed portions of the original level rose like hills on either side, rose to quite considerable mountains.

The chickens wakened her as usual that Sabbath morning from dreams of her absent husband, from whom she had not heard for weeks. The shadows drifted over the hills, down the slopes, across the wheat, and up the opposite wall in leisurely way, as if, being Sunday, they could take it easy also. The fowls clustered about the housewife as she went out into the yard. Fuzzy little chickens swarmed out from the coops, where their clucking and perpetually disgruntled mothers tramped about, petulantly thrusting their heads through the spaces between the slats.

A cow called in a deep, musical bass, and a calf answered from a little pen near by, and a pig scurried guiltily out of the cabbages. Seeing all this, seeing the pig in the cabbages, the tangle of grass in the garden, the broken fence which she had mended again and again — the little woman, hardly more than a girl, sat down and cried. The bright Sabbath morning was only a mockery without him!

A few years ago they had bought this farm, paying part, mortgaging the rest in the usual way. Edward Smith was a man of terrible energy. He worked "nights and Sundays," as the saying goes, to clear the farm of its brush and of its insatiate mortgage! In the midst of his Herculean struggle came the call for volunteers, and with the grim and unselfish devotion to his country which made the Eagle Brigade able to "whip its weight in wild-cats," he threw down his scythe and grub-axe, turned his cattle loose, and became a blue-coated cog in a vast machine for killing men, and not thistles. While the millionaire sent his money to England for safe-keeping, this man, with his girl-wife and three babies, left them on a mortgaged farm, and went away to fight for an idea. It was foolish, but it was sublime for all that.

That was three years before, and the young wife, sitting on the well-curb on this bright Sabbath harvest morning, was righteously rebellious. It seemed to her that she had borne her share of the country's sorrow. Two brothers had been killed, the renter in whose hands her husband left the farm had proved a villain; one year the farm had been without crops, and now the overripe grain was waiting the tardy hand of the neighbor who had rented it, and who was cutting his own grain first.

About six weeks before, she had received a letter saying, "We'll be discharged in a little while." But no other word had come from him.

She had seen by the papers that his army was being discharged, and from day to day other soldiers slowly percolated in blue streams back into the State and county, but still *her* hero did not return.

Each week she had told the children that he was coming, and she had watched the road so long that it had become unconscious; and as she stood at the well, or by the kitchen door, her eyes were fixed unthinkingly on the road that wound down the coolly.

Nothing wears on the human soul like waiting. If the stranded mariner, searching the sun-bright seas, could once give up hope of a ship, that horrible grinding on his brain would cease. It was this waiting, hoping, on the edge of despair, that gave Emma Smith no rest.

Neighbors said, with kind intentions: "He's sick, maybe, an' can't start north just yet. He'll come along one o' these days."

"Why don't he write?" was her question, which silenced them all. This Sunday morning it seemed to her as if she could not stand it longer. The house seemed intolerably lonely. So she dressed the little ones in their best calico dresses and home-made jackets, and, closing up the house, set off down the coolly to old Mother Gray's.

"Old Widder Gray" lived at the "mouth of the coolly." She was a widow woman with a large family of stalwart boys and laughing girls. She was the visible incarnation of hospitality and optimistic poverty. With Western open-heartedness she fed every mouth that asked food of her, and worked herself to death as cheerfully as her girls danced in the neighborhood harvest dances.

She waddled down the path to meet Mrs. Smith with a broad smile on her face.

"Oh, you little dears! Come right to your granny. Gimme a kiss! Come right in, Mis' Smith. How are yeh, anyway? Nice mornin', ain't it? Come in an' set down. Everything's in a clutter, but that won't scare you any."

She led the way into the best room, a sunny, square room, carpeted with a faded and patched rag carpet, and papered with white-and-green-striped wall-paper, where a few faded effigies of dead members of the family hung in variously sized oval walnut frames. The house resounded with singing, laughter, whistling, tramping of heavy boots, and riotous scufflings. Half-grown boys came to the door and crooked their fingers at the children, who ran out, and were soon heard in the midst of the fun.

"Don't s'pose you've heard from Ed?" Mrs. Smith shook her head. "He'll turn up some day, when you ain't lookin' for 'm." The good old soul had said that so many times that poor Mrs. Smith derived no comfort from it any longer.

"Liz heard from Al the other day. He's comin' some day this week. Anyhow, they expect him."

"Did he say anything of — "

"No, he didn't," Mrs. Gray admitted. "But then it was only a short letter, anyhow. Al ain't much for writin', anyhow. — But come out and see my new cheese. I tell yeh, I don't believe I ever had better luck in my life. If Ed should come, I want you should take him up a piece of this cheese."

It was beyond human nature to resist the influence of that noisy, hearty, loving household, and in the midst of the singing and laughing the wife forgot her anxiety, for the time at least, and laughed and sang with the rest.

About eleven o'clock a wagon-load more drove up to the door, and Bill Gray, the widow's oldest son, and his whole family, from Sand Lake Coolly, piled out amid a good-natured uproar. Every one talked at once, except Bill, who sat in the wagon with his wrists on his knees, a straw in his mouth, and an amused twinkle in his blue eyes.

"Ain't heard nothin' o' Ed, I s'pose?" he asked in a kind of bellow. Mrs. Smith shook her head. Bill, with a delicacy very striking in such a great giant, rolled his quid in his mouth, and said:

"Didn't know but you had. I hear two or three of the Sand Lake boys are comin.' Left New Orleenes some time this week. Didn't write nothin' about Ed, but no news is good news in such cases, mother always says."

"Well, go put out yer team," said Mrs. Gray, "an' go'n bring me in some taters, an', Sim, you go see if you c'n find some corn. Sadie, you put on the water to bile. Come now, hustle yer boots, all o' yeh. If I feed this yer crowd, we've got to have some raw materials. If y' think I'm goin' to feed yeh on pie — you're jest mightily mistaken."

The children went off into the fields, the girls put dinner on to boil, and then went to change their dresses and fix their hair. "Somebody might come," they said.

"Land sakes, I hope not! I don't where in time I'd set 'em, 'less they'd eat at the second table," Mrs. Gray laughed, in pretended dismay.

The two older boys, who had served their time in the army, lay out on the grass before the house, and whittled and talked desultorily about the war and the crops, and planned buying a threshing-machine. The older girls and Mrs. Smith helped enlarge the table and put on the dishes, talking all the time in that cheery, incoherent, and meaningful way a group of such women have, — a conversation to be taken for its spirit rather than for its letter, though Mrs. Gray at last got the ear of them all and dissertated at length on girls.

"Girls in love ain't no use in the whole blessed week," she said. "Sundays they're a-lookin' down the road, expectin' he'll *come*. Sunday afternoons they can't think o' nothin' else, 'cause he's *here*. Monday mornin' they're sleepy and kind o' dreamy and slimpsy, and good f'r nothin' on Tuesday and Wednesday. Thursday they git absent-minded, an' begin to look off toward Sunday agin, an' mope aroun' and let the dishwater git cold, right under their noses. Friday they break dishes, an' go off in the best room an' snivel, an' look out o' the winder. Saturdays they have queer spurts o' workin' like all p'ssessed, an' spurts o' frizzin' their hair. An' Sunday they begin it all over again."

The girls giggled and blushed, all through this tirade from their mother, their broad faces and powerful frames anything but suggestive of lackadaisical sentiment. But Mrs. Smith said:

"Now, Mrs. Gray, I hadn't ought to stay to dinner. You've got — "

"Now you set right down! If any of them girls' beaus comes, they'll have to take what's left, that's all. They ain't s'posed to have much appetite, nohow. No, you're goin' to stay if they starve, an' they ain't no danger o' that."

At one o'clock the long table was piled with boiled potatoes, cords of boiled corn on the cob, squash and pumpkin pies, hot biscuit, sweet pickles, bread and butter, and honey. Then one of the girls took down a conch-shell from a nail, and going to the door, blew a long, fine, free blast, that showed there was no weakness of lungs in her ample chest.

Then the children came out of the forest of corn, out of the creek, out of the loft of the barn, and out of the garden.

"They come to their feed f'r all the world jest like the pigs when y' holler 'poo-ee!' See 'em scoot!" laughed Mrs. Gray, every wrinkle on her face shining with delight.

The men shut up their jack-knives, and surrounded the horse-trough to souse their faces in the cold, hard water, and in a few moments the table was filled with a merry crowd, and a row of wistful-eyed youngsters circled the kitchen wall, where they stood first on one leg and then on the other, in impatient hunger.

"Now pitch in, Mrs. Smith," said Mrs. Gray, presiding over the table. "You know these men critters. They'll eat every grain of it, if yeh give 'em a chance. I swan, they're made o' Indian-rubber, their stoachs is, I know it."

"Haf to eat to work," said Bill, gnawing a cob with a swift, circular motion that rivalled a corn-sheller in results.

"More like workin' to eat," put in one of the girls, with a giggle. "More eat 'n work with you."

"*You* needn't say anything, Net. Any one that'll eat seven ears — "

"I didn't, no such thing. You piled your cobs on my plate."

"That'll do to tell Ed Varney. It won't go down here where we know yeh."

"Good land! Eat all yeh want! They's plenty more in the fiel's, but I can't afford to give you young uns tea. The tea is for us women-folks, and 'specially f'r Mis' Smith an' Bill's wife. We're a-goin' to tell fortunes by it."

One by one the men filled up and shoved back, and one by one the children slipped into their places, and by two o'clock the women alone remained around the debris-covered table, sipping their tea and telling fortunes.

As they got well down to the grounds in the cup, they shook them with a circular motion in the hand, and then turned them bottom-side-up quickly in the saucer, then twirled them three or four times one way, and three or four times the other, during a breathless pause. Then Mrs. Gray lifted the cup, and, gazing into it with profound gravity, pronounced the impending fate.

It must be admitted that, to a critical observer, she had abundant preparation for hitting close to the mark, as when she told the girls that "somebody was comin'." "It's a man," she went on gravely. "He is cross-eyed — "

"Oh, you hush!" cried Nettie.

"He has red hair, and is death on b'iled corn and hot biscuit."

The others shrieked with delight.

"But he's goin' to get the mitten, that red-haired feller is, for I see another feller comin' up behind him."

"Oh, lemme see, lemme see!" cried Nettie.

"Keep off," said the priestess, with a lofty gesture. "His hair is black. He don't eat so much, and he works more."

The girls exploded in a shriek of laughter, and pounded their sister on the back.

At last came Mrs. Smith's turn, and she was trembling with excitement as Mrs. Gray again composed her jolly face to what she considered a proper solemnity of expression.

"Somebody is comin' to *you*," she said, after a long pause. "He's got a musket on his back. He's a soldier. He's almost here. See?"

She pointed at two little tea-stems, which really formed a faint suggestion of a man with a musket on his back. He had climbed nearly to the edge of the cup. Mrs. Smith grew pale with excitement. She trembled so she could hardly hold the cup in her hand as she gazed into it.

"It's Ed," cried the old woman. "He's on the way home. Heavens an' earth! There he is now!" She turned and waved her hand out toward the road. They rushed to the door to look where she pointed.

A man in a blue coat, with a musket on his back, was toiling slowly up the hill on the sun-bright, dusty road, toiling slowly, with bent head half hidden by a heavy knapsack. So tired it seemed that walking was indeed a process of falling. So eager to get home he would not stop, would not look aside, but plodded on, amid the cries of the locusts, the welcome of the crickets, and the rustle of the yellow wheat. Getting back to God's country, and his wife and babies!

Laughing, crying, trying to call him and the children at the same time; the little wife, almost hysterical, snatched her hat and ran out into the yard. But the soldier had disappeared over the hill into the hollow beyond, and, by the time she had found the children, he was too far away for her voice to reach him. And, besides, she was not sure it was her husband, for he had not turned his head at their shouts. This seemed so strange. Why didn't he stop to rest at his old neighbor's house? Tortured by hope and doubt, she hurried up the coolly as fast as she could push the baby wagon, the blue-coated figure just ahead pushing steadily, silently forward up the coolly.

When the excited, panting little group came in sight of the gate they saw the blue-coated figure standing, leaning upon the rough rail fence, his chin on his palms, gazing at the empty house. His knapsack, canteen, blankets, and musket lay upon the dusty grass at his feet.

He was like a man lost in a dream. His wide, hungry eyes devoured the scene. The rough lawn, the little unpainted house, the field of clear yellow wheat behind it, down across which streamed the sun, now almost ready to touch the high hill to the west, the crickets crying merrily, a cat on the fence near by, dreaming, unmindful of the stranger in blue —

How peaceful it all was. O God! How far removed from all camps, hospitals, battle lines. A little cabin in a Wisconsin coolly, but it was majestic in its peace. How did he ever leave it for those years of tramping, thirsting, killing?

Trembling, weak with emotion, her eyes on the silent figure, Mrs. Smith hurried up to the fence. Her feet made no noise in the dust and grass, and they were close upon him before he knew of them. The oldest boy ran a little ahead. He will never forget that figure, that face. It will always remain as something epic, that return of the private. He fixed his eyes on the pale face covered with a ragged beard.

"Who *are* you, sir?" asked the wife, or, rather, started to ask, for he turned, stood a moment, and then cried:

"Emma!"

"Edward!"

The children stood in a curious row to see their mother kiss this bearded, strange man, the elder girl sobbing sympathetically with her mother. Illness had left the soldier partly deaf, and this added to the strangeness of his manner.

But the youngest child stood away, even after the girl had recognized her father and kissed him. The man turned then to the baby, and said in a curiously unpaternal tone:

"Come here, my little man; don't you know me?" But the baby backed away under the fence and stood peering at him critically.

"My little man!" What meaning in those words! This baby seemed like some other woman's child, and not the infant he had left in his wife's arms. The war had come between him and his baby — he was only a strange man to him, with big eyes; a soldier, with mother hanging to his arm, and talking in a loud voice.

"And this is Tom," the private said, drawing the oldest boy to him. "*He'll* come and see me. *He* knows his poor old pap when he comes home from the war."

The mother heard the pain and reproach in his voice and hastened to apologize.

"You've changed so, Ed. He can't know yeh. This is papa, Teddy; come and kiss him — Tom and Mary do. Come, won't you?" But Teddy still peered through the fence with solemn eyes, well out of reach. He resembled a half-wild kitten that hesitates, studying the tones of one's voice.

"I'll fix him," said the soldier, and sat down to undo his knapsack, out of which he drew three enormous and very red apples. After giving one to each of the older children, he said:

"*Now* I guess he'll come. Eh, my little man? Now come see your pap."

Teddy crept slowly under the fence, assisted by the overzealous Tommy, and a moment later was kicking and squalling in his father's arms. Then they entered the house, into the sitting room, poor, bare, art-forsaken little room, too, with its rag carpet, its square clock, and its two or three chromos and pictures from *Harper's Weekly* pinned about.

"Emma, I'm all tired out," said Private Smith, as he flung himself down on the carpet as he used to do, while his wife brought a pillow to put under his head, and the children stood about munching their apples.

"Tommy, you run and get me a pan of chips, and Mary, you get the tea-kettle on, and I'll go and make some biscuit."

And the soldier talked. Question after question he poured forth about the crops, the cattle, the renter, the neighbors. He slipped his heavy government brogan shoes off his poor, tired, blistered feet, and lay out with utter, sweet relaxation. He was a free man again, no longer a soldier under command. At supper he stopped once, listened and smiled. "That's old Spot. I know her voice. I s'pose that's her calf out there in the pen. I can't milk her to-night, though. But I tell you, I'd like a drink o' her milk. What's become of old Rove?"

"He died last winter. Poisoned, I guess." There was a moment of sadness for them all. It was some time before the husband spoke again, in a voice that trembled a little.

"Poor old feller! He'd 'a' known me half a mile away. I expected him to come down the hill to meet me. It 'ud 'a' been more like comin' home if I could 'a' seen him comin' down the road an' waggin' his tail, an' laughin' that way he has. I tell yeh, it kind o' took hold o' me to see the blinds down an' the house shut up."

"But, yeh see, we — we expected you'd write again 'fore you started. And then we thought we'd see you if you *did* come," she hastened to explain.

"Well, I ain't worth a cent on writin'. Besides, it's just as well yeh didn't know when I was comin'. I tell you, it sounds good to hear them chickens out there, an' turkeys, an' the crickets. Do you know they don't have just the same kind o' crickets down South? Who's Sam hired t' help cut yer grain?"

"The Ramsey boys."

"Looks like a good crop; but I'm afraid I won't do much gettin' it cut. This cussed fever an' ague has got me down pretty low. I don't know when I'll get rid of it. I'll bet I've took twenty-five pounds of quinine if I've taken a bit. Gimme another biscuit. I tell yeh, they taste good, Emma. I ain't had anything like it — Say, if you'd 'a' hear'd me braggin' to the boys about your butter 'n' biscuits I'll bet your ears 'ud 'a' burnt."

The private's wife colored with pleasure. "Oh, you're always a-braggin' about your things. Everybody makes good butter."

"Yes; old lady Snyder, for instance."

"Oh, well, she ain't to be mentioned. She's Dutch."

"Or old Mis' Snively. One more cup o' tea, Mary. That's my girl! I'm feeling better already. I just b'lieve the matter with me is, I'm *starved*."

This was a delicious hour, one long to be remembered. They were like lovers again. But their tenderness, like that of a typical American family, found utterance in tones, rather than in words. He was praising her when praising her biscuit, and she knew it. They grew soberer when he showed where he had been struck, one ball burning the back of his hand, one cutting away a lock of hair from his temple, and one passing through the calf of his leg. The wife shuddered to think how near she had come to being a soldier's widow. Her waiting no longer seemed hard. This sweet, glorious hour effaced it all.

Then they rose, and all went out into the garden and down to the barn. He stood beside her while she milked old Spot. They began to plan fields and crops for next year.

His farm was weedy and encumbered, a rascally renter had run away with his machinery (departing between two days), his children needed clothing, the years were coming upon him, he was sick and emaciated, but his heroic soul did not quail. With the same courage with which he had faced his Southern march he entered upon a still more hazardous future.

Oh, that mystic hour! The pale man with big eyes standing there by the well, with his young wife by his side. The vast moon swinging above the eastern peaks, the cattle winding down the pasture slopes with jangling bells, the crickets singing, the stars blooming out sweet and far and serene; the katydids rhythmically calling, the little turkeys crying querulously, as they settled to roost in the poplar tree near the open gate. The voices at the well drop lower, the little ones nestle in their father's arms at last, and Teddy falls asleep there.

The common soldier of the American volunteer army had returned. His war with the South was over, and his fight, his daily running fight with nature and against the injustice of his fellow-men, was begun again.

# Henry James (1843–1916)

HENRY JAMES was born into an extraordinary family. His radical father, Henry James, Sr., lectured on religion, society, and literature and was a friend of Emerson and Carlyle. His older brother, William, was America's most famous philosopher. Henry's early education was private and unorthodox although he later attended Harvard Law School. Because he considered America hostile to artists, he spent most of his mature years in Europe but called Cambridge, Massachusetts, home. His first published writings were stories and reviews in magazines. *The Passionate Pilgrim* in 1871 was his first full novel and established him as a leading writer. All his many short stories, novels, and criticism that followed are important. His only failure and bitterest disappointment was in playwriting where success was his dearest desire. None of his four plays succeeded, and at one he was booed off the stage. To show his sympathy for the Allied cause, James became a British citizen in 1915.

"The Real Thing" is one of the most interesting short stories ever written. "It should be a little gem of bright quick vivid form," James said when writing it. It is that but has other fascinating dimensions. Does life make art or art make life? "Art makes life," James insisted. For years he and H. G. Wells, a close friend, became at times almost enemies when Wells accused him of being like "a hippopotamus trying to pick up a pea." Based on an anecdote he heard, James is pursuing in "The Real Thing" his favorite thesis about art. All the characters in "The Real Thing," the artist, the embarrassed once "high-society" couple, the Cockney woman, and the Italian ice-cream peddler, are beautifully drawn. But did James unconsciously defeat himself? Which of his models are more memorable? His imitators of real life? Or the sad, aging couple? This reader is still trying to decide.


# *The Real Thing*

WHEN the porter's wife who used to answer the house-bell announced, "A gentleman and a lady, sir," I had, as I often had in those days — the wish being father to the thought — an immediate vision of sitters. Sitters my visitors in this case proved to be; but not in the sense I should have preferred. There was nothing at first however to indicate that they mightn't have come for a portrait. The gentleman, a man of fifty, very high and very straight, with a moustache slightly grizzled and a dark grey walking-coat admirably fitted, both of which I noted professionally — I don't mean as a barber or yet as a tailor — would have struck me as a celebrity if celebrities often were striking. It was a truth of which I had for some time been conscious that a figure with a good deal of frontage was, as one might say, almost never a public institution. A glance at the lady helped to remind me of this paradoxical law: she also looked too distinguished to be a "personality." Moreover one would scarcely come across two variations together.

Neither of the pair immediately spoke — they only prolonged the preliminary gaze suggesting that each wished to give the other a chance. They were visibly shy; they stood there letting me take them in — which, as I afterwards perceived, was the most practical thing they could have done. In this way their embarrassment served their cause. I had seen people painfully reluctant to mention that they desired anything so gross as to be represented on canvas; but the scruples of my new friends appeared amost insurmountable. Yet the gentleman might have said "I should like a portrait of my wife," and the lady might have said "I should like a portrait of my husband." Perhaps they weren't husband and wife — this naturally would make the matter more delicate. Perhaps they wished to be done together — in which case they ought to have brought a third person to break the news.

"We come from Mr. Rivet," the lady finally said with a dim smile that had the effect of a moist sponge passed over a "sunk" piece of painting, as well as of a vague allusion to vanished beauty. She was as tall and straight, in her degree, as her companion, and with ten years less to carry. She looked as sad as a woman could look whose face was not charged with expression; that is her tinted oval mask showed waste as an exposed surface shows friction. The hand of time had played over her freely, but to an effect of elimination. She was slim and stiff, and so well-dressed, in dark blue cloth, with lappets and pockets and buttons, that it was clear she employed the same tailor as her husband. The couple had an indefinable air of prosperous thrift — they evidently got a good deal of luxury for their money. If I was to be one of their luxuries, it would behoove me to consider my terms.

"Ah, Claude Rivet recommended me?" I echoed; and I added that it was very kind of him, though I could reflect that, as he only painted landscape, this wasn't a sacrifice.

The lady looked very hard at the gentleman, and the gentleman looked round the room. Then, staring at the door a moment and stroking his moustache, he rested his pleasant eyes on me with the remark: "He said you were the right one."

"I try to be, when people want to sit."

"Yes, we should like to," said the lady anxiously.

"Do you mean together?"

My visitors exchanged a glance. "If you could do anything with *me* I suppose it would be double," the gentleman stammered.

"Oh yes, there's naturally a higher charge for two figures than for one."

"We should like to make it pay," the husband confessed.

"That's very good of you," I returned, appreciating so unwonted a sympathy — for I supposed he meant pay the artist.

A sense of strangeness seemed to dawn on the lady. "We mean for the illustrations — Mr. Rivet said you might put one in."

"Put in — an illustration?" I was equally confused.

"Sketch her off, you know," said the gentleman, colouring.

It was only then that I understood the service Claude Rivet had rendered me; he had told them how I worked in black and white, for magazines, for story books, for sketches of contemporary life, and consequently had copious employment for models. These things were true, but it was not less true — I may confess it now; whether because the aspiration was to lead to everything or to nothing I leave the reader to guess — that I couldn't get the honours, to say nothing of the emoluments, of a great painter of portraits out of my head. My "illustrations" were my pot-boilers; I looked to a different branch of art — far and away the most interesting it had always seemed to me — to perpetuate my fame. There was no shame in looking to it also to make my fortune; but that fortune was by so much further from being made from the moment my visitors wished to be "done" for something. I was disappointed; for in the pictorial sense I had immediately seen them. I had seized their type — I had already settled what I would do with it. Something that wouldn't absolutely have pleased them, I afterwards reflected.

"Ah, you're — you're — a — ?" I began as soon as I had mastered my surprise. I couldn't bring out the dingy word "models": it seemed so little to fit the case.

"We haven't had much practice," said the lady.

"We've got to *do* something, and we've thought that an artist in your line might perhaps make something of us," her husband threw off. He further mentioned that they didn't know many artists and that they had gone first, on the off chance — he painted views of course, but sometimes put in figures; perhaps I remembered — to Mr. Rivet, whom they had met a few years before at a place in Norfolk where he was sketching.

"We used to sketch a little ourselves," the lady hinted.

"It's very awkward, but we absolutely *must* do something," her husband went on.

"Of course we're not so *very* young," she admitted with a wan smile.

With the remark that I might as well know something more about them the husband had handed me a card extracted from a neat new pocket-book — their appurtenances were all of the freshest — and inscribed with the words "Major Monarch." Impressive as these words were they didn't carry my knowledge much further; but my visitor presently added: "I've left the army and we've had the misfortune to lose our money. In fact our means are dreadfully small."

"It's awfully trying — a regular strain," said Mrs. Monarch.

They evidently wished to be discreet — to take care not to swagger because they were gentlefolk. I felt them willing to recognise this as something of a drawback, at the same time that I guessed at an under-lying sense — their consolation in adversity — that they *had* their points. They certainly had; but these advantages struck me as pre-ponderantly social; such, for instance, as would help to make a drawing-room look well. However, a drawing-room was always, or ought to be, a picture.

In consequence of his wife's allusion to their age Major Monarch observed: "Naturally it's more for the figure that we thought of going in. We can still hold ourselves up." On the instant I saw that the figure was indeed their strong point. His "naturally" didn't sound vain, but it lighted up the question. "*She* has the best one," he continued, nodding at his wife with a pleasant after-dinner absence of circum-locution. I could only reply, as if we were in fact sitting over our wine, that this didn't prevent his own from being very good; which led him in turn to make answer: "We thought that if you ever have to do people like us we might be something like it. *She* particularly — for a lady in a book, you know."

I was so amused by them that, to get more of it, I did my best to take their point of view; and though it was an embarrassment to find myself appraising physically, as if they were animals on hire or useful blacks, a pair whom I should have expected to meet only in one of the relations in which criticism is tacit, I looked at Mrs. Monarch judicially enough to be able to exclaim after a moment with conviction: "Oh, yes, a lady in a book!" She was singularly like a bad illustration.

"We'll stand up, if you like," said the Major; and he raised himself before me with a really grand air.

I could take his measure at a glance — he was six feet two and a perfect gentleman. It would have paid any club in process of formation and in want of a stamp to engage him at a salary to stand in the principal window. What struck me at once was that in coming to me they had rather missed their vocation; they could surely have been turned to better account for advertising purposes. I couldn't of course see the thing in detail, but I could see them make somebody's fortune — I don't mean their own. There was something in them for a waistcoat-maker, an hotel-keeper or a soap-vendor. I could imagine "We always use it" pinned on their bosoms with the greatest effect; I had a vision of the brilliancy with which they would launch a table d'hote.

Mrs. Monarch sat still, not from pride but from shyness, and presently her husband said to her: "Get up, my dear, and show how smart you are." She obeyed, but she had no need to get up to show it. She walked to the end of the studio and then came back blushing, her fluttered eyes on the partner of her appeal. I was reminded of an incident I had accidentally had a glimpse of in Paris — being with a friend there, a dramatist about to produce a play, when an actress came to him to ask to be entrusted with a part. She went through her paces before him, walked up and down as Mrs. Monarch was doing. Mrs. Monarch did it quite as well, but I abstained from applauding. It was very odd to see such people apply for such poor pay. She looked as if she had ten thousand a year. Her husband had used the word that described her: she was in the London current jargon essentially and typically "smart." Her figure was, in the same order of ideas, conspicuously and irreproachably "good." For a woman of her age her waist was surprisingly small; her elbow moreover had the orthodox crook. She held her head at the conventional angle, but why did she come to *me*? She ought to have tried on jackets at a big shop. I feared my visitors were not only destitute but "artistic" — which would be a great complication. When she sat down again I thanked her, observing that what a draughtsman most valued in his model was the faculty of keeping quiet.

"Oh, *she* can keep quiet," said Major Monarch. Then he added jocosely: "I've always kept her quiet."

"I'm not a nasty fidget, am I?" It was going to wring tears from me, I felt, the way she hid her head, ostrich-like, in the other broad bosom.

The owner of this expanse addressed his answer to me. "Perhaps it isn't out of place to mention — because we ought to be quite business-like, oughtn't we? — that when I married her she was known as the Beautiful Statue."

"Oh dear!" said Mrs. Monarch ruefully.

"Of course I should want a certain amount of expression," I rejoined.

"Of *course*!" — and I had never heard such unanimity.

"And then I suppose you know that you'll get awfully tired."

"Oh, we *never* get tired!" they eagerly cried.

"Have you had any kind of practice?"

They hesitated — they looked at each other. "We've been photographed — *immensely*," said Mrs. Monarch.

"She means the fellows have asked us themselves," added the Major.

"I see — because you're so good-looking."

"I don't know what they thought, but they were always after us."

"We always got our photographs for nothing," smiled Mrs. Monarch.

"We might have brought some, my dear," her husband remarked.

"I'm not sure we have any left. We've given quantities away," she explained to me.

"With our autographs and that sort of thing," said the Major.

"Are they to be got in the shops?" I inquired as a harmless pleasantry.

"Oh, yes, *hers* — they used to be."

"Not now," said Mrs. Monarch with her eyes on the floor.

## II

I could fancy the "sort of thing" they put on the presentation copies of their photographs, and I was sure they wrote a beautiful hand. It was odd how quickly I was sure of everything that concerned them. If they were now so poor as to have to earn shillings and pence they could never have had much of a margin. Their good looks had been their capital, and they had good-naturedly made the most of the career that this resource marked out for them. It was in their faces, the blankness, the deep intellectual repose of the twenty years of country-house visiting that had given them pleasant intonations. I could see the sunny drawing-rooms, sprinkled with periodicals she didn't read, in which Mrs. Monarch had continuously sat; I could see the wet shrubberies in which she had walked, equipped to admiration for either exercise. I could see the rich coveys the Major had helped to shoot and the wonderful garments in which, late at night, he repaired to the smoking-room to talk about them. I could imagine their leggings and water-proofs, their knowing tweeds and rugs, their rolls of sticks and cases of tackle and neat umbrellas; and I could evoke the exact appearance of their servants and the compact variety of their luggage on platforms of country stations.

They gave small tips, but they were liked; they didn't do anything themselves, but they were welcome. They looked so well everywhere; they gratified the general relish for stature, complexion and "form." They knew it without fatuity or vulgarity, and they respected themselves in consequence. They weren't superficial; they were thorough and kept themselves up — it had been their line. People with such a taste for activity had to have some line. I could feel how even in a dull house they could have been counted on for the joy of life. At present something had happened — it didn't matter what, their little income had grown less, it had grown least — and they had to do something for pocket-money. Their friends could like them, I made out, without liking to support them. There was something about them that represented credit — their clothes, their manners, their type; but if credit is a large empty pocket in which an occasional chink reverberates, the chink at least must be audible. What they wanted of me was help to make it so. Fortunately they had no children — I soon divined that. They would also perhaps wish our relations to be kept secret: this was why it was "for the figure" — the reproduction of the face would betray them.

I liked them — I felt, quite as their friends must have done — they were so simple; and I had no objection to them if they would suit. But somehow with all their perfections I didn't easily believe in them. After all they were amateurs, and the ruling passion of my life was the detestation of the amateur. Combined with this was another perversity — an innate preference for the represented subject over the real one: the defect of the real one was so apt to be a lack of representation. I liked things that appeared; then one was sure. Whether they *were* or not was a subordinate and almost always profitless question. There were other considerations, the first of which was that I already had two or three recruits in use, notably a young person with big feet, in alpaca, from Kilburn, who for a couple of years had come to me regularly for my illustrations and with whom I was still — perhaps ignobly — satisfied. I frankly explained to my visitors how the case stood, but they had taken more precautions than I supposed. They had reasoned out their opportunity, for Claude Rivet had told them of the projected *édition de luxe* of one of the writers of our day — the rarest of the novelists — who, long neglected by the multitudinous vulgar and dearly prized by the attentive (need I mention Philip Vincent?), had had the happy fortune of seeing, late in life, the dawn and then the full light of a higher criticism; an estimate in which on the part of the public there was something really of expiation. The edition preparing, planned by a publisher of taste, was practically an act of high reparation; the woodcuts with which it was to be enriched were the homage of English art to one of the most independent representatives of English letters. Major and Mrs. Monarch confessed to me they had hoped I might be able to work *them* into my branch of the enterprise. They knew I was to do the first of the books, *Rutland Ramsay*, but I had to make clear to them that my participation in the rest of the affair — this first book was to be a test — must depend on the satisfaction I should give. If this should be limited my employers would drop me with scarce common forms. It was therefore a crisis for me, and naturally I was making special preparations, looking about for new people, should they be necessary, and securing the best types. I admitted however that I should like to settle down to two or three good models who would do for everything.

"Should we have often to — a — put on special clothes?" Mrs. Monarch timidly demanded.

"Dear, yes — that's half the business."

"And should we be expected to supply our own costumes?"

"Oh, no; I've got a lot of things. A painter's models put on — or put off — anything he likes."

"And you mean — a — the same?"

"The same?"

Mrs. Monarch looked at her husband again.

"Oh, she was just wondering," he explained, "if the costumes are in *general* use." I had to confess that they were, and I mentioned further that some of them — I had a lot of genuine greasy last-century things — had served their time, a hundred years ago, on living world-stained men and women; on figures not perhaps so far removed, in that vanished world, from *their* type, the Monarchs', *quoi*! of a breeched and bewigged age. "We'll put on anything that *fits*," said the Major.

"Oh, I arrange that — they fit in the pictures."

"I'm afraid I should do better for the modern books. I'd come as you like," said Mrs. Monarch.

"She has got a lot of clothes at home: they might do for contemporary life," her husband continued.

"Oh, I can fancy scenes in which you'd be quite natural." And indeed I could see the slipshod rearrangements of stale properties — the stories I tried to produce pictures for without the exasperation of reading them — whose sandy tracts the good lady might help to people. But I had to return to the fact that for this sort of work — the daily mechanical grind — I was already equipped: the people I was working with were fully adequate.

"We only thought we might be more like *some* characters," said Mrs. Monarch mildly, getting up.

Her husband also rose; he stood looking at me with a dim wistfulness that was touching in so fine a man. "Wouldn't it be rather a pull sometimes to have — a — to have — ?" He hung fire; he wanted me to help him by phrasing what he meant. But I couldn't — I didn't know. So he brought it out awkwardly: "The *real* thing; a gentleman, you know, or a lady." I was quite ready to give a general assent — I admitted that there was a great deal in that. This encouraged Major Monarch to say, following up his appeal with an unacted gulp: "It's awfully hard — we've tried everything." The gulp was communicative; it proved too much for his wife. Before I knew it Mrs. Monarch had dropped again upon a divan and burst into tears. Her husband sat down beside her, holding one of her hands; whereupon she quickly dried her eyes with the other, while I felt embarrassed as she looked up at me. "There isn't a confounded job I haven't applied for — waited for — prayed for. You can fancy we'd be pretty bad first. Secretaryships and that sort of thing? You might as well ask for a peerage. I'd be *anything* — I'm strong; a messenger or a coal-heaver. I'd put on a gold-laced cap and open carriage-doors in front of the haberdasher's; I'd hang about a station to carry portmanteaus; I'd be a postman. But they won't *look* at you; there are thousands as good as yourself already on the ground. *Gentlemen*, poor beggars, who've drunk their wine, who've kept their hunters!"

I was as reassuring as I knew how to be, and my visitors were presently on their feet again while, for the experiment, we agreed on an hour. We were discussing it when the door opened and Miss Churm came in with a wet umbrella. Miss Churm had to take the omnibus to Maida Vale and then walk half a mile. She looked a trifle blowsy and slightly splashed. I scarcely ever saw her come in without thinking afresh how odd it was that, being so little in herself, she should yet be so much in others. She was a meagre little Miss Churm, but was such an ample heroine of romance. She was only a freckled cockney, but she could represent everything, from a fine lady to a shepherdess; she had the faculty as she might have had a fine voice or long hair. She couldn't spell and she loved beer, but she had two or three "points," and practice, and a knack, and mother-wit, and a whimsical sensibility, and a love of the theatre, and seven sisters, and not an ounce of respect, especially for the *h.* The first thing my visitors saw was that her umbrella was wet, and in their spotless perfection they visibly winced at it. The rain had come on since their arrival.

"I'm all in a soak; there *was* a mess of people in the 'bus. I wish you lived near a styion," said Miss Churm. I requested her to get ready as quickly as possible, and she passed into the room in which she always changed her dress. But before going out she asked me what she was to get into this time.

"It's the Russian princess, don't you know?" I answered; "the one with the 'golden eyes,' in black velvet, for the long thing in the *Cheapside.*"

"Golden eyes? I *say!*" cried Miss Churm, while my companions watched her with intensity as she withdrew. She always arranged herself, when she was late, before I could turn round; and I kept my visitors a little on purpose, so that they might get an idea, from seeing her, what would be expected of themselves. I mentioned that she was quite my notion of an excellent model — she was really very clever.

"Do you think she looks like a Russian princess?" Major Monarch asked with lurking alarm.

"When I make her, yes."

"Oh, if you have to *make* her — !" he reasoned, not without point.

"That's the most you can ask. There are so many who are not makeable."

"Well, now, *here's* a lady" — and with a persuasive smile he passed his arm into his wife's — "who's already made!"

"Oh, I'm not a Russian princess," Mrs. Monarch protested a little coldly. I could see she had known some and didn't like them. There at once was a complication of a kind I never had to fear with Miss Churm.

This young lady came back in black velvet — the gown was rather rusty and very low on her lean shoulders — and with a Japanese fan in her red hands. I reminded her that in the scene I was doing she had to look over someone's head. "I forget whose it is; but it doesn't matter. Just look over a head."

"I'd rather look over a stove," said Miss Churm; and she took her station near the fire. She fell into position, settled herself into a tall attitude, gave a certain backward inclination to her head and a certain forward droop to her fan, and looked, at least to my prejudiced sense, distinguished and charming, foreign and dangerous. We left her looking so while I went downstairs with Major and Mrs. Monarch.

"I believe I could come about as near it as that," said Mrs. Monarch.

"Oh, you think she's shabby, but you must allow for the alchemy of art."

However, they went off with an evident increase of comfort founded on their demonstrable advantage in being the real thing. I could fancy them shuddering over Miss Churm. She was very droll about them when I went back, for I told her what they wanted.

"Well, if *she* can sit I'll tyke to bookkeeping," said my model.

"She's very ladylike," I replied as an innocent form of aggravation.

"So much the worse for *you*. That means she can't turn round."

"She'll do for the fashionable novels."

"Oh, yes, she'll *do* for them!" my model humorously declared. "Ain't they bad enough without her?" I had often sociably denounced them to Miss Churm.

### III

It was for the elucidation of a mystery in one of these works that I first tried Mrs. Monarch. Her husband came with her, to be useful if necessary — it was sufficiently clear that as a general thing he would prefer to come with her. At first I wondered if this were for "propriety's" sake — if he were going to be jealous and meddling. The idea was too tiresome, and if it had been confirmed it would speedily have brought our acquaintance to a close. But I soon saw there was nothing in it and that if he accompanied Mrs. Monarch it was — in addition to the chance of being wanted — simply because he had nothing else to do. When they were separate his occupation was gone, and they never *had* been separate. I judged rightly that in their awkward situation their close union was their main comfort and that this union had no weak spot. It was a real marriage, an encouragement to the hesitating, a nut for pessimists to crack. Their address was humble — I remember afterwards thinking it had been the only thing about them that was really professional — and I could fancy the lamentable lodgings in which the Major would have been left alone.. He could sit there more or less grimly with his wife — he couldn't sit there anyhow without her.

He had too much tact to try and make himself agreeable when he couldn't be useful; so when I was too absorbed in my work to talk he simply sat and waited. But I liked to hear him talk — it made my work, when not interrupting it, less mechanical, less special. To listen to him was to combine the excitement of going out with the economy of staying at home. There was only one hindrance — that I seemed not to know any of the people this brilliant couple had known. I think he wondered extremely, during the term of our intercourse, whom the deuce I *did* know. He hadn't a stray sixpence of an idea to fumble for, so we didn't spin it very fine; we confined ourselves to questions of leather and even of liquor — saddlers and breeches-makers and how to get excellent claret cheap — and matters like "good trains" and the habits of small game. His lore on these last subjects was astonishing — he managed to interweave the station-master with the ornithologist. When he couldn't talk about greater things he could talk cheerfully about small, and since I couldn't accompany him into reminiscences of the fashionable world he could lower the conversation without a visible effort to my level.

So earnest a desire to please was touching in a man who could so easily have knocked one down. He looked after the fire and had an opinion on the draught of the stove without my asking him, and I could see that he thought many of my arrangements not half knowing. I remember telling him that if I were only rich I'd offer him a salary to come and teach me how to live. Sometimes he gave a random sigh of which the essence might have been: "Give me even such a bare old barrack as *this*, and I'd do something with it!" When I wanted to use him he came alone; which was an illustration of the superior courage of women. His wife could bear her solitary second floor, and she was in general more discreet; showing by various small reserves that she was alive to the propriety of keeping our relations markedly professional — not letting them slide into sociability. She wished it to remain clear that she and the Major were employed, not cultivated, and if she approved of me as a superior, who could be kept in his place, she never thought me quite good enough for an equal.

She sat with great intensity, giving the whole of her mind to it, and was capable of remaining for an hour almost as motionless as before a photographer's lens. I could see she had been photographed often, but somehow the very habit that made her good for that purpose unfitted her for mine. At first I was extremely pleased with her ladylike air, and it was a satisfaction, on coming to follow her lines to see how good they were and how far they could lead the pencil. But after a little skirmishing I began to find her too insurmountably stiff; do what I would with it my drawing looked like a photograph or a copy of a photograph. Her figure had no variety of expression — she herself had no sense of variety. You may say that this was my business and was only a question of placing her. Yet I placed her in every conceivable position and she managed to obliterate their differences. She was always a lady certainly, and into the bargain was always the same lady. She was the real thing, but always the same thing. There were moments when I rather writhed under the serenity of her confidence that she *was* the real thing. All her dealings with me and all her husband's were an implication that this was lucky for *me*. Meanwhile I found myself trying to invent types that approached her own, instead of making her own transform itself — in the clever way that was not impossible for instance to poor Miss Churm. Arrange as I would and take the precautions I would, she always came out, in my pictures, too tall — landing me in the dilemma of having represented a fascinating woman as seven feet high, which (out of respect perhaps to my own very much scantier inches) was far from my idea of such a personage.

The case was worse with the Major — nothing I could do would keep *him* down, so that he became useful only for representation of brawny giants. I adored variety and range, I cherished human accidents, the illustrative note; I wanted to characterise closely, and the thing in the world I most hated was the danger of being ridden by a type. I had quarrelled with some of my friends about it; I had parted company with them for maintaining that one *had* to be, and that if the type was beautiful — witness Raphael and Leonardo — the servitude was only a gain. I was neither Leonardo nor Raphael — I might only be a presumptuous young modern searcher; but I held that everything was to be sacrificed sooner than character. When they claimed that the obsessional form could easily *be* character I retorted, perhaps superficially, "Whose?" It couldn't be everybody's — it might end in being nobody's.

After I had drawn Mrs. Monarch a dozen times I felt surer even than before that the value of such a model as Miss Churm resided precisely in the fact that she had no positive stamp, combined of course with the other fact that what she did have was a curious and inexplicable talent for imitation. Her usual appearance was like a curtain which she could draw up at request for a capital performance. This performance was simply suggestive; but it was a word to the wise — it was vivid and pretty. Sometimes even I thought it, though she was plain herself, too insipidly pretty; I made it a reproach to her that the figures drawn from her were monotonously (*bêtement,* as we used to say) graceful. Nothing made her more angry: it was so much her pride to feel she could sit for characters that had nothing in common with each other. She would accuse me at such moments of taking away her "reputytion."

It suffered a certain shrinkage, this queer quantity, from the repeated visits of my new friends. Miss Churm was greatly in demand, never in want of employment, so I had no scruple in putting her off occasionally, to try them more at my ease. It was certainly amusing at first to do the real thing — it was amusing to do Major Monarch's trousers. They *were* the real thing, even if he did come out colossal. It was amusing to do his wife's back hair — it was so mathematically neat — and the particular "smart" tension of her tight stays. She lent herself especially to positions in which the face was somewhat averted or blurred; she abounded in ladylike back views and *profils perdus.* When she stood erect she took naturally one of the attitudes in which court painters represent queens and princesses; so that I found myself wondering whether, to draw out this accomplishment, I couldn't get the editor of the *Cheapside* to publish a really royal romance, "A Tale of Buckingham Palace." Sometimes, however, the real thing and the make-believe came into contact; by which I mean that Miss Churm, keeping an appointment or coming to make one on days when I had much work in hand, encountered her invidious rivals. The encounter was not on their part, for they noticed her no more than if she had been the housemaid; not from intentional loftiness, but simply because as yet, professionally, they didn't know how to fraternise, as I could imagine they would have liked — or at least that the Major would. They couldn't talk about the omnibus — they always walked; and they didn't know what else to try — she wasn't interested in good trains or cheap claret. Besides, they must have felt — in the air — that she was amused at them, secretly derisive of their ever knowing how. She wasn't a person to conceal the limits of her faith if she had had a chance to show them. On the other hand Mrs. Monarch didn't think her tidy; for why else did she take pains to say to me — it was going out of the way, for Mrs. Monarch — that she didn't like dirty women?

One day when my young lady happened to be present with my other sitters — she even dropped in, when it was convenient, for a chat — I asked her to be so good as to lend a hand in getting tea, a service with which she was familiar and which was one of a class that, living as I did in a small way, with slender domestic resources, I often appealed to my models to render. They liked to lay hands on my property, to break the sitting, and sometimes the china — it made them feel Bohemian. The next time I saw Miss Churm after this incident she surprised me greatly by making a scene about it — she accused me of having wished to humiliate her. She hadn't resented the outrage at the time, but had seemed obliging and amused, enjoying the comedy of asking Mrs. Monarch, who sat vague and silent, whether she would have cream and sugar, and putting an exaggerated simper into the question. She had tried intonations — as if she too wished to pass for the real thing — till I was afraid my other visitors would take offence.

Oh, they were determined not to do this, and their touching patience was the measure of their great need. They would sit by the hour, uncomplaining, till I was ready to use them; they would come back on the chance of being wanted and would walk away cheerfully if it failed. I used to go to the door with them to see in what magnificent order they retreated. I tried to find other employment for them — I introduced them to several artists. But they didn't "take," for reasons I could appreciate, and I became rather anxiously aware that after such disappointments they fell back upon me with a heavier weight. They did me the honour to think me most *their* form. They weren't romantic enough for the painters, and in those days there were few serious workers in black-and-white. Besides, they had an eye to the great job I had mentioned to them — they had secretly set their hearts on supplying the right essence for my pictorial vindication of our fine novelist. They knew that for this undertaking I should want no costume effects, none of the frippery of past ages — that it was a case in which everything would be contemporary and satirical and presumably genteel. If I could work them into it their future would be assured, for the labour would of course be long and the occupation steady.

One day Mrs. Monarch came without her husband — she explained his absence by his having had to go to the City. While she sat there in her usual relaxed majesty there came at the door a knock which I immediately recognised as the subdued appeal of a model out of work. It was followed by the entrance of a young man whom I at once saw to be a foreigner and who proved in fact an Italian acquainted with no English word but my name, which he uttered in a way that made it seem to include all others. I hadn't then visited his country, nor was I proficient in his tongue; but as he was not so meanly constituted — what Italian is? — as to depend only on that member for expression he conveyed to me, in familiar but graceful mimicry, that he was in search of exactly the employment in which the lady before me was engaged. I was not struck with him at first, and while I continued to draw I dropped few signs of interest or encouragement. He stood his ground, however — not importunately, but with a dumb dog-like fidelity in his eyes that amounted to innocent impudence, the manner of a devoted servant — he might have been in the house for years — unjustly suspected. Suddenly it struck me that this very attitude and expression made a picture; whereupon I told him to sit down and wait till I should be free. There was another picture in the way he obeyed me, and I observed as I worked that there were others still in the way he looked wonderingly, with his head thrown back, about the high studio. He might have been crossing himself in Saint Peter's. Before I finished I said to myself, "The fellow's a bankrupt orange-monger, but a treasure."

When Mrs. Monarch withdrew he passed across the room like a flash to open the door by her, standing there with the rapt, pure gaze of the young Dante spellbound by the young Beatrice. As I never insisted, in such situations, on the blankness of the British domestic, I reflected that he had the making of a servant — and I needed one, but couldn't pay him to be only that — as well as of a model; in sort I resolved to adopt my bright adventurer if he would agree to officiate in the double capacity. He jumped at my offer, and in the event my rashness — for I had really known nothing about him — wasn't brought home to me. He proved a sympathetic though a desultory ministrant, and had in a wonderful degree the *sentiment de la pose*. It was uncultivated, instinctive, a part of the happy instinct that had guided him to my door and helped him to spell out my name on the card nailed to it. He had had no other introduction to me than a' guess, from the shape of my high north window, seen outside, that my place was a studio and that as a studio it would contain an artist. He had wandered to England in search of fortune, like other itinerants, and had embarked, with a partner and a small green handcart, on the sale of penny ices. The ices had melted away and the partner had dissolved in their train. My young man wore tight yellow trousers with reddish stripes and his name was Oronte. He was sallow but fair, and when I put him into some old clothes of my own he looked like an Englishman. He was as good as Miss Churm, who could look, when requested, like an Italian.

## IV

I thought Mrs. Monarch's face slightly convulsed when, on her coming back with her husband, she found Oronte installed. It was strange to have to recognise in a scrap of a lazzarone a competitor to her magnificent Major. It was she who scented danger first, for the Major was anecdotically unconscious. But Oronte gave us tea, with a hundred eager confusions — he had never been concerned in so queer a process — and I think she thought better of me for having at last an "establishment." They saw a couple of drawings that I had made of the establishment, and Mrs. Monarch hinted that it never would have struck her he had sat for them. "Now the drawings you make from *us*, they look exactly like us," she reminded me, smiling in triumph; and I recognised that this was indeed just their defect. When I drew the Monarchs I couldn't anyhow get away from them — get into the character I wanted to represent; and I hadn't the least desire my model should be discoverable in my picture. Miss Churm never was, and Mrs. Monarch thought I hid her, very properly, because she was vulgar; whereas if she was lost it was only as the dead who go to heaven are lost — in the gain of an angel the more.

But this time I had got a certain start with *Rutland Ramsay*, the first novel in the great projected series; that is, I had produced a dozen drawings, several with the help of the Major and his wife, and I had sent them in for approval. My understanding with the publishers, as I have already hinted, had been that I was to be left to do my work, in this particular case, as I liked, with the whole book committed to me; but my connexion with the rest of the series was only contingent. There were moments when, frankly, it *was* a comfort to have the real thing under one's hand; for there were characters in *Rutland Ramsay* that were very much like it. There were people presumably as erect as the Major and women of as good a fashion as Mrs. Monarch. There was a great deal of country-house life — treated, it is true, in a fine fanciful ironical generalised way — and there was a considerable implication of knickerbockers and kilts. There were certain things I had to settle at the outset; such things for instance as the exact appearance of the hero and the particular bloom and figure of the heroine. The author of course gave me a lead, but there was a margin for interpretation. I took the Monarchs into my confidence, I told them frankly what I was about, I mentioned my embarrassments and alternatives. "Oh, take *him*!" Mrs. Monarch murmured sweetly, looking at her husband; and "What could you want better than my wife?" the Major inquired with the comfortable candour that now prevailed between us.

I wasn't obliged to answer these remarks — I was only obliged to place my sitters. I wasn't easy in mind, and I postponed a little timidly perhaps the solving of my question. The book was a large canvas, the other figures were numerous, and I worked off at first some of the episodes in which the hero and the heroine were not concerned. When once I had set *them* up I should have to stick to them — I couldn't make my young man seven feet high in one place and five feet nine in another. I inclined on the whole to the latter measurement, though the Major more than once reminded me that *he* looked about as young as any one. It was indeed quite possible to arrange him, for the figure, so that it

would have been difficult to detect his age. After the spontaneous
Oronte had been with me a month, and after I had given him to understand several times over that his native exuberance would presently
constitute an insurmountable barrier to our further intercourse, I waked
to a sense of his heroic capacity. He was only five feet seven, but the
remaining inches were latent. I tried him almost secretly at first, for
I was really rather afraid of the judgment my other models would pass
on such a choice. If they regarded Miss Churm as little better than
a snare what would they think of the representation of a person so little
the real thing as an Italian street-vendor of a protagonist formed by a
public school?

If I went a little in fear of them it wasn't because they bullied me,
because they had got an oppressive foothold, but because in their really
pathetic decorum and mysteriously permanent newness they counted
on me so intensely. I was therefore very glad when Jack Hawley came
home: he was always of such good counsel. He painted badly himself,
but there was no one like him for putting his finger on the place. He
had been absent from England for a year; he had been somewhere — I
don't remember where — to get a fresh eye. I was in a good deal of dread
of any such organ, but we were old friends; he had been away for months
and a sense of emptiness was creeping into my life. I hadn't dodged a
missile for a year.

He came back with a fresh eye, but with the same old black velvet
blouse, and the first evening he spent in my studio we smoked cigarettes
till the small hours. He had done no work himself, he had only got the
eye; so the field was clear for the production of my little things. He
wanted to see what I had produced for the *Cheapside*, but he was
disappointed in the exhibition. That at least seemed the meaning of
two or three comprehensive groans which, as he lounged on my big
divan, his leg folded under him, looking at my latest drawings, issued
from his lips with the smoke of the cigarette.

"What's the matter with you?" I asked.

"What's the matter with *you*?"

"Nothing save that I'm mystified."

"You are indeed. You're quite off the hinge. What's the meaning
of this new fad?" And he tossed me, with visible irreverence, a drawing
in which I happened to have depicted both my elegant models. I asked
if he didn't think it good, and he replied that it struck him as execrable,
given the sort of thing I had always represented myself to him as wishing
to arrive at; but I let that pass — I was so anxious to see exactly what
he meant. The two figures in the picture looked colossal, but I
supposed this was *not* what he meant, inasmuch as, for aught he knew
to the contrary, I might have been trying for some such effect. I

maintained that I was working exactly in the same way as when he last had done me the honour to tell me I might do something some day. "Well, there's a screw loose somewhere," he answered; "wait a bit and I'll discover it." I depended upon him to do so: where else was the fresh eye? But he produced at last nothing more luminous than "I don't know — I don't like your types." This was lame for a critic who had never consented to discuss with me anything but the question of execution, the direction of strokes and the mystery of values.

"In the drawings you've been looking at I think my types are very handsome."

"Oh, they won't do!"

"I've been working with new models."

"I see you have. *They* won't do."

"Are you very sure of that?"

"Absolutely — they're stupid."

"You mean *I* am — for I ought to get round that."

"You *can't* — with such people. Who are they?"

I told him, so far as was necessary, and he concluded heartlessly: *"Ce sont des gens qu'il faut mettre à la porte."*

"You've never seen them; they're awfully good" — I flew to their defence.

"Not seen them? Why all this recent work of yours drops to pieces with them. It's all I want to see of them."

"No one else has said anything against it — the *Cheapside* people are pleased."

"Every one else is an ass, and the *Cheapside* people the biggest asses of all. Come, don't pretend at this time of day to have pretty illusions about the public, especially about publishers and editors. It's not for *such* animals you work — it's for those who know, *coloro che sanno*; so keep straight for *me* if you can't keep straight for yourself. There was a certain sort of thing you used to try for — and a very good thing it was. But this twaddle isn't *in* it." When I talked with Hawley later about *Rutland Ramsay* and its possible successors he declared that I must get back into my boat again or I should go to the bottom. His voice in short was the voice of warning.

I noted the warning, but I didn't turn my friends out of doors. They bored me a good deal; but the very fact that they bored me admonished me not to sacrifice them — if there was anything to be done with them — simply to irritation. As I look back at this phase they seem to me to have pervaded my life not a little. I have a vision of them as most of the time in my studio, seated against the wall on an old velvet bench to be out of the way, and resembling the while a pair of patient courtiers in a royal ante-chamber. I'm convinced that during the coldest weeks of the winter they held their ground because it saved them fire. Their newness was losing its gloss, and it was impossible not to feel them objects of charity. Whenever Miss Churm arrived they went away, and after I was fairly launched in *Rutland Ramsay* Miss Churm arrived pretty often. They managed to express to me tacitly that they supposed I wanted her for the low life of the book, and I let them suppose it, since they had attempted to study the work — it was lying about the studio — without discovering that it dealt only with the highest circles. They had dipped into the most brilliant of our novelists without deciphering many passages. I still took an hour from them, now and again, in spite of Jack Hawley's warning: it would be time enough to dismiss them, if dismissal should be necessary, when the rigour of the season was over. Hawley had made their acquaintance — he had met them at my fireside — and thought them a ridiculous pair. Learning that he was a painter they tried to approach him, to show him too that they were the real thing; but he looked at them, across the big room, as if they were miles away: they were a compendium of everything he most objected to in the social system of his country. Such people as that, all convention and patent-leather, with ejaculations that stopped conversation, had no business in a studio. A studio was a place to learn to see, and how could you see through a pair of feather-beds?

The main inconvenience I suffered at their hands was that at first I was shy of letting it break upon them that my artful little servant had begun to sit to me for *Rutland Ramsay*. They knew I had been odd enough — they were prepared by this time to allow oddity to artists — to pick a foreign vagabond out of the streets when I might have had a person with whiskers and credentials; but it was some time before they learned how high I rated his accomplishments. They found him in an attitude more than once, but they never doubted I was doing him as an organ-grinder. There were several things they never guessed, and one of them was that for a striking scene in the novel, in which a footman briefly figured, it occurred to me to make use of Major Monarch as the menial. I kept putting this off, I didn't like to ask him to don the livery — besides the difficulty of finding a livery to fit him. At last, one day late in the winter, when I was at work on the despised Oronte, who caught one's idea on the wing, and was in the glow of feeling myself go very straight, they came in, the Major and his wife, with their society laugh about nothing (there was less and less to laugh at); came in like country-callers — they always reminded me of that — who have walked across the park after church and are presently persuaded to stay to luncheon. Luncheon was over, but they could stay to tea — I knew they wanted it. The fit was on me, however, and I couldn't let my ardour cool and my work wait, with the fading daylight, while my model prepared it. So I asked Mrs.

Monarch if she would mind laying it out — a request which for an instant brought all the blood to her face. Her eyes were on her husband's for a second, and some mute telegraphy passed between them. Their folly was over the next instant; his cheerful shrewdness put an end to it. So far from pitying their wounded pride, I must add, I was moved to give it as complete a lesson as I could. They bustled about together and got out the cups and saucers and made the kettle boil. I know they felt as if they were waiting on my servant, and when the tea was prepared I said: "He'll have a cup, please — he's tired." Mrs. Monarch brought him one where he stood, and he took it from her as if he had been a gentleman at a party squeezing a crush-hat with an elbow.

Then it came over me that she had made a great effort for me — made it with a kind of nobleness — and that I owed her a compensation. Each time I saw her after this I wondered what the compensation could be. I couldn't go on doing the wrong thing to oblige them. Oh, it *was* the wrong thing, the stamp of the work for which they sat — Hawley was not the only person to say it now. I sent in a large number of the drawings I had made for *Rutland Ramsay,* and I received a warning that was more to the point than Hawley's. The artistic adviser of the house for which I was working was of opinion that many of my illustrations were not what had been looked for. Most of these illustrations were the subjects in which the Monarchs had figured. Without going into the question of what *had* been looked for, I had to face the fact that at this rate I shouldn't get the other books to do. I hurled myself in despair on Miss Churm — I put her through all her paces. I not only adopted Oronte publicly as my hero, but one morning when the Major looked in to see if I didn't require him to finish a *Cheapside* figure for which he had begun to sit the week before, I told him I had changed my mind — I'd do the drawing from my man. At this my visitor turned pale and stood looking at me. "Is *he* your idea of an English gentleman?" he asked.

I was disappointed, I was nervous, I wanted to get on with my work; so I replied with irritation: "Oh my dear Major — I can't be ruined for *you!*"

It was a horrid speech, but he stood another moment — after which, without a word, he quitted the studio. I drew a long breath, for I said to myself that I shouldn't see him again. I hadn't told him definitely that I was in danger of having my work rejected, but I was vexed at his not having felt the catastrophe in the air, read with me the moral of our fruitless collaboration, the lesson that in the deceptive atmosphere of art even the highest respectability may fail of being plastic.

I didn't owe my friends money, but I did see them again. They reappeared together three days later, and, given all the other facts, there was something tragic in that one. It was a clear proof they could find nothing else in life to do. They had threshed the matter out in a dismal conference — they had digested the bad news that they were not in for the series. If they weren't useful to me even for the *Cheapside*, their function seemed difficult to determine, and I could only judge at first that they had come, forgivingly, decorously, to take a last leave. This made me rejoice in secret that I had little leisure for a scene; for I had placed both my other models in position together and I was pegging away at a drawing from which I hoped to derive glory. It had been suggested by the passage in which Rutland Ramsay, drawing up a chair to Artemisia's piano-stool, says extraordinary things to her while she ostensibly fingers out a difficult piece of music. I had done Miss Churm at the piano before — it was an attitude in which she knew how to take on an absolutely poetic grace. I wished the two figures to "compose" together with intensity, and my little Italian had entered perfectly into my conception. The pair were vividly before me, the piano had been pulled out; it was a charming show of blended youth and murmured love, which I had only to catch and keep. My visitors stood and looked at it, and I was friendly to them over my shoulder.

They made no response, but I was used to silent company and went on with my work, only a little disconcerted — even though exhilarated by the sense that *this* was at least the ideal thing — at not having got rid of them after all. Presently I heard Mrs. Monarch's sweet voice beside or rather above me: "I wish her hair were a little better done." I looked up and she was staring with a strange fixedness at Miss Churm, whose back was turned to her. "Do you mind my just touching it?" she went on — a question which made me spring up for an instant as with the instinctive fear that she might do the young lady a harm. But she quieted me with a glance I shall never forget — I confess I should like to have been able to paint *that* — and went for a moment to my model. She spoke to her softly, laying a hand on her shoulder and bending over her; and as the girl, understanding, gratefully assented, she disposed her rough curls, with a few quick passes, in such a way as to make Miss Churm's head twice as charming. It was one of the most heroic personal services I've ever seen rendered. Then Mrs. Monarch turned away with a low sigh and, looking about her as if for something to do, stooped to the floor with a noble humility and picked up a dirty rag that had dropped out of my paint-box.

The Major meanwhile had also been looking for something to do, and, wandering to the other end of the studio, saw before him my breakfast-things neglected, unremoved. "I say, can't I be useful *here*?" he called out to me with an irrepressible quaver. I assented with a laugh that I fear was awkward, and for the next ten minutes, while I worked, I heard the light clatter of china and the tinkle of spoons and glass. Mrs. Monarch assisted her husband — they washed up my crockery, they put it away. They wandered off into my little scullery, and I afterwards found that they had cleaned my knives and that my slender stock of plate had an unprecedented surface. When it came over me, the latent eloquence of what they were doing, I confess that my drawing was blurred for a moment — the picture swam. They had accepted their failure, but they couldn't accept their fate. They had bowed their head in bewilderment to the perverse and cruel law in virtue of which the real thing could be so much less precious than the unreal; but they didn't want to starve. If my servants were my models, then my models might be my servants. They would reverse the parts — the others would sit for the ladies and gentlemen and *they* would do the work. They would still be in the studio — it was an intense dumb appeal to me not to turn them out. "Take us on," they wanted to say — "we'll do *anything*."

My pencil dropped from my hand; my sitting was spoiled and I got rid of my sitters, who were also evidently rather mystified and awe-struck. Then, alone with the Major and his wife I had a most uncomfortable moment. He put their prayer into a single sentence: "I say, you know — just let *us* do for you, can't you?" I couldn't — it was dreadful to see them emptying my slops; but I pretended I could, to oblige them, for about a week. Then I gave them a sum of money to go away, and I never saw them again. I obtained the remaining books, but my friend Hawley repeats that Major and Mrs. Monarch did me a permanent harm, got me into false ways. If it be true I'm content to have paid the price — for the memory.

# Sarah Orne Jewett (1849–1909)

OFTEN CALLED the best of the New England regional writers, Sarah Orne Jewett grew up in South Berwick, Maine, where she was born in 1849. She accompanied her father, a doctor, on his rounds and the people she met as his patients were to be characters in many of her stories. Her first story was accepted by the *Atlantic Monthly* when she was nineteen. It was the beginning of a series that was to constitute her first book, *Deephaven*, published in 1877. Her novels *A Country Doctor*, about a woman who refuses marriage to become a doctor, and *A Marsh Island*, the romance of an artist and a farm woman, are regional. Primarily, she was a short-story writer, and six volumes of her stories were published. The masterpiece is considered to be *The Country of the Pointed Firs* (1896), a collection laid in a Maine seaport. This reader spent summers in the area and, although Jewett was a common family name there, could find no one who knew her work. But Willa Cather said her desire to write was inspired by the beauty of Sarah Orne Jewett's stories.

Reticent in content, understated in manner, the story reprinted here is a good example of the way Sarah Orne Jewett wrote. It is permeated by her quiet sensitivity to people and places. Her evocation of her characters makes them as alive as real people that one knows intimately, and her description of the Maine countryside is as rewarding as a trip there. She exemplifies the truth of what Edward J. O'Brien meant when he wrote, "American literature began when the writer learned to discover the expression on the face of the man next door."

# *The Courting of Sister Wisby*

ALL the morning there had been an increasing temptation to take an out-door holiday, and early in the afternoon the temptation outgrew my power of resistance. A far-away pasture on the long southwestern slope of a high hill was persistently present to mind, yet there seemed to be no particular reason why I should think of it. I was not sure that I wanted anything from the pasture, and there was no sign, except the temptation, that the pasture wanted anything of me. But I was on the farther side of as many as three fences before I stopped to think again where I was going, and why.

There is no use in trying to tell another person about that afternoon unless he distinctly remembers weather exactly like it. No number of details concerning an Arctic ice-blockade will give a single shiver to a child of the tropics. This was one of those perfect New England days in late summer, when the spirit of autumn takes a first stealthy flight, like a spy, through the ripening country-side, and, with feigned sympathy for those who droop with August heat, puts her cool cloak of bracing air about leaf and flower and human shoulders. Every living thing grows suddenly cheerful and strong; it is only when you catch sight of a horror-stricken little maple in swampy soil, — a little maple that has second sight and foreknowledge of coming disaster to her race, — only then does a distrust of autumn's friendliness dim your joyful satisfaction.

In midwinter there is always a day when one has the first foretaste of spring; in late August there is a morning when the air is for the first time autumnlike. Perhaps it is a hint to the squirrels to get in their first supplies for the winter hoards, or a reminder that summer will soon end, and everybody had better make the most of it. We are always looking forward to the passing and ending of winter, but when summer is here it seems as if summer must always last. As I went across the fields that day, I found myself half lamenting that the world must fade again, even that the best of her budding and bloom was only a preparation for another spring-time, for an awakening beyond the coming winter's sleep.

The sun was slightly veiled; there was a chattering group of birds, which had gathered for a conference about their early migration. Yet, oddly enough, I heard the voice of a belated bobolink, and presently saw him rise from the grass and hover leisurely, while he sang a brief tune. He was much behind time if he were still a housekeeper; but as for the other birds, who listened, they cared only for their own notes. An old crow went sagging by, and gave a croak at his despised neighbor, just as a black reviewer croaked at Keats: so hard it is to be just to one's contemporaries. The bobolink was indeed singing out of season, and it was impossible to say whether he really belonged most to this summer or to the next. He might have been delayed on his northward journey; at any rate, he had a light heart now, to judge from his song, and I wished that I could ask him a few questions, — how he liked being the last man among the bobolinks, and where he had taken singing lessons in the South.

Presently I left the lower fields, and took a path that led higher, where I could look beyond the village to the northern country mountainward. Here the sweet fern grew, thick and fragrant, and I also found myself heedlessly treading on pennyroyal. Nearby, in a field corner, I long ago made a most comfortable seat by putting a stray piece of board and bit of rail across the angle of the fences. I have spent many a delightful hour there, in the shade and shelter of a young pitch-pine and a wild-cherry tree, with a lovely outlook toward the village, just far enough away beyond the green slopes and tall elms of the lower meadows. But that day I still had the feeling of being outward bound, and did not turn aside nor linger. The high pasture land grew more and more enticing.

I stopped to pick some blackberries that twinkled at me like beads among their dry vines, and two or three yellow-birds fluttered up from the leaves of a thistle, and then came back again, as if they had complacently discovered that I was only an overgrown yellow-bird, in strange disguise but perfectly harmless. They made me feel as if I were an intruder, though they did not offer to peck at me, and we parted company very soon. It was good to stand at last on the great shoulder of the hill. The wind was coming in from the sea, there was a fine fragrance from the pines, and the air grew sweeter every moment. I took new pleasure in the thought that in a piece of wild pasture land like this one may get closest to Nature, and subsist upon what she gives of her own free will. There have been no drudging, heavy-shod ploughmen to overturn the soil, and vex it into yielding artificial crops. Here one has to take just what Nature is pleased to give, whether one is a yellow-bird or a human being. It is very good entertainment for a summer wayfarer, and I am asking my reader now to share the winter provision which I harvested that day. Let us hope that the small birds are also faring well after their fashion, but I give them an anxious thought while the snow goes hurrying in long waves across the buried fields, this windy winter night.

I next went farther down the hill, and got a drink of fresh cool water from the brook, and pulled a tender sheaf of sweet flag beside it. The mossy old fence just beyond was the last barrier between me and the pasture which had sent an invisible messenger earlier in the day, but I saw that somebody else had come first to the rendezvous: there was a brown gingham cape-bonnet and a sprigged shoulder-shawl bobbing up and down, a little way off among the junipers. I had taken such uncommon pleasure in being alone that I instantly felt a sense of disappointment; then a warm glow of pleasant satisfaction rebuked my selfishness. This could be no one but dear old Mrs. Goodsoe, the friend of my childhood and fond dependence of my maturer years. I had not seen her for many weeks, but here she was, out on one of her famous campaigns for herbs, or perhaps just returning from a blueberrying expedition. I approached with care, so as not to startle the gingham bonnet; but she heard the rustle of the bushes against my dress, and looked up quickly, as she knelt, bending over the turf. In that position she was hardly taller than the luxuriant junipers themselves.

"I'm a-gittin' in my mulleins," she said briskly, "an' I've been thinking o' you these twenty times since I come out o' the house. I begun to believe you must ha' forgot me at last."

"I have been away from home," I explained. "Why don't you get in your pennyroyal too? There's a great plantation of it beyond the next fence but one."

"Pennyr'yal!" repeated the dear little old woman, with an air of compassion for inferior knowledge; "'t ain't the right time, darlin'. Pennyr'yal's too rank now. But for mulleins this day is prime. I've got a dreadful graspin' fit for 'em this year; seems if I must be goin' to need 'em extry. I feel like the squirrels must when they know a hard winter's comin'." And Mrs. Goodsoe bent over her work again, while I stood by and watched her carefully cut the best full-grown leaves with a clumsy pair of scissors, which might have served through at least half a century of herb-gathering. They were fastened to her apron-strings by a long piece of list.

"I'm going to take my jack-knife and help you," I suggested, with some fear of refusal. "I just passed a flourishing family of six or seven heads that must have been growing on purpose for you."

"Now be keerful, dear heart," was the anxious response; "choose 'em well. There's odds in mulleins same's there is in angels. Take a plant that's all run up to stalk, and there ain't but little goodness in the leaves. This one I'm at now must ha' been stepped on by some creatur' and blighted of its bloom, and the leaves is han'some! When I was small I used to have a notion that Adam an' Eve must a took mulleins fer their winter wear. Ain't they just like flannel, for all the world? I've had experience, and I know there's plenty of sickness might be saved to folks if they'd quit horse-radish and such fiery, exasperating things, and use mullein drarves in proper season. Now I shall spread these an' dry 'em nice on my spare floor in the garrit, an' come to steam 'em for use along in the winter there 'll be the vally of the whole summer's goodness in 'em, sartin." And she snipped away with the dull scissors, while I listened respectfully, and took great pains to have my part of the harvest present a good appearance.

"This is most too dry a head," she added presently, a little out of breath. "There! I can tell you there's win'rows o' young doctors, bilin' over with book-larnin', that is truly ignorant of what to do for the sick, or how to p'int out those paths that well people foller toward sickness. Book-fools I call 'em, them young men, an' some on 'em never'll live to know much better, if they git to be Methuselahs. In my time every middle-aged woman, who had brought up a family, had some proper ideas o' dealin' with complaints. I won't say but there was some fools amongst *them*, but I'd rather take my chances, unless they'd forsook herbs and gone to dealin' with patent stuff. Now my mother really did sense the use of herbs and roots. I never see anybody that come up to her. She was a meek-looking woman, but very understandin', mother was."

"Then that's where you learned so much yourself, Mrs. Goodsoe," I ventured to say.

"Bless your heart, I don't hold a candle to her; 't is but little I can recall of what she used to say. No, her l'arnin' died with her," said my friend, in a self-depreciating tone. "Why, there was as many as twenty kinds of roots alone that she used to keep by her, that I forget the use of; an' I'm sure I shouldn't know where to find the most of 'em, any. There was an herb" — *airb*, she called it — "an herb called masterwort, that she used to get way from Pennsylvany; and she used to think everything of noble liverwort, but I never could seem to get the right effects from it as she could. Though I don't know as she ever really did use masterwort where somethin' else wouldn't a served. She had a cousin married out in Pennsylvany that used to take pains to get it to her every year or two, and so she felt 't was important to have it. Some set more by such things as come from a distance, but I rec'lect mother always used to maintain that folks was meant to be doctored with the stuff that grew right about 'em; 't was sufficient, an' so ordered. That was before the whole population took to livin' on wheels, the way they do now. 'T was never my idee that we was meant to know what's goin' on all over the world to once. There's goin' to be some sort of a set-back one o' these days, with these telegraphs an' things, an' letters comin' every hand's turn, and folks leavin' their proper work to answer 'em. I may not live to see it. 'T was allowed to be difficult for folks to git about in old times, or to git word across the country, and they stood in their lot an' place, and weren't all just alike, either, same as pine-spills."

We were kneeling side by side now, as if in penitence for the march of progress, but we laughed as we turned to look at each other.

"Do you think it did much good when everybody brewed a cracked quart mug of herb-tea?" I asked, walking away on my knees to a new mullein.

"I've always lifted my voice against the practice, far 's I could," declared Mrs. Goodsoe; "an' I won't deal out none o' the herbs I save for no such nonsense. There was three houses along our road, — I call no names, — where you couldn't go into the livin' room without findin' a mess o' herb-tea drorin' on the stove or side o' the fireplace, winter or summer, sick or well. One was thoroughwut, one would be camomile, and the other, like as not, yellow dock; but they all used to put in a little new rum to git out the goodness, or keep it from spilin'." (Mrs. Goodsoe favored me with a knowing smile.) "Land, how mother used to laugh! But, poor creaturs, they had to work hard, and I guess it never done 'em a mite o' harm; they was all good herbs. I wish you could hear the quawkin' there used to be when they was indulged with a real case o' sickness. Everybody would collect from far an' near; you'd see 'em coming along the road and across the pastures then; everybody clamorin' that nothin' wouldn't do no kind o' good but her choice o' teas or drarves to the feet. I wonder there was a babe lived to grow up in the whole lower part o' the town; an' if nothin' else 'peared to ail 'em, word was passed about that 't was likely Mis' So-and-So's last young one was goin' to be foolish. Land, how they'd gather! I know one day the doctor come to Widder Peck's and the house was crammed so 't he could scercely git inside the door; and he says, just as polite, 'Do send for some of the neighbors!' as if there wa'n't a soul to turn to, right or left. You'd ought to seen 'em begin to scatter."

"But don't you think the cars and telegraphs have given people more to interest them, Mrs. Goodsoe? Don't you believe people's lives were narrower then, and more taken up with little things?" I asked, unwisely, being a product of modern times.

"Not one mite, dear," said my companion stoutly. "There was as big thoughts then as there is now; these times was born o' them. The difference is in folks themselves; but now, instead o' doin' their own housekeepin' and watchin' their own neighbors, — though that was carried to excess, — they git word that a niece's child is ailin' the other side o' Massachusetts, and they drop everything and git on their best clothes, and off they jiggit in the cars. 'T is a bad sign when folks wears out their best clothes faster 'n they do their every-day ones. The other side o' Massachusetts has got to look after itself by rights. An' besides that, Sunday-keepin' 's all gone out o' fashion. Some lays it to one thing an' some another, but some o' them old ministers that folks are all a-sighin' for did preach a lot o' stuff that wa'n't nothin' but chaff; 't wa'nt' the word o' God out o' either Old Testament or New. But everybody went to meetin' and heard it, and come home, and was set to fightin' with their next door neighbor over it. Now I'm a believer, and I try to live a Christian life, but I'd as soon hear a surveyor's book read out, figgers an' all, as try to get any simple truth out o' most sermons. It's them as is most to blame."

"What was the matter that day at Widow Peck's?" I hastened to ask, for I knew by experience that the good, clear-minded soul beside me was apt to grow unduly vexed and distressed when she contemplated the state of religious teaching.

"Why, there wa'n't nothin' the matter, only a gal o' Miss Peck's had met with a dis'pointment and had gone into screechin' fits. 'T was a rovin' creatur' that had come along hayin' time, and he'd gone off an' forsook her betwixt two days; nobody ever knew what become of him. Them Pecks was 'Good Lord, anybody!' kind o' gals, and took up with whoever they could get. One of 'em married Heron, the Irishman; they lived in that little house that was burnt this summer, over on the edge o' the plains. He was a good-hearted creatur', with a laughin' eye and a clever word for everybody. He was the first Irishman that ever came this way, and we was all for gettin' a look at him, when he first used to go by. Mother's folks was what they call Scotch-Irish, though; there was an old race of 'em settled about here. They could foretell events, some on 'em, and had the second sight. I know folks used to say mother's grandmother had them gifts, but mother was never free to speak about it to us. She remembered her well, too.''

"I suppose that you mean old Jim Heron, who was such a famous fiddler?" I asked with great interest, for I am always delighted to know more about that rustic hero, parochial Orpheus that he must have been!

"Now, dear heart, I suppose you don't remember him, do you?" replied Mrs. Goodsoe, earnestly. "Fiddle! He'd about break your heart with them tunes of his, or else set your heels flying up the floor in a jig, though you was minister o' the First Parish and all wound up for a funeral prayer. I tell ye there ain't no tunes sounds like them used to. It used to seem to me summer nights when I was comin' along the plains road, and he set by the window playin', as if there was a bewitched human creatur' in that old red fiddle o' his. He could make it sound just like a woman's voice tellin' somethin' over and over, as if folks could help her out o' her sorrows if she could only make 'em understand. I've set by the stone-wall and cried as if my heart was broke, and dear knows it wa'n't in them days. How he would twirl off them jigs and dance tunes! He used to make somethin' han'some out of 'em in fall an' winter, playin' at huskins and dancin' parties; but he was unstiddy by spells, as he got along in years, and never knew what it was to be forehanded. Everybody felt bad when he died; you couldn't help likin' the creatur'. He'd got the gift — that 's all you could say about it.

"There was a Mis' Jerry Foss, that lived over by the brook bridge, on the plains road, that had lost her husband early, and was left with three child'n. She set the world by 'em, and was a real pleasant, ambitious little woman, and was workin' on as best she could with that little farm, when there come a rage o' scarlet fever, and her boy and two girls was swept off and laid dead within the same week. Every one o' the neighbors did what they could, but she'd had no sleep since they was taken sick, and after the funeral she set there just like a piece o' marble, and would only shake her head when you spoke to her. They all thought her reason would go; and 't would certain, if she couldn't have shed tears. An' one o' the neighbors — 't was like mother's sense, but it might have been somebody else — spoke o' Jim Heron. Mother an' one or two o' the women that knew her best was in the house with her. 'T was right in the edge of the woods and some of us younger ones was over by the wall on the other side of the road where there was a couple of old willows, —I remember just how the brook damp felt; and we kept quiet 's we could, and some other folks come along down the road, and stood waitin' on the little bridge, hopin' somebody 'd come out, I suppose, and they'd git news. Everybody was wrought up, and felt a good deal for her, you know. By an' by Jim Heron come stealin' right out o' the shadows an' set down on the doorstep, an' 't was a good while before we heard a sound; then, oh, dear me! 't was what the whole neighborhood felt for that mother all spoke in the notes, an' they told me afterwards that Mis' Foss's face changed in a minute, and she come right over an' got into my mother's lap, — she was a little woman, — an' laid her head down, and there she cried herself into a blessed sleep. After awhile one o' the other women stole out an' told the folks, and we all went home. He only played that one tune.

"But there!" resumed Mrs. Goodsoe, after a silence, during which my eyes were filled with tears. "His wife always complained that the fiddle made her nervous. She never 'peared to think nothin' o' poor Heron after she'd once got him."

"That's often the way," said I, with harsh cynicism, though I had no guilty person in my mind at the moment; and we went straying off, not very far apart, up through the pasture. Mrs. Goodsoe cautioned me that we must not get so far off that we could not get back the same day. The sunshine began to feel very hot on our backs, and we both turned toward the shade. We had already collected a large bundle of mullein leaves, which were carefully laid into a clean, calico apron, held together by the four corners, and proudly carried by me, though my companion regarded them with anxious eyes. We sat down together at the edge of the pine woods, and Mrs. Goodsoe proceeded to fan herself with her limp cape-bonnet.

"I declare, how hot it is! The east wind's all gone again," she said. "It felt so cool this forenoon that I overburdened myself with as thick a petticoat as any I've got. I'm despri't afeared of having a chill, now that I ain't so young as once. I hate to be housed up."

"It's only August, after all," I assured her unnecessarily, confirming my statement by taking two peaches out of my pocket, and laying them side by side on the brown pine needles between us.

"Dear sakes alive!" exclaimed the old lady, with evident pleasure. "Where did you get them, now? Doesn't anything taste twice better out-o'-doors? I ain't had such a peach for years. Do le's keep the stones, an' I'll plant 'em; it only takes four year for a peach pit to come to bearing, an' I guess I'm good for four year, 'thout I meet with some accident."

I could not help agreeing, or taking a fond look at the thin little figure, and her wrinkled brown face and kind, twinkling eyes. She looked as if she had properly dried herself, by mistake, with some of her mullein leaves, and was likely to keep her goodness, and to last the longer in consequence. There never was a truer, simple-hearted soul made out of the old-fashioned country dust than Mrs. Goodsoe. I thought, as I looked away from her across the wide country, that nobody was left in

any of the farm-houses so original, so full of rural wisdom and reminiscence, so really able and dependable, as she. And nobody had made
better use of her time in a world foolish enough to sometimes under-
value medicinal herbs.

When we had eaten our peaches we still sat under the pines, and I
was not without pride when I had poked about in the ground with a
little twig, and displayed to my crony a long fine root, bright yellow to
the eye, and a wholesome bitter to the taste.

"Yis, dear, goldthread," she assented indulgently. "Seems to me
there's more of it than anything except grass an' hardhack. Good for
canker, but no better than two or three other things I can call to mind;
but I always lay in a good wisp of it, for old times' sake. Now, I want
to know why you should a bit it, and took away all the taste o' your nice
peach? I was just thinkin' what a han'some entertainment we've had.
I've got so I 'sociate certain things with certain folks, and goldthread
was somethin' Lizy Wisby couldn't keep house without, no ways whatever. I believe she took so much it kind o' puckered her disposition."

"Lizy Wisby?" I repeated inquiringly.

"You knew her, if ever, by the name of Mis' Deacon Brimblecom,"
answered my friend, as if this were only a brief preface to further information, so I waited with respectful expectation. Mrs. Goodsoe had
grown tired out in the sun, and good story would be an excuse for
sufficient rest. It was a most lovely place where we sat, halfway up the
long hillside; for my part, I was perfectly contented and happy. "You've
often heard of Deacon Brimblecom?" she asked, as if a great deal
depended upon his being properly introduced.

"I remember him," said I. "They called him Deacon Brimfull, you
know, and he used to go about with a witch-hazel branch to show people
where to dig wells."

"That's the one," said Mrs. Goodsoe, laughing. "I didn't know's
you could go so far back. I'm always divided between whether you can
remember everything I can, or are only a babe in arms."

"I have a dim recollection of there being something strange about
their marriage," I suggested, after a pause, which began to appear
dangerous. I was so much afraid the subject would be changed.

"I can tell you all about it," I was quickly answered. "Deacon
Brimblecom was very pious accordin' to his lights in his early years.
He lived way back in the country then, and there come a rovin' preacher
along, and set everybody up that way all by the ears. I've heard the old
folks talk it over, but I forget most of his doctrine, except some of his
followers was persuaded they could dwell among the angels while yet on
airth, and this Deacon Brimfull, as you call him, felt sure he was called
by the voice of a spirit bride. So he left a good, deservin' wife he had,

an' four children, and built him a new house over to the other side of the land he'd had from his father. They didn't take much pains with the buildin', because they expected to be translated before long, and then the spirit brides and them folks was goin' to appear and divide up the airth amongst 'em, and the world's folks and onbelievers was goin' to serve 'em or be sent to torments. They had meetins about in the school-houses, an' all sorts o' goins on; some on 'em went crazy, but the deacon held on to what wits he had, an' by an' by the spirit bride didn't turn out to be much of a housekeeper, an' he had always been used to good livin', so he sneaked home ag'in. One o' mother's sisters married up to Ash Hill, where it all took place; that's how I come to have the particulars."

"Then how did he come to find his Eliza Wisby?" I inquired. "Do tell me the whole story; you've got mullein leaves enough."

"There's all yesterday's at home, if I haven't," replied Mrs. Goodsoe. "The way he come a-courtin' o' Sister Wisby was this: she went a-courtin' o' him.

"There was a spell he lived to home, and then his poor wife died, and he had a spirit bride in good earnest, an' the child'n was placed about with his folks and hers, for they was both out o' good families; and I don't know what come over him, but he had another pious fit that looked for all the world like the real thing. He hadn't no family cares, and he lived with his brother's folks, and turned his land in with theirs. He used to travel to every meetin' an' conference that was within reach of his old sorrel hoss's feeble legs; he j'ined the Christian Baptists that was just in their early prime, and he was a great exhorter, and got to be called deacon, though I guess he wa'n't deacon, 'less it was for a spare hand when deacon timber was scercer 'n usual. An' one time there was a four days' protracted meetin' to the church in the lower part of the town. 'T was a real solemn time; something more'n usual was goin' forward, an' they collected from the whole country round. Women folks liked it, an' the men too; it give 'em a change, an' they was quartered round free, same as conference folks now. Some on 'em, for a joke, sent Silas Brimblecom up to Lizy Wisby's, though she'd give out she couldn't accommodate nobody, because of expectin' her cousin's folks. Everybody knew 't was a lie; she was amazin' close considerin' she had plenty to do with. There was a streak that wa'n't just right somewheres in Lizy's wits, I always thought. She was very kind in case o' sickness, I'll say that for her.

"You know where the house is, over there on what they call Windy Hill? There the deacon went, all unsuspectin', and 'stead o' Lizy's resentin' of him she put in her own hoss, and they come back together to evenin' meetin'. She was prominent among the sect herself, an' he

bawled and talked, and she bawled and talked, an' took up more 'n
the time allotted in the exercises, just as if they was showin' off to each
other what they was able to do at expoundin'. Everybody was laughin'
at 'em after the meetin' broke up, and that next day an' the next, an' all
through, they was constant, and seemed to be havin' a beautiful occasion.
Lizy had always give out she scorned the men, but when she got a chance
at a particular one 't was altogether different, and the deacon seemed to
please her somehow or 'nother, and — There! you don't want to listen
to this old stuff that 's past an' gone?''

"Oh yes, I do,'' said I.

"I run on like a clock that's onset her striking hand,'' said Mrs.
Goodsoe mildly. "Sometimes my kitchen timepiece goes on half the
forenoon, and I says to myself the day before yisterday I would let it be a
warnin', and keep it in mind for a check on my own speech. The next
news that was heard was that the deacon an' Lizy — well, opinions
differed which of 'em had spoke first, but them fools settled it before the
protracted meetin' was over, and give away their hearts before he started
for home. They considered 't would be wise, though, considerin' their
short acquaintance, to take one another on trial a spell; 't was Lizy's
notion, and she asked him why he would n't come over and stop with her
till spring, and then, if they both continued to like, they could git married
any time 't was convenient. Lizy, she come and talked it over with
mother, and mother disliked to offend her, but she spoke pretty plain;
and Lizy felt hurt, and' thought they was showin' excellent judgment, so
much harm come from hasty unions and folks comin' to a realizin' sense
of each other's failin's when 't was too late.

"So one day our folks saw Deacon Brimfull a-ridin' by with a gre't
coopful of hens in the back o' his wagon, and bundles o' stuff tied on
top and hitched to the exes underneath; and he riz a hymn just as he
passed the house, and was speedin' the old sorrel with a willer switch.
'T was most Thanksgivin' time, an' sooner 'n she expected him. New
Year's was the time she set; but he thought he'd better come while the
roads was fit for wheels. They was out to meetin' together Thanksgivin' Day, an' that used to be a gre't season for marryin'; so the young
folks nudged each other, and some on 'em ventured to speak to the couple
as they come down the aisle. Lizy carried it off real well; she wa'n't afraid
o' what nobody said or thought, and so home they went. They'd got
out her yaller sleigh and her hoss; she never would ride after the deacon's
poor old creatur', and I believe it died long o' the winter from stiffenin'
up.

"Yes,'' said Mrs. Goodsoe emphatically, after we had silently
considered the situation for a short space of time, — "yes, there was
consider'ble talk, now I tell you! The raskil boys pestered 'em just

about to death for a while. They used to collect up there an' rap on the winders, and they'd turn out all the deacon's hens 'long at nine o'clock 'o night, and chase 'em all over the dingle; an' one night they even lugged the pig right out o' the sty, and shoved it into the back entry, an' run for their lives. They'd stuffed its mouth full o' somethin', so it couldn't squeal till it got there. There wa'n't a sign o' nobody to be seen when Lizy hasted out with the light, and she an' the deacon had to persuade the creatur' back as best they could; 't was a cold night, and they said it took 'em till towards mornin'. You see the deacon was just the kind of man that a hog wouldn't budge for; it takes a masterful man to deal with a hog. Well, there was no end to the works nor the talk, but Lizy left 'em pretty much alone. She did 'pear kind of dignified about it, I must say!"

"And then, were they married in the spring?"

"I was tryin' to remember whether it was just before Fast Day or just after," responded my friend, with a careful look at the sun, which was nearer the west than either of us had noticed. "I think likely 't was along in the last o' April, any way some of us looked out o' the window one Monday mornin' early, and says, 'For goodness' sake! Lizy's sent the deacon home again!' His old sorrel havin' passed away, he was ridin' in Ezry Welsh's hoss-cart, with his hen-coop and more bundles than he had when he come, and he looked as meechin' as ever you see. Ezry was drivin', and he let a glance fly swiftly round to see if any of us was lookin' out; an' then I declare if he didn't have the malice to turn right in towards the barn, where he see my oldest brother, Joshuay, an' says he real natural, 'Joshuay, just step out with your wrench. I believe I hear my kingbolt rattlin' kind o' loose.' Brother, he went out an' took in the sitooation, an' the deacon bowed kind of stiff. Joshuay was so full o' laugh, and Ezry Welsh, that they couldn't look one another in the face. There wa'n't nothing ailed the kingbolt, you know, an' when Josh riz up he says, 'Goin' up country for a spell, Mr. Brimblecom?'

" 'I be,' says the deacon, lookin' dreadful mortified and cast down.

" 'Ain't things turned out well with you an' Sister Wisby?' says Joshuay. 'You had ought to remember that the woman is the weaker vessel.'

" 'Hang her, let her carry less sail, then!' the deacon bu'st out, and he stood right up an' shook his fist there by the hen-coop, he was so mad; an' Ezry's hoss was a young creatur', an' started up an set the deacon right over backwards into the chips. We didn't know but he'd broke his neck; but when he see the women folks runnin' out, he jumped up quick as a cat, an' clim' into the cart, an' off they went. Ezry said he told him that he couldn't git along with Lizy, she was so fractious in thundery weather; if there was a rumble in the daytime she must go right to bed an' screech, and if 't was night she must git right up an' go an' call him out of a sound sleep. But everybody knew he'd never a gone home unless she'd sent him.

"Somehow they made it up agin right away, him an' Lizy, and she had him back. She'd been countin' all along on not havin' to hire nobody to work about the gardin an' so on, an' she said she wa'n't goin' to let him have a whole winter's board for nothin'. So the old hens was moved back, and they was married right off fair an' square, an' I don't know but they got along well as most folks. He brought his youngest girl down to live with 'em after a while, an' she was a real treasure to Lizy; everybody spoke well o' Phebe Brimblecom. The deacon got over his pious fit, and there was consider'ble work in him if you kept right after him. He was an amazin' cider-drinker, and he airn't the name you know him by in his latter days. Lizy never trusted him with nothin', but she kep' him well. She left everything she owed to Phebe, when she died, 'cept somethin' to satisfy the law. There, they're all gone now: seems to me sometimes, when I get thinkin,' as if I'd lived a thousand years!"

I laughed, but I found that Mrs. Goodsoe's thoughts had taken a serious turn.

"There, I come by some old graves down here in the lower edge of the pasture," she said as we rose to go. "I couldn't help thinking how I should like to be laid right out in the pasture ground, when my time comes; it looked sort o' comfortable, and I have ranged these slopes so many summers. Seems as if I could see right up through the turf and tell when the weather was pleasant and get the goodness o' the sweet fern. Now, dear, just hand me my apernful o' mulleins out o' the shade. I hope you won't come to need none this winter, but I'll dry some special for you."

"I'm going home by the road," said I "or else by the path across the meadows, and I will walk as far as the house with you. Aren't you pleased with my company?" for she demurred at my going the least bit out of the way.

So we strolled toward the little gray house, with our plunder of mullein leaves slung on a stick which we carried between us. Of course I went in to make a call, as if I had not seen my hostess before; she is the last maker of muster-gingerbread, and before I came away I was kindly measured for a pair of mittens.

"You'll be sure to come an' see them two peach-trees after I get 'em well growin'!" Mrs. Goodsoe called after me when I had said good-by, and was almost out of hearing down the road.

# Stephen Crane (1871–1900)

STEPHEN CRANE was only twenty-nine years old when he died of tuberculosis, "the literary disease." His writing has been destined for a far longer life. He was born in New Jersey, grew up in New York State, attended Lafayette College and Syracuse University for a year each, and became a part-time newspaper reporter in New York City. His first book, *Maggie: A Girl of the Streets*, was considered too grim and Crane printed it privately on borrowed money. As a child he had absorbed the stories told him by Civil War veterans and, inspired by Tolstoy's *War and Peace*, he wrote the masterpiece, *Red Badge of Courage* (1895), which established his reputation once and for all. It resulted in the rescue from obscurity of *Maggie*. From then on a book by him was published nearly every year. When the Spanish-American War was imminent, he accompanied as correspondent an arms-smuggling expedition to Cuba. Later he covered briefly the Greco-Turkish War. Like Poe, Crane was the target of malicious gossip accusing him of immorality and drug addiction. He went to live permanently in England, but became sick and sought a cure in Germany, where he died.

The impact of war on Crane's writing was continuous. On the filibustering expedition his ship was sunk and for fifty hours he struggled for his life in the sea. Out of this experience grew "The Open Boat," one of the magnificent short stories in the collection *The Open Boat and Other Tales of Adventures*. At times "The Open Boat" reminds a reader of "The Ancient Mariner" when a shark accompanies the small craft and when there is the tense waiting for rescue. Impressive, too, is the way Crane tells the gentle consideration the four wrecked men show one another.

# *The Open Boat*

## A Tale Intended to be after the Fact: Being the Experience of Four Men from the Sunk Steamer *Commodore*

NONE of them knew the color of the sky. Their eyes glanced level, and were fastened upon the waves that swept toward them. These waves were of the hue of slate, save for the tops, which were of foaming white, and all of the men knew the colors of the sea. The horizon narrowed and widened, and dipped and rose, and at all times its edge was jagged with waves that seemed thrust up in points like rocks.

Many a man ought to have a bathtub larger than the boat which here rode upon the sea. These waves were most wrongfully and barbarously abrupt and tall, and each froth-top was a problem in small-boat navigation.

The cook squatted in the bottom, and looked with both eyes at the six inches of gunwale which separated him from the ocean. His sleeves were rolled over his fat forearms, and the two flaps of his unbuttoned vest dangled as he bent to bail out the boat. Often he said, "Gawd! that was a narrow clip." As he remarked it he invariably gazed eastward over the broken sea.

The oiler, steering with one of the two oars in the boat, sometimes raised himself suddenly to keep clear of water that swirled in over the stern. It was a thin little oar, and it seemed often ready to snap.

The correspondent, pulling at the other oar, watched the waves and wondered why he was there.

The injured captain, lying in the bow, was at this time buried in that profound dejection and indifference which comes, temporarily at least, to even the bravest and most enduring when, willy-nilly, the firm fails, the army loses, the ship goes down. The mind of the master of a vessel is rooted deep in the timbers of her, though he command for a day or a decade; and this captain had on him the stern impression of a scene in the grays of dawn of seven turned faces, and later a stump of a topmast with a white ball on it, that slashed to and fro at the waves, went low and lower, and down. Thereafter there was something strange in his voice. Although steady, it was deep with mourning, and of a quality beyond oration or tears.

"Keep'er a little more south, Billie," said he.

"A little more south, sir," said the oiler in the stern.

A seat in this boat was not unlike a seat upon a bucking broncho, and by the same token a broncho is not much smaller. The craft pranced and reared and plunged like an animal. As each wave came, and she rose for it, she seemed like a horse making at a fence outrageously high. The manner of her scramble over these walls of water is a mystic thing, and, moreover, at the top of them were ordinarily these problems in white water, the foam racing down from the summit of each wave requiring a new leap, and a leap from the air. Then, after scornfully bumping a crest, she would slide and race and splash down a long incline, and arrive bobbing and nodding in front of the next menace.

A singular disadvantage of the sea lies in the fact that after successfully surmounting one wave you discover that there is another behind it just as important and just as nervously anxious to do something effective in the way of swamping boats. In a ten-foot dinghy one can get an idea of the resources of the sea in the line of waves that is not probable to the average experience, which is never at sea in a dinghy. As each slaty wall of water approached, it shut all else from the view of the men in the boat and it was not difficult to imagine that this particular wave was the final outburst of the ocean, the last effort of the grim water. There was a terrible grace in the move of the waves, and they came in silence, save for the snarling of the crests.

In the wan light the faces of the men must have been gray. Their eyes must have glinted in strange ways as they gazed steadily astern. Viewed from a balcony, the whole thing would doubtless have been weirdly picturesque. But the men in the boat had no time to see it, and if they had had leisure, there were other things to occupy their minds. The sun swung steadily up the sky, and they knew it was broad day because the color of the sea changed from slate to emerald-green streaked with amber lights, and the foam was like tumbling snow. The process of the breaking day was unknown to them. They were aware only of this effect upon the color of the waves that rolled toward them.

In disjointed sentences the cook and the correspondent argued as to the difference between a life-saving station and a house of refuge. The cook had said: "There's a house of refuge just north of the Mosquito Inlet Light, and as soon as they see us they'll come off in their boat and pick us up."

"As soon as who see us?" said the correspondent.

"The crew," said the cook.

"Houses of refuge don't have crews," said the correspondent. "As I understand them, they are only places where clothes and grub are stored for the benefit of shipwrecked people. They don't carry crews."

"Oh, yes, they do," said the cook.

"No, they don't," said the correspondent.

"Well, we're not there yet, anyhow," said the oiler, in the stern.

"Well," said the cook, "perhaps it's not a house of refuge that I'm thinking of as being near Mosquito Inlet Light; perhaps it's a lifesaving station."

"We're not there yet," said the oiler in the stern.

## II

As the boat bounced from the top of each wave the wind tore through the hair of the hatless men, and as the craft plopped her stern down again the spray splashed past them. The crest of each of these waves was a hill, from the top of which the men surveyed for a moment a broad tumultuous expanse, shining and wind-riven. It was probably splendid, it was probably glorious, this play of the free sea, wild with lights of emerald and white and amber.

"Bully good thing it's an onshore wind," said the cook. "If not, where would we be? Wouldn't have a show."

"That's right," said the correspondent.

The busy oiler nodded his assent.

Then the captain, in the bow, chuckled in a way that expressed humor, contempt, tragedy, all in one. "Do you think we've got much of a show now, boys?" said he.

Whereupon the three were silent, save for a trifle of hemming and hawing. To express any particular optimism at this time they felt to be childish and stupid, but they all doubtless possessed this sense of the situation in their minds. A young man thinks doggedly at such times. On the other hand, the ethics of their condition were decidedly against any open suggestion of hopelessness. So they were silent.

"Oh, well," said the captain, soothing his children, "we'll get ashore all right."

But there was that in his tone which made them think; so the oiler quoth, "Yes! if this wind holds."

The cook was bailing. "Yes! if we don't catch hell in the surf."

Canton-flannel gulls flew near and far. Sometimes they sat down on the sea, near patches of brown seaweed that rolled over the waves with a movement like carpets on a line in a gale. The birds sat comfortably in groups, and they were envied by some in the dinghy, for the wrath of the sea was no more to them than it was to a covey of prairie chickens a thousand miles inland. Often they came very close and stared at the men with black bead-like eyes. At these times they were uncanny and sinister in their unblinking scrutiny, and the men hooted angrily at them, telling them to be gone. One came, and evidently decided to alight on the top of the captain's head. The bird flew parallel to the boat and did not circle, but made short sidelong jumps in the air in chicken fashion. His black eyes were wistfully fixed upon the captain's head. "Ugly brute," said the oiler to the bird. "You look as if you were made with a jackknife." The cook and the correspondent swore darkly at the creature. The captain naturally wished to knock it away with the end of the heavy painter, but he did not dare do it, because anything resembling an emphatic gesture would have capsized this freighted boat; and so, with his open hand, the captain gently and carefully waved the gull away. After it had been discouraged from the pursuit the captain breathed easier on account of his hair, and others breathed easier because the bird struck their minds at this time as being somehow gruesome and ominous.

In the meantime the oiler and the correspondent rowed. And also they rowed. They sat together in the same seat, and each rowed an oar. Then the oiler took both oars; then the correspondent took both oars; then the oiler; then the correspondent. They rowed and they rowed. The very ticklish part of the business was when the time came for the reclining one in the stern to take his turn at the oars. By the very last star of truth, it is easier to steal eggs from under a hen than it was to change seats in the dinghy. First the man in the stern slid his hand along the thwart and moved with care, as if he were of Sevres. Then the man in the rowing-seat slid his hand along the other thwart. It was all done with the most extraordinary care. As the two sidled past each other, the whole party kept watchful eyes on the coming wave, and the captain cried: "Look out, now! Steady, there!"

The brown mats of seaweed that appeared from time to time were like islands, bits of earth. They were traveling, apparently, neither one way nor the other. They were, to all intents, stationary. They informed the men in the boat that it was making progress slowly toward the land.

The captain, rearing cautiously in the bow after the dinghy soared on a great swell, said that he had seen the lighthouse at Mosquito Inlet. Presently the cook remarked that he had seen it. The correspondent was at the oars then, and for some reason he too wished to look at the lighthouse; but his back was toward the far shore, and the waves were important, and for some time he could not seize an opportunity to turn his head. But at last there came a wave more gentle than the others, and when at the crest of it he swiftly scoured the western horizon.

"See it?" said the captain.

"No," said the correspondent, slowly; "I didn't see anything."

"Look again," said the captain. He pointed. "It's exactly in that direction."

At the top of another wave the correspondent did as he was bid, and this time his eyes chanced on a small, still thing on the edge of the swaying horizon. It was precisely like the point of a pin. It took an anxious eye to find a lighthouse so tiny.

"Think we'll make it, Captain?"

"If this wind holds and the boat don't swamp, we can't do much else," said the captain.

The little boat, lifted by each towering sea and splashed viciously by the crests, made progress that in the absence of seaweed was not apparent to those in her. She seemed just a wee thing wallowing, miraculously top up, at the mercy of five oceans. Occasionally a great spread of water, like white flames, swarmed into her.

"Bail her, cook," said the captain, serenely.

"All right, Captain," said the cheerful cook.

### III

It would be difficult to describe the subtle brotherhood of men that was here established on the seas. No one said that it was so. No one mentioned it. But it dwelt in the boat, and each man felt it warm him. They were a captain, an oiler, a cook, and a correspondent, and they were friends — friends in a more curiously ironbound degree than may be common. The hurt captain, lying against the water jar in the bow, spoke always in a low voice and calmly; but he could never command a more ready and swiftly obedient crew than the motley three of the dinghy. It was more than a mere recognition of what was best for the common safety. There was surely in it a quality that was personal and heartfelt. And after this devotion to the commander of the boat, there was this comradeship, that the correspondent, for instance, who had been taught to be cynical of men, knew even at the time was the best experience of his life. But no one said that it was so. No one mentioned it.

"I wish we had a sail," remarked the captain. "We might try my overcoat on the end of an oar, and give you two boys a chance to rest." So the cook and the correspondent held the mast and spread wide the overcoat; the oiler steered; and the little boat made good way with her new rig. Sometimes the oiler had to scull sharply to keep a sea from breaking into the boat, but otherwise sailing was a success.

Meanwhile the lighthouse had been growing slowly larger. It had now almost assumed color, and appeared like a little gray shadow on the sky. The man at the oars could not be prevented from turning his head rather often to try for a glimpse of this little gray shadow.

At last, from the top of each wave, the men in the tossing boat could see land. Even as the lighthouse was an upright shadow on the sky, this land seemed but a long black shadow on the sea. It certainly was thinner than paper. "We must be about opposite New Smyrna," said the cook, who had coasted this shore often in schooners. "Captain, by the way, I believe they abandoned that lifesaving station there about a year ago."

"Did they?" said the captain.

The wind slowly died away. The cook and the correspondent were not now obliged to slave in order to hold high the oar. But the waves continued their old impetuous swooping at the dinghy, and the little craft, no longer under way, struggled woundily over them. The oiler or the correspondent took the oars again.

Shipwrecks are *apropos* of nothing. If men could only train for them and have them occur when the men had reached pink condition, there would be less drowning at sea. Of the four in the dinghy none had slept any time worth mentioning for two days and two nights previous to embarking in the dinghy, and in the excitement of clambering about the deck of a foundering ship they had also forgotten to eat heartily.

For these reasons, and for others, neither the oiler nor the correspondent was fond of rowing at this time. The correspondent wondered ingenuously how in the name of all that was sane could there be people who thought it amusing to row a boat. It was not an amusement; it was a diabolical punishment, and even a genius of mental aberrations could never conclude that it was anything but a horror to the muscles and a crime against the back. He mentioned to the boat in general how the amusement of rowing struck him, and the weary-faced oiler smiled in full sympathy. Previously to the foundering, by the way, the oiler had worked a double watch in the engine room of the ship.

"Take her easy now, boys," said the captain. "Don't spend yourselves. If we have to run a surf you'll need all your strength, because we'll sure have to swim for it. Take your time."

Slowly the land arose from the sea. From a black line it became a line of black and a line of white — trees and sand. Finally the captain said that he could make out a house on the shore. "That's the house of refuge, sure," said the cook. "They'll see us before long, and come out after us."

The distant lighthouse reared high. "The keeper ought to be able to make us out now, if he's looking through a glass," said the captain. "He'll notify the lifesaving people."

"None of those other boats could have got ashore to give word of this wreck," said the oiler, in a low voice, "else the lifeboat would be out hunting us."

Slowly and beautifully the land loomed out of the sea. The wind came again. It had veered from the northeast to the southeast. Finally a new sound struck the ears of the men in the boat. It was the low thunder of the surf on the shore. "We'll never be able to make the lighthouse now," said the captain. "Swing her head a little more north, Billie."

"A little more north, sir," said the oiler.

Whereupon the little boat turned her nose once more down the wind, and all but the oarsman watched the shore grow. Under the influence of this expansion doubt and direful apprehension were leaving the minds of the men. The management of the boat was still most absorbing, but it could not prevent a quiet cheerfulness. In an hour, perhaps, they would be ashore.

Their backbones had become thoroughly used to balancing in the boat, and they now rode this wild colt of a dinghy like circus men. The correspondent thought that he had been drenched to the skin, but happening to feel in the top pocket of his coat, he found therein eight cigars. Four of them were soaked with seawater; four were perfectly scatheless. After a search, somebody produced three dry matches; and thereupon the four waifs rode impudently in their little boat and, with an assurance of an impending rescue shining in their eyes, puffed at the big cigars, and judged well and ill of all men. Everybody took a drink of water.

## IV

"Cook," remarked the captain, "there don't seem to be any signs of life about your house of refuge."

"No," replied the cook. "Funny they don't see us!"

A broad stretch of lowly coast lay before the eyes of the men. It was of low dunes topped with dark vegetation. The roar of the surf was plain, and sometimes they could see the white lip of a wave as it spun up the beach. A tiny house was blocked out black upon the sky. Southward, the slim lighthouse lifted its little gray length.

Tide, wind, and waves were swinging the dinghy northward. "Funny they don't see us," said the men.

The surf's roar was here dulled, but its tone was nevertheless thunderous and mighty. As the boat swam over the great rollers the men sat listening to this roar. "We'll swamp sure," said everybody.

It is fair to say here that there was not a lifesaving station within twenty miles in either direction; but the men did not know this fact, and in consequence they made dark and opprobrious remarks concerning the eyesight of the nation's lifesavers. Four scowling men sat in the dinghy and surpassed records in the invention of epithets.

"Funny they don't see us."

The light-heartedness of a former time had completely faded. To their sharpened minds it was easy to conjure pictures of all kinds of incompetency and blindness and, indeed, cowardice. There was the shore of the populous land, and it was bitter and bitter to them that from it came no sign.

"Well," said the captain, ultimately, "I suppose we'll have to make a try for ourselves. If we stay out here too long, we'll none of us have strength left to swim after the boat swamps."

And so the oiler, who was at the oars, turned the boat straight for the shore. There was a sudden tightening of muscles. There was some thinking.

"If we don't all get ashore," said the captain — "if we don't all get ashore, I suppose you fellows know where to send news of my finish?"

They then briefly exchanged some addresses and admonitions. As for the reflections of the men, there was a great deal of rage in them. Perchance they might be formulated thus: "If I am going to be drowned — if I am going to be drowned — if I am going to be drowned, why, in the name of the seven mad gods who rule the sea, was I allowed to come thus far and contemplate sand and trees? Was I brought here merely to have my nose dragged away as I was about to nibble the sacred cheese of life? It is preposterous. If this old ninny-woman, Fate, cannot do better than this, she should be deprived of the management of men's fortunes. She is an old hen who knows not her intention. If she has decided to drown me, why did she not do it in the beginning and save me all this trouble? The whole affair is absurd . . . But no; she cannot mean to drown me. She dare not drown me. She cannot drown me. Not after all this work." Afterward the man might have had an impulse to shake his fist at the clouds.. "Just you drown me, now, and then hear what I call you!"

The billows that came at this time were more formidable. They seemed always just about to break and roll over the little boat in a turmoil of foam. There was a preparatory and long growl in the speech of them. No mind unused to the sea would have concluded that the dinghy could ascend these sheer heights in time. The shore was still afar. The oiler was a wily surfman. "Boys," he said swiftly, "she won't live three minutes more, and we're too far out to swim. Shall I take her to sea again, Captain?"

"Yes; go ahead!" said the captain.

This oiler, by a series of quick miracles and fast and steady oarsmanship, turned the boat in the middle of the surf and took her safely to sea again.

There was a considerable silence as the boat bumped over the furrowed sea to deeper water. Then somebody in gloom spoke: "Well, anyhow, they must have seen us from the shore by now."

The gulls went in slanting flight up the wind toward the gray, desolate east. A squall, marked by dingy clouds and clouds brick-red, like smoke from a burning building, appeared from the southeast.

"What do you think of those lifesaving people? Ain't they peaches?"

"Funny they haven't seen us."

"Maybe they think we're out here for sport! Maybe they think we're fishin'. Maybe they think we're damned fools."

It was a long afternoon. A changed tide tried to force them southward, but wind and wave said northward. Far ahead, where coastline, sea, and sky formed their mighty angle, there were little dots which seemed to indicate a city on the shore.

"St. Augustine?"

The captain shook his head. "Too near Mosquito Inlet."

And the oiler rowed, and then the correspondent rowed; then the oiler rowed. It was a weary business. The human back can become the seat of more aches and pains than are registered in books for the composite anatomy of a regiment. It is limited area, but it can become the theater of innumerable muscular conflicts, tangles, wrenches, knots, and other comforts.

"Did you ever like to row, Billie?" asked the correspondent.

"No," said the oiler; "hang it!"

When one exchanged the rowing-seat for a place in the bottom of the boat, he suffered a bodily depression that caused him to be careless of everything save an obligation to wiggle one finger. There was cold seawater swashing to and fro in the boat, and he lay in it. His head, pillowed on a thwart, was within an inch of the swirl of a wave-crest, and sometimes a particularly obstreperous sea came inboard and drenched him once more. But these matters did not annoy him. It is almost certain that if the boat had capsized he would have tumbled comfortably out upon the ocean as if he felt sure that it was a great soft mattress.

"Look! There's a man on the shore!"

"Where?"

"There! See 'im? See 'im?"

"Yes, sure! He's walking along."

"Now he's stopped. Look! He's facing us!"

"He's waving at us!"

"So he is! By thunder!"

"Ah, now we're all right! Now we're all right! There'll be a boat out here for us in half an hour."

"He's going on. He's running. He's going up to that house there."

The remote beach seemed lower than the sea, and it required a searching glance to discern the little black figure. The captain saw a floating stick, and they rowed to it. A bath towel was by some weird chance in the boat, and, tying this on the stick, the captain waved it. The oarsman did not dare turn his head, so he was obliged to ask questions.

"What's he doing now?"

"He's standing still again. He's looking, I think . . . There he goes again — toward the house . . . Now he's stopped again."

"Is he waving at us?"

"No, not now; he was, though."

"Look! There comes another man!"

"He's running."

"Look at him go, would you!"

"Why, he's on a bicycle. Now he's met the other man. They're both waving at us. Look!"

"There comes something up the beach."

"What the devil is that thing?"

"Why, it looks like a boat."

"Why, certainly, it's a boat."

"No; it's on wheels."

"Yes, so it is. Well, that must be the lifeboat. They drag them along shore on a wagon."

"That's the lifeboat, sure."

"No, by God, it's — it's an omnibus."

"I tell you it's a lifeboat."

"It is not! It's an omnibus. I can see it plain. See? One of these big hotel omnibuses."

"By thunder, you're right. It's an omnibus, sure as fate. What do you suppose they are doing with an omnibus? Maybe they are going around collecting the life-crew, hey?"

"That's it, likely. Look! There's a fellow waving a little black flag. He's standing on the steps of the omnibus. There come those other two fellows. Now they're all talking together. Look at the fellow with the flag. Maybe he ain't waving it!"

"That ain't a flag, is it? That's his coat. Why, certainly, that's his coat."

"So it is; it's his coat. He's taken it off and is waving it around his head. But would you look at him swing it!"

"Oh, say, there isn't any lifesaving station there. That's just a winter-resort hotel omnibus that has brought over some of the boarders to see us drown."

"What's that idiot with the coat mean? What's he signaling, anyhow?"

"It looks as if he were trying to tell us to go north. There must be a lifesaving station up there."

"No; he thinks we're fishing. Just giving us a merry hand. See? Ah, there, Willie!"

"Well, I wish I could make something out of those signals. What do you suppose he means?"

"He don't mean anything; he's just playing."

"Well, if he'd just signal us to try the surf again, or to go to sea and wait, or go north, or go south, or go to hell, there would be some reason in it. But look at him! He just stands there and keeps his coat revolving like a wheel. The ass!"

"There come more people."

"Now there's quite a mob. Look! Isn't that a boat?"

"Where? Oh, I see where you mean. No, that's no boat."

"That fellow is still waving his coat."

"He must think we like to see him do that. Why don't he quit it? It don't mean anything."

"I don't know. I think he is trying to make us go north. It must be that there's a lifesaving station there somewhere."

"Say, he ain't tired yet. Look at 'im wave!"

"Wonder how long he can keep that up. He's been revolving his coat ever since he caught sight of us. He's an idiot. Why aren't they getting men to bring a boat out? A fishing boat — one of those big yawls — could come out here all right. Why don't he do something?"

"Oh, it's all right now."

"They'll have a boat out here for us in less than no time, now that they've seen us."

A faint yellow tone came into the sky over the low land. The shadows on the sea slowly deepened. The wind bore coldness with it, and the men began to shiver.

"Holy smoke!" said one, allowing his voice to express his impious mood, "if we keep on monkeying out here! If we've got to flounder out here all night!"

"Oh, we'll never have to stay here all night! Don't you worry. They've seen us now, and it won't be long before they'll come chasing out after us."

The shore grew dusky. The man waving a coat blended gradually into this gloom, and it swallowed in the same manner the omnibus and the group of people. The spray, when it dashed uproariously over the side, made the voyagers shrink and swear like men who were being branded.

"I'd like to catch the chump who waved the coat. I feel like socking him one, just for luck."

"Why? What did he do?"

"Oh, nothing, but then he seemed so damned cheerful."

In the meantime the oiler rowed, and then the correspondent rowed, and then the oiler rowed. Gray-faced and bowed forward, they mechanically, turn by turn, plied the leaden oars. The form of the lighthouse had vanished from the southern horizon, but finally a pale star appeared, just lifting from the sea. The streaked saffron in the west passed before the all-merging darkness, and the sea to the east was black. The land had vanished, and was expressed only by the low and drear thunder of the surf.

"If I am going to be drowned — if I am going to be drowned — if I am going to be drowned, why, in the name of the seven mad gods who rule the sea, was I allowed to come thus far and contemplate sand and trees? Was I brought here merely to have my nose dragged away as I was about to nibble the sacred cheese of life?"

The patient captain, drooped over the water jar, was sometimes obliged to speak to the oarsman.

"Keep her head up! Keep her head up!"

"Keep her head up, sir." The voices were weary and low.

This was surely a quiet evening. All save the oarsman lay heavily and listlessly in the boat's bottom. As for him, his eyes were just capable of noting the tall black waves that swept forward in a most sinister silence, save for an occasional subdued growl of a crest.

The cook's head was on a thwart, and he looked without interest at the water under his nose. He was deep in other scenes. Finally he spoke. "Billie," he murmured, dreamfully, "what kind of pie do you like best?"

## V

"Pie!" said the oiler and the correspondent, agitatedly. "Don't talk about those things, blast you!"

"Well," said the cook, "I was just thinking about ham sandwiches, and — "

A night on the sea in an open boat is a long night. As darkness settled finally, the shine of the light, lifting from the sea in the south, changed to full gold. On the northern horizon a new light appeared, a small bluish gleam on the edge of the waters. These two lights were the furniture of the world. Otherwise there was nothing but waves.

Two men huddled in the stern, and distances were so magnificent in the dinghy that the rower was enabled to keep his feet partly warm by thrusting them under his companions. Their legs indeed extended far under the rowing-seat until they touched the feet of the captain forward. Sometimes, despite the efforts of the tired oarsman, a wave came piling into the boat, an icy wave of the night, and the chilling water soaked them anew. They would twist their bodies for a moment and groan, and sleep the dead sleep once more, while the water in the boat gurgled about them as the craft rocked.

The plan of the oiler and the correspondent was for one to row until he lost he ability, and then arouse the other from his sea-water couch in the bottom of the boat.

The oiler plied the oars until his head drooped forward and the overpowering sleep blinded him; and he rowed yet afterward. Then he touched a man in the bottom of the boat, and called his name. "Will you spell me for a little while?" he said meekly.

"Sure, Billie," said the correspondent, awaking and dragging himself to a sitting position. They exchanged places carefully, and the oiler, cuddling down in the seawater at the cook's side, seemed to go to sleep instantly.

The particular violence of the sea had ceased. The waves came without snarling. The obligation of the man at the oars was to keep the boat headed so that the tilt of the rollers would not capsize her, and to preserve her from filling when the crests rushed past. The black waves were silent and hard to be seen in the darkness. Often one was almost upon the boat before the oarsman was aware.

In a low voice the correspondent addressed the captain. He was not sure that the captain was awake, although this iron man seemed to be always awake. "Captain, shall I keep her making for that light north, sir?"

The same steady voice answered him. "Yes. Keep it about two points off the port bow."

The cook had tied a lifebelt around himself in order to get even the warmth which this clumsy cork contrivance could donate, and he seemed almost stove-like when a rower, whose teeth invariably chattered wildly as soon as he ceased his labor, dropped down to sleep.

The correspondent, as he rowed, looked down at the two men sleeping underfoot. The cook's arm was around the oiler's shoulder, and, with their fragmentary clothing and haggard faces, they were the babes of the sea — a grotesque rendering of the old babes in the wood.

Later he must have grown stupid at his work, for suddenly there was a growling of water, and a crest came with a roar and a swash into the boat, and it was a wonder that it did not set the cook afloat in his lifebelt. The cook continued to sleep, but the oiler sat up, blinking his eyes and shaking with the new cold.

"Oh, I'm awful sorry, Billie," said the correspondent, contritely.

"That's all right, old boy," said the oiler, and lay down again and was asleep.

Presently it seemed that even the captain dozed, and the correspondent thought that he was the one man afloat on all the oceans. The wind had a voice as it came over the waves, and it was sadder than the end.

There was a long, loud swishing astern of the boat, and a gleaming trail of phosphorescence, like blue flame, was furrowed on the black waters. It might have been made by a monstrous knife.

Then there came a stillness, while the correspondent breathed with open mouth and looked at the sea.

Suddenly there was another swish and another long flash of bluish light, and this time it was alongside the boat, and might almost have been reached with an oar. The correspondent saw an enormous fin speed like a shadow through the water, hurling the crystalline spray and leaving the long glowing trail.

The correspondent looked over his shoulder at the captain. His face was hidden, and he seemed to be asleep. He looked at the babes of the sea. They certainly were asleep. So, being bereft of sympathy, he leaned a little way to one side and swore softly into the sea.

But the thing did not then leave the vicinity of the boat. Ahead or astern, on one side of the other, at intervals long or short, fled the long sparkling streak, and there was to be heard the *whirroo* of the dark fin. The speed and power of the thing was greatly to be admired. It cut the water like a gigantic and keen projectile.

The presence of this biding thing did not affect the man with the same horror that it would if he had been a picnicker. He simply looked at the sea dully and swore in an undertone.

Nevertheless, it is true that he did not wish to be alone with the thing. He wished one of his companions to awake by chance and keep him company with it. But the captain hung motionless over the water jar, and the oiler and the cook in the bottom of the boat were plunged in slumber.

## VI

"If I am going to be drowned — if I am going to be drowned — if I am going to be drowned, why, in the name of the seven mad gods who rule the sea, was I allowed to come thus far and contemplate sand and trees?"

During this dismal night, it may be remarked that a man would conclude that it was really the intention of the seven gods to drown him, despite the abominable injustice of it. For it was certainly an abominable injustice to drown a man who had worked so hard, so hard. The man felt it would be a crime most unnatural. Other people had drowned at sea since galleys swarmed with painted sails, but still —

When it occurs to a man that nature does not regard him as important, and that she feels she would not maim the universe by disposing of him, he at first wishes to throw bricks at the temple, and he hates deeply the fact that there was no bricks and no temples. Any visible expression of nature would surely be pelleted with his jeers.

Then, if there be no tangible thing to hoot, he feels, perhaps, the desire to confront a personification and indulge in pleas, bowed to one knee, and with hands supplicant, saying, "Yes, but I love myself."

A high cold star on a winter's night is the word he feels that she says to him. Thereafter he knows the pathos of his situation.

The men in the dinghy had not discussed these matters, but each had, no doubt, reflected upon them in silence and according to his mind. There was seldom any expression upon their faces save the general one of complete weariness. Speech was devoted to the business of the boat.

To chime the notes of his emotion, a verse mysteriously entered the correspondent's head. He had even forgotten that he had forgotten this verse, but it suddenly was in his mind.

> A soldier of the Legion lay dying in Algiers;
> There was lack of woman's nursing, there was dearth of woman's tears;
> But a comrade stood beside him, and he took that comrade's hand,
> And he said, "I never more shall see my own, my native land."

In his childhood the correspondent had been made acquainted with the fact that a soldier of the Legion lay dying in Algiers, but he had never regarded the fact as important. Myriads of his schoolfellows had informed him of the soldier's plight, but the dinning had naturally ended by making him perfectly indifferent. He had never considered it his affair that a soldier of the Legion lay dying in Algiers, nor had it appeared to him as a matter for sorrow. It was less to him than the breaking of a pencil's point.

Now, however, it quaintly came to him as a human, living thing. It was no longer merely a picture of a few throes in the breast of a poet, meanwhile drinking tea and warming his feet at the grate; it was an actuality — stern, mournful, and fine.

The correspondent plainly saw the soldier. He lay on the sand with his feet out straight and still. While his pale left hand was upon his chest in an attempt to thwart the going of his life, the blood came between his fingers. In the far Algerian distance, a city of low square forms was set against a sky that was faint with the last sunset hues. The correspondent, plying the oars and dreaming of the slow and slower movements of the lips of the soldier, was moved by a profound and perfectly impersonal comprehension. He was sorry for the soldier of the Legion who lay dying in Algiers.

The thing which had followed the boat and waited had evidently grown bored at the delay. There was no longer to be heard the slash of the cut-water, and there was no longer the flame of the long trail. The light in the north still glimmered, but it was apparently no nearer to the boat. Sometimes the boom of the surf rang in the correspondent's ears, and he turned the craft seaward then and rowed harder. Southward, some one had evidently built a watch fire on the beach. It was too low and too far to be seen, but it made a shimmering, roseate reflection upon the bluff in back of it, and this could be discerned from the boat. The wind came stronger, and sometimes a wave suddenly raged out like a mountain cat, and there was to be seen the sheen and sparkle of a broken crest.

The captain, in the bow, moved on his water jar and sat erect. "Pretty long night," he observed to the correspondent. He looked at the shore. "Those lifesaving people take their time."

"Did you see that shark playing around?"

"Yes, I saw him. He was a big fellow, all right."

"Wish I had known you were awake."

Later the correspondent spoke into the bottom of the boat. "Billie!" There was a slow and gradual disentanglement. "Billie, will you spell me?"

"Sure," said the oiler.

As soon as the correspondent touched the cold, comfortable seawater in the bottom of the boat and had huddled close to the cook's lifebelt he was deep in sleep, despite the fact that his teeth played all the popular airs. This sleep was so good to him that it was but a moment before he heard a voice call his name in a tone that demonstrated the last stages of exhaustion. "Will you spell me?"

"Sure, Billie."

The light in the north had mysteriously vanished, but the correspondent took his course from the wide-awake captain.

Later in the night they took the boat farther out to sea, and the captain directed the cook to take one oar at the stern and keep the boat facing the seas. He was to call out if he should hear the thunder of the surf. This plan enabled the oiler and the correspondent to get respite together. "We'll give those boys a chance to get into shape again," said the captain. They curled down and, after a few preliminary chatterings and trembles, slept once more the dead sleep. Neither knew they had bequeathed to the cook the company of another shark, or perhaps the same shark.

As the boat caroused on the waves, spray occasionally bumped over the side and gave them a fresh soaking, but this had no power to break their repose. The ominous slash of the wind and the water affected them as it would have affected mummies.

"Boys," said the cook, with the notes of every reluctance in his voice, "she's drifted in pretty close. I guess one of you had better take her to sea again." The correspondent, aroused, heard the crash of the toppled crests.

As he was rowing, the captain gave him some whiskey-and-water, and this steadied the chills out of him. "If I ever get ashore and anybody shows me even a photograph of an oar — "

At last there was a short conversation.

"Billie! . . . Billie, will you spell me?"

"Sure," said the oiler.

## VII

When the correspondent again opened his eyes, the sea and the sky were each of the gray hue of the dawning. Later, carmine and gold was painted upon the waters. The morning appeared finally, in its splendor, with a sky of pure blue, and the sunlight flamed on the tips of the waves.

On the distant dunes were set many little black cottages, and a tall white windmill reared above them. No man, nor dog, nor bicycle appeared on the beach. The cottages might have formed a deserted village.

The voyagers scanned the shore. A conference was held in the boat. "Well," said the captain, "if no help is coming, we might better try a run through the surf right away. If we stay out here much longer we will be too weak to do anything for ourselves at all." The others silently acquiesced in this reasoning. The boat was headed for the beach. The correspondent wondered if none ever ascended the tall wind-tower, and if then they never looked seaward. This tower was a giant, standing with its back to the plight of the ants. It represented in a degree, to the correspondent, the serenity of nature amid the struggles of the individual — nature in the wind, and nature in the vision of men. She did not seem cruel to him then, nor beneficent, nor treacherous, nor wise. But she was indifferent, flatly indifferent. It is, perhaps, plausible that a man in this situation, impressed with the unconcern of the universe, should see the innumerable flaws of his life, and have them taste wickedly in his mind, and wish for another chance. A distinction between right and wrong seems absurdly clear to him, then, in this new ignorance of the grave-edge, and he understands that if he were given another opportunity he would mend his conduct and his words, and be better and brighter during an introduction or at a tea.

"Now, boys," said the captain, "she is going to swamp sure. All we can do is to work her in as far as possible, and then when she swamps, pile out and scramble for the beach. Keep cool now, and don't jump until she swamps sure."

The oiler took the oars. Over his shoulders he scanned the surf. "Captain," he said, "I think I'd better bring her about and keep her head-on to the seas and back her in."

"All right, Billie," said the captain. "Back her in." The oiler swung the boat then, and, seated in the stern, the cook and the correspondent were obliged to look over their shoulders to contemplate the lonely and indifferent shore.

The monstrous inshore rollers heaved the boat high until the men were again enabled to see the white sheets of water scudding up the slanted beach. "We won't get in very close," said the captain. Each time a man could wrest his attention from the rollers, he turned his glance toward the shore, and in the expression of the eyes during this contemplation there was a singular quality. The correspondent, observing the others, knew that they were not afraid, but the full meaning of their glances was shrouded.

As for himself, he was too tired to grapple fundamentally with the fact. He tried to coerce his mind into thinking of it, but the mind was dominated at this time by the muscles, and the muscles said they did not care. It merely occurred to him that if he should drown it would be a shame.

There were no hurried words, no pallor, no plain agitation. The men simply looked at the shore. "Now, remember to get well clear of the boat when you jump," said the captain.

Seaward the crest of a roller suddenly fell with a thunderous crash, and the long white comber came roaring down upon the boat.

"Steady now," said the captain. The men were silent. They turned their eyes from the shore to the comber and waited. The boat slid up the incline, leaped at the furious top, bounced over it, and swung down the long back of the wave. Some water had been shipped, and the cook bailed it out.

But the next crest crashed also. The tumbling, boiling flood of white water caught the boat and whirled it almost perpendicular. Water swarmed in from all sides. The correspondent had his hands on the gunwale at this time, and when the water entered at that place he swiftly withdrew his fingers, as if he objected to wetting them.

The little boat, drunken with this weight of water, reeled and snuggled deeper into the sea.

"Bail her out, cook! Bail her out!" said the captain.

"All right, Captain," said the cook.

"Now, boys, the next one will do for us sure," said the oiler. "Mind to jump clear of the boat."

The third wave moved forward, huge, furious, implacable. It fairly swallowed the dinghy, and almost simultaneously the men tumbled into the sea. A piece of lifebelt had lain in the bottom of the boat, and as the correspondent went overboard he held this to his chest with his left hand.

The January water was icy, and he reflected immediately that it was colder than he had expected to find it off the coast of Florida. This appeared to his dazed mind as a fact important enough to be noted at the time. The coldness of the water was sad; it was tragic. This fact was somehow mixed and confused with his opinion of his own situation, so that it seemed almost a proper reason for tears. The water was cold.

When he came to the surface he was conscious of little but the noisy water. Afterward he saw his companions in the sea. The oiler was ahead in the race. He was swimming strongly and rapidly. Off to the correspondent's left, the cook's great white and corked back bulged out of the water; and in the rear the captain was hanging with his one good hand to the keel of the overturned dinghy.

There is a certain immovable quality to a shore, and the correspondent wondered at it amid the confusion of the sea.

It seemed also very attractive; but the correspondent knew that it was a long journey, and he paddled leisurely. The piece of life preserver lay under him, and sometimes he whirled down the incline of a wave as if he were on a hand-sled.

But finally he arrived at a place in the sea where travel was beset with difficulty. He did not pause swimming to inquire what manner of current had caught him, but there his progress ceased. The shore was set before him like a bit of scenery on a stage, and he looked at it and understood with his eyes each detail of it.

As the cook passed, much farther to the left, the captain was calling to him, "Turn over on your back, cook! Turn over on your back and use the oar."

"All right, sir." The cook turned on his back, and, paddling with an oar, went ahead as if he were a canoe.

Presently the boat also passed to the left of the correspondent, with the captain clinging with one hand to the keel. He would have appeared like a man raising himself to look over a board fence if it were not for the extraordinary gymnastics of the boat. The correspondent marveled that the captain could still hold to it.

They passed on nearer to shore — the oiler, the cook, the captain — and following them went the water jar, bouncing gaily over the seas.

The correspondent remained in the grip of this strange new enemy — a current. The shore, with its white slope of sand and its green bluff topped with little silent cottages, was spread like a picture before him. It was very near to him then, but he was impressed as one who, in a gallery, looks at a scene from Brittany or Algiers.

He thought: "I am going to drown? Can it be possible? Can it be possible? Can it be possible?" Perhaps an individual must consider his own death to be the final phenomenon of nature.

But later a wave perhaps whirled him out of this small deadly current, for he found suddenly that he could again make progress toward the shore. Later still he was aware that the captain, clinging with one hand to the keel of the dinghy, had his face turned away from the shore and toward him, and was calling his name. "Come to the boat! Come to the boat!"

In his struggle to reach the captain and boat, he reflected that when one gets properly wearied drowning must really be a comfortable arrangement — a cessation of hostilities accompanied by a large degree of relief; and he was glad of it, for the main thing in his mind for some moments had been horror of the temporary agony. He did not wish to be hurt.

Presently he saw a man running along the shore. He was undressing with most remarkable speed. Coat, trousers, shirt, everything flew magically off him.

"Come to the boat!" called the captain.

"All right, Captain." As the correspondent paddled, he saw the captain let himself down to bottom and leave the boat. Then the correspondent performed his one little marvel of the voyage. A large wave caught him and flung him with ease and supreme speed completely over the boat and far beyond it. It struck him even then as an event in gymnastics and a true miracle of the sea. An overturned boat in the surf is not a plaything to a swimming man.

The correspondent arrived in water that reached only to his waist, but his condition did not enable him to stand for more than a moment. Each wave knocked him into a heap, and the undertow pulled at him.

Then he saw the man who had been running and undressing, and undressing and running, come bounding into the water. He dragged ashore the cook, and then waded toward the captain; but the captain waved him away and sent him to the correspondent. He was naked — naked as a tree in winter, but a halo was about his head, and he shone like a saint. He gave a strong pull, and a long drag, and a bully heave at the correspondent's hand. The correspondent, schooled in the minor formulae, said, "Thanks, old man." But suddenly the man cried, "What's that?" He pointed a swift finger. The correspondent said, "Go."

In the shallows, face downward, lay the oiler. His forehead touched sand that was periodically, between each wave, clear of the sea.

The correspondent did not know all that transpired afterward. When he achieved safe ground he fell, striking the sand with each particular part of his body. It was as if he had dropped from a roof, but the thud was grateful to him.

It seems that instantly the beach was populated with men with blankets, clothes, and flasks, and women with coffeepots and all the remedies sacred to their minds. The welcome of the land to the men from the sea was warm and generous; but a still and dripping shape was carried slowly up the beach, and the land's welcome for it could only be the different and sinister hospitality of the grave.

When it came night, the white waves paced to and fro in the moonlight, and the wind brought the sound of the great sea's voice to the men on the shore, and they felt that they could then be interpreters.

# Samuel Langhorne Clemens (1835–1910)

SAMUEL LANGHORNE CLEMENS, better known as Mark Twain, America's most famous humorist, and one of its bitterest cynics, was born in Florida and grew up in Hannibal, Missouri. The son of a restless Virginian constantly questing in vain for riches, Sam became a school dropout at twelve when his father died. His first writing was for a newspaper after he had been apprenticed to it as a journeyman printer. Frustrated in a plan to seek his fortune in South America, he became a Mississippi steamboat pilot, later taking as a pseudonym the call pilots used to signify "two fathoms deep!" As a sympathizer with the South he volunteered for the Confederate Army in which he served briefly. Afterward he went West where his life as a miner and newspaperman gave him the material for his first fiction, *The Celebrated Jumping Frog of Calaveras County and Other Sketches* (1867). His frontier humor won him immediate popularity, further enhanced by his second book, *Innocents Abroad* (1869), lampooning the ancient culture of Europe, Egypt, and the Holy Land. In 1870 Clemens married Olivia Langdon, a conservative society woman, and settled in genteel surroundings in Hartford, Connecticut. Although he was to write many of his most important books thereafter, especially *The Adventures of Tom Sawyer* (1876) and *The Adventures of Huckleberry Finn* (1884), the effect on Clemens of the change from the rough and bawdy frontier to the Puritanical atmosphere of a small New England city has caused much critical debate. Quixotic investments forced him to take on uncongenial lecturing tours. The deaths of his wife and two daughters saddened his last years.

"The Man That Corrupted Hadleyburg" is considered the tour de force among Clemens's short stories. His first short story, "The Celebrated Jumping Frog of Calaveras County," which made him famous, was written in 1865 and "The Man That Corrupted Hadleyburg" in 1900. Much more than thirty-five years separates the two tales. The first mirrors the rollicking carefreeness and good nature of pioneer life in the old West. Bitterness and cynicism permeate the second. It also is written in startling contrast to *Tom Sawyer* and *Huckleberry Finn*. A reader can wonder who really was corrupted — the people of Hadleyburg or Sam Clemens, not through sin but by the mores of his time? Four years before, he had endured a bitter bankruptcy due to failures of rash investments that he, already comfortably well-off, hoped would make him fabulously rich. Did he see a moral for himself in Hadleyburg? Or, perhaps, it was as Van Wyck Brooks wrote in his celebrated *Ordeal of Mark Twain*, the blackness in his later writing was due to the frustrations of the Puritan New England society into which he had married. And when he escaped it into such occasional ribald outbursts as the notorious "1601," he was quickly suppressed.

# The Man That Corrupted Hadleyburg

IT WAS many years ago. Hadleyburg was the most honest and upright town in all the region round about. It had kept that reputation unsmirched during three generations, and was prouder of it than of any other of its possessions. It was so proud of it, and so anxious to insure its perpetuation, that it began to teach the principles of honest dealing to its babies in the cradle, and made the like teachings the staple of their culture thenceforward through all the years devoted to their education. Also, throughout the formative years temptations were kept out of the way of the young people, so that their honesty could have every chance to harden and solidify, and become a part of their very bone. The neighboring towns were jealous of this honorable supremacy, and affected to sneer at Hadleyburg's pride in it and call it vanity; but all the same they were obliged to acknowledge that Hadleyburg was in reality an incorruptible town; and if pressed they would also acknowledge that the mere fact that a young man hailed from Hadleyburg was all the recommendation he needed when he went forth from his natal town to seek for responsible employment.

But at last, in the drift of time, Hadleyburg had the ill luck to offend a passing stranger — possibly without knowing it, certainly without caring, for Hadleyburg was sufficient unto itself, and cared not a rap for strangers or their opinions. Still, it would have been well to make an exception in this one's case, for he was a bitter man and revengeful. All through his wanderings during a whole year he kept his injury in mind, and gave all his leisure moments to trying to invent a compensating satisfaction for it. He contrived many plans, and all of them were good, but none of them was quite sweeping enough; the poorest of them would hurt a great many individuals, but what he wanted was a plan which would comprehend the entire town, and not let so much as one person escape unhurt. At last he had a fortunate idea, and when it fell into his brain it lit up his whole head with an evil joy. He began to form a plan at once, saying to himself, "That is the thing to do — I will corrupt the town."

Six months later he went to Hadleyburg, and arrived in a buggy at the house of the old cashier of the bank about ten at night. He got a sack out of the buggy, shouldered it, and staggered with it through the cottage yard, and knocked at the door. A woman's voice said "Come in," and he entered, and set his sack behind the stove in the parlor, saying politely to the old lady who sat reading the *Missionary Herald* by the lamp:

"Pray keep your seat, madam, I will not disturb you. There — now it is pretty well concealed; one would hardly know it was there. Can I see your husband a moment, madam?"

No, he was gone to Brixton, and might not return before morning.

"Very well, madam, it is no matter. I merely wanted to leave that sack in his care, to be delivered to the rightful owner when he shall be found. I am a stranger; he does not know me; I am merely passing through the town to-night to discharge a matter which has been long in my mind.

My errand is now completed, and I go pleased and a little proud, and you will never see me again. There is a paper attached to the sack which will explain everything. Good-night, madam."

The old lady was afraid of the mysterious big stranger, and was glad to see him go. But her curiosity was roused, and she went straight to the sack and brought away the paper. It began as follows:

> "*TO BE PUBLISHED: or, the right man sought out by private inquiry — either will answer. This sack contains gold coin weighing a hundred and sixty pounds four ounces —*"

"Mercy on us, and the door not locked!"

Mrs. Richards flew to it all in a tremble and locked it, then pulled down the window-shades and stood frightened, worried, and wondering if there was anything else she could do toward making herself and the money more safe. She listened awhile for burglars, then surrendered to curiosity and went back to the lamp and finished reading the paper:

> "*I am a foreigner, and am presently going back to my own country, to remain there permanently. I am grateful to America for what I have received at her hands during my long stay under her flag; and to one of her citizens — a citizen of Hadleyburg — I am especially grateful for a great kindness done me a year or two ago. Two great kindnesses, in fact. I will explain. I was a gambler. I say I WAS. I was a ruined gambler. I arrived in this village at night, hungry and without a penny. I asked for help — in the dark; I was ashamed to beg in the light. I begged of the right man. He gave me twenty dollars — that it to say, he gave me life, as I considered it. He also gave me a fortune; for out of that money I have made myself rich at the gaming-table. And finally, a remark which he made to me has remained with me to this day, and has at last conquered me; and in conquering has saved the remnant of my morals: I shall gamble no more. Now I have no idea who that man was, but I want him found, and I want him to have this money, to give away, throw away, or keep, as he pleases. It is merely my way of testifying my gratitude to him. If I could stay, I would find him myself; but no matter, he will be found. This is an honest town, an incorruptible town, and I know I can trust it without fear. This man can be identified by the remark which he made to me; I feel persuaded that he will remember it.*
>
> "*And now my plan is this: If you prefer to conduct the inquiry privately, do so. Tell the contents of this present writing to any one who is likely to be the right man. If he shall answer, 'I am the man; the remark I made was so-and-so,' apply the test — to wit: open the sack, and in it you will find a sealed envelope containing that remark. If the remark mentioned by the candidate tallies with it, give him the money, and ask no further questions, for he is certainly the right man.*
>
> "*But if you shall prefer a public inquiry, then publish this present*

*writing in the local paper — with these instructions added, to wit: Thirty days from now, let the candidate appear at the town-hall at eight in the evening (Friday), and hand his remark, in a sealed envelope, to the Rev. Mr. Burgess (if he will be kind enough to act); and let Mr. Burgess there and then destroy the seals of the sack, open it, and see if the remark is correct; if correct, let the money be delivered, with my sincere gratitude, to my bene-factor thus identified."*

Mrs. Richards sat down, gently quivering with excitement, and was soon lost in thinkings — after this pattern: "What a strange thing it is! . . . And what a fortune for that kind man who set his bread afloat upon the waters! . . . If it had only been my husband that did it! . . . for we are so poor, so old and poor! . . ." Then, with a sigh — "But it was not my Edward; no, it was not he that gave a stranger twenty dollars. It is a pity, too; I see it now . . ." Then, with a shudder — "But it is *gambler's* money! the wages of sin: we couldn't take it; we couldn't touch it. I don't like to be near it; it seems a defilement." She moved to a farther chair . . . "I wish Edward would come, and take it to the bank; a bur-glar might come at any moment; it is dreadful to be here all alone with it."

At eleven Mr. Richards arrived, and while his wife was saying, "I am *so* glad you've come!" he was saying, "I'm so tired — tired clear out; it is dreadful to be poor, and have to make these dismal journeys at my time of life. Always at the grind, grind, grind, on a salary — another man's slave, and he sitting at home in his slippers, rich and comfortable."

"I am so sorry for you, Edward, you know that; but be comforted: we have our livelihood; we have our good name —"

"Yes, Mary, and that is everything. Don't mind my talk — it's just a moment's irritation and doesn't mean anything. Kiss me — there, it's all gone now, and I am not complaining any more. What have you been getting? What's in the sack?"

Then his wife told him the great secret. It dazed him for a moment; then he said:

"It weighs a hundred and sixty pounds? Why, Mary, it's for-ty thou-sand dollars — think of it — a whole fortune! Not ten men in this village are worth that much. Give me the paper."

He skimmed through it and said:

"Isn't it an adventure! Why, it's a romance; it's like the impossible things one reads about in books, and never sees in life." He was well stirred up now, cheerful, even gleeful. He tapped his old wife on the cheek, and said, humorously, "Why, we're rich, Mary, rich; all we've got to do is to bury the money and burn the papers. If the gambler ever comes to inquire, we'll merely look coldly upon him and say: 'What is this nonsense you are talking? We have never heard of you and your sack of gold before'; and then he would look foolish, and — "

"And in the meantime, while you are running on with your jokes, the money is still here, and it is fast getting along toward burglar-time."

"True. Very well, what shall we do — make the inquiry private? No, not that: it would spoil the romance. The public method is better. Think what a noise it will make! And it will make all the other towns jealous; for no stranger would trust such a thing to any town but Hadleyburg, and they know it. It's a great card for us. I must get to the printing-office, now, or I shall be too late."

"But stop — stop — don't leave me here alone with it, Edward!"

But he was gone. For only a little while, however. Not far from his own house he met the editor-proprietor of the paper, and gave him the document, and said, "Here is a good thing for you, Cox — put it in!"

"It may be too late, Mr. Richards, but I'll see."

At home again he and his wife sat down to talk the charming mystery over; they were in no condition for sleep. The first question was, "Who could the citizen have been who gave the stranger the twenty dollars?" It seemed a simple one; both answered it in the same breath—

"Barclay Goodson."

"Yes," said Richards, "he would have done it, and it would have been like him, but there's not another in the town."

"Everybody will grant that, Edward — grant it privately, anyway. For six months, now, the village has been its own proper self once more — honest, narrow, self-righteous, and stingy."

"It's what he always called it, to the day of his death — said it right out publicly, too."

"Yes, and he was hated for it."

"Oh, of course; but he didn't care. I reckon he was the best-hated man among us, except the Reverend Burgess."

"Well, Burgess deserves it — he will never get another congregation here. Mean as the town is, it knows how to estimate *him*. Edward, doesn't it seem odd that the stranger should appoint Burgess to deliver the money?"

"Well, yes — it does. That is — that is —"

"Why so much that-*is*-ing? Would *you* select him?"

"Mary, maybe the stranger knows him better than this village does."

"Much *that* would help Burgess!"

The husband seemed perplexed for an answer; the wife kept a steady eye upon him, and waited. Finally Richards said, with the hesitancy of one who is making a statement which is likely to encounter doubt,

"Mary, Burgess is not a bad man."

His wife was certainly surprised.

"Nonsense!" she exclaimed.

"He is not a bad man. I know. The whole of his unpopularity had its foundation in that one thing — the thing that made so much noise."

"That 'one thing,' indeed! As if that 'one thing' wasn't enough, all by itself."

"Plenty. Plenty. Only he wasn't guilty of it."

"How you talk! Not guilty of it! Everybody knows he *was* guilty."

"Mary, I give you my word — he was innocent."

"I can't believe it, and I don't. How do you know?"

"It is a confession. I am ashamed, but I will make it. I was the only man who knew he was innocent. I could have saved him, and — and — well, you know how the town was wrought up — I hadn't the pluck to do it. It would have turned everybody against me. I felt mean, ever so mean; but I didn't dare; I hadn't the manliness to face that."

Mary looked troubled, and for a while was silent. Then she said, stammeringly:

"I — I don't think it would have done for you to — to — One mustn't — er — public opinion — one has to be so careful — so — " It was a difficult road, and she got mired; but after a little she got started again. "It was a great pity, but — Why, we couldn't afford it, Edward — we couldn't indeed. Oh, I wouldn't have had you do it for anything!"

"It would have lost us the good-will of so many people, Mary; and then — and then —"

"What troubles me now is, what *he* thinks of us, Edward."

"He? *He* doesn't suspect that I could have saved him."

"Oh," exclaimed the wife, in a tone of relief, "I am glad of that. As long as he doesn't know that you could have saved him, he — he — well, that makes it a great deal better. Why, I might have known he didn't know, because he is always trying to be friendly with us, as little encouragement as we give him. More than once people have twitted me with it. There's the Wilsons, and the Wilcoxes, and the Harknesses, they have a mean pleasure in saying, '*Your friend* Burgess,' because they know it pesters me. I wish he wouldn't persist in liking us so; I can't think why he keeps it up."

"I can explain it. It's another confession. When the thing was new and hot, and the town made a plan to ride him on a rail, my conscience hurt me so that I couldn't stand it, and I went privately and gave him notice, and he got out of the town and staid out till it was safe to come back."

"Edward! If the town had found it out —"

"*Don't!* It scares me yet, to think of it. I repented of it the minute it was done; and I was even afraid to tell you, lest your face might betray it to somebody. I didn't sleep any that night, for worrying. But after a few days I saw that no one was going to suspect me, and after that I got to feeling glad I did it. And I feel glad yet, Mary — glad through and through."

"So do I, now, for it would have been a dreadful way to treat him. Yes, I'm glad; for really you did owe him that, you know. But, Edward, suppose it should come out yet, some day!"

"It won't."

"Why?"

"Because everybody thinks it was Goodson."

"Of course they would!"

"Certainly. And of course *he* didn't care. They persuaded poor old Sawlsberry to go and charge it on him, and he went blustering over there and did it. Goodson looked him over, like as if he was hunting for a place on him that he could despise the most, then he says, 'So you are the Committee of Inquiry, are you?' Sawlsberry said that was about what he was. 'Hm. Do they require particulars, or do you reckon a kind of a *general* answer will do?' 'If they require particulars, I will come back, Mr. Goodson; I will take the general answer first.' 'Very well, then, tell them to go to hell — I reckon that's general enough. And I'll give you some advice, Sawlsberry; when you come back for the particulars, fetch a basket to carry the relics of yourself home in.' "

"Just like Goodson; it's got all the marks. He had only one vanity: he thought he could give advice better than any other person."

"It settled the business, and saved us, Mary. The subject was dropped."

"Bless you, I'm not doubting *that*."

Then they took up the gold-sack mystery again, with strong interest. Soon the conversation began to suffer breaks — interruptions caused by absorbed thinkings. The breaks grew more and more frequent. At last Richards lost himself wholly in thought. He sat long, gazing vacantly at the floor, and by and by he began to punctuate his thoughts with little nervous movements of his hands that seemed to indicate vexation. Meantime his wife too had relapsed into a thoughtful silence, and her movements were beginning to show a troubled discomfort. Finally Richards got up and strode aimlessly about the room, plowing his hands through his hair, much as a somnambulist might do who was having a bad dream. Then he seemed to arrive at a definite purpose; and without a word he put on his hat and passed quickly out of the house. His wife sat brooding, with a drawn face, and did not seem to be aware that she was alone. Now and then she murmured, "Lead us not into t— . . . but — but — we are so poor, so poor! . . . Lead us not into . . . Ah, who would be hurt by it? — and no one would ever know . . . Lead us . . ." The voice died out in mumblings. After a little she glanced up and muttered in a half-frightened, half-glad way —

"He is gone! But, oh dear, he may be too late — too late . . . Maybe not — maybe there is still time." She rose and stood thinking, nervously clasping and unclasping her hands. A slight shudder shook her frame, and she said, out of a dry throat, "God forgive me — it's awful to think such things — but . . . Lord, how we are made — how strangely we are made!"

She turned the light low, and slipped stealthily over and kneeled down by the sack and felt of it ridgy sides with her hands, and fondled them lovingly; and there was a gloating light in her poor old eyes. She fell into fits of absence; and came half out of them at times to mutter, "If we had only waited! — oh, if we had only waited a little, and not been in such a hurry!"

Meantime Cox had gone home from his office and told his wife all about the strange things that had happened, and they had talked it over eagerly, and guessed that the late Goodson was the only man in the town who could have helped a suffering stranger with so noble a sum as twenty dollars. Then there was a pause, and the two became thoughtful and silent. And by and by nervous and fidgety. At last the wife said, as if to herself,

"Nobody knows this secret but the Richardses . . . and us . . . nobody."

The husband came out of his thinkings with a slight start, and gazed wistfully at his wife, whose face was become very pale; then he hesitatingly rose, and glanced furtively at his hat, then at his wife — a sort of mute inquiry. Mrs. Cox swallowed once or twice, with her hand at her throat, then in place of speech she nodded her head. In a moment she was alone, and mumbling to herself.

And now Richards and Cox were hurrying through the deserted streets, from opposite directions. They met, panting, at the foot of the printing-office stairs; by the night-light there they read each other's face. Cox whispered,

"Nobody knows about this but us?"

The whispered answer was,

"Not a soul — on honor, not a soul!"

"If it isn't too late to —"

The men were starting up-stairs; at this moment they were overtaken by a boy, and Cox asked,

"Is that you, Johnny?"

"Yes, sir."

"You needn't ship the early mail — nor *any* mail; wait till I tell you."

"It's already gone, sir."

"*Gone?*" It had the sound of an unspeakable disappointment in it.

"Yes, sir. Time-table for Brixton and all the towns beyond changed to-day, sir — had to get the papers in twenty minutes earlier than common. I had to rush; if I had been two minutes later —"

The men turned and walked slowly away, not waiting to hear the rest. Neither of them spoke during ten minutes; then Cox said, in a vexed tone,

"What possessed you to be in such a hurry, I can't make out."

The answer was humble enough:

"I see it now, but somehow I never thought, you know, until it was too late. But the next time — "

"Next time be hanged! It won't come in a thousand years."

Then the friends separated without a good-night, and dragged themselves home with the gait of mortally stricken men. At their homes their wives sprang up with an eager "Well?" — then saw the answer with their eyes and sank down sorrowing, without waiting for it to come in words. In both houses a discussion followed of a heated sort — a new thing; there had been discussions before, but not heated ones, not ungentle ones. The discussions to-night were a sort of seeming plagiarisms of each other. Mrs. Richard said,

"If you had only waited, Edward — if you had only stopped to think; but no, you must run straight to the printing-office and spread it all over the world."

"It *said* publish it."

"That is nothing; it also said do it privately, if you liked. There, now — is that true, or not?"

"Why, yes — yes, it is true; but when I thought what a stir it would make, and what a compliment it was to Hadleyburg that a stranger should trust it so —"

"Oh, certainly, I know all that; but if you had only stopped to think, you would have seen that you *couldn't* find the right man, because he is in his grave, and hasn't left chick nor child nor relation behind him; and as long as the money went to somebody that awfully needed it, and nobody would be hurt by it, and — and —"

She broke down crying. Her husband tried to think of some comforting thing to say, and presently came out with this:

"But after all, Mary, it must be for the best — it *must* be; we know that. And we must remember that it was so ordered —"

"Ordered! Oh, everything's *ordered*, when a person has to find some way out when he has been stupid. Just the same, it was *ordered* that the money should come to us in this special way, and it was you that must take it on yourself to go meddling with the designs of Providence — and who gave you the right? It was wicked, that is what is was — just blasphemous presumption, and no more becoming to a meek and humble professor of —"

"But, Mary, you know how we have been trained all our lives long, like the whole village, till it is absolutely second nature to us to stop not a single moment to think when there's an honest thing to be done —"

"Oh, I know it, I know it — it's been one everlasting training and training and training in honesty — honesty shielded, from the very cradle, against every possible temptation, and so it's *artificial* honesty, and weak as water when temptation comes, as we have seen this night. God knows I never had shade nor shadow of a doubt of my petrified and indestructible honesty until now — and now, under the very first big and real temptation, I — Edward, it is my belief that this town's honesty is as rotten as mine is; as rotten as yours is. It is a mean town, a hard, stingy town, and hasn't a virtue in the world but this honesty it is so celebrated for and so conceited about; and so help me, I do believe that if ever the day comes that its honesty falls under great temptation, its grand reputation will go to ruin like a house of cards. There, now, I've made confession, and I feel better; I am a humbug, and I've been one all my life, without knowing it. Let no man call me honest again — I will not have it."

"I — well, Mary, I feel a good deal as you do; I certainly do. It seems strange, too, so strange. I never could have believed it — never."

A long silence followed; both were sunk in thought. At last the wife looked up and said,

"I know what you are thinking, Edward."

Richards had the embarrassed look of a person who is caught.

"I am ashamed to confess it, Mary, but —"

"It's no matter, Edward, I was thinking the same question myself."

"I hope so. State it."

"You were thinking, if a body could only guess out *what the remark was* that Goodson made to the stranger.

"It's perfectly true. I feel guilty and ashamed. And you?"

"I'm past it. Let us make a pallet here, we've got to stand watch till the bank vault opens in the morning and admits the sack . . . Oh dear, oh dear — if we hadn't made the mistake!"

The pallet was made, and Mary said:

"The open sesame — what could it have been? I do wonder what that remark could have been? But come; we will get to bed now."

"And sleep?"

"No: think."

"Yes, think."

By this time the Coxes too had completed their spat and their reconciliation, and were turning in — to think, to think, and toss, and fret, and worry over what the remark could possibly have been which Goodson made to the stranded derelict; that golden remark; that remark worth forty thousand dollars, cash.

The reason that the village telegraph office was open later than usual that night was this: The foreman of Cox's paper was the local representative of the Associated Press. One might say its honorary representative, for it wasn't four times a year that he could furnish thirty words that would be accepted. But this time it was different. His dispatch stating what he had caught got an instant answer:

*"Send the whole thing — all the details — twelve hundred words."*

A colossal order! The foreman filled the bill; and he was the proudest man in the State. By breakfast-time the next morning the name of Hadleyburg the Incorruptible was on every lip in America, from Montreal to the Gulf, from the glaciers of Alaska to the orange-groves of Florida; and millions and millions of people were discussing the stranger and his money-sack, and wondering if the right man would be found, and hoping some more news about the matter would come soon — right away.

## II

Hadleyburg village woke up world-celebrated — astonished — happy — vain. Vain beyond imagination. Its nineteen principal citizens and their wives went about shaking hands with each other, and beaming, and smiling, and congratulating, and saying *this* thing adds a new word to the dictionary — *Hadleyburg*, synonym for *incorruptible* — destined to live in dictionaries forever! And the minor and unimportant citizens and their wives went around acting in much the same way. Everybody ran to the bank to see the gold-sack; and before noon grieved and envious crowds began to flock in from Brixton and all neighboring towns; and that afternoon and next day reporters began to arrive from everywhere to verify the sack and its history and write the whole thing up anew, and make dashing free-hand pictures of the sack, and of Richards's house, and the bank, and the Presbyterian church, and the Baptist church, and the public square, and the town-hall where the test would be applied and the money delivered; and damnable portraits of the Richardses, and Pinkerton the banker, and Cox, and the foreman, and Reverend Burgess, and the postmaster — and even of Jack Halliday, who was the loafing, good-natured, no-account, irreverent fisherman, hunter, boys' friend, stray-dogs' friend, typical "Sam Lawson" of the town. The little mean, smirking, oily Pinkerton showed the sack to all comers, and rubbed his sleek palms together pleasantly, and enlarged upon the town's fine old reputation for honesty and upon this wonderful endorsement of it, and hoped and believed that the example would now spread far and wide over the American world, and be epoch-making in the matter of moral regeneration. And so on, and so on.

By the end of the week things had quieted down again; the wild intoxication of pride and joy had sobered to a soft, sweet, silent delight — a sort of deep, nameless, unutterable content. All faces bore a look of peaceful, holy happiness.

Then a change came. It was a gradual change: so gradual that its beginnings were hardly noticed; maybe were not noticed at all, except by Jack Halliday, who always noticed everything; and always made fun of it, too, no matter what it was. He began to throw out chaffing remarks about people not looking quite so happy as they did a day or two ago; and next he claimed that the new aspect was deepening to positive sadness; next, that it was taking on a sick look; and finally he said that everybody was become so moody, thoughtful, and absent-minded that he could rob the meanest man in town of a cent out of the bottom of his breeches pocket and not disturb his revery.

At this stage — or at about this stage — a saying like this was dropped at bedtime — with a sigh, usually — by the head of each of the nineteen principal households: "Ah, what *could* have been the remark that Goodson made?"

And straightway — with a shudder — came this, from the man's wife:

"Oh, *don't!* What horrible thing are you mulling in your mind? Put it away from you, for God's sake!"

But that question was wrung from those men again the next night — and got the same retort. But weaker.

And the third night the men uttered the question yet again — with anguish, and absently. This time — and the following night — the wives fidgeted feebly, and tried to say something. But didn't.

And the night after that they found their tongues and responded — longingly,

"Oh, if we *could* only guess!"

Halliday's comments grew daily more and more sparklingly disagreeable and disparaging. He went diligently about, laughing at the town, individually and in mass. But his laugh was the only one left in the village: it fell upon a hollow and mournful vacancy and emptiness. Not even a smile was findable anywhere. Halliday carried a cigar-box around on a tripod, playing that it was a camera, and halted all passers and aimed the thing and said, "Ready! — now look pleasant, please," but not even this capital joke could surprise the dreary faces into any softening.

So three weeks passed — one week was left. It was Saturday evening — after supper. Instead of the aforetime Saturday-evening flutter and bustle and shopping and larking, the streets were empty and desolate. Richards and his old wife sat apart in their little parlor — miserable and thinking. This was become their evening habit now: the lifelong habit which had preceded it, of reading, knitting, and contented chat, or receiving or paying neighborly calls, was dead and gone and forgotten, ages ago — two or three weeks ago; nobody talked now, nobody read, nobody visited — the whole village sat at home, sighing, worrying, silent. Trying to guess out that remark.

The postman left a letter. Richards glanced listlessly at the superscription and the postmark — unfamiliar, both — and tossed the letter on the table and resumed his might-have-beens and his hopeless dull miseries where he had left them off. Two or three hours later his wife got wearily up and was going away to bed without a good-night — custom now — but she stopped near the letter and eyed it awhile with a dead interest, then broke it open, and began to skim it over. Richards, sitting there with his chair tilted back against the wall and his chin between his knees, heard something fall. It was his wife. He sprang to her side, but she cried out:

"Leave me alone, I am too happy. Read the letter — read it!"

He did. He devoured it, his brain reeling. The letter was from a distant State, and it said:

*"I am a stranger to you, but no matter: I have something to tell. I have just arrived home from Mexico, and learned about that episode. Of course you do not know who made that remark, but I know, and I am the only person living who does know. It was* GOODSON. *I knew him well, many years ago. I passed through your village that very night, and was his guest till the midnight train came along. I overheard him make that remark to the stranger in the dark — it was in Hale Alley. He and I talked of it the rest of the way home, and while smoking in his house. He mentioned many of your villagers in the course of his talk — most of them in a very uncomplimentary way, but two or three favorably; among these latter yourself. I say 'favorably' — nothing stronger. I remember his saying he did not actually* LIKE *any person in the town — not one; but that you — I* THINK *he said you — am almost sure — had done him a very great service once, possibly without knowing the full value of it, and he wished he had a fortune, he would leave it to you when he died, and a curse apiece for the rest of the citizens. Now, then, if it was you that did him that service, you are his legitimate heir, and entitled to the sack of gold. I know that I can trust to your honor and honesty, for in a citizen of Hadleyburg these virtues are an unfailing inheritance, and so I am going to reveal to you the remark, well satisfied that if you are not the right man you will seek and find the right one and see that poor Goodson's debt of gratitude for the service referred to is paid. This is the remark:* 'YOU ARE FAR FROM BEING A BAD MAN: GO AND REFORM.'*

"HOWARD L. STEPHENSON."*

"Oh, Edward, the money is ours, and I am so grateful, *oh*, so grateful — kiss me, dear, it's forever since we kissed — and we needed it so — the money — and now you are free of Pinkerton and his bank, and nobody's slave any more; it seems to me I could fly for joy."

It was a happy half-hour that the couple spent there on the settee caressing each other; it was the old days come again — days that had begun with their courtship and lasted without a break till the stranger brought the deadly money. By and by the wife said:

"Oh, Edward, how lucky it was you did him that grand service, poor Goodson! I never liked him, but I love him now. And it was fine and beautiful of you never to mention it or brag about it." Then, with a touch of reproach, "But you ought to have told *me*, Edward, you ought to have told your wife, you know."

"Well, I — er — well, Mary, you see —"

"Now stop hemming and hawing, and tell me about it, Edward. I always loved you, and now I'm proud of you. Everybody believes there was only one good generous soul in this village, and now it turns out that you — Edward, why don't you tell me?"

"Well — er — er — Why, Mary, I can't!"

"You *can't*? *Why* can't you?"

"You see, he — well, he — he made me promise I wouldn't."

The wife looked him over, and said, very slowly,

"Made — you — promise? Edward, what do you tell me that for?"

"Mary, do you think I would lie?"

She was troubled and silent for a moment, then she laid her hand within his and said:

"No . . . no. We have wandered far enough from our bearings — God spare us that! In all your life you have never uttered a lie. But now — now that the foundations of things seem to be crumbling from under us, we — we —" She lost her voice for a moment, then said, brokenly, "Lead us not into temptation . . . I think you made the promise, Edward. Let it rest so. Let us keep away from that ground. Now — that is all gone by; let us be happy again; it is no time for clouds."

Edward found it something of an effort to comply, for his mind kept wandering — trying to remember what the service was that he had done Goodson.

The couple lay awake the most of the night, Mary happy and busy, Edward busy but not so happy. Mary was planning what she would do with the money. Edward was trying to recall that service. At first his conscience was sore on account of the lie he had told Mary — if it was a lie. After much reflection — suppose it *was* a lie? What then? Was it such a great matter? Aren't we always *acting* lies? Then why not *tell* them? Look at Mary — look what she had done. While he was hurrying off on his honest errand, what was she doing? Lamenting because the papers hadn't been destroyed and the money kept! Is theft better than lying?

*That* point lost its sting — the lie dropped into the background and left comfort behind it. The next point came to the front: *Had* he rendered that service? Well, here was Goodson's own evidence as reported in Stephenson's letter, there could be no better evidence than that — it was even *proof* that he had rendered it. Of course. So that point was settled . . .No, not quite. He recalled with a wince that this unknown Mr. Stephenson was just a trifle unsure as to whether the performer of it was Richards or some other — and, oh dear, he had put Richards on his honor! He must himself decide whither that money must go — and Mr. Stephenson was not doubting that if he was the wrong man he would go honorably and find the right one. Oh, it was odious to put a man in such a situation — ah, why couldn't Stephenson have left out that doubt! What did he want to intrude that for?

Further reflection. How did it happen that *Richards's* name remained in Stephenson's mind as indicating the right man, and not some other man's name? That looked good. Yes, that looked very good. In fact, it went on looking better and better, straight along — until by and by it grew into positive *proof*. And then Richards put the matter at once out of his mind, for he had a private instinct that a proof once established is better left so.

He was feeling reasonably comfortable now, but there was still one other detail that kept pushing itself on his notice: of course he had done that service — that was settled; but what *was* that service? He must recall it — he would not go to sleep till he had recalled it; it would make his peace of mind perfect. And so he thought and thought. He thought of a dozen things — possible services, even probable services — but none of them seemed adequate, none of them seemed large enough, none of them seemed worth the money — worth the fortune Goodson had wished he could leave in his will. And besides, he couldn't remember having done them, anyway. Now, then — now, then — what *kind* of a service would it be that would make a man so inordinately grateful? Ah — the saving of his soul! That must be it. Yes, he could remember, now, how he once set himself the task of converting Goodson, and labored at it as much as — he was going to say three months; but upon closer examination it shrunk to a month, then to a week, then to a day, then to nothing. Yes, he remembered now, and with unwelcome vividness, that Goodson had told him to go to thunder and mind his own business — *he* wasn't hankering to follow Hadleyburg to heaven!

So that solution was a failure — he hadn't saved Goodson's soul. Richards was discouraged. Then after a little came another idea: had he saved Goodson's property? No, that wouldn't do — he hadn't any. His life? That is it! Of course. Why, he might have thought of it before. This time he was on the right track, sure. His imagination-mill was hard at work in a minute, now.

Thereafter during a stretch of two exhausting hours he was busy saving Goodson's life. He saved it in all kinds of difficult and perilous ways. In every case he got it saved satisfactorily up to a certain point; then, just as he was beginning to get well persuaded that it had really happened, a troublesome detail would turn up which made the whole thing impossible. As in the matter of drowning, for instance. In that case he had swum out and tugged Goodson ashore in an unconscious state with a great crowd looking on and applauding, but when he had got it all thought out and was just beginning to remember all about it, a whole swarm of disqualifying details arrived on the ground; the town would have known of the circumstance, Mary would have known of it, it would glare like a limelight in his own memory instead of being an inconspicuous service which he had possibly rendered "without knowing its full value." And at this point he remembered that he couldn't swim, anyway.

Ah — *there* was a point which he had been overlooking from the start: it had to be a service which he had rendered "possibly without knowing the full value of it." Why, really, that ought to be an easy hunt — much easier than those others. And sure enough, by and by he found it. Goodson, years and years ago, came near marrying a very sweet and pretty girl, named Nancy Hewitt, but in some way or other the match had been broken off; the girl died; Goodson remained a bachelor, and by and by became a soured one and a frank despiser of the human species. Soon after the girl's death the village found out, or thought it had found out, that she carried a spoonful of negro blood in her veins. Richards worked at these details a good while, and in the end he thought he remembered things concerning them which must have gotten mislaid in his memory through long neglect. He seemed to dimly remember that it was *he* that found out about the negro blood; that it was he that told the village; that the village told Goodson where they got it; that he thus saved Goodson from marrying the tainted girl; that he had done him this great service "without knowing the full value of it," in fact without knowing that he *was* doing it; but that Goodson knew the value of it, and what a narrow escape he had had, and so went to his grave grateful to his benefactor and wishing he had a fortune to leave him. It was all clear and simple now, and the more he went over it the more luminous and certain it grew; and at last, when he nestled to sleep satisfied and happy, he remembered the whole thing just as if it had been yesterday. In fact, he dimly remembered Goodson's *telling* him his gratitude once.

Meantime Mary had spent six thousand dollars on a new house for herself and a pair of slippers for her pastor, and then had fallen peacefully to rest.

That same Saturday evening the postman had delivered a letter to each of the other principal citizens — nineteen letters in all. No two of the envelopes were alike, and no two of the superscriptions were in the same hand, but the letters inside were just like each other in every detail but one. They were exact copies of the letter received by Richards — handwriting and all — and were all signed by Stephenson, but in place of Richards's name each receiver's own name appeared.

All night long eighteen principal citizens did what their caste-brother Richards was doing at the same time — they put in their energies trying to remember what notable service it was that they had unconsciously done Barclay Goodson. In no case was it a holiday job; still they succeeded.

And while they were at this work, which was difficult, their wives put in the night spending the money, which was easy. During that one night the nineteen wives spent an average of seven thousand dollars each out of the forty thousand in the sack — a hundred and thirty-three thousand altogether.

Next day there was a surprise for Jack Halliday. He noticed that the faces of the nineteen chief citizens and their wives bore that expression of peaceful and holy happiness again. He could not understand it, neither was he able to invent any remarks about it that could damage it or disturb it. And so it was his turn to be dissatisfied with life. His private guesses at the reasons for the happiness failed in all instances, upon examination. When he met Mrs. Wilcox and noticed the placid ecstasy in her face, he said to himself, "Her cat has had kittens" — and went and asked the cook: but it was not so; the cook had detected the happiness, but did not know the cause. When Halliday found the duplicate ecstasy in the face of "Shadbelly" Billson (village nickname), he was sure some neighbor of Billson's had broken his leg, but inquiry showed that this had not happened. The subdued ecstasy in Gregory Yates's face could mean but one thing — he was a mother-in-law short: it was another mistake. "And Pinkerton — Pinkerton — he has collected ten cents that he thought he was going to lose." And so on, and so on. In some cases the guesses had to remain in doubt, in the others they proved distinct errors. In the end Halliday said to himself, "Anyway it foots up that there's nineteen Hadleyburg families temporarily in heaven: I don't know how it happened; I only know Providence is off duty to-day."

An architect and builder from the next State had lately ventured to set up a small business in this unpromising village, and his sign had now been hanging out a week. Not a customer yet; he was a discouraged man, and sorry he had come. But his weather changed suddenly now. First one and then another chief citizen's wife said to him privately:

"Come to my house Monday week — but say nothing about it for the present. We think of building."

He got eleven invitations that day. That night he wrote his daughter and broke off her match with her student. He said she could marry a mile higher than that.

Pinkerton the banker and two or three other well-to-do men planned country-seats — but waited. That kind don't count their chickens until they are hatched.

The Wilsons devised a grand new thing — a fancy-dress ball. They made no actual promises, but told all their acquaintanceship in confidence that they were thinking the matter over and thought they should give it — "and if we do, you will be invited, of course." People were surprised, and said, one to another, "Why they are crazy, those poor Wilsons, they can't afford it." Several among the nineteen said privately to their husbands, "It is a good idea: we will keep still till their cheap thing is over, then *we* will give one that will make it sick."

The days drifted along, and the bill of future squanderings rose higher and higher, wilder and wilder, more and more foolish and reckless. It began to look as if every member of the nineteen would not only spend his whole forty thousand dollars before receiving-day, but be actually in debt by the time he got the money. In some cases light-headed people did not stop with planning to spend, they really spent — on credit. They bought land, mortgages, farms, speculative stocks, fine clothes, horses, and various other things, paid down the bonus, and made themselves liable for the rest — at ten days. Presently the sober second thought came, and Halliday noticed that a ghastly anxiety was beginning to show up in a good many faces. Again he was puzzled, and didn't know what to make of it. "The Wilcox kittens aren't dead, for they weren't born; nobody's broken a leg; there's no shrinkage in mother-in-laws; *nothing* has happened — it is an unsolvable mystery."

There was another puzzled man, too — the Rev. Mr. Burgess. For days, wherever he went, people seemed to follow him or to be watching out for him; and if he ever found himself in a retired spot, a member of the nineteen would be sure to appear, thrust an envelope privately into his hand, whisper "To be opened at the town-hall Friday evening," then vanish away like a guilty thing. He was expecting that there might be one claimant for the sack, — doubtful, however, Goodson being dead, — but it never occurred to him that all this crowd might be claimants. When the great Friday came at last, he found that he had nineteen envelopes.

## III

The town-hall had never looked finer. The platform at the end of it was backed by a showy draping of flags; at intervals along the walls were festoons of flags; the gallery fronts were clothed in flags; the supporting columns were swathed in flags; all this was to impress the stranger, for he would be there in considerable force, and in a large degree he would be connected with the press. The house was full. The 412 fixed seats were occupied; also the 68 extra chairs which had been packed into the aisles; the steps of the platform were occupied; some distinguished strangers were given seats on the platform; at the horseshoe of tables which fenced the front and sides of the platform sat a strong force of special correspondents who had come from everywhere. It was the best-dressed house the town had ever produced. There were some tolerably expensive toilets there, and in several cases the ladies who wore them had the look of being unfamiliar with that kind of clothes. At least the town thought they had that look, but the notion could have arisen from the town's knowledge of the fact that these ladies had never inhabited such clothes before.

The gold-sack stood on a little table at the front of the platform where all the house could see it. The bulk of the house gazed at it with a burning interest, a mouth-watering interest, a wistful and pathetic interest; a minority of nineteen couples gazed at it tenderly, lovingly, proprietarily, and the male half of this minority kept saying over to themselves the moving little impromptu speeches of thankfulness for the audience's applause and congratulations which they were presently going to get up and deliver. Every now and then one of these got a piece of paper out of his vest pocket and privately glanced at it to refresh his memory.

Of course there was a buzz of conversation going on — there always is; but at last when the Rev. Mr. Burgess rose and laid his hand on the sack he could hear his microbes gnaw, the place was so still. He related the curious history of the sack, then went on to speak in warm terms of Hadleyburg's old and well-earned reputation for spotless honesty, and of the town's pride in this reputation. He said that this reputation was a treasure of priceless value; that under Providence its value had now become inestimably enhanced, for the recent episode had spread this fame far and wide, and thus had focused the eyes of the American world upon this village, and made its name for all time, as he hoped and believed, a synonym for commercial incorruptibility. [*Applause.*] "And who is to be the guardian of this noble treasure — the community as a whole? No! The responsibility is individual, not communal. From this day forth each and every one of you is in his own person its special guardian, and individually responsible that no harm shall come of it. Do you — does each of you — accept this great trust? [*Tumultuous assent.*] Then all is well. Transmit it to your children and to your children's children. To-day your purity is beyond reproach — see to it that it shall remain so. To-day there is not a person in your community who could be beguiled to touch a penny not his own — see to it that you abide in this grace. ["*We will! We will!*"] This is not the place to make comparisons between ourselves and other communities — some of them ungracious toward us; they have their ways, we have ours; let us be content. [*Applause.*] I am done. Under my hand, my friends, rests a stranger's eloquent recognition of what we are; through him the world will always henceforth know what we are. We do not know who he is, but in your name I utter your gratitude, and ask you to raise your voices in endorsement."

The house rose in a body and made the walls quake with the thunders of its thankfulness for the space of a long minute. Then it sat down, and Mr. Burgess took an envelope out of his pocket. The house held its breath while he slit the envelope open and took from it a slip of paper. He read its contents — slowly and impressively — the audience listening with tranced attention to this magic document, each of whose words stood for an ingot of gold:

"'*The remark which I made to the distressed stranger was this:* "*You are very far from being a bad man: go, and reform.*"'" Then he continued:

"We shall know in a moment now whether the remark here quoted corresponds with the one concealed in the sack; and if that shall prove to be so — and it undoubtedly will — this sack of gold belongs to a fellow-citizen who will henceforth stand before the nation as a symbol of the special virtue which has made our town famous throughout the land — Mr. Billson!"

The house had gotten itself all ready to burst into the proper tornado of applause; but instead of doing it, it seemed stricken with a paralysis; there was a deep hush for a moment or two, then a wave of whispered murmurs swept the place — of about this tenor: "*Billson!* oh, come, this is *too* thin! Twenty dollars to a stranger — or anybody — *Billson!* tell it to the marines!" And now at this point the house caught its breath all of a sudden in a new access of astonishment, for it discovered that whereas in one part of the hall Deacon Billson was standing up with his head meekly bowed, in another part of it Lawyer Wilson was doing the same. There was a wondering silence now for a while.

Everybody was puzzled, and nineteen couples were surprised and indignant.

Billson and Wilson turned and stared at each other. Billson asked, bitingly,

"Why do *you* rise, Mr. Wilson?"

"Because I have a right to. Perhaps you will be good enough to explain to the house why *you* rise?"

"With great pleasure. Because I wrote that paper."

"It is an impudent falsity! I wrote it myself."

It was Burgess's turn to be paralyzed. He stood looking vacantly at first one of the men and then the other, and did not seem to know what to do. The house was stupefied. Lawyer Wilson spoke up, now, and said,

"I ask the Chair to read the name signed to that paper."

That brought the Chair to itself, and it read out the name,

" 'John Wharton *Billson.*' "

"There!" shouted Billson, "what have you got to say for yourself, now? And what kind of apology are you going to make to me and to this insulted house for the imposture which you have attempted to play here?"

"No apologies are due, sir; and as for the rest of it, I publicly charge you with pilfering my note from Mr. Burgess and substituting a copy of it signed with your own name. There is no other way by which you could have gotten hold of the test-remark; I alone, of living men, possessed the secret of its wording."

There was likely to be a scandalous state of things if this went on; everybody noticed with distress that the short-hand scribes were scribbling like mad; many people were crying "Chair, Chair! Order! order!" Burgess rapped with his gavel, and said:

"Let us not forget the proprieties due. There has evidently been a mistake somewhere, but surely that is all. If Mr. Wilson gave me an envelope — and I remember now that he did — I still have it."

He took one out of his pocket, opened it, glanced at it, looked surprised and worried, and stood silent a few moments. Then he waved his hand in a wandering and mechanical way, and made an effort or two to say something, then gave it up, despondently. Several voices cried out:

"Read it! read it! What is it?"

So he began in a dazed and sleep-walker fashion:

" '*The remark which I made to the unhappy stranger was this: "You are far from being a bad man.* [The house gazed at him, marveling.] *Go, and reform."* ' [*Murmurs*: "Amazing! what can this mean?"] This one," said the Chair, "is signed Thurlow G. Wilson."

"There!" cried Wilson, "I reckon that settles it! I knew perfectly well my note was purloined."

"Purloined!" retorted Billson. "I'll let you know that neither you nor any man of your kidney must venture to — "

*The Chair.* "Order, gentlemen, order! Take your seats, both of you, please."

They obeyed, shaking their heads and grumbling angrily. The house was profoundly puzzled; it did not know what to do with this curious emergency. Presently Thompson got up. Thompson was the hatter. He would have liked to be a Nineteener; but such was not for him: his stock of hats was not considerable enough for the position. He said:

"Mr. Chairman, if I may be permitted to make a suggestion, can both of these gentlemen be right? I put it to you, sir, can both have happened to say the very same words to the stranger? It seems to me — "

The tanner got up and interrupted him. The tanner was a disgruntled man; he believed himself entitled to be a Nineteener, but he couldn't get recognition. It made him a little unpleasant in his ways and speech. Said he:

"Sho, *that's* not the point! *That* could happen — twice in a hundred years — but not the other thing. *Neither* of them gave the twenty dollars!"

[*A ripple of applause.*]

*Billson.* "I did!"

*Wilson.* "I did!"

Then each accused the other of pilfering.

*The Chair.* "Order! Sit down, if you please — both of you. Neither of the notes has been out of my possession at any moment."

*A Voice.* "Good — that settles *that!*"

*The Tanner.* "Mr. Chairman, one thing is now plain: one of these men has been eavesdropping under the other one's bed, and filching family secrets. If it is not unparliamentary to suggest it, I will remark that both are equal to it. [*The Chair.* "Order! order!"] I withdraw the remark, sir, and will confine myself to suggesting that *if* one of them has overheard the other reveal the test-remark to his wife, we shall catch him now."

*A Voice.* "How?"

*The Tanner.* "Easily. The two have not quoted the remark in exactly the same words. You would have noticed that, if there hadn't been a considerable stretch of time and an exciting quarrel inserted between the two readings."

*A Voice.* "Name the difference."

*The Tanner.* "The word *very* is in Billson's note, and not in the other."

*Many Voices.* "That's so — he's right!"

*The Tanner.* "And so, if the Chair will examine the test-remark in the sack, we shall know which of these two frauds — [*The Chair.* "Order!"] — which of these two adventurers — [*The Chair.* "Order! order!"] — which of these two gentlemen — [*laughter and applause*] — is entitled to wear the belt as being the first dishonest blatherskite ever bred in this town — which he has dishonored, and which will be a sultry place for him from now out!" [*Vigorous applause.*]

*Many Voices.* "Open it! — open the sack!"

Mr. Burgess made a slit in the sack, slid his hand in and brought out an envelope. In it were a couple of folded notes. He said:

"One of these is marked, 'Not to be examined until all written communications which have been addressed to the Chair — if any — shall have been read.' The other is marked '*The Test.*' Allow me. It is worded — to wit:

" 'I do not require that the first half of the remark which was made to me by my benefactor shall be quoted with exactness, for it was not striking, and could be forgotten; but its closing fifteen words are quite striking, and I think easily rememberable; unless *these* shall be accurately reproduced, let the applicant be regarded as an impostor. My benefactor began by saying he seldom gave advice to any one, but that it always bore the hall-mark of high value when he did give it. Then he said this — and it has never faded from my memory: "*You are far from being a bad man* — " ' "

*Fifty Voices.* "That settles it — the money's Wilson's! Wilson! Wilson! Speech! Speech!"

People jumped up and crowded around Wilson, wringing his hand and congratulating fervently — meantime the Chair was hammering with the gavel and shouting:

"Order, gentlemen! Order! Order! Let me finish reading, please." When quiet was restored, the reading was resumed — as follows:

> " ' "Go, and reform — or, mark my words — some day, for your sins, you will die and go to hell or Hadleyburg — TRY AND MAKE IT THE FORMER." ' "

A ghastly silence followed. First an angry cloud began to settle darkly upon the faces of the citizenship; after a pause the cloud began to rise, and a tickled expression tried to take its place; tried so hard that it was only kept under with great and painful difficulty; the reporters, the Brixtonites, and other strangers bent their heads down and shielded their faces with their hands, and managed to hold in by main strength and heroic courtesy. At this most inopportune time burst upon the stillness the roar of a solitary voice — Jack Halliday's:

"*That's* got the hall-mark on it!"

Then the house let go, strangers and all. Even Mr. Burgess's gravity broke down presently, then the audience considered itself officially absolved from all restraint, and it made the most of its privilege. It was a good long laugh, and a tempestuously whole-hearted one, but it ceased at last — long enough for Mr. Burgess to try to resume, and for the people to get their eyes partially wiped; then it broke out again; and afterward yet again; then at last Mr. Burgess was able to get out these serious words:

"It is useless to try to disguise the fact — we find ourselves in the presence of a matter of grave import. It involves the honor of your town, it strikes at the town's good name. The difference of a single word between the test-remarks offered by Mr. Wilson and Mr. Billson was itself a serious thing, since it indicated that one or the other of these gentlemen had committed a theft — "

The two men were sitting limp, nerveless, crushed; but at these words both were electrified into movement, and started to get up —

"Sit down!" said the Chair, sharply, and they obeyed. "That, as I have said, was a serious thing. And it was — but for only one of them. But the matter has become graver; for the honor of *both* is now in formidable peril. Shall I go even further, and say in inextricable peril? *Both* left out the crucial fifteen words." He paused. During several moments he allowed the pervading stillness to gather and deepen its impressive effects, then added: "There would seem to be but one way whereby this could happen. I ask these gentlemen — Was there *collusion? — agreement!*"

A low murmur sifted through the house; its import was, "He's got them both."

Billson was not used to emergencies; he sat in a helpless collapse. But Wilson was a lawyer. He struggled to his feet, pale and worried, and said:

"I ask the indulgence of the house while I explain this most painful matter. I am sorry to say what I am about to say, since it must inflict irreparable injury upon Mr. Billson, whom I have always esteemed and respected until now, and in whose invulnerability to temptation I entirely believed — as did you all. But for the preservation of my *own* honor I must speak — and with frankness. I confess with shame — and I now beseech your pardon for it — that I said to the ruined stranger all of the words contained in the test-remark, including the disparaging fifteen. [*Sensation.*] When the late publication was made I recalled them, and I resolved to claim the sack of coin, for by every right I was entitled to it. Now I will ask you to consider this point, and weigh it well: that stranger's gratitude to me that night knew no bounds; he said himself that he could find no words for it that were adequate, and that if he should ever be able he would repay me a thousand fold. Now, then, I ask you this: Could I expect — could I believe — could I even remotely imagine — that, feeling as I did, he would do so ungrateful a thing as to add those quite unnecessary fifteen words to his test? — set a trap for me? — expose me as a slanderer of my own town before my own people assembled in a public hall? It was preposterous; it was impossible. His test would contain only the kindly opening clause of my remark. Of that I had no shadow of doubt. You would have thought as I did. You would not have expected a base betrayal from one whom you had befriended and against whom you had committed no offense. And so, with perfect confidence, perfect trust, I wrote on a piece of paper the opening words — ending with 'Go, and reform,' — and signed it. When I was about to put it in an envelope I was called into my back office, and without thinking I left the paper lying open on my desk." He stopped, turned his head slowly toward Billson, waited a moment, then added: "I ask you to note this: when I returned, a little later, Mr. Billson was retiring by my street door." [*Sensation.*]

In a moment Billson was on his feet and shouting:

"It's a lie! It's an infamous lie!"

*The Chair.* "Be seated, sir! Mr. Wilson has the floor."

Billson's friends pulled him into his seat and quieted him, and Wilson went on:

"Those are the simple facts. My note was now lying in a different place on the table from where I had left it. I noticed that, but attached no importance to it, thinking a draught had blown it there. That Mr. Billson would read a private paper was a thing which could not occur to me; he was an honorable man, and he would be above that. If you will allow me to say it, I think his extra word '*very*' stands explained; it is attributable to a defect of memory. I was the only man in the world who could furnish here any detail of the test-remark — by *honorable* means. I have finished."

There is nothing in the world like a persuasive speech to fuddle the mental apparatus and upset the convictions and debauch the emotions of an audience not practiced in the tricks and delusions of oratory. Wilson sat down victorious. The house submerged him in tides of approving applause; friends swarmed to him and shook him by the hand and congratulated him, and Billson was shouted down and not allowed to say a word. The Chair hammered and hammered with its gavel, and kept shouting,

"But let us proceed, gentlemen, let us proceed!"

At last there was a measurable degree of quiet, and the hatter said:

"But what is there to proceed with, sir, but to deliver the money?"

*Voices.* "That's it! That's it! Come forward, Wilson!"

*The Hatter.* "I move three cheers for Mr. Wilson, Symbol of the special virtue which —"

The cheers burst forth before he could finish; and in the midst of them — and in the midst of the clamor of the gavel also — some enthusiasts mounted Wilson on a big friend's shoulder and were going to fetch him in triumph to the platform. The Chair's voice now rose above the noise —

"Order! To your places! You forget that there is still a document to read." When quiet had been restored he took up the document, and was going to read it, but laid it down again, saying, "I forgot; this is not to be read until all written communications received by me have first been read." He took an envelope out of his pocket, removed its enclosure, glanced at it — seemed astonished — held it out and gazed at it — stared at it.

Twenty or thirty voices cried out:

"What is it? Read it! read it!

And he did — slowly, and wondering:

" 'The remark which I made to the stranger — [*Voices.* "Hello! how's this?"] — was this: "You are far from being a bad man. [*Voices.* "Great Scott!"] Go, and reform." ' [*Voice.* "Oh, saw my leg off!"] Signed by Mr. Pinkerton the banker."

The pandemonium of delight which turned itself loose now was of a sort to make the judicious weep. Those whose withers were unwrung laughed till the tears ran down; the reporters, in throes of laughter, set down disordered pot-hooks which would never in the world be decipherable; and a sleeping dog jumped up, scared out of its wits, and barked itself crazy at the turmoil. All manner of cries were scattered through the din: "We're getting rich — *two* Symbols of Incorruptibility! — without counting Billson!" "*Three!* — count Shadbelly in — we can't have too many!" "All right — Billson's elected!" "Alas, poor Wilson — victim of *two* thieves!"

*A Powerful Voice.* "Silence! The Chair's fished up something more out of its pocket."

*Voices.* "Hurrah! Is it something fresh? Read it! read it! read!"

*The Chair* [*reading.*] " 'The remark which I made,' etc.: ' "You are far from being a bad man. Go," ' etc. Signed, 'Gregory Yates.' "

*Tornado of Voices* . "Four symbols!" " 'Rah for Yates!" "Fish again!"

The house was in a roaring humor now, and ready to get all the fun out of the occasion that might be in it. Several Nineteeners, looking pale and distressed, got up and began to work their way toward the aisles, but a score of shouts went up:

"The doors, the doors — close the doors; no Incorruptible shall leave this place! Sit down, everybody!"

The mandate was obeyed.

"Fish again! Read! read!"

The Chair fished again, and once more the familiar words began to fall from its lips — " 'You are far from being a bad man — ' "

"Name! name! What's his name?"

" 'L. Ingoldsby Sargent.' "

"Five elected! Pile up the Symbols! Go on, go on!"

" 'You are far from being a bad — ' "

"Name! name!"

" 'Nicholas Whitworth.' "

"Hooray! hooray! it's a symbolical day!"

Somebody wailed in, and began to sing this rhyme (leaving out "it's") to the lovely "Mikado" tune of "When a man's afraid, a beautiful maid — "; the audience joined in, with joy; then, just in time, somebody contributed another line —

"And don't you this forget —"

The house roared it out. A third line was at once furnished —

"Corruptibles far from Hadleyburg are —"

The house roared that one too. As the last note died, Jack Halliday's voice rose high and clear, freighted with a final line —

"But the Symbols are here, you bet!"

That was sung with booming enthusiasm. Then the happy house started in at the beginning and sang the four lines through twice, with immense swing and dash, and finished up with a crashing three-times-three and a tiger for "Hadleyburg the Incorruptible and all Symbols of it which we shall find worthy to receive the hall-mark to-night."

Then the shouting at the Chair began again, all over the place:

"Go on! go on! Read! read some more! Read all you've got!"

"That's it — go on! We are winning eternal celebrity!"

A dozen men got up now and began to protest. They said that this farce was the work of some abandoned joker, and was an insult to the whole community. Without a doubt these signatures were all forgeries —

"Sit down! sit down! Shut up! You are confessing. We'll find *your* names in the lot."

"Mr. Chairman, how many of those envelopes have you got?"

The Chair counted.

"Together with those that have been already examined, there are nineteen."

A storm of derisive applause broke out.

"Perhaps they all contain the secret. I move that you open them all and read every signature that is attached to a note of that sort — and read also the first eight words of the note."

"Second the motion!"

It was put and carried — uproariously. Then poor old Richards got up, and his wife rose and stood at his side. Her head bent down, so that none might see that she was crying. Her husband gave her his arm, and so supporting her, he began to speak in a quavering voice:

"My friends, you have known us two — Mary and me — all our lives, and I think you have liked us and respected us —"

The Chair interrupted him:

"Allow me. It is quite true — that which you are saying, Mr. Richards: this town *does* know you two; it *does* like you; it *does* respect you; more — it honors you and *loves* you —"

Halliday's voice rang out:

"That's the hall-marked truth, too! If the Chair is right, let the house speak up and say it. Rise! Now, then — hip! hip! hip! — all together!"

The house rose in mass, faced toward the old couple eagerly, filled the air with a snowstorm of waving handkerchiefs, and delivered the cheers with all its affectionate heart.

The Chair then continued:

"What I was going to say is this: We know your good heart, Mr. Richards, but this is not a time for the exercise of charity toward offenders. [*Shouts of "Right! right!"*] I see your generous purpose in your face, but I cannot allow you to plead for these men —"

"But I was going to —"

"Please take your seat, Mr. Richards. We must examine the rest of these notes — simple fairness to the men who have already been exposed requires this. As soon as that has been done — I give you my word for this — you shall be heard."

*Many Voices.* "Right! — the Chair is right — no interruption can be permitted at this stage! Go on! — the names! the names! — according to the terms of the motion!"

The old couple sat reluctantly down, and the husband whispered to the wife, "It is pitifully hard to have to wait; the shame will be greater than ever when they find we were only going to plead for *ourselves.*"

Straightway the jollity broke loose again with the reading of the names.

" 'You are far from being a bad man —' Signature, 'Robert J. Titmarsh.'

" 'You are far from being a bad man —' Signature, 'Eliphalet Weeks.'

" 'You are far from being a bad man —' Signature, 'Oscar B. Wilder.' "

At this point the house lit upon the idea of taking the eight words out of the Chairman's hands. He was not unthankful for that. Thenceforward he held up each note in its turn, and waited. The house droned out the eight words in a massed and measured and musical deep volume of sound (with a daringly close resemblance to a well-known church chant) — " 'You are f-a-r from being a b-a-a-a-d man.' " Then the Chair said, "Signature, 'Archibald Wilcox.' " And so on, and so on, name after name, and everybody had an increasingly and gloriously good time except the wretched Nineteen. Now and then, when a particularly shining name was called, the house made the Chair wait while it changed the whole of the test-remark from the beginning to the closing words, "And go to hell or Hadleyburg — try and make it the for-or-m-e-r!" and in these special cases they added a grand and agonized and imposing "A-a-a-a-*men*!"

The list dwindled, dwindled, dwindled, poor old Richards keeping tally of the count, wincing when a name resembling his own was pronounced, and waiting in miserable suspense for the time to come when it would be his humiliating privilege to rise with Mary and finish his plea, which he was intending to word thus: ". . . for until now we have never done any wrong thing, but have gone our humble way unreproached. We are very poor, we are old, and have no chick nor child to help us; we were sorely tempted, and we fell. It was my purpose when I got up before to make confession and beg that my name might not be read out in this public place, for it seemed to us that we could not bear it; but I was prevented. It was just; it was our place to suffer with the rest. It has been hard for us. It is the first time we have ever heard our name fall from any one's lips — sullied. Be merciful — for the sake of the better days; make our shame as light to bear as in your charity you can." At this point in his revery Mary nudged him, perceiving that his mind was absent. The house was chanting, "You are f-a-r," etc.

"Be ready," Mary whispered. "Your name comes now; he has read eighteen."

The chant ended.

"Next! next! next!" came volleying from all over the house.

Burgess put his hand into his pocket. The old couple, trembling, began to rise. Burgess fumbled a moment, then said,

"I find I have read them all."

Faint with joy and surprise, the couple sank into their seats, and Mary whispered,

"Oh, bless God, we are saved! — he has lost ours — I wouldn't give this for a hundred of those sacks!"

The house burst out with its "Mikado" travesty, and sang it three times with ever-increasing enthusiasm, rising to its feet when it reached for the third time the closing line —

"But the Symbols are here, you bet!"

and finishing up with cheers and a tiger for "Hadleyburg purity and our eighteen immortal representatives of it."

Then Wingate, the saddler, got up and proposed cheers "for the cleanest man in town, the one solitary important citizen in it who didn't try to steal that money — Edward Richards."

They were given with great and moving heartiness; then somebody proposed that Richards be elected sole guardian and Symbol of the now Sacred Hadleyburg Tradition, with power and right to stand up and look the whole sarcastic world in the face.

Passed, by acclamation; then they sang the "Mikado" again, and ended it with,

"And there's *one* Symbol left, you bet!"

There was a pause; then —

*A Voice.* "Now, then, who's to get the sack?"

*The Tanner (with bitter sarcasm).* "That's easy. The money has to be divided among the eighteen Incorruptibles. They gave the suffering stranger twenty dollars apiece — and that remark — each in his turn — it took twenty-two minutes for the procession to move past. Staked the stranger — total contribution, $360. All they want is just the loan back — and interest — forty thousand dollars altogether."

*Many Voices [derisively.]* "That's it! Divvy! divvy! Be kind to the poor — don't keep them waiting!"

*The Chair.* "Order! I now offer the stranger's remaining document. It says: 'If no claimant shall appear [*grand chorus of groans*], I desire that you open the sack and count out the money to the principal citizens of your town, they to take it in trust [*cries of "Oh! Oh! Oh!"*], and use it in such ways as to them shall seem best for the propagation and preservation of your community's noble reputation for incorruptible honesty [*more cries*] — a reputation to which their names and their efforts will add a new and far-reaching lustre.' [*Enthusiastic outburst of sarcastic applause.*] That seems to be all. No — here is a postscript:

" 'P. S. — CITIZENS OF HADLEYBURG: There *is* no test-remark — nobody made one. [*Great sensation.*] There wasn't any pauper stranger, nor any twenty-dollar contribution, nor any accompanying benediction and compliment — these are all inventions. [*General buzz and hum of astonishment and delight.*] Allow me to tell my story — it will take but a word or two. I passed through your town at a certain time, and received a deep offense which I had not earned. Any other man would have been content to kill one or two of you and call it square, but to me that would have been a trivial revenge, and inadequate; for the dead do not *suffer*. Besides, I could not kill you all — and, anyway, made as I am, even that would not have satisfied me. I wanted to damage every man in the place, and every woman — and not in their bodies or in their estate, but in their vanity — the place where feeble and foolish people are most vulnerable. So I disguised myself and came back and studied you. You were easy game. You had an old and lofty reputation for honesty, and naturally you were proud of it — it was your treasure of treasures, the very apple of your eye. As soon as I found out that you carefully and vigilantly kept yourselves and your children *out of temptation*, I knew how to proceed. Why, you simple creatures, the weakest of all weak things is a virtue which has not been tested in the fire. I laid a plan, and gathered a list of names. My project was to corrupt Hadleyburg the Incorruptible. My idea was to make liars and thieves of nearly half a hundred smirchless men and women who had never in their lives uttered a lie or stolen a penny. I was afraid of Goodson. He was neither born nor reared in Hadleyburg. I was afraid that if I started to operate my scheme by getting my letter laid before you, you would say to yourselves, "Goodson is the only man among us who would give away twenty dollars to a poor devil" — and then you might not bite at my bait. But Heaven took Goodson; then I knew I was safe, and I set my trap and baited it. It may be that I shall not catch all the men to whom I mailed the pretended test secret, but I shall catch the most of them, if I know Hadleyburg nature. [*Voices.* "Right — he got every last one of them."] I believe they will even steal ostensible *gamble*-money, rather than miss, poor, tempted, and mistrained fellows. I am hoping to eternally and everlastingly squelch your vanity and give Hadleyburg a new renown — one that will *stick* — and spread far. If I have succeeded, open the sack and summon the Committee on Propagation and Preservation of the Hadleyburg Reputation.' "

*A Cyclone of Voices.* "Open it! Open it! The Eighteen to the front! Committee on Propagation of the Tradition! Forward — the Incorruptibles!"

The Chair ripped the sack wide, and gathered up a handful of bright, broad, yellow coins, shook them together, then examined them —

"Friends, they are only gilded disks of lead!"

There was a crashing outbreak of delight over this news, and when the noise had subsided, the tanner called out:

"By right of apparent seniority in this business, Mr. Wilson is Chairman of the Committee on Propagation of the Tradition. I suggest that he step forward on behalf of his pals, and receive in trust the money."

*A Hundred Voices.* "Wilson! Wilson! Wilson! Speech! Speech!"

*Wilson* [*in a voice trembling with anger.*] "You will allow me to say, and without apologies for my language, *damn* the money!"

*A Voice.* "Oh, and him a Baptist!"

*A Voice.* "Seventeen Symbols left! Step up, gentlemen, and assume your trust!"

There was a pause — no response.

*The Saddler.* "Mr. Chairman, we've got *one* clean man left, anyway, out of the late aristocracy; and he needs money, and deserves it. I move that you appoint Jack Halliday to get up there and auction off that sack of gilt twenty-dollar pieces, and give the result to the right man — the man whom Hadleyburg delights to honor — Edward Richards."

This was received with great enthusiasm, the dog taking a hand again; the saddler started the bids at a dollar, the Brixton folk and Barnum's representative fought hard for it, the people cheered every jump that the bids made, the excitement climbed moment by moment higher and higher, the bidders got on their mettle and grew steadily more and more daring, more and more determined, the jumps went from a dollar up to five, then to ten, then to twenty, then fifty, then to a hundred, then —

At the beginning of the auction Richards whispered in distress to his wife: "O Mary, can we allow it? It — it — you see, it is an honor-reward, a testimonial to purity of character, and — and — can we allow it? Hadn't I better get up and — O Mary, what ought we to do? — what do you think we — [*Halliday's voice.* "Fifteen I'm bid! — fifteen for the sack! — twenty! — ah, thanks! — thirty — thanks again! Thirty, thirty, thirty! — do I hear forty? — forty it is! Keep the ball rolling, gentlemen, keep it rolling! —fifty! — thanks, noble Roman! going at fifty, fifty, fifty! — seventy! — ninety! — splendid! — a hundred! — pile it up, pile it up! — hundred and twenty! — forty! — just in time! — hundred and fifty! — two hundred! — superb! Do I hear two h — thanks! — two hundred and fifty! — "*]

"It is another temptation, Edward — I'm all in a tremble — but, oh, we've escaped *one* temptation, and that ought to warn us to — [*"Six did I hear? — thanks! — six fifty, six f —* SEVEN *hundred!"*] And yet, Edward, when you think — nobody susp — [*"Eight hundred dollars!*

*— hurrah! — make it nine! — Mr. Parsons, did I hear you say —
thanks — nine! — this noble sack of virgin lead going at only nine hundred dollars, gilding and all — come! do I hear — a thousand! — gratefully yours! — did some one say eleven? — a sack which is going to be
the most celebrated in the whole Uni —*"]O Edward" (beginning to
sob), "we are *so* poor! — but — but — do as you think best — do as
you think best."

Edward fell — that is, he sat still; sat with a conscience which was
not satisfied, but which was overpowered by circumstances.

Meantime a stranger, who looked like an amateur detective gotten
up as an impossible English earl, had been watching the evenings's proceedings with manifest interest, and with a contented expression in his
face; and he had been privately commenting to himself. He was now
soliloquizing somewhat like this: "None of the Eighteen are bidding;
that is not satisfactory; I must change that — the dramatic unities require
it; they must buy the sack they tried to steal; they must pay a heavy price,
too — some of them are rich. And another thing, when I make a mistake in Hadleyburg nature the man that puts that error upon me is
entitled to a high honorarium, and some one must pay it. This poor
old Richards has brought my judgment to shame; he is an honest man:
— I don't understand it, but I acknowledge it. Yes, he saw my deuces
*and* with a straight flush, and by rights the pot is his. And it shall be
a jack-pot, too, if I can manage it. He disappointed me, but let that pass."

He was watching the bidding. At a thousand, the market broke;
the prices tumbled swiftly. He waited — and still watched. One competitor dropped out, then another, and another. He put in a bid or two,
now. When the bids had sunk to ten dollars, he added a five; some one
raised him a three; he waited a moment, then flung in a fifty-dollar jump,
and the sack was his — at $1,282. The house broke out in cheers — then
stopped; for he was on his feet, and had lifted his hand. He began to
speak.

"I desire to say a word, and ask a favor. I am a speculator in rarities,
and I have dealings with persons interested in numismatics all over the
world. I can make a profit on this purchase, just as it stands; but there is
a way, if I can get your approval, whereby I can make every one of these
leaden twenty-dollar pieces worth its face in gold, and perhaps more.
Grant me that approval, and I will give part of my gains to your Mr.
Richards, whose invulnerable probity you have so justly and so cordially
recognized to-night; his share shall be ten thousand dollars, and I will
hand him the money to-morrow. [*Great applause from the house.* But
the "invulnerable probity" made the Richardses blush prettily; however,
it went for modesty, and did no harm.] If you will pass my proposition

by a good majority — I would like a two-thirds vote — I will regard that as the town's consent, and that is all I ask. Rarities are always helped by any device which will rouse curiosity and compel remark. Now if I may have your permission to stamp upon the faces of each of these ostensible coins the names of the eighteen gentlemen who —"

Nine-tenths of the audience were on their feet in a moment — dog and all — and the proposition was carried with a whirlwind of approving applause and laughter.

They sat down, and all the Symbols except "Dr." Clay Harkness got up, violently protesting against the proposed outrage, and threatening to —

"I beg you not to threaten me," said the stranger, calmly. "I know my legal rights, and am not accustomed to being frightened at bluster." [*Applause.*] He sat down. "Dr." Harkness saw an opportunity here. He was one of the two very rich men of the place, and Pinkerton was the other. Harkness was proprietor of a mint; that is to say, a popular patent medicine. He was running for the Legislature on one ticket, and Pinkerton on the other. It was a close race and a hot one, and getting hotter every day. Both had strong appetites for money; each had bought a great tract of land, with a purpose; there was going to be a new railway, and each wanted to be in the Legislature and help locate the route to his own advantage; a single vote might make the decision, and with it two or three fortunes. The stake was large, and Harkness was a daring speculator. He was sitting close to the stranger. He leaned over while one or another of the other Symbols was entertaining the house with protests and appeals, and asked, in a whisper,

"What is your price for the sack?"

"Forty thousand dollars."

"I'll give you twenty."

"No."

"Twenty-five."

"No."

"Say thirty."

"The price is forty thousand dollars; not a penny less."

"All right, I'll give it. I will come to the hotel at ten in the morning. I don't want it known; will see you privately."

"Very good." Then the stranger got up and said to the house:

"I find it late. The speeches of these gentlemen are not without merit, not without interest, not without grace; yet if I may be excused I will take my leave. I thank you for the great favor which you have shown me in granting my petition. I ask the Chair to keep the sack for me until to-morrow, and to hand these three five-hundred-dollar notes to Mr. Richards." They were passed up to the Chair. "At nine I will call for the sack, and at eleven will deliver the rest of the ten thousand to Mr. Richards in person, at his home. Good night."

Then he slipped out, and left the audience making a vast noise, which was composed of a mixture of cheers, the "Mikado" song, dog-disapproval, and the chant, "You are f-a-r from being a b-a-a-d man — a-a-a a-men!"

IV

At home the Richardses had to endure congratulations and compliments until midnight. Then they were left to themselves. They looked a little sad, and they sat silent and thinking. Finally Mary sighed and said,

"Do you think we are to blame, Edward — *much* to blame?" and her eyes wandered to the accusing triplet of big bank notes lying on the table, where the congratulators had been gloating over them and reverently fingering them. Edward did not answer at once; then he brought out a sigh and said, hesitatingly:

"We — we couldn't help it, Mary. It — well, it was ordered. *All* things are."

Mary glanced up and looked at him steadily, but he didn't return the look. Presently she said:

"I thought congratulations and praises always tasted good. But — it seems to me, now — Edward?"

"Well?"

"Are you going to stay in the bank?"

"N-no."

"Resign?"

"In the morning — by note."

"It does seem best."

Richards bowed his head in his hands and muttered:

"Before, I was not afraid to let oceans of people's money pour through my hands, but — Mary, I am so tired, so tired —"

"We will go to bed."

At nine in the morning the stranger called for the sack and took it to the hotel in a cab. At ten Harkness had a talk with him privately. The stranger asked for and got five checks on a metropolitan bank — drawn to "Bearer," — four for $1,500 each, and one for $34,000. He put one of the former in his pocketbook, and the remainder, representing $38,500, he put in an envelope, and with these he added a note, which he wrote after Harkness was gone. At eleven he called at the Richards house and knocked. Mrs. Richards peeped through the shutters, then went and received the envelope, and the stranger disappeared without a word. She came back flushed and a little unsteady on her legs, and gasped out:

"I am sure I recognized him! Last night it seemed to me that maybe I had seen him somewhere before."

"He is the man that brought the sack here?"

"I am almost sure of it."

"Then he is the ostensible Stephenson, too, and sold every important citizen in this town with his bogus secret. Now if he has sent checks instead of money, we are sold, too, after we thought we had escaped. I was beginning to feel fairly comfortable once more, after my night's rest, but the look of that envelope makes me sick. It isn't fat enough; $8,500 in even the largest bank notes makes more bulk than that."

"Edward, why do you object to checks?"

"Checks signed by Stephenson! I am resigned to take the $8,500 if it could come in bank notes — for it does seem that it was so ordered, Mary — but I have never had much courage, and I have not the pluck to try to market a check signed with that disastrous name. It would be a trap. That man tried to catch me; we escaped somehow or other; and now he is trying a new way. If it is checks —"

"Oh, Edward, it is *too* bad!" and she held up the checks and began to cry.

"Put them in the fire! quick! we musn't be tempted. It is a trick to make the world laugh at *us*, along with the rest, and — Give them to *me*, since you can't do it!" He snatched them and tried to hold his grip till he could get to the stove; but he was human, he was a cashier, and he stopped a moment to make sure of the signature. Then he came near to fainting.

"Fan me, Mary, fan me! They are the same as gold!"

"Oh, how lovely, Edward! Why?"

"Signed by Harkness. What can the mystery of that be, Mary?"

"Edward, do you think —"

"Look here — look at this! Fifteen — fifteen — fifteen — thirty-four. Thirty-eight thousand five hundred! Mary, the sack isn't worth twelve dollars, and Harkness — apparently — has paid about par for it."

"And does it all come to us, do you think — instead of the ten thousand?"

"Why, it looks like it. And the checks are made to 'Bearer,' too."

"Is that good, Edward? What is it for?"

"A hint to collect them at some distant bank, I reckon. Perhaps Harkness doesn't want the matter known. What is that — a note?"

"Yes. It was with the checks."

It was in the "Stephenson" handwriting, but there was no signature. It said:

*"I am a disappointed man. Your honesty is beyond the reach of tempta-
tion. I had a different idea about it, but I wronged you in that and I beg
pardon, and do it sincerely. I honor you — and that is sincere too. This
town is not worthy to kiss the hem of your garment. Dear sir, I made a
square bet with myself that there were nineteen debauchable men in your
self-righteous community. I have lost. Take the whole pot, you are entitled to it."*

Richards drew a deep sigh, and said:
"It seems written with fire — it burns so. Mary — I am miserable
again."
"I, too. Ah, dear, I wish —"
"To think, Mary — he *believes* in me."
"If those beautiful words were deserved, Mary — and God knows
I believed I deserved them once — I think I could give the forty thousand
dollars for them. And I would put that paper away, as representing more
than gold and jewels, and keep it always. But now — We could not
live in the shadow of its accusing presence, Mary."
He put it in the fire.
A messenger arrived and delivered an envelope.
Richards took from it a note and read it; it was from Burgess.

*"You saved me in a difficult time. I saved you last night. It was at cost of a
lie, but I made the sacrifice freely, and out of a grateful heart. None in this
village knows so well as I know how brave and good and noble you are.
At bottom you cannot respect me, knowing as you do of that matter of
which I am accused, and by the general voice condemned; but I beg that
you will at least believe that I am a grateful man; it will help me to bear
my burden.*

[*Signed*]          "Burgess."

"Saved, once more. And on such terms!" He put the note in the
fire. "I — I wish I were dead, Mary, I wish I were out of it all."
"Oh, these are bitter, bitter days, Edward. The stabs, through their
very generosity, are so deep — and they come so fast!"
Three days before the election each of two thousand voters suddenly
found himself in possession of a prized memento — one of the renowned
bogus double-eagles. Around one of its faces was stamped these words:
"THE REMARK I MADE TO THE POOR STRANGER WAS —" Around the other face
was stamped these: "GO AND REFORM. [SIGNED] PINKERTON." Thus the
entire remaining refuse of the renowned joke was emptied upon a single
head, and with calamitous effect. It revived the recent vast laugh and
concentrated it upon Pinkerton; and Harkness's election was a walkover.
Within twenty-four hours after the Richardses had received their

checks their consciences were quieting down, discouraged; the old couple were learning to reconcile themselves to the sin which they had committed. But they were to learn, now, that a sin takes on new and real terrors when there seems a chance that it is going to be found out. This gives it a fresh and most substantial and important aspect. At church the morning sermon was of the usual pattern; it was the same old things said in the same old way; they had heard them a thousand times and found them innocuous, next to meaningless, and easy to sleep under; but now it was different: the sermon seemed to bristle with accusations; it seemed aimed straight and specially at people who were concealing deadly sins. After church they got away from the mob of congratulators as soon as they could, and hurried homeward, chilled to the bone at they did not know what — vague, shadowy, indefinite fears. And by chance they caught a glimpse of Mr. Burgess as he turned a corner. He paid no attention to their nod of recognition! He hadn't seen it; but they did not know that. What could his conduct mean? It might mean — it might mean — oh, a dozen dreadful things. Was it possible that he knew that Richards could have cleared him of guilt in that bygone time, and had been silently waiting for a chance to even up accounts? At home, in their distress they got to imagining that their servant might have been in the next room listening when Richards revealed the secret to his wife that he knew of Burgess's innocence; next, Richards began to imagine that he had heard the swish of a gown in there at that time; next, he was sure he *had* heard it. They would call Sarah in, on a pretext, and watch her face: if she had been betraying them to Mr. Burgess, it would show in her manner. They asked her some questions — questions which were so random and incoherent and seemingly purposeless that the girl felt sure that the old people's minds had been affected by their sudden good fortune; the sharp and watchful gaze which they bent upon her frightened her, and that completed the business. She blushed, she became nervous and confused, and to the old people these were plain signs of guilt — guilt of some fearful sort or other — without doubt she was a spy and a traitor. When they were alone again they began to piece many unrelated things together and get horrible results out of the combination. When things had got about to the worst, Richards was delivered of a sudden gasp, and his wife asked,

"Oh, what is it? — what is it?"

"The note — Burgess's note! Its language was sarcastic, I see it now." He quoted: " 'At bottom you cannot respect me, *knowing*, as you do, of *that matter* of which I am accused' — oh, it is perfectly plain, now, God help me! He knows that I know! You see the ingenuity of the phrasing. It was a trap — and like a fool, I walked into it. And Mary —?"

"Oh, it is dreadful — I know what you are going to say — he didn't return your transcript of the pretended test-remark."

"No — kept it to destroy us with. Mary, he has exposed us to some already. I know it — I know it well. I saw it in a dozen faces after church. Ah, he wouldn't answer our nod of recognition — *he* knew what he had been doing!"

In the night the doctor was called. The news went around in the morning that the old couple were rather seriously ill — prostrated by the exhausting excitement growing out of their great windfall, the congratulations, and the late hours, the doctor said. The town was sincerely distressed; for these old people were about all it had left to be proud of, now.

Two days later the news was worse. The old couple were delirious, and were doing strange things. By witness of the nurses, Richards had exhibited checks — for $8,500? No — for an amazing sum — $38,500! What could be the explanation of this gigantic piece of luck?

The following day the nurses had more news — and wonderful. They had concluded to hide the checks, lest harm come to them; but when they searched they were gone from under the patient's pillow — vanished away. The patient said:

"Let the pillow alone; what do you want?"

"We thought it best that the checks —"

"You will never see them again — they are destroyed. They came from Satan. I saw the hell-brand on them, and I knew they were sent to betray me to sin." Then he fell to gabbling strange and dreadful things which were not clearly understandable, and which the doctor admonished them to keep to themselves.

Richards was right; the checks were never seen again.

A nurse must have talked in her sleep, for within two days the forbidden gabblings were the property of the town; and they were of a surprising sort. They seemed to indicate that Richards had been a claimant for the sack himself, and that Burgess had concealed that fact and then maliciously betrayed it.

Burgess was taxed with this and stoutly denied it. And he said it was not fair to attach weight to the chatter of a sick old man who was out of his mind. Still, suspicion was in the air, and there was much talk.

After a day or two it was reported that Mrs. Richards's delirious deliveries were getting to be duplicates of her husband's. Suspicion flamed up into conviction, now, and the town's pride in the purity of its one undiscredited important citizen began to dim down and flicker toward extinction.

Six days passed, then came more news. The old couple were dying.

Richards's mind cleared in his latest hour, and he sent for Burgess.
Burgess said:

"Let the room be cleared. I think he wishes to say something in
privacy."

"No!" said Richards: "I want witnesses. I want you all to hear
my confession, so that I may die a man, and not a dog. I was clean —
artificially — like the rest; and like the rest I fell when temptation came.
I signed a lie, and claimed the miserable sack. Mr. Burgess remembered
that I had done him a service, and in gratitude (and ignorance) he suppressed my claim and saved me. You know the thing that was charged
against Burgess years ago. My testimony, and mine alone, could have
cleared him, and I was a coward, and left him to suffer disgrace —"

"No — no — Mr. Richards, you —"

"My servant betrayed my secret to him —"

"No one has betrayed anything to me —"

— "and then he did a natural and justifiable thing, he repented
of the saving kindness which he had done me, and he *exposed* me — as
I deserved —"

"Never! — I make oath —"

"Out of my heart I forgive him."

Burgess's impassioned protestations fell upon deaf ears; the dying
man passed away without knowing that once more he had done poor
Burgess a wrong. The old wife died that night.

The last of the sacred Nineteen had fallen a prey to the fiendish
sack; the town was stripped of the last rag of its ancient glory. Its
mourning was not showy, but it was deep.

By act of the Legislature — upon prayer and petition — Hadleyburg was allowed to change its name to (never mind what — I will not
give it away), and leave one word out of the motto that for many generations had graced the town's official seal.

It is an honest town once more, and the man will have to rise early
that catches it napping again.

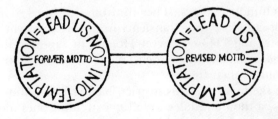

# O. Henry (1862–1910)

THE COUNTRY'S most popular short-story writer at the turn of the century, William Sydney Porter, better known as O. Henry, was born in Greensboro, North Carolina, where, after a brief schooling, he worked as a clerk in a drugstore. At twenty he went to Texas, becoming a ranch hand and later a bank teller. He wrote for a Houston newspaper and founded a humorous weekly, *The Rolling Stone* (1894). Unjustly accused of embezzling bank funds, he fled to Honduras but returned to Texas to see his dying wife. He was arrested and sentenced to three years in prison. There his real literary career began with the "banana republic" stories that were to be collected in his first book *Cabbages and Kings* (1904). Hundreds more short stories rapidly followed. Within the seven years before his death he turned out ten volumes of stories and left so many more that four collections of them were published posthumously. His story of a reformed burglar was dramatized by Paul Armstrong into the tremendously successful play, *Alias Jimmy Valentine.* The stories laid in New York, the city he labeled "Baghdad-upon-the-Subway," and published in *The Four Million* (1906), are considered his best.

"Be concise and familiar and punch when your adversary (the reader) is off guard. This stuns him and you may then disappear." O. Henry thus defined his suicidal formula for writing that has led to most of his stories also disappearing from serious literary esteem. The "punch," of course, is the famous surprise ending that he reduced to a boring repetitiousness. A surprise can be a surprise only once. A twin weakness was his fondness for the *deus ex machina* of a coincidence. But his genuine love for the ordinary people of whom he wrote and called "The Four Million" in contradistinction to "The Four Hundred," as favored by the society pages of the period, endeared him to his hundreds of thousands of readers. There are bona fide nuggets to be mined from his voluminous writings, of which "The Furnished Room" is an example, and they entitle him to a place in America's literary Pantheon.

# *The Furnished Room*

RESTLESS, shifting, fugacious as time itself is a certain vast bulk of the population of the red brick district of the lower West Side. Homeless, they have a hundred homes. They flit from furnished room to furnished room, transients forever — transients in abode, transients in heart and mind. They sing "Home, Sweet Home" in ragtime; they carry their *lares et penates* in a bandbox; their vine is entwined about a picture hat; a rubber plant is their fig tree.

Hence the houses of this district, having had a thousand dwellers, should have a thousand tales to tell, mostly dull ones, no doubt; but it would be strange if there could not be found a ghost or two in the wake of all these vagrant guests.

One evening after dark a young man prowled among these crumbling red mansions, ringing their bells. At the twelfth he rested his lean hand-baggage upon the step and wiped the dust from his hatband and forehead. The bell sounded faint and far away in some remote, hollow depths.

To the door of this, the twelfth house whose bell he had rung, came a housekeeper who made him think of an unwholesome, surfeited worm that had eaten its nut to a hollow shell and now sought to fill the vacancy with edible lodgers.

He asked if there was a room to let.

"Come in," said the housekeeper. Her voice came from her throat; her throat seemed lined with fur. "I have the third-floor back, vacant since a week back. Should you wish to look at it?"

The young man followed her up the stairs. A faint light from no particular source mitigated the shadows of the halls. They trod noiselessly upon a stair carpet that its own loom would have forsworn. It seemed to have become vegetable; to have degenerated in that rank, sunless air to lush lichen or spreading moss that grew in patches to the stair-case and was viscid under the foot like organic matter. At each turn of the stairs were vacant niches in the wall. Perhaps plants had once been set within them. If so they had died in that foul and tainted air. It may be that statues of the saints had stood there, but it was not difficult to conceive that imps and devils had dragged them forth in the darkness and down to the unholy depths of some furnished pit below.

"This is the room," said the housekeeper, from her furry throat. "It's a nice room. It ain't often vacant. I had some most elegant people in it last summer — no trouble at all, and paid in advance to the minute. The water's at the end of the hall. Sprowls and Mooney kept it three months. They done a vaudeville sketch. Miss B'retta Sprowls — you may have heard of her — Oh, that was just the stage names — right there over the dresser is where the marriage certificate hung, framed. The gas is here, and you see there is plenty of closet room. It's a room everybody likes. It never stays idle long."

"Do you have many theatrical people rooming here?" asked the young man.

"They comes and goes. A good proportion of my lodgers is connected with the theatres. Yes, sir, this is the theatrical district. Actor people never stays long anywhere. I get my share. Yes, they comes and they goes."

He engaged the room, paying for a week in advance. He was tired, he said, and would take possession at once. He counted out the money. The room had been made ready, she said, even to towels and water. As the housekeeper moved away he put, for the thousandth time, the question that he carried at the end of his tongue.

"A young girl — Miss Vashner — Miss Eloise Vashner — do you remember such a one among your lodgers? She would be singing on the stage, most likely. A fair girl, of medium height and slender, with reddish, gold hair and dark mole near her left eyebrow."

"No, I don't remember the name. Them stage people has names they change as often as their rooms. They comes and they goes. No, I don't call that one to mind."

No. Always no. Five months of ceaseless interrogation and the inevitable negative. So much time by days in questioning managers, agents, schools and choruses; by night among the audiences of theatres from all-star casts down to music halls so low that he dreaded to find what he most hoped for. He who had loved her best had tried to find her. He was sure that since her disappearance from home this great, water-girt city held her somewhere, but it was like a monstrous quicksand, shifting its particles constantly, with no foundation, its upper granules of to-day buried to-morrow in ooze and slime.

The furnished room received its latest guest with a first glow of pseudo-hospitality, a hectic, haggard, perfunctory welcome like the specious smile of a demirep. The sophistical comfort came in reflected gleams from the decayed furniture, the ragged brocade upholstery of a couch and two chairs, a foot-wide cheap pier glass between the two windows, from one or two gilt picture frames and a brass bedstead in a corner.

The guest reclined, inert, upon a chair, while the room, confused in speech as though it were an apartment in Babel, tried to discourse to him of its divers tenantry.

A polychromatic rug like some brilliant-flowered rectangular, tropical islet lay surrounded by a billowy sea of soiled matting. Upon the gay-papered wall were those pictures that pursue the homeless one from house to house — The Huguenot Lovers, The First Quarrel, The Wedding Breakfast, Psyche at the Fountain. The mantel's chastely severe outline was ingloriously veiled behind some pert drapery drawn rakishly askew like the sashes of the Amazonian ballet. Upon it was some desolate flotsam cast aside by the room's marooned when a lucky sail had borne them to a fresh port — a trifling vase or two, pictures of actresses, a medicine bottle, some stray cards out of a deck.

One by one, as the characters of a cryptograph became explicit, the little signs left by the furnished room's procession of guests developed a significance. The threadbare space in the rug in front of the dresser told that lovely women had marched in the throng. The tiny fingerprints on the wall spoke of little prisoners trying to feel their way to sun and air. A splattered stain, raying like the shadow of a bursting bomb, witnessed where a hurled glass or bottle had splintered with its contents against the wall. Across the pier glass had been scrawled with a diamond in staggering letters the name "Marie." It seemed that the succession of dwellers in the furnished room had turned in fury — perhaps tempted beyond forbearance by its garish coldness — and wreaked upon it their passions. The furniture was chipped and bruised; the couch, distorted by bursting springs, seemed a horrible monster that had been slain during the stress of some grotesque convulsion. Some more potent upheaval had cloven a great slice from the marble mantel. Each plank in the floor owned its particular cant and shriek as from a separate and individual agony. It seemed incredible that all this malice and injury had been wrought upon the room by those who had called it for a time their home; and yet it may have been the cheated home instinct surviving blindly, the resentful rage at false household gods that had kindled their wrath. A hut that is our own we can sweep and adorn and cherish.

The young tenant in the chair allowed these thoughts to file, soft-shod, through his mind, while there drifted into the room furnished sounds and furnished scents. He heard in one room a tittering and incontinent, slack laughter; in others the monologue of a scold, the rattling of dice, a lullaby, and one crying dully; above him a banjo tinkled with spirit. Doors banged somewhere; the elevated trains roared intermittently; a cat yowled miserably upon a back fence. And he breathed the breath of the house — a dank savor rather than a smell — a cold, musty effluvium as from underground vaults mingled with the reeking exhalations of linoleum and mildewed and rotten woodwork.

Then suddenly, as he rested there, the room was filled with the strong, sweet odor of mignonette. It came as upon a single buffet of wind with such sureness and fragrance and emphasis that it almost seemed a living visitant. And the man cried aloud: "What, dear?" as if he had been called, and sprang up and faced about. The rich odor clung to him and wrapped him around. He reached out his arms for it, all his senses for the time confused and commingled. How could one be peremptorily called by an odor? Surely it must have been a sound. But, was it not the sound that had touched, that had caressed him?

"She has been in this room," he cried, and he sprang to wrest from it a token, for he knew he would recognize the smallest thing that had belonged to her or that she had touched. This enveloping scent of mignonette, the odor that she had loved and made her own — whence came it?

The room had been but carelessly set in order. Scattered upon the flimsy dresser scarf were a half a dozen hairpins — those discreet, indistinguishable friends of womankind, feminine of gender, infinite of mood and uncommunicative of tense. These he ignored, conscious of their triumphant lack of identity. Ransacking the drawers of the dresser he came upon a discarded, tiny, ragged handkerchief. He pressed it to his face. It was racy and insolent with heliotrope; he hurled it to the floor. In another drawer he found odd buttons, a theatre programme, a pawn-broker's card, two lost marshmallows, a book on the divination of dreams. In the last was a woman's black satin hair bow, which halted him, poised between ice and fire. But the black satin hair bow also is femininity's demure, impersonal common ornament and tells no tales.

And then he traversed the room like a hound on the scent, skimming the walls, considering the corners of the bulging matting on his hands and knees, rummaging mantel and tables, the curtains and hangings, the drunken cabinet in the corner, for a visible sign, unable to perceive that she was there beside, around, against, within, above him, clinging to him, wooing him, calling him so poignantly through the finer senses that even his grosser ones became cognizant of the call. Once again he answered loudly: "Yes, dear!" and turned, wild-eyed, to gaze on vacancy, for he could not yet discern form and color and love and outstretched arms in the odor of mignonette. Oh, God! whence that odor, and since when have odors had a voice to call? Thus he groped.

He burrowed in crevices and corners, and found corks and cigarettes. These he passed in passive contempt. But once he found in a fold of the matting a half-smoked cigar, and this he ground beneath his heel with a green and trenchant oath. He sifted the room from end to end. He found dreary and ignoble small records of many a peripatetic tenant; but of her whom he sought, and who may have lodged there, and whose spirit seemed to hover there, he found no trace.

And then he thought of the housekeeper.

He ran from the haunted room downstairs and to a door that showed a crack of light. She came out to his knock. He smothered his excitement as best he could.

"Will you tell me, madam," he besought her, "who occupied the room I have before I came?"

"Yes, sir. I can tell you again. 'Twas Sprowls and Mooney, as I said. Miss B'retta Sprowls it was in the theatres, but Missis Mooney she was. My house is well known for respectability. The marriage certificate hung, framed, on a nail over — "

"What kind of a lady was Miss Sprowls — in looks, I mean?"

"Why, black-haired, sir, short, and stout, with a comical face. They left a week ago Tuesday."

"And before they occupied it?"

"Why, there was a single gentleman connected with the draying business. He left owing me a week. Before him was Missis Crowder and her two children, that stayed four months; and back of them was old Mr. Doyle, whose sons paid for him. He kept the room six months. That goes back a year, sir, and further I do not remember."

He thanked her and crept back to his room. The room was dead. The essence that had vivified it was gone. The perfume of mignonette had departed. In its place was the old, stale odor of mouldy house furniture, of atmosphere in storage.

The ebbing of his hope drained his faith. He sat staring at the yellow, singing gaslight. Soon he walked to the bed and began to tear the sheets into strips. With the blade of his knife he drove them tightly into every crevice around windows and door. When all was snug and taut he turned out the light, turned the gas full on again and laid himself gratefully upon the bed.

It was Mrs. McCool's night to go with the can for beer. So she fetched it and sat with Mrs. Purdy in one of those subterranean retreats where housekeepers foregather and the worm dieth seldom.

"I rented out my third-floor-back this evening," said Mrs. Purdy, across a fine circle of foam. "A young man took it. He went up to bed two hours ago."

"Now, did ye, Mrs. Purdy, ma'am?" said Mrs. McCool, with intense admiration. "You do be a wonder for rentin' rooms of that kind. And did ye tell him, then?" she concluded in a husky whisper laden with mystery.

"Rooms," said Mrs. Purdy, in her furriest tones, "are furnished for to rent. I did not tell him, Mrs. McCool."

" 'Tis right ye are, ma'am; 'tis by renting rooms we kape alive. Ye have the rale sense for business, ma'am. There be many people will rayjict the rentin' of a room if they be tould a suicide has been after dyin' in the bed of it."

"As you say, we has our living to be making," remarked Mrs. Purdy.

"Yis, ma'am; 'tis true. 'Tis just one wake ago this day I helped ye lay out the third-floor-back. A pretty slip of a colleen she was to be killin' herself wid the gas — a swate little face she had, Mrs. Purdy, ma'am."

"She'd a-been called handsome, as you say," said Mrs. Purdy, assenting but critical, "but for that mole she had a-growin' by her left eyebrow. Do fill up your glass again, Mrs. McCool."

# Jack London (1876–1916)

AFTER HIS BIRTH, in San Francisco in 1876, the reputed bastard son of a wandering astrologer, London lived only forty years, but in those years he packed more hard-living action and hard-hitting writing than most authors could manage in a dozen normal lifetimes. A school dropout at fourteen, he lived by selling oysters he stole from Oakland Bay beds. At twenty-one he shipped on a sealing cruise to Japan; returned to become a tramp; got interested in sociology and literature and, with a unique ambivalence, worshipped those two extremes, Nietzsche and Marx. His first book, published in 1900, *The Son of the Wolf*, was an instant success. From then on there was an unending stream of books: short-story collections, novels, social treatises, memoirs, and travel observations. In addition he went on foreign correspondence assignments and lecture tours, became rich and famous and, in his eagerness for wealth, became an artist manqué. His life ended in suicide. But he did leave some fine works, among them *The Call of the Wild*, *The Sea-Wolf*, *Martin Eden*, and *The Iron Heel*.

Unlike many man-and-dog stories, "To Build a Fire" is unsentimental and because of that all the more effective. Both animal and human come off here as distinctly individual creatures, one reacting to the sharp pain of the Yukon cold with instinct, the other with reasoning. So vividly does London make one feel that seventy-five-below-zero frigidity that even in the tropics a reader could want to hug a fire. The story emphasizes, as does most of the author's fiction, individual struggle in primitive circumstances. The short story was London's favorite form of writing. Shortly before his death he wrote a magazine editor: "I do not mind telling you that, had the United States been as kindly toward the short story writer as France has always been kindly, from the beginning of my writing career I would have written many a score of short stories quite different from the ones I have written."

# To Build a Fire

DAY had broken cold and gray, exceedingly cold and gray, when the man turned aside from the main Yukon trail and climbed the high earth-bank, where a dim and little-travelled trail led eastward through the fat spruce timberland. It was a steep bank, and he paused for breath at the top, excusing the act to himself by looking at his watch. It was nine o'clock. There was no sun nor hint of sun, though there was not a cloud in the sky. It was a clear day, and yet there seemed an intangible pall over the face of things, a subtle gloom that made the day dark, and that was due to the absence of sun. This fact did not worry the man. He was used to the lack of sun. It had been days since he had seen the sun, and he knew that a few more days must pass before that cheerful orb, due south, would just peep above the sky-line and dip immediately from view.

The man flung a look back along the way he had come. The Yukon lay a mile wide and hidden under three feet of ice. On top of this ice were as many feet of snow. It was all pure white, rolling in gentle undulations where the ice-jams of the freeze-up had formed. North and south, as far as his eye could see, it was unbroken white, save for a dark hair-line that curved and twisted from around the spruce-covered island to the south, and that curved and twisted away into the north, where it disappeared behind another spruce-covered island. This dark hair-line was the trail — the main trail — that led south five hundred miles to the Chilcoot Pass, Dyea, and salt water; and that led north seventy miles to Dawson, and still on to the north a thousand miles to Nulato, and finally to St. Michael on Bering Sea, a thousand miles and half a thousand more.

But all this — the mysterious, far-reaching hair-line trail, the absence of sun from the sky, the tremendous cold, and the strangeness and weirdness of it all — made no impression on the man. It was not because he was long used to it. He was a newcomer in the land, a *chechaquo*, and this was his first winter. The trouble with him was that he was without imagination. He was quick and alert in the things of life, but only in the things, and not in the significances. Fifty degrees below zero meant eighty-odd degrees of frost. Such fact impressed him as being cold and uncomfortable, and that was all. It did not lead him to meditate upon his frailty as a creature of temperature, and upon man's frailty in general, able only to live within certain narrow limits of heat and cold; and from there on it did not lead him to the conjectural field of immortality and man's place in the universe. Fifty degrees below zero stood for a bite of frost that hurt and that must be guarded against by the use of mittens, ear-flaps, warm moccasins, and thick socks. Fifty degrees below zero was to him just precisely fifty degrees below zero. That there should be anything more to it than that was a thought that never entered his head.

As he turned to go on, he spat speculatively. There was a sharp, explosive crackle that startled him. He spat again. And again, in the air, before it could fall to the snow, the spittle crackled. He knew that at fifty below spittle crackled on the snow, but this spittle had crackled in the air. Undoubtedly it was colder than fifty below — how much colder he did not know. But the temperature did not matter. He was bound for the old claim on the left fork of Henderson Creek, where the boys were already. They had come over across the divide from the Indian Creek country, while he had come the roundabout way to look at the possibilities of getting out logs in the spring from the islands in the Yukon. He would be in to camp by six o'clock; a bit after dark, it was true, but the boys would be there, a fire would be going, and a hot supper would be ready. As for lunch, he pressed his hand against the protruding bundle under his jacket. It was also under his shirt, wrapped up in a handkerchief and lying against the naked skin. It was the only way to keep the biscuits from freezing. He smiled agreeably to himself as he thought of those biscuits, each cut open and sopped in bacon grease, and each enclosing a generous slice of fried bacon.

He plunged in among the big spruce trees. The trail was faint. A foot of snow had fallen since the last sled had passed over, and he was glad he was without a sled, travelling light. In fact he carried nothing but the lunch wrapped in the handkerchief. He was surprised, however, at the cold. It certainly was cold, he concluded, as he rubbed his numb nose and cheek-bones with his mittened hand. He was a warm-whiskered man, but the hair on his face did not protect the high cheek-bones and the eager nose that thrust itself aggressively into the frosty air.

At the man's heels trotted a dog, a big native husky, the proper wolf-dog, gray-coated and without any visible or temperamental difference from its brother, the wild wolf. The animal was depressed by the tremendous cold. It knew that it was no time for travelling. Its instinct told it a truer tale than was told to the man by the man's judgment. In reality, it was not merely colder than fifty below zero; it was colder than sixty below, than seventy below. It was seventy-five below zero. Since the freezing-point is thirty-two above zero, it meant that one hundred and seven degrees of frost obtained. The dog did not know anything about thermometers. Possibly in its brain there was no sharp consciousness of a condition of very cold such as was in the man's brain. But the brute had its instinct. It experienced a vague but menacing apprehension that subdued it and made it slink along at the man's heels, and that made it question eagerly every unwonted movement of the man as if expecting him to go into camp or to seek shelter somewhere and build a fire. The dog had learned fire, and it wanted fire, or else to burrow under the snow and cuddle its warmth away from the air.

The frozen moisture of its breathing had settled on its fur in a fine powder of frost, and especially were its jowls, muzzle, and eyelashes whitened by its crystalled breath. The man's red beard and mustache were likewise frosted, but more solidly, the deposit taking the form of ice and increasing with every warm, moist breath he exhaled. Also, the man was chewing tobacco, and the muzzle of ice held his lips so rigidly that he was unable to clear his chin when he expelled the juice. The result was that a crystal beard of the color and solidity of amber was increasing its length on his chin. If he fell down it would shatter itself, like glass, into brittle fragments. But he did not mind the appendage. It was the penalty all tobacco-chewers paid in that country, and he had been out before in two cold snaps. They had not been so cold as this, he knew, but by the spirit thermometer at Sixty Mile he knew they had been registered at fifty below and at fifty-five.

He held on through the level stretch of woods for several miles, crossed a wide flat of nigger-heads, and dropped down a bank to the frozen bed of a small stream. This was Henderson Creek, and he knew he was ten miles from the forks. He looked at his watch. It was ten o'clock. He was making four miles an hour, and he calculated that he would arrive at the forks at half-past twelve. He decided to celebrate that event by eating his lunch there.

The dog dropped in again at his heels, with a tail drooping discouragement, as the man swung along the creek-bed. The furrow of the old sled-trail was plainly visible, but a dozen inches of snow covered the marks of the last runners. In a month no man had come up or down that silent creek. The man held steadily on. He was not much given to thinking, and just then particularly he had nothing to think about save that he would eat lunch at the forks and that at six o'clock he would be in camp with the boys. There was noboby to talk to; and, had there been, speech would have been impossible because of the ice-muzzle on his mouth. So he continued monotonously to chew tobacco and to increase the length of his amber beard.

Once in a while the thought reiterated itself that it was very cold and that he had never experienced such cold. As he walked along he rubbed his cheek-bones and nose with the back of his mittened hand. He did this automatically, now and again changing hands. But rub as he would, the instant he stopped his cheek-bones went numb, and the following instant the end of his nose went numb. He was sure to frost his cheeks; he knew that, and experienced a pang of regret that he had not devised a nose-strap of the sort Bud wore in cold snaps. Such a strap passed across the cheeks, as well, and saved them. But it didn't matter much, after all. What were frosted cheeks? A bit painful, that was all; they were never serious.

Empty as the man's mind was of thoughts, he was keenly observant, and he noticed the changes in the creek, the curves and bends and timber-jams, and always he sharply noted where he placed his feet. Once, coming around a bend, he shied abruptly, like a startled horse, curved away from the place where he had been walking, and retreated several paces back along the trail. The creek he knew was frozen clear to the botton, — no creek could contain water in that arctic winter, — but he knew also that there were springs that bubbled out from the hillsides and ran along under the snow and on top the ice of the creek. He knew that the coldest snaps never froze these springs, and he knew likewise their danger. They were traps. They hid pools of water under the snow that might be three inches deep, or three feet. Sometimes a skin of ice half an inch thick covered them, and in turn was covered by the snow.

Sometimes there were alternate layers of water and ice-skin, so that when one broke through he kept on breaking through for a while, sometimes wetting himself to the waist.

That was why he had shied in such panic. He had felt the give under his feet and heard the crackle of a snow-hidden ice-skin. And to get his feet wet in such a temperature meant trouble and danger. At the very least it meant delay, for he would be forced to stop and build a fire, and under its protection to bare his feet while he dried his socks and moccasins. He stood and studied the creek-bed and its banks, and decided that the flow of water came from the right. He reflected awhile, rubbing his nose and cheeks, then skirted to the left, stepping gingerly and testing the footing for each step. Once clear of the danger, he took a fresh chew of tobacco and swung along at his four-mile gait.

In the course of the next two hours he came upon several similar traps. Usually the snow above the hidden pools had a sunken, candied appearance that advertised the danger. Once, again, however, he had a close call; and once, suspecting danger, he compelled the dog to go on in front. The dog did not want to go. It hung back until the man shoved it forward, and then it went quickly across the white, unbroken surface. Suddenly it broke through, floundered to one side, and got away to firmer footing. It had wet its forefeet and legs, and almost immediately, the water that clung to it turned to ice. It made quick efforts to lick the ice off its legs, then dropped down in the snow and began to bite out the ice that had formed between the toes. This was a matter of instinct. To permit the ice to remain would mean sore feet. It did not know this. It merely obeyed the mysteriously prompting that arose from the deep crypts of its being. But the man knew, having achieved a judgment on the subject, and he removed the mitten from his right hand and helped tear out the ice-particles. He did not expose his fingers more than a minute, and was astonished at the swift numbness that smote them. It certainly was cold. He pulled on the mitten hastily, and beat the hand savagely across his chest.

At twelve o'clock the day was at its brightest. Yet the sun was too far south on its winter journey to clear the horizon. The bulge of the earth intervened between it and Henderson Creek, where the man walked under a clear sky at noon and cast no shadow. At half-past twelve, to the minute, he arrived at the forks of the creek. He was pleased at the speed he had made. If he kept it up, he would certainly be with the boys by six. He unbuttoned his jacket and shirt and drew forth his lunch. The action consumed no more than a quarter of a minute, yet in that brief moment the numbness laid hold of the exposed fingers. He did not put the mitten on, but, instead, struck the fingers a dozen sharp smashes against his leg. Then he sat down on a snow-covered log to eat. The sting that followed upon the striking of his fingers against his leg ceased so quickly that he was startled. He had no chance to take a bite of biscuit. He struck the fingers repeatedly and returned them to the mitten, baring the other hand for the purpose of eating. He tried to take a mouthful, but the ice-muzzle prevented. He had forgotten to build a fire and thaw out. He chuckled at his foolishness, and as he chuckled he noted the numbness creeping into the exposed fingers. Also, he noted that the stinging which had first come to his toes when he sat down was already passing away. He wondered whether the toes were warm or numb. He moved them inside the moccasins and decided that they were numb.

He pulled the mitten on hurriedly and stood up. He was a bit frightened. He stamped up and down until the stinging returned into the feet. It certainly was cold, was his thought. That man from Sulphur Creek had spoken the truth when telling how cold it sometimes got in the country. And he had laughed at him at the time! That showed one must not be too sure of things. There was no mistake about it, it *was* cold. He strode up and down, stamping his feet and threshing his arms, until reassured by the returning warmth. Then he got out matches and proceeded to make a fire. From the undergrowth where high water of the previous spring had lodged a supply of seasoned twigs, he got his firewood. Working carefully from a small beginning, he soon had a roaring fire, over which he thawed the ice from his face and in the protection of which he ate his biscuits. For the moment the cold of space was outwitted. The dog took satisfaction in the fire stretching out close enough for warmth and far enough away to escape being singed.

When the man had finished, he filled his pipe and took his comfortable time over a smoke. Then he pulled on his mittens, settled the ear-flaps on his cap firmly about this ears, and took the creek trail up the left fork. The dog was disappointed and yearned back toward the fire. This man did not know cold. Possibly all the generations of his ancestry had been ignorant of cold, of real cold, of cold one hundred and seven degrees below freezing-point. But the dog knew; all its ancestry knew, and it had inherited the knowledge. And it knew that it was not good to walk abroad in such fearful cold. It was the time to lie snug in a hole in the snow and wait for a curtain of cloud to be drawn across the face of outer space whence this cold came. On the other hand, there was no keen intimacy between the dog and the man. The one was the toil-slave of the other, and the only caresses it had ever received were the caresses of the whip-lash and of harsh and menacing throat-sounds that threatened the whip-lash. So the dog made no effort to communicate its apprehension to the man. It was not concerned in the welfare of the man; it was for its own sake that it yearned back toward the fire. But the man whistled, and spoke to it with the sound of whip-lashes, and the dog swung in at the man's heels and followed after.

The man took a chew of tobacco and proceeded to start a new amber beard. Also, his moist breath quickly powdered with white his mustache, eyebrows, and lashes. There did not seem to be so many springs on the left fork of the Henderson, and for half an hour the man saw no signs of any. And then it happened. At a place where there were no signs, where the soft, unbroken snow seemed to advertise solidity beneath, the man broke through. It was not deep. He wet himself halfway to the knees before he floundered out to the firm crust.

He was angry, and cursed his luck aloud. He had hoped to get into camp with the boys at six o'clock, and this would delay him an hour, for he would have to build a fire and dry out his foot-gear. This was imperative at that low temperature — he knew that much; and he turned aside to the bank, which he climbed. On top, tangled in the underbrush about the trunks of several small spruce trees, was a high-water deposit of dry firewood — sticks and twigs, principally, but also larger portions of seasoned branches and fine, dry, last-year's grasses. He threw down several large pieces on top of the snow. This served for a foundation and prevented the young flame from drowning itself in the snow it otherwise would melt. The flame he got by touching a match to a small shred of birch-bark that he took from his pocket. This burned even more readily than paper. Placing it on the foundation, he fed the young flame with wisps of dry grass and with the tiniest dry twigs.

He worked slowly and carefully, keenly aware of his danger. Gradually, as the flame grew stronger, he increased the size of the twigs with which he fed it. He squatted in the snow, pulling the twigs out from their entanglement in the brush and feeding directly to the flame. He knew there must be no failure. When it is seventy-five below zero, a man must not fail in his first attempt to build a fire — that is, if his feet are wet. If his feet are dry, and he fails, he can run along the trail for half a mile and restore his circulation. But the circulation of wet and freezing feet cannot be restored by running when it is seventy-five below. No matter how fast he runs, the wet feet will freeze the harder.

All this the man knew. The old-timer on Sulphur Creek had told him about it the previous fall, and now he was appreciating the advice. Already all sensation had gone out of his feet. To build a fire he had been forced to remove his mittens, and the fingers had quickly gone numb. His pace of four miles an hour had kept his heart pumping blood to the surface of his body and to all the extremities. But the instant he stopped, the action of the pump eased down. The cold of space smote the unprotected tip of the planet, and he, being on that unprotected tip, received the full force of the blow. The blood of his body recoiled before it. The blood was alive, like the dog, and like the dog it wanted to hide away and cover itself up from the fearful cold. So long as he walked four miles an hour, he pumped that blood, willy-nilly, to the surface; but now it ebbed away and sank down into the recesses of his body. The extremities were the first to feel its absence. His wet feet froze the faster, and his exposed fingers numbed the faster, though they had not yet begun to freeze. Nose and cheeks were already freezing, while the skin of all his body chilled as it lost its blood.

But he was safe. Toes and nose and cheeks would be only touched by the frost, for the fire was beginning to burn with strength. He was feeding it with twigs the size of his finger. In another minute he would be able to feed it with branches the size of his wrist, and then he could remove his wet foot-gear and, while it dried, he could keep his naked feet warm by the fire, rubbing them at first, of course, with snow. The fire was a success. He was safe. He remembered the advice of the old-timer on Sulphur Creek, and smiled. The old-timer had been very serious in laying down the law that no man must travel alone in the Klondike after fifty below. Well, here he was; he had had the accident; he was alone; and he had saved himself. Those old-timers were rather womanish, some of them, he thought. All a man had to do was to keep his head, and he was all right. Any man who was a man could travel alone. But it was surprising, the rapidity with which his cheeks and nose were freezing. And he had not thought his fingers could go lifeless in so short a time. Lifeless they were, for he could scarcely make them move together to grip a twig, and they seemed remote from his body and from him. When he touched a twig, he had to look and see whether or not he had hold of it. The wires were pretty well down between him and his finger-ends.

All of which counted for little. There was the fire, snapping and crackling and promising life with every dancing flame. He started to untie his moccasins. They were coated with ice; the thick German socks were like sheaths of iron halfway to the knees; and the moccasin strings were like rods of steel all twisted and knotted as by some conflagration. For a moment he tugged with his numb fingers, then, realizing the folly of it, he drew his sheath-knife.

But before he could cut the strings, it happened. It was his own fault or, rather, his mistake. He should not have built the fire under the spruce tree. He should have built it in the open. But it had been easier to pull the twigs from the brush and drop them directly on the fire. Now the tree under which he had done this carried a weight of snow on its boughs. No wind had blown for weeks, and each bough was fully weighted. Each time he had pulled a twig he had communicated a slight agitation to the tree — an imperceptible agitation, so far as he was concerned, but an agitation sufficient to bring about the disaster. High up in the tree one bough capsized its load of snow. This fell on the boughs beneath, capsizing them. This process continued spreading out and involving the whole tree. It grew like an avalanche, and it descended without warning upon the man and the fire, and the fire was blotted out! Where it had burned was a mantle of fresh and disordered snow.

The man was shocked. It was as though he had just heard his own sentence of death. For a moment he sat and stared at the spot where the fire had been. Then he grew very calm. Perhaps the old-timer on Sulphur Creek was right. If he had only a trail-mate he would have been in no danger now. The trail-mate could have built the fire. Well, it was up to him to build the fire over again, and this second time there must be no failure. Even if he succeeded, he would most likely lose some toes. His feet must be badly frozen by now, and there would be some time before the second fire was ready.

Such were his thoughts, but he did not sit and think them. He was busy all the time they were passing through his mind. He made a new foundation for a fire, this time in the open, where no treacherous tree could blot it out. Next, he gathered dry grasses and tiny twigs from the high-water flotsam. He could not bring his fingers together to pull them out, but he was able to gather them by the handful. In this way he got many rotten twigs and bits of green moss that were undesirable, but it was the best he could do. He worked methodically, even collecting an armful of the larger branches to be used later when the fire gathered strength. And all the while the dog sat and watched him, a certain yearning wistfulness in its eyes, for it looked upon him as the fire-provider, and the fire was slow in coming.

When all was ready, the man reached in his pocket for a second piece of birch-bark. He knew the bark was there, and, though he could not feel it with his fingers, he could hear its crisp rustling as he fumbled for it. Try as he would, he could not clutch hold of it. And all the time, in his consciousness, was the knowledge that each instant his feet were freezing. This thought tended to put him in a panic, but he fought against it and kept calm. He pulled on his mittens with his teeth, and threshed his arms back and forth, beating his hands with all his might against his sides. He did this sitting down, and he stood up to do it; and all the while the dog sat in the snow, its wolf-brush of a tail curled around warmly over its forefeet, its sharp wolf-ears pricked forward intently as it watched the man. And the man, as he beat and threshed with his arms and hands felt a great surge of envy as he regarded the creature that was warm and secure in its natural covering.

After a time he was aware of the first far-away signals of sensation in his beaten fingers. The faint tingling grew stronger till it evolved into a stinging ache that was excruciating, but which the man hailed with satisfaction. He stripped the mitten from his right hand and fetched forth the birch-bark. The exposed fingers were quickly going numb again. Next he brought out his bunch of sulphur matches. But the tremendous cold had already driven the life out of his fingers. In his effort to separate one match from the others, the whole bunch fell in the snow. He tried to pick it out of the snow, but failed. The dead fingers could neither touch nor clutch. He was very careful. He drove the thought of freezing feet, and nose, and cheeks out of his mind, devoting his whole soul to the matches. He watched, using the sense of vision in place of that of touch, and when he saw his fingers on each side the bunch, he closed them — that is, he willed to close them, for the wires were down, and the fingers did not obey. He pulled the mitten on the right hand, and beat it fiercely against his knee. Then, with both mittened hands, he scooped the bunch of matches, along with much snow, into his lap. Yet he was no better off.

After some manipulation he managed to get the bunch between the heels of his mittened hands. In this fashion he carried it to his mouth. The ice crackled and snapped when by a violent effort he opened his mouth. He drew the lower jaw in, curled the upper lip out of the way, and scraped the bunch with his upper teeth in order to separate a match. He succeeded in getting one, which he dropped on his lap. He was no better off. He could not pick it up. Then he devised a way. He picked it up in his teeth and scratched it on his leg. Twenty times he scratched before he succeeded in lighting it. As it flamed he held it with his teeth to the birch-bark. But the burning brimstone went up his nostrils and into his lungs, causing him to cough spasmodically. The match fell into the snow and went out.

The old-timer on Sulphur Creek was right, he thought in the moment of controlled despair that ensued: after fifty below, a man should travel with a partner. He beat his hands, but failed in exciting any sensation. Suddenly he bared both hands, removing the mittens with his teeth. He caught the whole bunch between the heels of his hands. His arm-muscles not being frozen enabled him to press the hand-heels tightly against the matches. Then he scratched the bunch along his leg. It flared into flame, seventy sulphur matches at once! There was no wind to blow them out. He kept his head to one side to escape the strangling fumes, and held the blazing bunch to the birch-bark. As he so held it, he became aware of sensation in his hand. His flesh was burning. He could smell it. Deep down below the surface he could feel it. The sensation developed into pain that grew acute. And still he endured it, holding the flame of the matches clumsily to the bark that would not light readily because his own burning hands were in the way, absorbing most of the flame.

At last, when he could endure no more, he jerked his hands apart. The blazing matches fell sizzling into the snow, but the birch-bark was alight. He began laying dry grasses and the tiniest twigs on the flame. He could not pick and choose, for he had to lift the fuel between the heels of his hands. Small pieces of rotten wood and green moss clung to the twigs, and he bit them off as well as he could with his teeth. He cherished the flame carefully and awkwardly. It meant life, and it must not perish. The withdrawal of blood from the surface of his body now made him begin to shiver, and he grew more awkward. A large piece of green moss fell squarely on the little fire. He tried to poke it out with his fingers, but his shivering frame made him poke too far, and he disrupted the nucleus of the little fire, the burning grasses and tiny twigs separating and scattering. He tried to poke them together again, but in spite of the tenseness of the effort, his shivering got away with him, and the twigs gushed a puff of smoke and went out. The fire-provider had failed. As he looked apathetically about him, his eyes chanced on the dog, sitting across the ruins of the fire from him, in the snow, making restless, hunching movements, slightly lifting one forefoot and then the other, shifting its weight back and forth on them with wistful eagerness.

The sight of the dog put a wild idea into his head. He remembered the tale of the man, caught in a blizzard, who killed a steer and crawled inside the carcass, and so was saved. He would kill the dog and bury his hands in the warm body until the numbness went out of them. Then he could build another fire. He spoke to the dog, calling it to him; but in his voice was a strange note of fear that frightened the animal, who had never known the man to speak in such a way before. Something was the matter, and its suspicious nature sensed danger — it knew not what danger, but somewhere, somehow, in its brain arose an apprehension of the man. It flattened its ears down at the sound of the man's voice, and its restless, hunching movements and the liftings and shiftings of its forefeet became more pronounced; but it would not come to the man. He got on his hands and knees and crawled toward the dog. This unusual posture again excited suspicion, and the animal sidled mincingly away.

The man sat up in the snow for a moment and struggled for calmness. Then he pulled on his mittens, by means of his teeth, and got upon his feet. He glanced down at first in order to assure himself that he was really standing up, for the absence of sensation in his feet left him unrelated to the earth. His erect position in itself started to drive the webs of suspicion from the dog's mind; and when he spoke peremptorily, with the sound of whip-lashes in his voice, the dog rendered its customary allegiance and came to him. As it came within reaching distance, the man lost his control. His arms flashed out to the dog, and he experienced genuine surprise when he discovered that his hands could not clutch, that there was neither bend nor feeling in the fingers. He had forgotten for the moment that they were frozen and that they were freezing more and more. All this happened quickly, and before the animal could get away, he encircled its body with his arms. He sat down in the snow, and in this fashion held the dog, while it snarled and whined and struggled.

But it was all he could do, hold its body encircled in his arms and sit there. He realized that he could not kill the dog. There was no way to do it. With his helpless hands he could neither draw nor hold his sheath-knife nor throttle the animal. He released it, and it plunged wildly away, with tail between its legs, and still snarling. It halted forty feet away and surveyed him curiously, with ears sharply pricked forward. The man looked down at his hands in order to locate them, and found them hanging on the ends of his arms. It struck him as curious that one should have to use his eyes in order to find out where his hands were. He began threshing his arms back and forth, beating the mittened hands against his sides. He did this for five minutes, violently, and his heart pumped enough blood up to the surface to put a stop to his shivering. But no sensation was aroused in the hands. He had an impression that they hung like weights on the ends of his arms, but when he tried to run the impression down, he could not find it.

A certain fear of death, dull and oppressive, came to him. This fear quickly became poignant as he realized that it was no longer a mere matter of freezing his fingers and toes, or of losing his hands and feet, but that it was a matter of life and death with the chances against him. This threw him into a panic, and he turned and ran up the creek-bed along the old, dim trail. The dog joined in behind and kept up with him. He ran blindly, without intention, in fear such as he had never known in his life. Slowly, as he ploughed and floundered through the snow, he began to see things again, — the banks of the creek, the old timber-jams, the leafless aspens, and the sky. The running made him feel better. He did not shiver. Maybe, if he ran on, his feet would thaw out; and, anyway, if he ran far enough, he would reach camp and the boys. Without doubt he would lose some fingers and toes and some of his face; but the boys would take care of him, and save the rest of him when he got there. And at the same time there was another thought in his mind that said he would never get to the camp and the boys; that it was too many miles away, that the freezing had too great a start on him, and that he would soon be stiff and dead. This thought he kept in the background and refused to consider. Sometimes it pushed itself forward and demanded to be heard, but he thrust it back and strove to think of other things.

It struck him as curious that he could run at all on feet so frozen that he could not feel them when they struck the earth and took the weight of his body. He seemed to himself to skim along above the surface, and to have no connection with the earth. Somewhere he had once seen a winged Mercury, and he wondered if Mercury felt as he felt when skimming over the earth.

His theory of running until he reached camp and the boys had one flaw in it: he lacked the endurance. Several times he stumbled, and finally he tottered, crumpled up, and fell. When he tried to rise, he failed. He must sit and rest, he decided, and next time he would merely walk and keep on going. As he sat and regained his breath, he noted that he was feeling quite warm and comfortable. He was not shivering, and it even seemed that a warm glow had come to his chest and trunk. And yet, when he touched his nose or cheeks, there was no sensation. Running would not thaw them out. Nor would it thaw out his hands and feet. Then the thought came to him that the frozen portions of his body must be extending. He tried to keep this thought down, to forget it, to think of something else; he was aware of the panicky feeling that it caused, and he was afraid of the panic. But the thought asserted itself, and persisted, until it produced a vision of his body totally frozen. This was too much, and he made another wild run along the trail. Once he slowed down to a walk, but the thought of the freezing extending itself made him run again.

And all the time the dog ran with him, at his heels. When he fell down a second time, it curled its tail over its forefeet and sat in front of him, facing him, curiously eager and intent. The warmth and security of the animal angered him, and he cursed it till it flattened down its ears appeasingly. This time the shivering came more quickly upon the man. He was losing in his battle with the frost. It was creeping into his body from all sides. The thought of it drove him on but he ran no more than a hundred feet, when he staggered and pitched headlong. It was his last panic. When he had recovered his breath and control he sat up and entertained in his mind the conception of meeting death with dignity. However, the conception did not come to him in such terms. His idea of it was that he had been making a fool of himself, running around like a chicken with its head cut off — such was the simile that occurred to him. Well, he was bound to freeze anyway, and he might as well take it decently. With this new-found peace of mind came the first glimmerings of drowsiness. A good idea, he thought, to sleep off to death. It was like taking an anaesthetic. Freezing was not so bad as people thought. There were lots worse ways to die.

He pictured the boys finding his body next day. Suddenly he found himself with them, coming along the trail and looking for himself. And, still with them, he came around a turn in the trail and found himself lying in the snow. He did not belong with himself any more, for even then he was out of himself, standing with the boys and looking at himself in the snow. It certainly was cold, was his thought. When he got back to the States he could tell the folks what real cold was. He drifted on from this to a vision of the old-timer on Sulphur Creek. He could see him quite clearly, warm and comfortable, and smoking a pipe.

"You were right, old hoss; you were right," the man mumbled to the old-timer of Sulphur Creek.

Then the man drowsed off into what seemed to him the most comfortable and satisfying sleep he had ever known. The dog sat facing him and waiting. The brief day drew to a close in a long, slow twilight. There were no signs of a fire to be made, and, besides, never in the dog's experience had it known a man to sit like that in the snow and make no fire. As the twilight drew on, its eager yearning for the fire mastered it, and with a great lifting and shifting of forefeet, it whined softly, then flattened its ears down in anticipation of being chidden by the man. But the man remained silent. Later, the dog whined loudly. And still later it crept close to the man and caught the scent of death. This made the animal bristle and back away. A little longer it delayed, howling under the stars that leaped and danced and shone brightly in the cold sky. Then it turned and trotted up the trail in the direction of the camp it knew, where were the other food-providers and fire-providers.

# Sherwood Anderson (1876–1941)

THE TWO THINGS those who knew him remember most about the life of Sherwood Anderson is his suddenly walking out in the middle of dictating a letter to his secretary, leaving behind the paint factory he managed, his family, and all the life he had known until then, never to return. The second is how he was never able to recover from the blow dealt him by a man he had helped, Ernest Hemingway, in *Torrents of Spring*, which ridiculed Anderson's own writing. Anderson was born in the scene of his most important book, *Winesburg, Ohio* (1919), a collection of short stories that was an immediate sensation. After leaving Ohio, he worked as an advertising copy writer in Chicago and wrote his first novel, *Windy McPherson's Son* (1916). This and all his other fiction stresses "the quiet desperation" of men in modern small towns. In 1927 he retired to Virginia where he edited two newspapers, one Republican, the other Democratic. His death in 1941, on a boat cruise to South America, was caused by a bizarre accident, his swallowing a toothpick in a cocktail appetizer. His short stories have immortalized him to all lovers of good writing.

So taken for granted today is the simple, straightforward style of Sherwood Anderson's short stories, it is hard to realize the impact they made on other American writers when first published. *Winesburg, Ohio*, marks the Great Divide, the watershed between the modern uncontrived story and the old heavily plotted story. The style is consciously naive but far from primitive, and packs terrific emotional force. "Influence" is a word too casually used about writers and painters. Is it "influence" or *zeitgeist*, the spirit of the times, that accounts for the similarity of much writing produced in the same period? It happens all the time in science, too. Sinclair Lewis based his *Arrowsmith* on such a medical discovery coincidence. "The Strength of God" and "The Teacher," twin stories of the frustrated small town minister and a school teacher, belong together: an excellent example of the kind of writing that has made Anderson's fiction so noteworthy.

# *The Strength of God*

# and

# *The Teacher*

## *The Strength of God*

THE Reverend Curtis Hartman was pastor of the Presbyterian Church of Winesburg, and had been in that position ten years. He was forty years old, and by his nature very silent and reticent. To preach, standing in the pulpit before the people, was always a hardship for him and from Wednesday morning until Saturday evening he thought of nothing but the two sermons that must be preached on Sunday. Early on Sunday morning he went into a little room called a study in the bell tower of the church and prayed. In his prayers there was one note that always predominated. "Give me strength and courage for Thy work, O Lord!" he pleaded, kneeling on the bare floor and bowing his head in the presence of the task that lay before him.

The Reverend Hartman was a tall man with a brown beard. His wife, a stout, nervous woman, was the daughter of a manufacturer of underwear at Cleveland, Ohio. The minister himself was rather a favorite in the town. The elders of the church liked him because he was quiet and unpretentious and Mrs. White, the banker's wife, thought him scholarly and refined.

The Presbyterian Church held itself somewhat aloof from the other churches of Winesburg. It was larger and more imposing and its minister was better paid. He even had a carriage of his own and on summer evenings sometimes drove about town with his wife. Through Main Street and up and down Buckeye Street he went, bowing gravely to the people, while his wife, afire with secret pride, looked at him out of the corners of her eyes and worried lest the horse become frightened and run away.

For a good many years after he came to Winesburg things went well with Curtis Hartman. He was not one to arouse keen enthusiasm among the worshippers in his church but on the other hand he made no enemies. In reality he was much in earnest and sometimes suffered prolonged periods of remorse because he could not go crying the word of God in the highways and byways of the town. He wondered if the flame of the spirit really burned in him and dreamed of a day when a strong sweet new current of power would come like a great wind into his voice and his soul and the people would tremble before the spirit of God made manifest in him. "I am a poor stick and that will never really happen to me," he mused dejectedly and then a patient smile lit up his features. "Oh well, I suppose I'm doing well enough," he added philosophically.

The room in the bell tower of the church, where on Sunday mornings the minister prayed for an increase in him of the power of God, had but one window. It was long and narrow and swung outward on a hinge like a door. On the window, made of little leaded panes, was a design showing the Christ laying his hand upon the head of a child. One Sunday morning in the summer as he sat by his desk in the room with a large Bible opened before him, and the sheets of his sermon scattered about, the minister was shocked to see, in the upper room of the house next door, a woman lying in her bed and smoking a cigarette while she read a book. Curtis Hartman went on tiptoe to the window and closed it softly. He was horror stricken at the thought of a woman smoking and trembled also to think that his eyes, just raised from the pages of the book of God, had looked upon the bare shoulders and white throat of a woman. With his brain in a whirl he went down into the pulpit and preached a long sermon without once thinking of his gestures or his voice. The sermon attracted unusual attention because of its power and clearness. "I wonder if she is listening, if my voice is carrying a message into her soul," he thought and began to hope that on future Sunday mornings he might be able to say words that would touch and awaken the woman apparently far gone in secret sin.

The house next door to the Presbyterian Church, through the windows of which the minister had seen the sight that had so upset him, was occupied by two women. Aunt Elizabeth Swift, a grey competent-looking widow with money in the Winesburg National Bank, lived there with her daughter Kate Swift, a school teacher. The school teacher was thirty years old and had a neat trim-looking figure. She had few friends and bore a reputation of having a sharp tongue. When he began to think about her, Curtis Hartman remembered that she had been to Europe and had lived for two years in New York City. "Perhaps after all her smoking means nothing," he thought. He began to remember that when he was a student in college and occasionally read novels, good, although somewhat worldly women, had smoked through the pages of a book that had once fallen into his hands. With a rush of new determination he worked on his sermons all through the week and forgot, in his zeal to reach the ears and the soul of this new listener, both his embarrassment in the pulpit and the necessity of prayer in the study on Sunday mornings.

Reverend Hartman's experience with women had been somewhat limited. He was the son of a wagon maker from Muncie, Indiana, and had worked his way through college. The daughter of the underwear manufacturer had boarded in a house where he lived during his school days and he had married her after a formal and prolonged courtship, carried on for the most part by the girl herself. On his marriage day the underwear manufacturer had given his daughter five thousand dollars and he promised to leave her at least twice that amount in his will. The minister had thought himself fortunate in marriage and had never permitted himself to think of other women. He did not want to think of other women. What he wanted was to do the work of God quietly and earnestly.

In the soul of the minister a struggle awoke. From wanting to reach the ears of Kate Swift, and through his sermons to delve into her soul, he began to want also to look again at the figure lying white and quiet in the bed. On a Sunday morning when he could not sleep because of his thoughts he arose and went to walk in the streets. When he had gone along Main Street almost to the old Richmond place he stopped and picking up a stone rushed off to the room in the bell tower. With the stone he broke out a corner of the window and then locked the door and sat down at the desk before the open Bible to wait. When the shade of the window to Kate Swift's room was raised he could see, through the hole, directly into her bed, but she was not there. She also had arisen and had gone for a walk and the hand that raised the shade was the hand of Aunt Elizabeth Swift.

The minister almost wept with joy at this deliverance from the carnal desire to "peep" and went back to his own house praising God. In an ill moment he forgot, however, to stop the hole in the window. The piece of glass broken out at the corner of the window just nipped off the bare heel of the boy standing motionless and looking with rapt eyes into the face of the Christ.

Curtis Hartman forgot his sermon on that Sunday morning. He talked to his congregation and in his talk said that it was a mistake for people to think of their minister as a man set aside and intended by nature to lead a blameless life. "Out of my own experience I know that we, who are the ministers of God's word, are beset by the same temptations that assail you," he declared. "I have been tempted and have surrendered to temptation. It is only the hand of God, placed beneath my head, that has raised me up. As he has raised me so also will he raise you. Do not despair. In your hour of sin raise your eyes to the skies and you will be again and again saved."

Resolutely the minister put the thoughts of the woman in the bed out of his mind and began to be something like a lover in the presence of his wife. One evening when they drove out together he turned the horse out of Buckeye Street and in the darkness on Gospel Hill, above Waterworks Pond, put his arm about Sarah Hartman's waist. When he had eaten breakfast in the morning and was ready to retire to his study at the back of his house he went around the table and kissed his wife on the cheek. When thoughts of Kate Swift came into his head, he smiled and raised his eyes to the skies. "Intercede for me, Master," he muttered, "keep me in the narrow path intent on Thy work."

And now began the real struggle in the soul of the brown-bearded minister. By chance he discovered that Kate Swift was in the habit of lying in her bed in the evenings and reading a book. A lamp stood on a table by the side of the bed and the light streamed down upon her white shoulders and bare throat. On the evening when he made the discovery the minister sat at the desk in the study from nine until after eleven and when her light was put out stumbled out of the church to spend two more hours walking and praying in the streets. He did not want to kiss the shoulders and the throat of Kate Swift and had not allowed his mind to dwell on such thoughts. He did not know what he wanted. "I am God's child and he must save me from myself," he cried in the darkness under the trees as he wandered in the streets. By a tree he stood and looked at the sky that was covered with hurrying clouds. He began to talk to God intimately and closely. "Please, Father, do not forget me. Give me power to go to-morrow and repair the hole in the window. Lift my eyes again to the skies. Stay with me, Thy servant, in his hour of need."

Up and down through the silent streets walked the minister and for days and weeks his soul was troubled. He could not understand the temptation that had come to him nor could he fathom the reason for its coming. In a way he began to blame God, saying to himself that he had tried to keep his feet in the true path and had not run about seeking sin. "Through my days as a young man and all through my life here I have gone quietly about my work," he declared. "Why now should I be tempted? What have I done that this burden should be laid on me?"

Three times during the early fall and winter of that year Curtis Hartman crept out of his house to the room in the bell tower to sit in the darkness looking at the figure of Kate Swift lying in her bed and later went to walk and pray in the streets. He could not understand himself. For weeks he would go along scarcely thinking of the school teacher and telling himself that he had conquered the carnal desire to look at her body. And then something would happen. As he sat in the study of his own house, hard at work on a sermon, he would become nervous and begin to walk up and down the room. "I will go out into the streets," he told himself and even as he let himself in at the church door he persistently denied to himself the cause of his being there. "I will not repair the hole in the window and I will train myself to come here at night and sit in the presence of this woman without raising my eyes. I will not be defeated in this thing. The Lord has devised this temptation as a test of my soul and I will grope my way out of darkness into the light of righteousness."

One night in January when it was bitter cold and snow lay deep on the streets of Winesburg Curtis Hartman paid his last visit to the room in the bell tower of the church. It was past nine o'clock when he left his own house and he set out so hurriedly that he forgot to put on his overshoes. In Main Street no one was abroad but Hop Higgins the night watchman and in the whole town no one was awake but the watchman and young George Willard, who sat in the office of the *Winesburg Eagle* trying to write a story. Along the street to the church went the minister, plowing through the drifts and thinking that this time he would utterly give way to sin. "I want to look at the woman and to think of kissing her shoulders and I am going to let myself think what I choose," he declared bitterly and tears came into his eyes. He began to think that he would get out of the ministry and try some other way of life. "I shall go to some city and get into business," he declared. "If my nature is such that I cannot resist sin, I shall give myself over to sin. At least I shall not be a hypocrite, preaching the word of God with my mind thinking of the shoulders and neck of a woman who does not belong to me." It was cold in the room of the bell tower of the church on that January night and almost as soon as he came into the room Curtis Hartman knew that if he stayed he would be ill. His feet were wet from tramping in the snow and there was no fire. In the room in the house next door Kate Swift had not yet appeared. With grim determination the man sat down to wait. Sitting in the chair and gripping the edge of the desk on which lay the Bible he stared into the darkness thinking the blackest thoughts of his life. He thought of his wife and for the moment almost hated her. "She has always been ashamed of passion and has cheated me," he thought. "Man has a right to expect living passion and beauty in a woman. He has no right to forget that he is an animal and in me there is something that is Greek. I will throw off the woman of my bosom and seek other women. I will besiege this school teacher. I will fly in the face of all men and if I am a creature of carnal lusts I will live then for my lusts."

The distracted man trembled from head to foot, partly from cold, partly from the struggle in which he was engaged. Hours passed and a fever assailed his body. His throat began to hurt and his teeth chattered. His feet on the study floor felt two cakes of ice. Still he would not give up. "I will see this woman and will think the thoughts I have never dared to think," he told himself, gripping the edge of the desk and waiting.

Curtis Hartman came near dying from the effects of that night of waiting in the church, and also he found in the thing that happened what he took to be the way of life for him. On other evenings when he had waited he had not been able to see, through the little hole in the glass, any part of the school teacher's room except that occupied by her bed. In the darkness he had waited until the woman suddenly appeared sitting in the bed in her white nightrobe. When the light was turned up she propped herself up among the pillows and read a book. Sometimes she smoked one of the cigarettes. Only her bare shoulders and throat were visible.

On the January night, after he had come near dying with cold and after his mind had two or three times actually slipped away into an odd land of fantasy so that he had by an exercise of will power to force himself back into consciousness, Kate Swift appeared. In the room next door a lamp was lighted and the waiting man stared into an empty bed. Then upon the bed before his eyes a naked woman threw herself. Lying face downward she wept and beat with her fists upon the pillow. With a final outburst of weeping she half arose, and in the presence of the man who had waited to look and to think thoughts the woman of sin began to pray. In the lamplight her figure, slim and strong, looked like the figure of the boy in the presence of the Christ on the leaded window.

Curtis Hartman never remembered how he got out of the church. With a cry he arose, dragging the heavy desk along the floor. The Bible fell, making a great clatter in the silence. When the light in the house next door went out he stumbled down the stairway and into the street. Along the street he went and ran in at the door of the *Winesburg Eagle*. To George Willard, who was tramping up and down in the office undergoing a struggle of his own, he began to talk incoherently. "The ways of God are beyond human understanding," he cried, running in quickly and closing the door. He began to advance upon the young man, his eyes glowing and his voice ringing with fervor. "I have found the light," he cried. "After ten years in this town, God has manifested himself to me in the body of a woman." His voice dropped and he began to whisper. "I did not understand," he said. "What I took to be a trial of my soul was only a preparation for a new and more beautiful fervor of the spirit. God has appeared to me in the person of Kate Swift, the school teacher, kneeling naked on a bed. Do you know Kate Swift? Although she may not be aware of it, she is an instrument of God, bearing the message of truth."

Reverend Curtis Hartman turned and ran out of the office. At the door he stopped, and after looking up and down the deserted street, turned again to George Willard. "I am delivered. Have no fear." He held up a bleeding fist for the young man to see. "I smashed the glass of the window," he cried. "Now it will have to be wholly replaced. The strength of God was in me and I broke it with my fist."

# The Teacher

Snow lay deep in the streets of Winesburg. It had begun to snow about ten o'clock in the morning and a wind sprang up and blew the snow in clouds along Main Street. The frozen mud roads that led into town were fairly smooth and in places ice covered the mud. "There will be good sleighing," said Will Henderson, standing by the bar in Ed Griffith's saloon. Out of the saloon he went and met Sylvester West the druggist stumbling along in the kind of heavy overshoes called arctics. "Snow will bring the people into town on Saturday," said the druggist. The two men stopped and discussed their affairs. Will Henderson, who had on a light overcoat and no overshoes, kicked the heel of his left foot with the toe of the right. "Snow will be good for the wheat," observed the druggist sagely.

Young George Willard, who had nothing to do, was glad because he did not feel like working that day. The weekly paper had been printed and taken to the post office on Wednesday evening and the snow began to fall on Thursday. At eight o'clock, after the morning train had passed, he put a pair of skates in his pocket and went up to Waterworks Pond but did not go skating. Past the pond and along a path that followed Wine Creek he went until he came to a grove of beech trees. There he built a fire against the side of a log and sat down at the end of the log to think. When the snow began to fall and the wind to blow he hurried about getting fuel for the fire.

The young reporter was thinking of Kate Swift who had once been his school teacher. On the evening before he had gone to her house to get a book she wanted him to read and had been alone with her for an hour. For the fourth or fifth time the woman had talked to him with great earnestness and he could not make out what she meant by her talk. He began to believe she might be in love with him and the thought was both pleasing and annoying.

Up from the log he sprang and began to pile sticks on the fire. Looking about to be sure he was alone he talked aloud pretending he was in the presence of the woman. "Oh, you're just letting on, you know you are," he declared. "I am going to find out about you. You wait and see."

The young man got up and went back along the path toward town leaving the fire blazing in the wood. As he went through the streets the skates clanked in his pocket. In his own room in the New Willard House he built a fire in the stove and lay down on top of the bed. He began to have lustful thoughts and pulling down the shade of the window closed his eyes and turned his face to the wall. He took a pillow into his arms and embraced it thinking first of the school teacher, who by her words had stirred something within him, and later of Helen White, the slim daughter of the town banker, with whom he had been a long time half in love.

By nine o'clock of that evening snow lay deep in the streets and the weather had become bitter cold. It was difficult to walk about. The stores were dark and the people had crawled away to their houses. The evening train from Cleveland was very late but nobody was interested in its arrival. By ten o'clock all but four of the eighteen hundred citizens of the town were in bed.

Hop Higgins, the night watchman, was partially awake. He was lame and carried a heavy stick. On dark nights he carried a lantern. Between nine and ten o'clock he went his rounds. Up and down Main Street he stumbled through the drifts trying the doors of the stores. Then he went into alleyways and tried the back doors. Finding all tight he hurried around the corner to the New Willard House and beat on the door. Through the rest of the night he intended to stay by the stove. "You go to bed. I'll keep the stove going," he said to the boy who slept on a cot in the hotel office.

Hop Higgins sat down by the stove and took off his shoes. When the boy had gone to sleep he began to think of his own affairs. He intended to paint his house in the spring and sat by the stove calculating the cost of paint and labor. That led him into other calculations. The night watchman was sixty years old and wanted to retire. He had been soldier in the Civil War and drew a small pension. He hoped to find some new method of making a living and aspired to become a professional breeder of ferrets. Already he had four of the strangely shaped savage little creatures, that are used by sportsmen in the pursuit of rabbits, in the cellar of his house. "Now I have one male and three females," he mused. "If I am lucky by spring I shall have twelve or fifteen. In another year I shall be able to begin advertising ferrets for sale in the sporting papers."

The night watchman settled into his chair and his mind became a blank. He did not sleep. By years of practice he had trained himself to sit for hours through the long nights neither asleep nor awake. In the morning he was almost as refreshed as though he had slept.

With Hop Higgins safely stowed away in the chair behind the stove only three people were awake in Winesburg. George Willard was in the office of the *Eagle* pretending to be at work on the writing of a story but in reality continuing the mood of the morning by the fire in the wood. In the bell tower of the Presbyterian Church the Reverend Curtis Hartman was sitting in the darkness preparing himself for a revelation from God, and Kate Swift, the school teacher, was leaving her house for a walk in the storm.

It was past ten o'clock when Kate Swift set out and the walk was unpremediated. It was as though the man and the boy, by thinking of her, had driven her forth into the wintry streets. Aunt Elizabeth Swift had gone to the county seat concerning some business in connection with mortgages in which she had money invested and would not be back until the next day. By a huge stove, called a base burner, in the living room of the house sat the daughter reading a book. Suddenly she sprang to her feet and, snatching a clock from a rack by the front door, ran out of the house.

At the age of thirty Kate Swift was not known in Winesburg as a pretty woman. Her complexion was not good and her face was covered with blotches that indicated ill health. Alone in the night in the winter streets she was lovely. Her back was straight, her shoulders square and her features were as the features of a tiny goddess on a pedestal in a garden in the dim light of a summer evening.

During the afternoon the school teacher had been to see Dr. Welling concerning her health. The doctor had scolded her and had declared she was in danger of losing her hearing. It was foolish for Kate Swift to be abroad in the storm, foolish and perhaps dangerous.

The woman in the streets did not remember the words of the doctor and would not have turned back had she remembered. She was very cold but after walking for five minutes no longer minded the cold. First she went to the end of her own street and then across a pair of hay scales set in the ground before a feed barn and into Trunion Pike. Along Trunion Pike she went to Ned Winter's barn and turning east followed a street of low frame houses that led over Gospel Hill and into Sucker Road that ran down a shallow valley past Ike Smead's chicken farm to Waterworks Pond. As she went along, the bold, excited mood that had driven her out of doors passed and then returned again.

There was something biting and forbidding in the character of Kate Swift. Everyone felt it. In the schoolroom she was silent, cold, and stern, and yet in an odd way very close to her pupils. Once in a long while something seemed to have come over her and she was happy. All of the children in the schoolroom felt the effect of her happiness. For a time they did not work but sat back in their chairs and looked at her.

With hands clasped behind her back the school teacher walked up and down in the schoolroom and talked very rapidly. It did not seem to matter what subject came into her mind. Once she talked to the children of Charles Lamb and made up strange intimate little stories concerning the life of the dead writer. The stories were told with the air of one who had lived in a house with Charles Lamb and knew all the secrets of his private life. The children were somewhat confused, thinking Charles Lamb must be someone who had once lived in Winesburg.

On another occasion the teacher talked to the children of Benevenuto Cellini. That time they laughed. What a bragging, blustering, brave, lovable fellow she made of the old artist! Concerning him also she invented anecdotes. There was one of a German music teacher who had a room above Cellini's lodgings in the city of Milan that made the boys guffaw. Sugars McNutts, a fat boy with red cheeks, laughed so hard that he became dizzy and fell off his seat and Kate Swift laughed with him. Then suddenly she became again old and stern.

On the winter night when she walked through the deserted snow-covered streets, a crisis had come into the life of the school teacher. Although no one in Winesburg would have suspected it, her life had been very adventurous. It was still adventurous. Day by day as she worked in the schoolroom or walked in the streets, grief, hope, and desire fought within her. Behind a cold exterior the most extraordinary events transpired in her mind. The people of the town thought of her as a confirmed old maid and because she spoke sharply and went her own way thought her lacking in all the human feeling that did so much to make and mar their own lives. In reality she was the most eagerly passionate soul among them, and more than once, in the five years since she had come back from her travels to settle in Winesburg and become a school teacher, had been compelled to go out of the house and walk half through the night fighting out some battle raging within. Once on a night when it rained she had stayed out six hours and when she came home had a quarrel with Aunt Elizabeth Swift. "I am glad you're not a man," said the mother sharply. "More than once I've waited for your father to come home, not knowing what new mess he had got into. I've had my share of uncertainty and you cannot blame me if I do not want to see the worst side of him reproduced in you."

Kate Swift's mind was ablaze with thoughts of George Willard. In something he had written as a school boy she thought she had recognized the spark of genius and wanted to blow on the spark. One day in the summer she had gone to the *Eagle* office and finding the boy unoccupied had taken him out Main Street to the fair ground, where the two sat on a grassy bank and talked. The school teacher tried to bring home to the mind of the boy some conception of the difficulties he would have to face as a writer. "You will have to know life," she declared, and her voice trembled with earnestness. She took hold of George Willard's shoulders and turned him about so that she could look into his eyes. A passer-by might have thought them about to embrace. "If you are to become a writer you'll have to stop fooling with words," she explained. "It would be better to give up the notion of writing until you are better prepared. Now it's time to be living. I don't want to frighten you, but I would like to make you understand the import of what you think of attempting. You must not become a mere peddler of words. The thing to learn is to know what people are thinking about, not what they say."

On the evening before that stormy Thursday night, when the Reverend Curtis Hartman sat in the bell tower of the church waiting to look at her body, young Willard had gone to visit the teacher and to borrow a book. It was then the thing happened that confused and puzzled the boy. He had the book under his arm and was preparing to depart. Again Kate Swift talked with great earnestness. Night was coming on and the light in the room grew dim. As he turned to go she spoke his name softly and with an impulsive movement took hold of his hand. Because the reporter was rapidly becoming a man something of his man's appeal, combined with the winsomeness of the boy, stirred the heart of the lonely woman. A passionate desire to have him understand the import of life, to learn to interpret it truly and honestly, swept over her. Leaning forward, her lips brushed his cheek. At the same moment he for the first time became aware of the marked beauty of her features. They were both embarrassed, and to relieve her feeling she became harsh and domineering. "What's the use? It will be ten years before you begin to understand what I mean when I talk to you," she cried passionately.

On the night of the storm and while the minister sat in the church waiting for her Kate Swift went to the office of the *Winesburg Eagle*, intending to have another talk with the boy. After the long walk in the snow she was cold, lonely, and tired. As she came through Main Street she saw the light from the print shop window shining on the snow and on an impulse opened the door and went in. For an hour she sat by the stove in the office talking of life. She talked with passionate earnestness. The impulse that had driven her out into the snow poured itself out into talk. She became inspired as she sometimes did in the presence of the children in school. A great eagerness to open the door of life to the boy, who had been her pupil and who she thought might possess a talent for the understanding of life, had possession of her. So strong was her passion that it became something physical. Again her hands took hold of his shoulders and she turned him about. In the dim light her eyes blazed. She arose and laughed, not sharply as was customary with her, but in a queer, hesitating way. "I must be going," she said. "In a moment, if I stay, I'll be wanting to kiss you."

In the newspaper office a confusion arose. Kate Swift turned and walked to the door. She was a teacher but she was also a woman. As she looked at George Willard, the passionate desire to be loved by a man, that had a thousand times before swept like a storm over her body, took possession of her. In the lamplight George Willard looked no longer a boy, but a man ready to play the part of a man.

The school teacher let George Willard take her into his arms. In the warm little office the air became suddenly heavy and the strength went out of her body. Leaning against a low counter by the door she waited. When he came and put a hand on her shoulder she turned and let her body fall heavily against him. For George Willard the confusion was immediately increased. For a moment he held the body of the woman tightly against his body and then it stiffened. Two sharp little fists began to beat on his face. When the school teacher had run away and left him alone, he walked up and down in the office swearing furiously.

It was into this confusion that the Reverend Curtis Hartman protruded himself. When he came in George Willard thought the town had gone mad. Shaking a bleeding fist in the air, the minister proclaimed the woman George had only a moment before held in his arms an instrument of God bearing a message of truth.

George blew out the lamp by the window and locking the door of the print shop went home. Through the hotel office, past Hop Higgins lost in his dreams of the raising of ferrets, he went and up into his own room. The fire in the stove had gone out and he undressed in the cold. When he got into bed the sheets were like blankets of dry snow.

George Willard rolled about in the bed on which he had lain in the afternoon hugging the pillow and thinking thoughts of Kate Swift. The words of the minister, who he thought had gone suddenly insane, rang in his ears. His eyes stared about the room. The resentment, natural to the baffled male, passed and he tried to understand what had happened. He could not make it out. Over and over he turned the matter in his mind. Hours passed and he began to think it must be time for another day to come. At four o'clock he pulled the covers up about his neck and tried to sleep. When he became drowsy and closed his eyes, he raised a hand and with it groped about in the darkness. "I have missed something. I have missed something Kate Swift was trying to tell me," he muttered sleepily. Then he slept and in all Winesburg he was the last soul on that winter night to go to sleep.

# F. Scott Fitzgerald (1896–1940)

"By brooks too broad for leaping
The lightfoot boys are laid
The rose-lipt girls are sleeping
In fields where roses fade."

WITH ZELDA, his wife, F. Scott Fitzgerald incarnated the glamor of the twenties. Leaping in public fountains, reveling in Paris and on the Riviera, dancing the nights away at Long Island parties, but — and it is a most important *but* — Fitzgerald was no mere charming, giddy "golden boy"; he had genius. Born in St. Paul, Minnesota, he entered Princeton at seventeen where he was a close friend of Edmund Wilson and John Peale Bishop, also to become distinguished writers. He left to join the army when the United States entered the First World War in 1917. In boot camp he wrote his first novel, *This Side of Paradise* (1920), which brilliantly captures the moods and mores of the period's youth. His next two books were collections of his short stories, *Flappers and Philosophers* (1920) and *Tales of the Jazz Age* (1922). Of his later books, the most important are *The Great Gatsby* (1925) and *The Last Tycoon* (1941), the latter left unfinished because of his premature death. Tragedy overwhelmed Fitzgerald in mid-career when Zelda, who wrote a number of the stories signed by Fitzgerald for financial reasons, had a mental collapse. He himself became ill and poverty-stricken. This ordeal he described with heart-breaking honesty in *The Crack-Up* (1945), edited by Edmund Wilson. Fitzgerald vainly struggled to put his life together again by toiling at commercial screen-writing in Hollywood where he was scorned as a "has-been." Of the only two mourners at his funeral one was Dorothy Parker who, looking down at him in his coffin, exclaimed, "You poor son-of-a-bitch!"

A satirical fantasy, "The Diamond as Big as the Ritz" reveals a side of Fitzgerald usually overlooked. It is worth noting as an indication of the blighting effects McCarthyism once had on the arts that in 1950 a prominent American composer seeking an opera libretto rejected "The Diamond as Big as the Ritz" as being subversive. Fitzgerald's early short stories in the twenties often anticipated the social consciousness that was to be associated with the writing of the thirties. Those knowing the author's life may see this story as a kind of nightmarish wish-fulfillment that might have grown out of his frantic straining to make money. Another Fitzgerald story, "Babylon Revisited," provides an interesting parallel in its account of a man surveying the ruins of the period after the twenties boom had collapsed. Fitzgerald was not only the best fictional historian of the Jazz Age, he was one of its best social critics.

# *The Diamond as Big as the Ritz*

JOHN T. UNGER came from a family that had been well known in Hades — a small town on the Mississippi River — for several generations. John's father had held the amateur golf championship through many a heated contest; Mrs. Unger was known "from hot-box to hot-bed" as the local phrase went, for her political addresses; and young John T. Unger, who had just turned sixteen, had danced all the latest dances from New York before he put on long trousers. And now, for a certain time, he was to be away from home. That respect for a New England education which is the bane of all provincial places, which drains them yearly of their most promising young men, had seized upon his parents. Nothing would suit them but that he should go to St. Midas' School near Boston — Hades was too small to hold their darling and gifted son.

Now in Hades — as you know if you ever have been there — the names of the more fashionable preparatory schools and colleges mean very little. The inhabitants have been so long out of the world that, though they make a show of keeping up to date in dress and manners and literature, they depend to a great extent on hearsay, and a function that in Hades would be considered elaborate would doubtless be hailed by a Chicago beef-princess as "perhaps a little tacky."

John T. Unger was on the eve of departure. Mrs. Unger, with maternal fatuity, packed his trunks full of linen suits and electric fans, and Mr. Unger presented his son with an asbestos pocket-book stuffed with money.

"Remember, you are always welcome here," he said. "You can be sure, boy, that we'll keep the home fires burning."

"I know," answered John huskily.

"Don't forget who you are and where you come from," continued his father proudly, "and you can do nothing to harm you. You are an Unger — from Hades."

So the old man and the young shook hands and John walked away with tears streaming from his eyes. Ten minutes later he had passed outside the city limits, and he stopped to glance back for the last time. Over the gates the old-fashioned Victorian motto seemed strangely attractive to him. His father had tried time and time again to have it changed to something with a little more push and verve about it, such as "Hades — Your Opportunity," or else a plain "Welcome" sign set over a hearty handshake pricked out in electric lights. The old motto was a little depressing, Mr. Unger had thought — but now . . .

St. Midas' School is half an hour from Boston in a Rolls-Pierce motor-car. The actual distance will never be known, for no one, except John T. Unger, had ever arrived there save in a Rolls-Pierce and probably no one ever will again. St. Midas' is the most expensive and the most exclusive boys' preparatory school in the world.

John's first two years there passed pleasantly. The fathers of all the boys were money-kings and John spent his summers visiting at fashionable resorts. While he was very fond of all the boys he visited, their fathers struck him as being much of a piece, and in his boyish way he often wondered at their exceeding sameness. When he told them where his home was they would ask jovially, "Pretty hot down there?" and John would muster a faint smile and answer, "It certainly is." His response would have been heartier had they not all made this joke — at best varying it with, "Is it hot enough for you down there?" which he hated just as much.

In the middle of his second year at school, a quiet, handsome boy named Percy Washington had been put in John's form. The newcomer was pleasant in his manner and exceedingly well dressed even for St. Midas', but for some reason he kept aloof from the other boys. The only person with whom he was intimate was John T. Unger, but even to John he was entirely uncommunicative concerning his home or his family. That he was wealthy went without saying, but beyond a few such deductions John knew little of his friend, so it promised rich confectionery for his curiosity when Percy invited him to spend the summer at his home "in the West." He accepted, without hesitation.

It was only when they were in the train that Percy became, for the first time, rather communicative. One day while they were eating lunch in the dining-car and discussing the imperfect characters of several of the boys at school, Percy suddenly changed his tone and made an abrupt remark.

"My father," he said, "is by far the richest man in the world."

"Oh," said John, politely. He could think of no answer to make to this confidence. He considered "That's very nice," but it sounded hollow and was on the point of saying, "Really?" but refrained since it would seem to question Percy's statement. And such an astounding statement could scarcely be questioned.

"By far the richest," repeated Percy.

"I was reading in the *World Almanac*," began John, "that there was one man in America with an income of over five million a year and four men with incomes of over three million a year, and — "

"Oh, they're nothing," Percy's mouth was a half-moon of scorn. "Catch-penny capitalists, financial small-fry, petty merchants and money-lenders. My father could buy them out and not know he'd done it."

"But how does he —"

"Why haven't they put down *his* income tax? Because he doesn't pay any. At least he pays a little one — but he doesn't pay any on his *real* income."

"He must be very rich," said John simply. "I'm glad. I like very rich people.

"The richer a fella is, the better I like him." There was a look of passionate frankness upon his dark face. "I visited the Schnlitzer-Murphys last Easter. Vivian Schnlitzer-Murphy had rubies as big as hen's eggs, and sapphires that were like globes with lights inside them —"

"I love jewels," agreed Percy enthusiastically. "Of course I wouldn't want any one at school to know about it, but I've got quite a collection myself. I used to collect them instead of stamps."

"And diamonds," continued John eagerly. "The Schnlitzer-Murphys had diamonds as big as walnuts —"

"That's nothing." Percy had leaned forward and dropped his voice to a low whisper. "That's nothing at all. My father has a diamond bigger than the Ritz-Carlton Hotel."

## II

The Montana sunset lay between two mountains like a gigantic bruise from which dark arteries spread themselves over a poisoned sky. An immense distance under the sky crouched the village of Fish, minute, dismal, and forgotten. There were twelve men, so it was said, in the village of Fish, twelve sombre and inexplicable souls who sucked a lean milk from the almost literally bare rock upon which a mysterious populatory force had begotten them. They had become a race apart, these twelve men of Fish, like some species developed by an early whim of nature, which on second thought had abandoned them to struggle and extermination.

Out of the blue-black bruise in the distance crept a long line of moving lights upon the desolation of the land, and the twelve men of Fish gathered like ghosts at the shanty depot to watch the passing of the seven o'clock train, the Transcontinental Express from Chicago. Six times or so a year the Transcontinental Express, through some inconceivable jurisdiction, stopped at the village of Fish, and when this occurred a figure or so would disembark, mount into a buggy that always appeared from out of the dusk, and drive off toward the bruised sunset. The observation of this pointless and preposterous phenomenon had become a sort of cult among the men of Fish. To observe, that was all; there remained in them none of the vital quality of illusion which would make them wonder or speculate, else a religion might have grown up around these mysterious visitations. But the men of Fish were beyond all religion — the barest and most savage tenets of even Christianity could gain no foothold on that barren rock — so there was no altar, no priest, no sacrifice; only each night at seven the silent concourse by the shanty depot, a congregation who lifted up a prayer of dim, anaemic wonder.

On this June night, the Great Brakeman, whom, had they deified any one, they might well have chosen as their celestial protagonist, had ordained that the seven o'clock train should leave its human (or inhuman) deposit at Fish. At two minutes after seven Percy Washington and John T. Unger disembarked, hurried past the spellbound, the agape, the fearsome eyes of the twelve men of Fish, mounted into a buggy which had obviously appeared from nowhere, and drove away.

After half an hour, when the twilight had coagulated into dark, the silent negro who was driving the buggy hailed an opaque body somewhere ahead of them in the gloom. In response to his cry, it turned upon them a luminous disk which regarded them like a malignant eye out of the unfathomable night. As they came closer, John saw that it was the taillight of an immense automobile, larger and more magnificent than any he had ever seen. Its body was of gleaming metal richer than nickel and lighter than silver, and the hubs of the wheels were studded with iridescent geometric figures of green and yellow — John did not dare to guess whether they were glass or jewel.

Two negroes, dressed in glittering livery such as one sees in pictures of royal processions in London, were standing at attention beside the car and as the two young men dismounted from the buggy they were greeted in some language which the guest could not understand, but which seemed to be an extreme form of the Southern negro's dialect.

"Get in," said Percy to his friend, as their trunks were tossed to the ebony roof of the limousine. "Sorry we had to bring you this far in that buggy, but of course it wouldn't do for the people on the train or those Godforsaken fellas in Fish to see this automobile."

"Gosh! What a car!" This ejaculation was provoked by its interior. John saw that the upholstery consisted of a thousand minute and exquisite tapestries of silk, woven with jewels and embroideries, and set upon a background of cloth of gold. The two armchair seats in which the boys luxuriated were covered with stuff that resembled duvetyn, but seemed woven in numberless colors of the ends of ostrich feathers.

"What a car!" cried John again, in amazement.

"This thing?" Percy laughed. "Why, it's just an old junk we use for a station wagon."

By this time they were gliding along through the darkness toward the break between the two mountains.

"We'll be there in an hour and a half," said Percy, looking at the clock. "I may as well tell you it's not going to be like anything you ever saw before."

If the car was any indication of what John would see, he was prepared to be astonished indeed. The simple piety prevalent in Hades has the earnest worship of and respect for riches as the first article of its creed — had John felt otherwise than radiantly humble before them, his parents would have turned away in horror at the blasphemy.

They had now reached and were entering the break between the two mountains and almost immediately the way became much rougher.

"If the moon shone down here, you'd see that we're in a big gulch," said Percy, trying to peer out of the window. He spoke a few words into the mouthpiece and immediately the footman turned on a searchlight and swept the hillsides with an immense beam.

"Rocky, you see. An ordinary car would be knocked to pieces in half an hour. In fact, it'd take a tank to navigate it unless you knew the way. You notice we're going uphill now."

They were obviously ascending, and within a few minutes the car was crossing a high rise, where they caught a glimpse of a pale moon newly risen in the distance. The car stopped suddenly and several figures took shape out of the dark beside it — these were negroes also. Again the two young men were saluted in the same dimly recognizable dialect; then the negroes set to work and four immense cables dangling from overhead were attached with hooks to the hubs of the great jeweled wheels. At a resounding "Hey-yah!" John felt the car being lifted slowly from the ground — up and up — clear of the tallest rocks on both sides — then higher, until he could see a wavy, moonlit valley stretched out before him in sharp contrast to the quagmire of rocks that they had just left. Only on one side was there still rock — and then suddenly there was no rock beside them or anywhere around.

It was apparent that they had surmounted some immense knife-blade of stone, projecting perpendicularly into the air. In a moment they were going down again, and finally with a soft bump they were landed upon the smooth earth.

"The worst is over," said Percy, squinting out the window. "It's only five miles from here, and our own road — tapestry brick — all the way. This belongs to us. This is where the United States ends, father says."

"Are we in Canada?"

"We are not. We're in the middle of the Montana Rockies. But you are now on the only five square miles of land in the country that's never been surveyed."

"Why hasn't it? Did they forget it?"

"No," said Percy, grinning, "they tried to do it three times. The first time my grandfather corrupted a whole department of the State survey; the second time he had the official maps of the United States tinkered with — that held them for fifteen years. The last time was harder. My father fixed it so that their compasses were in the strongest magnetic field ever artificially set up. He had a whole set of surveying instruments made with a slight defection that would allow for this territory not to appear, and he substituted them for the ones that were to be used. Then he had a river deflected and he had what looked like a village built up on its banks — so that they'd see it, and think it was a town ten miles farther up the valley. There's only one thing my father's afraid of," he concluded, "only one thing in the world that could be used to find us out."

"What's that?"

Percy sank his voice to a whisper.

"Aeroplanes," he breathed. "We've got half a dozen anti-aircraft guns and we've arranged it so far — but there've been a few deaths and a great many prisoners. Not that we mind *that*, you know, father and I, but it upsets mother and the girls, and there's always the chance that some time we won't be able to arrange it."

Shreds and tatters of chinchilla, courtesy clouds in the green moon's heaven, were passing the green moon like precious Eastern stuffs paraded for the inspection of some Tartar khan. It seemed to John that it was day, and that he was looking at some lads sailing above him in the air, showering down tracts and patent medicine circulars, with their messages of hope for despairing, rockbound hamlets. It seemed to him that he could see them look down out of the clouds and stare — and stare at whatever there was to stare at in this place whither he was bound — What then? Were they induced to land by some insidious device there to be immured far from patent medicines and from tracts until the judgment day — or, should they fail to fall into the trap, did a quick puff of smoke and the sharp round of a splitting shell bring them drooping to earth — and "upset" Percy's mother and sisters. John shook his head and the wraith of a hollow laugh issued silently from his parted lips. What desperate transaction lay hidden here? What a moral expedient of a bizarre Croesus? What terrible and golden mystery? . . .

The chinchilla clouds had drifted past now and outside the Montana night was bright as day. The tapestry brick of the road was smooth to the tread of the great tires as they rounded a still, moonlit lake; they passed into darkness for a moment, a pine grove, pungent and cool, then they came out into a broad avenue of lawn and John's exclamation of pleasure was simultaneous with Percy's taciturn "We're home."

Full in the light of the stars, an exquisite château rose from the borders of the lake, climbed in marble radiance half the height of an adjoining mountain, then melted in grace, in perfect symmetry, in translucent feminine languor, into the massed darkness of a forest of pine. The many towers, the slender tracery of the sloping parapets, the chiselled wonder of a thousand yellow windows with their oblongs and hectagons and triangles of golden light, the shattered softness of the intersecting planes of star-shine and blue shade, all trembled on John's spirit like a chord of music. On one of the towers, the tallest, the blackest at its base, an arrangement of exterior lights at the top made a sort of floating fairy-land — and as John gazed up in warm enchantment the faint acciaccare sound of violins drifted down in a rococo harmony that was like nothing he had ever heard before. Then in a moment the car stopped before wide, high marble steps around which the night air was fragrant with a host of flowers. At the top of the steps two great doors swung silently open and amber light flooded out upon the darkness, silhouetting the figure of an exquisite lady with black, high-piled hair, who held out her arms toward them.

"Mother," Percy was saying, "this is my friend, John Unger, from Hades."

Afterward John remembered that first night as a daze of many colors, of quick sensory impressions, of music soft as a voice in love, and of the beauty of things, lights and shadows, and motions and faces. There was a white-haired man who stood drinking a many-hued cordial from a crystal thimble set on a golden stem. There was a girl with a flowery face, dressed like Titania with braided sapphires in her hair. There was a room where the solid, soft gold of the walls yielded to the pressure of his hand, and a room that was like a platonic conception of the ulti-mate prison — ceiling, floor, and all, it was lined with an unbroken mass of diamonds, diamonds of every size and shape, until, lit with tall violet lamps in the corners, it dazzled the eyes with a whiteness that could be compared only with itself, beyond human wish or dream.

Through a maze of these rooms the two boys wandered. Sometimes the floor under their feet would flame in brilliant patterns from lighting below, patterns of barbaric clashing colors, of pastel delicacy, of sheer whiteness, or of subtle and intricate mosaic, surely from some mosque on the Adriatic Sea. Sometimes beneath layers of thick crystal he would see blue or green water swirling, inhabited by vivid fish and growths of rainbow foliage. Then they would be treading on furs of every tex-ture and color or along corridors of palest ivory, unbroken as though carved complete from the gigantic tusks of dinosaurs extinct before the age of man . . .

Then a hazily remembered transition, and they were at dinner — where each plate was of two almost imperceptible layers of solid diamond between which was curiously worked a filigree of emerald design, a shaving sliced from green air. Music, plangent and unobtrusive, drifted down through far corridors — his chair, feathered and curved insid-iously to his back, seemed to engulf and overpower him as he drank his first glass of port. He tried drowsily to answer a question that had been asked him, but the honeyed luxury that clasped his body added to the illusion of sleep — jewels, fabrics, wines, and metals blurred before his eyes into a sweet mist . . .

"Yes," he replied with a polite effort, "it certainly is hot enough for me down there."

He managed to add a ghostly laugh; then, without movement, without resistance, he seemed to float off and away, leaving an iced dessert that was pink as a dream . . . He fell asleep.

When he awoke he knew that several hours had passed. He was in a great quiet room with ebony walls and a dull illumination that was too faint, too subtle, to be called a light. His young host was standing over him.

"You fell asleep at dinner," Percy was saying. "I nearly did, too — it was such a treat to be comfortable again after this year of school. Servants undressed and bathed you while you were sleeping."

"Is this a bed or a cloud?" sighed John. "Percy, Percy — before you go, I want to apologize."

"For what?"

"For doubting you when you said you had a diamond as big as the Ritz-Carlton Hotel."

Percy smiled.

"I thought you didn't believe me. It's that mountain, you know."

"What mountain?"

"The mountain the château rests on. It's not very big for a mountain. But except for fifty feet of sod and gravel on top it's solid diamond. *One* diamond, one cubic mile without a flaw. Aren't you listening? Say —"

But John T. Unger had again fallen asleep.

### III

Morning. As he awoke he perceived drowsily that the room had at the same moment become dense with sunlight. The ebony panels of one wall had slid aside on a sort of track, leaving his chamber half open to the day. A large negro in a white uniform stood beside his bed.

"Good-evening," muttered John, summoning his brains from the wild places.

"Good-morning, sir. Are you ready for your bath, sir? Oh, don't get up — I'll put you in, if you'll just unbutton your pajamas — there. Thank you, sir."

John lay quietly as his pajamas were removed — he was amused and delighted; he expected to be lifted like a child by this black Gargantua who was tending him, but nothing of the sort happened; instead he felt the bed tilt up slowly on its side — he began to roll, startled at first, in the direction of the wall, but when he reached the wall its drapery gave way, and sliding two yards farther down a fleecy incline he plumped gently into water the same temperature as his body.

He looked about him. The runway or rollway on which he had arrived had folded gently back into place. He had been projected into another chamber and was sitting in a sunken bath with his head just above the level of the floor. All about him, lining the walls of the room and the sides and bottom of the bath itself, was a blue aquarium, and gazing through the crystal surface on which he sat, he could see fish swimming among amber lights and even gliding without curiosity past his outstretched toes, which were separated from them only by the thickness of the crystal. From overhead, sunlight came down through sea-green glass.

"I suppose, sir, that you'd like hot rosewater and soapsuds this morning, sir — and perhaps cold salt water to finish."

The negro was standing beside him.

"Yes," agreed John, smiling inanely, "as you please." Any idea of ordering this bath according to his own meagre standards of living would have been priggish and not a little wicked.

The negro pressed a button and a warm rain began to fall, apparently from overhead, but really, so John discovered after a moment, from a fountain arrangment near by. The water turned to a pale rose color and jets of liquid soap spurted into it from four miniature walrus heads at the corners of the bath. In a moment a dozen little paddle-wheels, fixed to the sides, had churned the mixture into a radiant rainbow of pink foam which enveloped him softly with its delicious lightness, and burst in shining, rosy bubbles here and there about him.

"Shall I turn on the moving-picture machine, sir?" suggested the negro deferentially. "There's a good one-reel comedy in this machine to-day, or I can put in a serious piece in a moment, if you prefer it."

"No, thanks," answered John, politely but firmly. He was enjoying his bath too much to desire any distraction. But distraction came. In a moment he was listening intently to the sound of flutes from just outside, flutes dripping a melody that was like a waterfall, cool and green as the room itself, accompanying a frothy piccolo, in play more fragile than the lace of suds that covered and charmed him.

After a cold salt-water bracer and a cold fresh finish, he stepped out and into a fleecy robe, and upon a couch covered with the same material he was rubbed with oil, alcohol, and spice. Later he sat in a voluptuous chair while he was shaved and his hair was trimmed.

"Mr. Percy is waiting in your sitting-room," said the negro, when these operations were finished. "My name is Gygsum, Mr. Unger, sir. I am to see to Mr. Unger every morning."

John walked out into the brisk sunshine of his living-room, where he found breakfast waiting for him and Percy, gorgeous in white kid knickerbockers, smoking in an easy chair.

## IV

This is the story of the Washington family as Percy sketched it for John during breakfast.

The father of the present Mr. Washington had been a Virginian, a direct descendant of George Washington, and Lord Baltimore. At the close of the Civil War he was a twenty-five-year-old Colonel with a played-out plantation and about a thousand dollars in gold.

Fitz-Norman Culpepper Washington, for that was the young Colonel's name, decided to present the Virginia estate to his younger brother and go West. He selected two dozen of the most faithful blacks, who, of course, worshipped him, and bought twenty-five tickets to the West, where he intended to take out land in their names and start a sheep and cattle ranch.

When he had been in Montana for less than a month and things were going very poorly indeed, he stumbled on his great discovery. He had lost his way when riding in the hills, and after a day without food he began to grow hungry. As he was without rifle, he was forced to pursue a squirrel, and in the course of the pursuit he noticed that it was carrying something shiny in its mouth. Just before it vanished into its hole — for Providence did not intend that this squirrel should alleviate his hunger — it dropped its burden. Sitting down to consider the situation Fitz-Norman's eye was caught by a gleam in the grass beside him. In ten seconds he had completely lost his appetite and gained one hundred thousand dollars. The squirrel, which had refused with annoying persistence to become food, had made him a present of a large and perfect diamond.

Late that night he found his way to camp and twelve hours later all the males among his darkies were back by the squirrel hole digging furiously at the side of the mountain. He told them he had discovered a rhinestone mine, and, as only one or two of them had ever seen a small diamond before, they believed him, without question. When the magnitude of his discovery became apparent to him, he found himself in a quandary. The mountain was *a* diamond — it was literally nothing else but solid diamond. He filled four saddle bags full of glittering samples and started on horseback for St. Paul. There he managed to dispose of half a dozen small stones — when he tried a larger one a storekeeper fainted and Fitz-Norman was arrested as a public disturber. He escaped from jail and caught the train for New York, where he sold a few medium-sized diamonds and received in exchange about two hundred thousand

dollars in gold. But he did not dare to produce any exceptional gems —
in fact, he left New York just in time. Tremendous excitement had been
created in jewelry circles, not so much by the size of his diamonds as
by their appearance in the city from mysterious sources. Wild rumors
became current that a diamond mine had been discovered in the Cats-
kills, on the Jersey coast, on Long Island, beneath Washington Square.
Excursion trains, packed with men carrying picks and shovels, began to
leave New York hourly, bound for various neighboring El Dorados. But
by that time young Fitz-Norman was on his way back to Montana.

By the end of a fortnight he had estimated that the diamond in the
mountain was approximately equal in quantity to all the rest of the
diamonds known to exist in the world. There was no valuing it by any
regular computation, however, for it was *one solid diamond* — and if it
were offered for sale not only would the bottom fall out of the market,
but also, if the value should vary with its size in the usual arithmetical
progression, there would not be enough gold in the world to buy a tenth
part of it. And what could any one do with a diamond that size?

It was an amazing predicament. He was, in one sense, the richest
man that ever lived — and yet was he worth anything at all? If his
secret should transpire there was no telling to what measures the Government might resort in order to prevent a panic, in gold as well as in jewels.
They might take over the claim immediately and institute a monopoly.

There was no alternative — he must market his mountain in secret.
He sent South for his younger brother and put him in charge of his
colored following — darkies who had never realized that slavery was
abolished. To make sure of this, he read them a proclamation that he
had composed, which announced that General Forrest had reorganized
the shattered Southern armies and defeated the North in one pitched
battle. The negroes believed him implicity. They passed a vote declaring
it a good thing and held revival services immediately.

Fitz-Norman himself set out for foreign parts with one hundred
thousand dollars and two trunks filled with rough diamonds of all sizes.
He sailed for Russia in a Chinese junk and six months after his departure
from Montana he was in St. Petersburg. He took obscure lodgings and
called immediately upon the court jeweller, announcing that he had a
diamond for the Czar. He remained in St. Petersburg for two weeks, in
constant danger of being murdered, living from lodging to lodging,
and afraid to visit his trunks more than three or four times during the
whole fortnight.

On his promise to return in a year with larger and finer stones, he was
allowed to leave for India. Before he left, however, the Court Treasurers
had deposited to his credit, in American banks, the sum of fifteen million
dollars — under four different aliases.

He returned to America in 1868, having been gone a little over two years. He had visited the capitals of twenty-two countries and talked with five emperors, eleven kings, three princes, a shah, a khan, and a sultan. At that time Fitz-Norman estimated his own wealth at one billion dollars. One fact worked consistently against the disclosure of his secret. No one of his larger diamonds remained in the public eye for a week before being invested with a history of enough fatalities, amours, revolutions, and wars to have occupied it from the days of the first Babylonian Empire.

From 1870 until his death in 1900, the history of Fitz-Norman Washington was a long epic in gold. There were side issues, of course — he evaded the surveys, he married a Virginia lady, by whom he had a single son, and he was compelled, due to a series of unfortunate complications, to murder his brother, whose unfortunate habit of drinking himself into an indiscreet stupor had several times endangered their safety. But very few other murders stained these happy years of progress and expansion.

Just before he died he changed his policy, and with all but a few million dollars of his outside wealth bought up rare minerals in bulk, which he deposited in the safety vaults of banks all over the world, marked as bric-à-brac. His son, Braddock Tarleton Washington, followed this policy on an even more tensive scale. The minerals were converted into the rarest of all elements — radium — so that the equivalent of a billion dollars in gold could be placed in a receptacle no bigger than a cigar box.

When Fitz-Norman had been dead three years, his son, Braddock, decided that the business had gone far enough. The amount of wealth that he and his father had taken out of the mountain was beyond all exact computation. He kept a note-book in cipher in which he set down the approximate quantity of radium in each of the thousand banks he patronized, and recorded the alias under which it was held. Then he did a very simple thing — he sealed up the mine.

He sealed up the mine. What had been taken out of it would support all the Washingtons yet to be born in unparalleled luxury for generations. His one care must be the protection of his secret, lest in the possible panic attendant on its discovery he should be reduced with all the property-holders in the world to utter poverty.

This was the family among whom John T. Unger was staying. This was the story he heard in his silver-walled living-room the morning after his arrival.

## V

After breakfast, John found his way out the great marble entrance, and looked curiously at the scene before him. The whole valley, from the diamond mountain to the steep granite cliff five miles away, still gave off a breath of golden haze which hovered idly above the fine sweep of lawns and lakes and gardens. Here and there clusters of elms made delicate groves of shade, contrasting strangely with the tough masses of pine forest that held the hills in a grip of dark-blue green. Even as John looked he saw three fawns in single file patter out from one clump about a half mile away and disappear with awkward gayety into the black-ribbed half-light of another. John would not have been surprised to see a goat-foot piping his way among the trees or to catch a glimpse of pink nymph-skin and flying yellow hair between the greenest of the green leaves.

In some such cool hope he descended the marble steps, disturbing faintly the sleep of two silky Russian wolfhounds at the bottom, and set off along a walk of white and blue brick that seemed to lead in no particular direction.

He was enjoying himself as much as he was able. It is youth's felicity as well as its insufficiency that it can never live in the present, but must always be measuring up the day against its own radiantly imagined future — flowers and gold, girls and stars, they are only prefigurations and prophecies of that incomparable, unattainable young dream.

John rounded a soft corner where the massed rosebushes filled the air with heavy scent, and struck off across a park toward a patch of moss under some trees. He had never lain upon moss, and he wanted to see whether it was really soft enough to justify the use of its name as an adjective. Then he saw a girl coming toward him over the grass. She was the most beautiful person he had ever seen.

She was dressed in a white little gown that came just below her knees, and a wreath of mignonettes clasped with blue slices of sapphire bound up her hair. Her pink bare feet scattered the dew before them as she came. She was younger than John — not more than sixteen.

"Hello," she cried softly, "I'm Kismine."

She was much more than that to John already. He advanced toward her, scarcely moving as he drew near lest he should tread on her bare toes.

"You haven't met me," said her soft voice. Her blue eyes added, "Oh, but you've missed a great deal!" . . . "You met my sister, Jasmine, last night. I was sick with lettuce poisoning," went on her soft voice, and her eyes continued, "and when I'm sick I'm sweet — and when I'm well."

"You have made an enormous impression on me," said John's eyes, "and I'm not so slow myself" — "How do you do?" said his voice. "I hope you're better this morning." — "You darling," added his eyes tremulously.

John observed that they had been walking along the path. On her suggestion they sat down together upon the moss, the softness of which he failed to determine.

He was critical about women. A single defect — a thick ankle, a hoarse voice, a glass eye — was enough to make him utterly indifferent. And here for the first time in his life he was beside a girl who seemed to him the incarnation of physical perfection.

"Are you from the East?" asked Kismine with charming interest.

"No," answered John simply. "I'm from Hades."

Either she had never heard of Hades, or she could think of no pleasant comment to make upon it, for she did not discuss it further.

"I'm going East to school this fall," she said. "D'you think I'll like it? I'm going to New York to Miss Bulge's. It's very strict, but you see over the weekends I'm going to live at home with the family in our New York house, because father heard that the girls had to go walking two by two."

"Your father wants you to be proud," observed John.

"We are," she answered, her eyes shining with dignity. "None of us has ever been punished. Father said we never should be. Once when my sister Jasmine was a little girl she pushed him down-stairs and he just got up and limped away.

"Mother was — well, a little startled," continued Kismine, "when she heard that you were from — from where you *are* from, you know. She said that when she was a young girl — but then, you see, she's a Spaniard and old-fashioned."

"Do you spend much time out here?" asked John, to conceal the fact that he was somewhat hurt by this remark. It seemed an unkind allusion to his provincialism.

"Percy and Jasmine and I are here every summer, but next summer Jasmine is going to Newport. She's coming out in London a year from this fall. She'll be presented at court."

"Do you know," began John hesitantly, "you're much more sophisticated than I thought you were when I first saw you?"

"Oh, no, I'm not," she exclaimed hurriedly. "Oh, I wouldn't think of being. I think that sophisticated young people are terribly common, don't you? I'm not at all, really. If you say I am, I'm going to cry."

She was so distressed that her lip was trembling. John was impelled to protest:

"I didn't mean that; I only said it to tease you."

"Because I wouldn't mind if I *were*," she persisted "but I'm *not*. I'm very innocent and girlish. I never smoke, or drink, or read anything except poetry. I know scarcely any mathematics or chemistry. I dress *very* simply — in fact, I scarcely dress at all. I think sophisticated is the last thing you can say about me. I believe that girls ought to enjoy their youths in a wholesome way."

"I do too," said John heartily.

Kismine was cheerful again. She smiled at him, and a still-born tear dripped from the corner of one blue eye.

"I like you," she whispered, intimately. "Are you going to spend all your time with Percy while you're here, or will you be nice to me? Just think — I'm absolutely fresh ground. I've never had a boy in love with me in all my life. I've never been allowed even to *see* boys alone — except Percy. I came all the way out here into this grove hoping to run into you, where the family wouldn't be around."

Deeply flattered, John bowed from the hips as he had been taught at dancing school in Hades.

"We'd better go now," said Kismine sweetly. "I have to be with mother at eleven. You haven't asked me to kiss you once. I thought boys always did that nowadays."

John drew himself up proudly.

"Some of them do," he answered, "but not me. Girls don't do that sort of thing — in Hades."

Side by side they walked back toward the house.

## VI

John stood facing Mr. Braddock Washington in the full sunlight. The elder man was about forty with a proud, vacuous face, intelligent eyes, and a robust figure. In the mornings he smelt of horses — the best horses. He carried a plain walking-stick of gray birch with a single large opal for a grip. He and Percy were showing John around.

"The slaves' quarters are there." His walking-stick indicated a cloister of marble on their left that ran in graceful Gothic along the side of the mountain. "In my youth I was distracted for a while from the business of life by a period of absurd idealism. During that time they lived in luxury. For instance, I equipped every one of the rooms with a tile bath."

"I suppose," ventured John, with an ingratiating laugh, "that they used the bathtubs to keep coal in. Mr. Schnlitzer-Murphy told me that once he —"

"The opinions of Mr. Schnlitzer-Murphy are of little importance, I should imagine," interrupted Braddock Washington, coldly. "My slaves did not keep coal in their bathtubs. They had orders to bathe every day, and they did. If they hadn't I might have ordered a sulphuric acid shampoo. I discontinued the baths for quite another reason. Several of them caught cold and died. Water is not good for certain races — except as a beverage."

John laughed, and then decided to nod his nead in sober agreement. Braddock Washington made him uncomfortable.

"All these negroes are descendants of the ones my father brought North with him. There are about two hundred and fifty now. You notice that they've lived so long apart from the world that their original dialect has become an almost indistinguishable patois. We bring a few of them up to speak English — my secretary and two or three of the house servants.

"This is the golf course," he continued, as they strolled along the velvet winter grass. "It's all a green, you see — no fairway, no rough, no hazards."

He smiled pleasantly at John.

"Many men in the cage, father?" asked Percy suddenly.

Braddock Washington stumbled, and let forth an involuntary curse.

"One less than there should be," he ejaculated darkly — and then added after a moment, "We've had difficulties."

"Mother was telling me," exclaimed Percy, "that Italian teacher —"

"A ghastly error," said Braddock Washington angrily. "But of course there's a good chance that we may have got him. Perhaps he fell somewhere in the woods or stumbled over a cliff. And then there's always the probability that if he did get away his story wouldn't be believed. Nevertheless, I've had two dozen men looking for him in different towns around here."

"And no luck?"

"Some. Fourteen of them reported to my agent that they'd each killed a man answering to that description, but of course it was probably only the reward they were after —"

He broke off. They had come to a large cavity in the earth about the circumference of a merry-go-round and covered by a strong iron grating. Braddock Washington beckoned to John, and pointed his cane down through the grating. John stepped to the edge and gazed. Immediately his ears were assailed with a wild clamor from below.

"Come on down to Hell!"

"Hello, kiddo, how's the air up there?"

"Hey! Throw us a rope!"

"Got an old doughnut, Buddy, or a couple of second-hand sandwiches?"

"Say, fella, if you'll push down that guy you're with, we'll show you a quick disappearance scene."

"Paste him one for me, will you?"

It was too dark to see clearly into the pit below, but John could tell from the coarse optimism and rugged vitality of the remarks and voices that they proceeded from middle-class Americans of the more spirited type. Then Mr. Washington put out his cane and touched a button in the grass, and the scene below sprang into light.

"These are some adventurous mariners who had the misfortune to discover El Dorado," he remarked.

Below them there had appeared a large hollow in the earth shaped like the interior of a bowl. The sides were steep and apparantly of polished glass, and on its slightly concave surface stood about two dozen men clad in the half costume, half uniform, of aviators. Their upturned faces, lit with wrath, with malice, with despair, with cynical humor, were covered with long growths of beard, but with the exception of a few who had pined perceptibly away, they seemed to be a well-fed, healthy lot.

Braddock Washington drew a garden chair to the edge of the pit and sat down.

"Well, how are you, boys?" he inquired genially.

A chorus of execration in which all joined except a few too dispirited to cry out, rose up into the sunny air, but Braddock Washington heard it with unruffled composure. When its last echo had died away he spoke again.

"Have you thought up a way out of your difficulty?"

From here and there among them a remark floated up.

"We decided to stay here for love!"

"Bring us up there and we'll find us a way!"

Braddock Washington waited until they were again quiet. Then he said:

"I've told you the situation. I don't want you here. I wish to heaven I'd never seen you. Your own curiosity got you here, and any time that you can think of a way out which protects me and my interests I'll be glad to consider it. But so long as you confine your efforts to digging tunnels — yes, I know about the new one you've started — you won't get very far. This isn't as hard on you as you make it out, with all your howling for the loved ones at home. If you were the type who worried much about the loved ones at home, you'd never have taken up aviation."

A tall man moved apart from the others, and held up his hand to call his captor's attention to what he was about to say.

"Let me ask you a few questions!" he cried. "You pretend to be a fair-minded man."

"How absurd. How could a man of *my* position be fair-minded toward *you*? You might as well speak of a Spaniard being fair-minded toward a piece of steak."

At this harsh observation the faces of the two dozen steaks fell, but the tall man continued:

"All right!" he cried. "We've argued this out before. You're not a humanitarian and you're not fair-minded, but you're human — at least you say you are — and you ought to be able to put yourself in our place for long enough to think how — how — how — "

"How what?" demanded Washington, coldly.

" — how unnecessary — "

"Not to me."

"Well, — how cruel — "

"We've covered that. Cruelty doesn't exist where self-preservation is involved. You've been soldiers: you know that. Try another."

"Well, then, how stupid."

"There," admitted Washington, "I grant you that. But try to think of an alternative. I've offered to have all or any of you painlessly executed if you wish. I've offered to have your wives, sweethearts, children, and mothers kidnapped and brought out here. I'll enlarge your place down there and feed and clothe you the rest of your lives. If there was some method of producing permanent amnesia I'd have all of you operated on and released immediately, somewhere outside of my preserves. But that's as far as my ideas go."

"How about trusting us not to peach on you?" cried someone.

"You don't proffer that suggestion seriously," said Washington, with an expression of scorn. "I did take out one man to teach my daughter Italian. Last week he got away."

A wild yell of jubilation went up suddenly from two dozen throats and a pandemonium of joy ensued. The prisoners clog-danced and cheered and yodled and wrestled with one another in a sudden up-rush of animal spirits. They even ran up the glass sides of the bowl as far as they could, and slid back to the bottom upon the natural cushions of their bodies. The tall man started a song in which they all joined —

> *"Oh, we'll hang the kaiser*
> *On a sour apple tree — "*

Braddock Washington sat in inscrutable silence until the song was over.

"You see," he remarked, when he could gain a modicum of attention, "I bear you no ill-will. I like to see you enjoying yourselves. That's why

I didn't tell you the whole story at once. The man — what was his name? Critchtichiello? — was shot by some of my agents in fourteen different places."

Not guessing that the places referred to were cities, the tumult of rejoicing subsided immediately.

"Nevertheless," cried Washington with a touch of anger, "he tried to run away. Do you expect me to take chances with any of you after an experience like that?"

Again a series of ejaculations went up.

"Sure!"

"Would your daughter like to learn Chinese?"

"Hey, I can speak Italian! My mother was a wop."

"Maybe she'd like t'learna speak N'Yawk!"

"If she's the little one with the big blue eyes I can teach her a lot of things better than Italian."

"I knew some Irish songs — and I could hammer brass once't."

Mr. Washington reached forward suddenly with his cane and pushed the button in the grass so that the picture below went out instantly, and there remained only that great dark mouth covered dismally with the black teeth of the grating.

"Hey!" called a single voice from below, "you ain't goin' away without givin' us your blessing?"

But Mr. Washington, followed by the two boys, was already strolling on toward the ninth hole of the golf course, as though the pit and its contents were no more than a hazard over which his facile iron had triumphed with ease.

### VII

July under the lee of the diamond mountain was a month of blanket nights and of warm, glowing days. John and Kismine were in love. He did not know that the little gold football (inscribed with her legend *Pro deo et patria et St. Mida*) which he had given her rested on a platinum chain next to her bosom. But it did. And she for her part was not aware that a large sapphire which had dropped one day from her simple coiffure was stowed away tenderly in John's jewel box.

Late one afternoon when the ruby and ermine music room was quiet, they spent an hour there together. He held her hand and she gave him such a look that he whispered her name aloud. She bent toward him — then hesitated.

"Did you say 'Kismine'?" she asked softly, "or —"

She had wanted to be sure. She thought she might have misunderstood.

Neither of them had ever kissed before, but in the course of an hour it seemed to make little difference.

The afternoon drifted away. That night when a last breath of music drifted down from the highest tower, they each lay awake, happily dreaming over the separate minutes of the day. They had decided to be married as soon as possible.

## VIII

Every day Mr. Washington and the two young men went hunting or fishing in the deep forests or played golf around the somnolent course — games which John diplomatically allowed his host to win — or swam in the mountain coolness of the lake. John found Mr. Washington a somewhat exacting personality — utterly uninterested in any ideas or opinions except his own. Mrs. Washington was aloof and reserved at all times. She was apparently indifferent to her two daughters, and entirely absorbed in her son Percy, with whom she held interminable conversations in rapid Spanish at dinner.

Jasmine, the elder daughter, resembled Kismine in appearance — except that she was somewhat bow-legged, and terminated in large hands and feet — but was utterly unlike her in temperament. Her favorite books had to do with poor girls who kept house for widowed fathers. John learned from Kismine that Jasmine had never recovered from the shock and disappointment caused her by the termination of the World War, just as she was about to start for Europe as a canteen expert. She had even pined away for a time, and Braddock Washington had taken steps to promote a new war in the Balkans — but she had seen a photograph of some wounded Serbian soldiers and lost interest in the whole proceedings. But Percy and Kismine seemed to have inherited the arrogant attitude in all its harsh magnificence from their father. A chaste and consistent selfishness ran like a pattern through their every idea.

John was enchanted by the wonders of the château and the valley. Braddock Washington, so Percy told him, had caused to be kidnapped a landscape gardener, an architect, a designer of state settings, and a French decadent poet left over from the last century. He had put his entire force of negroes at their disposal, guaranteed to supply them with any materials that the world could offer, and left them to work out some ideas of their own. But one by one they had shown their uselessness. The decadent poet had at once begun bewailing his separation from the boulevards in spring — he made some vague remarks about spices, apes, and ivories, but said nothing that was of any practical value. The stage designer on his part wanted to make the whole valley a series of tricks and sensational effects — a state of things that the Washingtons would soon have grown tired of. And as for the architect and the landscape gardener, they thought only in terms of convention. They must make this like this and that like that.

But they had, at least, solved the problem of what was to be done with them — they all went mad early one morning after spending the night in a single room trying to agree upon the location of a fountain, and were now confined comfortably in an insane asylum at Westport, Connecticut.

"But," inquired John curiously, "who did plan all your wonderful reception rooms and halls, and approaches and bathrooms — ?"

"Well," answered Percy, "I blush to tell you, but it was a moving-picture fella. He was the only man we found who was used to playing with an unlimited amount of money, though he did tuck his napkin in his collar and couldn't read or write."

As August drew to a close John began to regret that he must soon go back to school. He and Kismine had decided to elope the following June.

"It would be nicer to be married here," Kismine confessed, "but of course I could never get father's permission to marry you at all. Next to that I'd rather elope. It's terrible for wealthy people to be married in America at present — they always have to send out bulletins to the press saying that they're going to be married in remnants, when what they mean is just a peck of old second-hand pearls and some used lace worn once by the Empress Eugenie."

"I know," agreed John fervently. "When I was visiting the Schnlitzer-Murphys, the eldest daughter, Gwendolyn, married a man whose father owns half of West Virginia. She wrote home saying what a tough struggle she was carrying on on his salary as a bank clerk — and then she ended up saying that 'Thank God, I have four good maids anyhow, and that helps a little.' "

"It's absurd," commented Kismine. "Think of the millions and millions of people in the world, laborers and all, who get along with only two maids."

One afternoon late in August a chance remark of Kismine's changed the face of the entire situation, and threw John into a state of terror.

They were in their favorite grove, and between kisses John was indulging in some romantic forebodings which he fancied added poignancy to their relations.

"Sometimes I think we'll never marry," he said sadly. "You're too wealthy, too magnificent. No one as rich as you are can be like other girls. I should marry the daughter of some well-to-do wholesale hardware man from Omaha or Sioux City, and be content with her half-million."

"I knew the daughter of a wholesale hardware man once," remarked

Kismine. "I don't think you'd have been contented with her. She was a friend of my sister's. She visited here."

"Oh, then you've had other guests?" exclaimed John in surprise.

Kismine seemed to regret her words.

"Oh, yes," she said hurriedly, "we've had a few."

"But aren't you — wasn't your father afraid they'd talk outside?"

"Oh, to some extent, to some extent," she answered. "Let's talk about something pleasanter."

But John's curiosity was aroused.

"Something pleasanter!" he demanded. "What's unpleasant about that? Weren't they nice girls?"

To his great surprise Kismine began to weep.

"Yes — th — that's the — the whole t-trouble. I grew qu-quite attached to some of them. So did Jasmine, but she kept inv-viting them anyway. I couldn't under*stand* it."

A dark suspicion was born in John's heart.

"Do you mean that they *told,* and your father had them — removed?"

"Worse than that," she muttered brokenly. "Father took no chances — and Jasmine kept writing them to come, and they had *such* a good time!"

She was overcome by a paroxysm of grief.

Stunned with the horror of this revelation, John sat there open-mouthed feeling the nerves of his body twitter like so many sparrows perched upon his spinal column.

"Now, I've told you, and I shouldn't have," she said, calming suddenly and drying her dark blue eyes.

"Do you mean to say that your father had them *murdered* before they left?"

She nodded.

"In August usually — or early in September. It's only natural for us to get all the pleasure out of them that we can first."

"How abominable! How — why, I must be going crazy! Did you really admit that —"

"I did," interrupted Kismine, shrugging her shoulders. "We can't very well imprison them like those aviators, where they'd be a continual reproach to us every day. And it's always been made easier for Jasmine and me, because father had it done sooner than we expected. In that way we avoided any farewell scene —"

"So you murdered them! Uh!" cried John.

"It was done very nicely. They were drugged while they were asleep — and their families were always told that they died of scarlet fever in Butte."

"But — I fail to understand why you kept on inviting them!"

"I didn't," burst out Kismine. "I never invited one. Jasmine did. And they always had a very good time. She'd give them the nicest presents toward the last. I shall probably have visitors too — I'll harden up to it. We can't let such an inevitable thing as death stand in the way of enjoying life while we have it. Think how lonesome it'd be out here if we never had *any* one. Why, father and mother have sacrificed some of their best friends just as we have."

"And so," cried John accusingly, "and so you were letting me make love to you and pretending to return it, and talking about marriage, all the time knowing perfectly well that I'd never get out of here alive —"

"No," she protested passionately. "Not any more. I did at first. You were here. I couldn't help that, and I thought your last days might as well be pleasant for both of us. But then I fell in love with you, and — I'm honestly sorry you're going to — going to be put away — though I'd rather you'd be put away than ever kiss another girl."

"Oh, you would, would you?" cried John ferociously.

"Much rather. Besides, I've always heard that a girl can have more fun with a man whom she knows she can never marry. Oh, why did I tell you? I've probably spoiled your whole good time now, and we were really enjoying things when you didn't know it. I knew it would make things sort of depressing for you."

"Oh, you did, did you?" John's voice trembled with anger. "I've heard about enough of this. If you haven't any more pride and decency than to have an affair with a fellow that you know isn't much better than a corpse, I don't want to have any more to do with you!"

"You're not a corpse!" she protested in horror. "You're not a corpse! I won't have you saying that I kissed a corpse!"

"I said nothing of the sort!"

"You did! You said I kissed a corpse!"

"I didn't!"

Their voices had risen, but upon a sudden interruption they both subsided into immediate silence. Footsteps were coming along the path in their direction, and a moment later the rose bushes were parted displaying Braddock Washington, whose intelligent eyes set in his good-looking vacuous face were peering in at them.

"Who kissed a corpse?" he demanded in obvious disapproval.

"Nobody," answered Kismine quickly. "We were just joking."

"What are you two doing here, anyhow?" he demanded gruffly. "Kismine, you ought to be — to be reading or playing golf with your sister. Go read! Go play golf! Don't let me find you here when I come back!"

Then he bowed at John and went up the path.

"See?" said Kismine crossly, when he was out of hearing. "You've spoiled it all. We can never meet any more. He won't let me meet you. He'd have you poisoned if he thought we were in love."

"We're not, any more!" cried John fiercely, "so he can set his mind at rest upon that. Moreover, don't fool yourself that I'm going to stay around here. Inside of six hours I'll be over those mountains if I have to gnaw a passage through them, and on my way East."

They had both got to their feet, and at this remark Kismine came close and put her arm through his.

"I'm going, too."

"You must be crazy —"

"Of course I'm going," she interrupted impatiently.

"You most certainly are not. You —"

"Very well," she said quietly, "we'll catch up with father now and talk it over with him."

Defeated, John mustered a sickly smile.

"Very well, dearest," he agreed, with pale and unconvincing affection, "we'll go together."

His love for her returned and settled placidly on his heart. She was his — she would go with him to share his dangers. He put his arms about her and kissed her fervently. After all she loved him; she had saved him, in fact.

Discussing the matter, they walked slowly back toward the château. They decided that since Braddock Washington had seen them together they had best depart the next night. Nevertheless, John's lips were unusually dry at dinner, and he nervously emptied a great spoonful of peacock soup into his left lung. He had to be carried into the turquoise and sable card-room and pounded on the back by one of the under-butlers, which Percy considered a great joke.

## IX

Long after midnight John's body gave a nervous jerk, and he sat suddenly upright, staring into the veils of somnolence that draped the room. Through the squares of blue darkness that were his open windows, he heard a faint far-away sound that died upon a bed of wind before identifying itself on his memory, clouded with uneasy dreams. But the sharp noise that had succeeded it was nearer, was just outside the room — the click of a turned knob, a footstep, a whisper, he could not tell; a hard lump gathered in the pit of his stomach, and his whole body ached in the moment that he strained agonizingly to hear. Then one of the veils seemed to dissolve, and he saw a vague figure standing by the door, a figure only faintly limned and blocked in upon the darkness, mingled so with the folds of the drapery as to seem distorted, like a reflection seen in a dirty pane of glass.

With a sudden movement of fright or resolution John pressed the button by his bedside, and the next moment he was sitting in the great sunken bath of the adjoining room, waked into alertness by the shock of the cold water which half filled it.

He sprang out, and, his wet pajamas scattering a heavy trickle of water behind him, ran for the aquamarine door which he knew led out onto the ivory landing of the second floor. The door opened noiselessly. A single crimson lamp burning in a great dome above lit the magnificent sweep of the carved stairways with a poignant beauty. For a moment John hesitated, appalled by the silent splendor massed about him, seeming to envelop in its gigantic folds and contours the solitary drenched little figure shivering upon the ivory landing. Then simultaneously two things happened. The door of his own sitting-room swung open, precipitating three naked negroes into the hall — and, as John swayed in wild terror toward the stairway, another door slid back in the wall on the other side of the corridor, and John saw Braddock Washington standing in the lighted lift, wearing a fur coat and a pair of riding boots which reached to his knees and displayed, above, the glow of his rose-colored pajamas.

On the instant the three negroes — John had never seen any of them before, and it flashed through his mind that they must be the professional executioners — paused in their movement toward John, and turned expectantly to the man in the lift, who burst out with an imperious command:

"Get in here! All three of you! Quick as hell!"

Then, within the instant, the three negroes darted into the cage, the oblong of light was blotted out as the lift door slid shut, and John was again alone in the hall. He slumped weakly down against an ivory stair.

It was apparent that something portentous had occurred, something which, for the moment at least, had postponed his own petty disaster. What was it? Had the negroes risen in revolt? Had the aviators forced aside the iron bars of the grating? Or had the men of Fish stumbled blindly through the hills and gazed with bleak, joyless eyes upon the gaudy valley? John did not know. He heard a faint whir of air as the lift whizzed up again, and then, a moment later, as it descended. It was probable that Percy was hurrying to his father's assistance, and it occurred to John that this was his opportunity to join Kismine and plan an immediate escape. He waited until the lift had been silent for several minutes;

shivering a little with the night cool that whipped in through his wet pajamas, he returned to his room and dressed himself quickly. Then he mounted a long flight of stairs and turned down the corridor carpeted with Russian sable which led to Kismine's suite.

The door of her sitting-room was open and the lamps were lighted. Kismine, in an angora kimono, stood near the window of the room in a listening attitude, and as John entered noiselessly, she turned toward him.

"Oh, it's you!" she whispered, crossing the room to him. "Did you hear them?"

"I heard your father's slaves in my —"

"No," she interrupted excitedly. "Aeroplanes!"

"Aeroplanes? Perhaps that was the sound that woke me."

"There's at least a dozen. I saw one a few moments ago dead against the moon. The guard back by the cliff fired his rifle and that's what roused father. We're going to open on them right away."

"Are they here on purpose?"

"Yes — it's that Italian who got away —"

Simultaneously with her last word, a succession of sharp cracks tumbled in through the open window. Kismine uttered a little cry, took a penny with fumbling fingers from a box on her dresser, and ran to one of the electric lights. In an instant the entire château was in darkness — she had blown out the fuse.

"Come on!" she cried to him. "We'll go up to the roof garden, and watch it from there!"

Drawing a cape about her, she took his hand, and they found their way out the door. It was only a step to the tower lift, and as she pressed the button that shot them upward he put his arms around her in the darkness and kissed her mouth. Romance had come to John Unger at last. A minute later they had stepped out upon the star-white platform. Above, under the misty moon, sliding in and out of the patches of cloud that eddied below it, floated a dozen dark-winged bodies in a constant circling course. From here and there in the valley flashes of fire leaped toward them, followed by sharp detonations. Kismine clapped her hands with pleasure, which a moment later turned to dismay as the aeroplanes, at some pre-arranged signal, began to release their bombs and the whole of the valley became a panorama of deep reverberate sound and lurid light.

Before long the aim of the attackers became concentrated upon the points where the anti-aircraft guns were situated, and one of them was almost immediately reduced to a giant cinder to lie smouldering in a park of rose bushes.

"Kismine," begged John, "you'll be glad when I tell you that this attack came on the eve of my murder. If I hadn't heard that guard shoot off his gun back by the pass I should now be stone dead —"

"I can't hear you!" cried Kismine, intent on the scene before her. "You'll have to talk louder!"

"I simply said," shouted John, "that we'd better get out before they begin to shell the château!"

Suddenly the whole portico of the negro quarters cracked asunder, a geyser of flame shot up from under the colonnades, and great fragments of jagged marble were hurled as far as the borders of the lake.

"There go fifty thousand dollars' worth of slaves," cried Kismine, "at prewar prices. So few Americans have any respect for property."

John renewed his efforts to compel her to leave. The aim of the aeroplanes was becoming more precise minute by minute, and only two of the anti-aircraft guns were still retaliating. It was obvious that the garrison, encircled with fire, could not hold out much longer.

"Come on!" cried John, pulling Kismine's arm, "we've got to go. Do you realize that those aviators will kill you without question if they find you?"

She consented reluctantly.

"We'll have to wake Jasmine!" she said, as they hurried toward the lift. Then she added in a sort of childish delight: "We'll be poor, won't we? Like people in books. And I'll be an orphan and utterly free. Free and poor! What fun!" She stopped and raised her lips to him in a delighted kiss.

"It's impossible to be both together," said John grimly. "People have found that out. And I should choose to be free as preferable of the two. As an extra caution you'd better dump the contents of your jewel box into your pockets."

Ten minutes later the two girls met John in the dark corridor and they descended to the main floor of the château. Passing for the last time through the magnificence of the splendid halls, they stood for a moment out on the terrace, watching the burning negro quarters and the flaming embers of two planes which had fallen on the other side of the lake. A solitary gun was still keeping up a sturdy popping, and the attackers seemed timorous about descending lower, but sent their thunderous fireworks in a circle around it, until any chance shot might annihilate its Ethiopian crew.

John and the two sisters passed down the marble steps, turned sharply to the left, and began to ascend a narrow path that wound like a garter around the diamond mountain. Kismine knew a heavily wooded spot half-way up where they could lie concealed and yet be able to observe the wild night in the valley — finally to make an escape, when it should be necessary, along a secret path laid in a rocky gully.

## X

It was three o'clock when they attained their destination. The obliging and phlegmatic Jasmine fell off to sleep immediately, leaning against the trunk of a large tree, while John and Kismine sat, his arm around her, and watched the desperate ebb and flow of the dying battle among the ruins of a vista that had been a garden spot that morning. Shortly after four o'clock the last remaining gun gave out a clanging sound and went out of action in a swift tongue of red smoke. Though the moon was down, they saw that the flying bodies were circling closer to the earth. When the planes had made certain that the beleaguered possessed no further resources, they would land and the dark and glittering reign of the Washingtons would be over.

With the cessation of the firing the valley grew quiet. The embers of the two aeroplanes glowed like the eyes of some monster crouching in the grass. The château stood dark and silent, beautiful without light as it had been beautiful in the sun, while the woody rattles of Nemesis filled the air above with a growing and receding complaint. Then John perceived that Kismine, like her sister, had fallen sound asleep.

It was long after four when he became aware of footsteps along the path they had lately followed, and he waited in breathless silence until the persons to whom they belonged had passed the vantage-point he occupied. There was a faint stir in the air now that was not of human origin, and the dew was cold; he knew that the dawn would break soon. John waited until the steps had gone a safe distance up the mountain and were inaudible. Then he followed. About half-way to the steep summit the trees fell away and a hard saddle of rock spread itself over the diamond beneath. Just before he reached this point he slowed down his pace, warned by an animal sense that there was life just ahead of him. Coming to a high boulder, he lifted his head gradually above its edge. His curiosity was rewarded; this is what he saw:

Braddock Washington was standing there motionless, silhouetted against the gray sky without sound or sign of life. As the dawn came up out of the east, lending a cold green color to the earth, it brought the solitary figure into insignificant contrast with the new day.

While John watched, his host remained for a few moments absorbed in some inscrutable contemplation; then he signalled to the two negroes who crouched at his feet to lift the burden which lay between them. As they struggled upright, the first yellow beam of the sun struck through the innumerable prisms of an immense and exquisitely chiselled diamond — and a white radiance was kindled that glowed upon the air like a fragment of the morning star. The bearers staggered beneath its weight for a moment — then their rippling muscles caught and hardened under the wet shine of the skins and the three figures were again motionless in their defiant impotency before the heavens.

After a while the white man lifted his head and slowly raised his arms in a gesture of attention, as one who would call a great crowd to hear — but there was no crowd, only the vast silence of the mountain and the sky, broken by faint bird voices down among the trees. The figure on the saddle of rock began to speak ponderously and with an inextinguishable pride.

"You out there — " he cried in a trembling voice. "You — there — !" He paused, his arms still uplifted, his head held attentively as though there might be men coming down the mountain, but the mountain was bare of human life. There was only sky and a mocking flute of wind along the tree-tops. Could Washington be praying? For a moment John wondered. Then the illusion passed — there was something in the man's whole attitude antithetical to prayer.

"Oh, you above there!"

The voice was become strong and confident. This was no forlorn supplication. If anything, there was in it a quality of monstrous condescension.

"You there —"

Words too quickly uttered to be understood, flowing one into the other . . . John listened breathlessly, catching a phrase here and there, while the voice broke off, resumed, broke off again — now strong and argumentative, now colored with a slow, puzzled impatience. Then a conviction commenced to dawn on the single listener, and as realization crept over him a spray of quick blood rushed through his arteries. Braddock Washington was offering a bribe to God!

That was it — there was no doubt. The diamond in the arms of his slaves was some advance sample, a promise of more to follow.

That, John perceived after a time, was the thread running through his sentences. Prometheus Enriched was calling to witness forgotten sacrifices, forgotten rituals, prayers obsolete before the birth of Christ. For a while his discourse took the form of reminding God of this gift or that which Divinity had deigned to accept from men — great churches if he would rescue cities from the plague, gifts of myrrh and gold, of human lives and beautiful women and captive armies, of children and queens, of beasts of the forest and field, sheep and goats, harvests and cities, whole conquered lands that had been offered up in lust or blood for His appeasal, buying a meed's worth of alleviation from the Divine wrath — and now he, Braddock Washington, Emperor of Diamonds, king and priest of the age of gold, arbiter of splendor and luxury, would offer up a treasure such as princes before him had never dreamed of, offer it up not in suppliance, but in pride.

He would give to God, he continued, getting down to specifications, the greatest diamond in the world. This diamond would be cut with many more thousand facets than there were leaves on a tree, and yet the whole diamond would be shaped with the perfection of a stone no bigger than a fly. Many men would work upon it for many years. It would be set in a great dome of beaten gold, wonderfully carved and equipped with gates of opal and crusted sapphire. In the middle would be hollowed out a chapel presided over by an altar of iridescent, decomposing, ever-changing radium which would burn out the eyes of any worshipper who lifted up his head from prayer — and on this altar there would be slain for the amusement of the Divine Benefactor any victim He should choose, even though it should be the greatest and most powerful man alive.

In return he asked only a simple thing, a thing that for God would be absurdly easy — only that matters should be as they were yesterday at this hour and that they should so remain. So very simple! Let but the heavens open, swallowing these men and their aeroplanes — and then close again. Let him have his slaves once more, restored to life and well.

There was no one else with whom he had ever needed to treat or bargain.

He doubted only whether he had made his bribe big enough. God had His price, of course. God was made in man's image, so it had been said: He must have His price. And the price would be rare — no cathedral whose building consumed many years, no pyramid constructed by ten thousand workmen, would be like this cathedral, this pyramid.

He paused here. That was his proposition. Everything would be up to specifications and there was nothing vulgar in his assertion that it would be cheap at the price. He implied that Providence could take it or leave it.

As he approached the end his sentences became broken, became short and uncertain, and his body seemed tense, seemed strained to catch the slightest pressure or whisper of life in the spaces around him. His hair had turned gradually white as he talked, and now he lifted his head high to the heavens like a prophet of old — magnificently mad.

Then, as John stared in giddy fascination, it seemed to him that a curious phenomenon took place somewhere around him. It was as though the sky had darkened for an instant, as though there had been a sudden murmur in a gust of wind, a sound of far-away trumpets, a sighing like the rustle of a great silken robe — for a time the whole of nature round about partook of this darkness: the birds' song ceased; the trees were still, and far over the mountain there was a mutter of dull, menacing thunder.

That was all. The wind died along the tall grasses of the valley. The dawn and the day resumed their place in a time, and the risen sun sent hot waves of yellow mist that made its path bright before it. The leaves laughed in the sun, and their laughter shook the trees until each bough was like a girls' school in fairyland. God had refused to accept the bribe.

For another moment John watched the triumph of the day. Then, turning, he saw a flutter of brown down by the lake, then another flutter, then another, like the dance of golden angels alighting from the clouds. The aeroplanes had come to earth.

John slid off the boulder and ran down the side of the mountain to the clump of trees, where the two girls were awake and waiting for him. Kismine sprang to her feet, the jewels in her pockets jingling, a question on her parted lips, but instinct told John that there was no time for words. They must get off the mountain without losing a moment. He seized a hand of each, and in silence they threaded the tree-trunks, washed with light now and with the rising mist. Behind them from the valley came no sound at all, except the complaint of the peacocks far away and the pleasant undertone of morning.

When they had gone about half a mile, they avoided the park land and entered a narrow path that led over the next rise of ground. At the highest point of this they paused and turned around. Their eyes rested upon the mountainside they had just left — oppressed by some dark sense of tragic impendency.

Clear against the sky a broken, white-haired man was slowly descending the steep slope, followed by two gigantic and emotionless negroes, who carried a burden between them which still flashed and glittered in the sun. Half-way down two other figures joined them — John could see that they were Mrs. Washington and her son, upon whose arm she leaned. The aviators had clambered from their machines to the sweeping lawn in front of the chateau, and with rifles in hand were starting up the diamond mountain in skirmishing formation.

But the little group of five which had formed farther up and was engrossing all the watchers' attention had stopped upon a ledge of rock. The negroes stooped and pulled up what appeared to be a trap-door in the side of the mountain. Into this they all disappeared, the white-haired man first, then his wife and son, finally the two negroes, the glittering tips of whose jeweled head-dresses caught the sun for a moment before the trap-door descended and engulfed them all.

Kismine clutched John's arm.

"Oh," she cried wildly, "where are they going? What are they doing to do?"

"It must be some underground way of escape —"

A little scream from the two girls interrupted his sentence.

"Don't you see?" sobbed Kismine hysterically. "The mountain is wired!"

Even as she spoke John put up his hands to shield his sight. Before their eyes the whole surface of the mountain had changed suddenly to a dazzling burning yellow, which showed up through the jacket of turf as light shows through a human hand. For a moment the intolerable glow continued, and then like an extinguished filament it disappeared, revealing a black waste from which blue smoke arose slowly, carrying off with it what remained of vegetation and of human flesh. Of the aviators there was left neither blood nor bone — they were consumed as completely as the five souls who had gone inside.

Simultaneously, and with an immense concussion, the château literally threw itself into the air, bursting into flaming fragments as it rose, and then tumbling back upon itself in a smoking pile that lay projecting half into the water of the lake. There was no fire — what smoke there was drifted off mingling with the sunshine, and for a few minutes longer a powdery dust of marble drifted from the great featureless pile that had once been the house of jewels. There was no more sound and the three people were alone in the valley.

## XI

At sunset John and his two companions reached the high cliff which had marked the boundaries of the Washingtons' dominion, and looking back found the valley tranquil and lovely in the dusk. They sat down to finish the food which Jasmine had brought with her in a basket.

"There!" she said, as she spread the table-cloth and put the sandwiches in a neat pile upon it. "Don't they look tempting? I always think that food tastes better outdoors."

"With that remark," remarked Kismine, "Jasmine enters the middle class."

"Now," said John eagerly, "turn out your pocket and let's see what jewels you brought along. If you made a good selection we three ought to live comfortably all the rest of our lives."

Obediently Kismine put her hand in her pocket and tossed two handfuls of glittering stones before him.

"Not so bad," cried John, enthusiastically. "They aren't very big, but — Hello!" His expression changed as he held one of them up to the declining sun. "Why, these aren't diamonds! There's something the matter!"

"By golly!" exclaimed Kismine, with a startled look. "What an idiot I am!"

"Why, these are rhinestones!" cried John.

"I know." She broke into a laugh. "I opened the wrong drawer. They belonged on the dress of a girl who visited Jasmine. I got her to give them to me in exchange for diamonds. I'd never seen anything but precious stones before."

"And this is what you brought?"

"I'm afraid so." She fingered the brilliants wistfully. "I think I like these better. I'm a little tired of diamonds."

"Very well," said John gloomily. "We'll have to live in Hades. And you will grow old telling incredulous women that you got the wrong drawer. Unfortunately your father's bank-books were consumed with him."

"Well, what's the matter with Hades?"

"If I come home with a wife at my age my father is just as liable as not to cut me off with a hot coal, as they say down there."

Jasmine spoke up.

"I love washing," she said quietly. "I have always washed my own handkerchiefs. I'll take in laundry and support you both."

"Do they have washwomen in Hades?" asked Kismine innocently.

"Of course," answered John. "It's just like anywhere else."

"I thought — perhaps it was too hot to wear any clothes."

John laughed.

"Just try it!" he suggested. "They'll run you out before you're half started."

"Will father be there?" she asked.

John turned to her in astonishment.

"Your father is dead," he replied somberly. "Why should he go to Hades? You have it confused with another place that was abolished long ago."

After supper they folded up the table-cloth and spread their blankets for the night.

"What a dream it was," Kismine sighed, gazing up at the stars. "How strange it seems to be here with one dress and a penniless fiancé!

"Under the stars," she repeated. "I never noticed the stars before. I always thought of them as great big diamonds that belonged to some one. Now they frighten me. They make me feel that it was all a dream, all my youth."

"It *was* a dream," said John quietly. "Everybody's youth is a dream, a form of chemical madness."

"How pleasant then to be insane!"

"So I'm told," said John gloomily. "I don't know any longer. At any rate, let us love for a while, for a year or so, you and me. That's a form of divine drunkenness that we can all try. There are only diamonds in the whole world, diamonds and perhaps the shabby gift of disillusion. Well, I have that last and I will make the usual nothing of it." He shivered. "Turn up your coat collar, little girl, the night's full of chill

and you'll get pneumonia. His was a great sin who first invented consciousness. Let us lose it for a few hours."

So wrapping himself in his blanket he fell off to sleep.

# Ring Lardner (1885–1933)

RINGGOLD WILMER LARDNER, an appellation he quickly discarded as a free-wheeling newspaperman, was born in Niles, Michigan. He was a popular sports writer and editor on Chicago and New York papers where he acquired his wonderful command of idiomatic American as spoken by the man in the street. Although he was one of the most prolific of short-story writers, his first book was a collection of verse, *Bib Ballads* (1917). His first fiction was *You Know Me Al: A Busher's Letters* (1916), a story of a baseball rookie. Three more books followed but it was not until *How to Write Short Stories* (1924) that he was recognized as an important writer. Altogether he wrote eight volumes of short stories. One of the most important was *The Love Nest* (1926) which included "Haircut" and was dramatized by Robert Sherwood. With George S. Kaufman, he collaborated on a comedy about Tin Pan Alley song writers, *June Moon* (1929). He also wrote one novel, *The Big Town* (1921), and a satirical "autobiography," *Story of a Wonder Man* (1927).

Ring Lardner wrote during the days of that "Noble Experiment," Prohibition, and, like the rest of the journalistic craft, was at home in all the best speakeasies. Thus he became a crony of prizefighters, stock brokers, stenographers, barbers, actors, salesmen, and the rest of the wonderful assortment of characters who people his short stories. Groucho Marx, in a *Playboy* interview, tells how when Lardner wanted to write, he rented a hotel room and pulled all the shades down so no one could see him. It was a significant action. Hiding behind the seeming good humor of light entertainment, just as the author himself hid behind those drawn hotel shades, is a terrific bitterness. Lardner hates his people. He cynically strips them to show them as cruel, vicious, and stupid. "Haircut" is a marvelous example with the genial barber and the other small town people laughing at cruel practical jokes, and the horror of the end. It is not an easy kind of writing to accomplish, this coupling of laughter with the macabre, but Lardner was a master of black humor.

# *Haircut*

I GOT another barber that comes over from Carterville and helps me out Saturdays, but the rest of the time I can get along all right alone. You can see for yourself that this ain't no New York City and besides that, the most of the boys works all day and don't have no leisure to drop in here and get themselves prettied up.

You're a newcomer, ain't you? I thought I hadn't seen you round before. I hope you like it good enough to stay. As I say, we ain't no New York City or Chicago, but we have pretty good times. Not as good, though, since Jim Kendall got killed. When he was alive, him and Hod Meyers used to keep this town in an uproar. I bet they was more laughin' done here than any town its size in America.

Jim was comical, and Hod was pretty near a match for him. Since Jim's gone, Hod tries to hold his end up just the same as ever, but it's tough goin' when you ain't got nobody to kind of work with.

They used to be plenty fun in here Saturdays. This place is jam-packed Saturdays, from four o'clock on. Jim and Hod would show up right after their supper, round six o'clock. Jim would set himself down in that big chair, nearest the blue spittoon. Whoever had been settin' in that chair, why they'd get up when Jim come in and give it to him.

You'd have thought it was a reserved seat like they have sometimes in a theayter. Hod would generally always stand or walk up and down, or some Saturdays, of course, he'd be settin' in this chair part of the time, gettin' a haircut.

Well, Jim would set there a w'ile without openin' his mouth only to spit, and then finally he'd say to me, "Whitey," — my right name, that is, my right first name, is Dick, but everybody round here calls me Whitey — Jim would say, "Whitey, your nose looks like a rosebud to-night. You must of been drinkin' some of your aw de cologne."

So I'd say, "No, Jim, but you look like you'd been drinkin' somethin' of that kind or somethin' worse."

Jim would have to laugh at that, but then he'd speak up and say, "No, I ain't had nothin' to drink, but that ain't sayin' I wouldn't like somethin'. I wouldn't even mind if it was wood alcohol."

Then Hod Meyers would say, "Neither would your wife." That would set everybody to laughin' because Jim and his wife wasn't on very good terms. She'd of divorced him only they wasn't no chance to get alimony and she didn't have no way to take care of herself and the kids. She couldn't never understand Jim. He *was* kind of rough, but a good fella at heart.

Him and Hod had all kinds of sport with Milt Sheppard. I don't suppose you've seen Milt. Well, he's got an Adam's apple that looks more like a mushmelon. So I'd be shavin' Milt and when I start to shave down here on his neck, Hod would holler, "Hey, Whitey. wait a minute! Before you cut into it, let's make up a pool and see who can guess closest to the number of seeds."

And Jim would say, "If Milt hadn't of been so hoggish, he'd of ordered a half a cantaloupe instead of a whole one and it might not of stuck in his throat."

All the boys would roar at this and Milt himself would force a smile, though the joke was on him. Jim certainly was a card!

There's his shavin' mug, settin' on the shelf, right next to Charley Vail's. "Charles M. Vail." That's the druggist. He comes in regular for his shave, three times a week. And Jim's is the cup next to Charley's. "James H. Kendall." Jim won't need no shavin' mug no more, but I'll leave it there just the same for old time's sake. Jim certainly was a character!

Years ago, Jim used to travel for a canned goods concern over in Carterville. They sold canned goods. Jim had the whole northern half of the State and was on the road five days out of every week. He'd drop in here Saturdays and tell his experiences for that week. It was rich.

I guess he paid more attention to playin' jokes than makin' sales. Finally the concern let him out and he come right home here and told everybody he'd been fired instead of sayin' he'd resigned like most fellas would of.

It was a Saturday and the shop was full and Jim got up out of that chair and says, "Gentlemen, I got an important announcement to make. I been fired from my job."

Well, they asked him if he was in earnest and he said he was and nobody could think of nothin' to say till Jim finally broke the ice himself. He says, "I been sellin' canned goods and now I'm canned goods myself."

You see, the concern he'd been workin' for was a factory that made canned goods. Over in Carterville. And now Jim said he was canned himself. He was certainly a card!

Jim had a great trick that he used to play w'ile he was travelin'. For instance, he'd be ridin' on a train and they'd come to some little town like, well, like, we'll say, like Benton. Jim would look out the train window and read the signs on the stores.

For instance, they'd be a sign, "Henry Smith, Dry Goods." Well Jim would write down the name and the name of the town and when he got to wherever he was goin' he'd mail back a postal card to Henry Smith at Benton and not sign no name to it, but he'd write on the card, well, somethin' like "Ask your wife about that book agent that spent the afternoon last week," or "Ask your Missus who kept her from gettin' lonesome the last time you was in Carterville." And he'd sign the card, "A Friend."

Of course, he never knew what really come of none of these jokes, but he could picture what *probably* happened and that was enough.

Jim didn't work very steady after he lost his position with the Carterville people. What he did earn, doin' odd jobs round town, why he spent pretty near all of it on gin and his family might of starved if the stores hadn't of carried them along. Jim's wife tried her hand at dressmakin', but they ain't nobody goin' to get rich makin' dresses in this town.

As I say, she'd of divorced Jim, only she seen that she couldn't support herself and the kids and she was always hopin' that some day Jim would cut out his habits and give her more than two or three dollars a week.

They was a time when she would go to whoever he was workin' for and ask them to give her his wages, but after she done this once or twice, he beat her to it by borrowin' most of his pay in advance. He told it all around town, how he had outfoxed his Missus. He certainly was a caution!

But he wasn't satisfied with just outwittin' her. He was sore the way she acted, tryin' to grab off his pay. And he made up his mind he'd get even. Well, he waited till Evans's Circus was advertised to come to town. Then he told his wife and two kiddies that he was goin' to take them to the circus. The day of the circus, he told them he would get the tickets and meet them outside the entrance to the tent.

Well, he didn't have no intentions of bein' there or buyin' tickets or nothin'. He got full of gin and laid round Wright's poolroom all day. His wife and the kids waited and waited and of course he didn't show up. His wife didn't have a dime with her, or nowhere else, I guess. So she finally had to tell the kids it was all off and they cried like they wasn't never goin' to stop.

Well, it seems, w'ile they was cryin', Doc Stair came along and he asked what was the matter, but Mrs. Kendall was stubborn and wouldn't tell him, but the kids told him and he insisted on takin' them and their mother in the show. Jim found this out afterwards and it was one reason why he had it in for Doc Stair.

Doc Stair come here about a year and a half ago. He's a mighty handsome young fella and his clothes always look like he has them made to order. He goes to Detroit two or three times a year and w'ile he's there he must have a tailor take his measure and then make him a suit to order. They cost pretty near twice as much, but they fit a whole lot better than if you just bought them in a store.

For a w'ile everybody was wonderin' why a young doctor like Doc Stair should come to a town like this where we already got old Doc Gamble and Doc Foote that's both been here for years and all the practice in town was always divided between the two of them.

Then they was a story got round that Doc Stair's gal had throwed him over, a gal up in the Northern Peninsula somewheres, and the reason he come here was to hide himself away and forget it. He said himself that he thought they wasn't nothin' like general practice in a place like ours to fit a man to be a good all round doctor. And that's why he'd came.

Anyways, it wasn't long before he was makin' enough to live on, though they tell me that he never dunned nobody for what they owed him, and the folks here certainly has got the owin' habit, even in my business. If I had all that was comin' to me for just shaves alone, I could go Carterville and put up at the Mercer for a week and see a different picture every night. For instance, they's old George Purdy — but I guess I shouldn't ought to be gossipin'.

Well, last year, our coroner died, died of the flu. Ken Beatty, that was his name. He was the coroner. So they had to choose another man to be coroner in his place and they picked Doc Stair. He laughed at first and said he didn't want it, but they made him take it. It ain't no job that anybody would fight for and what a man makes out of it in a year would just about buy seeds for their garden. Doc's the kind, though, that can't say no to nothin' if you keep at him long enough.

But I was goin' to tell you about a poor boy we got here in town — Paul Dickson. He fell out of a tree when he was about ten years old. Lit on his head and it done somethin' to him and he ain't never been right. No harm in him, but just silly. Jim Kendall used to call him cuckoo; that's a name Jim had for anybody that was off their head, only he called people's head their bean. That was another of his gags, callin' head bean and callin' crazy people cuckoo. Only poor Paul ain't crazy, but just silly.

You can imagine that Jim used to have all kinds of fun with Paul. He'd send him to the White Front Garage for a left-handed monkey wrench. Of course they ain't no such a thing as a left-handed monkey wrench.

And once we had a kind of a fair here and they was a baseball game between the fats and the leans and before the game started Jim called Paul over and sent him way down to Schrader's hardware store to get a key for the pitcher's box.

They wasn't nothin' in the way of gags that Jim couldn't think up, when he put his mind to it.

Poor Paul was always kind of suspicious of people, maybe on account of how Jim had kept foolin' him. Paul wouldn't have much to do with anybody only his own mother and Doc Stair and a girl here in town named Julie Gregg. That is, she ain't a girl no more, but pretty near thirty or over.

When Doc first came to town, Paul seemed to feel like here was a real friend and he hung round Doc's office most of the w'ile; the only time he wasn't there was when he'd go home to eat or sleep or when he seen Julie Gregg doin' her shoppin'.

When he looked out Doc's window and seen her, he'd run downstairs and join her and tag along with her to the different stores. The poor boy was crazy about Julie and she always treated him mighty nice and made him feel like he was welcome, though of course it wasn't nothin' but pity on her side.

Doc done all he could to improve Paul's mind and he told me once that he really thought the boy was gettin' better, that they was times when he was as bright and sensible as anybody else.

But I was goin' to tell you about Julie Gregg. Old Man Gregg was in the lumber business, but got to drinkin' and lost the most of his money and when he died, he didn't leave nothin' but the house and just enough insurance for the girl to skimp along on.

Her mother was a kind of a half invalid and didn't hardly ever leave the house. Julie wanted to sell the place and move somewheres else after the old man died, but the mother said she was born here and would die here. It was tough on Julie, as the young people round this town — well, she's too good for them.

She's been away to school and Chicago and New York and different places and they ain't no subject she can't talk on, where you take the rest of the young folks here and you mention anything to them outside of Gloria Swanson or Tommy Meighan and they think you're delirious. Did you see Gloria in *Wages of Virtue?* You missed somethin'!

Well, Doc Stair hadn't been here more than a week when he come in one day to get shaved and I recognized who he was as he had been pointed out to me, so I told him about my old lady. She's been ailin' for a couple years and either Doc Gamble or Doc Foote, neither one, seemed to be helpin' her. So he said he would come out and see her, but if she was able to get out herself, it would be better to bring her to his office where he could make a completer examination.

So I took her to his office and w'ile I was waitin' for her in the reception room, in come Julie Gregg. When somebody comes in Doc Stair's office, they's a bell that rings in his inside office so as he can tell they's somebody to see him.

So he left my old lady inside and come out to the front office and that's the first time him and Julie met and I guess it was what they call love at first sight. But it wasn't fifty-fifty. This young fella was the slickest lookin' fella she'd ever seen in this town and she went wild over him. To him she was just a young lady that wanted to see the doctor.

She'd came on about the same business I had. Her mother had been doctorin' for years with Doc Gamble and Doc Foote and without no results. So she'd heard they was a new doc in town and decided to give him a try. He promised to call and see her mother that same day.

I said a minute ago that it was love at first sight on her part. I'm not only judgin' by how she acted afterwards but how she looked at him that first day in his office. I ain't no mind reader, but it was wrote all over her face that she was gone.

Now Jim Kendall, besides bein' a jokesmith and a pretty good drinker, well, Jim was quite a lady-killer. I guess he run pretty wild durin' the time he was on the road for them Carterville people, and besides that, he'd had a couple little affairs of the heart right here in town. As I say, his wife could of divorced him only she couldn't.

But Jim was like the majority of men, and women, too, I guess. He wanted what he couldn't get. He wanted Julie Gregg and worked his head off tryin' to land her. Only he'd of said bean instead of head.

Well, Jim's habits and his jokes didn't appeal to Julie and of course he was a married man, so he didn't have no more chance than, well, than a rabbit. That's an expression of Jim's himself. When somebody didn't have no chance to get elected or somethin', Jim would always say they didn't have no more chance than a rabbit.

He didn't make no bones about how he felt. Right in here, more than once, in front of the whole crowd, he said he was stuck on Julie and anybody that could get her for him was welcome to his house and his wife and kids included. But she wouldn't have nothin' to do with him; wouldn't even speak to him on the street. He finally seen he wasn't gettin' nowheres with his usual line so he decided to try the rough stuff. He went right up to her house one evenin' and when she opened the door he forced his way in and grabbed her. But she broke loose and before he could stop her, she run in the next room and locked the door and phoned to Joe Barnes. Joe's the marshal. Jim could hear who she was phonin' to and he beat it before Joe got there.

Joe was an old friend of Julie's pa. Joe went to Jim the next day and told him what would happen if he ever done it again.

I don't know how the news of this little affair leaked out. Chances is that Joe Barnes told his wife and she told somebody else's wife and they told their husband. Anyways, it did leak out and Hod Meyers had the nerve to kid Jim about it, right here in this shop. Jim didn't deny nothin' and kind of laughed it off and said for us all to wait; that lots of people had tried to make a monkey out of him, but he always got even.

Meanw'ile everybody in town was wise to Julie's bein' wild mad over the Doc. I don't suppose she had any idear how her face changed when him and her was together; of course she couldn't of, or she'd of kept away from him. And she didn't know that we was all noticin' how many times she made excuses to go up to his office or pass it on the other side of the street and look up in his window to see if he was there. I felt sorry for her and so did most other people.

Hod Meyers kept rubbin' it into Jim about how the Doc had cut him out. Jim didn't pay no attention to the kiddin' and you could see he was plannin' one of his jokes.

One trick Jim had was the knack of changin' his voice. He could make you think he was a girl talkin' and he could mimic any man's voice. To show you how good he was along this line, I'll tell you the joke he played on me once.

You know, in most towns of any size, when a man is dead and needs a shave, why the barber that shaves him soaks him five dollars for the job; that is, he don't soak *him*, but whoever ordered the shave. I just charge three dollars because personally I don't mind much shavin' a dead person. They lay a whole lot stiller than live customers. The only thing is that you don't feel like talkin' to them and you get kind of lonesome.

Well, about the coldest day we ever had here, two years ago last winter, the phone rung at the house w'ile I was home to dinner and I answered the phone and it was a woman's voice and she said she was Mrs. John Scott and her husband was dead and would I come out and shave him.

Old John had always been a good customer of mine. But they live seven miles out in the country, on the Streeter road. Still I didn't see how I could say no.

So I said I would be there, but would have to come in a jitney and it might cost three or four dollars besides the price of the shave. So she, or the voice, it said that was all right, so I got Frank Abbott to drive me out to the place and when I got there, who should open the door but old John himself! He wasn't no more dead than, well, than a rabbit.

It didn't take no private detective to figure out who had played me this little joke. Nobody could of thought it up but Jim Kendall. He certainly was a card!

I tell you this incident just to show you how he could disguise his voice and make you believe it was somebody else talkin'. I'd of swore it was Mrs. Scott had called me. Anyways, some woman.

Well, Jim waited till he had Doc Stair's voice down pat; then he went after revenge.

He called Julie up on a night when he knew Doc was over in Carterville. She never questioned but what it was Doc's voice. Jim said he must see her that night; he couldn't wait no longer to tell her somethin'. She was all excited and told him to come to the house. But he said he was expectin' an important long distance call and wouldn't she please forget her manners for once and come to his office. He said they couldn't nothin' hurt her and nobody would see her and he just *must* talk to her a little w'ile. Well, poor Julie fell for it.

Doc always keeps a night light in his office, so it looked to Julie like they was somebody there.

Meanw'ile Jim Kendall had went to Wright's poolroom, where they was a whole gang amusin' themselves. The most of them had drank plenty of gin, and they was a rough bunch even when sober. They was always strong for Jim's jokes and when he told them to come with him and see some fun they give up their card games and pool games and followed along.

Doc's office is on the second floor. Right outside his door they's a flight of stairs leadin' to the floor above. Jim and his gang hid in the dark behind these stairs.

Well, Julie come up to Doc's door and rung the bell and they was nothin' doin'. She rung it again and she rung it seven or eight times. Then she tried the door and found it locked. Then Jim made some kind of noise and she heard it and waited a minute, and then she says, "Is that you, Ralph?" Ralph is Doc's first name.

They was no answer and it must of come to her all of a sudden that she'd been bunked. She pretty near fell downstairs and the whole gang after her. They chased her all the way home, hollerin', "Is that you, Ralph?" and "Oh, Ralphie, dear, is that you?" Jim says he couldn't holler it himself, as he was laughin' too hard.

Poor Julie! She didn't show up here on Main Street for a long, long time afterward.

And of course Jim and his gang told everybody in town, everybody but Doc Stair. They was scared to tell him, and he might of never knowed only for Paul Dickson. The poor cuckoo, as Jim called him, he was here in the shop one night while Jim was still gloatin' yet over what he'd done to Julie. And Paul took in as much of it as he could understand and he run to Doc with the story.

It's a cinch Doc went up in the air and swore he'd make Jim suffer. But it was a kind of a delicate thing, because if it got out that he had beat Jim up, Julie was bound to hear of it and then she'd know that Doc knew and of course knowin' that he knew would make it worse for her than ever. He was goin' to do somethin', but it took a lot of figurin'.

Well, it was a couple days later when Jim was here in the shop again, and so was the cuckoo. Jim was goin' duck-shootin' the next day and had came in lookin' for Hod Meyers to go with him. I happened to know that Hod had went over to Carterville and wouldn't be home till the end of the week. So Jim said he hated to go alone and he guessed he would call if off. Then poor Paul spoke up and said if Jim would take him he would go along. Jim thought a w'ile and then he said, well, he guessed a half-wit was better than nothin'.

I suppose he was plottin' to get Paul out in the boat and play some joke on him, like pushin' him in the water. Anyways, he said Paul could go. He asked him had he ever shot a duck and Paul said no, he'd never even had a gun in his hands. So Jim said he could set in the boat and watch him and if he behaved himself, he might lend him his gun for a couple of shots. They made a date to meet in the mornin' and that's the last I seen of Jim alive.

Next mornin', I hadn't been open more than ten minutes when Doc Stair came in. He looked kind of nervous. He asked me had I seen Paul Dickson. I said no, but I knew where he was, out duck-shootin' with Jim Kendall. So Doc says that's what he had heard, and he couldn't understand it because Paul had told him he wouldn't never have no more to do with Jim as long as he lived.

He said Paul had asked him what he thought of the joke and the Doc had told him that anybody that would do a thing like that ought not to be let live.

I said it had been a kind of a raw thing, but Jim just couldn't resist no kind of joke, no matter how raw. I said I thought he was all right at heart, but just bubblin' over with mischief. Doc turned and walked out.

At noon he got a phone call from old John Scott. The lake where Jim and Paul had went shootin' is on John's place. Paul had came runnin' up to the house a few minutes before and said they'd been an accident. Jim had shot a few ducks and then give the gun to Paul and told him to try his luck. Paul hadn't never handled a gun and he was nervous. He was shakin' so hard that he couldn't control the gun. He let fire and Jim sunk back in the boat, dead.

Doc Stair, bein' the coroner, jumped in Frank Abbott's flivver and rushed out to Scott's farm. Paul and old John was down on the shore of the lake. Paul had rowed the boat to shore, but they'd left the body in it, waitin' for Doc to come.

Doc examined the body and said they might as well fetch it back to town. They was no use leavin' it there or callin' a jury, as it was a plain case of accidental shootin'.

Personally I wouldn't never leave a person shoot a gun in the same boat I was in unless I was sure they knew somethin' about guns. Jim was a sucker to leave a new beginner have his gun, let alone a half-wit. It probably served Jim right, what he got. But still we miss him around here. He certainly was a card!

Comb it wet or dry?

# Willa Cather (1876–1947)

DEFINITELY a major American writer, Willa Cather was born in Winchester, Virginia, but grew up in Nebraska among immigrant farmer settlers who provided her with rich literary material. After graduation from the University of Nebraska she taught high school and published her first book, *April Twilights* (1903), a collection of poems. In 1905 came her first published prose, *The Troll Garden*, a collection of short stories. For the next six years she was an editor of *McClure's Magazine* in New York. Her first novel was *Alexander's Bridge* (1912) but it was with *O Pioneers!* (1913), a novel about Swedish immigrants, that she was established once and for all as an important writer. Outstanding among her other novels are *The Song of the Lark, My Antonia, The Professor's House, Death Comes for the Archbishop, Shadows on the Rock, Lucy Gayheart, Sapphira and the Slave Girl,* and *A Lost Lady.* One of her books, *Youth and the Bright Medusa* (1920), was a volume of short stories about artists, who had always fascinated her as characters.

The short stories of Sarah Orne Jewett inspired her to become a writer, Willa Cather said. Both women were primarily regional writers but whereas Jewett stayed close to her native New England, Cather in her life went venturing far from her Nebraska prairies to the Southwest and Canada for her later fiction. Both women grew up among simple and not rich farm people and the Jewett stories were laid in the years of Cather's youth. "Double Birthday" exhibits the author's power in depicting the foreigner in America and that most difficult of all characters to write about, the artist. Also difficult to achieve in a short story is a changing point of view, which the author does here in a masterly way.

# *Double Birthday*

EVEN in American cities, which seem so much alike, where people seem all to be living the same lives, striving for the same things, thinking the same thoughts, there are still individuals a little out of tune with the times — there are still survivals of a past more loosely woven, there are disconcerting beginnings of a future yet unforeseen.

Coming out of the grey stone Court House in Pittsburgh on a dark November afternoon, Judge Hammersley encountered one of these men whom one does not readily place, whom one is, indeed, a little embarrassed to meet, because they have not got on as they should. The Judge saw him mounting the steps outside, leaning against the wind, holding his soft felt hat on with his hand, his head thrust forward — hurrying with a light, quick step, and so intent upon his own purposes that the Judge could have gone out by a side door and avoided the meeting. But that was against his principles.

"Good day, Albert," he muttered, seeming to feel, himself, all the embarrassment of the encounter, for the other snatched off his hat with a smile of very evident pleasure, and something like pride. His gesture bared an attractive head — small, well-set, definite and smooth — one of those heads that look as if they had been turned out of some hard, rich wood by a workman deft with the lathe. His smooth-shaven face was dark — a warm coffee colour — and his hazel eyes were warm and lively. He was not young, but his features had a kind of quicksilver mobility. His manner toward the stiff, frowning Judge was respectful and admiring — not in the least self-conscious.

The Judge inquired after his health and that of his uncle.

"Uncle Albert is splendidly preserved for his age. Frail, and can't stand any strain, but perfectly all right if he keeps to his routine. He's going to have a birthday soon. He will be eighty on the first day of December, and I shall be fifty-five on the same day. I was named after him because I was born on his twenty-fifth birthday."

"Umph." The Judge glanced from left to right as if this announcement were in bad taste, but he put a good face on it and said with a kind of testy heartiness, "That will be an — occasion. I'd like to remember it in some way. Is there anything your uncle would like, any — recognition?" He stammered and coughed.

Young Albert Engelhardt, as he was called, laughed apologetically, but with confidence. "I think there is, Judge Hammersley. Indeed, I'd thought of coming to you to ask a favour. I am going to have a little supper for him, and you know he likes good wine. In these dirty bootlegging times, it's hard to get."

"Certainly, certainly." The Judge spoke up quickly, and for the first time looked Albert squarely in the eye. "Don't give him any of that bootleg stuff. I can find something in my cellar. Come out tomorrow night after eight, with a gripsack of some sort. Very glad to help you out, Albert. Glad the old fellow holds up so well. Thank'ee, Albert," as Engelhardt swung the heavy door open and held it for him to pass.

Judge Hammersley's car was waiting for him, and on the ride home to Squirrel Hill he thought with vexation about the Engelhardts. He really was a sympathetic man, and though so stern of manner, he had deep affections; was fiercely loyal to old friends, old families, and old ideals. He didn't think highly of what is called success in the world to-day, but such as it was he wanted his friends to have it, and was vexed with them when they missed it. He was vexed with Albert for unblushingly, almost proudly, declaring that he was fifty-five years old, when he had nothing whatever to show for it. He was the last of the Engelhardt boys, and they had none of them had anything to show. They all died much worse off in the world than they began. They began with a flourishing glass factory up the river, a comfortable fortune, a fine old house on the park in Allegheny, a good standing in the community; and it was all gone, melted away.

Old August Engelhardt was a thrifty, energetic man, though pig-headed — Judge Hammersley's friend and one of his first clients. August's five sons had sold the factory and wasted the money in fantastic individual enterprises, lost the big house, and now they were all dead except Albert. They ought all to be alive, with estates and factories and families. To be sure, they had that queer German streak in them; but so had old August, and it hadn't prevented his amounting to something. Their bringing-up was wrong; August had too free a hand, he was too proud of his five handsome boys, and too conceited. Too much tennis, Rhine wine punch, music, and silliness. They were always running over to New York, like this Albert. Somebody, when asked what in the world young Albert had ever done with his inheritance, had laughingly replied that he had spent it on the Pennsylvania Railroad.

Judge Hammersley didn't see how Albert could hold his head up. He had some small job in the County Clerk's office, was dependent upon it, had nothing else but the poor little house on the South Side where he lived with his old uncle. The county took care of him for the sake of his father, who had been a gallant officer in the Civil War, and afterwards a public-spirited citizen and a generous employer of labour. But, as Judge Hammersley had bitterly remarked to Judge Merriman when Albert's name happened to come up: "If it weren't for his father's old friends seeing that he got something, that fellow wouldn't be able to make a living." Next to a charge of dishonesty, this was the worst that could be said of any man.

Judge Hammersley's house out on Squirrel Hill sat under a grove of very old oak trees. He lived alone, with his daughter, Marjorie Par-menter, who was a widow. She had a great many engagements, but she usually managed to dine at home with her father, and that was about as much society as he cared for. His house was comfortable in an old-fashioned way, well appointed — especially the library, the room in which he lived when he was not in bed or at the Court House. To-night, when he came down to dinner, Mrs. Parmenter was already at the table, dressed for an evening party. She was tall, handsome, with a fine, easy carriage, and her face was both hard and sympathetic, like her father's. She had not, however, his stiffness of manner, that contraction of the muscles which was his unconscious protest at any irregularity in the machinery of life. She accepted blunders and accidents smoothly if not indifferently.

As the old coloured man pulled back the Judge's chair for him, he glanced at his daughter from under his eyebrows.

"I saw that son of old Gus Engelhardt's this afternoon," he said in an angry, challenging tone.

As a young girl his daughter had used to take up the challenge and hotly defend the person who had displeased or disappointed her father. But as she grew older she was conscious of that same feeling in herself when people fell short of what she expected; and she understood now that when her father spoke as if he were savagely attacking someone, it merely meant that he was disappointed or sorry for them; he never spoke thus of persons for whom he had no feeling. So she said calmly:

"Oh, did you really? I haven't seen him for years, not since the war. How was he looking? Shabby?"

"Not so shabby as he ought to. That fellow's likely to be in want one of these days."

"I'm afraid so," Mrs. Parmenter sighed. "But I believe he would be rather plucky about it."

The Judge shrugged. "He's coming out here to-morrow night, on some business for his uncle."

"Then I'll have a chance to see for myself. He must look much older. I can't imagine his ever looking really old and settled, though."

"See that you don't ask him to stay. I don't want the fellow hanging around. He'll transact his business and get it over. He had the face to admit to me that he'll be fifty-five years old on the first of December. He's giving some sort of birthday party for old Albert, a-hem." The Judge coughed formally, but was unable to check a smile; his lips sarcastic, but his eyes full of sly humour.

"Can he be as old as that? Yes, I suppose so. When we were both at Mrs. Sterrett's in Rome, I was fifteen, and he must have been about thirty."

Her father coughed. "He'd better have been in Homestead!"

Mrs. Parmenter looked up; that was rather commonplace, for her father. "Oh, I don't know. Albert would never have been much use in Homestead, and he was very useful to Mrs. Sterrett in Rome."

"What did she want the fellow hanging around for? All the men of her family amounted to something."

"To too much! There must be some butterflies if one is going to give house parties, and the Sterretts and Dents were all heavyweights. He was in Rome a long while; three years, I think. He had a gorgeous time. Anyway, he learned to speak Italian very well, and that helps him out now, doesn't it? You still send for him at the Court House when you need an interpreter?"

"That's not often. He picks up a few dollars. Nice business for his father's son."

After dinner the Judge retired to his library, where the gas-fire was lit, and his book at hand, with a paper-knife inserted to mark the place where he had left off reading last night at exactly ten-thirty. On his way he went to the front door, opened it, turned on the porch light, and looked at the thermometer, making an entry in a little note-book. In a few moments his daughter, in an evening cloak, stopped at the library door to wish him good night and went down the hall. He listened for the closing of the front door; it was a reassuring sound to him. He liked the feeling of an orderly house, empty for himself and his books all evening. He was deeply read in divinity, philosophy, and in the early history of North America.

## II

While Judge Hammersley was settling down to his book, Albert Engelhardt was sitting at home in a garnet velvet smoking-jacket, at an upright piano, playing Schumann's *Kreisleriana* for his old uncle. They lived, certainly, in a queer part of the city, on one of the dingy streets that run uphill off noisy Carson Street, in a little two-story brick house, a working man's house, that Albert's father had taken over long ago in satisfaction of a bad debt. When his father had acquired this building, it was a mere nothing — the Engelhardts were then living in their big, many-gabled, so-German house on the Park, in Allegheny; and they owned many other buildings, besides the glass factory up the river. After the father's death, when the sons converted houses and lands into cash, this forgotten little house on the South Side had somehow never been sold or mortgaged. A day came when Albert, the last surviving son, found this piece of property the only thing he owned in the world besides his personal effects. His uncle, having had a crushing disappointment, wanted at that time to retire from the practice of medicine, so Albert settled in the South Side house and took his uncle with him.

He had not gone there in any mood of despair. His impoverishment had come about gradually, and before he took possession of these quarters he had been living in a boarding house; the change seemed going up instead of going down in the world. He was delighted to have a home again, to unpack his own furniture and his books and pictures — the most valuable in the world to him, because they were full of his own history and that of his family, were like part of his own personality. All the years and the youth which had slipped away from him still clung to these things.

At his piano, under his Degas drawing in black and red — three ballet girls at the bar — or seated at his beautiful inlaid writing table, he was still the elegant young man who sat there long ago. His rugs were fine ones, his collection of books was large and very personal. It was full of works which, though so recent, were already immensely far away and diminished. The glad, rebellious excitement they had once caused in the world he could recapture only in memory. Their power to seduce and stimulate the young, the living, was utterly gone. There was a complete file of the *Yellow Book*, for instance; who could extract sweet poison from these volumes now? A portfolio of the drawings of Aubrey Beardsley — decadent, had they been called? A slender, padded volume — the complete works of a great new poet, Ernest Dowson. Oscar Wilde, whose wickedness was now so outdone that he looked like the poor old hat of some Victorian belle, wired and feathered and garlanded and faded.

Albert and his uncle occupied only the upper floor of their house. The ground floor was let to an old German glass engraver who had once been a workman in August Engelhardt's factory. His wife was a good cook, and every night sent their dinner up hot on the dumb waiter. The house opened directly upon the street and to reach Albert's apartment one went down a narrow paved alley at the side of the building and mounted an outside flight of wooden stairs at the back. They had only four rooms — two bedrooms, a snug sitting-room in which they dined, and a small kitchen where Albert got breakfast every morning. After he had gone to work, Mrs. Rudder came up from downstairs to wash the dishes and do the cleaning, and to cheer up old Doctor Engelhardt.

At dinner this evening Albert had told his uncle about meeting Judge Hammersley, and of his particular inquiries after his health. The old man was very proud and received this intelligence as his due, but could not conceal a certain gratification.

"The daughter, she still lives with him? A damned fine-looking woman!" he muttered between his teeth. Uncle Albert, a bachelor, had been a professed connoisseur of ladies in his day.

Immediately after dinner, unless he were going somewhere, Albert always played for his uncle for an hour. He played extremely well. Doctor Albert sat by the fire smoking his cigar. While he listened, the look of wisdom and professional authority faded, and many changes went over his face, as if he were playing a little drama to himself; moods of scorn and contempt, of rakish vanity, sentimental melancholy . . . and something remote and lonely. The Doctor had always flattered himself that he resembled a satyr, because the tops of his ears were slightly pointed; and he used to hint to his nephews that his large pendulous nose was the index of an excessively amorous disposition. His mouth was full of long, yellowish teeth, all crowded irregularly, which he snapped and ground together when he uttered denunciations of modern art or the Eighteenth Amendment. He wore his moustache short and twisted up at the corners. His thick grey hair was cut close and upright, in the bristling French fashion. His hands were small and fastidious, high-knuckled, quite elegant in shape.

Across the Doctor's throat ran a long, jagged scar. He used to mutter to his young nephews that it had been justly inflicted by an out-raged husband — a pistol shot in the dark. But his brother August always said that he had been cut by glass, when, wandering about in the garden one night after drinking too much punch, he had fallen into the cold-frames.

After playing Schumann for some time, Albert, without stopping, went into Stravinsky.

Doctor Engelhardt by the gas-fire stirred uneasily, turned his impor-tant head towards his nephew, and snapped his teeth. "Br-r-r, that stuff! Poverty of imagination, poverty of musical invention; *fin-de-siècle*!"

Albert laughed. "I thought you were asleep. Why will you use that phrase? It shows your vintage. Like this any better?" He began the second act of *Pelleas et Melisande*.

The Doctor nodded. "Yes, that is better, though I'm not fooled by it." He wrinkled his nose as if he were smelling out something, and squinted with superior discernment. "To this *canaille* that is all very new; but to me it goes back to Bach."

"Yes, if you like."

Albert, like Judge Hammersley, was jealous of his solitude — liked a few hours with his books. It was time for Uncle Doctor to be turning in. He ended the music by playing half a dozen old German songs which the old fellow always wanted but never asked for. The Doctor's chin sank into his shirt front. His face took on a look of deep, resigned sad-ness; his features, losing their conscious importance, seemed to shrink a good deal. His nephew knew that this was the mood in which he would most patiently turn to rest and darkness. Doctor Engelhardt had had a heavy loss late in life. Indeed, he had suffered the same loss twice.

As Albert left the piano, the Doctor rose and walked a little stiffly across the room. At the door of his chamber he paused, brought his hand up in a kind of military salute and gravely bowed, so low that one saw only the square upstanding grey brush on the top of his head and the long pear-shaped nose. After this he closed the door behind him. Albert sat down to his book. Very soon he heard the bath water running. Having taken his bath, the Doctor would get into bed immediately to avoid catching cold. Luckily, he usually slept well. Perhaps he dreamed of that unfortunate young singer whom he sometimes called, to his nephew and himself, "the lost Lenore."

## III

Long years ago, when the Engelhardt boys were still living in the old house in Allegheny with their mother, after their father's death, Doctor Engelhardt was practising medicine, and had an office on the Park, five minutes' walk from his sister-in-law. He usually lunched with the family, after his morning office hours were over. They always had a good cook, and the Allegheny market was one of the best in the world. Mrs. Engelhardt went to market every morning of her life; such vegetables and poultry, such cheeses and sausages and smoked and pickled fish as one could buy there! Soon after she had made her rounds, boys in white aprons would come running across the Park with her purchases. Everyone knew the Engelhardt house, built of many-coloured bricks, with gables and turrets and, on the west, a large stained-glass window representing a scene on the Grand Canal in Venice, the Church of Santa Maria della Salute in the background, in the foreground a gondola with a slender gondolier. People said August and Mrs. Engelhardt should be solidly seated in the prow to make the picture complete.

Doctor Engelhardt's especial interest was the throat, preferably the singing throat. He had studied every scrap of manuscript that Manuel Garcia had left behind him, every reported conversation with him. He had doctored many singers, and imagined he had saved many voices. Pittsburgh air is not good for the throat, and travelling artists often had need of medical assistance. Conductors of orchestras and singing societies recommended Doctor Engelhardt because he was very lax about collecting fees from professionals, especially if they sent him a photograph floridly inscribed. He had been a medical student in New York while Patti was still singing; his biography fell into chapters of great voices as a turfman's falls into chapters of fast horses. This passion for the voice had given him the feeling of distinction, of being unique in his profession, which had made him all his life a well-satisfied and happy man, and had left him a poor one.

One morning when the Doctor was taking his customary walk about the Park before office hours, he stopped in front of the Allegheny High School building because he heard singing — a chorus of young voices. It was June, and the chapel windows were open. The Doctor listened for a few moments, then tilted his head on one side and laid his forefinger on his pear-shaped nose with an anxious, inquiring squint. Among the voices he certainly heard one Voice. The final bang of the piano was followed by laughter and buzzing. A boy ran down the steps. The Doctor stopped him and learned that this was a rehearsal for Class Day exercises. Just then the piano began again, and in a moment he heard the same voice alone:

"Still wie die Nacht, tief wie das Meer."

No, he was not mistaken; a full, rich, soprano voice, so easy, so sure; a golden warmth, even in the high notes. Before the second verse was over he went softly into the building, into the chapel, and for the first time laid eyes on Marguerite Thiesinger. He saw a sturdy, blooming German girl standing beside the piano; good-natured one knew at a glance, glowing with health. She looked like a big peony just burst into bloom and full of sunshine — sunshine in her auburn hair, in her rather small hazel eyes. When she finished the song, she began waltzing on the platform with one of the boys.

Doctor Albert waited by the door, and accosted her as she came out carrying her coat and schoolbooks. He introduced himself and asked her if she would go over to Mrs. Engelhardt's for lunch and sing for him.

Oh, yes! she knew one of the Engelhardt boys, and she'd always wanted to see that beautiful window from the inside.

She went over at noon and sang for them before lunch, and the family took stock of her. She spoke a very ordinary German, and her English was still worse; her people were very ordinary. Her flat, slangy speech was somehow not vulgar because it was so naive — she knew no other way. The boys were delighted with her because she was jolly and interested in everything. She told them about the glorious good times she had going to dances in suburban Turner halls, and to picnics in the damp, smoke-smeared woods up the Allegheny. The boys roared with laughter at the unpromising places she mentioned. But she had the warm bubble in her blood that makes everything fair; even being a junior in the Allegheny High School was "glorious," she told them!

She came to lunch with them again and again, because she liked the boys, and she thought the house magnificent. The Doctor observed her narrowly all the while. Clearly she had no ambition, no purpose; she sang to be agreeable. She was not very intelligent, but she had a kind of personal warmth that, to his way of thinking, was much better than brains. He took her over to his office and poked and pounded her. When he had finished his examination, he stood before the foolish, happy young thing and inclined his head in his peculiar fashion.

"Miss Thiesinger, I have the honour to announce to you that you are on the threshold of a brilliant, possibly a great career."

She laughed her fresh, ringing laugh. "Aren't you nice, though, to take so much trouble about me!"

The Doctor lifted a forefinger. "But for that you must turn your back on this childishness, these snivelling sapheads you play marbles with. You must uproot this triviality." He made a gesture as if he were wringing a chicken's neck, and Marguerite was thankful she was able to keep back a giggle.

Doctor Engelhardt wanted her to go to New York with him at once, and begin her studies. He was quite ready to finance her. He had made up his mind to stake everything upon this voice.

But not at all. She thought it was lovely of him, but she was very fond of her classmates, and she wanted to graduate with her class next year. Moreover, she had just been given a choir position in one of the biggest churches in Pittsburgh, though she was still a schoolgirl; she was going to have money and pretty clothes for the first time in her life and wouldn't miss it all for anything.

All through the next school year Doctor Albert went regularly to the church where she sang, watched and cherished her, expostulated and lectured, trying to awaken fierce ambition in his big peony flower. She was very much interested in other things just then, but she was patient with him; accepted his devotion with good nature, respected his wisdom, and bore with his "stagey" manners as she called them. She graduated in June, and immediately after Commencement, when she was not quite nineteen, she eloped with an insurance agent and went to Chicago to live. She wrote Doctor Albert: "I do appreciate all your kindness to me, but I guess I will let my voice rest for the present."

He took it hard. He burned her photographs and the foolish little scrawls she had written to thank him for presents. His life would have been dull and empty if he hadn't had so many reproaches to heap upon her in his solitude. How often and how bitterly he arraigned her for betrayal of so beautiful a gift. Where did she keep it hidden now, that jewel, in the sordid life she had chosen?

Three years after her elopement, suddenly, without warning, Marguerite Thiesinger walked into his office on Arch Street one morning and told him she had come back to study! Her husband's "affairs were involved"; he was now quite willing that she should make as much as possible of her voice — and out of it.

"My voice is better than it was," she said, looking at him out of her rather small eyes — greenish-yellow, with a glint of gold in them. He believed her. He suddenly realized how uncommonly truthful she had always been. Rather stupid, unimaginative, but carried joyously along on a flood of warm vitality, and truthful to a degree he had hardly known in any woman or in any man. And now she was a woman.

He took her over to his sister-in-law's. Albert, who chanced to be at home, was sent to the piano. She was not mistaken. The Doctor kept averting his head to conceal his delight, to conceal, once or twice, a tear — the moisture that excitement and pleasure brought to his eyes.

The voice, after all, he told himself, is a physical thing. She had been growing and ripening like fruit in the sun, and the voice with the body. Doctor Engelhardt stepped softly out of the music-room into the conservatory and addressed a potted palm, his lips curling back from his teeth: "So we get that out of you, *Monsieur le commis-voyageur,* and now we throw you away like a squeezed lemon."

When he returned to his singer, she addressed him very earnestly from under her spring hat covered with lilacs: "Before my marriage, Doctor Englehardt, you offered to take me to New York to a teacher, and lend me money to start on. If you still feel like doing it, I'm sure I could repay you before very long. I'll follow your instructions. What was it you used to tell me I must have — application and ambition?"

He glared at her: "Take note, Gretchen, that I change the prescription. There is something vulgar about ambition. Now we will play for higher stakes; for *ambition* read *aspiration!*" His index finger shot upward.

In New York he had no trouble in awakening the interest of his friends and acquaintances. Within a week he had got his protégée to a very fine artist, just then retiring from the Opera, a woman who had been a pupil of Pauline Garcia Viardot. In short, Doctor Engelhardt had realized the dream of a lifetime; he had discovered a glorious voice, backed by a rich vitality. Within a year Marguerite had one of the best church positions in New York; she insisted upon repaying her benefactor before she went abroad to complete her studies. Doctor Engelhardt went often to New York to counsel and advise, to gloat over his treasure. He often shivered as he crossed the Jersey ferry, he was afraid of Fate. He would tell over her assets on his fingers to reassure himself. You might have seen a small, self-important man of about fifty, standing by the rail of the ferry boat, his head impressively inclined as if he were addressing an amphitheatre full of students, gravely counting upon his fingers.

But Fate struck, and from the quarter least under suspicion — through that blooming, rounded, generously moulded young body, from the abundant, glowing health which the Doctor proudly called peasant vigour. Marguerite's success had brought to his office many mothers of singing daughters. He was not insensible to the compliment, but he usually dismissed them by dusting his fingers delicately in the air and growling: "Yes, she can sing a little, she has a voice; *aber kleine, kleine!*" He exulted in the opulence of his cabbage rose. To his nephews he used to match her possibilities with the singers of that period. Emma Eames he called *die Puritan,* Geraldine Farrar *la voix blanche,* another was *trop raffinée.*

Marguerite had been in New York two years, her path one of uninterrupted progress, when she wrote the Doctor about a swelling of some sort; the surgeons wanted to operate. Doctor Albert took the next train for New York. An operation revealed that things were very bad indeed; a malignant growth, so far advanced that the knife could not check it. Her mother and grandmother had died of the same disease.

Poor Marguerite lived a year in a hospital for incurables. Every week-end when Doctor Albert went over to see her he found great changes — it was rapid and terrible. That winter and spring he lived like a man lost in a dark morass, the Slave in the Dismal Swamp. He suffered more than his Gretchen, for she was singularly calm and hopeful to the very end, never doubting that she would get well.

The last time he saw her she had given up. But she was noble and sweet in mood, and so piteously apologetic for disappointing him — like a child who has broken something precious and is sorry. She was wasted, indeed, until she was scarcely larger than a child, her beautiful hair cut short, her hands like shadows, but still a stain of colour in her cheeks.

"I'm so sorry I didn't do as you wanted instead of running off with Phil," she said. "I see now how little he cared about me — and you've just done everything. If I had my twenty-six years to live over, I'd live them very differently."

Doctor Albert dropped her hand and walked to the window, the tears running down his face. *"Pourquoi, pourquoi?"* he muttered, staring blindly at that brutal square of glass. When he could control himself and come back to the chair at her bedside, she put her poor little sheared head out on his knee and lay smiling and breathing softly.

"I expect you don't believe in the hereafter," she murmured. "Scientific people hardly ever do. But if there is one, I'll not forget you. I'll love to remember you."

When the nurse came to give her her hypodermic, Doctor Albert went out into Central Park and wandered about without knowing where or why, until he smelled something which suddenly stopped his breath, and he sat down under a flowering linden tree. He dropped his face in his hands and cried like a woman. Youth, art, love, dreams, true-heartedness — why must they go out of the summer world into darkness? *Warum, warum?* He thought he had already suffered all that man could, but never had it come down on him like this. He sat on that bench like a drunken man or like a dying man, muttering Heine's words: "God is a grimmer humorist than I. Nobody but God could have perpetrated anything so cruel." She was ashamed, he remembered it afresh and struck his bony head with his clenched fist — ashamed at having been used like this; she was apologetic for the power, whatever it was, that had tricked her. "Yes, by God, she apologized for God!"

The tortured man looked up through the linden branches at the blue arch that never answers. As he looked, his face relaxed, his breathing grew regular. His eyes were caught by puffy white clouds like the cherub-heads in Raphael's pictures, and something within him seemed to rise and travel with those clouds. The moment had come when he could bear no more . . . When he went back to the hospital that evening, he learned that she had died very quietly between eleven and twelve, the hour when he was sitting on the bench in the park.

Uncle Doctor now sometimes spoke to Albert out of a long silence: "Anyway, I died for her; that was given to me. She never knew a death-struggle — she went to sleep. That struggle took place in my body. Her dissolution occurred within me."

## IV

Old Doctor Engelhardt walked abroad very little now. Sometimes on a fine Sunday his nephew would put him aboard a street car that climbs the hills beyond Mount Oliver and take him to visit an old German graveyard and a monastery. Every afternoon, in good weather, he walked along the pavement which ran past the front door, as far as the first corner, where he bought his paper and cigarettes. If Elsa, the pretty little granddaughter of his housekeeper, ran out to join him and see him over the crossings, he would go a little farther. In the morning, while Mrs. Rudder did the sweeping and dusting, the Doctor took the air on an upstairs back porch, overhanging the court.

The court was bricked, and had an old-fashioned cistern and hydrant, and three ailanthus trees — the last growing things left to the Engelhardts, whose flowering shrubs and greenhouses had once been so well known in Allegheny. In these trees, which he called *les Chinoises*, the Doctor took a great interest. The clothes line ran about their trunks in a triangle, and on Monday he looked down upon the washing. He was too nearsighted to be distressed by the sooty flakes descending from neighbouring chimneys upon the white sheets. He enjoyed the full green leaves of his *Chinoises* in summer, scarcely moving on breathless, sticky nights, when the moon came up red over roofs and smoke-stacks. In autumn he watched the yellow fronds drop down upon the brick pavement like great ferns. Now, when his birthday was approaching, the trees were bare; and he thought he liked them best so, especially when all the knotty, curly twigs were outlined by a scurf of snow.

As he sat there, wrapped up in rugs, a stiff felt hat on his head — he would never hear to a cap — and woollen gloves on his hands, Elsa, the granddaughter, would bring her cross-stitch and chatter to him. Of late she had been sewing on her trousseau, and that amused the Doctor highly — though it meant she would soon go to live in Lower Allegheny, and he would lose her. Her young man, Carl Abberbock, had now a half-interest in a butcher stall in the Allegheny market, and was in a hurry to marry.

When Mrs. Rudder had quite finished her work and made the place neat, she would come and lift the rug from his knees and say: "Time to go in, Herr Doctor."

## V

The next evening after dinner Albert left the house with a suitcase, the bag that used to make so many trips to New York in the opera season. He stopped downstairs to ask Elsa to carry her sewing up and sit with his uncle for a while; then he took the street car across the Twenty-Second Street Bridge by the blazing steel mills. As he waited on Soho Hill to catch a Fifth Avenue car, the heavy, frosty air suddenly began to descend in snowflakes. He wished he had worn his old overcoat; didn't like to get this one wet. He had to consider such things now. He was hesitating about a taxi when his car came, bound for the East End.

He got off at the foot of one of the streets running up Squirrel Hill, and slowly mounted. Everything was white with the softly falling snow. Albert knew all the places; old school friends lived in many of them. Big, turreted stone houses, set in ample grounds with fine trees and shrubbery and driveways. He stepped aside now and then to avoid a car, rolling from the gravel drives on to the stone-block pavement. If the occupants had recognized Albert, they would have felt sorry for him. But he did not feel sorry for himself. He looked up at the lighted windows, the red gleam on the snowy rhododendron bushes, and shrugged. His old schoolfellows went to New York now as often as he had done in his youth; but they went to consult doctors, to put children in school, or to pay the bills of incorrigible sons.

He thought he had had the best of it; he had gone a-Maying while it was May. This solid comfort, this iron-bound security, didn't appeal to him much. These massive houses, after all, held nothing but the heavy domestic routine; all the frictions and jealousies and discontents of family life. Albert felt light and free, going up the hill in his thin overcoat. He believed he had had a more interesting life than most of his friends who owned real estate. He could still amuse himself, and he had lived to the full all the revolutions in art and music that his period covered. He wouldn't at this moment exchange his life and his memories — his memories of his teacher, Rafael Joseffy, for instance — for any one of these massive houses and the life of the man who paid the upkeep. If Mephistopheles were to emerge from the rhododendrons and stand behind his shoulder with such an offer, he wouldn't hesitate. Money? Oh, yes, he would like to have some, but not what went with it.

He turned in under Judge Hammersley's fine oak trees. A car was waiting in the driveway, near the steps by which he mounted to the door. The coloured man admitted him, and just as he entered the hall Mrs. Parmenter came down the stairs.

"Ah, it's you, Albert! Father said you were coming in this evening, and I've kept the car waiting, to have a glimpse of you."

Albert had dropped his hat and bag, and stood holding her hand with the special grace and appreciation she remembered in him.

"What a pleasure to see you!" he exclaimed, and she knew from his eyes it was. "It doesn't happen often, but it's always such a surprise and pleasure." He held her hand as if he wanted to keep it there. "It's a long while since the Villa Scipione, isn't it?"

They stood for a moment in the shrouded hall light. Mrs. Parmenter was looking very handsome, and Albert was thinking that she had all her father's authority, with much more sweep and freedom. She was impulsive and careless, where he was strong and shrinking — a powerful man terribly afraid of little annoyances. His daughter, Albert believed, was not afraid of anything. She had proved more than once that if you aren't afraid of gossip, it is harmless. She did as she pleased. People took it. Even Parmenter had taken it, and he was rather a stiff sort.

Mrs. Parmenter laughed at his allusion to their summer at Mrs. Sterrett's, in Rome, and gave him her coat to hold.

"You remember, Albert, how you and I used to get up early on fete days, and go down to the garden gate to see the young king come riding in from the country at the head of the horse guards? How the sun flashed on his helmet! Heavens, I saw him last summer! So grizzled and battered."

"And we were always going to run away to Russia together, and now there is no Russia. Everything has changed but you, Mrs. Parmenter."

"Wish I could think so. But you don't know any Mrs. Parmenter. I'm Marjorie, please. How often I think of those gay afternoons I had with you and your brothers in the garden behind your old Allegheny house. There's such a lot I want to talk to you about. And this birthday — when is it? May I send your uncle some flowers? I always remember his goodness to poor Marguerite Thiesinger. He never got over that, did he? But I'm late, and father is waiting. Good night, you'll have a message from me."

Albert bent and kissed her hand in the old-fashioned way, keeping it a moment and breathing in softly the fragrance of her clothes, her furs, her person, the fragrance of that other world to which he had once belonged and out of which he had slipped so gradually that he scarcely realized it, unless suddenly brought face to face with something in it that was charming. Releasing her, he caught up his hat and opened the door to follow her, but she pushed him back with her arm and smiled over her shoulder. "No, no, father is waiting for you in the library. Good night."

Judge Hammersley stood in the doorway, fingering a bunch of keys and blinking with impatience to render his service and have done with it. The library opened directly into the hall; he couldn't help overhearing his daughter, and he disliked her free and unreproachful tone with this man who was young when he should be old, single when he should be married, and penniless when he should be well fixed.

Later, as Albert came down the hill with two bottles of the Judge's best champagne in his bag, he was thinking that the greatest disadvantage of being poor and dropping out of the world was that he didn't meet attractive women any more. The men he could do without, Heaven knew! But the women, the ones like Marjorie Hammersley, were always grouped where the big fires burned — money and success and big houses and fast boats and French cars; it was natural.

Mrs. Parmenter, as she drove off, resolved that she would see more of Albert and his uncle — wondered why she had let an old friendship lapse for so long. When she was a little girl, she used often to spend a week with her aunt in Allegheny. She was fond of the aunt, but not of her cousins, and she used to escape whenever she could to the Engelhardts' garden only a few doors away. No grass in that garden—in Allegheny grass was always dirty — but glittering gravel, and lilac hedges beautiful in spring, and barberry hedges red in the fall, and flowers and bird cages and striped awnings, boys lying about in tennis clothes, making mint juleps before lunch, having coffee under the sycamore trees after dinner. The Engelhardt boys were different, like people in a book or a play. All the young men in her set were scornful of girls until they wanted one; then they grabbed her rather brutally and it was over. She had felt that the Engelhardt boys admired her without in the least wanting to grab her, that they enjoyed her aesthetically, so to speak, and it pleased her to be liked in that way.

## VI

On the afternoon of the first of December, Albert left his desk in the County Clerk's office at four o'clock, feeling very much as he used to when school was dismissed in the middle of the afternoon just before the Christmas holidays. It was his uncle's birthday that was in his mind; his own, of course, gave him no particular pleasure. If one stopped to think of that, there was a shiver waiting around the corner. He walked over the Smithfield Street Bridge. A thick brown fog made everything dark, and there was a feeling of snow in the air. The lights along the sheer cliffs of Mount Washington, high above the river, were already lighted. When Albert was a boy, those cliffs, with the row of lights far up against the sky, always made him think of some far-away, cloud-set city in Asia; the forbidden city, he used to call it. Well, that was a long time ago; a lot of water had run under this bridge since then, and kingdoms and empires had fallen. Meanwhile, Uncle Doctor was still hanging on, and things were not so bad with them as they might be. Better not reflect too much. He hopped on board a street car, and old women with market baskets shifted to make room for him.

When he reached home, the table was already set in the living-room. Beautiful table linen had been one of his mother's extravagances (he had boxes of it; meant to give some to Elsa on her marriage), and Mrs. Rudder laundered it with pious care. She had put out the best silver. He had forgotten to order flowers, but the old woman had brought up one of her blooming geraniums for a centrepiece. Uncle Albert was dozing by the fire in his old smoking jacket, a volume of Schiller on his knee.

"I'll put the studs in your shirt for you. Time to dress, Uncle Doctor."

The old man blinked and smiled drolly. "So? *Die* claw-hammer?"

"Of course *die* claw-hammer! Elsa is going to a masquerade with Carl, and they are coming up to see us before they go. I promised her you would dress."

"Albert," the Doctor called him back, beckoned with a mysterious smile; "where did you get that wine now?"

"Oh, you found it when she put it on ice, did you? That's Judge Hammersley's, the best he had. He insisted on sending it to you, with his compliments and good wishes."

Uncle Albert rose and drew up his shoulders somewhat pompously. "From my own kind I still command recognition." Then dropping into homely vulgarity he added, with a sidelong squint at his nephew, "By God, some of that will feel good, running down the gullet."

"You'll have all you want for once. It's a great occasion. Did you shave carefully? I'll take my bath, and then you must be ready for me."

In half an hour Albert came out in his dress clothes and found his uncle still reading his favourite poet. "The trousers are too big," the Doctor complained. "Why not *die* claw-hammer and my old trousers? Elsa wouldn't notice."

"Oh, yes, she would! She's seen these every day for five years. Quick change!"

Doctor Engelhardt submitted, and when he was dressed, surveyed himself in his mirror with satisfaction, though he slyly slipped a cotton handkerchief into his pocket instead of the linen one Albert had laid out. When they came back to the sitting-room, Mrs. Rudder had been up again and had put on the wine glasses. There was still half an hour before dinner, and Albert sat down to play for his uncle. He was beginning to feel that it was all much ado about nothing, after all.

A gentle tap at the door, and Elsa came in with her young man. She was dressed as a Polish maiden, and Carl Abberbock was in a Highlander's kilt.

"Congratulations on your birthday, Herr Doctor, and I've brought you some flowers." She went to his chair and bent down to be kissed, putting a bunch of violets in his hand.

The Doctor rose and stood looking down at the violets. "Hey, you take me for a Bonapartist? What is Mussolini's flower, Albert? Advise your friends in Rome that a Supreme Dictator should always have a flower." He turned the young girl around in the light and teased her about her thin arms — such an old joke, but she laughed for him.

"But that's the style now, Herr Doctor. Everybody wants to be as thin as possible."

"Bah, there are no styles in such things! A man will always want something to take hold of, till Hell freezes over! Is dat so, Carl?"

Carl, a very broad-faced, smiling young man with outstanding ears, was suddenly frightened into silence by the entrance of a fine lady, and made for the door to get his knotty knees into the shadow. Elsa, too, caught her breath and shrank away.

Without knocking, Mrs. Parmenter, her arms full of roses, appeared in the doorway, and just behind her was her chauffeur, carrying a package. "Put it down there and wait for me," she said to him, then swept into the room and lightly embraced Doctor Engelhardt without waiting to drop the flowers or take off her furs. "I wanted to congratulate you in person. They told me below that you were receiving. Please take these flowers, Albert. I want a moment's chat with Doctor Engelhardt."

The Doctor stood with singular gravity, like someone in a play, the violets still in his hand. "To what," he muttered with his best bow, "to what am I indebted for such distinguished consideration?"

"To your own distinction, my dear sir — always one of the most distinguished men I ever knew."

The Doctor, to whom flattery was thrice dearer than to ordinary men, flushed deeply. But he was not so exalted that he did not notice his little friend of many lonely hours slipping out of the entry-way — the bare-kneed Highland chief had already got down the wooden stairs. "Elsa," he called commandingly, "come here and kiss me good night." He pulled her forward. "This is Elsa Rudder, Mrs. Parmenter, and my very particular friend. You should have seen her beautiful hair before she cut it off." Elsa reddened and glanced up to see whether the lady understood. Uncle Doctor kissed her on the forehead and ran his hand over her shingled head. "Nineteen years," he said softly. "If the next nineteen are as happy, we won't bother about the rest. *Behüt' dich, Gott!*"

"Thank you, Uncle Doctor. Good night."

After she fluttered out, he turned to Mrs. Parmenter. "That little girl," he said impressively, "is the rose in winter. She is my heir. Everything I have, I leave to her."

"Everything but my birthday present, please! You must drink that. I've brought you a bottle of champagne."

Both Alberts began to laugh. "But your father has already given us two!"

Mrs. Parmenter looked from one to the other. "My father? Well, that is a compliment! It's unheard of. Of course he and I have different lockers. We could never agree when to open them. I don't think he's opened his since the Chief Justice dined with him. Now I must leave you. Be as jolly as the night is long; with three bottles you ought to do very well! The good woman downstairs said your dinner would be served in half an hour."

Both men started towards her. "Don't go. Please, please, stay and dine with us! It's the one thing we needed." Albert began to entreat her in Italian, a language his uncle did not understand. He confessed that he had been freezing up for the last hour, couldn't go on with it alone. "One can't do such things without a woman — a beautiful woman."

"Thank you, Albert. But I've a dinner engagement; I ought to be at the far end of Ellsworth Avenue this minute."

"But this is once in a lifetime — for him! Still, if your friends are waiting for you, you can't. Certainly not." He took up her coat and held it for her. But how the light had gone out of his face; he looked so different, so worn, as he stood holding her coat at just the right height. She slipped her arms into it, then pulled them out. "I can't, but I just will! Let me write a note, please. I'll send Henry on with it and tell them I'll drop in after dinner." Albert pressed her hand gratefully and took her to his desk. "Oh, Albert, your Italian writing-table, and all the lovely things on it, just as it stood in your room at the Villa Scipione! You used to let me write letters at it. You had the nicest way with young girls. If I had a daughter, I'd want you to do it all over again."

She scratched a note, and Albert put a third place at the table. He noticed Uncle Doctor slip away, and come back with his necktie set straight, attended by a wave of eau de Cologne. While he was lighting the candles and bringing in the wine cooler, Mrs. Parmenter sat down beside the Doctor, accepted one of his cigarettes, and began to talk to him simply and naturally about Marguerite Thiesinger. Nothing could have been more tactful, Albert knew; nothing could give the old man more pleasure on his birthday. Albert himself couldn't do it any more; he had worn out his power of going over that sad story. He tried to make up for it by playing the songs she had sung.

"Albert," said Mrs. Parmenter when they sat down to dinner, "this is the only spot I know in the world that is before-the-war. You've got a period shut up in here; the last ten years of one century, and the first ten of another. Sitting here, I don't believe in aeroplanes, or jazz, or Cubists. My father is nearly as old as Doctor Engelhardt, and we never buy anything new; yet we haven't kept it out. How do you manage."

Albert smiled a little ruefully. "I suppose it's because we never have any young people about. They bring it in."

"Elsa," murmured the Doctor. "But I see; she is only a child."

"I'm sorry for the young people now," Mrs. Parmenter went on. "They seem to me coarse and bitter. There's nothing wonderful left for them, poor things; the war destroyed it all. Where could any girl find such a place to escape to as your mother's house, full of chests of linen like this? All houses now are like hotels; nothing left to cherish. Your house was wonderful! And what music we used to have. Do you remember the time you took me to hear Joseffy play the second Brahms, with Gericke? It was the last time I ever heard him. What did happen to him, Albert? Went to pieces in some way, didn't he?"

Albert sighed and shook his head; wine was apt to plunge him into pleasant, poetic melancholy. "I don't know if anyone knows. I stayed in Rome too long to know, myself. Before I went abroad, I'd been taking lessons with him right along — I saw no change in him, though he gave fewer and fewer concerts. When I got back, I wrote him the day I landed in New York — he was living up the Hudson then. I got a reply from his housekeeper, saying that he was not giving lessons, was ill and was seeing nobody. I went out to his place at once. I wasn't asked to come into the house. I was told to wait in the garden. I waited a long while. At last he came out, wearing white clothes, as he often did, a panama hat, carrying a little cane. He shook hands with me, asked me about Mrs. Sterrett — but he was another man, that's all. He was gone; he wasn't there. I was talking to his picture."

"Drugs!" muttered the Doctor out of one corner of his mouth.

"Nonsense!" Albert shrugged in derision. "Or if he did, that was secondary; a result, not a cause. He'd seen the other side of things; he'd let go. Something had happened in his brain that was not paresis."

Mrs. Parmenter leaned forward. "Did he *look* the same? Surely, he had the handsomest head in the world. Remember his forehead? Was he grey? His hair was a reddish chestnut as I remember."

"A little grey; not much. There was no change in his face, except his eyes. The bright spark had gone out, and his body had a sort of trailing languor when he moved."

"Would he give you a lesson?"

"No. Said he wasn't giving any. Said he was sorry, but he wasn't seeing people at all any more. I remember he sat making patterns in the gravel with his cane. He frowned and said he simply couldn't see people; said the human face had become hateful to him — and the human voice! 'I am sorry,' he said, 'but that is the truth.' I looked at his left hand, lying on his knee. I wonder, Marjorie, that I had the strength to get up and go away. I felt as if everything had been drawn out of me. He got up and took my hand. I understood that I must leave. In desperation I asked him whether music didn't mean anything to him still. 'Music,' he said slowly, with just a ghost of his old smile, 'yes — some music.' He went back into the house. Those were the last words I ever heard him speak."

"Oh, dear! And he had everything that is beautiful — and the name of an angel! But we're making the Doctor melancholy. Open another bottle, Albert — father did very well by you. We've not drunk a single toast. Many returns, we take for granted. Why not each drink a toast of our own, to something we care for?" She glanced at Doctor Engelhardt, who lifted the bunch of violets by his plate and smelled them absently. "Now, Doctor Englehardt, a toast."

The Doctor put down his flowers, delicately took up his glass and held it directly in front of him; everything he did with his hands was deft and sure. A beautiful, a wonderful look came over his face as she watched him.

"I drink," he said slowly, "to a memory; to the last Lenore."

"And I," said young Albert softly, "to my youth, to my beautiful youth!"

Tears flashed into Mrs. Parmenter's eyes. "Ah," she thought, "that's what liking people amounts to; it's liking their silliness and absurdities. That's what it really is."

"And I," she said aloud, "will drink to the future; to our renewed friendship, and many dinners together. I like you two better than anyone I know."

When Albert came back from seeing Mrs. Parmenter down to her car, he found his uncle standing by the fire, his elbow on the mantel, thoughtfully rolling a cigarette. "Albert," he said in a deeply confidential tone, "good wine, good music, beautiful women; that is all there is worth turning over the hand for."

Albert began to laugh. The old man wasn't often banal. "Why, Uncle, you and Martin Luther . . ."

The Doctor lifted a hand imperiously to stop him, and flushed darkly. He evidently hadn't been aware that he was quoting — it came from the heart. "Martin Luther," he snapped, "was a vulgarian of the first water; cabbage soup." He paused a moment to light his cigarette. "But don't fool yourself; one like her always knows when a man has had success with women!"

Albert poured a last glass from the bottle and sipped it critically. "Well, you had success to-night, certainly. I could see that Marjorie was impressed. She's coming to take you for a ride to-morrow, after your nap, so you must be ready."

The Doctor passed his flexible, nervous hand lightly over the thick bristles of his French hair-cut. *"Even in our ashes,"* he muttered haughtily.

# James T. Farrell (1904–    )

FIRST an outstanding writer of the socially conscious thirties, James T. Farrell continues to be an important author. He was born on the South Side of Chicago, the scene of most of his writing, attended Catholic parish schools, studied at the University of Chicago, and worked as clerk, salesman, and reporter. His first novel, *Young Lonigan* (1932), was an immediate sensation with its utterly realistic picture of the harsh life in Chicago slums. It appeared when the entire country was feeling the first impact of the Depression and shared his indignation. It was the first volume of a noteworthy trilogy, *Studs Lonigan*, and was succeeded by many other novels centering around Lonigan. His short stories have been collected in ten excellent volumes. His nonfiction includes literary criticism and poems.

Appearing in 1932, the same year as *Young Lonigan*, and like it a study of thwarted youth, "Spring Evening" typifies the lyricism that underlies even the most "hard-boiled" passages in Farrell's writing. It is an added dimension that makes more poignant the blank, desperate lives to which these boys are being conditioned. What is being conveyed between the lines here is that not just the Lucullan life of "Mr. and Mrs. Richbitch" is being yearned after but Life — escape from the deadly frustration to which the poor are condemned. James T. Farrell's writing has been compared to Dreiser's. His style is much closer, however, to that of another James — James Joyce of *The Dubliners*.

# Spring Evening

GEORGE walked down Euclid Avenue with Jack, his good old pal from those never-to-be-forgotten high school days. It was a tree-arched street, reposeful in the accumulating spring twilight. Both its sidewalks were rowed with low and spectacular specimens of American suburban architecture, which were, principally, red-brick affairs rising above neat lawns and clipped shrubbery. Automobiles lined the curbs. Dozy, slippered people were on front porches and benches. Here and there a potbelly stood, ruminating while he played the hose across grass which sparkled when wet; sprinklers were gurgling. George and Jack strolled along.

Wouldn't it be swell tuh be out in the country? George said.

It ud be the nuts, Jack said.

Yeh! It ud be the nuts all right. Jus' think! Tuh be able to go up tuh Maine, Bar Harbor or one uh them joints, and tuh park yere fanny at a swell resort where Mr. and Mrs. Richbitch always stay. That's the cat's nuts, and I don't mean maybe. No sir!

Yeah! That ud be the nuts. It ud be nothing at all the same as stayin' at a lousy joint like Cedar Lake. Why do you know, there actually wasn't a decent lookin' mama up there las' summer. They all looked like they forgot to take dere false faces off, said Jack.

They walked along, and George thought of the office. He saw it plainly, the cramped room with his desk in a corner, the clatter of type-writers and adding machines, the roar of the loop crashing dustily through the opened window, himself at his desk, sweating like a bastard, cooped up on grand spring days, adding, adding, adding columns and columns of figures. It was lousy work all right. He looked wistfully at the sky, and told himself that Nature was a grand thing all right. If he ever got a break in the luck, he would certainly give the job the goby just like that, and get himself a swell joint somewhere in the country, close to Nature. Nature must be a pretty swell affair all right, out there in the country, where a guy could sit in the shade of a big tree, or go fishing, or take a broad in the forest where it would be all alone and quiet, and not have to bring her to a hotel where it was all dark and stuffy and hot; and in the country, the sunlight would be warmer and clearer and more shiny, the stars brighter, and the moon bigger; the air would be sweeter and give a guy a better appetite, and he would get healthier. It would be the nuts to go to the country and get closer to Nature. If only he would get a break, have some rich bimbo go gagga over him, clean up heavy on the ponies, or maybe enter and win a dance marathon and get signed up for Hollywood.

Gee, it ud be the nuts to be a big shot; and just loll about on the beach on these nice warm days, said George. Yuh could have a swell broad by yere side, and have yere Marmon roadster parked waitin' for yuh with James tuh spin yuh to wherever yuh wanted uh go, an after a swim yuh could take some mama along, and dash out to a roadhouse and get a real chicken feed.

Yeh, wouldn't it be the nuts? said Jack.

It wouldn't be no ordinary beach where, what the hell do yuh call 'em, the hoipolloi go. No sirreee. It would be a private beach of some ritzy joint like the South Shore Country Club, an exclusive dive whose members ud all be filthy with dough.

I'd get 'em off these hot days, sittin' in my white flannels with some rich bim on the veranda of the South Shore Country Club, sippin' my Martini, said Jack.

Well I'd be sippin' a Johnny Walker, said George.

Then wouldn't life be the nuts. You could live like uh royal king, and I don' mean maybe. You could play a round uh golf early in the mornin' before it got too hot, and then have James drive yuh some place for a nice breakfast, and then rest a while, and then take a dip in the lake, and then dine like the King of Italy, and then just loll away the afternoon, or maybe go to the races and play for some small change, you know a thousand bucks or so, and maybe have yere own stable uh nags, and have a harem uh mamas, and keep them each in a swell apartment, and take turns sleepin' with yuh. I tell yuh life ud be the nuts then, said Jack.

And yuh could winter in Florida, and now and then take a littull airplane hop over to London and to see yere foreign banker, and tuh take a few turns out uh the London stock exchange, and then dash over to Paris for some French mamas, and yuh could take in the season at Deauville, and then finish it off by jazzing some hot Spanish senoritas, said George.

It ud be the nuts, Jack said.

Yeh, said George.

They strolled along in silence, puffing away at their Camels. George had, or believed that he had a pain in his heart. Heartburn! He would have to cut down on his smoking. But he might just as well finish the one he was having. No use wasting them. He wasn't getting enough exercise either. He would have to watch that, and get a lotta tennis and golf and swimming this summer, and then next winter join the Y. He would get up early in the morning, and take a little hike before breakfast. Goddamn it, it was lousy; getting up, dashing for a train, and half the time not getting a seat. And at noon a guy had to dash out, and eat at the counter in a place jammed with jabbering broads. And then having to work all day too. He wished that he had a job working outside. But then, most outside jobs were common laborers' jobs, and they had no future. It would be the nuts though if he could land a good selling job, maybe travelling, seeing America, riding swell on Pullmans, stopping at good hotels, and getting himself some brand new broad every night. That would be the nuts all right. Tomorrow morning, he would be getting up early, and dashing for the train, and then he'd be sweating all day in the office. Jesus Christ! Some guys just didn't know how lucky they were.

I'm gonna play Blood'l-Tell tomorrow, said George.

That goddamn nag, said Jack.

You watch! I'm playin' it tuh place. You watch and see, becuz I got my system, and it don't go wrong, said George.

Well, if yuh wanna real tip, take this. Play Mickey Gallagher in the fourth, said Jack.

That bitch! said George.

I got my system, said George

Coming to Jackson Park, they entered a path through the bushes and came out upon the golf course. It was already dark, and the scene was deserted, except for a few passing golfers. A foursome passed homeward; two of the group were girls whom Jack and George agreed were swell lays with grand toilets. They slowly passed on along the grass stretch. Looking back, they could see the rising hulk of the Southmore Hotel at Sixty-seventh and Stoney Island, and further along, the ugly red pyramid of the Balaban and Katz Tower Theatre at Sixty-third. They discussed going to a movie, but decided not to, because it was too hot, and too swell a night to be wasted on the movies. It was nice out all right, they agreed, and they walked on. Jack said that he would like to have five percent of what the guys got in Jackson Park in the summer time. George said that if he did, he wouldn't have a backbone. Jack said that he had a lot of stuff. It made George secretly worried over one of his recurrent fears: was he sterile? He had never got a jane in trouble. Maybe he was. But he couldn't tell anyone, expose his fear, even to Jack. Jack would laugh at him. There was no real reason to suspect that he was. But he was afraid, and the fear was always drumming away at him.

Jack told an anecdote about a pig he had picked up once. She was too lousy and and scummy to take a chance on, but he said he let her go ahead and do you know and when he got home he'd washed his mouth out with soap because he'd kissed her. He said he gave her half a buck. George spoke of the lousy bitch he had gotten one night at the Midway Gardens a couple of years ago when the Gardens was the place to go to if you wanted to dance or pick up some easy broads and they had that hot band, the Memphis Melody Boys with Volley La Forge (a swell guy, Jack knew him) in the orchestra. That was one red hot band all right, you bet. Well, George said, he had taken this bim over to the island in Washington Park, and they had gotten along nice, and she had seemed to be one blazing party and he was beginning to think that he was going to get something pretty nice when damnit if she didn't turn out to be a muff diver. Of course he had let her do her stuff, but the lousy bitch, to think of being that way, anyway. He had felt like busting her teeth down her throat, and he still couldn't understand why he didn't let her have one. Jack said that when broads were low, they were low, like no fellow could be low, except maybe a fairy.

They sat under a tree at the edge of the golf course.

That's a nice sky, said George.

Yeh, said Jack.

You know, I wish I hada lotta bucks, said George.

Who don't? said Jack.

Now if I was in some racket like Al Capone? said George.

You'd get yere ears shot off, said Jack.

It ud be worth the chance, said George.

Boloney, said Jack.

They lit cigarettes, and George tried to convince Jack that he wouldn't mind taking the chances that go with being a big shot in the gang wars. Then the conversation drifted back to the good old days, when they were at St. Cyril High School.

Remember the time Van Der Shans kicked us out of geometry, and we went to the music room, and organized a band with all the instruments, George said.

And Jumps was one of the gang, Jack said.

Yeh, it was too bad about Jumps. He was such a swell guy. And yah know, he woulda been a dandy athlete. He got too smart. He wasn't so smart like Lusk and those guys in school. Why Christ he was the biggest drunkard in the class, outside of Jimmy. And then he went and got goofy. I hear he's a communist, and married some rich broad.

Well, that's not so bad, said Jack.

He always ustuh come to dances with a new broad everytime, and he usually had a keen one.

Yeh, he was a good guy, said Jack.

But now he's writin' a lotta goofy junk, and he's went and lost his religion, said George.

It all goes tuh show that yuh never know what a guy's gonna become. Now there was Jumps a great football player, winning more letters than any guy in school, becoming too smart and an atheist, said Jack. Now who would uh ever thought he'd uh turned out like that, he added.

You never kin tell, said George.

And say, remember the time we went down to play De La Salle of Joliet, and we broke the surburban car window out in Argo? said Jack.

And remember the trolley car at Bourbonais, when we got skunked at St. Viator's? said Jack.

Yeh, said Jack.

And at Joliet when Bud walked into the railroad station with a cigar bigger'n he was, and there was coach Harry watching him. Jesus that was a scream! said George.

And the surprise party on Jimmy before we played St. Mel's in our senior years, when we all got drunk and Jumps slept in Mac's hallway, and they called the paddywagon on him, and then we all hadda play the next afternoon, said Jack.

Yeh, said George.

Them was the days, said Jack, with an audible sigh.

I wish we had 'em back, said George.

Don't I, said Jack.

Nostalgia ached inside of George. He recalled things, events with a sentimental pain, and he started singing the popular songs of other days as an outlet for and a stimulus to his unravelling memories. He sang the choruses of Oogie Oogie Wa Wa that Waring's Pennsylvanians had played at the Tivoli, The Sheik, Saw Mill River Road that Isham Jones' orchestra had played when they were at Trianon, Mean Mean Mama, Oh Gee, Oh Gosh, Oh Golly, I'm In Love; Three O'clock In The Morning, I Hear You Calling Yoo Hoo that they were playing at Teresa Dolan's the first time he had danced with that broad Sally Schmalski who had taken him over to Jackson Park, and I'm Runnin' Wild that he had heard the time he had taken Coletta to College Inn. Thinking of Coletta, he started singing:

> I don't know why I should cry over you,
> Sigh over you,
> Or even feel blue.

Then he sang:

> You know you belong to somebody else,
> So why don't you leave me alone?

And then:

> You're the kind of girl that men forget;
> Just a toy to enjoy for a while;
> For when men settle down, they'll always find,
> An old fashioned girl with an old fashioned smile;
> And you'll soon realize that you're not so wise,
> When the years bring you tears of regret.
> When they play Here Comes The Bride,
> You'll stand outside.
> You're the kind of a girl that men forget.

He grew soft and sentimental. Jack complimented him on his memory of old songs, and George swelled with pride. They sat, revelling in the commonplace anecdotes of the past.

George was tired, and he thought of the morning, and the day's work. To erase the unpleasant anticipations caused by these thoughts, he turned his mind to Coletta. He had met her at his class' Senior Prom. When anyone mentioned her, he always said: Why that goddamn bitch! Yet he loved her. Coletta! He loved her. He got goofy everytime he thought of her. He looked at the stars, and soulgazing, he was thrilled and inspired with a new and, to him, a devout and sacred love for her. Once he had been walking home with her, after they had been to Cocoanut Grove, and he had seemed excited and mushy. That night, she had danced close to him, and he had thought that she had shimmied a little; and going home, she had allowed him to put his arm around her. They had been walking home, and it had been a swell night, like the present one, and he had been thrilled and happy and all exalted, walking with her down the street with trees casting deep shadows, and the wind making little noises in the leaves, and the sky over them so blue, and the stars all lit up like a carnival, and the moon big and silver, and himself with his arm around Coletta; and he had said: Coletta, do you get inspired by the stars? After that, things hadn't gone so well with them, and she had treated him like dirt. The next time she had a date with him, she had broken it. Finally, she had given him the air. She liked college boys in frats; she still went with them. But Coletta was a damn fine, and a damn decent girl; it was just that he had never been able to make her understand just how he felt, and what he really thought of her, and how he loved her, and how he had hoped for a future so different and full of love, different from the life he had lived when he went with her, with its parties, and wise-cracks and its flirting and things like that. He would like to settle down and marry a girl, a decent girl like Coletta. Really, he was too lousy for a decent girl like her; him, playing the races and gambling and drinking, and picking up bums from public dance halls and taking them in entrance ways and taxicabs and going to can houses. He wished that he was up in the bucks, and settling down, marrying a girl like Coletta, marrying her . . . And there he was with nothing, and now he was twenty-four, and in the morning he would go down to the office and work. He had been there four years. Yet he didn't have such a right to kick. Wasn't he making his forty-five bucks a week; and having a pretty good time at that. He was getting on better than most of the guys from his graduating class. Yes sir! But to be really up in the bucks! That would be the nuts all right. Maybe someday!

Sa-ay, I saw Coletta the other day, Jack said, interrupting a long silence.

That bitch! said George.

Come on now. Don't goof yere grandpa. I know different. Lissen, remember the time you broke down and confessed that she was the kind of a girl a guy would like to marry, said Jack.

Yeh, but that was a long time ago.

Don't krap me. Yere still in love with ur, said Jack.

George said: No! Don't krap me, said Jack. George was finally forced into admitting that he still cared for her, and his admittance stirred rays of hope that he might still get her. Jack started to kid him, saying that she was a three-way whore and all that sort of thing; and George started kidding Jack about his girl, Ann, saying how she used to love

niggers, and they kept dwelling upon the many abnormalities and per-
versions and indecencies of the two girls, just kidding, and having a good
time like they always did, and not meaning no offense, and knowing that
each was only kidding and trying to get the other's goat.

It's a swell night, said George.

Wouldn't it be the nuts to go out now and have a drive in the country,
said Jack.

Yeh, said George.

I say! Isn't that a swell sky, said Jack.

Yeh, and the moon's nice, said George.

You know these guys that got bucks don't know how lucky they are.
I know that if something don't happen for me soon, I'm gonna get my old
man tuh get me on the force. You know, it's not a bad racket. My old
man made plenty. And then there's his friend, Pat O'Shaughnessy. Can
yah tell me how a plain ordinary cop kin keep a family of six, and save
enough dough tuh own a six story apartment building in South Shore?
No, sir! He had a beat down in the red light district, and then, he cashed
in a lotta graft from bootleggers. My old man said so, said Jack.

Sure they all get it, said George.

But don't say I said so, or my old man did, becuz you know how
gossip flies, said Jack.

Ain't I yere buddy? said George.

An' yessir, I'm gonna have my old man get me on the force. If he
slips the right guys a few bucks, I'll get on. Maybe I kin be a secretary
to some big shot. It ud be the nuts to be a secretary like that guy was
in City Hall.

I didn't see it, said George.

It was the nuts of a show. A real one. This guy Herbert Rawlings
or something like that who used tuh be in the movies was the mayor,
and he was one smart gee. But you know in politics or on the force, a
guy kin get his. They all do, said Jack.

Well if I didn't have a good jobber, I wouldn't mind gettin' on,
said George.

If a guy gets on with a drag like I would, it ud be the nuts, said Jack.

George said yeh.

They sat, puffing cigarettes, watching the frail lines of smoke waver
out of sight. A fellow passed with a girl. She had little on underneath,
and as she walked through a moonlit patch, they could see right through
her dress. Jack said that there was a guy that had a nice mama, and that
he probably wasn't taking her out to the golf course for nix. George
said no, particularly since the guy had some newspapers. Jack said that
she made him anxious and suggested that they go down to the Rex at

Twenty-second and Wabash. George said he didn't mind going down
to 22, but when they took an inventory of their money, they didn't have
enough. It was tough all right, them feeling like they did.

George thought of work in the morning. Every night it was the
same. The thought of going to work the next day spoiled things. It
was the same with his vacation. He was getting tired too; he said he
guessed he had better blow. They walked back to Seventy-first Street,
and had a chocolate malted milk in the crowded Walgreen Drug Store
at Jeffery. Then, they parted. George said for Jack to watch Blood'l-
Tell because he had his system. Jack said the nag was lousy, but that
George should keep his eyes peeled on Mickey Gallagher in the fourth.
Then he told him not to take any wooden nickels. George told Jack
not to do anything he wouldn't do. George went home. He thought
of Coletta, and hummed I'm Runnin' Wild, and then, You're The Kind
Of A Girl That Men Forget. He told himself that it ud be the nuts if
he was only up in the bucks.

# Erskine Caldwell (1903–    )

No PERIOD in American history, including that of the Civil War, has produced as grim literature as that coming out of the Depression, and one of its most uncompromising authors is Erskine Caldwell. His birthplace was White Oak, in Georgia, the state that is the scene of his most powerful stories and plays. In a time of scarce jobs, he worked when he could get them at cotton-picking, and as a stage hand and professional football player. He was educated at Erskine College, the University of Virginia, and the University of Pennsylvania. The sensational *Tobacco Road* (1932), his first novel about starving sharecroppers, dramatized by Jack Kirkland, had a continuous run of three thousand, one hundred and eighty-two Broadway performances. His second novel, *God's Little Acre* (1933), was prosecuted for obscenity but was acquitted in a landmark judicial decision. *You Have Seen Their Faces*, with photos by his former wife, Margaret Bourke-White, is still considered an important documentary of the sufferings of Southern sharecroppers. Caldwell's many novels have been tremendously popular. Critics, however, generally agree that Caldwell's best writing is in his early stories.

It couldn't happen here, but it did, and people were starving to death in America in the thirties, with once prosperous businessmen selling apples on street corners; soup lines for blocks and "Brother, Can You Spare a Dime?" a popular song. Erskine Caldwell illustrates the Depression in this powerful story of a frantic mother's desperate effort to keep her starving children alive. The story caused no shock when published in a magazine in 1933, for the degradation caused by extreme poverty was all around. Earthy humor and sexual frankness in *Tobacco Road* and *God's Little Acre* accounted for much of their best-selling popularity, but in most of his writing Caldwell's social indignation was deadly serious.

# Masses of Men

HUGH MILLER worked for the street railway company. Hugh had a silver button, a gold button, a bronze watch-fob made like a trolley-car, and a small tin disk with the numeral 7 almost worn off. He had worked for the company twenty-six years repairing tracks, and the company had once told him that some day he would be retired with a comfortable pension.

After all those years, Hugh was still trying to get along in the world. He still hoped to be made superintendent of construction. For some reason, though, he had never got far. He was still repairing tracks. Even though there were other men who were stepped ahead when the time came to fill up the ranks, Hugh kept his job as a laborer, repairing the tracks year after year, and hoped he would be made superintendent before he got too old to work any longer.

"I'll get it yet," he told himself. "I'll get it as sure as shooting. They've got to promote me some day, and I've been working long enough now to get it. I'll get it as sure as shooting."

Hugh had put off marrying Cora until he was promoted. Cora told him that she did not mind waiting a little longer, because she was working then in a store in town and earning as much as Hugh himself was. But after the twelfth year, Hugh decided that if he ever was going to get married, he ought to do it without further delay. He was growing old, and, although Cora was still as youthful in appearance as she was when they became engaged, she was beginning to complain of the long hours she was compelled to stand on her feet behind the counter in the notion store.

"We'll get married right now," Hugh told her one Saturday night while they were riding home on his company pass. "There's no sense in waiting any longer. If you are ready, we'll be married next week. I've been thinking about it a long time, and there's no sense in waiting till I get promoted."

"I'd love to, Hugh," she said, clutching his arm in the crowded car. "I think it's silly to put it off any longer. I've been hoping for it to happen for I don't know how long. We don't have to wait until you get promoted."

They got off the car at the boulevard stop and walked slowly home. They lived next door to each other, in boarding houses, and there was no hurry since it was Saturday night.

That was the beginning. They walked slowly down the dark street talking about next week, and Hugh kept saying to himself under his breath that he would surely be promoted the next time the company filled up the ranks. He was certain of it. He told Cora he was. She believed him.

After they were married, Hugh rented a five-room house not far from the car-barn. It was just a step down the alley from the tree-lined street where the trollies passed all day long. It was a good house, for the money, and it was comfortable. Having their door-step in an alley did not really matter so much after all. They did not mind that. The house was almost on the corner, and the upstairs windows looked out over the tree-lined street. They could step out the front door, walk a few steps, and be in the street. It was not a bad place to live, and Cora liked it.

First there was a girl; they named her Pearl. Later there was a boy, John; after another year there was another girl, and they named her Ruby.

Hugh still looked forward to the time when he would be made superintendent of construction for the street railway company, but after Ruby was born, he did not think about it any more. Cora had stopped working in the notion store; she stayed at home and attended to the house and cared for the children. She was beginning to wonder what she could do to her skin to keep it from turning so dark; in the meantime, she hid her face when people for some reason or another came to the door. She knew there was nothing wrong with her skin; it was merely becoming darker and darker every day. But she wished she knew what to do about it. Her hair already had a streak of gray in it.

She would have mentioned it to Hugh, but Hugh never talked any more. When he came home from work, he ate his supper and went to bed. She did not have a chance to tell Hugh anything like that. He was too tired to listen to her.

When Pearl, the oldest child, was nine, Hugh was knocked down by an automobile one day while he was jacking up a rail to replace a rotted cross-tie, and run over and killed. The company sent his body home that evening, when the rest of the workers got off at five o'clock, and Cora did not know what to do. After she had put the children to bed, she went out and walked down the street until she saw a policeman. She told him what had happened to Hugh, and he said he would have the body taken away the next morning. She went back home and looked at Hugh, but she could not notice any difference in him; at home, he was always asleep.

Cora knew there would be a little money coming in from the company. She was certain there would be something, but she was afraid it would not be enough to pay for Hugh's funeral and burial, and leave enough for them to live on until she could find work of some kind.

The policeman had the body taken away the next morning, and it was buried somewhere. Cora did not know where, but she did know it was the only thing she could do about it. The children had to have food, and they had to have a little heat in the house.

She waited a month for the money to come from the street railway company, and still it did not come. After that she went to the office and asked for it. There was no one there who seemed to know anything about the matter. Nobody in the big brick building had ever heard of Hugh Miller, and when they looked up the name, no one was certain which Hugh Miller she had inquired about. Cora stayed there all day, but when the people in the building went home at dark, she did not know what else to do except to go home, too.

After that she did not bother the people at the street railway company any more. She did not have time to go there, for one thing; and she had a lot to do at home. The three children had to be taken care of, and she had to go out every day and find enough food to keep them from being hungry. Sometimes it took her all day long to get enough just for one small meal; other times she could find nothing at all for them to eat, but she kept on walking because the children had to be fed.

Pearl was going on ten. She was the oldest, and Ruby was still just a baby. But Pearl was growing up. She had long yellow hair and a blue gingham dress, and she tried to help her mother all she could. She cared for the other children while Cora was out trying to get some food, and at night she helped her mother put them to bed. After they were asleep, Cora would tell her about her father, Hugh.

"Your father worked for the street railway company," she told Pearl. "The company would help us out, but they are so busy up there they can't seem to find time to do anything about it. They would help us if they could get all the Hugh Millers who have worked for them straight in their minds. Your father was just one of them."

"I can work," Pearl told her mother. "I'm old enough now. I'll see if I can find something to do. You take me with you, Mama, and I'll ask about it. John and Ruby can take care of each other if we lock them in a room before we go out."

"You're not very big for your age," Cora said. "People wouldn't believe you when you told them you are going on ten."

"But I can work. I'll show them how much I can do."

"Hugh worked for the street railway company, Pearl. He was your father. Some day the company will help us. They're busy right now. I don't like to bother them so much."

Pearl went to bed telling her mother that she was old enough to work. Cora did not say anything else to her, but she could not think of any kind of work that Pearl was capable of doing.

The next morning John and Ruby went out early to bring back some wood for the stove. They had no shoes to wear, and their coats were not warm enough. It was mid-winter, but the ground was bare of snow. When they came back that afternoon, their feet were bleeding around the toes and their heels had cracked open in several places.

"Where's the fire-wood, John?" Cora asked him.

"We couldn't find any."

Cora put her cloak around her head and shoulders and went out into the alley. There was no wood of any kind there, but up at the other end there was a coal bin that sometimes overflowed into the narrow way. She filled her apron with coal and ran back to the house. The children huddled around the stove, shivering and whimpering, while she kindled the fire.

"I'm hungry, Mama," Ruby said.

"I'll get you something to eat," Cora promised her.

"When are we going to have something to eat again?" John asked her.

"I'll bring you something when I come back."

Pearl piled the quilts on the floor beside the stove and held John and Ruby close beside her in the warmth. Her gingham dress was torn, but her long yellow hair was thick and warm over her shoulders. She held the children close to her and rubbed their toes and heels.

Cora put on her cloak and went out into the alley. She ran to the street and stood there indecisively for a moment until she could make up her mind which direction she would take. She turned down the street this time, instead of going up it.

After she had run and walked for five or six blocks, she came to a cluster of one-story suburban stores. There were several men standing at the curb in front of the buildings. They were waiting for a street car to take them into town. The men turned and looked at Cora when they saw that she was running towards them.

"Mister, give me half a dollar for my children," she pleaded.

The men turned all the way around and looked her up and down. One of them laughed at her.

"Sister," one of them said, "I wouldn't give a dime for you and a dozen more like you."

The others laughed at what he had said. The trolley was coming down the street; it was two or three blocks away, and its bell was clanging. The men stepped out into the street and stood beside the tracks waiting for it to stop. Cora followed them into the street.

"Mister," she said to the man who had spoken to her, "Mister, what would you —"

"Don't call me 'Mister,' " he said angrily. "My name's Johnson."

The others laughed at her again. Johnson stepped forward and looked down at her while his friends continued laughing at her.

"Mr. Johnson," Cora said, "what would you give me half a dollar for?"

"What would I give you half a dollar for?" he asked.

"Yes, Mr. Johnson. What would you give it to me for?"

He turned around and winked at the other men before answering her. They urged him on.

"Have you got a girl at home?" he asked her.

"Yes, sir. I've got Pearl, and Ruby, too."

"Well, I couldn't give you half a dollar, but I might be able to give you a quarter."

The street car stopped and the door sprang open. The other two men hopped on, calling to Johnson to hurry. He looked at Cora for a moment longer, but when she continued to stand there with her mouth open, unable to say anything, he ran and jumped aboard.

Cora was left standing beside the tracks. When the car started, she stood on her toes and tried to see the man inside. She called to him frantically, trying to make him understand her; and she waved her arms excitedly, attempting to attract his attention. All three of them ran to the rear end of the car and pressed their faces against the glass to see her better. Cora ran down the middle of the street, calling to them and waving her arms to stop them, but the car was soon out of sight and she was left alone on the car tracks. She went to the sidewalk and walked back up the street until she reached the corner in front of the stores where the men had been standing when she first saw them. When she got to the corner, she sat down on the curb to wait.

Cora did not know how long she had waited, but she had promised the children she would bring back some food when she returned, and she had to wait no matter how long the time was. But Johnson finally came back. He got off the street car and walked towards her at the curb. He was surprised to see her there, and he stopped before her and looked at her in amazement. Cora was glad the other men had not come back with him.

She led him up the street, running ahead and urging him to hurry. Even though he followed her without protest, he did not walk fast enough to please Cora, and she was continually asking him to hurry. He stopped once and struck a match for his cigarette against an iron street-light pole, and Cora ran back and pulled at his coat, begging him to follow her as fast as he could walk.

When the got inside the house, Cora awakened Pearl. The man stood close to the door, debating within himself whether to remain or to leave. Cora got behind him and held the door shut so he could not leave.

"How old is she?" he asked Cora.

"She's almost ten now."

"It's cold as hell in this house. Why don't you have some heat in here? You've got a stove there."

"Give me the quarter, and I'll try to get a little coal somewhere."

"Tell her to stand up."

"Stand up, Pearl," Cora told her.

Pearl shrank against the foot of the bed; she was bewildered and frightened. She wished to run to her mother, but the strange man was between them. She was afraid he would catch her before she could reach the door where Cora stood.

"You're lying to me," Johnson said. "She's nowhere near ten."

"I swear to God, Mr. Johnson, she's almost ten. Please, Mr. Johnson, don't go off now."

Johnson looked around the room and saw John and Ruby asleep under the quilts on the bed.

"How old is the other girl?"

"She's eight."

"I don't believe you. You're lying to me. Neither of them is over eight."

"Pearl's almost ten, Mr. Johnson. I swear before God, she is. Please give me the quarter."

He walked across the room towards Pearl. She tried to run away, but Cora caught her and made her stand beside the foot of the bed. Cora waited behind Johnson.

"Tell her to turn around," he said.

"Turn around, Pearl," Cora told her.

"It's too damn cold in here," he said, his hands trembling. "My feet are frozen. Why don't you make a fire in that stove?"

"If you'll give me the quarter, I'll try to get a little coal somewhere."

"How do I know you're on the level?" he asked her. "I'm afraid of you. You don't look right to me. How do I know you won't go yelling for a cop the first thing?"

"I wouldn't do that. Give me the quarter."

"I'd be in a pretty fix, caught like that. They'd give me twenty years at hard labor. I'd never come out alive."

"I won't tell anybody, Mr. Johnson. I swear to God, I won't. Just give me the quarter."

Johnson pushed his hands into his pockets and looked at Pearl again. His hands were cold, and his feet were, too. His breath looked like smoke in the cold house.

"Tell her to let me see her," he said.

"Let him see you, Pearl," Cora said.

Johnson waited, looking at her and at Cora. He could not stand still while he watched her against the foot of the bed.

"Hurry up, Pearl, and let him see you," Cora urged.

Pearl began to cry.

"They'd give me life for that," Johnson said, backing towards the door. "You'd get a cop after me before I could get out of the house. I don't like the way you look. Why don't you have some heat in here? You've got a stove."

"Honest to God, Mr. Johnson, I wouldn't tell on you. Give me the quarter, and you can trust me."

"Get some heat in here first," he said. "My feet are freezing."

"I can't get any coal till you give me the quarter."

"You can go steal some, can't you?"

"Give me the quarter first, Mr. Johnson."

"How do I know you're on the level? I don't like the way you look."

"I swear to God, I won't tell on you, Mr. Johnson."

Johnson lit a cigarette and inhaled the smoke in the manner of a man gasping for breath. With his lungs and mouth and nostrils dense with smoke, he dropped the stub into the stove and thrust his hands back into his pockets.

"Tell her to come over here," he said.

"Go over there, Pearl."

Johnson bent down and looked at Pearl in the dim light. He straightened up once for a moment, and bent down again and looked at her more closely.

"They'd hang me before tomorrow night if they caught me," he said jerkily.

"Give me the quarter, Mr. Johnson, and I swear to God I won't tell anybody."

"Tell her to stand still."

"Stand still, Pearl."

"For God's sake get some heat in here."

"Give me the quarter first, Mr. Johnson," Cora begged.

"And then go out and tell a cop," he said shrilly.

"Just give me the quarter first."

"You're crazy," he shouted at her. "I don't like the looks of you. How do I know what you'll do? You might run out of here the first thing yelling for a cop."

"Give me the quarter, and I'll get a little coal."

"And tell a cop."

"I swear I won't do that, Mr. Johnson. Give me the quarter, and I'll get some coal."

Johnson turned his back on Cora and went closer to Pearl. He took his hands out of his pockets and blew into them.

"Tell her to stop that crying."

"Stop crying, Pearl."

Johnson reached down and put his hands under Pearl's thick yellow hair, but the moment he touched her, she whirled around and ran to Cora.

"They'd screw my head off of my neck so quick I wouldn't have a chance to think about it."

"Give me the quarter, Mr. Johnson, and I swear to God I won't tell on you."

He hesitated a moment; looking at Pearl, he shoved his hands into his pants pocket and brought out a twenty-five cent piece. Cora grabbed it from his hand and bolted for the door.

"Wait a minute!" he shouted, running and catching her. "Come back here and tell her to keep still before you go."

"Keep still, Pearl," her mother told her.

"Hurry up and get some coal before I freeze to death. And if you tell a policeman, I'll kill the last one of you before they take me. I ought to have better sense than to let you go. I don't like the way you look."

Cora ran out the door and into the alley before he could say anything more to her. She slammed the door and ran with all her might to the end of the alley. Without losing a moment, she raced down the street towards the one-story stores. After she had gone a block, she stopped and carefully laid the quarter on her tongue and closed her lips tightly so she would be sure not to drop it or lose it on the dark street.

One of the grocery stores was still open. She took the coin out of her mouth, pointing at bread and pressed meat, and placed it in the clerk's hand. He dropped the wet silver piece as though it were white-hot steel and wiped his hands on his apron.

When Cora got back, the children were asleep. John and Ruby were rolled tightly in the quilts, and Pearl was lying on the bed with the coat over her. She had been crying, and the tears had not fully dried on her cheeks; her eyes were inflamed, and her face was swollen across the bridge of her nose. Cora went to the side of the bed and threw the coat from her and looked down at her. Pearl had doubled herself into a knot, with her arms locked around her knees, and her head was thrust forward over her chest. Cora looked at her for a while, and then she carefully replaced the coat over her.

After unwrapping the bread and pressed meat, she stuffed the paper into the stove and struck a match to it. She drew her chair closer and bent forward so she could stretch her arms around the sides of the stove and feel the heat as much as possible before it burned out.

When the stove became cold again, Cora laid the bread and pressed meat on a chair beside her and rolled up in her quilt to wait for day. When the children woke up, the food would be there for them.

# Zora Neale Hurston (1903–1960)

ZORA NEALE HURSTON was black and beautiful. Beautiful in appearance, in personality, and in her writing, she was born in Florida and graduated from Barnard College (1938) where she majored in anthropology, an interest that was to underlie much of her literary work. At North Carolina College for Negroes she was a greatly beloved teacher. The first of her many short stories, "The Gilded Six-Bits" (1933), is reprinted here. Her *Mules and Men* (1935) was a collection of voodoo tales about blacks in the Southern United States. *Tell My Horse* (1938) was based on her researches among Haitians and other West Indian peoples. Among her novels are *Jonah's Gourd Vine* (1934), *Their Eyes Were Watching God* (1937) and *Moses: Man of the Mountain* (1939). Her autobiography is called *Dust Tracks on a Road* (1942).

The rarest kind of fiction, whether it be a short story or a novel, is a well-written, happy, love story and "The Gilded Six-Bits" is one of those rare few from many stories this reader knows. The intimate picture of the life of Missie May and Joe, highlighted by the homely details of their little house, the merry play of their love-making, and the skillful way in which are handled the effects on a saddened man of Missie May's temporary lapse makes this story a joy. And oh, what a plea for racial understanding Hurston makes with her no-comment recording of the white clerk's empty-headed remark: "Wisht I could be like these darkies. Laughin' all the time. Nothin' worries 'em"!

# *The Gilded Six-Bits*

IT WAS a Negro yard around a Negro house in a Negro settlement that looked to the payroll of the G and G Fertilizer works for its support. But there was something happy about the place. The front yard was parted in the middle by a sidewalk from gate to door-step, a sidewalk edged on either side by quart bottles driven neck down into the ground on a slant. A mess of homey flowers planted without a plan but blooming cheerily from their helter-skelter places. The fence and house were whitewashed. The porch and steps scrubbed white.

The front door stood open to the sunshine so that the floor of the front room could finish drying after its weekly scouring. It was Saturday. Everything clean from the front gate to the privy house. Yard raked so that the strokes of the rake would make a pattern. Fresh newspaper cut in fancy edge on the kitchen shelves.

Missy May was bathing herself in the galvanized washtub in the bedroom. Her dark-brown skin glistened under the soapsuds that skittered down from her wash rag. Her stiff young breasts thrust forward aggressively like broad-based cones with the tips lacquered in black.

She heard men's voices in the distance and glanced at the dollar clock on the dresser.

"Humph! Ah'm way behind time t'day! Joe gointer be heah 'fore Ah git mah clothes on if Ah don't make haste."

She grabbed the clean meal sack at hand and dried herself hurriedly and began to dress. But before she could tie her slippers, there came the ring of singing metal on wood. Nine times.

Missie May grinned with delight. She had not seen the big tall man come stealing in the gate and creep up the walk grinning happily at the joyful mischief he was about to commit. But she knew that it was her husband throwing silver dollars in the door for her to pick up and pile beneath her plate at dinner. It was this way every Saturday afternoon. The nine dollars hurled into the open door, he scurried to a hiding place behind the cape jasmine bush and waited.

Missie May promptly appeared at the door in mock alarm.

"Who dat chuckin' money in mah do'way?" she demanded. No answer from the yard. She leaped off the porch and began to search the shrubbery. She peeped under the porch and hung over the gate to look up and down the road. While she did this, the man behind the jasmine darted to the china berry tree. She spied him and gave chase.

"Nobody ain't gointer be chunkin' money at me and Ah not do 'em nothin'," she shouted in mock anger. He ran around the house with Missie May at his heels. She overtook him at the kitchen door. He ran inside but could not close it after him before she crowded in and locked with him in a rough and tumble. For several minutes the two were a furious mass of male and female energy. Shouting, laughing, twisting, turning, tussling, tickling each other in the ribs; Missie May clutching Joe and Joe trying, but not too hard, to get away.

"Missie May, take yo' hand out mah pocket!" Joe shouted out between laughs.

"Ah ain't, Joe, not lessen you gwine gimme whateve' it is good you got in yo' pocket. Turn it go, Joe, do Ah'll tear yo' clothes."

"Go on tear 'em. You de one dat pushes de needles around heah. Move yo' hand, Missie May."

"Lemme git dat paper sack out yo' pocket. Ah bet it's candy kisses."

"Tain't. Move yo' hand. Woman ain't got no business in a man's clothes nohow. Go way."

Missie May gouged way down and gave an upward jerk and triumphed.

"Unhhunh! Ah got it. It 'tis so candy kisses. Ah knowed you had somethin' for me in yo' clothes. Now Ah got to see whut's in every pocket you got."

Joe smiled indulgently and let his wife go through all of his pockets
and take out the things that he had hidden there for her to find. She
bore off the chewing gum, the cake of sweet soap, the pocket handkerchief as if she had wrested them from him, as if they had not been
bought for the sake of this friendly battle.

"Whew! dat play-fight done got me all warmed up," Joe exclaimed.
"Got me some water in de kittle?"

"Yo' water is on de fire and yo' clean things is cross de bed. Hurry
up and wash yo'self and git changed so we kin eat. Ah'm hongry."
As Missie said this, she bore the steaming kettle into the bedroom.

"You ain't hongry, sugar," Joe contradicted her. "Youse jes' a
little empty. Ah'm de one whut's hongry. Ah could eat up camp
meetin', back off 'ssociation, and drink Jurdan dry. Have it on de table
when Ah git out de tub."

"Don't you mess wid mah business, man. You git in yo' clothes.
Ah'm a real wife, not no dress and breath. Ah might not look lak one,
but if you burn me, you won't git a thing but wife ashes."

Joe splashed in the bedroom and Missie May fanned around in the
kitchen. A fresh red and white checked cloth on the table. Big pitcher
of buttermilk beaded with pale drops of butter from the churn. Hot
fried mullet, crackling bread, ham hock atop a mound of string beans
and new potatoes, and perched on the window-sill a pone of spicy potato
pudding.

Very little talk during the meal but that little consisted of banter
that pretended to deny affection but in reality flaunted it. Like when
Missie May reached for a second helping of the tater pone. Joe snatched
it out of her reach.

After Missie May had made two or three unsuccessful grabs at the
pan, she begged, "Aw, Joe, gimme some mo' dat tater pone."

"Nope, sweetenin' is for us men-folks. Y'all pritty lil frail eels
don't need nothin' lak dis. You too sweet already."

"Please, Joe."

"Naw, naw. Ah don't want you to git no sweeter than whut you is
already. We goin' down de road a lil piece t'night so you go put on
yo' Sunday-go-to-meetin' things."

Missie May looked at her husband to see if he was playing some
prank. "Sho nuff, Joe?"

"Yeah. We goin' to de ice cream parlor."

"Where de ice cream parlor at, Joe?"

"A new man done come heah from Chicago and he done got a place
and took and opened it up for a ice cream parlor, and bein' as it's real
swell, Ah wants you to be one de first ladies to walk in dere and have
some set down."

"Do Jesus, Ah ain't knowed nothin' 'bout it. Who de man done it?"

"Mister Otis D. Slemmons, of spots and places — Memphis, Chicago, Jacksonville, Philadelphia and so on."

"Dat heavy-set man wid his mouth full of gold teethes?"

"Yeah. Where did you see 'im at?"

"Ah went down to de sto' tuh git a box of lye and Ah seen 'im standin' on de corner talkin' to some of de mens, and Ah come on back and went to scrubbin' de floor, and he passed and tipped his hat whilst Ah was scourin' de steps. Ah thought Ah never seen *him* befo'."

Joe smiled pleasantly. "Yeah, he's up to date. He got de finest clothes Ah ever seen on a colored man's back."

"Aw, he don't look no better in his clothes than you do in yourn. He got a puzzle gut on 'im and he so chuckle-headed, he got a pone behind his neck."

Joe looked down at his own abdomen and said wistfully, "Wisht Ah had a build on me lak he got. He ain't puzzle-gutted, honey. He jes' got a corperation. Dat make 'm look lak a rich white man. All rich mens is got some belly on 'em."

"Ah seen de pitchers of Henry Ford and he's a spare-built man and Rockefeller look lak he ain't got but one gut. But Ford and Rockefeller and dis Slemmons and all de rest kin be as many-gutted as dey please, Ah'm satisfied wid you jes' lak you is, baby. God took pattern after a pine tree and built you noble. Youse a pritty man, and if Ah knowed any way to make you mo' pritty still Ah'd take and do it."

Joe reached over gently and toyed with Missie May's ear. "You jes' say dat cause you love me, but Ah know Ah can't hold no light to Otis D. Slemmons. Ah ain't never been nowhere and Ah ain't got nothin' but you."

Missie May got on his lap and kissed him and he kissed back in kind. Then he went on. "All de womens is crazy 'bout 'im everywhere he go."

"How do you know dat, Joe?"

"He tole us so hisself."

"Dat don't make it so. His mouf is cut cross-ways, ain't it? Well, he kin lie jes' lak anybody else."

"Good Lawd, Missie! You womens sho is hard to sense into things. He's got a five-dollar gold piece for a stick-pin and he got a ten-dollar gold piece on his watch chain and his mouf is jes' crammed full of gold teethes. Sho wisht it wuz mine. And whut make it so cool, he got money 'cumulated. And womens give it all to 'im."

"Ah don't see whut de womens see on 'im. Ah wouldn't give 'im a wink if de sheriff wuz after 'im."

"Well, he tole us how de white womens in Chicago give 'im all dat gold money. So he don't 'low nobody to touch it at all. Not even put dey finger on it. Dey tole 'im not to. You kin make 'miration at it, but don't tetch it.''

"Whyn't he stay up dere where dey so crazy 'bout 'im?''

"Ah reckon dey done made 'im vast-rich and he wants to travel some. He say dey wouldn't leave 'im hit a lick of work. He got mo' lady people crazy 'bout him than he kin shake a stick at.''

"Joe, Ah hates to see you so dumb. Day stray nigger jes' tell y'all anything and y'all b'lieve it.''

"Go 'head on now, honey and put on yo' clothes. He talkin' 'bout his pritty womens — Ah want 'im to see *mine*.''

Missie May went off to dress and Joe spent the time trying to make his stomach punch out like Slemmons' middle. He tried the rolling swagger of the stranger, but found that his tall bone-and-muscle stride fitted ill with it. He just had time to drop back into his seat before Missie May came in dressed to go.

On the way home that night Joe was exultant. "Didn't Ah say ole Otis was swell? Can't he talk Chicago talk? Wuzn't dat funny whut he said when great big fat ole Ida Armstrong come in? He asted me, 'Who is dat broad wid de forte shake?' Dat's a new word. Us always thought forty was a set of figgers but he showed us where it means a whole heap of things. Sometimes he don't say forty, he jes' say thirty-eight and two and dat mean de same thing. Know whut he tole me when Ah wuz payin' for our ice cream? He say, 'Ah have to hand it to you, Joe. Dat wife of yours is jes' thirty-eight and two. Yessuh, she's forte!' Ain't he killin'?''

"He'll do in case of a rush. But he sho is got uh heap uh gold on 'im. Dats de first time Ah ever seed gold money. It lookted good on him sho nuff, but it'd look a whole heap better on you.''

"Who, me? Missie May youse crazy! Where would a po' man lak me git gold money from?''

Missie May was silent for a time, then she said, "Us might find some goin' long de road some time. Us could.''

"Who would be losin' gold money round heah? We ain't even seen none dese white folks wearin' no gold money on dey watch chain. You must be figgerin' Mister Packard or Mister Cadillac goin' pass through heah.''

"You don't know whut been lost 'round heah. Maybe somebody way back in memorial times lost they gold money and went on off and it ain't never been found. And then if we wuz to find it, you could wear some 'thout havin' no gang of womens lak dat Slemmons say he got.''

Joe laughed and hugged her. "Don't be so wishful 'bout me. Ah'm satisfied de way Ah is. So long as Ah be yo' husband, Ah don't keer 'bout nothin' else. Ah'd ruther all de other womens in de world to be dead than for you to have de toothache. Less we go to bed and git our night rest."

It was Saturday night once more before Joe could parade his wife in Slemmons' ice cream parlor again. He worked the night shift and Saturday was his only night off. Every other evening around six o'clock he left home, and dying dawn saw him hustling home around the lake where the challenging sun flung a flaming sword from east to west across the trembling water.

That was the best part of life — going home to Missie May. Their white-washed house, the mock battle on Saturday, the dinner and ice cream parlor afterwards, church on Sunday nights when Missie out-dressed any woman in town — all, everything was right.

One night around eleven the acid ran out at the G. and G. The foreman knocked off the crew and let the steam die down. As Joe rounded the lake on his way home, a lean moon rode the lake in a silver boat. If anybody had asked Joe about the moon on the lake, he would have said he hadn't paid it any attention. But he saw it with his feelings. It made him yearn painfully for Missie. Creation obsessed him. He thought about children. They had been married more than a year now. They had money put away. They ought to be making little feet for shoes. A little boy child would be about right.

He saw a dim light in the bedroom and decided to come in through the kitchen door. He could wash the fertilizer dust off himself before presenting himself to Missie May. It would be nice for her not to know that he was there until he slipped into his place in bed and hugged her back. She always liked that.

He eased the kitchen door open slowly and silently, but when he went to set his dinner bucket on the table he bumped it into a pile of dishes, and something crashed to the floor. He heard his wife gasp in fright and hurried to reassure her.

"Iss me, honey. Don't git skeered."

There was a quick, large movement in the bedroom. A rustle, a thud and a stealthy silence. The light went out.

What? Robbers? Murderers? Some varmit attacking his help-less wife, perhaps. He struck a match, threw himself on guard and stepped over the door-sill into the bedroom.

The great belt on the wheel of Time slipped and eternity stood still. By the match light he could see the man's legs fighting with his breeches in his frantic desire to get them on. He had both chance and time to kill the intruder in his helpless condition — half in and half out of his pants — but he was too weak to take action. The shapeless enemies of humanity that live in the hours of Time had waylaid Joe. He was assaulted in his weakness. Like Samson awakening after his haircut. So he just opened his mouth and laughed.

The match went out and he struck another and lit the lamp. A howling wind raced across his heart, but underneath its fury he heard his wife sobbing and Slemmons pleading for his life. Offering to buy it with all that he had. "Please, suh, don't kill me. Sixty-two dollars at de sto'. Gold money."

Joe just stood. Slemmons looked at the window, but it was screened. Joe stood like a rough-backed mountain between him and the door. Barring him from escape, from sunrise, from life.

He considered a surprise attack upon the big clown that stood there laughing like a chessy cat. But before his fist could travel an inch, Joe's own rushed out to crush him like a battering ram. Then Joe stood over him.

"Git into yo' damn rags, Slemmons, and dat quick."

Slemmons scrambled to his feet and into his vest and coat. As he grabbed his hat, Joe's fury overrode his intentions and he grabbed at Slemmons with his left hand and struck at him with his right. The right landed. The left grazed the front of his vest. Slemmons was knocked a somersault into the kitchen and fled through the open door. Joe found himself alone with Missie May, with the golden watch charm clutched in his left fist. A short bit of broken chain dangled between his fingers.

Missie May was sobbing. Wails of weeping without words. Joe stood, and after awhile he found out that he had something in his hand. And then he stood and felt without thinking and without seeing with his natural eyes. Missie May kept on crying and Joe kept on feeling so much and not knowing what to do with all his feelings, he put Slemmons watch charm in his pants pocket and took a good laugh and went to bed.

"Missie May, whut you cryin' for?"

"Cause Ah love you so hard and Ah know you don't love *me* no mo'."

Joe sank his face into the pillow for a spell then he said huskily, "You don't know de feelings of dat yet, Missie May."

"Oh Joe, honey, he said he wuz gointer give me dat gold money and he jes' kept on after me —"

Joe was very still and silent for a long time. Then he said, "Well, don't cry no mo', Missie May. Ah got yo' gold piece for you."

The hours went past on their rusty ankles. Joe still and quiet on one bed-rail and Missie May wrung dry of sobs on the other. Finally the sun's tide crept upon the shore of night and drowned all its hours. Missie May with her face stiff and streaked towards the window saw the dawn come into her yard. It was day. Nothing more. Joe wouldn't be coming home as usual. No need to fling open the front door and sweep off the porch, making it nice for Joe. Never no more breakfast to cook; no more washing and starching of Joe's jumper-jackets and pants. No more nothing. So why get up?

With this strange man in her bed, she felt embarrassed to get up and dress. She decided to wait till he had dressed and gone. Then she would get up, dress quickly and be gone forever beyond reach of Joe's looks and laughs. But he never moved. Red light turned to yellow, then white.

From beyond the no-man's land between them came a voice. A strange voice that yesterday had been Joe's.

"Missie May, ain't you gonna fix me no breakfus'?"

She sprang out of bed. "Yeah, Joe. Ah didn't reckon you wuz hongry."

No need to die today. Joe needed her for a few more minutes anyhow.

Soon there was a roaring fire in the cook stove. Water bucket full and two chickens killed. Joe loved fried chicken and rice. She didn't deserve a thing and good Joe was letting her cook him some breakfast. She rushed hot biscuits to the table as Joe took his seat.

He ate with his eyes in his plate. No laughter, no banter.

"Missie May, you ain't eatin' yo' breakfus'."

"Ah don't choose none, Ah thank yuh."

His coffee cup was empty. She sprang to refill it. When she turned from the stove and bent to set the cup beside Joe's plate, she saw the yellow coin on the table between them.

She slumped into her seat and wept into her arms.

Presently Joe said calmly, "Missie May, you cry too much. Don't look back lak Lot's wife and turn to salt."

The sun, the hero of every day, the impersonal old man that beams as brightly on death as on birth, came up every morning and raced across the blue dome and dipped into the sea of fire every evening. Water ran down hill and birds nested.

Missie knew why she didn't leave Joe. She couldn't. She loved him too much, but she could not understand why Joe didn't leave her. He was polite, even kind at times, but aloof.

There were no more Saturday romps. No ringing silver dollars to stack beside her plate. No pockets to rifle. In fact the yellow coin in his trousers was like a monster hiding in the cave of his pockets to destroy her.

She often wondered if he still had it, but nothing could have induced her to ask nor yet to explore his pockets to see for herself. Its shadow was in the house whether or no.

One night Joe came home around midnight and complained of pains in the back. He asked Missie to rub him down with liniment. It had been three months since Missie had touched his body and it all seemed strange. But she rubbed him. Grateful for the chance. Before morning, youth triumphed and Missie exulted. But the next day, as she joyfully made up their bed, beneath her pillow she found the piece of money with the bit of chain attached.

Alone to herself, she looked at the thing with loathing, but look she must. She took it into her hands with trembling and saw first thing that it was no gold piece. It was a gilded half dollar. Then she knew why Slemmons had forbidden anyone to touch his gold. He trusted village eyes at a distance not to recognize his stick-pin as a gilded quarter, and his watch charm as a four-bit piece.

She was glad at first that Joe had left it there. Perhaps he was through with her punishment. They were man and wife again. Then another thought came clawing at her. He had come home to buy from her as if she were any woman in the long house. Fifty cents for her love. As if to say that he could pay as well as Slemmons. She slid the coin into his Sunday pants pocket and dressed herself and left his house.

Half way between her house and the quarters she met her husband's mother, and after a short talk she turned and went back home. Never would she admit defeat to that woman who prayed for it nightly. If she had not the substance of marriage she had the outside show. Joe must leave *her*. She let him see she didn't want his old gold four-bits too.

She saw no more of the coin for some time though she knew that Joe could not help finding it in his pocket. But his health kept poor, and he came home at least every ten days to be rubbed.

The sun swept around the horizon, trailing its robes of weeks and days. One morning as Joe came in from work, he found Missie May chopping wood. Without a word he took the ax and chopped a huge pile before he stopped.

"You ain't got no business choppin' wood, and you know it."

"How come? Ah been choppin' it for de last longest."

"Ah ain't blind. You makin' feet for shoes."

"Won't you be glad to have a lil baby chile, Joe?"

"You know dat 'thout astin' me."

"Iss gointer be a boy chile and de very spit of you."

"You reckon, Missie May?"

"Who else could it look lak?"

Joe said nothing, but he thrust his hand deep into his pocket and fingered something there.

It was almost six months later Missie May took to bed and Joe went and got his mother to come wait on the house.

Missie May was delivered of a fine boy. Her travail was over when Joe came in from work one morning. His mother and the old women were drinking great bowls of coffee around the fire in the kitchen.

The minute Joe came into the room his mother called him aside. "How did Missie May make out?" he asked quickly.

"Who, dat gal? She strong as a ox. She gointer have plenty mo'. We done fixed her wid de sugar and lard to sweeten her for de nex' one."

Joe stood silent awhile.

"You ain't ast 'bout de baby, Joe. You oughter be mighty proud cause he sho is de spittin' image of yuh, son. Dat's yourn all right, if you never git another one, dat un is yourn. And you know Ah'm mighty proud too, son, cause Ah never thought well of you marryin' Missie May cause her ma used tuh fan her foot round right smart and Ah been mighty skeered dat Missie May wuz gointer git misput on her road."

Joe said nothing. He fooled around the house till late in the day then just before he went to work, he went and stood at the foot of the bed and asked his wife how she felt. He did this every day during the week.

On Saturday he went to Orlando to make his market. It had been a long time since he had done that.

Meat and lard, meal and flour, soap and starch. Cans of corn and tomatoes. All the staples. He fooled around town for a while and bought bananas and apples. Way after while he went around to the candy store.

"Hello, Joe," the clerk greeted him. "Ain't seen you in a long time."

"Nope, Ah ain't been heah. Been round in spots and places."

"Want some of them molasses kisses you always buy?"

"Yessuh." He threw the gilded half dollar on the counter. "Will dat spend?"

"Whut is it, Joe? Well, I'll be doggone! A gold-plated four-bit piece. Where'd you git it, Joe?"

"Offen a stray nigger dat come through Eatonville. He had it on his watch chain for a charm — goin' round making out iss gold money. Ha ha! He had a quarter on his tie pin and it wuz all golded up too. Tryin' to fool people. Makin' out he so rich and everything. Ha! Ha! Tryin' to tole off folkses wives from home."

"How did you git it, Joe? Did he fool you, too?"

"Who, me? Naw suh! He ain't fooled me none. Know what Ah done? He come round me wid his smart talk. Ah hauled off and knocked 'im down and took his old four-bits way from 'im. Gointer buy my wife some good ole lasses kisses wid it. Gimme fifty cents worth of dem candy kisses."

"Fifty cents buys a mighty lot of candy kisses, Joe. Why don't you split it up and take some chocolate bars, too. They eat good, too."

"Yessuh, dey do, but Ah wants all dat in kisses. Ah got a lil boy chile home now. Tain't a week old yet, but he kin suck a sugar tit and maybe eat one them kisses hisself."

Joe got his candy and left the store. The clerk turned to the next customer. "Wisht I could be like these darkies. Laughin' all the time. Nothin' worries 'em."

Back in Eatonville, Joe reached his own front door. There was the ring of singing metal on wood. Fifteen times. Missie May couldn't run to the door, but she crept there as quickly as she could.

"Joe Banks, Ah hear you chunkin' money in mah do'way. You wait till Ah got mah strength back and Ah'm gointer fix you for dat."

# Conrad Aiken (1889–1973)

WHEN HE was a small boy Conrad Aiken saw his father shoot his mother to death and then kill himself. The shock of such a terrible tragedy on a child was bound to mark him and it did, both in his life and his writing. Aiken was born in Savannah, Georgia, but on his parents' death taken to Massachusetts where he was reared by relatives. He graduated from Harvard University with the celebrated class of 1910, which included such literary figures as T. S. Eliot and John Reed. Aiken was a splendid poet, writing metaphysical verse, epics, and sonnets. Beginning in 1914, twenty-seven books of his poems were published. He also wrote novels and three volumes of short stories. His "Mr. Arcularis" was dramatized as a play in 1957. An autobiography, *Ushant*, was published in 1952 with Malcolm Lowry, the English writer who was a close friend figuring prominently in it.

There are two theories as to how the modern short story evolved. One is that it grew out of the essay of the kind written by Addison and Steele. The other is that it is a close relative of the poem. If ever a short story confirmed the second theory it is "Silent Snow, Secret Snow." And it breaks the heart when one understands that the child hungry for the peace all-enveloping snow might give him had been a witness to his mother's murder and his father's suicide. It is a cliché, the admonition to a writer "to write out of his own knowing and feeling" but that was what Aiken was doing here and exquisitely. Clues are plentiful, especially during his inquisition, when the three adults stared hard at him "as if he had done something monstrous, or was himself some kind of monster." How often Conrad Aiken as a child must have known himself to be an object of morbid curiosity! And how grateful we must be to him for this lovely legacy of his pain.

# Silent Snow, Secret Snow

JUST WHY it should have happened, or why it should have happened just when it did, he could not, of course, possibly have said; nor perhaps would it even have occurred to him to ask. The thing was above all a secret, something to be preciously concealed from Mother and Father; and to that very fact it owed an enormous part of its deliciousness. It was like a peculiarly beautiful trinket to be carried unmentioned in one's trouser pocket — a rare stamp, an old coin, a few tiny gold links found trodden out of shape on the path in the park, a pebble of carnelian, a seashell distinguishable from all others by an unusual spot or stripe — and, as if it were any one of these, he carried around with him everywhere a warm and persistent and increasingly beautiful sense of possession. Nor was it only a sense of possession — it was also a sense of protection. It was as if, in some delightful way, his secret gave him a fortress, a wall behind which he could retreat into heavenly seclusion. This was almost the first thing he had noticed about it — apart from the oddness of the thing itself — and it was this that now again, for the fiftieth time, occurred to him, as he sat in the little schoolroom. It was the half-hour for geography. Miss Buell was revolving with one finger, slowly, a huge terrestrial globe which had been placed on her desk. The green and yellow continents passed and repassed, questions were asked and answered, and now the little girl in front of him, Deirdre, who had a funny little constellation of freckles on the back of her neck, exactly like the Big Dipper, was standing up and telling Miss Buell that the equator was the line that ran round the middle.

Miss Buell's face, which was old and grayish and kindly, with gray stiff curls beside the cheeks, and eyes that swam very brightly, like little minnows, behind thick glasses, wrinkled itself into a complication of amusements.

"Ah! I see. The earth is wearing a belt, or a sash. Or someone drew a line round it!"

"Oh no — not that — I mean — "

In the general laughter, he did not share, or only a very little. He was thinking about the Arctic and Antarctic regions, which of course, on the globe, were white. Miss Buell was now telling them about the tropics, the jungles, the steamy heat of equatorial swamps, where the birds and butterflies, and even the snakes, were like living jewels. As he listened to these things, he was already, with a pleasant sense of half-effort, putting his secret between himself and the words. Was it really an effort at all? For effort implied something voluntary, and perhaps even something one did not especially want; whereas this was distinctly pleasant, and came almost of its own accord. All he needed to do was to think of that morning, the first one, and then of all the others —

But it was all so absurdly simple! It had amounted to so little. It was nothing, just an idea — and just why it should have become so wonderful, so permanent, was a mystery — a very pleasant one, to be sure, but also, in an amusing way, foolish. However, without ceasing to listen to Miss Buell, who had now moved up to the north temperate zones, he deliberately invited his memory of the first morning. It was only a moment or two after he had waked up — or perhaps the moment itself. But was there, to be exact, an exact moment? Was one awake all at once? or was it gradual? Anyway, it was after he had stretched a lazy hand up toward the headrail, and yawned, and then relaxed again among his warm covers, all the more grateful on a December morning, that the thing had happened. Suddenly, for no reason, he had thought of the postman, he remembered the postman. Perhaps there was nothing so odd in that. After all, he heard the postman almost every morning in his life — his heavy boots could be heard clumping round the corner at the top of the little cobbled hill-street, and then, progressively nearer, progressively louder, the double knock at each door, the crossings and re-crossings of the street, till finally the clumsy steps came stumbling across to the very door, and the tremendous knock came which shook the house itself.

(Miss Buell was saying, "Vast wheat-growing areas in North America and Siberia."

Deirdre had for the moment placed her left hand across the back of her neck.)

But on this particular morning, the first morning, as he lay there with his eyes closed, he had for some reason *waited* for the postman. He wanted to hear him come round the corner. And that was precisely the joke — he never did. He never came. He never had come — *round the corner* — again. For when at last the steps *were* heard, they had already, he was quite sure, come a little down the hill, to the first house; and even so, the steps were curiously different — they were softer, they had a new secrecy about them, they were muffled and indistinct; and while the rhythm of them was the same, it now said a new thing — it said peace, it said remoteness, it said cold, it said sleep. And he had understood the situation at once — nothing could have seemed simpler — there had been snow in the night, such as all winter he had been longing for; and it was this which had rendered the postman's first footsteps inaudible, and the later ones faint. Of course! How lovely! And even now it must be snowing — it was going to be a snowy day — the long white ragged lines were drifting and sifting across the street, across the faces of the old houses, whispering and hushing, making little triangles of white in the corners between cobblestones, seething a little when the wind blew them over the ground to a drifted corner; and so it would be all day, getting deeper and silenter and silenter.

(Miss Buell was saying, "Land of perpetual snow.")

All this time, of course (while he lay in bed), he had kept his eyes closed, listening to the nearer progress of the postman, the muffled footsteps thumping and slipping on the snow-sheathed cobbles; and all the other sounds — the double knocks, a frosty far-off voice or two, a bell ringing thinly and softly as if under a sheet of ice — had the same slightly abstracted quality, as if removed by one degree from actuality — as if everything in the world had been insulated by snow. But when at last, pleased, he opened his eyes, and turned them toward the window, to see for himself this long-desired and now so clearly imagined miracle — what he saw instead was brilliant sunlight on a roof; and when, astonished, he jumped out of bed and stared down into the street, expecting to see the cobbles obliterated by the snow, he saw nothing but the bare bright cobbles themselves.

Queer, the effect this extraordinary surprise had had upon him — all the following morning he had kept with him a sense as of snow falling about him, a secret screen of new snow between himself and the world. If he had not dreamed such a thing — and how could he have dreamed it while awake? — how else could one explain it? In any case, the delusion had been so vivid as to affect his entire behavior. He could not now remember whether it was on the first or the second morning — or was it even the third — that his mother had drawn attention to some oddness in his manner.

"But my darling" — she had said at the breakfast table — "what has come over you? You don't seem to be listening . . ."

And how often that very thing had happened since!

(Miss Buell was now asking if anyone knew the difference between the North Pole and the Magnetic Pole. Deirdre was holding up her flickering brown hand, and he could see the four white dimples that marked the knuckles.)

Perhaps it hadn't been either the second or third morning — or even the fourth or fifth. How could he be sure? How could he be sure just when the delicious *progress* had become clear? Just when it had really *begun*? The intervals weren't very precise . . . All he now knew was, that at some point or other — perhaps the second day, perhaps the sixth — he had noticed that the presence of the snow was a little more insistent, the sound of it clearer; and, conversely, the sound of the postman's footsteps more indistinct. Not only could he not hear the steps come round the corner, he could not even hear them at the first house. It was below the first house that he heard them; and then, a few days later, it was below the second house that he heard them; and a few days later again, below the third. Gradually, gradually, the snow was becoming heavier, the sound of its seething louder, the cobblestones more and more muffled. When he found, each morning, on going to the window, after the ritual of listening, that the roofs and cobbles were as bare as ever, it made no difference. This was, after all, only what he had expected. It was even what pleased him, what rewarded him: the thing was his own, belonged to no one else. No one else knew about it, not even his mother and father. There, outside, were the bare cobbles; and here, inside, was the snow. Snow growing heavier each day, muffling the world, hiding the ugly, and deadening increasingly — above all — the steps of the postman.

"But my darling" — she had said at the luncheon table — "what has come over you? You don't seem to listen when people speak to you. That's the third time I've asked you to pass your plate . . ."

How was one to explain this to Mother? or to Father? There was, of course, nothing to be done about it: nothing. All one could do was laugh embarrassedly, pretend to be a little ashamed, apologize, and take a sudden and somewhat disingenuous interest in what was being done or said. The cat had stayed out all night. He had a curious swelling on his left cheek — perhaps somebody had kicked him, or a stone had struck him. Mrs. Kempton was or was not coming to tea. The house was going to be housecleaned, or "turned out," on Wednesday instead of Friday. A new lamp was provided for his evening work — perhaps it was eyestrain which accounted for this new and so peculiar vagueness of his — Mother was looking at him with amusement as she said this, but with something else as well. A new lamp? A new lamp. Yes, Mother, No, Mother, Yes, Mother. School is going very well. The geometry is very easy. The history is very dull. The geography is very interesting — particularly when it takes one to the North Pole. Why the North Pole? Oh, well, it would be fun to be an explorer. Another Peary or Scott or Shackleton. And then abruptly he found his interest in the talk at an end, stared at the pudding on his plate, listened, waited, and began once more — ah, how heavenly, too, the first beginnings — to hear or feel — for could he actually hear it? — the silent snow, the secret snow.

(Miss Buell was telling them about the search for the Northwest Passage, about Hendrik Hudson, the *Half Moon*.)

This had been, indeed, the only distressing feature of the new experience; the fact that it so increasingly had brought him into a kind of mute misunderstanding, or even conflict, with his father and mother. It was as if he were trying to lead a double life. On the one hand, he had to be Paul Hasleman, and keep up the appearance of being that person — dress, wash, and answer intelligently when spoken to —; on the other, he had to explore this new world which had been opened to him. Nor could there be the slightest doubt — not the slightest — that the new world was the profounder and more wonderful of the two. It was irresistible. It was miraculous. Its beauty was simply beyond anything — beyond speech as beyond thought — utterly incommunicable. But how then, between the two worlds, of which he was thus constantly aware, was he to keep a balance? One must get up, one must go to breakfast, one must talk with Mother, go to school, do one's lessons — and, in all this, try not to appear too much of a fool. But if all the while one was also trying to extract the full deliciousness of another and quite separate existence, one which could not easily (if at all) be spoken of — how was one to manage? How was one to explain? Would it be safe to explain? Would it be absurd? Would it merely mean that he would get into some obscure kind of trouble?

These thoughts came and went, came and went, as softly and secretly as the snow; they were not precisely a disturbance, perhaps they were even a pleasure; he liked to have them; their presence was something almost palpable, something he could stroke with his hand, without closing his eyes, and without ceasing to see Miss Buell and the school-room and the globe and the freckles on Deirdre's neck; nevertheless he did in a sense cease to see, or to see the obvious external world, and sub-stituted for this vision the vision of snow, the sound of snow, and the slow, almost soundless, approach of the postman. Yesterday, it had been only at the sixth house that the postman had become audible; the snow was much deeper now, it was falling more swiftly and heavily, the sound of its seething was more distinct, more soothing, more persistent. And this morning, it had been — as nearly as he could figure — just above the seventh house — perhaps only a step or two above; at most, he had heard two or three footsteps before the knock had sounded . . . And with each such narrowing of the sphere, each nearer approach of the limit at which the postman was first audible, it was odd how sharply was increased the amount of illusion which had to be carried into the ordinary business of daily life. Each day, it was harder to get out of bed, to go to the window, to look out at the — as always — perfectly empty and snowless street. Each day it was more difficult to go through the perfunctory motions of greeting Mother and Father at breakfast, to reply to their questions, to put his books together and go to school. And at school, how extraordinarily hard to conduct with success simultan-eously the public life and the life that was secret! There were times when he longed — positively ached — to tell everyone about it — to burst out with it — only to be checked almost at once by a far-off feeling as of some faint absurdity which was inherent in it — but *was* it absurd? — and more importantly by a sense of mysterious power in his very secrecy. Yes; it must be kept secret. That, more and more, became clear. At whatever cost to himself, whatever pain to others —

(Miss Buell looked straight at him, smiling, and said, "Perhaps we'll ask Paul. I'm sure Paul will come out of his daydream long enough to be able to tell us. Won't you, Paul?" He rose slowly from his chair, resting one hand on the brightly varnished desk, and deliberately stared through the snow toward the blackboard. It was an effort, but it was amusing to make it. "Yes," he said slowly, "it was what we now call the Hudson River. This he thought to be the Northwest Passage. He was disappointed." He sat down again, and as he did so Deirdre half turned in her chair and gave him a shy smile, of approval and admiration.)

At whatever pain to others.

This part of it was very puzzling, very puzzling. Mother was very nice, and so was Father. Yes, that was all true enough. He wanted to be nice to them, to tell them everything — and yet, was it really wrong of him to want to have a secret place of his own?

At bed-time, the night before, Mother had said, "If this goes on, my lad, we'll have to see a doctor, we will! We can't have our boy —" But

what was it she had said? "Live in another world"? "Live so far
away"? The word "far" had been in it, he was sure, and then Mother
had taken up a magazine again and laughed a little, but with an expression which wasn't mirthful. He had felt sorry for her . . .

The bell rang for dismissal. The sound came to him through long
curved parallels of falling snow. He saw Deirdre rise, and had himself
risen almost as soon — but not quite as soon — as she.


## II

On the walk homeward, which was timeless, it pleased him to see
through the accompaniment, or counterpoint, of snow, the items of mere
externality on his way. There were many kinds of brick in the sidewalks,
and laid in many kinds of pattern. The garden walls, too, were various,
some of wooden palings, some of plaster, some of stone. Twigs of bushes
leaned over the walls: the little hard green winter-buds of lilac, on gray
stems, sheathed and fat; other branches very thin and fine and black and
desiccated. Dirty sparrows huddled in the bushes, as dull in color as
dead fruit left in leafless trees. A single starling creaked on a weather
vane. In the gutter, beside a drain, was a scrap of torn and dirty newspaper, caught in a little delta of filth; the word ECZEMA appeared in
large capitals, and below it was a letter from Mrs. Amelia D. Cravath,
2100 Pine Street, Fort Worth, Texas, to the effect that after being a suf-
ferer for years she had been cured by Caley's Ointment. In the little delta,
beside the fan-shaped and deeply runneled continent of brown mud, were
lost twigs, descended from their parent trees, dead matches, a rusty
horse-chestnut burr, a small concentration of eggshell, a streak of yellow
sawdust which had been wet and now was dry and congealed, a brown
pebble, and a broken feather. Farther on was a cement sidewalk, ruled
into geometrical parallelograms, with a brass inlay at one end commem-
orating the contractors who had laid it, and, halfway across, an irregular
and random series of dog-tracks, immortalized in synthetic stone. He
knew these well, and always stepped on them; to cover the little hollows
with his own foot had always been a queer pleasure; today he did it once
more, but perfunctorily and detachedly, all the while thinking of something else. That was a dog, a long time ago, who had made a mistake
and walked on the cement while it was still wet. He had probably
wagged his tail, but that hadn't been recorded. Now, Paul Hasleman,
aged twelve, on his way home from school, crossed the same river, which
in the meantime had frozen into rock. Homeward through the snow,
the snow falling in bright sunshine. Homeward?

Then came the gateway with the two posts surmounted by egg-
shaped stones which had been cunningly balanced on their ends, as if

by Columbus, and mortared in the very act of balance; a source of perpetual wonder. On the brick wall just beyond, the letter H had been stenciled, presumably for some purpose. H? H.

The green hydrant, with a little green-painted chain attached to the brass screw-cap.

The elm tree, with the great gray wound in the bark, kidney-shaped, into which he always put his hand — to feel the cold but living wood. The injury, he had been sure, was due to the gnawings of a tethered horse. But now it deserved only a passing palm, a merely tolerant eye. There were more important things. Miracles. Beyond the thoughts of trees, mere elms. Beyond the thoughts of sidewalks, mere stone, mere brick, mere cement. Beyond the thoughts even of his own shoes, which trod these sidewalks obediently, bearing a burden — far above — of elaborate mystery. He watched them. They were not very well polished; he had neglected them, for a very good reason: they were one of the many parts of the increasing difficulty of the daily return to daily life, the morning struggle. To get up, having at last opened one's eyes, to go to the window, and discover no snow, to wash, to dress, to descend the curving stairs to breakfast —

At whatever pain to others, nevertheless, one must persevere in severance, since the incommunicability of the experience demanded it. It was desirable, of course, to be kind to Mother and Father, especially as they seemed to be worried, but it was also desirable to be resolute. If they should decide — as appeared likely — to consult the doctor, Doctor Howells, and have Paul inspected, his heart listened to through a kind of dictaphone, his lungs, his stomach — well, that was all right. He would go through with it. He would give them answer for question, too — perhaps such answers as they hadn't expected? No. That would never do. For the secret world must, at all costs, be preserved.

The bird-house in the apple tree was empty — it was the wrong time of year for wrens. The little round black door had lost its pleasure. The wrens were enjoying other houses, other nests, remoter trees. But this too was a notion which he only vaguely and grazingly entertained — as if, for the moment, he merely touched an edge of it; there was something further on, which was already assuming a sharper importance; something which already teased at the corners of his eyes, teasing also at the corner of his mind. It was funny to think that he so wanted this, so awaited it — and yet found himself enjoying this momentary dalliance with the bird-house, as if for a quite deliberate postponement and enhancement of the approaching pleasure. He was aware of his delay, of his smiling and detached and now almost uncomprehending gaze at the little bird-house; he knew what he was going to look at next: it was his own little cobbled hill-street, his own house, the little river at the bottom of the hill, the grocer's shop with the cardboard man in the window — and now, thinking of all this, he turned his head, still smiling, and looking quickly right and left through the snow-laden sunlight.

And the mist of snow, as he had foreseen, was still on it — a ghost of snow falling in the bright sunlight, softly and steadily floating and turning and pausing, soundlessly meeting the snow that covered, as with a transparent mirage, the bare bright cobbles. He loved it — he stood still and loved it. Its beauty was paralyzing — beyond all words, all experience, all dream. No fairy story he had ever read could be compared with it — none had ever given him this extraordinary combination of ethereal loveliness with a something else, unnameable, which was faintly and deliciously terrifying. What was this thing? As he thought of it, he looked upward toward his own bedroom window, which was open — and it was as if he looked straight into the room and saw himself lying half awake in his bed. There he was — at this very instant he was still perhaps actually there — more truly there than standing here at the edge of the cobbled hill-street, with one hand lifted to shade his eyes against the snow-sun. Had he indeed ever left his room, in all this time? since that very first morning? Was the whole progress still being enacted there, was it still the same morning, and himself not yet wholly awake? And even now, had the postman not yet come round the corner? . . .

This idea amused him, and automatically, as he thought of it, he turned his head and looked toward the top of the hill. There was, of course, nothing there — nothing and no one. The street was empty and quiet. And all the more because of its emptiness it occurred to him to count the houses — a thing which, oddly enough, he hadn't before thought of doing. Of course, he had known there weren't many — many, that is, on his own side of the street, which were the ones that figured in the postman's progress — but nevertheless it came as something of a shock to find that there were precisely *six*, above his own house — his own house was the seventh.

Six!

Astonished, he looked at his own house — looked at the door, on which was the number thirteen — and then realized that the whole thing was exactly and logically and absurdly what he ought to have known. Just the same, the realization gave him abruptly, and even a little frighteningly, a sense of hurry. He was being hurried — he was being rushed. For — he knit his brow — he couldn't be mistaken — it was just above the *seventh* house, his *own* house, that the postman had first been audible this very morning. But in that case — in that case — did it mean that tomorrow he would hear nothing? The knock he had heard must have been the knock of their own door. Did it mean — and this was an idea which gave him a really extraordinary feeling of surprise — that he would never hear the postman again? — that tomorrow morning the postman would already have passed the house, in a snow so deep as to render his footsteps completely inaudible? That he would have made his approach down the snow-filled street so soundlessly, so secretly, that he, Paul Hasleman, there lying in bed, would not have waked in time, or waking, would have heard nothing?

But how could that be? Unless even the knocker should be muffled in the snow — frozen tight, perhaps? . . . But in that case —

A vague feeling of disappointment came over him; a vague sadness as if he felt himself deprived of something which he had long looked forward to, something much prized. After all this, all this beautiful progress, the slow delicious advance of the postman through the silent and secret snow, the knock creeping closer each day, and the footsteps nearer, the audible compass of the world thus daily narrowed, narrowed, narrowed, as the snow soothingly and beautifully encroached and deepened, after all this, was he to be defrauded of the one thing he had so wanted — to be able to count, as it were, the last two or three solemn footsteps, as they finally approached his own door? Was it all going to happen, at the end, so suddenly? or indeed, had it already happened? with no slow and subtle gradations of menace, in which he could luxuriate?

He gazed upward again, toward his own window which flashed in the sun; and this time almost with a feeling that it would be better if he *were* still in bed, in that room; for in that case this must still be the first morning, and there would be six more mornings to come — or, for that matter, seven or eight or nine — how could he be sure? — or even more.

III

After supper, the inquisition began. He stood before the doctor, under the lamp, and submitted silently to the usual thumpings and tappings.

"Now will you please say 'Ah!'?"

"Ah!"

"Now again, please, if you don't mind."

"Ah."

"Say it slowly, and hold it if you can —"

"Ah-h-h-h-h-h —"

"Good."

How silly all this was. As if it had anything to do with his throat! Or his heart, or lungs!

Relaxing his mouth, of which the corners, after all this absurd stretching, felt uncomfortable, he avoided the doctor's eyes, and stared toward the fireplace, past his mother's feet (in gray slippers) which projected from the green chair, and his father's feet (in brown slippers) which stood neatly side by side on the hearth rug.

"Hm. There is certainly nothing wrong there . . . ?"

He felt the doctor's eyes fixed upon him, and, as if merely to be polite, returned the look, but with a feeling of justifiable evasiveness.

"Now, young man, tell me — do you feel all right?"

"Yes, sir, quite all right."

"No headaches? no dizziness?"

"No, I don't think so."

"Let me see. Let's get a book, if you don't mind — yes, thank you, that will do splendidly — and now, Paul, if you'll just read it, holding it as you would normally hold it —"

He took the book and read:

"And another praise have I to tell for this the city our mother, the gift of a great god, a glory of the land most high; the might of horses, the might of young horses, the might of the sea . . . For thou, son of Cronus, our lord Poseidon, hath throned herein this pride, since in these roads first thou didst show forth the curb that cures the rage of steeds. And the shapely oar, apt to men's hands, hath a wondrous speed on the brine, following the hundred-footed Nereids . . . O land that art praised above all lands, now is it for thee to make those bright praises seen in deeds."

He stopped, tentatively, and lowered the heavy book.

"No — as I thought — there is certainly no superficial sign of eyestrain."

Silence thronged the room, and he was aware of the focused scrutiny of the three people who confronted him . . .

"We could have his eyes examined — but I believe it is something else."

"What could it be?" That was his father's voice.

"It's only this curious absent-mindedness —" This was his mother's voice.

In the presence of the doctor, they both seemed irritatingly apologetic.

"I believe it is something else. Now Paul — I would like very much to ask you a question or two. You will answer them, won't you — you know I'm an old, old friend of yours, eh? That's right! . . ."

His back was thumped twice by the doctor's fat fist — then the doctor was grinning at him with false amiability, while with one fingernail he was scratching the top button of his waistcoat. Beyond the doctor's shoulder was the fire, the fingers of flame making light presti-digitation against the sooty fireback, the soft sound of their random flutter the only sound.

"I would like to know — is there anything that worries you?"

The doctor was again smiling, his eyelids low against the little black pupils, in each of which was a tiny white bead of light. Why answer him? why answer him at all? "At whatever pain to others" — but it was all a nuisance, this necessity for resistance, this necessity for attention; it was as if one had been stood up on a brilliantly lighted stage, under a great round blaze of spotlight; as if one were merely a trained seal, or a performing dog, or a fish, dipped out of an aquarium and held up by the tail. It would serve them right if he were merely to bark or growl. And meanwhile, to miss these last few precious hours, these hours of which each minute was more beautiful than the last, more menacing — ! He still looked, as if from a great distance, at the beads of light in the doctor's eyes, at the fixed false smile, and then, beyond, once more at his mother's slippers, his father's slippers, the soft flutter of the fire. Even here, even amongst these hostile presences, and in this arranged light, he could see the snow, he could hear it — it was in the corners of the room, where the shadow was deepest, under the sofa, behind the half-opened door which led to the dining room. It was gentler here, softer, its seethe the quietest of whispers, as if, in deference to a drawing room, it had quite deliberately put on its "manners"; it kept itself out of sight, oblit-erated itself, but distinctly with an air of saying, "Ah, but just wait! Wait till we are alone together! Then I will begin to tell you something new! Something white! something cold! something sleepy! something of cease, and peace, and the long bright curve of space! Tell them to go away. Banish them. Refuse to speak. Leave them, go upstairs to your room, turn out the light and get into bed — I will go with you, I will be waiting for you, I will tell you a better story than Little Kay of the Skates, or The Snow Ghost — I will surround your bed, I will close the windows, pile a deep drift against the door, so that none will ever again be able to enter. Speak to them! . . ." It seemed as if the little hissing voice came from a slow white spiral of falling flakes in the corner by the front window — but he could not be sure. He felt himself smiling, then, and said to the doctor, but without looking at him, looking beyond him still —

"Oh no, I think not —"

"But are you sure, my boy?"

His father's voice came softly and coldly then — the familiar voice of silken warning.

"You needn't answer at once, Paul — remember we're trying to help you — think it over and be quite sure, won't you?"

He felt himself smiling again, at the notion of being quite sure. What a joke! As if he weren't so sure that reassurance was no longer necessary, and all this cross-examination a ridiculous farce, a grotesque parody! What could they know about it? these gross intelligences, these humdrum minds so bound to the usual, the ordinary? Impossible to tell them about it! Why, even now, even now, with the proof so abundant, so formidable, so imminent, so appallingly present here in this very room, could they believe it? — could even his mother believe it? No — it was only too plain that if anything were said about it, the merest hint given, they would be incredulous — they would laugh — they would say "Absurd!" — think things about him which weren't true . . .

"Why no, I'm not worried — why should I be?"

He looked then straight at the doctor's low-lidded eyes, looked from one of them to the other, from one bead of light to the other, and gave a little laugh.

The doctor seemed to be disconcerted by this. He drew back in his chair, resting a fat white hand on either knee. The smile faded slowly from his face.

"Well, Paul!" he said, and paused gravely, "I'm afraid you don't take this quite seriously enough. I think you perhaps don't quite realize — don't quite realize —" He took a deep quick breath and turned, as if helplessly, at a loss for words, to the others. But Mother and Father were both silent — no help was forthcoming.

"You must surely know, be aware, that you have not been quite yourself, of late? Don't you know that? . . ."

It was amusing to watch the doctor's renewed attempt at a smile, a queer disorganized look, as of confidential embarrassment.

"I feel all right, sir," he said, and again gave the little laugh.

"And we're trying to help you." The doctor's tone sharpened.

"Yes, sir, I know. But why? I'm all right. I'm just *thinking*, that's all."

His mother made a quick movement forward, resting a hand on the back of the doctor's chair.

"Thinking?" she said. "But my dear, about what?"

This was a direct challenge — and would have to be directly met. But before he met it, he looked again into the corner by the door, as if for reassurance. He smiled again at what he saw, at what he heard. The little spiral was still there, still softly whirling, like the ghost of a white kitten chasing the ghost of a white tail, and making as it did so the faintest of whispers. It was all right! If only he could remain firm, everything was going to be all right.

"Oh, about anything, about nothing — you know the way you do!"

"You mean — daydreaming?"

"Oh, no — thinking!"

"But thinking about *what?*"

"Anything."

He laughed a third time — but this time, happening to glance upward toward his mother's face, he was appalled at the effect his laughter seemed to have upon her. Her mouth had opened in an expression of horror . . . This was too bad! Unfortunate! He had known it would cause pain, of course — but he hadn't expected it to be quite so bad as this. Perhaps — perhaps if he just gave them a tiny gleaming hint —?

"About the snow," he said.

"What on earth?" This was his father's voice. The brown slippers came a step nearer on the hearth-rug.

"But my dear, what do you mean?" This was his mother's voice. The doctor merely stared.

"Just *snow*, that's all. I like to think about it."

"Tell us about it, my boy."

"But that's all it is. There's nothing to tell. *You* know what snow is?"

This he said almost angrily, for he felt that they were trying to corner him. He turned sideways so as no longer to face the doctor, and the better to see the inch of blackness between the window-sill and the lowered curtain — the cold inch of beckoning and delicious night. At once he felt better, more assured.

"Mother — can I go to bed, now, please? I've got a headache."

"But I thought you said —"

"It's just come. It's all these questions — ! Can I, mother?"

"You can go as soon as the doctor has finished."

"Don't you think this thing ought to be gone into thoroughly, and *now?*" This was Father's voice. The brown slippers again came a step nearer, the voice was the well-known "punishment" voice, resonant and cruel.

"Oh, what's the use, Norman —"

Quite suddenly, everyone was silent. And without precisely facing them, nevertheless he was aware that all three of them were watching him with an extraordinary intensity — staring hard at him — as if he had done something monstrous, or was himself some kind of monster. He could hear the soft irregular flutter of the flames, the cluck-click-cluck-click of the clock; far and faint, two sudden spurts of laughter from the kitchen, as quickly cut off as begun; a murmur of water in the pipes; and then, the silence seemed to deepen, to spread out, to become world-long and world-wide, to become timeless and shapeless, and to center inevitably and rightly, with a slow and sleepy but enormous concentration of all power, on the beginning of a new sound. What this new sound was going to be, he knew perfectly well. It might begin with a hiss, but it would end with a roar — there was no time to lose — he must escape. It mustn't happen here —

Without another word, he turned and ran up the stairs.


## IV

Not a moment too soon. The darkness was coming in long white waves. A prolonged sibilance filled the night — a great seamless seethe of wild influence went abruptly across it — a cold low humming shook the windows. He shut the door and flung off his clothes in the dark. The bare black floor was like a little raft tossed in waves of snow, almost overwhelmed, washed under whitely, up again, smothered in curled billows of feather. The snow was laughing; it spoke from all sides at once; it pressed closer to him as he ran and jumped exulting into his bed.

"Listen to us!" it said. "Listen! We have come to tell you the story we told you about. You remember? Lie down. Shut your eyes, now — you will no longer see much — in this white darkness who could see, or want to see? We will take the place of everything . . . Listen —"

A beautiful varying dance of snow began at the front of the room, came forward and then retreated, flattened out toward the floor, then rose fountain-like to the ceiling, swayed, recruited itself from a new stream of flakes which poured laughing in through the humming window, advanced again, lifted long white arms. It said peace, it said remoteness, it said cold — it said —

But then a gash of horrible light fell brutally across the room from the opening door — the snow drew back hissing — something alien had come into the room — something hostile. This thing rushed at him, clutched at him, shook him — and he was not merely horrified, he was filled with such a loathing as he had never known. What was this? this cruel disturbance? this act of anger and hate? It was as if he had to reach up a hand toward another world for any understanding of it — an effort of which he was only barely capable. But of that other world he still remembered just enough to know the exorcising words. They tore themselves from his other life suddenly —

"Mother! Mother! Go away! I hate you!"

And with that effort, everything was solved, everything became all right: the seamless hiss advanced once more, the long white wavering lines rose and fell like enormous whispering sea-waves, the whisper becoming louder, the laughter more numerous.

"Listen!" it said. "We'll tell you the last, the most beautiful and secret story — shut your eyes — it is a very small story — a story that gets smaller and smaller — it comes inward instead of opening like a flower — it is a flower becoming a seed — a little cold seed — do you hear? we are leaning closer to you —"

This hiss was now becoming a roar — the whole world was a vast moving screen of snow — but even now it said peace, it said remoteness, it said cold, it said sleep.

# William Faulkner (1897–1962)

A TOWERING FIGURE in American literature, William Faulkner was born in New Albany, Mississippi, and grew up in Oxford, Mississippi, in the heart of the region he made famous as "Yoknapatawpha County." He was the great-grandson of William Faulkner, army officer, railroad builder, and author of a tremendously popular novel, *The White Rose of Memphis*. His education was irregular. Turned down as too small by the United States Army in the First World War, he joined the British Royal Air Force but saw no action. After publishing a book of poems, *The Marble Faun* (1924), he became a newspaperman in New Orleans and a close friend of Sherwood Anderson, who helped him publish his first novel, *Soldier's Pay* (1926). There followed a long series of distinguished novels, short stories, and poems. In 1950 when he received the Nobel Award he spoke the memorable words, "I decline to accept the end of man . . . I believe that man will not merely endure: he will prevail. He is immortal not because he alone among creatures has an inexhaustible voice but because he has a soul, a spirit capable of compassion and sacrifice and endurance. The poet's, the writer's duty, is to write about these things."

Originally called "The Unvanquished," the story reprinted here is one of Faulkner's earlier stories and was combined with others to make a Civil War novel of that title. Its period was a terrible time for the South, immediately after the Civil War when Reconstruction was beginning, carpetbaggers were scavenging, and memory of the cruel and bloody conflict still tortured the survivors. In its recreation of the atmosphere of the times and the distraught reactions of the people, "An Odor of Verbena" is one of Faulkner's finest achievements in the short-story form.

# An Odor of Verbena

IT WAS just after supper. I had just opened my *Coke* on the table beneath the lamp; I heard Professor Wilkins' feet in the hall and then the instant of silence as he put his hand to the door knob, and I should have known. People talk glibly of presentiment, but I had none. I heard his feet on the stairs and then in the hall approaching and there was nothing in the feet because although I had lived in his house for three college years now and although both he and Mrs. Wilkins called me Bayard in the house, he would no more have entered my room without knocking than I would have entered his — or hers. Then he flung the door violently inward against the doorstop with one of those gestures with or by which an almost painfully unflagging preceptory of youth ultimately aberrates, and stood there saying, "Bayard. Bayard, my son, my dear son."

I should have known; I should have been prepared. Or maybe I was prepared because I remember how I closed the book carefully, even marking the place, before I rose. He (Professor Wilkins) was doing something, bustling at something; it was my hat and cloak which he handed me and which I took although I would not need the cloak, unless even then I was thinking (although it was October, the equinox had not occurred) that the rains and the cool weather would arrive before I should see this room again and so I would need the cloak anyway to return to it if I returned, thinking "God, if he had only done this last night, flung that door crashing and bouncing against the stop last night, without knocking so I could have gotten there before it happened, been there when it did, beside him on whatever spot, wherever it was that he would have to fall and lie in the dust and dirt."

"Your boy is downstairs in the kitchen," he said. It was not until years later that he told me (someone did; it must have been Judge Wilkins) how Ringo had apparently flung the cook aside and come on into the house and into the library where he and Mrs. Wilkins were sitting and said without preamble and already turning to withdraw: "They shot Colonel Sartoris this morning. Tell him I be waiting in the kitchen" and was gone before either of them could move. "He had ridden forty miles yet he refuses to eat anything." We were moving toward the door now — the door on my side of which I had lived for three years now with what I knew, what I knew now I must have believed and expected, yet beyond which I had heard the approaching feet yet heard nothing in the feet. "If there was just anything I could do."

"Yes, sir," I said. "A fresh horse for my boy. He will want to go back with me."

"By all means take mine — Mrs. Wilkins'," he cried. His tone was no different yet he did cry it and I suppose that at the same moment we both realised that was funny — a short-legged deep-barreled mare who looked exactly like a spinster music teacher, which Mrs. Wilkins drove to a basket phaeton — which was good for me, like being doused with a pail of cold water would have been good for me.

"Thank you, sir," I said. "We won't need it. I will get a fresh horse for him at the livery stable when I get my mare." Good for me, because even before I finished speaking I knew that would not be necessary either, that Ringo would have stopped at the livery stable before he came out to the college and attended to that and that the fresh horse for him and my mare both would be saddled and waiting now at the side fence and we would not have to go through Oxford at all. Loosh would not have thought of that if he had come for me, he would have come straight to the college, to Professor Wilkins', and told his news and then sat down and let me take charge from then on. But not Ringo.

He followed me from the room. From now until Ringo and I rode away into the hot thick dusty darkness quick and strained for the over-due equinox like a laboring delayed woman, he would be somewhere either just beside me or just behind me and I never to know exactly nor care which. He was trying to find the words with which to offer me his pistol too. I could almost hear him: "Ah, this unhappy land, not ten years recovered from the fever yet still men must kill one another, still we must pay Cain's price in his own coin." But he did not actually say it. He just followed me, somewhere beside or behind me as we descended the stairs toward where Mrs. Wilkins waited in the hall beneath the chandelier — a thin gray woman who reminded me of Granny, not that she looked like Granny probably but because she had known Granny — a lifted anxious still face which was thinking *Who lives by the sword shall die by it* just as Granny would have thought, toward which I walked, had to walk not because I was Granny's grandson and had lived in her house for three college years and was about the age of her son when he was killed in almost the last battle nine years ago, but because I was now The Sartoris. (The Sartoris: that had been one of the concomitant flashes, along with the *at last it has happened* when Professor Wilkins opened my door.) She didn't offer me a horse and pistol, not because she liked me any less than Professor Wilkins but because she was a woman and so wiser than any man, else the men would not have gone on with the War for two years after they knew they were whipped. She just put her hands (a small woman, no bigger than Granny had been) on my shoulders and said, "Give my love to Drusilla and your Aunt Jenny. And come back when you can."

"Only I don't know when that will be," I said. "I don't know how many things I will have to attend to." Yes, I lied even to her; it had not been but a minute yet since he had flung that door bouncing into the stop yet already I was beginning to realize, to become aware of that which I still had no yardstick to measure save that one consisting of what, despite myself, despite my raising and background (or maybe because of them) I had for some time known I was becoming and had feared the test of it; I remember how I thought while her hands still rested on my shoulders: *At least this will be my chance to find out if I am what I think I am or if I just hope; if I am going to do what I have taught myself is right or if I am just going to wish I were.*

We went on to the kitchen, Professor Wilkins still somewhere beside me or behind me and still offering me the pistol and horse in a dozen different ways. Ringo was waiting; I remember how I thought then that no matter what might happen to either of us, I would never be The Sartoris to him. He was twenty-four too, but in a way he had changed even less than I had since that day when we had nailed Grumby's body to the door of the old compress. Maybe it was because he had outgrown me, had changed so much that summer while he and Granny traded mules with the Yankees that since then I had had to do most of the changing just to catch up with him. He was sitting quietly in a chair beside the cold stove, spent-looking too who had ridden forty miles (at one time, either in Jefferson or when he was alone at last on the road somewhere, he had cried; dust was now caked and dried in the tear-channels on his face) and would ride forty more yet would not eat, looking up at me a little red-eyed with weariness (or maybe it was more than just weariness and so I would never catch up with him) then rising without a word and going on toward the door and I following and Professor Wilkins still offering the horse and the pistol without speaking the words and still thinking (I could feel that too) *Dies by the sword. Dies by the sword.*

Ringo had the two horses saddled at the side gate, as I had known he would — the fresh one for himself and my mare father had given me three years ago, that could do a mile under two minutes any day and a mile every eight minutes all day long. He was already mounted when I realised that what Professor Wilkins wanted was to shake my hand. We shook hands; I knew he believed he was touching flesh which might not be alive tomorrow night and I thought for a second how if I told him what I was going to do, since we had talked about it, about how if there was anything at all in the Book, anything of hope and peace for His blind and bewildered spawn which He had chosen above all others to offer immortality, *Thou shalt not kill* must be it, since maybe he even believed that he had taught it to me except that he had not, nobody had, not even myself since it went further than just having been learned. But I did not tell him. He was too old to be forced so, to condone even in principle such a decision; he was too old to have to stick to principle in the face of blood and raising and background, to be faced without warning and made to deliver like by a highwayman out of the dark: only the young could do that — one still young enough to have his youth supplied him gratis as a reason (not an excuse) for cowardice.

So I said nothing. I just shook his hand and mounted too, and Ringo and I rode on. We would not have to pass through Oxford now and so soon (there was a thin sickle of moon like the heel print of a boot in wet sand) the road to Jefferson lay before us, the road which I had travelled for the first time three years ago with Father and travelled twice at Christmas time and then in June and September and twice at Christmas time again and then June and September again each college term since alone on the mare, not even knowing that this was peace; and now this time and maybe last time who would not die (I knew that) but who maybe forever after could never again hold up his head. The horses took the gait which they would hold for forty miles. My mare knew the long road ahead and Ringo had a good beast too, had talked Hilliard at the livery stable out of a good horse too. Maybe it was the tears, the channels of dried mud across which his strain-reddened eyes had looked at me, but I rather think it was that same quality which used to enable him to replenish his and Granny's supply of United States Army letterheads during that time — some outrageous assurance gained from too long and too close association with white people: the one whom he called Granny, the other with whom he had slept from the time we were born until Father rebuilt the house. We spoke one time, then no more:

"We could bushwhack him," he said. "Like we done Grumby that day. But I reckon that wouldn't suit that white skin you walks around in."

"No," I said. We rode on; it was October; there was plenty of time still for verbena although I would have to reach home before I would realise there was a need for it; plenty of time for verbena yet from the garden where Aunt Jenny puttered beside old Joby, in a pair of Father's old cavalry gauntlets, among the coaxed and ordered beds, the quaint and odorous old names, for though it was October no rain had come yet and hence no frost to bring (or leave behind) the first half-warm half-chill nights of Indian Summer — the drowsing air cool and empty for geese yet languid still with the old hot dusty smell of fox grape and sassafras — the nights when before I became a man and went to college to learn law Ringo and I, with lantern and axe and crokersack and six dogs (one to follow the trail and five more just for the tonguing, the music) would hunt possum in the pasture where, hidden, we had seen our first Yankee that afternoon on the bright horse, where for the last year now you could hear the whistling of the trains which had no longer belonged to Mr. Redmond for a long while now and which at some instant, some second during the morning Father too had relinquished along with the pipe which Ringo said he was smoking, which slipped from his hand as he fell. We rode on, toward the house where he would be lying in the parlor now, in his regimentals (sabre too) and where Drusilla would be waiting for me beneath all the festive glitter of the chandeliers, in the yellow ball gown and the sprig of verbena in her hair, holding the two loaded pistols (I could see that too, who had had no presentiment; I could see her, in the formal brilliant room arranged formally for obsequy, not tall, not slender as a woman is but as a youth, a boy, is motionless, in yellow, the face calm, almost bemused, the head simple and severe, the balancing sprig of verbena above each ear, the two arms bent at the elbows, the two hands shoulder high, the two identical duelling pistols lying up, not clutched in, one to each: the Greek amphora priestess of a succinct and formal violence).

## II

Drusilla said that he had a dream. I was twenty then and she and I would walk in the garden in the summer twilight while we waited for Father to ride in from the railroad. I was twenty then: that summer before I entered the University to take the law degree which Father decided I should have and four years after the one, the day, the evening when Father and Drusilla had kept old Cash Benbow from becoming United States Marshal and returned home still unmarried and Mrs. Habersham herded them into her carriage and drove them back to town and dug her husband out of his little dim hole in the new bank and made him sign Father's peace bond for killing the two carpet baggers, and took Father and Drusilla to the minister herself and saw that they were married. And Father had rebuilt the house too, on the same blackened spot, over the same cellar, where the other had burned, only larger, much larger: Drusilla said that the house was the aura of Father's dream just as a bride's trousseau and veil is the aura of hers. And Aunt Jenny had come to live with us now so we had the garden (Drusilla would no more have bothered with flowers than Father himself would have, who even now, even four years after it was over, still seemed to exist, breathe, in that last year of it while she had ridden in man's clothes and with her hair cut short like any other member of Father's troop, across Georgia and both Carolinas in front of Sherman's army) for her to gather sprigs of verbena from to wear in her hair because she said verbena was the only scent you could smell above the smell of horses and courage and so it was the only one that was worth wearing. The railroad was hardly begun then and Father and Mr. Redmond were not only still partners, they were still friends, which as George Wyatt said was easily a record for Father, and he would leave the house at daybreak on Jupiter, riding up and down the unfinished line with two saddlebags of gold coins borrowed on Friday to pay the men on Saturday, keeping just two cross-ties ahead of the sheriff as Aunt Jenny said. So we walked in the dusk, slowly between Aunt Jenny's flower beds while Drusilla (in a dress now, who still would have worn pants all the time if Father had let her) leaned lightly on my arm and I smelled the verbena in her hair as I had smelled the rain in it and in Father's beard that night four years ago when he and Drusilla and Uncle Buck McCaslin found Grumby and then came home and found Ringo and me more than just asleep: escaped into that oblivion which God or Nature or whoever it was had supplied us with for the time being, who had had to perform more than should be required of children because there should be some limit to the age, the youth at least below which one should not have to kill. This was just after the Saturday night when he returned and I watched him clean the derringer and reload it and we learned that the dead man was almost a neighbor, a hill man who had been in the first infantry regiment when it voted Father out of command: and we never to know if the man actually intended to rob Father or not because Father had shot too quick, but only that he had a wife and several children in a dirt-floored cabin in the hills, to whom Father the next day sent some money and she (the wife) walked into the house two days later while we were sitting at the dinner table and flung the money at Father's face.

"But nobody could have more of a dream than Colonel Sutpen," I said. He had been Father's second-in-command in the first regiment and had been elected colonel when the regiment deposed Father after Second Manassas, and it was Sutpen and not the regiment whom Father never forgave. He was underbred, a cold ruthless man who had come into the country about thirty years before the War, nobody knew from where except Father said you could look at him and know he would not dare to tell. He had got some land and nobody knew how he did that either, and he got money from somewhere — Father said they all believed he robbed steamboats, either as a card sharper or as an out-and-out highwayman — and built a big house and married and set up as a gentleman. Then he lost everything in the War like everybody else, all hope of descendants too (his son killed his daughter's fiancé on the eve of the wedding and vanished) yet he came back home and set out singlehanded to rebuild the plantation. He had no friends to borrow from and he had nobody to leave it to and he was past sixty years old, yet he set out to rebuild the place like it used to be; they told how he was too busy to bother with politics or anything; how when Father and the other men organised the nightriders to keep the carpet baggers from organising the Negroes into an insurrection, he refused to have anything to do with it. Father stopped hating him long enough to ride out to see Sutpen himself and he (Sutpen) came to the door with a lamp and did not even invite them to come in and discuss it; Father said, "Are you with us or against us?" and he said, "I'm for my land. If every man of you would rehabilitate his own land, the country will take care of itself" and Father challenged him to bring the lamp out and set it on a stump where they could both see to shoot and Sutpen would not. "Nobody could have more of a dream than that."

"Yes. But his dream is just Sutpen. John's is not. He is thinking of this whole country which he is trying to raise by its bootstraps, so that all the people in it, not just his kind nor his old regiment, but all the people, black and white, the women and children back in the hills who don't even own shoes — Don't you see?"

"But how can they get any good from what he wants to do for them if they are — after he has —"

"Killed some of them? I suppose you include those two carpet baggers he had to kill to hold that first election, don't you?"

"They were men. Human beings."

"They were Northerners, foreigners who had no business here. They were pirates." We walked on, her weight hardly discernible on my arm, her head just reaching my shoulder. I had always been a little taller than she, even on that night at Hawkhurst while we listened to the niggers passing in the road, and she had changed but little since — the same boy-hard body, the close implacable head with its savagely cropped hair which I had watched from the wagon above the tide of crazed singing niggers as we went down into the river — the body not slender as women are but as boys are slender. "A dream is not a very safe thing to be near, Bayard. I know; I had one once. It's like a loaded pistol with a hair trigger: if it stays alive long enough, somebody is going to be hurt. But if it's a good dream, it's worth it. There are not many dreams in the world, but there are a lot of human lives. And one human life or two dozen —"

"Are not worth anything?"

"No. Not anything — Listen. I hear Jupiter. I'll beat you to the house." She was already running, the skirts she did not like to wear lifted almost to her knees, her legs beneath it running as boys run just as she rode like men ride.

I was twenty then. But the next time I was twenty-four; I had been three years at the University and in another two weeks I would ride back to Oxford for the final year and my degree. It was just last summer, last August, and Father had just beat Redmond for the State legislature. The railroad was finished now and the partnership between Father and Redmond had been dissolved so long ago that most people would have forgotten they were ever partners if it hadn't been for the enmity between them. There had been a third partner but nobody hardly remembered his name now; he and his name both had vanished in the fury of the conflict which set up between Father and Redmond almost before they began to lay the rails, between Father's violent and ruthless dictatorialness and will to dominate (the idea was his; he did think of the railroad first and then took Redmond in) and that quality in Redmond (as George Wyatt said, he was not a coward or Father would never have teamed with him) which permitted him to stand as much as he did from Father, to bear and bear and bear until something (not his will nor his courage) broke in him. During the War Redmond had not been a soldier, he had had something to do with cotton for the Government; he could have made money himself out of it but he had not and everybody knew he had not, Father knew it, yet Father would even taunt him with not having smelled powder. He was wrong; he knew he was when it was too late for him to stop just as a drunkard reaches a point where it is too late for him to stop, where he promises himself that he will and maybe believes he will or can but it is too late. Finally they reached the point (they had both put everything they could mortgage or borrow into it for Father to ride up and down the line, paying the workmen and the waybills on the rails at the last possible instant) where even Father realised that one of them would have to get out. So (they were not speaking then; it was arranged by Judge Benbow) they met and agreed to buy or sell, naming a price which, in reference to what they had put into it, was ridiculously low but which each believed the other could not raise — at least Father claimed that Redmond did not believe he could raise it. So Redmond accepted the price, and found out that Father had the money. And according to Father, that's what started it, although Uncle Buck McCaslin said Father could not have owned a half interest in even one hog, let alone a railroad, and not dissolve the business either sworn enemy or death-pledged friend to his recent partner. So they parted and Father finished the road. By that time, seeing that he was going to finish it, some Northern people sold him a locomotive on credit which he named for Aunt Jenny, with a silver oil can in the cab with her name engraved on it; and last summer the first train ran into Jefferson, the engine decorated with flowers and Father in the cab blowing blast after blast on the whistle when he passed Redmond's house; and there were speeches at the station, with more flowers and a Confederate flag and girls in white dresses and red sashes and a band, and Father stood on the pilot of the engine and made a direct and absolutely needless allusion to Mr. Redmond. That was it. He wouldn't let him alone. George Wyatt came to me right afterward and told me. "Right or wrong," he said, "us boys and most of the other folks in this county know John's right. But he ought to let Redmond alone. I know what's wrong: he's had to kill too many folks, and that's bad for a man. We all know Colonel's brave as a lion, but Redmond ain't no coward either and there ain't any use in making a brave man that made one mistake eat crow all the time. Can't you talk to him?"

"I don't know," I said. "I'll try." But I had no chance. That is, I could have talked to him and he would have listened, but he could not have heard me because he had stepped straight from the pilot of that engine into the race for the legislature. Maybe he knew that Redmond would have to oppose him to save his face even though he (Redmond) must have known that, after that train ran into Jefferson, he had no chance against Father, or maybe Redmond had already announced his candidacy and Father entered the race just because of that, I don't remember. Anyway they ran, a bitter contest in which Father continued to badger

Redmond without reason or need, since they both knew it would be a landslide for Father. And it was, and we thought he was satisfied. Maybe he thought so himself, as the drunkard believes that he is done with drink; and it was that afternoon and Drusilla and I walked in the garden in the twilight and I said something about what George Wyatt had told me and she released my arm and turned me to face her and said, "This from you? You? Have you forgotten Grumby?"

"No," I said. "I never will forget him."

"You never will. I wouldn't let you. There are worse things than killing men, Bayard. There are worse things than being killed. Sometimes I think the finest thing that can happen to a man is to love something, a woman preferably, well, hard hard hard, then to die young because he believed what he could not help but believe and was what he could not (could not? would not) help but be." Now she was looking at me in a way she never had before. I did not know what it meant then and was not to know until tonight since neither of us knew then that two months later Father would be dead. I just knew that she was looking at me as she never had before and that the scent of the verbena in her hair seemed to have increased a hundred times, to have got a hundred times stronger, to be everywhere in the dusk in which something was about to happen which I had never dreamed of. Then she spoke. "Kiss me, Bayard."

"No. You are Father's wife."

"And eight years older than you are. And your fourth cousin too. And I have black hair. Kiss me, Bayard."

"No."

"Kiss me, Bayard." So I leaned my face down to her. But she didn't move, standing so, bent lightly back from me from the waist, looking at me; now it was she who said, "No." So I put my arms around her. Then she came to me, melted as women will and can, the arms with the wrist- and elbow-power to control horses about my shoulders, using the wrists to hold my face to hers until there was no longer need for the wrists; I thought then of the woman of thirty, the symbol of the ancient and eternal Snake and of the men who have written of her, and I realised then the immitigable chasm between all life and all print — that those who can, do, those who cannot and suffer enough because they can't, write about it. Then I was free, I could see her again, I saw her still watching me with that dark inscrutable look, looking up at me now across her down-slanted face; I watched her arms rise with almost the exact gesture with which she had put them around me as if she were repeating the empty and formal gesture of all promises so that I should never forget it, the elbows angling outward as she put her hands to the sprig of verbena in her hair, I standing straight and rigid facing the slightly bent head, the short jagged hair, the rigid curiously formal angle of the bare arms gleaming faintly in the last of light as she removed the verbena sprig and put it into my lapel, and I thought how the War had tried to stamp all the women of her generation and class in the South into a type and how it had failed — the suffering, the identical experience (hers and Aunt Jenny's had been almost the same except that Aunt Jenny had spent a few nights with her husband and before they brought him back home in an ammunition wagon while Gavin Breckbridge was just Drusilla's fiancé) was there in the eyes, yet beyond that was the incorrigibly individual woman: not like so many men who return from wars to live on Government reservations like so many steers, emasculate and empty of all save an identical experience which they cannot forget and dare not, else they would cease to live at that moment, almost interchangeable save for the old habit of answering to a given name.

"Now I must tell Father," I said.

"Yes," she said. "You must tell him. Kiss me." So again it was like it had been before. No. Twice, a thousand times and never like — the eternal and symbolical thirty to a young man, a youth, each time both cumulative and retroactive, immitigably unrepetitive, each wherein remembering excludes experience, each wherein experience antedates remembering; the skill without weariness, the knowledge virginal to surfeit, the cunning secret muscles to guide and control just as within the wrists and elbows lay slumbering the mastery of horses: she stood back, already turning, not looking at me when she spoke, never having looked at me, already moving swiftly on in the dusk: "Tell John. Tell him tonight."

I intended to. I went to the house and into the office at once; I went to the center of the rug before the cold hearth, I don't know why, and stood there rigid like soldiers stand, looking at eye level straight across the room and above his head and said "Father" and then stopped. Because he did not even hear me. He said, "Yes, Bayard?" but he did not hear me although he was sitting behind the desk doing nothing, immobile, as still as I was rigid, one hand on the desk with a dead cigar in it, a bottle of brandy and a filled and untasted glass beside his hand, clothed quiet and bemused in whatever triumph it was he felt since the last overwhelming return of votes had come in late in the afternoon. So I waited until after supper. We went to the diningroom and stood side by side until Aunt Jenny entered and then Drusilla, in the yellow ball gown, who walked straight to me and gave me one fierce inscrutable look then went to her place and waited for me to draw her chair while Father drew Aunt Jenny's. He had roused by then, not to talk himself but rather to sit at the head of the table and reply to Drusilla as she talked with a sort of feverish and glittering volubility — to reply now and then to her with that courteous intolerant pride which had lately become a little forensic, as if merely being in a political contest filled with fierce and empty oratory had retroactively made a lawyer of him who was anything and everything except a lawyer. Then Drusilla and Aunt Jenny rose and left us and he said, "Wait" to me who had made no move to follow and directed Joby to bring one of the bottles of wine which he had fetched back from New Orleans when he went there last to borrow money to liquidate his first private railroad bonds. Then I stood again like soldiers stand, gazing at eye level above his head while he sat half-turned from the table, a little paunchy now though not much, a little grizzled too in the hair though his beard was as strong as ever, with that spurious forensic air of lawyers and the intolerant eyes which in the last two years had acquired that transparent film which the eyes of carnivorous animals have and from behind which they look at a world which no ruminant ever sees, perhaps dares to see, which I have seen before on the eyes of men who have killed too much, who have killed so much that never again as long as they live will they ever be alone. I said again, "Father," then I told him.

"Hah?" he said. "Sit down." I sat down, I looked at him, watched him fill both glasses and this time I knew it was worse with him than not hearing: it didn't even matter. "You are doing well in the law, Judge Wilkins tells me. I am pleased to hear that. I have not needed you in my affairs so far, but from now on I shall. I have now accomplished the active portion of my aims in which you could not have helped me; I acted as the land and the time demanded and you were too young for that, I wished to shield you. But now the land and the time too are changing; what will follow will be a matter of consolidation, of pettifogging and doubtless chicanery in which I would be a babe in arms but in which you, trained in the law, can hold your own — our own. Yes, I have accomplished my aim, and now I shall do a little moral housecleaning. I am tired of killing men, no matter what the necessity nor the end. Tomorrow, when I go to town and meet Ben Redmond, I shall be unarmed."


### III

We reached home just before midnight; we didn't have to pass through Jefferson either. Before we turned in the gates I could see the lights, the chandeliers — hall, parlor, and what Aunt Jenny (without any effort or perhaps even design on her part) had taught even Ringo to call the drawing room, the light falling outward across the portico, past the columns. Then I saw the horses, the faint shine of leather and buckle-glints on the black silhouettes and then the men too — Wyatt and others of Father's old troop — and I had forgot that they would be there. I had forgot that they would be there; I remember how I thought, since I was tired and spent with strain, *Now it will have to begin tonight. I won't even have until tomorrow in which to begin to resist.* They had a watchman, a picquet out, I suppose, because they seemed to know at once that we were in the drive. Wyatt met me, I halted the mare, I could look down at him and at the others gathered a few yards behind him with that curious vulture-like formality which Southern men assume in such situations.

"Well, boy," George said.

"Was it —" I said. "Was he —"

"It was all right. It was in front. Redmond ain't no coward. John had the derringer inside his cuff like always, but he never touched it, never made a move toward it." I have seen him do it, he showed me once: the pistol (it was not four inches long) held flat inside his left wrist by a clip he made himself of wire and an old clock spring; he would raise both hands at the same time, cross them, fire the pistol from beneath his left hand almost as if he were hiding from his own vision what he was doing; when he killed one of the men he shot a hole through his own coat sleeve. "But you want to get on to the house," Wyatt said. He began to stand aside, then he spoke again: "We'll take this off your hands, any of us. Me." I hadn't moved the mare yet and I had made no move to speak, yet he continued quickly, as if he had already rehearsed all this, his speech and mine, and knew what I would say and only spoke himself as he would have removed his hat on entering a house or used "sir" in conversing with a stranger: "You're young, just a boy, you ain't had any experience in this kind of thing. Besides, you got them two ladies in the house to think about. He would understand, all right."

"I reckon I can attend to it," I said.

"Sure," he said; there was no surprise, nothing at all, in his voice because he had already rehearsed this: "I reckon we all knew that's what you would say." He stepped back then; almost it was as though he and not I bade the mare to move on. But they all followed, still with that unctuous and voracious formality. Then I saw Drusilla standing at the top of the front steps, in the light from the open door and the windows like a theatre scene, in the yellow ball gown and even from here I believed that I could smell the verbena in her hair, standing there motionless yet emanating something louder than the two shots must have been — something voracious too and passionate. Then, although I had dismounted and someone had taken the mare, I seemed to be still in the saddle and to watch myself enter that scene which she had postulated like another actor while in the background for chorus Wyatt and the others stood with the unctuous formality which the Southern man shows in the presence of death — that Roman holiday engendered by mist-born Protestantism grafted onto this land of violent sun, of violent alteration from snow to heat-stroke which has produced a race impervious to both. I mounted the steps toward the figure straight and yellow and immobile as a candle which moved only to extend one hand; we stood together and looked down at them where they stood clumped, the horses too gathered in a tight group beyond them at the rim of light from the brilliant door and windows. One of them stamped and blew his breath and jangled his gear.

"Thank you, gentlemen," I said. "My aunt and my — Drusilla thank you. There's no need for you to stay. Goodnight." They murmured, turning. George Wyatt paused, looking back at me.

"Tomorrow?" he said.

"Tomorrow." Then they went on, carrying their hats and tiptoeing, even on the ground, the quiet and resilient earth, as though anyone in that house awake would try to sleep, anyone already asleep in it whom they could have awakened. Then they were gone and Drusilla and I turned and crossed the portico, her hand lying light on my wrist yet discharging into me with a shock like electricity that dark and passionate voracity, the face at my shoulder — the jagged hair with a verbena sprig above each ear, the eyes staring at me with that fierce exaltation. We entered the hall and crossed it, her hand guiding me without pressure, and entered the parlor. Then for the first time I realised it — the alteration which is death — not that he was now just clay but that he was lying down. But I didn't look at him yet because I knew that when I did I would begin to pant; I went to Aunt Jenny who had just risen from a chair behind which Louvinia stood. She was Father's sister, taller than Drusilla but no older, whose husband had been killed at the very beginning of the War, by a shell from a Federal frigate at Fort Moultrie, come to us from Carolina six years ago. Ringo and I went to Tennessee Junction in the wagon to meet her. It was January, cold and clear and with ice in the ruts; we returned just before dark with Aunt Jenny on the seat beside me holding a lace parasol and Ringo in the wagon bed nursing a hamper basket containing two bottles of old sherry and the two jasmine cuttings which were bushes in the garden now, and the panes of colored glass which she had salvaged from the Carolina house where she and Father and Uncle Bayard were born and which Father had set in a fanlight about one of the drawing room windows for her — who came up the drive and Father (home now from the railroad) went down the steps and lifted her from the wagon and said, "Well, Jenny," and she said, "Well, Johnny," and began to cry. She stood too, looking at me as I approached — the same hair, the same high nose, the same eyes as Father's except that they were intent and very wise instead of intolerant. She said nothing at all, she just kissed me, her hands light on my shoulders. Then Drusilla spoke, as if she had been waiting with a sort of dreadful patience for the empty ceremony to be done, in a voice like a bell: clear, unsentient, on a single pitch, silvery and triumphant: "Come, Bayard."

"Hadn't you better go to bed now?" Aunt Jenny said.

"Yes," Drusilla said in that silvery ecstatic voice, "Oh, yes. There will be plenty of time for sleep." I followed her, her hand again guiding me without pressure; now I looked at him. It was just as I had imagined it — sabre, plumes, and all — but with that alteration, that irrevocable difference which I had known to expect yet had not realised, as you can put food into your stomach which for a while the stomach declines to assimilate — the illimitable grief and regret as I looked down at the face which I knew — the nose, the hair, the eyelids closed over the intolerance — the face which I realised I now saw in repose for the first time in my life; the empty hands still now beneath the invisible stain of what had been (once, surely) needless blood, the hands now appearing clumsy in their very inertness, too clumsy to have performed the fatal actions which forever afterward he must have waked and slept with and maybe was glad to lay down at last — those curious appendages clumsily conceived to begin with yet with which man has taught himself to do so much, so much more than they were intended to do or could be forgiven for doing, which had now surrendered that life to which his intolerant heart had fiercely held; and then I knew that in a minute I would begin to pant. So Drusilla must have spoken twice before I heard her and turned and saw in the instant Aunt Jenny and Louvinia watching us, hearing Drusilla now, the unsentient bell quality gone now, her voice whispering into that quiet death-filled room with a passionate and dying fall: "Bayard." She faced me, she was quite near; again the scent of the verbena in her hair seemed to have increased a hundred times as she stood holding out to me, one in either hand, the two duelling pistols. "Take them, Bayard," she said, in the same tone in which she had said "Kiss me" last summer, already pressing them into my hands, watching me with that passionate and voracious exaltation, speaking in a voice fainting and passionate with promise: "Take them. I have kept them for you. I give them to you. Oh you will thank me, you will remember me who put into your hands what they say is an attribute only of God's, who took what belongs to heaven and gave it to you. Do you feel them? the long true barrels true as justice, the triggers (you have fired them) quick as retribution, the two of them slender and invincible and fatal as the physical shape of love?" Again I watched her arms angle out and upward as she removed the two verbena sprigs from her hair in two motions faster than the eye could follow, already putting one of them into my lapel and crushing the other in her other hand while she still spoke in that rapid passionate voice not much louder than a whisper: "There. One I give to you to wear tomorrow (it will not fade), the other I cast away, like this — " dropping the crushed bloom at her feet. "I abjure it. I abjure verbena forever more; I have smelled it above the odor of courage; that was all I wanted. Now let me look at you." She stood back, staring at me — the face tearless and exalted, the feverish eyes brilliant and voracious. "How beautiful you are: do you know it? How beautiful: young, to be permitted to kill, to be permitted vengeance, to take into your bare hands the fire of heaven that cast down Lucifer. No; I. I gave it to you; I put it into your hands; Oh you will thank me, you will remember me when I am dead and you are an old man saying to himself, 'I have tasted all things.' — It will be the right hand, won't it?" She moved; she had taken my right hand which still held one of the pistols before I knew what she was about to do; she had bent and kissed it before I comprehended why she took it. Then she stopped dead still, still stooping in that attitude of fierce exultant humility, her hot lips and her hot hands still touching my flesh, light on my flesh as dead leaves yet communicating to it that battery charge dark, passionate and damned forever of all peace. Because they are wise, women are — a touch, lips or fingers, and the knowledge, even clairvoyance, goes straight to the heart without bothering the laggard brain at all. She stood erect now, staring at me with intolerable and amazed incredulity which occupied her face alone for a whole minute while her eyes were completely empty; it seemed to me that I stood there for a full minute while Aunt Jenny and Louvinia watched us, waiting for her eyes to fill. There was no blood in her face at all, her mouth open a little and pale as one of those rubber rings women seal fruit jars with. Then her eyes filled with an expression of bitter and passionate betrayal. "Why, he's not —" she said. "He's not — And I kissed his hand," she said in an aghast whisper; "*I kissed his hand!*" beginning to laugh, the laughter, rising, becoming a scream yet still remaining laughter, screaming with laughter, trying herself to deaden the sound by putting her hand over her mouth, the laughter spilling between her fingers like vomit, the incredulous betrayed eyes still watching me across the hand.

"Louvinia!" Aunt Jenny said. They both came to her. Louvinia touched and held her and Drusilla turned her face to Louvinia.

"I kissed his hand, Louvinia!" she cried. "Did you see it? *I kissed his hand!*" the laughter rising again, becoming the scream again yet still remaining laughter, she still trying to hold it back with her hand like a small child who has filled its mouth too full.

"Take her upstairs," Aunt Jenny said. But they were already moving toward the door, Louvinia half-carrying Drusilla, the laughter diminishing as they neared the door as though it waited for the larger space of the empty and brilliant hall to rise again. Then it was gone; Aunt Jenny and I stood there and I knew soon that I would begin to pant. I could feel it beginning like you feel regurgitation beginning, as though there were not enough air in the room, the house, not enough air anywhere under the heavy hot low sky where the equinox couldn't seem to accomplish, nothing in the air for breathing, for the lungs. Now it was Aunt Jenny who said "Bayard" twice before I heard her. "You are not going to try to kill him. All right."

"All right?" I said.

"Yes. All right. Don't let it be Drusilla, a poor hysterical young woman. And don't let it be him, Bayard, because he's dead now. And don't let it be George Wyatt and those others who will be waiting for you tomorrow morning. I know you are not afraid."

"But what good will that do?" I said. "What good will that do?" It almost began then; I stopped it just in time. "I must live with myself, you see."

"Then it's not just Drusilla? Not just him? Not just George Wyatt and Jefferson?"

"No," I said.

"Will you promise to let me see you before you go to town tomorrow?" I looked at her; we looked at one another for a moment. Then she put her hands on my shoulders and kissed me and released me, all in one motion. "Goodnight, son," she said. Then she was gone too and now it could begin. I knew that in a minute I would look at him and it would begin and I did look at him, feeling the long-held breath, the hiatus before it started, thinking how maybe I should have said, "Goodbye, Father" but did not. Instead I crossed to the piano and laid the pistols carefully on it, still keeping the panting from getting too loud too soon. Then I was outside on the porch and (I don't know how long it had been) I looked in the window and saw Simon squatting on a stool beside him. Simon had been his body servant during the War and when they came home Simon had a uniform too — a Confederate private's coat with a Yankee brigadier's star on it and he had put it on now too, like they had dressed Father, squatting on the stool beside him, not crying, not weeping the facile tears which are the white man's futile trait and which Negroes know nothing about but just sitting there, motionless, his lower lip slacked down a little; he raised his hand and touched the coffin, the black hand rigid and fragile-looking as a clutch of dead twigs, then dropped the hand; once he turned his head and I saw his eyes roll red and unwinking in his skull like those of a cornered fox. It had begun by that time; I panted, standing there and this was it — the regret and grief, the despair out of which the tragic mute insensitive bones stand up that can bear anything, anything.

## IV

After a while the whippoorwills stopped and I heard the first day bird, a mockingbird. It had sung all night too but now it was the day song, no longer the drowsy moony fluting. Then they all began — the sparrows from the stable, the thrush that lived in Aunt Jenny's garden, and I heard a quail too from the pasture and now there was light in the room. But I' didn't move at once. I still lay on the bed (I hadn't undressed) with my hands under my head and the scent of Drusilla's verbena faint from where my coat lay on a chair, watching the light grow, watching it turn rosy with the sun. After a while I heard Louvinia come up across the back yard and go into the kitchen; I heard the door and then the long crash of her armful of stovewood into the box. Soon they would begin to arrive — the carriages and buggies in the drive — but not for a while yet because they too would wait first to see what I was going to do. So the house was quiet when I went down to the diningroom, no sound in it except Simon snoring in the parlor, probably still sitting on the stool though I didn't look in to see. Instead I stood at the diningroom window and drank the coffee which Louvinia brought me, then I went to the stable; I saw Joby watching me from the kitchen door as I crossed the yard and in the stable Loosh looked up at me across Betsy's head, a curry comb in his hand, though Ringo didn't look at me at all. We curried Jupiter then. I didn't know if we would be able to without trouble or not, since always Father would come in first and touch him and tell him to stand and he would stand like a marble horse (or pale bronze rather) while Loosh curried him. But he stood for me too, a little restive but he stood, then that was done and now it was almost nine o'clock and soon they would begin to arrive and I told Ringo to bring Betsy on to the house.

I went on to the house and into the hall. I had not had to pant in some time now but it was there, waiting, a part of the alteration, as though by being dead and no longer needing air he had taken all of it, all that he had compassed and claimed and postulated between the walls which he had built, along with him. Aunt Jenny must have been waiting; she came out of the diningroom at once, without a sound, dressed, the hair that was like Father's combed and smooth above the eyes that were different from Father's eyes because they were not intolerant but just intent and grave and (she was wise too) without pity. "Are you going now?" she said.

"Yes." I looked at her. Yes, thank God, without pity. "You see, I want to be thought well of."

"I do," she said. "Even if you spend the day hidden in the stable loft, I still do."

"Maybe if she knew that I was going. Was going to town anyway."

"No," she said. "No, Bayard." We looked at one another. Then she said quietly, "All right. She's awake." So I mounted the stairs. I mounted steadily, not fast because if I had gone fast the panting would have started again or I might have had to slow for a second at the turn or at the top and I would not have gone on. So I went slowly and steadily, across the hall to her door and knocked and opened it. She was sitting at the window, in something soft and loose for morning in her bedroom only she never did look like morning in a bedroom because here was no hair to fall about her shoulders. She looked up, she sat there looking at me with her feverish brilliant eyes and I remembered I still had the verbena sprig in my lapel and suddenly she began to laugh again. It seemed to come not from her mouth but to burst out all over her face like sweat does and with a dreadful and painful convulsion as when you have vomited until it hurts you yet still you must vomit again — burst out all over her face except her eyes, the brilliant incredulous eyes looking at me out of the laughter as if they belonged to somebody else, as if they were two inert fragments of tar or coal lying on the bottom of a receptacle filled with turmoil: "I kissed his hand! *I kissed his hand!*" Louvinia entered, Aunt Jenny must have sent her directly after me; again I walked slowly and steadily so it would not start yet, down the stairs where Aunt Jenny stood beneath the chandelier in the hall as Mrs. Wilkins had stood yesterday at the University. She had my hat in her hand. "Even if you hid all day in the stable, Bayard," she said. I took the hat; she said quietly, pleasantly, as if she were talking to a stranger, a guest: "I used to see a lot of blockade runners in Charleston. They were heroes in a way, you see — not heroes because they were helping to prolong the Confederacy but heroes in the sense that David Crockett or John Sevier would have been to small boys or fool young women. There was one of them, an Englishman. He had no business there; it was the money of course, as with all of them. But he was the Davy Crockett to us because by that time we had all forgot what money was, what you could do with it. He must have been a gentleman once or associated with gentlemen before he changed his name, and he had a vocabulary of seven words, though I must admit he got along quite well with them. The first four were, 'I'll have rum, thanks,' and then, when he had the rum, he would use the other three — across the champagne, to whatever ruffled bosom or low gown: 'No bloody moon.' No bloody moon, Bayard."

Ringo was waiting with Betsy at the front steps. Again he did not look at me, his face sullen, downcast even while he handed me the reins. But he said nothing, nor did I look back. And sure enough I was just in time; I passed the Compson carriage at the gates, General Compson lifted his hat as I did mine as we passed. It was four miles to town but I had not gone two of them when I heard the horse coming up behind me and I did not look back because I knew it was Ringo. I did not look back; he came up on one of the carriage horses, he rode up beside me and looked me full in the face for one moment, the sullen determined face, the eyes rolling at me defiant and momentary and red; we rode on. Now we were in town — the long shady street leading to the square, the new courthouse at the end of it; it was eleven o'clock now: long past breakfast and not yet noon so there were only women on the street, not to recognise me perhaps or at least not the walking stopped sudden and dead in mid-walking as if the legs contained the sudden eyes, the caught breath, that not to begin until we reached the square and I thinking *If I could only be invisible until I reach the stairs to his office and begin to mount.* But I could not, I was not; we rode up to the Holston House and I saw the row of feet along the gallery rail come suddenly and quietly down and I did not look at them, I stopped Betsy and waited until Ringo was down then I dismounted and gave him the reins. "Wait for me here," I said.

"I'm going with you," he said, not loud; we stood there under the still circumspect eyes and spoke quietly to one another like two conspirators. Then I saw the pistol, the outline of it inside his shirt, probably the one we had taken from Grumby that day we killed him.

"No you ain't," I said.

"Yes I am."

"No you ain't." So I walked on, along the street in the hot sun. It was almost noon now and I could smell nothing except the verbena in my coat, as if it had gathered all the sun, all the suspended fierce heat in which the equinox could not seem to occur and were distilling it so that I moved in a cloud of verbena as I might have moved in a cloud of smoke from a cigar. Then George Wyatt was beside me (I don't know where he came from) and five or six others of Father's old troop a few yards behind, George's hand on my arm, drawing me into a doorway out of the avid eyes like caught breaths.

"Have you got that derringer?" George said.

"No," I said.

"Good," George said. "They are tricky things to fool with. Couldn't nobody but Colonel ever handle one right; I never could. So you take this. I tried it this morning and I know it's right. Here." He was already fumbling the pistol into my pocket, then the same thing seemed to happen to him that happened to Drusilla last night when she kissed my hand — something communicated by touch straight to the simple code by which he lived, without going through the brain at all: so that he too stood suddenly back, the pistol in his hand, staring at me

with his pale outraged eyes and speaking in a whisper thin with fury:
"Who are you? Is your name Sartoris? By God, if you don't kill
him, I'm going to." Now it was not panting, it was a terrible desire
to laugh, to laugh as Drusilla had, and say, "That's what Drusilla said."
But I didn't. I said,

"I'm tending to this. You stay out of it. I don't need any help."
Then his fierce eyes faded gradually, exactly as you turn a lamp down.

"Well," he said, putting the pistol back into his pocket. "You'll
have to excuse me, son. I should have knowed you wouldn't do anything
that would keep John from laying quiet. We'll follow you and wait at
the foot of the steps. And remember: he's a brave man, and he's been
sitting in that office by himself since yesterday morning waiting for you
and his nerves are on edge."

"I'll remember," I said. "I don't need any help." I had started on
when suddenly I said it without having any warning that I was going
to: "No bloody moon."

"What?" he said. I didn't answer. I went on across the square
itself now, in the hot sun, they following though not close so that I never
saw them again until afterward, surrounded by the remote still eyes not
following me yet either, just stopped where they were before the stores
and about the door to the courthouse, waiting. I walked steadily on
enclosed in the now fierce odor of the verbena sprig. Then shadow fell
upon me; I did not pause, I looked once at the small faded sign nailed to
the brick *B. J. Redmond. Atty at Law* and began to mount the stairs,
the wooden steps scuffed by the heavy bewildered boots of countrymen
approaching litigation and stained by tobacco spit, on down the dim
corridor to the door which bore the name again, *B. J. Redmond* and
knocked once and opened it. He sat behind the desk, not much taller
than Father but thicker as a man gets who spends most of his time sitting
and listening to people, freshly shaven and with fresh linen; a lawyer
yet it was not a lawyer's face — a face much thinner than the body would
indicate, strained (and yes, tragic; I know that now) and exhausted beneath
the neat recent steady strokes of the razor, holding a pistol flat on the
desk before him, loose beneath his hand and aimed at nothing. There
was no smell of drink, not even of tobacco in the neat clean dingy room
although I knew he smoked. I didn't pause. I walked steadily toward
him. It ws not twenty feet from door to desk yet I seemed to walk in a
dreamlike state in which there was neither time nor distance, as though
the mere act of walking was no more intended to encompass space than
was his sitting. We didn't speak. It was as if we both knew what the
passage of words would be and the futility of it; how he might have said,
"Go out, Bayard. Go away, boy" and then, "Draw then. I will allow
you to draw" and it would have been the same as if he had never said it.

So we did not speak; I just walked steadily toward him as the pistol rose from the desk. I watched it, I could see the foreshortened slant of the barrel and I knew it would miss me though his hand did not tremble. I walked toward him, toward the pistol in the rocklike hand, I heard no bullet. Maybe I didn't even hear the explosion though I remember the sudden orange bloom and smoke as they appeared against his white shirt as they had appeared against Grumby's greasy Confederate coat; I still watched that foreshortened slant of barrel which I knew was not aimed at me and saw the second orange flash of smoke and heard no bullet that time either. Then I stopped; it was done then. I watched the pistol descend to the desk in short jerks; I saw him release it and sit back, both hands on the desk, I looked at his face and I knew too what it was to want air when there was nothing in the circumambience for the lungs. He rose, shoved the chair back with a convulsive motion and rose, with a queer ducking motion of his head; with his head still ducked aside and one arm extended as though he couldn't see and the other hand resting on the desk as if he couldn't stand alone, he turned and crossed to the wall and took his hat from the rack and with his head still ducked aside and one hand extended he blundered along the wall and passed me and reached the door and went through it. He was brave; no one denied that. He walked down those stairs and out onto the street where George Wyatt and the other six of Father's old troop waited and where the other men had begun to run now; he walked through the middle of them with his hat on and his head up (they told me how someone shouted at him: "Have you killed that boy too?"), saying no word, staring straight ahead and with his back to them, on to the station where the south-bound train was just in and got on it with no baggage, nothing, and went away from Jefferson and from Mississippi and never came back.

I heard their feet on the stairs then in the corridor then in the room, but for a while yet (it wasn't that long, of course) I still sat behind the desk as he had sat, the flat of the pistol still warm under my hand, my hand growing slowly numb between the pistol and my forehead. Then I raised my head; the little room was full of men. "My God!" George Wyatt cried. "You took the pistol away from him and then missed him, missed him *twice*?" Then he answered himself — that same rapport for violence which Drusilla had and which in George's case was actual character judgment: "No; wait. You walked in here without even a pocket knife and let him miss you twice. My God in heaven." He turned, shouting: "Get to hell out of here! You, White, ride out to Sartoris and tell his folks it's all over and he's all right. Ride!" So they departed, went away; presently only George was left, watching me with that pale bleak stare which was speculative yet not at all ratiocinative. "Well by God," he said. " — Do you want a drink?"

"No," I said. "I'm hungry. I didn't eat any breakfast."

"I reckon not, if you got up this morning aiming to do what you did. Come on. We'll go to the Holston House."

"No," I said. "No. Not there."

"Why not? You ain't done anything to be ashamed of. I wouldn't have done it that way, myself. I'd a shot at him once, anyway. But that's your way or you wouldn't have done it."

"Yes," I said. "I would do it again."

"Be damned if I would. — You want to come home with me? We'll have time to eat and then ride out there in time for the — " But I couldn't do that either.

"No," I said. "I'm not hungry after all. I think I'll go home."

"Don't you want to wait and ride out with me?"

"No. I'll go on."

"You don't want to stay here, anyway." He looked around the room again, where the smell of powder smoke still lingered a little, still lay somewhere on the hot dead air though invisible now, blinking a little with his fierce pale unintroverted eyes. "Well by God," he said again. "Maybe you're right, maybe there has been enough killing in your family without — Come on." We left the office. I waited at the foot of the stairs and soon Ringo came up with the horses. We crossed the square again. There were no feet on the Holston House railing now (it was twelve o'clock) but a group of men stood before the door who raised their hats and I raised mine and Ringo and I rode on.

We did not go fast. Soon it was one, maybe after; the carriages and buggies would begin to leave the square soon, so I turned from the road at the end of the pasture and I sat the mare, trying to open the gate without dismounting, until Ringo dismounted and opened it. We crossed the pasture in the hard fierce sun; I could have seen the house now but I didn't look. Then we were in the shade, the close thick airless shade of the creek bottom; the old rails still lay in the undergrowth where we had built the pen to hide the Yankee mules. Presently I heard the water, then I could see the sunny glints. We dismounted. I lay on my back, I thought *Now it can begin again if it wants to.* But it did not. I went to sleep. I went to sleep almost before I had stopped thinking. I slept for almost five hours and I didn't dream anything at all yet I waked myself up crying, crying too hard to stop it. Ringo was squatting beside me and the sun was gone though there was a bird of some sort still singing somewhere and the whistle of the north-bound evening train sounded and the short broken puffs of starting where it had evidently stopped at our flag station. After a while I began to stop and Ringo brought his hat full of water from the creek but instead I went down to the water myself and bathed my face.

There was still a good deal of light in the pasture, though the whip-poorwills had begun, and when we reached the house there was a mock-ingbird singing in the magnolia, the night song now, the drowsy moony one, and again the moon like the rim print of a heel in wet sand. There was just one light in the hall now and so it was all over though I could smell the flowers even above the verbena in my coat. I had not looked at him again. I had started to before I left the house but I did not, I did not see him again and all the pictures we had of him were bad ones because a picture could no more have held him dead than the house could have kept his body. But I didn't need to see him again because he was there, he would always be there; maybe what Drusilla meant by his dream was not something which he possessed but something which he had be-queathed us which we could never forget, which would even assume the corporeal shape of him whenever any of us, black or white, closed our eyes. I went into the house. There was no light in the drawing room except the last of the afterglow which came through the western window where Aunt Jenny's colored glass was; I was about to go on upstairs when I saw her sitting there beside the window. She didn't call me and I didn't speak Drusilla's name, I just went to the door and stood there. "She's gone," Aunt Jenny said. "She took the evening train. She has gone to Montgomery, to Dennison." Denny had been married about a year now; he was living in Montgomery, reading law.

"I see," I said. "Then she didn't —" But there wasn't any use in that either; Jed White must have got there before one o'clock and told them. And besides, Aunt Jenny didn't answer. She could have lied to me but she didn't, she said,

"Come here." I went to her chair. "Kneel down. I can't see you."

"Don't you want the lamp?"

"No. Kneel down." So I knelt beside the chair. "So you had a perfectly splendid Saturday afternoon, didn't you? Tell me about it." Then she put her hands on my shoulders. I watched them come up as though she were trying to stop them; I felt them on my shoulders as if they had a separate life of their own and were trying to do something which for my sake she was trying to restrain, prevent. Then she gave up or she was not strong enough because they came up and took my face between them, hard, and suddenly the tears sprang and streamed down her face like Drusilla's laughing had. "Oh, damn you Sartorises!" she said. "Damn you! Damn you!"

As I passed down the hall the light came up in the diningroom and I could hear Louvinia laying the table for supper. So the stairs were lighted quite well. But the upper hall was dark. I saw her open door (that unmistakable way in which an open door stands open when nobody lives in the room any more) and I realised I had not believed that she was really gone. So I didn't look into the room. I went on to mine and entered. And then for a long moment I thought it was the verbena in my lapel which I still smelled. I thought that until I had crossed the room and looked down at the pillow on which it lay — a single sprig of it (without looking she would pinch off a half dozen of them and they would be all of a size, almost all of a shape, as if a machine had stamped them out) filling the room, the dusk, the evening with that odor which she said you could smell alone above the smell of horses.

# William Saroyan (1908–     )

AN ARMENIAN-AMERICAN ORIGINAL, William Saroyan is a law unto himself as an important writer. He was born in the San Joaquin Valley, California, where his family had settled after fleeing the Turkish invasion of Armenia. In 1934 he was working as a telegraph messenger boy when *Story Magazine* published his first story, "The Daring Young Man on the Flying Trapeze," which excited immediate national attention. A number of other stories, which he wrote at the rate of one a day, followed rapidly and were collected in his book, also called *The Daring Young Man on the Flying Trapeze.* Twelve volumes of his short stories have been published. His novels include *The Human Comedy* (1943) and *The Adventures of Wesley Jackson* (1946). The two most memorable of his many plays are *My Heart's in the Highlands* (1939) and *The Time of Your Life* (1939) for which he refused a Pulitzer Prize.

"William Saroyan has invented a new form successfully for the short story," is the tribute Edward J. O'Brien paid him in 1935. "It is a free fantasia in which he pours forth his thoughts and feelings about America and himself with extraordinary brilliance and perceptive power." His writing also is an exuberant forty-year-long love letter to the world and everybody in it. There is tragedy in the writing but no bitterness and not a single villain. Not even in this Depression story of a dying young man.

# The Daring Young Man
# on the Flying Trapeze

## I. Sleep

HORIZONTALLY wakeful amid universal widths, practicing laughter and mirth, satire, the end of all, of Rome and yes of Babylon, clenched teeth, remembrance, much warmth volcanic, the streets of Paris, the plains of Jericho, much gliding as of reptile in abstraction, a gallery of watercolors, the sea and the fish with eyes, symphony, a table in the corner of the Eiffel Tower, jazz at the opera house, alarm clock and the tap-dancing of doom, conversation with a tree, the river Nile, Cadillac coupe to Kansas, the roar of Dostoyevsky, and the dark sun.

This earth, the face of one who lived, the form without the weight, weeping upon snow, white music, the magnified flower twice the size of the universe, black clouds, the caged panther staring, deathless space, Mr. Eliot with rolled sleeves baking bread, Flaubert and Guy de Maupassant, a wordless rhyme of early meaning, Finlandia, mathematics highly polished and slick as a green onion to the teeth, Jerusalem, the path to paradox.

The deep song of man, the sly whisper of someone unseen but vaguely known, hurricane in the cornfield, a game of chess, hush the queen, the king, Karl Franz, black Titanic, Mr. Chaplin weeping, Stalin, Hitler, a multitude of Jews, tomorrow is Monday, no dancing in the streets.

O swift moment of life: it is ended, the earth is again now.

## II. Wakefulness

He (the living) dressed and shaved, grinning at himself in the mirror. Very unhandsome, he said; where is my tie? (He had but one.) Coffee and a gray sky, Pacific Ocean fog, the drone of a passing streetcar, people going to the city, time again, the day, prose and poetry. He moved swiftly down the stairs to the street and began to walk, thinking suddenly, *It is only in sleep that we may know that we live. There only, in that living death, do we meet ourselves and the far earth, God and the saints, the names of our fathers, the substance of remote moments; it is there that the centuries merge in the moment, that the vast becomes the tiny, tangible atom of eternity.*

He walked into the day as alertly as might be, making a definite noise with his heels, perceiving with his eyes the superficial truth of streets and structures, the trivial truth of reality. Helplessly his mind sang, *He flies through the air with the greatest of ease; the daring young man on the flying trapeze*; then laughed with all the might of his being. It was really a splendid morning: gray, cold, and cheerless, a morning for inward vigor; ah, Edgar Guest, he said, how I long for your music.

In the gutter he saw a coin which proved to be a penny dated 1923, and placing it in the palm of his hand he examined it closely, remembering that year and thinking of Lincoln whose profile was stamped upon the coin. There was almost nothing a man could do with a penny. I will purchase a motorcar, he thought. I will dress myself in the fashion of a fop, visit the hotel strumpets, drink and dine, and then return to the quiet. Or I will drop the coin into a slot and weigh myself.

It was good to be poor, and the Communists — but it was dreadful to be hungry. What appetites they had, how fond they were of food! Empty stomachs. He remembered how greatly he needed food. Every meal was bread and coffee and cigarettes, and now he had no more bread. Coffee without bread could never honestly serve as supper, and there were no weeds in the park that could be cooked as spinach is cooked.

If the truth were known, he was half starved, and yet there was still no end of books he ought to read before he died. He remembered the young Italian in a Brooklyn hospital, a small sick clerk named Mollica, who had said desperately, I would like to see California once before I die. And he thought earnestly, I ought at least to read *Hamlet* once again; or perhaps *Huckleberry Finn*.

It was then that he became thoroughly awake: at the thought of dying. Now wakefulness was a state in the nature of a sustained shock. A young man could perish rather unostentatiously, he thought; and already he was very nearly starved. Water and prose were fine, they filled much inorganic space, but they were inadequate. If there were only some work he might do for money, some trivial labor in the name of commerce. If they would only allow him to sit at a desk all day and add trade figures, subtract and multiply and divide, then perhaps he would not die. He would buy food, all sorts of it: untasted delicacies from Norway, Italy, and France; all manner of beef, lamb, fish, cheese; grapes, figs, pears, apples, melons, which he would worship when he had satisfied his hunger. He would place a bunch of red grapes on a dish beside two black figs, a large yellow pear, and a green apple. He would buy great brown loaves of French bread, vegetables of all sorts, meat; he would buy life.

From a hill he saw the city standing majestically in the east, great towers, dense with his kind, and there he was suddenly outside of it all, almost definitely certain that he should never gain admittance, almost positive that somehow he had ventured upon the wrong earth, or perhaps into the wrong age, and now a young man of twenty-two was to be permanently ejected from it. This thought was not saddening. He said to himself, sometime soon I must write *An Application for Permission to Live*. He accepted the thought of dying without pity for himself or for man, believing that he would at least sleep another night. His rent for another day was paid; there was yet another tomorrow. And after that he might go where other homeless men went. He might even visit the Salvation Army — sing to God and Jesus (unlover of my soul), be saved, eat and sleep. But he knew that he would not. His life was a private life. He did not wish to destroy this fact. Any other alternative would be better.

*Through the air on the flying trapeze,* his mind hummed. Amusing it was, astoundingly funny. A trapeze to God, or to nothing, a flying trapeze to some sort of eternity; he prayed objectively for strength to make the flight with grace.

I have one cent, he said. It is an American coin. In the evening I shall polish it until it glows like a sun and I shall study the words.

He was now walking in the city itself, among living men. There were one or two places to go. He saw his reflection in the plate-glass windows of stores and was disappointed with his appearance. He seemed not at all as strong as he felt; he seemed, in fact, a trifle infirm in every part of his body, in his neck, his shoulders, arms, trunk, and knees. This will never do, he said, and with an effort he assembled all his disjointed parts and became tensely, artificially erect and solid.

He passed numerous restaurants with magnificent discipline, refusing even to glance into them, and at last reached a building which he entered. He rose in an elevator to the seventh floor, moved down a hall, and, opening a door, walked into the office of an employment agency. Already there were two dozen young men in the place; he found a corner where he stood waiting his turn to be interviewed. At length he was granted this great privilege and was questioned by a thin, scatterbrained miss of fifty.

Now tell me, she said; what can you do?

He was embarrassed. I can write, he said pathetically.

You mean your penmanship is good? Is that is? said the elderly maiden.

Well, yes, he replied. But I mean that I can write.

Write what? said the miss, almost with anger.

Prose, he said simply.

There was a pause. At last the lady said:

Can you use a typewriter?

Of course, said the young man.

All right, went on the miss, we have your address; we will get in touch with you. There is nothing this morning, nothing at all.

It was much the same at the other agency, except that he was questioned by a conceited young man who closely resembled a pig. From the agencies he went to the large department stores: there was a good deal of pomposity, some humiliation on his part, and finally the report that work was not available. He did not feel displeased, and strangely did not even feel that he was personally involved in all the foolishness. He was a living young man who was in need of money with which to go on being one, and there was no way of getting it except by working for it; and there was no work. It was purely an abstract problem which he wished for the last time to attempt to solve. Now he was pleased that the matter was closed.

He began to perceive the definiteness of the course of his life. Except for moments, it had been largely artless, but now at the last minute he was determined that there should be as little imprecision as possible.

He passed countless stores and restaurants on his way to the Y.M.C.A., where he helped himself to paper and ink and began to compose his *Application.* For an hour he worked on this document, then suddenly, owing to the bad air in the place and to hunger, he became faint. He semed to be swimming away from himself with great strokes, and hurriedly left the building. In the Civic Center Park, across from the

Public Library Building, he drank almost a quart of water and felt himself refreshed. An old man was standing in the center of the brick boulevard surroundered by sea gulls, pigeons, and robins. He was taking handfuls of bread crumbs from a large paper sack and tossing them to the birds with a gallant gesture.

Dimly he felt impelled to ask the old man for a portion of the crumbs, but he did not allow the thought even nearly to reach consciousness; he entered the Public Library and for an hour read Proust, then, feeling himself to be swimming away again, he rushed outdoors. He drank more water at the fountain in the park and began the long walk to his room.

I'll go and sleep some more, he said; there is nothing else to do. He knew now that he was much too tired and weak to deceive himself about being all right, and yet his mind seemed somehow still lithe and alert. It, as if it were a separate entity, persisted in articulating impertinent pleasantries about his very real physical suffering. He reached his room early in the afternoon and immediately prepared coffee on the small gas range. There was no milk in the can, and the half pound of sugar he had purchased a week before was all gone; he drank a cup of the hot black fluid, sitting on his bed and smiling.

From the Y.M.C.A. he had stolen a dozen sheets of letter paper upon which he hoped to complete his document, but now the very notion of writing was unpleasant to him. There was nothing to say. He began to polish the penny he had found in the morning, and this absurd act somehow afforded him great enjoyment. No American coin can be made to shine so brilliantly as a penny. How many pennies would he need to go on living? Wasn't there something more he might sell? He looked about the bare room. No. His watch was gone; also his books. All those fine books; nine of them for eighty-five cents. He felt ill and ashamed for having parted with his books. His best suit he had sold for two dollars, but that was all right. He didn't mind at all about clothes. But the books. That was different. It made him very angry to think that there was no respect for men who wrote.

He placed the shining penny on the table, looking upon it with the delight of a miser. How prettily it smiles, he said. Without reading them he looked at the words, *E Pluribus Unum One Cent United States of America*, and turning the penny over, he saw Lincoln and the words, *In God We Trust 1923*. How beautiful it is, he said.

He became drowsy and felt a ghastly illness coming over his blood, a feeling of nausea and disintegration. Bewildered, he stood beside his bed, thinking there *is nothing to do but sleep*. Already he felt himself making great strides through the fluid of the earth, swimming away to the beginning. He fell face down upon the bed, saying, I ought first at least to give the coin to some child. A child could buy any number of things with a penny.

Then swiftly, neatly, with the grace of the young man on the trapeze, he was gone from his body. For an eternal moment he was all things at once: the bird, the fish, the rodent, the reptile, and man. An ocean of print undulated endlessly and darkly before him. The city burned. The herded crowd rioted. The earth circled away, and knowing that he did so, he turned his lost face to the empty sky and became dreamless, unalive, perfect.

# Ernest Hemingway (1899–1961)

WARRIOR, bullfight aficionado, big game hunter, deep sea fisherman, and writer, Ernest Hemingway, a leading American exponent of *machismo*, was born in Oak Park, Illinois. He was educated in public schools and worked as a reporter in Kansas City. After serving with the Italian infantry in the First World War, he became one of the Paris expatriates of the twenties. His first published work, "My Old Man," a short story, was published in *The Best American Short Stories 1923* after he told Edward J. O'Brien, the editor, he was abandoning writing because all his work had been rejected. It is the only story in the series that did not first appear in a magazine. A small Paris firm, The Three Mountains Press, published his first book, *Three Stories and Ten Poems* (1923). Sherwood Anderson persuaded his own American publisher to bring out the short stories *In Our Time* (1925), Hemingway's first book to appear in the United States. His second book and first novel was *Torrents of Spring* (1926) lampooning Anderson's writing. Among his best known novels are *The Sun Also Rises* (1926) about American and English expatriates, and *For Whom the Bell Tolls* (1940), which grew out of his Spanish Civil War experience. His novel of the First World War, *A Farewell to Arms* (1929), is generally considered his finest. He was awarded the Nobel Prize for *The Old Man and the Sea* (1952), which was a return to and in some ways a re-writing of his earlier short stories.

"Out of Stein by Anderson" was a New York newspaper's headline for a review of Hemingway that featured three parallel columns of writing samples by the three authors. Whereupon Stein disowned such parentage and Hemingway wrote *Torrents of Spring* lampooning Anderson, to show independence of him. Ironically for years any number of writers have been charged since with imitating Hemingway. Instead of an over-worked "literary" influence, however, it may be the *zeitgeist*, the spirit of the time, which results in a similarity. Authors, too, can be victims of the environment. The repetitive rhythm of Hemingway's simple declarative sentences evokes Stein and his spare dialogue and freedom from plotted contrivance is like Anderson's. Ornate periodic sentences bored, and tricky plots and surprise endings no longer enticed a war-weary, disillusioned "lost generation." There is, however, more unabashed emotion in "The Snows of Kilimanjaro," about a dying writer, than in most of Hemingway's work and it is considered his most important story.

# *The Snows of Kilimanjaro*

THE MARVELLOUS thing is that it's painless," he said. "That's how you know when it starts."

"Is it really?"

"Absolutely. I'm awfully sorry about the odor though. That must bother you."

"Don't! Please don't."

"Look at them," he said. "Now is it sight or is it scent that brings them like that?"

The cot the man lay on was in the wide shade of a mimosa tree and as he looked out past the shade onto the glare of the plain there were three of the big birds squatted obscenely, while in the sky a dozen more sailed, making quick-moving shadows as they passed.

"They've been there since the truck broke down," he said. "Today's the first time any have lit on the ground. I watched the way they sailed very carefully at first in case I ever wanted to use them in a story. That's funny now."

"I wish you wouldn't," she said.

"I'm only talking," he said. "It's much easier if I talk. But I don't want to bother you."

"You know it doesn't bother me," she said. "It's that I've gotten so very nervous not being able to do anything. I think we might make it as easy as we can until the plane comes."

"Or until the plane doesn't come."

"Please tell me what I can do. There must be something I can do."

"You can take the leg off and that might stop it, though I doubt it. Or you can shoot me. You're a good shot now. I taught you to shoot didn't I."

"Please don't talk that way. Couldn't I read to you?"

"Read what?"

"Anything in the book bag that we haven't read."

"I can't listen to it," he said. "Talking is the easiest. We quarrel and that makes the time pass."

"I don't quarrel. I never want to quarrel. Let's not quarrel any more. No matter how nervous we get. Maybe they will be back with another truck today. Maybe the plane will come."

"I don't want to move," the man said. "There is no sense in moving now except to make it easier for you."

"That's cowardly."

"Can't you let a man die as comfortably as he can without calling him names? What's the use of slanging me?"

"You're not going to die."

"Don't be silly. I'm dying now. Ask those bastards." He looked over to where the huge, filthy birds sat, their naked heads sunk in the hunched feathers. A fourth planed down, to run quick-legged and then waddle slowly toward the others.

"They are around every camp. You never notice them. You can't die if you don't give up."

"Where did you read that? You're such a bloody fool."

"You might think about someone else."

"For Christ's sake," he said, "that's been my trade." He lay then and was quiet for a while and looked across the heat shimmer of the plain to the edge of the bush. There were a few Tommies that showed minute and white against the yellow and, far off, he saw a herd of zebra, white against the green of the bush. This was a pleasant camp under big trees against a hill, with good water, and, close by, a nearly dry water hole where sand grouse flighted in the mornings.

"Wouldn't you like me to read?" she asked. She was sitting on a canvas chair beside his cot. "There's a breeze coming up."

"No thanks."

"Maybe the truck will come."

"I don't give a damn about the truck."

"I do."

"You give a damn about so many things that I don't."

"Not so many, Harry."

"What about a drink?"

"It's supposed to be bad for you. It said in Black's to avoid all alcohol. You shouldn't drink."

"Molo!" he shouted.

"Yes Bwana."

"Bring whiskey-soda."

"Yes Bwana."

"You shouldn't," she said. "That's what I mean by giving up. It says it's bad for you. I know it's bad for you."

"No," he said. "It's good for me."

So now it was all over, he thought. So now he would never have a chance to finish it. So this was the way it ended in a bickering over a drink. Since the gangrene started in his right leg he had no pain and with the pain the horror had gone and all he felt now was a great tiredness and anger that this was the end of it. For this, that now was coming, he had very little curiosity. For years it had obsessed him; but now it meant nothing in itself. It was strange how easy being tired enough made it.

Now he would never write the things that he had saved to write until he knew enough to write about them well. Well, he would not have to fail at trying to write them either. Maybe you could never write them, and that was why you put them off and delayed the starting. Well he would never know, now.

"I wish we'd never come," the woman said. She was looking at him holding the glass and biting her lip. "You never would have gotten anything like this in Paris. You always said you loved Paris. We could have stayed in Paris or gone anywhere. I'd have gone anywhere. I said I'd go anywhere you wanted. If you wanted to shoot we could have gone shooting in Hungary and been comfortable."

"Your bloody money," he said.

"That's not fair," she said. "It was always yours as much as mine. I left everything and I went wherever you wanted to go and I've done what you wanted to do. But I wish we'd never come here."

"You said you loved it."

"I did when you were all right. But now I hate it. I don't see why that had to happen to your leg. What have we done to have that happen to us?"

"I suppose what I did was to forget to put iodine on it when I first scratched it. Then I didn't pay any attention to it because I never infect. Then, later, when it got bad, it was probably using that weak carbolic solution when the other antiseptics ran out that paralyzed the minute blood vessels and started the gangrene." He looked at her, "What else?"

"I don't mean that."

"If we would have hired a good mechanic instead of a half baked kikuyu driver, he would have checked the oil and never burned out that bearing in the truck."

"I don't mean that."

"If you hadn't left your own people, your goddamned old Westbury, Saratoga, Palm Beach people to take me on —"

"Why I loved you. That's not fair. I love you now. I'll always love you. Don't you love me?"

"No," said the man. "I don't think so. I never have."

"Harry, what are you saying? You're out of your head."

"No. I haven't any head to go out of."

"Don't drink that," she said. "Darling, please don't drink that. We have to do everything we can."

"You do it," he said. "I'm tired."

*Now in his mind he saw a railway station at Karagatch and he was standing with his pack and that was the headlight of the Simplon-Orient cutting the dark now and he was leaving Thrace then after the retreat. That was one of the things he had saved to write, with, in the morning at breakfast, looking out the window and seeing snow on the mountains in Bulgaria and Nansen's Secretary asking the old man if it were snow and the old man looking at it and saying, No, that's not snow. It's too early for snow. And the Secretary repeating to the other girls, No, you see. It's not snow and them all saying, It's not snow we were mistaken. But it was the snow all right and he sent them on into it when he evolved exchange of populations. And it was snow they tramped along in until they died that winter.*

*It was snow too that fell all Christmas week that year up in the Gauertal, that year they lived in the woodcutter's house with the big square porcelain stove that filled half the room, and they slept on mattresses filled with beech leaves, the time the deserter came with his feet bloody in the snow. He said the police were right behind him and they gave him woolen socks and held the gendarmes talking until the tracks had drifted over. In Schruns, on Christmas day, the snow was so bright it hurt your eyes when you looked out from the weinstube and saw every-one coming home from church. That was where they walked up the sleigh-smoothed urine-yellowed road along the river with the steep pine hills, skis heavy on the shoulder, and where they ran that great run down the glacier above the Madlener-haus, the snow as smooth to see as cake frosting and as light as powder and he remembered the noiseless rush the speed made as you dropped down like a bird. They were snowbound a week in the Madlener-haus that time in the blizzard playing cards in the smoke by the lantern light and the stakes were higher all the time as Herr Lent lost more. Finally he lost it all. Everything, the ski-schule money and all the season's profit and then his capital. He could see him with his long nose, picking up the cards and then opening, "Sans Voir." There was always gambling then. When there was no snow you gambled and when there was too much you gambled. He thought of all the time in his life he had spent gambling. But he had never written a line of that, nor of that cold, bright Christmas day with the mountains showing across the plain that Barker had flown across the lines to bomb the Au-strian officers' leave train, machine-gunning them as they scattered and ran. He remembered Barker afterwards coming into the mess and starting to tell about it. And how quiet it got and then somebody saying, "You bloody, murderous bastard." Those were the same Austrians they killed then that he skied with later. No not the same. Hans, that he skied with all that year, had been in the Kaiser-Jagers and when they went hunting hares together up the little valley above the saw-mill they had talked of the fighting on Pasubio and of the attack on Pertica and Asalone and he had never written a word of that. Nor of Monte Corno, nor the Siete Communi, nor of Arsiero. How many winters had he lived in the Vorarlberg and the Arlberg? It was four and then he remembered the man who had the fox to sell when they had walked into Bludenz, that time to buy presents, and the cherry pit taste of good kirsch, the fast-slipping rush of running powder-snow on crust, singing "Hi Ho said Rolly!" as you ran down the last stretch to the steep drop, taking it straight, then running the orchard in three turns and out across the ditch and onto the icy road behind the inn. Knocking your bindings loose, kicking the skis free and leaning them up against the wooden wall of the inn, the lamplight coming from the window where inside, in the smoky, new-wine smelling warmth, they were playing the accordion.*

"Where did we stay in Paris?" he asked the woman who was sitting by him in a canvas chair, now, in Africa.

"At the Crillon. You know that."

"Why do I know that?"

"That's where we always stayed."

"No. Not always."

"There and at the Pavillion Henri-Quatre in St. Germain. You said you loved it there."

"Love is a dunghill," said Harry. "And I'm the cock that gets on it to crow."

"If you have to go away," she said, "is it absolutely necessary to kill everything you leave behind? I mean do you have to take away everything? Do you have to kill your horse, and your wife and burn your saddle and your armour?"

"Yes," he said. "Your damned money was my armour. My Swift and my Armour."

"Don't."

"All right. I'll stop that. I don't want to hurt you."

"It's a little bit late now."

"All right then. I'll go on hurting you. It's more amusing. The only thing I ever really liked to do with you I can't do now."

"No, that's not true. You liked to do many things and everything you wanted to do I did."

"Oh for Christ's sake stop bragging will you?"

He looked at her and saw her crying.

"Listen," he said. "Do you think that it is fun to do this? I don't know why I'm doing it. It's trying to kill to keep yourself alive I imagine. I was all right when we started talking. I didn't mean to start this, and now I'm crazy as a coot and being as cruel to you as I can be. Don't pay any attention, darling, to what I say. I love you, really. You know I love you. I've never loved anyone else the way I love you." He slipped into the familiar lie he made his bread and butter by.

"You're sweet to me."

"You bitch," he said. "You rich bitch. That's poetry. I'm full of poetry now. Rot and poetry. Rotten poetry."

"Stop it. Harry, why do you have to turn into a devil now?"

"I don't like to leave anything," the man said. "I don't like to leave things behind."

It was evening now and he had been asleep. The sun was gone behind the hill and there was a shadow all across the plain and the small animals were feeding close to camp; quick dropping heads and switching tails, he watched them keeping well out away from the bush now. The birds no longer waited on the ground. They were all perched heavily in a tree. There were many more of them. His personal boy was sitting by the bed.

"Memsahib's gone to shoot," the boy said. "Does Bwana want?"
"Nothing."

She had gone to kill a piece of meat and, knowing how he liked to watch the game, she had gone well away so she would not disturb this little pocket of the plain that he could see. She was always thoughtful, he thought. On anything she knew about, or had read, or that she had ever heard.

It was not her fault that when he went to her he was already over. How could a woman know that you meant nothing that you said; that you spoke only from habit and to be comfortable. After he no longer meant what he said, his lies were more successful with women than when he had told them the truth.

It was not that he lied as that there was no truth to tell. He had had his life and it was over and then he went on living it again with different people and more money, with the best of the same places, and some new ones. You kept from thinking and it was all marvellous. You were equipped with good insides so that you did not go to pieces that way, the way most of them had, and you made an attitude that you cared nothing for the work you used to do, now that you could no longer do it. But, in yourself, you said that you would write about these people; about the very rich; that you were really not of them but a spy in their country; that you would leave it and write of it and for once it would be written by someone who knew what he was writing of. But he would never do it, because each day of not writing, of comfort, of being that which he despised, dulled his ability and softened his will to work so that, finally, he did no work at all. The people he knew now were all much more comfortable when he did not work. Africa was where he had been happiest in the good time of his life so he had come out here to start again. They had made this safari with the minimum of comfort. There was no hardship; but there was no luxury and he had thought that he could get back into training that way. That in some way he could work the fat off his soul the way a fighter went into the mountains to work and train in order to burn it out of his body.

She had liked it. She said she loved it. She loved anything that was exciting, that involved a change of scene, where there were new people and where things were pleasant. And he had felt the illusion of returning strength of will to work. Now if this was how it ended, and he knew it was, he must not turn like some snake biting itself because its back was broken. It wasn't this woman's fault. If it had not been she it would have been another. If he lived by a lie he should try to die by it. He heard a shot beyond the hill.

She shot very well this good, this rich bitch, this kindly caretaker and destroyer of his talent. Nonsense. He had destroyed his talent himself. Why should he blame this woman because she kept him well? He had destroyed his talent by not using it, by betrayals of himself and what he believed in, by drinking so much that he blunted the edge of his perceptions, by laziness, by sloth, and by snobbery, by pride and by prejudice, by hook and by crook. What was this? A catalogue of old books? What was his talent anyway? It was a talent all right but instead of using it, he had traded on it. It was never what he had done, but always what he could do. And he had chosen to make his living with something else instead of a pen or a pencil. It was strange too, wasn't it, that when he fell in love with another woman, that woman should always have more money than the last one? But when he no longer was in love, when he was only lying, as to this woman, now, who had the most money of all, who had all the money there was, who had had a husband and children, who had taken lovers and been dissatisfied with them, and who loved him dearly as a writer, as a man, as a companion and as a proud possession; it was strange that when he did not love her at all and was lying, that he should be able to give her more for her money than when he had really loved. We must all be cut out for what we do, he thought. However you make your living is where your talent lies. He had sold vitality, in one form or another, all his life and when your affections are not too involved you give much better value for the money. He had found that out but he would never write that, now, either. No, he would not write that, although it was well worth writing.

Now she came in sight, walking across the open toward the camp. She was wearing jodhpurs and carrying her rifle. The two boys had a Tommy slung and they were coming along behind her. She was still a good looking woman, he thought, and she had a pleasant body. She had a great talent and appreciation for the bed, she was not pretty, but he liked her face, she read enormously, liked to ride and shoot and, certainly, she drank too much. Her husband had died when she was still a comparatively young woman and for a while she had devoted herself to her two just-grown children, who did not need her and were embarrassed at having her about, to her stable of horses, to books, and to bottles. She liked to read in the evening before dinner and she drank scotch and soda while she read. By dinner she was fairly drunk and after a bottle of wine at dinner she was usually drunk enough to sleep.

That was before the lovers. After she had the lovers she did not drink so much because she did not have to be drunk to sleep. But the lovers bored her. She had been married to a man who had never bored her and these people bored her very much.

Then one of her two children was killed in a plane crash and after that was over she did not want the lovers, and drink being no anaesthetic she had to make another life. Suddenly she had been acutely frightened of being alone. But she wanted someone that she respected with her.

It had begun very simply. She liked what he wrote and she had always envied the life he led. She thought he did exactly what he wanted to. The steps by which she had acquired him and the way in which she had finally fallen in love with him were all part of a regular progression in which she had built herself a new life and he had traded away what remained of his old life. He had traded it for security, for comfort too, there was no denying that, and for what else? He did not know. She would have bought him anything he wanted. He knew that. She was a damned nice woman too. He would as soon be in bed with her as anyone; rather with her, because she was richer, because she was very pleasant and appreciative and because she never made scenes. And now this life that she had built again was coming to a term because he had not used iodine two weeks ago when a thorn had scratched his knee as they moved forward trying to photogtaph a herd of waterbuck standing, their heads up, peering while their nostrils searched the air, their ears spread wide to hear the first noise that would send them rushing into the bush. They had bolted, too, before he got the picture.

Here she came now.

He turned his head on the cot to look toward her. "Hello," he said.

"I shot a Tommy ram," she told him. "He'll make you good broth and I'll have them mash some potatoes with the Klim. How do you feel?"

"Much better."

"Isn't that lovely. You know I thought perhaps you would. You were sleeping when I left."

"I had a good sleep. Did you walk far?"

"No. Just around behind the hill. I made quite a good shot on the Tommy."

"You shoot marvellously you know."

"I love it. I've loved Africa. Really. If *you're* all right it's the most fun that I've ever had. You don't know the fun it's been to shoot with you. I've loved the country."

"I love it too."

"Darling you don't know how marvellous it is to see you feeling better. I couldn't stand it when you felt that way. You won't talk to me like that again, will you? Promise me?"

"No," he said. "I don't remember what I said."

"You don't have to destroy me. Do you? I'm only a middle-aged woman who loves you and wants to do what you want to do. I've been destroyed two or three times already. You wouldn't want to destroy me again, would you?"

"I'd like to destroy you a few times in bed," he said.

"Yes. That's the good destruction. That's the way we're made to be destroyed. The plane will be here tomorrow."

"How do you know?"

"I'm sure. It's bound to come. The boys have the wood all ready and the grass to make the smudge. I went down and looked at it again today. There's plenty of room to land and we have the smudges ready at both ends."

"What makes you think it will come tomorrow?"

"I'm sure it will. It's overdue now. Then, in town, they will fix up your leg and then we will have some good destruction. Not that dreadful talking kind."

"Should we have a drink? The sun is down."

"Do you think you should?"

"I'm having one."

"We'll have one together. *Molo, letti dui whiskey-soda!*" she called.

"You'd better put on your mosquito boots," he told her.

"I'll wait till I bathe . . ."

While it grew dark they drank and just before it was dark and there was no longer enough light to shoot, a hyena crossed the open on his way around the hill.

"That bastard crosses there every night," the man said. "Every night for two weeks."

"He's the one makes the noise at night. I don't mind it. They're a filthy animal though."

Drinking together, with no pain now except the discomfort of lying in the one position, the boys lighting a fire, its shadow jumping on the tents, he could feel the return of acquiescence in this life of pleasant surrender. She *was* very good to him. He had been cruel and unjust in the afternoon. She was a fine woman, marvellous really. And just then it occurred to him that he was going to die.

It came with a rush; not as a rush of water nor of wind; but of a sudden evil smelling emptiness and the odd thing was that the hyena slipped lightly along the edge of it.

"What is it, Harry?" she asked him.

"Nothing," he said. "You had better move over to the other side. To windward."

"Did Molo change the dressing?"

"Yes. I'm just using the boric now."

"How do you feel?"

"A little wobbly."

"I'm going in to bathe," she said. "I'll be right out. I'll eat with you and then we'll put the cot in."

So, he said to himself, we did well to stop the quarreling. He had never quarreled much with this woman, while with the women that he loved he had quarreled so much they had finally, always, with the corrosion of the quarreling, killed what they had together. He had loved too much, demanded too much, and he wore it all out.

    *He thought about alone in Constantinople that time, having quarreled in Paris before he had gone out. He had whored the whole time and then, when that was over, and he had failed to kill his loneliness, but only made it worse, he had written her, the first one, the one who left him, a letter telling her how he had never been able to kill it . . . How when he thought he saw her outside the* Regence *one time it made him go all faint and sick inside, and that he would follow a woman who looked like her in some way, along the Boulevard, afraid to see it was not she, afraid to lose the feeling it gave him. How everyone he had slept with had only made him miss her more. How what she had done could never matter since he knew he could not cure himself of loving her. He wrote this letter at the Club, cold sober, and mailed it to New York asking her to write him at the office in Paris. That seemed safe. And that night missing her so much it made him feel hollow sick inside, he wandered up past Taxim's, picked a girl up and took her out to supper. He had gone to a place to dance with her afterward, she danced badly, and left her for a hot Armenian slut, that swung her belly against him so it almost scalded. He took her away from a British gunner subaltern after a row. The gunner asked him outside and they fought in the street on the cobbles in the dark. He'd hit him twice, hard, on the side of the jaw and when he didn't go down he knew he was in for a fight. The gunner hit him in the body, then beside his eye. He swung with his left again and landed and the gunner fell on him and grabbed his coat and tore the sleeve off and he clubbed him twice behind the ear and then smashed him with his right as he pushed him away. When the gunner went down his head hit first and he ran with the girl because they heard the M.P.'s coming. They got into a taxi and drove out to Rimmily Hissa along the Bosphorus, and around, and back in the cool night and went to bed and she felt as overripe as she looked but smooth, rose-petal, syrupy, smooth-bellied, big-breasted and needed no pillow under her, and he left her before she was awake looking blowzy enough in the first daylight and turned up at the Pera Palace with a black eye, carrying his coat because one sleeve was missing. That same night he left for Anatolia and he remembered, later on that trip, riding all day through fields of the poppies that they raised for opium and how strange it made you feel finally and all the distances seemed wrong, to where they had made the attack with the newly arrived Constantine officers, that did not know a goddamned thing, and the artillery had fired into the troops and the British observer had cried like a child. That was the day he'd first seen dead men wearing white ballet skirts and upturned shoes with pompons on them. The Turks had come steadily and lumpily and he had seen the skirted men running and the officers shooting into them and running then themselves and he and the British observer had run too until his lungs ached and his mouth was full of the taste of pennies and they stopped behind some rocks and there were the Turks coming as lumpily as ever. Later he had seen the things that he could never think of and later still he had seen much worse. So when he got back to Paris that time he could not talk about it or stand to have it mentioned. And there in the café as he passed was that American poet with a pile of saucers in front of him and a stupid look on his potato face talking about the Dada movement with a Roumanian who said his name was Tristan Tzara, who always wore a monocle and had a headache, and, back at the apartment with his wife that now he loved again, the quarrel all over, the madness all over, glad to be home, the office sent his mail up to the flat. So when the letter in answer to the one he'd written came in on a platter one morning and when he saw the handwriting he went cold all over and tried to slip the letter underneath another. But his wife said, "Who is that letter from, dear?" and that was the end of the beginning of that. He remembered the good times with them all, and the quarrels. They always picked the finest places to have the quarrels. And why had they always quarreled when he was feeling best? He had never written any of that because, at first, he never wanted to hurt anyone and then it seemed as though there was enough to write without it. But he had always thought that he would write it finally. There was so much to write. He had seen the world change; not just the events; although he had seen many of them and had watched the people, but he had seen the subtler change and he could remember how the people were at different times. He had been in it and he had watched it and it was his duty to write of it; but now he never would.*

"How do you feel?" she said. She had come out from the tent now after her bath.

"All right."

"Could you eat now?" He saw Molo behind her with the folding table and the other boy with the dishes.

"I want to write," he said.

"You ought to take some broth to keep your strength up."

"I'm going to die tonight." he said. "I don't need my strength up."

"Don't be melodramatic, Harry, please," she said.

"Why don't you use your nose? I'm rotted half way up my thigh now. What the hell should I fool with broth for? Molo bring whisky-soda."

"Please take the broth," she said gently.

"All right."

The broth was too hot. He had to hold it in the cup until it cooled enough to take it and then he just got it down without gagging.

"You're a fine woman," he said. "Don't pay any attention to me."

She looked at him with her well known, well loved face from *Spur* and *Town and Country*, only a little the worse for drink, only a little the worse for bed, but *Town and Country* never showed those good breasts and those useful thighs and those lightly small-of-back caressing hands, and as he looked and saw her well known pleasant smile, he felt death come again. This time there was no rush. It was a puff, as of a wind that makes a candle flicker and the flame go tall.

"They can bring my net out later and hang it from the tree and build the fire up. I'm not going in the tent tonight. It's not worth moving. It's a clear night. There won't be any rain."

So this was how you died, in whispers that you did not hear. Well, there would be no more quarreling. He could promise that. The one experience that he had never had he was not going to spoil now. He probably would. You spoiled everything. But perhaps he wouldn't.

"You can't take dictation, can you?"

"I never learned," she told him.

"That's all right."

There wasn't time, of course, although it seemed as though it telescoped so that you might put it all into one paragraph if you could get it right.

*There was a log house, chinked white with mortar, on a hill above the lake. There was a bell on a pole by the door to call the people to meals. Behind the house were fields and behind the fields was the timber. A line of lombardy poplars ran from the house to the dock. Other poplars ran along the point. A road went up to the hills along the edge of the timber and along that road he picked blackberries. Then that log house was burned down and all the guns that had been on deer foot racks above the open fire place were burned and afterwards their barrels, with the lead melted in the magazines, and the stocks burned away, lay out on the heap of ashes that were used to make lye for the big iron soap kettles, and you asked Grandfather if you could have them to play with, and he said, no. You see they were his guns still and he never bought any others. Nor did he hunt any more. The house was rebuilt in the same place out of lumber now and painted white and from its porch you saw the poplars and the lake beyond; but there were never any more guns. The barrels of the guns that had hung on the deer feet on the wall of the log house lay out there on the heap of ashes and no one ever touched them.*

In the Black Forest, after the war, we rented a trout stream and there were two ways to walk to it. One was down the valley from Triberg and around the valley road in the shade of the trees that bordered the white road, and then up a side road that went up through the hills past many small farms, with the big Schwartzwald houses, until that road crossed the stream. That was where our fishing began. The other way was to climb steeply up to the edge of the woods and then go across the top of the hills through the pine woods, and then out to the edge of a meadow and down across this meadow to the bridge. There were birches along the stream and it was not big, but narrow, clear and fast, with pools where it had cut under the roots of the birches. At the Hotel in Triberg the proprietor had a fine season. It was very pleasant and we were all great friends. The next year came the inflation and the money he had made the year before was not enough to buy supplies to open the hotel and he hanged himself.

You could dictate that, but you could not dictate the Place Contrescarpe where the flower sellers dyed their flowers in the street and the dye ran over the paving where the autobus started and the old men and the women, always drunk on wine and bad marc; and the children with their noses running in the cold; the smell of dirty sweat and poverty and drunkenness at the Café des Amateurs and the whores at the Bal Musette they lived above. The Concierge who entertained the trooper of the Garde Republicaine in her loge, his horsehair plumed helmet on a chair. The locataire across the hall whose husband was a bicycle racer and her joy that morning at the Cremerie when she had opened L'Auto and seen where he placed third in Paris-Tours, his first big race. She had blushed and laughed and then gone upstairs crying with the yellow sporting paper in her hand. The husband of the woman who ran the Bal Musette drove a taxi and when he, Harry, had to take an early plane the husband knocked upon the door to wake him and they each drank a glass of white wine at the Zinc of the bar before they started. He knew his neighbors in that quarter then because they were all poor. Around that Place there were two kinds; the drunkards and the sportifs. The drunkards killed their poverty that way; the sportifs took it out in exercise. They were the descendants of the Communards and it was no struggle for them to know their politics. They knew who had shot their fathers, their relatives, their brothers, and their friends when the Versailles troops came in and took the town after the Commune and executed anyone they could catch with calloused hands, or who wore a cap, or carried any other sign he was a working man. And in that poverty, and in that quarter across the street from Boucherie Chevaline and a wine co-operative he had written the start of all he was to do. There never was another part of Paris that he loved like that, the sprawl-

ing trees, the old white plastered houses painted brown below, the long
green of the autobus in that round square, the purple flower dye upon
the paving, the sudden drop down the hill of the rue Cardinal Lemoine to
the River, and the other way the narrow crowded world of the rue Mouffe-
tard. The street that ran up toward the Pantheon and the other that he
always took with the bicycle, the only asphalted street in all that quarter,
smooth under the tires, with the high narrow houses and the cheap tall
hotel where Paul Verlaine had died. There were only two rooms in the
apartment where they lived and he had a room on the top floor of that
hotel that cost him sixty francs a month where he did his writing, and
from it he could see the roofs and chimney pots and all the hills of Paris.

From the apartment you could only see the wood and coal man's
place. He sold wine too, bad wine. The golden horse's head outside
the Boucherie Chevaline where the carcasses hung yellow gold and red
in the open window, and the green painted co-operative where they bought
their wine; good wine and cheap. The rest was plaster walls and the
windows of the neighbors. The neighbors who, at night, when someone
lay drunk in the street, moaning and groaning in that typical French
ivresse that you were propaganded to believe did not exist, would open
their windows and then the murmur of talk.

"Where is the policeman? When you don't want him the bugger is
always there. He's sleeping with some concierge. Get the Agent."
Till someone threw a bucket of water from a window and the moaning
stopped. "What's that? Water. Ah, that's intelligent." And the
windows shutting. Marie, his femme de ménage, protesting against the
eight hour day saying, "If a husband works until six he gets only a little
drunk on the way home and does not waste too much. If he works only
until five he is drunk every night and one has no money. It is the wife of
the working man who suffers from this shortening of hours."

"Wouldn't you like some more broth?" the woman asked him now.

"No thank you very much. It is awfully good."

"Try just a little."

"I would like a whiskey-soda."

"It's not good for you."

"No. It's bad for me. Cole Porter wrote the words and the music.
This knowledge that you're going mad for me."

"You know I like you to drink."

"Oh yes. Only it's bad for me."

When she goes, he thought. I'll have all I want. Not all I want
but all there is. Ayee he was tired. Too tired. He was going to sleep
a little while. He lay still and death was not there. It must have gone
around another street. It went in pairs, on bicycles, and moved absolutely silently on the pavements.

*No, he had never written about Paris. Not the Paris that he cared about. But what about the rest that he had never written.*

*What about the ranch and the silvered gray of the sage brush, the quick, clear water in the irrigation ditches, and the heavy green of the alfalfa. The trail went up into the hills and the cattle in the summer were shy as deer. The bawling and the steady noise and slow moving mass raising a dust as you brought them down in the fall. And behind the mountains, the clear sharpness of the peak in the evening light and riding down along the trail in the moonlight, bright across the valley. Now he remembered coming down through the timber in the dark holding the horse's tail when you could not see and all the stories that he meant to write.*

*About the half-wit chore boy who was left at the ranch that time and told not to let anyone get any hay, and that old bastard from the Forks who had beaten the boy when he had worked for him stopping to get some feed. The boy refusing and the old man saying he would beat him again. The boy got the rifle from the kitchen and shot him when he tried to come into the barn and when they came back to the ranch he'd been dead a week, frozen in the corral, and the dogs had eaten a big part of him. But what was left you packed on a sled wrapped in a blanket and roped on and you got the boy to help you haul it, and the two of you took it out over the road on skis, and sixty miles down to town to turn the boy over. He having no idea he would be arrested. Thinking he had done his duty and that you were his friend and he would be rewarded. He'd helped to haul the old man in so everybody could know how bad the old man had been and how he'd tried to steal some feed that didn't belong to him, and when the sheriff put the handcuffs on the boy he couldn't believe it. Then he'd started to cry. That was one story he had saved to write. He knew at least twenty good stories from out there and he had never written one. Why?*

"You tell them why," he said.

"Why what, dear?"

"Why nothing."

She didn't drink so much, now, since she had him. But if he lived he would never write about her, he knew that now. Nor about any of them. The rich were dull and they drank too much, or they played too much backgammon. They were dull and they were repetitious. He remembered poor Scott Fitzgerald and his romantic awe of them and how he had started a story once that began, "The very rich are different from you and me." And how someone had said to Scott, Yes they have more money. But that was not humorous to Scott. He thought they were a special glamorous race and when he found they weren't it wrecked him just as much as any other thing that wrecked him.

He had been contemptuous of those who wrecked. You did not have to like it because you understood it. He could beat anything, he thought, because no thing could hurt him if he did not care.

All right. Now he would not care for death. One thing he had always dreaded was the pain. He could stand pain as well as any man, until it went on too long, and wore him out, but here he had something that had hurt frightfully and just when he had felt it breaking him, the pain had stopped.

*He remembered long ago when Williamson, the bombing officer, had been hit by a stick bomb someone in a German patrol had thrown as he was coming in through the wire that night and, screaming, had begged everyone to kill him. He was a fat man, very brave, and a good officer, although addicted to fantastic shows. But that night he was caught in the wire, with a flare lighting him up and his bowels spilled out into the wire, so when they brought him in, alive, they had to cut him loose. Shoot me, Harry. For Christ's sake shoot me. They had had an argument one time about our Lord never sending you anything you could not bear and someone's theory had been that meant that at a certain time the pain passed you out automatically. But he had always remembered William-son that night. Nothing passed out Williamson until he gave him all his morphine tablets that he had always saved to use himself and then they did not work right away.*

Still this now, that he had, was very easy; and if it was no worse as it went on there was nothing to worry about. Except that he would rather be in better company.

He thought a little about the company that he would like to have.

No, he thought, when everything you do, you do too long, and do too late, you can't expect to find the people still there. The people all are gone. The party's over and you are with your hostess now.

I'm getting as bored with dying as with everything else, he thought.

"It's a bore," he said out loud.

"What is, my dear?"

"Anything you do too bloody long."

He looked at her face between him and the fire. She was leaning back in the chair and the firelight shone on her pleasantly lined face and he could see that she was sleepy. He heard the hyena make a noise just outside the range of the fire.

"I've been writing," he said. "But I got tired."

"Do you think you will be able to sleep?"

"Pretty sure. Why don't you turn in?"

"I like to sit here with you."

"Do you feel anything strange?" he asked her.

"No. Just a little sleepy."

"I do," he said.

He had just felt death come by again.

"You know the only thing I've never lost is curiosity," he said to her.

"You've never lost anything. You're the most complete man I've ever known."

"Christ," he said. "How little a woman knows. What is that? Your intuition?"

Because, just then, death had come and rested its head on the foot of the cot and he could smell its breath.

"Never believe any of that about a scythe and a skull," he told her. "It can be two bicycle policemen as easily, or be a bird. Or it can have a wide snout like a hyena."

It had moved up on him now, but it had no shape any more. It simply occupied space.

"Tell it to go away."

It did not go away but moved a little closer.

"You've got a hell of a breath," he told it. "You stinking bastard."

It moved up closer to him still and now he could not speak to it, and when it saw he could not speak it came a little closer, and now he tried to send it away without speaking, but it moved in on him so its weight was all upon his chest, and while it crouched there and he could not move, or speak, he heard the woman say, "Bwana is asleep now. Take the cot up very gently and carry it into the tent."

He could not speak to tell her to make it go away and it crouched now, heavier, so he could not breathe. And then, while they lifted the cot, suddenly it was all right and the weight went from his chest.

It was morning and had been morning for some time and he heard the plane. It showed very tiny and then made a wide circle and the boys ran out and lit the fires, using kerosene, and piled on grass so there were two big smudges at each end of the level place and the morning breeze blew them toward the camp and the plane circled twice more, low this time, and then glided down and levelled off and landed smoothly and, coming walking toward him, was old Compton in slacks, a tweed jacket and a brown felt hat.

"What's the matter, old cock?" Compton said.

"Bad leg," he told him. "Will you have some breakfast?"

"Thanks. I'll just have some tea. It's the Puss Moth you know. I won't be able to take the Memsahib. There's only room for one. Your lorry is on the way."

Helen had taken Compton aside and was speaking to him. Compton came back more cheery than ever.

"We'll get you right in," he said. "I'll be back for the Mem. Now

I'm afraid I'll have to stop at Arusha to refuel. We'd better get going."

"What about the tea?"

"I don't really care about it you know."

The boys had picked up the cot and carried it around the green tents and down along the rock and out onto the plain and along past the smudges that were burning brightly now, the grass all consumed, and the wind fanning the fire, to the little plane. It was difficult getting him in, but once in he lay back in the leather seat, and the leg was stuck straight out to one side of the seat where Compton sat. Compton started the motor and got in. He waved to Helen and to the boys and, as the clatter moved into the old familiar roar, they swung around with Compie watching for warthog holes and roared, bumping, along the stretch between the fires and with the last bump rose and he saw them all standing below, waving, and the camp beside the hill, flattening now, and the plain spreading, clumps of trees, and the bush flattening, while the game trails ran now smoothly to the dry waterholes, and there was a new water that he had never known of. The zebra, small rounded backs now, and the wildebeeste, big headed dots seeming to climb as they moved in long fingers across the plain, now scattering as the shadow came toward them, they were tiny now, and the movement had no gallop, and the plain as far as you could see, gray-yellow now and ahead old Compie's tweed back and the brown felt hat. Then they were over the first hills and the wildebeeste were trailing up them, and then they were over mountains with sudden depths of green-rising forest and the solid bamboo slopes, and then the heavy forest again, sculptured into peaks and hollows until they crossed, and hills sloped down and then another plain, hot now, and purple brown, bumpy, with heat and Compie looking back to see how he was riding. Then there were other mountains dark ahead. And then instead of going on to Arusha they turned left, he evidently figured that they had the gas, and looking down he saw a pink sifting cloud, moving over the ground, and in the air, like the first snow in a blizzard, that comes from nowhere, and he knew the locusts were coming up from the South. Then they began to climb and they were going to the East it seemed, and then it darkened and they were in a storm, the rain so thick it seemed like flying through a waterfall, and then they were out and Compie turned his head and grinned and pointed and there, ahead, all he could see, as wide as all the world, great, high, and unbelievably white in the sun, was the square top of Kilimanjaro. And then he knew that there was where he was going.

Just then the hyena stopped whimpering in the night and started to make a strange, human, almost crying sound. The woman heard it and stirred uneasily. She did not wake. In her dream she was at the house on Long Island and it was the night before her daughter's début. Somehow her father was there and he had been very rude. Then the noise the hyena made was so loud she woke and for a moment she did not know where she was and she was very afraid. Then she took the flashlight and shone it on the other cot that they had carried in after Harry had gone to sleep. She could see his bulk under the mosquito bar but somehow he had gotten his leg out and it hung down alongside the cot. The dressings had all come down and she could not look at it.

"Molo," she called. "Molo! Molo!"

Then she said, "Harry, Harry!" Then her voice rising, "Harry! Please, Oh Harry!"

There was no answer and she could not hear him breathing.

Outside the tent the hyena made the same strange noise that had awakened her. But she did not hear him for the beating of her heart.

# Stephen Vincent Benét (1898–1943)

ONE OF THE TWO poetry-writing Benét brothers — the other was William Rose — Stephen Vincent was a native of Pennsylvania and a Yale graduate (1919). Two books of his poems were published while he was still a student and a novel soon after his graduation, but it was not until he wrote about America that his work became of permanent interest. *John Brown's Body* (1928), a long narrative poem of the Civil War, won a Pulitzer Prize, and he based a successful folk opera on one of his best-known short stories, "The Devil and Daniel Webster" (1937). His intense hatred of Fascism then on the rise in Europe was voiced in *Nightmare at Noon* (1940), poetry warning America of its danger. A collection of his short stories is *Tales Before Midnight* (1939).

It is both interesting and amusing to compare "A Tooth for Paul Revere" with another narrative on the same theme, Longfellow's "Midnight Ride of Paul Revere." Both are historically inaccurate although Benét's account is nearer to the truth. Revere was never guided by signals from lanterns in a church tower and he never went to Concord that night. He went to Lexington, Lige Butterwick's home town, as in this story. It was a Dr. Samuel Prescott who raised the alarm "The British are coming!" when he, and not Revere, went to Concord. But who cares? Both are exciting stories that can arouse patriotic fervor.

# A Tooth for Paul Revere

SOME SAY it all happened because of Hancock and Adams (said the old man, pulling at his pipe), and some put it back to the Stamp Act and before. Then there's some hold out for Paul Revere and his little silver box. But the way I heard it, it broke loose because of Lige Butterwick and his tooth.

What's that? Why, the American Revolution, of course. What else would I be talking about? Well, your story about the land down South that they had to plow with alligators reminded me.

No, this is a true story — or at least that's how I heard it told. My great-aunt was a Butterwick, and I heard it from her. And every now and then she'd write it out and want to get it put in the history books. But they'd always put her off with some trifling sort of excuse. Till finally she got her dander up and wrote direct to the President of the United States. Well, no, he didn't answer himself exactly — the President's apt to be a pretty busy man. But the letter said he'd received her interesting communication and thanked her for it, so that shows you. We've got it framed, in the trailer — the ink's a little faded, but you can make out the man's name who signed it. It's either Bowers or Thorpe, and he wrote a very nice hand.

You see, my great-aunt, she wasn't very respectful to the kind of history that does get into the books. What she liked was the queer corners of it and the tales that get handed down in families. Take Paul Revere, for instance — all most folks think about, with him, is his riding a horse. But when she talked about Paul Revere — why, you could just see him in his shop, brewing the American Revolution in a silver teapot and waiting for it to settle. Oh, yes, he was a silversmith by trade — but she claimed he was something more. She claimed there was a kind of magic in that quick, skillful hand of his — and that he was one of the kind of folks that can see just a little bit farther into a millstone than most. But it was when she got to Lige Butterwick that she really turned herself loose.

For she claimed that it took all sorts to make a country — and that meant the dumb ones, too. I don't mean ijits or nincompoops — just the ordinary folks that live along from day to day. And that day may be a notable day in history — but it's just Tuesday to them till they read all about it in the papers. Oh, the heroes and the great men — they can plan and contrive and see ahead, but it isn't till the Lige Butterwicks get stirred up that things really start to happen. Or so she claimed. And the way that they do get stirred up is often curious, as she'd tell this story to prove.

For, now you take Lige Butterwick — and before his tooth started aching he was just like you and me. He lived on a farm about eight miles from Lexington, Massachusetts, and he was a peaceable man. It was troubled times in the American colonies, what with British warships in Boston Harbor and British soldiers in Boston and Sons of Liberty hooting the British soldiers — not to speak of Boston tea parties and such. But Lige Butterwick, he worked his farm and didn't pay much attention. There's lots of people like that, even in troubled times.

When he went into town, to be sure, there was high talk at the tavern. But he bought his goods and came home again — he had ideas about politics, but he didn't talk about them much. He had a good farm and it kept him busy — he had a wife and five children and they kept him humping. The young folks could argue about King George and Sam Adams — he wondered how the corn was going to stand that year. Now and then, if somebody said that this and that was a burning shame, he'd allow as to how it might be, just to be neighborly. But, inside, he was wondering whether next year he mightn't make an experiment and plant the west field in rye.

Well, everything went along for him the way that it does for most folks with good years and bad years, till one April morning, in 1775, he woke up with a toothache. Being the kind of man he was, he didn't pay much attention to it at first. But he mentioned it that evening at supper, and his wife got a bag of hot salt for him. He held it to his face and it seemed to ease him, but he couldn't hold it there all night, and next morning the tooth hurt worse than ever.

Well, he stood it the next day and the next, but it didn't improve any. He tried tansy tea and other remedies — he tried tying a string to it and having his wife slam the door, but when it came to the pinch he couldn't quite do it. So finally he took the horse and rode into Lexington town to have it seen to. Mrs. Butterwick made him — she said it might be an expense, but anything was better than having him act as if he wanted to kick the cat across the room every time she put her feet down hard.

When he got into Lexington, he noticed that folks there seemed kind of excited. There was a lot of talk about muskets and powder and a couple of men called Hancock and Adams who were staying at Parson Clarke's. But Lige Butterwick had his own business to attend to — and, besides, his tooth was jumping so he wasn't in any mood for conversation. He set off for the local barber's, as being the likeliest man he knew to pull a tooth.

The barber took one look at it and shook his head.

"I can pull her, Lige," he said. "Oh, I can pull her, all right. But she's got long roots and strong roots, and she's going to leave an awful gap when she's gone. Now, what you really need," he said, kind of excited, for he was one of those perky little men who's always interested in the latest notion, "what you really need — though it's taking away my business — is one of these-here artificial teeth to go in the hole."

"Artificial teeth!" said Lige. "It's flying in the face of Nature!"

The barber shook his head. "No, Lige," he said. "That's where you're wrong. Artificial teeth is all the go these days, and Lexington ought to keep up with the times. It would do me good to see you with an artificial tooth — it would so."

"Well, it might do *you* good," said Lige, rather crossly, for his tooth was jumping; "but supposing I did want one — how in tunket will I get one in Lexington?"

"Now you just leave that to me," said the barber, all excited, and he started to rummage around. "You'll have to go to Boston for it, but I know just the man." He was one of those men who can always tell you where to go and it's usually wrong. "See here," he went on. "There's a fellow called Revere in Boston that fixes them and they say he's a boss workman. Just take a look at this prospectus" — and he started to read from a paper: "Whereas many persons are so unfortunate as to lose their fore-teeth" — that's you, Lige — "to their great detriment, not only in looks but in speaking, both in public and private, this is to inform all such that they may have them replaced by artificial ones" — see? — "that look as well as the natural and answer the end of speaking to all intents" — and then he's got his name — Paul Revere, goldsmith, near the head of Doctor Clarke's wharf, Boston."

"Sounds well enough," said Lige, "but what's it going to cost?"

"Oh, I know Revere," said the barber, swelling up like a robin. "Comes through here pretty often, as a matter of fact. And he's a decent fellow, if he is a pretty big bug in the Sons of Liberty. You just mention my name."

"Well, it's something I hadn't thought of," said Lige, as his tooth gave another red-hot jounce, "but in for a penny, in for a pound. I've missed a day's work already, and that tooth's got to come out before I go stark, staring mad. But what sort of man is this Revere, anyway?"

"Oh, he's a regular wizard!" said the barber. "A regular wizard with his tools."

"Wizard!" said Lige. "Well, I don't know about wizards. But if he can fix my tooth I'll call him one."

"You'll never regret it," said the barber — and that's the way folks always talk when they're sending someone else to the dentist. So Lige Butterwick got on his horse again and started out for Boston. A couple of people shouted at him as he rode down the street, but he didn't pay any attention. And going by Parson Clarke's he caught a glimpse of two men talking in the Parson's front room. One was a tallish, hand-somish man in pretty fine clothes and the other was shorter and untidy, with a kind of bulldog face. But they were strangers to him and he didn't really notice them — just rode ahead.

## II

But as soon as he got into Boston he started to feel queer — and it wasn't only his tooth. He hadn't been there in four years and he'd expected to find it changed, but it wasn't that. It was a clear enough day, and yet he kept feeling there was thunder in the air. There'd be knots of people talking and arguing on street corners, and then, when you got closer to them, they'd kind of melt away. Or if they stayed, they'd look at you out of the corners of their eyes. And there in the Port of Boston were the British warships, black and grim. He'd known they'd be there, of course, but it was different seeing them. It made him feel queer to see their guns pointed at the town. He'd known there was trouble and dispute in Boston, but the knowledge had passed over him like rain and hail. But now here he was in the middle of it — and it smelt like earthquake weather. He couldn't make head or tail of it, but he wanted to be home.

All the same, he'd come to get his tooth fixed, and being New England he was bound to do it. But first he stopped at a tavern for a bite and a sup, for it was long past his dinnertime. And there, it seemed to him, things got even more curious.

"Nice weather we're having these days," he said in a friendly way to the barkeep.

"It's bitter weather for Boston," said the barkeep in an unfriendly voice, and a sort of low growl went up from the boys at the back of the room and every eye fixed on Lige.

Well, that didn't help the toothache any, but being a sociable person, Lige kept on.

"May be for Boston," he said, "but out in the country we'd call it good planting weather."

The barkeep stared at him hard.

"I guess I was mistaken in you," he said. "It *is* good planting weather — for some kinds of trees."

"And what kind of trees were you thinking of?" said a sharp-faced man at Lige's left, and squeezed his shoulder.

"There's trees and trees, you know," said a red-faced man at Lige's right, and gave him a dig in the ribs.

"Well, now that you ask me — " said Lige, but he couldn't even finish before the red-faced man dug him hard in the ribs again.

"The liberty tree!" said the red-faced man. "And may it soon be watered in the blood of tyrants!"

"The royal oak of England!" said the sharp-faced man. "And God save King George and loyalty!"

Well, with that it seemed to Lige Butterwick as if the whole tavern kind of riz up at him. He was kicked and pummeled and mauled and thrown into a corner and yanked out of it again, with the red-faced man and all the rest of them dancing quadrilles over his prostrate form. Till finally he found himself out in the street with half his coat gone galley-west.

"Well," said Lige to himself, "I always heard city folks were crazy. But politics must be getting serious in these American colonies when they start fighting about trees!"

Then he saw the sharp-faced man was beside him, trying to shake his hand. He noticed with some pleasure that the sharp-faced man had the beginnings of a beautiful black eye.

"Nobly done, friend," said the sharp-faced man, "and I'm glad to find another true-hearted loyalist in this pestilent, rebellious city."

"Well, I don't know as I quite agree with you about that," said Lige. "But I came here to get my tooth fixed, not to talk politics. And as long as you've spoken so pleasant, I wonder if you could help me out. You see, I'm from Lexington way — and I'm looking for a fellow named Paul Revere — "

"Paul Revere!" said the sharp-faced man, as if the name hit him like a bullet. Then he began to smile again — not a pleasant smile.

"Oh, it's Paul Revere you want, my worthy and ingenuous friend from the country," he said. "Well, I'll tell you how to find him. You go up to the first British soldier you see and ask the way. But you better give the password first."

"Password?" said Lige Butterwick, scratching his ear.

"Yes," said the sharp-faced man, and his smile got wider. "You say to that British soldier, 'Any lobsters for sale today?' Then you ask about Revere."

"But why do I talk about lobsters first?" said Lige Butterwick, kind of stubborn.

"Well, you see," said the sharp-faced man, "the British soldiers wear red coats. So they like being asked about lobsters. Try it and see." And he went away, with his shoulders shaking.

Well, that seemed queer to Lige Butterwick, but no queerer than the other things that had happened that day. All the same, he didn't quite trust the sharp-faced man, so he took care not to come too close to the British patrol when he asked them about the lobsters. And it was lucky he did, for no sooner were the words out of his mouth than the British soldiers took after him and chased him clear down to the wharves before he could get away. At that, he only managed it by hiding in an empty tar-barrel, and when he got out he was certainly a sight for sore eyes.

"Well, I guess that couldn't have been the right password," he said to himself, kind of grimly, as he tried to rub off some of the tar. "All the same, I don't think soldiers ought to act like that when you ask them a civil question. But city folks or soldiers, they can't make a fool out of me. I came here to get my tooth fixed and get it fixed I will, if I have to surprise the whole British Empire to do it."

And just then he saw a sign on a shop at the end of the wharf. And, according to my great-aunt, this was what was on the sign. It said "PAUL REVERE, SILVERSMITH" at the top, and then, under it, in smaller letters: "Large and small bells cast to order, engraving and printing done in job lots, artificial teeth sculptured and copper boilers mended, all branches of goldsmith and silversmith work and revolutions put up to take out. Express Service, Tuesdays and Fridays, to Lexington, Concord and Points West."

"Well," said Lige Butterwick, "kind of a jack-of-all-trades. Now maybe I can get my tooth fixed." And he marched up to the door.

## III

Paul Revere was behind the counter when Lige came in, turning a silver bowl over and over in his hands. A man of forty-odd he was, with a quick, keen face and snapping eyes. He was wearing Boston clothes, but there was a French look about him — for his father was Apollos Rivoire from the island of Guernsey, and good French Huguenot stock. They'd changed the name to Revere when they crossed the water.

It wasn't such a big shop, but it had silver pieces in it that people have paid thousands for since. And the silver pieces weren't all. There were prints and engravings of the Port of Boston and caricatures of the British and all sorts of goldsmith work, more than you could put a name to. It was a crowded place, but shipshape. And Paul Revere moved about it, quick and keen, with his eyes full of life and hot temper — the kind of man who knows what he wants to do and does it the next minute.

There were quite a few customers there when Lige Butterwick first came in — so he sort of scrooged back in a corner and waited his chance. For one thing, after the queer sign and the barber's calling him a wizard, he wanted to be sure about this fellow Revere, and see what kind of customers came to his shop.

Well, there was a woman who wanted a christening mug for a baby and a man who wanted a print of the Boston Massacre. And then there was a fellow who passed Revere some sort of message under cover — Lige caught the whisper, "powder" and "Sons of Liberty," though he couldn't make out the rest. And finally there was a very fine silk-dressed lady who seemed to be giving Revere considerable trouble. Lige peeked at her round the corner of his chair, and somehow or other she reminded him of a turkey-gobbler, especially the strut.

She was complaining about some silver that Paul Revere had made for her — expensive silver it must have been. And "Oh, Master Revere, I'm so disappointed!" she was saying. "When I took the things from the box, I could just have cried!"

Revere drew himself up a little at that, Lige noticed, but his voice was pleasant.

"It is I who am disappointed, madam," he said, with a little bow. "But what was the trouble? It must have been carelessly packed. Was it badly dented? I'll speak to my boy."

"Oh, no, it wasn't dented," said the turkey-gobbler lady. "But I wanted a really impressive silver service — something I can use when the Governor comes to dinner with us. I certainly *paid* for the best. And what have you given me?"

Lige waited to hear what Paul Revere would say. When he spoke, his voice was stiff.

"I have given you the best work of which I am capable, madam," he said. "It was in my hands for six months — and I think they are skillful hands."

"Oh," said the woman, and rustled her skirts, "I know you're a competent artisan, Master Revere — "

"Silversmith, if you please," said Paul Revere, and the woman rustled again.

"Well, I don't care what you call it," she said, and then you could see her fine accent was put on like her fine clothes. "But I know I wanted a real service — something I could show my friends. And what have you given me? Oh, it's silver, if you choose. But it's just as plain and simple as a picket fence!"

Revere looked at her for a moment and Lige Butterwick thought he'd explode.

"Simple?" he said. "And plain? You pay me high compliments, madam!"

"Compliments, indeed!" said the woman, and now she was getting furious. "I'm sending it back tomorrow! Why, there isn't as much as a lion or a unicorn on the cream jug. And I told you I wanted the sugar bowl covered with silver grapes! But you've given me something as bare as the hills of New England! And I won't stand it, I tell you! I'll send to England instead."

Revere puffed his cheeks and blew, but his eyes were dangerous.

"Send away, madam," he said. "We're making new things in this country — new men — new silver — perhaps, who knows, a new nation. Plain, simple, bare as the hills and rocks of New England — graceful as the boughs of her elm trees — if my silver were only like that, indeed! But that is what I wish to make it. And, as for you, madam" — he stepped toward her like a cat — "with your lions and unicorns and grape leaves and your nonsense of bad ornament done by bad silversmiths — your imported bad taste and your imported British manners — puff!" And he blew at her, just the way you blow at a turkey-gobbler, till she fairly picked up her fine silk skirts and ran. Revere watched her out of the door and turned back, shaking his head.

"William!" he called to the boy who helped him in the shop. "Put up the shutters — we're closing for the day. And William — no word yet from Doctor Warren?"

"Not yet, sir," said the boy, and started to put up the shutters. Then Lige Butterwick thought it was about time to make his presence known.

So he coughed, and Paul Revere whirled and Lige Butterwick felt those quick, keen eyes boring into his. He wasn't exactly afraid of them, for he was stubborn himself, but he knew this was an unexpected kind of man.

"Well, my friend," said Revere, impatiently, "and who in the world are you?"

"Well, Mr. Revere," said Lige Butterwick. "It is Mr. Revere, isn't it? It's kind of a long story. But, closing or not, you've got to listen to me. The barber told me so."

"The barber!" said Revere, kind of dumbfounded.

"Uh-huh," said Lige, and opened his mouth. "You see, it's my tooth."

"Tooth!" said Revere, and stared at him as if they were both crazy. "You'd better begin at the beginning. But wait a minute. You don't talk like a Boston man. Where do you come from?"

"Oh, around Lexington way," said Lige. "And, you see — "

But the mention of Lexington seemed to throw Revere into a regular excitement. He fairly shook Lige by the shoulders.

"Lexington!" he said. "Were you there this morning?"

"Oh course I was," said Lige. "That's where the barber I told you about — "

"Never mind the barber!" said Revere. "Were Mr. Hancock and Mr. Adams still at Parson Clarke's?"

"Well, they might have been for all I know," said Lige. "But I couldn't say."

"Great heaven!" said Revere. "Is there a man in the American colonies who doesn't know Mr. Hancock and Mr. Adams?"

"There seems to be me," said Lige. "But speaking of strangers — there *was* two of them staying at the parsonage, when I rode past. One was a handsomish man and the other looked more like a bulldog — "

"Hancock and Adams!" said Revere. "So they are still there." He took a turn or two up and down the room. "And the British ready to march!" he muttered to himself. "Did you see many soldiers as you came to my shop, Mr. Butterwick?"

"See them?" said Lige. "They chased me into a tar-barrel. And there was a whole passel of them up by the Common with guns and flags. Looked as if they meant business."

Revere took his hand and pumped it up and down.

"Thank you, Mr. Butterwick," he said. "You're a shrewd observer. And you have done me — and the colonies — an invaluable service."

"Well, that's nice to know," said Lige. "But, speaking about this tooth of mine — "

Revere looked at him and laughed, while his eyes crinkled.

"You're a stubborn man, Mr. Butterwick," he said. "All the better. I like stubborn men. I wish we had more of them. Well, one good turn deserves another — you've helped me and I'll do my best to help you.

I've made artificial teeth — but drawing them is hardly my trade. All the same, I'll do what I can for you."

So Lige sat down in a chair and opened his mouth.

"Whew!" said Revere, with his eyes dancing. His voice grew solemn. "Mr. Butterwick," he said, "it seems to be a compound, agglutinated infraction of the upper molar. I'm afraid I can't do anything about it tonight."

"But — " said Lige.

"But here's a draught — that will ease the pain for a while," said Revere, and poured some medicine into a cup. "Drink!" he said, and Lige drank. The draught was red and spicy, with a queer, sleepy taste, but pungent. It wasn't like anything Lige had ever tasted before, but he noticed it eased the pain.

"There," said Revere. "And now you go to a tavern and get a good night's rest. Come back to see me in the morning — I'll find a tooth-drawer for you, if I'm here. And — oh, yes — you'd better have some liniment."

He started to rummage in a big cupboard at the back of the shop. It was dark now, with the end of day and the shutters up, and whether it was the tooth, or the tiredness, or the draught Paul Revere had given him, Lige began to feel a little queer. There was a humming in his head and a lightness in his feet. He got up and stood looking over Paul Revere's shoulder, and it seemed to him that things moved and scampered in that cupboard in a curious way, as Revere's quick fingers took down this box and that. And the shop was full of shadows and murmurings.

"It's a queer kind of shop you've got here, Mr. Revere," he said, glad to hear the sound of his own voice.

"Well, some people think so," said Revere — and that time Lige was almost sure he saw something move in the cupboard. He coughed. "Say — what's in that little bottle?" he said, to keep his mind steady.

"That?" said Paul Revere, with a smile, and held the bottle up. "Oh, that's a little chemical experiment of mine. I call it Essence of Boston. But there's a good deal of East Wind in it."

"Essence of Boston," said Lige, with his eyes bulging. "Well, they did say you was a wizard. It's gen-u-wine magic, I suppose?"

"Genuine magic, of course," said Revere, with a chuckle. "And here's the box with your liniment. And here — "

He took down two little boxes — a silver and a pewter one — and placed them on the counter. But Lige's eyes went to the silver one — they were drawn to it, though he couldn't have told you why.

"Pick it up," said Paul Revere, and Lige did so and turned it in his hands. It was a handsome box. He could make out a growing tree and an eagle fighting a lion. "It's mighty pretty work," he said.

"It's my own design," said Paul Revere. "See the stars around the edge — thirteen of them? You could make a very pretty design with stars — for a new country, say — if you wanted to. I've sometimes thought of it."

"But what's in it?" said Lige.

"What's in it?" said Paul Revere, and his voice was light but steely. "Why, what's in the air around us? Gunpowder and war and the making of a new nation. But the time isn't quite ripe yet — not quite ripe."

"You mean," said Lige — and he looked at the box very respectful — "that this-here revolution folks keep talking about — "

"Yes," said Paul Revere, and he was about to go on. But just then his boy ran in, with a letter in his hand.

"Master!" he said. "A message from Doctor Warren!"

## IV

Well, with that Revere started moving, and, when he started to move, he moved fast. He was calling for his riding boots in one breath and telling Lige Butterwick to come back tomorrow in another — and what with all the bustle and confusion, Lige Butterwick nearly went off without his liniment after all. But he grabbed up a box from the counter just as Revere was practically shoving him out of the door — and it wasn't till he'd got to his tavern and gone to bed for the night that he found out he'd taken the wrong box.

He found it out then because when he went to bed he couldn't get to sleep. It wasn't his tooth that bothered him — that had settled to a kind of dull ache and he could have slept through that — but his mind kept going over all the events of the day — the two folks he'd seen at Parson Clarke's and being chased by the British and what Revere had said to the turkey-gobbler woman — till he couldn't get any peace. He could feel something stirring in him, though he didn't know what it was.

" 'Tain't right to have soldiers chase a fellow down the street," he said to himself. "And 'tain't right to have people like that woman run down New England. No, it ain't. Oh, me — I better look for that liniment of Mr. Revere's."

So he got up from his bed and went over and found his coat. Then he reached his hand in the pocket and pulled out the silver box.

Well, at first he was so flustrated that he didn't know rightly what to do. For here, as well as he could remember it, was gun-powder and war and the makings of a new nation — the revolution itself, shut up in a silver box by Paul Revere. He mightn't have believed there could be such things before he came to Boston. But now he did.

The draught was still humming in his head, and his legs felt a mite wobbly. But, being human, he was curious. "Now, I wonder what *is* inside that box," he said.

He shook the box and handled it, but that seemed to make it warmer, as if there was something alive inside it, so he stopped that mighty quick. Then he looked all over it for a keyhole, but there wasn't any keyhole, and if there had been, he didn't have a key.

Then he put his ear to the box and listened hard. And it seemed to him that he heard, very tiny and far away, inside the box, the rolling fire of thousands of tiny muskets and the tiny, far-away cheers of many men. "Hold your fire!" he heard a voice say. "Don't fire till you're fired on — but if they want a war, let it begin here!" And then there was a rolling of drums and a squeal of fifes. It was small, still, and far away, but it made him shake all over, for he knew he was listening to something in the future — and something that he didn't have a right to hear. He sat down on the edge of his bed with the box in his hands.

"Now, what am I going to do with this?" he said. "It's too big a job for one man."

Well, he thought, kind of scared, of going down to the river and throwing the box in, but, when he thought of doing it, he knew he couldn't. Then he thought of his farm near Lexington and the peaceful days. Once the revolution was out of the box, there'd be an end to that. But then he remembered what Revere had said when he was talking with the woman about the silver — the thing about building a new country and building it clean and plain. "Why, I'm not a Britisher," he thought. "I'm a New Englander. And maybe there's something beyond that — something people like Hancock and Adams know about. And if it has to come with a revolution — well, I guess it has to come. We can't stay Britishers forever, here in this country."

He listened to the box again, and now there wasn't any shooting in it — just a queer tune played on a fife. He didn't know the name of the tune, but it lifted his heart.

He got up, sort of slow and heavy. "I guess I'll have to take this back to Paul Revere," he said.

Well, the first place he went was Doctor Warren's, having heard Revere mention it, but he didn't get much satisfaction there. It took quite a while to convince them that he wasn't a spy, and when he did, all they'd tell him was that Revere had gone over the river to Charlestown. So he went down to the waterfront to look for a boat. And the first person he met was a very angry woman.

"No," she said. "You don't get any boats from me. There was a crazy man along here an hour ago and he wanted a boat too, and my husband was crazy enough to take him. And then do you know what he did?"

"No, mam," said Lige Butterwick.

"He made my husband take my best petticoat to muffle the oars so they wouldn't make a splash when they went past that Britisher ship," she said, pointing out where the man-of-war *Somerset* lay at anchor. "My best petticoat, I tell you! And when my husband comes back he'll get a piece of my mind!"

"Was his name Revere?" said Lige Butterwick. "Was he a man of forty-odd, keen-looking and kind of Frenchy?"

"I don't know what his right name is," said the woman, "but his name's mud with me. My best petticoat tore into strips and swimming in that nasty river!" And that was all he could get out of her.

All the same, he managed to get a boat at last — the story doesn't say how — and row across the river. The tide was at young flood and the moonlight bright on the water, and he passed under the shadow of the *Somerset*, right where Revere had passed. When he got to the Charlestown side he could see the lanterns in North Church, though he didn't know what they signified. Then he told the folks at Charlestown he had news for Revere, and they got him a horse, and so he started to ride. And all the while the silver box was burning his pocket.

Well, he lost his way more or less, as you well might in the darkness, and it was dawn when he came into Lexington by a side road. The dawn in that country's pretty, with the dew still on the grass. But he wasn't looking at the dawn. He was feeling the box burn his pocket and thinking hard.

Then, all of a sudden, he reined up his tired horse. For there on the side road were two men carrying a trunk — and one of them was Paul Revere.

They looked at each other and Lige began to grin. For Revere was just as dirty and mud-splashed as he was — he'd warned Hancock and Adams all right, but then, on his way to Concord, he'd got caught by the British and turned loose again. So he'd gone back to Lexington to see how things were there — and now he and the other fellow were saving a trunk of papers that Hancock had left behind, so they wouldn't fall into the hands of the British.

Lige swung off his horse. "Well, Mr. Revere," he said, "you see I'm on time for that little appointment about my tooth. And by the way, I've got something for you." He took the box from his pocket. And then he looked over toward Lexington Green and caught his breath. For on the Green there was a little line of Minute Men — neighbors of his, as he knew — and in front of them the British regulars.

And, even as he looked there was the sound of a gunshot, and suddenly smoke wrapped the front of the British line and he heard them shout as they ran forward.

Lige Butterwick took the silver box and stamped on it with his heel. And with that the box broke open — and there was a dazzle in his eyes for a moment and a noise of men shouting — and then it was gone.

"Do you know what you've done?" said Revere. "You've let out the American Revolution!"

"Well," said Lige Butterwick, "I guess it was about time. And I guess I'd better be going home, now. I've got a gun on the wall there, and I'll need it."

"But what about your tooth?" said Paul Revere.

"Oh, a tooth's a tooth," said Lige Butterwick. "But a country's a country. And, anyhow, it's stopped aching."

All the same, they say Paul Revere made a silver tooth for him, after the war. But my great-aunt wasn't quite sure of it, so I won't vouch for that.

# Katherine Anne Porter (1890–    )

A SHORT-STORY WRITER, pure, simple, and powerful, Katherine Anne Porter resisted, with one exception, the tremendous pressure on short-story writers to produce novels. She was born in Texas, had a convent education and lived abroad for many years, mainly in Mexico and in Germany and France. *Flowering Judas* (1930), a short-story collection, was her first published book and the beauty of its writing won her immediate recognition as a great literary artist. Other books of hers are *Pale Horse, Pale Rider* (1939), *The Leaning Tower* (1944) and *Collected Stories* (1965). In 1962, thirty-two years after her first book of short stories appeared, her only novel, *A Ship of Fools*, was published. An allegory about the entanglement of good and evil, it was not considered by critics as important as her short stories.

There are so many splendid facets to "Noon Wine" that a seminar on literature could be based on it alone. First, there are the characters. The saucy little boys, the farmer who hated his dairy, his frail wife, the harmonica-playing Swede, his callous pursuer, every single one emerges and stays in the memory as vital, living persons. And the way the Texas farm becomes a familiar place because of the way the author, bit by bit, gives little descriptions of the milk house, the hired man's shack, and all the other parts of the farm, subtly yet vividly. But Porter did not learn such art out of a seminar or textbook, she achieved it because she knew that Texas farm so well and the kind of people who would live on it, she knew what they would do and what would happen when they did it, shattering the pastoral peace with violence. A student once wrote her asking what a small silver dove, found by children playing in a graveyard in another of her stories, was supposed to symbolize. She answered it did not symbolize anything, that it was in the story because she herself as a child playing in a graveyard had once found a small silver dove.

# Noon Wine

THE TWO GRUBBY small boys with tow-colored hair who were digging among the ragweed in the front yard sat back on their heels and said "Hello," when the tall bony man with straw-colored hair turned in at their gate. He did not pause at the gate; it had swung back, conveniently half open, long ago, and was now sunk so firmly on its broken hinges no one thought of trying to close it. He did not even glance at the small boys, much less give them good-day. He just clumped down his big square dusty shoes one after the other steadily, like a man following a plow, as if he knew the place well and knew where he was going and what he would find there. Rounding the right-hand corner of the house under the row of chinaberry trees, he walked up to the side porch where Mr. Thompson was pushing a big swing churn back and forth.

Mr. Thompson was a tough weather-beaten man with stiff black hair and a week's growth of black whiskers. He was a noisy proud man who held his neck so straight his whole face stood level with his Adam's apple, and the whiskers continued down his neck and disappeared into a black thatch under his open collar. The churn rumbled and swished like the belly of a trotting horse, and Mr. Thompson seemed somehow to be driving a horse with one hand, reining it in and urging it forward; and every now and then he turned half way around and squirted a tremendous spit of tobacco juice out over the steps. The door stones were brown and gleaming with fresh tobacco juice. Mr. Thompson had been churning quite a while and he was tired of it. He was just fetching a mouthful of juice to squirt again when the stranger came around the corner and stopped. Mr. Thompson saw a narrow-chested man with blue eyes so pale they were almost white, looking and not looking at him from a long gaunt face, under white eyebrows. Mr. Thompson judged him to be another of these Irishmen, by his long upper lip.

"Howdy do, sir," said Mr. Thompson politely, swinging his churn.

"I need work," said the man, clearly enough but with some kind of foreign accent Mr. Thompson couldn't place. It wasn't Cajun and it wasn't Nigger and it wasn't Dutch, so it had him stumped. "You need a man here?"

Mr. Thompson gave the churn a great shove and it swung back and forth several times on its own momentum. He sat on the steps, shot his quid into the grass, and said, "Set down. Maybe we can make a deal. I been kinda lookin round for somebody. I had two niggers but they got into a cutting scrape up the creek last week, one of 'em dead now and the other in the hoosegow at Cold Springs. Neither one of 'em worth killing, come right down to it. So it looks like I'd better get somebody. Where'd you work last?"

"North Dakota," said the man, folding himself down on the other end of the steps, but not as if he were tired. He folded up and settled down as if it would be a long time before he got up again. He never had looked at Mr. Thompson, but there wasn't anything sneaking in his eye, either. He didn't seem to be looking anywhere else. His eyes sat in his head and let things pass by them. They didn't seem to be expecting to see anything worth looking at. Mr. Thompson waited a long time for the man to say something more, but he had gone into a brown study.

"North Dakota," said Mr. Thompson, trying to remember where that was. "That's a right smart distance off, seems to me."

"I can do everything on farm," said the man, "cheap. I need work."

Mr. Thompson settled himself to get down to business. "My name's Thompson, Mr. Royal Earle Thompson," he said.

"I'm Mr. Helton," said the man, "Mr. Olaf Helton." He did not move.

"Well now," said Mr. Thompson in his most carrying voice, "I guess we'd better talk turkey."

When Mr. Thompson expected to drive a bargain he always grew very hearty and jovial. There was nothing wrong with him except that he hated like the devil to pay wages. He said so himself. "You furnish grub and a shack," he said, "and then you got to pay 'em besides. It aint right. Besides the wear and tear on your implements," he said, "they just let everything go to rack and ruin." So he began to laugh and shout his way through the deal.

"Now what I want to know is, how much you fixing to gouge outa me?" he brayed, slapping his knee. After he had kept it up as long as he could, he quieted down, feeling a little sheepish, and cut himself a chew. Mr. Helton was staring out somewhere between the barn and the orchard, and seemed to be sleeping with his eyes open.

"I'm good worker," said Mr. Helton as from the tomb. "I get dollar a day."

Mr. Thompson was so shocked he forgot to start laughing again at the top of his voice until it was nearly too late to do any good. "Haw, haw," he bawled. "Why, for a dollar a day I'd hire out myself. What kinda work is it where they pay you a dollar a day?"

"Wheatfields, North Dakota," said Mr. Helton, not even smiling.

Mr. Thompson stopped laughing. "Well, this aint any wheatfield by a long shot. This is more of a dairy farm," he said, feeling apologetic. "My wife, she was set on a dairy, she seemed to like working around with cows and calves, so I humored her. But it was a mistake," he said, "I got nearly everything to do, anyhow. My wife aint very strong. She's sick today, that's a fact. She's been porely for the last few days. We plant a little feed, and a corn patch, and there's the orchard, and a few pigs and chickens, but our main hold is the cows. Now just speakin as one man to another, there aint any money in it. Now I can't give you no dollar a day because ackshally I don't make that much out of it. No sir, we get along on a lot less than a dollar a day, I'd say, if we figger up everything in the long run. Now, I paid seven dollars a month to the two niggers, three-fifty each, and grub, but what I say is, one middlin-good white man ekals a whole passel of niggers any day in the week, so I'll give you seven dollars and you eat at the table with us, and you'll be treated like a white man, as the feller says — "

"That's all right," said Mr. Helton. "I take it."

"Well, now I guess we'll call it a deal, hey?" Mr. Thompson jumped up as if he had remembered important business. "Now, you just take hold of that churn and give it a few swings, will you, while

I ride to town on a coupla little errands. I aint been able to leave the place all week. I guess you know what to do with butter after you get it, don't you?"

"I know," said Mr. Helton without turning his head. "I know butter business." He had a strange drawling voice, and even when he spoke only two words his voice waved slowly up and down and the emphasis was in the wrong place. Mr. Thompson wondered what kind of foreigner Mr. Helton could be.

"Now just where did you say you worked last?" he asked, as if he expected Mr. Helton to contradict himself.

"North Dakota," said Mr. Helton.

"Well, one place is good as another once you get used to it," said Mr. Thompson amply. "You're a forriner, aint you?"

"I'm a Swede," said Mr. Helton, beginning to swing the churn.

Mr. Thompson let forth a booming laugh, as if this was the best joke on somebody he'd ever heard. "Well, I'll be damned," he said at the top of his voice. "A Swede: well now, I'm afraid you'll get pretty lonesome around here. I never seen any Swedes in this neck of the woods."

"That's all right," said Mr. Helton. He went on swinging the churn as if he had been working on the place for years.

"In fact, I might as well tell you, you're practically the first Swede I ever laid eyes on."

"That's all right," said Mr. Helton.

Mr. Thompson went into the front room where Mrs. Thompson was lying down, with the green shades drawn. She had a bowl of water by her on the table and a wet cloth over her eyes. She took the cloth off at the sound of Mr. Thompson's boots and said, "What's all the noise out there? Who is it?"

"Got a feller out there says he's a Swede, Ellie," said Mr. Thompson. "Says he knows how to make butter."

"I hope it turns out to be the truth," said Mrs. Thompson. "Looks like my head will never get any better."

"Don't you worry," said Mr. Thompson. "You fret too much. Now I'm gointa ride into town and get a little order of groceries."

"Don't you linger, now, Mr. Thompson," said Mrs. Thompson. "Don't go to the hotel." She meant the saloon; the proprietor also had rooms for rent upstairs.

"Just a coupla little toddies," said Mr. Thompson, laughing loudly, "never hurt anybody."

"I never took a dram in my life," said Mrs. Thompson, "and what's more I never will."

"I wasn't talking about the womenfolks," said Mr. Thompson.

The sound of the swinging churn rocked Mrs. Thompson first into a gentle doze, then a deep drowse from which she waked suddenly knowing that the swinging had stopped a good while ago. She sat up shading her weak eyes from the flat strips of late summer sunlight between the sill and the lower shades. There she was, thank God, still alive, with supper to cook but no churning on hand, and her head still bewildered, but easy. Slowly she realized she had been hearing a new sound even in her sleep. Somebody was playing a tune on the harmonica, not merely shrilling up and down making a sickening noise, but really playing a pretty tune, merry and sad.

She went out through the kitchen, stepped off the porch, and stood facing the east, shading her eyes. When her vision cleared and settled, she saw a long, pale-haired man in blue jeans sitting in the doorway of the hired man's shack, tilted back in a kitchen chair, blowing away at the harmonica with his eyes shut. Mrs. Thompson's heart fluttered and sank. Heavens, he looked lazy and worthless, he did, now. First a lot of no-count fiddling darkies and then a no-count white man. It was just like Mr. Thompson to take on that kind. She did wish he would be more considerate, and take a little trouble with his business. She wanted to believe in her husband, and there were too many times when she couldn't. She wanted to believe that tomorrow, or at least the day after, life, such a battle at best, was going to be easier.

She walked past the shack without glancing aside, stepping carefully, bent at the waist because of the nagging pain in her side, and went to the spring house, trying to harden her mind to speak very plainly to that new hired man if he had not done his work.

The milk house was only another shack, of weatherbeaten boards nailed together hastily years before they needed a milk house; it was meant to be temporary, and it was; already shapeless, leaning this way and that over a perpetual cool trickle of water that fell from a little grot, almost choked with pallid ferns. No one else in the whole countryside had such a spring on his land. Mr. and Mrs. Thompson felt they had a fortune in that spring, if ever they got around to doing anything with it.

Rickety wooden shelves clung at hazard in the square around the small pool where the larger pails of milk and butter stood, fresh and sweet in the cold water. One hand supporting her flat, pained side, the other shading her eyes, Mrs. Thompson leaned over and peered into the pails. The cream had been skimmed and set aside, there was a rich roll of butter, the wooden molds and shallow pans had been scrubbed and scalded for the first time in who knows when, the barrel was full of buttermilk ready for the pigs and the weanling calves, the hard packed-dirt floor had been swept smooth. Mrs. Thompson straightened up again, smiling tenderly. She had been ready to scold him, a poor man who needed a job, who had just come there and who might not have been expected to do things properly at first. There was nothing she could do to make up for the injustice she had done him in her thoughts but to tell him how she appreciated his good clean work, finished already, in no time at all. She ventured near the door of the shack with her careful steps; Mr. Helton opened his eyes, stopped playing, and brought his chair down straight, but did not look at her, or get up. She was a little frail woman with long thick brown hair in a braid, a suffering patient mouth and diseased eyes which cried easily. She wove her fingers into an eyeshade, thumbs on temples, and, winking her tearful lids, said with a polite little manner, "Howdy do, sir. I'm Miz Thompson, and I wanted to tell you I think you did real well in the milk house. It's always been a hard place to keep."

He said, "That's all right," in a slow voice, without moving.

Mrs. Thompson waited a moment. "That's a pretty tune you're playing. Most folks don't seem to get much music out of a harmonica."

Mr. Helton sat humped over, long legs sprawling, his spine in a bow, running his thumb over the square mouth-stops; except for his moving hand he might have been asleep. The harmonica was a big shiny new one, and Mrs. Thompson, her gaze wandering about, counted five others, all good and expensive, standing in a row on the shelf beside his cot. He must carry them around in his jumper pocket, she thought, and noted there was not a sign of any other possession lying about. "I see you're mighty fond of music," she said. "We used to have an old accordion, and Mr. Thompson could play it right smart, but the little boys broke it up."

Mr. Helton stood up rather suddenly, the chair clattered under him, his knees straightened though his shoulders did not, and he looked at the floor, but as if he were hearing what she said. "You know how little boys are," said Mrs. Thompson. "You'd better set them harmonicas on a high shelf or they'll be after them. They're great hands for getting into things. I try to learn 'em, but it don't do much good."

Mr. Helton, in one wide gesture of his long arms, swept his harmonicas up against his chest, and from there transferred them in a row to the ledge where the roof joined to the wall. He pushed them back almost out of sight.

"That'll do, maybe," said Mrs. Thompson. "Now I wonder," she said, turning and closing her eyes helplessly against the stronger western light, "I wonder what became of them little tads. I can't keep up with them." She had a way of speaking about her children as if they were rather troublesome nephews on a prolonged visit.

"Down by the creek," said Mr. Helton, in his hollow voice. Mrs. Thompson, listening confusedly, decided he had answered her question. He stood in silent patience, not exactly waiting for her to go, perhaps, but pretty plainly not waiting for anything else. Mrs. Thompson was perfectly accustomed to all kinds of men full of all kinds of cranky ways. The point was, to find out just how Mr. Helton's crankiness was different from any other man's, and then get used to it, and let him feel at home. Her father had been cranky, her brothers and uncles had all been set in their ways and none of them alike; and every hired man she'd ever seen had quirks and crochets of his own. Now here was Mr. Helton, who was a Swede, who wouldn't talk, and who played the harmonica besides.

"They'll be needing something to eat," said Mrs. Thompson in a vague friendly way, "pretty soon. Now I wonder what I ought to be thinking about for supper? Now what do you like to eat, Mr. Helton? We always have plenty of good butter and milk and cream, that's a blessing. Mr. Thompson says we ought to sell all of it, but I say my family comes first." Her little face went all out of shape in a pained, blind smile.

"I eat anything," said Mr. Helton, his words wandering up and down.

He *can't* talk, for one thing, thought Mrs. Thompson; it's a shame to keep at him when he don't know the language good. She took a slow step away from the shack, looking back over her shoulder. "We usually have cornbread except on Sundays," she told him. "I suppose in your part of the country you don't get much good cornbread."

Not a word from Mr. Helton. She saw from her eye-corner that he had sat down again, looking at his harmonica, chair tilted. She hoped he would remember it was getting near milking time. As she moved away, he started playing again, the same tune.

Milking time came and went. Mrs. Thompson saw Mr. Helton going back and forth between the cow barn and the milk house. He swung along in an easy lope, shoulders bent, head hanging, the big buckets balancing like a pair of scales at the ends of his bony arms. Mr. Thompson rode in from town sitting straighter than usual, chin in, a towsack full of supplies swung behind the saddle. After a trip to the barn, he came into the kitchen full of good will, and gave Mrs. Thompson a hearty smack on the cheek after dusting her face off with his tough whiskers. He had been to the hotel, that was plain. "Took a look around the premises, Ellie," he shouted. "That Swede sure is grinding out the labor. But he is the closest mouthed feller I ever met up with in all my days. Looks like he's scared he'll crack his jaw if he opens his front teeth."

Mrs. Thompson was stirring up a big bowl of buttermilk cornbread. "You smell like a toper, Mr. Thompson," she said with perfect dignity. "I wish you'd get one of the little boys to bring me in an extra load of firewood. I'm thinking about baking a batch of cookies tomorrow."

Mr. Thompson, all at once smelling the liquor on his own breath, sneaked out, justly rebuked, and brought in the firewood himself. Arthur and Herbert, grubby from thatched head to toes, from skin to shirt, came stamping in yelling for supper. "Go wash your faces and comb your hair," said Mrs. Thompson, automatically. They retired to the porch. Each one put his hand under the pump and wet his forelock, combed it down with his fingers, and returned at once to the kitchen, where all the fair prospects of life were centered. Mrs. Thompson set an extra plate and commanded Arthur, the eldest, eight years old, to call Mr. Helton for supper.

Arthur, without moving from the spot, bawled like a bull calf, "Saaaaaay, Helllllllton, suuuuuupper's ready!" and added in a lower voice, "You big Swede!"

"Listen to me," said Mrs. Thompson, "that's no way to act. Now you go out there and ask him decent, or I'll get your Daddy to give you a good licking."

Mr. Helton loomed, long and gloomy, in the doorway. "Sit right there," boomed Mr. Thompson, waving his arm. Mr. Helton swung his square shoes across the kitchen in two steps, slumped onto the bench and sat. Mr. Thompson occupied his chair at the head of the table, the two boys scrambled into place opposite Mr. Helton, and Mrs. Thompson sat at the end nearest the stove. Mrs. Thompson clasped her hands, bowed her head and said aloud hastily, "Lord for all these and thy other blessings we thank Thee in Jesus' name amen," trying to finish before Herbert's rusty little paw reached the nearest dish. Otherwise she would be duty-bound to send him away from the table, and growing children need their meals. Mr. Thompson and Arthur always waited, but Herbert, aged six, was too young to take training yet.

Mr. and Mrs. Thompson tried to engage Mr. Helton in conversation, but it was a failure. They tried first the weather, and then the crops, and then the cows, but Mr. Helton simply did not reply. Mr. Thompson then told something funny he had seen in town. It was about some of the other old grangers at the hotel, friends of his, giving beer to a goat, and the goat's subsequent behavior. Mr. Helton did not seem to hear. Mrs. Thompson laughed dutifully, but she didn't think it was very funny. She had heard it often before, though Mr. Thompson, each time he told it, pretended it had happened that self-same day. It must have happened years ago if it ever happened at all, and it had never been a story that Mrs. Thompson thought suitable for mixed company. The whole thing came of Mr. Thompson's weakness for a dram too much now and then, though he voted for local option at every election. She passed the food to Mr. Helton, who took a helping of everything, but not much, not enough to keep him up to his full powers if he expected to go on working the way he had started.

At last, he took a fair-sized piece of cornbread, wiped his plate up as clean as if it had been licked by a hound dog, stuffed his mouth full, and, still chewing, slid off the bench and started for the door.

"Good night, Mr. Helton," said Mrs. Thompson, and the other Thompsons took it up in a scattered chorus. "Good night, Mr. Helton!"

"Good night," said Mr. Helton's wavering voice grudgingly from the darkness.

"Gude not," said Arthur, imitating Mr. Helton.

"Gude not," said Herbert, the copy-cat.

"You don't do it right," said Arthur. "Now listen to me. Guuu-uuude naht," and he ran a hollow scale in a luxury of successful inpersonation. Herbert almost went into a fit with joy.

"Now you *stop* that," said Mrs. Thompson. "He can't help the way he talks. You ought to be ashamed of yourselves, both of you, making fun of a poor stranger like that. How'd you like to be a stranger in a strange land?"

"I'd like it," said Arthur. "I think it would be fun."

"They're both regular heathens, Ellie," said Mr. Thompson. "Just plain ignoramusses." He turned the face of awful fatherhood upon his young. "You're both going to get sent to school next year, and that'll knock some sense into you."

"I'm going to git sent to the 'formatory when I'm old enough," piped up Herbert. "That's where I'm goin."

"Oh, you are, are you?" asked Mr. Thompson. "Who says so?"

"The Sunday School Supintendent," said Herbert, a bright boy showing off.

"You see?" said Mr. Thompson, staring at his wife. "What did I tell you?" He became a hurricane of wrath. "Get to bed, you two," he roared until his Adam's apple shuddered. "Get now before I take the hide off you!" They got, and shortly from their attic bedroom the sounds of scuffling and snorting and giggling and growling filled the house and shook the kitchen ceiling.

Mrs. Thompson held her head and said in a small uncertain voice, "It's no use picking on them when they're so young and tender. I can't stand it."

"My goodness, Ellie," said Mr. Thompson, "we've got to raise 'em. We can't just let 'em grow up hog wild."

She went on in another tone. "That Mr. Helton seems all right, even if he can't be made to talk. Wonder how he comes to be so far from home."

"Like I said, he isn't no whamper-jaw," said Mr. Thompson, "but he sure knows how to lay out the work. I guess that's the main thing around here. Country's full of fellows tramping round looking for work."

Mrs. Thompson was gathering up the dishes. She now gathered up Mr. Thompson's plate from under his chin. "To tell you the honest truth," she remarked, "I think it's a mighty good change to have a man round the place who knows how to work and keep his mouth shut. Means he'll keep out of our business. Not that we've got anything to hide, but it's convenient."

"That's a fact," said Mr. Thompson. "Haw, haw," he shouted suddenly. "Means you can do all the talking, huh?"

"The only thing," went on Mrs. Thompson, "is this, he don't eat hearty enough to suit me. I like to see a man sit down and relish a good meal. My Granma used to say, it was no use putting dependence on a man who won't set down and make out his dinner. I hope it won't be that way this time."

"Tell *you* the truth, Ellie," said Mr. Thompson, picking his teeth with a fork and leaning back in the best of good humors, "I always thought your Granma was a ter'ble ole fool. She'd just say the first thing that popped into her head and call it God's wisdom."

"My Granma wasn't anybody's fool. Nine times out of ten she knew what she was talking about. I always say the first thing you think is the best thing you can say."

"Well," said Mr. Thompson, going into another shout, "you're so *ree*fined about that goat story, you just try speaking out in mixed company sometime! You just try it. S'pose you happened to be thinking about a hen and a rooster, hey? I reckon you'd shock the Babtist preacher!" He gave her a good pinch on her thin little rump. "No more meat on you than a rabbit," he said fondly. "Now I like 'em cornfed."

Mrs. Thompson looked at him open-eyed and blushed. She could see better by lamplight. "Why Mr. Thompson, sometimes I think you're the evilest-minded man that ever lived." She took a handful of hair on the crown of his head and gave it a good, slow pull. "That's to show you how it feels, pinching so hard when you're supposed to be playing," she said, gently.

In spite of his situation in life, Mr. Thompson had never been able to outgrow his deep conviction that running a dairy and chasing after chickens was woman's work. He was fond of saying that he could plough a furrow, cut sorghum, shuck corn, handle a team, build a corn crib, as well as any man. Buying and selling, too, was man's work. Twice a week he drove the spring wagon to market with the fresh butter, a few eggs, fruits in their proper season, sold them, pocketed the change, and spent it as it seemed best, being careful not to dig into Mrs. Thompson's pin money.

But from the first the cows worried him, coming up regularly twice a day to be milked, standing there reproaching him with their smug female faces. Calves worried him, fighting the rope and strangling themselves until their eyes bulged, trying to get at the teat. Wrestling with a calf unmanned him, like having to change a baby's diaper. Milk worried him, coming bitter sometimes, drying up, turning sour. Hens worried him, cackling, clucking, hatching out when you least expected it and leading their broods into the barnyard where the horses could step on them; dying of roup and wryneck and getting plagues of chicken lice, laying eggs all over God's creation so that half of them were spoiled before a man could find them, in spite of a rack of nests Mrs. Thompson had set out for them in the feed room. Hens were a blasted nuisance.

Slopping hogs was hired man's work, in Mr. Thompson's opinion. Killing hogs was a job for the boss, but skinning them and cutting them up was for the hired man again; and again woman's proper work was dressing meat, smoking, pickling, and making lard and sausage. All his carefully limited fields of activity were related somehow to Mr. Thompson's feeling for the appearance of things, his own appearance in the sight of God and man. "It don't *look* right" was his final reason for not doing anything he did not wish to do.

It was his dignity and his reputation that he cared about, and there were only a few kinds of work manly enough for Mr. Thompson to undertake with his own hands. Mrs. Thompson, to whom so many forms of work would have been becoming, had simply gone down on him early. He saw, after a while, how short-sighted it had been of him to expect much from Mrs. Thompson; he had fallen in love with her delicate waist and lace-trimmed petticoats and big blue eyes, and, though all those charms had disappeared, she had in the meantime become Ellie to him, not at all the same person as Miss Ellen Bridges, popular Sunday School teacher in the Mountain City First Baptist Church, but his dear wife, Ellie, who was not strong. Deprived as he was, however, of the main support in life which a man might expect in marriage, he had almost without knowing it resigned himself to failure. Head erect, a prompt payer of taxes, yearly subscriber to the preacher's salary, land owner and father of a family, employer, a hearty good fellow among men, Mr. Thompson knew, without putting it into words, that he had been going steadily down hill. God amighty, it did look like somebody around the place might take a rake in hand now and then and clear up the clutter around the barn and the kitchen steps. The wagon shed was so full of broken-down machinery and ragged harness and old wagon wheels and battered milk pails and rotting lumber you could hardly drive in there any more. Not a soul on the place would raise a hand to it, and as for him, he had all he could do with his regular work. He would sometimes in the slack season sit for hours worrying about it, squirting tobacco on the ragweeds growing in a thicket against the wood pile, wondering what a fellow could do, handicapped as he was. He looked forward to the boys growing up soon; he was going to put them through the mill just as his own father had done with him when he was a boy; they were going to learn how to take hold and run the place right. He wasn't going to overdo it, but those two boys were going to earn their salt, or he'd know why. Great big lubbers sitting around whittling! Mr. Thompson sometimes grew quite enraged with them, when imagining their possible future, big lubbers sitting arnd whittling or thinking about fishing trips. Well, he'd put a stop to that, mighty damn quick.

As the seasons passed, and Mr. Helton took hold more and more, Mr. Thompson began to relax in his mind a little. There seemed to be nothing the fellow couldn't do, all in the day's work and as a matter of course. He got up at five o'clock in the morning, boiled his own coffee and fried his own bacon and was out in the cow lot before Mr. Thompson had even begun to yawn, stretch, groan, roar and thump around looking for his jeans. He milked the cows, kept the milk house, and churned the butter; rounded the hens up and somehow persuaded them to lay in the nests, not under the house and behind the haystacks; he fed them regularly and they hatched out until you couldn't set a foot down for them. Little by little the piles of trash around the barns and house disappeared. He carried buttermilk and corn to the hogs, and curried cockle burs out of the horses' manes. He was gentle with the calves, if a little grim with the cows and hens; judging by his conduct Mr. Helton had never heard of the difference between man's and woman's work on a farm.

In the second year, he showed Mr. Thompson the picture of a cheese press in a mail order catalogue, and said, "This is a good thing. You buy this, I make cheese." The press was bought and Mr. Helton did make cheese, and it was sold, along with the increased butter and the crates of eggs. Sometimes Mr. Thompson felt a little contemptuous of Mr. Helton's ways. It did seem kind of picayune for a man to go around picking up half a dozen ears of corn that had fallen off the wagon on the way from the field, gathering up fallen fruit to feed to the pigs, storing up old nails and stray parts of machinery, spending good time stamping a fancy pattern on the butter before it went to market. Mr. Thompson, sitting up high on the spring-wagon seat, with the decorated butter in a five-gallon lard can wrapped in wet towsack, driving to town, chirruping to the horses and snapping the reins over their backs, sometimes thought that Mr. Helton was a pretty meeching sort of fellow; but he never gave way to these feelings, he knew a good thing when he had it. It was a fact the hogs were in better shape and sold for more money. It was a fact that Mr. Thompson stopped buying feed, Mr. Helton managed the crops so well. When beef- and hog-slaughtering time came, Mr. Helton knew how to save the scraps that Mr. Thompson had thrown away, and wasn't above scraping guts and filling them with sausages that he made by his own methods. In all, Mr. Thompson had no grounds for complaint. In the third year, he raised Mr. Helton's wages, though Mr. Helton had not asked for a raise. The fourth year, when Mr. Thompson was not only out of debt but had a little cash in the bank, he raised Mr. Helton's wages again, two dollars and a half a month each time.

"The man's worth it, Ellie," said Mr. Thompson, in a glow of self-justification for his extravagance. "He's made this place pay, and I want him to know I appreciate it."

Mr. Helton's silence, the pallor of his eyebrows and hair, his long, glum jaw and eyes that refused to see anything, even the work under his hands, had grown perfectly familiar to the Thompsons. At first, Mr. Thompson complained a little. "It's like sitting down at the table with a disembodied spirit," she said. "You'd think he'd find something to say, sooner or later."

"Let him alone," said Mr. Thompson. "When he gets ready to talk, he'll talk."

The years passed, and Mr. Helton never got ready to talk. After his work was finished for the day, he would come up from the barn or the milk house or the chicken house, swinging his lantern, his big shoes clumping like pony hoofs on the hard path. They, sitting in the kitchen in the winter, or on the back porch in summer, would hear him drag out his wooden chair, hear the creak of it tilted back, and then for a little while he would play his single tune on one or another of his harmonicas. The harmonicas were in different keys, some lower and sweeter than the others, but the same changeless tune went on, a strange tune, with sudden turns in it, night after night, and sometimes even in the afternoons when Mr. Helton sat down to catch his breath. At first the Thompsons liked it very much, and always stopped to listen. Later there came a time when they were fairly sick of it, and began to wish to each other that he would learn a new one. At last they did not hear it any more, it was as natural as the sound of the wind rising in the evenings, or the cows lowing, or their own voices.

Mrs. Thompson pondered now and then over Mr. Helton's soul. He didn't seem to be a church-goer, and worked straight through Sunday as if it were any common day of the week. "I think we ought to invite him to go to hear Dr. Martin," she told Mr. Thompson. "It isn't very Christian of us not to ask him. He's not a forward kind of man, he'd wait to be asked."

"Let him alone," said Mr. Thompson. "The way I look at it, his religion is every man's own business. Besides, he ain't got any Sunday clothes. He wouldn't want to go to church in them jeans and jumpers of his. I don't know what he does with his money. He certainly don't spend it foolishly."

Still, once the notion got into her head, Mrs. Thompson could not rest until she invited Mr. Helton to go to church with the family next Sunday. He was pitching hay into neat little piles in the field back of the orchard; Mrs. Thompson put on smoked glasses and a sunbonnet and walked all the way down there to speak to him. He stopped and leaned on his pitchfork, listening, and for a moment Mrs. Thompson was almost frightened at his face. The pale eyes seemed to glare past her, the eyebrows frowned, the long jaw hardened. "I got work," he said bluntly, and lifting his pitchfork he turned from her and began to toss the hay. Mrs. Thompson, her feelings hurt, walked back thinking that by now she should be used to Mr. Helton's ways, but it did seem like a man, even a foreigner, could be just a little polite when you gave him a Christian invitation. "He's not polite, that's the only thing I've got against him," she said to Mr. Thompson. "He just can't seem to behave like other people. You'd think he had a grudge against the world," she said. "I sometimes don't know what to make of it."

In the second year something had happened that made Mrs. Thompson uneasy, the kind of thing she could not put into words, hardly into thoughts, and if she had tried to explain to Mr. Thompson it would have sounded worse than it was, or not bad enough. It was that kind of queer thing that seems to be giving a warning, and yet, nearly always nothing comes of it. It was on a hot, still spring day, and Mrs. Thompson had been down to the garden patch to pull some new carrots and green onions and string beans for dinner. As she worked, sunbonnet low over her eyes, putting each kind of vegetable in a pile by itself in her basket, she noticed how neatly Mr. Helton weeded, and how rich the soil was. He had spread it all over with manure from the barns, and worked it in, in the fall, and the vegetables were coming up fine and full. She walked back under the nubbly little fig trees where the unpruned branches leaned almost to the ground, and the thick leaves made a cool screen. Mrs. Thompson was always looking for shade to save her eyes. So she, looking idly about, saw through the screen a sight that struck her as very strange. If it had been a noisy spectacle, it would have been quite natural. It was the silence that struck her. Mr. Helton was shaking Arthur by the shoulders, ferociously, his face most terribly fixed and pale. Arthur's head snapped back and forth and he had not stiffened in resistance, as he did when Mrs. Thompson tried to shake him. His eyes were rather frightened, but surprised, too, probably more surprised than anything else. Herbert stood by meekly, watching. Mr. Helton dropped Arthur, and seized Herbert, and shook him with the same methodical ferocity, the same face of hatred. Herbert's mouth crumpled as if he would cry, but he made no sound. Mr. Helton let him go, turned and strode into the shack, and the little boys ran, as if for their lives, without a word. They disappeared around the corner to the front of the house.

Mrs. Thompson took time to set her basket on the kitchen table, to push her sunbonnet back on her head and draw it forward again, to look in the stove and make certain the fire was going, before she followed the boys. They were sitting huddled together under a clump of china-berry trees in plain sight of her bedroom window, as if it were a safe place they had discovered.

"What are you doing?" asked Mrs. Thompson.

They looked hang-dog from under their foreheads and Arthur mumbled, "Nothin."

"Nothing *now*, you mean," said Mrs. Thompson, severely. "Well, I have plenty for you to do. Come right in here this minute and help me fix vegetables. This minute."

They scrambled up very eagerly and followed her close. Mrs. Thompson tried to imagine what they had been up to; she did not like the notion of Mr. Helton taking it on himself to correct her little boys, but she was afraid to ask them for reasons. They might tell her a lie, and she would have to overtake them in it, and whip them. Or she would have to pretend to believe them, and they would get in the habit of lying. Or they might tell her the truth, and it would be something she would have to whip them for. The very thought of it gave her a headache. She supposed she might ask Mr. Helton, but it was not her place to ask. She would wait and tell Mr. Thompson, and let him get at the bottom of it. While her mind ran on, she kept the little boys hopping. "Cut those carrot tops closer, Herbert, you're just being careless. Arthur, stop breaking up the beans so little. They're little enough already. Herbert, you go get an armload of wood. Arthur, you take these onions and wash them under the pump. Herbert, as soon as you're done here, you get a broom and sweep out this kitchen. Arthur, you get a shovel and take up the ashes. Stop picking your nose, Herbert. How often must I tell you? Arthur, you go look in the top drawer of my bureau, left-hand side, and bring me the Vaseline for Herbert's nose. Herbert, come here to me — "

They galloped through their chores, their animal spirits rose with activity, and shortly they were out in the front yard again, engaged in a wrestling match. They sprawled and fought, scrambled, clutched, rose and fell shouting, as aimlessly, noisily, monotonously as two puppies. They imitated various animals, not a human sound from them, and their dirty faces were streaked with sweat. Mrs. Thompson, sitting at her window, watched them with baffled pride and tenderness, they were so sturdy and healthy and growing so fast; but uneasily too, with her pained little smile and the tears rolling from her eyelids that clinched themselves against the sunlight. They were so idle and careless, as if they had no future in this world, and no immortal souls to save, and oh, what had they been up to that Mr. Helton had shaken them, with his face positively dangerous?

In the evening before supper, without a word to Mr. Thompson of the curious fear the sight had caused her, she told him that Mr. Helton had shaken the little boys for some reason. He stepped out to the shack and spoke to Mr. Helton. In five minutes he was back, glaring at his young. "He says them brats been fooling with his harmonicas, Ellie, blowing in them and getting them all dirty and full of spit and they don't play good."

"Did he say all that?" asked Mrs. Thompson. "It doesn't seem possible."

"Well, that's what he meant, anyhow," said Mr. Thompson. "He didn't say it just that way. But he acted pretty worked up about it."

"That's a shame," said Mrs. Thompson, "a perfect shame. Now we've got to do something so they'll remember they mustn't go into Mr. Helton's things."

"I'll tan their hides for them," said Mr. Thompson. "I'll take a calf rope to them if they don't look out."

"Maybe you'd better leave the whipping to me," said Mrs. Thompson. "You haven't got a light enough hand for children."

"That's just what's the matter with them now," shouted Mr. Thompson, "rotten spoiled and they'll wind up in the penitentiary. You don't half whip 'em. Just little love taps. My Pa used to knock me down with a stick of stove wood or anything else that came handy."

"Well, that's not saying it's right," said Mrs. Thompson. "I don't hold with that way of raising children. It makes them run away from home. I've seen too much of it."

"I'll break every bone in 'em," said Mr. Thompson, simmering down, "if they don't mind you better and stop being so bull-headed."

"Leave the table and wash your face and hands," Mrs. Thompson commanded the boys, suddenly. They slunk out and dabbled at the pump and slunk in again, trying to make themselves small. They had learned long ago that their mother always made them wash when there was trouble ahead. They looked at their plates. Mr. Thompson opened up on them.

"Well, now, what you got to say for yourselves about going into Mr. Helton's shack and ruining his harmonicas?"

The two little boys wilted, their faces dropped into the grieved hopeless lines of children's faces when they are brought to the terrible bar of blind adult justice; their eyes telegraphed each other in panic, "Now we're really going to catch a licking"; in despair, they dropped their buttered cornbread on their plates, their hands lagged on the edge of the table.

"I ought to break your ribs," said Mr. Thompson, "and I'm a good mind to do it."

"Yes, sir," whispered Arthur, faintly.

"Yes, sir," said Herbert, his lip trembling.

"Now papa," said Mrs. Thompson in a warning tone. The children did not glance at her. They had no faith in her good will. She had betrayed them in the first place. There was no trusting her. Now she might save them and she might not. No use depending on her.

"Well, you ought to get a good thrashing, you deserve it, don't you, Arthur?"

Arthur hung his head. "Yes, sir."

"And the next time I catch either of you hanging around Mr. Helton's shack, I'm going to take the hide off *both* of you, you hear me, Herbert?"

Herbert mumbled and choked, scattering his cornbread. "Yes, sir."

"Well, now sit up and eat your supper and not another word out of you," said Mr. Thompson, beginning on his own food. The little boys perked up somewhat and started chewing, but every time they looked around they met their parents' eyes, regarding them steadily. There was no telling when they would think of something new. The boys ate warily, trying not to be seen or heard, the cornbread sticking, the butter-milk gurgling, as it went down their gullets.

"And something else, Mr. Thompson," said Mrs. Thompson after a pause. "Tell Mr. Helton he's to come straight to us when they bother him, and not to trouble shaking them himself. Tell him we'll look after that."

"They're so mean," answered Mr. Thompson, staring at them. "It's a wonder he don't just kill 'em off and be done with it." But there was something in the tone that told Arthur and Herbert that nothing more worth worrying about was going to happen this time. Heaving deep sighs, they sat up, reaching for the food nearest them.

"Listen," said Mrs. Thompson, suddenly. The little boys stopped eating. "Mr. Helton hasn't come for his supper. Arthur, go and tell Mr. Helton he's late for supper. Tell him nice, now."

Arthur, miserably depressed, slid out of his place and made for the door, without a word.

There were no miracles of fortune to be brought to pass on a small dairy farm. The Thompsons did not grow rich, but they kept out of the poor house, as Mr. Thompson was fond of saying, meaning he had got a little foothold in spite of Ellie's poor health, and unexpected weather, and strange declines in market prices, and his own mysterious handicaps which weighed him down. Mr. Helton was the hope and the prop of the family, and all the Thompsons became fond of him, or at any rate they ceased to regard him as in any way peculiar, and looked upon him, from a distance they did not know how to bridge, as a good man and a good friend. Mr. Helton went his way, worked, played his tune. Nine years passed. The boys grew up and learned to work. They could not remember the time when Ole Helton hadn't been there: a grouchy cuss, Brother Bones; Mr. Helton, the dairy maid; that Big Swede. If he had heard them, he might have been annoyed at some of the names they called him. But he did not hear them, and besides they meant no harm — or at least such harm as existed was all there, in the names; the boys referred to their father as the Old Man, or the Old Geezer, but not to his face. They lived through by main strength all the grimy, secret, oblique phases of growing up and got past the crisis safely if anyone does. Their parents could see they were good solid boys with hearts of gold in spite of their rough ways. Mr. Thompson was relieved to find that, without knowing how he had done it, he had succeeded in raising a set of boys who were not trifling whittlers. They were such good boys Mr. Thompson began to believe they were born that way, and that he had never spoken a harsh word to them in their lives, much less thrashed them. Herbert and Arthur never disputed his word.

Mr. Helton, his hair wet with sweat, plastered to his dripping forehead, his jumper streaked dark and light blue and clinging to his ribs, was chopping a little firewood. He chopped slowly, struck the axe into the end of the chopping log, and piled the wood up neatly. He then disappeared round the house into his shack, which shared with the wood pile a good shade from a row of mulberry trees. Mr. Thompson was lolling in a swing chair on the front porch, a place he rarely frequented. The chair was new, and Mrs. Thompson had wanted it on the front porch, though the side porch was the place for it, being cooler; and Mr. Thompson wanted to sit in the chair, so there he was. As soon as the new wore off of it, and Ellie's pride in it was exhausted, he would move it round to the side porch. Meantime the August heat was almost unbearable, the air so thick you could poke a hole in it. The dust was inches thick on everything, though Mr. Helton sprinkled the whole yard regularly every night. He even shot the hose upward and washed the tree tops and the roof of the house. They had laid waterpipes to the kitchen and an outside faucet.

Mr. Thompson must have dozed, for he opened his eyes and shut his mouth just in time to save his face before a stranger who had driven up to the front gate. Mr. Thompson stood up, put on his hat, pulled up his jeans, and watched while the stranger tied his team, attached to a light spring wagon, to the hitching post. Mr. Thompson recognized the team and wagon. They were from a livery stable in Buda. While the stranger was opening the gate, a strong gate that Mr. Helton had built and set firmly on its hinges several years back, Mr. Thompson strolled down the path to greet him and find out what in God's world a man's business might be that would bring him out at this time of day, in all this dust and welter.

He wasn't exactly a fat man. He was more like a man who had been fat recently. His skin was baggy and his clothes were too big for him, and he somehow looked like a man who should be fat, ordinarily, but who might have just got over a spell of sickness. Mr. Thompson didn't take to his looks at all, he couldn't say why.

The stranger took off his hat. He said in a loud hearty voice, "Is this Mr. Thompson, Mr. Royal Earle Thompson?"

"That's my name," said Mr. Thompson, almost quietly, he was so taken aback by the free manner of the stranger.

"My name is Hatch," said the stranger, "Mr. Homer T. Hatch, and I've come to see you about buying a horse."

"I reckon you've been misdirected," and Mr. Thompson. "I haven't got a horse for sale. Usually if I've got anything like that to sell," he said, "I tell the neighbors and tack up a little sign on the gate."

The fat men opened his mouth and roared with joy, showing rabbit teeth brown as shoeleather. Mr. Thompson saw nothing to laugh at, for once. The stranger shouted, "That's just an old joke of mine." He caught one of his hands in the other and shook hands with himself heartily. "I always say something like that when I'm calling on a stranger, because I've noticed that when a feller says he's come to buy something nobody takes him for a suspicious character. You see? Haw, haw, haw."

His joviality made Mr. Thompson nervous, because the expression in the man's eyes didn't match the sounds he was making. "Haw, haw," laughed Mr. Thompson obligingly, still not seeing the joke.

"Well, that's all wasted on me because I never take any man for a suspicious character til he shows hisself to be one. Says or does something," he explained. "Until that happens, one man's as good as another, so far's *I'm* concerned."

"Well," said the stranger, suddenly very sober and sensible, "I ain't come neither to buy nor sell. Fact is, I want to see you about something that's of interest to us both. Yes, sir, I'd like to have a little talk with you, and it won't cost you a cent."

"I guess that's fair enough," said Mr. Thompson, reluctantly. "Come on around the house where there's a little shade."

They went round and seated themselves on two stumps under a chinaberry tree.

"Yes, sir, Homer T. Hatch is my name and America is my nation," said the stranger. "I reckon you must know the name? I used to have a cousin named Jameson Hatch lived up the country a ways."

"Don't think I know the name," said Mr. Thompson. "There's some Hatchers settled somewhere around Mountain City."

"Don't know the old Hatch family," cried the man in deep concern. He seemed to be pitying Mr. Thompson's ignorance. "Why, we came over from Georgia fifty years ago. Been here long yourself?"

"Just all my whole life," said Mr. Thompson, beginning to feel peevish. "And my pa and my grampap before me. Yes sir, we've been right here all along. Anybody wants to find a Thompson knows where to look for him. My grampap immigrated in 1836."

"From Ireland, I reckon?" said the stranger.

"From Pennsylvania," said Mr. Thompson. "Now what makes you think we came from Ireland?"

The stranger opened his mouth and began to shout with merriment, and he shook hands with himself as if he hadn't met himself for a long time. "Well, what I always says is, a feller's got to come from *somewhere*, ain't he?"

While they were talking, Mr. Thompson kept glancing at the face near him. He certainly did remind Mr. Thompson of somebody, or maybe he really had seen the man himself somewhere. He couldn't just place the features. Mr. Thompson finally decided it was just that all rabbit-teethed men looked alike.

"That's right," acknowledged Mr. Thompson, rather sourly, "but what I always say is, Thompsons have been settled here for so long it don't make much difference any more *where* they come from. Now a course, this is the slack season, and we're all just laying round a little, but nevertheless we've all got our chores to do, and I don't want to hurry you, and so if you've come to see me on business maybe we'd better get down to it."

"As I said, it's not business in a way, and again in a way it is," said the fat man. "Now I'm looking for a man named Helton, Mr. Olaf Eric Helton, from North Dakota, and I was told up around the country a ways that I might find him here, and I wouldn't mind having a little talk with him. No, siree, I sure wouldn't mind, if it's all the same to you."

"I never knew his middle name," said Mr. Thompson, "but Mr. Helton is right here, and been here now for going on nine years. He's a mighty steady man, and you can tell anybody I said so."

"I'm glad to hear that," said Mr. Homer T. Hatch. "I like to hear of a feller mending his ways and settling down. Now when I knew Mr. Helton he was pretty wild, yes sir, wild is what he was, he didn't know his own mind a tall. Well, now, it's going to be a great pleasure to me to meet up with an old friend and find him all settled down and doing well by hisself."

"We've all got to be young once," said Mr. Thompson. "It's like the measles, it breaks out all over you, and you're a nuisance to yourself and everybody else, but it don't last, and it usually don't leave no ill effects." He was so pleased with this notion he forgot and broke into a guffaw. The stranger folded his arms over his stomach and went into a kind of fit, roaring until he had tears in his eyes. Mr. Thompson stopped shouting and eyed the stranger uneasily. Now he liked a good laugh as well as any man, but there ought to be a little moderation. Now this feller laughed like a perfect lunatic, that was a fact. And he wasn't laughing because he really thought things were funny, either. He was laughing for reasons of his own. Mr. Thompson fell into a moody silence, and waited until Mr. Hatch settled down a little.

Mr. Hatch got out a very dirty blue cotton bandana and wiped his eyes. "That joke just about caught me where I live," he said, almost apologetically. "Now I wish I could think up things as funny as that to say. It's a gift. It's . . ."

"If you want to speak to Mr. Helton, I'll go and round him up," said Mr. Thompson, making motions as if he might get up. "He may be in the milk house and he may be setting in his shack this time of day." It was drawing toward five o'clock. "It's right around the corner," he said.

"Oh, well, there ain't no special hurry," said Mr. Hatch. "I've been wanting to speak to him for a good long spell now and I guess a few minutes more won't make no difference. I just more wanted to locate him, like. That's all."

Mr. Thompson stopped beginning to stand up, and unbuttoned one more button of his shirt, and said, "Well, he's here, and he's this kind of man, that if he had any business with you he'd like to get it over. He don't dawdle, that's one thing you can say for him."

Mr. Hatch appeared to sulk a little at these words. He wiped his face with the bandana and opened his mouth to speak, when round the house there came the music of Mr. Helton's harmonica. Mr. Thompson raised a finger. "There he is," said Mr. Thompson. "Now's your time."

Mr. Hatch cocked an ear toward the east side of the house and listened for a few seconds, a very strange expression on his face.

"I know that tune like I know the palm of my own hand," said Mr. Thompson, "but I never heard Mr. Helton say what it was."

"That's a kind of Scandahoovian song," said Mr. Hatch. "Where I come from they sing it a lot. In North Dakota, they sing it. It says something about starting out in the morning feeling so good you can't hardly stand it, so you drink up all your likker before noon. All the likker, y' understand, that you was saving for the noon lay-off. The words ain't much, but it's a pretty tune. It's a kind of drinking song." He sat there drooping a little, and Mr. Thompson didn't like his expression. It was a satisfied expression, but it was more like the cat that eat the canary.

"So far as I know," said Mr. Thompson, "he ain't touched a drop since he's been on the place, and that's nine years this coming September. Yes sir, nine years, so far as I know, he ain't whetted his whistle once. And that's more than I can say for myself," he said, meekly proud.

"Yes, that's a drinking song," said Mr. Hatch. "I used to play Little Brown Jug on the fiddle when I was younger than I am now," he went on, "but this Helton, he just keeps it up. He just sits and plays it by himself."

"He's been playing it off and on for nine years right here on the place," said Mr. Thompson, feeling a little proprietary.

"And he was certainly singing it as well, fifteen years before that, in North Dakota," said Mr. Hatch. "He used to sit up in a straitjacket, practically, when he was in the asylum —."

"What's that you say?" said Mr. Thompson. "What's that?"

"Shucks, I didn't mean to tell you," said Mr. Hatch, a faint leer of regret in his drooping eyelids. "Shucks, that just slipped out. Funny, now I'd made up my mind I wouldn't say a word, because it would just make a lot of excitement, and what I say is, if a man has lived harmless and quiet for nine years it don't matter if he *is* loony, does it? So long's he keeps quiet and don't do nobody harm."

"You mean they had him in a straitjacket?" asked Mr. Thompson, uneasily. "In a lunatic asylum?"

"They sure did," said Mr. Hatch, "that's right where they had him, from time to time."

"They put my Aunt Ida in one of them things in the State asylum," said Mr. Thompson. "She got vi'lent, and they put her in one of these jackets with long sleeves and tied her to an iron ring in the wall, and Aunt Ida got so wild she broke a blood vessel and when they went to look after her she was dead. I'd think one of them things was dangerous."

"Mr. Helton used to sing his drinking song when he was in a straitjacket," said Mr. Hatch. "Nothing ever bothered him, except if you tried to make him talk. That bothered him, and he'd get vi'lent, like your Aunt Ida. He'd get vi'lent, and then they'd put him in the jacket and go off and leave him, and he'd lay there perfickly contented, so far's you could see, singing his song. Then one night he just disappeared. Left, you might say, just went, and nobody ever saw hide or hair of him again. And then I come along and find him here!" said Mr. Hatch, "all settled down and playing the same song."

"He never acted crazy to me," said Mr. Thompson. "He always acted like a sensible man, to me. He never got married, for one thing, and he works like a horse, and I bet he's got the first cent I paid him when he landed here, and he don't drink, and he never says a word, much less swear, and he don't waste time runnin' around Saturday nights, and if he's crazy," said Mr. Thompson, "why, I think I'll go crazy myself for a change."

"Haw, ha," said Mr. Hatch, "heh, he, that's good! Ha, ha, ha, I hadn't thought of it jes like that. Yeah, that's right! Let's all go crazy and get rid of our wives and save our money, hey?" He smiled unpleasantly, showing his little rabbit teeth.

Mr. Thompson felt he was being misunderstood. He turned around and motioned toward the open window back of the honeysuckle trellis. "Let's move off down here a little," he said. "I oughta thought of that before." His visitor bothered Mr. Thompson. He had a way of taking the words out of Mr. Thompson's mouth, turning them around and mixing them up until Mr. Thompson didn't know himself what he had said. "My wife's not very strong," said Mr. Thompson. "She's been kind of invalid now goin' on fourteen years. It's mighty tough on a poor man, havin sickness in the family. She had four operations," he said proudly, "one right after the other, but they didn't do any good. For five years handrunnin, I just turned every nickel I made over to the doctors. Upshot is, she's a might delicate woman."

"My old woman," said Mr. Homer T. Hatch, "had a back like a mule, yes sir. That woman could have moved the barn with her bare hands if she'd ever took the notion. I used to say, it was a good thing she didn't know her own stren'th. She's dead now, though. That kind wear out quicker than the puny ones. I never had much use for a woman always complainin. I'd get rid of her mighty quick, yes sir, mighty quick. It's just as you say: a dead loss, keeping one of 'em up."

This was not at all what Mr. Thompson had heard himself say; he had been trying to explain that a wife as expensive as his was a credit to a man. "She's a mighty reasonable woman," said Mr. Thompson, feeling baffled, "but I wouldn't answer for what she'd say or do if she found out we'd had a lunatic on the place all this time." They had moved away from the window; Mr. Thompson took Mr. Hatch the front way, because if he went the back way they would have to pass Mr. Helton's shack. For some reason he didn't want the stranger to see or talk to Mr. Helton. It was strange, but that was the way Mr. Thompson felt.

Mr. Thompson sat down again, on the chopping log, offering his guest another tree stump. "Now, I mighta got upset myself at such a thing, once," said Mr. Thompson, "but now I *deefy* anything to get me lathered up." He cut himself an enormous plug of tobacco with his horn-handled pocketknife, and offered it to Mr. Hatch, who then produced his own plug and, opening a huge bowie knife with a long blade sharply whetted, cut off a large wad and put it in his mouth. They then compared plugs and both of them were astonished to see how different men's ideas of good chewing tobacco were.

"Now, for instance," said Mr. Hatch, "mine is lighter colored. That's because, for one thing, there ain't any sweetenin in this plug. I like it dry, natural leaf, medium strong."

"A little sweetenin don't do no harm so far as I'm concerned," said Mr. Thompson, "but it's got to be mighty little. But with me, now, I want a strong leaf, I want it heavy-cured, as the feller says. There's a man near here, named Williams, Mr. John Morgan Williams, who chews a plug — well, sir, it's black as your hat and soft as melted tar. It fairly drips with molasses, jus plain molasses, and it chews like licorice. Now, I don't call that a good chew."

"One man's meat," said Mr. Hatch, "is another man's poison. Now, such a chew would simply gag me, I couldn't begin to put it in my mouth."

"Well," said Mr. Thompson, a tinge of apology in his voice, "I just barely tasted it myself, you might say. Just took a little piece in my mouth and spit it out again."

"I'm dead sure I couldn't even get that far," said Mr. Hatch. "I like a dry natural chew without any artificial flavorin of any kind."

Mr. Thompson began to feel that Mr. Hatch was trying to make out he had the best judgment in tobacco, and was going to keep up the argument until he proved it. He began to feel seriously annoyed with the fat man. After all, who was he and where did he come from? Who was he to go around telling other people what kind of tobacco to chew?

"Artificial flavorin," Mr. Hatch went on, doggedly, "is jes put in to cover up a cheap leaf and make a man think he's gettin somethin more than he *is* gettin. Even a little sweetenin is a sign of a cheap leaf, you can mark my words."

"I've always paid a fair price for my plug," said Mr. Thompson, stiffly. "I'm not a rich man and I don't go round settin myself up for one, but I'll say this, when it comes to such things as tobacco, I buy the best on the market."

"Sweetenin, even a little," began Mr. Hatch, shifting his plug and squirting tobacco juice at a dry-looking little rose bush that was having a hard enough time as it was, standing all day in the blazing sun, its roots clenched in the baked earth, "is the sign of — "

"About this Mr. Helton, now," said Mr. Thompson, determinedly, "I don't see no reason to hold it against a man because he went loony once or twice in his lifetime and so I don't expect to take no steps about it. Not a step. I've got nothin against the man, he's always treated me fair. They's things and people," he went on, "nough to drive any man loony. The wonder to me is, more men don't wind up in straitjackets, the way things are going these days and times."

"That's right," said Mr. Hatch, promptly, entirely too promptly, as if he were turning Mr. Thompson's meaning back on him. "You took the words right out of my mouth. There ain't every man in a strait-jacket that ought to be there. Ha, ha, you're right all right. You got the idea."

Mr. Thompson sat silent and chewed steadily and stared at a spot on the ground about six feet away and felt a slow muffled resentment climbing from somewhere deep down in him, climbing and spreading all through him. What was this fellow driving at? What was he trying to say? It wasn't so much his words, but his looks and his way of talking: that droopy look in the eye, that tone of voice, as if he were trying to mortify Mr. Thompson about something. Mr. Thompson didn't like it, but he couldn't get hold of it either. He wanted to turn around and shove the fellow off the stump, but it wouldn't look reasonable. Suppose something happened to the fellow when he fell off the stump, just for instance, if he fell on the axe and cut himself, and then someone should ask Mr. Thompson why he shoved him, and what could a man say? It would look mighty funny, it would sound mighty strange to say, Well, him and me fell out over a plug of tobacco. He might just shove him anyhow and then tell people he was a fat man not used to the heat and while he was talking he got dizzy and fell off by himself, or something like that, and it wouldn't be the truth either, because it wasn't the heat and it wasn't the tobacco. Mr. Thompson made up his mind to get the fellow off the place pretty quick, without seeming to be anxious, and watch him sharp till he was out of sight. It doesn't pay to be friendly with strangers from another part of the country. They're always up to something, or they'd stay at home where they belong.

"And they's some people," said Mr. Hatch, "would jus as soon have a loonatic around their house as not, they can't see no difference between them and anybody else. I always say, if that's the way a man feels, don't care who he associates with, why, why, that's his business, not mine. I don't want to have a thing to do with it. Now back home in North Dakota, we don't feel that way. I'd like to a seen anybody hiring a loonatic there, a specially after what he done."

"I didn't understand your home was North Dakota," said Mr. Thompson, "I thought you said Georgia."

"I've got a married sister in North Dakota," said Mr. Hatch, "married a Swede, but a white man if ever I saw one. So I say *we* because we got into a little business together out that way. And it seems like home, kind of."

"What did he do?" asked Mr. Thompson, feeling very uneasy again.

"Oh, nothin to speak of," said Mr. Hatch, jovially, "just went loony one day in the hayfield and shoved a pitchfork right square through his brother, when they was makin hay. They was goin to execute him, but they found out he had went crazy with the heat, as the feller says, and so they put him in the asylum. That's all he done. Nothin to get lathered up about, ha, ha, ha!" he said, and taking out his sharp knife he began to slice off a chew as carefully as if he were cutting cake.

"Well," said Mr. Thompson, "I don't deny that's news. Yes, sir, news. But I still say somethin must have drove him to it. Some men make you feel like giving 'em a good killing just by lookin at you. His brother may a been a mean ornery cuss."

"Brother was going to get married," said Mr. Hatch, "used to go courtin his girl nights. Borrowed Mr. Helton's harmonica to give her a serenade one evenin, and lost it. Brand new harmonica."

"He thinks a heap of his harmonicas," said Mr. Thompson. "Only money he ever spends, now and then he buys hisself a new one. Must have a dozen in that shack, all kinds and sizes."

"Brother wouldn't buy him a new one," said Mr. Hatch, "so Mr. Helton just ups, as I says, and runs his pitchfork through his brother. Now you know he musta been crazy to get all worked up over a little thing like that."

"Sounds like it," said Mr. Thompson, reluctant to agree in anything with this intrusive and disagreeable fellow. He kept thinking he couldn't remember when he had taken such a dislike to a man on first sight.

"Seems to me you'd get pretty sick of hearin the same tune year in, year out," said Mr. Hatch.

"Well, sometimes I think it wouldn't do no harm if he learned a new one," said Mr. Thompson, "but he don't, so there's nothin to be done about it. It's a pretty good tune, though."

"One of the Scandahoovians told me what it meant, that's how I come to know," said Mr. Hatch. "Especially that part about getting so gay you jus go ahead and drink up all the likker you got on hand before noon. It seems like up in them Swede countries a man carries a bottle of wine around with him as a matter of course, at least that's the way I understood it. Those fellers will tell you anything, though — " He broke off and spat.

The idea of drinking any kind of liquor in this heat made Mr. Thompson dizzy. The idea of anybody feeling good on a day like this, for instance, made him tired. He felt he was really suffering from the heat. The fat man looked as if he had grown to the stump; he slumped there in his damp, dark clothes too big for him, his belly slack in his pants, his wide black felt hat pushed off his narrow forehead red with prickly heat. A bottle of good cold beer, now, would be a help, thought Mr. Thompson, remembering the four bottles sitting deep in the pool at the spring house, and his dry tongue squirmed in his mouth. He wasn't going to offer this man anything, though, not even a drop of water. He wasn't even going to chew any more tobacco with him. He shot out his quid suddenly, and wiped his mouth on the back of his hand, and studied the head near him attentively. The man was no good, and he was there for no good, but what was he up to? Mr. Thompson made up his mind he'd give him a little more time to get his business, whatever it was, with Mr. Helton over, and then if he didn't get off the place he'd kick him off.

Mr. Hatch, as if he suspected Mr. Thompson's thoughts, turned his eyes, wicked and pig-like, on Mr. Thompson. "Fact is," he said, as if he had made up his mind about something, "I might need your help in the little matter I've got on hand, but it won't cost you any trouble. Now, this Mr. Helton here, like I tell you, he's a dangerous escaped loonatic, you might say. Now fact is, in the last twelve years or so I must a rounded up twenty-odd escaped loonatics, besides a couple of escaped convicts that I just run into by accident, like. I don't made a business of it, but if there's a reward, and there usually is a reward, of course, I get it. It amounts to a tidy little sum in the long run, but that ain't the main question. Fact is, I'm for law and order, I don't like to see lawbreakers and loonatics at large. It ain't the place for them. Now I reckon you're bound to agree with me on that, aren't you?"

Mr. Thompson said, "Well, circumstances alters cases, as the feller says. Now, what I know of Mr. Helton, he ain't dangerous, as I told you." Something serious was going to happen, Mr. Thompson could see that. He stopped thinking about it. He'd just let this fellow shoot off his head and then see what could be done about it. Without thinking he got out his knife and plug and started to cut a chew, then remembered himself and put them back in his pocket.

"The law," said Mr. Hatch, "is solidly behind me. Now this Mr. Helton, he's been one of my toughest cases. He's kept my record from being practically one hundred per cent. I knew him before he went loony, and I know the fam'ly, so I undertook to help out rounding him up. Well, sir he was gone slick as a whistle, for all we knew the man was as good as dead long while ago. Now we never might have caught up with him, but do you know what he did? Well sir, about two weeks ago his old mother gets a letter from him, and in that letter what do you reckon she found? Well, it was a post-office money order for eight hundred and fifty dollars, just like that; the letter wasn't nothing much, just said he was sending her a few little savings, she might need something, but there it was, name, postmark, date, everything. The old woman practically lost her mind with joy. She's gettin childish, and it looked like she kinda forgot that her only living son killed his brother and went loony. Mr. Helton said he was getting along all right, and for her not to tell nobody. Well, natchally, she couldn't keep it to herself, with that money order to cash and everything. So that's how I come to know." His feelings got the better of him. "You could a knocked me down with a feather." He shook hands with himself and rocked, wagging his head, going "Heh, heh," in his throat. Mr. Thompson felt the corners of his mouth turning down. Why, the dirty low-down hound, sneaking around spying into other people's business like that. Collecting blood money, that's what it was! Let him talk!

"Yea, well, that must a been a surprise all right," he said, trying to hold his voice even. "I'd say a surprise."

"Well, siree," said Mr. Hatch, "the more I got to thinking about it, the more I just come to the conclusion that I'd better look into the matter a little, and so I talked to the old woman. She's pretty decrepit, now, half blind and all, but she was all for taking the first train out and going to see her son. I put it up to her square — how she was too feeble for the trip, and all. So, just as a favor to her, I told her for my expenses I'd come down and see Mr. Helton and bring her back all the news about him. She gave me a new shirt she made herself by hand, and a big Swedish kind of cake to bring to him, but I musta mislaid them along the road somewhere. It don't reely matter, though, he prob'ly ain't in any state of mind to appreciate 'em.''

Mr. Thompson sat up and turning round on the log looked at Mr. Hatch and asked as quietly as he could, "And now what are you aiming to do? That's the question.''

Mr. Hatch slouched up to his feet and shook himself. "Well, I come all prepared for a little scuffle," he said. "I got the handcuffs," he said, "but I don't want no violence if I can help it. I didn't want to say nothing around the countryside, making an uproar. I figured the two of us could overpower him." He reached into his big inside pocket and pulled them out. Handcuffs, for God's sake, thought Mr. Thompson. Coming round on a peacable afternoon worrying a man, making trouble, and fishing handcuffs out of his pocket on a decent family homestead, as if it was all in the day's work.

Mr. Thompson, his head buzzing, got up too. "Well," he said, roundly, "I want to tell you I think you've got a mighty sorry job on hand, you sure must be hard up for something to do, and now I want to give you a good piece of advice. You just drop the idea that you're going to come here and make trouble for Mr. Helton, and the quicker you drive that hired rig away from my front gate the better I'll be satisfied."

Mr. Hatch put one handcuff in his outside pocket, the other dangling down. He pulled his hat down over his eyes, and reminded Mr. Thompson of a sheriff, somehow. He didn't seem in the least nervous, and didn't take up Mr. Thompson's words. He said, "Now listen just a minute, it ain't reasonable to suppose that a man like yourself is going to stand in the way of getting an escaped loonatic back to the asylum where he belongs. Now I know it's enough to throw you off, coming sudden like this, but fact is I counted on your being a respectable man and helping me out to see that justice is done. Now a course, if you won't help, I'll have to look around for help somewheres else. It won't look very good to your neighbors that you was harbring an escaped loonatic who killed his own brother, and then you refused to give him up. It will look mighty funny."

Mr. Thompson knew almost before he heard the words that it would look funny. It would put him in a mighty awkward position. He said,

"But I've been trying to tell you all along that the man ain't loony now. He's been perfectly harmless for nine years. He's — he's — "

Mr. Thompson couldn't think how to describe how it was with Mr. Helton. "Why, he's been like one of the family," he said, "the best standby a man ever had." Mr. Thompson tried to see his way out. It was a fact Mr. Helton might go loony again any minute, and now this fellow talking around the country would put Mr. Thompson in a fix. It was a terrible position. He couldn't think of any way out. "You're crazy," Mr. Thompson roared suddenly, "you're the crazy one around here, you're crazier than he ever was! You get off this place or I'll handcuff you and turn you over to the law. You're trespassing," shouted Mr. Thompson. "Get out of here before I knock you down!"

He took a step toward the fat man, who backed off, shrinking. "Try it, try it, go ahead!" and then something happened that Mr. Thompson tried hard afterward to piece together in his mind, and in fact it never did come straight. He saw the fat man with his long bowie knife in his hand, he saw Mr. Helton come round the corner on the run, his long jaw dropped, his arms swinging, his eyes wild. Mr. Helton came in between them, fists doubled up, then stopped short, glaring at the fat man, his big frame seemed to collapse, he trembled like a shied horse; and then the fat man drove at him, knife in one hand, handcuffs in the other. Mr. Thompson saw it coming, he saw the blade going into Mr. Helton's stomach, he knew he had the axe out of the log in his own hands, felt his arms go up over his head and bring the axe down on Mr. Hatch's head as if he were stunning a beef.

Mrs. Thompson had been listening uneasily for some time to the voices going on, one of them strange to her, but she was too tired at first to get up and come out to see what was going on. The confused shouting that rose so suddenly brought her up to her feet and out across the front porch without her slippers, hair half-braided. Shading her eyes, she saw first Mr. Helton, running all stooped over through the orchard, running like a man with dogs after him; and Mr. Thompson supporting himself on the axe handle was leaning over shaking by the shoulder a man Mrs. Thompson had never seen, who lay doubled up with the top of his head smashed and the blood running away in a greasy-looking puddle. Mr. Thompson without taking his hand from the man's shoulder said in a thick voice, "He killed Mr. Helton, he killed him, I saw him do it. I had to knock him out," he called loudly, "but he won't come to."

Mrs. Thompson said in a faint scream, "Why yonder goes Mr. Helton," and she pointed. Mr. Thompson pulled himself up and looked where she pointed. Mrs. Thompson sat down slowly against the side of the house and began to slide forward on her face; she felt as if she were drowning, she couldn't rise to the top somehow, and her only thought was she was glad the boys were not there, they were out, fishing at Halifax. Oh God, she was glad the boys were not here.

Mr. and Mrs. Thompson drove up to their barn about sunset. Mr. Thompson handed the reins to his wife, got out to open the big door, and Mrs. Thompson guided old Jim in under the roof. The buggy was gray with dust and age, Mrs. Thompson's face was gray with dust and weariness, and Mr. Thompson's face, as he stood at the horse's head and began unhitching, was gray except for the dark blue of his freshly shaven jaws and chin, gray and blue and caved in, but patient, like a dead man's face.

Mrs. Thompson stepped down to the hard packed manure of the barn floor, and shook out her light flower-sprigged dress. She wore her smoked glasses, and her wide shady leghorn hat with the wreath of exhausted pink and blue forgetmenots hid her forehead, fixed in a knot of distress.

The horse hung his head, raised a huge sigh and flexed his stiffened legs. Mr. Thompson's words came up muffled and hollow. "Poor ole Jim," he said, clearing his throat, "he looks pretty sunk in the ribs. I guess he's had a hard week." He lifted the harness up in one piece, slid it off, and Jim walked out of the shafts halting a little. "Well, this is the last time," Mr. Thompson said talking to Jim. "Now you can get a good rest."

Mrs. Thompson closed her eyes behind her smoked glasses. The last time, and high time, and they should never have gone at all. She did not need her glasses any more, now the good darkness was coming down again, but her eyes ran full of tears steadily, though she was not crying, and she felt better with the glasses, safer, hidden away behind them. She took out her handkerchief with her hands shaking as they had been shaking ever since *that day*, and blew her nose. She said, "I see the boys have lighted the lamps. I hope they've started the stove going."

She stepped along the rough path holding her thin dress and starched petticoats around her, feeling her way between the sharp small stones, leaving the barn because she could hardly bear to be near Mr. Thompson, advancing slowly toward the house because she dreaded going there. Life was all one dread, the faces of her neighbors, of her boys, of her husband, the face of the whole world, the shape of her own house in the darkness, the very smell of the grass and the trees were horrible to her. There was no place to go, only one thing to do, bear it somehow — but how? She asked herself that question often. How was she going to keep on living now? Why had she lived at all? She wished now she had died one of those times when she had been so sick, instead of living on for this.

The boys were in the kitchen, Herbert was looking at the funny pictures from last Sunday's newspapers, the Katzenjammer Kids and Happy Hooligan. His chin was in his hands and his elbows on the table, and he was really reading and looking at the pictures, but his face was unhappy. Arthur was building the fire, adding kindling a stick at a time, watching it catch and blaze. His face was heavier and darker than Herbert's but he was a little sullen by nature; Mrs. Thompson thought, he takes things harder, too. Arthur said, "Hello, Momma," and went on with his work. Herbert swept the papers together and moved over on the bench. They were big boys — fifteen and seventeen, and Arthur as tall as his father. Mrs. Thompson sat down beside Herbert, taking off her hat. She said, "I guess you're hungry. We were late today. We went the Log Hollow road, it's rougher than ever." Her pale mouth drooped with a sad fold on either side.

"I guess you saw the Mannings, then," said Herbert.

"Yes, and the Fergusons, and the Allbrights, and that new family McClellan."

"Anybody say anything?" asked Herbert.

"Nothing much, you know how it's been all along, some of them keeps saying, yes, they know it was a clear case and a fair trial and they say how glad they are your Papa came out so well, and all that, some of 'em do, anyhow, but it looks like they don't really take sides with him. I'm about wore out," she said, the tears rolling again from under her dark glasses, "I don't know what good it does, but your Papa can't seem to rest unless he's telling how it happened. I don't know."

"I don't think it does any good, not a speck," said Arthur, moving away from the stove. "It just keeps the whole question stirred up in people's minds. Everybody will go round telling what he heard, and the whole thing is going to get worse mixed up than ever. It just makes matters worse. I wish you could get Papa to stop driving round the country talking like that."

"Your Papa knows best," said Mrs. Thompson. "You oughtn't to criticize him. He's got enough to put up with without that."

Arthur said nothing, his jaw stubborn. Mr. Thompson came in, his eyes hollowed out and dead-looking, his thick hands gray-white and seamed from washing them clean every day before he started out to see the neighbors to tell them his side of the story. He was wearing his Sunday clothes, a thick pepper-and-salt-colored suit with a black string tie.

Mrs. Thompson stood up, her head swimming. "Now you-all get

out of the kitchen, it's too hot in here and I need room. I'll get us a little bite of supper, if you'll just get out and give me some room."

They went as if they were glad to go, the boys outside, Mr. Thompson into his bedroom. She heard him groaning to himself as he took off his shoes, and heard the bed creak as he lay down. Mrs. Thompson opened the icebox and felt the sweet coldness flow out of it; she had never expected to have an icebox, much less did she hope to afford to keep it filled with ice. It still seemed like a miracle, after two or three years. There was the food, cold and clean, all ready to be warmed over. She would never have had that icebox if Mr. Helton hadn't happened along one day, just by the strangest luck; so saving, and so managing, so good, thought Mrs. Thompson, her heart swelling until she feared she would faint again, standing there with the door open and leaning her head upon it. She simply could not bear to remember Mr. Helton, with his long sad face and silent ways, who had always been so quiet and harmless, who had worked so hard and helped Mr. Thompson so much, running through the hot fields and woods, being hunted like a mad dog, everybody turning out with ropes and guns and sticks to catch and tie him. Oh, God, said Mrs. Thompson in a long dry moan, kneeling before the icebox and fumbling inside for the dishes, even if they did pile mattresses all over the jail floor and against the walls, and five men there to hold him to keep him from hurting himself any more, he was already hurt too badly, he couldn't have lived anyway. Mr. Barbee, the sheriff, told her about it. He said, well, they didn't aim to harm him but they had to catch him, he was crazy as a loon; he picked up rocks and tried to brain every man that got near him. He had two harmonicas in his jumper pocket, said the sheriff, but they fell out in the scuffle, and Mr. Helton tried to pick 'em up again, and that's when they finally got him. "They *had* to be rough, Miz Thompson, he fought like a wildcat." Yes, thought Mrs. Thompson again with the same bitterness, of course, they had to be rough. They always have to be rough. Mr. Thompson can't argue with a man and get him off the place peaceably; no, she thought, standing up and shutting the icebox, he has to kill somebody, he has to be a murderer and ruin his boys' lives and cause Mr. Helton to be killed like a mad dog.

Her thoughts stopped with a little soundless explosion, cleared and began again. The rest of Mr. Helton's harmonicas were still in the shack, his tune ran in Mrs. Thompson's head at certain times of the day. She missed it in the evenings. It seemed so strange she had never known the name of that song, nor what it meant, until after Mr. Helton was gone. Mrs. Thompson, trembling in the knees, took a drink of water at the sink and poured the red beans into the baking dish, and began to roll the pieces of chicken in flour to fry them. There was a time, she said to herself, when I thought I had neighbors and friends, there was a time when we could hold up our heads, there was a time when my husband hadn't killed a man and I could tell the truth to anybody about anything.

Mr. Thompson, turning on his bed, figured that he had done all he could, he'd just try to let the matter rest from now on. His lawyer, Mr. Burleigh, had told him right at the beginning, "Now you keep calm and collected. You've got a fine case, even if you haven't got witnesses. Your wife must sit in court, she'll be a powerful argument with the jury. You just plead not guilty and I'll do the rest. The trial is going to be a mere formality, you haven't got a thing to worry about. You'll be clean out of this before you know it." And to make talk Mr. Burleigh had got to telling about all the men he knew around the country who for one reason or another had been forced to kill somebody, always in self defense, and there just wasn't anything to it at all. He even told about how his own father in the old days had shot and killed a man just for setting foot inside his gate when he told him not to. "Sure, I shot the scoundrel," said Mr. Burleigh's father, "in self defense; I *told* him I'd shoot him if he set his foot in my yard, and he did, and I did." There had been bad blood between them for years, Mr. Burleigh said, and his father had waited a long time to catch the other fellow in the wrong, and when he did he certainly made the most of his opportunity.

"But Mr. Hatch, as I told you," Mr. Thompson had said, "made a pass at Mr. Helton with his bowie knife. That's why I took a hand."

"All the better," said Mr. Burleigh. "That stranger hadn't any right coming to your house on such an errand. Why, hell," said Mr. Burleigh, "that wasn't even manslaughter you committed. So now you just hold your horses and keep your shirt on. And don't say one word without I tell you."

Wasn't even manslaughter. Mr. Thompson had to cover Mr. Hatch with a piece of wagon canvas and ride to town to tell the sheriff. It had been hard on Ellie. When they got back, the sheriff and the coroner and two deputies, they found her sitting beside the road, on a low bridge over a gully, about half a mile from the place. He had taken her up behind his saddle and got her back to the house. He had already told the sheriff that his wife had witnessed the whole business, and now he had time, getting her to her room and in bed, to tell her what to say if they asked anything. He had left out the part about Mr. Helton being crazy all along, but it came out at the trial. By Mr. Burleigh's advice Mr. Thompson had pretended to be perfectly ignorant; Mr. Hatch hadn't said a word about that. Mr. Thompson pretended to believe that Mr. Hatch had just come looking for Mr. Helton to settle old scores, and the two members of

Mr. Hatch's family who had come down to try to get Mr. Thompson convicted didn't get anywhere at all. It hadn't been much of a trial, Mr. Burleigh saw to that. He had charged a reasonable fee, and Mr. Thompson had paid him and felt grateful, but after it was over Mr. Burleigh didn't seem pleased to see him when he got to dropping into the office to talk it over, telling him things that had slipped his mind at first: trying to explain what an ornery low hound Mr. Hatch had been, anyhow. Mr. Burleigh seemed to have lost his interest; he looked sour and upset when he saw Mr. Thompson at the door. Mr. Thompson kept saying to himself that he'd got off, all right, just as Mr. Burleigh had predicted, but, but — and it was right there that Mr. Thompson's mind stuck, squirming like an angle-worm on a fishhook: he had killed Mr. Hatch, and he was a murderer. That was the truth about himself that Mr. Thompson couldn't grasp, even when he said the word to himself. Why, he had not even once *thought* of killing anybody, much less Mr. Hatch, and if Mr. Helton hadn't come out so unexpectedly, hearing the row, why, then — but then, Mr. Helton had come on the run that way to help him. What he couldn't understand was what happened next. He had seen Mr. Hatch go after Mr. Helton with the knife, he had seen the point, blade up, go into Mr. Helton's stomach and slice up like you slice a hog, but when they finally caught Mr. Helton there wasn't a knife scratch on him. Mr. Thompson knew he had the axe in his own hands and felt himself lifting it, but he couldn't remember hitting Mr. Hatch. He couldn't remember it. He couldn't. He remembered only that he had been determined to stop Mr. Hatch from cutting Mr. Helton. If he was given a chance he could explain the whole matter. At the trial they hadn't let him talk. They just asked questions and he answered yes or no, and they never did get to the core of the matter. Since the trial, now, every day for a week he had washed and shaved and put on his best clothes and had taken Ellie with him to tell every neighbor he had that he never killed Mr. Hatch on purpose, and what good did it do? Nobody believed him. Even when he turned to Ellie and said, "You was there, you saw it, didn't you?" and Ellie spoke up saying, "Yes, that's the truth. Mr. Thompson was trying to save Mr. Helton's life," and he added, "If you don't believe me, you can believe my wife. She won't lie." Mr. Thompson saw something in all their faces that disheartened him, made him feel empty and tired out. They didn't believe he was not a murderer.

Even Ellie never said anything to comfort him. He hoped she would say finally, "I remember now, Mr. Thompson, I really did come around the corner in time to see everything. It's not a lie, Mr. Thompson. Don't you worry." But as they drove together in silence, with the days still hot and dry, shortening for fall, day after day, the buggy jolting in the ruts, she said nothing; they grew to dread the sight of another

house, and the people in it: all houses looked alike now, and the people
— old neighbors or new — had the same expression when Mr. Thompson
told them why he had come and began his story. Their eyes looked as if
some one had pinched the eyeball at the back; they shrivelled and the
light went out of them. Some of them sat with fixed tight smiles trying
to be friendly. "Yes, Mr. Thompson, we know how you must feel. It
must be terrible for you, Mrs. Thompson. Yes, you know, I've about
come to the point where I believe in such a thing as killing in self
defense. Why, certainly, we believe you, Mr. Thompson, why shouldn't
we believe you? Didn't you have a perfectly fair and above-board trial?
Well, now natchally, Mr. Thompson, we think you done right."

Mr. Thompson was satisfied they didn't think so. Sometimes the
air around him was so thick with their blame he fought and pushed with
his fists, and the sweat broke out all over him, he shouted his story in a
dust-choked voice, he would fairly bellow at last: "My wife, here, you
know her, she was there, and saw and heard it all, if you don't believe me,
ask her, she won't lie!" and Mrs. Thompson, with her hands knotted
together, aching, her chin trembling, would never fail to say: "Yes, that's
right, that's the truth — "

The last straw had been laid on today, Mr. Thompson decided. Tom
Allbright, an old beau of Ellie's, why, he had squired Ellie around a
whole summer, had come out to meet them when they drove up, and
standing there bareheaded had stopped them from getting out. He had
looked past them with an embarrassed frown on his face, telling them his
wife's sister was there with a raft of young ones, and the house was pretty
full and everything upset, or he'd ask them to come in. "We've been
thinking of trying to get up to your place one of these days," said Mr.
Allbright, moving away trying to look busy, "we've been mighty occupied up here of late." So they had to say, "Well, we just happened to be
driving this way," and go on. "The Allbrights," said Mrs. Thompson,
"always was fair-weather friends." "They look out for number one, that's
a fact," said Mr. Thompson. But it was cold comfort to them both.

Finally Mrs. Thompson had given up. "Let's go home," she said.
"Old Jim's tired and thirsty, and we've gone far enough."

Mr. Thompson said, "Well, while we're out thu way, we might as
well stop at the McClellans." They drove in, and asked a little cotton-
haired boy if his mama and papa were at home. Mr. Thompson wanted
to see them. The little boy stood gazing with his mouth open, then
galloped into the house shouting, "Mommer, Popper, come out hyah.
That man that kilt Mr. Hatch has come ter see yer!"

The man came out in his sock feet, with one gallus up, the other
broken and dangling, and said, "Light down, Mr. Thompson, and come
in. The old woman's washing but she'll git here."

Mrs. Thompson, feeling her way, stepped down and sat in a broken rockingchair on the porch that sagged under her feet. The woman of the house, barefooted, in a calico wrapper, sat on the edge of the porch, her fat sallow face full of curiosity. Mr. Thompson began, "Well, as I reckon you happen to know, I've had some strange troubles lately, and, as the feller says, it's not the kind of trouble that happens to a man every day in the year, and there's some things I don't want no misunderstanding about in the neighbors' minds, so — " He halted and stumbled forward and the two listening faces took on a mean look, a greedy, despising look, a look that said plain as day, "My you must be a purty sorry feller to come round worrying what *we* think, *we* know you wouldn't be here if you had anybody else to turn to — my, I wouldn't lower myself that much, myself." Mr. Thompson was ashamed of himself, he was suddenly in a rage, he'd like to knock their dirty skunk heads together, the low-down white trash — but he held himself down and went on to the end. "My wife will tell you," he said, and this was the hardest place, because Ellie always without moving a muscle seemed to stiffen as if somebody had threatened to hit her, "ask my wife, she won't lie."

"It's true, I saw it — "

"Well now," said the man, drily, scratching his ribs inside his shirt, "that sholy is too bad. Well, now, I kaint see what we've got to do with all this here, however. I kaint see no good reason for us to git mixed up in these murder matters, I shore kaint. Whichever way you look at it, it ain't none of my business. However, it's mighty nice of you-all to come around and give us the straight of it, fur we've heerd some mighty queer yarns about it, mighty queer, I golly you couldn't hardly make head ner tail of it."

"Evveybody goin round shootin they heads off," said the woman, "now we don't hold with killin, the Bible says — "

"Shet yer trap," said the man, "and keep it shet r I'll shet it fer yer. Now it shore looks like to me — "

"We mustn't linger," said Mrs. Thompson, unclasping her hands. "We've lingered too long now. It's getting late, and we've far to go." Mr. Thompson took the hint and followed her. The man and the woman lolled against their rickety porch poles and watched them go.

Now lying on his bed, Mr. Thompson knew the end had come. Now, this minute, lying in the bed where he had slept with Ellie for eighteen years; under this roof where he had laid the shingles when he was waiting to get married; there as he was with his whiskers already sprouting since his shave that morning; with his fingers feeling his bony chin, Mr. Thompson felt he was a dead man. He was dead to his other life, he had got to the end of something without knowing why, and he had to make a fresh start, he did not know how. Something different was going to begin, he didn't know what. It was in some way not his business. He didn't feel he was going to have much to do with it. He got up, aching, hollow, and went out to the kitchen where Mrs. Thompson was just taking up the supper.

"Call the boys," said Mrs. Thompson. They had been down to the barn, and Arthur put out the lantern before hanging it on a nail near the door. Mr. Thompson didn't like their silence. They had hardly said a word about anything to him since that day. They seemed to avoid him, they ran the place together as if he wasn't there, and attended to everything without asking him for any advice. "What you boys been up to?" he asked, trying to be hearty, "Finishing your chores?"

"No, sir," said Arthur, "there ain't much to do. Just greasing some axles." Herbert said nothing. Mrs. Thompson bowed her head: "For these and all Thy blessings . . . Amen," she whispered weakly, and the Thompsons sat there with their eyes down and their faces sorrowful, as if they were at a funeral.

Every time he shut his eyes, trying to sleep, Mr. Thompson's mind started up and began to run like a rabbit. It jumped from one thing to another, trying to pick up a trail here or there that would straighten out what had happened that day he killed Mr. Hatch. Try as he might, Mr. Thompson's mind would not go anywhere that it had not already been, he could not see anything but what he had seen once, and he knew that was not right. If he had not seen straight that first time, then everything about his killing Mr. Hatch was wrong from start to finish, and there was nothing more to be done about it, he might just as well give up. It still seemed to him that he had done, maybe not the right thing, but the only thing he could do, that day, but had he? *Did he have to kill Mr. Hatch?* He had never seen a man he hated more, the minute he laid eyes on him. He knew in his bones the fellow was there for trouble, what seemed so funny now was this: why hadn't he just told Mr. Hatch to get out before he ever even hardly got in?

Mrs. Thompson, her arms crossed on her breast, was lying beside him, perfectly still, but she seemed awake, somehow. "Asleep, Ellie?"

After all, he might have got rid of him peaceably, or maybe he might have had to overpower him and put those handcuffs on him and turn him over to the sheriff for disturbing the peace. The most they could have done was to lock Mr. Hatch up while he cooled off for a few days, or fine him a little something. He would try to think of things he might have said to Mr. Hatch. Why, let's see, I could just have said, Now look here, Mr. Hatch, I want to talk to you as man to man. But his brain would go empty. What could he have said or done? But if he *could* have done anything else almost except kill Mr. Hatch, then nothing would have happened to Mr. Helton. Mr. Thompson hardly ever thought of Mr. Helton. His mind just skipped over him and went on. If he stopped to think about Mr. Helton he'd never in God's world get anywhere. He tried to imagine how it might all have been, this very night even, if Mr. Helton were still safe and sound out in his shack playing his tune about feeling so good in the morning, drinking up all the wine so you'd feel even better; and Mr. Hatch safe in jail somewhere, mad as hops, maybe, but out of harm's way and ready to listen to reason and to repent of his meanness, the dirty, yellow-livered hound coming around persecuting an innocent man and ruining a whole family that never harmed him! Mr. Thompson felt the veins of his forehead start up, his fists clutched as if they seized an axe handle, the sweat broke out on him, he bounded up from the bed with a yell smothered in his throat, and Ellie started up after him crying out, "Oh, oh, don't! Don't! Don't!" as if she were having a nightmare. He stood shaking until his bones rattled in him, crying hoarsely, "Light the lamp, light the lamp, Ellie."

Instead, Mrs. Thompson gave a shrill weak scream, almost the same scream he had heard on that day she came around the house when he was standing there with the axe in his hand. He could not see her in the dark, but she was on the bed, rolling violently. He felt for her in horror, and his groping hands found her arms, up, and her own hands pulling her hair straight out from her head, her neck strained back, and the tight screams strangling her. He shouted out for Arthur, for Herbert. "Your mother!" he bawled, his voice cracking. As he held Mrs. Thompson's arms, the boys came tumbling in, Arthur with the lamp above his head. By this light Mr. Thompson saw Mrs. Thompson's eyes, wide open, staring dreadfully at him, the tears pouring. She sat up at sight of the boys, and held out one arm toward them, the hand wagging in a crazy circle, then dropped on her back again, and suddenly went limp. Arthur set the lamp on the table and turned on Mr. Thompson. "She's scared," he said, "she's scared to death." His face was in a knot of rage, his fists were doubled up, he faced his father as if he meant to strike him. Mr. Thompson's jaw fell, he was so surprised he stepped back from the bed. Herbert went to the other side. They stood on each side of Mrs. Thompson and watched Mr. Thompson as if he were a dangerous wild beast. "What did you do to her?" shouted Arthur, in a grown man's voice. "You touch her again and I'll blow your heart out!" Herbert was pale and his cheek twitched, but he was on Arthur's side; he would do what he could to help Arthur.

Mr. Thompson had no fight left in him. His knees bent as he stood, his chest collapsed. "Why, Arthur," he said, his words crumbling and his breath coming short. "She's fainted again. Get the ammonia."

Arthur did not move. Herbert brought the bottle, and handed it, shrinking, to his father.

Mr. Thompson held it under Mrs. Thompson's nose. He poured a little in the palm of his hand and rubbed it on her forehead. She gasped and opened her eyes and turned her head away from him. Herbert began a doleful hopeless sniffling. "Mama," he kept saying, "mama, don't die."

"I'm all right," Mrs. Thompson said. "Now don't you worry around. Now Herbert, you mustn't do that. I'm all right." She closed her eyes. Mr. Thompson began pulling on his best pants; he put on his socks and shoes. The boys sat on each side of the bed, watching Mrs. Thompson's face. Mr. Thompson put on his shirt and coat. He said, "I reckon I'll ride over and get the doctor. Don't look like all this fainting is a good sign. Now you just keep watch until I get back." They listened, but said nothing. He said, "Don't you get any notions in your head. I never did your mother any harm in my life, on purpose." He went out, and, looking back, saw Herbert staring at him from under his brows, like a stranger. "You'll know how to look after her," said Mr. Thompson.

Mr. Thompson went through the kitchen. There he lighted the lantern, took a thin pad of scratch paper and a stub pencil from the shelf where the boys kept their schoolbooks. He swung the lantern on his arm and reached into the cupboard where he kept the guns. The shotgun was there to his hand, primed and ready, a man never knows when he may need a shotgun. He went out of the house without looking around, or looking back when he had left it, passed his barn without seeing it, and struck out to the farthest end of his fields, which ran for half a mile to the east. So many blows had been struck at Mr. Thompson and from so many directions he couldn't stop any more to find out where he was hit. He walked on, over ploughed ground and over meadow, going through barbed wire fences cautiously, putting his gun through first; he could almost see in the dark, now his eyes were used to it. Finally he came to the last fence; here he sat down, back against a post, lantern at his side, and, with the pad on his knee, moistened the stub pencil and began to write:

"Before Almighty God, the great judge of all before who I am about to appear, I do hereby solemnly swear that I did not take the life of Mr. Homer T. Hatch on purpose. It was done in defense of Mr. Helton. I did not aim to hit him with the axe but only to keep him off Mr. Helton. He aimed a blow at Mr. Helton who was not looking for it. It was my belief at the time that Mr. Hatch would of taken the life of Mr. Helton if I did not interfere. I have told all this to the judge and the jury and they let me off but nobody believes it. This is the only way I can prove I am not a cold-blooded murderer like everybody seems to think. If I had been in Mr. Helton's place he would of done the same for me. I still think I done the only thing there was to do. My wife — "

Mr. Thompson stopped here to think a while. He wet the pencil point with the tip of his tongue and marked out the last two words. He sat a while blacking out the words until he had made a neat oblong patch where they had been, and started again:

"It was Mr. Homer T. Hatch who came to do wrong to a harmless man. He caused all this trouble and he deserved to die but I am sorry it was me who had to kill him."

He licked the point of his pencil again, and signed his full name carefully, folded the paper and put it in his outside pocket. Taking off his right shoe and sock, he set the butt of the shotgun along the ground with the twin barrels pointed toward his head. It was very awkward. He thought about this a little, leaning his head against the gun mouth. He was trembling and his head was drumming until he was deaf and blind, but he lay down on the earth on his side, drew the barrel under his chin and fumbled for the trigger with his great toe. That way he could work it.

# John Steinbeck (1902–1968)

ONE OF THE SEVEN American authors to win the Nobel Prize, John Steinbeck was born in Salinas, California, and attended Stanford University. *Cup of Gold* (1929), a historical romance of piratical adventure, was his first novel. Steinbeck's later novels were more realistic, dealing with migrant workers and their struggles of the Depression years in California. Important among these were *In Dubious Battle* (1936), *Of Mice and Men* (1937), and *The Grapes of Wrath* (1939). His finest short stories are to be found in *The Long Valley* (1938). Steinbeck's last book concerned his tour of forty states with his dog and was called *Travels with Charley in Search of America* (1962).

Steinbeck was a restless author writing about many periods, places, and peoples, but only when he wrote about the life he had known in his native California was he successful. It was true of his proletarian novels and it is so in this emotional story of an old pioneer. And a reader senses also Steinbeck's great love for California in his pictures of the countryside. But most impressive is the way he tells the pioneer's story. "It wasn't Indians that were important, nor adventures, nor even getting out here . . . We carried life out here and set it down the way those ants carry eggs. And I was the leader. The westering was as big as God, and the slow steps that made the movement piled up and piled up until the continent was crossed. Then we came down to the sea, and it was done." There, in a few words, Steinbeck has written an epic.

# *The Leader of the People*

ON SATURDAY AFTERNOON Billy Buck, the ranch-hand, raked together the last of the old year's haystack and pitched small forkfuls over the wire fence to a few mildly interested cattle. High in the air small clouds like puffs of cannon smoke were driven eastward by the March wind. The wind could be heard whishing in the brush on the ridge crests, but no breath of it penetrated down into the ranch-cup.

The little boy, Jody, emerged from the house eating a thick piece of buttered bread. He saw Billy working on the last of the haystack. Jody tramped down scuffling his shoes in a way he had been told was destructive to good shoe-leather. A flock of white pigeons flew out of the black cypress tree as Jody passed, and circled the tree and landed again. A half-grown tortoise-shell cat leaped from the bunkhouse porch, galloped on stiff legs across the road, whirled and galloped back again. Jody picked up a stone to help the game along, but he was too late, for the cat was under the porch before the stone could be discharged. He threw the stone into the cypress tree and started the white pigeons on another whirling flight.

Arriving at the used-up haystack, the boy leaned against the barbed wire fence. "Will that be all of it, do you think?" he asked.

The middle-aged ranch-hand stopped his careful raking and stuck his fork into the ground. He took off his black hat and smoothed down his hair. "Nothing left of it that isn't soggy from ground moisture," he said. He replaced his hat and rubbed his dry leathery hands together.

"Ought to be plenty mice," Jody suggested.

"Lousy with them," said Billy. "Just crawling with mice."

"Well, maybe, when you get all through, I could call the dogs and hunt the mice."

"Sure, I guess you could," said Billy Buck. He lifted a forkful of the damp ground-hay and threw it into the air. Instantly three mice leaped out and burrowed frantically under the hay again.

Jody sighed with satisfaction. Those plump, sleek, arrogant mice were doomed. For eight months they had lived and multiplied in the haystack. They had been immune from cats, from traps, from poison and from Jody. They had grown smug in their security, overbearing and fat. Now the time of disaster had come; they would not survive another day.

Billy looked up at the top of the hills that surrounded the ranch. "Maybe you better ask your father before you do it," he suggested.

"Well, where is he? I'll ask him now."

"He rode up to the ridge ranch after dinner. He'll be back pretty soon."

Jody slumped against the fence post. "I don't think he'd care."

As Billy went back to his work he said ominously, "You'd better ask him anyway. You know how he is."

Jody did know. His father, Carl Tiflin, insisted upon giving permission for anything that was done on the ranch, whether it was important or not. Judy sagged farther against the post until he was sitting on the ground. He looked up at the little puffs of wind-driven cloud. "Is it like to rain, Billy?"

"It might. The wind's good for it, but not strong enough."

"Well, I hope it don't rain until after I kill those damn mice." He looked over his shoulder to see whether Billy had noticed the mature profanity. Billy worked on without comment.

Jody turned back and looked at the side-hill where the road from the outside world came down. The hill was washed with lean March sunshine. Silver thistles, blue lupins and a few poppies bloomed among the sagebushes. Halfway up the hill Jody could see Doubletree Mutt, the black dog, digging in a squirrel hole. He paddled for a while and then paused to kick bursts of dirt out between his hind legs, and he dug with an earnestness which belied the knowledge he must have had that no dog had ever caught a squirrel by digging in a hole.

Suddenly, while Jody watched, the black dog stiffened, and backed out of the hole and looked up the hill toward the cleft in the ridge where the road came through. Jody looked up too. For a moment Carl Tiflin on horseback stood out against the pale sky and then he moved down the road toward the house. He carried something white in his hand.

The boy started to his feet. "He's got a letter," Jody cried. He trotted away toward the ranch house, for the letter would probably be read aloud and he wanted to be there. He reached the house before his father did, and ran in. He heard Carl dismount from his creaking saddle and slap the horse on the side to send it to the barn where Billy would unsaddle it and turn it out.

Jody ran into the kitchen. "We got a letter!" he cried.

His mother looked up from a pan of beans. "Who has?"

"Father has. I saw it in his hand."

Carl strode into the kitchen then, and Jody's mother asked, "Who's the letter from, Carl?"

He frowned quickly. "How did you know there was a letter?"

She nodded her head in the boy's direction. "Big-Britches Jody told me."

Jody was embarrassed.

His father looked down at him contemptuously. "He *is* getting to be a Big-Britches," Carl said. "He's minding everybody's business but his own. Got his big nose into everything."

Mrs. Tiflin relented a little. "Well, he hasn't enough to keep him busy. Who's the letter from?"

Carl still frowned on Jody. "I'll keep him busy if he isn't careful." He held out a sealed letter. "I guess it's from your father."

Mrs. Tiflin took a hairpin from her head and slit open the flap. Her lips pursed judiciously. Jody saw her eyes snap back and forth over the lines. "He says," she translated, "he says he's going to drive out Saturday to stay for a little while. Why, this is Saturday. The letter must have been delayed." She looked at the postmark. "This was mailed day before yesterday. It should have been here yesterday." She looked up questioningly at her husband, and then her face darkened angrily. "Now what have you got that look on you for? He doesn't come often."

Carl turned his eyes away from her anger. He could be stern with her most of the time, but when occasionally her temper arose, he could not combat it.

"What's the matter with you?" she demanded again.

In his explanation there was a tone of apology Jody himself might have used. "It's just that he talks," Carl said lamely. "Just talks."

"Well, what of it? You talk yourself."

"Sure I do. But your father only talks about one thing."

"Indians!" Jody broke in excitedly. "Indians and crossing the plains!"

Carl turned fiercely on him. "You get out, Mr. Big-Britches! Go on, now! Get out!"

Jody went miserably out the back door and closed the screen with elaborate quietness. Under the kitchen window his shamed, downcast eyes fell upon a curiously shaped stone, a stone of such fascination that he squatted down and picked it up and turned it over in his hands.

The voices came clearly to him through the open kitchen window. "Jody's damn well right," he heard his father say. "Just Indians and crossing the plains. I've heard that story about how the horses got driven off about a thousand times. He just goes on and on, and he never changes a word in the things he tells."

When Mrs. Tiflin answered her tone was so changed that Jody, outside the window, looked up from his study of the stone. Her voice had become soft and explanatory. Jody knew how her face would have changed to match the tone. She said quietly, "Look at it this way, Carl. That was the big thing in my father's life. He led a wagon train clear across the plains to the coast, and when it was finished, his life was done. It was a big thing to do, but it didn't last long enough. Look!" she continued, "it's as though he was born to do that, and after he finished it, there wasn't anything more for him to do but think about it and talk about it. If there'd been any farther west to go, he'd have gone. He's told me so himself. But at last there was the ocean. He lives right by the ocean where he had to stop."

She had caught Carl, caught him and entangled him in her soft tone.

"I've seen him," he agreed quietly. "He goes down and stares off west over the ocean." His voice sharpened a little. "And then he goes up to the Horseshoe Club in Pacific Grove, and he tells people how the Indians drove off the horses."

She tried to catch him again. "Well, it's everything to him. You might be patient with him and pretend to listen."

Carl turned impatiently away. "Well, if it gets too bad, I can always go down to the bunkhouse and sit with Billy," he said irritably. He walked through the house and slammed the front door after him.

Jody ran to his chores. He dumped the grain to the chickens without chasing any of them. He gathered the eggs from the nests. He trotted into the house with the wood and interlaced it so carefully in the wood-box that two armloads seemed to fill it to overflowing.

His mother had finished the beans by now. She stirred up the fire and brushed off the stove-top with a turkey wing. Jody peered cautiously at her to see whether any rancor toward him remained. "Is he coming today?" Jody asked.

"That's what his letter said."

"Maybe I better walk up the road to meet him."

Mrs. Tiflin clanged the stove-lid shut. "That would be nice," she said. "He'd probably like to be met."

"I guess I'll just do it then."

Outside, Jody whistled shrilly to the dogs. "Come on up the hill," he commanded. The two dogs waved their tails and ran ahead. Along the roadside the sage had tender new tips. Jody tore off some pieces and rubbed them on his hands until the air was filled with the sharp wild smell. With a rush the dogs leaped from the road and yapped into the brush after a rabbit. That was the last Jody saw of them, for when they failed to catch the rabbit, they went back home.

Jody plodded on up the hill toward the ridge top. When he reached the little cleft where the road came through, the afternoon wind struck him and blew up his hair and ruffled his shirt. He looked down on the little hills and ridges below and then out at the huge green Salinas Valley. He could see the white town of Salinas far out in the flat and the flash of its windows under the waning sun. Directly below him, in an oak tree, a crow congress had convened. The tree was black with crows all cawing at once. Then Jody's eyes followed the wagon road down from the ridge where he stood, and lost it behind a hill, and picked it up again on the other side. On that distant stretch he saw a cart slowly pulled by a bay horse. It disappeared behind the hill. Jody sat down on the ground and watched the place where the cart would reappear again. The wind sang on the hilltops and the puff-ball clouds hurried eastward.

Then the cart came into sight and stopped. A man dressed in black dismounted from the seat and walked to the horse's head. Although it was so far away, Jody knew he had unhooked the check-rein, for the horse's head dropped forward. The horse moved on, and the man walked slowly up the hill beside it. Jody gave a glad cry and ran down the road toward them. The squirrels bumped along off the road, and a road-runner flirted its tail and raced over the edge of the hill and sailed out like a glider.

Jody tried to leap into the middle of his shadow at every step. A stone rolled under his foot and he went down. Around a little bend he raced, and there, a short distance ahead, were his grandfather and the cart. The boy dropped from his unseemly running and approached at a dignified walk.

The horse plodded stumble-footedly up the hill and the old man walked beside it. In the lowering sun their giant shadows flickered darkly behind them. The grandfather was dressed in a black broadcloth suit and he wore kid congress gaiters and a black tie on a short, hard collar. He carried his black slouch hat in his hand. His white beard was cropped close and his white eyebrows overhung his eyes like mustaches. The blue eyes were sternly merry. About the whole face and figure there was a granite dignity, so that every motion seemed an impossible thing. Once at rest, it seemed the old man would be stone, would never move again. His steps were slow and certain. Once made, no step could ever be retraced; once headed in a direction, the path would never bend nor the pace increase nor slow.

When Jody appeared around the bend, Grandfather waved his hat slowly in welcome, and he called, "Why, Jody! Come down to meet me, have you?"

Jody sidled near and turned and matched his step to the old man's step and stiffened his body and dragged his heels a little. "Yes, sir," he said. "We got your letter only today."

"Should have been here yesterday," said Grandfather. "It certainly should. How are all the folks?"

"They're fine, sir." He hesitated and then suggested shyly, "Would you like to come on a mouse hunt tomorrow, sir?"

"Mouse hunt, Jody?" Grandfather chuckled. "Have the people of this generation come down to hunting mice? They aren't very strong, the new people, but I hardly thought mice would be game for them."

"No, sir. It's just play. The haystack's gone. I'm going to drive out the mice to the dogs. And you can watch, or even beat the hay a little."

The stern, merry eyes turned down on him. "I see. You don't eat them, then. You haven't come to that yet."

Jody explained, "The dogs eat them, sir. It wouldn't be much like hunting Indians, I guess."

"No, not much — but then later, when the troops were hunting Indians and shooting children and burning teepees, it wasn't much different from your mouse hunt."

They topped the rise and started down into the ranch-cup, and they lost the sun from their shoulders. "You've grown," Grandfather said. "Nearly an inch, I should say."

"More," Jody boasted. "Where they mark me on the door, I'm up more than an inch since Thanksgiving even."

Grandfather's rich throaty voice said, "Maybe you're getting too much water and turning to pith and stalk. Wait until you head out, and then we'll see."

Jody looked quickly into the old man's face to see whether his feelings should be hurt, but there was no will to injure, no punishing nor putting-in-your-place light in the keen blue eyes. "We might kill a pig," Jody suggested.

"Oh, no! I couldn't let you do that. You're just humoring me. It isn't the time and you know it."

"You know Riley, the big boar, sir?"

"Yes. I remember Riley well."

"Well, Riley ate a hole into that same haystack, and it fell down on him and smothered him."

"Pigs do that when they can," said Grandfather.

"Riley was a nice pig, for a boar, sir. I rode him sometimes, and he didn't mind."

A door slammed at the house below them, and they saw Jody's mother standing on the porch waving her apron in welcome. And they saw Carl Tiflin walking up from the barn to be at the house for the arrival.

The sun had disappeared from the hills by now. The blue smoke from the house chimney hung in flat layers in the purpling ranch-cup. The puff-ball clouds, dropped by the falling wind, hung listlessly in the sky.

Billy Buck came out of the bunkhouse and flung a wash basin of soapy water on the ground. He had been shaving in mid-week, for Billy held Grandfather in reverence, and Grandfather said that Billy was one of the few men of the new generation who had not gone soft. Although Billy was in middle age, Grandfather considered him a boy. Now Billy was hurrying toward the house too.

When Jody and Grandfather arrived, the three were waiting for them in front of the yard gate.

Carl said, "Hello, sir. We've been looking for you."

Mrs. Tiflin kissed Grandfather on the side of his beard, and stood still while his big hand patted her shoulder. Billy shook hands solemnly, grinning under his straw mustache. "I'll put up your horse," said Billy, and he led the rig away.

Grandfather watched him go, and then, turning back to the group, he said as he had said a hundred times before, "There's a good boy. I knew his father, old Mule-tail Buck. I never knew why they called him Mule-tail except he packed mules."

Mrs. Tiflin turned and led the way into the house. "How long are you going to stay, Father? Your letter didn't say."

"Well, I don't know. I thought I'd stay about two weeks. But I never stay as long as I think I'm going to."

In a short while they were sitting at the white oilcloth table eating their supper. The lamp with the tin reflector hung over the table.

Outside the dining-room windows the big moths battered softly against the glass.

Grandfather cut his steak into tiny pieces and chewed slowly. "I'm hungry," he said. "Driving out here got my appetite up. It's like when we were crossing. We all got so hungry every night we could hardly wait to let the meat get done. I could eat about five pounds of buffalo meat every night."

"It's moving around does it," said Billy. "My father was a government packer. I helped him when I was a kid. Just the two of us could about clean up a deer's ham."

"I knew your father, Billy," said Grandfather. "A fine man he was. They called him Mule-tail Buck. I don't know why except he packed mules."

"That was it," Billy agreed. "He packed mules."

Grandfather put down his knife and fork and looked around the table. "I remember one time we ran out of meat — " His voice dropped to a curious low sing-song, dropped into a tonal groove the story had worn for itself. "There was no buffalo, no antelope, not even rabbits. The hunters couldn't even shoot a coyote. That was the time for the leader to be on the watch. I was the leader, and I kept my eyes open. Know why? Well, just the minute the people began to get hungry they'd start slaughtering the team oxen. Do you believe that? I've heard of parties that just ate up their draft cattle. Started from the middle and worked toward the ends. Finally they'd eat the lead pair, and then the wheelers. The leader of a party had to keep them from doing that."

In some manner a big moth got into the room and circled the hanging kerosene lamp. Billy got up and tried to clap it between his hands. Carl struck with a cupped palm and caught the moth and broke it. He walked to the window and dropped it out.

"As I was saying," Grandfather began again, but Carl interrupted him. "You'd better eat some more meat. All the rest of us are ready for our pudding."

Jody saw a flash of anger in his mother's eyes. Grandfather picked up his knife and fork. "I'm pretty hungry, all right," he said. "I'll tell you about that later."

When supper was over, when the family and Billy Buck sat in front of the fireplace in the other room, Jody anxiously watched Grandfather. He saw the signs he knew. The bearded head leaned forward; the eyes lost their sternness and looked wonderingly into the fire; the big lean fingers laced themselves on the black knees.

"I wonder," he began, "I just wonder whether I ever told you how those thieving Piutes drove off thirty-five of our horses."

"I think you did," Carl interrupted. "Wasn't it just before you went up into the Tahoe country?"

Grandfather turned quickly toward his son-in-law. "That's right. I guess I must have told you that story."

"Lots of times," Carl said cruelly, and he avoided his wife's eyes. But he felt the angry eyes on him, and he said, " 'Course I'd like to hear it again."

Grandfather looked back at the fire. His fingers unlaced and laced again. Jody knew how he felt, how his insides were collapsed and empty. Hadn't Jody been called a Big-Britches that very afternoon? He arose to heroism and opened himself to the term Big-Britches again. "Tell about Indians," he said softly.

Grandfather's eyes grew stern again. "Boys always want to hear about Indians. It was a job for men, but boys want to hear about it. Well, let's see. Did I ever tell you how I wanted each wagon to carry a long iron plate?"

Everyone but Jody remained silent. Jody said, "No. You didn't."

"Well, when the Indians attacked, we always put the wagons in a circle and fought from between the wheels. I thought that if every wagon carried a long plate with rifle holes, the men could stand the plates on the outside of the wheels when the wagons were in the circle and they would be protected. It would save lives and that would make up for the extra weight of the iron. But of course the party wouldn't do it. No party had done it before and they couldn't see why they should go to the expense. They lived to regret it, too."

Jody looked at his mother, and knew from her expression that she was not listening at all. Carl picked at a callus on his thumb and Billy Buck watched a spider crawling up the wall.

Grandfather's tone dropped into its narrative groove again. Jody knew in advance exactly what words would fall. The story droned on, speeded up for the attack, grew sad over the wounds, struck a dirge at the burials on the great plains. Jody sat quietly watching Grandfather. The stern blue eyes were detached. He looked as though he were not very interested in the story himself.

When it was finished, when the pause had been politely respected as the frontier of the story, Billy Buck stood up and stretched and hitched his trousers. "I guess I'll turn in," he said. Then he faced Grandfather. "I've got an old powder horn and a cap and ball pistol down to the bunkhouse. Did I ever show them to you?"

Grandfather nodded slowly. "Yes, I think you did, Billy. Reminds me of a pistol I had when I was leading the people across." Billy stood politely until the little story was done, and then he said, "Good night," and went out of the house.

Carl Tiflin tried to turn the conversation then. "How's the country between here and Monterey? I've heard it's pretty dry."

"It is dry," said Grandfather. "There's not a drop of water in the Laguna Seca. But it's a long pull from '87. The whole country was powder then, and in '61 I believe all the coyotes starved to death. We had fifteen inches of rain this year."

"Yes, but it all came too early. We could do with some now." Carl's eye fell on Jody. "Hadn't you better be getting to bed?"

Jody stood up obediently. "Can I kill the mice in the old haystack, sir?"

"Mice? Oh! Sure, kill them all off. Billy said there isn't any good hay left."

Jody exchanged a secret and satisfying look with Grandfather. "I'll kill every one tomorrow," he promised.

Jody lay in his bed and thought of the impossible world of Indians and buffaloes, a world that had ceased to be forever. He wished he could have been living in the heroic time, but he knew he was not of heroic timber. No one living now, save possibly Billy Buck, was worthy to do the things that had been done. A race of giants had lived then, fearless men, men of a staunchness unknown in this day. Jody thought of the wide plains and of the wagons moving across like centipedes. He thought of Grandfather on a huge white horse, marshaling the people. Across his mind marched the great phantoms, and they marched off the earth and they were gone.

He came back to the ranch for a moment, then. He heard the dull rushing sound that space and silence make. He heard one of the dogs, out in the doghouse, scratching a flea and bumping his elbow against the floor with every stroke. Then the wind arose again and the black cypress groaned and Jody went to sleep.

He was up half an hour before the triangle sounded for breakfast. His mother was rattling the stove to make the flames roar when Jody went through the kitchen. "You're up early," she said. "Where are you going?"

"Out to get a good stick. We're going to kill the mice today."

"Who is 'we'?"

"Why, Grandfather and I."

"So you've got him in it. You always like to have some one in with you in case there's blame to share."

"I'll be right back," said Jody. "I just want to have a good stick ready for after breakfast."

He closed the screen door after him and went out into the cool blue morning. The birds were noisy in the dawn and the ranch cats came down from the hill like blunt snakes. They had been hunting gophers in the dark, and although the four cats were full of gopher meat, they sat in a semi-circle at the back door and mewed piteously for milk. Doubletree Mutt and Smasher moved sniffing along the edge of the brush, performing the duty with rigid ceremony, but when Jody whistled, their heads jerked up and their tails waved. They plunged down to him, wriggling their skins and yawning. Jody patted their heads seriously, and moved on to the weathered scrap pile. He selected an old broom handle and a short piece of inch-square scrap wood. From his pocket he took a shoelace and tied the ends of the sticks loosely together to make a flail. He whistled his new weapon through the air and struck the ground experimentally, while the dogs leaped aside and whined with apprehension.

Jody turned and started down past the house toward the old hay-stack ground to look over the field of slaughter, but Billy Buck, sitting patiently on the back steps, called to him, "You better come back. It's only a couple of minutes till breakfast."

Jody changed his course and moved toward the house. He leaned his flail against the steps. "That's to drive the mice out," he said. "I'll bet they're fat. I'll bet they don't know what's going to happen to them today."

"No, nor you either," Billy remarked philosophically, "nor me, nor anyone."

Jody was staggered by this thought. He knew it was true. His imagination twitched away from the mouse hunt. Then his mother came out on the back porch and struck the triangle, and all thoughts fell in a heap.

Grandfather hadn't appeared at the table when they sat down. Billy nodded at this empty chair. "He's all right? He isn't sick?"

"He takes a long time to dress," said Mrs. Tiflin. "He combs his whiskers and rubs up his shoes and brushes his clothes."

Carl scattered sugar on his mush. "A man that's led a wagon train across the plains has got to be pretty careful how he dresses."

Mrs. Tiflin turned on him. "Don't do that, Carl! Please don't!" There was more of threat than of request in her tone. And the threat irritated Carl.

"Well, how many times do I have to listen to the story of the iron plates, and the thirty-five horses? That time's done. Why can't he forget it, now it's done?" He grew angrier while he talked, and his voice rose. "Why does he have to tell them over and over? He came across the plains. All right! Now it's finished. Nobody wants to hear about it over and over."

The door into the kitchen closed softly. The four at the table sat frozen. Carl laid his mush spoon on the table and touched his chin with his fingers.

Then the kitchen door opened and Grandfather walked in. His mouth smiled tightly and his eyes were squinted. "Good morning," he said, and he sat down and looked at his mush dish.

Carl could not leave it there. "Did — did you hear what I said?" Grandfather jerked a little nod.

"I don't know what got into me, sir. I didn't mean it. I was just being funny."

Jody glanced in shame at his mother, and he saw that she was looking at Carl, and that she wasn't breathing. It was an awful thing that he was doing. He was tearing himself to pieces to talk like that. It was a terrible thing to him to retract a word, but to retract it in shame was infinitely worse.

Grandfather looked sidewise. "I'm trying to get right side up," he said gently. "I'm not being mad. I don't mind what you said, but it might be true, and I would mind that."

"It isn't true," said Carl. "I'm not feeling well this morning. I'm sorry I said it."

"Don't be sorry, Carl. An old man doesn't see things sometimes. Maybe you're right. The crossing is finished. Maybe it should be forgotten, now it's done."

Carl got up from the table. "I've had enough to eat. I'm going to work. Take your time, Billy!" He walked quickly out of the dining-room. Billy gulped the rest of his food and followed soon after. But Jody could not leave his chair.

"Won't you tell any more stories?" Jody asked.

"Why, sure I'll tell them, but only when — I'm sure people want to hear them."

"I like to hear them, sir."

"Oh! Of course you do, but you're a little boy. It was a job for men, but only little boys like to hear about it."

Jody got up from his place. "I'll wait outside for you, sir. I've got a good stick for those mice."

He waited by the gate until the old man came out on the porch. "Let's go down and kill the mice now," Jody called.

"I think I'll just sit in the sun, Jody. You go kill the mice."

"You can use my stick if you like."

"No, I'll just sit here a while."

Jody turned disconsolately away, and walked down toward the old haystack. He tried to whip up his enthusiasm with thoughts of the fat juicy mice. He beat the ground with his flail. The dogs coaxed and whined about him, but he could not go. Back at the house he could see Grandfather sitting on the porch, looking small and thin and black.

Jody gave up and went to sit on the steps at the old man's feet.

"Back already? Did you kill the mice?"

"No, sir. I'll kill them some other day."

The morning flies buzzed close to the ground and the ants dashed about in front of the steps. The heavy smell of sage slipped down the hill. The porch boards grew warm in the sunshine.

Jody hardly knew when Grandfather started to talk. "I shouldn't stay here, feeling the way I do." He examined his strong old hands. "I feel as though the crossing wasn't worth doing." His eyes moved up the side-hill and stopped on a motionless hawk perched on a dead limb. "I tell those old stories, but they're not what I want to tell. I only know how I want people to feel when I tell them.

"It wasn't Indians that were important, nor adventures, nor even getting out here. It was a whole bunch of people made into one big crawling beast. And I was the head. It was westering and westering. Every man wanted something for himself, but the big beast that was all of them wanted only westering. I was the leader, but if I hadn't been there, someone else would have been the head. The thing had to have a head.

"Under the little bushes the shadows were black at white noonday. When we saw the mountains at last, we cried — all of us. But it wasn't getting here that mattered, it was movement and westering.

"We carried life out here and set it down the way those ants carry eggs. And I was the leader. The westering was as big as God, and the slow steps that made the movement piled up and piled up until the continent was crossed.

"Then we came down to the sea, and it was done," He stopped and wiped his eyes until the rims were red. "That's what I should be telling instead of stories."

When Jody spoke, Grandfather started and looked down at him. "Maybe I could lead the people some day," Jody said.

The old man smiled. "There's no place to go. There's the ocean to stop you. There's a line of old men along the shore hating the ocean because it stopped them."

"In boats I might, sir."

"No place to go, Jody. Every place is taken. But that's not the worst — no, not the worst. Westering has died out of the people. Westering isn't a hunger any more. It's all done. Your father is right. It is finished." He laced his fingers on his knee and looked at them.

Jody felt very sad. "If you'd like a glass of lemonade I could make it for you."

Grandfather was about to refuse, and then he saw Jody's face. "That would be nice," he said. "Yes, it would be nice to drink a lemonade."

Jody ran into the kitchen where his mother was wiping the last of the breakfast dishes. "Can I have a lemon to make a lemonade for Grandfather?"

His mother mimicked — "And another lemon to make a lemonade for you."

"No, ma'am. I don't want one."

"Jody! You're sick!" Then she stopped suddenly. "Take a lemon out of the cooler," she said softly. "Here, I'll reach the squeezer down to you."

# Eudora Welty (1909–    )

GENTLER, less macabre in her presentation of grotesque characters than many of her regional contemporaries, Mississippi-born Eudora Welty is one of our most admired Southern writers. The bulk of her work has been in the short-story form. Four collections of her stories have been published: *A Curtain of Green* (1941), *The Wide Net* (1943), *The Golden Apples* (1949), and *The Bride of the Innisfallen* (1955). A novella, *The Robber Bridegroom* (1942) recounted in fairy tale style the romance of a planter's daughter and a bandit chief. Life on a modern Mississippi plantation is the material of her novel, *Delta Wedding* (1946). *The Ponder Heart* (1954) was dramatized in 1957 by Jerome Chodorov and Joseph Fields.

The wonderful quality in most of Eudora Welty's writing as revealed in "Lily Daw and the Three Ladies," a comic fantasy of small town life, is the author's smile implicit in it. The busybody ladies could have been shown as irksome fools, which of course they were, and slow-witted Lily tedious as most simpletons are, but the author's warm-hearted tolerance of such characters makes for joyous reading.

# Lily Daw and the Three Ladies

MRS. Watts and Mrs. Carson were both in the post office in Victory when the letter came from the Ellisville Institute for the Feeble-minded of Mississippi. Aimee Slocum, with her hand still full of mail, ran out in front and handed it straight to Mrs. Watts and they all three read it together. Mrs. Watts held it taut between her pink hands and Mrs. Carson underscored each line slowly with her thimbled finger. Everybody else in the post office wondered what was up now.

"What will Lily say," beamed Mrs. Carson at last, "when we tell her we're sending her to Ellisville!"

"She'll be tickled to death," said Mrs. Watts, and added in a guttural voice to a deaf lady, "Lily Daw's getting in at Ellisville!"

"Don't you-all dare go off and tell Lily without me!" called Aimee Slocum, trotting back to finish putting up the mail.

"Do you suppose they'll look after her down there?" Mrs. Carson began to carry on a conversation with a group of Baptist ladies waiting in the post office. She was the Baptist preacher's wife.

"I've always heard it was lovely down there, but crowded," said one.

"Lily lets people walk over her so," said another.

"Last night at the tent show — " said another, and then popped her hand over her mouth.

"Don't mind me; I know there are such things in the world," said Mrs. Carson, looking down and fingering the tape-measure which hung over her bosom.

"Oh, Mrs. Carson. Well, anyway, last night at the tent show, why, the man was just before making Lily buy a ticket to get in."

"A ticket!"

"Till my husband went up and explained she wasn't bright, and so did everybody else."

The ladies all clicked their tongues.

"Oh, it was a very nice show," said the lady who had gone. "And Lily acted very nice. She was a perfect lady — she just set in her seat and stared."

"Oh, she can be, she can be," said Mrs. Carson, shaking her head and turning her eyes up.

"Yes'm, she kept her eyes on what's that thing makes all the commotion? The xylophone," said the lady. "Didn't turn her head to the right or left the whole time. Sat in front of me."

"The point is, what did she do after the show?" asked Mrs. Watts practically. "Lily has gotten so she is very mature for her age."

"Oh, Hermine!" protested Mrs. Carson, looking at her wildly for a moment.

"And that's how come we are sending her to Ellisville," finished Mrs. Watts.

"I'm ready, you-all," said Aimee Slocum, running out with white powder all over her face. "Mail's up."

"Well, of course, I do hope it's for the best," said several of the other ladies. They did not go at once to take their mail out of their boxes; they felt a little left out.

The three women stood at the foot of the water tank.

"To find Lily is a different thing," said Aimee Slocum. "Where in the wide world do you suppose she'd be?"

"I don't see a sign of her either on this side of the street or on the other side," said Mrs. Carson as they walked along.

Ed Newton was stringing Redbird school tablets on the wire across the store.

"If you're looking for Lily, she come in here an' tole me she was goin' to git married, while ago," he said.

"Ed Newton!" cried the ladies, clutching one another. Mrs. Watts began to fan herself at once with the letter from Ellisville. She wore widow's black and the least thing made her hot.

"Why, she's not, she's going to Ellisville, Ed," said Mrs. Carson gently. "Mrs. Watts and I and Aimee Slocum are sending her, out of our own pockets. Besides, the boys of Victory are on their honor — Lily's not going to get married, that's just an idea she's got in her head."

"More power to you, ladies," said Ed Newton, spanking himself with a tablet.

They saw Estelle Mabers sitting on the rail of the bridge over the railroad track, slowly drinking a Ne-Hi orange drink. "Have you seen Lily?" they asked her.

"I'm supposed to be out here watching for her now," said the Mabers girl, as though she weren't there yet. "For Jewel. Jewel says Lily come in the store while ago and took a two-ninety-eight hat and wore it off. Jewel wants to swap her something else for it."

"Oh, Estelle, Lily says she's going to get married!" cried Aimee Slocum.

"Well, I declare," said Estelle; she never understood anything.

Loralee Adkins came riding by in her Willys-Knight, blowing the horn to find out what they were talking about.

Aimee ran waving out into the street and yelled: "Loralee, you got to ride us up to Lily Daw's. She's up yonder fixing to git married!"

"Well, that just shows you right now," said Mrs. Watts, groaning as she was helped into the back seat. "What we've got to do is persuade Lily it will be nicer to go to Ellisville."

"Just to think." While they rode around the corner Mrs. Carson was going on in her sad voice, like soft noises in the henhouse at twilight. "We buried Lily's poor defenseless mother. We gave Lily all her food and kindling and every stitch she had on. Sent her to Sunday school to learn the Lord's teachings, had her baptized a Baptist. And when her old father commenced beating her and tried to cut her head off with the butcher-knife, why, we took her away from him and gave her a place to stay."

The paintless frame house was three stories high in places and had red and green stained-glass windows in front and gingerbread around the porch. It leaned steeply to one side and the front steps were gone. The car drew up under the cedar tree.

"Now Lily's almost grown up," Mrs. Carson continued; "in fact, she's grown," she concluded, getting out.

"Talking about getting married," said Mrs. Watts disgustedly. "Thanks, Loralee, you run on home."

They climbed over the dusty zinnias onto the porch and walked through the open door without knocking.

Lily was there, in the empty dark center hall, kneeling on the floor beside a small open trunk. ("There certainly is always a funny smell in this house. I say it every time I come," said Aimee Slocum.)

When Lily saw them she put a zinnia in her mouth.

"Hello, Lily," said Mrs. Carson reproachfully.

"Hello," said Lily, and gave a suck on the zinnia stem that sounded exactly like a jay-bird. She was wearing a petticoat for a dress, one of the things Mrs. Carson kept after her about. Her milky-yellow hair streamed freely down from under a new hat. You could see the wavy scar on her throat if you knew it was there.

Mrs. Carson and Mrs. Watts, the two fattest, sat in the double rocker. Aimee Slocum sat on the wire chair donated from the drugstore that burned.

"Well, what are you doing, Lily?" asked Mrs. Watts.

Lily smiled.

The trunk was old and lined with yellow and brown paper with an asterisk pattern showing in darker circles and rings. The ladies indicated mutely that they did not know where in the world it had come from. It was empty except for two bars of soap and a green washcloth, which Lily was trying to arrange in the bottom.

"Go on and tell us what you're doing, Lily," said Aimee Slocum.

"Packing, silly," said Lily.

"Where are you going?"

"Going to get married, and I bet you wish you was me now," said Lily. But shyness overcame her suddenly and she popped the zinnia back in her mouth.

"Talk to me, dear," said Mrs. Carson. "Tell old Mrs. Carson why you want to get married."

"No," said Lily, after a moment's hesitation.

"Well, we've thought of something that will be so much nicer," said Mrs. Carson. "You can go to Ellisville."

"Won't that be lovely?" said Mrs. Watts. "Why, yes."

"It's a lovely place," said Aimee Slocum uncertainly.

"You've got bumps on your face," said Lily.

"Aimee, dear, you stay out of this if you don't mind," said Mrs. Carson anxiously. "I don't know what it is comes over Lily when you come around her."

Lily stared at Aimee Slocum meditatively.

"There — wouldn't you like to go to Ellisville now?" asked Mrs. Carson.

"No'm," said Lily.

"Why not?" All the ladies looked down at her in impressive astonishment.

" 'Cause I'm goin' to git married," said Lily.

"Well, and who are you going to marry, dear?" said Mrs. Watts.

She knew how to pin people down and made them deny what they'd already said.

Lily bit her lip and began to smile. She reached into the trunk and held up both cakes of soap and wagged them.

"Tell us," said Mrs. Watts, "who you're going to marry, now?"

"A man last night."

There was a gasp from each lady. The possible reality of a lover descended suddenly like a summer hail over their heads. Mrs. Watts stood up.

"One of those show fellows! A musician!" she cried.

Lily looked up in admiration.

"Did he — did he do anything to you?" It was still only Mrs. Watts who could take charge.

"Oh, yes'm," said Lily. She patted the cakes of soap fastidiously with the tips of her small fingers and tucked them in with the washcloth.

"What?" demanded Aimee Slocum, tottering before her scream.

"Don't ask her what," said Mrs. Carson. "Tell me, Lily, are you the same as you were?"

"He had a red coat, too," said Lily graciously. "He took little sticks and went ping-pong! ding-dong!"

"Oh, I think I'm going to faint, " said Aimee Slocum.

"The xylophone!" cried Mrs. Watts. "The xylophone player they talked about! Why, the coward, he ought to be run out of town on a rail."

"Oh, he is out of town by now," cried Aimee. "Don't you know — the sign in the café — Victory on the ninth and Como on the tenth? He's in Como! Como!"

"Then we'll bring him back!" cried Mrs. Watts. "He can't get away from me!"

"Hush," said Mrs. Carson. "I don't think it's any use following that line of reasoning at all. It's better in the long run for him to be gone out of our lives for good and all. That kind of a man. He wanted Lily's body alone. He wouldn't make the poor little thing happy, even if we was to force him to marry her like he ought, at the point of a gun."

"Still," began Aimee.

"Shut up," said Mrs. Watts. "Mrs. Carson, you're right, I suppose."

"This is my hope chest, see?" said Lily. "You haven't looked at it. I've already got soap and a washrag. And I have my hat — on. What are you-all going to give me?"

"Lily," said Mrs. Watts, starting over, "we'll give you lots of gorgeous things if you'll only go to Ellisville instead of getting married."

"What will you give me?" asked Lily.

"I'll give you a pair of hem-stitched pillowcases," said Mrs. Carson.

"I'll give you a big caramel cake," said Mrs. Watts.

"I'll give you a souvenir from Jackson, a little toy bank," said Aimee Slocum. "Now will you go?"

"No'm," said Lily.

"I'll give you a pretty little Bible with your name on it in real gold," said Mrs. Carson.

"What if I was to give you a pink crepe-de-chine brassière with adjustable shoulder straps?" asked Mrs. Watts grimly.

"Oh, Hermine."

"Well, she needs it," said Mrs. Watts. "Unless she'll wear dresses in Ellisville."

"I wish *I* could go to Ellisville!" said Aimee Slocum luringly.

"What will they have for me down there?" asked Lily softly.

"Oh! Lots of things. You'll weave baskets, I expect . . ." Mrs. Carson looked vaguely at the others.

"Oh, yes, they'll let you make all sorts of baskets," said Mrs. Watts; then her voice too trailed off.

"No'm, I'd rather git married," said Lily.

"Lily Daw! Now that's just plain stubbornness!" cried Mrs. Watts. "You almost said you'd go and then took it back."

"We've all asked God, Lily," said Mrs. Carson finally, "and God seemed to tell us — Mr. Carson too — that the place where you ought to be, so as to be happy, was Ellisville."

"We've really just got to get her there — now!" screamed Aimee Slocum suddenly. "Suppose — ! She can't stay here! *You* know — *you* know!"

"Oh, no, no, no," said Mrs. Carson hurriedly. "We mustn't think that."

"Could I take my hope chest — for Ellisville?" asked Lily shyly, looking at them sidewise.

"Why, yes," said Mrs. Carson blankly.

"If I could just take my hope chest!"

"All the time it was just her hope chest!" cried Aimee Slocum.

"It's settled!" Mrs. Watts struck her palms together.

"Praise the fathers," murmured Mrs. Carson.

"O.K. — Toots!" said Lily, her eyes gleaming with the triumph of a quotation.

The ladies were backing away to the door. "I think I'd better stay," said Mrs. Carson, stopping in her tracks. "Where — where could she have learned that terrible expression?"

"Pack her things," said Mrs. Watts. "Make the 12:35."

In the station the train was puffing. Nearly everyone in Victory was hanging around waiting for it to leave. The Victory Civic Band was scattered through the crowd. Ed Newton gave false signals to start on his bass horn. Everybody wanted to see Lily all dressed up, but Mrs. Carson and Mrs. Watts had sneaked her into the train from the other side of the tracks. The two ladies were going to travel as far as Jackson to help Lily change trains.

Lily sat between them with her hair combed and pinned up into a figure-eight knot under a small blue hat without flowers. She wore a thin made-over black dress from Mrs. Watts's last summer's mourning. Pink straps glowed through. She had a purse and a Bible and a cake in a tin box, all in her lap.

Aimee Slocum had been getting the outgoing mail stamped and bundled. She stood in the aisle of the coach now, tears shaking from her eyes. "Good-bye, Lily," she said. She was the one who felt things.

"Good-bye, silly," said Lily.

"Oh, dear, I hope they get our telegram to meet her in Ellisville!" Aimee cried suddenly, as she thought how far away it was. "And it was so hard to get it all in ten words, too."

"Get off, Aimee," said Mrs. Watts, all settled and waving her dressy fan from the funeral parlor. "I declare I'm so hot, as soon as we get a few miles out of town I'm going to slip my corset down."

"Oh, Lily, be good down there, weave baskets and do anything else they tell you — it's all because they love you." Aimee drew her mouth down and backed down the aisle.

Lily laughed. She pointed across Mrs. Carson out the window toward a man who had stepped off the train and stood there in the dust. He was a stranger and wore a cap. "Look," she said, laughing softly through her fingers.

"Don't look," said Mrs. Carson, very distinctly, as if to impress these two solemn words out of all she had ever spoken upon Lily's soft little brain. "Just don't look at anything till you get to Ellisville."

Outside, Aimee Slocum was crying and almost ran into the stranger. He wore a cap and was short and seemed to have on perfume.

"Could you tell me, lady," he said, "where a little lady lives in this burg name of Miss Lily Daw?" He lifted his cap; he had red hair.

"What do you want to know for?" asked Aimee.

"Talk louder," said the stranger. He almost whispered, himself.

"She's gone away — she's gone to Ellisville!"

"Gone?"

"Gone to Ellisville!"

"Well, I like that!" breathed the man.

"What business did you have with the lady?" cried Aimee suddenly.

"We was only going to get married, that's all," said the man. He laid the cap back on his hair and gave an agitated pat to the plaid-covered button.

Aimee Slocum started to scream in front of all those people. She almost pointed to the long black box she saw lying on the ground at the man's feet. Then she jumped back in fright. "The xylophone! The xylophone!" she cried, looking back and forth from the man to the hissing train. The bell began to ring hollowly and the man was talking.

"Did you say Ellisville — that in the state of Mississippi?" He was writing in a red notebook entitled *Permanent Facts & Data.* "I don't hear well."

Aimee nodded her head up and down.

Under "Ellis-Ville Miss" he was drawing a line; now he was flicking it with two little marks. "Maybe she didn't say she would. Maybe she said she wouldn't." He suddenly laughed very loudly, after the way he had whispered. Aimee cringed. "Women! — Well, if we play anywheres near Ellisville, Miss., in the future, I may look her up, and I may not," he said.

The bass horn sounded the true signal for the band to begin.

"Wait!" Aimee Slocum did scream. "Wait, Mister! I can get her for you!"

Then there she was back on the train screaming in Mrs. Carson's and Mrs. Watts's faces. "The xylophone player! He meant it! He wants to marry her! There he is!"

"Nonsense," murmured Mrs. Watts, peering over the others to look where Aimee pointed. "If he's there I don't see him. Where is he? You're looking at One-Eye Beasley."

"That little man with the cap — no, with the red hair! Hurry — the train — "

"Is that really him?" Mrs. Carson asked Mrs. Watts in wonder. "Mercy! He's small, isn't he?"

"Never saw him before in my life," cried Mrs. Watts.

"Come on!" cried Aimee Slocum. Her nerves were all unstrung.

"All right. Hold your horses, girl," said Mrs. Watts. "Come on," she cried thickly to Mrs. Carson.

"Where are we going now?" asked Lily as they struggled down the aisle.

"We're taking you to get married," said Mrs. Watts. "Mrs. Carson, you'd better call up your husband from the station."

"But I don't want to git married," said Lily, beginning to whimper. "I'm going to Ellisville."

"Hush, and we'll all have some ice cream cones later," whispered Mrs. Carson.

Just as they appeared on the steps of the train the band went into the "Independence March."

The xylophone player was still there. He came up and said, "Hello, Toots. What's up — tricks?" and kissed Lily with a smack, after which she hung her head.

"So you're the young man we've heard so much about," said Mrs. Watts. Her smile was brilliant. "Here's your little Lily."

"What say?" asked the xylophone player.

"My husband happens to be the Baptist preacher of Victory," said Mrs. Carson, in a louder voice. "Isn't that lucky? I can get him here in five minutes."

They were in a circle around the xylophone player, all going into the white waiting-room.

"Oh, I feel just like crying, at a time like this," said Aimee Slocum. She looked back and saw the train moving slowly away, going under the bridge at Main Street. Then it disappeared around the curve.

"And whom have we the pleasure of addressing?" Mrs. Watts was shouting.

The band went on playing. Some of the people thought Lily was on the train, and some swore she wasn't. Everybody cheered, though, and a straw hat was thrown into the telephone wires.

# Richard Wright (1908–1960)

SIX THOUSAND six hundred unemployed writers, journalists, and editors worked on the Federal Writers' Project during the Depression. Many since have become among our best known authors. Richard Wright was definitely one who proves its immense value. He was born near Natchez, Mississippi, and worked during his growing years at menial jobs in that state and in Chicago. When jobs vanished he had to go on relief, from which the Project rescued him. In 1939, *Uncle Tom's Children*, a collection of his stories, won *Story Magazine's* prize for the best book by a Project author. His second book, *Native Son* (1940), a novel that was dramatized by Paul Green, has become a classic as has *Black Boy* (1945), an autobiography of his youth. After the Second World War he became an expatriate in Europe and wrote many more novels and short stories, but those mentioned above are considered his most important.

Two things make "Fire and Cloud" memorable: the Biblical nobility of the black preacher and the fervor with which the author has written. It is seldom heard in recent years but during the Depression the old revolutionary song, "Internationale," was heard often at street demonstrations with its opening cry of "Arise, ye prisoners of starvation!" "Proletarian" fiction was popular. Much of it was weakened by a quickie conversion ending in which a reactionary character suddenly sees the error of his ways and becomes a Communist. "Fire and Cloud" has a conversion ending but Wright has skillfully built his story and given his characters time enough to develop so that the preacher's action at the end is completely logical. And so are the actions of all the others, even those of the bigoted mayor.

# *Fire and Cloud*

"A NAUGHTS *a naught . . .*"

As he walked his eyes looked vacantly on the dusty road, and the words rolled without movement from his lips, each syllable floating softly up out of the depth of his body.

"*N fives a figger . . .*"

He pulled out his pocket handkerchief and mopped his brow without lessening his pace.

"*All fer the white man . . .*"

He reached the top of the slope and paused, head down.

"*N none fer the nigger . . .*"

His shoulders shook in half-laugh and half-shudder. He finished mopping his brow and spat, as though to rid himself of some bitter thing. He thought, Thas the way its awways been! Wistfully he turned and looked back at the dim buildings of the town lying sprawled mistily on the crest of a far hill. Seems like the white folks jus erbout own this whole worl! Looks like they done conquered *everything*. We black folks is jus los in one big white fog . . . With his eyes still on the hazy buildings, he flexed his lips slowly and spoke under his breath:

"They could do something! They could do *something*, awright! Mabbe ef five er six thousan of us marched downtown we could *scare* em inter doin something! Lawd knows, mabbe them Reds *is* right!"

He walked again and tucked his handkerchief back into his pocket. He could feel the heat of the evening over all his body, not strongly, but closely and persistently, as though he were holding his face over a tub of steaming suds. Far below him, at the bottom of the valley, lay a cluster of bleak huts with window panes red-lit from dying sunlight. Those huts were as familiar to his eyes as a nest is to the eyes of a bird, for he had lived among them all his life. He knew by sight or sound every black man, woman and child living within those huddled walls. For a moment an array of soft black faces hovered before his eyes. N whut kin Ah tell em? Whut kin Ah say t em ? He stopped, looked at the ground and sighed. And then he saw himself as he had stood but a few minutes ago, facing the white woman who sat behind the brown, gleaming desk: her arms had been round, slender, snow-white, like cold marble; her hair had been the color of flowing gold and had glinted in the sunlight; her eyes had been wide and gray behind icily white spectacles. It seemed he could hear her saying in her dry, metallic voice: I'm sorry, Taylor. You'll just have to do the best you can. Explain it to them, make them understand that we cant do anything. Everybodys hongry, and after all, it's no harder on your people than it is on ours. Tell them theyll just have to wait . . .

He wagged his head and his lips broke in a slow sick smile. Whut she know erbout bein hongry? Whut she know erbout it? He walked again, thinking, Here Ah is a man called by Gawd t preach n whut kin Ah do? Hongry folks lookin t me fer hep n whut kin Ah do? Ah done tried everything n cant do *nuthin*! Shucks, mabbe Hadley n Greens right? They *might* be right. Gawd knows, they *might* be right.

He lifted his head and saw the wide fields plunging before him, down the hillside. The grass was dark and green. All this he thought. All *this* n folks hongry! Good Gawd, whuts *wrong*! He saw the road running before him, winding, vanishing, the soft yellow dust filled with the ruts of wagon wheels and tiny threads of auto tires. He threw back his head and spoke out loud:

"The good Lawds gonna clean up this ol worl some day! Hes gonna make a new Heaven n a new Earth! N Hes gonna do it in a eye-twinkle change! Hes gotta do it! Things cant go on like this ferever! Gawd knows they cant!" He pulled off his coat and slung it under his left arm. "Waal, there ain nothin t do but go back n tell em . . . Tell em the white folks wont let em eat . . ."

The road curved, descending among the green fields that tumbled to a red sky. This was the land on which the Great God Almighty had first let him see the light of His blessed day. This was the land on which he had first taken unto himself a wife, leaving his mother and father to cleave to her. And it was on the green slopes of these struggling hills that his first-born son, Jimmy, had romped and played, growing to a strong, upright manhood. He wagged his head, musing, Lawd, them wuz the good ol days . . . There had been plenty to eat; the blessings of God had been overflowing. He had toiled from sunup to sundown, and in the cool of the evenings his wife, May, had taught him to read and write. Then God had spoken to him, a quiet, deep voice coming out of the black night; God had called him to preach His word, to spread it to the four corners of the earth, to save His black people. And he had obeyed God and had built a church on a rock which the very gates of Hell could not prevail against. Yes, he had been like Moses, leading his people out of the wilderness into the Promised Land. He sighed, walking and taking his coat from his left arm and tucking it under his right. Yes, things had been clear-cut then. In those days there had stretched before his eyes a straight and narrow path and he had walked in it, with the help of a Gracious God. On Sundays he had preached God's Word, and on Mondays and Tuesdays and Wednesdays and Thursdays and Fridays and Saturdays he had taken old Bess, his mule, and his plow and had broke God's ground. For a moment while walking through the dust and remembering his hopes of those early years he seemed to feel again the plow handles trembling in his calloused hands and hear the earth cracking and breaking open, black, rich and damp; it seemed he could see old Bess straining forward with the plow, swishing her tail and tossing her head and snorting now and then. Yes, there had been something in those good old days when he had walked behind his plow, between the broad green earth and a blue sweep of sunlit sky; there had been in it all a surge of will, clean, full, joyful; the earth was his and he was the earth's; they were one; and it was that joy and will and oneness in him that God had spoken to when He had called him to preach His Word, to save His black people, to lead them, to guide them, to be a shepherd to His flock. But now the whole thing was giving way, crumbling in his hands, right before his eyes. And every time he tried to think of some way out, of some way to stop it, he saw wide gray eyes behind icily white spectacles. He mopped his brow again. Mabbe Hadley n Greens right . . . Lawd, Ah don know what t do! Ef Ah fight fer things the white folk say Ahma a bad nigger stirrin up trouble. N ef Ah don do nothin, we starve . . . But somethings *gotta* be done! Mabbe ef we hada demonstration like Hadley n Green said, we could *scare* them white folks inter doin something . . .

He looked at the fields again, half-wistfully, half-curiously. Lawd,

we could make them ol fiels bloom ergin. We could make em feed us.
Thas whut Gawd put em there fer. Plows could break and hoes could
chop and hands could pick and arms could carry . . . On and on that
could happen and people could eat and feel as he had felt with the plow
handles trembling in his hands, following old Bess, hearing the earth
cracking and breaking because he wanted it to crack and break; because he
willed it, because the earth was his. And they could sing as he had sung
when he and May were first married; sing about picking cotton, fishing,
hunting, about sun and rain. They could . . . But whuts the usa
thinkin erbout stuff like this? Its all gone now . . . And he had to go
and tell his congregation, the folks the Great God Almighty had called
him to lead to the Promised Land — he had to tell them that relief would
give them no food.

That morning he had sent a committee of ten men and a woman
from his congregation to see the mayor. Wondah how they come out?
The mayor tol em something, sho! So fer hes been pretty wid me even ef
he is a white man. As his feet sank softly into the dust he saw Mayor
Bolton; he saw the red chin that always had a short, black stubble of
beard; he saw the cigar glowing red in front of a pink, fat face. But he
needs something t scare im now, he thought. Hes been running over us
too long . . .

He reached the bottom of the slope, turned into a cinder path, and
approached the huts. N Lawd, when Ah do try t do somethin mah own
folks wont stan by me, wont stick wid me. Theres ol Deacon Smith
a-schemin n a-plottin, just a-watchin me like a hawk, jus a-waitin fer me
t take mah eyes off the groun sos he kin trip me up, sos he kin run t the
white folks n tell em Ahm doin somethin wrong! A black snake in the
grass! A black Judas! Thas all he is! Lawd, the Devils sho busy in
this worl . . .

He was walking among the crowded huts now.

*hello reveren*

"How yuh tonight, sonny!" Let ol Deacon Smith tell it, no mattah
whut Ah do Ahm wrong . . .

*good evenin, reveren*

"Good evenin, Sistah!" Hes been a-tryin t cheat me outta mah
church ever since hes been erroun here . . .

*how yuh tonight, reveren taylor?*

"Jus fine. N how yuh tonight, Brother?" Hes awways a-whisperin
berhin mah back, a-tryin t take mah congregation erway from me . . .
N when he ain doin tha hes a-tryin his bes t give me wrong advice, jus
like the Devil a-tryin t tempt Jesus. But Ahm gonna march on wida
hepa Gawd . . . Yeah, Ah might preach a sermon erbout tha nex
Sunday.

As he turned into the street leading to his home and church, he saw a tall brown-skinned boy hurrying toward him. Here comes Jimmy! Ah bet hes lookin fer me . . . Lawd, Ah hope ain nothin wrong . . .

## II

"Pa!" said Jimmy breathlessly when he was some twenty feet away. Taylor stopped.

"Whuts the mattah, son?"

Jimmy came close.

"The mayors at home, waitin t see yuh," he whispered.

"The *mayor*?"

"Yeah, n two mo white men. One of em is the Chiefa Police."

"They there *now*?"

"Yeah; in the parlor."

"How long they been there?"

"Bout two-three minutes, Ah reckon. N lissen, Pa . . . Sam wuz by jus now. He say the white folks is ridin up n down the streets in their cars warnin all the black folks t stay off the streets cause theres gonna be trouble . . ."

"Sam say tha?"

"Thas whut he tol me. N lissen, Pa . . . Ahma git Sam n Pete n Bob n Jack n some mo boys together sos ef anything happens . . ."

Taylor gripped Jimmy's shoulders.

"Naw, son! Yuh fixin t git us *all* inter trouble now! Yuh cant do nothin like tha! Yuh gotta be careful! Ef them white folks jus *thought* we wuz doin something like tha theyd crack down on us! Wed hava riot!"

"But we cant let em ride erroun n talk big n we do nothin!"

"Lissen here, son! Yuh do whut Ah tell you t do!" He shook Jimmy's shoulders and his voice was husky. "Yuh go tell them boys t do *nuthin* till Ah see em, yuh hear me? Yuh young fools fixin t git us *all* murdered!"

"We just as waal git killed fightin as t git killed doin nothin," said Jimmy sullenly.

"Yuh go n do whut Ah tol yuh, *hear* me? Ah gotta go n see tha mayor . . ."

"Hes here t see yuh erbout tha demonstration," said Jimmy.

"How yuh know?"

"Cause thas whut everybodys sayin."

"Who yuh hear say tha?"

"Deacon Smiths spreadin the word."

Taylor winced as though struck by a blow and looked at the dust.

"Hes tellin alla deacons n the church membahs tha the mayors here t stop yuh," said Jimmy. "Hes tellin em yuhs mixed up wid the Reds."

"Deacon Smith there now, *too?*"

"Yeah; hes in the basement wida other deacons. Theys waitin t see yuh."

"How long they been there?"

"Bout hafa hour. N Hadley n Greens in the Bible Room, waitin t talk wid yuh, too . . ."

Fear gripped Taylor and he stammered:

"Ddddid the mmmmayor sssee em?"

"Naw, ain nobody seen em yit. Ah brought em in thu the back do and tol em t wait fer yuh. Ahm mighty scared wid them Reds waitin fer yuh in the Bible Room and tha Chiefa Police waitin fer yuh in the parlor. Ef 'ol Deacon Smith knowed tha he sho would make a lotta trouble . . ."

"Where yo ma?"

"She upstairs, sewin."

"She know whuts happenin?"

"Naw, Pa."

Taylor stood still, barely breathing.

"Whut yuh gonna do, Pa?" asked Jimmy.

"Yuh go n tell them boys not t do nothin wrong, son. Go on n tell em now! Ah got too much on mah hans now widout yuh boys stirrin up mo trouble!"

"Yessuh."

"Yuh bettah go n do it *now!*"

"Yessuh."

He watched Jimmy hurry down the street. Lawd, Ah hope tha boy don go n git inter trouble . . .

"Yuh do whut Ah tol you, Jimmy!" he yelled.

"Yessuh!" Jimmy hollered back.

He saw Jimmy turn a dusty corner, and go out of sight. Hadley n Greens there in the Bible Room n the Chiefa Police is waitin in the parlor! Ah cant let them white folks see them Reds! N ef Deacon Smith tells on me theyll lynch me . . . Ah gotta git em out of tha church widout em seein each other . . . Good Gawd, whut a mess!

### III

No sooner had he opened the door of his church than he heard a crescendo of voices. They back awready! Tha committees back! Aw, Ah bet the mayor followed em here . . . He walked down the hall, turned into the church's waiting room, and saw a roomful of black faces.

"Reveren Taylor! The mayor run us out!"

"He put the police on us!"

The black brothers and sisters ran to Taylor and surrounded him.

"The mayor tol us t git out n don come back no mo!"

A thin black woman swung onto Taylor's arm, crying:

"Whut Ahm gonna do? Ah ain gotta mouthful bread at home!"

"Sistahs n Brothers, jusa minute," said Taylor. "Firs, tell me whut the mayor said . . ."

"He say he cant do *nuthin*! N say fer us not t come back t his office no *mo*! N say ef we do hes gonna put us in jail!"

"In *jail*?" asked Taylor.

"Thas whut he said."

"N he tol us not t march, Reveren. He said ef we demonstrated hed put us *all* in jail."

"Who tol em yuh wuz gonna march?" asked Taylor.

"Ah bet it wuz the ol Deacon Smith," said Sister Harris.

"The Bible says testify whut yuh see n speak whut yuh know," said Sister Davis to Sister Harris.

"Ah knows whut Ahm talkin erbout!" blazed Sister Harris.

"Sistahs n Brothers, les don start no fuss," said Taylor, sighing and dropping his shoulders.

"Whut they tell yuh at the relief station, Reveren Taylor?" asked Sister James.

"They say they cant do nothin," said Taylor.

The thin black woman came and knelt at Taylor's feet, her face in her hands.

"Reveren Taylor, it ain fer me Ahm astin! Its fer mah chillun! Theys hongry! It ain fer me, its fer them! Gawd, have mercy, theys hongry . . ."

Taylor stepped back, ran his hand into his pocket and pulled out a palmful of loose coins.

"Here, Sistahs n Brothers, split this up between yuh all. Its ever cent Ah got in this worl, so hep me Gawd!"

He laid the coins on a small table. Brother Booker divided them as far as they would go. Then they swarmed around him again.

"Reveren, whut we gonna do?"

"Cant we make the white folks do something fer us?"

"Ahm tireda bein hongry!"

"Reveren, mah babys sick n Ah cant git her no milk!"

"Reveren, whut kin Ah tell mah wife?"

"Lawd knows, Ahm just erbout sick of this!"

"Whut kin we do, Reveren?"

Taylor looked at them and was ashamed of his own helplessness and theirs.

"Sistahs n Brothers, les call on the great Gawd who made us n put us in this worl . . ."

He clasped his hands in front of him, closed his eyes, and bowed his head. The room grew still and silent.

"Lawd Gawd Awmighty, Yuh made the sun n the moon n the stars n the earth n the seas n mankind n the beasts of the fiels!"

*yes jesus*

"Yuh made em all, Lawd, n Yuh tol em whut t do!"

*yuh made em lawd*

"Yuhs strong n powerful n Yo will rules this worl!"

*yuh rules it lawd*

"Yuh brought the chillun of Israel outta the lan of Egypt!"

*yuh sho did*

"Yuh made the dry bones rise up outta the valley of death n live!"

*yuh made em live lawd*

"Yuh saved the Hebrew chillun in the fiery furnace!"

*yes jesus*

"Yuh stopped the storm n yuh made the sun stan still!"

*yuh stopped it lawd*

"Yuh knocked down the walls of Jericho n Yuh kept Jona in the belly of the whale!"

*yuh kept im lawd*

"Yuh let Yo son Jesus walk on watah n Yuh brought Im back from the dead!"

*have mercy jesus*

"Yuh made the lame walk!"

*yuh did it lawd*

"Yuh made the blin see!"

*hep us now lawd*

"Yuh made the deaf hear!"

*glory t the mos high*

"Lawd, Yuhs a rock in the tima trouble n Yuhs a shelter in the tima storm!"

*he is he is*

"Lawd, Yuh said Yudh strike down the wicked men who plagued yo chillun!"

*glory t gawd*

"Yuh said Yud destroy this old worl n create a new Heaven n a new Earth!"

*wes waitin on yuh jesus*

"Lawd, Yuh said call on Yo name n Yuhd answer!"

*yuh said it lawd n now wes callin*

"Yuh made us n put the breatha life in us!"

*yuh did lawd*

"Now look down on us, Lawd! Speak t our hearts n let us know whut Yo will is! Speak t us like Yuh spoke t Jacob!"

*speak lawd n our souls will be clay in yo hans*

"Lawd, ack in us n well obey! Try us, lawd, try us n watch us move t Yo will! Wes helpless at Yo feet a-waitin fer Yo sign!"

*send it lawd*

"The white folks say we cant raise nothin on yo earth! They done put the lans of the worl in their pockets! They done fenced em off n nailed em down! Theys a-tryin t take Yo place, Lawd!"

*speak t em lawd*

"Yuh put us in this worl n said we could live in it! Yuh said this worl wuz Yo own! Now show us the sign like Yuh showed Saul! Show us the sign n well ack! We ast this in the name of Yo son Jesus who died tha we might live! Amen!"

*amen amen*

Taylor stopped and opened his eyes. The room was quiet; he could hear the clock ticking softly above his head, and from the rear came the sound of children playing back of the church. The sisters and brothers rose from their knees and began talking in subdued tones.

"But, Reveren, whut kin we *do*?"

"The issues wid Gawd now, Sistahs n Brothers."

"Is we gonna march?"

"Is yuh goin wid us t the mayor?"

"Have faith, Sistahs n Brothers. Gawd takes care of His own."

"But Ahm hongry, Reveren . . ."

"Now, Sistahs n Brothers, Ah got t go. Ah got business t tend t . . ."

He pushed ahead of the black hands that clung to his sleeve.

"Reveren Taylor . . ."

The thin black woman wailed, kneeling:

"Please, Reveren, cant yuh do *somethin* . . ."

He pushed through the door, closed it, and stood for a moment with his eyes shut and with his fingers slowly loosening on the knob, his ears filled with the sound of wailing voices.


## IV

How come all this gotta happen at *once*? Folks a-beggin fer bread n the mayor here t see me n them Reds a-waitin in the Bible Room . . . Ef Deacon Smith knowed tha hed ruin me sho! Ah cant let the mayor see them Reds . . . Naw, Gawd! He looked at a door at the far end of the room, then hurried to it and opened it softly.

"May!" he called in a hoarse whisper.

"Hunh?"

"C mere, quick!"

"Whutcha wan, Dan?"

"C mon in the *room*, May!"

She edged through the half-opened door and stood in front of him, wide-eyed.

"Whutcha wan, Dan?"

"Now, lissen . . ."

"Ain nothin wrong, is it, Dan? Ain nothin happened, is it?"

He grabbed her arm.

"Naw, n don git scared!"

"Ah ain scared!"

"Yuh cant do whut Ah wan yuh t do ef yuhs scared!"

"Ah *ain* scared, Dan!"

"Lissen . . ."

"Yeah?"

"The mayors here, in the parlor. N the Chiefa Police . . ."

She stood stock still and seemed not to breathe.

"The *mayor?*"

"Yeah . . ."

"*Ain* nothin wrong, is it, Dan?"

"There wont be ef yuh lissen n try t do right."

"Be careful, Dan!"

"Yeah," he said, his voice low and husky. "Go in and tell them white folks Ahm sick, hear?"

She stepped back from him and shook her head.

"Gawd *ain* wid yuh when yuh lie, Dan!"

"We *gotta* lie t white folks! Theys on our necks? They *make* us lie t them! Whut kin we do but lie?"

"*Dan!*"

"Lissen t whut Ahm tellin yuh, May! Tell the mayor Ahm gittin outta bed t see im. Tell im Ahm dressin, see? Tell im t wait a few minutes."

"Yeah?"

"Then go t the basement n tell Deacon Smith Ahm wid the mayor. Tell im n the other deacons t wait."

"Now?"

"Yeah; but Ah ain thu yit. Yuh know Hadley n Green?"

"Them *Reds?*"

"Yeah . . ."

"Dan!" said May, her lungs suspiring in one gasp of amazed helplessness.

"May, fer Chrissakes!"

She began to cry.

"Don do nothin wrong, Dan, please! Don fergit Jimmy! Hes jus a young boy n hes gotta grow up in this town wid these white folks. Don go n do nothin n fix it so he wont hava chance . . . Me n yuh don mattah, but thinka him, Dan, please . . ."

Taylor swallowed and looked hard at her.

"May, yuh do whut *Ah* tell yuh t do! Ah know whut Ahm doin. Hadley n Greens downstairs, in the Bible Room. Tell em so nobody kin hear yuh, hear? — tell em aftah yuh done tol the others — tell em t come in here. Let em in thu *yo* room . . ."

"Naw!"

She tried to get through the door. He ran to her and caught her hand again.

"Yuh do whut Ah tell yuh, May!"

"Ah ain gonna have them Reds in *here* wid tha mayor n Chiefa Police out *there*! Ah *ain*!"

"Go on n do whut Ah tell yuh, May!"

"Dan!"

"Go *erhead*, May!"

He pushed her. She went through the door, slowly, looking back at him. When the door was closed he rammed his hands deep into his pants' pockets, turned to the open window, and looked out into the street. It was profoundly quiet, save for the silvery sound of children's voices back of the church. The air was soft, warm, and full of the scent of magnolias and violets. Window panes across the street were blood-red from dying sunlight. A car sped past, lifting a great cloud of yellow-brown dust. He went to the center of the room and stood over a table littered with papers. He cocked his head, listening. He heard a door slam; footsteps echoed and ceased. A big eight-day clock above his head boomed six times; he looked and his eyes strayed up and rested on a gleaming, brass cross. Gawd, hep me now! Jus hep me t go thu wid this! Again he heard a door slam. Lawd, Ah hope May do right now . . . N Ah hope Jimmy don go n ack a fool . . . He crossed the floor on tiptoe, opened the door, and peeped into May's room. It was empty. A slender prism of dust-filled sunlight cut across the air. He closed the door, turned, pulled off his coat and threw it across the table. Then he loosened his collar and tie. He went to the window again and leaned with his back against the ledge, watching the door of May's room. He heard a hoarse voice rise and die. Footsteps again sounded and ceased. He frowned, listening. How come its takin May so long? He started when a timid knock came. He hurried to the door and cracked it.

## V

"Hello, Reverend Taylor!" said Hadley, a white man.

"How yuh, Brother Hadley?"

"N how yuh, Reveren?" asked Green, a black man.

"Ahm fine, Brother Green. C mon in, yuh all."

Hadley and Green edged through the door.

"Say, whuts alla mystery?" asked Green.

"Ssssh! Don talk so loud," cautioned Taylor. "The mayor n the Chiefa Police is out there."

The Negro and the white man stood stone still.

"Do they know wes here?" asked Green.

"Naw, n don git scared. They done come t see me erbout tha demonstration . . ."

Hadley and Green looked at each other.

"Pull down tha shade," whispered Green, pointing a shaking, black finger.

Quickly, Hadley moved to one side, out of range of the window. His cheeks flushed pink. Taylor lowered the shade and faced them in the semi-darkness. The eyes of the white man and the black man were upon him steadily.

"Waal?" said Green.

"Ah spose yuh know whuts up," said Taylor.

"Theyre here to scare you," said Hadley.

"Ahm trustin Gawd," sighed Taylor.

"Whut yuh gonna tell em?" asked Green.

"Thas whut Ah wanna see yuh all erbout," said Taylor.

"O.K. Whut kin we do?" asked Green.

Taylor looked around and motioned toward two chairs.

"Set down, Brothers."

"Naw, this is awright," said Green, still standing.

"Come on," said Hadley. "What's on your mind?"

Taylor folded his arms and half-sat and half-leaned on the edge of the table.

"Yuh all think wes gonna have many folks out in the mawnin fer the demonstration?"

"Whut yuh mean?" asked Green.

"When Ahm talkin wid the mayor and Chiefa Police Ah wanna know how many folks Ahm talkin fer. There ain no use in us havin a demonstration ef ain but a few of us is gonna be out there. The police will try t kill us then . . ."

"How many folks we can get out tomorrow depends a great deal on you, Reverend," said Hadley.

"Hows tha?" asked Taylor.

"If you had let us use your name on those handbills, we could say five thousand easily . . ."

Taylor turned sharply to Hadley.

"Lissen, Brother. Ah done tol yuh Ah cant do tha! N there ain no use in us talkin erbout it no mo! Ah done tol yuh Ah cant let them white folks know Ahm callin folks t demonstrate. After all, Ahma preacher . . ."

"Its yo duty, Reveren," said Green. "We owes it our black folks."

"Ahm doin mah duty as Gawd lets me see it," said Taylor.

"All right, Reverend," said Hadley. "Heres what happened: Weve covered the city with fifteen thousand leaflets. Weve contacted every organization we could think of, black and white. In other words, weve done all *we* could. The rest depends on the leaders of each group. If we had their active endorsement, none of us would have to worry about a crowd tomorrow. And if we had a crowd we would not have to worry about the police. If they see the whole town turning out, theyll not start any trouble. Now, youre known. White and black in this town respect you. If you let us send out another leaflet with your name on it calling for . . ."

Taylor turned from them and drew his hand nervously across his face. Hadley and Green were silent, watching him. Taylor went to the window and pulled back the curtain slightly and peeped out. Without turning he said softly:

"Ah done tol yuh all Ah ain scareda lettin yuh use mah name."

"We don mean *tha*," said Green hastily.

"Ef it wuz jus me who wuz takin the chance," said Taylor, "Ah wouldnt care none. But Gawd knows it ain right fer me to send them po folks out inter the streets in fronta police. Gawd knows, Ah cant do tha!"

"Honest, Reveren," said Green touching Taylor's arm. "Ah don understan. Yuh done been thu harder things than this befo."

"N Ahll go thu wid em ergin." said Taylor proudly.

"All right!" said Hadley. "You can say the word that can make this thing a success. If you dont and we have no crowd, then youre to blame . . ."

Taylor's eyes narrowed and when he spoke there was a note of anger in his voice.

"Gawd hep yuh ef yuhs a-tryin t say yuh gonna blame me ef things don go right!"

"Naw, Reveren!" said Green, coming hurriedly forward and spreading his black palms softly upon the air. "Don feel tha way! Wes all jus in a jam. We got t do either two things: Call off this demonstration and let the folks stay hongry, er git as many as we kin together n go downtown in the mawnin. Ef we git five thousan down there the police wont bother us. Ef yuh let us send out yo name tellin the black folks . . ."

"Naw, Brother!" said Taylor emphatically.

"Then the demonstrations going to be smashed," said Hadley. "*You* can stop it! You have the responsibility and the blame!"

Taylor sighed.

"Gawd knows Ah ain t blame. Ahm doin whut mah heart tells me t do . . ."

"Then whats keeping you from working with us?" asked Hadley. "Im a white man and Im here willing to fight for your peoples rights!"

"Ahm wid yuh, Brother!" said Taylor in a voice which carried a deep note of pleading. "Ahm wid yuh no matter whut yuh *think*! But yuh *cant* use mah name! Ef them white folks knowed Ah wuz callin mah folks in the streets t demonstrate, they wouldnt never gimme a chance t git something fer mah folks ergin . . ."

"Thats just it, Reverend," said Hadley. "Don't be afraid of their turning you down because youre fighting for your people. If they knew youd really fight, theyd dislike you; yes? But you can *make* them give something to *all* of your people, not just to *you*. Don't you see, Taylor, youre standing *between* your people and the white folks. You can make them give something to *all* of them. And the poor, hungry white folks will be with you."

"Ah cant lead mah folks to go ergin them white folks like tha," said Taylor. "Thas *war*!"

Hadley came close to Taylor.

"Reverend, cant you see thats just the way the white folks *want* you to feel? Are you leading your folks just because the white folks *say* you should, or are you leading them because you *want* to? Dont you believe in what youre doing? What kind of leaders are black people to have if the white folks pick them and tell them what to do?"

"Brothers, Ahma Christian, n whut yuhs astin fer is something tha makes blood!" thundered Taylor.

Hadley and Green looked at each other.

"Waal, whut yuh gonna tell the mayor?" asked Green.

Taylor stood in the center of the room with his hands in his pockets,

looking down at his feet. His voice came low, as though he were talking
to himself, trying to convince himself.

"Ahma tell em mah folks is hongry. Ahma tell em they wanna
march. Ahma tell em ef they march Ahma march wid em. Ahma tell
em they wan bread . . ."

"Reverend," asked Hadley, "why do you feel that this is so different
from all the other times youve gone straight to the white folks and
*demanded* things for your people?"

"It is different!" said Taylor.

"You didnt say that when you saved Scott from that *mob*!"

"Tha wuz different, Brother Hadley."

"I dont see it."

Taylor's voice came low.

"Ah feels differently erbout it, Brothers."

"You saved Scotts life. All right, youre saving the lives of your
congregation now. Scott was one man, but there are five hundred
starving people in your church."

"We ain facin no mob now, Brother Hadley."

"Then what in Gods name are we facing, Reverend? If those police
wholl be out there in the morning with their guns and clubs arent a
*legal* mob, then what . . ."

"It more than a mob, Brother Hadley."

Hadley and Green shook their heads.

"Ah don understan yuh, Reveren," said Green.

"When Ah saved Scott from tha mob, Ah wuz going erginst *some*
of the white folks. But this thing is going ergin em *all*! This is too
much like war!"

"You mean youre going against the ones with *money* now!" said
Hadley. "Over three thousand of the poor white folks will be with
*us* . . ."

"But, Brother Hadley, the white folks whos got moneys got *everthing*! This is jus like civil war!"

"Reverend," said Hadley, "cant you see that if they were not afraid
they wouldnt be here asking to *talk* with you? Go in and talk with them,
speak to them in the name of five thousand hungry people. Tell the
mayor and the Chief of Police that if they dont give the relief back we will
demonstrate."

"Ah cant do tha, Brothers. Ah cant let these white folks think Ahm
leadin mah folks tha way. Ah tol yuh brothers when Ah ergreed t work
wid yuh Ahd go as fer as Ah could. Waal, Ah done done tha. Now, yuh
here astin me t threaten this whole town n Ah ain gonna do tha!" said
Taylor.

"Yuh astin fer bread, Reveren," said Green.

"Its threatenin, Brothers," said Taylor. "N tha ain Gawds way!"

"So youll let your folks starve before youll stand up and talk to those white folks?" asked Hadley.

"Ahm ackin as Gawd gives me the light t see," said Taylor.

There was silence. Then Hadley laughed, noiselessly.

"Well," he said. "I didn't know you felt this way, Reverend. I thought we could count on you. You know the Party will stand behind you no matter what happens."

"Ahm sorry, Brother Hadley," said Taylor.

"When kin we see yuh t fin out whut the mayor n Chiefa Police say?" asked Green.

Taylor looked at his watch.

"Its a little aftah six now. Make it haf-pas six. Thall gimme time t see the Deacon Board."

Green sighed.

"O.K."

"O.K."

Taylor held the door for them. Then he stood in the center of the room and looked miles through the floor. *Lawd, Ah hope Ahm doin right. N they think Ahm scared* . . . He flushed hot with shame and anger. He sat in a chair for a moment, then got right up. He drummed his fingers on the corner of the table. *Shucks, Ah jus as waal see them white folks now n git it over wid. Ah knowed this wuz comin up! Ah knowed it!* He went through May's room, walking slowly, softly, seeing in his mind the picture of the fat, pink face of Mayor Bolton and the lean, red face of Chief of Police Bruden. As he turned into the narrow hall that led to the parlor he heard children yelling in the playground. He went down a stairway, opened a door and walked through his hushed, dim-lit church. Pale rose light fell slantwise through stained windows and glinted on mahogany pews. He lifted his eyes and saw the figure of Christ on a huge snow-white cross. *Gawd, hep me now! Lemme do the right thing!* He followed a red carpet to a door that opened into the parlor. He paused and passed his tongue over his dry lips. He could feel his heart beating. *Ahll let them do all the talkin. Ahll jus tell em mah folks is hongry. Thas all Ah kin do.* Slowly, he turned the knob, his lips half-parted in dread.

## VI

"Why, hello, Dan!"

"Good evenin, Mistah Mayor."

"Howve you been, Dan?"

"Fairly well, wid the hepa Gawd, suh."

Taylor shook hands with a tall, fat white man in a blue serge suit.

"Its been a long time since Ive seen you, Dan."

"Yessuh. It sho has, yo Honah."

"Hows Jimmy?"

"Jus fine, suh."

"Thats a fine boy youve got, Dan."

"Ahm sho glad yuh think so, suh."

"If you raise that boy right he will be a leader of his people some day, Dan."

"Thas the one hope of mah life, suh," said Taylor with deep emotion.

"May was tellin me youre sick," said the mayor.

"Aw, it ain nothin, suh. Jusa summer col, suh."

"I didnt mean to bother you if youre sick, Dan."

"Thas awright, suh. Ahm feelin much bettah now, suh."

"Oh, youll pull through all right; itll take a lot more than a summer cold to kill old war-horses like you and me, eh, Dan?"

The mayor laughed and winked.

"Ahm hopin Gawd spares me a few mo years, suh," said Taylor.

"But at least you look all right now," said the mayor. "Say, Dan, I want you to meet Chief Bruden. This is Dan, Chief, the boy I was telling you about."

"How yuh, Mistah Chief?" asked Taylor.

A black cigar burned red in Bruden's mouth. He shifted his thin body and growled:

"Hello, boy."

"And, Dan, this is Mr. Lowe, head of our fine Industrial Squad."

"How yuh, suh?" asked Taylor.

Lowe nodded with half-closed eyes.

"Sit down, Dan," said the mayor.

"Yessuh."

Taylor sat on the edge of a chair and rested his palms lightly on his knees.

"Maybe our little visit is a surprise, hunh?" asked the mayor.

"Yessuh. It is. But Ahm glad to be of any hep Ah kin, suh."

"Good! I knew youd talk that way. Now, Dan, we want you to help us. Youre a responsible man in this community; thats why we are here."

"Ah tries t do mah duty as Gawd shows it t me, suh."

"Thats the spirit, Dan!" The mayor patted Taylor's knee. "Now, Im going to be perfectly frank with you. Dan." The mayor peeled a wrapper from a black cigar. "Here, have one."

"Thank yuh, suh." Taylor put the cigar into his vest pocket. "Ahll smoke it aftah dinner, suh."

There was a silence during which the three white men looked at Taylor.

"Dan," began the mayor, "its not every nigger Id come to and talk this way. Its not every nigger Id trust as Im about to trust you." The mayor looked straight at Taylor. "Im doing this because Ive faith in you. Ive known you for twenty-five years, Dan. During that time I think Ive played pretty fair with you, havent I?"

Taylor swallowed.

"Ahll have t say yuh have, yo Honah."

"Mister Lowe and the Chief here had another plan," said the mayor. "But I wouldnt hear of it. I told them Id work this thing *my* way. I thought *my* way would be much better. After all, Dan, you and I have worked together in the past and I dont see why we cant work together now. Ive backed you up in a lot of things, Dan. Ive backed you even when other white folks said you were wrong. But I believe in doing the right thing. After all, we are human beings, arent we?"

"Yessuh."

"What Ive done for you in the past Im willing to do again. You remember Scott, dont you?"

"Yessuh. Yuhs been a big hep t me n mah folks, suh."

"Well, Dan, my office is always open to you when you want to see me about any of your problems or the problems of your people," said the mayor.

"N Gawd knows Ah sho thanks yuh, suh!"

The mayor bit off the tip of his cigar and spat it into a brass spittoon.

"I'm not going to beat about the bush, Dan."

The mayor paused again. There was silence. Taylor felt called upon to say something.

"Yessuh. Ah sho preciates tha, suh."

"You know these Goddam Reds are organizing a demonstration for to-morrow, dont you?" asked the mayor.

Taylor licked his lips before he answered.

"Yessuh. Ah done heard a lotta folks talkin erbout it, suh."

"Thats too bad, Dan," said the mayor.

"Folks is talking erbout it everywhere . . ." began Taylor.

"What *folks*?" interjected Bruden.

"Waal, mos everybody, suh."

Bruden leaned forward and shook his finger in Taylor's face.

"Listen, boy! I want you to get this straight! Reds aint *folks*! Theyre Goddam sonofabitching lousy bastard rats trying to wreck our country, see? Theyre stirring up race hate! Youre old enough to understand that!"

"Hes telling you straight, boy," said Lowe. "And furthermore . . ."

"Say, whats all this?" demanded the mayor, turning to Lowe and Bruden. "Wait a minute! Whats the big idea of talking to Dan like that? Hes not mixed up in anything like that. Save that kind of talk for bad niggers . . ."

"The quicker all you niggers get sense enough in your Goddam thick skulls to keep away from them Reds the better off youll be!" said Bruden, ignoring the mayor.

"Aw, c mon," said the mayor. "Dans all right. Aint that right, Dan?"

Taylor looked down and saw at his feet a sharp jutting angle of sunshine falling obliquely through a window. His neck felt hot. This is the show-down, he thought. Theys tryin t trap me . . . He cleared his throat and looked up slowly and saw the mayor gazing at him with cold gray eyes. He shifted his body slightly and saw the glint of Chief Bruden's police star; he saw Lowe's red lips twisted in half-smile and half-leer.

"Isnt that right, Dan?" the mayor asked again.

"Yessuh. Whut yuh white folks say is right. N Ah ergrees wid yuh. But Ah ain foolin wid nobody thas tryin t stir up race hate; naw, *suh!* Ah ain never done nothin like tha n Ah never will, so hep me Gawd! Now, erbout this demonstration: Yessuh, Ah heard erbout it. Thas all everbodys been talkin erbout erroun here fer a week, yo Honah. Waal, suh, Ahll tell yuh. Theys jus hongry! Theys marchin cause they don know whut else t do, n thas the truth from here t Heaven! Mistah Mayor, theys hongry! Just plain *hongry!* Ah give mah las dime today t a woman wid eight chillun . . ."

"We know all about that, Dan," said the mayor.

"Everybodys hungry," said Bruden.

"Boy, cant you see we are all in the *same* boat?" asked Lowe.

"Waal . . ." drawled Taylor.

"Thingsll be straightened out soon, Dan," interjected the mayor soothingly. "We will see that nobody starves."

"Ah beg yo pardon, suh. A man died jus the other day from starvation . . ."

Taylor's voice died in his throat and he looked at the floor. He knew that he had said too much.

"I reckon that makes you out a liar, don't it?" Bruden asked the mayor.

"Aw, naw, suh!" said Taylor eagerly. "Ah ain disputin nobodys word, suh. Ah jus thought yuh hadnt heard erbout it . . ."

"We know all about it," said Bruden, turning his head away and looking out of the window; as though he was through with the conversation, as though his mind was made up.

"What do they think theyre going to get by marching?" asked Lowe.

"They think they kin git some bread," said Taylor.

"It wont get em a Goddam crumb!" said Lowe.

There was silence. Taylor looked again at the jutting angle of sunshine and heard the mayor's shoes shifting uneasily on the brown carpet. A match struck; he heard it drop with an angry hiss into the spittoon.

"I dont see why we cant get along, Dan," drawled the mayor.

"Ahm willin t git erlong, Mistah Mayor!" protested Taylor.

"Dan, here we all are, living in good old Dixie. There are twenty-five thousand people in this town. Ten thousand of those people are black, Dan. Theyre your people. Now, its our job to keep order among the whites, and we would like to think of you as being a responsible man to keep order among the blacks. Lets get together, Dan. You know these black people better than we do. We want to feel we can depend on you. Why dont you look at this thing the right way? You know Ill never turn you down if you do the right thing . . ."

"Mistah Mayor, as Gawds mah judge, Ahm doin right when Ah tell you mah folks is hongry . . ."

"Youre not doing right when you act like a Goddam Red!" said Lowe.

"These niggers around here trust you, Dan," said the mayor. "Theyll do what you tell them to do."

"Speak to them," urged Lowe. "Tell them whats right."

"Mistah Mayor, Gawd in Heaven knows mah people is hongry," said Taylor humbly.

The mayor threw his body forward in the chair and rested his hands on his knees.

"Listen, Dan. I know just how you feel. We *all* feel that way. White people are hungry, too. But weve got to be prudent and do this thing right. Dan, youre a leader and youve got great influence over your congregation here." The mayor paused to let the weight of his words sink in. "Dan, I helped you to get that influence by doing your people a lot of favors through *you* when you came into my office a number of times." The mayor looked at Taylor solemnly. "I'm asking you now to use that influence and tell your people to stay *off* the streets tomorrow!"

When Taylor spoke he seemed to be outside of himself, listening to his own words, aghast and fearful.

"Ahm sho thankful as Gawd knows fer all yuh done done fer me n

mah people, suh. But mah word don go so fer in times like these, yo
Honah. These folks is lookin t me fer bread an Ah cant give it t em.
They hongry n Ah cant tell em where t eat. Theys gonna march no
mattah whut Ah say . . ."

"You've got influence here, Dan, and you can use it!"

"They wouldnt be marchin ef they wuznt hongry, yo Honah!"

"Thats Red talk, nigger!" said Lowe, standing.

"Aw, thats all right, Lowe," said the mayor, placatingly.

"Im not going to sit here and let this Goddam nigger insult me to
my face!" said Lowe.

Taylor stood up.

"Ahm sorry, suh!"

"You *will* be sorry when you find a Goddam rope around your
neck!" said Lowe.

"Now, now," said the mayor, laying his hand on Lowe's arm. He
turned to Taylor. "You dont mean you wont speak to em, do you, Dan?"

"There ain nothin Ah kin say t em, Mistah Mayor . . ."

"Youre doing the wrong thing, Dan!"

"Ahm lettin Gawd be mah judge, suh!"

"If you dont do the right thing *we* will be your judges!" said Lowe.

"Ahm trustin Gawd, suh."

"Well, Goddammit, you better let Him guide you right!" said Bruden, jumping to his feet.

"But white folks!" pleaded Taylor. "Mah folks cant plant nothin!
Its erginst the law! They cant git no work! Whut they gonna do?
They don want no trouble . . ."

"Youre heading for a plenty right now!" said Bruden.

The mayor spoke and his voice was low and resigned.

"Ive done all I could, Dan. You wouldnt follow my advice, now
the rest is up to Mister Lowe and Chief Bruden here."

Bruden's voice came with a shout:

"A niggers a nigger! I was against coming here talking to this
nigger like he was a white man in the first place. He needs his teeth
kicked down his throat!" Bruden poked the red tip of his cigar at
Taylor's face. "Im the Chief of Police of this town, and Im here to see
that orders kept! The Chamber of Commerce says therell be no demonstration tomorrow. Therell be three hundred police downtown in the
morning to see that thats done! If you send them niggers down there, or
if you let these Goddam Reds fool you into it, Ill not be responsible for
whatll happen! Weve never had a riot in this town, but youre plotting
one right now when you act like this! And you know wholl get the
worst of it!"

"Cant yuh do something, Mistah Mayor? Cant yuh fix it sos we kin git some relief!"

The mayor did not answer; Lowe came close to him.

"We know youve been seeing Hadley and Green! We know whats going on! So watch yourself, nigger!"

"Suh?"

They went out. Taylor stood at the window and saw them get into their car and disappear in a cloud of dust around a corner. He sat down, feeling sweat over all his body. Gawd knows whut t do . . . He brought Lowe n Bruden here t threaten me . . . N they know erbout Hadley n Green . . . Somebody tol . . . He looked up, hearing the soft boom of a clock. Hadley n Greens comin back here at six-thirty . . . He went down the hall, thinking, Lawd, ef Ah only knowed whut t do . . .

## VII

May met him in the hall.

"Whut they say, Dan?" she asked with suppressed hysteria.

"Don bother me now, May!"

"There wont be no trouble, will it, Dan?"

"Naw, May! Now, please! Yuh worryin me!"

"Yuhll spoil things fer Jimmy, Dan! Don do nothin wrong! Its fer Jimmy Ahm astin!"

"Itll be awright! Now, lemme go!"

He hurried down the hallway, leaving her crying. Good Gawd! How come she wont leave me erlone? Firs, its Jimmy; then its her . . . Ef it ain one its the other . . . He went to the end of the hall, down the steps, turned, and came to the door of the Deacon Room. He heard subdued voices. He knew that the deacons were waiting for him, waiting for some definite word. Shucks, Ahm willin t go thu wid tha march ef they is. Them white folks cant kill us *all* . . . He pushed the door in. The voices ceased. He saw a dense cloud of tobacco smoke and a circle of black faces. He forced a wan smile.

"Good evenin, Brothers!" he said.

"How yuh, Reveren?" asked Deacon Bonds.

"Ahm sorry Ahm late," said Taylor.

"Wuz tha the mayor out there?" asked Deacon Williams.

Taylor paused and pulled out his handkerchief.

"Yeah, Brothers, it wuz the mayor. N the Chiefa Police n tha man Lowe from the Red Squad . . ."

"RED SQUAD!" shouted Deacon Smith, jumping to his feet with an outraged look.

"Whut they say, Reveren?" asked Deacon Williams quietly, ignoring Deacon Smith.

Taylor sighed and looked at the floor. For a moment he loathed them because he knew they were expecting an answer to their questions. They were expecting him to speak now as he had always spoken, to the point, confidently, and finally. He had wanted them to do the talking, and now they were silent, waiting for him to speak. Lawd, Ah hope Ahm doin right. Ah don wanna lead these folks wrong . . .

"They know all erbout tha demonstration," he said.

"But whut they *say?*" asked Deacon Bonds.

"Shucks, man! Yuh *know* whut they said!" said Deacon Smith. "Yuh *know* how them white folks feel erbout this thing!"

"They don wan us t march," said Taylor. "They said ef we march theyll put the police on us . . ."

Deacon Smith leveled his forefinger at Taylor and intoned:

"AH TOL YUH SO!"

"They said therell be a riot," Taylor went on stubbornly.

"Yessuh! Brothers, wes gotta do *right!*" said Deacon Smith, banging his open palm down on the table. "Ah awways said wes gotta do *right*, Reveren!"

"Ahm prayin t Gawd t guide us right," said Taylor.

"Yuh sho don ack like it!" said Deacon Smith.

"Let the Reveren finish, will yuh?" asked Deacon Bonds.

"Wes gotta do right!" said Deacon Smith again, sitting down, folding his arms, crossing his legs and turning his face sternly away.

"Whut else they say, Reveren?" asked Deacon Bonds.

Taylor sighed.

"They say wes mixed up wid the Reds . . ."

"N by Gawd we *is!*" bawled Deacon Smith. "At least *yuh* is! Ah tol yuh t leave them Reds erlone! They don mean *no*body *no* good! When men starts t deny Gawd, nothin good kin come from em!"

"Brother Smith, let the Reveren talk, will yuh?" asked Deacon Williams.

"He ain talkin *sense!*" said Deacon Smith.

"They say therell be three hundred police downtown in the mawnin," said Taylor, ignoring Smith. "They say only Washington kin do something erbout relief, n tha we must wait . . ."

"N Gawd Awmighty knows thas all we kin do: wait!" said Deacon Smith.

"Fer Chrissakes, Brother Smith, let im talk!" said Deacon Williams. "We all knows *yuhs* scared!"

"Ah ain scared! Ah got sense! Ah . . ."

"Yuh sho don ack like it, the way yuh shoot off yo mouth!" said Deacon Williams.

Deacon Smith stood up.

"Yuh cant talk tha way t me!"

"Then keep yo big mouth shut!" said Deacon Williams.

"Whos gonna make me?"

"Brothers, please!" begged Taylor.

"A fool kin see tha the white folks is scared!" said Deacon Williams.

"N jus cause theys *scared*, theyll kill *any*body whuts fool ernuff t go downtown in the mawnin," said Deacon Smith.

"Shucks, Ahm willin t taka chance," said Deacon Hilton.

"Me too!"

"We ain got nothin t lose!"

"Any *fool* kin git his head busted!" said Deacon Smith.

"Brothers, fer the lova Gawd, quit fussin!" said Taylor.

They were silent. Taylor looked at them, letting his eyes rove from face to face.

"Brothers, this is the case," he said finally. "They threatenin us not t march, but they ain sayin our folks kin git no relief. Now, Ah figgers ef we hada big crowd downtown in the mawnin they wont bother us . . ."

"Thas whut *yuh* think," sneered Deacon Smith.

"N ef we don hava big crowd, theyll smash us. Now, its up t us . . ."

"Reveren, do the *po* white folks say they gonna be *wid* us?" asked Deacon Jones.

"Brother Hadley tol me theys gonna be wid us," said Taylor.

"Tha Hadley is a lie n the trutha Gawd ain in im!" shouted Deacon Smith. "Tha white man is jus tryin t trick yuh, Ahm tellin yuh!"

"Waal, we kin never know less we try n see," said Deacon Bonds.

"Yeah, they ain gonna let yuh try but *once*," said Deacon Smith.

"Waal, Ah ain got but *one* time t die!" said Deacon Bonds.

"Ah think the white folksll be there," said Taylor. "Theys hongry, too . . ."

"Yuhll wake up *some* day!" said Deacon Smith.

"Whut yuh gonna do, Reveren?" asked Deacon Williams.

"Do the congregation wanna march?" asked Taylor.

"They say theys *gonna* march!"

"Waal, Ahll march wid em," said Taylor quietly. "They wont march erlone . . ."

Deacon Smith waved his arms and screamed:

"Yeah, yuhll march! But yuhs scared t let em use yo name! Whut kinda leader *is* yuh? If yuhs gonna ack a fool n be a *Red*, then how come yuh wont come on out n say so sos we kin all hear it? Naw, yuh ain man ernuff t say whut yuh is! Yuh wanna stan in wid the white folks! Yuh wanna stan in wid the Reds! Yuh wanna stan in wid the congregation! Yuh wanna stan in wid the Deacon Board! Yuh wanna stan in wid *every*body n yuh stan in wid *no*body!"

"Ahm ackin accordin t mah lights!" said Taylor.

"Waal, they ain lettin yuh see fer!" said Deacon Smith.

"Ef yuh gotta plan bettah than mine, Brother Smith, tell us erbout it!"

"AH SAY WE OUGHTNT MARCH!"

"Then, whut we gonna do?"

"Wait n see how things come out!"

"Ahm tireda waitin," said Taylor.

"How come yuh didnt send yo name out on them leaflets?" demanded Deacon Smith. Without waiting for Taylor to answer, he flared: "Ahll tell yuh why yuh didn't! Yuh *scared*! Yuh didnt wan them white folks t know yuhs mixed up in this demonstration. Yuh wanted em t think yuh wuz being pushed erlong by other folks n yuh couldnt hep whut wuz happenin! But, Reveren, as sho as theres a Gawd in Heaven yuh ain foolin nobody!"

Taylor stood up.

"Brother Smith, Ah knows whut yuhs up t! Yuh tryin t run me outta mah church, but yuh cant! Gawd Awmighty Himself put me here n Ahm stayin till He says fer me t go! Yuh been schemin t git me out, but yuh cant do it this way! It ain right n Gawd knows it ain! Yeah; ef mah folks marches in the mawnin Ahm marchin wid em!"

"Thas the time, Reveren!"

"We kin show tha ol mayor something!"

"N therell be white folks wid us, too!"

"Ahll go wid the Reveren n the congregation!"

"Ahll go!"

"N me too!"

"Gawd ain wid yuh when yuh ain in the right!" said Deacon Smith.

"Gawd didnt mean fer folks t be hongry!" said Deacon Bonds.

"But He ain wid yuh when yuh stirrin up trouble, makin blood n riots!" said Deacon Smith. 'N any man whut sets here n calls himself a leader called by Gawd t preach n leads his folks the wrong way is a fool n the spirita Gawd ain in im!"

"Now, wait a minute there, Brother Smith!" said Taylor. "Yuhs talkin *dangerous*!"

"Ah say any man whut leads his folks inter guns n police . . ."

"Ain nobody leadin us *nowhere*!" said Deacon Bonds.

"We gwine *ourselves*!" said Deacon Williams.

"Ah ain in this!" said Deacon Smith, jumping again to his feet. "Ah ain in this n Ahm gonna do whut Ah kin t hep mah people!"

The room grew quiet.

"Whut yuh mean, Brother Smith?" asked Taylor.

"Ah say Ahm gonna hep mah people!" said Deacon Smith again.

Taylor walked over to him.

"Is yuh gonna tell the white folks on us?"

Deacon Smith did not answer.

"Talk, Brother Smith!" said Taylor. "Tell us whut yuh mean!"

"Ah means whut Ah means!" said Deacon Smith; and he clamped his teeth tight, sat again, crossed his legs, folded his arms and stared at the blank wall.

Taylor swallowed and looked at the floor. Lawd, Ah don know whut t do! Ah wish this wuz over . . . This niggers gonna tell on us! Hes gonna tell the white folks sos he kin stan in wid em . . .

"Brother Smith . . ." began Taylor.

The door opened and Jimmy stepped into the room.

"Say, Pa!"

"Whut yuh wan, son?"

"Somebodys out front t see yuh. Theys in a car. Theys white folks."

"Scuse me, Brothers," said Taylor. "Ahll be right back."

"Wes gonna set right here till yuh git back," said Deacon Smith.

When outside the door, Taylor turned to Jimmy.

"Who is they, Jimmy? How come they wouldnt come in?"

"Ah dunno, Pa. The car drove up jus as Ah wuz comin thu the gate. They white men. They said fer yuh t come right out."

"Awright. N, son, yuh better go see bout yo ma."

"Whuts the mattah?"

"Shes jus upset erbout the demonstration."

"Is they gonna march, Pa?"

"Ah reckon so."

"Is many gonna be out?"

"Ah dunno, son. Ah hope so. Yuh bettah go see erbout yo ma now."

"Yessuh."

"Yuh tell them boys whut Ah tol yuh?"

"Yessuh."

Taylor paused at the front door and peeped out from behind a curtain. In front of his gate was a long black car. Who kin tha be? For a moment he thought the mayor had come back. But his cars gray . . . He opened the door and walked slowly down the steps. Lawd, mabbe we oughtnt go thu wid this demonstration aftah all? We might all be sorry ef somebodys killed in the mawnin . . . He walked along a flower-bordered path that smelt of violets and magnolias. Dust rested filmily on tree leaves. The sun was almost gone. As he came to the car a white face looked out.

"You Taylor?"

"Yessuh," answered Taylor, smiling.

The rear door of the car opend and the white man stepped to the ground.

"So youre Taylor, hunh?"

"Yessuh," said Taylor again, still smiling, but puzzled. "Kin Ah be of service t yuh, suh?"

Taylor saw it coming, but could do nothing. He remembered afterward that he had wanted to ask, Whut yuh doin? The blow caught him flush on the point of the jaw, sending him flying backward. His head struck the edge of the running-board; a flash of red shot before his eyes. He rolled, face downward, into a bed of thick violets. Dazed, he turned his head, trying to speak. He felt a hand grab the back of his collar and jerk him up.

"Get in the car, nigger!"

"Say, whut yuh . . ."

"Shut up and get in the car, Goddam you!"

A blow came to his right' eye. There were three white men now. They lifted him and rammed him down on the floor in the back of the car.

"Say, you cant do this!"

"Get your Goddam mouth shut, you bastard!"

A hard palm slappéd him straight across his face. He struggled up, protesting.

"You . . ."

The heel of a shoe came hard into his solar plexus. He doubled up, like a jack-knife. His breath left, and he was rigid, half-paralyzed.

"You think you can run this whole Goddam town, don't you? You think a nigger can run over white folks and get away with it?"

He lay still, barely breathing, looking at blurred white faces in the semi-darkness of the roaring car.

## VIII

The moment he tried to tell the direction in which the car was moving he knew he had waited too long. He remembered dimly that they had turned corners at least three times. He lay with closed eyes and wondered what they were going to do with him. She gonna be worried t death, he thought, thinking of May. And then he thought of Jimmy and said to himself, *Ah hope he don go n ack a fool now* . . . The numbness which had deadened most of his stomach and chest was leaving. He felt sweat on his back and forehead. The car slowed, turned; then it ran fast again. He knew by the way the rocks crunched beneath the humming rubber tires that they were speeding over gravel. *Whut roads this?* He could not tell. There were so many gravel roads leading out of town. He tried to recall how long he had lain there half-paralyzed from that kick in the solar plexus. He was confused; it might have been five minutes or it might have been a hour. The car slowed again, turning. He smelt the strong scent of a burning cigarette and heard the toll of a far off church bell. The car stopped; he heard the sound of other cars, gears shifting and motors throbbing. *We mus be at some crossroads.* But he could not guess which one. He had an impulse to call for help. But there would not be any use in his doing that now. *Mabbe they white folks anyhow.* He would be better off as he was; even six white men were better than a mob of white men. The car was speeding again, lurching. He smelt dust, clay dust. Then he heard a hard, rasping voice:

"How is he?"

"O.K."

"Keep im quiet!"

"O.K."

He said nothing. He began to wonder how many of them were in the car. *Yes, he should have been watching for something like this. They been threatenin me fer a long time. Now this is it.* The car was gradually slowing with that long slow slowing preceding a final stop. He felt the rubber tires turning over rough ground; his head rocked from side to side, hitting against the lower back of the front seat. Then the car stopped; the motor stopped; for a moment there was complete silence. Then he heard wind sighing in trees. *Wes out in the country somewhere. In the woods,* he thought.

"O.K.?"

"O.K.?"

He heard a door open.

"C mon, nigger! Get up and watch yourself!"

He pulled up and caught a glimpse of starry sky. As his feet hit the ground his head began to ache. He had lain cramped so long the blood had left his limbs; he took a step, kicking out his legs to restore circulation. His arms were grabbed from behind and he felt the pressure of a kneecap in the center of his spine. He gasped and reeled backward.

"Where you think youre goin?"

He rested on his knees, his body full of pain. He heard a car door slam.

"Awright, nigger! Lets go! Straight ahead!"

He got up and twisted his head about to see who had spoken. He saw four blurred white faces and then they were blotted out. He reeled backward again, his head striking the ground. A pain knotted in his temple.

"Get up, nigger! Keep your eyes in front, and walk, Goddammit!"

He pulled up and limped off, his head down. Mabbe they gonna shoot me? His feet and the feet behind him made a soft *cush-cush* in the dew-wet grass and leaves.

"All right, nigger!"

He stopped. Slowly he raised his eyes; he saw a tall white man holding a plaited leather whip in his hand, hitting it gently against his trousers' leg.

"You know what this is, nigger?"

He said nothing.

"Wont talk, hunh? Well, this is a nigger-lesson!"

The whip flashed in faint starlight. The blow numbed his lips. He tasted blood.

"You know what this is? Im asking you again, nigger?"

"Nawsuh," he whispered.

"This is a nigger-whip!"

The leather whacked across his shoulders.

"Mistah, Ah ain done nothin!"

"Aw, naw! You aint done nothing! You aint never done a Goddam thing, have you?" White men were standing close around him now. "All you ever do is play around with Reds, dont you? All you ever do is get crowds of niggers together to threaten white folks, dont you? When we get through with you tonight youll know how to stay in a niggers place! C mon! Get that Goddam vest off!"

He did not move. The whip wrapped itself around his neck, leaving a ring of fire.

"You want me to *beat* it off you?"

He pulled off the vest and held it in his hands.

"C mon! Get that shirt and undershirt off!"

He stripped to his waist. A night wind cooled his sweaty body; he was conscious of his back as he had never been before, conscious of every square inch of black skin there. One of the white men walked off a few paces and stopped.

"Bring im over here!"

"O.K.!"

They guided him with prods and kicks.

"On your knees, nigger!"

He did not move. Again his arms were caught from behind and a kneecap came into the center of his back. Breathless, he dropped, his hands and knees cooling in the wet grass. He lifted his fingers to feel his swelling lips; he felt his wrists being grabbed and carried around the trunk of a tree. He held stiffly and struggled against a rope.

"Let go!"

His arms went limp. He rested his face against a cold tree trunk. A rope cut into his wrists. They tied his feet together, drawing the rope tight about his ankles. He looked around; they stood watching.

"Well, nigger, what do you know?"

"Nothin, suh."

"Youre a preacher, aint you?"

"Yessuh."

"Well, lets hear you pray some!"

He said nothing. The whip lashed across his bare back, *whick*! He flinched and struggled against the rope that cut his wrists to the bone. The leather thong hummed again, *whick*! and his spine arched inward, like a taut bow.

"Goddam your black soul, pray!"

He twisted his face around, pleading:

"Please, Mistah! Don whip me! Ah ain done nothin . . ."

Another lash came across his half-turned cheek, *whick*! He jerked around and sheltered his face against the tree trunk. The lash hit his back, *whick*!

"*Hit* that black bastard, Bob!"

"Let me have that whip!"

"Naw, wait a minute!"

He said nothing. He clenched his teeth, his whole body quivering and waiting. A split second after each blow his body would lurch, as though absorbing the shock.

"You going to pray? You want me to beat you till you *cant* pray?"

He said nothing. He was expecting each blow now; he could almost feel them before they came, stinging, burning. Each flick came straight on his back and left a streak of fire, a streak that merged with the last streak, making his whole back a sheet of living flame. He felt his strength ebbing; he could not clench his teeth any more. His mouth hung open.

"Let me have it, Bob?"

"Naw, its my turn!"

There was a pause. Then the blows came again; the pain burned its way into his body, wave upon wave. It seemed that when he held his muscles taut the blows hurt less; but he could not hold taut long. Each blow weakened him; each blow told him that soon he would give out. Warm blood seeped into his trousers, ran down his thighs. He felt he could not stand it any longer; he held his breath. his lungs swelling. Then he sagged, his back a leaping agony of fire; leaping as of itself, as though it were his but he could not control it any longer. The weight of his body rested on his arms; his head dropped to one side.

"Ahhlll pppprray," he sobbed.

"Pray, then! Goddam you, pray!"

He tried to get his breath, tried to form words, hearing trees sighing somewhere. The thong flicked again, *whick*!

"Aint you going to pray!"

"Yyyyyessuh . . ."

He struggled to draw enough air into his lungs to make his words sound.

"Ooour ffather . . ."

The whip cut hard, *whick*! pouring fire and fire again.

"Have mercy, Lawd!" he screamed.

"Pray, nigger! Pray like you *mean* it!"

". . . wwwhich aaaaart in hheaven . . . hhhallowed bbe Ttthy nname . . ." The whip struck, *whick*! "Ahm prayin, Mmmmistah!"

"Goddam your black heart, *pray*!"

". . . Ttthine kkkindon ccome . . . Ttthy wwill bbe ddddone . . ."

He sobbed, his breath leaving his lungs, going out from him, not wanting to stay to give sound to his words. The whip brought more fire and he could not stand it any longer; his heart seemed about to burst. He screamed, stretched his knees out and twisted his arms till he lay sideways, half on his stomach. The whip came into his stomach, *whick*! He turned over; it came on his back again, *whick*! He stopped struggling and hung limply, his weight suspended on arms he could not feel. Then fire flamed over all his body; he stiffened, glaring upward, wild-eyed.

"Whats the matter, nigger? You hurt?"

"Awright, kill me! Tie me n kill me! Yuh white trash cowards, kill me!"

"Youre tough, aint you? Just wait! We'll kill you, you black sonofabitch!"

"Lemme have that whip!"

"C mon, now! Its my turn!"

"Give me that whip, Ellis!"

He was taut, but not feeling the effort to be taut.

"We'll git yuh white trash some day! So hep me Gawd, we'll git yuh!"

The whip stopped.

"Say that again, Goddam you!"

The whip lashed, *whick*! but there was no streak of fire now;

there was only one sheet of pain stretching all over his body, leaping, jumping, blazing in his flesh.

"Say it!"

He relaxed and closed his eyes. He stretched his legs out, slowly, not listening, not waiting for the whip to fall. *say it whick! say it whick! say it whick!* He groaned. Then he dropped his head and could not feel any more.


## IX

Moonlight pained his eyeballs and the rustle of tree leaves thundered in his ears. He seemed to have only a head that hurt, a back that blazed, and eyes that ached. In him was a feeling that some power had sucked him deep down into the black earth, had drained all strength from him. He was waiting for that power to go away so he could come back to life, to light. His eyes were half-open, but his lids did not move. He was thirsty; he licked his lips, wanting water. Then the thunder in his ears died, rolling away. He moved his hand and touched his forehead; his arm fell limply in the wet grass and he lay waiting to feel that he wanted to move. As his blood began to flow swiftly again he felt sweat breaking out over his body. It seemed he could hear a tiny, faraway sound whispering over and over like a voice in an empty room: Ah got fever . . . His back rested on a bed of fire, the imprint of leaves and grass searing him with a scalding persistence. He turned over on his stomach and groaned. Then he jerked up, half-sitting. He was fully conscious now, fighting for his strength, remembering the curses, the prayer and the whip. The voice whispered again, this time louder: Ah gotta git home . . . With fumbling fingers he untied the rope from his wrists and ankles. They didnt kill me, he thought. He stood up and the dark earth swayed and the stars blurred. Lawd, have mercy! He found himself on his knees; he had not known when he had started falling; he just found himself on his knees. Lawd, Ahm weak! He stood up again, more slowly this time, holding onto a tree. He would have to get his shirt; he could not go through the streets with a naked and bleeding back. He put one foot in front of the other with conscious effort, holding his body stiffly. Each slight twist of his shoulders sent a wave of liquid metal over him. In the grass at his feet his shirt was smeared like a white blur. He touched it; it was wet. He held it, instinctively fearing to put it on. When it did touch, his whole back blazed with a pain so intense that it seemed to glow white hot. No, he could not put it on now. Stiffly, he went among the trees, holding the shirt in his hands, looking at the ground.

He stopped at the edge of a dirt road, conscious of the cool steady stars and the fire that smouldered in his back. Whut roads this? He could not tell. Then he heard a clock striking so faintly that it seemed to be tolling in his own mind. He counted, Wun, Tuh . . . Its tuh erclock, he thought. He could not stay here all night; he had to go in one direction or another. He watched the brown dusty road winding away in the darkness, like a twisting ribbon. Then he ducked his head, being seared again with fire and feeling a slight rush of air brush across his face. A small bird wheeled past his eyes and fluttered dizzily in the starlight. He watched it veer and dip, then crash softly into a tree limb. It fell to the ground, flapping tiny wings blindly. Then the bird twittered in fright and sailed straight upward into the starlight, vanishing. He walked northward, not going anywhere in particular, but walked northward because the bird had darted in the direction.

The road curved, turned to gravel, crunching under his shoes. This mus be the way, he thought. There were fences along the sides of the road now. He went faster, holding his legs stiffly to avoid pulling the muscles in his back. A church steeple loomed in the starlight, slender and faint. Yeah, thas Houstons church. N Ah gotta go thu a white neighborhod, he thought with despair. He saw houses, white, serene and cool in the night. Spose Ah go to Houston? Naw, hes white. *White* . . . Even tho he preaches the gospel Ah preaches, he might not take me in . . . He passed a small graveyard surrounded by a high iron picket fence. A *white* graveyard, he thought and snickered bitterly. Lawd Gawd in Heaven, even the dead cant be together! He stopped and held his shirt in his hands. He dreaded trying to put it on, but he had to. Ah cant go thu the streets like this. Gingerly, he draped the shirt over his shoulders; the whole mass of bruised and mangled flesh flamed, glowed white. With a convulsive movement he rammed his arms into the sleeves, thinking that the faster he did it the less pain there would be. The fire raged so he had a wild impulse to run, feeling that he would have no time then to suffer. But he could not run in a white neighborhood. To run would mean to be shot, for a burglar, or anything. Stiff-legged, he went down a road that turned from brown dust to black asphalt. Ahead street lamps glowed in round, rosy hazes.

Far down the shadow-dappled pavement he heard the sound of feet. He walked past a white man, then he listened to the white man's footsteps dying away behind him. He stopped at a corner and held on to a telephone pole. It would be better to keep in the residential district than to go through town. He would be stopped and questioned in town surely. And jailed maybe. Three blocks later on a white boy came upon him so softly and suddenly that he started in panic. After the boy had gone he turned to look; he saw the boy turning, looking at him. He walked on hurriedly. A block later a white woman appeared. When she was some fifty feet away she crossed to the other side of the street. Hate tightened his throat, then he emptied his lungs in a short, silent, bitter laugh. Ah ain gonna bother yuh, white lady. Ah only wan t git home . . .

Like a pillar of fire he went through the white neighborhood. Some day theys gonna burn! Some day theys gonna burn in Gawds Awmighty fire! How come they make us suffer so? The worls got too mucha everything! Yit they bleed us! They fatten on us like leeches! There ain no groun yuh kin walk on tha they don own! N Gawd knows tha ain right! He made the earth fer us all! He ain tol no lie when He put us in this worl n said be fruitful n multiply . . . Fire fanned his hate; he stopped and looked at the burning stars. "Gawd, ef yuh gimme the strength Ahll tear this ol buildin down! Tear it down, Lawd! Tear it down like ol Samson tore the temple down!" He walked again, mumbling. "Lawd, tell me whut t do! Speak t me, Lawd!" He caught his breath; a dark figure came out of the shadows in front of him. He saw a glint of metal; it was a policeman. He held erect and walked rapidly. Ahll stop, he thought. He wont have t ast me t stop . . . He saw the white face drawing closer. He stopped and waited.

"Put your hands up, nigger!"

"Yessuh."

He lifted his arms. The policeman patted his hips, his sides. His back blazed, but he bit his lips and held still.

"Who you work for?"

"Ahma preacher, suh."

"A *preacher*?"

"Yessuh."

"What you doing out here this time of night?"

"Ah wuz visitin a sick man, a janitah, suh, whut comes t mah church. He works fer Miz Harvey . . ."

"Who?"

"Miz Harvey, suh."

"Never heard of her, and Ive been on this beat for ten years."

"She lives right back there, suh," he said, half-turning and pointing.

"Well, you look all right. You can go on. But keep out of here at night."

"Yessuh."

He was near his own people now. Across a grassy square he could see the top of the round-house glinting dully in the moonlight. The black asphalt turned to cinders and the houses were low, close together, squatting on the ground as though hiding in fear. He saw his church and relaxed. He came to the steps, caught hold of a bannister and rested a moment.

When inside he went quietly down a hall, mounted the stairs, and came to the door of his room. He groped in the dark and felt the bed. He tried to pull off the shirt. It had stuck. He peeled it. Then he eased onto the bed and lay on his stomach. In the darkness his back seemed to take new fire. He went to the kitchen and wet a cloth with cold water. He lay down again with the cloth spread over him. That helped some. Then he began to shake. He was crying.

X

The door creaked.

"Tha yuh, Pa?"

"Son?"

"Good Gawd, wes been lookin all over fer yuh! Where yuh been? Mas worried t death!"

"C mon in, son, n close the do."

"Don yuh wanna light?"

"Naw; close the do."

There was a short silence.

"Whuts the mattah, Pa? Yuh sick?"

"Close the do n set down, son!"

Taylor could hear Jimmy's breathing, then a chair scraping over the floor and the soft rustle of Jimmy's clothes as he sat.

"Whuts the mattah, Pa? Whut happened?"

Taylor stared in the darkness and slowly licked his swollen lips. He wanted to speak, but somehow could not. Then he stiffened, hearing Jimmy rise.

"Set *down*, son!"

"But, Pa . . ."

Fire seethed not only in Taylor's back, but all over, inside and out. It was the fire of shame. The questions that fell from Jimmy's lips burned as much as the whip had. There rose in him a memory of all the times he had given advice, counsel, and guidance to Jimmy. And he wanted to talk to him now as he had in the past. But his impulses were dead-locked. Then suddenly he heard himself speaking, hoarsely, faintly. His voice was like a whisper rising from his whole body.

"They whipped me, son . . ."

"Whipped yuh? Who?"

Jimmy ran to the bed and touched him.

"Son, set *down*!"

Taylor's voice was filled with a sort of tense despair. He felt Jimmy's fingers leaving him slowly. There was a silence in which he could hear only his own breath struggling in his throat.

"Yuh mean the *white* folks?"

Taylor buried his face in his pillow and tried to still the heaving in his chest.

"They beat me, son . . ."

"Ahll git a doctah!"

"Naw!"

"But yuhs hurt!"

"Naw; lock the do! Don let May in here . . ."

"Goddam them white bastards!"

"Set down, son!"

"Who wuz they, Pa?"

"Yuh cant do nothin, son. Yuhll have t wait . . ."

"Wes been waitin too long! All we do is wait, *wait!*"

Jimmy's footsteps scuffed across the floor. Taylor sat up.

"Son?"

"Ahma git mah gun n git Pete n Bob n Joe n Sam! Theyll see they cant do this t us!"

Taylor groped in the darkness; he found Jimmy's shoulders.

"C mon, son! Ahm awright . . ."

"Thas the reason why they kill us! We take everything they put on us! We take everthing! *Everthing!*"

"Yuh cant do nothin *erlone*, Jimmy!"

Jimmy's voice was tense, almost hysterical.

"But we kin *make* em know they cant do this t us widout us doin *some*thing! Aw, hell, Pa! Is we gonna be dogs *all* the time?"

"But theyll kill yuh, son!"

"Somebody *has* t die!"

Taylor wanted to tell Jimmy something, but he could not find the words. What he wanted to say boiled in him, but it seemed too big to come out. He flinched from pain, pressing his fingers to his mouth, holding his breath.

"Pa?"

"Yeah, son?"

"Hadley n Green wuz here t see yuh three-fo times."

"Yeah?"

Jimmy said nothing. Taylor twisted around, trying to see his son's face in the darkness.

"Whut they say, son?"

"Aw, hell! It don mattah . . ."

"Tell me whut they *said!*"

"Ttthey ssaid . . . Aw, Pa, they didn't know!"

"Whut they *say?*"

"They said yuh had done run out on em . . ."

"Run *out?*"

"Everybody wuz astin where yuh wuz," said Jimmy. "Nobody knowed. So they tol em yuh run out. N Brother Smith had the Deacon Board t vote yuh outta the church . . ."

"Vote me *out?*"

"They said they didn't wan yuh fer pastah no mo. It wuz Smith who made em do it. He tol em yuh had planned a demonstration n lef em holdin the bag. He fussed n stormed at em. They thought they wuz doin right . . ."

Taylor lay on his bed of fire in the darkness and cried. He felt Jimmy's fingers again on his face.

"Its awright, Pa. We'll git erlong somehow . . ."

"Seems like Gawds done lef me! Ahd die fer mah people ef Ah only knowed how . . ."

"Pa . . ."

"How come Ah cant never do nothin? All mah life Ah done tried n cant do nothin! *Nothin!*"

"Its awright, Pa!"

"Ah done lived all mah life on mah knees, a-beggin n a-pleadin wid the white folks. N all they gimme wuz crumbs! All they did wuz kick me! N then they come wida gun n ast me t give mah own soul! N ef Ah so much as talk lika man they try t kill me . . ."

He buried his face in the pillow, trying to sink himself into something so deeply that he could never feel again. He heard Jimmy turning the key in the lock.

"Son!"

Again he ran to Jimmy and held him.

"Don do tha, son!"

"Thingsll awways be like this less we *fight!*"

"Set down, son! Yo po ol pas *a-beggin* yuh to set down!"

He pulled Jimmy back to the bed. But even then it did not seem he could speak as he wanted to. He felt what he wanted to say, but it was elusive and hard to formulate.

"Son . . ."

"Ah ain gonna live this way, Pa!"

He groped for Jimmy's shoulders in the darkness and squeezed them till the joints of his fingers cracked. And when words came they seemed to be tearing themselves from him, as though they were being pushed upward like hot lava out of a mountain from deep down.

"Don be a fool, son! Don thow yo life erway! We cant do nothin erlone."

"But theys gonna treat us this way as long as we *let* em!"

He had to make Jimmy understand; for it seemed that in making him understand, in telling him, he, too, would understand.

"We gotta git wid the *people*, son. Too long we done tried t do this thing our way n when we failed we wanted t run out n pay-off the white folks. Then they kill us up like flies. Its the *people*, son! Wes too much erlone this way! Wes los when wes erlone! Wes gotta be wid our folks . . ."

"But theys killin us!"

"N theyll keep on killin us less we learn how t fight! Son, its the people we mus git wid us! Wes empty n weak this way! The reason we cant do nothin is cause wes so much erlone . . ."

"Them Reds wuz right," said Jimmy.

"Ah dunno," said Taylor. "But let nothin come tween yuh n *yo* people. Even the Reds cant do nothin ef yuh lose yo people . . ." Fire burned him as he talked, and he talked as though trying to escape it. "Membah whut Ah tol yuh prayer wuz, son?"

There was silence, then Jimmy answered slowly:

"Yuh mean lettin Gawd be so real in yo life tha everthing yuh do is cause of Im?"

"Yeah, but its different now, son. Its the *people!* Theys the ones whut mus be real t us! Gawds wid the people! N the peoples gotta be real as Gawd t us! We cant hep ourselves er the people when wes erlone. Ah been wrong erbout a lotta things Ah tol yuh, son. Ah tol yuh them things cause Ah though they wuz right. Ah tol yuh t work hard n climb t the top. Ah tol yuh folks would lissen t yuh then. But they wont, son! All the will, all the strength, all the power, all the numbahs is in the people! Yuh cant live by yoself! When they beat me tonight, they beat *me* . . . There wuznt nothing Ah could do but lay there n hate n pray n cry . . . Ah couldnt *feel* mah people, Ah couldnt *see* mah people, Ah couldnt *hear* mah people . . . All Ah could feel wuz tha whip cuttin mah blood out . . ."

In the darkness he imagined he could see Jimmy's face as he had seen it a thousand times, looking eagerly, his eyes staring before him, fashioning his words into images, into life. He hoped Jimmy was doing that now.

"Ahll awways hate them bastards! Ahll *aw*ways hate em!"

"Theres other ways, son."

"Yuhs sick, Pa . . ."

"Wes all sick, son. Wes gotta think erbout the people, night n day, think erbout em so hard tha our po selves is fergotten . . . Whut they suffer is whut Ah suffered las night when they whipped me. Wes gotta keep the people wid us."

Jimmy was silent. A soft knock came at the door.


## XI

"Dan!"

"Thas ma," said Jimmy.

Taylor heard Jimmy rise to his feet; he gripped Jimmy's hands.

"Please, Pa! Let her come in n hep yuh!"

"Naw."

"Dan!"

Jimmy broke from him; he heard the key turn in the lock. The door opened.

"Dan! Fer Gawds sake, whuts the mattah?"

Jimmy switched on the light. Taylor lay blinking at May's anxious face. He felt shame again, knowing that he should not feel it, but feeling it anyway. He turned over and buried his face in his hands.

"Dan!"

She ran and knelt at the side of the bed.

"They tried t kill im, Ma! They beat im!" said Jimmy.

"Ah knowed them white folks wuz gonna do something like this! Ah knowed it," sobbed May.

Taylor sat up.

"Yuh be still! Lay down!" said May. She pushed him back onto the bed.

"Cant yuh do something fer im, Ma? Hes sufferin tha way."

Taylor heard May leave the room and come back.

"Hol still, Dan. This ain gonna hurt yuh . . ."

He felt warm water laving him, then something cool that smelled of oil. He heard Jimmy moving to and fro, getting things for May. When his back was dressed he felt the bed sink as May sat on the edge of it. The heavy odors of violets and magnolias came to him; he was slowly coming back to the world again. He was the same man, but he was coming back somehow changed. He wondered at the strange peace that seeped into his mind and body there in the room with May and Jimmy, with the white folks far off in the darkness.

"Feel bettah, Dan?"

"Ahm awright."

"Yuh hongry?"

"Naw."

He wanted to talk to Jimmy again, to tell him about the black people. But he could not think of words that would say what he wanted to say. He would tell it somehow later on. He began to toss, moving jerkily, more now from restlessness of mind than from the dying fire that still lingered in his body.

## XII

Suddenly the doorbell pealed. Taylor turned and saw May and Jimmy looking at each other.

"Somebody at the do," said Jimmy in a tense voice.

"Yuh reckon they white folks?" asked May.

"Yuh bettah go down, Jimmy," said Taylor.

"Ef its any white folks tell em Dans out," said May.

Jimmy's footsteps died away on the stairs. A door slammed. There were faint sound of voices. Footsteps echoed, came on the stairs, grew loud. Taylor knew that more than one person was coming up. He lifted himself and sat on the edge of the bed.

"Dan, yuh cant git up! Yuhll make yoself sick!"

He ignored her. The door opened and Jimmy ran in.

"Its Brother Bonds, Pa!"

Bonds stood in the doorway with his head wrapped in blood-stained bandages. His face twitched and his eyes stared at something beyond the walls of the room, as though his attention had been riveted once and for always upon one fixed spot.

"Whut happened, Brother?" asked Taylor.

Bonds stared, dazed, with hunched and beaten shoulders. Then he sank to the floor, sobbing softly:

"They beat me! They beat mah chillun! They beat mah wife! They beat us all cause Ah tol em t git outta mah house! Lawd, how long Yuh gonna let em treat us this way? How long Yuh gonna let em make us suffer?"

May sobbed. Jimmy ran out of the room. Taylor caught him on the stairs.

"Don be a fool, boy! Yuh c mon back here, *now!*"

Jimmy flopped on the edge of a chair and mumbled to himself. The room was quiet save for the rustle of tree leaves that drifted in from the outside and the sound of Bonds sobbing on the floor. As Taylor stood his own suffering was drowned in a sense of widening horror. There was in his mind a vivid picture of all the little dingy huts where black men and women were crouched, afraid to stir out of doors. Bonds stopped crying and looked at Taylor; again that sense of shame spread over Taylor, inside and out. It stirred him to speech.

"Who else they beat, Brother?"

"Seem like everybody, Reveren! Them two Commoonists got beat something terrible n they put em in jail. N Ah heard they kilt one black man whut tried t fight back. They ketchin everbody they kin on the streets n lettin em have it. They ridin up n down in cars . . ."

Jimmy cursed. The doorbell pealed again.

"Git me a shirt, May!"

"Dan, yuh ain able t do nothin!"

The doorbell pealed again, then again. Taylor started toward the dresser; but May got there before he did and gave him a shirt.

"Dan, be careful!"

"C mon downstairs, Brother Bonds. N yuh, too, Jimmy," said Taylor.


## XIII

The church's waiting room was full. Black men and women sat and stood, saying nothing, waiting. Arms were in slings; necks were wrapped in white cloth; legs were bound in blood-stained rags.

"LOOK AT WHUT YUH DONE DONE!" a voice bawled.

It was Deacon Smith. Taylor's eyes went from face to face; he knew them all. Every Sunday they sat in the pews of his church, praying, singing, and trusting the God he gave them. The mute eyes and silent lips pinned him to a fiery spot of loneliness. He wanted to protest that loneliness, wanted to break it down; but he did not know how. No parables sprang to his lips now to give form and meaning to his words; alone and naked, he stood ashamed. Jimmy came through the door and placed his hand on his shoulder.

"Its daylight, Pa. The folks is gatherin in the playgroun; theys waitin fer yuh . . ."

Taylor went into the yard with the crowd at his heels. It was broad daylight and the sun shone. The men in their overalls and the women with children stood about him on all sides, silent. A fat black woman elbowed her way in and faced him.

"Well, Reveren, we done got beat up. Now, is we gonna march?"

"Yuh wanna march?" asked Taylor.

"It don make no difference wid me," she said. "Them white folks cant do no mo than theys aweady done."

The crowd chimed in.

"N Gawd knows they cant!"

"Ahll go ef the nex one goes!"

"Ah gotta die sometime, so Ah jus as waal die now!"

"They cant kill us but once!"

"Ahm tired anyhow! Ah don care!"

"The white folks says theys gonna meet us at the park!"

Taylor turned to Jimmy.

"Son, git yo boys together n tell em t roun up everbody!"

"Yessuh!"

May was pulling at his sleeve.

"Dan, yuh *cant* do this . . ."

Deacon Smith pushed his way in and faced him.

"Yuhll never set foot in a church ergin ef yuh lead them po black folks downtown t be killed!"

The crowd surged.

"Ain nobody leadin us nowhere!"

"We goin ourselves!"

"Is we gonna march, Reveren?"

"Yeah; soon as the crowd gits together," said Taylor.

"Ain nobody t blame but yuh ef yuh carry em t their *death!*" warned Deacon Smith.

"How come yuh don shut yo old big mouth n let the Reveren talk?" asked the fat woman.

"Sistah, Ah got as much right t speak as yuh!"

"Well, don speak to me, yuh hear!"

"Somebody has t say something when ain *nobody* got no sense!"

"Man, don yuh tell me Ah ain got no sense!"

"Yuh sho don ack like it!"

"Ah got as much sense as yuh got!"

"How come yuh don use it?"

The fat sister slapped Deacon Smith straight across his face. Taylor ran between them and pried them apart. The crowd surged and screamed.

"Ef he touches Sistah Henry ergin Ahll kill im!"

"He ain got no bisness talkin tha way t a woman!"

Taylor dragged the fat woman toward the gate. The crowd followed, yelling. He stopped and faced them. They circled around, tightly, asking questions. May had hold of his sleeve. Jimmy came to him.

"Pa, theys comin!"

Taylor turned and walked across the yard with the crowd following. He took two planks and laid them upon the ends of two saw-horses and made a solid platform. He climbed up and stood in the quiet sunshine. He did not know exactly what it was he wanted to say, but whatever it was he would say it when they were quiet. He felt neither fear nor joy, just an humble confidence in himself, as though he were standing before his mirror in his room. Then he was conscious that they were quiet;

he took one swift look over their heads, heads that stretched away to the street and beyond, a solid block of black, silent faces; then he looked down, not to the dust, but just a slight lowering of eyes, as though he were no longer looking at them, but at something within himself.

"Sistahs n Brothers, they tell me the Deacon Boards done voted me outta the church. Ef thas awright wid yuh, its awright wid me. The white folks says Ahma bad nigger n they don wanna have nothin else t do wid me. N thas awright, too. But theres one thing Ah wanna say. Ah knows how yuh feel erbout bein hongry. N how yuh feel is no different from how Ah feel. Yuh been waitin a week fer me t say whut yuh ought t do. Yuh been wonderin how come Ah didnt tell yuh whut yuh oughta do. Waal . . ."

He paused and looked over the silent crowd; then again his eyes, his gaze, went inward.

"Sistahs n Brothers, the reason Ah didnt say nothin is cause Ah didnt know *whut* t say. N the only reason Ahm speakin now is cause Ah *do* know. Ah know whut t do . . ."

He paused again, swallowing. The same feeling which had gripped him so hard last night when he had been talking to Jimmy seized him. He opened his mouth to continue; his lips moved several times before words came; and when they did come they fell with a light and hoarse whisper.

"Sistahs n Brothers, las night the white folks took me out t the woods. They took me out cause Ah tol em yuh wuz hongry. They ast me t tell yuh not t march, n Ah tol em Ah wouldnt. Then they beat me. They tied me t a tree n beat me till Ah couldnt feel no mo. They beat me cause Ah wouldnt tell yuh not t ast fer bread. They said yuhd blieve everthing Ah said. All the time they wuz hepin me, all the time they been givin me favors, they wuz doin it sos *they* could tell *me* t tell *yuh* how t ack! Sistahs n Brothers, as Gawds mah judge, Ah thought Ah wuz doin right when Ah did tha. Ah thought Ah wuz doin right when Ah tol yuh t do the things they said. N cause Ah wouldnt do it this time, they tied me t a tree n beat me till mah blood run . . ."

Mist covered his eyes. He heard the crowd murmuring; but he did not care if they were murmuring for or against him; he wanted to finish, to say what he had been trying so hard to say for many long hours.

"Sistahs n Brothers, they whipped me n made me take the name of *Gawd* in vain! They made me say mah prayers n beat me n laughed! They beat me till Ah couldnt membah nothin! All las night Ah wuz lyin stretched out on the groun wid mah back burnin . . . All this mawnin befo day Ah wuz limpin thu white folks streets. Sistahs n Brothers, Ah *know* now! Ah done seen the *sign!* Wes gotta git together. Ah know whut yo life is! Ah done felt it! Its *fire!* Its like

the fire tha burned me las night! Its sufferin! Its hell! Ah cant bear
this fire erlone! Ah know now whut t do! Wes gotta git close t one
ernother! Gawds done spoke! Gawds done sent His sign. Now its
fer us t *ack . . .*"

The crowd started yelling:

"We'll go ef yuh go!"

"Wes ready!"

"The white folks says theyll meet us at the park!"

The fat black woman started singing:

> *"So the sign of the fire by night*
> *N the sign of the cloud by day*
> *A-hoverin oer*
> *Jus befo*
> *As we journey on our way . . ."*

Taylor got down. He moved with the crowd slowly toward the
street. May went with him, looking, wondering, saying nothing.
Jimmy was at his side. They sang as they marched. More joined along
the way. When they reached the park that separated the white district
from the black, the poor whites were waiting. Taylor trembled when
he saw them join, swelling the mass that moved toward the town. He
looked ahead and saw black and white marching; he looked behind and
saw black and white marching. And still they sang:

*"So the sign of the fire by night . . ."*

They turned into the street that led to town.

*"N the sign of the cloud by day . . ."*

Talor saw blue-coated policemen standing lined along the curb.

*"A-hoverin oer . . ."*

Taylor felt himself moving between the silent lines of blue-coated
white men, moving with a sea of placards and banners, moving under
the sun like a pregnant cloud. He said to himself, They ain gonna
bother us! They bettah *not* bother us . . .

*"Jus befo . . ."*

Across a valley, in front of him, he could see the buildings of the
town sprawled on a hill.

*"As we journey on our way . . ."*

They were tramping on pavement now. And the blue-coated men
stood still and silent. Taylor saw Deacon Smith standing on the curb,
and Smith's face merged with the faces of the others, meaningless, lost.
Ahead was the City Hall, white and clean in the sunshine. The autos
stopped at the street corners while the crowd passed; and as they entered
the downtown section people massed quietly on the sidewalks. Then

the crowd began to slow, barely moving. Taylor looked ahead and wondered what was about to happen; he wondered without fear; as though whatever would or could happen could not hurt this many-limbed, many-legged, many-handed crowd that was he. He felt May clinging to his sleeve. Jimmy was peering ahead. A policeman came running up to him.

"You Taylor?"

"Yessuh," he said quietly, his gaze straight and steady.

"The mayors down front; he wants to see you!"

"Tell im Ahm back here," said Taylor.

"But he wants to see the leader up front!"

"Tell im Ahm back here," said Taylor again.

The man hesitated, then left; they waited quiet, still. Then the crowd parted. Taylor saw Mayor Bolton hurrying toward him, his face beet-red.

"Dan, tell your people not to make any trouble! We dont want any trouble, Dan . . ."

"There ain gonna be no trouble, yo Honah!"

"Well, tell them they can get food if they go back home, peacefully . . ."

"Yuh tell em, yo Honah!"

They looked at each other for a moment. Then the mayor turned and walked back. Taylor saw him mount the rear seat of an auto and lift his trembling hands high above the crowd, asking for silence, his face a pasty white.

A baptism of clean joy swept over Taylor. He kept his eyes on the sea of black and white faces. The song swelled louder and vibrated through him. This is the way! he thought. Gawd ain no lie! He ain no lie! His eyes grew wet with tears, blurring his vision: the sky trembled; the buildings wavered as if about to topple; and the earth shook . . . He mumbled out loud, exultingly:

*"Freedom belongs t the strong!"*

# William Maxwell (1908–      )

AFTER GRADUATING from the State University in Illinois, where he was born, and receiving a Master's degree from Harvard, William Maxwell taught for a short time at the latter institution. He became an editor at *The New Yorker* where he has remained ever since. He was twenty-two years old when his first book, *Bright Center of Heaven* (1934), was published. This novel was followed by another, *They Came Like Swallows* (1937). The utter charm and sensitivity of his *The Folded Leaf* (1945), two boys developing through adolescence to maturity, endeared the author's writing permanently to a wide reading public. The titles of his two later novels are *Time Will Darken It* (1948) and *The Chateau* (1961). Mr. Maxwell has also published a number of short stories, a children's book, and a book about fiction.

William Maxwell has written a lovely idyll in "The Patterns of Love." Its serenity is an interesting contrast to the violent scenes and turbulent emotions in so many modern American short stories. The utter simplicity of the writing is deceptive and quite beyond the abilities of many an author. Can you imagine Norman Mailer, for instance, excellent writer though he is, being able to achieve a story like this? And what happens here? Nothing really and at the same time an awful lot: a pleasant weekend in the country with some nice people, and the contentment that comes with a deep breath of sweet fresh air.


# *The Patterns of Love*


KATE TALBOT's bantam rooster, awakened by the sudden appearance of the moon from behind a cloud on a white June night, began to crow. There were three bantams — a cock and two hens — and their roost was in a tree just outside the guest-room windows. The guest room was on the first floor and the Talbots' guest that weekend was a young man by the name of Arnold, a rather light sleeper. He got up and closed the windows and went back to bed. In the sealed room he slept, but was awakened at frequent intervals until daylight Saturday morning.

Arnold had been coming to the Talbots' place in Wilton sometime during the spring or early summer for a number of years. His visits were, for the children, one of a thousand seasonal events that could be counted on, less exciting than the appearance of the first robin or the arrival of violets in the marsh at the foot of the Talbots' hill but akin to them. Sometimes Duncan, the Talbots' older boy, who for a long time was under the impression that Arnold came to see *him*, slept in the guest room when Arnold was there. Last year, George, Duncan's younger brother, had been given that privilege. This time, Mrs. Talbot, knowing how talkative the boys were when they awoke in the morning, had left Arnold to himself.

When he came out of his room, Mrs. Talbot and George, the apple of her eye, were still at breakfast. George was six, small and delicate and very blond, not really interested in food at any time, and certainly not now, when there was a guest in the house. He was in his pajamas and a pink quilted bathrobe. He smiled at Arnold with his large and very gentle eyes and said, "Did you miss me?"

"Yes, of course," Arnold said. "I woke up and there was the other bed, flat and empty. Nobody to talk to while I looked at the ceiling. Nobody to watch me shave."

George was very pleased that his absence had been felt. "What is your favorite color?" he asked.

"Red," Arnold said, without having to consider.

"Mine, too," George said, and his face became so illuminated with pleasure at this coincidence that for a moment he looked angelic.

"No matter how much we disagree about other things," Arnold said, "we'll always have that in common, won't we?"

"Yes," George said.

"You'd both better eat your cereal," Mrs. Talbot said.

Arnold looked at her while she was pouring his coffee and wondered if there wasn't something back of her remark — jealousy, perhaps. Mrs. Talbot was a very soft-hearted woman, but for some reason she seemed to be ashamed — or perhaps afraid — to let other people know it. She took refuge continually behind a dry humor. There was probably very little likelihood that George would be as fond of anyone else as he was of his mother, Arnold decided, for many years to come. There was no real reason for her to be jealous.

"Did the bantams keep you awake?" she asked.

Arnold shook his head.

"Something tells me you're lying," Mrs. Talbot said. "John didn't wake up, but he felt his responsibilities as a host even so. He cried 'Oh!' in his sleep every time a bantam crowed. You'll have to put up with them on Kate's account. She loves them more than her life."

Excluded from the conversation of the grownups, George finished his cereal and ate part of a soft-boiled egg. Then he asked to be excused and, with pillows and pads which had been brought in from the garden furniture the night before, he made a train right across the dining-room floor. The cook had to step over it when she brought a fresh pot of coffee, and Mrs. Talbot and Arnold had to do likewise when they went out through the dining-room door to look at the bantams. There were only two — the cock and one hen — walking around under the Japanese cherry tree on the terrace. Kate was leaning out of an upstairs window, watching them fondly.

"Have you made your bed?" Mrs. Talbot asked.

The head withdrew.

"Kate is going to a houseparty," Mrs. Talbot said, looking at the bantams. "A sort of houseparty. She's going to stay all night at Mary Sherman's house and there are going to be some boys and they're going to dance to the victrola."

"How old is she, for heaven's sake?" Arnold asked.

"Thirteen," Mrs. Talbot said. "She had her hair cut yesterday and it's too short. It doesn't look right, so I have to do something about it."

"White of egg?" Arnold asked.

"How did you know that?" Mrs. Talbot asked in surprise.

"I remembered it from the last time," Arnold said. "I remembered it because it sounded so drastic."

"It only works with blonds," Mrs. Talbot said. "Will you be able to entertain yourself for a while?"

"Easily," Arnold said. "I saw *Anna Karenina* in the library and I think I'll take that and go up to the little house."

"Maybe I'd better come with you," Mrs. Talbot said.

The little house was a one-room studio halfway up the hill, about a hundred feet from the big house, with casement windows on two sides and a Franklin stove. It have been built several years before, after Mrs. Talbot had read *A Room of One's Own*, and by now it had a slightly musty odor which included lingering traces of wood smoke.

"Hear the wood thrush?" Arnold asked, as Mrs. Talbot threw open the windows for him. They both listened.

"No," she said. "All birds sound alike to me."

"Listen," he said.

This time there was no mistaking it — the liquid notes up and then down the same scale.

"Oh, that," she said. "Yes, I love that," and went off to wash Kate's hair.

From time to time Arnold raised his head from the book he was reading and heard not only the wood thrush but also Duncan and George, quarrelling in the meadow. George's voice was shrill and unhappy and sounded as if he were on the verge of tears. Both boys appeared at the window eventually and asked for permission to come in. The little house was out of bounds to them. Arnold nodded. Duncan, who was nine, crawled in without much difficulty, but George had to be hoisted. No sooner were they inside than they began to fight over a wooden gun which had been broken and mended and was rightly George's, it seemed, though Duncan had it and refused to give it up.

He refused to give it up one moment, and the next moment, after a sudden change of heart, pressed it upon George — *forced* George to take it, actually, for by that time George was more concerned about the Talbots' dog, who also wanted to come in.

The dog was a Great Dane, very mild but also very enormous. He answered to the name of Satan. Once Satan was admitted to the little house, it became quite full and rather noisy, but John Talbot appeared and sent the dog out and made the children leave Arnold in peace. They left as they had come, by the window. Arnold watched them and was touched by the way Duncan turned and helped George, who was too small to jump. Also by the way George accepted this help. It was as if their hostility had two faces and one of them was the face of love. Cain and Abel, Arnold thought, and the wood thrush. All immortal.

John Talbot lingered outside the little house. Something had been burrowing in the lily-of-the-valley bed, he said, and had also uprooted several lady slippers. Arnold suggested that it might be moles.

"More likely a rat," John Talbot said, and his eyes wandered to a two-foot espaliered pear tree. "That pear tree," he said, "we put in over a year ago."

Mrs. Talbot joined them. She had shampooed not only Kate's hair but her own as well.

"It's still alive," John Talbot said, staring at the pear tree, "but it doesn't put out any leaves."

"I should think it would be a shock to a pear tree to be espaliered," Mrs. Talbot said. "Kate's ready to go."

They all piled into the station wagon and took Kate to her party. Her too-short blond hair looked quite satisfactory after the egg shampoo, and Mrs. Talbot had made a boutonniere out of a pink geranium and some little blue and white flowers for Kate to wear on her coat. She got out of the car with her suitcase and waved at them from the front steps of the house.

"I hope she has a good time," John Talbot said uneasily as he shifted gears. "It's her first dance with boys. It would be terrible if she didn't have any partners." In his eyes there was a vague threat toward the boys who, in their young callowness, might not appreciate his daughter.

"Kate always has a good time," Mrs. Talbot said. "By the way, have you seen both of the bantam hens today?"

"No," John Talbot said.

"One of them is missing," Mrs. Talbot said.

One of the things that impressed Arnold whenever he stayed with the Talbots was the number and variety of animals they had. Their place was not a farm, after all, but merely a big white brick house in the country, and yet they usually had a dog and a cat, kittens, rabbits, and chickens, all actively involved in the family life. This summer the Talbots weren't able to go in and out by the front door, because a phoebe had built a nest in the porch light. They used the dining-room door instead, and were careful not to leave the porch light on more than a minute or two, lest the eggs be cooked. Arnold came upon some turtle food in his room, and when he asked about it, Mrs. Talbot informed him that there were turtles in the guest room, too. He never came upon the turtles.

The bantams were new this year, and so were the two very small ducklings that at night were put in a paper carton in the sewing room, with an electric light bulb to keep them warm. In the daytime they hopped in and out of a saucer of milk on the terrace. One of them was called Mr. Rochester because of his distinguished air. The other had no name.

All the while that Mrs. Talbot was making conversation with Arnold, after lunch, she kept her eyes on the dog, who, she explained, was jealous of the ducklings. Once his great head swooped down and he pretended to take a nip at them. A nip would have been enough. Mrs. Talbot spoke to him sharply and he turned his head away in shame.

"They probably smell the way George did when he first came home from the hospital," she said.

"What did George smell like?" Arnold asked.

"Sweetish, actually. Actually awful."

"Was Satan jealous of George when he was a baby?"

"Frightfully," Mrs. Talbot said. "Call Satan!" she shouted to her husband, who was up by the little house. He had found a rat hole near the ravaged lady slippers and was setting a trap. He called the dog, and the dog went bounding off, devotion in every leap.

While Mrs. Talbot was telling Arnold how they found Satan at the baby's crib one night, Duncan, who was playing only a few yards away with George, suddenly, and for no apparent reason, made his younger brother cry. Mrs. Talbot got up and separated them.

"I wouldn't be surprised if it wasn't time for your nap, George," she said, but he was not willing to let go of even a small part of the day. He wiped his tears away with his fist and ran from her. She ran after him, laughing, and caught him at the foot of the terrace.

Duncan wandered off into a solitary world of his own, and Arnold, after yawning twice, got up and went into the house. Stretched out on the bed in his room, with the Venetian blinds closed, he began to compare the life of the Talbots with his own well-ordered but childless and animalless life in town. Everywhere they go, he thought, they leave tracks behind them, like people walking in the snow. Paths crisscrossing, lines that are perpetually meeting: the mother's loving pursuit of her youngest, the man's love for his daughter, the dog's love for the man, the two boys' preoccupation with each other. Wheels and diagrams, Arnold said to himself. The patterns of love.

That night Arnold was much less bothered by the crowing, which came to him dimly, through dreams. When he awoke finally and was fully awake, he was conscious of the silence and the sun shining in his eyes. His watch had stopped and it was later than he thought. The Talbots had finished breakfast and the Sunday *Times* was waiting beside his place at the table. While he was eating, John Talbot came in and sat down for a minute, across the table. He had been out early that morning, he said, and had found a chipmunk in the rat trap and also a nest with three bantam eggs in it. The eggs were cold.

He was usually a very quiet, self-contained man. This was the first time Arnold had ever seen him disturbed about anything. "I don't know how we're going to tell Kate," he said. "She'll be very upset."

Kate came home sooner than they expected her, on the bus. She came up the driveway, lugging her suitcase.

"Did you have a good time?" Mrs. Talbot called to her from the terrace.

"Yes," she said, "I had a beautiful time."

Arnold looked at the two boys, expecting them to blurt out the tragedy as soon as Kate put down her suitcase, but they didn't. It was her father who told her, in such a roundabout way that she didn't seem to understand at all what he was saying. Mrs. Talbot interrupted him with the flat facts; the bantam hen was not on her nest and therefore, in all probability, had been killed, maybe by the rat.

Kate went into the house. The others remained on the terrace. The dog didn't snap at the ducklings, though his mind was on them still, and the two boys didn't quarrel. In spite of the patterns on which they seem so intent, Arnold thought, what happens to one of them happens to all. They are helplessly involved in Kate's loss.

At noon other guests arrived, two families with children. There was a picnic, with hot dogs and bowls of salad, cake, and wine, out under the grape arbor. When the guests departed, toward the end of the afternoon, the family came together again on the terrace. Kate was lying on the ground, on her stomach, with her face resting on her arms, her head practically in the ducklings' saucer of milk. Mrs. Talbot, who had stretched out on the garden chaise longue, discovered suddenly that Mr. Rochester was missing. She sat up in alarm and cried, "Where is he?"

"Down my neck," Kate said.

The duck emerged from her crossed arms. He crawled around them and climbed up on the back of her neck. Kate smiled. The sight of the duck's tiny downy head among her pale ash-blond curls made them all burst out laughing. The cloud that had been hanging over the household evaporated into bright sunshine, and Arnold seized that moment to glance surreptitiously at his watch.

They all went to the train with him, including the dog. At the last moment Mrs. Talbot, out of a sudden perception of his lonely life, tried to give him some radishes, but he refused them. When he stepped out of the car at the station, the boys were arguing and were with difficulty persuaded to say goodbye to him. He watched the station wagon drive away and then stood listening for the sound of the wood thrush. But, of course, in the center of South Norwalk there was no such sound.

# Carson McCullers (1917–1967)

In 1936 Sylvia Chatfield Bates, creative writing teacher at New York University, sent *Story Magazine* a manuscript by a teen-age girl in her class with a wildly enthusiastic letter predicting a magnificent literary future for her. Professor Bates was a good prophet, for the girl from Columbus, Georgia, was Carson McCullers. The story, "Wunderkind," was published and became a cornerstone for many short stories and novels. Her first novel, *The Heart Is a Lonely Hunter* (1940), occupies a permanent place in American literature. Another, *The Member of the Wedding* (1946), was equally successful as a novel and a play. "The Ballad of the Sad Café" (1943) was dramatized by Edward Albee in 1963. A collection of her short stories was published under the same title.

Many a reader feels as if he had been in a trance on finishing this strange, hypnotic story of strange Miss Amelia, Marvin Macy, an ex-convict, and Cousin Lymon, a hunchbacked dwarf, entangled in a love-hate web. As a background the sluggish Southern mill town and its slow inhabitants add to the illusory effect. It is a macabre lullaby McCullers sings here even at the story's most violent moments. All of the author's work is Southern either in locale or mood, yet she is not to be classified as "regional," so universal is its appeal.

# *The Ballad of the Sad Café*

THE TOWN itself is dreary; not much is there except the cotton mill, the two-room houses where the workers live, a few peach trees, a church with two colored windows, and a miserable main street only a hundred yards long. On Saturdays the tenants from the near-by farms come in for a day of talk and trade. Otherwise the town is lonesome, sad, and like a place that is far off and estranged from all other places in the world. The nearest train stop is Society City, and the Greyhound and White Bus Lines use the Forks Falls Road which is three miles away. The winters here are short and raw, the summers white with glare and fiery hot.

If you walk along the main street on an August afternoon there is nothing whatsoever to do. The largest building, in the very center of the town, is boarded up completely and leans so far to the right that it seems bound to collapse at any minute. The house is very old. There is about it a curious, cracked look that is very puzzling until you suddenly realize that at one time, and long ago, the right side of the front porch had been painted, and part of the wall — but the painting was left unfinished and one portion of the house is darker and dingier than the other. The building looks completely deserted. Nevertheless, on the second floor there is one window which is not boarded; sometimes in the late afternoon when the heat is at its worst a hand will slowly open the shutter and a face will look down on the town. It is a face like the terrible dim faces known in dreams — sexless and white, with two gray crossed eyes which are turned inward so sharply that they seem to be exchanging with each other one long and secret gaze of grief. The face lingers at the window for an hour or so, then the shutters are closed once more, and as likely as not there will not be another soul to be seen along the main street. These August afternoons — when your shift is finished there is absolutely nothing to do; you might as well walk down to the Forks Falls Road and listen to the chain gang.

However, here in this very town there was once a café. And this old boarded-up house was unlike any other place for many miles around. There were tables with cloths and paper napkins, colored streamers from the electric fans, great gatherings on Saturday nights. The owner of the place was Miss Amelia Evans. But the person most responsible for the success and gaiety of the place was a hunchback called Cousin Lymon. One other person had a part in the story of this café — he was the former husband of Miss Amelia, a terrible character who returned to the town after a long term in the penitentiary, caused ruin, and then went on his way again. The café has long since been closed, but it is still remembered.

The place was not always a café. Miss Amelia inherited the building from her father, and it was a store that carried mostly feed, guano, and staples such as meal and snuff. Miss Amelia was rich. In addition to the store she operated a still three miles back in the swamp, and ran out the best liquor in the county. She was a dark, tall woman with bones and muscles like a man. Her hair was cut short and brushed back from the forehead, and there was about her sunburned face a tense, haggard quality. She might have been a handsome woman if, even then, she was not slightly cross-eyed. There were those who would have courted her, but Miss Amelia cared nothing for the love of men and was a solitary person. Her marriage had been unlike any other marriage ever contracted in this county — it was a strange and dangerous marriage, lasting only for ten days, that left the whole town wondering and shocked. Except for this queer marriage Miss Amelia had lived her life alone. Often she spent whole nights back in her shed in the swamp, dressed in overalls and gum boots, silently guarding the low fire of the still.

With all things which could be made by the hands Miss Amelia prospered. She sold chitterlins and sausage in the town near-by. On fine autumn days she ground sorghum, and the syrup from her vats was dark golden and delicately flavored. She built the brick privy behind her store in only two weeks and was skilled in carpentering. It was only with people that Miss Amelia was not at ease. People, unless they are nilly-willy or very sick, cannot be taken into the hands and changed overnight to something more worthwhile and profitable. So that the only use that Miss Amelia had for other people was to make money out of them. And in this she succeeded. Mortgages on crops and property, a sawmill, money in the bank — she was the richest woman for miles around. She would have been rich as a congressman if it were not for her one great failing, and that was her passion for lawsuits and the courts. She would involve herself in long and bitter litigation over just a trifle. It was said that if Miss Amelia so much as stumbled over a rock in the road she would glance around instinctively as though looking for something to sue about it. Aside from these lawsuits she lived a steady life and every day was very much like the day that had gone before. With the exception of her ten-day marriage, nothing happened to change this until the spring of the year that Miss Amelia was thirty years old.

It was toward midnight on a soft quiet evening in April. The sky was the color of a blue swamp iris, the moon clear and bright. The crops that spring promised well and in the past weeks the mill had run a night shift. Down by the creek the square brick factory was yellow with light, and there was the faint, steady hum of the looms. It was such a night when it is good to hear from faraway, across the dark fields, the slow song of a Negro on his way to make love. Or when it is pleasant to sit quietly and pick a guitar, or simply to rest alone and think of nothing at all. The street that evening was deserted, but Miss Amelia's store was lighted and on the porch outside there were five people. One of these was Stumpy MacPhail, a foreman with a red face and dainty, purplish hands. On the top step were two boys in overalls, the Rainey twins — both of them lanky and slow, with white hair and sleepy green eyes. The other man was Henry Macy, a shy and timid person with gentle manners and nervous ways, who sat on the edge of the bottom step. Miss Amelia herself stood leaning against the side of the open door, her feet crossed in their big swamp boots, patiently untying knots in a rope she had come across. They had not talked for a long time.

One of the twins, who had been looking down the empty road, was the first to speak. "I see something coming," he said.

"A calf got loose," said his brother.

The approaching figure was still too distant to be clearly seen. The moon made dim, twisted shadows of the blossoming peach trees along the side of the road. In the air the odor of blossoms and sweet spring grass mingled with the warm, sour smell of the near-by lagoon.

"No. It's somebody's youngun," said Stumpy MacPhail.

Miss Amelia watched the road in silence. She had put down her rope and was fingering the straps of her overalls with her brown bony hand. She scowled, and a dark lock of hair fell down on her forehead. While they were waiting there, a dog from one of the houses down the road began a wild, hoarse howl that continued until a voice called out and hushed him. It was not until the figure was quite close, within the range of the yellow light from the porch, that they saw clearly what had come.

The man was a stranger, and it is rare that a stranger enters the town on foot at that hour. Besides, the man was a hunchback. He was scarcely more than four feet tall and he wore a ragged, dusty coat that reached only to his knees. His crooked little legs seemed too thin to carry the weight of his great warped chest and the hump that sat on his shoulders. He had a very large head, with deep-set blue eyes and a sharp little mouth. His face was both soft and sassy — at the moment his pale skin was yellowed by dust and there were lavender shadows beneath his eyes. He carried a lopsided old suitcase which was tied with a rope.

"Evening," said the hunchback, and he was out of breath.

Miss Amelia and the men on the porch neither answered his greeting nor spoke. They only looked at him.

"I am hunting for Miss Amelia Evans."

Miss Amelia pushed back her hair from her forehead and raised her chin. "How come?"

"Because I am kin to her," the hunchback said.

The twins and Stumpy MacPhail looked up at Miss Amelia.

"That's me," she said. "How do you mean 'kin'?"

"Because — " the hunchback began. He looked uneasy, almost as though he was about to cry. He rested the suitcase on the bottom step, but did not take his hand from the handle. "My mother was Fanny Jesup and she come from Cheehaw. She left Cheehaw some thirty years ago when she married her first husband. I remember hearing her tell how she had a half-sister named Martha. And back in Cheehaw today they tell me that was your mother."

Miss Amelia listened with her head turned slightly aside. She ate her Sunday dinners by herself; her place was never crowded with a flock of relatives, and she claimed kin with no one. She had had a great-aunt who owned the livery stable in Cheehaw, but that aunt was now dead. Aside from her there was only one double first cousin who lived in a town twenty miles away, but this cousin and Miss Amelia did not get on so well, and when they chanced to pass each other they spat on the side of the road. Other people had tried very hard, from time to time, to work out some kind of far-fetched connection with Miss Amelia, but with absolutely no success.

The hunchback went into a long rigmarole, mentioning names and places that were unknown to the listeners on the porch and seemed to have nothing to do with the subject. "So Fanny and Martha Jesup were half-sisters. And I am the son of Fanny's third husband. So that would make you and I — " He bent down and began to unfasten his suitcase. His hands were like dirty sparrow claws and they were trembling. The bag was full of all manner of junk — ragged clothes and odd rubbish that looked like parts out of a sewing machine, or something just as worthless. The hunchback scrambled among these belongings and brought out an old photograph. "This is a picture of my mother and her half-sister."

Miss Amelia did not speak. She was moving her jaw slowly from side to side, and you could tell from her face what she was thinking about. Stumpy MacPhail took the photograph and held it out toward the light. It was a picture of two pale, withered-up little children of about two and three years of age. The faces were tiny white blurs, and it might have been an old picture in anyone's album.

Stumpy MacPhail handed it back with no comment. "Where you come from?" he asked.

The hunchback's voice was uncertain. "I was traveling."

Still Miss Amelia did not speak. She just stood leaning against the side of the door, and looked down at the hunchback. Henry Macy winked nervously and rubbed his hands together. Then quietly he left the bottom step and disappeared. He is a good soul, and the hunchback's situation had touched his heart. Therefore he did not want to wait and watch Miss Amelia chase this newcomer off her property and run him out of town. The hunchback stood with his bag open on the bottom step; he sniffled his nose, and his mouth quivered. Perhaps he began to feel his dismal predicament. Maybe he realized what a miserable thing it was to be a stranger in the town with only a suitcase full of junk, and claiming kin with Miss Amelia. At any rate he sat down on the steps and suddenly began to cry.

It was not a common thing to have an unknown hunchback walk to the store at midnight and then sit down and cry. Miss Amelia rubbed back her hair from her forehead and the men looked at each other uncomfortably. All around the town was very quiet.

At last one of the twins said: "I'll be damned if he ain't a regular Morris Finestein."

Everyone nodded and agreed, for that is an expression having a certain special meaning. But the hunchback cried louder because he could not know what they were talking about. Morris Finestein was a person who had lived in the town years before. He was only a quick, skipping little Jew who cried if you called him Christ-killer, and ate light bread and canned salmon every day. A calamity had come over him and he had moved away to Society City. But since then if a man were prissy in any way, or if a man ever wept, he was known as a Morris Finestein. Some times Henry Macy was referred to as a Morris Finestein.

"Well, he is afflicted," said Stumpy MacPhail. "There is some cause."

Miss Amelia crossed the porch with two slow, gangling strides. She went down the steps and stood looking thoughtfully at the stranger. Gingerly, with one long brown forefinger, she touched the hump on his back. The hunchback still wept, but he was quieter now. The night was silent and the moon still shone with a soft, clear light — it was getting colder. Then Miss Amelia did a rare thing; she pulled out a bottle from her hip pocket and after polishing off the top with the palm of her hand she handed it to the hunchback to drink. Miss Amelia could seldom be persuaded to sell her liquor on credit, and for her to give so much as a drop away free was almost unknown.

"Drink," she said. "It will liven your gizzard."

The hunchback stopped crying, neatly licked the tears from around his mouth, and did as he was told. When he was finished, Miss Amelia took a slow swallow, warmed and washed her mouth with it, and spat. Then she also drank. The twins and the foreman had their own bottle they had paid for.

"It is smooth liquor," Stumpy MacPhail said. "Miss Amelia, I have never known you to fail."

The whisky they drank that evening (two big bottles of it) is important. Otherwise, it would be hard to account for what followed. Perhaps without it there would never have been a cafe. For the liquor of Miss Amelia has a special quality of its own. It is clean and sharp on the tongue, but once down a man it glows inside him for a long time afterward. And that is not all. It is known that if a message is written with lemon juice on a clean sheet of paper there will be no sign of it. But if the paper is held for a moment to the fire then the letters turn brown and the meaning becomes clear. Imagine that the whisky is the fire and that the message is that which is known only in the soul of a man — then the worth of Miss Amelia's liquor can be understood. Things that have gone unnoticed, thoughts that have been harbored far back in the dark mind, are suddenly recognized and comprehended. A spinner who has thought only of the loom, the dinner pail, the bed, and then the loom again — this spinner might drink some on a Sunday and come across a marsh lily. And in his palm he might hold this flower, examining the golden dainty cup, and in him suddenly might come a sweetness keen as pain. A weaver might look up suddenly and see for the first time the cold, weird radiance of midnight January sky, and a deep fright at his own smallness stop his heart. Such things as these, then, happen when a man has drunk Miss Amelia's liquor. He may suffer, or he may be spent with joy — but the experience has shown the truth; he has warmed his soul and seen the message hidden there.

They drank until it was past midnight, and the moon was clouded over so that the night was cold and dark. The hunchback still sat on the bottom steps, bent over miserably with his forehead resting on his knee. Miss Amelia stood with her hands in her pockets, one foot resting on the second step of the stairs. She had been silent for a long time. Her face had the expression often seen in slightly cross-eyed persons who are thinking deeply, a look that appears to be both very wise and very crazy. At last she said: "I don't know your name."

"I'm Lymon Willis," said the hunchback.

"Well, come on in," she said. "Some supper was left in the stove and you can eat."

Only a few times in her life had Miss Amelia invited anyone to eat with her, unless she were planning to trick them in some way, or make money out of them. So the men on the porch felt there was something wrong. Later, they said among themselves that she must have been drinking back in the swamp the better part of the afternoon. At any rate she left the porch, and Stumpy MacPhail and the twins went on off home. She bolted the front door and looked all around to see that her goods were in order. Then she went to the kitchen, which was at the back of the store. The hunchback followed her, dragging his suitcase, sniffling and wiping his nose on the sleeve of his dirty coat.

"Sit down," said Miss Amelia. "I'll just warm up what's here."

It was a good meal they had together on that night. Miss Amelia was rich and she did not grudge herself food. There was fried chicken (the breast of which the hunchback took on his own plate), mashed roota-beggars, collard greens, and hot, pale golden, sweet potatoes. Miss Amelia ate slowly and with the relish of a farm hand. She sat with both elbows on the table, bent over the plate, her knees spread wide apart and her feet braced on the rungs of the chair. As for the hunchback, he gulped down his supper as though he had not smelled food in months. During the meal one tear crept down his dingy cheek — but it was just a little leftover tear and meant nothing at all. The lamp on the table was well-trimmed, burning blue at the edges of the wick, and casting a cheerful light in the kitchen. When Miss Amelia had eaten her supper she wiped her plate carefully with a slice of light bread, and then poured her own clear, sweet syrup over the bread. The hunchback did likewise — except that he was more finicky and asked for a new plate. Having finished, Miss Amelia tilted back her chair, tightened her fist, and felt the hard, supple muscles of her right arm beneath the clean, blue cloth of her shirtsleeves — an unconscious habit with her, at the close of a meal. Then she took the lamp from the table and jerked her head toward the staircase as an invitation for the hunchback to follow after her.

Above the store there were the three rooms where Miss Amelia had lived during all her life — two bedrooms with a large parlor in between. Few people had ever seen these rooms, but it was generally known that they were well-furnished and extremely clean. And now Miss Amelia was taking up with her a dirty little hunchback stranger, come from God knows where. Miss Amelia walked slowly, two steps at a time, holding the lamp high. The hunchback hovered so close behind her that the swinging light made on the staircase wall one great, twisted shadow of the two of them. Soon the premises above the store were dark as the rest of the town.

The next morning was serene, with a sunrise of warm purple mixed with rose. In the fields around the town the furrows were newly plowed, and very early the tenants were at work setting out the young, deep green tobacco plants. The wild crows flew down close to the fields, making swift blue shadows on the earth. In town the people set out early with their dinner pails, and the windows of the mill were blinding gold in the sun. The air was fresh and the peach trees light as March clouds with their blossoms.

Miss Amelia came down at about dawn, as usual. She washed her head at the pump and very shortly set about her business. Later in the morning she saddled her mule and went to see about her property, planted with cotton, up near the Forks Falls Road. By noon, of course, everybody had heard about the hunchback who had come to the store in the middle of the night. But no one as yet had seen him. The day soon grew hot and the sky was a rich, midday blue. Still no one had laid an eye on this strange guest. A few people remembered that Miss Amelia's mother had had a half-sister — but there was some difference of opinion as to whether she had died or had run off with a tobacco stringer. As for the hunchback's claim, everyone thought it was a trumped-up business. And the town, knowing Miss Amelia, decided that surely she had put him out of the house after feeding him. But toward evening, when the sky had whitened, and the shift was done, a woman claimed to have seen a crooked face at the window of one of the rooms up over the store. Miss Amelia herself said nothing. She clerked in the store for a while,

argued for an hour with a farmer over a plow shaft, mended some chicken
wire, locked up near sundown, and went to her rooms. The town was
left puzzled and talkative.

The next day Miss Amelia did not open the store, but stayed locked
up inside her premises and saw no one. Now this was the day that the
rumor started — the rumor so terrible that the town and all the county
about were stunned by it. The rumor was started by a weaver called
Merlie Ryan. He is a man of not much account — sallow, shambling,
and with no teeth in his head. He has the three-day malaria, which
means that every third day the fever comes on him. So on two days he
is dull and cross, but on the third day he livens up and sometimes has
an idea or two, most of which are foolish. It was while Merlie Ryan
was in his fever that he turned suddenly and said:

"I know what Miss Amelia done. She murdered that man for
something in that suitcase."

He said this in a calm voice, as a statement of fact. And within an
hour the news had swept through the town. It was a fierce and sickly
tale the town built up that day. In it were all the things which cause
the heart to shiver — a hunchback, a midnight burial in the swamp, the
dragging of Miss Amelia through the streets of the town on the way to
prison, the squabbles over what would happen to her property — all
told in hushed voices and repeated with some fresh and weird detail.
It rained and women forgot to bring in the washing from the lines. One
or two mortals, who were in debt to Miss Amelia, even put on Sunday
clothes as though it were a holiday. People clustered together on the
main street, talking and watching the store.

It would be untrue to say that all the town took part in this evil
festival. There were a few sensible men who reasoned that Miss Amelia,
being rich, would not go out of her way to murder a vagabond for a few
trifles of junk. In the town there were even three good people, and they
did not want this crime, not even for the sake of the interest and the
great commotion it would entail; it gave them no pleasure to think of
Miss Amelia holding to the bars of the penitentiary and being elec-
trocuted in Atlanta. These good people judged Miss Amelia in a different way from what the others judged her. When a person is as
contrary in every single respect as she was, and when the sins of a
person have mounted to such a point that they can hardly be remembered all at once — then this person plainly requires a special judgment.
They remembered that Miss Amelia had been born dark and somewhat
queer of face, raised motherless by her father who was a solitary man,
that early in youth she had grown to be six feet two inches tall which
in itself is not natural for a woman, and that her ways and habits of life
were too peculiar ever to reason about. Above all, they remembered her

puzzling marriage, which was the most unreasonable scandal ever to happen in this town.

So these good people felt toward her something near to pity. And when she was out on her wild business, such as rushing in a house to drag forth a sewing machine in payment for a debt, or getting herself worked up over some matter concerning the law — they had toward her a feeling which was a mixture of exasperation, a ridiculous little inside tickle, and a deep, unnamable sadness. But enough of the good people, for there were only three of them; the rest of the town was making a holiday of this fancied crime the whole of the afternoon.

Miss Amelia herself, for some strange reason, seemed unaware of all of this. She spent most of her day upstairs. When down in the store, she prowled around peacefully, her hands deep in the pockets of her overalls and head bent so low that her chin was tucked inside the collar of her shirt. There was no bloodstain on her anywhere. Often she stopped and just stood somberly looking down at the cracks in the floor, twisting a lock of her short-cropped hair, and whispering something to herself. But most of the day was spent upstairs.

Dark came on. The rain that afternoon had chilled the air, so that the evening was bleak and gloomy as in wintertime. There were no stars in the sky, and a light, icy drizzle had set in. The lamps in the houses made mournful, wavering flickers when watched from the street. A wind had come up, not from the swamp side of the town but from the cold, black pinewoods to the north.

The clocks in the town struck eight. Still nothing had happened. The bleak night, after the gruesome talk of the day, put a fear in some people, and they stayed home close to the fire. Others were gathered in groups together. Some eight or ten men had convened on the porch of Miss Amelia's store. They were silent and were indeed just waiting about. They themselves did not know what they were waiting for, but it was this: in times of tension, when some great action is impending, men gather and wait in this way. And after a time there will come a moment when all together they will act in unison, not from thought or from the will of any one man, but as though their instincts had merged together so that the decision belongs to no single one of them, but to the group as a whole. At such a time no individual hesitates. And whether the matter will be settled peaceably, or whether the joint action will result in ransacking, violence, and crime, depends on destiny. So the men waited soberly on the porch of Miss Amelia's store, not one of them realizing what they would do, but knowing inwardly that they must wait, and that the time had almost come.

Now the door to the store was open. Inside it was bright and natural-looking. To the left was the counter where slabs of white meat, rock candy, and tobacco were kept. Behind this were shelves of salted white meat and meal. The right side of the store was mostly filled with farm implements and such. At the back of the store, to the left, was the door leading up the stairs, and it was open. And at the far right of the store there was another door which led to a little room that Miss Amelia called her office. This door was also open. And at eight o'clock that evening Miss Amelia could be seen there sitting before her rolltop desk, figuring with a fountain pen and some pieces of paper.

The office was cheerfully lighted, and Miss Amelia did not seem to notice the delegation on the porch. Everything around her was in great order, as usual. This office was a room well-known, in a dreadful way, throughout the country. It was there Miss Amelia transacted all business. On the desk was a carefully covered typewriter which she knew how to run, but used only for the most important documents. In the drawers were literally thousands of papers, all filed according to the alphabet. This office was also the place where Miss Amelia received sick people, for she enjoyed doctoring and did a great deal of it. Two whole shelves were crowded with bottles and various paraphernalia. Against the wall was a bench where the patients sat. She could sew up a wound with a burnt needle so that it would not turn green. For burns she had a cool, sweet syrup. For unlocated sicknesses there were any number of different medicines which she had brewed herself from unknown recipes. They wrenched loose the bowels very well, but they could not be given to small children, as they caused bad convulsions; for them she had an entirely separate draught, gentler and sweet-flavored. Yes, all in all, she was considered a good doctor. Her hands, though very large and bony, had a light touch about them. She possessed great imagination and used hundreds of different cures. In the face of the most dangerous and extraordinary treatment she did not hesitate, and no disease was so terrible but what she would undertake to cure it. In this there was one exception. If a patient came with a female complaint she could do nothing. Indeed at the mere mention of the words her face would slowly darken with shame, and she would stand there craning her neck against the collar of her shirt, or rubbing her swamp boots together, for all the world like a great, shamed, dumb-tongued child. But in other matters people trusted her. She charged no fees whatsoever and always had a raft of patients.

On this evening Miss Amelia wrote with her fountain pen a good deal. But even so she could not be forever unaware of the group waiting out there on the dark porch, and watching her. From time to time she looked up and regarded them steadily. But she did not holler out to them to demand why they were loafing around her property like a sorry bunch of gabbies. Her face was proud and stern, as it always was when she sat at the desk of her office. After a time their peering in like that seemed to annoy her. She wiped her cheek with a red handkerchief, got up, and closed the office door.

Now to the group on the porch this gesture acted as a signal. The time had come. They had stood for a long while with the night raw and gloomy in the street behind them. They had waited long and just at that moment the instinct to act came on them. All at once, as though moved by one will, they walked into the store. At that moment the eight men looked very much alike — all wearing blue overalls, most of them with whitish hair, all pale of face, and all with a set, dreaming look in the eye. What they would have done next no one knows. But at that instant there was a noise at the head of the staircase. The men looked up and then stood dumb with shock. It was the hunchback, whom they had already murdered in their minds. Also, the creature was not at all as he had been pictured to them — not a pitiful and dirty little chatterer, alone and beggared in this world. Indeed, he was like nothing any man among them had ever beheld until that time. The room was still as death.

The hunchback came down slowly with the proudness of one who owns every plank of the floor beneath his feet. In the past days he had greatly changed. For one thing he was clean beyond words. He still wore his little coat, but it was brushed off and neatly mended. Beneath this was a fresh red and black checked shirt belonging to Miss Amelia. He did not wear trousers such as ordinary men are meant to wear, but a pair of tight-fitting little knee-length breeches. On his skinny legs he wore black stockings, and his shoes were of a special kind, being queerly shaped, laced up over the ankles, and newly cleaned and polished with wax. Around his neck, so that his large, pale ears were almost completely covered, he wore a shawl of lime-green wool, the fringes of which almost touched the floor.

The hunchback walked down the store with his stiff little strut and then stood in the center of the group that had come inside. They cleared a space about him and stood looking with hands loose at their sides and eyes wide open. The hunchback himself got his bearings in an odd manner. He regarded each person steadily at his own eye level, which was about belt line for an ordinary man. Then with shrewd deliberation he examined each man's lower regions — from the waist to the sole of the shoe. When he had satisfied himself he closed his eyes for a moment and shook his head, as though in his opinion what he had seen did not amount to much. Then with assurance, only to reconfirm himself, he tilted back his head and took in the halo of faces around him with one long, circling stare. There was a half-filled sack of guano on the left side of the store, and when he had found his bearings in this way, the hunchback sat down upon it. Cozily settled, with his little legs crossed, he took from his coat pocket a certain object.

Now it took some moments for the men in the store to regain their ease. Merlie Ryan, he of the three-day fever who had started the rumor that day, was the first to speak. He looked at the object which the hunchback was fondling, and said in a hushed voice:

"What is it you have there?"

Each man knew well what it was the hunchback was handling. For it was the snuffbox which had belonged to Miss Amelia's father. The snuffbox was of blue enamel with a dainty embellishment of wrought gold on the lid. The group knew it well and marveled. They glanced warily at the closed office door, and heard the low sound of Miss Amelia whistling to herself.

"Yes, what is it, Peanut?"

The hunchback looked up quickly and sharpened his mouth to speak. "Why, this is a lay-low to catch meddlers."

The hunchback reached in the box with his scrambly little fingers and ate something, but he offered no one around him a taste. It was not even proper snuff which he was taking, but a mixture of sugar and cocoa. This he took, though, as snuff, pocketing a little wad of it beneath his lower lip and licking down neatly into this with a flick of his tongue which made a frequent grimace come over his face.

"The very teeth in my head have always tasted sour to me," he said in explanation. "That is the reason why I take this kind of sweet snuff."

The group still clustered around, feeling somewhat gawky and bewildered. This sensation never quite wore off, but it was soon tempered by another feeling — an air of intimacy in the room and a vague festivity. Now the names of the men of the group there on that evening were as follows: Hasty Malone, Robert Calvert Hale, Merlie Ryan, Reverend T. M. Willin, Rosser Cline, Rip Wellborn, Henry Ford Crimp, and Horace Wells. Except for Reverend Willin, they are all alike in many ways, as has been said — all having taken pleasure from something or other, all having wept and suffered in some way, most of them tractable unless exasperated. Each of them worked in the mill, and lived with others in a two- or three-room house for which the rent was ten dollars or twelve dollars a month. All had been paid that afternoon, for it was Saturday. So, for the present, think of them as a whole.

The hunchback, however, was already sorting them out in his mind. Once comfortably settled he began to chat with everyone, asking questions such as if a man was married, how old he was, how much his wages came to in an average week, et cetera — picking his way along to inquiries which were downright intimate. Soon the group was joined by others in the town, Henry Macy, idlers who had sensed something extraordinary, women come to fetch their men who lingered on, and even one loose, towhead child who tiptoed into the store, stole a box of animal crackers, and made off very quietly. So the premises of Miss Amelia were soon crowded, and she herself had not yet opened her office door.

There is a type of person who has a quality about him that sets him apart from other and more ordinary human beings. Such a person has an instinct which is usually found only in small children, an instinct to establish immediate and vital contact between himself and all things in the world. Certainly the hunchback was of this type. He had only been in the store half an hour before an immediate contact had been established between him and each other individual. It was as though he had lived in the town for years, was a well-known character, and had been sitting and talking there on that guano sack for countless evenings. This, together with the fact that it was Saturday night, could account for the air of freedom and illicit gladness in the store. There was a tension, also, partly because of the oddity of the situation and because Miss Amelia was still closed off in her office and had not yet made her appearance.

She came out that evening at ten o'clock. And those who were expecting some drama at her entrance were disappointed. She opened the door and walked in with her slow, gangling swagger. There was a streak of ink on one side of her nose, and she had knotted the red hand-kerchief about her neck. She seemed to notice nothing unusual. Her gray, crossed eyes glanced over to the place where the hunchback was sitting, and for a moment lingered there. The rest of the crowd in her store she regarded with only a peaceable surprise.

"Does anyone want waiting on?" she asked quietly.

There were a number of customers, because it was Saturday night, and they all wanted liquor. Now Miss Amelia had dug up an aged barrel only three days past and had siphoned it into bottles back by the still. This night she took the money from the customers and counted it beneath the bright light. Such was the ordinary procedure. But after this what happened was not ordinary. Always before, it was necessary to go around to the dark back yard, and there she would hand out your bottle through the kitchen door. There was no feeling of joy in the transaction. After getting his liquor the customer walked off into the night. Or, if his wife would not have it in the home, he was allowed to come back around to the front porch of the store and guzzle there or in the street. Now, both the porch and the street before it were the property of Miss Amelia, and no mistake about it — but she did not regard them as her premises; the premises began at the front door and took in the entire inside of the building. There she had never allowed liquor to be opened or drunk by anyone but herself. Now for the first time she broke this rule. She went to the kitchen, with the hunchback close at her heels, and she brought back the bottles into the warm, bright store. More than that she furnished some glasses and opened two boxes of crackers so that they were there hospitably in a platter on the counter and anyone who wished could take one free.

She spoke to no one but the hunchback, and she only asked him in a somewhat harsh and husky voice: "Cousin Lymon, will you have yours straight, or warmed in a pan with water on the stove?"

"If you please, Amelia," the hunchback said. (And since what time had anyone presumed to address Miss Amelia by her bare name, without a title of respect? — Certainly not her bridegroom and her husband of ten days. In fact, not since the death of her father, who for some reason had always called her Little, had anyone dared to address her in such a familiar way.) "If you please, I'll have it warmed."

Now, this was the beginning of the café. It was as simple as that. Recall that the night was gloomy as in wintertime, and to have sat around the property outside would have made a sorry celebration. But inside there was company and a genial warmth. Someone had rattled up the stove in the rear, and those who bought bottles shared their liquor with friends. Several women were there and they had twists of licorice, a Nehi, or even a swallow of the whisky. The hunchback was still a novelty and his presence amused everyone. The bench in the office was brought in, together with several extra chairs. Other people leaned against the counter or made themselves comfortable on barrels and sacks. Nor did the opening of liquor on the premises cause any rambunctiousness, indecent giggles, or misbehavior whatsoever. On the contrary the company was polite even to the point of a certain timidity. For people in this town were then unused to gathering together for the sake of pleasure. They met to work in the mill. Or on Sunday there would be an all-day camp meeting — and though that is a pleasure, the intention of the whole affair is to sharpen your view of Hell and put into you a keen fear of the Lord Almighty. But the spirit of a café is altogether different. Even the richest, greediest old rascal will behave himself, insulting no one in a proper café. And poor people look about them gratefully and pinch up the salt in a dainty and modest manner. For the atmosphere of a proper café implies these qualities: fellowship, the satisfactions of the belly, and a certain gaiety and grace of behavior. This had never been told to the gathering in Miss Amelia's store that night. But they knew it of themselves, although never, of course, until that time had there been a café in the town.

Now, the cause of all this, Miss Amelia, stood most of the evening in the doorway leading to the kitchen. Outwardly she did not seem changed at all. But there were many who noticed her face. She watched all that went on, but most of the time her eyes were fastened lonesomely on the hunchback. He strutted about the store, eating from his snuffbox, and being at once sour and agreeable. Where Miss Amelia stood, the light from the chinks of the stove cast a glow, so that her brown, long face was somewhat brightened. She seemed to be looking inward. There was in her expression pain, perplexity, and uncertain joy. Her lips were not so firmly set as usual, and she swallowed often. Her skin had paled and her large empty hands were sweating. Her look that night, then, was the lonesome look of the lover.

This opening of the café came to an end at midnight. Everyone said good-bye to everyone else in a friendly fashion. Miss Amelia shut the front door of her premises, but forgot to bolt it. Soon everything — the main street with its three stores, the mill, the houses — all the town, in fact — was dark and silent. And so ended three days and nights in which had come an arrival of a stranger, an unholy holiday, and the start of the café.

Now time must pass. For the next four years are much alike. There are great changes, but these changes are brought about bit by bit, in simple steps which in themselves do not appear to be important. The hunchback continued to live with Miss Amelia. The café expanded in a gradual way. Miss Amelia began to sell her liquor by the drink, and some tables were brought into the store. There were customers every evening, and on Saturday a great crowd. Miss Amelia began to serve fried catfish suppers at fifteen cents a plate. The hunchback cajoled her into buying a fine mechanical piano. Within two years the place was a store no longer, but had been converted into a proper café, open every evening from six until twelve o'clock.

Each night the hunchback came down the stairs with the air of one who has a grand opinion of himself. He always smelled slightly of turnip greens, as Miss Amelia rubbed him night and morning with pot liquor to give him strength. She spoiled him to a point beyond reason, but nothing seemed to strengthen him; food only made his hump and his head grow larger while the rest of him remained weakly and deformed. Miss Amelia was the same in appearance. During the week she still wore swamp boots and overalls, but on Sunday she put on a dark red dress that hung on her in a most peculiar fashion. Her manners, however, and her way of life were greatly changed. She still loved a fierce lawsuit, but she was not so quick to cheat her fellow man and to exact cruel payments. Because the hunchback was so extremely sociable she even went about a little — to revivals, to funerals, and so forth. Her doctoring was as successful as ever, her liquor even finer than before, if that were possible. The cafe itself proved profitable and was the only place of pleasure for many miles around.

So for the moment regard these years from random and disjointed views. See the hunchback marching in Miss Amelia's footsteps when on a red winter morning they set out for the pinewoods to hunt. See them working on her properties — with Cousin Lymon standing by and doing absolutely nothing, but quick to point out any laziness among the hands. On autumn afternoons they sat on the back steps chopping sugar cane. The glaring summer days they spent back in the swamp where the water cypress is a deep black green, where beneath the tangled swamp trees there is a drowsy gloom. When the path leads through a bog or a stretch of blackened water see Miss Amelia bend down to let Cousin Lymon scramble on her back — and see her wading forward with the hunchback settled on her shoulders, clinging to her ears or to her broad forehead. Occasionally Miss Amelia cranked up the Ford which she had bought and treated Cousin Lymon to a picture-show in Cheehaw, or to some distant fair or cockfight; the hunchback took a passionate delight in spectacles. Of course, they were in their café every evening. And late at night, or rather early in the morning, they would often sit for hours together by the fireplace in the parlor upstairs. For the hunchback was sickly at night and dreaded to lie looking into the dark. He had a deep fear of death. And Miss Amelia would not leave him by himself to suffer with this fright. It may even be reasoned that the growth of the café came about mainly on this account; it was a thing that brought him company and pleasure and that helped him through the night. So compose from such flashes an image of these years as a whole. And for a moment let it rest.

Now some explanation is due for all this behavior. The time has come to speak about love. For Miss Amelia loved Cousin Lymon. So much was clear to everyone. They lived in the same house together and were never seen apart. Therefore, according to Mrs. Stumpy MacPhail, a warty-nosed old busybody who is continually moving her sticks of furniture from one part of the front room to another; according to her and to certain others, these two were living in sin. If they were related, they were only a cross between first and second cousins, and even that could in no way be proved. Now, of course Miss Amelia was a powerful blunderbuss of a person, more than six feet tall — and Cousin Lymon a weakly little hunchback reaching only to her waist. But so much the better for Mrs. Stumpy MacPhail and her cronies, for they and their kind glory in conjunctions which are ill-matched and pitiful. So let them be. The good people thought that if those two had found some satisfaction of the flesh between themselves, then it was a matter concerning them and God alone. All sensible people agreed in their opinion about this conjecture — and their answer was a plain, flat *no*. What sort of thing, then, was this love?

First of all, love is a joint experience between two persons — but the fact that it is a joint experience does not mean that it is a similar experience to the two people involved. There are the lover and the beloved, but these two come from different countries. Often the beloved is only a stimulus for all the stored-up love which has lain quiet within the lover for a long time hitherto. And somehow every lover knows this. He feels in his soul that his love is a solitary thing. He comes to know a new, strange loneliness and it is this knowledge which makes him suffer. So there is only one thing for the lover to do. He must house his love within himself as best he can; he must create for himself a whole new inward world — a world intense and strange, complete in himself. Let it be added here that this lover about whom we speak need not necessarily be a young man saving for a wedding ring — this lover can be man, woman, child, or indeed any human creature on this earth.

Now, the beloved can also be of any description. The most outlandish people can be the stimulus for love. A man may be a doddering great-grandfather and still love only a strange girl he saw in the streets of Cheehaw one afternoon two decades past. The preacher may love a fallen woman. The beloved may be treacherous, greasy-headed, and given to evil habits. Yes, and the lover may see this as clearly as anyone else — but that does not affect the evolution of his love one whit. A most mediocre person can be the object of a love which is wild, extravagant, and beautiful as the poison lilies of the swamp. A good man may be the stimulus for a love both violent and debased, or a jabbering madman may bring about in the soul of someone a tender and simple idyll. Therefore, the value and quality of any love is determined solely by the lover himself.

It is for this reason that most of us would rather love than be loved. Almost everyone wants to be the lover. And the curt truth is that, in a deep secret way, the state of being beloved is intolerable to many people. The beloved fears and hates the lover, and with the best of reasons. For the lover is forever trying to strip bare his beloved. The lover craves any possible relation with the beloved, even if this experience can cause him only pain.

It has been mentioned before that Miss Amelia was once married. And this curious episode might as well be accounted for at this point. Remember that it all happened long ago, and that it was Miss Amelia's only personal contact, before the hunchback came to her, with this phenomenon — love.

The town then was the same as it is now, except there were two stores instead of three and the peach trees along the street were more crooked and smaller than they are now. Miss Amelia was nineteen years old at the time, and her father had been dead many months. There was in the town at that time a loom-fixer named Marvin Macy. He was the brother of Henry Macy, although to know them you would never guess that those two could be kin. For Marvin Macy was the hand-somest man in this region — being six feet one inch tall, hard-muscled, and with slow gray eyes and curly hair. He was well off, made good wages, and had a gold watch which opened in the back to show a picture of a waterfall. From the outward and worldly point of view Marcy Macy was a fortunate fellow; he needed to bow and scrape to no one and always got just what he wanted. But from a more serious and thoughtful viewpoint Marvin Macy was not a person to be envied, for he was an evil character. His reputation was as bad, if not worse, than that of any young man in the county. For years, when he was a boy, he had carried about with him the dried and salted ear of a man he had killed in a razor fight. He had chopped off the tails of squirrels in the pinewoods just to please his fancy, and in his left hip pocket he carried the forbidden marijuana weed to tempt those who were dis-couraged and drawn toward death. Yet in spite of his well-known reputation he was the beloved of many females in this region — and there were at the time several young girls who were clean-haired and soft-eyed, with tender sweet little buttocks and charming ways. These gentle young girls he degraded and shamed. Then finally, at the age of twenty-two, this Marvin Macy chose Miss Amelia. That solitary, gangling, queer-eyed girl was the one he longed for. Nor did he want her because of her money, but solely out of love.

And love changed Marvin Macy. Before the time when he loved Miss Amelia it could almost be questioned if such a person had within him a heart and soul. Yet there is some explanation for the ugliness of his character, for Marvin Macy had had a hard beginning in this world. He was one of seven unwanted children whose parents could hardly be called parents at all; these parents were wild younguns who liked to fish and roam around the swamp. Their own children, and there was a new one almost every year, were only a nuisance to them. At night when they came home from the mill they would look at the children as though they did not know wherever they had come from. If the children cried they were beaten, and the first thing they learned in this world was to seek the darkest corner of the room and try to hide themselves as best they could. They were as thin as little whitehaired ghosts, and they did not speak, not even to each other. Finally, they were abandoned by their parents altogether and left to the mercies of the town. It was a hard winter, with the mill closed down almost three months, and much misery everywhere. But this is not a town to let white orphans perish in the road before your eyes. So here is what came about: the eldest child, who was eight years old, walked into Cheehaw and disappeared — perhaps he took a freight train somewhere and went out into the world, nobody knows. Three other children were boarded out amongst the town, being sent around from one kitchen to another, and as they were delicate they died before Easter time. The last two children were Marvin Macy and Henry Macy, and they were taken into a home. There was a good woman in the town named Mrs. Mary Hale, and she took Marvin Macy and Henry Macy and loved them as her own. They were raised in her household and treated well.

But the hearts of small children are delicate organs. A cruel beginning in this world can twist them into curious shapes. The heart of a hurt child can shrink so that forever afterward it is hard and pitted as the seed of a peach. Or again, the heart of such a child may fester and swell until it is a misery to carry within the body, easily chafed and hurt by the most ordinary things. This last is what happened to Henry Macy, who is so opposite to his brother, is the kindest and gentlest man in town. He lends his wages to those who are unfortunate, and in the old days he used to care for the children whose parents were at the café on Saturday night. But he is a shy man, and he has the look of one who has a swollen heart and suffers. Marvin Macy, however, grew to be bold and fearless and cruel. His heart turned tough as the horns of Satan, and until the time when he loved Miss Amelia he brought to his brother and the good woman who raised him nothing but shame and trouble.

But love reversed the character of Marvin Macy. For two years he loved Miss Amelia, but he did not declare himself. He would stand near the door of her premises, his cap in his hand, his eyes meek and longing and misty gray. He reformed himself completely. He was good to his brother and foster mother, and he saved his wages and learned thrift. Moreover, he reached out toward God. No longer did he lie around on the floor of the front porch all day Sunday, singing and playing his guitar; he attended church services and was present at all religious meetings. He learned good manners: he trained himself to rise and give his chair to a lady, and he quit swearing and fighting and using holy names in vain. So for two years he passed through this transformation and improved his character in every way. Then at the end of the two years he went one evening to Miss Amelia, carrying a bunch of swamp flowers, a sack of chitterlins, and a silver ring — that night Marvin Macy declared himself.

And Miss Amelia married him. Later everyone wondered why. Some said it was because she wanted to get herself some wedding presents. Others believed it came about through the nagging of Miss Amelia's great-aunt in Cheehaw, who was a terrible old woman. Anyway, she strode with great steps down the aisle of the church wearing her dead mother's bridal gown, which was of yellow satin and at least twelve inches too short for her. It was a winter afternoon and the clear sun shone through the ruby windows of the church and put a curious glow on the pair before the altar. As the marriage lines were read Miss Amelia kept making an odd gesture — she would rub the palm of her right hand down the side of her satin wedding gown. She was reaching for the pocket of her overalls, and being unable to find it her face became impatient, bored, and exasperated. At last when the lines were spoken and the marriage prayer was done Miss Amelia hurried out of the church, not taking the arm of her husband, but walking at least two paces ahead of him.

The church is no distance from the store so the bride and groom walked home. It is said that on the way Miss Amelia began to talk about some deal she had worked up with a farmer over a load of kindling wood. In fact, she treated her groom in exactly the same manner she would have used with some customer who had come into the store to buy a pint from her. But so far all had gone decently enough; the town was gratified, as people had seen what this love had done to Marvin Macy and hoped that it might also reform his bride. At least, they counted on the marriage to tone down Miss Amelia's temper, to put a bit of bride-fat on her, and to change her at last into a calculable woman.

They were wrong. The young boys who watched through the window on that night said that this is what actually happened: The bride and groom ate a grand supper prepared by Jeff, the old Negro who cooked for Miss Amelia. The bride took second servings of everything, but the groom picked with his food. Then the bride went about her ordinary business — reading the newspaper, finishing an inventory of the stock in the store, and so forth. The groom hung about in the doorway with a loose, foolish, blissful face and was not noticed. At eleven o'clock the bride took a lamp and went upstairs. The groom followed close behind her. So far all had gone decently enough, but what followed after was unholy.

Within half an hour Miss Amelia had stomped down the stairs in breeches and a khaki jacket. Her face had darkened so that it looked quite black. She slammed the kitchen door and gave it an ugly kick.

Then she controlled herself. She poked up the fire, sat down, and put her feet up on the kitchen stove. She read the Farmer's Almanac, drank coffee, and had a smoke with her father's pipe. Her face was hard, stern, and had now whitened to its natural color. Sometimes she paused to jot down some information from the Almanac on a piece of paper. Toward dawn she went into her office and uncovered her typewriter, which she had recently bought and was only just learning how to run. That was the way in which she spent the whole of her wedding night. At daylight she went out to her yard as though nothing whatsoever had occurred and did some carpentering on a rabbit hutch which she had begun the week before and intended to sell somewhere.

A groom is in a sorry fix when he is unable to bring his well-loved bride to bed with him, and when the whole town knows it. Marvin Macy came down that day still in his wedding finery, and with a sick face. God knows how he had spent the night. He moped about the yard, watching Miss Amelia, but keeping some distance away from her. Then toward noon an idea came to him and he went off in the direction of Society City. He returned with presents — an opal ring, a pink enamel doreen of the sort which was then in fashion, a silver bracelet with two hearts on it, and a box of candy which had cost two dollars and a half. Miss Amelia looked over these fine gifts and opened the box of candy, for she was hungry. The rest of the presents she judged shrewdly for a moment to sum up their value — then she put them in the counter out for sale. The night was spent in much the same manner as the preceding one — except that Miss Amelia brought her feather mattress to make a pallet by the kitchen stove, and she slept fairly well.

Things went on like this for three days. Miss Amelia went about her business as usual, and took great interest in some rumor that a bridge was to be built some ten miles down the road. Marvin Macy still followed her about around the premises, and it was plain from his face how he suffered. Then on the fourth day he did an extremely simple-minded thing: he went to Cheehaw and came back with a lawyer. Then in Miss Amelia's office he signed over to her the whole of his worldly goods, which was ten acres of timberland which he had bought with the money he had saved. She studied the paper sternly to make sure there was no possibility of a trick and filed it soberly in the drawer of her desk. That afternoon Marvin Macy took a quart bottle of whisky and went with it alone out in the swamp while the sun was still shining. Toward evening he came in drunk, went up to Miss Amelia with wet wide eyes, and put his hand on her shoulder. He was trying to tell her something, but before he could open his mouth she had swung once with her fist and hit his face so hard that he was thrown back against the wall and one of his front teeth was broken.

The rest of this affair can only be mentioned in bare outline. After this first blow Miss Amelia hit him whenever he came within arm's reach of her, and whenever he was drunk. At last she turned him off the premises altogether, and he was forced to suffer publicly. During the day he hung around just outside the boundary line of Miss Amelia's property and sometimes with a drawn crazy look he would fetch his rifle and sit there cleaning it, peering at Miss Amelia steadily. If she was afraid she did not show it, but her face was sterner than ever, and often she spat on the ground. His last foolish effort was to climb in the window of her store one night and to sit there in the dark, for no purpose whatsoever, until she came down the stairs next morning. For this Miss Amelia set off immediately to the courthouse in Cheehaw with some notion that she could get him locked in the penitentiary for trespassing. Marvin Macy left the town that day, and no one saw him go, or knew just where he went. On leaving he put a long curious letter, partly written in pencil and partly with ink, beneath Miss Amelia's door. It was a wild love letter — but in it were also included threats, and he swore that in this life he would get even with her. His marriage had lasted for ten days. And the town felt the special satisfaction that people feel when someone has been thoroughly done in by some scandalous and terrible means.

Miss Amelia was left with everything that Marvin Macy had ever owned — his timberwood, his gold watch, every one of his possessions. But she seemed to attach little value to them and that spring she cut up his Klansman's robe to cover her tobacco plants. So all that he had ever done was to make her richer and to bring her love. But, strange to say, she never spoke of him but with a terrible and spiteful bitterness. She never once referred to him by name but always mentioned him scornfully as "that loom-fixer I was married to."

And later, when horrifying rumors concerning Marvin Macy reached the town, Miss Amelia was very pleased. For the true character of Marvin Macy finally revealed itself, once he had freed himself of his love. He became a criminal whose picture and whose name were in all the papers in the state. He robbed three filling stations and held up the A & P store of Society City with a sawed-off gun. He was suspected of the murder of Slit-Eye Sam who was a noted highjacker. All these crimes were connected with the name of Marvin Macy, so that his evil became famous through many counties. Then finally the law captured him, drunk, on the floor of a tourist cabin, his guitar by his side, and fifty-seven dollars in his right shoe. He was tried, sentenced, and sent off to the penitentiary near Atlanta. Miss Amelia was deeply gratified.

Well, all this happened a long time ago, and it is the story of Miss

Amelia's marriage. The town laughed a long time over this grotesque affair. But though the outward facts of this love are indeed sad and ridiculous, it must be remembered that the real story was that which took place in the soul of the lover himself. So who but God can be the final judge of this or any other love? On the very first night of the café there were several who suddenly thought of this broken bridegroom, locked in the gloomy penitentiary, many miles away. And in the years that followed, Marvin Macy was not altogether forgotten in the town. His name was never mentioned in the presence of Miss Amelia or the hunchback. But the memory of his passion and his crimes, and the thought of him trapped in his cell in the penitentiary, was like a troubling undertone beneath the happy love of Miss Amelia and the gaiety of the café. So do not forget this Marvin Macy, as he is to act a terible part in the story which is yet to come.

During the four years in which the store became a café the rooms upstairs were not changed. This part of the premises remained exactly as it had been all of Miss Amelia's life, as it was in the time of her father, and most likely his father before him. The three rooms, it is already known, were immaculately clean. The smallest object had its exact place, and everything was wiped and dusted by Jeff, the servant of Miss Amelia, each morning. The front room belonged to Cousin Lymon — it was the room where Marvin Macy had stayed during the few nights he was allowed on the premises, and before that it was the bedroom of Miss Amelia's father. The room was furnished with a large chifforobe, a bureau covered with a stiff white linen cloth crocheted at the edges, and a marble-topped table. The bed was immense, an old four-poster made of carved, dark rosewood. On it were two feather mattresses, bolsters, and a number of handmade comforts. The bed was so high that beneath it were two wooden steps — no occupant had ever used these steps before, but Cousin Lymon drew them out each night and walked up in state. Beside the steps, but pushed modestly out of view, there was a china chamberpot painted with pink roses. No rug covered the dark, polished floor and the curtains were of some white stuff, also crocheted at the edges.

On the other side of the parlor was Miss Amelia's bedroom, and it was smaller and very simple. The bed was narrow and made of pine. There was a bureau for her breeches, shirts, and Sunday dress, and she had hammered two nails in the closet wall on which to hang her swamp boots. There were no curtains, rugs, or ornaments of any kind.

The large middle room, the parlor, was elaborate. The rosewood sofa, upholstered in threadbare green silk, was before the fireplace. Marble-topped tables, two Singer sewing machines, a big vase of pampas grass — everything was rich and grand. The most important piece of furniture in the parlor was a big, glass-doored cabinet in which was kept a number of treasures and curios. Miss Amelia had added two objects to this collection — one was a large acorn from a water oak, the other a little velvet box holding two small, grayish stones. Sometimes when she had nothing much to do, Miss Amelia would take out this velvet box and stand by the window with the stones in the palm of her hand, looking down at them with a mixture of fascination, dubious respect, and fear. They were the kidney stones of Miss Amelia herself, and had been taken from her by the doctor in Cheehaw some years ago. It had been a terrible experience, from the first minute to the last, and all she had got out of it were those two little stones; she was bound to set great store by them, or else admit to a mighty sorry bargain. So she kept them and in the second year of Cousin Lymon's stay with her she had them set as ornaments in a watch chain which she gave to him. The other object she had added to the collection, the large acorn, was precious to her — but when she looked at it her face was always saddened and perplexed.

"Amelia, what does it signify?" Cousin Lymon asked her.

"Why, it's just an acorn," she answered. "Just an acorn I picked up on the afternoon Big Papa died."

"How do you mean?" Cousin Lymon insisted.

"I mean it's just an acorn I spied on the ground that day. I picked it up and put it in my pocket. But I don't know why."

"What a peculiar reason to keep it," Cousin Lymon said.

The talks of Miss Amelia and Cousin Lymon in the rooms upstairs, usually in the first few hours of the morning when the hunchback could not sleep, were many. As a rule, Miss Amelia was a silent woman, not letting her tongue run wild on any subject that happened to pop into her head. There were certain topics of conversation, however, in which she took pleasure. All these subjects had one point in common — they were interminable. She liked to contemplate problems which could be worked over for decades and still remain insoluble. Cousin Lymon, on the other hand, enjoyed talking on any subject whatsoever, as he was a great chatterer. Their approach to any conversation was altogether different. Miss Amelia always kept to the broad, rambling generalities of the matter, going on endlessly in a low, thoughtful voice and getting nowhere — while Cousin Lymon would interrupt her suddenly to pick up, magpie fashion, some detail which, even if unimportant, was at least concrete and bearing on some practical facet close at hand. Some of the favorite subjects of Miss Amelia were: the stars, the reason why Negroes are black, the best treatment for cancer, and so forth. Her father was also an interminable subject which was dear to her.

"Why, Law," she would say to Lymon. "Those days I slept. I'd go to bed just as the lamp was turned on and sleep — why, I'd sleep like I was drowned in warm axle grease. Then come daybreak Big Papa would walk in and put his hand down on my shoulder. 'Get stirring, Little,' he would say. Then later he would holler up the stairs from the kitchen when the stove was hot. 'Fried grits,' he would holler. 'White meat and gravy. Ham and eggs.' And I'd run down the stairs and dress by the hot stove while he was out washing at the pump. Then off we'd go to the still or maybe — "

"The grits we had this morning was poor," Cousin Lymon said. "Fried too quick so that the inside never heated."

"And when Big Papa would run off the liquor in those days — " The conversation would go on endlessly, with Miss Amelia's long legs stretched out before the hearth; for winter or summer there was always a fire in the grate, as Lymon was cold-natured. He sat in a low chair across from her, his feet not quite touching the floor and his torso usually well-wrapped in a blanket or the green wool shawl. Miss Amelia never mentioned her father to anyone else except Cousin Lymon.

That was one of the ways in which she showed her love for him. He had her confidence in the most delicate and vital matters. He alone knew where she kept the chart that showed where certain barrels of whisky were buried on a piece of property near by. He alone had access to her bankbook and the key to the cabinet of curios. He took money from the cash register, whole handfuls of it, and appreciated the loud jingle it made inside his pockets. He owned almost everything on the premises, for when he was cross Miss Amelia would prowl about and find some present — so that now there was hardly anything left close at hand to give him. The only part of her life that she did not want Cousin Lymon to share with her was the memory of her ten-day marriage. Marvin Macy was the one subject that was never, at any time, discussed between the two of them.

So let the slow years pass and come to a Saturday evening six years after the time when Cousin Lymon came first to the town. It was August and the sky had burned above the town like a sheet of flame all day. Now the green twilight was near and there was a feeling of repose. The street was coated an inch deep with dry golden dust and the little children ran about half-naked, sneezed often, sweated, and were fretful. The mill had closed down at noon. People in the houses along the main street sat resting on their steps and the women had palmetto fans. At Miss Amelia's there was a sign at the front of the premises saying CAFÉ. The back porch was cool with latticed shadows and there Cousin Lymon sat turning the ice-cream freezer — often he unpacked the salt and ice and removed the dasher to lick a bit and see how the work was coming on. Jeff cooked in the kitchen. Early that morning Miss Amelia had put a notice on the wall of the front porch reading: Chicken Dinner — Twenty Cents Tonite. The café was already open and Miss Amelia had just finished a period of work in her office. All the eight tables were occupied and from the mechanical piano came a jingling tune.

In a corner, near the door and sitting at a table with a child, was Henry Macy. He was drinking a glass of liquor, which was unusual for him, as liquor went easily to his head and made him cry or sing. His face was very pale and his left eye worked constantly in a nervous tic, as it was apt to do when he was agitated. He had come into the café sidewise and silent, and when he was greeted he did not speak. The child next to him belonged to Horace Wells, and he had been left at Miss Amelia's that morning to be doctored.

Miss Amelia came out from her office in good spirits. She attended to a few details in the kitchen and entered the café with the pope's nose of a hen between her fingers, as that was her favorite piece. She looked about the room, saw that in general all was well, and went over to the corner table by Henry Macy. She turned the chair around and sat straddling the back, as she only wanted to pass the time of day and was not yet ready for her supper. There was a bottle of Kroup Kure in the hip pocket of her overalls — a medicine made from whisky, rock candy, and a secret ingredient. Miss Amelia uncorked the bottle and put it to the mouth of the child. Then she turned to Henry Macy and, seeing the nervous winking of his left eye, she asked:

"What ails you?"

Henry Macy seemed on the point of saying something difficult, but, after a long look into the eyes of Miss Amelia, he swallowed and did not speak.

So Miss Amelia returned to her patient. Only the child's head showed above the table top. His face was very red, with the eyelids half-closed and the mouth partly open. He had a large, hard, swollen boil on his thigh, and had been brought to Miss Amelia so that it could be opened. But Miss Amelia used a special method with children; she did not like to see them hurt, struggling, and terrified. So she had kept the child around the premises all day, giving him licorice and frequent doses of the Kroup Kure, and toward evening she tied a napkin around his neck and let him eat his fill of the dinner. Now as he sat at the table his head wobbled slowly from side to side and sometimes as he breathed there came from him a little worn-out grunt.

There was a stir in the café and Miss Amelia looked around quickly. Cousin Lymon had come in. The hunchback strutted into the café as he did every night, and when he reached the exact center of the room he stopped short and looked shrewdly around him, summing up the people and making a quick pattern of the emotional material at hand that night. The hunchback was a great mischief-maker. He enjoyed any kind of to-do, and without saying a word he could set people at each other in a way that was miraculous. It was due to him that the Rainey twins had quarreled over a jackknife two years past, and had not spoken one word to each other since. He was present at the big fight between Rip Wellborn and Robert Calvert Hale, and every other fight for that matter since he had come into the town. He nosed around everywhere, knew the intimate business of everybody, and trespassed every waking hour. Yet, queerly enough, in spite of this it was the hunchback who was most responsible for the great popularity of the café. Things were never so gay as when he was around. When he walked into the room there was always a quick feeling of tension, because with this busybody about there was never any telling what might descend on you, or what might suddenly be brought to happen in the room. People are never so free with themselves and so recklessly glad as when there is some possibility of commotion or calamity ahead. So when the hunchback marched into the café everyone looked around at him and there was a quick outburst of talking and a drawing of corks.

Lymon waved his hand to Stumpy MacPhail who was sitting with Merlie Ryan and Henry Ford Crimp. "I walked to Rotten Lake today to fish," he said. "And on the way I stepped over what appeared at first to be a big fallen tree. But then as I stepped over I felt something stir and I taken this second look and there I was straddling this here alligator long as from the front door to the kitchen and thicker than a hog."

The hunchback chattered on. Everyone looked at him from time to time, and some kept track of his chattering and others did not. There were times when every word he said was nothing but lying and bragging. Nothing he said tonight was true. He had lain in bed with a summer quinsy all day long, and had only got up in the late afternoon in order to turn the ice-cream freezer. Everybody knew this, yet he stood there in the middle of the café and held forth with such lies and boasting that it was enough to shrivel the ears.

Miss Amelia watched him with her hands in her pockets and her head turned to one side. There was a softness about her gray, queer eyes and she was smiling gently to herself. Occasionally she glanced from the hunchback to the other people in the café — and then her look was proud, and there was in it the hint of a threat, as though daring anyone to try to hold him to account for all his foolery. Jeff was bringing in the suppers, already served on the plates, and the new electric fans in the café made a pleasant stir of coolness in the air.

"The little youngun is asleep," said Henry Macy finally.

Miss Amelia looked down at the patient beside her, and composed her face for the matter in hand. The child's chin was resting on the table edge and a trickle of spit or Kroup Kure had bubbled from the corner of his mouth. His eyes were quite closed, and a little family of gnats had clustered peacefully in the corners. Miss Amelia put her hand on his head and shook it roughly, but the patient did not awake. So Miss Amelia lifted the child from the table, being careful not to touch the sore part of his leg, and went into the office. Henry Macy followed after her and they closed the office door.

Cousin Lymon was bored that evening. There was not much going on, and in spite of the heat the customers in the café were good-humored. Henry Ford Crimp and Horace Wells sat at the middle table with their arms around each other, sniggering over some long joke — but when he approached them he could make nothing of it as he had missed the beginning of the story. The moonlight brightened the dusty road, and the dwarfed peach trees were black and motionless: there was no breeze. The drowsy buzz of swamp mosquitoes was like an echo of the silent night. The town seemed dark, except far down the road to the right there was the flicker of a lamp. Somewhere in the darkness a woman sang in a high wild voice and the tune had no start and no finish and was made up of only three notes which went on and on and on. The hunchback stood leaning against the banister of the porch, looking down the empty road as though hoping that someone would come along.

There were footsteps behind him, then a voice: "Cousin Lymon, your dinner is set out upon the table."

"My appetite is poor tonight," said the hunchback, who had been eating sweet snuff all the day. "There is a sourness in my mouth."

"Just a pick," said Miss Amelia. "The breast, the liver, and the heart."

Together they went back into the bright café, and sat down with Henry Macy. Their table was the largest one in the café, and on it there was a bouquet of swamp lilies in a Coca-Cola bottle. Miss Amelia had finished with her patient and was satisfied with herself. From behind the closed office door there had come only a few sleepy whimpers, and before the patient could wake up and become terrified it was all over. The child was now slung across the shoulder of his father, sleeping deeply, his little arms dangling loose along his father's back and his puffed-up face very red — they were leaving the café to go home.

Henry Macy was still silent. He ate carefully, making no noise when he swallowed, and was not a third as greedy as Cousin Lymon who had claimed to have no appetite and was now putting down helping after helping of the dinner. Occasionally Henry Macy looked across at Miss Amelia and again seemed to be on the point of saying something. But he held his peace.

It was a typical Saturday night. An old couple who had come in from the country hesitated for a moment at the doorway, holding each other's hand, and finally decided to come inside. They had lived together so long, this old country couple, that they looked as similar as twins. They were brown, shriveled, and like two little walking peanuts. They left early, and by midnight most of the other customers were gone. Rosser Cline and Merlie Ryan still played checkers, and Stumpy MacPhail sat with a liquor bottle on his table (his wife would not allow it in the home) and carried on peaceable conversations with himself. Henry Macy had not yet gone away, and this was unusual, as he almost always went to bed soon after nightfall. Miss Amelia yawned sleepily, but Lymon was restless and she did not suggest that they close up for the night.

Finally, at one o'clock, Henry Macy looked up at the corner of the ceiling and said quietly to Miss Amelia: "I got a letter today."

Miss Amelia was not one to be impressed by this, because all sorts of business letters and catalogues came addressed to her.

"I got a letter from my brother," said Henry Macy.

The hunchback, who had been goose-stepping about the café with his hands clasped behind his head, stopped suddenly. He was quick to sense any change in the atmosphere of a gathering. He glanced at each face in the room and waited.

Miss Amelia scowled and hardened her right fist. "You are welcome to it," she said.

"He is on parole. He is out of the penitentiary."

The face of Miss Amelia was very dark, and she shivered although the night was warm. Stumpy MacPhail and Merlie Ryan pushed aside their checker game. The café was very quiet.

"Who?" asked Cousin Lymon. His large, pale ears seemed to grow on his head and stiffen. "What?"

Miss Amelia slapped her hands palm down on the table. "Because Marvin Macy is a — " But her voice hoarsened and after a few moments she only said: "He belongs to be in that penitentiary the balance of his life."

"What did he do?" asked Cousin Lymon.

There was a long pause, as no one knew exactly how to answer this. "He robbed three filling stations," said Stumpy MacPhail. But his words did not sound complete and there was a feeling of sins left unmentioned.

The hunchback was impatient. He could not bear to be left out of anything, even a great misery. The name Marvin Macy was unknown to him, but it tantalized him as did any mention of subjects which others knew about and of which he was ignorant — such as any reference to the old sawmill that had been torn down before he came, or a chance word about poor Morris Finestein, or the recollection of any event that had occurred before his time. Aside from this inborn curiosity, the hunchback took a great interest in robbers and crimes of all varieties. As he strutted around the table he was muttering the words "released on parole" and "penitentiary" to himself. But although he questioned insistently, he was unable to find anything, as nobody would dare to talk about Marvin Macy before Miss Amelia in the café.

"The letter did not say very much," said Henry Macy. "He did not say where he was going."

"Humph!" said Miss Amelia, and her face was still hardened and very dark. "He will never set his split hoof on my premises."

She pushed back her chair from the table, and made ready to close the café. Thinking about Marvin Macy may have set her to brooding, for she hauled the cash register back to the kitchen and put it in a private place. Henry Macy went off down the dark road. But Henry Ford Crimp and Merlie Ryan lingered for a time on the front porch. Later Merlie Ryan was to make certain claims, to swear that on that night he had a vision of what was to come. But the town paid no attention, for that was just the sort of thing that Merlie Ryan would claim. Miss Amelia and Cousin Lymon talked for a time in the parlor. And when at last the hunchback thought that he could sleep she arranged the mosquito netting over his bed and waited until he had finished with his prayers. Then she put on her long nightgown, smoked two pipes, and only after a long time went to sleep.

That autumn was a happy time. The crops around the country-side were good, and over at the Forks Falls market the price of tobacco held firm that year. After the long hot summer the first cool days had a clean bright sweetness. Goldenrod grew along the dusty roads, and the sugar cane was ripe and purple. The bus came each day from Cheehaw to carry off a few of the younger children to the consolidated school to get an education. Boys hunted foxes in the pinewoods, winter quilts were aired out on the wash lines, and sweet potatoes bedded in the ground with straw against the colder months to come. In the evening, delicate shreds of smoke rose from the chimneys, and the moon was round and orange in the autumn sky. There is no stillness like the quiet of the first cold nights in the fall. Sometimes, late in the night when there was no wind, there could be heard in the town the thin wild whistle of the train that goes through Society City on its way far off to the North.

For Miss Amelia Evans this was a time of great activity. She was at work from dawn until sundown. She made a new and bigger condenser for her still, and in one week ran off enough liquor to souse the whole county. Her old mule was dizzy from grinding so much sorghum, and she scalded her Mason jars and put away pear preserves. She was looking forward greatly to the first frost, because she had traded for threee tremendous hogs, and intended to make much barbecue, chitterlins, and sausage.

During these weeks there was a quality about Miss Amelia that many people noticed. She laughed often, with a deep ringing laugh, and her whistling had a sassy, tuneful trickery. She was forever trying out her strength, lifting up heavy objects, or poking her tough biceps with her finger. One day she sat down to her typewriter and wrote a story — a story in which there were foreigners, trap doors, and millions of dollars. Cousin Lymon was with her always, traipsing along behind her coat-tails, and when she watched him her face had a bright, soft look, and when she spoke his name there lingered in her voice the undertone of love.

The first cold spell came at last. When Miss Amelia awoke one morning there were frost flowers on the windowpanes, and rime had silvered the patches of grass in the yard. Miss Amelia built a roaring fire in the kitchen stove, then went out of doors to judge the day. The air was cold and sharp, the sky pale green and cloudless. Very shortly people began to come in from the country to find out what Miss Amelia thought of the weather; she decided to kill the biggest hog, and word got round the countryside. The hog was slaughtered and a low oak fire started in the barbecue pit. There was the warm smell of pig blood and smoke in the back yard, the stamp of footsteps, the ring of voices in the winter air. Miss Amelia walked around giving orders and soon most of the work was done.

She had some particular business to do in Cheehaw that day, so after making sure that all was going well, she cranked up her car and got ready to leave. She asked Cousin Lymon to come with her, in fact, she asked him seven times, but he was loath to leave the commotion and wanted to remain. This seemed to trouble Miss Amelia, as she always liked to have him near to her, and was prone to be terribly homesick when she had to go any distance away. But after asking him seven times, she did not urge him any further. Before leaving she found a stick and drew a heavy line all around the barbecue pit, about two feet back from the edge, and told him not to trespass beyond that boundary. She left after dinner and intended to be back before dark.

Now, it is not so rare to have a truck or an automobile pass along the road and through the town on the way from Cheehaw to somewhere else. Every year the tax collector comes to argue with rich people such as Miss Amelia. And if somebody in the town, such as Merlie Ryan, takes a notion that he can connive to get a car on credit, or to pay down three dollars and have a fine electric icebox such as they advertise in the store windows of Cheehaw, then a city man will come out asking meddlesome questions, finding out all his troubles, and ruining his chances of buying anything on the installment plan. Sometimes, especially since they are working on the Forks Falls highway, the cars hauling the chain gang come through the town. And frequently people in automobiles get lost and stop to inquire how they can find the right road again. So, late that afternoon it was nothing unusual to have a truck pass the mill and stop in the middle of the road near the café of Miss Amelia. A man jumped down from the back of the truck, and the truck went on its way.

The man stood in the middle of the road and looked about him. He was a tall man, with brown curly hair, and slow-moving, deep-blue eyes. His lips were red and he smiled the lazy, half-mouthed smile of the braggart. The man wore a red shirt, and a wide belt of tooled leather; he carried a tin suitcase and a guitar. The first person in the town to see this newcomer was Cousin Lymon, who had heard the shifting of gears and come around to investigate. The hunchback stuck his head around the corner of the porch, but did not step out altogether into full view. He and the man stared at each other, and it was not the look of two strangers meeting for the first time and swiftly summing up each other. It was a peculiar stare they exchanged between them, like the look of two criminals who recognize each other. Then the man in the red shirt shrugged his left shoulder and turned away. The face of the hunchback was very pale as he watched the man go down the road, and after a few moments he began to follow along carefully, keeping many paces away.

It was immediately known throughout the town that Marvin Macy had come back again. First, he went to the mill, propped his elbows lazily on a window sill and looked inside. He liked to watch others hard at work, as do all born loafers. The mill was thrown into a sort of numb confusion. The dyers left the hot vats, the spinners and weavers forgot about their machines, and even Stumpy MacPhail, who was foreman, did not know exactly what to do. Marvin Macy still smiled his wet half-mouthed smiles, and when he saw his brother, his bragging expression did not change. After looking over the mill Marvin Macy went down the road to the house where he had been raised, and left his suitcase and guitar on the front porch. Then he walked around the millpond, looked over the church, the three stores, and the rest of the town. The hunchback trudged along quietly at some distance behind him, his hands in his pockets, and his little face still very pale.

It had grown late. The red winter sun was setting, and to the west the sky was deep gold and crimson. Ragged chimney swifts flew to their nests; lamps were lighted. Now and then there was the smell of smoke, and the warm rich odor of the barbecue slowly cooking in the pit behind the café. After making the rounds of the town Marvin Macy stopped before Miss Amelia's premises and read the sign above the porch. Then, not hesitating to trespass, he walked through the side yard. The mill whistle blew a thin, lonesome blast, and the day's shift was done. Soon there were others in Miss Amelia's back yard beside Marvin Macy — Henry Ford Crimp, Merlie Ryan, Stumpy MacPhail, and any number of children and people who stood around the edges of the property and looked on. Very little was said. Marvin Macy stood by himself on one side of the pit, and the rest of the people clustered together on the other side. Cousin Lymon stood somewhat apart from everyone, and he did not take his eyes from the face of Marvin Macy.

"Did you have a good time in the penitentiary?" asked Merlie Ryan, with a silly giggle.

Marvin Macy did not answer. He took from his hip pocket a large knife, opened it slowly, and honed the blade on the seat of his pants. Merlie Ryan grew suddenly very quiet and went to stand directly behind the broad back of Stumpy MacPhail.

Miss Amelia did not come home until almost dark. They heard the rattle of her automobile while she was still a long distance away, then the slam of the door and a bumping noise as though she were hauling something up the front steps of her premises. The sun had already set, and in the air there was the blue smoky glow of early winter evenings. Miss Amelia came down the back steps slowly, and the group in her yard waited very quietly. Few people in this world could stand up to Miss Amelia, and against Marvin Macy she had this special and bitter hate. Everyone waited to see her burst into a terrible holler, snatch up some dangerous object, and chase him altogether out of town. At first she did not see Marvin Macy, and her face had the relieved and dreamy expression that was natural to her when she reached home after having gone some distance away.

Miss Amelia must have seen Marvin Macy and Cousin Lymon at the same instant. She looked from one to the other, but it was not the wastrel from the penitentiary on whom she finally fixed her gaze of sick amazement. She, and everyone else, was looking at Cousin Lymon, and he was a sight to see.

The hunchback stood at the end of the pit, his pale face lighted by the soft glow from the smoldering oak fire. Cousin Lymon had a very peculiar accomplishment, which he used whenever he wished to ingratiate himself with someone. He would stand very still, and with just a little concentration, he could wiggle his large pale ears with marvelous quickness and ease. This trick he always used when he wanted to get something special out of Miss Amelia, and to her it was irresistible. Now as he stood there the hunchback's ears were wiggling furiously on his head, but it was not Miss Amelia at whom he was looking this time. The hunchback was smiling at Marvin Macy with an entreaty that was near to desperation. At first Marvin Macy paid no attention to him, and when he did finally glance at the hunchback it was without any appreciation whatsoever.

"What ails this Brokeback?" he asked with a rough jerk of his thumb.

No one answered. And Cousin Lymon, seeing that his accomplishment was getting him nowhere, added new efforts of persuasion. He fluttered his eyelids, so that they were like pale, trapped moths in his sockets. He scraped his feet around on the ground, waved his hands about, and finally began doing a little trotlike dance. In the last gloomy light of the winter afternoon he resembled the child of a swamp-haunt.

Marvin Macy, alone of all the people in the yard, was unimpressed.

"Is the runt throwing a fit?" he asked, and when no one answered he stepped forward and gave Cousin Lymon a cuff on the side of his head. The hunchback staggered, then fell back on the ground. He sat where he had fallen, still looking up at Marvin Macy, and with great effort his ears managed one last forlorn little flap.

Now everyone turned to Miss Amelia to see what she would do. In all these years no one had so much as touched a hair of Cousin Lymon's head, although many had had the itch to do so. If anyone even spoke crossly to the hunchback, Miss Amelia would cut off this rash mortal's credit and find ways of making things go hard for him a long time afterward. So now if Miss Amelia had split open Marvin Macy's head with the ax on the back porch no one would have been surprised. But she did nothing of the kind.

There were times when Miss Amelia seemed to go into a sort of trance. And the cause of these trances was usually known and understood. For Miss Amelia was a fine doctor, and did not grind up swamp roots and other untried ingredients and give them to the first patient who came along; whenever she invented a new medicine she always tried it out first on herself. She would swallow an enormous dose and spend the following day walking thoughtfully back and forth from the café to the brick privy. Often, when there was a sudden keen gripe, she would stand quite still, her queer eyes staring down at the ground and her fists clenched; she was trying to decide which organ was being worked upon, and what misery the new medicine might be most likely to cure. And now as she watched the hunchback and Marvin Macy, her face wore this same expression, tense with reckoning some inward pain, although she had taken no new medicine that day.

"That will learn you, Brokeback," said Marvin Macy.

Henry Macy pushed back his limp whitish hair from his forehead and coughed nervously. Stumpy MacPhail and Merlie Ryan shuffled their feet, and the children and black people on the outskirts of the property made not a sound. Marvin Macy folded the knife he had been honing, and after looking about him fearlessly he swaggered out of the yard. The embers in the pit were turning to gray feathery ashes and it was now quite dark.

That was the way Marvin Macy came back from the penitentiary. Not a living soul in all the town was glad to see him. Even Mrs. Mary Hale, who was a good woman and had raised him with love and care — at the first sight of him even this old foster mother dropped the skillet she was holding and burst into tears. But nothing could faze that Marvin Macy. He sat on the back steps of the Hale house, lazily picking his guitar, and when the supper was ready, he pushed the children of the household out of the way and served himself a big meal, although there had been barely enough hoecakes and white meat to go round. After eating he settled himself in the best and warmest sleeping place in the front room and was untroubled by dreams.

Miss Amelia did not open the café that night. She locked the doors and all the windows very carefully, nothing was seen of her and Cousin Lymon, and a lamp burned in her room all the night long.

Marvin Macy brought with him bad fortune, right from the first, as could be expected. The next day the weather turned suddenly, and it became hot. Even in the early morning there was a sticky sultriness in the atmosphere, the wind carried the rotten smell of the swamp, and delicate shrill mosquitoes webbed the green millpond. It was unseasonable, worse than August, and much damage was done. For nearly everyone in the county who owned a hog had copied Miss Amelia and slaughtered the day before. And what sausage could keep in such weather at this? After a few days there was everywhere the smell of slowly spoiling meat, and an atmosphere of dreary waste. Worse yet, a family reunion near the Forks Falls highway ate pork roast and died, every one of them. It was plain that their hog had been infected — and who could tell whether the rest of the meat was safe or not? People were torn between the longing for the good taste of pork, and the fear of death. It was a time of waste and confusion.

The cause of all this, Marvin Macy, had no shame in him. He was seen everywhere. During work hours he loafed about the mill, looking in at the windows, and on Sundays he dressed in his red shirt and paraded up and down the road with his guitar. He was still handsome — with his brown hair, his red lips, and his broad strong shoulders; but the evil in him was now too famous for his good looks to get him anywhere. And this evil was not measured only by the actual sins he had committed. True, he had robbed those filling stations. And before that he had ruined the tenderest girls in the county and laughed about it. Any number of wicked things could be listed against him, but quite apart from these crimes there was about him a secret meanness that clung to him almost like a smell. Another thing — he never sweated, not even in August, and that surely is a sign worth pondering over.

Now it seemed to the town that he was more dangerous than he had ever been before, as in the penitentiary in Atlanta he must have learned the method of laying charms. Otherwise how could his effect on Cousin Lymon be explained? For since first setting eyes on Marvin Macy the hunchback was possessed by an unnatural spirit. Every minute he wanted to be following along behind this jailbird, and he was full of silly schemes to attract attention to himself. Still Marvin Macy either treated him hatefully or failed to notice him at all. Sometimes the hunchback would give up, perch himself on the banister of the front porch much as a sick bird huddles on a telephone wire, and grieve publicly.

"But why?" Miss Amelia would ask, staring at him with her crossed, gray eyes, and her fists closed tight.

"Oh, Marvin Macy," groaned the hunchback, and the sound of the name was enough to upset the rhythm of his sobs so that he hiccuped. "He has been to Atlanta."

Miss Amelia would shake her head and her face was dark and hardened. To begin with she had no patience with any traveling; those who had made the trip to Atlanta or traveled fifty miles from home to see the ocean — those restless people she despised. "Going to Atlanta does no credit to him."

"He has been to the penitentiary," said the hunchback, miserable with longing.

How are you going to argue against such envies as these? In her perplexity Miss Amelia did not herself sound any too sure of what she was saying. "Been to the penitentiary, Cousin Lymon? Why, a trip like that is no travel to brag about."

During these weeks Miss Amelia was closely watched by everyone. She went about absent-mindedly, her face remote as though she had lapsed into one of her gripe trances. For some reason, after the day of Marvin Macy's arrival, she put aside her overalls and wore always the red dress she had before this time reserved for Sundays, funerals, and sessions of the court. Then as the weeks passed she began to take some steps to clear up the situation. But her efforts were hard to understand. If it hurt her to see Cousin Lymon follow Marvin Macy about the town, why did she not make the issues clear once and for all, and tell the hunchback that if he had dealings with Marvin Macy she would turn him off the premises? That would have been simple, and Cousin Lymon would have had to submit to her, or else face the sorry business of finding himself loose in the world. But Miss Amelia seemed to have lost her will; for the first time in her life she hesitated as to just what course to pursue. And, like most people in such a position of uncertainty, she did the worst thing possible — she began following several courses at once, all of them contrary to each other.

The café was opened every night as usual, and, strangely enough, when Marvin Macy came swaggering through the door, with the hunchback at his heels, she did not turn him out. She even gave him free drinks and smiled at him in a wild, crooked way. At the same time she set a terrible trap for him out in the swamp that surely would have killed him if he had got caught. She let Cousin Lymon invite him to Sunday dinner, and then tried to trip him up as he went down the steps. She began a great campaign of pleasure for Cousin Lymon — making exhausting trips to various spectacles being held in distant places, driving the automobile thirty miles to a Chautauqua, taking him to Forks Falls to watch a parade. All in all it was a distracting time for Miss Amelia. In the opinion of most people she was well on her way in the climb up fools' hill, and everyone waited to see how it would all turn out.

The weather turned cold again, the winter was upon the town, and night came before the last shift in the mill was done. Children kept on all their garments when they slept, and women raised the backs of their skirts to toast themselves dreamily at the fire. After it rained, the mud in the road made hard frozen ruts, there were faint flickers of lamplight from the windows of the houses, the peach trees were scrawny and bare. In the dark, silent nights of wintertime the café was the warm center point of the town, the lights shining so brightly that they could be seen a quarter of a mile away. The great iron stove at the back of the room roared, crackled, and turned red. Miss Amelia had made red curtains for the windows, and from a salesman who passed through the town she bought a great bunch of paper roses that looked very real.

But it was not only the warmth, the decorations, and the brightness, that made the café what it was. There is a deeper reason why the café was so precious to this town. And this deeper reason has to do with a certain pride that had not hitherto been known in these parts. To understand this new pride the cheapness of human life must be kept in mind. There were always plenty of people clustered around a mill — but it was seldom that every family had enough meal, garments, and fat back to go the rounds. Life could become one long dim scramble just to get the things needed to keep alive. And the confusing point is this: All useful things have a price, and are bought only with money, as that is the way the world is run. You know without having to reason about it the price of a bale of cotton, or a quart of molasses. But no value has been put on human life; it is given to us free and taken without being paid for. What is it worth? If you look around, at times the value may seem to be little or nothing at all. Often after you have sweated and tried and things are not better for you, there comes a feeling deep down in the soul that you are not worth much.

But the new pride that the café brought to this town had an effect on almost everyone, even the children. For in order to come to the café you did not have to buy the dinner, or a portion of liquor. There were cold bottled drinks for a nickel. And if you could not even afford that, Miss Amelia had a drink called Cherry Juice which sold for a penny a glass, and was pink-colored and very sweet. Almost everyone, with the exception of Reverend T. M. Willin, came to the café at least once during the week. Children love to sleep in houses other than their own, and to eat at a neighbor's table; on such occasions they behave themselves decently and are proud. The people in the town were likewise proud when sitting at the tables in the café. They washed before coming to Miss Amelia's, and scraped their feet very politely on the threshold as they entered the café. There, for a few hours at least, the deep bitter knowing that you are not worth much in this world could be laid low.

The café was a special benefit to bachelors, unfortunate people, and consumptives. And here it may be mentioned that there was some reason to suspect that Cousin Lymon was consumptive. The brightness of his gray eyes, his insistence, his talkativeness, and his cough — these were all signs. Besides, there is generally supposed to be some connection between a hunched spine and consumption. But whenever this subject had been mentioned to Miss Amelia she had become furious; she denied these symptoms with bitter vehemence, but on the sly she treated Cousin Lymon with hot chest plasters, Kroup Kure, and such. Now this winter the hunchback's cough was worse, and sometimes even on cold days he would break out in a heavy sweat. But this did not prevent him from following along after Marvin Macy.

Early every morning he left the premises and went to the back door of Mrs. Hale's house, and waited and waited — as Marvin Macy was a lazy sleeper. He would stand there and call out softly. His voice was just like the voices of children who squat patiently over those tiny little holes in the ground where doodlebugs are thought to live, poking the hole with a broom straw, and calling plaintively: "Doodlebug, Doodlebug — fly away home. Mrs. Doodlebug, Mrs. Doodlebug. Come out, come out. Your house is on fire and all your children are burning up." In just such a voice — at once sad, luring, and resigned — would the hunchback call Marvin Macy's name each morning. Then when Marvin Macy came out for the day, he would trail him about the town, and sometimes they would be gone for hours together out in the swamp.

And Miss Amelia continued to do the worst thing possible: that is, to try to follow several courses at once. When Cousin Lymon left the house she did not call him back, but only stood in the middle of the road and watched lonesomely until he was out of sight. Nearly every day Marvin Macy turned up with Cousin Lymon at dinnertime, and ate at her table. Miss Amelia opened the pear preserves, and the table was well-set with ham or chicken, great bowls of hominy grits, and winter peas. It is true that on one occasion Miss Amelia tried to poison Marvin Macy — but there was a mistake, the plates were confused, and it was she herself who got the poisoned dish. This she quickly realized by the slight bitterness of the food, and that day she ate no dinner. She sat tilted back in her chair, feeling her muscle, and looking at Marvin Macy.

Every night Marvin Macy came to the café and settled himself at the best and largest table, the one in the center of the room. Cousin Lymon brought him liquor, for which he did not pay a cent. Marvin Macy brushed the hunchback aside as if he were a swamp mosquito, and not only did he show no gratitude for these favors, but if the hunchback got in his way he would cuff him with the back of his hand, or say: "Out of my way, Brokeback — I'll snatch you bald-headed." When this happened Miss Amelia would come out from behind her counter and approach Marvin Macy very slowly, her fists clenched, her peculiar red dress hanging awkwardly around her bony knees. Marvin Macy would also clench his fists and they would walk slowly and meaningfully around each other. But, although everyone watched breathlessly, nothing ever came of it. The time for the fight was not yet ready.

There is one particular reason why this winter is remembered and still talked about. A great thing happened. People woke up on the second of January and found the whole world about them altogether changed. Little ignorant children looked out of the windows, and they were so puzzled that they began to cry. Old people harked back and could remember nothing in these parts to equal the phenomenon. For in the night it had snowed. In the dark hours after midnight the dim flakes started falling softly on the town. By dawn the ground was covered, and the strange snow banked the ruby windows of the church, and whitened the roofs of the houses. The snow gave the town a drawn, bleak look. The two-room houses near the mill were dirty, crooked, and seemed about to collapse, and somehow everything was dark and shrunken. But the snow itself — there was a beauty about it few people around here had ever known before. The snow was not white, as Northerners had pictured it to be; in the snow there were soft colors of blue and silver, the sky was a gentle shining gray. And the dreamy quietness of falling snow — when had the town been so silent?

People reacted to the snowfall in various ways. Miss Amelia, on looking out of her window, thoughtfully wiggled the toes of her bare feet, gathered close to her neck the collar of her nightgown. She stood there for some time, then commenced to draw the shutters and lock every window on the premises. She closed the place completely, lighted the lamps, and sat solemnly over her bowl of grits. The reason for this was not that Miss Amelia feared the snowfall. It was simply that she was unable to form an immediate opinion of this new event, and unless she knew exactly and definitely what she thought of a matter (which was nearly always the case) she preferred to ignore it. Snow had never fallen in this county in her lifetime, and she had never thought about it one way or the other. But if she admitted this snowfall she would have to come to some decision, and in those days there was enough distraction in her life as it was already. So she poked about the gloomy, lamp-lighted house and pretended that nothing had happened. Cousin Lymon, on the contrary, chased around in the wildest excitement, and when Miss Amelia turned her back to dish him some breakfast he slipped out of the door.

Marvin Macy laid claim to the snowfall. He said that he knew snow, had seen it in Atlanta, and from the way he walked about the town that day it was as though he owned every flake. He sneered at the little children who crept timidly out of the houses and scooped up handfuls of snow to taste. Reverend Willin hurried down the road with a furious face, as he was thinking deeply and trying to weave the snow into his Sunday sermon. Most people were humble and glad about this marvel; they spoke in hushed voices and said "thank you" and "please" more than was necessary. A few weak characters, of course, were demoralized and got drunk — but they were not numerous. To everyone this was an occasion and many counted their money and planned to go to the café that night.

Cousin Lymon followed Marvin Macy about all day, seconding his claim to the snow. He marveled that snow did not fall as does rain, and stared up at the dreamy, gently falling flakes until he stumbled from dizziness. And the pride he took on himself, basking in the glory of Marvin Macy — it was such that many people could not resist calling out to him: " 'Oho,' said the fly on the chariot wheel. 'What a dust we do raise.' "

Miss Amelia did not intend to serve a dinner. But when, at six o'clock, there was the sound of footsteps on the porch she opened the front door cautiously. It was Henry Ford Crimp, and though there was no food, she let him sit at a table and served him a drink. Others came. The evening was blue, bitter, and though the snow fell no longer there was a wind from the pine trees that swept up delicate flurries from the ground. Cousin Lymon did not come until after dark, with him Marvin Macy, and he carried his tin suitcase and his guitar.

"So you mean to travel?" said Miss Amelia quickly.

Marvin Macy warmed himself at the stove. Then he settled down at his table and carefully sharpened a little stick. He picked his teeth, frequently taking the stick out of his mouth to look at the end and wipe it on the sleeve of his coat. He did not bother to answer.

The hunchback looked at Miss Amelia, who was behind the counter. His face was not in the least beseeching; he seemed quite sure of himself. He folded his hands behind his back and perked up his ears confidently. His cheeks were red, his eyes shining, and his clothes were soggy wet. "Marvin Macy is going to visit a spell with us," he said.

Miss Amelia made no protest. She only came out from behind the counter and hovered over the stove, as though the news had made her suddenly cold. She did not warm her backside modestly, lifting her skirt only an inch or so, as do most women when in public. There was not a grain of modesty about Miss Amelia, and she frequently seemed to forget altogether that there were men in the room. Now as she stood warming herself, her red dress was pulled up quite high in the back so that a piece of her strong, hairy thigh could be seen by anyone who cared to look at it. Her head was turned to one side; and she had begun talking with herself, nodding and wrinkling her forehead, and there was the tone of accusation and reproach in her voice although the words were not plain. Meanwhile, the hunchback and Marvin Macy had gone upstairs — up to the parlor with the pampas grass and the two sewing machines, to the private rooms where Miss Amelia had lived the whole of her life. Down in the café you could hear them bumping around, unpacking Marvin Macy, and getting him settled.

That is the way Marvin Macy crowded into Miss Amelia's home. At first Cousin Lymon, who had given Marvin Macy his own room, slept on the sofa in the parlor. But the snowfall had a bad effect on him; he caught a cold that turned into a winter quinsy, so Miss Amelia gave up her bed to him. The sofa in the parlor was much too short for her, her feet lapped over the edges, and often she rolled off onto the floor. Perhaps it was this lack of sleep that clouded her wits; everything she tried to do against Marvin Macy rebounded on herself. She got caught in her own tricks, and found herself in many pitiful positions. But still she did not put Marvin Macy off the premises, as she was afraid that she would be left alone. Once you have lived with another, it is a great torture to have to live alone. The silence of a firelit room when suddenly the clock stops ticking, the nervous shadows in an empty house — it is better to take in your mortal enemy than face the terror of living alone.

The snow did not last. The sun came out and within two days the town was just as it had always been before. Miss Amelia did not open her house until every flake had melted. Then she had a big house cleaning and aired everything out in the sun. But before that, the very first thing she did on going out again into her yard, was to tie a rope to the largest branch of the chinaberry tree. At the end of the rope she tied a crocus sack tightly stuffed with sand. This was the punching bag she made her herself, and from that day on she would box with it out in her yard every morning. Already she was a fine fighter — a little heavy on her feet, but knowing all manner of mean holds and squeezes to make up for this.

Miss Amelia, as has been mentioned, measured six feet two inches in height. Marvin Macy was one inch shorter. In weight they were about even — both of them weighing close to a hundred and sixty pounds. Marvin Macy had the advantage in slyness of movement, and in toughness of chest. In fact from the outward point of view the odds were altogether in his favor. Yet almost everyone in the town was betting on Miss Amelia; scarcely a person would put up money on Marvin Macy. The town remembered the great fight between Miss Amelia and a Forks Falls lawyer who had tried to cheat her. He had been a huge strapping fellow, but he was left three-quarters dead when she had finished with him. And it was not only her talent as a boxer that had impressed everyone — she could demoralize her enemy by making terrifying faces and fierce noises, so that even the spectators were sometimes cowed. She was brave, she practiced faithfully with her punching bag, and in this case she was clearly in the right. So people had confidence in her, and they waited. Of course there was no set date for this fight. There were just the signs that were too plain to be overlooked.

During these times the hunchback strutted around with a pleased little pinched-up face. In many delicate and clever ways he stirred up trouble between them. He was constantly plucking at Marvin Macy's trouser leg to draw attention to himself. Sometimes he followed in Miss Amelia's footsteps — but these days it was only in order to imitate her awkward, long-legged walk; he crossed his eyes and aped her gestures in a way that made her appear to be a freak. There was something so terrible about this that even the silliest customers of the café, such as Merlie Ryan, did not laugh. Only Marvin Macy drew up the left corner of his mouth and chuckled. Miss Amelia, when this happened, would be divided between two emotions. She would look at the hunchback with a lost, dismal reproach — then turn toward Marvin Macy with her teeth clamped.

"Bust a gut!" she would say bitterly.

And Marvin Macy, most likely, would pick up the guitar from the floor beside his chair. His voice was wet and slimy, as he always had too much spit in his mouth. And the tunes he sang glided slowly from his throat like eels. His strong fingers picked the strings with dainty skill, and everything he sang both lured and exasperated. This was usually more than Miss Amelia could stand.

"Bust a gut!" she would repeat, in a shout.

But always Marvin Macy had the answer ready for her. He would cover the strings to silence the quivering leftover tones, and reply with slow, sure insolence.

"Everything you holler at me bounces back on yourself. Yah! Yah!"

Miss Amelia would have to stand there helpless, as no one has ever invented a way out of this trap. She could not shout out abuse that would bounce back on herself. He had the best of her, there was nothing she could do.

So things went on like this. What happened between the three of them during the nights in the rooms upstairs nobody knows. But the café became more and more crowded every night. A new table had to be brought in. Even the Hermit, the crazy man named Rainer Smith, who took to the swamp years ago, heard something of the situation, and came one night to look in at the window and brood over the gathering in the bright café. And the climax each evening was the time when Miss Amelia and Marvin Macy doubled their fists, squared up, and glared at each other. Usually this did not happen after any especial argument, but it seemed to come about mysteriously, by means of some instinct on the part of both of them. At these times the café would become so quiet that you could hear the bouquet of paper roses rustling in the draft. And each night they held this fighting stance a little longer than the night before.

The fight took place on Ground Hog Day, which is the second of February. The weather was favorable, being neither rainy nor sunny, and with a neutral temperature. There were several signs that this was the appointed day, and by ten o'clock the news spread all over the county. Early in the morning Miss Amelia went out and cut down her punching bag. Marvin Macy sat on the back step with a tin can of hog fat between his knees and carefully greased his arms and his legs. A hawk with a bloody breast flew over the town and circled twice around the property of Miss Amelia. The tables in the café were moved out to the back porch, so that the whole big room was cleared for the fight. There was every sign. Both Miss Amelia and Marvin Macy ate four helpings of half-raw roast for dinner, and then lay down in the afternoon to store up strength. Marvin Macy rested in the big room upstairs, while Miss Amelia stretched herself out on the bench in her office. It was plain from her white stiff face what a torment it was for her to be lying still and doing nothing, but she lay there quiet as a corpse with her eyes closed and her hands crossed on her chest.

Cousin Lymon had a restless day, and his little face was drawn and tightened with excitement. He put himself up a lunch, and set out to find the ground hog — within an hour he returned, the lunch eaten, and said that the ground hog had seen his shadow and there was to be bad weather ahead. Then, as Miss Amelia and Marvin Macy were both resting to gather strength, and he was left to himself, it occurred to him that he might as well paint the front porch. The house had not been painted for years — in fact, God knows if it had ever been painted at all. Cousin Lymon scrambled around, and soon he had painted half the floor of the porch a gay bright green. It was a loblolly job, and he smeared himself all over. Typically enough he did not even finish the floor, but changed over to the walls, painting as high as he could reach and then standing on a crate to get up a foot higher. When the paint ran out, the right side of the floor was bright green and there was a jagged portion of wall that had been painted. Cousin Lymon left it at that.

There was something childish about his satisfaction with his painting. And in this respect a curious fact should be mentioned. No one in the town, not even Miss Amelia, had any idea how old the hunchback was. Some maintained that when he came to town he was about twelve years old, still a child — others were certain that he was well past forty. His eyes were blue and steady as a child's, but there were lavender crepy shadows beneath these blue eyes that hinted of age. It was impossible to guess his age by his hunched queer body. And even his teeth gave no clue — they were all still in his head (two were broken from cracking a pecan), but he had stained them with so much sweet snuff that it was impossible to decide whether they were old teeth or young teeth. When questioned directly about his age the hunchback professed to know absolutely nothing — he had no idea how long he had been on the earth, whether for ten years or a hundred! So his age remained a puzzle.

Cousin Lymon finished his painting at five-thirty o'clock in the afternoon. The day had turned colder and there was a wet taste in the air. The wind came up from the pinewoods, rattling windows, blowing an old newspaper down the road until at last it caught upon a thorn tree. People began to come in from the country; packed automobiles that bristled with the poked-out heads of children, wagons drawn by old mules who seemed to smile in a weary, sour way and plodded along with their tired eyes half-closed. Three young boys came from Society City. All three of them wore yellow rayon shirts and caps put on backward — they were as much alike as triplets, and could always be seen at cockfights and camp meetings. At six o'clock the mill whistle sounded the end of the day's shift and the crowd was complete. Naturally, among the newcomers there were some riffraff, unknown characters, and so forth — but even so the gathering was quiet. A hush was on the town and the faces of people were strange in the fading light. Darkness hovered softly; for a moment the sky was a pale clear yellow against which the gables of the church stood out in dark and bare outline, then the sky died slowly and the darkness gathered into night.

Seven is a popular number, and especially it was a favorite with Miss Amelia. Seven swallows of water for hiccups, seven runs around the millpond for cricks in the neck, seven doses of Amelia Miracle Mover as a worm cure — her treatment nearly always hinged on this number. It is a number of mingled possibilities, and all who love mystery and charms set store by it. So the fight was to take place at seven o'clock. This was known to everyone, not by announcement or words, but understood in the unquestioning way that rain is understood, or an evil odor from the swamp. So before seven o'clock everyone gathered gravely around the property of Miss Amelia. The cleverest got into the café itself and stood lining the walls of the room. Others crowded onto the front porch, or took a stand in the yard.

Miss Amelia and Marvin Macy had not yet shown themselves. Miss Amelia, after resting all afternoon on the office bench, had gone upstairs. On the other hand Cousin Lymon was at your elbow every minute, threading his way through the crowd, snapping his fingers nervously, and batting his eyes. At one minute to seven o'clock he squirmed his way into the café and climbed up on the counter. All was very quiet.

It must have been arranged in some manner beforehand. For just at the stroke of seven Miss Amelia showed herself at the head of the stairs. At the same instant Marvin Macy appeared in front of the café and the crowd made way for him silently. They walked toward each other with no haste, their fists already gripped, and their eyes like the eyes of dreamers. Miss Amelia had changed her red dress for her old overalls, and they were rolled up to the knees. She was barefooted and she had an iron strengthband around her right wrist. Marvin Macy had also rolled his trouser legs — he was naked to the waist and heavily greased; he wore the heavy shoes that had been issued him when he left the penitentiary. Stumpy MacPhail stepped forward from the crowd and slapped their hip pockets with the palm of his hand to make sure there would be no sudden knives. Then they were alone in the cleared center of the bright café.

There was no signal, but they both struck out simultaneously. Both blows landed on the chin, so that the heads of Miss Amelia and Marvin Macy bobbed back and they were left a little groggy. For a few seconds after the first blows they merely shuffled their feet around on the bare floor, experimenting with various positions, and making mock fists. Then, like wildcats, they were suddenly on each other. There was the sound of knocks, panting, and thumpings on the floor. They were so fast that it was hard to take in what was going on — but once Miss Amelia was hurled backward so that she staggered and almost fell, and another time Marvin Macy caught a knock on the shoulder that spun him round like a top. So the fight went on in this wild violent way with no sign of weakening on either side.

During a struggle like this, when the enemies are as quick and strong as these two, it is worthwhile to turn from the confusion of the fight itself and observe the spectators. The people had flattened back as close as possible against the walls. Stumpy MacPhail was in a corner, crouched over and with his fists tight in sympathy, making strange noises. Poor Merlie Ryan had his mouth so wide open that a fly buzzed into it, and was swallowed before Merlie realized what had happened. And Cousin Lymon — he was worth watching. The hunchback still stood on the counter, so that he was raised up above everyone else in the café. He had his hands on his hips, his big head thrust forward, and his little legs bent so that the knees jutted outward. The excitement had made him break out in a rash, and his pale mouth shivered.

Perhaps it was half an hour before the course of the fight shifted. Hundreds of blows had been exchanged, and there was still a deadlock. Then suddenly Marvin Macy managed to catch hold of Miss Amelia's left arm and pinion it behind her back. She struggled and got a grasp around his waist; the real fight was now begun. Wrestling is the natural way of fighting in this county — as boxing is too quick and requires much thinking and concentration. And now that Miss Amelia and Marvin Macy were locked in a hold together the crowd came out of its daze and pressed in closer. For a while the fighters grappled muscle to muscle, their hipbones braced against each other. Backward and forward, from side to side, they swayed in this way. Marvin Macy still had not sweated, but Miss Amelia's overalls were drenched and so much sweat had trickled down her legs that she left wet footprints on the floor. Now the test had come, and in these moments of terrible effort, it was Miss Amelia who was the stronger. Marvin Macy was greased and slippery, tricky to grasp, but she was stronger. Gradually she bent him over backward, and inch by inch she forced him to the floor. It was a terrible thing to watch and their deep hoarse breaths were the only sound in the café. At last she had him down, and straddled; her strong big hands were on his throat.

But at that instant, just as the fight was won, a cry sounded in the café that caused a shrill bright shiver to run down the spine. And what took place has been a mystery ever since. The whole town was there to testify what happened, but there were those who doubted their own eyesight. For the counter on which Cousin Lymon stood was at least twelve feet from the fighters in the center of the café. Yet at the instant Miss Amelia grasped the throat of Marvin Macy the hunchback sprang forward and sailed through the air as though he had grown hawk wings. He landed on the broad strong back of Miss Amelia and clutched at her neck with his clawed little fingers.

The rest is confusion. Miss Amelia was beaten before the crowd could come to their senses. Because of the hunchback the fight was won by Marvin Macy, and at the end Miss Amelia lay sprawled on the floor, her arms flung outward and motionless. Marvin Macy stood over her, his face somewhat popeyed, but smiling his old half-mouthed smile. And the hunchback, he had suddenly disappeared. Perhaps he was frightened about what he had done, or maybe he was so delighted that he wanted to glory with himself alone — at any rate he slipped out of the café and crawled under the back steps. Someone poured water on Miss Amelia, and after a time she got up slowly and dragged herself into her office. Through the open door the crowd could see her sitting at her desk, her head in the crook of her arm, and she was sobbing with the last of her grating, winded breath. Once she gathered her right fist together and knocked it three times on the top of her office desk, then her hand opened feebly and lay palm upward and still. Stumpy Mac-Phail stepped forward and closed the door.

The crowd was quiet, and one by one the people left the café. Mules were waked up and untied, automobiles cranked, and the three boys from Society City roamed off down the road on foot. This was not a fight to hash over and talk about afterward; people went home and pulled the covers up over their heads. The town was dark, except for the premises of Miss Amelia, but every room was lighted there the whole night long.

Marvin Macy and the hunchback must have left the town an hour or so before daylight. And before they went away this is what they did:

They unlocked the private cabinet of curios and took everything in it.

They broke the mechanical piano.

They carved terrible words on the café tables.

The found the watch that opened in the back to show a picture of a waterfall and took that also.

They poured a gallon of sorghum syrup all over the kitchen floor and smashed the jars of preserves.

They went out in the swamp and completely wrecked the still, ruining the big new condenser and the cooler, and setting fire to the shack itself.

They fixed a dish of Miss Amelia's favorite food, grits with sausage, seasoned it with enough poison to kill off the county, and placed this dish temptingly on the café counter.

They did everything ruinous they could think of without actually breaking into the office where Miss Amelia stayed the night. Then they went off together, the two of them.

That was how Miss Amelia was left alone in the town. The people would have helped her if they had known how, as people in this town will as often as not be kindly if they have a chance. Several housewives nosed around with brooms and offered to clear up the wreck. But Miss Amelia only looked at them with lost crossed eyes and shook her head. Stumpy MacPhail came in on the third day to buy a plug of Queenie tobacco, and Miss Amelia said the price was one dollar. Everything in the café had suddenly risen in price to be worth one dollar. And what sort of a café is that? Also, she changed very queerly as a doctor. In all the years before she had been much more popular than the Cheehaw doctor. She had never monkeyed with a patient's soul, taking away from him such real necessities as liquor, tobacco, and so forth. Once in a great while she might carefully warn a patient never to eat fried watermelon or some such dish it had never occurred to a person to want in the first place. Now all this wise doctoring was over. She told one-half of her patients that they were going to die outright, and to the remaining half she recommended cures so farfetched and agonizing that no one in his right mind would consider them for a moment.

Miss Amelia let her hair grow ragged, and it was turning gray. Her face lengthened, and the great muscles of her body shrank until she was thin as old maids are thin when they go crazy. And those gray eyes — slowly day by day they were more crossed, and it was as though they sought each other out to exchange a little glance of grief and lonely recognition. She was not pleasant to listen to; her tongue had sharpened terribly.

When anyone mentioned the hunchback she would say only this: "Ho! If I could lay hand to him I would rip out his gizzard and throw it to the cat!" But it was not so much the words that were terrible, but the voice in which they were said. Her voice had lost its old vigor; there was none of the ring of vengeance it used to have when she would mention "that loom-fixer I was married to," or some other enemy. Her voice was broken, soft, and sad as the wheezy whine of the church pump-organ.

For three years she sat out on the front steps every night, alone and silent, looking down the road and waiting. But the hunchback never returned. There were rumors that Marvin Macy used him to climb into windows and steal, and other rumors that Marvin Macy had sold him into a side show. But both these reports were traced back to Merlie Ryan. Nothing true was ever heard of him. It was in the fourth year that Miss Amelia hired a Cheehaw carpenter and had him board up the premises, and there in those closed rooms she has remained ever since.

Yes, the town is dreary. On August afternoons the road is empty, white with dust, and the sky above is bright as glass. Nothing moves — there are no children's voices, only the hum of the mill. The peach trees seem to grow more crooked every summer, and the leaves are dull gray and of a sickly delicacy. The house of Miss Amelia leans so much to the right that it is now only a question of time when it will collapse completely, and people are careful not to walk around the yard. There is no good liquor to be bought in the town; the nearest still is eight miles away, and the liquor is such that those who drink it grow warts on their livers the size of goobers, and dream themselves into a dangerous inward world. There is absolutely nothing to do in the town. Walk around the millpond, stand kicking at a rotten stump, figure out what you can do with the old wagon wheel by the side of the road near the church. The soul rots with boredom. You might as well go down to the Forks Falls highway and listen to the chain gang.

# The Twelve Mortal Men

The Forks Falls highway is three miles from the town, and it is here the chain gang has been working. The road is of macadam, and the county decided to patch up the rough places and widen it at a certain dangerous place. The gang is made up of twelve men, all wearing black and white striped prison suits, and chained at the ankles. There is a guard, with a gun, his eyes drawn to red slits by the glare. The gang works all the day long, arriving huddled in the prison cart soon after daybreak, and being driven off again in the gray August twilight. All day there is the sound of the picks striking into the clay earth, hard sunlight, the smell of sweat. And every day there is music. One dark voice will start a phrase, half-sung, and like a question. And after a moment another voice will join in, soon the whole gang will be singing. The voices are dark in the golden glare, the music intricately blended, both somber and joyful. The music will swell until at last it seems that the sound does not come from the twelve men on the gang, but from the earth itself, or the wide sky. It is music that causes the heart to broaden and the listener to grow cold with ecstasy and fright. Then slowly the music will sink down until at last there remains one lonely voice, then a great hoarse breath, the sun, the sound of the picks in the silence.

And what kind of gang is this that can make such music? Just twelve mortal men, seven of them black and five of them white boys from this county. Just twelve mortal men who are together.

# Robert Penn Warren (1905–     )

POET, short-story writer, novelist, biographer, essayist, teacher, and editor, Robert Penn Warren is one of the most versatile as well as distinguished of our Southern writers. He was born in Kentucky, graduated from Vanderbilt University, where he was associated with the famous *Fugitive* magazine, received a Master's degree from the University of California, and was a Rhodes Scholar at Oxford. In 1935 he founded *The Southern Review* of which he was an editor for seven years. He was a prominent member of the New Critics group. His first book was a biography, *John Brown: The Making of a Martyr* (1929), and his first novel *Night Rider* (1939). Two of his books have won Pulitzer Prizes: *All the King's Men* in 1946, a novel, and *Promises* in 1957, poetry.

Although a tragic love story beginning and ending in the present, "Cass Mastern's Wedding Ring" gives a finely distilled sense of Kentucky life immediately before and after the War between the States. The sharply contrasting attitudes of various Southern whites in their behavior toward slaves, some indifferent to their suffering, others aware and trying to ameliorate it, gives a historical perspective on the whole abomination. Robert Penn Warren has achieved a psychological triumph by making Cass Mastern understand his own "humanitarian" behavior toward slaves when he learns why the woman he loves sold "down river" her slave woman. It also confronts a reader with a delicate problem in his own ethics.

# Cass Mastern's Wedding Ring

LONG AGO Jack Burden was a graduate student, working for his Ph.D. in American History, in the State University of his native state. This Jack Burden (of whom the present Jack Burden, *Me*, is a legal, biological, and perhaps even metaphysical continuator) lived in a slatternly apartment with two other graduate students, one industrious, stupid, unlucky, and alcoholic, and the other idle, intelligent, lucky, and alcoholic. At least they were alcoholic for a period after the first of the month, when they received the miserable check paid them by the University for their miserable work as assistant teachers. The industry and ill luck of one cancelled out against the idleness and luck of the other and they both amounted to the same thing, and they drank what they could get when they could get it. They drank because they didn't really have the slightest interest in what they were doing now and didn't have the slightest hope for the future. They could not even bear the thought of pushing on to finish their degrees, for that would mean leaving the University (leaving the first-of-the-month drunks, the yammer about "work" and "ideas" in smoke-blind rooms, the girls who staggered slightly and giggled indiscreetly on the dark stairs leading to the apartment) to go to some normal school on a sun-baked cross-roads or a junior college long on Jesus and short on funds, to go to face the stark reality of drudgery and dry-rot and prying eyes and the slow withering of the green wisp of dream which had, like some window-plant in an invalid's room, grown out of a bottle. Only the bottle hadn't had water in it. It had had something which looked like water, smelled like kerosene, and tasted like carbolic acid: one-run corn whisky.

Jack Burden lived with them, in the slatternly apartment among the unwashed dishes in the sink and on the table, the odor of stale tobacco smoke, the dirty shirts and underwear piled in corners. He even took a relish in the squalor, in the privilege of letting a last crust of buttered toast fall to the floor to lie undisturbed until the random heel should grind it into the mud-colored carpet, in the spectacle of the fat roach moving across the cracked linoleum of the bathroom floor while he steamed in the tub. Once he had brought his mother to the apartment for tea, and she had sat on the edge of the overstuffed chair, holding a cracked cup and talking with a brittle and calculated charm out of a face which was obviously being held in shape by a profound exercise of will. She saw a roach venture out from the kitchen door. She saw one of Jack Burden's friends crush an ant on the inner lip of the sugar bowl and flick the carcass from his finger. The nail of the finger itself was not very clean. But she kept right on delivering the charm, out of the rigid face. He had to say that for her.

But afterwards, as they walked down the street, she had said: "Why do you live like that?"

"It's what I'm built for, I reckon," Jack Burden said.

"With those people," she said.

"They're all right," he said, and wondered if they were, and wondered if he was.

His mother didn't say anything for a minute, making a sharp, bright clicking on the pavement with her heels as she walked along, holding her small shoulders trimly back, carrying her famished-cheeked, blue-eyed, absolutely innocent face slightly lifted to the pulsing sunset world of April like a very expensive present the world ought to be glad even to have a look at. And back then, fifteen years ago, it was still something to look at, too. Sometimes Jack Burden (who was *Me* or what *Me* was fifteen years ago) would be proud to go into a place with her, and have people stare the way they would, and just for a minute he would be happy. But there is a lot more to everything than just walking into a hotel lobby or restaurant.

Walking along beside him, she said meditatively: "That dark-haired one — if he'd get cleaned up — he wouldn't be bad looking."

"That's what a lot of other women think," Jack Burden said, and suddenly felt a nauseated hatred of the dark-haired one, the one who had killed the ant on the sugar bowl, who had the dirty nails. But he had to go on, something in him made him go on: "Yes, and a lot of them don't even care about cleaning him up. They'll take him like he is. He's the great lover of the apartment. He put the sag in the springs of that divan we got."

"Don't be vulgar," she said, because she definitely did not like what is known as vulgarity in conversation.

"It's the truth," he said.

She didn't answer, and her heels did the bright clicking. Then she said, "If he'd throw those awful clothes away — and get something decent."

"Yeah," Jack Burden said, "on his seventy-five dollars a month."

She looked at him now, down at his clothes. "Yours are pretty awful, too," she said.

"Are they?" Jack Burden demanded.

"I'll send you money for some decent clothes," she said.

A few days later the check came and a note telling him to get a "couple of decent suits and accessories." The check was for two hundred and fifty dollars. He did not even buy a necktie. But he and the two other men in the apartment had a wonderful blow-out, which lasted for five days, and as a result of which the industrious and unlucky one lost his job and the idle and lucky one got too sociable and, despite his luck, contracted what is quaintly known as a social disease. But nothing happened to Jack Burden, for nothing ever happened to Jack Burden, who was invulnerable. Perhaps that was the curse of Jack Burden: he was invulnerable.

So, as I have said, Jack Burden lived in the slatternly apartment with the two other graduate students, for even after being fired the unlucky, industrious one still lived in the apartment. He simply stopped paying anything, but he stayed. He borrowed money for cigarettes. He sullenly ate the food the others brought in and cooked. He lay around during the day, for there was no reason to be industrious any more, ever again. Once at night, Jack Burden woke up and thought he heard the sounds of sobs from the living room, where the unlucky, industrious one slept on a wall-bed. Then one day the unlucky, industrious one was not there. They never did know where he had gone, and they never heard from him again.

But before that they lived in the apartment, in an atmosphere of brotherhood and mutual understanding. They had this in common: they were all hiding. The difference was in what they were hiding from. The two others were hiding from the future, from the day when they would get degrees and leave the University. Jack Burden, however, was hiding from the present. The other two took refuge in the present.

Jack Burden took refuge in the past. The other two sat in the living room and argued and drank or played cards or read, but Jack Burden was sitting, as like as not, back in his bedroom before a little pine table, with the notes and papers and books before him, scarcely hearing the voices. He might come out and take a drink or take a hand of cards or argue or do any of the other things they did, but what was real was back in that bedroom on the pine table.

What was back in the bedroom on the pine table?

A large packet of letters, eight tattered, black-bound account books tied together with faded red tape, a photograph, 5 x 8 inches, mounted on cardboard and stained in its lower half by water, and a plain gold ring, mansized, with some engraving on it, on a loop of string. The past. Or that part of the past which had gone by the name of Cass Mastern.

Cass Mastern was one of Jack Burden's father's two maternal uncles, a brother of his mother, Lavinia Mastern, a great-uncle to Jack Burden. The other great-uncle was named Gilbert Mastern, who died in 1914, at the age of ninety-four or -five, rich, a builder of railroads, a sitter on boards of directors, and left the packet of letters, the black account books, and the photograph, and a great deal of money to a grandson (and not a penny to Jack Burden). Some ten years later the heir of Gilbert Mastern, recollecting that his cousin Jack Burden, with whom he had no personal acquaintance, was a student of history, or something of the sort, sent him the packet of letters, the account books, and the photograph, asking if he, Jack Burden, thought that the enclosures were of any "financial interest" since he, the heir, had heard that libraries sometimes would pay a "fair sum for old papers and ante-bellum relics and keep-sakes." Jack Burden replied that, since Cass Mastern had been of no historical importance as an individual, it was doubtful that any library would pay more than a few dollars, if anything, for the material, and asked for instructions as to the disposition of the parcel. Their heir replied that under the circumstances Jack Burden might keep the things for "sentimental reasons."

So Jack Burden made the acquaintance of Cass Mastern, his great-uncle, who had died in 1864 at a military hospital in Atlanta, who had been only a heard but forgotten name to him, and who was the pair of dark, wide-set, deep eyes which burned out of the photograph, through the dinginess and dust and across more than fifty years. The eyes, which were Cass Mastern, stared out of a long, bony face, but a young face with full lips above a rather thin, curly black beard. The lips did not seem to belong to that bony face and the burning eyes.

The young man in the picture, standing visible from the thighs up, wore a loose-fitting, shapeless jacket, too large in the collar, short in the sleeves, to show strong wrists and bony hands clasped at the waist. The thick dark hair, combed sweepingly back from the high brow, came down long and square-cut, after the fashion of time, place, and class, almost to brush the collar of the coarse, hand-me-down-looking jacket, which was the jacket of an infantryman in the Confederate Army.

But everything in the picture, in contrast with the dark, burning eyes, seemed accidental. That jacket, however, was not accidental. It was worn as the result of calculation and anguish, in pride and self-humiliation, in the conviction that it would be worn in death. But death was not to be that quick and easy. It was to come slow and hard, in a stinking hospital in Atlanta. The last letter in the packet was not in Cass Mastern's hand. Lying in the hospital with his rotting wound, he dictated his farewell letter to his brother, Gilbert Mastern. The letter, and the last of the account books in which Cass Mastern's journal was kept, were eventually sent back home to Mississippi, and Cass Mastern was buried somewhere in Atlanta, nobody had ever known where.

It was, in a sense, proper that Cass Mastern — in the gray jacket, sweat-stiffened, and prickly like a hair shirt, which it was for him at the same time that it was the insignia of a begrudged glory — should have gone back to Georgia to rot slowly to death. For he had been born in Georgia, he and Gilbert Mastern and Lavinia Mastern, Jack Burden's grandmother, in the red hills up toward Tennessee. "I was born," the first page of the first volume of the journal said, "in a log cabin in north Georgia, in circumstances of poverty, and if in later years I have lain soft and have supped from silver, may the Lord not let die in my heart the knowledge of frost and of coarse diet. For all men come naked into the world, and in prosperity 'man is prone to evil as the sparks fly upward.'" The lines were written when Cass was a student at Transylvania College, up in Kentucky, after what he called his "darkness and trouble" had given place to the peace of God. For the journal began with an account of the "darkness and trouble" — which was a perfectly real trouble, with a dead man and a live woman and long nailscratches down Cass Mastern's bony face. "I write this down," he said in the journal, "with what truthfulness a sinner may attain unto that if ever pride is in me, of flesh or spirit, I can peruse these pages and know with shame what evil has been in me, and may be in me, for who knows what breeze may blow upon the charred log and fan up flame again?"

The impulse to write the journal sprang from the "darkness and trouble," but Cass Mastern apparently had a systematic mind, and so he went back to the beginning, to the log cabin in the red hills of Georgia. It was the older brother, Gilbert, some fifteen years older than Cass, who lifted the family from the log cabin. Gilbert, who had run away from home when a boy and gone West to Mississippi, was well on the way to being "a cotton-snob" by the time he was twenty-seven or -eight, that is, by 1850. The penniless and no doubt hungry boy walking barefoot onto the black soil of Mississippi was to become, ten or twelve years later, the master sitting the spirited roan stallion (its name was Powhatan — that from the journal) in front of the white veranda. How did Gilbert make his first dollar? Did he cut the throat of a traveller in the cane-brake? Did he black boots at an inn? It is not recorded. But he made his fortune, and sat on the white veranda and voted Whig. After the war when the white veranda was a pile of ashes and the fortune was gone, it was not surprising that Gilbert, who had made one fortune with his bare hands, out of the very air, could now, with all his experience and cunning and hardness (the hardness harder now for the four years of riding and short rations and disappointment), snatch another one, much greater than the first. If in later years he ever remembered his brother Cass and took out the last letter, the one dictated in the hospital in Atlanta, he must have mused over it with a tolerant irony. For it said: "Remember me, but without grief. If one of us is lucky, it is I. I shall have rest and I hope in the mercy of the Everlasting and in His blessed election. But you, my dear brother, are condemned to eat bread in bitterness and build on the place where the charred embers and ashes are and to make bricks without straw and to suffer in the ruin and guilt of our dear land and in the common guilt of man. In the next bed to me there is a young man from Ohio. He is dying. His moans and curses and prayers are not different from any others to be heard in this tabernacle of pain. He marched hither in his guilt as I in mine. And in the guilt of his land. May a common Salvation lift us both from the dust. And dear brother, I pray God to give you strength for what is to come." Gilbert must have smiled, looking back, for he had eaten little bread in bitterness. He had had his own kind of strength. By 1870 he was again well off. By 1875 he was rich. By 1880 he had a fortune, was living in New York, was a name, a thick, burly man, slow of move-ment, with a head like a block of bare granite. He had lived out of one world into another. Perhaps he was even more at home in the new than the old. Or perhaps the Gilbert Masterns are always at home in any world. As the Cass Masterns are never at home in any world.

But to return: Jack Burden came into possession of the papers from the grandson of Gilbert Mastern. When the time came for him to select a subject for his dissertation for his Ph.D., his professor suggested that he edit the journal and letters of Cass Mastern, and write a biographical essay, a social study based on those and other materials. So Jack Burden began his first journey into the past.

It seemed easy at first. It was easy to reconstruct the life of the log cabin in the red hills. There were the first letters back from Gilbert, after he had begun his rise (Jack Burden managed to get possession of the other Gilbert Mastern papers of the period before the Civil War). There was the known pattern of that life, gradually altered toward comfort as Gilbert's affluence was felt at that distance. Then, in one season, the mother and father died, and Gilbert returned to burst, no doubt, upon Cass and Lavinia as an unbelievable vision, a splendid imposter in black broadcloth, varnished boots, white linen, heavy gold ring. He put Lavinia in a school in Atlanta, bought her trunks of dresses, and kissed her good-bye. ("Could you not have taken me with you, dear Brother Gilbert? I would have been ever so dutiful and affectionate a sister," so she wrote to him, in the copy-book hand, in brown ink, in a language not her own, a language of school-room propriety. "May I not come to you now? Is there no little task which I — " But Gilbert had other plans. When the time came for her to appear in his house she would be ready.) But he took Cass with him, a hobbledehoy now wearing black and mounted on a blooded mare.

At the end of three years Cass was not a hobbledehoy. He had spent three years of monastic rigor at *Valhalla*, Gilbert's house, under the tuition of a Mr. Lawson and of Gilbert himself. From Gilbert he learned the routine of plantation management. From Mr. Lawson, a turbercular and vague young man from Princeton, New Jersey, he learned some geometry, some Latin, and a great deal of Presbyterian theology. He liked the books, and once Gilbert (so the journal said) stood in the doorway and watched him bent over the table and then said, "At least you may be good for *that.*"

But he was good for more than that. When Gilbert gave him a small plantation, he managed it for two years with such astuteness (and such luck, for both season and market conspired in his behalf) that at the end of the time he could repay Gilbert a substantial part of the purchase price. Then he went, or was sent, to Transylvania. It was Gilbert's idea. He came into the house on Cass's plantation one night to find Cass at his books. He walked across the room to the table where the books lay, by which Cass now stood. Gilbert stretched out his arm and tapped the open book with his riding crop. "You might make something out of that," he said. The journal reported that, but it did not report what book it was that Gilbert's riding crop tapped. It is not important what book it was. Or perhaps it is important, for something in our mind, in our imagination, wants to know the fact. We see the red, square, strong hand ("My brother is strong-made and florid") protruding from the white cuff, grasping the crop which in that grasp looks fragile like a twig. We see the flick of the little leather loop on the open page, a flick brisk, not quite contemptuous, but we cannot make out the page.

In any case, it probably was not a book on theology, for it seems doubtful that Gilbert, in such a case, would have used the phrase "make something out of that." It might have been a page of the Latin poets, however, for Gilbert would have discovered that, in small doses, they went well with politics or the law. So Transylvania College it was to be, suggested, it developed, by Gilbert's neighbor and friend, Mr. Davis, Mr. Jefferson Davis, who had once been a student there. Mr. Davis had studied Greek.

At Transylvania, in Lexington, Cass discovered pleasure. "I discovered that there is an education for vice as well as for virtue, and I learned what was to be learned from the gaming table, the bottle, and the racecourse, and from the illicit sweetness of the flesh." He had come out of the poverty of the cabin and the monastic regime of *Valhalla* and the responsibilities of his own little plantation; and he was tall and strong and, to judge from the photograph, well favored, with the burning dark eyes. It was no wonder that he "discovered pleasure" — or that pleasure discovered him. For though the journal does not say so, in the events leading up to the "darkness and trouble," Cass seems to have been, in the beginning at least, the pursued rather than the pursuer.

The pursuer is referred to in the journal as "She" and "Her." But I learned the name. "She" was Annabelle Trice, Mrs. Duncan Trice, and Mr. Duncan Trice was a prosperous young banker of Lexington, Kentucky, who was an intimate of Cass Mastern and apparently one of those who led him into the paths of pleasure. I learned the name by going back to the files of the Lexington newspapers for the middle 1850's to locate the story of a death. It was the death of Mr. Duncan Trice. In the newspaper it was reported as an accident. Duncan Trice had shot himself by accident, the newspaper said, while cleaning a pair of pistols. One of the pistols, already cleaned, lay on the couch where he had been sitting, in his library, at the time of the accident. The other, the lethal instrument, had fallen to the floor. I had known, from the journal, the nature of the case, and when I had located the special circumstances, I had learned the identity of "She." Mr. Trice, the newspaper said, was survived by his widow, née Annabelle Puckett, of Washington, D.C.

Shortly after Cass had come to Lexington, Annabelle Trice met him. Duncan Trice brought him home, for he had received a letter from Mr. Davis, recommending the brother of his good friend and neighbor, Mr. Gilbert Mastern. (Duncan Trice had come to Lexington from Southern Kentucky, where his own father had been a friend of Samuel Davis, the father of Jefferson, when Samuel lived at Fairview and bred racers.) So Duncan Trice brought the tall boy home, who was no longer a hobbledehoy, and set him on a sofa and thrust a glass into his hand and called in his pretty, husky-voiced wife, of whom he was so proud, to greet the stranger. "When she first entered the room, in which the shades of approaching twilight were gathering though the hour for the candles to be lit had scarcely come, I thought that her eyes were black, and the effect was most striking, her hair being of such a fairness. I noticed, too, how softly she trod and with a gliding motion which, though she was perhaps of a little less than moderate stature, gave an impression of regal dignity —

> *et avertens rosea cervice refulsit*
> *ambrosiaeque comae divinum vertice odorem*
> *spiravere, pedes vestis defluxit ad imos,*
> *et vera incessu patuit dea.*

So the Mantuan said, when Venus appeared and the true goddess was revealed by her gait. She came into the room and was the true goddess as revealed in her movement, and was, but for Divine Grace (if such be granted to a parcel of corruption such as I), my true damnation. She gave me her hand and spoke with a tingling huskiness which made me think of rubbing my hand upon a soft deep-piled cloth, like velvet, or upon a fur. It would not have been called a musical voice such as is generally admired. I know that, but I can only set down what effect it worked upon my own organs of bearing."

Was she beautiful? Well, Cass set down a very conscientious description of every feature and proportion, a kind of tortured inventory, as though in the midst of the "darkness and trouble," at the very moment of his agony and repudiation, he had to take one last backward look even at the risk of being turned into the pillar of salt. "Her face was not large though a little given to fullness. Her mouth was strong but the lips were red and moist and seemed to be slightly parted or about to part themselves. The chin was short and firmly moulded. Her skin was of a great whiteness, it seemed then before the candles were lit, but afterwards I was to see that it had a bloom of color upon it. Her hair, which was in a remarkable abundance and of great fairness was drawn back from her face and worn in large coils low down to the neck. Her waist was very small and her breasts, which seemed naturally high and round and full, were the higher for the corseting. Her dress, of a dark blue silk, I remember, was cut low to the very downward curve of the shoulders, and in the front showed how the breasts were lifted like twin orbs."

Cass described her that way. He admitted that her face was not beautiful. "Though agreeable in its proportions," he added. But the hair was beautiful, and "of an astonishing softness, upon your hand softer and finer than your thought of silk." So even in that moment, in the midst of the "darkness and trouble," the recollection intrudes into the journal of how that abundant, fair hair had slipped across his fingers. "But," he added, "her beauty was her eyes."

He had remarked how, when she first came in, into the shadowy room, her eyes had seemed black. But he had been mistaken, he was to discover, and that discovery was the first step toward his undoing. After the greeting ("she greeted me with great simplicity and courtesy and bade me again take my seat"), she remarked on how dark the room was and how the autumn always came to take one unawares. Then she touched a bell-pull and a Negro boy entered. "She commanded him to bring light and to mend the fire, which was sunk to ash, or near so. He came back presently with a seven-branched candlestick which he put upon the table back of the couch on which I sat. He struck a lucifer but she said, 'Let me light the candles.' I remember it as if yesterday. I was sitting on the couch. I had turned my head idly to watch her light the candles. The little table was between us. She leaned over the candles and applied the lucifer to the wicks, one after another. She was leaning over, and I saw how the corset lifted her breasts together, but because she was leaning the eyelids shaded her eyes from my sight. Then she raised her head a little and looked straight at me over the new candle flames, and I saw all at once that her eyes were not black. They were blue, but a blue so deep that I can only compare it to the color of the night sky in autumn when the weather is clear and there is no moon and the stars have just well come out. And I had not known how large they were. I remember saying that to myself with perfect clearness, "I had not known how large they were," several times, slowly, like a man marvelling. Then I knew that I was blushing and I felt my tongue dry like ashes in my mouth and I was in the manly state.

"I can see perfectly clearly the expression on her face even now, but I cannot interpret it. Sometimes I have thought of it as having a smiling hidden in it, but I cannot be sure. (I am only sure of this: that man is never safe and damnation is ever at hand, O God and my Redeemer!) I sat there, one hand clenched upon my knee and the other holding an empty glass, and I felt that I could not breathe. Then she said to her husband, who stood in the room behind me, 'Duncan, do you see that Mr. Mastern is in need of refreshment?' "

The year passed. Cass, who was a good deal younger than Duncan Trice, and as a matter of fact several years younger than Annabelle Trice, became a close companion of Duncan Trice and learned much from him, for Duncan Trice was rich, fashionable, clever, and high-spirited ("much given to laughter and full-blooded"). Duncan Trice led Cass to the bottle, the gaming table and the racecourse, but not to "the illicit sweetness of the flesh." Duncan Trice was passionately and single-mindedly devoted to his wife. ("When she came into a room, his eyes would fix upon her without shame, and I have seen her avert her face and blush for the boldness of his glance when company was present. But I think that it was done by him unawares, his partiality for her was so great.") No, the other young men, members of the Trice circle, led Cass first to the "illicit sweetness." But despite the new interests and gratifications, Cass could work at his books. There was even time for that, for he had great strength and endurance.

So the year passed. He had been much in the Trice house, but no word beyond the words of merriment and civility had passed between him and Annabelle Trice. In June, there was a dancing party at the house of some friend of Duncan Trice. Duncan Trice, his wife, and Cass happened to stroll at some moment into the garden and so sit in a little arbor, which was covered with a jasmine vine. Duncan Trice returned to the house to get punch for the three of them, leaving Annabelle and Cass seated side by side in the arbor. Cass commented on the sweetness of the scent of jasmine. All at once, she burst out ("her voice low-pitched and with its huskiness, but in a vehemence which astonished me"), "Yes, yes, it is too sweet. It is suffocating. I shall suffocate." And she laid her right hand, with the fingers spread, across the bare swell of her bosom above the pressure of the corset.

"Thinking her taken by some sudden illness," Cass recorded in the journal, "I asked if she were faint. She said no, in a very low, husky voice. Nevertheless I rose, with the expressed intention of getting a glass of water for her. Suddenly she said, quite harshly and to my amazement, because of her excellent courtesy, 'Sit down, sit down, I don't want water!' So somewhat distressed in mind that unwittingly I might have offended, I sat down. I looked across the garden where in the light of the moon several couples promenaded down the paths between the low hedges. I could hear the sound of her breathing beside me. It was disturbed and irregular. All at once she said, 'How old are you, Mr. Mastern?' I said twenty-two. Then she said, 'I am twenty-nine.' I stammered something, in my surprise. She laughed as though at my confusion, and said, 'Yes, I am seven years older than you, Mr. Mastern. Does that surprise you, Mr. Mastern?' I replied in the affirmative. Then she said, 'Seven years is a long time. Seven years ago you were a child, Mr. Mastern.' Then she laughed, with a sudden sharpness, but quickly stopped herself to add, 'But I wasn't a child. Not seven years ago, Mr. Mastern.' I did not answer her, for there was no thought clear in my head. I sat there in confusion, but in the middle of my confusion I was trying to see what she would have looked like as a child. I could call up no image. Then her husband returned from the house."

A few days later Cass went back to Mississippi to devote some months to his plantation, and, under the guidance of Gilbert, to go once to Jackson, the capital, and one to Vicksburg. It was a busy summer. Now Cass could see clearly what Gilbert intended: to make him rich and to put him into politics. It was a flattering and glittering prospect, and one not beyond reasonable expectation for a young man whose brother was Gilbert Mastern. ("My brother is a man of great taciturnity and strong mind, and when he speaks, though he practices no graces and ingratiations, all men, especially those of the sober sort who have responsibility and power, weigh his words with respect.") So the summer passed, under the strong hand and cold eye of Gilbert. But toward the end of the season, when already Cass was beginning to give thought to his return to Transylvania, an envelope came addressed to him from Lexington, in an unfamiliar script. When Cass unfolded the single sheet of paper a small pressed blossom, or what he discovered to be such, slipped out. For a moment he could not think what it was, or why it was in his hand. Then he put it to his nostrils. The odor, now faint and dusty, was the odor of jasmine.

The sheet of paper had been folded twice, to make four equal sections. In one section, in a clean, strong, not large script, he read; "Oh, Cass!" That was all.

It was enough.

One drizzly autumn afternoon, just after his return to Lexington, Cass called at the Trice house to pay his respects. Duncan Trice was not there, having sent word that he had been urgently detained in the town and would be home for a late dinner. Of that afternoon, Cass wrote: "I found myself in the room alone with her. There were shadows, as there had been that afternoon, almost a year before, when I first saw her in that room, and when I had thought that her eyes were black. She greeted me civilly, and I replied and stepped back after having shaken her hand. Then I realized that she was looking at me fixedly, as I at her. Suddenly, her lips parted slightly and gave a short exhalation, like a sigh or suppressed moan. As of one accord, we moved toward each other and embraced. No words were passed between us as we stood there. We stood there for a long time, or so it seemed. I held her body close to me in a strong embrace, but we did not exchange a kiss, which upon recollection has since seemed strange. But was it strange? Was it strange that some remnant of shame should forbid us to look each other in the face? I felt and heard my heart racing within my bosom, with a loose feeling as though it were unmoored and were leaping at random in a great cavity within me, but at the same time I scarcely accepted the fact of my situation. I was somehow possessed by incredulity, even as to my identity, as I stood there and my nostrils were filled with the fragrance of her hair. It was not to be believed that I was Mastern, who stood thus in the house of a friend and benefactor. There was no remorse or horror at the turpitude of the act, but only the incredulity which I have referred to. (One feels incredulity at observing the breaking of a habit, but horror at the violation of a principle. Therefore what virtue and honor I had known in the past had been an accident of habit and not the fruit of will. Or can virtue be the fruit of human will? The thought is pride.)

"As I have said, we stood there for a long time in a strong embrace, but with her face lowered against my chest, and the deepening obscurity of the evening. When she finally raised her face, I saw that she had been silently weeping. Why was she weeping? I have asked myself that question. Was it because even on the verge of committing an irremediable wrong she could weep at the consequence of an act which she felt powerless to avoid? Was it because the man who held her was much younger than she and his embrace gave her the reproach of youth and seven years? Was it because he had come seven years too late and could not come in innocence? It does not matter what the cause. If it was the first, then the tears can only prove that sentiment is no substitute for obligation, if the second, then they only prove that pity of the self is no substitute for wisdom. But she shed the tears and finally lifted her face to mine with those tears bright in her large eyes, and even now, though those tears were my ruin, I cannot wish them unshed, for they testify to the warmth of her heart and prove that whatever her sin (and mine) she did not step to it with a gay foot and with the eyes hard with lust and fleshly cupidity.

"The tears were my ruin, for when she lifted her face to me some streak of tenderness was mixed into my feelings and my heart seemed to flood itself into my bosom to fill that great cavity wherein it had been leaping. She said, 'Cass' — the first time she had ever addressed me by my Christian name. 'Yes,' I replied. 'Kiss me,' she said very simply, 'you can do it now.' So I kissed her. And thereupon in the blindness of our mortal blood and in the appetite of our hearts we performed the act. There in that very room with the servants walking with soft feet somewhere in the house and with the door to the room open and with her husband expected, and not yet in the room the darkness of evening. But we were secure in our very recklessness, as though the lustful heart could give forth a cloud of darkness in which we were shrouded, even as Venus once shrouded Aeneas in a cloud so that he passed unspied among men to approach the city of Dido. In such cases as ours the very recklessness gives security as the strength of the desire seems to give the sanction of justice and righteousness.

"Though she had wept and had seemed to perform the act in a sadness and desperation, immediately afterward she spoke cheerfully to me. She stood in the middle of the room pressing her hair into place, and I stumblingly ventured some remark about our future, a remark very vague for my being was still confused, but she responded, 'Oh, let us not think about it now,' as though I had broached a subject of no consequence. She promptly summoned a servant and asked for lights. They were brought and thereupon I inspected her face to find it fresh and unmarked. When her husband came, she greeted him familiarly and affectionately, and as I witnessed it my own heart was wrenched, but not, I must confess, with compunction. Rather with a violent jealousy. When he spoke to me, so great was my disturbance that I was sure that my face could but betray it."

So began the second phase of the story of Cass Mastern. All that year, as before, he was often in the house of Duncan Trice, and as before he was often with him in field sports, gambling, drinking, and race-going. He learned, he says, to "wear his brow unwrinkled," to accept the condition of things. As for Annabelle Trice, he says that sometimes looking back, he could scarcely persuade himself that "she had shed tears." She was, he says, "of a warm nature, reckless and passionate of disposition, hating all mention of the future (she would never let me mention times to come), agile, resourceful, and cheerful in devising to gratify our appetites, but with a womanly tenderness such as any man might prize at a sanctified hearthside." She must indeed have been agile and resourceful, for to carry on such a liaison undetected in that age and place must have been a problem. There was a kind of summer house at the foot of the Trice garden, which one could enter unobserved from an alley. Some of their meetings occurred there. A half-sister of Annabelle Trice, who lived in Lexington, apparently assisted the lovers or winked at their relationship, but, it seems, only after some pressure by Annabelle, for Cass hints at "a stormy scene." So some of the meetings were there. But now and then Duncan Trice had to be out of town on business, and on those occasions Cass would be admitted, late at night, to the house, even during a period when Annabelle's mother and father were staying there; so he actually lay in the very bed belonging to Duncan Trice.

There were, however, other meetings, unplanned and unpredictable moments snatched when they found themselves left alone together. "Scarce a corner, cranny, or protected nook or angle of my friend's trusting house did we not at one time or another defile, and that even in the full and shameless light of day," Cass wrote in the journal, and when Jack Burden, the student of history, went to Lexington and went to see the old Trice home he remembered the sentence. The town had grown up around the house, and the gardens, except for a patch of lawn, were gone. But the house was well maintained (some people named Miller lived there and by and large respected the place) and Jack Burden was permitted to inspect the premises. He wandered about the room where the first meeting had taken place and she had raised her eyes to Cass Mastern above the newly lighted candles and where, a year later, she had uttered the sigh, or suppressed moan, and stepped to his arms; and out into the hall, which was finely proportioned and with a graceful stair; and into a small, shadowy library; and to a kind of back hall, which was a well "protected nook or angle" and had, as a matter of fact, furniture adequate to the occasion. Jack Burden stood in the main hall, which was cool and dim, with dully glittering floors, and in the silence of the house, recalled that period, some seventy years before, of the covert glances, the guarded whispers, the abrupt rustling of silk in the silence (the costume of the period certainly had not been designed to encourage casual vice), the sharp breath, the reckless sighs. Well, all of that had been a hell of a long time before, and Annabelle Trice and Cass Mastern were long since deader than mackerel, and Mrs. Miller, who came down to give Jack Burden a cup of tea (she was flattered by the "historical" interest in her house, though she didn't guess the exact nature of the case), certainly was not "agile" and didn't look "resourceful" and probably had used up all her energy in the Ladies Altar Guild of Saint Luke's Episcopal Church and in the D.A.R.

The period of the intrigue, the second phase of the story of Cass Mastern, lasted all of one academic year, part of the summer (for Cass was compelled to go back to Mississippi for his plantation affairs and to attend the wedding of his sister Lavinia, who married a well-connected young man named Willis Burden), and well through the next winter, when Cass was back in Lexington. Then, on March 19, 1854, Duncan died, in his library (which was a "protected nook or angle" of his house), with a lead slug nearly the size of a man's thumb in his chest. It was quite obviously an accident.

The widow sat in church, upright and immobile. When she once raised her veil to touch at her eyes with a handkerchief, Cass Mastern saw that the cheek was "pale as marble but for a single flushed spot, like the flush of fever." But even when the veil was lowered he detected the fixed, bright eyes glittering "within that artificial shadow."

Cass Mastern, with five other young men of Lexington, cronies and boon companions of the dead man, carried the coffin. "The coffin which I carried seemed to have no weight, although my friend had been of large frame and had inclined to stoutness. As we proceeded with it, I marvelled at the fact of its lightness, and once the fancy flitted into my mind that he was not in the coffin at all, that it was empty, and that all the affair was a masquerade or mock-show carried to ludicrous and blasphemous length, for no purpose, as in a dream. Or to deceive me, the fancy came. I was the object of the deception, and all the other people were in league and conspiracy against me. But when that thought came, I suddenly felt a sense of great cunning and a wild exhilaration. I had been too sharp to be caught so. I had penetrated the deception. I had the impulse to hurl the coffin to the ground and see its emptiness burst open and to laugh in triumph. But I did not, and I saw the coffin sink beneath the level of the earth on which we stood and receive the first clods.

"As soon as the sound of the first clods striking the coffin came to me, I felt a great relief, and then a most overmastering desire. I looked toward her. She was kneeling at the foot of the grave, with what thoughts I could not know. Her head was inclined slightly and the veil was over her face. The bright sun poured over her black-clad figure. I could not take my eyes from the sight. The posture seemed to accentuate the charms of her person and to suggest to my inflamed senses the suppleness of her members. Even the funereal tint of her costume seemed to add to the provocation. The sunshine was hot upon my neck and could be felt through the stuff of my coat upon my shoulders. It was preternaturally bright so that I was blinded by it and my eyes were blinded and my senses swam. But all the while I could hear, as from a great distance, the scraping of the spades upon the piled earth and the muffled sound of earth falling into the excavation."

That evening Cass went to the summer house in the garden. It was not by appointment, simply on impulse. He waited there a long time, but she finally appeared, dressed in black "which was scarce darker than the night." He did not speak, or make any signs as she approached, "gliding like a shadow among shadows," but remained standing where he had been, in the deepest obscurity of the summer house. Even when she entered, he did not betray his presence. "I cannot be certain that any premeditation was in my silence. It was prompted by an overpowering impulse which gripped me and sealed my throat and froze my limbs. Before that moment, and afterwards, I knew that it is dishonorable to spy upon another, but at the moment no such considerations presented themselves. I had to keep my eyes fixed upon her as she stood there thinking herself alone in the darkness of the structure. I had the fancy that since she thought herself alone I might penetrate into her being, that I might learn what change, what effect, had been wrought by the death of her husband. The passion which had seized me to the very extent of paroxysm that afternoon at the very brink of my friend's grave was gone. I was perfectly cold now. But I had to know, to try to know. It was as though I might know myself by knowing her. (It is the human defect — to try to know oneself by the self of another. One can only know oneself in God and in His great eye.)

"She entered the summer house and sank upon one of the benches, not more than a few feet from my own location. For a long time I stood there, peering at her. She sat perfectly upright and rigid. At last I whispered her name, as low as might be. If she heard it, she gave no sign. So I repeated her name, in the same fashion, and again. Upon the third utterance, she whispered, "yes," but she did not change her posture or turn her head. Then I spoke more loudly, again uttering her name, and instantly, with a motion of wild alarm she rose, with a strangled cry, and her hands lifted toward her face. She reeled, and it seemed that she would collapse to the floor, but she gained control of herself and stood there staring at me. Stammeringly, I made my apology, saying that I had not wanted to startle her, that I had understood her to answer yes to my whisper before I spoke, and I asked her, 'Did you not answer to my whisper?'

"She replied that she had.

" 'Then why were you distressed when I spoke again?' I asked her.

" 'Because, I did not know that you were here,' she said.

" 'But," I said, 'you say that you had just heard my whisper and had answered to it, and now you say that you did not know I was here.'

" 'I did not know that you were here,' she repeated, in a low voice, and the import of what she was saying dawned upon me.

" 'Listen,' I said, 'when you heard the whisper — did you recognize it was my voice?'

"She stared at me, not answering.

" 'Answer me,' I demanded, for I had to know.

"She continued to stare, and finally replied hesitantly, 'I do not know.'

" 'You thought it was — ' I began, but before I could utter the words she had flung herself upon me, clasping me in desperation like a person frantic with drowning, and ejaculated: 'No, no, it does not matter what I thought, you are here, you are here!' And she drew my face down and pressed her lips against mine to stop my words. Her lips were cold, but they hung upon mine.

"I too was perfectly cold, as of a mortal chill. And the coldness was the final horror of the act which we performed, as though two dolls should parody the shame and filth of man to make it doubly shameful.

"After, she said to me, 'Had I not found you here tonight, it could never have been between us again.'

" 'Why?' I demanded.

" 'It was a sign,' she said.

" 'A sign?' I asked.

" 'A sign that we cannot escape, that we — ' and she interrupted herself, to resume, whispering fiercely in the dark, 'I do not want to escape — it is a sign — whatever I have done is done.' She grew quiet for a moment, then she said, 'Give me your hand.'

"I gave her my right hand. She grasped it, dropped it, and said, 'The other, the other hand.'

"I held it out, across my own body, for I was sitting on her left. She seized it with her own left hand, bringing her hand upward from below to press my hand flat against her bosom. Then, fumblingly, she slipped a ring upon my finger, the finger next to the smallest.

" 'What is that?' I asked.

" 'A ring,' she answered, paused, and added, 'It is his ring.'

"Then I recalled that he, my friend, had always worn a wedding ring, and I felt the metal cold upon my flesh. 'Did you take it off of his finger?' I asked, and the thought shook me.

" 'No,' she said.

" 'No?' I questioned.

" 'No,' she said, 'he took it off. It was the only time he ever took it off.'

"I sat beside her, waiting for what, I did not know, while she held my hand pressed against her bosom. I could feel it rise and fall. I could say nothing.

"Then she said, 'Do you want to know how — how he took it off?'

" 'Yes,' I said in the dark, and waiting for her to speak, I moved my tongue out upon my dry lips.

" 'Listen,' she commanded me in an imperious whisper, 'that evening after — after it happened — after the house was quiet again, I sat in my room, in the little chair by the dressing table, where I always sit for Phebe to let down my hair. I had sat there out of habit, I suppose, for I was numb all over. I watched Phebe preparing the bed for the night.' (Phebe was her waiting maid, a comely yellow wench somewhat given to the fits and sulks.) 'I saw Phebe remove the bolster and then look down at a spot where the bolster had lain, on my side of the bed. She picked something up and came toward me. She stared at me — and her eyes, they are yellow, you look into them and you can't see what is in them — she stared at me — a long time — and then she held out her hand, clenched shut and she watched me — and then — slow, so slow — she opened up the fingers — and there lay the ring on the palm of her hand — and I knew it was his ring, but all I thought was, it is gold and it is lying in a gold hand. For Phebe's hand was gold — I had never noticed how her hand is the color of pure gold. Then I looked up and she was still staring at me, and her eyes were gold, too, and bright and hard like gold. And I knew that she knew.'

" 'Knew?' I echoed, like a question, for I knew, too, now. My friend had learned the truth — from the coldness of his wife, from the gossip of servants — and had drawn the gold ring from his finger and carried it to the bed where he had lain with her and had put it beneath her pillow and had gone down and shot himself but under such circumstances that no one save his wife would ever guess it to be more than an accident. But he had made one fault of calculation. The yellow wench had found the ring.

" 'She knows,' she whispered, pressing my hand hard against her bosom, which heaved and palpitated with a new wildness. 'She knows — and she looks at me — she will always look at me.' Then suddenly her voice dropped, and a wailing intonation came into it: 'She will tell. All of them will know. All of them in the house will look at me and know — when they hand me the dish — when they come into the room — and their feet don't make any noise!' She rose abruptly, dropping my hand. I remained seated, and she stood there beside me, her back toward me, the whiteness of her face and hands no longer visible, and to my sight the blackness of her costume faded into the shadow, even in such proximity. Suddenly, in a voice which I did not recognize for its hardness, she said in the darkness above me, 'I will not abide it, I will not abide it!' Then she turned, and with a swooping motion leaned to kiss me upon the mouth. Then she was gone from my side and I heard her feet running up the gravel of the path. I sat there in the darkness for a time longer, turning the ring upon my finger."

After that meeting in the summer house, Cass did not see Annabelle Trice for some days. He learned that she had gone to Louisville, where, he recalled, she had close friends. She had, as was natural, taken Phebe with her. Then he heard that she had returned, and that night, late, went to the summer house in the garden. She was there, sitting in the dark. She greeted him. She seemed, he wrote later, peculiarly cut off, remote, and vague in manner, like a somnambulist or a person drugged. He asked about her trip to Louisville, and she replied briefly that she had been down the river to Paducah. He remarked that he had not known that she had friends in Paducah, and she said that she had none there. Then, all at once, she turned on him, the vagueness changing to violence, and burst out, "You are prying — you are prying into my affairs — and I will not tolerate it." Cass stammered out some excuse before she cut in to say, "But if you must know, I'll tell you. I took her there."

For a moment Cass was genuinely confused, "Her?" he questioned. "Phebe," she replied. "I took her to Paducah, and she's gone."

"Gone — gone where?"

"Down the river," she answered, repeated, "down the river," and laughed abruptly, and added, "and she won't look at me any more like that."

"You sold her?"

"Yes, I sold her. In Paducah, to a man who was making up a coffle of Negroes for New Orleans. And nobody knows me in Paducah, nobody knew I was there, nobody knows I sold her, for I shall say she ran away into Illinois. But I sold her. For thirteen hundred dollars."

"You got a good price," Cass said, "even for a yellow girl as sprightly as Phebe." And, as he reports in the journal, he laughed with some "bitterness and rudeness," though he does not say why.

"Yes," she replied, "I got a good price. I made him pay every penny she was worth. And then do you know what I did with the money, do you?"

"No."

"When I came off the boat at Louisville, there was an old man, a nigger, sitting on the landing stage, and he was blind and picking on a guitar and singing 'Old Dan Tucker.' I took the money out of my bag and walked to him and laid it in his old hat."

"If you were going to give the money away — if you felt the money was defiled — why didn't you free her?" Cass asked.

"She'd stay right here, she wouldn't go away, she would stay right here and look at me. Oh, no, she wouldn't go away, for she's the wife of a man the Motleys have, their coachman. Oh, she'd stay right here and look at me and tell, tell what she knows, and I'll not abide it!"

Then Cass said: "If you had spoken to me I would have bought the man from Mr. Motley and set him free, too."

"He wouldn't have sold," she said. "The Motleys won't sell a servant."

"Even to be freed?" Cass continued, and she cut in, "I tell you I won't have you interfering with my affairs, do you understand that?" And she rose from his side and stood in the middle of the summer house, and, he reports, he saw the glimmer of her face in the shadow and heard her agitated breathing. "I thought you were fond of her," Cass said.

"I was," she said, "until — until she looked at me like that."

"You know why you got that price for her?" Cass asked, and without waiting for an answer, went on: "Because she's yellow and comely and well-made. Oh, the drovers wouldn't take her down chained in a coffle. They wouldn't wear her down. They'll take her down the river soft. And you know why?"

"Yes, I know why," she said, "and what is it to you? Are you so charmed by her?"

"That is unfair," Cass said.

"Oh, I see, Mr. Mastern," she said, "oh, I see, you are concerned for the honor of a black coachman. It is very delicate sentiment, Mr. Mastern. Why — " and she came to stand above him as he still sat on the bench, "why did you not show some such delicate concern for the honor of your friend? Who is now dead."

According to the journal, there was, at this moment, "a tempest of feeling" in his breast. He wrote: "Thus I heard put into words for the first time the accusation which has ever, in all climes, been that most calculated to make wince a man of proper nurture or natural rectitude. What the hardened man can bear to hear from the still small voice within, may yet be when spoken by an external tongue an accusation dire enough to drain his very cheeks of blood. But it was not only that accusation in itself, for in very truth I had supped full of that horror and made it my long familiar. It was not merely the betrayal of my friend. It was not merely the death of my friend, at whose breast I had leveled the weapon. I could have managed somehow to live with those facts. But I suddenly felt that the world outside of me was shifting and the substance of things, and that the process had only begun of a general disintegration of which I was the center. At that moment of perturbation, when the cold sweat broke on my brow, I did not frame any sentence distinctly to my mind. But I have looked back and wrestled to know the truth. It was not the fact that a slave woman was being sold away from the house where she had had protection and kindness and away from the arms of her husband into debauchery. I knew that such things had happened in fact, and I was no child, for after my arrival in Lexington and my acquaintance with the looser sort of companions, the sportsmen and the followers of the races, I had myself enjoyed such diversions. It was not only the fact that the woman for whom I had sacrificed my friend's life and my honor could, in her new suffering, turn on me with a cold rage and the language of insult so that I did not recognize her. It was, instead, the fact that all of these things — the death of my friend, the betrayal of Phebe, the suffering and rage and great change of the woman I had loved — all had come from my single act of sin and perfidy, as the boughs from the bole and the leaves from the bough. Or to figure the matter differently, it was as though the vibration set up in the whole fabric of the world by my act had spread infinitely and with ever-increasing power and no man could know the end. I did not put it into words in such fashion, but I stood there shaken by a tempest of feeling."

When Cass had somewhat controlled his agitation, he said, "To whom did you sell the girl?"

"What's it to you?" she answered.

"To whom did you sell the girl?" he repeated.

"I'll not tell you," she said.

"I will find out," he said. "I will go to Paducah and find out."

She grasped him by the arm, driving her fingers deep into the flesh, "like talons," and demanded, "Why — why are you going?"

"To find her," he said. "To find her and buy her and set her free."

He had not premeditated this. He heard the words, he wrote in the journal, and knew that that was his intention. "To find her and buy her and let her free," he said, and felt the grasp on his arm released and then in the dark suddenly felt the rake of her nails down his cheek, and heard her voice in a kind of "wild sibilance" saying, "If you do — if you do — oh, I'll not abide it — I will not!"

She flung herself from his side and to the bench. He heard her gasp and sob, "a hard dry sob like a man's." He did not move. Then he heard her voice, "If you do — if you do — she looked at me that way, and I'll not abide it — if you do — " Then after a pause, very quietly: "If you do, I shall never see you again."

He made no reply. He stood there for some minutes, he did not know how long, then he left the summer house, where she still sat, and walked down the alley.

The next morning he left for Paducah. He learned the name of the trader, but he also learned that the trader had sold Phebe (a yellow wench who answered to Phebe's description) to a "private party" who happened to be in Paducah at the time, but who had gone on down river. His name was unknown in Paducah. The trader had presumably sold Phebe so that he would be free to accompany his coffle when it had been made up. He had now headed, it was said, into South Kentucky, with a few bucks and wenches, to pick up more. As Cass had predicted, he had not wanted to wear Phebe down by taking her in the coffle. So getting a good figure of profit in Paducah, he had sold her there. Cass went south as far as Bowling Green, but lost track of his man there. So, rather hopelessly, he wrote a letter to the trader, in care of the market at New Orleans, asking for the name of the purchaser and any information about him. Then he swung back north to Lexington.

At Lexington he went down to West Short Street, to the Lewis C. Robards barracoon, which Mr. Robards had converted from the old Lexington Theatre a few years earlier. He had a notion that Mr. Robards, the leading trader of the section, might be able, through his down-river connections, to locate Phebe, if enough of a commission was in sight. At the barracoon there was no one in the office except a boy, who said that Mr. Robards was down river but that Mr. Simms was "holding things down" and was over at the "house" at an "inspection." So Cass went next door to the house. (When Jack Burden was in

Lexington investigating the life of Cass Mastern, he saw the "house" still standing, a two-story brick building of the traditional residential type, roof running lengthwise, door in center of front, window on each side, chimney at each end, lean-to in back. Robards had kept his "choice stock" there and not in the coops, to wait for "inspection.")

Cass found the main door unlocked at the house, entered the hall, saw no one, but heard laughter from above. He mounted the stairs and discovered, at the end of the hall, a small group of men gathered at an open door. He recognized a couple of them, young hangers-on he had seen about town and at the track. He approached and asked if Mr. Simms was about. "Inside," one of the men said, "showing." Over the heads, Cass could see into the room. First he saw a short, strongly made man, a varnished looking man, with black hair, black neck-cloth, large bright eyes, and black coat, with a crop in his hand. Cass knew immediately that he was a French "speculator," who was buying "fancies" for Louisiana. The Frenchman was staring at something beyond Cass's range of vision. Cass moved farther and could see within.

There he saw the man whom he took to be Mr. Simms, a nondescript fellow in a plug hat, and beyond him the figure of a woman. She was a very young woman, some twenty years old perhaps, rather slender, with skin slightly darker than ivory, probably an octoroon, and hair crisp rather than kinky, and deep dark liquid eyes, slightly bloodshot, which stared at a spot above and beyond the Frenchman. She did not wear the ordinary plaid osnaburg and kerchief of the female slave up for sale, but a white, loosely cut dress, with elbow-length sleeves, and skirts to the floor and no kerchief, only a band to her hair. Beyond her, in the neatly furnished room ("quite genteel," the journal called it, while noting the barred windows), Cass saw a rocking chair and little table, and on the table a sewing basket with a piece of fancy needlework lying there with the needle stuck in it, "as though some respectable young lady or householder had dropped it casually aside upon rising to greet a guest." Cass recorded that somehow he found himself staring at the needlework.

"Yeah," Mr. Simms was saying, "yeah." And grasped the girl by the shoulder to swing her slowly around for a complete view. Then he seized one of her wrists and lifted the arm to shoulder level and worked it back and forth a couple of times to show the supple articulation, saying, "yeah." That done, he drew the arm forward, holding it toward the Frenchman, the hand hanging limply from the wrist which he held. (The hand was, according to the journal, "well moulded, and the fingers tapered.") "Yeah," Mr. Simms said, "Look at that-air hand. Ain't no lady got a littler, teensier hand. And round and soft, yeah?"

"Ain't she got nuthen else round and soft?" one of the men at the door called, and the others laughed.

"Yeah," Mr. Simms said, and leaned to take the hem of her dress, which with a delicate flirting motion he lifted higher than her waist, while he reached out with his other hand to wad the cloth and draw it into a kind of "awkward girdle" about her waist. Still holding the wad of cloth he walked around her, forcing her to turn (she turned "without resistance and as though in a trance") with his motion until her small buttocks were toward the door. "Round and soft, boys," Mr. Simms said, and gave her a good whack on the near buttock to make the flesh tremble. "Ever git yore hand on anything rounder ner softer, boys?" he demanded. "Hit's a cushion, I declare. And shake like sweet jelly."

"God-a-mighty and got on stockings," one of the men said.

While the other men laughed, the Frenchman stepped to the side of the girl, reached out to lay the tip of his riding crop at the little depression just above the beginning of the swell of the buttocks. He held the tip delicately there for a moment, then flattened the crop across the back and moved it down slowly, evenly across each buttock, to trace the fullness of the curve. "Turn her," he said in his foreign voice.

Mr. Simms obediently carried the wad around, and the body followed in the half revolution. One of the men at the door whistled. The Frenchman laid his crop across the woman's belly as though he were a "carpenter measuring something or as to demonstrate its flatness," and moved it down as before, tracing the structure, until he came to rest across the thighs, below the triangle. Then he let his hand fall to his side, with the crop. "Open your mouth," he said to the girl.

She did so, and he peered earnestly at her teeth. The he leaned and whiffed her breath. "It is a good breath," he admitted, as though grudgingly.

"Yeah," Mr. Simms said, "yeah, you ain't a-finden no better breath."

"Have you any others?" the Frenchman demanded. "On hand?"

"We got 'em," Mr. Simms said.

"Let me see," the Frenchman said, and moved toward the door with, apparently, the "insolent expectation" that the group there would dissolve before him. He went out into the hall, Mr. Simms following. While Mr. Simms locked the door, Cass said to him, "I wish to speak to you, if you are Mr. Simms."

"Huh?" Mr. Simms said ("grunted" according to the journal), but looking at Cass became suddenly civil for he could know from dress and bearing that Cass was not one of the casual hangers-on. So Mr. Simms admitted the Frenchman to the next room to inspect its occupant, and returned to Cass. Cass remarked in the journal that trouble might have been avoided if he had been more careful to speak in private, but he wrote that at the time the matter was so much upon his mind that the men who stood about were as shadows to him.

He explained his wish to Mr. Simms, described Phebe as well as possible, gave the name of the trader in Paducah, and offered a liberal commission. Mr. Simms seemed dubious, promised to do what he could, and then said, "But nine outa ten you won't git her, Mister. And we got sumthen here better. You done seen Delphy, and she's nigh white as airy woman, and a sight more juicy, and that gal you talk about is nuthen but yaller. Now Delphy — "

"But the young gemmun got a hankeren fer yaller," one of the hangers-on said, and laughed, and the others laughed too.

Cass struck him across the mouth. "I struck him with the side of my fist," Cass wrote, "to bring blood. I struck him without thought, and I recollect the surprise which visited me when I saw the blood on his chin and saw him draw a bowie from his shirt-front. I attempted to avoid his first blow, but received it upon my left shoulder. Before he could withdraw, I had grasped his wrist in my right hand, forced it down so that I could also use my left hand, which still had some strength left at that moment, and with a turning motion of my body I broke his arm across my right hip, and then knocked him to the floor. I recovered the bowie from the floor, and with it faced the man who seemed to be the friend of the man who was now prostrate. He had a knife in his hand, but he seemed disinclined to pursue the discussion."

Cass declined the assistance of Mr. Simms, pressed a handkerchief over his wound, walked out of the building and toward his lodgings, and collapsed on West Short Street. He was carried home. The next day he was better. He learned that Mrs. Trice had left the city, presumably for Washington. A couple of days later his wound infected, and for some time he lay in delirium between life and death. His recovery was slow, presumably retarded by what he termed in the journal his "will toward darkness." But his constitution was stronger than his will, and he recovered, to know himself as the "chief of sinners and a plague-spot on the body of the human world." He would have committed suicide except for the fear of damnation for that act, for though "hopeless of Grace I yet clung to the hope of Grace." But sometimes the very fact of damnation because of suicide seemed to be the very reason for suicide: he had brought his friend to suicide and the friend, by that act, was eternally damned; therefore he, Cass Mastern, should, in justice, insure his own damnation by the same act. "But the Lord preserved me from self-slaughter for ends which are His and beyond my knowledge."

Mrs. Trice did not come back to Lexington.

He returned to Mississippi. For two years he operated his plantation, read the Bible, prayed, and, strangely enough, prospered greatly, almost as though against his will. In the end he repaid Gilbert his debt, and set free his slaves. He had some notion of operating the plantation with the same force on a wage basis. "You fool," Gilbert said to him, "be a private fool if you must, but in God's name don't be a public one. Do you think you can work them and them free? One day work, one day loaf. Do you think you can have a passell of free niggers next door to a plantation with slaves? If you did have to set them free, you don't have to spend the rest of your natural life nursing them. Get them out of this country, and take up law or medicine. Or preach the Gospel and at least make a living out of all this praying." Cass tried for more than a year to operate the plantation with his free Negroes, but was compelled to confess that the project was a failure. "Get them out of the country," Gilbert said to him. "And why don't you go with them. Why don't you go North?"

"I belong here," Cass replied.

"Well, why don't you preach Abolition right here?" Gilbert demanded. "Do something, do anything, but stop making a fool of yourself trying to raise cotton with free niggers."

"Perhaps I shall preach Abolition," Cass said, "someday. Even here. But not now. I am not worthy to instruct others. Not now. But meanwhile there is my example. If it is good, it is not lost. Nothing is ever lost."

"Except your mind," Gilbert said, and flung heavily from the room.

There was a sense of trouble in the air. Only Gilbert's great wealth and prestige and scarcely concealed humorous contempt for Cass saved Cass from ostracism, or worse. ("His contempt for me is a shield," Cass wrote. "He treats me like a wayward and silly child who may learn better and who does not have to be taken seriously. Therefore my neighbors do not take me seriously.") But trouble did come. One of Cass's Negroes had a broad-wife on a plantation near by. After she had had some minor trouble with the overseer, the husband stole her from the plantation and ran away. Toward the Tennessee border the pair were taken. The man, resisting officers, was shot; the woman was brought back. "See," Gilbert said, "all you have managed to do is get one nigger killed and one nigger whipped. I offer my congratulations." So Cass put his free Negroes on a boat bound up river, and never heard of them again.

"I saw the boat head out into the channel, and watched the wheels churn against the strong current, and my spirit was troubled. I knew that the Negroes were passing from one misery to another, and that the hopes they now carried would be blighted. They had kissed my hands and wept for joy, but I could take no part in their rejoicing. I had not flattered myself that I had done anything for them. What I had done I had done for myself, to relieve my spirit of a burden, the burden of their misery and their eyes upon me. The wife of my dead friend had found the eyes of the girl Phebe upon her and had gone wild and had ceased to be herself and had sold the girl into misery. I had found their eyes upon me and had freed them into misery, lest I should do worse. For many cannot bear their eyes upon them, and enter into evil and cruel ways in their desperation. There was in Lexington a decade and more before my stay in that city, a wealthy lawyer named Fielding L. Turner, who had married a lady of position from Boston. This lady, Caroline Turner, who had never had blacks around her and who had been nurtured in sentiments opposed to the institution of human servitude, quickly became notorious for her abominable cruelties performed in her fits of passion. All persons of the community reprehended her floggings, which she performed with her own hands, uttering meanwhile little cries in her throat, according to report. Once while she was engaged in flogging a servant in an apartment on the second floor of her palatial home, a small Negro boy entered the room and began to whimper. She seized him and bodily hurled him through the window of the apartment so that he fell upon a stone below and broke his back to become a cripple for his days. To protect her from the process of law and the wrath of the community, Judge Turner committed her to a lunatic asylum. But later the physicians said her to be of sound mind and released her. Her husband in his will left her no slaves, for to do so would, the will said, be to doom them to misery in life and a speedy death. But she procured slaves, among them a yellow coachman named Richard, mild of manner, sensible, and of plausible disposition. One day she had him chained and proceeded to flog him. But he tore himself from the chains that held him to the wall and seized the woman by the throat and strangled her. Later he was captured and hanged for murder, though many wished that his escape had been contrived. This story was told me in Lexington. One lady said to me: "Mrs. Turner did not understand Negroes." And another: "Mrs. Turner did it because she was from Boston where the Abolitionists are." But I did not understand. Then, much later, I began to understand. I understood that Mrs. Turner flogged her Negroes for the same reason that the wife of my friend sold Phebe down the river: she could not bear their eyes upon her. I understand, for I can no longer bear their eyes upon me. Perhaps only a man like my brother Gilbert can in the midst of evil retain enough of innocence and strength to bear their eyes upon him and to do a little justice in the terms of the great injustice."

So Cass, who had a plantation with no one to work it, went to Jackson, the capital of the state, and applied himself to the law. Before he left, Gilbert came to him and offered to take over the plantation and work it with a force of his people from his own great place on a share basis. Apparently he was still trying to make Cass rich. But Cass declined, and Gilbert said: "You object to my working it with slaves, is that it? Well, let me tell you, if you sell it, it will be worked with slaves.

It is black land and will be watered with black sweat. Does it make any difference then, which black sweat falls on it?" And Cass replied that he was not going to sell the plantation. Then Gilbert, in an apoplectic rage, bellowed: "My God, man, it is land, don't you understand, it is land, and land cries out for man's hand!" But Cass did not sell. He installed a caretaker in the house, and rented a little land to a neighbor for pasture.

He went to Jackson, sat late with his books, and watched trouble gathering over the land. For it was the autumn of 1858 when he went to Jackson. On January 8, 1861, Mississippi passed the Ordinance of Secession. Gilbert had opposed secession, writing to Cass: "The fools, there is not a factory for arms in the state. Fools not to have prepared themselves if they have foreseen the trouble. Fools, if they have not foreseen, to act thus in the face of facts. Fools not to temporize now and, if they must, prepare themselves to strike a blow. I have told responsible men to prepare. All fools." To which Cass replied: "I pray much for peace." But later, he wrote: "I have talked with Mr. French, who is, as you know, the Chief of Ordnance, and he says that they have only old muskets for troops, and those but flintlocks. The agents have scraped the state for shotguns, at the behest of Governor Pettus. Shotguns, Mr. French said, and curled his lips. And what shotguns, he added, and then told me of a weapon contributed to the cause, an old musket barrel strapped with metal to a piece of cypress rail crooked at one end. An old slave gave this treasure to the cause, and does one laugh or weep?" (One can guess what Gilbert would have done, reading the letter.) After Jefferson Davis had come back to Mississippi, having resigned from the Senate, and had accepted the command of the troops of Mississippi with the rank of Major-General, Cass called upon him, at the request of Gilbert. He wrote to Gilbert: "The General says that they have given him 10,000 men, but not a stand of modern rifles. But the General also said, they have given me a very fine coat with fourteen brass buttons in front and a black velvet collar. Perhaps we can use the buttons in our shotguns, he said, and smiled."

Cass saw Mr. Davis once more, for he was with Gilbert on the steamboat *Natchez* which carried the new President of the Confederacy on the first stage of his journey from his plantation, *Brierfield*, to Montgomery. "We were on old Mr. Tom Leather's boat," Cass wrote in the journal, "which had been supposed to pick up the President at a landing a few miles below Brierfield. But Mr. Davis was delayed in leaving his house and was rowed out to us. I leaned on the rail and saw the little black skiff proceeding toward us over the red water. A man waved from the skiff to us. The captain of the *Natchez* observed the signal, and gave a great blast of his boat's whistle which made our ears tingle and shivered out over the expanse of waters. Our boat stopped and the skiff approached. Mr. Davis was received on board. As the steamboat moved on, Mr. Davis looked back and lifted his hand in salute to the Negro servant (Isaiah Montgomery whom I had known at Brierfield) who stood in the skiff, which rocked in the wash of the steamboat, and waved his farewell. Later, as we proceeded upriver toward the bluffs of Vicksburg, he approached my brother, with whom I was standing on the deck. We had previously greeted him. My brother again, and more intimately, congratulated Mr. Davis, who replied that he could take no pleasure in the honor. 'I have,' he said, 'always looked upon the Union with a superstitious reverence and have freely risked my life for its dear flag on more than one battlefield, and you, gentlemen, can conceive the sentiment now in me that the object of my attachment for many years has been withdrawn from me.' And he continued, 'I have in the present moment only the melancholy pleasure of an easy conscience.' Then he smiled, as he did rarely. Thereupon he took his leave of us and retired within. I had observed how worn to emaciation was his face with illness and care, and how thin the skin lay over the bone. I remarked to my brother that Mr. Davis did not look well. He replied, a sick man, it is a fine how-de-do to have a sick man for a president. I responded that there might be no war, that Mr. Davis hoped for peace. But my brother said, make no mistake, the Yankees will fight and they will fight well and Mr. Davis is a fool to hope for peace. I replied, all good men hope for peace. At this my brother uttered an indistinguishable exclamation and said, what we want now that they've got into this is not a good man but a man who can win, and I am not interested in the luxury of Mr. Davis' conscience. Then my brother and I continued our promenade in silence, and I reflected that Mr. Davis was a good man. But the world is full of good men, I reflect as I write these lines, and yet the world drives hard into darkness and the blindness of blood, even as now late at night I sit in this hotel room in Vicksburg, and I am moved to ask the meaning of our virtue. May God hear our prayer!"

Gilbert received a commission as colonel in a cavalry regiment. Cass enlisted as a private in the Second Mississippi Rifles. "You could be a captain," Gilbert said, "or a major. You've got brains enough for that. And," he added, "damned few of them have." Cass replied that he preferred to be a private soldier, "marching with other men." But he could not tell his brother why, or tell his brother that, though he would march with other men and would carry a weapon in his hand, he would never take the life of an enemy. "I must march with these men who march," he wrote in the journal, "for they are my people and I must partake with them of all bitterness, and that more fully. But I cannot take the life of another man. How can I, who have taken the life of my friend, take the life of an enemy, for I have used up my right to blood?" So Cass marched away to war, carrying the musket which was, for him, but a meaningless burden, and wearing on a string, against the flesh of his chest, beneath the fabric of the gray jacket, the ring which had once been Duncan Trice's wedding ring and which Annabelle Trice, that night in the summer house, had slipped onto his finger as his hand lay on her bosom.

Cass marched to Shiloh, between the fresh fields, for it was early April, and then into the woods that screened the river. (Dogwood and redbud would have been out then.) He marched into the woods, heard the lead whistle by his head, saw the dead men on the ground, and the next day came out of the woods and moved in the sullen withdrawal toward Corinth. He had been sure that he would not survive the battle. But he had survived, and moved down the crowded road "as in a dream." And he wrote: "And I felt that henceforward I should live in that dream." The dream took him into Tennessee again — Chickamauga, Knoxville, Chattanooga, and the nameless skirmishes, and the bullet for which he waited did not find him. He became known as a man of extreme courage. At Chickamauga, when his company wavered in the enemy fire and seemed about to break in its attack, he moved steadily up the slope and could not understand his own inviolability. And the men regrouped, and followed. "It seemed strange to me," he wrote, "that I who in God's will sought death and could not find it, should in my seeking lead men to it who did not seek." When Colonel Hickman congratulated him, he could "find no words" for answer.

But if he had put on the gray jacket in anguish of spirit and in hope of expiation, he came to wear it in pride, for it was a jacket like those worn by the men with whom he marched. "I have seen men do brave things," he wrote, "and they ask for nothing." More and more into the journals crept the comments of the professional soldier, between the prayers and the scruples — criticism of command (of Bragg after Chicka- mauga), satisfaction and an impersonal pride in manoeuvre or gunnery ("the practice of Marlowe's battery excellent"), and finally the admira- tion for the feints and delays executed by Johnston's virtuosity on the approaches to Atlanta, at Buzzard's Roost, Snake Creek Gap, New Hope Church, Kenesaw Mountain ("there is always a kind of glory, however stained or obscured, in whatever man's hand does well, and General Johnston does well").

Then, outside Atlanta, the bullet found him. He lay in the hospital and rotted slowly to death. But even before the infection set it, when the wound in the leg seemed scarcely serious, he knew that he would die. "I shall die," he wrote in the journal, "and shall be spared the end and the last bitterness of war. I have lived to do no man good, and have seen others suffer for my sin. I do not question the Justice of God, that others have suffered for my sin, for it may be that only by the suffering of the innocent does God affirm that men are brothers, and brothers in His

Holy Name. And in this room with me now, men suffer for sins not theirs, as for their own. It is a comfort to know that I suffer only for my own." He knew not only that he was to die, but that the war was over. "It is over. It is all over but the dying, which will go on. Though the boil has come to a head and has burst, yet must the pus flow. Men shall yet come together and die in the common guilt of man and in the guilt that sent them hither from far places and distant firesides. But God in His Mercy has spared me the end. Blessed be His Name."

There was no more in the journal. There was only the letter to Gilbert, written in the strange hand, dictated by Cass after he had grown too weak to write. "Remember me, but without grief. If one of us is lucky, it is I . . . ."

Atlanta fell. In the last confusion, the grave of Cass Mastern was not marked. Someone at the hospital, a certain Albert Calloway, kept Cass's papers and the ring which he had carried on the cord around his neck, and much later, after the war in fact, sent them to Gilbert Mastern with a courteous note. Gilbert preserved the journal, the letters from Cass, the picture of Cass, and the ring on its cord, and after Gilbert's death, the heir finally sent the packet to Jack Burden, the student of history and the grand-nephew of Cass and Gilbert Mastern. So they came to rest on the little pine table in Jack Burden's bedroom in the slatternly apartment which he occupied with the two other graduate students, the unlucky, industrious, and alcoholic one, and the lucky, idle, and alcoholic one.

Jack Burden lived with the Mastern papers for a year and a half. He wanted to know all the facts of the world in which Cass and Gilbert Mastern had lived, and he did know many of the facts. And he felt that he knew Gilbert Mastern. Gilbert Mastern had kept no journal, but he felt that he knew him, the man with the head like the block of bare granite, who had lived through one world into another and had been at home in both. But the day came when Jack Burden sat down at the pine table and realized that he did not know Cass Mastern. He did not have to know Cass Mastern to get the degree; he only had to know the facts about Cass Mastern's world. But without knowing Cass Mastern, he could not put down the facts about Cass Mastern's world. Not that Jack Burden said that to himself. He simply sat there at the pine table, night after night, staring at the papers before him, twisting the ring on its cord, staring at the photograph, and writing nothing. Then he would get up to get a drink of water, and would stand in the dark kitchen, holding an old jelly glass in his hand, waiting for the water to run cold from the tap.

# Jean Stafford (1915–    )

SHE WAS BORN in California and raised in Colorado but most of Jean Stafford's life and writing has centered in the Eastern part of the United States. After graduation from the University of Colorado, where her literary ability was already being highly praised, she went to Germany for post-graduate study. Her letters from Heidelberg recorded her horror at the Nazi threat long before most Americans realized it and she cut short her stay there. As is the case with most American authors her first published work was short stories in magazines. Then came her first novel, *Boston Adventure* (1944), and *The Mountain Lion* (1947) and other novels. Collections of Stafford's short stories are *Children Are Bored on Sunday* (1953) and *Bad Characters* (1964). Her writing has won the National Book Award.

Boston was, of course, settled by the English in 1630. In the many years that have passed since then, although many other nationalities have settled there, Boston has never quite lost its English flavor. Perhaps that is why "The Wedding: Beacon Hill" has such Jane Austen overtones. No greater compliment can be paid any writer. Stafford does not have the sly humor that was one of Austen's glories but her sharp depiction of people in a social setting is akin to it. Also very much in the English eighteenth-century literary tradition is the story's narration by a woman secretary in the household of a rich woman. But the secretary's sympathetic awareness of the bride's predicament, told with fine empathy by the author, is definitely not eighteenth but twentieth century.

# The Wedding: Beacon Hill

THE DRESSMAKER who had been imported from New York to make Hopestill's trousseau was known by her trade name, Mamselle Therese, which she herself always substituted for the nominative case of the first person as though she were her own interpreter. "Mamselle Therese does not touch the potatoes," she said on her first evening in Louisburg Square, as she and I dined alone. She said to me, "Mamselle Therese goes to a nightclub twice a week in New York," by which I understood she wanted me, as Miss Pride's deputy, to supply her with the Boston equivalent of this diversion, but I did not respond as she had hoped and thereafter she made no more such overtures but amused herself (and presumably me) in designing costumes which she said would "bring out" my personality. She spoke of Chanel, Lilly Daché, Mainbocher, as though they were Brahms, Bach, Mozart, or Plato, Descartes, and Hegel. "Daché composed a superb number for an archduchess last month, a really revolutionary turban. People were simply swept off their feet."

Like the bald barber recommending a hair restorer, like the dentist whose teeth are false, Mamselle Therese dressed most frumpishly. She wore a strange assemblage of seedy garments, too large for her spare, nimble frame, out-of-date, soiled, frayed. And it was not only that the little modiste had clothed herself out of a rag bag, but that she had very bad taste, burdening herself like a fancy woman with gimcracks from the five-and-ten-cent stores; wooden brooches in the unreasonable shape of a Scotty or of an ice skate or of a Dutch shoe or a football; enameled beetles or dragon flies or cobras made of tin, with blinding rhinestone eyes; earrings in the shape of oak leaves or candlesticks; and, with any costume, upon her right arm she wore nine thin silver bracelets which she clanked interminably. Her shabbiness could not be explained by poverty, for she had a flourishing business, and the expensive dresses of her two assistants, who had been lodged in a house on Joy Street, suggested that she could afford to be generous in their salaries. She was charging Miss Pride a shocking price for her niece's trousseau, as I knew from her estimate she had handed in on the day she arrived. She spoke quite openly of this as "a good thing."

"Now for you, angel," she said, "Mamselle Therese would sew for next to nothing, but for them, the price is in the hundreds, sometimes in the thousands. It is an art, *n'est-ce pas?* Wouldn't they pay ten thousand for a picture by Rousseau? Then why shouldn't they pay ten thousand for a dress by Chanel? Mainbocher? Mamselle Therese don't kid herself. She knows she isn't in that class yet, but she works slow and sure like a mole. Five years from now Mamselle Therese will be in the movies like Adrian."

Her ruling passion was business, and she could see nothing except in terms of its commercial value. Thus, when she learned that I had gone to a secretarial school, she said, "You must keep your eyes open and when the time comes, rush in and nab yourself a plum. Mamselle Therese's advice to a young girl like you that has a good head on her shoulders is: be a secretary to a big-time lawyer. There's the money! There's the prestige! I'm telling you. What good are you doing yourself fooling around up here with that *vieille furie* when you could be on Fifth Avenue, New York? Mamselle Therese has a girl-friend working at Number One Wall Street on the thirty-fourth floor and she makes fifty dollars a week. I'm telling you."

But she was not, as she seemed, out of touch with human affairs. She was not especially interested in them, but nothing escaped her shrewd French eye. Knowing me to be Miss Pride's secretary, she spoke unguardedly of the household. *"Mon dieu,* that bridegroom! Angel, he is a fool, I'm telling you. Mamselle Therese don't need to make his acquaintance to know that like she knows the palm of her own hand.

She only has to contact the fiancée, *n'est-ce pas?* That rich *renarde.*"

"Why do you say he is *renarde?*" I asked.

"You can tell by the eyes. They are subzero. You know? It is on her part a *mariage de convenance.*"

"And how do you know that?"

"Because they haven't slept together. And how does Mamselle Therese know that?" She tapped her forehead. "*Par intuition.*"

"But perhaps it is a *mariage de convenance* on his part too?" I suggested.

"Maybe. Yes, maybe. It is a cold place, this Boston. He marries her because she is rich, beautiful, whatnot. Because a doctor should have a wife. She marries him because she is *enceinte, n'est-ce pas?*"

I should have laughed and denied the charge, but I was so astounded at the woman's wizardry that I could not gather my wits together, for a moment, and when I did, knowing that her conviction was not only right but that I could in no way shake her from it, I said, "You. may be right, but I beg you to say nothing to anyone. It would kill Miss Pride."

Mamselle Therese was offended. "Why should Mamselle Therese gossip? She is here for the money. She don't care a damn about the *mariage.* Angel, it is a dirty business and not for me. This little up-and-coming *couturière* stays single. I'm telling you. Plenty of boy-friends and not a husband. Don't mix business with pleasure, angel. So why should she interfere with someone else's *mariage?* Mamselle Therese won't talk to the interested parties. She is interested only in the money from the interested parties."

We were sitting in my room at the time of this conversation and it was rather late, perhaps eleven o'clock. Both Miss Pride and Hopestill had gone out for the evening. Presently we heard light footsteps coming up the last flight of stairs and Hopestill's door was opened. Evidently she had come back to get something, for in ten minutes she went out again and back down the stairs. Mamselle Therese, not so much through the fear of being overheard as through boredom with the subject, dropped it instantly on hearing the footsteps and began telling me about a new costume she had designed for nuns which would be at once more sanitary and more beautiful than their present ones.

But her soliloquy did not prevent me from hearing through the wall which separated our rooms, the soft collapse of the girl's body on the chaise longue and a sob, stifled at once as though she had pressed her face into a pillow. The sound would probably have escaped me if I had not heard it before and had not come to expect it as the expression, in a sense, of the reason for her visits to her room during the evening. Almost every night when there were dinner guests she came up two or three times, and usually I heard that secret, frustrated outburst like a checked curse. On such evenings she might stay as long as a quarter of an hour, and hearing her footsteps back and forth across the carpet, muted so that I could not be sure if I really heard them or only felt the vibrations of the floor, I sat at my typewriter unable to strike a key, embarrassed because she must have heard the clatter of the machine which stopped as her doorknob turned.

I could not immunize myself to her misery and pitied her for whatever punishment her conscience was meting out to her. I was impelled to go in to her in the way one may start, hearing a human cry in the night, and thinking it is someone lost or hurt and in need of help. Beside a warm fire in a light room, an impression of the night's cold and darkness superimposes itself upon the altruistic impulse, and one rationalizes, says the cry comes from the throat of a drunk or of a cat that can sound like a woman or even that it is the lure of a thief. I would wait until I heard her going down the stairs again and then I would shrug my shoulders with a resolute indifference and say aloud, "It's her affair, not mine."

Still, I could not help feeling that I was somehow better equipped to endure than Hopestill. She, the frail sheep lost from the herd, could not find her way back nor could she make her way alone. She knew already, as these flights to the privacy of her room showed, that she could not carry it off, for even if the discovery of her deception were long postponed or never made at all or made only by a few people who would not blame her or, if they did, would keep silent, she had nevertheless ruined herself in the only milieu for which she was trained. She had ruined herself even though there might never be suspicions or rumors, for she would never be *sure* that she was not suspected: she would hear the most innocent remark as a *double entendre*, the most amiable question as put with an ulterior design. It was possible, too, I thought, that after the secret gratitude to Philip for unknowingly saving her from disgrace had expired, she would commence to hate him.

By day our house was the scene of what Miss Pride crossly called "a needless hullabaloo" for which, as a matter of fact, she was largely responsible, for while Hopestill and Philip had wanted a small wedding, she had insisted that a step of this kind be taken with public pomp. It was typical of her to speak of it as "a step of this kind" as though it were some sort of sensible negotiation which had been undertaken after several other "kinds" had been discarded. It was she who had wired Mamselle Therese, and she who had sent out invitations to three hundred guests for the wedding breakfast, and she who had persuaded a notable clergyman who had left Boston several years before to perform the ceremony. There had been some argument about this last detail. Both Miss Pride and Dr. McAllister's father were Unitarians and did their best to dissuade Hopestill from being married in the Episcopal church in which, adopting her father's rather than her mother's sect, she had been confirmed. She was adamant and requested, moreover, that the minister from whom she had received the Eucharist at her first communion be brought back for the occasion. In only one other particular had she insisted on having her own way. She refused to be given away by her Uncle Arthur Hornblower or any other relative, and before even consulting her aunt conferred the honor upon her aunt's old admirer, Admiral Nephews.

I thought that she wanted to be married in the Episcopal church out of a nostalgic attachment to her childhood as having been a better and happier time. I could find no other reason, for she was altogether without religious conviction and never went to any services. I divined, too, that in denying any member of her family the right to participate actively in the ritual, she was relieving them, symbolically, of any accessory responsibility.

In the week before the wedding, my duties were many and complex. I acted as the intermediary between Miss Pride and the representatives of florists, liquor dealers, caterers, and took great pleasure in ordering such things as twelve cases of champagne and thirty pounds of filet of sole. Miss Pride would have preferred to attend to these matters herself because all tradespeople were scoundrels and I was both gullible and extravagant, but she was occupied with other things, among them with ridding the house of kinsfolk who came in droves beginning at nine o'clock in the morning, expecting to be asked to luncheon and then tea and even dinner.

They infuriated her by telling her that she looked "worn out" and that they were going to make her go to bed while they themselves took over, lock, stock, and barrel. To such a suggestion, Miss Pride would say, turning her eyes like pistols on the offender, "If I want crutches, I'll *buy* them, Sally Hornblower." They were full of plans for what she would wear to the wedding (I knew what she would wear: a new black broadcloth suit and a green beaver hat) and for the most decorative way of arranging the display of gifts. She would nod her head and say, "I daresay that would be nice. But I shall just muddle on in my old way. You can't teach an old dog new tricks." Once, after this cliché, she gave a mirthless, "Ha, ha!" and sounded, indeed, like the dog that could not be taught but had learned in his youth the trick of biting trespassers.

The continual stir of the house was intoxicating. On my way out of the house to run some important errand, I would glance into the upstairs sitting room where the presents gradually were accumulating. Hopestill might, as I passed, be unwrapping something that had just come. She would hold up for me to see a blue plum-blossom jar or a silver pitcher. We could hear the beelike flurry of the sewing machine and the animated conversation of Mamselle Therese and her two assistants. The doorbell and the telephone reiterated their clamorous demands until the servants were beside themselves. Leaving Hopestill surrounded by her treasure, I would go downstairs to receive a final instruction from Miss Pride.

Nearly always, on one of the tables in the hall, there was a silver bowl half-filled with water on whose surface floated the disintegrating but still fragrant flowers that Hopestill had worn the night before. I was curiously moved at the sight of them, and imagined her coming in late, the dangers of another day behind her, Philip's car already pulling away from the curb. I wondered if she would not ponder her face in the mirror above the table as she unpinned the orchid or the gardenias.

The churchly odor of old wood and stone was sweetened with the perfume and boutonnieres of the wedding guests assembled twenty minutes early. A beam of sunshine came through the open door and extended the length of the central aisle until, at the sanctuary, it joined in a pool of opaline light with another laden shaft sifted through the stained-glass windows, of which the three segments were so detailed that I could read in them no narrative but saw only brilliant colors throwing off the glitter of jewels.

From where I sat at the back of the chapel, I could see Miss Pride in the front row sitting between the Reverend McAllister and his wife. She was wearing a new suit, but as it was made in the same pattern as all her others and cut from the same wool, perhaps I alone knew that it was new, for I had seen the tailor's bill. She had made one concession to her relatives, and in place of her green beaver wore a small hat planted with red posies which caused her so much consternation, because she thought it would fall off, that during the ceremony, as she told everyone later, she could think of nothing but the moment when she might take it off.

Philip's mother, although she would have preferred to wear black as a sign of mourning for her son, had finally decided that it would be too much of a good thing if all four of the chief relatives were attired as for a funeral, and was dressed in pale blue, becoming to her rosy cheeks and her white hair and her blue eyes, which had not been reddened but made only prettily clouded by the incessant stream of tears they had released ever since the engagement was announced. She had lost her appetite, had been unable to sleep a night through, and had not appeared at any of the prenuptial parties. It was said by her husband that her heart was temporarily "out of kilter." She had several times written Hopestill begging her to come to Concord: "We have so much to talk about," she wrote. "I feel there are many things you must know about Philip which only I can tell you. The hastiness of your wedding has prevented us from getting really well acquainted, but perhaps we can make up for lost time if only you will agree to spend two or three days with me." Hopestill, either because she was harassed by the business which the wedding involved or because she could think of no way to refuse the invitation graciously, did not answer, a breach of manners that had already had serious consequences. The elder Mrs. McAllister had told the story everywhere, and making use of her daughter's unwittingly accurate phrase, repeated often, "The wedding is too hasty for me. Marian and I both wish they'd wait until June."

Sitting at the aisle in the middle of the church, casually dressed in tweeds, Mr. Harry Morgan slouched against the side of the pew, his chin in his hand, his eyes closed. He had not been invited, as I well enough knew because I had checked over the list of guests. But I was not in the least surprised to see him although I could not be certain of his motive, whether he had come to tease Hopestill or if he was in love with her and wished to torment himself, or if it was that, desiring to escape suspicion, he had thought it the better policy not to hide himself away. He had, if this last was his intention, made a serious mistake in his costume, and continued, throughout the ceremony, to make an even graver error in his indolent attitude and his drowsy grin, for he was most conspicuous in that church full of people whose dress was all so similar it was virtually a uniform, and thus he was set down by everyone who saw him — and he escaped the notice of very few — as vain and impudent, for in gainsaying the decrees of custom he was usurping custom's power. His presence relieved me on one point and troubled me on another. Evidently Hopestill had not been seeing him, as I had suspected from time to time, for if she had she would have told him not to come. What disturbed me was that since he apparently thought there was nothing odd in his coming this morning and coming with so blatant an air of indifference, there was no reason to suppose that Hopestill and Philip and their friends would be deprived of his company in the future. Perhaps he had come today for the simple reason that he wanted to see Hopestill, to refresh his memory of her beauty and to determine, from the expression on her face and the way she walked, whether his further siege of her would be rewarding.

In the hush that forewarned the wedding march, a hush that fell upon the flesh as well as on the ears so that the guests froze briefly in their postures of kneeling or leaning toward their neighbors, tears of excitement boiled over my eyelids and half-screened the four bridesmaids in their green tulle dresses, preceding the maid of honor whose medieval velvet gown, a deeper shade than theirs, was like the outer leaf and theirs the paler inside ones.

The dazzled guests watched the proud flower for whose protection and enhancement the leaves had been created: a chaste and perfect column draped in satin as pure as the wax of the tapers on the altar and outdoing their flame with the hair that blazed through a calotte of pearls. Her face, white as her finery and her lilies, wore an expression of solemnity befitting the occasion, although, as I heard someone whisper, there should have been something of a smile in her countenance, if not upon her lips then at least within her eyes, for joy should be in proportion equal to the other feelings of the partaker of this particular sacrament. Her look, to me, was one instinct with death, yet death less chill than that which now like a layer beneath her skin gave off a waxen luminosity and imparted to her movement a brittleness as though the soft integuments of skin and cloth concealed a metal mechanism. Her thin fingers were tightly curled on the Admiral's arm. Harry Morgan had turned, with all the others, and while I could not see her face, I knew by his, when she had passed by, that a sign had passed between them, for his mouth curved into a serene smile as if he had half-won his battle.

It seemed to me, as they joined before the minister, that Hopestill shuddered. If this was seen by anyone else — indeed, if it occurred at all — it was attributed to her nervousness, the understandable and appropriate reluctance of a girl about to relinquish her virginity by so public a ritual. With a tidal rustling, the audience sat down, arranged their hands in their laps, and adjusted their spectacles like people anticipating a well-known and beloved piece of music. It was, to be sure, an artistic performance, for the minister, wreathed in benign smiles, posed his literary questions and offered up his prayers with the intonations of a Shakespearean actor, which grace of pitch and diction was afterward to evoke from Reverend McAllister the remark that the service had been "nothing but rhetoric." I was astonished at the brevity of the cross-examination, and before I had accustomed myself to the idea that something of great importance was going on, the whole thing was over and the man and wife were coming back down the aisle, arm in arm, smiling to their well-wishers, their faces illuminated by the sunlight into which they were walking. Hopestill did not fail to include her husband in her dispensation of impartial smiles, but her hand that clutched the bouquet of flowers was clenched like stone.

The drawing room, the library, the dining room overflowed with cawing guests and the stairs were packed with two lanes, one ascending to view the wedding presents, the other coming down. As soon as I had offered my congratulations, I pushed my way through the throngs to Miss Pride, who had got rid of her hat and looked refreshed.

"There are two or three things I want you to attend to," she said to me. "Come along with me and I'll show you."

I followed her docilely down the hall to the door of the pantry, where she instructed me to post myself in order to see that the dirty dishes were immediately sent down on the dumbwaiter to be washed and sent up again so that everyone might be served. The waiters, who were perfectly capable of managing by themselves, regarded me with such wounded displeasure that for the half hour I stood on guard I did not utter a word, but leaned against the window where the sunlight was warm, drinking the remains of the champagne in the glasses that came out from the other rooms. Once I closed my eyes to feel the sun on my lids and when I opened them again saw Harry Morgan lounging up against the door giving me what I could only call a once-over. Fearing that if Miss Pride chanced to come into the pantry and saw us there together she might surmise that I was responsible for this intrusion, and being, moreover, greatly perturbed by his prowling eyes, I exclaimed, "My God!" and he, straightening up, extended his hand as he said, "May I share your quiet inglenook, dear, just we two?" One of the accommodators, a portly middle-aged man with a bald head and a frowning face turned on him a look of avuncular disapproval as he pushed past with a tray of glasses and I said, "It's very crowded in here."

"Well, then, let's find a place that isn't crowded. I can't go back into that crush."

"Nobody asked you to," I said, so nervous that I was obliged to put down the glass I was holding for fear of dropping it. "Nobody asked you to come in the first place."

"What kind of talk is that? I am guest Number One. I came at the urgent invitation of the doctor himself. No one asked me, indeed!"

He laughed openly at my perplexity. "Well, in that case," I said, "you ought to join the party."

I myself, feeling that my services in the pantry were dispensable, went out, taking up a place between the long buffet table and the doors to the drawing room which had been slid back all the way, there to examine the implications of the conversation I had just had. I was prevented from a long study by the Admiral who, with old Mrs. McAllister, appeared slowly making his way toward the refreshment table. "Ah," he cried, spotting me, "here we have an ally. Sonie, what could you do in the way of a hot bird and a cold bottle for two old fellows? I'm hungry as a bear. I tell you, giving away a young lady is hard work. It's a strain on the heart! Particularly if you wanted her for your granddaughter-in-law." He winked at his companion. "Well, all's well that ends well, as they say. And while I'm about consoling myself, ma'am, let me congratulate you on getting a pippin for the boy."

"Much obliged," said Mrs. McAllister coldly. "I think Hope looks ill."

"Ill? Why, ma'am, though you're a woman, you don't know women. What female creature ever looked well on her wedding day? I always say the expression shouldn't be 'white as a ghost' but 'white as a bride.' And the whiter they are, the prettier, what?"

Mrs. McAllister received a plate of sole and salad and a glass of champagne from me. Refusing from that moment forward to discuss the wedding, the wedding breakfast, or the bride and groom, she commenced on an analysis of Amy Brooks's water colors, in which she displayed more affection than intelligence, Amy being the bride she had coveted for her grandson. "The sweet thing, knowing that I don't get about, brought a whole portfolio full of them to me yesterday and I was perfectly charmed. She has real talent." She went on to describe in particular a little scene Amy had done of the hemlocks in the Arboretum. While I nodded with interest and even volunteered a few comments ("How much I should like to see the picture. No, I have never been to the Arboretum, but I hope to go on Lilac Sunday," et cetera), Reverend McAllister edged his way up to us. "How much champagne would you say Lucy Pride ordered for this collation?" he asked me. I told him exactly: twelve cases. He raised his eyebrows, appalled. "If all the money spent on drink were handed over to the missionaries, we would have a Christian world."

Mrs. McAllister, who had wanted her son to go into the Navy, had often been heard to speak like a pagan. She snapped at him, "I hope that time never comes, Son, for I feel that there are times when one *needs* alcohol. Now, for example. At weddings and at funerals." Her voice had risen to an impassioned shriek and her son put his finger to his solemn lips. "Hush, Mother, they say it takes very little to go to one's head when one is advanced in years."

The Admiral snorted, "Your mother can take care of herself, old man. She hasn't had enough to drink, that's her trouble. Hand me your glass, ma'am, and let me refill it."

"Good afternoon," said Miss Pride crisply from behind us. "Ah, Sonie, I see you're taking over out here. I don't know what I would do without you. Well, and have you seen our poor lambs, Sarah? They're complaining that their arms ache from shaking hands and their faces hurt from smiling. They groaned when I told them they must stay another hour at least."

"At least," rejoined the old lady staring hard at Miss Pride. "Why, I daresay that less than half of Boston has had a chance to congratulate them. My dear Lucy, you have outdone yourself!"

By this time, however, the crowd was beginning to thin. Hopestill beckoned to me. "Go up with me, will you, Sonie?" she whispered. I glanced toward her maid-of-honor and she said impatiently, "I've arranged that, don't worry." Philip's face was fixed in a smile that revealed his teeth which were so regular and white they looked almost false. The adjective "sanitary" flashed across my mind as I took in his clear intellectual eyes, his fair hair, his meticulously cared-for person, and in that moment, I preferred his bride upon whose cheek there was a light streak of dirt and who was frankly exhausted and was making no attempts to conceal the fact. I told her that I would meet her in her room and she left when she had said something to Philip who, looking at me as if he had never seen me before, formally shook my hand, not altering his grin in the least. I laughed uneasily and said, "I've already congratulated you once, don't you remember?" and he replied, "How stingy you are! Can't you congratulate a man twice on the happiest day of his life?" But there was in his voice a note of such staggering unhappiness, so taut an irony that I could make only a feeble rejoinder, told him I must hurry up to Hopestill, that I wished him all the happiness, that I . . .

Hopestill had flung her bouquet down the stair well, but one flower, limp and ragged at the edges, was caught in the pointed cuff of her wedding dress. She was waiting in her sitting room for me and she could have been waiting ten years, she had changed so much. The structure of her face was loose, as though the sagging muscles had weakened the mortised bones. There was a starched pallor on her thin lips, a narrow canniness in her eyes, and the skin, in the brief time since I had seen her in the church, had lost that shimmer which had seemed to be touched by the moon rather than the sun, and was ashen now, darkening to a bruised blue beneath her eyes. She had had a drink and, when I came in, put down her glass. There was a newly opened bottle of whisky on the table near where she stood.

"By God, he can wait for me!" she cried. "I'll go down when I'm God damned good and ready." And she sank into one of the winged chairs and poured herself another drink.

"It was a very nice wedding," I said.

"Lock the door, Sonie. I won't have any of them coming in here! I won't! I wish I were dead!"

I locked the door as she ordered me and reluctantly returned. She directed me to sit down opposite her and she said, "I really mean it: I wish I were dead. All I've accomplished today, all I've accomplished in my whole life, is that I've transferred myself from one martinet to another."

"You didn't have to marry him."

She got to her feet and glared at me. "I'm sure I don't know why I've taken you into my confidence, and you can jolly well forget this. Now I'm going to dress."

The crowd had thinned considerably when I went down. In the vestibule, I heard a woman remark, "I wouldn't mind if my income were cut to fifteen thousand. I'd just go out to my farm for the whole year." And another voice replied, "Of course it wouldn't go hard with you, Augusta. Why, you have a fortune in your roses if you'd only do something about it." Augusta, whom I immediately knew to be Philip's aunt, laughed heartily, "That's what my nephew tells me, but he's a pipe dreamer. I'm so glad that at least one of his pipe dreams has come true. Hope is the sweetest girl in Boston, I've always felt."

Hopestill was coming down the stairs and in her carefully composed face there was no sign of the fright and anger that had made her burst out to me in her room. She joined Philip at the door and they went out, sped on by the uproar of the guests who had lingered.

"At any rate," Miss Pride was saying at my elbow, "I haven't lost this one," and she slipped her arm through mine. She linked her other in the Admiral's, and three abreast, we went down the hall toward the library. "We'll quickly get rid of Ichabod," whispered Miss Pride nodding in the direction of Reverend McAllister, "and then we three can have a nice talk."

"Right-o," said the Admiral. "Ain't it a pity my wife had to miss this! I'm gay as a lark. Aren't you, Sonie?"

"Oh, yes, sir!" I cried. Miss Pride released us both and after she had gently closed the door behind us, switched off the ceiling light.

The sun had gone behind a cloud and the library was shadowy and cold. "There now," she said. "It's cozy. It's just right to have this sort of *Dämmerung* follow a wedding. It is the anticlimax to these affairs that I like most."

## Peter Taylor (1917–    )

ONE MORE glowing testimonial to the South as rich soil for splendid literature is the writing of Peter Taylor. He was born in Tennessee, a state that has been the background for many of his short stories. As a professor of English he has taught at the University of North Carolina and the University of Virginia. Volumes of his stories are *A Long Fourth* (1948), *The Widows of Thornton* (1954), *Happy Families Are All Alike* (1959), and *Miss Leonora When Last Seen* (1963). His *A Woman of Means* (1950) is a novel.

Love and lust — the words sound like a Jane Austen title if Jane had lived in this more outspoken twentieth century but their contrast in "Rain in the Heart" is like that in her *Pride and Prejudice* or *Sense and Sensibility*. The ribaldry of the soldiers here is common to all barracks but is heightened in conjunction with the newly married sergeant's love for his wife. The encounter with the sordid-minded woman at a bus stop is a further trial. There is extraordinary sensitivity in the description of the reunion of the sergeant with his wife and the fading of his weariness with the world's drosser ways as the rain falls among the leaves and he makes love.


# *Rain in the Heart*

WHEN the drilling was over, they stopped at the edge of the field and the drill sergeant looked across the flat valley toward the woods on Peavine Ridge. Among the shifting lights on the treetops there in the late afternoon, the drill sergeant visualized pointed roofs of houses that were on another, more thickly populated ridge seven miles to the west.

Lazily the sergeant rested the butt end of his rifle in the mud and turned to tell the squad of rookies to return to their own barracks. But they had already gone on without him and he stood a moment watching them drift back toward the rows of squat buildings, some with their rifles thrown over their shoulders, others toting them by the leather slings in suitcase fashion.

On the field behind the sergeant were the tracks which he and the twelve men had made during an hour's drilling. He turned and studied the tracks for a moment, wondering whether or not he could have told how many men had been tramping there if that had been necessary for telling the strength of an enemy. Then with a shrug of his shoulders he turned his face toward Peavine Ridge again, thinking once more of that other ridge in the suburban area where his bride had found furnished rooms. And seeing how the ridge before him stretched out endlessly north and south, he was reminded of a long streetcar ride that was before him on his journey to their rooms this night. Suddenly throwing the rifle over his shoulder, he began to make his way back toward his own barrack.

The immediate approach to the barrack of the non-commissioned officers was over a wide asphalt area where all formations were held. As the sergeant crossed the asphalt, it required a special effort for him to raise his foot each time. Since his furlough and wedding trip to the mountains, this was the first night the sergeant had been granted leave to go in to see his wife. When he reached the stoop before the entrance to the barrack, he lingered by the bulletin board. He stood aimlessly examining the notices posted there. But finally drawing himself up straight he turned and walked erectly and swiftly inside. He knew that the barrack would be filled with men ready with stale, friendly, evil jokes.

As he hurried down the aisle of the barrack he removed his blue denim jacket, indicating his haste. It seemed at first that no one had noticed him. Yet he was still filled with a dread of the jokes which must inevitably be directed at him today. At last a copper-headed corporal who sat on the bunk next to his own, whittling his toenails with his knife, had begun to sing:

> "Yes, she jumped in bed
> And she covered up her head — "

Another voice across the aisle took up the song here:

> "And she vowed he couldn't find her."

Then other voices, some faking soprano, others simulating the deepest choir bass, from all points of the long room joined in:

> "But she knew damned well
> That she lied like hell
> When he jumped right in behind her."

The sergeant blushed a little, pretended to be very angry, and began to undress for his shower. Silently he reminded himself that when he started for town, he must take with him the big volume of Civil War history, for it was past due at the city library. *She* could have it renewed for him tomorrow.

In the shower, too, the soldiers pretended at first to take no notice of him. They were talking of their own plans for the evening in town. One tall and bony sergeant with a head of wiry black hair was saying, "I've got a strong deal on tonight with a WAC from Vermont. But of course we'll have to be in by midnight."

Now the copper-headed corporal had come into the shower. He

was smaller than most of the other soldiers, and beneath his straight
copper-colored hair were a pair of bright gray-green eyes. He had a
hairy pot-belly that looked like a football. "My deal's pretty strong
tonight, too," he said, addressing the tall soldier beside him. "She lives
down the road a way with her family, so I'll have to be in early too. But
then you and me won't be all fagged out tomorrow, eh, Slim?"

"No," the tall and angular soldier said, "we'll be able to hold our
backs up straight and sort of carry ourselves like soldiers, as some won't
feel like doing."

The lukewarm shower poured down over the chest and back of the
drill sergeant. This was his second year in the army and now he found
himself continually surprised at the small effect that the stream of words
of the soldiers had upon him.

Standing in the narrow aisle between his own bunk and that of the
copper-headed corporal, he pulled on his clean khaki clothes before an
audience of naked soldiers who lounged on the two bunks.

"When I marry," the wiry-headed sergeant was saying, "I'll marry
me a WAC who I can take right to the front with me."

"You shouldn't do that," the corporal replied, "she might be
wounded in action." He and the angular, wiry-headed sergeant laughed
so bawdily and merrily that the drill sergeant joined in, hardly knowing
what were the jokes they'd been making. But the other naked soldiers, of
more regular shapes, found the jokes not plain enough, and they began to
ask literally:

"Can a WAC and a soldier overseas get married?"

"If a married WAC gets pregnant, what happens?"

"When I get married," said one soldier who was stretched out
straight on his back with his eyes closed and a towel thrown across his
loins, "it'll be to a nice girl like the sergeant here's married."

The sergeant looked at him silently.

"But where ever," asked Slim, "are *you* going to meet such a girl
like that in such company as you keep?"

The soldier lying on his back opened one eye: "I wouldn't talk about
my company if I was you. I've saw you and the corporal here with them
biddy-dolls at midway twiest."

The corporal's eyes shone. He laughed aloud and fairly shouted.
"And *he* got *me* the date both times, Buck."

"Well," said Buck, with his eyes still closed and his hands folded
over his bare chest, "when I marry it won't be to one of them sort. Nor
not to one of your WACs neither, Slim."

Slim said, "Blow it out your barracks bag."

One of those more regularly shaped soldiers seemed to rouse himself
as from sleep to say, "That's why y'like 'em, ain't it, Slim? Y'like 'em

because they know how?" His joke was sufficiently plain to bring laughter from all. They all looked toward Slim. Even the soldier who was lying down opened one eye and looked at him. And Slim, who was rubbing his wiry mop of black hair with a white towel, muttered, "At least I don't pollute little kids from the roller rink like some present."

The naked soldier named Buck who was stretched out on the cot opened his eyes and rolled them in the direction of Slim. Then he closed his eyes meditatively and suddenly opened them again. He sat up and swung his feet around to the floor. "Well, I did meet an odd number the other night," he said. "She was drinking beer alone in Conner's Café when I comes in and sits on her right, like this." He patted his hand on the olive-drab blanket, and all the while he talked he was not looking at the other soldiers. Rather his face was turned toward the window at the end of his cot, and with his lantern jaw raised and his small, round eyes squinting, he peered into the rays of sunlight. "She was an odd one and wouldn't give me any sort of talk as long as I sit there. Then I begun to push off and she says out of the clear, 'Soldier, what did the rat say to the cat?' I said that I don't know and she says, 'This pussy's killin' me.' " Now all the other soldiers began to laugh and hollo. But Buck didn't even smile. He continued to squint up into the light and to speak in the same monotone. "So I said, 'Come on,' and jerked her up by the arm. But, you know, she was odd. She never did say much but tell a nasty joke now and then. She didn't have a bunch of small talk, but she come along and did all right. But I do hate to hear a woman talk nasty."

The pot-bellied corporal winked at the drill sergeant and said: "Listen to him. He says he going to marry a nice girl like yours, but I bet you didn't run up on yours in Conner's Café or the roller rink."

Buck whisked the towel from across his lap and drawing it back he quickly snapped it at the corporal's little, hairy pot-belly. The drill sergeant laughed with the rest and watched for a moment the patch of white that the towel made on the belly which was otherwise still red from the hot shower.

Now the drill sergeant was dressed. He combed his sandy-colored hair before a square hand mirror which he had set on the window sill. The sight of himself reminded him of her who would already be waiting for him on that other ridge. She with her soft, Southern voice, her small hands forever clasping a handkerchief. This was what his own face in the tiny mirror brought to mind. How unreal to him were these soldiers and their hairy bodies and all their talk and their rough ways. How temporary. How different from his own life, from his real life with her.

He opened his metal foot locker and took out the history book in which he had been reading of battles that once took place on this camp

site and along the ridge where he would ride the bus tonight. He pulled
his khaki overseas cap onto the right side of his head and slipped away,
apparently unnoticed, from the soldiers gathered there. They were all
listening now to Slim who was saying, "Me and Pat McKenzie picked up
a pretty little broad one night who was deaf and dumb. But when me
and her finally got around to shacking up, she made the most mawkish
noises you ever heard."

With the book clasped under his arm the drill sergeant passed down
the aisle between the rows of cots, observing here a half-dressed soldier
picking up a pair of dirty socks, there another soldier shining a pair of
prized garrison shoes or tying a khaki tie with meticulous care. The drill
sergeant's thoughts were still on her whose brown curls fell over the
white collar of her summer dress. And he could dismiss the soldiers as he
passed them as good fellows each, saying, "So long, Smoky Joe," to one
who seemed to be retiring even before sundown, and "So long, Happy
Jack," to another who scowled at him. They were good rough-and-
ready fellows all, Smoky Joe, Happy Jack, Slim, Buck, and the copper-
headed one. But one of them called to him as he went out the door,
"I wouldn't take no book along. What you think you want with a book
this night?" And the laughter came through the open windows after
he was outside on the asphalt.

The bus jostled him and rubbed him against the civilian workers
from the camp and the mill workers who climbed aboard with their
dinner pails at the first stop. He could feel the fat thighs of middle-aged
women rubbing against the sensitive places of his body, and they —
unaware of such personal feelings — leaned toward one another and
swapped stories about their outrageous bosses. One of the women
said that for a little she'd quit this very week. The men, also mostly
middle-aged and dressed in overalls and shirtsleeves, seemed sensible of
nothing but that this suburban bus somewhere crossed Lake Road,
Pidgeon Street, Jackson Boulevard, and that at some such intersection
they must be ready to jerk the stop cord and alight. "The days are
getting a little shorter," one of them said.

The sergeant himself alighted at John Ross Road and transferred
to the McFarland Gap bus. The passengers on this bus were not as
crowded as on the first. The men were dressed in linen and seersucker
business suits, and the women carried purses and wore little tailored
dresses and straw hats. Those that were crowded together did not make
any conversation among themselves. Even those who seemed to know
one another talked in whispers. The sergeant was standing in the aisle,
but he bent over now and again and looked out the windows at the neat
bungalows and larger dwelling houses along the roadside. He would
one day have a house such as one of those for his own. His own father's

house was the like of these, with a screened porch on the side and a fine tile roof. He could hear his father saying, "A house is only as good as the roof over it." But weren't these the things that had once seemed prosaic and too binding for his notions? Before he went into the army had there not been moments when the thought of limiting himself to a genteel suburban life seemed intolerable by its restrictions and confine-ment? Even by the confinement to the company of such people as those here on the bus with him? And yet now, when he sometimes lay wakeful and lonesome at night in the long dark barrack among the carefree and garrulous soldiers or when he was kneed and elbowed by the worried and weary mill hands on a bus, he dreamed longingly of the warm com-panionship he would find with her and their sober neighbors in a house with a fine roof.

The rattling, bumping bus pulled along for several miles over the road atop the steep ridge which it had barely managed to climb in first gear. At the end of the bus line he stepped out to the roadside and waited for his streetcar. The handful of passengers that were still on the bus climbed out too and scattered to all parts of the neighborhood, dis-appearing into the doorways of brick bungalows or clapboard two-storied that were perched among evergreens and oak trees and maple and wild sumac on the crest and on the slopes of the ridge. *This* would be a good neighborhood to settle down in. The view was surely a prize — any way you chose to look.

But the sergeant had hardly more than taken his stand in the grass to wait for the streetcar, actually leaning a little against a low wall that bordered a sloping lawn, when he observed the figure of a woman standing in the shadow of a small chinaberry tree which grew beside the wall.

The woman came from behind the tree and stood by the wall. She was within three or four steps of the sergeant. He looked at her candidly, and her plainness from the very first made him want to turn his face away toward the skyline of the city in the valley. Her flat-chested and generally ill-shaped figure was clothed with a bag-like gingham dress that hung at an uneven knee-length. On her feet was a man's pair of brown oxfords. She wore white, ankle-length socks that emphasized the hairiness of her muscular legs. On her head a dark felt hat was drawn down almost to her eyebrows. Her hair was straight and of a dark color less rich than brown and yet more brown than black, and it was cut so that a straight and not wholly greaseless strand hung over each cheek and turned upward just the slightest bit at the ends.

And in her hands before her the woman held a large bouquet of white and lavender sweetpeas. She held them, however, as though they were a bunch of mustard greens. Or perhaps she held them more as a small boy holds flowers, half ashamed to be seen holding anything so delicate. Her eyes did not rest on them. Rather her eyes roved nervously up and down the car tracks. At last she turned her colorless, long face to the sergeant and asked with an artificial smile that showed her broad gums and small teeth, "Is this where the car stops?"

"I think so," he said. Then he did look away toward the city.

"I saw the yellow mark up there on the post, but I wasn't real sure," she pursued. He had to look back at her, and as he did so she said, "Don't that uniform get awful hot?"

"Oh, yes," he said. He didn't want to say more. But finally a thought of his own good fortune and an innate kindness urged him to speak again. "I sometimes change it two or three times a day."

"I'd sure say it would get hot."

After a moment's silence the sergeant observed, "This is mighty hot weather."

"It's awful hot here in the summer," she said. "But it's always awful here in some way. Where are you from?"

He still wanted to say no more. "I'm from West Tennessee."

"What part?" she almost demanded.

"I'm from Memphis. It gets mighty hot there."

"I onct know somebody from there."

"Memphis gets awfully hot in the summer too."

"Well," she said drawing in a long breath, "you picked an awful hot place to come to. I don't mind heat so much. It's just an awful place to be. I've lived here all my life and I hate it here."

The sergeant walked away up the road and leaned forward looking for the streetcar. Then he walked back to the wall because he felt that she would think him a snob. Unable to invent other conversation, he looked at the flowers and said, "They're very pretty."

"Well, if you like 'em at all," she said, "you like 'em a great lot more than I do. I hate flowers. Only the other day I say to Mother that if I get sick and go to the hospital don't bring any flowers around me. I don't want any. I don't like 'em."

"Why, those are pretty," he said. He felt for some reason that he must defend their worth. "I like all flowers. Those are especially hard to grow in West Tennessee."

"If you like 'em you like 'em more than I do. Only the other day I say to my Sunday School teacher that if I would die it'd save her a lot of money because I don't want anybody to send no flowers. I hate 'em. And it ain't just these. I hate all flowers."

"I think they're pretty," he insisted. "Did you pick 'em down there in the valley?"

"They was growing wild in a field and I picked them because I didn't have nothin' else to do. Here," she said, pushing the flowers into his hands, "you take 'em. I hate 'em."

"No, no, I wouldn't think of taking your flowers. Here, you must take them back."

"I don't want 'em. I'll just throw 'em away."

"Why, I can't take your flowers."

"You have 'em, and I ain't going to take 'em back. They'll just lay there and die if you put them on the wall."

"I feel bad accepting them. You must have gone to a lot of trouble to pick them."

"They was just growing wild at the edge of a field, and the lady said they was about to take her garden. I don't like flowers. I did her a favor, and you can do me one."

"There's nothing I like better," he said, feeling that he had been ungracious. "I guess I would like to raise flowers, and I used to work in the garden some." He leaned forward, listening for the sound of the streetcar.

For a minute or two neither of them spoke. She shifted from foot to foot and seemed to be talking to herself. From the corner of his eye he watched her lips moving. Finally she said aloud, "Some people act like they're doing you a favor to pay you a dollar a day."

"That's not much in these times," he observed.

"It's just like I was saying to a certain person the other day, If you are not willing to pay a dollar and a half a day you don't want nobody to work for you very bad. But I work for a dollar just the same. This is half of it right here." She held up a half dollar between her thumb and forefinger. "But last week I pay for all my insurance for next year. I put my money away instead of buying things I really want. You can't say that for many girls."

"You certainly can't."

"Not many girls do that."

"I don't know many that do."

"No, siree," she said, snapping the fingers of her right hand, "the girls in this place are awful. I hate the way they act with soldiers downtown. They go to the honky-tonks and drink beer. I don't waste anybody's money drinking beer. I put my own money away instead of buying things I might really want."

The sergeant stepped out into the middle of the road and listened for the streetcar. As he returned to the wall, a Negro man and woman rode by in a large blue sedan. The woman standing by the wall watched the automobile go over the streetcar tracks and down the hill. "There's no Negro in this town that will do housework for less than two and a half a day, and they pay us whites only a dollar."

"Why will they pay Negroes more?" he asked.

"Because-they-can-boss-'em," she said hastily. "Just because they can boss 'em around. I say to a certain person the other day, 'You can't boss me around like a Nigger, no ma'am.' "

"I suppose that's it." He now began to walk up and down in front of her, listening and looking for the streetcar and occasionally raising the flowers to his nose to smell them. She continued to lean against the wall, motionless and with her humorless face turned upward toward the car wire where were hanging six or eight rolled newspapers tied in pairs by long, dirty strings. "How y' reckon them papers come to be up there?" she asked.

"Some of the neighborhood kids or paper-boys did it, I guess."

"Yea. That's it. Rich people's kids's just as bad as anybody's."

"Well, the paper-boys probably did it whenever they had papers left over. I've done it myself when I was a kid."

"Yeea," she said through her nose. "But kids just make me nervous. And I didn't much like bein' a kid neither."

The sergeant looked along one of the steel rails that still glimmered a little in the late sunlight and remembered good times he had had walking along the railroad tracks as a child. Suddenly he hoped his first child would be a boy.

"I'll tell you one thing, soldier," the woman beside him was saying, "I don't spend my money on lipstick and a lot of silly clothes. I don't paint myself with a lot of lipstick and push my hair up on top of my head and walk around downtown so soldiers will look at me. You don't find many girls that don't do that in this awful place, do ya?"

"You certainly don't find many." The sergeant felt himself blushing.

"You better be careful, for you're going to drop some of them awful flowers. I don't know what you want with 'em."

"Why, they're pretty," he said as though he had not said it before.

Now the blue sedan came up the hill again and rolled quietly over the car tracks. Only the Negro man was in the sedan, and he was driving quite fast.

"How can a Nigger like that own a car like that?"

"He probably only drives for some of the people who live along here."

"Yea. That's it. That's it. Niggers can get away with anything. I guess you've heard about 'em attacking that white girl down yonder."

"Yes . . . Yes."

"They ought to kill 'em all or send 'em all back to Africa."

"It's a real problem, I think."

"I don't care if no man black nor white never looks at me if I have to put on a lot of lipstick and push my hair up and walk around without a hat."

The sergeant leaned forward, craning his neck.

"I'm just going to tell you what happened to me downtown the other day," she persisted. "I was standing looking in a store window on Broad when a soldier comes up behind me, and I'm just going to tell you what he said. He said he had a hotel room, and he asked me if I didn't want to go up to the room with him and later go somewhere to eat and that he'd give me some money too."

"I know," the sergeant said. "There's a mighty rough crowd in town now."

"But I just told him, 'No, thanks. If I can't make money honest I don't want it,' is what I told him. I says, 'There's a girl on that corner yonder at Main that wants ya. Just go down there.' "

The sergeant stood looking down the track, shaking his head.

"He comes right up behind me, you understand, and tells me that he has a room in a hotel and that we can go there and do what we want to do and then go get something to eat and he will give me some money besides. And I just told him, 'No, thanks. There's a girl on that corner yonder at Main that wants ya. Just go down there.' So where I was looking at a lot of silly clothes, and a man in a blue shirt who was standing there all the time says that the soldier had come back looking for me."

The sergeant stretched out his left arm so that his wrist watch appeared from under his sleeve. Then he crooked his elbow and looked at the watch.

"Oh, you have *some* wait yet," she said.

"How often do they run?"

"I don't know," she said without interest, "just every so often. I told him, y' see, if I can't make money honest I don't want it. You can't say that for many girls." Whenever his attention seemed to lag, her speech grew louder.

"No, you can't," he agreed.

"I save my money. Soldier, I've got two hundred and seven dollars in the bank, besides my insurance paid up for next year." She said nothing during what seemed to be several minutes. Then she asked, "Where do your mother and daddy live?"

"In West Tennessee."

"Where do you stay? Out at the camp?" She hardly gave him time to answer her questions now.

"Well, I stay out at camp some nights."

"*Some* nights? Where do you stay other nights?" She was grinning.

"I'm married and stay with my wife. I've just been married a little while, but we have rooms up the way here."

"Oh, are you a married man? Where is she from? I hope she ain't from here."

"She's from Memphis. She's just finished school."

The woman frowned, blushed deeply, then she grinned again showing her wide gums. "I'd say you are goin' to take her the flowers. You won't have to buy her any."

"I do wish you'd take some of them back."

The woman didn't answer him for a long time. Finally, when he had almost forgotten what he had said last, she said without a sign of a grin, "I don't want 'em. I hate 'em. The sight of 'em makes me sick."

And at last the streetcar came.

It was but a short ride now to the sergeant's stop. The car stopped just opposite the white two-story house. The sergeant alighted and had to stand on the other side of the track until the long yellow streetcar had rumbled away. It was as though an ugly, noisy curtain had at last been drawn back. He saw her face through an upstairs window of the white house with its precise cupola rising even higher than the tall brick chimneys and with fantastic lacy woodwork ornamenting the tiny porches and the cornices. He saw her through the only second-story window that was clearly visible between the foliage of trees that grew in the yard.

The house was older than most of the houses in the suburban neighborhood along this ridge top, and an old-fashioned iron fence enclosed its yard. He had to stop a moment to unlatch the iron gate, and there he looked directly up into the smiling countenance at the open window. She spoke to him in a voice even softer than he remembered.

Now he had to pass through his landlady's front hall and climb a crooked flight of stairs before reaching his rooms, and an old-fashioned bell had tinkled when he opened the front door. At this tinkling sound an old lady's voice called from somewhere in the back of the house, "Yes?" But he made no answer. He hurried up the steps and was at last in the room with his wife.

They sat on the couch with their knees touching and her hand in his.

Just as her voice was softer, her appearance was fairer even than he had remembered. He told her that he had been rehearsing this moment during every second of the past two hours, and simultaneously he realized that what he was saying was true, that during all other conversations and actions his imagination had been going over and over the present scene.

She glanced at the sweetpeas lying beside his cap on the table and said that when she had seen him in the gateway with the flowers she had felt that perhaps during the time they were separated she had not remembered him even as gentle and fine as he was. Yet she had been afraid until that moment by the window that in her heart she had exaggerated these virtues of his.

The sergeant did not tell her then how he had come into possession of the flowers. He knew that the incident of the cleaning woman would depress her good spirits as it had his own. And while he was thinking of the complete understanding and sympathy between them he heard her saying, "I know you are tired. You're probably not so tired from soldiering as from dealing with people of various sorts all day. I went to the grocery myself this morning, and coming home on the bus I thought of how tiresome and boring the long ride home would be for you this evening when the buses are so crowded." He leaned toward her and kissed her, holding her until he realized that she was smiling. He released her, and she drew away with a laugh and said that she had supper to tend to and that she must put the sweetpeas in water.

While she was stirring about the clean, closet-like kitchen, he surveyed in the late twilight the living-room that was still a strange room to him, and without lighting the table- or floor-lamps he wandered into the bedroom which was the largest room and from which an old-fashioned bay window overlooked the valley. He paused at the window and raised the shade. And he was startled by a magnificent view of the mountains that rose up on the other side of the city. And there he witnessed the last few seconds of a sunset — brilliant orange and brick red — beyond the blue mountains.

They ate at a little table that she drew out from the wall in the living-room. "How have I merited such a good cook for a wife?" he said and smiled when the meal was finished. They stacked the dishes unwashed in the sink, for she had put her arms about his neck and whispered, "Why should I waste one moment of the time I have you here when the days are so lonesome and endless?"

They sat in the living-room and read aloud the letters that had come during the past few days.

For a little while she worked on the hem of a tablecloth, and they talked. They spoke of their friends at home. She showed him a few of their wedding presents that had arrived late. And they kept saying how fortunate they were to have found an apartment so comfortable as this. Here on the ridge it was cool almost every night.

Afterward he took out his pen and wrote a letter to his father. He read the letter aloud to her.

Still later it rained. The two of them hurried about putting down windows. Then they sat and heard it whipping and splashing against the window glass when the wind blew.

By the time they were both in their nightclothes the rain had stopped. He sat on a footstool by the bed reading in the heavy, dark history book. Once he read aloud a sentence which he though impressive: "I have never seen the Federal dead lie so thickly on the ground save in front of the sunken wall at Fredericksburg." This was a Southern general writing of the battle fought along this ridge top.

"What a very sad-sounding sentence," she said. She was brushing her hair in long, even strokes.

Finally he put down the book, but remained sitting on the stool to polish his low-quartered military shoes. She at her dressing-table looked at his reflection in the mirror before her, said, "It's stopped raining."

"It stopped a good while ago," he said. And he looked up attentively, for there had seemed to be some regret in her voice.

"I'm sorry it stopped," she said, returning his gaze.

"You should be glad," he said. "I'd have to drill in all that mud tomorrow."

"Of course I'm glad," she said. "But hasn't the rain made us seem even more alone up here?"

The sergeant stood up. The room was very still and close. There was not even the sound of a clock. A light was burning on her dressing-table, and through the open doorway he could see the table-lamp that was still burning in the living-room. The table there was a regular part of the furnishing of the apartment. But it was a piece of furniture they might have chosen themselves. He went to the door and stood a moment studying the effect she had achieved in her arrangement of objects on the table. On the dark octagonal top was the white lamp with the urn-shaped base. The light the lamp shed contrasted the shape of the urn with the global shape of a crystal vase from which sprigs of ivy mixed with periwinkle sprang in their individual wiriness. And a square, crystal ash tray reflecting its exotic lights was placed at an angle to a small round silver dish.

He went to the living-room to put out the light. Yet with his hand on the little switch he hesitated because it was such a pleasing isolated arrangement of objects.

Once the light was out, he turned immediately to go back into the bedroom. And now he halted in the doorway again, for as he entered the bedroom his eyes fell on the vase of sweetpeas she had arranged. It was placed on top of a high bureau and he had not previously noticed it. Up there the flowers looked somehow curiously artificial and not like the real sweetpeas he had seen in the rough hands of the woman this afternoon. While he was gazing thus, he felt his wife's eyes upon him. Yet without turning to her he went to the window, for he was utterly preoccupied with the impression he had just received and he had a strange desire to sustain the impression long enough to examine it. He kept thinking of that woman's hands.

Now he raised the shade and threw open the big window in the bay, and standing there barefoot on a small hooked rug he looked out at the dark mountains and at the lines and splotches of light that burned on her dressing table. He knew that it had disturbed her to see him so suddenly preoccupied, and it was as though he tried to cram all of a whole day's reflections into a few seconds. Had it really been the pale flowers that had impressed him so? Or had it been the setting of his alarm clock a few minutes before and the realization that after a few more hours here with her he must take up again that other life that the yellow streetcar had carried away with it this afternoon? He could hear the voices of the boys in the barracks, and he saw the figure of the woman by the stone wall under the chinaberry tree.

Now he could hear his wife moving to switch off the overhead light. There was a click. The room was dark and he could hear her moving toward him. And the room being dark things outside seemed much brighter. On the slope of the ridge that dropped off steeply behind the house the dark tree tops became visible. And again there were the voices of the boys in the barracks. Their crudeness, their hardness, even their baseness — qualities that seemed to be taking root in the very hearts of those men — kept passing like objects through his mind. And the bitterness of the woman waiting by the streetcar tracks pressed upon him.

His wife had come up beside him in the dark and slipped her arm about his waist. He folded his arms tightly about her. She spoke his name. Then she said, "These hours we have together are so isolated and few that they must sometimes not seem quite real to you when you are away." She too, he realized, felt a terrible unrelated diversity in things. In the warmth of her companionship, he felt a sudden contrast with the cold fighting he might take part in on a battlefield that was now distant and almost abstract.

The sergeant's eyes had now grown so accustomed to the darkness inside and outside that he could look down between the trees on the slope of the ridge. He imagined there the line after line of Union soldiers that had once been thrown into the battle to take this ridge at all cost. The Confederate general's headquarters were not more than two blocks away. If he and she had been living in those days he would have seen ever so clearly the Cause for that fighting. And *this* battlefield would not be abstract. He would have stood here holding back the enemy from the very land which was his own, from the house in which she awaited him.

But here the sergeant stopped and smiled at himself. He examined the sergeant he had just imagined in the Confederate ranks and it was not himself at all. He compared the Confederate sergeant to the sergeant on the field this afternoon who had stood a moment puzzling over the tracks that twelve rookies had made. *The sergeant is I,* he said to himself desperately, *but it is not that morning in September of sixty-three when the Federal dead were lying so thick on the ground.* He leaned down and kissed his wife's forehead, and taking her up in his arms he carried her to their bed. *It is only a vase of flowers,* he remarked silently, rhetorically, to himself as his wife drew her arms tighter about his neck. *Three bunches from a stand of sweetpeas that had taken the lady's garden.* As he let her down gently on the bed, she asked, "Why did you look so strangely at the vase of flowers? What did they make you think about so long by the window?"

For a moment the sergeant was again overwhelmed by his wife's perception and understanding. He would tell her everything he had in his mind. What great fortune it was to have a wife who could under-stand and to have her here beside him to hear and to comprehend every-thing that was in his heart and mind. But as he lay in the dark trying to make out the line of her profile against the dim light of the window, there came through the rain-washed air outside the rumbling of a street-car. And before he could even speak the thoughts which he had been thinking, all those things no longer seemed to matter. The noise of the streetcar, the irregular rumble and uncertain clanging, brought back to him once more all the incidents of the day. He and his wife were here beside each other, but suddenly he was hopelessly distracted by this new sensation. The streetcar had moved away now beyond his hearing, and he could visualize it casting its diffused light among the dark foliage and over the white gravel between the tracks. He was left with the sense that no moment in his life had any relation to another. It was as though he were living a thousand lives. And the happiness and completeness of his marriage could not now seem so large a thing.

Impulsively, almost without realizing what he was doing, he sat up on the other side of the bed. "I wasn't really thinking about the flowers," he said. "I guess I was thinking of how nicely you had arranged things on the living-room table."

"Oh," she said, for by his very words, *I guess,* it was apparent that she felt him minimizing the importance of his own impressions this evening and of their own closeness. In the dark he went to the small rocking chair on which his clothes were hanging and drew a cigarette from his shirt pocket. He lit it and sat on the edge of the little rocker, facing the open window, and he sat smoking his cigarette until quite suddenly the rain began to fall again. At the very first sound of the rain, he stood up. He moved quickly to the window and put out his cigarette on the sill near the wire screen. The last bit of smoke sifted through the wire mesh. The rain was very noisy among the leaves. He stumbled hurriedly back through the dark and into the bed where he clasped his wife in his arms.

"It's begun to rain again," she said.

"Yes," the sergeant said. "It's much better now."

# Irwin Shaw (1913–    )

AT THE EARLY AGE of twenty-three, Irwin Shaw had a tremendous success with his pacifist play, *Bury the Dead* (1936). Ever since he has been one of our most noteworthy authors. He was born in Brooklyn, that seedbed for so many of our recent writers, and like them he has great social awareness. He has written a number of plays and novels, including *The Young Lions* (1948), one of the best American novels about the Second World War. Shaw, however, is preeminent as a short-story writer. Excellent collections of his stories in book form are *Sailor Off the Bremen* (1939), *Welcome to the City* (1941), *Act of Faith* (1946), *Mixed Company* (1950), and *Tip on a Dead Jockey* (1964).

It depends upon one's viewpoint as to whether "Gunners' Passage" is primarily patriotic or primarily pacifist. The love for their own land as voiced by these homesick men on the African coast in the Second World War is more stirring than the most martial of patriotic hymns. At the same time Gunner Whitejack's memories of the woods around his native Blue Ridge Mountains, his mother's cooking, and his dog, or what Novak, the Oklahoma boy, is saying in a letter to his girl on Long Island, makes a reader loathe war and the pain it forces young people to suffer. Especially sad is Novak saying to the others that, although he knows she is now going around with someone else, "I still like to think of her as my girl."

# *Gunners' Passage*

"IN BRAZIL," Whitejack was saying, "the problem was girls. American girls."

They were lying on the comfortable cots, with the mosquito netting looped gracefully over their heads and the barracks quiet and empty, except for the two of them, and shaded and cool, when you remembered that outside the full sun of Africa stared down.

"Three months in the jungle, on rice and monkey meat." Whitejack lit a large, long, nickel cigar and puffed deeply, squinting up at the tin roof. "When we got to Rio, we felt we deserved an American girl. So the lieutenant and Johnny Moffat and myself, we got the telephone directory of the American Embassy and we went down the list, calling up likely names — secretaries, typists, interpreters, filing clerks — " Whitejack grinned up at the ceiling. He had a large, sun-burned, rough face that was broken into good looks by his smile, and his speech was Southern, but not the kind of Southern that puts a Northerner's teeth on edge.

"It was the lieutenant's idea, and by the time we got to the Q's, he was ready to give up. But we hit pay dirt on the S's." Slowly he blew out a long column of cigar smoke. "Uh-uh," he said, closing his eyes reflectively. "Two months and eleven days of honey and molasses.

Three tender and affectionate American girls, as loving as the day is long, with their own flat. Beer in the icebox from Sunday to Sunday, steaks big enough to saddle a mule with, and nothing to do — just lie on the beach in the afternoon and go swimmin' when the mood seized yuh. On per diem."

"How were the girls?" Stais asked. "Pretty?"

"Well, Sergeant." Whitejack paused thoughtfully and pursed his lips. "To tell you the truth, Sergeant, the girls the lieutenant and Johnny had were as smart and pretty as chipmunks. Mine . . ." Once more he paused. "Ordinarily, my girl would find herself hard put to collect a man in the middle of a full division of infantry soldiers. She was small and runty and she had less curves than a rifle barrel and she wore glasses. But from the first time she looked at me, I could see she wasn't interested in Johnny or the lieutenant. She looked at me, and behind her glasses her eyes were soft and hopeful and humble and appealing." Whitejack flicked the cigar ash off into a little tin can which was resting on his bare chest. "Sometimes," he said slowly, "a man feels mighty small if he just thinks of himself and turns down an appeal like that. Let me tell you something, Sergeant. I was in Rio two months and eleven days and I didn't look at another woman. All those dark-brown women walkin' along the beach, three-quarters out of their bathing suits, just wavin' it in front of your face — I didn't look at them. This runty, skinny little thing with glasses was the most lovin' and satisfactory and decent little person a man could possibly conceive of and a man'd just have to be hog-greedy with sex to have winked an eye at another woman." Whitejack doused his cigar, took the tin can off his chest, and rolled over on his belly. "Now," he said, "I'm going to get myself a little sleep."

In a moment Whitejack was snoring gently, his tough mountaineer's face tucked childishly into the crook of one arm. Outside, on the shady side of the building, a native boy hummed low and wild to himself as he ironed a pair of sun-tan trousers. From the field, two hundred yards away, again and again came the sliding roar of engines climbing or descending the afternoon sky.

Stais closed his eyes wearily. Ever since he'd got into Accra, he had done nothing but sleep and lie on his cot daydreaming, listening to Whitejack talk.

"Hi," Whitejack had said as Stais had come slowly into the barracks two days before. "Which way you going?"

"Home," Stais had said, smiling wearily, as he did every time he said it. "Going home. Which way you going?"

"Not home." Whitejack had grinned a little. "Not home at all."

Stais liked to listen to Whitejack. Whitejack talked about America, about the woods of the Blue Ridge Mountains, where he had been in the forestry service, about his mother's cooking and how he had owned great dogs who had been extraordinary at finding a trail and holding it, about how they had tried hunting deer in the hills from the medium bomber (no good because of the swirling winds rising from the gorges), about pleasant, indiscriminate weekend parties in the woods with his friend Johnny Moffat and the girls from the mill in the next town. Stais had been away from America for nineteen months now, and Whitejack's talk made his native country seem present and pleasantly real to him.

"There was a man in my town by the name of Thomas Wolfe," Whitejack had said irrelevantly that morning. "He was a great big feller and he went away to New York to be an author. Maybe you heard of him?"

"Yes," said Stais. "I read two books of his."

"Well, I read that book of his," said Whitejack, "and the people in town were yellin' to lynch him for a while, but I read that book, and he got that town down fair and proper, and when they brought him back dead, I came down from the hills and I went to his funeral. There were a lot of important people from New York and over to Chapel Hill down for the funeral and it was a hot day, too, and I'd never met the feller, but I felt it was only right to go to his funeral after readin' his book. And the whole town was there, very quiet, although just five years before they were yellin' to lynch him, and it was a sad and impressive sight and I'm glad I went."

And another time, the slow, deep voice rolling between sleep and sleep in the shaded heat, "My mother takes a quail and bones it, then she scoops out a great big sweet potato and lays some bacon on it, then she puts the quail in and cooks it slow for three hours, bastin' it with butter all the time. You got to try that sometime."

"Yes," said Stais, "I will."

Stais did not have a high-priority number and there seemed to be a flood of colonels surging toward America, taking all the seats on the C-54s setting out westward, so he'd had to wait. It hadn't been bad. Just to lie down, stretched full out, unbothered, these days, was holiday enough after Greece, and anyway he didn't want to arrive home, in front of his mother, until he'd stopped looking like a tired old man. And the barracks usually were empty and quiet and the chow good at the transient mess and you could get Coca-Cola and chocolate milk at the PX. The rest of the enlisted men in Whitejack's crew were young and ambitious and were out swimming all day and going to the movies or playing poker in another barracks all night, and Whitejack's talk was smooth and amusing in the periods between sleep and dreams. Whitejack was an aerial photographer and gunner in a mapping and survey squadron and he'd been in Alaska and Brazil and back to the

States and now was on his way to India, full of conversation. He was in a Mitchell squadron and the whole squadron was supposed to be on its way together, but two of the Mitchells had crashed and burned on the takeoff at Natal as Whitejack's plane had circled the field, waiting to form up. The rest of the squadron had been held at Natal and Whitejack's plane had been sent on to Accra, across the ocean, by itself.

Vaguely and slowly, lying on the warm cot, with the wild song of the Negro boy outside the window, Stais thought of the two Mitchells burning between sea and jungle three thousand miles away, and of other planes burning elsewhere, and of what it was going to be like sitting down in the armchair of his own house and looking across the room at his mother, and of the pretty Viennese girl in Jerusalem, and of the DC-3 coming down slowly, like an angel in the dusk, to the rough, secret pasture in the Peloponnesian hills.

He fell asleep. His bones knit gently into dreams on the soft cot, with the sheets, in the quiet barracks, and he was over Athens again, with the ruins pale and shining on the hills, and the fighters boring in, and Lathrop saying, over the intercom, as they persisted into a hundred, fifty yards, twisting, swift and shifty, in the bright Greek sky, "They grounded all the students today. They have the instructors up this afternoon." And, suddenly and wildly, fifty feet over Ploesti, with Liberators going down into the filth in dozens, flaming . . . Then swimming off the white beach at Benghasi with the dead boys playing in the mild, tideless swell, then the parachute pulling at every muscle in his body, then the green and forest blue of Minnesota woods and his father, fat and small, sleeping on pine needles on his Sunday off, then Athens again, Athens . . .

"I don't know what's come over the lieutenant," a new voice was saying as Stais came out of his dream. "He passes us on the field and he just don't seem to see us."

Stais opened his eyes. Novak, a farm boy from Oklahoma, was sitting on the edge of Whitejack's bed, talking. "It has all the guys real worried." He had a high, shy, rather girlish voice. "I used to think they never came better than the lieutenant. Now — " Novak shrugged. "If he does see you, he snaps at you like he was General Ulysses S. Grant."

"Maybe," Whitejack said, "maybe seeing Lieutenant Brogan go down in Natal . . . He and Brogan were friends since they were ten years old. Like as if I saw Johnny Moffat go down."

"It's not that." Novak went over to his own cot and got out his writing pad. "It began back in Miami, four weeks ago. Didn't you notice it?"

"I noticed it," Whitejack said slowly.

"You ought to ask him about it." Novak started writing a letter. "You and him are good friends. After all, going into combat now, it's bad — the lieutenant just lookin' through us when he passes us on the field. You don't think he's drunk all the time, do you?"

"He's not drunk."

"You ought to ask him."

"Maybe I will." Whitejack sat up. "Maybe I will." He looked forlornly down at his stomach. "Since I got into the Army, I've turned pig-fat. On the day I took the oath, I was twenty-eight and one-half inches around the waist. Today I'm thirty-two and three-quarters if I'm an inch. The Army . . . Maybe I shouldn't've joined. I was in a reserved profession, and I was the sole support of an ailing mother."

"Why did you join?" Stais asked.

"Oh." Whitejack smiled at him. "You're awake. Feeling any better, Sergeant?"

"Feeling fine, thanks. Why did you join?"

"Well — " Whitejack rubbed the side of his jaw. "Well, I waited and I waited. I sat up in my cabin in the hills and I tried to avoid listenin' to the radio, and I waited and I waited, and finally I went downtown to my mother and I said, "Ma'am, I just can't wait any longer," and I joined up."

"When was that?" Stais asked.

"Eight days" — Whitejack lay down again, plumping the pillow under his head — "eight days after Pearl Harbor."

"Sergeant," Novak said. "Sergeant Stais, you don't mind if I tell my girl you're a Greek, do you?"

"No," Stais said gravely. "I don't mind. You know, I was born in Minnesota."

"I know," said Novak, writing industriously. "But your parents came from Greece and you bombing Greece and being shot down there."

"What do you mean, your girl?" Whitejack asked. "I thought you said she was going around with a technical sergeant in Flushing, Long Island."

"That's true," Novak said apologetically. "But I still like to think of her as my girl."

"It's the ones that stay at home," said Whitejack darkly, "that get all the stripes and all the girls. My motto is, don't write to a girl once you get out of pillowcase distance from her."

"I like to write to this girl in Flushing, Long Island," Novak said, his voice shy but stubborn. Then to Stais, "How many days were you in the hills before the Greek farmers found you?"

"Fourteen," said Stais.

"And how many of you were wounded?"

"Three. Out of seven. The others were dead."

"Maybe he doesn't like to talk about it, Charlie," Whitejack said.

"Oh, I'm sorry." Novak looked up, his young, unlined face crossed with concern.

"That's all right," Stais said. "I don't mind."

"Did you tell them you were a Greek, too?" Novak asked.

"When one finally showed up who could speak English."

"That must be funny," Novak said reflectively. "Being a Greek, bombing Greece, not speaking the language. Can I tell my girl they had a radio and they radioed to Cairo?"

"It's the girl of a technical sergeant in Flushing, Long Island," Whitejack chanted. "Why don't you look facts in the face?"

"I prefer it this way," Novak said, with dignity.

"I guess you can tell about the radio," Stais said. "It was pretty long ago. Three days later, the DC-3 came down through a break in the clouds. It'd been raining all the time and it just stopped for about thirty minutes at dusk and that plane came down, throwin' water fifteen feet in the air. We cheered, but we couldn't get up from where we were sitting, any of us, because we were too weak to stand."

"I got to write that to my girl," Novak said. "Too weak to stand."

"Then it started to rain again and the field was hip-deep in mud and when we all got into the DC-3, we couldn't get it started." Stais spoke calmly and thoughtfully, as though he were alone, reciting to himself. "We were just bogged down in that Greek mud. Then the pilot got out — he was a captain — and he looked around, with the rain coming down and all those farmers just standing there, sympathizing with him, and nothing anyone could do, and he just cursed for ten minutes. He was from San Francisco and he really knew how to curse. Then everybody started breaking branches off the trees in the woods around the pasture, even those of us who couldn't stand an hour before, and we just covered that big DC-3 complete with branches and waited for the rain to stop. We just sat in the woods and prayed no German patrols would come out in weather like that. In those three days I learned five words of Greek."

"What are they?" Novak asked.

"*Vouno*," Stais said. "That means 'mountain.' *Vrohi*: rain. *Theos*: God. *Avrion*: tomorrow. And *yassou*. That means 'Farewell.'"

"*Yassou*," Novak said. "Farewell."

"Then the sun came out and the field started to steam and nobody said anything. We just sat there, watching the water dry off the grass, then the puddles started to go, here and there, then the mud to cake a little. Then we got into the DC-3 and the Greeks pushed and hauled for a while and we broke loose and got out. And those farmers just standing below waving at us, as though they were seeing us off at Grand Central Station. Ten miles further on we went right over a German camp. They fired at us a couple of times, but they didn't come anywhere close. The best moment of my whole life was getting into that hospital bed in Cairo. I just stood there and looked at it for a whole minute, looking at the sheets. Then I got in, very slow."

"Did you ever find out what happened to those Greeks?" Novak asked.

"No," said Stais. "I guess they're still there waiting for us to come back someday."

There was silence, broken only by the slow scratching of Novak's pen. Stais thought of the thin, dark mountain faces of the men he had last seen, fading away, waving, standing in the scrub and short silver grass of the hill pasture near the Aegean Sea. They had been cheerful and anxious to please, and there was a look on their faces that made you feel they expected to die.

"How many missions were you on?" Novak asked.

"Twenty-one and a half," Stais said. He smiled. "I count the last one as half."

"How old are you?" Novak was obviously keeping the technical sergeant's girl carefully posted on all points of interest.

"Nineteen."

"You look older," said Whitejack.

"Yes," said Stais.

"A lot older."

"Yes."

"Did you shoot down any planes?" Novak peered at him shyly, his red face uncertain and embarrassed, like a little boy asking a doubtful question about girls. "Personally?"

"Two," Stais said. "Personally."

"What did you feel?"

"Why don't you leave him alone?" Whitejack said. "He's too tired to keep his eyes open as it is."

"I felt — relieved," Stais said. He tried to think of what he'd really felt when the tracers went in and the Focke-Wulf started to smoke like a crazy smudge pot and the German pilot fought wildly for half a second with the cowling and then didn't fight wildly any more. There was no way of telling these men, no way of remembering, in words, himself. "You'll find out," he said. "Soon enough. The sky's full of Germans."

"Japs," Whitejack said. "We're going to India."

"The sky's full of Japs."

There was silence once more, with the echo of the word "Japs" rustling thinly in the long, quiet room, over the empty rows of cots. Stais felt the old waving dizziness starting behind his eyes that the doctor in Cairo had said came from shock or starvation or exposure or all of these things, and lay back, still keeping his eyes open, because it became worse and waved more violently when he closed his eyes.

"One more question," Novak said. "Are — are guys afraid?"

"You'll be afraid," Stais said.

"Do you want to send that back to your girl in Flushing?" White-jack asked sardonically.

"No," said Novak quietly. "I wanted that for myself."

"If you want to sleep," said Whitejack, "I'll shut this farmer up."

"Oh, no," said Stais. "I'm pleased to talk."

"If you're not careful," Whitejack said, "he'll talk about his girl in Flushing."

"I'd be pleased to hear it," said Stais.

"It's only natural I should want to talk about her," Novak said. "She was the best girl I ever knew in my whole life. I'd've married her if I could."

"My motto," said Whitejack, "is never marry a girl who goes to bed with you the first time out. The chances are she isn't pure. The second time — that, of course, is different." He winked at Stais.

"I was in Flushing, Long Island, taking a five-week course in aerial cameras," Novak said, "and I was living at the Y.M.C.A."

"This is where I leave." Whitejack got off the bed and put on his pants.

"The Y.M.C.A. was very nice. There were bathrooms for every two rooms, and the food was very good," said Novak, talking earnestly to Stais, "but I must confess, I was lonely in Flushing, Long Island."

"I'll be back" — Whitejack was buttoning up his shirt — "for the ninth installment."

"As long as you're going out," Novak said to him, "I wish you'd talk to the lieutenant. It really makes me feel queer, passing him and him just looking through me like I was a window pane."

"Maybe I'll talk to the lieutenant," Whitejack said. "And leave the Sergeant alone. Remember, he's a tired man who's been to the war and he needs his rest." He went out.

Novak stared after Whitejack. "There's something wrong with him, too," he said. "Just lying on his back here for ten days, reading and sleeping. He never did that before. He was the liveliest man in the United States Air Force. Seeing those two planes go down . . . It's a funny thing, you fly with fellers all over the world, over America,

Brazil, Alaska, you watch them shoot porpoises and sharks in gunnery practice over the Gulf Stream, you get drunk with them, go to their weddings, talk to them over the radio with their planes maybe a hundred feet away, in the air, and after all that flying, in one minute, for no reason, two planes go down. Fourteen fellers you've been livin' with for over a year." Novak shook his head. "There was a particular friend of Whitejack's in one of those planes. Frank Sloan. Just before we left Miami, they had a big fight. Frank went off and married a girl that Whitejack'd been going with off and on for a year, every time we hit Miami. Whitejack told him he was crazy, half the squadron had slept with the lady, and that was true, too, and just to teach him a lesson he'd sleep with her himself after they'd been married. And he did, too." Novak sighed. "A lot of funny things happen in the Army when fellers've been together a long time and get to know each other real well. And then, one minute, the Mitchell goes down. I guess Whitejack must've felt sort of queer, watching Frankie burn." Novak had put his writing pad down and now he screwed the top of his fountain pen. "The truth is," he said, "I don't feel so solid myself. That's why I like to talk. Especially to you. You've been through it. You're young, but you've been through it. But if it's any bother to you, I'll keep quiet."

"No," said Stais, still lying back, abstractedly wondering whether the waving would get worse or better, "not at all,"

"This girl in Flushing, Long Island," Novak said slowly. "It's easy for Whitejack to make fun of me. The girls fall all over themselves chasing after him. He has no real conception of what it's like to be a man like me. Not very good-looking. Not much money. Not an officer. Not humorous. Shy."

Stais couldn't help grinning. "You're going to have a tough time in India."

"I know," Novak said. "I've resigned myself to not having a girl until the armistice. How did you do with the girls in the Middle East?" he asked politely.

"There was a nice Viennese girl in Jerusalem," Stais said dreamily. "But otherwise zero. You have to be very good, unless you're an officer, in the Middle East."

"That's what I heard," Novak said sorrowfully. "Well, it won't be so different to me from Oklahoma. That was the nice thing about this girl in Flushing, Long Island. She saw me come into the jewelry store where she worked and I was in my fatigues and I was with a very smooth feller who made a date with her for that night. But she smiled at me and I knew if I had the guts I could ask her for a date, too. But of course I didn't. But then later than night I was sitting in my room in the Y.M.C.A. and my phone rang. It was this girl. The other feller had stood her up, she said, and would I take her out." Novak smiled dimly, thinking of that tremulous moment of glory in the small Y.M.C.A. room far away. "I got my fatigues off in one minute and shaved and showered and I picked her up. We went to Coney Island. It was the first time in my entire life I had ever seen Coney Island. It took three and a half weeks for me to finish my course and I went out with that girl every single night. Nothing like that ever happened to me before in my life — a girl who just wanted to see me every night of the week. Then, the night before I was due to leave to join my squadron, she told me she had got permission to take the afternoon off and she would like to see me down to the train, if I let her. I called at the jewelry shop at noon and her boss shook my hand and she had a package under her arm and we got into the subway and we rode to New York City. Then we went into a cafeteria and had a wonderful lunch and she saw me off and gave me the package. It was Schrafft's candy, and she was crying at the gate there, crying for me, and she said she would like me to write, no matter what." Novak paused and Stais could tell that the scene at the gate, the hurrying crowds, the package of Schrafft's chocolates, the weeping young girl, were as clear as the afternoon sunlight to Novak, there on the coast of Africa. "So I keep writing," Novak said. "She's written me she has a technical sergeant now, but I keep writing. I haven't seen her in a year and a half and what's a girl to do? Do you blame her?"

"No," said Stais. "I don't blame her."

"I hope I haven't bored you," Novak said.

"Not at all," Stais smiled at him. Suddenly the dizziness had gone and he could close his eyes. As he drifted down into that weird and ever-present pool of sleep in which he half lived these days, he heard Novak say, "Now I have to write my mother."

Outside, the Negro boy sang, and the planes grumbled down from the Atlantic and laboriously set out across the Sahara Desert.

Dreams again: Arabs, bundled in rags, driving camels along the perimeter of the field, outlined against the parked Liberators and waiting bombs; two Mitchells still burning on the shores of Brazil and Frank Sloan burning there and, circling above him, Whitejack, who had told him he'd sleep with his wife and had; the hills around Jerusalem, gnarled, rocky, dusty, with the powdered green of olive groves set on slopes here and there, clinging against the desert wind; Mitchells slamming along the gorges of the Blue Ridge Mountains, bucking in the updrafts, their guns going, hunting deer; the Mediterranean, bluer than anything in America, below them on the way home from Italy, coming down below oxygen level, with the boys singing dirty songs over the intercom, and leave in Alexandria ahead of them. The girl from Flushing, Long Island, quietly going hand in hand with Novak to Coney Island on a summer's night.

It was Whitejack who awakened him. He woke slowly. It was dark outside and the electric light was shining in his eyes and Whitejack was standing over him, shaking him gently.

"I thought you'd like to know," Whitejack was saying, "your name's on the bulletin board. You're leaving tonight."

"Thanks," Stais said, dimly grateful at being shaken out of the broken and somehow sorrowful dreams.

"I took the liberty of initialling it for you, opposite your name," Whitejack said. "Save you a trip up to the field."

"Thanks," said Stais. "Very kind of you."

"Also," said Whitejack, "there's fried chicken for chow."

Stais pondered over the fried chicken. He was a little hungry, but the effort of getting up and putting on his shoes and walking the hundred yards to the mess hall had to be weighed in the balance. "Thanks. I'll just lie right here," he said. "Any news of your boys?" he asked.

"Yes," said Whitejack. "The squadron came in."

"That's good."

"All except one plane." Whitejack sat down on the end of Stais's cot. His voice was soft and expressionless. "Johnny Moffat's plane."

In all the months that Stais had been in the Air Forces, on fields to which planes had failed to return, he had learned that there was nothing to say. He was only nineteen years old, but he had learned that. So he lay quiet.

"They got separated in clouds on the way out of Ascension, and they never picked them up again. There's still a chance," Whitejack said, "that they'll drop in any minute." He looked at his watch. "Still a chance for another hour and forty minutes."

There was still nothing to say, so Stais lay silent.

"Johnny Moffat," said Whitejack, "at one time looked as though he was going to marry my sister. In a way, it's a good thing he didn't. It'd be a little hard, being brothers-in-law, on some of the parties the Air Force goes on in one place and another." Whitejack fell silent and looked down at his belly. Deliberately, he let his belt out a notch, then pulled it to, with a severe little click. "That fried chicken was mighty good," he said. "You sure you want to pass it up?"

"I'm saving my appetite for my mother's cooking," Stais said.

"My sister was passing fond of Johnny," said Whitejack, "and I have a feeling when he gets home from the war and settles down, she's going to snag him. She came to me right before I left and she asked me if I would let her have ten acres on the north side of my property and three acres of timber to build their house. I said it was O.K. with me." He was silent again, thinking of the rolling ten acres of upland meadow in North Carolina and the three tall acres of standing timber, oak and pine, from which it would be possible to build a strong country house. "There's nobody in the whole world I'd rather have living on my property than Johnny Moffat. I've known him for twenty years and I've had six fist fights with him and won them all, and been alone with him in the woods for two months at a time, and I still say that." He got up and went over to his own cot, then turned and came back. "By the way," he said softly, "this is between you and me, Sergeant."

"Sure," said Stais.

"My sister said she'd murder me for my hide and taller if I ever let Johnny know what was in store for him." He grinned a little. "Women're very confident in certain fields," he said. "And I never did tell Johnny, not even when I was so drunk I was singing 'Casey Jones' naked in the middle of the city of Tampa at three o'clock in the morning." He went over to his musette bag and got out a cigar and lit it thoughtfully. "You'd be surprised," he said, "how fond you become of nickel cigars in the Army."

"I tried smoking," said Stais. "I think I'll wait until I get a little older."

Whitejack sat heavily on his own cot. "Do you think they'll send you out to fight again?" he asked.

Stais stared up at the ceiling. "I wouldn't be surprised," he said. "There's nothing really wrong with me. I'm just tired."

Whitejack nodded, smoking slowly. "By the way," he said, "you heard us talking about the lieutenant, didn't you?"

"Yes."

"I went out to the field and had a little conversation with him. He's just been sittin' there all day and most of the night since we got here, outside the Operations room, just lookin' and starin' across at the planes comin' in. Him and me, we've been good friends for a long time and I asked him point-blank. I said, 'Freddie,' I said, 'there's a question the boys're askin' themselves these days about you.' And he said, 'What's the matter?' And I said, 'The boys're asking if you've turned bad. You pass 'em and you don't even look at them as though you recognize 'em. What is it, you turn G.I. after a year?' I said. He looked at me and then he looked at the ground and he didn't say anything for maybe a minute. Then he said, 'I beg your pardon, Arnold. It never occurred to me.' Then he told me what was on his mind." Whitejack looked at his watch, almost automatically, then lifted his head again. "Ever since we got the order to go overseas, he's been worrying.

You know Simpson, in our crew. Well, he's worrying about him and his navigator."

"What's he worrying about?" For a moment a crazy list of all the thousand things you can worry about in the crew of one airplane flashed through Stais's head.

"They're not fighting men," Whitejack said slowly. "They're both good fellers, you wouldn't want better, but the lieutenant's been watchin' 'em for a long time on the ground, in the air, at their guns, and he's convinced they won't measure. And he feels he's responsible for taking the Mitchell in and getting it out with as many of us alive as possible and he feels Simpson and the navigator're dangerous to have in the plane. And he's makin' up his mind to put in a request for two new men when we get to India, and he can't bear to think of what it'll do to Simpson and the navigator when they find out he's asked to have 'em grounded. That's why he just sits there outside Operations, not even seein' us when we go by." Whitejack sighed. "He's twenty-two years old, the lieutenant. It's a strain, something like that, for a man twenty-two years old. If you see Simpson or Novak, you won't tell them anything, will you?"

"No," said Stais.

"I suppose things like this come up all the time in any army."

"All the time," said Stais.

Whitejack looked at his watch. Outside there was the growing and lapsing roar of engines that had been the constant sound of both their lives for so many months.

"Ah," said Whitejack, "they should've put me in the infantry. I can hit a rabbit at three hundred yards with a rifle. They put me in the Air Force and give me a camera. Well, Sergeant, I think it's about time you were movin'."

Slowly, Stais got up. He put on his shoes and put his shaving kit into his musette bag and slung it over one shoulder.

"You ready?" asked Whitejack.

"Yes," said Stais.

"That all the baggage you got, that little musette bag?"

"Yes," said Sais. "I was listed as missing, presumed dead, and they sent all my stuff into the supply room and all my personal belongings home to my mother."

Stais looked around the barracks. They shone in the harsh Army light of barracks at night all over the world, by now familiar, homelike, to all the men who passed through them. He had left nothing.

They walked out into the soft, engine-filled night. A beacon flashed nervously across the sky, dimming the enormous pale twinkle of southern stars for a moment.

As they passed the Operations room, Stais saw a young lieutenant slumped down in a wobbly old wicker chair, staring out across the field.

"They come yet?" Whitejack asked.

"No," said the lieutenant, without looking up.

Stais went into the building and into the room where they had the rubber raft and the patented radio and the cloth painted blue on one side and yellow on the other. A fat, middle-aged A.T.C. captain wearily told them about ditching procedure. There were more than thirty people in the room, all passengers on Stais's plane. There were two small, yellow Chinamen and five bouncing fat Red Cross women and three sergeants with a lot of Air Force medals, trying not to seem excited about going home, and two colonels in the Engineers, looking too old for this war. Stais only half listened as the fat captain explained how to inflate the raft, what strings to pull, what levers to move, where to find the waterproofed Bible.

Whitejack was standing outside when Stais started for his plane. He gave Stais a slip of paper. "It's my home address," he said. "After the war, just come down sometime in October and I'll take you hunting."

"Thank you very much," said Strais gravely. Over Whitejack's shoulder he saw the lieutenant, still slumped in the wicker chair, still staring fixedly out across the dark field.

Whitejack walked out to the great plane with Stais, along the oil-spattered concrete of the runway, among the Chinamen and loud Red Cross women and the sergeants. The two men stopped without a word at the steps going up to the doorway of the plane and the other passengers filed past them.

They stood there, silently, with the two days of random conversation behind them, and Brazil and Athens behind them, and five hundred flights behind them, and Jerusalem and Miami behind them, and the girls from Vienna and the American Embassy and Flushing, Long Island, behind them, and the Greek mountaineers behind them, and Thomas Wolfe's funeral, and friends burning like torches, and dogs under treed raccoons in the Blue Ridge Mountains behind them, and a desperate twenty-two-year-old lieutenant painfully staring across a dusty airfield for ten days behind them, and the Mediterranean and the hospital bed in Cairo and Johnny Moffat wandering that night over the southern Atlantic, with ten acres of meadow and three acres of timber for his house and Whitejack's sister waiting for him, all behind them. And, ahead of Stais, home, and a mother who had presumed him dead and wept over his personal belongings, and ahead of Whitejack the cold, bitter mountains of India and China, and the tearing dead sound of the fifties and the sky full of Japs.

"All right, Sergeant," the voice of the lieutenant checking the passengers said. "Get on."

Stais waved, a little broken wave, at Whitejack standing there. "See you," he said, "in North Carolina."

"Some October." Whitejack smiled a little, in the light of the flood lamps.

The door closed and Stais sat down in the seat in front of the two Chinamen.

"I think these planes are absolutely charming," one of the Red Cross women was saying loudly. "Don't you?"

The engines started and the big plane began to roll. Stais looked out of the window. A plane was landing. It came slowly into the light of the runway lamps and set down heavily, bumping wearily. Stais stared. It was a Mitchell. Stais sighed. As the big C-54 wheeled at the head of the runway, then started clumsily down, Stais put the slip of paper with "Arnold Whitejack" written on it, and the address, in scrawling, childlike handwriting, into his pocket. And as he saw the Mitchell pull to a stop near the Operations room, he felt for the moment a little less guilty for going home.

# Shirley Jackson (1919–1965)

ONE SHORT STORY, "The Lottery," made Shirley Jackson instantly famous and although she wrote many novels and other short stories, it is "The Lottery" people attach to her name. She was born in California, studied at Syracuse University and lived most of her life thereafter in Vermont. New England folkways fascinated her and she found much material in the lives of her neighbors. Her novels include *The Road Through the Wall* (1948) and *Hangsaman* (1951). Later she turned to writing about the occult in such books as *The Sundial* (1958) and *The Haunting of Hill House* (1959). She also wrote two autobiographies about her family.

As the author of "The Lottery" Shirley Jackson is a lineal literary descendant of Nathaniel Hawthorne. The story continues the strain of Gothic writing that so paradoxically emerges every now and then in the supposedly most pragmatic of modern societies, the American. There is, however, a distinct difference between the two. Hawthorne evoked an aura of the unworldly. The impact of the horror in "The Lottery" is the matter-of-fact everyday atmosphere. Here are ordinary people, neighbors gathering in friendly fashion for what might be a ball game or political rally. And the reader wonders who will be the lucky person who wins the lottery?

# The Lottery

THE MORNING of June 27th was clear and sunny, with the fresh warmth of a full-summer day; the flowers were blossoming profusely and the grass was richly green. The people of the village began to gather in the square, between the post office and the bank, around ten o'clock; in some towns there were so many people that the lottery took two days and had to be started on June 26th, but in this village, where there were only about three hundred people, the whole lottery took less than two hours, so it could begin at ten o'clock in the morning and still be through in time to allow the villagers to get home for noon dinner.

The children assembled first, of course. School was recently over for the summer, and the feeling of liberty sat uneasily on most of them; they tended to gather quietly for a while before they broke into boisterous play, and their talk was still of the classroom and the teacher, of books and reprimands. Bobby Martin had already stuffed his pockets full of stones, and the other boys soon followed his example, selecting the smoothest and roundest stones; Bobby and Harry Jones and Dickie Delacroix — the villagers pronounced this name "Dellacroy" — eventually made a great pile of stones in one corner of the square and guarded it against the raids of the other boys. The girls stood aside, talking among themselves, looking over their shoulders at the boys, and the very small children rolled in the dust or clung to the hands of their older brothers or sisters.

Soon the men began to gather, surveying their own children, speaking of planting and rain, tractors and taxes. They stood together, away from the pile of stones in the corner, and their jokes were quiet and they smiled rather than laughed. The women, wearing faded house dresses and sweaters, came shortly after their menfolk. They greeted one another and exchanged bits of gossip as they went to join their husbands. Soon the women, standing by their husbands, began to call to their children, and the children came reluctantly, having to be called four or five times. Bobby Martin ducked under his mother's grasping hand and ran, laughing, back to the pile of stones. His father spoke up sharply, and Bobby came quickly and took his place between his father and his oldest brother.

The lottery was conducted — as were the square dances, the teen-age club, the Halloween program — by Mr. Summers, who had time and energy to devote to civic activities. He was a round-faced, jovial man and he ran the coal business, and people were sorry for him, because he had no children and his wife was a scold. When he arrived in the square, carrying the black wooden box, there was a murmur of conversation among the villagers, and he waved and called, "Little late today, folks." The postmaster, Mr. Graves, followed him, carrying a three-legged stool, and the stool was put in the center of the square and Mr. Summers set the black box down on it. The villagers kept their distance, leaving a space between themselves and the stool, and when Mr. Summers said, "Some of you fellows want to give me a hand?" there was a hesitation before two men, Mr. Martin and his oldest son, Baxter, came forward to hold the box steady on the stool while Mr. Summers stirred up the papers inside it.

The original paraphernalia for the lottery had been lost long ago, and the black box now resting on the stool had been put into use even before Old Man Warner, the oldest man in town, was born. Mr. Summers spoke frequently to the villagers about making a new box, but no one liked to upset even as much tradition as was represented by the black box. There was a story that the present box had been made with some pieces of the box that had preceded it, the one that had been constructed when the first people settled down to make a village here. Every year, after the lottery, Mr. Summers began talking again about a new box, but every year the subject was allowed to fade off without anything's being done. The black box grew shabbier each year; by now it was no longer completely black but splintered badly along one side to show the original wood color, and in some places faded or stained.

Mr. Martin and his oldest son, Baxter, held the black box securely on the stool until Mr. Summers had stirred the papers thoroughly with his hand. Because so much of the ritual had been forgotten or discarded, Mr. Summers had been successful in having slips of paper substituted for the chips of wood that had been used for generations. Chips of wood, Mr. Summers had argued, had been all very well when the village was tiny, but now that the population was more than three hundred and likely to keep on growing, it was necessary to use something that would fit more easily into the black box. The night before the lottery, Mr. Summers and Mr. Graves made up the slips of paper and put them in the box, and it was then taken to the safe of Mr. Summers' coal company and locked up until Mr. Summers was ready to take it to the square next morning. The rest of the year, the box was put away, sometimes one place, sometimes another; it had spent one year in Mr. Graves's barn and another year underfoot in the post office, and sometimes it was set on a shelf in the Martin grocery and left there.

There was a great deal of fussing to be done before Mr. Summers declared the lottery open. There were the lists to make up — of heads of families, heads of households in each family, members of each household in each family. There was the proper swearing-in of Mr. Summers by the postmaster, as the official of the lottery; at one time, some people remembered, there had been a recital of some sort, performed by the official of the lottery, a perfunctory, tuneless chant that had been rattled off duly each year; some people believed that the official of the lottery used to stand just so when he said or sang it, others believed that he was supposed to walk among the people, but years and years ago this part of the ritual had been allowed to lapse. There had been, also, a ritual salute, which the official of the lottery had had to use in addressing each person who came up to draw from the box, but this also had changed with time, until now it was felt necessary only for the official to speak to each person approaching. Mr. Summers was very good at all this; in his clean white shirt and blue jeans, with one hand resting carelessly on the black box, he seemed very proper and important as he talked interminably to Mr. Graves and the Martins.

Just as Mr. Summers finally left off talking and turned to the assembled villagers, Mrs. Hutchinson came hurriedly along the path to the square, her sweater thrown over her shoulders, and slid into place in the back of the crowd. "Clean forgot what day it was," she said to Mrs. Delacroix, who stood next to her, and they both laughed softly. "Thought my old man was out back stacking wood," Mrs. Hutchinson went on, "and then I looked out the window and the kids was gone, and then I remembered it was the twenty-seventh and came a-running." She dried her hands on her apron, and Mrs. Delacroix said, "You're in time, though. They're still talking away up there."

Mrs. Hutchinson craned her neck to see through the crowd and found her husband and children standing near the front. She tapped Mrs. Delacroix on the arm as a farewell and began to make her way through the crowd. The people separated good-humoredly to let her through; two or three people said, in voices just loud enough to be heard across the crowd, "Here comes your Missus, Hutchinson," and "Bill, she made it after all." Mrs. Hutchinson reached her husband, and Mr. Summers, who had been waiting, said cheerfully, "Thought we were going to have to get on without you, Tessie." Mrs. Hutchinson said, grinning, "Wouldn't have me leave m'dishes in the sink, now, would you, Joe?," and soft laughter ran through the crowd as the people stirred back into position after Mrs. Hutchinson's arrival.

"Well, now," Mr. Summers said soberly, "guess we better get started, get this over with, so's we can go back to work. Anybody ain't here?"

"Dunbar," several people said. "Dunbar, Dunbar."

Mr. Summers consulted his list. "Clyde Dunbar," he said. "That's right. He's broke his leg, hasn't he? Who's drawing for him?"

"Me, I guess," a woman said, and Mr. Summers turned to look at her. "Wife draws for her husband," Mr. Summers said. "Don't you have a grown boy to do it for you, Janey?" Although Mr. Summers and everyone else in the village knew the answer perfectly well, it was the business of the official of the lottery to ask such questions formally. Mr. Summers waited with an expression of polite interest while Mrs. Dunbar answered.

"Horace's not but sixteen yet," Mrs. Dunbar said regretfully. "Guess I gotta fill in for the old man this year."

"Right," Mr. Summers said. He made a note on the list he was holding. Then he asked, "Watson boy drawing this year?"

A tall boy in the crowd raised his hand. "Here," he said. "I'm drawing for m'mother and me." He blinked his eyes nervously and ducked his head as several voices in the crowd said things like "Good fellow, Jack," and "Glad to see your mother's got a man to do it."

"Well," Mr. Summers said, "guess that's everyone. Old Man Warner make it?"

"Here," a voice said, and Mr. Summers nodded.

A sudden hush fell on the crowd as Mr. Summers cleared his throat and looked at the list. "All ready?" he called. "Now, I'll read the names — heads of families first — and the men come up and take a paper out of the box. Keep the paper folded in your hand without looking at it until everyone has had a turn. Everything clear?"

The people had done it so many times that they only half listened to the directions; most of them were quiet, wetting their lips, not looking around. Then Mr. Summers raised one hand high and said, "Adams." A man disengaged himself from the crowd and came forward. "Hi, Steve," Mr. Summers said, and Mr. Adams said, "Hi, Joe." They grinned at one another humorlessly and nervously. Then Mr. Adams reached into the black box and took out a folded paper. He held it firmly by one corner as he turned and went hastily back to his place in the crowd, where he stood a little apart from his family, not looking down at his hand.

"Allen," Mr. Summers said. "Anderson . . . Bentham."

"Seems like there's no time at all between lotteries any more," Mrs. Delacroix said to Mrs. Graves in the back row. "Seems like we got through with the last one only last week."

"Time sure goes fast," Mrs. Graves said.

"Clark . . . Delacroix."

"There goes my old man," Mrs. Delacroix said. She held her breath while her husband went forward.

"Dunbar," Mr. Summers said, and Mrs. Dunbar went steadily to the box while one of the women said, "Go on, Janey," and another said, "There she goes."

"We're next," Mrs. Graves said. She watched while Mr. Graves came around from the side of the box, greeted Mr. Summers gravely, and selected a slip of paper from the box. By now, all through the crowd there were men holding the small folded papers in their large hands, turning them over and over nervously. Mrs. Dunbar and her two sons stood together, Mrs. Dunbar holding the slip of paper.

"Harburt . . . Hutchinson."

"Get up there, Bill," Mrs. Hutchinson said, and the people near her laughed.

"Jones."

"They do say," Mr. Adams said to Old Man Warner, who stood next to him, "that over in the north village they're talking of giving up the lottery."

Old Man Warner snorted. "Pack of crazy fools," he said. "Listening to the young folks, nothing's good enough for *them*. Next thing you know, they'll be wanting to go back to living in caves, nobody work any more, live *that* way for a while. Used to be a saying about 'Lottery in June, corn be heavy soon.' First thing you know, we'd all be eating stewed chickweed and acorns. There's *always* been a lottery," he added petulantly. "Bad enough to see young Joe Summers up there joking with everybody."

"Some places have already quit lotteries," Mrs. Adams said.

"Nothing but trouble in *that*," Old Man Warner said stoutly. "Pack of young fools."

"Martin." And Bobby Martin watched his father go forward. "Overdyke . . . Percy."

"I wish they'd hurry," Mrs. Dunbar said to her older son. "I wish they'd hurry."

"They're almost through," her son said.

"You get ready to run tell Dad," Mrs. Dunbar said.

Mr. Summers called his own name and then stepped forward precisely and selected a slip from the box. Then he called, "Warner."

"Seventy-seventh year I been in the lottery," Old Man Warner said as he went through the crowd. "Seventy-seventh time."

"Watson." The tall boy came awkwardly through the crowd. Someone said, "Don't be nervous, Jack," and Mr. Summers said, "Take your time, son."

"Zanini."

After that, there was a long pause, a breathless pause, until Mr. Summers, holding his slip of paper in the air, said, "All right, fellows." For a minute, no one moved, and then all the slips of paper were opened. Suddenly, all the women began to speak at once, saying, "Who is it?" "Who's got it?" "Is it the Dunbars?" "Is it the Watsons?" Then the voices began to say, "It's Hutchinson. It's Bill." "Bill Hutchinson's got it."

"Go tell your father," Mrs. Dunbar said to her older son.

People began to look around to see the Hutchinsons. Bill Hutchinson was standing quiet, staring down at the paper in his hand. Suddenly, Tessie Hutchinson shouted to Mr. Summers, "You didn't give him time enough to take any paper he wanted. I saw you. It wasn't fair!"

"Be a good sport, Tessie," Mrs. Delacroix called, and Mrs. Graves said, "All of us took the same chance."

"Shut up, Tessie," Bill Hutchinson said.

"Well, everyone," Mr. Summers said, "that was done pretty fast, and now we've got to be hurrying a little more to get done in time." He consulted his next list. "Bill," he said, "you draw for the Hutchinson family. You got any other households in the Hutchinsons?"

"There's Don and Eva," Mrs. Hutchinson yelled. "Make *them* take their chance!"

"Daughters draw with their husbands' families, Tessie," Mr. Summers said gently. "You know that as well as anyone else."

"It wasn't *fair*," Tessie said.

"I guess not, Joe," Bill Hutchinson said regretfully. "My daughter draws with her husband's family, that's only fair. And I've got no other family except the kids."

"Then, as far as drawing for families is concerned, it's you," Mr. Summers said in explanation, "and as far as drawing for households is concerned, that's you, too. Right?"

"Right," Bill Hutchinson said.

"How many kids, Bill?" Mr. Summers asked formally.

"Three," Bill Hutchinson said. "There's Bill, Jr., and Nancy, and little Dave. And Tessie and me."

"All right, then," Mr. Summers said. "Harry, you got their tickets back?"

Mr. Graves nodded and held up the slips of paper. "Put them in the box, then," Mr. Summers directed. "Take Bill's and put it in."

"I think we ought to start over," Mrs. Hutchinson said, as quietly as she could. "I tell you it wasn't *fair*. You didn't give him time enough to choose. *Every*body saw that."

Mr. Graves had selected the five slips and put them in the box, and he dropped all the papers but those onto the ground, where the breeze caught them and lifted them off.

"Listen, everybody," Mrs. Hutchinson was saying to the people around her.

"Ready, Bill?" Mr. Summers asked, and Bill Hutchinson, with one quick glance around at his wife and children, nodded.

"Remember," Mr. Summers said, "take the slips and keep them folded until each person has taken one. Harry, you help little Dave." Mr. Graves took the hand of the little boy, who came willingly with him up to the box. "Take a paper out of the box, Davy," Mr. Summers said. Davy put his hand into the box and laughed. "Take just *one* paper," Mr. Summers said. "Harry, you hold it for him." Mr. Graves took the child's hand and removed the folded paper from the tight fist and held it while little Dave stood next to him and looked up at him wonderingly.

"Nancy next," Mr. Summers said. Nancy was twelve, and her school friends breathed heavily as she went forward, switching her skirt, and took a slip daintily from the box. "Bill, Jr.," Mr. Summers said, and Billy, his face red and his feet overlarge, nearly knocked the box over as he got a paper out. "Tessie," Mr. Summers said. She hesitated for a minute, looking around defiantly, and then set her lips and went up to the box. She snatched a paper out and held it behind her.

"Bill," Mr. Summers said, and Bill Hutchinson reached into the box and felt around, bringing his hand out at last with the slip of paper in it.

The crowd was quiet. A girl whispered, "I hope it's not Nancy," and the sound of the whisper reached the edges of the crowd.

"It's not the way it used to be," Old Man Warner said clearly. "People ain't the way they used to be."

"All right," Mr. Summers said. "Open the papers. Harry, you open little Dave's."

Mr. Graves opened the slip of paper and there was a general sigh through the crowd as he held it up and everyone could see that it was blank. Nancy and Bill, Jr., opened theirs at the same time, and both beamed and laughed, turning around to the crowd and holding their slips of paper above their heads.

"Tessie," Mr. Summers said. There was a pause, and then Mr. Summers looked at Bill Hutchinson, and Bill unfolded his paper and showed it. It was blank.

"It's Tessie," Mr. Summers said, and his voice was hushed. "Show us her paper, Bill."

Bill Hutchinson went over to his wife and forced the slip of paper out of her hand. It had a black spot on it, the black spot Mr. Summers had made the night before with the heavy pencil in the coal-company office. Bill Hutchinson held it up, and there was a stir in the crowd.

"All right, folks," Mr. Summers said. "Let's finish quickly."

Although the villagers had forgotten the ritual and lost the original black box, they still remembered to use stones. The pile of stones the boys had made earlier was ready; there were stones on the ground with the blowing scraps of paper that had come out of the box. Mrs. Delacroix selected a stone so large she had to pick it up with both hands and turned to Mrs. Dunbar. "Come on," she said. "Hurry up."

Mrs. Dunbar had small stones in both hands, and she said, gasping for breath, "I can't run at all. You'll have to go ahead and I'll catch up with you."

The children had stones already, and someone gave little Davy Hutchinson a few pebbles.

Tessie Hutchinson was in the center of a cleared space by now, and she held her hands out desperately as the villagers moved in on her. "It isn't fair," she said. A stone hit her on the side of the head.

Old Man Warner was saying, "Come on, come on, everyone." Steve Adams was in the front of the crowd of villagers, with Mrs. Graves beside him.

"It isn't fair, it isn't right," Mrs. Hutchinson screamed, and then they were upon her.

# Ray Bradbury (1920–      )

BEST KNOWN as one of our most important science fiction writers, Ray Bradbury has also written many fine stories with other themes. He was born in Illinois but has spent most of his life in Los Angeles. His first published work was potboilers for pulp magazines. Unlike too many young writers who resort to potboiling and later try to escape only to find they are forever trapped, Bradbury was able to surmount hack work and win recognition as a serious writer. His science fiction includes the books, *Dark Carnival* (1947), *The Martian Chronicles* (1950), and *The Illustrated Man* (1951), which stresses social questions. Of particular interest to writers themselves is Bradbury's *Fahrenheit 451* (1953) depicting a future state where people are forced to think and know only what is shown on television and books are destroyed and the people who read them are burned to death. Short-story volumes by Bradbury are *The Golden Apples of the Sun* (1953), *October Country* (1955), *A Medicine for Melancholy* (1959), and *Something Wicked This Way Comes* (1963). The great range of his writing is shown by the quiet charm of a novel, *Dandelion Wine* (1957). The script for the filming of *Moby Dick* was written by Bradbury.

Too often a science fiction story reads like a boring description of interplanetary life by a well-meaning but dull automobile mechanic. "Ylla," a story in Ray Bradbury's celebrated collection, *The Martian Chronicles*, shows his exceptional ability to blend fantasy, believable characters, and lyrical writing in science fiction. There is no pause here, for instance, to detail how crystal walls are seeded and cultivated to bear golden fruit or how the plumbing can send founts of steaming water leaping up to warm a room. Exotic as is their description, the Martian man and wife come off as sentient beings in their experience with the man from space. Interesting, too, that without ever stating it, Bradbury makes a reader feel while reading this story that he is actually a stupendous distance from Earth.

# *February 1999: Ylla*

THEY HAD a house of crystal pillars on the planet Mars by the edge of an empty sea, and every morning you could see Mrs. K eating the golden fruits that grew from the crystal walls, or cleaning the house with handfuls of magnetic dust which, taking all dirt with it, blew away on the hot wind. Afternoons, when the fossil sea was warm and motionless, and the wine trees stood stiff in the yard, and the little distant Martian bone town was all enclosed, and no one drifted out their doors, you could see Mr. K himself in his room, reading from a metal book with raised hieroglyphs over which he brushed his hand, as one might play a harp. And from the book, as his fingers stroked, a voice sang, a soft ancient voice, which told tales of when the sea was red steam on the shore and ancient men had carried clouds of metal insects and electric spiders into battle.

Mr. and Mrs. K had lived by the dead sea for twenty years, and their ancestors had lived in the same house, which turned and followed the sun, flower-like, for ten centuries.

Mr. and Mrs. K were not old. They had the fair, brownish skin of the true Martian, the yellow coin eyes, the soft musical voices. Once they had liked painting pictures with chemical fire, swimming in the canals in the seasons when the wine trees filled them with green liquors, and talking into the dawn together by the blue phosphorous portraits in the speaking room.

They were not happy now.

This morning Mrs. K stood between the pillars, listening to the desert sands heat, melt into yellow wax, and seemingly run on the horizon.

Something was going to happen.

She waited.

She watched the blue sky of Mars as if it might at any moment grip in on itself, contract, and expel a shining miracle down upon the sand.

Nothing happened.

Tired of waiting, she walked through the misting pillars. A gentle rain sprang from the fluted pillar tops, cooling the scorched air, falling gently on her. On hot days it was like walking in a creek. The floors of the house glittered with cool streams. In the distance she heard her husband playing his book steadily, his fingers never tired of the old songs. Quietly she wished he might one day again spend as much time holding and touching her like a little harp as he did his incredible books.

But no. She shook her head, an imperceptible, forgiving shrug. Her eyelids closed softly down upon her golden eyes. Marriage made people old and familiar, while still young.

She lay back in a chair that moved to take her shape even as she moved. She closed her eyes tightly and nervously.

The dream occurred.

Her brown fingers trembled, came up, grasped at the air. A moment later she sat up, startled, gasping.

She glanced about swiftly, as if expecting someone there before her. She seemed disappointed; the space between the pillars was empty.

Her husband appeared in a triangular door. "Did you call?" he asked irritably.

"No!" she cried.

"I thought I heard you cry out."

"Did I? I was almost asleep and had a dream!"

"In the daytime? You don't often do that."

She sat as if struck in the face by the dream. "How strange, how very strange," she murmured. "The dream."

"Oh?" He evidently wished to return to his book.

"I dreamed about a man."

"A man?"

"A tall man, six feet one inch tall."

"How absurd; a giant, a misshapen giant."

"Somehow" — she tried the words — "he looked all right. In spite of being tall. And he had — oh, I know you'll think it silly — he had *blue* eyes!"

"Blue eyes! Gods!" cried Mr. K. "What'll you dream next? I suppose he had *black* hair?"

"How did you *guess*?" She was excited.

"I picked the most unlikely color," he replied coldly.

"Well, black it was!" she cried. "And he had a very white skin; oh, he was *most* unusual! He was dressed in a strange uniform and he came down out of the sky and spoke pleasantly to me." She smiled.

"Out of the sky; what nonsense!"

"He came in a metal thing that glittered in the sun," she remembered. She closed her eyes to shape it again. "I dreamed there was the sky and something sparkled like a coin thrown into the air, and suddenly it grew large and fell down softly to land, a long silver craft, round and alien. And a door opened in the side of the silver object and this tall man stepped out."

"If you worked harder you wouldn't have these silly dreams."

"I rather enjoyed it," she replied, lying back. "I never suspected myself of such an imagination. Black hair, blue eyes, and white skin! What a strange man, and yet — quite handsome."

"Wishful thinking."

"You're unkind. I didn't think him up on purpose; he just came in my mind while I drowsed. It wasn't like a dream. It was so unexpected and different. He looked at me and he said, 'I've come from the third planet in my ship. My name in Nathaniel York — '"

"A stupid name; it's no name at all," objected the husband.

"Of course it's stupid, because it's a dream," she explained softly. "And he said, 'This is the first trip across space. There are only two of us in our ship, myself and my friend Bert.'"

"*Another* stupid name."

"And he said, 'We're from a city on *Earth*; that's the name of our planet,'" continued Mrs. K. "That's what he said. 'Earth' was the name he spoke. And he used another language. Somehow I understood him. With my mind. Telepathy, I suppose."

Mr. K turned away. She stopped him with a word. "Yll?" she called quietly. "Do you ever wonder if — well, if there *are* people living on the third planet?"

"The third planet is incapable of supporting life," stated the husband patiently. "Our scientists have said there's far too much oxygen in their atmosphere."

"But wouldn't it be fascinating if there *were* people? And they traveled through space in some sort of ship?"

"Really, Ylla, you know how I hate this emotional wailing. Let's get on with our work."


It was late in the day when she began singing the song as she moved among the whispering pillars of rain. She sang it over and over again.

"What's that song?" snapped her husband at last, walking in to sit at the fire table.

"I don't know." She looked up, surprised at herself. She put her hand to her mouth, unbelieving. The sun was setting. The house was closing itself in, like a giant flower, with the passing of light. A wind blew among the pillars; the fire table bubbled its fierce pool of silver lava. The wind stirred her russet hair, crooning softly in her ears. She stood silently looking out into the great sallow distances of sea bottom, as if recalling something, her yellow eyes soft and moist. "'Drink to me only with thine eyes, and I will pledge with mine,'" she sang, softly, quietly, slowly. "'Or leave a kiss within the cup, and I'll not ask for wine.'" She hummed now, moving her hands in the wind ever so lightly, her eyes shut. She finished the song.

It was very beautiful.

"Never heard that song before. Did you compose it?" he inquired, his eyes sharp.

"No. Yes. No, I don't know, really!" She hesitated wildly. "I don't even know what the words are; they're another language!"

"What language?"

She dropped portions of meat numbly into the simmering lava. "I don't know." She drew the meat forth a moment later, cooked, served on a plate for him. "It's just a crazy thing I made up, I guess. I don't know why."

He said nothing. He watched her drown meats in the hissing fire pool. The sun was gone. Slowly, slowly the night came in to fill the room, swallowing the pillars and both of them, like a dark wine poured to the ceiling. Only the silver lava's glow lit their faces.

She hummed the strange song again.

Instantly he leaped from his chair and stalked angrily from the room.


Later, in isolation, he finished supper.

When he arose he stretched, glanced at her, and suggested, yawning,

"Let's take the flame birds to town tonight to see an entertainment."

"You don't *mean* it?" she said. "Are you feeling well?"

"What's so strange about that?"

"But we haven't gone for an entertainment in six months!"

"I think it's a good idea."

"Suddenly you're so solicitous," she said.

"Don't talk that way," he replied peevishly. "Do you or do you not want to go?"

She looked out at the pale desert. The twin white moons were rising. Cool water ran softly about her toes. She began to tremble just the least bit. She wanted very much to sit quietly here, soundless, not moving until this thing occurred, this thing expected all day, this thing that could not occur but might. A drift of song brushed through her mind.

"I —"

"Do you good," he urged. "Come along now."

"I'm tired," she said. "Some other night."

"Here's your scarf." He handed her a phial. "We haven't gone anywhere in months."

"Except you, twice a week to Xi City." She wouldn't look at him.

"Business," he said.

"Oh?" She whispered to herself.

From the phial a liquid poured, turned to blue mist, settled about her neck, quivering.

The flame birds waited, like a bed of coals, glowing on the cool smooth sands. The white canopy ballooned on the night wind, flapping softly, tied by a thousand green ribbons to the birds.

Ylla laid herself back in the canopy and, at a word from her husband, the birds leaped, burning, toward the dark sky. The ribbons tautened, the canopy lifted. The sand slid whining under; the blue hills drifted by, drifted by, leaving their home behind, the raining pillars, the caged flowers, the singing books, the whispering floor creeks. She did not look at her husband. She heard him crying out to the birds as they rose higher, like ten thousand hot sparkles, so many red-yellow fireworks in the heavens, tugging the canopy like a flower petal, burning through the wind.

She didn't watch the dead, ancient bone-chess cities slide under, or the old canals filled with emptiness and dreams. Past dry rivers and dry lakes they flew, like a shadow of the moon, like a torch burning.

She watched only the sky.

The husband spoke.

She watched the sky.

"Did you hear what I said?"

"What?"

He exhaled. "You might pay attention."

"I was thinking."

"I never thought you were a nature lover, but you're certainly interested in the sky tonight," he said.

"It's very beautiful."

"I was figuring," said the husband slowly. "I thought I'd call Hulle tonight. I'd like to talk to him about us spending some time, oh, only a week or so, in the Blue Mountains. It's just an idea — "

"The Blue Mountains!" She held to the canopy rim with one hand, turning swiftly toward him.

"Oh, it's just a suggestion."

"When do you want to go?" she asked, trembling.

"I thought we might leave tomorrow morning. You know, an early start and all that," he said very casually.

"But we *never* go this early in the year!"

"Just this once, I thought — " He smiled. "Do us good to get away. Some peace and quiet. You know. You haven't anything *else* planned? We'll go, won't we?"

She took a breath, waited, and then replied, "No."

"What?" His cry startled the birds. The canopy jerked.

"No," she said firmly. "It's settled. I won't go."

He looked at her. They did not speak after that. She turned away. The birds flew on, ten thousand firebrands down the wind.

In the dawn the sun, through the crystal pillars, melted the fog that supported Ylla as she slept. All night she had hung above the floor, buoyed by the soft carpeting of mist that poured from the walls when she lay down to rest. All night she had slept on this silent river, like a boat upon a soundless tide. Now the fog burned away, the mist level lowered until she was deposited upon the shore of wakening.

She opened her eyes.

Her husband stood over her. He looked as if he had stood there for hours, watching. She did not know why, but she could not look him in the face.

"You've been dreaming again!" he said. "You spoke out and kept me awake. I *really* think you should see a doctor."

"I'll be all right."

"You talked a lot in your sleep!"

"Did I?" She started up.

Dawn was cold in the room. A gray light filled her as she lay there.

"What was your dream?"

She had to think a moment to remember. "The ship. It came from the sky again, landed, and the tall man stepped out and talked with me, telling me little jokes, laughing, and it was pleasant."

Mr. K touched a pillar. Founts of warm water leaped up, steaming; the chill vanished from the room. Mr. K's face was impassive.

"And then," she said, "this man, who said his strange name was Nathaniel York, told me I was beautiful and — and kissed me."

"Ha!" cried the husband, turning violently away, his jaw working.

"It's only a dream." She was amused.

"Keep your silly, feminine dreams to yourself!"

"You're acting like a child." She lapsed back upon the few remaining remnants of chemical mist. After a moment she laughed softly. "I thought of some *more* of the dream," she confessed.

"Well, what is it, what *is* it?" he shouted.

"Yll, you're so bad-tempered."

"Tell me!" he demanded. "You can't keep secrets from me!" His face was dark and rigid as he stood over her.

"I've never seen you this way," she replied, half shocked, half entertained. "All that happened was this Nathaniel York person told me — well, he told me that he'd take me away into his ship, into the sky with him, and take me back to his planet with him. It's really quite ridiculous."

"Ridiculous, is it!" he almost screamed. "You should have heard yourself, fawning on him, talking to him, singing with him, oh gods, all night; you should have *heard* yourself!"

"Yll!"

"When's he landing? Where's he coming down with his damned ship?"

"Yll, lower your voice."

"Voice be damned!" He bent stiffly over her. "And *in* this dream" — he seized her wrist — "didn't the ship land over in Green Valley, *didn't* it? Answer me!"

"Why, yes — "

"And it landed this afternoon, didn't it?" he kept at her.

"Yes, yes, I think so, yes, but only in a dream!"

"Well" — he flung her hand away stiffly — "it's good you're truthful! I heard every word you said in your sleep. You mentioned the valley and the time." Breathing hard, he walked between the pillars like a man blinded by a lightning bolt. Slowly his breath returned. She watched him as if he were quite insane. She arose finally and went to him. "Yll," she whispered.

"I'm all right."

"You're sick."

"No." He forced a tired smile. "Just childish. Forgive me, darling." He gave her a rough pat. "Too much work lately. I'm sorry, I think I'll lie down awhile — "

"You were so excited."

"I'm all right now. Fine." He exhaled. "Let's forget it. Say, I heard a joke about Uel yesterday, I meant to tell you. What do you say . you fix breakfast, I'll tell the joke, and let's not talk about all this."

"It was only a dream."

"Of course." He kissed her cheek mechanically. "Only a dream."

At noon the sun was high and hot and the hills shimmered in the light.

"Aren't you going to town?" asked Ylla.

"Town?" He raised his brows faintly.

"This is the day you *always* go." She adjusted a flower cage on its pedestal. The flowers stirred, opening their hungry yellow mouths.

He closed his book. "No. It's too hot, and it's late."

"Oh." She finished her task and moved toward the door. "Well, I'll be back soon."

"Wait a minute! Where are you going?"

She was in the door swiftly. "Over to Pao's. She invited me!"

"Today?"

"I haven't seen her in a long time. It's only a little way."

"Over in Green Valley, isn't it?"

"Yes, just a walk, not far, I thought I'd — " She hurried.

"I'm sorry, really sorry," he said, running to fetch her back, looking very concerned about his forgetfulness. "It slipped my mind. I invited Dr. Nlle out this afternoon."

"Dr. Nlle!" She edged toward the door.

He caught her elbow and drew her steadily in. "Yes."

"But Pao — "

"Pao can wait, Ylla. We must entertain Nlle."

"Just for a few minutes — "

"No, Ylla."

"No?"

He shook his head. "No. Besides, it's a terribly long walk to Pao's. All the way over through Green Valley and then past the big canal and down, isn't it? And it'll be very, very hot, and Dr. Nlle would be delighted to see you. Well?"

She did not answer. She wanted to break and run. She wanted to cry out. But she only sat in the chair, turning her fingers over slowly, staring at them expressionlessly, trapped.

"Ylla?" he murmured. "You *will* be here, won't you?"

"Yes," she said after a long time. "I'll be here."

"All afternoon?"

Her voice was dull. "All afternoon."

Late in the day Dr. Nlle had not put in an appearance. Ylla's husband did not seem overly surprised. When it was quite late he murmured something, went to a closet, and drew forth an evil weapon, a long yellowish tube ending in a bellows and a trigger. He turned, and upon his face was a mask, hammered from silver metal, expressionless, the mask that he always wore when he wished to hide his feelings, the mask which curved and hollowed so exquisitely to his thin cheeks and chin and brow. The mask glinted, and he held the evil weapon in his hands, considering it. It hummed constantly, an insect hum. From it hordes of golden bees could be flung out with a high shriek. Golden, horrid bees that stung, poisoned, and fell lifeless, like seeds on the sand.

"Where are you going?" she asked.

"What?" He listened to the bellows, to the evil hum. "If Dr. Nlle is late, I'll be damned if I'll wait. I'm going out to hunt a bit. I'll be back. You be sure to stay right here now, won't you?" The silver mask glimmered.

"Yes."

"And tell Dr. Nlle I'll return. Just hunting."

The triangular door closed. His footsteps faded down the hill.

She watched him walking through the sunlight until he was gone. Then she resumed her tasks with the magnetic dusts and the new fruits to be plucked from the crystal walls. She worked with energy and dispatch, but on occasion a numbness took hold of her and she caught herself singing that odd and memorable song and looking out beyond the crystal pillars at the sky.

She held her breath and stood very still, waiting.

It was coming nearer.

At any moment it might happen.

It was like those days when you heard a thunderstorm coming and there was the waiting silence and then the faintest pressure of the atmosphere as the climate blew over the land in shifts and shadows and vapors. And the change pressed at your ears and you were suspended in the waiting time of the coming storm. You began to tremble. The sky was stained and coloured; the clouds were thickened; the mountains took on an iron taint. The caged flowers blew with faint sighs of warning. You felt your hair stir softly. Somewhere in the house the voice-clock sang, "Time, time, time, time . . ." ever so gently, no more than water tapping on velvet.

And then the storm. The electric illumination, the engulfments of dark wash and sounding black fell down, shutting in, forever.

That's how it was now. A storm gathered, yet the sky was clear. Lightning was expected, yet there was no cloud.

Ylla moved through the breathless summer house. Lightning would strike from the sky any instant; there would be a thunderclap, a boll of smoke, a silence, footsteps on the path, a rap on the crystalline door, and her *running* to answer . . .

Crazy Ylla! she scoffed. Why think these wild things with your idle mind?

And then it happened.

There was a warmth as of a great fire passing in the air. A whirling, rushing sound. A gleam in the sky, of metal.

Ylla cried out.

Running through the pillars, she flung wide a door. She faced the hills. But by this time there was nothing.

She was about to race down the hill when she stopped herself. She was supposed to stay here, go nowhere. The doctor was coming to visit, and her husband would be angry if she ran off.

She waited in the door, breathing rapidly, her hand out.

She strained to see over toward Green Valley, but saw nothing.

Silly woman. She went inside. You and your imagination, she thought. That was nothing but a bird, a leaf, the wind, or a fish in the canal. Sit down. Rest.

She sat down.

A shot sounded.

Very clearly, sharply, the sound of the evil insect weapon.

Her body jerked with it.

It came from a long way off. One shot. The swift humming distant bees. One shot. And then a second shot, precise and cold, and far away.

Her body winced again and for some reason she started up, screaming, and screaming, and never wanting to stop screaming. She ran violently through the house and once more threw wide the door.

The echoes were dying away, away.

Gone.

She waited in the yard, her face pale, for five minutes.

Finally, with slow steps, her head down, she wandered about the pillared rooms, laying her hand to things, her lips quivering, until finally she sat alone in the darkening wine room, waiting. She began to wipe an amber glass with the hem of her scarf.

And then, from far off, the sound of footsteps crunching on the thin, small rocks.

She rose up to stand in the center of the quiet room. The glass fell from her fingers, smashing to bits.

The footsteps hesitated outside the door.

Should she speak? Should she cry out, "Come in, oh, come in"? She went forward a few paces.

The footsteps walked up the ramp. A hand twisted the door latch. She smiled at the door.

The door opened. She stopped smiling.

It was her husband. His silver mask glowed dully.

He entered the room and looked at her for only a moment. Then he snapped the weapon bellows open, cracked out two dead bees, heard them spat on the floor as they fell, stepped on them, and placed the empty bellows gun in the corner of the room as Ylla bent down and tried, over and over, with no success, to pick up the pieces of the shattered glass. "What were you doing?" she asked.

"Nothing," he said with his back turned. He removed the mask.

"But the gun — I heard you fire it. Twice."

"Just hunting. Once in a while you like to hunt. Did Dr. Nlle arrive?"

"No."

"Wait a minute." He snapped his fingers disgustedly. "Why, I remember *now*. He was supposed to visit us *tomorrow* afternoon. How stupid of me."

They sat down to eat. She looked at her food and did not move her hands. "What's wrong?" he asked, not looking up from dipping his meat in the bubbling lava.

"I don't know. I'm not hungry," she said.

"Why not?"

"I don't know; I'm just not."

The wind was rising across the sky; the sun was going down. The room was small and suddenly cold.

"I've been trying to remember," she said in the silent room, across from her cold, erect, golden-eyed husband.

"Remember what?" He sipped his wine.

"That song. That fine and beautiful song." She closed her eyes and hummed, but it was not the song. "I've forgotten it. And, some-how, I don't want to forget it. It's something I want always to remember." She moved her hands as if the rhythm might help her to remember all of it. Then she lay back in her chair. "I can't remember." She began to cry.

"Why are you crying?" he asked.

"I don't know, I don't know, but I can't help it. I'm sad and I don't know why, I cry and I don't know why, but I'm crying."

Her head was in her hands; her shoulders moved again and again.

"You'll be all right tomorrow," he said.

She did not look up at him; she looked only at the empty desert and the very bright stars coming out now on the black sky, and far away there was a sound of wind rising and canal waters stirring cold in the long canals. She shut her eyes, trembling.

"Yes," she said. "I'll be all right tomorrow."

# John Cheever (1912–    )

IT IS NOT every wayward student who achieves the triumph of Massachusetts-born John Cheever. He was expelled from Thayer Academy and wrote a story about it. That was the end of Cheever's unsuccessful academic career and the start of his brilliantly successful literary one. He has written many short stories since then, which have been published in book form. The first collection to appear was *The Way Some People Live* (1943) and was followed by *The Enormous Radio* (1953), *The Housebreaker of Shady Hill* (1958), *Some People, Places and Things That Will Not Appear in My Next Novel* (1961), and *The Brigadier and the Golf Widow* (1964). His novels include *The Wapshot Chronicle* (1957), which won the National Book Award, and *The Wapshot Scandal* (1964). Suburban life has been the setting for much of his writing.

When the short stories of John Cheever are mentioned one of those most often recalled admiringly is "The Country Husband." It is the story of an unhappy husband caught in the throes of the autumnal passion that so often catches a middle-aged man unawares. It is also a cross section of American twentieth-century middle-class life in striking contrast to that described in writing of the eighteenth and nineteenth centuries. Country club dances, baby sitters, city commuters, auto and plane travel, they are more than centuries apart from the minuets and Virginia reels, the sleep-in maids, the home-to-middle-of-the-day-dinner men, the travels by carriage and sleighs, but the husbands and wives and children in John Cheever's story remain the same. The American norm seems to be unchanging. Even the desperate words of the woeful passion-stricken husband are no exception. "I am in love, Doctor," would not have been said to a psychiatrist in the old days but to a minister.

# The Country Husband

TO BEGIN at the beginning, the airplane from Minneapolis in which Francis Weed was travelling East ran into heavy weather. The sky had been a hazy blue, with the clouds below the plane lying so close together that nothing could be seen of the earth. Then mist began to form outside the windows, and they flew into a white cloud of such density that it reflected the exhaust fires. The color of the cloud darkened to gray, and the plane began to rock. Francis had been in heavy weather before, but he had never been shaken up so much. The man in the seat beside him pulled a flask out of his pocket and took a drink. Francis smiled at his neighbor, but the man looked away; he wasn't sharing his painkiller with anyone. The plane had begun to drop and flounder wildly. A child was crying. The air in the cabin was overheated and stale, and Francis' left foot went to sleep. He read a little from a paper book that he had bought at the airport, but the violence of the storm divided his attention. It was black outside the ports. The exhaust fires blazed and shed sparks in the dark, and, inside, the shaded lights, the stuffiness, and the window curtains gave the cabin an atmosphere of intense and misplaced domesticity. Then the lights flickered and went out. "You know what I've always wanted to do?" the man beside Francis said suddenly. "I've always wanted to buy a farm in New Hampshire and raise beef cattle." The stewardess announced that they were going to make an emergency landing. All but the child saw in their minds the spreading wings of the Angel of Death. The pilot could be heard singing faintly, "I've got sixpence, jolly, jolly sixpence. I've got sixpence to last me all my life . . ." There was no other sound.

The loud groaning of the hydraulic valves swallowed up the pilot's song, and there was a shrieking high in the air, like automobile brakes, and the plane hit flat on its belly in a cornfield and shook them so violently that an old man up forward howled, "Me kidneys! Me kidneys!" The stewardess flung open the door, and someone opened an emergency door at the back, letting in the sweet noise of their continuing mortality — the idle splash and smell of a heavy rain. Anxious for their lives, they filed out of the doors and scattered over the cornfield in all directions, praying that the thread would hold. It did. Nothing happened. When it was clear that the plane would not burn or explode, the crew and the stewardess gathered the passengers together and led them to the shelter of a barn. They were not far from Philadelphia, and in a little while a string of taxis took them into the city. "It's just like the Marne," someone said, but there was surprisingly little relaxation of that suspiciousness with which many Americans regard their fellow-travellers.

In Philadelphia, Francis Weed got a train to New York. At the end of that journey, he crossed the city and caught, just as it was about to pull out, the commuting train that he took five nights a week to his home in Shady Hill.

He sat with Trace Bearden. "You know, I was in that plane that just crashed outside Philadelphia," he said. "We came down in a field . . ." He had travelled faster than the newspapers or the rain, and the weather in New York was sunny and mild. It was a day in late September, as fragrant and shapely as an apple. Trace listened to the story, but how could he get excited? Francis had no powers that would let him re-create a brush with death — particularly in the atmosphere of a commuting train, journeying through a sunny countryside where already, in the slum gardens, there were signs of harvest. Trace picked up his newspaper, and Francis was left alone with his thoughts. He said good night to Trace on the platform at Shady Hill and drove in his second-hand Volkswagen up to the Blenhollow neighborhood, where he lived.

The Weeds' Dutch Colonial house was larger than it appeared to be from the driveway. The living room was spacious and divided like Gaul into three parts. Around an ell to the left as one entered from the vestibule was the long table, laid for six, with candles and a bowl of fruit in the center. The sounds and smells that came from the open kitchen door were appetizing, for Julia Weed was a good cook. The largest part of the living room centered around a fireplace. On the right were some bookshelves and a piano. The room was polished and tranquil, and from the windows that opened to the west there was some late-summer sunlight, brilliant and as clear as water. Nothing here was neglected; nothing had not been burnished. It was not the kind of household where, after prying open a stuck cigarette box, you would find an old shirt button and a tarnished nickel. The hearth was swept, the roses on the piano were reflected in the polish of the broad top, and there was an album of Schubert waltzes on the rack. Louisa Weed, a pretty girl of nine, was looking out the western windows. Her younger brother Henry was standing beside her. Her still younger brother, Toby, was studying the figures of some tonsured monks drinking beer on the polished brass of the wood box. Francis, taking off his hat and putting down his paper, was not consciously pleased with the scene; he was not that reflective. It was his element, his creation, and he returned to it with that sense of lightness and strength with which any creature returns to its home. "Hi, everybody," he said. "The plane from Minneapolis . . ."

Nine times out of ten, Francis would be greeted with affection, but tonight the children are absorbed in their own antagonisms. Francis has not finished his sentence about the plane crash before Henry plants a kick in Louisa's behind. Louisa swings around, saying, *"Damn* you!" Francis makes the mistake of scolding Louisa for bad language before he punishes Henry. Now Louisa turns on her father and accuses him of favoritism. Henry is always right; she is persecuted and lonely; her lot is hopeless. Francis turns to his son, but the boy has justification for the kick — she hit him first; she hit him on the ear, which is dangerous. Louisa agrees with this passionately. She hit him on the ear, and she *meant* to hit him on the ear, because he messed up her china collection. Henry says that this is a lie. Little Toby turns away from the wood box to throw in some evidence for Louisa. Henry claps his hand over little Toby's mouth. Francis separates the two boys but accidentally pushes Toby into the wood box. Toby begins to cry. Louisa is already crying. Just then, Julia Weed comes into that part of the room where the table is laid. She is a pretty, intelligent woman, and the white in her hair is premature. She does not seem to notice the fracas. "Hello, darling," she says serenely to Francis. "Wash your hands, everyone. Dinner is ready." She strikes a match and lights the six candles in this vale of tears.

This simple announcement, like the war cries of the Scottish chieftains, only refreshes the ferocity of the combatants. Louisa gives Henry a blow on the shoulder. Henry, although he seldom cries, has pitched nine innings and is tired. He bursts into tears. Little Toby discovers a splinter in his hand and begins to howl. Francis says loudly that he has been in a plane crash and that he is tired. Julia appears again, from the kitchen, and, still ignoring the chaos, asks Francis to go upstairs and tell Helen that everything is ready. Francis is happy to go; it is like getting back to headquarters company. He is planning to tell his oldest daughter about the airplane crash, but Helen is lying on her bed reading a *True Romance* magazine, and the first thing Francis does is to take the magazine from her hand and remind Helen that he has forbidden her to buy it. She did not buy it, Helen replies. It was given to her by her best friend, Bessie Black. Everybody reads *True Romance*. Bessie Black's father reads *True Romance*. There isn't a girl in Helen's class who doesn't read *True Romance*. Francis expresses his detestation of the magazine and then tells her dinner is ready — although from the sounds downstairs it doesn't seem so. Helen follows him down the stairs. Julia has seated herself in the candlelight and spread a napkin over her lap. Neither Louisa nor Henry has come to the table. Little Toby is still howling, lying face down on the floor. Francis speaks to him gently: "Daddy was in a plane crash this afternoon,Toby. Don't you want to hear about it?" Toby goes on crying. "If you don't come to the table now, Toby," Francis says, "I'll have to send you to bed without any supper." The little boy rises, gives a cutting look, flies up the stairs to his bedroom, and slams the door. "Oh dear," Julia says, and starts to go after him. Francis says that she will spoil him. Julia says that Toby is ten pounds underweight and has to be encouraged to eat. Winter is coming, and he will spend the cold months in bed unless he has his dinner. Julia goes upstairs. Francis sits down at the table with Helen. Helen is suffering from the dismal feeling of having read too intently on a fine day, and she gives her father and the room a jaded look. She doesn't understand about the plane crash, because there wasn't a drop of rain in Shady Hill.

Julia returns with Toby, and they all sit down and are served. "Do I have to look at that big, fat slob?" Henry says, of Louisa. Everybody but Toby enters into this skirmish, and it rages up and down the table for five minutes. Toward the end, Henry puts his napkin over his head and, trying to eat that way, spills spinach all over his shirt. Francis asks Julia if the children couldn't have their dinner earlier. Julia's guns are loaded for this. She can't cook two dinners and lay two tables. She paints with lightning strokes that panorama of drudgery in which her youth, her beauty, and her wit have been lost. Francis says he must be understood; he was nearly killed in an airplane crash, and he doesn't like to come home every night to a battlefield. Now Julia is deeply

committed. Her voice trembles. He doesn't come home every night to
a battlefield. The accusation is stupid and mean. Everything was
tranquil until he arrived. She stops speaking, puts down her knife and
fork, and looks into her plate as if it is a gulf. She begins to cry. "Poor
Mummy!" Toby says, and when Julia gets up from the table, drying her
tears with a napkin, Toby goes to her side. "Poor Mummy," he says.
"Poor Mummy!" And they climb the stairs together. The other
children drift away from the battlefield, and Francis goes into the back
garden for a cigarette and some air.

It was a pleasant garden, with walks and flower beds and places
to sit. The sunset had nearly burned out, but there was still plenty
of light. Put into a thoughtful mood by the crash and the battle,
Francis listened to the evening sounds of Shady Hill. "Varmits!
Rascals!" old Mr. Nixon shouted to the squirrels in his bird-feeding
station. "Avaunt and quit my sight!" A door slammed. Someone
was playing tennis on the Babcocks' court; someone was cutting grass.
Then Donald Goslin, who lived at the corner, began to play the
"Moonlight Sonata." He did this nearly every night. He threw tempo out
the window and played it *rubato* from beginning to end, like an outpouring
of tearful petulance, lonesomeness, and self-pity — of everything it was
Beethoven's greatness not to know. The music rang up and down the
street beneath the trees like an appeal for love, for tenderness, aimed
at some lonely housemaid — some fresh-faced, homesick girl from
Galway, looking at old snapshots in her third-floor room. "Here,
Jupiter, here, Jupiter," Francis called to the Mercers' retriever. Jupiter
crashed through the tomato vines with the remains of a felt hat in his
mouth.

Jupiter was an anomaly. His retrieving instincts and his high spirits
were out of place in Shady Hill. He was as black as coal, with a long,
alert, intelligent, rakehell face. His eyes gleamed with mischief, and
he held his head high. It was the fierce, heavily collared dog's head that
appears in heraldry, in tapestry, and that used to appear on umbrella handles and walking sticks. Jupiter went where he pleased, ransacking waste-
baskets, clotheslines, garbage pails, and shoebags. He broke up garden
parties and tennis matches, and got mixed up in the processional at Christ's
Church on Sunday, barking at the men in red dresses. He crashed
through old Mr. Nixon's rose garden two or three times a day, cutting a
wide swath through the Condesa de Sastagos, and as soon as Donald
Goslin lighted his barbecue fire on Thursday nights, Jupiter would get
the scent. Nothing the Goslins did could drive him away. Sticks and
stones and rude commands only moved him to the edge of the terrace,
where he remained, with his gallant and heraldic muzzle, waiting for
Donald Goslin to turn his back and reach for the salt. Then he would

spring onto the terrace, lift the steak lightly off the fire, and run away with the Goslins' dinner. Jupiter's days were numbered. The Wrightsons' German gardener or the Farquarsons' cook would soon poison him. Even old Mr. Nixon might put some arsenic in the garbage that Jupiter loved. "Here, Jupiter, Jupiter!" Francis called, but the dog pranced off, shaking the hat in his white teeth. Looking in at the windows of his house, Francis saw that Julia had come down and was blowing out the candles.

Julia and Francis Weed went out a great deal. Julia was well liked and gregarious, and her love of parties sprang from a most natural dread of chaos and loneliness. She went through her morning mail with real anxiety, looking for invitations, and she usually found some, but she was insatiable, and if she had gone out seven nights a week, it would not have cured her of a reflective look — the look of someone who hears distant music — for she would always suppose that there was a more brilliant party somewhere else. Francis limited her to two week-night parties, putting a flexible interpretation on Friday, and rode through the weekend like a dory in a gale. The day after the airplane crash, the Weeds were to have dinner with the Farquarsons.

Francis got home late from town, and Julia got the sitter while he dressed, and then hurried him out of the house. The party was small and pleasant, and Francis settled down to enjoy himself. A new maid passed the drinks. Her hair was dark, and her face was round and pale and seemed familiar to Francis. He had not developed his memory as a sentimental faculty. Wood smoke, lilac, and other such perfumes did not stir him, and his memory was something like his appendix — a vestigial repository. It was not his limitation at all to be unable to escape the past; it was perhaps his limitation that he had escaped it so successfully. He might have seen the maid at other parties, he might have seen her taking a walk on Sunday afternoons, but in either case he would not be searching his memory now. Her face was, in a wonderful way, a moon face — Norman or Irish — but it was not beautiful enough to account for his feeling that he had seen her before, in circumstances that he ought to be able to remember. He asked Nellie Farquarson who she was. Nellie said that the maid had come through an agency, and that her home was Trénon, in Normandy — a small place with a church and a restaurant that Nellie had once visited. While Nellie talked on about her travels abroad, Francis realized where he had seen the woman before. It had been at the end of the war. He had left a replacement depot with some other men and taken a three-day pass in Trénon. On their second day, they had walked out to a crossroads to see the public chastisement of a young woman who had lived with the German commandant during the Occupation.

It was a cool morning in the fall. The sky was overcast, and poured down onto the dirt crossroads a very discouraging light. They were on high land and could see how like one another the shapes of the clouds and the hills were as they stretched off toward the sea. The prisoner arrived sitting on a three-legged stool in a farm cart. She stood by the cart while the mayor read the accusation and the sentence. Her head was bent and her face was set in that empty half smile behind which the whipped soul is suspended. When the mayor was finished, she undid her hair and let it fall across her back. A little man with a gray mustache cut off her hair with shears and dropped it on the ground. Then, with a bowl of soapy water and a straight razor, he shaved her skull clean. A woman approached and began to undo the fastenings of her clothes, but the prisoner pushed her aside and undressed herself. When she pulled her chemise over her head and threw it on the ground, she was naked. The women jeered; the men were still. There was no change in the falseness or the plaintiveness of the prisoner's smile. The cold wind made her white skin rough and hardened the nipples of her breasts. The jeering ended gradually, put down by the recognition of their common humanity. One woman spat on her, but some inviolable grandeur in her nakedness lasted through the ordeal. When the crowd was quiet, she turned — she had begun to cry — and, with nothing on but a pair of worn black shoes and stockings, walked down the dirt road alone away from the village. The round white face had aged a little, but there was no question but that the maid who passed his cocktails and later served Francis his dinner was the woman who had been punished at the crossroads.

The war seemed now so distant and that world where the cost of partisanship had been death or torture so long ago. Francis had lost track of the men who had been with him in Vésey. He could not count on Julia's discretion. He could not tell anyone. And if he had told the story now, at the dinner table, it would have been a social as well as a human error. The people in the Farquarsons' living room seemed united in their tacit claim that there had been no past, no war — that there was no danger or trouble in the world. In the recorded history of human arrangements, this extraordinary meeting would have fallen into place, but the atmosphere of Shady Hill made the memory unseemly and impolite. The prisoner withdrew after passing the coffee, but the encounter left Francis feeling languid; it had opened his memory and his senses, and left them dilated. He had Julia drove home when the party ended, and Julia went into the house. Francis stayed in the car to take the sitter home.

Expecting to see Mrs. Henlein, the old lady who usually stayed with the children, he was surprised when a young girl opened the door and came out onto the lighted stoop. She stayed in the light to count her textbooks. She was frowning and beautiful. Now, the world is full of beautiful young girls, but Francis saw here the difference between beauty and perfection. All those endearing flaws, moles, birthmarks, and healed wounds were missing, and he experienced in his consciousness that moment when music breaks glass, and felt a pang of recognition as strange, deep, and wonderful as anything in his life. It hung from her frown, from an impalpable darkness in her face — a look that impressed him as a direct appeal for love. When she had counted her books, she came down the steps and opened the car door. In the light, he saw that her cheeks were wet. She got in and shut the door.

"You're new," Francis said.

"Yes. Mrs. Henlein is sick. I'm Anne Murchison."

"Did the children give you any trouble?"

"Oh, no, no." She turned and smiled at him unhappily in the dim dashboard light. Her light hair caught on the collar of her jacket, and she shook her head to set it loose.

"You've been crying."

"Yes."

"I hope it was nothing that happened in our house."

"No, no, it was nothing that happened in your house." Her voice was bleak. "It's no secret. Everybody in the village knows. Daddy's an alcoholic, and he just called me from some saloon and gave me a piece of his mind. He thinks I'm immoral. He called just before Mrs. Weed came back."

"I'm sorry."

"Oh, *Lord!*" She gasped and began to cry. She turned toward Francis, and he took her in his arms and let her cry on his shoulder. She shook in his embrace, and this movement accentuated his sense of the fineness of her flesh and bone. The layers of their clothing felt thin, and when her shuddering began to diminish, it was so much like a paroxysm of love that Francis lost his head and pulled her roughly against him. She drew away. "I live on Belleview Avenue," she said. "You go down Lansing Street to the railroad bridge."

"All right." He started the car.

"You turn left at the traffic light . . . Now you turn right here and go straight on toward the tracks."

The road Francis took brought him out of his own neighborhood, across the tracks, and toward the river, to a street where the near-poor lived, in houses whose peaked gables and trimmings of wooden lace conveyed the purest feelings of pride and romance, although the houses themselves could not have offered much privacy or comfort, they were all so small. The street was dark, and, stirred by the grace and beauty of the troubled girl, he seemed, in turning in to it, to have come into the deepest part of some submerged memory. In the distance, he saw a porch light burning. It was the only one, and she said that the house with the light was where she lived. When he stopped the car, he could see beyond the porch light into a dimly lighted hallway with an old-fashioned clothes tree. "Well, here we are," he said, conscious that a young man would have said something different.

She did not move her hands from the books, where they were folded, and she turned and faced him. There were tears of lust in his eyes. Determinedly — not sadly — he opened the door on his side and walked around to open hers. He took her free hand, letting his fingers in between hers, climbed at her side the two concrete steps, and went up a narrow walk through a front garden where dahlias, marigolds, and roses — things that had withstood the light frosts — still bloomed, and made a bittersweet smell in the night air. At the steps, she freed her hand and then turned and kissed him swiftly. Then she crossed the porch and shut the door. The porch light went out, then the light in the hall. A second later, a light went on upstairs at the side of the house, shining into a tree that was still covered with leaves. It took her only a few minutes to undress and get into bed, and then the house was dark.

Julia was asleep when Francis got home. He opened a second window and got into bed to shut his eyes on that night, but as soon as they were shut — as soon as he had dropped off to sleep — the girl entered his mind, moving with perfect freedom through its shut doors and filling chamber after chamber with her light, her perfume, and the music of her voice. He was crossing the Atlantic with her on the old *Mauretania* and, later, living with her in Paris. When he woke from this dream, he got up and smoked a cigarette at the open window. Getting back into bed, he cast around in his mind for something he desired to do that would injure no one, and he thought of skiing. Up through the dimness in his mind rose the image of a mountain deep in snow. It was late in the day. Wherever his eyes looked, he saw broad and heartening things. Over his shoulder, there was a snow-filled valley, rising into wooded hills where the trees dimmed the whiteness like a sparse coat of hair. The cold deadened all sound but the loud, iron clanking of the lift machinery. The light on the trails was blue, and it was harder than it had been a minute or two earlier to pick the turns, harder to judge — now that the snow was all deep blue — the crust, the ice, the bare spots, and the deep piles of dry powder. Down the mountain he swung, matching his speed against the contours of a slope that had been formed in the first ice age, seeking with ardor some simplicity of feeling and circumstance. Night fell then, and he drank a Martini with some old friend in a dirty country bar.

In the morning, Francis' snow-covered mountain was gone, and

he was left with his vivid memories of Paris and the *Mauretania*. He
had been bitten gravely. He washed his body, shaved his jaws, drank
his coffee, and missed the seven-thirty-one. The train pulled out just
as he brought his car to the station, and the longing he felt for the
coaches as they drew stubbornly away from him reminded him of the
humors of love. He waited for the eight-two, on what was now an
empty platform. It was a clear morning; the morning seemed thrown
like a gleaming bridge of light over his mixed affairs. His spirits were
feverish and high. The image of the girl seemed to put him into a
relationship to the world that was mysterious and enthralling. Cars
were beginning to fill up the parking lot, and he noticed that those that
had driven down from the high land above Shady Hill were white with
hoarfrost. This first clear sign of autumn thrilled him. An express
train — a night train from Buffalo or Albany — came down the tracks
between the platforms, and he saw that the roofs of the foremost cars
were covered with a skin of ice. Struck by the miraculous physicalness
of everything, he smiled at the passengers in the dining car, who could
be seen eating eggs and wiping their mouths with napkins as they
travelled. The sleeping-car compartments, with their soiled bed linen,
trailed through the fresh morning like a string of rooming-house
windows. Then he saw an extraordinary thing; at one of the bedroom
windows sat an unclothed woman of exceptional beauty, combing her
golden hair. She passed like an apparition through Shady Hill,
combing and combing her hair, and Francis followed her with his eyes
until she was out of sight. Then old Mrs. Wrightson joined him on
the platform and began to talk.

"Well, I guess you must be surprised to see me here the third
morning in a row," she said, "but because of my window curtains I'm
becoming a regular commuter. The curtains I bought on Monday I
returned on Tuesday, and the curtains I bought on Tuesday I'm
returning today. On Monday, I got exactly what I wanted — it's a wool
tapestry with roses and birds — but when I got them home, I found
they were the wrong length. Well, I exchanged them yesterday, and
when I got them home, I found they were still the wrong length. Now
I'm praying to high Heaven that the decorator will have them in the
right length, because you know my house, you *know* my living-room
windows, and you can imagine what a problem they present. I don't
know what to do with them."

"I know what to do with them," Francis said.

"What?"

"Paint them black on the inside, and shut up."

There was a gasp from Mrs. Wrightson, and Francis looked down
at her to be sure that she knew he meant to be rude. She turned and

walked away from him, so damaged in spirit that she limped. A wonderful feeling enveloped him, as if light were being shaken about him, and he thought again of Venus combing and combing her hair as she drifted through the Bronx. The realization of how many years had passed since he had enjoyed being deliberately impolite sobered him. Among his friends and neighbors, there were brilliant and gifted people — he saw that — but many of them, also, were bores and fools, and he made the mistake of listening to them all with equal attention. He had confused a lack of discrimination with Christian love, and the confusion seemed general and destructive. He was grateful to the girl for this bracing sensation of independence. Birds were singing — cardinals and the last of the robins. The sky shone like enamel. Even the smell of ink from his morning paper honed his appetite for life, and the world that was spread out around him was plainly a paradise.

If Francis had believed in some hierarchy of love — in spirits armed with hunting bows, in the capriciousness of Venus and Eros — or even in magical potions, philtres, and stews, in scapulae and quarters of the moon, it might have explained his susceptibility and his feverish high spirits. The autumnal loves of middle age are well publicized, and he guessed that he was face to face with one of these, but there was not a trace of autumn in what he felt. He wanted to sport in the green woods, scratch where he itched, and drink from the same cup.

His secretary, Miss Rainey, was late that morning — she went to a psychiatrist three mornings a week — and when she came in, Francis wondered what advice a psychiatrist would have for him. But the girl promised to bring back into his life something like the sound of music. The realization that this music might lead him straight to a trial for statutory rape at the county courthouse collapsed his happiness. The photograph of his four children laughing into the camera on the beach at Gay Head reproached him. On the letterhead of his firm there was a drawing of the "Laocoön," and the figure of the priest and his sons in the coils of the snake appeared to him to have the deepest meaning.

He had lunch with Pinky Trabert, who told him a couple of dirty stories. At a conversational level, the mores of his friends were robust and elastic, but he knew that the moral card house would come down on them all — on Julia and the children as well — if he got caught taking advantage of a baby-sitter. Looking back over the recent history of Shady Hill for some precedent, he found there was none. There was no turpitude; there had not been a divorce since he lived there; there had not even been a breath of scandal. Things seemed arranged with more propriety even than in the Kingdom of Heaven. After leaving Pinky, Francis went to a jeweller's and bought the girl a bracelet. How happy this clandestine purchase made him, how stuffy and comical the jeweller's clerks seemed, how sweet the women who passed at his back smelled! On Fifth Avenue, passing Atlas with his shoulders bent under the weight of the world, Francis thought of the strenuousness of containing his physicalness within the patterns he had chosen.

He did not know when he would see the girl next. He had the bracelet in his inside pocket when he got home. Opening the door of his house, he found her in the hall. Her back was to him, and she turned when she heard the door close. Her smile was open and loving. Her perfection stunned him like a fine day — a day after a thunderstorm. He seized her and covered her lips with his, and she struggled but she did not have to struggle for long, because just then little Gertrude Flannery appeared from somewhere and said, "Oh, Mr. Weed . . ."

Gertrude was a stray. She had been born with a taste for exploration, and she did not have it in her to center her life with her affectionate parents. People who did not know the Flannerys concluded from Gertrude's behavior that she was the child of a bitterly divided family, where drunken quarrels were the rule. This was not true. The fact that little Gertrude's clothing was ragged and thin was her own triumph over her mother's struggle to dress her warmly and neatly. Garrulous, skinny, and unwashed, she drifted from house to house around the Blenhollow neighborhood, forming and breaking alliances based on an attachment to babies, animals, children her own age, adolescents, and sometimes adults. Opening your front door in the morning, you would find Gertrude sitting on your stoop. Going into the bathroom to shave, you would find Gertrude using the toilet. Looking into your son's crib, you would find it empty, and, looking further, you would find that Gertrude had pushed him in his baby carriage into the next village. She was helpful, pervasive, honest, hungry, and loyal. She never went home of her own choice. When the time to go arrived, she was indifferent to all its signs. "Go home, Gertrude," people could be heard saying in one house or another, night after night. "Go home, Gertrude." "It's time for you to go home now, Gertrude." "You had better go home and get your supper, Gertrude." "I told you to go home twenty minutes ago, Gertrude." "You mother will be worrying about you, Gertrude." "Go home, Gertrude, go home."

There are times when the lines around the human eye seem like shelves of eroded stone and when the staring eye itself strikes us with such a wilderness of animal feeling that we are at a loss. The look Francis gave the little girl was ugly and queer, and it frightened her. He reached into his pocket — his hands were shaking — and took out a quarter. "Go home, Gertrude, go home, and don't tell anyone,

Gertrude. Don't — " He choked and ran into the living room as Julia called down to him from upstairs to hurry and dress.

The thought that he would drive Anne Murchison home later that night ran like a golden thread through the events of the party that Francis and Julia went to, and he laughed uproariously at dull jokes, dried a tear when Mabel Mercer told him about the death of her kitten, and stretched, yawned, sighed, and grunted like any other man with a rendezvous at the back of his mind. The bracelet was in his pocket. As he sat talking, the smell of grass was in his nose, and he was wondering where he would park the car. Nobody lived in the old Parker mansion, and the driveway was used as a lover's lane. Townsend Street was a dead end, and he could park there, beyond the last house. The old lane that used to connect Elm Street to the riverbanks was overgrown, but he had walked there with his children, and he could drive his car deep enough into the brushwoods to be concealed.

The Weeds were the last to leave the party, and their host and hostess spoke of their own married happiness while they all four stood in the hallway saying good night. "She's my girl," their host said, squeezing his wife. "She's my blue sky. After sixteen years, I still bite her shoulders. She makes me feel like Hannibal crossing the Alps."

The Weeds drove home in silence. Francis brought his car up to the driveway and sat still, with the motor running. "You can put the car in the garage," Julia said as she got out. "I told the Murchison girl she could leave at eleven. Someone drove her home." She shut the door, and Francis sat in the dark. He would be spared nothing then, it seemed, that a fool was not spared: ravening, lewdness, jealousy, this hurt to his feelings that put tears in his eyes, even scorn — for he could see clearly the image he now presented, his arms spread over the steering wheel and his head buried in them for love. Francis had been a dedicated Boy Scout when he was young, and, remembering the precepts of his youth, he left his office early the next afternoon and played some round-robin squash, but, with his body toned up by exercise and a shower, he realized that he might better have stayed at his desk. It was a frosty night when he got home. The air smelled sharply of change. When he stepped into the house, he sensed an unusual stir. The children were in their best clothes, and when Julia came down she was wearing a lavender dress and her diamond sunburst. She explained the stir: Mr. Hubber was coming at seven to take their photograph for the Christmas card. She had put out Francis' blue suit and a tie with some color in it, because the picture was going to be in color this year. Julia was light-hearted at the thought of being photographed for Christmas. It was the kind of ceremony she enjoyed.

Francis went upstairs to change his clothes. He was tired from the day's work and tired with longing, and sitting on the edge of the bed had the effect of deepening his weariness. He thought of Anne Murchison, and the physical need to express himself, instead of being restrained by the pink lamps on Julia's dressing table, engulfed him. He went to Julia's desk, took a piece of writing paper, and began to write on it. "Dear Anne, I love you, I love you, I love you . . ." No one would see the letter, and he used no restraint. He used phrases like "Heavenly bliss," and "love nest." He salivated, sighed, and trembled. When Julia called him to come down, the abyss between his fantasy and the practical world opened so wide that he felt it affect the muscles of his heart.

Julia and the children were on the stoop, and the photographer and his assistant had set up a double battery of floodlights to show the family and architectural beauty of the entrance to their house. People who had come home on a late train slowed their cars to see the Weeds being photographed for their Christmas card. A few waved and called to the family. It took half an hour of smiling and wetting their lips before Mr. Hubber was satisfied. The heat of the lights made an unfresh smell in the frosty air, and when they were turned off, they lingered on the retina of Francis' eyes.

Later that night, while Francis and Julia were drinking their coffee in the living room, the doorbell rang. Julia answered the door and let in Clayton Thomas. He had come to pay her for some theatre tickets that she had given his mother some time ago, and that Helen Thomas had scrupulously insisted on paying for, though Julia had asked her not to. Julia invited him in to have a cup of coffee. "I won't have any coffee," Clayton said, "but I will come in for a minute." He followed her into the living room, said good evening to Francis, and sat down awkwardly in a chair.

Clayton's father had been killed in the war, and the young man's fatherlessness surrounded him like an element. This may have been conspicuous in Shady Hill because the Thomases were the only family that lacked a piece; all the other marriages were intact and productive. Clayton was in his second or third year of college, and he and his mother lived alone in a large house which she hoped to sell. Clayton had once made some trouble. Years ago, he had stolen some money and run away; he had got to California before they caught up with him. He was tall and homely, wore horn-rimmed glasses, and spoke in a deep voice.

"When do you go back to college, Clayton?" Francis asked.

"I'm not going back," Clayton said. "Mother doesn't have the money, and there's no sense in all this pretense. I'm going to get a job, and if we sell the house, we'll take an apartment in New York."

"Won't you miss Shady Hill?" Julia asked.

"No," Clayton said. "I don't like it."

"Why not?" Francis asked.

"Well, there's a lot here I don't approve of," Clayton said gravely. "Things like the club dances. Last Saturday night, I looked in toward the end and saw Mr. Granner trying to put Mrs. Minot into the trophy case. They were both drunk. I disapprove of so much drinking."

"It was Saturday night," Francis said.

"And all the dovecotes are phony," Clayton said. "And the way people clutter up their lives. I've thought about it a lot, and what seems to me to be really wrong with Shady Hill is that it doesn't have any future. So much energy is spent in perpetuating the place — in keeping out undesirables, and so forth — that the only idea of the future anyone has is just more and more commuting trains and more parties. I don't think that's healthy. I think people ought to be able to dream big dreams about the future. I think people ought to be able to dream great dreams."

"It's too bad you couldn't continue with college," Julia said.

"I wanted to go to divinity school," Clayton said.

"What's your church?" Francis asked.

"Unitarian, Theosophist, Transcendentalist, Humanist," Clayton said.

"Wasn't Emerson a transcendentalist?" Julia asked.

"I mean the English transcendentalists," Clayton said. "All the American transcendentalists were goops."

"What kind of a job do you expect to get?" Francis asked.

"Well, I'd like to work for a publisher," Clayton said, "but everyone tells me there's nothing doing. But it's the kind of thing I'm interested in. I'm writing a long verse play about good and evil. Uncle Charlie might get me into a bank, and that would be good for me. I need the discipline. I have a long way to go in forming my character. I have some terrible habits. I talk too much. I think I ought to take vows of silence. I ought to try not to speak for a week, and discipline myself. I've thought of making a retreat at one of the Episcopalian monasteries, but I don't like Trinitarianism."

"Do you have any girl friends?" Francis asked.

"I'm engaged to be married," Clayton said. "Of course, I'm not old enough or rich enough to have my engagement observed or respected or anything, but I bought a simulated emerald for Anne Murchison with the money I made cutting lawns this summer. We're going to be married as soon as she finishes school."

Francis recoiled at the mention of the girl's name. Then a dingy light seemed to emanate from his spirit, showing everything — Julia, the boy, the chairs — in their true colorlessness. It was like a bitter turn of the weather.

"We're going to have a large family," Clayton said. "Her father's a terrible rummy, and I've had my hard times, and we want to have lots of children. Oh, she's wonderful, Mr. and Mrs. Weed, and we have so much in common. We like all the same things. We sent out the same Christmas card last year without planning it, and we both have an allergy to tomatoes, and our eyebrows grow together in the middle. Well, good night."

Julia went to the door with him. When she returned, Francis said that Clayton was lazy, irresponsible, affected, and smelly. Julia said that Francis seemed to be getting intolerant; the Thomas boy was young and should be given a chance. Julia had noticed other cases where Francis had been short-tempered. "Mrs. Wrightson has asked everyone in Shady Hill to her anniversary party but us," she said.

"I'm sorry, Julia."

"Do you know why they didn't ask us?"

"Why?"

"Because you insulted Mrs. Wrightson."

"Then you know about it?"

"June Masterson told me. She was standing behind you."

Julia walked in front of the sofa with a small step that expressed, Francis knew, a feeling of anger.

"I did insult Mrs. Wrightson, Julia, and I meant to. I've never liked her parties, and I'm glad she's dropped us."

"What about Helen?"

"How does Helen come into this?"

"Mrs. Wrightson's the one who decides who goes to the assemblies."

"You mean she can keep Helen from going to the dances?"

"Yes."

"I hadn't thought of that."

"Oh, I knew you hadn't thought of it," Julia cried, thrusting hilt-deep into this chink of his armor. "And it makes me furious to see this kind of stupid thoughtlessness wreck everyone's happiness."

"I don't think I've wrecked anyone's happiness."

"Mrs. Wrightson runs Shady Hill and has run it for the last forty years. I don't know what makes you think that in a community like this you can indulge every impulse you have to be insulting, vulgar, and offensive."

"I have very good manners," Francis said, trying to give the evening a turn toward the light.

"Damn you, Francis Weed!" Julia cried, and the spit of her words struck him in the face. "I've worked hard for the social position we enjoy in this place, and I won't stand by and see you wreck it. You must have understood when you settled here that you couldn't expect to live like a bear in a cave."

"I've got to express my likes and dislikes."

"You can conceal your dislikes. You don't have to meet everything head-on, like a child. Unless you're anxious to be a social leper. It's no accident that we get asked out a great deal. It's no accident that Helen has so many friends. How would you like to spend your Saturday nights at the movies? How would you like to spend your Sundays raking up dead leaves? How would you like it if your daughter spent the assembly nights sitting at her window, listening to the music from the club? How would you like it — " He did something then that was, after all, not so unaccountable, since her words seemed to raise up between them a wall so deadening that he gagged: He struck her full in the face. She staggered and then, a moment later, seemed composed. She went up the stairs to their room. She didn't slam the door. When Francis followed, a few minutes later, he found her packing a suitcase.

"Julia, I'm very sorry."

"It doesn't matter," she said. She was crying.

"Where do you think you're going?"

"I don't know. I just looked at a timetable. There's an eleven-sixteen into New York. I'll take that."

"You can't go, Julia."

"I can't stay. I know that."

"I'm sorry about Mrs. Wrightson, Julia, and I'm — "

"It doesn't matter about Mrs. Wrightson. That isn't the trouble."

"What is the trouble?"

"You don't love me."

"I do love you, Julia."

"No, you don't."

"Julia, I do love you, and I would like to be as we were — sweet and bawdy and dark — but now there are so many people."

"You hate me."

"I don't hate you, Julia."

"You have no idea of how much you hate me. I think it's subconscious. You don't realize the cruel things you've done."

"What cruel things, Julia?"

"The cruel acts your subconscious drives you to in order to express your hatred of me."

"What, Julia?"

"I've never complained."

"Tell me."

"You don't know what you're doing."

"Tell me."

"Your clothes."

"What do you mean?"

"I mean the way you leave your dirty clothes around in order to express your subconscious hatred of me."

"I don't understand."

"I mean your dirty socks and your dirty pajamas and your dirty underwear and your dirty shirts!" She rose from kneeling by the suitcase and faced him, her eyes blazing and her voice ringing with emotion. "I'm talking about the fact that you've never learned to hang up anything. You just leave your clothes all over the floor where they drop, in order to humiliate me. You do it on purpose!" She fell on the bed, sobbing.

"Julia, darling!" he said, but when she felt his hand on her shoulder she got up.

"Leave me alone," she said. "I have to go." She brushed past him to the closet and came back with a dress. "I'm not taking any of the things you've given me," she said. "I'm leaving my pearls and the fur jacket."

"Oh, Julia!" Her figure, so helpless in its self-deceptions, bent over the suitcase made him nearly sick with pity. She did not understand how desolate her life would be without him. She didn't understand the hours that working women have to keep. She didn't understand that most of her friendships existed within the framework of their marriage, and that without this she would find herself alone. She didn't understand about travel, about hotels, about money. "Julia, I can't let you go! What you don't understand, Julia, is that you've come to be dependent on me."

She tossed her head back and covered her face with her hands. "Did you say that *I* was dependent on *you*?" she asked. "Is that what you said? And who is it that tells you what time to get up in the morning and when to go to bed at night? Who is it that prepares your meals and picks up your dirty closet and invites your friends to dinner? If it weren't for me, your neckties would be greasy and your clothing would be full of moth holes. You were alone when I met you, Francis Weed, and you'll be alone when I leave. When Mother asked you for a list to send out invitations to our wedding, how many names did you have to give her? Fourteen!"

"Cleveland wasn't my home, Julia."

"And how many of your friends came to the church? Two!"

"Cleveland wasn't my home, Julia."

"Since I'm not taking the fur jacket," she said quietly, "you'd better put it back into storage. There's an insurance policy on the pearls that comes due in January. The name of the laundry and the maid's telephone number — all those things are in my desk. I hope you won't drink too much, Francis. I hope that nothing bad will happen to you. If you do get into serious trouble, you can call me."

"Oh my darling, I can't let you go!" Francis said. "I can't let you go, Julia!" He took her in his arms.

"I guess I'd better stay and take care of you for a little while longer," she said.

Riding to work in the morning, Francis saw the girl walk down the aisle of the coach. He was surprised; he hadn't realized that the school she went to was in the city, but she was carrying books, she seemed to be going to school. His surprise delayed his reaction, but then he got up clumsily and stepped into the aisle. Several people had come between them, but he could see her ahead of him, waiting for someone to open the car door, and then, as the train swerved, putting out her hand to support herself as she crossed the platform into the next car. He followed her through that car and halfway through another before calling her name — "Anne! Anne!" — but she didn't turn. He followed her into still another car, and she sat down in an aisle seat. Coming up to her, all his feelings warm and bent in her direction, he put his hand on the back of her seat — even this touch warmed him — and, leaning down to speak to her, he saw that it was not Anne. It was an older woman wearing glasses. He went on deliberately into another car, his face red with embarrassment and the much deeper feeling of having his good sense challenged; for if he couldn't tell one person from another, what evidence was there that his life with Julia and the children had as much reality as his dreams of iniquity in Paris or the litter, the grass smell, and the cave-shaped trees in Lovers' Lane.

Late that afternoon, Julia called to remind Francis that they were going out for dinner. A few minutes later, Trace Bearden called. "Look, fellar," Trace said. "I'm calling for Mrs. Thomas. You know? Clayton, that boy of hers, doesn't seem able to get a job, and I wondered if you could help. If you'd call Charlie Bell — I know he's indebted to you — and say a good word for the kid, I think Charlie would — "

"Trace, I hate to say this," Francis said, "but I don't feel that I can do anything for that boy. The kid's worthless. I know it's a harsh thing to say, but it's a fact. Any kindness done for him would backfire in everybody's face. He's just a worthless kid, Trace, and there's nothing to be done about it. Even if we got him a job, he wouldn't be able to keep it for a week. I know that to be a fact. It's an awful thing, Trace, and I know it is, but instead of recommending that kid, I'd feel obliged to warn people against him — people who knew his father and would naturally want to step in and do something. I'd feel obliged to warn them. He's a thief . . ."

The moment this conversation was finished, Miss Rainey came in and stood by his desk. "I'm not going to be able to work for you any more, Mr. Weed," she said. "I can stay until the seventeenth if you need me, but I've been offered a whirlwind of a job, and I'd like to leave as soon as possible."

She went out, leaving him to face alone the wickedness of what he had done to the Thomas boy. His children in their photograph laughed and laughed, glazed with all the bright colors of summer, and he remembered that they had met a bagpiper on the beach that day and he had paid the piper a dollar to play them a battle song of the Black Watch. The girl would be at the house when he got home. He would spend another evening among his kind neighbors, picking and choosing dead-end streets, car tracks, and the driveways of abandoned houses. There was nothing to mitigate his feeling — nothing that laughter or a game of softball with the children would change — and, thinking back over the plane crash, the Farquarsons' new maid, and Anne Murchison's difficulties with her drunken father, he wondered how he could have avoided arriving at just where he was. He was in trouble. He had been lost once in his life, coming back from a trout stream in the north woods, and he had now the same bleak realization that no amount of cheerfulness or hopefulness or valor or perseverance could help him find, in the gathering dark, the path that he'd lost. He smelled the forest. The feeling of bleakness was intolerable, and he saw clearly that he had reached the point where he would have to make a choice.

He could go to a psychiatrist, like Miss Rainey; he could go to church and confess his lusts; he could go to a Danish massage parlor in the West Seventies that had been recommended by a salesman; he could rape the girl or trust that he would somehow be prevented from doing this; or he could get drunk. It was his life, his boat, and, like every other man, he was made to be the father of thousands, and what harm could there be in a tryst that would make them both feel more kindly toward the world? This was the wrong train of thought, and he came back to the first, the psychiatrist. He had the telephone number of Miss Rainey's doctor, and he called and asked for an immediate appointment. He was insistent with the doctor's secretary — it was his manner in business — and when she said that the doctor's schedule was full for the next few weeks, Francis demanded an appointment that day and was told to come at five.

The psychiatrist's office was in a building that was used mostly by doctors and dentists, and the hallways were filled with the candy smell of mouthwash and memories of pain. Francis' character had been formed upon a series of private resolves — resolves about cleanliness, about going off the high diving board or repeating any other feat that challenged his courage, about punctuality, honesty, and virtue. To abdicate the perfect loneliness in which he had made his most vital decisions shattered his concept of character and left him now in a condition that felt like shock. He was stupefied. The scene for his *miserere mei Deus* was, like the waiting room of so many doctors' offices, a crude token gesture toward the sweets of domestic bliss: a place arranged with antiques, coffee tables, potted plants, and etchings of snow-covered bridges and geese in flight, although there were no children, no marriage bed, no stove, even, in this travesty of a house, where no one had ever spent the night and where the curtained windows looked straight onto a dark air shaft. Francis gave his name and address to a secretary and then saw, at the side of the room, a policeman moving toward him. "Hold it, hold it," the policeman said. "Don't move. Keep your hands where they are."

"I think it's all right, Officer," the secretary began. "I think it will be — "

"Let's make sure," the policeman said, and he began to slap Francis' clothes, looking for what — pistols, knives, an icepick? Finding nothing, he went off, and the secretary began a nervous apology: "When you called on the telephone, Mr. Weed, you seemed very excited, and one of the doctor's patients has been threatening his life, and we have to be careful. If you want to go in now?" Francis pushed open a door connected to an electrical chime, and in the doctor's lair sat down heavily, blew his nose into a handkerchief, searched in his pockets for cigarettes, for matches, for something, and said hoarsely, with tears in his eyes, "I'm in love, Dr. Herzog."

It is a week or ten days later in Shady Hill. The seven-fourteen has come and gone, and here and there dinner is finished and the dishes are in the dishwashing machine. The village hangs, morally and economically, from a thread; but it hangs by its thread in the evening light. Donald Goslin has begun to worry the "Moonlight Sonata" again. *Marcato ma sempre pianissimo!* He seems to be wringing out a wet bath towel, but the housemaid does not heed him. She is writing a letter to Arthur Godfrey. In the cellar of his house, Francis Weed is building a coffee table. Dr. Herzog recommended woodwork as a therapy, and Francis finds some true consolation in the simple arithmetic involved and in the holy smell of new wood. Francis is happy. Upstairs, little Toby is crying, because he is tired. He puts off his cowboy hat, gloves, and fringed jacket, unbuckles the belt studded with gold and rubies, the silver bullets and holsters, slips off his suspenders, his checked shirt, and Levis, and sits on the edge of his bed to pull off his high boots. Leaving this equipment in a heap, he goes to the closet and takes his space suit off a nail. It is a struggle for him to get into the long tights, but he succeeds. He loops the magic cape over his shoulders and, climbing onto the footboard of his bed, he spreads his arms and flies the short distance to the floor, landing with a thump that is audible to everyone in the house but himself.

"Go home, Gertrude, go home," Mrs. Masterson says. "I told you to go home an hour ago, Gertrude. It's way past your suppertime, and your mother will be worried. Go home!" A door on the Babcocks' terrace flies open, and out comes Mrs. Babcock without any clothes on, pursued by her naked husband. (Their children are away at boarding school, and their terrace is screened by a hedge.) Over the terrace they go and in at the kitchen door, as passionate and handsome a nymph and satyr as you will find on any wall in Venice. Cutting the last of the roses in her garden, Julia hears old Mr. Nixon shouting at the squirrels in his bird-feeding station. "Rapscallions! Varmits! Avaunt and quit my sight!" A miserable cat wanders into the garden, sunk in spiritual and physical discomfort. Tied to its head is a small straw hat — a doll's hat — and it is securely buttoned into a doll's dress, from the skirts of which protrudes its long, hairy tail. As it walks, it shakes its feet, as if it had fallen into water.

"Here, pussy, pussy, pussy!" Julia calls.

"Here, pussy, here, poor pussy!" But the cat gives her a skeptical look and stumbles away in its skirts. The last to come is Jupiter. He prances through the tomato vines, holding in his generous mouth the remains of an evening slipper. Then it is dark; it is a night where kings in golden suits ride elephants over the mountains.

# Flannery O'Connor (1925–1964)

HER LIFE was brief but Flannery O'Connor was one of the most admired authors of her time. She was born in Georgia and lived on a farm that raised peacocks, in which she delighted. She studied at the Iowa University Writers' Workshop and, although she was terminally ill and knew it, continued to write until she died. She wrote two novels, *Wise Blood* (1952) and *The Violent Bear It Away* (1960), both tales of religious fanaticism. Two collections of her short stories, *A Good Man Is Hard to Find* (1955) and *Everything That Rises Must Converge* (1965), have been published.

Flannery O'Connor was a ruthless writer. In "A Good Man Is Hard to Find," as soon as the Florida-bound Georgia family in their wrecked car encounter The Misfit and his companions the reader knows what is going to happen, doesn't want it to happen, and prays to God that it won't. In the preceding few pages each of the family members has become so real that the reader cannot bear even to think of their fate. But it happens, and foresight and all, it packs a terrific wallop. O'Connor's writing has been described as macabre, grotesque. Hell, it is unearthly!

# *A Good Man Is Hard to Find*

THE GRANDMOTHER didn't want to go to Florida. She wanted to visit some of her connections in east Tennessee and she was seizing at every chance to change Bailey's mind. Bailey was the son she lived with, her only boy. He was sitting on the edge of his chair at the table, bent over the orange sports section of the *Journal*. "Now look here, Bailey," she said, "see here, read this," and she stood with one hand on her thin hip and the other rattling the newspaper at his bald head. "Here this fellow that calls himself The Misfit is aloose from the Federal Pen and headed toward Florida and you read here what it says he did to these people. Just you read it. I wouldn't take my children in any direction with a criminal like that aloose in it. I couldn't answer to my conscience if I did."

Bailey didn't look up from his reading so she wheeled around then and faced the children's mother, a young woman in slacks, whose face was as broad and innocent as a cabbage and was tied around with a green head-kerchief that had two points on the top like rabbit's ears. She was sitting on the sofa, feeding the baby his apricots out of a jar. "The children have been to Florida before," the old lady said. "You all ought to take them somewhere else for a change so they would see different parts of the world and be broad. They never have been to east Tennessee."

The children's mother didn't seem to hear her but the eight-year-old boy, John Wesley, a stocky child with glasses, said, "If you don't want to go to Florida, why dontcha stay at home?" He and the little girl, June Star, were reading the funny papers on the floor.

"She wouldn't stay at home to be queen for a day," June Star said without raising her yellow head.

"Yes and what would you do if this fellow, The Misfit, caught you?" the grandmother asked.

"I'd smack his face," John Wesley said.

"She wouldn't stay at home for a million bucks," June Star said. "Afraid she'd miss something. She has to go everywhere we go."

"All right, Miss," the grandmother said. "Just remember that the next time you want me to curl your hair."

June Star said her hair was naturally curly.

The next morning the grandmother was the first one in the car, ready to go. She had her big black valise that looked like the head of a hippopotamus in one corner, and underneath it she was hiding a basket with Pitty Sing, the cat, in it. She didn't intend for the cat to be left alone in the house for three days because he would miss her too much and she was afraid he might brush against one of the gas burners and accidentally asphyxiate himself. Her son, Bailey, didn't like to arrive at a motel with a cat.

She sat in the middle of the back seat with John Wesley and June Star on either side of her. Bailey and the children's mother and the baby sat in front and they left Atlanta at eight forty-five with the mileage on the car at 55,890. The grandmother wrote this down because she thought it would be interesting to say how many miles they had been when they got back. It took them twenty minutes to reach the outskirts of the city.

The old lady settled herself comfortably, removing her white cotton gloves and putting them up with her purse on the shelf in front of the back window. The children's mother still had on slacks and still had her head tied up in a green kerchief, but the grandmother had on a navy blue straw sailor hat with a bunch of white violets on the brim and a navy blue dress with a small white dot in the print. Her collars and cuffs were white organdy trimmed with lace and at her neckline she had pinned a purple spray of cloth violets containing a sachet. In case of an accident, anyone seeing her dead on the highway would know at once that she was a lady.

She said she thought it was going to be a good day for driving, neither too hot nor too cold, and she cautioned Bailey that the speed limit was fifty-five miles an hour and that the patrolmen hid themselves behind billboards and small clumps of trees and sped out after you before you had a chance to slow down. She pointed out interesting details of the scenery: Stone Mountain; the blue granite that in some places came up to both sides of the highway; the brilliant red clay banks slightly streaked with purple; and the various crops that made rows of green lace-work on the ground. The trees were full of silver-white sunlight and the meanest of them sparkled. The children were reading comic magazines and their mother had gone back to sleep.

"Let's go through Georgia fast so we won't have to look at it much," John Wesley said.

"If I were a little boy," said the grandmother, "I wouldn't talk about my native state that way. Tennessee has the mountains and Georgia has the hills."

"Tennessee is just a hillbilly dumping ground," John Wesley said, "and Georgia is a lousy state too."

"You said it," June Star said.

"In my time," said the grandmother, folding her thin veined fingers, "children were more respectful of their native states and their parents and everything else. People did right then. Oh look at the cute little pickaninny!" she said and pointed to a Negro child standing in the door of a shack. "Wouldn't that make a picture, now?" she asked and they all turned and looked at the little Negro out of the back window. He waved.

"He didn't have any britches on," June Star said.

"He probably didn't have any," the grandmother explained. "Little niggers in the country don't have things like we do. If I could paint, I'd paint that picture," she said.

The children exchanged comic books.

The grandmother offered to hold the baby and the children's mother passed him over the front seat to her. She set him on her knee and bounced him and told him about the things they were passing. She rolled her eyes and screwed up her mouth and stuck her leathery thin face into his smooth bland one. Occasionally he gave her a far-away smile. They passed a large cotton field with five or six graves fenced in the middle of it, like a small island. "Look at the graveyard!" the grandmother said, pointing it out. "That was the old family burying ground. That belonged to the plantation."

"Where's the plantation?" John Wesley asked.

"Gone With the Wind," said the grandmother. "Ha. Ha."

When the children finished all the comic books they had brought, they opened the lunch and ate it. The grandmother ate a peanut butter sandwich and an olive and would not let the children throw the box and the paper napkins out the window. When there was nothing else to do they played a game by choosing a cloud and making the other two guess what shape it suggested. John Wesley took one the shape of a cow and June Star guessed a cow and John Wesley said, no, an automobile, and June Star said he didn't play fair, and they began to slap each other over the grandmother.

The grandmother said she would tell them a story if they would keep quiet. When she told a story, she rolled her eyes and waved her head and was very dramatic. She said once when she was a maiden lady she had been courted by a Mr. Edgar Atkins Teagarden from Jasper, Georgia. She said he was a very good-looking man and a gentleman and that he brought her a watermelon every Saturday afternoon with his initials cut in it. E. A. T. Well, one Saturday, she said, Mr. Teagarden brought the watermelon and there was nobody at home and he left it on the front porch and returned in his buggy to Jasper, but she never got the watermelon, she said, because a nigger boy ate it when he saw the initials, E. A. T.! This story tickled John Wesley's funny bone and he giggled and giggled but June Star didn't think it was any good. She said she wouldn't marry a man that just brought her a watermelon on Saturday. The grandmother said she would have done well to marry Mr. Teagarden because he was a gentleman and had bought Coca-Cola stock when it first came out and that he had died only a few years ago, a very wealthy man.

They stopped at The Tower for barbecued sandwiches. The Tower was a part stucco and part wood filling station and dance hall set in a clearing outside of Timothy. A fat man named Red Sammy Butts ran it and there were signs stuck here and there on the building and for miles up and down the highway saying, TRY RED SAMMY'S FAMOUS BARBECUE. NONE LIKE FAMOUS RED SAMMY'S! RED SAM! THE FAT BOY WITH THE HAPPY LAUGH. A VETERAN! RED SAMMY'S YOUR MAN!

Red Sammy was lying on the bare ground outside The Tower with his head under a truck while a gray monkey about a foot high, chained to a small chinaberry tree, chattered nearby. The monkey sprang back into the tree and got on the highest limb as soon as he saw the children jump out of the car and run toward him.

Inside, The Tower was a long dark room with a counter at one end and tables at the other and dancing space in the middle. They all sat down at a board table next to the nickelodeon and Red Sam's wife, a tall burnt-brown woman with hair and eyes lighter than her skin, came and took their order. The children's mother put a dime in the machine and played "The Tennessee Waltz," and the grandmother said that tune always made her want to dance. She asked Bailey if he would like to dance but he only glared at her. He didn't have a naturally sunny disposition like she did and trips made him nervous. The grandmother's brown eyes were very bright. She swayed her head from side to side and pretended she was dancing in her chair. June Star said play something she could tap to so the children's mother put in another dime and played a fast number and June Star stepped out onto the dance floor and did her tap routine.

"Ain't she cute?" Red Sam's wife said, leaning over the counter. "Would you like to come be my little girl?"

"No I certainly wouldn't," June Star said. "I wouldn't live in a broken-down place like this for a million bucks!" and she ran back to the table.

"Ain't she cute?" the woman repeated, stretching her mouth politely.

"Aren't you ashamed?" hissed the grandmother.

Red Sam came in and told his wife to quit lounging on the counter and hurry up with these people's order. His khaki trousers reached just to his hip bones and his stomach hung over them like a sack of meal swaying under his shirt. He came over and sat down at a table nearby and let out a combination sigh and yodel. "You can't win," he said. "You can't win," and he wiped his sweating red face off with a gray handkerchief. "These days you don't know who to trust," he said. "Ain't that the truth?"

"People are certainly not nice like they used to be," said the grand-mother.

"Two fellers come in here last week," Red Sammy said, "driving a Chrysler. It was a old beat-up car but it was a good one and these boys looked all right to me. Said they worked at the mill and you know I let them fellers charge the gas they bought? Now why did I do that?"

"Because you're a good man!" the grandmother said at once.

"Yes'm, I suppose so," Red Sam said as if he were struck with this answer.

His wife brought the orders, carrying the five plates all at once without a tray, two in each hand and one balanced on her arm. "It isn't a soul in this green world of God's that you can trust," she said. "And I don't count nobody out of that, not nobody," she repeated, looking at Red Sammy.

"Did you read about that criminal, The Misfit, that's escaped?" asked the grandmother.

"I wouldn't be a bit surprised if he didn't attact this place right here," said the woman. "If he hears about it being here, I wouldn't be none surprised to see him. If he heard it's two cent in the cash register, I wouldn't be a tall surprised if he . . . ."

"That'll do," Red Sam said. "Go bring these people their Co'-Colas," and the woman went off to get the rest of the order.

"A good man is hard to find," Red Sammy said. "Everything is getting terrible. I remember the day you could go off and leave your screen door unlatched. Not no more."

He and the grandmother discussed better times. The old lady said that in her opinion Europe was entirely to blame for the way things were now. She said the way Europe acted you would think we were made of money and Red Sam said it was no use talking about it, she was exactly right. The children ran outside into the white sunlight and looked at the monkey in the lacy chinaberry tree. He was busy catching fleas on himself and biting each one carefully between his teeth as if it were a delicacy.

They drove off again into the hot afternoon. The grandmother took cat naps and woke up every few minutes with her own snoring. Outside of Toombsboro she woke up and recalled an old plantation that she had visited in this neighborhood once when she was a young lady. She said the house had six white columns across the front and that there was an avenue of oaks leading up to it and two little wooden trellis arbors on either side in front where you sat down with your suitor after a stroll in the garden. She recalled exactly which road to turn off to get to it. She knew that Bailey would not be willing to lose any time looking at an old house, but the more she talked about it, the more she wanted to see it once again and find out if the little twin arbors were still standing. "There was a secret panel in this house," she said craftily, not telling the truth but wishing that she were, "and the story went that all the family silver was hidden in it when Sherman came through but it was never found . . ."

"Hey!" John Wesley said. "Let's go see it! We'll find it! We'll poke all the woodwork and find it! Who lives there? Where do you turn off at? Hey Pop, can't we turn off there?"

"We never have seen a house with a secret panel!" June Star shrieked. "Let's go to the house with the secret panel! Hey Pop, can't we go see the house with the secret panel!"

"It's not far from here, I know," the grandmother said. "It wouldn't take over twenty minutes."

Bailey was looking straight ahead. His jaw was as rigid as a horseshoe. "No," he said.

The children began to yell and scream that they wanted to see the house with the secret panel. John Wesley kicked the back of the front seat and June Star hung over her mother's shoulder and whined desperately into her ear that they never had any fun even on their vacation, that they could never do what THEY wanted to do. The baby began to scream and John Wesley kicked the back of the seat so hard that his father could feel the blows in his kidney.

"All right!" he shouted and drew the car to a stop at the side of the road. "Will you all shut up? Will you all just shut up for one second? If you don't shut up, we won't go anywhere."

"It would be very educational for them," the grandmother murmured.

"All right," Bailey said, "but get this: this is the only time we're going to stop for anything like this. This is the one and only time."

"The dirt road that you have to turn down is about a mile back," the grandmother directed. "I marked it when we passed."

"A dirt road," Bailey groaned.

After they had turned around and were headed toward the dirt road, the grandmother recalled other points about the house, the beautiful glass over the front doorway and the candle-lamp in the hall. John Wesley said that the secret panel was probably in the fireplace.

"You can't go inside this house," Bailey said. "You don't know who lives there."

"While you all talk to the people in front, I'll run around behind and get in a window," John Wesley suggested.

"We'll all stay in the car," his mother said.

They turned onto the dirt road and the car raced roughly along in a swirl of pink dust. The grandmother recalled the times when there were no paved roads and thirty miles was a day's journey. The dirt road was hilly and there were sudden washes in it and sharp curves on dangerous embankments. All at once they would be on a hill, looking down over the blue tops of trees for miles around, then the next minute, they would be in a red depression with the dust-coated trees looking down on them.

"This place had better turn up in a minute," Bailey said, "or I'm going to turn around."

The road looked as if no one had traveled on it in months.

"It's not much farther," the grandmother said and just as she said it, a horrible thought came to her. The thought was so embarrassing that she turned red in the face and her eyes dilated and her feet jumped up, upsetting her valise in the corner. The instant the valise moved, the newspaper top she had over the basket under it rose with a snarl and Pitty Sing, the cat, sprang onto Bailey's shoulder.

The children were thrown to the floor and their mother, clutching the baby, was thrown out the door onto the ground; the old lady was thrown into the front seat. The car turned over once and landed right-side-up in a gulch off the side of the road. Bailey remained in the driver's seat with the cat — gray-striped with a broad white face and an orange nose — clinging to his neck like a caterpillar.

As soon as the children saw they could move their arms and legs, they scrambled out of the car, shouting, "We've had an ACCIDENT!" The grandmother was curled up under the dashboard, hoping she was injured so that Bailey's wrath would not come down on her all at once. The horrible thought she had had before the accident was that the house she had remembered so vividly was not in Georgia but in Tennessee.

Bailey removed the cat from his neck with both hands and flung it out the window against the side of a pine tree. Then he got out of the car and started looking for the children's mother. She was sitting against the side of the red gutted ditch, holding the screaming baby, but she only had a cut down her face and a broken shoulder. "We've had an ACCIDENT!" the children screamed in a frenzy of delight.

"But nobody's killed," June Star said with disappointment as the grandmother limped out of the car, her hat still pinned to her head but the broken front brim standing up at a jaunty angle and the violet spray hanging off the side. They all sat down in the ditch, except the children, to recover from the shock. They were all shaking.

"Maybe a car will come along," said the children's mother hoarsely.

"I believe I have injured an organ," said the grandmother, pressing her side, but no one answered her. Bailey's teeth were clattering. He had on a yellow sport shirt with bright blue parrots designed in it and his face was as yellow as the shirt. The grandmother decided that she would not mention that the house was in Tennessee.

The road was about ten feet above and they could see only the tops of the trees on the other side of it. Behind the ditch they were sitting in there were more woods, tall and dark and deep. In a few minutes they saw a car some distance away on top of a hill, coming slowly as if the occupants were watching them. The grandmother stood up and waved both arms dramatically to attract their attention. The car continued to come on slowly, disappeared around a bend and appeared again, moving even slower, on top of the hill they had gone over. It was a big black battered hearse-like automobile. There were three men in it.

It came to a stop just over them and for some minutes, the driver looked down with a steady expressionless gaze to where they were sitting, and didn't speak. Then he turned his head and muttered something to the other two and they got out. One was a fat boy in black trousers and a red sweat shirt with a silver stallion embossed on the front of it. He moved around on the right side of them and stood staring, his mouth partly open in a kind of loose grin. The other had on khaki pants and a blue striped coat and a gray hat pulled down very low, hiding most of his face. He came around slowly on the left side. Neither spoke.

The driver got out of the car and stood by the side of it, looking down at them. He was an older man than the other two. His hair was just beginning to gray and he wore silver-rimmed spectacles that gave him a scholarly look. He had a long creased face and didn't have on any shirt or undershirt. He had on blue jeans that were too tight for him and was holding a black hat and a gun. The two boys also had guns.

"We've had an ACCIDENT!" the children screamed.

The grandmother had the peculiar feeling that the bespectacled man was someone she knew. His face was as familiar to her as if she had known him all her life but she could not recall who he was. He moved away from the car and began to come down the embankment, placing his feet carefully so that he wouldn't slip. He had on tan and white shoes and no socks, and his ankles were red and thin. "Good afternoon," he said. "I see you all had you a little spill."

"We turned over twice!" said the grandmother.

"Oncet," he corrected. "We seen it happen. Try their car and see will it run, Hiram," he said quietly to the boy with the gray hat.

"What you got that gun for?" John Wesley asked. "Whatcha gonna do with that gun?"

"Lady," the man said to the children's mother, "would you mind calling them children to sit down by you? Children make me nervous. I want all you all to sit down right together there where you're at."

"What are you telling US what to do for?" June Star asked.

Behind them the line of woods gaped like a dark open mouth. "Come here," said their mother.

"Look here now," Bailey began suddenly, "we're in a predicament! We're in . . ."

The grandmother shrieked. She scrambled to her feet and stood staring. "You're The Misfit!" she said. "I recognized you at once!"

"Yes'm," the man said, smiling slightly as if he were pleased in spite of himself to be known, "but it would have been better for all of you, lady, if you hadn't of reckernized me."

Bailey turned his head sharply and said something to his mother that shocked even the children. The old lady began to cry and The Misfit reddened.

"Lady," he said, "don't you get upset. Sometimes a man says things he don't mean. I don't reckon he meant to talk to you thataway."

"You wouldn't shoot a lady, would you?" the grandmother said and removed a clean handkerchief from her cuff and began to slap at her eyes with it.

The Misfit pointed the toe of his shoe into the ground and made a little hole and then covered it up again. "I would hate to have to," he said.

"Listen," the grandmother almost screamed, "I know you're a good man. You don't look a bit like you have common blood. I know you must come from nice people!"

"Yes mam," he said, "finest people in the world." When he smiled he showed a row of strong white teeth. "God never made a finer woman than my mother and my daddy's heart was pure gold," he said. The boy with the red sweat shirt had come around behind them and was standing with his gun at his hip. The Misfit squatted down on the ground. "Watch them children, Bobby Lee," he said. "You know they make me nervous." He looked at the six of them huddled together in front of him and he seemed to be embarrassed as if he couldn't think of anything to say. "Ain't a cloud in the sky," he remarked, looking up at it. "Don't see no sun but don't see no cloud neither."

"Yes, it's a beautiful day," said the grandmother. "Listen," she said, "you shouldn't call yourself The Misfit because I know you're a good man at heart. I can just look at you and tell."

"Hush!" Bailey yelled. "Hush! Everybody shut up and let me handle this!" He was squatting in the position of a runner about to sprint forward but he didn't move.

"I pre-chate that, lady," The Misfit said and drew a little circle in the ground with the butt of his gun.

"It'll take a half a hour to fix this here car," Hiram called, looking over the raised hood of it.

"Well, first you and Bobby Lee get him and that little boy to step over yonder with you," The Misfit said, pointing to Bailey and John Wesley. "The boys want to ast you something," he said to Bailey. "Would you mind stepping back in them woods there with them?"

"Listen," Bailey began, "we're in a terrible predicament! Nobody realizes what this is," and his voice cracked. His eyes were as blue and intense as the parrots in his shirt and he remained perfectly still.

The grandmother reached up to adjust her hat brim as if she were going to the woods with him but it came off in her hand. She stood staring at it and after a second she let if fall on the ground. Hiram pulled Bailey up by the arm as if he were assisting an old man. John Wesley caught hold of his father's hand and Bobby Lee followed. They went off toward the woods and just as they reached the dark edge, Bailey turned and supporting himself against a gray naked pine trunk, he shouted, "I'll be back in a minute, Mamma, wait on me!"

"Come back this instant!" his mother shrilled but they all disappeared into the woods.

"Bailey Boy!" the grandmother called in a tragic voice but she found she was looking at The Misfit squatting on the ground in front of her. "I just know you're a good man," she said desperately. "You're not a bit common!"

"Nome, I ain't a good man," The Misfit said after a second as if he had considered her statement carefully, "but I ain't the worst in the world neither. My daddy said I was a different breed of dog from my brothers and sisters. 'You know,' Daddy said, 'it's some that can live their whole life out without asking about it and it's others has to know why it is, and this boy is one of the latters. He's going to be into everything!'" He put on his black hat and looked up suddenly and then away deep into the woods as if he were embarrassed again. "I'm sorry I don't have on a shirt before you ladies," he said, hunching his shoulders slightly. "We buried our clothes that we had on when we escaped and we're just making do until we can get better. We borrowed these from some folks we met," he explained.

"That's perfectly all right," the grandmother said. "Maybe Bailey has an extra shirt in his suitcase."

"I'll look and see terrectly," The Misfit said.

"Where are they taking him?" the children's mother screamed.

"Daddy was a card himself," The Misfit said. "You couldn't put anything over on him. He never got in trouble with the Authorities though. Just had the knack of handling them."

"You could be honest too if you'd only try," said the grandmother. "Think how wonderful it would be to settle down and live a comfortable life and not have to think about somebody chasing you all the time."

The Misfit kept scratching in the ground with the butt of his gun as if he were thinking about it. "Yes'm, somebody is always after you," he murmured.

The grandmother noticed how thin his shoulder blades were just behind his hat because she was standing up looking down on him. "Do you ever pray?" she asked.

He shook his head. All she saw was the black hat wiggle between his shoulder blades. "Nome," he said.

There was a pistol shot from the woods, followed closely by another. Then silence. The old lady's head jerked around. She could hear the wind move through the tree tops like a long satisfied insuck of breath. "Bailey Boy!" she called.

"I was a gospel singer for a while," The Misfit said. "I been most everything. Been in the arm service, both land and sea, at home and abroad, been twict married, been an undertaker, been with the railroads, plowed Mother Earth, been in a tornado, seen a man burnt alive oncet," and he looked up at the children's mother and the little girl who were sitting close together, their faces white and their eyes glassy; "I even seen a woman flogged," he said.

"Pray, pray," the grandmother began, "pray, pray . . ."

"I never was a bad boy that I remember of," The Misfit said in an almost dreamy voice, "but somewheres along the line I done something wrong and got sent to the penitenti.ry. I was buried alive," and he looked up and held her attention to him by a steady stare.

"That's when you should have started to pray," she said. "What did you do to get sent to the penitentiary that first time?"

"Turn to the right, it was a wall," The Misfit said, looking up again at the cloudless sky. "Turn to the left, it was a wall. Look up it was a ceiling, look down it was a floor. I forget what I done, lady. I set there and set there, trying to remember what it was I done and I ain't recalled it to this day. Oncet in a while, I would think it was coming to me, but it never come."

"Maybe they put you in by mistake," the old lady said vaguely.

"Nome," he said. "It wasn't no mistake. They had the papers on me."

"You must have stolen something," she said.

The Misfit sneered slightly. "Nobody had nothing I wanted," he said. "It was a head-doctor at the penitentiary said what I had done was kill my daddy but I known that for a lie. My daddy died in nineteen ought nineteen of the epidemic flu and I never had a thing to do with it. He was buried in the Mount Hopewell Baptist churchyard and you can go there and see for yourself."

"If you would pray," the old lady said, "Jesus would help you."

"That's right," The Misfit said.

"Well then, why don't you pray?" she asked trembling with delight suddenly.

"I don't want no hep," he said. "I'm doing all right by myself."

Bobby Lee and Hiram came ambling back from the woods. Bobby Lee was dragging a yellow shirt with bright blue parrots in it.

"Thow me that shirt, Bobby Lee," The Misfit said. The shirt came flying at him and landed on his shoulder and he put it on. The grandmother couldn't name what the shirt reminded her of. "No, lady," The Misfit said while he was buttoning it up, "I found out the crime don't matter. You can do one thing or you can do another, kill a man or take a tire off his car, because sooner or later you're going to forget what it was you done and just be punished for it."

The children's mother had begun to make heaving noises as if she couldn't get her breath. "Lady," he asked, "would you and that little girl like to step off yonder with Bobby Lee and Hiram and join your husband?"

"Yes, thank you," the mother said faintly. Her left arm dangled helplessly and she was holding the baby, who had gone to sleep, in the other. "Hep that lady up, Hiram," The Misfit said as she struggled to climb out of the ditch, "and Bobby Lee, you hold onto that little girl's hand."

"I don't want to hold hands with him," June Star said. "He reminds me of a pig."

The fat boy blushed and laughed and caught her by the arm and pulled her off into the woods after Hiram and her mother.

Alone with The Misfit, the grandmother found that she had lost her voice. There was not a cloud in the sky nor any sun. There was nothing around her but woods. She wanted to tell him that he must pray. She opened and closed her mouth several times before anything came out. Finally she found herself saying, "Jesus. Jesus," meaning, Jesus will help you, but the way she was saying it, it sounded as if she might be cursing.

"Yes'm," The Misfit said as if he agreed. "Jesus thown everything off balance. It was the same case with Him as with me except He hadn't committed any crime and they could prove I had committed one because they had the papers on me. Of course," he said, "they never shown me my papers. That's why I sign myself now. I said long ago, you get you a signature and sign everything you do and keep a copy of it. Then you'll know what you done and you can hold up the crime to the punishment and see do they match and in the end you'll have something to prove you ain't been treated right. I call myself The Misfit," he said, "because I can't make what all I done wrong fit what all I gone through in punishment."

There was a piercing scream from the woods, followed closely by a pistol report. "Does it seem right to you, lady, that one is punished a heap and another ain't punished at all?"

"Jesus!" the old lady cried. "You've got good blood! I know you wouldn't shoot a lady! I know you come from nice people! Pray! Jesus, you ought not to shoot a lady. I'll give you all the money I've got!"

"Lady," The Misfit said, looking beyond her far into the woods, "there never was a body that give the undertaker a tip."

There were two more pistol reports and the grandmother raised her head like a parched old turkey hen crying for water and called, "Bailey Boy, Bailey Boy!" as if her heart would break.

"Jesus was the only One that ever raised the dead," The Misfit continued, "and He shouldn't have done it. He thown everything off balance. If He did what He said, then it's nothing for you to do but thow away everything and follow Him, and if He didn't, then it's nothing for you to do but enjoy the few minutes you got left the best way you can — by killing somebody or burning down his house or doing some other meanness to him. No pleasure but meanness," he said and his voice had become almost a snarl.

"Maybe He didn't raise the dead," the old lady mumbled, not knowing what she was saying and feeling so dizzy that she sank down in the ditch with her legs twisted under her.

"I wasn't there so I can't say He didn't," The Misfit said. "I wisht

I had of been there," he said, hitting the ground with his fist. "It ain't right I wasn't there because if I had of been there I would of known. Listen lady," he said in a high voice, "if I had of been there I would of known and I wouldn't be like I am now." His voice seemed about to crack and the grandmother's head cleared for an instant. She saw the man's face twisted close to her own as if he were going to cry and she murmured, "Why you're one of my babies. You're one of my own children!" She reached out and touched him on the shoulder. The Misfit sprang back as if a snake had bitten him and shot her three times through the chest. Then he put his gun down on the ground and took off his glasses and began to clean them.

Hiram and Bobby Lee returned from the woods and stood over the ditch, looking down at the grandmother who half sat and half lay in a puddle of blood with her legs crossed under her like a child's and her face smiling up at the cloudless sky.

Without his glasses, The Misfit's eyes were red-rimmed and pale and defenseless-looking. "Take her off and thow her where you thown the others," he said, picking up the cat that was rubbing itself against his leg.

"She was a talker, wasn't she?" Bobby Lee said, sliding down the ditch with a yodel.

"She would of been a good woman," The Misfit said, "if it had been somebody there to shoot her every minute of her life."

"Some fun!" Bobby Lee said.

"Shut up, Bobby Lee," The Misfit said. "It's no real pleasure in life."

# Jack Kerouac (1922–1969)

WHAT F. Scott Fitzgerald was to the "Flaming Youth" of the twenties, Jack Kerouac was to the "Beats" of the fifties. Of French-Canadian parentage, his birthplace was Massachusetts, where he attended the public schools. He studied at Columbia University in New York for two years, then left it to wander about the country like so many young people of his generation, taking odd jobs, rebelling against the social mores of conventional society, and seeking spiritual fulfillment in Zen Buddhism. His first novel, *The Town and the City*, grew out of his French-Canadian background and was published in 1950. It was not until his novel, *On The Road* (1957), that his importance as a chronicler of the Beat generation was recognized. There followed in rapid succession *The Dharma Bums* (1958), inspired by his interest in Zen Buddhism; *The Subterraneans* (1958), about a Beat writer's love for a black girl; and seven more novels. *Big Sur* (1962) more or less heralded the end of the Beat movement. Kerouac's short stories have been collected in *Lonesome Traveler* (1960) and his poems in *Mexico City Blues* (1959).

"The Mexican Girl" is a vibrant story. Or, in the hipster language of the fifties, Jack Kerouac's "vibes" were doing all right when he wrote this piece. And what we get from them are the acutely sensitive impressions of an eagerly receptive youth seeing for the first time Mexican peasant life transplanted to Southern California. Plus the brief but pure love affair with a Mexican girl whose "eyes were great blue windows with timidities inside." From the loveliness of that description alone, the reader knows Kerouac was a poet. But vivid descriptions abound throughout "The Mexican Girl." There is a Breughel mastery in the way Kerouac pinpoints the many individuals thronging a Los Angeles city street. And the way he tells about the exhilaration Sal Paradise feels in the fresh sweetness of the California countryside air exhilarates the reader as well. The open sincerity of the style, free from the slightest affectation and warm in its appreciation of human values, makes one wish to have known the narrator personally.

# *The Mexican Girl*

I HAD BOUGHT my ticket and was waiting for the L.A. bus when all of a sudden I saw the cutest little Mexican girl in slacks come cutting across my sight. She was in one of the buses that had just pulled in with a big sigh of airbrakes and was discharging passengers for a rest stop. Her breasts stuck out straight; her little thighs looked delicious; her hair was long and lustrous black; and her eyes were great blue windows with timidities inside. I wished I was on her bus. A pain stabbed my heart, as it did every time I saw a girl I loved who was going the opposite direction in this too big world. "Los Angeles coach now loading in door two," says the announcer and I get on. I saw her sitting alone. I dropped right opposite her on the other window and began scheming right off. I was so lonely, so sad, so tired, so quivering, so broken, so beat that I got up my courage, the courage necessary to approach a strange girl, and acted. Even then I had to spend five minutes beating my thighs in the dark as the bus rolled down the road. "You gotta, you gotta or you'll die! Damn fool talk to her! What's wrong with you? Aren't you tired enough of yourself by now?" And before I knew what I was doing I leaned across the aisle to her (she was trying to sleep on the seat). "Miss, would you like to use my raincoat for a pillow?" She looked up with a smile and said, "No, thank you very much." I sat back trembling; I lit a butt. I waited till she looked at me, with a sad little sidelook of love, and I got right up and leaned over her. "May I sit with you, Miss?"

"If you wish."

And this I did. "Where going?"

"L.A." I loved the way she said L.A.; I love the way everybody says L.A. on the Coast; it's their one and only golden town when all is said and done.

"That's where I'm going too!" I cried. "I'm very glad you let me sit with you, I was very lonely and I've been traveling a hell of a long time." And we settled down to telling our stories. Her story was this; she had a husband and child. The husband beat her so she left him, back at Sabinal south of Fresno, and was going to L.A. to live with her sister awhile. She left her little son with her family, who were grape pickers and lived in a shack in the vineyards. She had nothing to do but brood and get mad. I felt like putting my arms around her right away. We talked and talked. She said she loved to talk with me. Pretty soon she was saying she wished she could go to New York too. "Maybe we could!" I laughed. The bus groaned up Grapevine Pass and then we were coming down into the great sprawls of light. Without coming to any particular agreement we began holding hands, and in the same way it was mutely and beautifully and purely decided that when I got my hotel room in L.A. she would be beside me. I ached all over for her; I leaned my face in her beautiful hair. Her little shoulders drove me mad, I hugged her and hugged her. And she loved it.

"I love love," she said closing her eyes. I promised her beautiful love. I gloated over her. Our stories were told, we subsided into silence and sweet anticipatory thoughts. It was as simple as that. You could have all your Peaches and Vi's and Ruth Glenarms and Marylous and Eleanors and Carmens in this world, this was my girl and my kind of girlsoul, and I told her that. She confessed she saw me watching from the bus station bench. "I thought you was a nice college boy."

"Oh I'm a college boy!" I assured her. The bus arrived in Hollywood. In the gray dirty dawn, like the dawn Joel McCrea met Veronica Lake in the diner in the picture *Sullivan's Travels*, she slept in my lap. I looked greedily out the window; stucco houses and palms and drive-ins, the whole mad thing, the ragged promised land, the fantastic end of

America. We got off the bus at Main Street which was no different than where you get off a bus in Kansas City or Chicago or Boston, redbrick, dirty, characters drifting by, trolleys grating in the hopeless dawn, the whorey smell of a big city.

And here my mind went haywire, I don't know why. I began getting foolish paranoiac visions that Teresa, or Terry, her name, was a common little hustler who worked the buses for a guy's bucks by making regular appointments like ours in L.A. where she brought the sucker first to a breakfast place, where her boy waited, and then to a certain hotel to which he had access with his gun or his whatever. I never confessed this to her. We ate breakfast and a pimp kept watching us; I fancied Terry was making secret eyes at him. I was tired and felt strange and lost in a faraway, disgusting place. The goof of terror took over my thoughts and made me act petty and cheap. "Do you know that guy?" I said.

"What guy you mean, ho-ney?" I let it drop. She was slow and hung up in everything she did; it took her a long time to eat, she chewed slowly and stared into space, and smoked a cigarette slowly, and kept talking, and I was like a haggard ghost suspicioning every move she made, thinking she was stalling for time. This was all a fit of sickness. I was sweating as we went down the street hand in hand. Fellows kept turning and looking at us. The first hotel we hit had a vacant room and before I knew it I was locking the door behind me and she was sitting on the bed taking off her shoes. I kissed her meekly. Better she'd never know. To relax our nerves I knew we needed whiskey, especially me. I ran out and fiddled all over for twelve blocks hurrying till I found a pint of whiskey for sale at a newsstand. I ran back all energy. Terry was in the bathroom fixing her face. I poured one big drink in a water-glass and we had slugs. Oh it was sweet and delicious and worth. my whole life and lugubrious voyage. I stood behind her at the mirror and we danced in the bathroom that way. I began talking about my friends back East. I said, "You oughta meet a great girl I know called Dorie. She's a sixfoot redhead. If you came to New York she'd show you where to get work."

"Who is this sixfoot redhead?" she demanded suspiciously. "Why do you tell me about her?" In her simple soul she couldn't fathom my kind of glad nervous talk. I let it drop. She began to get drunk in the bathroom.

"Come on to bed!" I kept saying.

"Sixfoot redhead, hey? And I thought you was a nice college boy, I saw you in your nice sweater and I said to myself, 'Hmm ain't he nice' — No! And no! And no! You have to be a goddam pimp like all of them!"

"What in the hell are you talking about?"

"Don't stand there and tell me that sixfoot redhead ain't a madam, 'cause I know a madam when I hear about one, and you, you're just a pimp like all the rest of 'em I meet, everybody's a pimp."

"Listen Terry, I am not a pimp. I swear to you on the Bible I am not a pimp. Why should I be a pimp. My only interest is you."

"All the time I thought I met a nice boy. I was so glad, I hugged myself and said, 'Hmm a real nice boy instead of a damn pimp!'"

"Terry," I pleaded with all my soul, "please listen to me and understand. I'm not a pimp, I'm just Sal Paradise, look at my wallet." And an hour ago I thought *she* was a hustler. How sad it was. Our minds with their store of madness had diverged. O gruesome life how I moaned and pleaded and then I got mad and realized I was pleading with a dumb little Mexican wench and I told her so; and before I knew it I picked up her red pumps and threw them at the bathroom door and told her to get out. "Go on, beat it!" I'd sleep and forget it; I had my own life; my own sad and ragged life forever. There was a dead silence in the bathroom. I took my clothes off and went to bed. Terry came out with tears of sorriness in her eyes. In her simple and funny little mind had been decided the fact that a pimp does not throw a woman's shoes against the door and does not tell her to get out. In reverent and sweet silence she took her things off and slipped her tiny body into the sheets with me. It was brown as grapes. Her hips were so narrow she couldn't bear a child without getting gashed open; a Caesarian scar crossed her poor belly. Her legs were like little sticks. She was only four-foot-ten. I made love to her in the sweetness of the weary morning. Then, two tired angels of some kind, hung up forlornly on an L.A. shelf, having found the closest and most delicious thing in life together, we fell asleep and slept till late afternoon.

For the next fifteen days we were together for better or worse. We decided to hitchhike to New York together; she was going to be my girl in town. I envisioned wild complexities, a season, a new season. First we had to work and earn enough money for the trip. Terry was all for starting at once with my twenty dollars. I didn't like it. And like a damnfool I considered the problem for two days reading the want ads of wild new L.A. papers I'd never seen before in my life, in cafeterias and bars, until my twenty'd dwindled to twelve. The situation was growing. We were happy as kids in our little hotel room. In the middle of the night I got up because I couldn't sleep, pulled the cover over baby's bare brown shoulder, and examined the L.A. night. What brutal, hot, siren-whining nights they are! Right across the street there was trouble. An old rickety rundown roominghouse was the scene of some kind of tragedy. The cruiser was pulled up below and the cops were questioning an old man with gray hair. Sobbings came from within. I could hear everything, together with the hum of my hotel neon. I never felt sadder in my life. L. A. is the loneliest and most brutal of American cities; New York gets godawful cold in the winter but there's a feeling of whacky comradeship somewhere in some streets. L.A. is a jungle.

South Main Street, where Terry and I took strolls with hotdogs, was a fantastic carnival of lights and wildness. Booted cops frisked people on practically every corner. The beatest characters in the country swarmed on the sidewalks — all of it under those soft Southern California stars that are lost in the brown halo of the huge desert encampment L.A. really is. You could smell tea, weed, I mean marijuana floating in the air, together with the chili beans and beer. That grand wild sound of bop floated from beerparlor jukes, Dizzy and Bird and Bags and early Miles; it mixed medleys with every kind of cowboy and boogie-woogie in the American night. Everybody looked like Hunkey. Wild Negroes with bop caps and goatees came laughing by; then longhaired brokendown hipsters straight off Route 66 from New York, then old desert rats carrying packs and heading for a park bench at the Plaza, then Methodist ministers with raveled sleeves, and an occasional Nature Boy saint in beard and sandals. I wanted to meet them all, talk to everybody, but Terry hurried along, we were busy trying to get a buck together, like everybody else.

We went to Hollywood to try to work in the drugstore at Sunset and Vine. The questions that were asked of us in upstairs offices to determine our fitness for the slime of the sodafountain greaseracks were so sinister that I had to laugh. It turned my gut. Sunset and Vine! — what a corner! Now there's a corner! Great families off jalopies from the hinterlands stood around the sidewalk gaping for sight of some movie star and the movie star never showed up. When a limousine passed they rushed eagerly to the curb and ducked to look: some character in dark glasses sat inside with a bejeweled blonde. "Don Ameche! Don Ameche!" "No George Murphy! George Murphy!" They milled around looking at one another. Luscious little girls by the thousands rushed around with drive-in trays; they'd come to Hollywood to be movie stars and instead got all involved in everybody's garbage, including Darryl Zanuck's. Handsome queer boys who had come to Hollywood to be cowboys walked around wetting their eyebrows with hincty fingertip. Those beautiful little gone gals cut by in slacks in a continuous unbelievable stream; you thought you were in heaven but it was only Purgatory and everybody was about to be pardoned, paroled, powdered and put down; the girls came to be starlets; they up-ended in drive-ins with pouts and goosepimples on their bare legs. Terry and I tried to find work at the drive-ins. It was no soap anywhere, thank God. Hollywood Boulevard was a great screaming frenzy of cars;

there were minor accidents at least once a minute; everybody was rushing off toward the farthest palm . . . and beyond that was the desert and nothingness. So they thought. You don't expect everybody to know that you can find water in a kopash cactus, or sweet taffy in your old mesquite. Hollywood Sams stood in front of swank restaurants arguing exactly, loudly and showoff the same way Broadway Sams argue on Jacobs Beach sidewalks, New York, only here they wore light-weight suits and their talk was even more dreary and unutterably cornier. Tall cadaverous preachers shuddered by. Seventy-year-old World Rosicrucian ladies with tiaras in their hair stood under palms signifying nothing. Fat screaming women ran across the Boulevard to get in line for the quiz shows. I saw Jerry Colonna buying a car at Buick Motors; he was inside the vast plateglass window fingering his mustachio, incredible, real, like seeing the Three Stooges seriously ashen-faced in a real room. Terry and I ate in a cafeteria downtown which was decorated to look like a grotto, with metal tits spurting everywhere and great impersonal stone buttoxes belonging to deities of fish and soapy Neptune. People ate lugubrious meals around the waterfalls, their faces green with marine sorrow. All the cops in L.A. looked like handsome gigolos; obviously, they'd come to L.A. to make the movies. Everybody had come to make the movies, even me. Terry and I were finally reduced to trying to get jobs on South Main Street among the beat countermen and dishgirls who made no bones about their beatness and even there it was no go. We still had twelve dollars.

"Man, I'm going to get my clothes from Sis and we'll hitchhike to New York," said Terry. "Come on man. Let's do it. If you can't boogie I know I'll show you how." That last part was a song of hers she kept singing, after a famous record. We hurried to her sister's house in the sliverous Mexican shacks somewhere beyond Alameda Avenue. I waited in a dark alley behind Mexican kitchens because her sister wasn't supposed to see me and like it. Dogs ran by. There were little lamps illuminating the little rat alleys. I stood there swigging from the bottle of wine and eying the stars and digging the sounds of the neighborhood. I could hear Terry and her sister arguing in the soft warm night. I was ready for anything. Terry came out and led me by the hand to Central Avenue, which is the colored main drag of L.A. And what a wild place it is, with chickenshacks barely big enough to house a jukebox and the jukebox blowing nothing but blues, bop and jump. We went up dirty tenement stairs and came to the room of Terry's friend, Margarina, a colored girl apparently named by her loving mother after the spelling on an oleo wrapper. Margarina, a lovely mulatto, owed Terry a skirt and a pair of shoes; her husband was black as spades and kindly. He went right out and bought a pint of whiskey to host me proper. I tried to pay part of it but he said no. They had two little children. The kids bounced on the bed, it was their play-place. They put their arms around me and looked at me with wonder. The wild humming night of Central Avenue, the night of Hamp's *Central Avenue Breakdown*, howled and boomed along outside. They were singing in the halls, singing from their windows, just hell be damned and lookout. Terry got her clothes and we said goodbye. We went down to a chickenshack and played records on the jukebox. Yakking with our beer we decided what to do: we decided to hitch to New York with our remaining monies. She had five dollars coming from her sister; we rushed back to the shacks. So before the daily room rent was due again we packed up and took off on a red car to Arcadia, California, where Santa Anita racetrack is located under snowcapped mountains as I well knew from boyhood pastings of horse-race pictures in sad old notebooks showing Azucar winning in 1935 the great $100,000 'Cap and you see dim snows heaped over the backstretch mountains. Route 66. It was night. We were pointed toward that enormity which is the American continent. Holding hands we walked several miles down the dark road to get out of the populated district. It was a Saturday night. We stood under a road-lamp thumbing when suddenly cars full of young kids roared by with streamers flying. "Yaah! yaah! we won! we won!" they all shouted. Then they yoo-hooed us and got great glee out of seeing a guy and a girl on the road. Dozens of them passed in successive jalopies, young faces and "throaty young voices" as the saying does. I hated every one of them. Who did they think they were yaahing at somebody on the road because they were little high school punks and their parents carved the roast beef on Sunday afternoons. Nor did we get a ride. We had to walk back to town and worst of all we needed coffee and had the misfortune of going into the same gaudy wood-laced place with old soda johns with beer-fountain mustaches out front. The same kids were there but we were still minding our own business. Terry and I sipped our coffee and cocoa. We had battered bags and all the world before us . . . all that ground out there, that desert dirt and rat tat tat. We looked like a couple of sullen Indians in a Navajo Springs sodafountain, black bent heads at a table. The schoolkids saw now that Terry was a Mexican, a Pachuco wildcat; and that her boy was worse than that. With her pretty nose in the air she cut out of there and we wandered together in the dark up along the ditches of highways. I carried the bags and wanted to carry more. We made tracks and cut along and were breathing fogs in the cold night air. I didn't want to go on another minute without a warm night's rest in a warm sack together. Morning be damned, let's hide from the world another night. I wanted to fold her up in my system of limbs under no light but stars in the window. We went to a motel court and asked if they had a cabin. Yes. We bought a comfortable little suite for four dollars. I was spending my money anyhow. Shower, bath towels, wall radio and all, just for one more night. We held each other tight. We had long serious talks and took baths and discussed things on the pillow with light on and then with light out. Something was being proved, I was convincing her of something, which she accepted, and we concluded the pact in the dark, breathless. Then pleased, like little lambs.

In the morning we boldly struck out on our new plan. Terry wore her dark glasses with authority. Her pretty little severe face beneath, with the noble nose, almost hawk-like Indian nose, but with upswerved cute hollow cheekbones to make an oval and a prettywoman blush, with red ruby full lips and Aunt Jemima skirt teeth, mud nowhere on her but was imprinted in the pigment of the Mongol skin. We were going to take a bus to Bakersfield with the last eight dollars and work picking grapes. "See instead of going to New York now we're all set to work awhile and get what we need, then we'll go, in a bus, we won't have to hitchhike, you see how no good it is . . ."

We arrived in Bakersfield in late afternoon, with our plan to hit every fruit wholesaler in town. Terry said we could live in tents on the job. The thought of me lying there in a tent, and picking grapes in the cool California mornings after nights of guitar music and wine with dipped grapes, hit me right. "Don't worry about a thing."

But there were no jobs to be had and much confusion with everybody giving confused Indian information and innumerable tips ("Go out to County Road you'll find Sacano") and no job materialized. So we went to a Chinese restaurant and had a dollar's worth of chow mein among the sad Saturday afternoon families, digging them, and set out with reinforced bodies. We went across the Southern Pacific tracks to Mexican town. Terry jabbered with her brethren asking for jobs. It was night now, we had a few dollars left, and the little Mextown street was one blazing bulb of lights: movie marquees, fruit stands, penny arcades, Five and Tens and hundreds of rickety trucks and mudspattered jalopies parked all over. Whole Mexican fruitpicking families wandered around eating popcorn. Terry talked to everybody. I was beginning to despair. What I needed, what Terry needed too, was a drink so we bought a quart of California port wine for 35 cents and went to the railyards to drink. We found a place where hoboes had drawn up crates to sit over fires. We sat there and drank the wine. On our left were the freight cars, sad and sooty red beneath the moon; straight ahead the lights and airport pokers of Bakersfield proper; to our right a tremendous aluminum Quonset warehouse. I remembered it later in passing. Ah it was a fine night, a warm night, a wine-drinking night, a moony night, and a night to hug your girl and talk and spit and be heavengoing. This we did. She was a drinking little fool and kept up with me and passed me and went right on talking till midnight. We never moved from those crates. Occasionally bums passed, Mexican mothers passed with children, and the prowl car came by and the cop got out to leak but most of the time we were alone and mixing up our souls more and ever more till it would be terribly hard to say goodbye. At midnight we got up and goofed toward the highway.

Terry had a new idea. We would hitch to Sabinal, her hometown up the San Joaquin Valley, and live in her brother's garage. Anything was all right to me, especially a nice garage. On the road I made Terry sit down on my bag to make her look like a woman in distress and right off a truck stopped and we ran for it all gleegiggles. The man was a good man, his truck was poor. He roared and crawled on up the Valley. We got to Sabinal in the wee hours of the morning not until after that tired sleepy beau' pushed his old rattle rig from Indian Ponce de Leon Springs of down-valley up the screaming cricket fields of grape and lemon four hours, to let us off, with a cheerful "So long pard," and here we were with the wine finished (I, while she slept in the truck). Now I'm stoned. The sky is gray in the east. "Wake, for morning in the bowl of night . . ." There was a quiet leafy square, we walked around it, past sleeping soda-fountains and barber shops, looking for some garage. There was no garage. Ghostly white houses. A whistle stop on the S.P. A California town of old goldbottle times. She couldn't find her brother's garage but now we were going to find her brother's buddy, who would know. Nobody home. It all went on in rickety alleys of little Mextown Sabinal, wrong side of the tracks. As dawn began to break I lay flat on my back in the lawn of the town square, and I'd done that once before when they thought I was drowned in an eastern resort, and I kept saying over and over, "You won't tell what he done up in Weed will you? What'd he do up in Weed? You won't tell will you? What'd he do up in Weed?" This was from the picture *Of Mice and Men* with Burgess Meredith talking to the big foreman of the ranch; I thought we were near Weed. Terry giggled. Anything I did was all right with her. I could lay there and go on saying "What'd he do up in Weed?" till the ladies come out for church and she wouldn't care.

Because her brother was in these parts I figured we'd be all set soon and I took her to an old hotel by the tracks and we went to bed comfortably. Five dollars left. It was all smelling of fresh paint in there, and old mahogany mirrors and creaky. In the bright sunny morning Terry got up early and went to find her brother. I slept till noon; when I looked out the window I suddenly saw an S.P. freight going by with hundreds of hoboes reclining on the flatcars and in gons and rolling merrily along with packs for pillows and funny papers before their noses and some munching on good California grapes picked up by the watertank. "Damn!" I yelled. "Hooee! It *is* the promised land." They were all coming from Frisco; in a week they'd all be going back in the same grand style.

Terry arrived with her brother, his buddy, and her child. Her brother was a wildbuck Mexican hotcat with a hunger for booze, a great good kid. His buddy was a big flabby Mexican who spoke English without much accent and was anxious to please and overconcerned to prove something. I could see he had always had eyes for Terry. Her little boy was Raymond, seven years old, darkeyed and sweet. Well there we were, and another wild day began.

Her brother's name was Freddy. He had a '38 Chevvy. We piled into that and took off to parts unknown. "Where we going?" I asked. The buddy did the explaining, Ponzo, that's what everybody called him. He stank. I found out why. His business was selling manure to farmers, he had a truck. We were going to check on that. Freddy always had three or four dollars in his pocket and was happygolucky about things. He always said "That's right man, there you go — dah you go, dah you go!" And he went. He drove 70 miles an hour in the old heap and we went to Madera beyond Fresno, throwing dust back of our tires, and saw farmers about manure. Their voices drawled to us from the hot sun open. Freddy had a bottle. "Today we drink, tomorrow we work. Dah you go man — take a shot." Terry sat in back with her baby; I looked back at her and saw a flush of homecoming joy on her face. She'd been driving around like this for years. The beautiful green countryside of October in California reeled by madly. I was guts and juice again and ready to go.

"Where do we go now man?"

"We go find a farmer with some manure layin around — tomorrow we drive back in the truck and pick up. Man we'll make a lot of money. Don't worry about nothing."

"We're all in this together!" yelled Ponzo, who wouldn't have got the manure by himself. I saw this was so — everywhere I went everybody was in it together. We raced through the crazy streets of Fresno and on up the Valley to some farmers in certain backroads. Ponzo got out of the car and conducted confused conversations with old Mexicans; nothing of course came of it.

"What we need is a drink!" yelled Freddy and off we went to a crossroads saloon. Americans are always drinking in crossroads saloons on Sunday afternoon; they bring their kids; there are piles of manure outside the screendoor; they gabble and brawl over brews and grow haggly baggly and you hear harsh laughter rising from routs and song, nobody's really having any fun but faces get redder and time flies fading

faster. But everything's fine. Come nightfall the kids come crying and
the parents are drunk. Around the jukebox they go weaving back to
the house. Everywhere in America I've been in crossroads saloons
drinking with whole families. The kids eat popcorn and chips and play
in back or sneak stale beers for all I know. Freddy and I and Ponzo and
Terry sat there drinking and shouting. Vociferous types. The sun
got red. Nothing had been accomplished. What was there to
accomplish? "Mañana," said Freddy, "mañana, man, we make it; have
another beer, man, dah you go, DAH YOU GO!" We staggered out and got
in the car; off we went to a highway bar. This one had blue neons and
pink lights. Ponzo was a big loud vociferous type who knew everybody
in San Joaquin Valley apparently from the way every time we clomped
into a joint he'd let out loud Ho-Yo's. Now I had a few bucks left and
ruefully counted them. Festooned all over my brain were the ideas of
going back home to New York at once with this handful of change,
hitching as I'd been doing at Bakersfield that night, leave Terry with her
wild brothers and mad Mexican manure piles and mañanas of crazy beer.
But I was having a hell of a time. From the highway bar I went with
Ponzo alone in the car to find some certain farmer; instead we wound
up in Madera Mextown digging the girls and trying to pick up a few
for him and Freddy; and then, as purple dusk descended over the grape
country, I found myself sitting dumbly in the car as he argued with some
old farmer at the kitchen door about the price of a watermelon the old
man grew in the backyard. We had a watermelon, ate it on the spot
and threw the rinds on the old Mexican's dirt sidewalk. All kinds of
pretty little girls were cutting down the darkening street. I said "Where
the hell are we?"

"Don't worry man," said big Ponzo, "tomorrow we make a lot of
money, tonight we don't worry." We went back and picked up Terry
and the others and wailed to Fresno in the highway lights of night.
We were all raving hungry. We bounced over the railroad tracks and hit
the wild streets of Fresno Mextown. Strange Chinamen hung out of
windows digging the Sunday night streets; groups of Mex chicks
swaggered around in slacks; mambo blasted from jukeboxes; the lights
were festooned around like Halloween. We went into a restaurant
and had tacos and mashed pinto beans rolled in tortillas; it was delicious.
I whipped out my last shining four dollars and change which stood
between me and the Atlantic shore and paid for the lot. Now I had
three bucks. Terry and I looked at each other. "Where we going to
sleep tonight baby?"

"I don't know." Freddy was drunk; now all he was saying was "Dah
you go man — dah you go man" in a tender and tired voice. It had been

a long day. None of us knew what was going on, or what the Good Lord appointed. Poor little Raymond fell asleep against my arm. We drove back to Sabinal. On the way we pulled up sharp at a roadhouse on the highway, 99, because Freddy wanted one last beer. In back were trailers and tents and a few rickety motel-style rooms. I inquired about the price and it was two bucks for a cabin. I asked Terry how about that and she said great, because we had the kid on our hands now and had to make him comfortable. So after a few beers in the saloon, where sullen Okies reeled to the music of a cowboy band and sprawled drawling at sticky tables where they'd been swiggling brew since one o'clock in the afternoon and here it was twelve hours later and all the stars out and long sleepy, Terry and I and Raymond went into a cabin and got ready to hit the sack. Ponzo kept hanging around, talking to us in the starry door; he had no place to sleep. Freddy slept at his father's house in the vineyard shack. "Where do you live, Ponzo?" I asked.

"Nowhere, man. I'm supposed to live with Big Rosey but she threw me out last night. I'm goin to get my truck and sleep in it tonight." Guitars tinkled. Terry and I gazed at the stars together from the tiny bathroom window and took a shower and dried each other.

"Mañana," she said, "everything'll be all right tomorrow, don't you think so Sal-honey man?"

"Sure baby, mañana." It was always mañana. For the next week that was all I heard, Mañana, a lovely word and one that probably means heaven. Little Raymond jumped in bed, clothes and all and went to sleep; sand spilled out of his shoes, Madera sand. Terry and I had to get up in the middle of the night and brush it off the sheets. In the morning I got up, washed and took a walk around the place. Sweet dew was making me breathe that human fog. We were five miles out of Sabinal in the cotton fields and grape vineyards along highway 99. I asked the big fat woman who owned the camp if any field tents were vacant. The cheapest one, a dollar a day, was vacant. I fished up that last dollar and moved into it. There was a bed, a stove and a cracked mirror hanging from a pole; it was delightful. I had to stoop to get in, and when I did there was my baby and my baby-boy. We waited for Freddy and Ponzo to arrive with the truck. They arrived with beer and started to get drunk in the tent. "Great tent!"

"How about the manure?"

"Too late today — tomorrow man we make a lot of money, today we have a few beers. What do you say, beer?" I didn't have to be prodded. "Dah you go — DAH YOU GO!" yelled Freddy. I began to see that our plans for making money with the manure truck would never materialize. The truck was parked outside the tent. It smelled like

Ponzo. That night Terry and I went to sleep in the sweet night air and made sweet old love. I was just getting ready go to sleep when she said, "You want to love me now?"

I said, "What about Raymond?"

"He don't mind. He's asleep." But Raymond wasn't asleep and he said nothing.

The boys came back the next day with the manure truck and drove off to find whiskey; they came back and had a big time in the tent. Talking about the great old times when they were kids here and when they were kids in Calexico and their eccentric old uncles from Old Mexico and the fabulous characters out of the past I missed. "You tink I'm crazy!" yelled Freddy wildeyed, his hair over his eyes. That night Ponzo said it was too cold and slept on the ground in our tent wrapped in a big tarpaulin smelling of cowflaps. Terry hated him; she said he hung around her brother just to be close to her. He was probably in love with her. I didn't blame him.

Nothing was going to happen except starvation for Terry and me, I had a dime left, so in the morning I walked around the countryside asking for cottonpicking work. Everybody told me to go to a farm across the highway from the camp. I went; the farmer was in the kitchen with his women. He came out, listened to my story, and warned me he was only paying so much per hundred pound of picked cotton. I pictured myself picking at least three hundred pounds a day and took the job. He fished out some old long canvas bags from the barn and told me the picking started at dawn. I rushed back to Terry all glee. On the way a grapetruck went over a bump in the road and threw off great bunches of grape on the hot tar. I picked it up and took it home. Terry was glad. "Raymond and me'll come with you and help."

"Pshaw!" I said. "No such thing!"

"You see, you see, it's very hard picking cotton. If you can't boogie I know I show you how." We ate the grapes and in the evening Freddy showed up with a loaf of bread and a pound of hamburg and we had a picnic. In a larger tent next to ours lived a whole family of Okie cottonpickers; the grandfather sat in a chair all day long, he was too old to work; the son and daughter, and their children, filed every dawn across the highway to my farmer's field and went to work. At dawn the next day I went with them. They said the cotton was heavier at dawn because of the dew and you could make more money than in the afternoon. Nevertheless they worked all day from dawn to sundown. The grandfather had come from Nebraska during the great plague of the thirties, that old selfsame dustcloud, with the entire family in a jalopy truck. They had been in California ever since. They loved to work. In the ten years the old man's son had increased his children to the number of four, some of whom were old enough now to pick cotton. And in that time they had progressed from ragged poverty in Simon Legree fields to a kind of smiling respectability in better tents, and that was all. They were extremely proud of their tent. "Ever going back to Nebraska?"

"Pshaw, there's nothing back there. What we want to do is buy a trailer." We bent down and began picking cotton. It was beautiful. Across the field were the tents, and beyond them the sere brown cottonfields that stretched out of sight, and over that the brown arroyo foothills and then as in a dream the snowcapped Sierras in the blue morning air. This was so much better than washing dishes on South Main Street. But I knew nothing about cottonpicking. I spent too much time disengaging the white ball from its crackly bed; the others did it in one flick. Moreover my fingertips began to bleed; I needed gloves, or more experience. There was an old Negro couple in the field with us. They picked cotton with the same Godblessed patience their grandfathers had practised in prewar Alabama: they moved right along their rows, bent and blue, and their bags increased. My back began to ache. But it was beautiful kneeling and hiding in that earth; if I felt like resting I just lay down with my face on the pillow of brown moist earth. Birds sang an accompaniment. I thought I had found my life's work. Terry and Raymond came waving at me across the field in the hot lullal noon and pitched in with me. Damn if he wasn't faster than I was!! — a child. And of course Terry was twice as fast. They worked ahead of me and left me piles of clean cotton to add to my bag, my long lugubrious nightmare bag that dragged after me like some serpent or some begraggled buttoned dragon in a Kafkean dream and worse. My mouth drops just to think of that deep bag. Terry left workmanlike piles, Raymond little childly piles. I stuck them in with sorrow. What kind of an old man was I that I couldn't support my own can let alone theirs. They spent all afternoon with me; the earth is an Indian thing. When the sun got red we trudged back together. At the end of the field I unloaded my burden on a scale, to my surprise it weighed a pound and a half only, and I got a buck fifty. Then I borrowed one of the Okie boys' bicycles and rode down 99 to a crossroads grocery where I bought cans of spaghetti and meatballs, bread, butter, coffee and five-cent cakes, and came back with the bag on the handlebars. L.A.-bound traffic zoomed by; Fresno-bound harassed my tail. I swore and swore. I looked up at the dark sky and prayed to God for a better break in life and a better chance to do something for the little people I loved. Nobody was paying any attention to me up there. I should have known better. It was Terry who brought my soul back; on the tent stove she warmed up the food and it was one of the greatest meals of my life I was so hungry and tired. Sighing like an old Negro cottonpicker, I reclined on the bed and smoked a cigarette. Dogs barked in the cool night. Freddy and

Ponzo had given up calling in the evenings. I was satisfied with that. Terry curled up beside me, Raymond sat on my chest, and they drew pictures of animals in my notebook. The light of our tent burned on the frightful plain. The cowboy music twanged in the roadhouse and carried across the fields all sadness. It was all right with me. I kissed my baby and we put out the lights.

In the morning the dew made the tent sag; I got up with my towel and toothbrush and went to the general motel toilet to wash; then I came back, put on my pants, which were all torn from kneeling in the earth and had been sewed by Terry in the evening; put on my ragged strawhat, which had originally been Raymond's toy hat; and went across the highway with my canvas cottonbag. The cotton was wet and heavy. The sun was red on moist earth.

Every day I earned approximately a dollar and a half. It was just enough to buy groceries in the evening on the bicycle. The days rolled by. I forgot all about the East and the ravings of the bloody road. Raymond and I played all the time: he liked me to throw him up in the air and down on the bed. Terry sat mending clothes. I was a man of the earth precisely as I had dreamed I would be in New York. There was talk that Terry's husband was back in Sabinal and out for me; I was ready for him. One night the Okies went berserk in the roadhouse and tied a man to a tree and beat him with two-by-fours. I was asleep at the time and only heard about it. From then on I carried a big stick with me in the tent in case they got the idea we Mexicans were fouling up their trailer camp. They thought I was a Mexican, of course; and I am.

But now it was getting on in October and getting much colder in the nights. The Okie family had a woodstove and planned to stay for the winter. We had no stove, and besides the rent for the tent was due. Terry and I bitterly decided we'd have to leave and try something else. "Go back to your family," I gnashed. "For God's sake you can't be batting around tents with a baby like Raymond; the poor little tyke is cold." Terry cried because I was criticizing her motherly instincts; I meant no such thing. When Ponzo came in the truck one gray afternoon we decided to see her family about the situation. But I mustn't be seen and would have to hide in the vineyard. "Tell your mother you'll get a job and help with the groceries. Anything's better than this."

"But you're going, I can hear you talk."

"Well I got to go *some*time —

"What do you mean, sometime. You said we'd stick together and go to New York together. Freddy wants to go to New York too! Now! We'll all go."

"I dunno, Terry, goddamit I dunno — "

We got in the truck and Ponzo started for Sabinal; the truck broke down in some backroad and simultaneously it started to rain wildly. We sat in the old truck cursing. Ponzo got out and toiled in the rain in his torn white shirt. He was a good old guy after all. We promised each other one big more bat. Off we went to a rickety bar in Sabinal Mextown and spent an hour sopping up the cerveza as the rain drove past the door and the jukebox boomed those brokenhearted campo love-songs from old Mexico, sad, incredibly sad like clouds going over the horizon like dogs on their hind legs, the singer breaking out his wild Ya Ya Henna like the sound of a coyote crying, broken, half laughter, half tears. I was through with my chores in the cottonfield, I could feel it as the beer ran through me like wildfire. We screamed happily our insane conversations. We'd do it, we'd do everything! I could feel the pull of my own whole life calling me back. I needed fifty dollars to get back to New York. While Terry and Ponzo drank I ran in the rain to the postoffice and scrawled a penny postcard request for $50 and sent it to my aunt; she'd do it. I was as good as saved; lazy butt was saved again. It was a secret from Terry.

The rain stopped and we drove to Terry's family shack. It was situated on an old road that ran between the vineyards. It was dark when we got there finally. They let me off a quarter-mile up the road and drove to the door. Light poured out of the door; Terry's six other brothers were playing their guitars and singing all together like a professional recording and beautiful. ". . . si tu corazon . . ." The old man was drinking wine. I heard shouts and arguments above the singing. They called her a whore because she'd left her no good husband and gone to L.A. and left Raymond with them. At intervals the brothers stopped singing to regroup their choruses. The old man was yelling. But the sad fat brown mother prevailed, as she always does among the great Fellaheen peoples of the world, and Terry was allowed to come back home. The brothers began to sing gay songs, fast. I huddled in the cold rainy wind and watched everything across the sad vineyards of October in the Valley. My mind was filled with that great song "Lover Man" as Billie Holiday sings it; I had my own concert in the bushes. "Someday we'll meet, and you'll dry all my tears, and whisper sweet little words in my ear, hugging and akissing, Oh what we've been missing, Lover Man Oh where can you be . . ." It's not the words so much as the great harmonic tune and the way Billie sings it, like a woman stroking her man's hair in soft lamplight. The winds howled. I got cold. Terry and Ponzo came back and we rattled off in the old truck to meet Freddy, who was now living with Ponzo's woman Big Rosey; we tooted the horn for him in woodfence alleys. Big Rosey threw him out, we heard yelling and saw Freddy running out with his head ducking. Everything was collapsing. Everybody was laughing.

That night Terry held me tight, of course, and told me not to leave. She said she'd work picking grapes and make enough money for both of us; meanwhile I could live in Farmer Heffelfinger's barn down the road from her family. I'd have nothing to do but sit in the grass all day and eat grapes. "You like that?"

I rubbed my jaw. In the morning her cousins came to the tent to get us in the truck. These were also singers. I suddenly realized thousands of Mexicans all over the countryside knew about Terry and I and that it must have been a juicy romantic topic for them. The cousins were very polite and in fact charming. I stood on the truck platform with them as we rattlebanged into town, hanging on to the rail and smiling pleasantries, talking about where we were in the war and what the pitch was. There were five cousins in all and every one of them was nice. They seemed to belong to the side of Terry's family that didn't act up like her brother Freddy. But I loved that wild Freddy. He swore he was coming to New York and join me. I pictured him in New York putting off everything till mañana. He was drunk in a field someplace today.

I got off the truck at the crossroads and the cousins drove Terry and Raymond home. They gave me the high-sign from the front of the house: the father and mother weren't home. So I had the run of the house for the afternoon, digging it and Terry's three giggling fat sisters and the crazy children sitting in the middle of the road with tortillas in their hands. It was a four-room shack; I couldn't imagine how the whole family managed to live in there, find room. Flies flew over the sink. There were no screens, just like in the song: "The window she is broken and the rain she's coming in . . ." Terry was at home now and puttering around pots. The sisters giggled over True Love magazines in Spanish showing daguerreotype brown covers of lovers in great, somehow darker more passionate throes, with long sideburns and huge worries and burning secret eyes. The little children screamed in the road, roosters ran around. When the sun came out red through the clouds of my last Valley afternoon Terry led me to Farmer Heffelfinger's barn. Farmer Heffelfinger had a prosperous farm up the road. We put crates together, she brought blankets from the house, and I was all set except for a great hairy tarantula that lurked at the pinpoint top of the barn-roof. Terry said it wouldn't harm me if I didn't bother it. I lay on my back and stared at it. I went out to the cemetery and climbed a tree. In the tree I sang "Blue Skies." Terry and Raymond sat in the grass; we had grapes. In California you chew the juice out of the grapes and spit the skin and pits away, the gist of the grape is always wine. Nightfall came. Terry went home for supper and came to the barn at nine o'clock with my secret supper of delicious tortillas and mashed beans. I lit a woodfire on the cement floor of the barn to make light. We made love on the crates. Terry got up and cut right back to the shack. Her father was yelling at her, I could hear him from the barn. "Where have you been? What you doing running around at night in the fields?" Words to that effect. She'd left me a cape to keep warm, some old Spanish garment, I threw it over my shoulder and skulked through the moonlit vineyard to see what was going on. I crept to the end of a row and kneeled in the warm dirt. Her five brothers were singing melodious songs in Spanish. The stars bent over the little roof; smoke poked from the stovepipe chimney. I smelled mashed beans and chili. The old man growled. The brothers kept right on singing. The mother was silent. Raymond and the kids were giggling on one vast bed in the bedroom. A California home; I hid in the grapevines digging it all. I felt like a million dollars; I was adventuring in the crazy American night. Terry came out slamming the door behind her. I accosted her on the dark road. "What's the matter?"

"Oh we fight all the time. He wants me to go to work tomorrow. He says he don't want me fooling around with boys. Sallie-boy I want to go to New York with you."

"But how?"

"I don't know honey. I'll miss you. I love you."

"But I can't stay here."

"You say what you like, I know what you mean. Yes  yes, we lay down one more time then you leave." We went back to the barn; I made love to her under the tarantula. What was the tarantula doing? We slept awhile on the crates as the fire died. She went back at midnight; her father was drunk; I could hear him roaring; then there was silence as he fell asleep. The stars folded over the sleeping countryside.

In the morning Father Heffelfinger stuck his head through the horse gate and said, "How you doing young fella?"

"Fine. I hope it's all right my staying here."

"Sure. You going with that little Mexican floozie?"

"She's a very nice girl."

"Pretty too. S'got blue eyes. I think the bull jumped the fence there . . ." We talked about his farm.

Terry brought my breakfast. I had my handbag all packed and ready to go back East, as soon as I picked up my money in Sabinal. I knew it was waiting there for me. I told Terry I was leaving. She had been thinking about it all night and was resigned to it. Emotionlessly she kissed me in the vineyards and walked off down the row. We turned at a dozen paces, for love is a duel, and looked at each other for the last time. "See you in New York Terry," I said. She was supposed to drive to New York in a month with her brother. But we both knew she wouldn't make it somehow. At a hundred feet I turned to look at her. She just walked on back to the shack, carrying my breakfast plate in one hand. I bowed my head and watched her. Well lackadaddy, I was on the road again. I walked down the highway to Sabinal eating black walnuts from the walnut tree, then on the railroad track balancing on the rail.

# William H. Gass (1924-    )

ONE of the most intriguing of the new writers who first emerged in the nine-
teen-sixties is William H. Gass. He is a graduate of Kenyon College and
received a Ph.D. from Cornell University. He became a professor of philosophy at Purdue University and at Washington University in St. Louis.
Novels of which he is the author are *Omensetter's Luck* (1966) and *Willie
Master's Lonesome Wife* (1968). His short stories have been collected in *In
the Heart of the Heart of the Country and Other Stories* (1968). His *Fiction
and Other Figures of Life* (1970) is a work of literary criticism.

From the moment "The Pedersen Kid" appeared in the little magazine
*MSS*, writing by Gass attracted much critical comment. It is easy to see why
on reading this story. Grisly and schizophrenic as a nightmare, the power
of the story lies in the many involutions that ensnare a reader. It is cerebrally
complex and utterly simple at the same time. Or, to put it in other words, it
is a highbrow story told in lowbrow style. Perhaps this is because its author
is a philosopher. The main characters, Pa, Hans, the Pedersen kid, and the
narrator, and what happens that bleak winter night in the wheat fields are
unforgettable because there is not only a philosopher but an artist at work
here.

# *The Pedersen Kid*

## PART ONE

BIG HANS yelled, so I came out. The barn was dark but the sun burned
on the snow. Hans was carrying something from the crib. I yelled
but Big Hans didn't hear. He was in the house with what he had before
I reached the steps.

It was the Pedersen kid. Hans had put the kid on the kitchen table
like you would a ham and started the kettle. He wasn't saying anything.
I guess he figured one yell from the crib was enough noise. Ma was
fumbling with the kid's clothes which were stiff with ice. She made a
sound like "whew" from every outgoing breath. The kettle filled and
Hans said,

"Get some snow and call your pa."

"Why?"

"Get some snow."

I took the big pail from under the sink and the shovel by the stove.
I didn't hurry and nobody said anything. There was a drift over the
edge of the porch and I spaded some out of that. When I brought the
pail in, Hans said,

"There's coal dust in that. Get more."

"A little coal won't hurt."

"Get more."

"Coal's warming."

"It's not enough. Shut your mouth and get your pa."

Ma had rolled out some dough on the table where Hans had dropped the Pedersen kid like a filling. Most of the kid's clothes lay on the floor where they were going to make a puddle. Hans began rubbing snow on the kid's face. Ma stopped undressing him for a moment and simply stood by the table with her hands held away from her as if they were wet, staring first at Big Hans and then at the kid.

"Get."

"Why?"

"I told you."

"It's Pa I mean — "

"I know what you mean. Get."

I found a cardboard box that condensed milk had come in and shoveled it full of snow. It was too small. I figured it would be. I found another with rags and an old sponge I threw out. Campbell's soup. I filled it too, using the rest of the drift. Snow would melt through the bottom of the boxes but that was all right with me. By now the kid was naked. I was satisfied mine was bigger.

"Looks like a sick shoat, don't he?"

"Shut up and get your pa."

"He's asleep."

"Yeah."

"He don't like to get waked."

"I know that. Don't I know that as good as you? Get him."

"What good'll he be?"

"We're going to need his whisky."

"He can fix that all right. He's good for fixing the crack in his face. If it ain't all gone."

The kettle was whistling.

"What are we going to do with these?" Ma said.

"Wait, Hed. Now I want you to get. I'm tired of talking. Get, you hear?"

"What are we going to do with them? They're all wet," she said.

I went to wake the old man. He didn't like being roused. It was too hard and far to come, the sleep he was in. He didn't give a damn about the Pedersen kid, any more than I did. Pedersen's kid was just a kid. He didn't carry any weight. Not like I did. And the old man would be mad, unable to see, coming that way from where he was asleep. I decided I hated Big Hans, though this was hardly something new for me. I hated Big Hans just then because I was thinking of how Pa's eyes would blink at me — as if I were the sun off the snow and burning to blind him.

His eyes were old and they never saw well, but heated with whisky they'd glare at my noise, growing red and raising up his rage. I decided I hated the Pedersen kid too, dying in our kitchen while I was away where I couldn't watch, dying just to entertain Hans and making me go up snapping steps and down a drafty hall, Pa lumped under the covers at the end like dung covered with snow, snoring and whistling. Oh he'd not care about the Pedersen kid. He'd not care about getting waked so he could give up some of his whisky to a slit of a kid and maybe lose one of his hiding places in the bargain. That would make him mad enough if he was sober. I didn't hurry though it was cold and the Pedersen kid was in the kitchen.

He was all shoveled up like I thought he'd be. I pushed at his shoulder, calling his name. I think his name stopped the snoring but he didn't move except to roll a little when I shoved him. The covers slid down his skinny neck so I saw his head, fuzzed like a dandelion gone to seed, but his face was turned to the wall — there was the pale shadow of his nose on the plaster — and I thought, Well you don't look much like a pig-drunk bully now. I couldn't be sure he was still asleep. He was a cagey sonofabitch. I shook him a little harder and made some noise. "Pap-pap-pap-hey," I said.

I was leaning too far over. I knew better. He always slept close to the wall so you had to lean to reach him. Oh he was smart. It put you off. I knew better but I was thinking of the Pedersen kid mother-naked in all that dough. When his arm came up I ducked away but it caught me on the side of the neck, watering my eyes, and I backed off to cough. Pa was on his side, looking at me, his eyes winking, the hand that had hit me a fist in the pillow.

"Get the hell out of here."

I didn't say anything, trying to get my throat clear, but I watched him. He was like a mean horse to come at from the rear. It was better, though, he'd hit me. He was bitter when he missed.

"Get the hell out of here."

"Big Hans sent me. He told me to wake you."

"A fat hell on Big Hans. Get out of here."

"He found the Pedersen kid by the crib."

"Get the hell out."

Pa pulled at the covers. He was tasting his mouth.

"The kid's froze good. Hans is rubbing him with snow. He's got him in the kitchen."

"Pedersen?"

"No, Pa. It's the Pedersen kid. The kid."

"Nothing to steal from the crib."

"Not stealing, Pa. He was just lying there. Hans found him froze. That's where he was when Hans found him."

Pa laughed.

"I ain't hid nothing in the crib."

"You don't understand, Pa. The Pedersen kid. The kid — "

"I god damn well understand."

Pa had his head up, glaring, his teeth gnawing at the place where he'd grown a mustache once.

"I god damn well understand. You know I don't want to see Pedersen. That cock. Why should I? What did he come for, hey? God dammit, get. And don't come back. Find out something. You're a fool. Both you and Hans. Pedersen. That cock. Don't come back. Out. Out."

He was shouting and breathing hard and closing his fist on the pillow. He had long black hairs on his wrist. They curled around the cuff of his nightshirt.

"Big Hans made me come. Big Hans said — "

"A fat hell on Big Hans. He's an even bigger fool than you are. Fat, hey? I taught him, dammit, and I'll teach you. Out. You want me to drop my pot?"

He was about to get up so I got out, slamming the door. He was beginning to see he was too mad to sleep. Then he threw things. Once he went after Hans and dumped his pot over the banister. Pa'd been shit-sick in that pot. Hans got an axe. He didn't even bother to wipe himself off and he chopped part of Pa's door down before he stopped. He might not have gone that far if Pa hadn't been locked in laughing fit to shake the house. That pot put Pa in an awful good humor whenever he thought of it. I always felt the memory was present in both of them, stirring in their chests like a laugh or a growl, as eager as an animal to be out. I heard Pa cursing all the way downstairs.

Hans had laid steaming towels over the kid's chest and stomach. He was rubbing snow on the kid's legs and feet. Water from the snow and water from the towels had run off the kid to the table where the dough was, and the dough was turning pasty, sticking to the kid's back and behind.

"Ain't he going to wake up?"

"What about your pa?"

"He was awake when I left."

"What'd he say? Did you get the whisky?"

"He said a fat hell on Big Hans."

"Don't be smart. Did you ask him about the whisky?"

"Yeah."

"Well?"

"He said a fat hell on Big Hans."

"Don't be smart. What's he going to do?"

"Go back to sleep most likely."

"You'd best get that whisky."

"You go. Take the axe. Pa's scared to hell of axes."

"Listen to me, Jorge, I've had enough to your sassing. This kid's froze bad. If I don't get some whisky down him he might die. You want the kid to die? Do you? Well, get your pa and get that whisky."

"Pa don't care about the kid."

"Jorge."

"Well he don't. He don't care at all, and I don't care to get my head busted neither. He don't care, and I don't care to have his shit flung on me. He don't care about anybody. All he cares about is his whisky and that dry crack in his face. Get pig-drunk — that's what he wants. He don't care about nothing else at all. Nothing. Not Pedersen's kid neither. That cock. Not the kid neither."

"I'll get the spirits," Ma said.

I'd wound Big Hans up tight. I was ready to jump but when Ma said she'd get the whisky it surprised him like it surprised me, and he ran down. Ma never went near the old man when he was sleeping it off. Not any more. Not for years. The first thing every morning when she washed her face she could see the scar on her chin where he'd cut her with a boot cleat, and maybe she saw him heaving it again, the dirty sock popping out as it flew. It should have been nearly as easy for her to remember that as it was for Big Hans to remember going after the axe while he was still spattered with Pa's yellow sick insides.

"No you won't," Big Hans said.

"Yes, Hans, if they're needed," Ma said.

Hans shook his head but neither of us tried to stop her. If we had, then one of us would have had to go instead. Hans rubbed the kid with more snow . . . rubbed . . . rubbed.

"I'll get more snow," I said. I took the pail and shovel and went out on the porch. I don't know where Ma went. I thought she'd gone upstairs and expected to hear she had. She had surprised Hans like she had surprised me when she said she'd go, and then she surprised him again when she came back so quick like she must have, because when I came in with the snow she was there with a bottle with three white feathers on its label and Hans was holding it angrily by the throat.

Oh, he was being queer and careful, pawing about in the drawer and holding the bottle like a snake at the length of his arm. He was awful angry because he'd thought Ma was going to do something big, something heroic even, especially for her . . . I know him . . . I know him . . . we felt the same sometimes . . . while Ma wasn't thinking about that at all, not anything like that. There was no way of getting even. It wasn't like getting cheated at the fair. They were always trying so you got to expect it. Now Hans had given Ma something of his — we both had when we thought she was going straight to Pa — something valuable; but since she didn't know we'd given it to her, there was no easy way of getting it back.

Hans cut the foil off finally and unscrewed the cap. He was put out too because there was only one way of understanding what she'd done. Ma had found one of Pa's hiding places. She'd found one and she hadn't said a word while Big Hans and I had hunted and hunted as we always did all winter, every winter since the spring that Hans had come and I had looked in the privy and found the first one. Pa had a knack for hiding. He knew we were looking and he enjoyed it. But now Ma. She'd found it by luck most likely but she hadn't said anything and we didn't know how long ago it'd been or how many other ones she'd found, saying nothing. Pa was sure to find out. Sometimes he didn't seem to because he hid them so well he couldn't find them himself or because he looked and didn't find anything and figured he hadn't hid one after all or had drunk it up. But he'd find out about this one because we were using it. A fool could see what was going on. If he found out Ma found it — that'd be bad. He took pride in his hiding. It was all the pride he had. I guess fooling Hans and me took doing. But he didn't figure Ma for much. He didn't figure her at all, and if he found out . . . a woman . . . it'd be bad.

Hans poured some in a tumbler.

"You going to put more towels on him?"

"No."

"Why not? That's what he needs, something warm to his skin, don't he?"

"Not where he's froze good. Heat's bad for frostbite. That's why I only put towels on his chest and belly. He's got to thaw slow. You ought to know that."

Colors on the towels had run.

Ma poked her toe in the kid's clothes.

"What are we going to do with these?"

Big Hans began pouring whisky in the kid's mouth but his mouth filled without any getting down his throat and in a second it was dripping from his chin.

"Here, help me prop him up. I got to hold his mouth open."

I didn't want to touch him and I hoped Ma would do it but she kept looking at the kid's clothes piled on the floor and the pool of water by them and didn't make any move to.

"Come on, Jorge."

"All right."

"Lift, don't shove . . . lift."

"O.K., I'm lifting."

I took him by the shoulders. His head flopped back. His mouth fell open. The skin on his neck was tight. He was cold all right.

"Hold his head up. He'll choke."

"His mouth is open."

"His throat's shut. He'll choke."

"He'll choke anyway."

"Hold his head up."

"I can't."

"Don't hold him like that. Put your arms around him."

"Well Jesus."

He was cold all right. I put my arm carefully around him. Hans had his fingers in the kid's mouth.

"Now he'll choke for sure."

"Shut up. Just hold him like I told you."

He was cold all right, and wet. I had my arm behind his back. He sure felt dead.

"Tilt his head back a bit . . . not too much."

He felt cold and slimy. He sure was dead. We had a dead body in our kitchen. All this time he'd been dead. When Hans had brought him in, he'd been dead. I couldn't see him breathing. He was awful skinny, sunk between the ribs. We were getting him ready to bake. Hans was basting him. I had my arm around him, holding him up. He was dead and I had hold of him. I could feel my muscles jumping.

"Well Jesus Christ."

"He's dead, Hans. He's dead."

"You dropped him."

"Dead?" Ma said.

"He's dead. I could feel. He's dead."

"Dead?"

"Ain't you got any sense? You let his head hit the table."

"Is he dead? Is he dead?" Ma said.

"Well Christ no, not yet, not yet he's not dead. Look what you done, Jorge, there's whisky all over."

"He *is* dead. He *is*."

"No he ain't. Not yet he ain't. Now stop yelling and hold him up."

"He ain't breathing."

"Yes he is, he *is* breathing. Hold him up."

"I ain't. I ain't holding any dead body. You can hold it if you want. You dribble whisky on it all you want. You can do anything you want to. I ain't. I ain't holding any dead body."

"If he's dead," Ma said, "what are we going to do with these?"

"Jorge, god damn you, come back here."

I went down to the crib where Big Hans had found him. There was still a hollow in the snow and some prints the wind hadn't sifted snow over. The kid must have been out on his feet, they wobbled so. I could see where he had walked smack into a drift and then backed off and lurched up beside the crib, maybe bumping into it before he fell, then lying quiet so the snow had time to curl around him, piling up until in no time it would have covered him completely. Who knows, I thought, the way it's been snowing, we mightn't have found him till spring. Even if he was dead in our kitchen, I was glad Big Hans had found him. I could see myself coming out of the house some morning with the sun high up and strong and the eaves dripping, the snow speckled with drops and the ice on the creek slushing up; coming out and walking down by the crib on the crusts of the drift . . . coming out to play my game with the drifts . . . and I could see myself losing, breaking through the big drift that was always sleeping up against the crib and running a foot right into him, right into the Pedersen kid curled up, getting soft.

That would have been worse than holding his body in the kitchen. The feeling would have come on quicker, and it would have been worse, happening in the middle of a game. There wouldn't have been any warning, any way of getting ready for it to happen, to know what I'd struck before I bent down, even though Old Man Pedersen would have come over between snows looking for the kid most likely and everybody would have figured that the kid was lying buried somewhere under the snow; that maybe after a high wind someday somebody would find him lying like a black stone uncovered in a field; but probably in the spring somebody would find him in some back pasture thawing out with the mud and have to bring him in and take him over to the Pedersen place and present him to Missus Pedersen. Even so: even with everyone knowing that, and hoping one of the Pedersens would find him first so they wouldn't have to pry him up out of the mud to fetch him out from a thicket and bring him in and give him to Missus Pedersen in soggy season-old clothes; even then, who would expect to stick a foot all of a sudden through the crust losing at the drift game and step on Pedersen's kid lying all crouched together right beside your own crib? It was a good thing Hans had come down this morning and found him, even if he was dead in our kitchen and I had held him up.

When Pedersen came over asking for his kid, maybe hoping that the kid had got to our place all right and stayed, waiting for the blizzard to quit before going home, Pa would meet him and bring him for a drink and tell him it was his fault for putting up all those snow fences. If I knew Pa, he'd tell Pedersen to look under the drifts his snow fences had made, and Pedersen would get so mad he'd go for Pa and stomp out calling for the vengeance of God like he was fond of doing. Now though, since Big Hans had found him, and he was dead in our kitchen, Pa might not say much when Pedersen came. He might just offer Pedersen a drink and keep his mouth shut about those snow fences. Pedersen might come yet this morning. That would be best because Pa would be still asleep. If Pa was asleep when Pedersen came he wouldn't have a chance to talk about those snow fences, or offer Pedersen a drink. Pedersen wouldn't have to refuse the drink then and could take his kid and go home. I hoped Pedersen would certainly come soon. I hoped he would come and take that cold damp body out of our kitchen. The way I felt I didn't think that today I'd be able to eat. I knew every time I'd see the Pedersen kid in the kitchen being fixed for the table.

The wind had dropped. The sun lay burning on the snow. I got cold just the same. I didn't want to go in but I could feel the cold crawling over me like it must have crawled over him while he was coming. It had slipped over him like a sheet, icy at first, especially around the feet, and he'd likely wiggled his toes in his boots and wanted to wrap his legs around each other like you do when you first come to bed. But then things would begin to warm up some, the sheet feeling warmer all the time until it felt real cozy and you went to sleep. Only when the kid went to sleep by our crib it wasn't like going to sleep in bed because the sheet never really got warm and he never really got warm either. Now he was just as cold in our kitchen with the kettle whistling and Ma getting ready to bake as I was out by the crib jigging my feet in our snow. I had to go in. I looked but I couldn't see anyone trying to come down where the road was. All I could see was a set of half-filled prints jiggling crazily away into the snow until they sank under a drift. There wasn't anything around. There wasn't anything: a tree or a stick or a rock whipped bare or a bush hugged by snow sticking up to mark the place where those prints came up out of the drift like somebody had come up from underground.

I decided to go around by the front though I wasn't allowed to track through the front room. I went back, thinking of where the kid lay on the kitchen table in all that dough, pasty with whisky and water, like spring had come all at once to our kitchen, and our all the time not knowing he was there, had thawed the top of his grave off and left him for us to find, stretched out cold and stiff and bare; and who was it that was going to have to take him to the Pedersen place and give him to Missus Pederson, naked, and flour on his bare behind?

## II

"Just his back. The green mackinaw. The black stocking cap. The yellow gloves. The gun."

Big Hans kept repeating it. He was letting the meaning have a chance to change. He'd look at me and shake his head and say it over.

"He put them down the cellar so I ran."

Hans filled the tumbler. It was spotted with whisky and flecks of flour.

"He didn't say nothing the whole time," Hans said.

He put the bottle on the table and the bottom sank unevenly in the paste, tilting heavily and queerly to one side — acting crazy, like everything else.

"That's all he says he saw," Hans said, staring at the mark of the kid's behind in the dough. "Just his back. The green mackinaw. The black stocking cap. The yellow gloves. The gun."

"That's all?"

He waited and waited.

"That's all."

He tossed the whisky off and peered at the bottom of the glass.

"Now why should he remember all them colors?"

He leaned over, his legs apart, his elbows on his knees, and held the glass between them with both hands, tilting it to watch the liquor that was left roll back and forth across the bottom.

"How does he know? I mean, for sure."

"He thinks he knows," Hans said in a tired voice. "He thinks he knows."

He picked up the bottle and a hunk of dough was stuck to it.

"Christ. That's all. It's how he feels. It's enough, ain't it?" Hans said.

"What a mess," Ma said.

"He was raving," Hans said. "He couldn't think of anything else. He had to talk. He had to get it out. You should have heard him grunt."

"Poor poor Stevie," Ma said.

"He was raving?"

"All right, is it something you dream?" Hans said.

"He must have been dreaming. Look — how could he have got there. Where'd he come from? Fall from the sky?"

"He came through the storm."

"That's just it, Hans, he'd have had to. It was blizzarding all day. It didn't let up, did it? till late afternoon. He'd have had to. Now what chance is there of that? What?"

"Enough a chance it happened," Hans said.

"But listen. Jesus. He's a stranger. If he's a stranger he's come a ways. He'd never make it in a blizzard, not even knowing the country."

"He came through the storm. He came out of the ground like a grub. He came."

Hans poured himself a drink, not me.

"He came through the storm," he said. "He came through just like the kid came through. The kid had no chance neither, but he came. He's here, ain't he? He's right upstairs, right now. You got to believe that."

"It wasn't blizzarding when the kid came."

"It was starting."

"That ain't the same."

"All right. The kid had forty-five minutes, maybe an hour before it started to come on good. That isn't enough. You need the whole time, not a start. In a blizzard you got to be where you're going if you're going to get there."

"That's what I mean. See, Hans? See? The kid had a chance. He knew the way. He had a head start. Besides, he was scared. He ain't going to be lazying. And he's lucky. He had a chance to be lucky. Now yellow gloves ain't got that chance. He has to come farther. He has to come through the storm all the way. But he don't know the way, and he ain't scared proper, except maybe by the storm. He hasn't got a chance to be lucky."

"The kid was scared, you said. Right. Now why? You tell me that."

Hans kept his eyes on the whisky that was shining in his glass. He didn't want to give in. He was holding on hard.

"And yellow — he ain't scared?" he said. "How do you know he ain't scared, by something else besides wind and snow and cold and howling, I mean?"

"All right, I don't know, but it's likely ain't it? Anyway, the kid, well, maybe he ain't scared at all, starting out. Maybe his pa was just looking to tan him and he lit out. Then first thing he knows it's blizzarding again and he's lost, and when he gets to our crib he don't know where he is."

Hans slowly shook his head.

"Yes yes, hell Hans, the kid's scared of having run away. He don't want to say he done a fool stunt like that. So he makes the whole thing up. He's just a little kid. He made the whole thing up."

Hans didn't like that. He didn't want to believe the kid any more than I did, but if he didn't then the kid had fooled him sure. He didn't want to believe that either.

"No," he said. "Is it something you make up? It is something you come to, raving with frostbite and fever and not knowing who's there or where you are or anything, and make up?"

"Yeah."

"No it ain't. You don't make up them colors neither. You don't make up putting your folks down cellar where they'll freeze. You don't make up his not saying anything the whole time or only seeing his back or exactly what he was wearing. It's like something you see once and it hits you so hard you never forget it even if you want to; like something that sticks to you like burs you try and brush off while you're doing something else, but they never brush off, just roll a little, and first thing you know you ain't doing what you set out to, you're just trying to get them burs off. I know. I got things stuck to me like that. Everybody has. Pretty soon you get tired trying to pick them off. If they was just burs, it wouldn't matter, but they ain't. They never is. The kid saw something that hit him hard like that; hit him so hard that probably all the time he was running over here he didn't see anything else but what hit him. Not really. It hit him so hard he couldn't do anything but spit it out raving when he come to. You don't make things like that up, Jorge. No. He came through the storm, just like the kid. He had no business coming, but he came. I don't know how or why or when exactly, except it must have been during the blizzard yesterday. He got to the Pedersen place just before or just after it stopped snowing. He got there and he shoved them all in the fruit cellar to freeze and I'll bet he had his reasons."

"You got dough stuck to the bottom of your bottle."

I couldn't think of anything else to say. It sounded right. It sounded right but it couldn't be right. It just couldn't be. Whatever was right, the Pedersen kid had run off from his pa's place probably late yesterday afternoon when the storm let up, and had turned up at our crib this morning. I knew he was here. I knew that much. I'd held him. I'd felt him dead in my hands, only I guess he wasn't dead now. Hans had put him to bed upstairs but I could still see him in the kitchen, so skinny naked, two towels steaming on him, whisky drooling from the corners of his mouth, lines of dirt between his toes, squeezing Ma's dough in the shape of his behind.

I reached for the bottle. Hans held it away.

"He didn't see him do it though," I said.

Hans shrugged.

"Then he ain't sure."

"He's sure, I told you. Do you run out in a blizzard unless you're sure?"

"It wasn't blizzarding."

"It was starting."

"I don't run out in blizzards."

"Crap."

Hans pointed the doughy end of the bottle at me.

"Crap."

He shook it.

"You come in from the barn — like this morning. As far as you know there ain't a gun in yellow gloves in a thousand miles. You come in from the barn not thinking anything special. You just get inside when you see a guy you never saw before, the guy that wasn't in a thousand miles, that wasn't in your mind even, he was so far away, and he's wearing them yellow gloves and that green mackinaw, and he's got me and your ma and pa lined up with our hands back of our necks like this — "

Hans hung the bottle and the glass behind his head.

" — he's got a rifle in between them yellow gloves and he's waving the point of it up and down in front of your ma's face real slow and quiet."

Hans got up and waved the bottle violently in Ma's face. She shivered and shooed it away. Hans stopped to come to me. He stood over me, his black eyes buttons on his big face, and I tried to look like I wasn't hunching down any in my chair.

"What do you do?" Hans roared. "You drop a little kid's head on the table."

"Like hell — "

Hans had the bottle in front of him again, smack in my face.

"Hans Esbyorn," Ma said, "don't pester the boy."

"Like hell — "

"Jorge."

"I wouldn't run, Ma."

Ma sighed. "I don't know. But don't yell."

"Well Christ almighty, Ma."

"Don't swear neither. Please. You been swearing too much — you and Hans both."

"But I wouldn't run."

"Yes, Jorgie, yes. I'm sure you wouldn't run," she said.

Hans went back and sat down and finished his drink and poured another. He could relax now he'd got me all strung up. He was a fancy bastard.

"You'd run all right," he said, running his tongue across his lips. "Maybe you'd be right to run. Maybe anybody would. With no gun, with nothing to stop him."

"Poor child. Whewee. And what are we going to do with these?"

"Hang them up, Hed, for Christ's sake."

"Where?"

"Well, where do you mostly?"

"Oh no," she said, "I wouldn't feel right doing that."

"Then Jesus, Hed, I don't know. Jesus."

"Please Hans, please. Those words are hard for me to bear."

She stared at the ceiling.

"Dear. The kitchen's such a mess. I can't bear to see it. And the baking's not done."

That's all she could think of. That's all she had to say. She didn't care about me. I didn't count. Not like her kitchen. I wouldn't have run.

"Stick the baking," I said.

"Shut your face."

He could look as mean as he liked, I didn't care. What was his meanness to me? A blister on my heel, another discomfort, a cold bed. Yet when he took his eyes off me to drink, I felt better. I was going to twist his balls.

"All right," I said. "All right. All right."

He was lost in his glass, thinking it out.

"They're awful cold in that cellar," I said.

There was a little liquor burning in the bottom. I was going to twist his balls like the neck of a sack.

"What are you going to do about it?"

He was putting his mean look back but it lacked enthusiasm. He was seeing things in his glass.

"I saved the kid, didn't I?" he finally said.

"Maybe you did."

"You didn't."

"No. I didn't."

"It's time you did something then, ain't it?"

"Why should I? I don't think they're freezing. You're the one who thinks that. You're the one who thinks he ran for help. You're the one. You saved him. All right. You didn't let his head hit the table. I did that. You didn't. No. It was you who rubbed him. All right. You saved him. That wasn't the kid's idea though. He came for help. According to you, that is. He didn't come to be saved. You saved him, but what are you going to do now to help him? You've been feeling mighty, ain't you? thinking how you did it. Still feel like a savior, Hans? How's it feel?"

"You little bastard."

"All right. Little or big. Never mind. You did it all. You found him. You raised the rumpus, ordering everybody around. He was as good as dead. I held him and I felt him. Maybe in your way he was alive, but it was a way that don't count. No, but you couldn't leave him alone. Rubbing. Well, I felt him . . . cold . . . God! Ain't you proud? He was dead, right here, dead. And there weren't no yellow gloves. Now, though, there is. That's what comes of rubbing. Rubbing . . . ain't you proud? You can't believe the kid was lying good enough to fool you. So he was dead. But now he ain't. Not for you. He ain't for you."

"He's alive for you too. You're crazy. He's alive for everybody."

"No he ain't. He ain't alive for me. He never was. I never seen him except he was dead. Cold . . . I felt him . . . God! He's in your bed. All right. You took him up there. It's your bed he's in, Hans. It was you he babbled to. You believe him too, so he's alive for you, then. Not for me. Not for me he ain't."

"You can't say that."

"I am saying it though. Rubbing . . . You didn't know what you was bringing to, did you? Something besides the kid came through the storm, Hans. I ain't saying yellow gloves did neither. He didn't. He couldn't. But something else did. While you was rubbing you didn't think of that."

"You little bastard."

"Hans, Hans, please," Ma said.

"Never mind that. Little or big, like I said. I'm asking what you're going to do. You believe it. You made it. What are you going to do about it? It'd be funny if right now while we're sitting here the kid's dying upstairs."

"Jorge," Ma said, "what an awful thing — in Hans's bed."

"All right. But suppose. Suppose you didn't rub enough — not long and hard enough, Hans. And suppose he dies up there in your bed. He might. He was cold, I know. That'd be funny because that yellow gloves — he won't die. It ain't going to be so easy, killing him."

Hans didn't move or say anything.

"I ain't no judge. I ain't no hand at saving, like you said. It don't make no difference to me. But why'd you start rubbing if you was going to stop? Seems like it'd be terrible if the Pedersen kid was to have come all that way through the storm, scared and freezing, and you was to have done all that rubbing and saving so he could come to and tell you his fancy tale and have you believe it, if you ain't going to do nothing now but sit and hold hands with that bottle. That ain't a bur so easy picked off."

Still he didn't say anything.

"Fruit cellars get mighty cold. Of course they ain't supposed to freeze."

I leaned back easy in my chair. Hans just sat.

The top of the kitchen table looked muddy where it showed. Patches of dough and pools of water were scattered all over it. There were rusty streaks through the paste and the towels had run. Everywhere there were little sandy puddles of whisky and water. Something, it looked like whisky, dripped slowly to the floor and with the water trickled to the puddle by the pile of clothes. The boxes sagged. There were thick black tracks around the table and the stove. I thought it was funny the boxes had gone so fast. The bottle and the glass were posts around which Big Hans had his hands.

Ma began picking up the kid's clothes. She picked them up one at a time, delicately, by their ends and corners, lifting a sleeve like you would the flat, burned, crooked leg of a frog dead of summer to toss it from the road. They didn't seem human things, the way her hands pinched together on them, but animal — dead and rotting things out of the ground. She took them away and when she came back I wanted to tell her to bury them — to hide them somehow quick under the snow — but she scared me, the way she came with her arms out, trembling, fingers coming open and closed, moving like a combine between rows.

I heard the dripping clearly, and Hans swallow. I heard the water and the whisky fall. I heard the frost on the window melt to the sill and drop into the sink. Hans poured whisky in his glass. I looked past Hans and Pa was watching from the doorway. His nose and eyes were red, his feet in red slipppers.

"What's this about the Pedersen kid?" he said.

Ma stood behind him with a mop.

## III

"Ever think of a horse?" Pa said.

"A horse? Where'd he get a horse?"

"Anywhere — on the way — anyplace."

"Could he make it on a horse?"

"He made it on something."

"Not on a horse, though."

"Not on his feet."

"I ain't saying he made it on anything."

"Horses can't get lost."

"Yes they can."

"They got a sense."

"That's a lot of manure about horses."

"In a blizzard a horse'll go home."

"That's so."

"You let them go and they go home."

"That's so."

"If you steal a horse, and let him go, he'll take you to the barn you stole him from."

"Couldn't give him his head then."

"Must have really rode him then."

"If he had a horse."

"Yeah, if he had a horse."

"If he hooked a horse before the storm and rode it a ways, then when the snow came, the horse would be too far off and wouldn't know how to head for home."

"They got an awful good sense."

"Manure."

"What difference does it make? He made it. What difference does it make how?" Hans said.

"I'm considering if he could have," Pa said.

"And I'm telling you he did," Hans said.

"And I've been telling you he didn't. The kid made the whole thing up," I said.

"The horse'd stop. He'd put his head into the wind and stop."

"I've seen them put their rears in."

"They always put their heads in."

"He could jockey him."

"If he was gentle and not too scared."

"A plower is gentle."

"Some are."

"Some don't like to be rid."

"Some don't like strangers neither."

"What the hell," Hans said.

Pa laughed. "I'm just considering," he said. "Just considering, Hans, that's all."

Pa'd seen the bottle right away. He'd been blinking but he hadn't missed that. He'd seen it and the glass in Hans's hand. I'd expected him to say something. So had Hans. He'd held on to the glass long enough so no one would get the idea he was afraid to, then he'd set it down casual, like he hadn't any reason to hold it or any reason to put it down, but was putting it down anyway, without thinking. I'd grinned but he hadn't seen me, or else he made out he hadn't. Pa'd kept his mouth shut about the bottle. I guess we had the Pedersen kid to thank for that, though we had him to thank for the bottle too.

"It's his own fault for putting out all them snow fences," Pa said. "You think, being here the time he has, he'd know the forces better."

"Pedersen just likes to be ready, Pa, that's all."

"Hell he does. He likes to *get* ready, that cock. Get, get, get, get. He's always getting ready, but he ain't never got ready. Not yet, he ain't. Last summer, instead of minding his crops, he got ready for hoppers. Christ. Who wants hoppers? Well, that's the way to get hoppers — that's the sure way — get ready for hoppers."

"Bull."

"Bull? You say bull, Hans, hey?"

"I say bull, yeah."

"You're one to get ready, ain't you? Like Pedersen, ain't you? Oh what a wrinkled scrotum you got, with all that thinking. You'd put out poison for a million, hey? You know what you'd get? Two million. Wise, oh the wise men, yeah. Pedersen asked for hoppers. He begged for hoppers. He went on his knees for hoppers. And he got hoppers. That just exactly how you get hoppers. So me? I got hoppers too. Now he's gone and asked for snow, gone on his knees for snow, wrung his fingers for snow. Is he ready, tell me? Hey? Snow? For real snow? Anybody ever ready for real snow? Oh Jesus, that fool. he should have kept his kid behind them fences. What business . . . what . . . what business . . . to send him here. Look — " Pa pointed out the window. "See . . . see . . . what did I tell you . . . snowing . . . always snowing . . ."

"You seen a winter it didn't snow?"

"You were ready, I guess."

"It always snows."

"You were ready for the Pedersen kid, too, I guess. You was just out there waiting for him, cooling your cod."

Pa laughed and Hans got red.

"Pedersen's a fool. Wise men can't be taught. Oh no, not old holy Pete. He never learned all the things that can fall out the sky and happen to wheat. His neck's bent all the time too, studying clouds, hah — that shit. He don't even keep an eye on his kid in a blizzard. But you'll keep an eye out for him, hey Hans? You're a bigger fool because you're fatter."

Hans's face was red and swollen like the skin around a splinter. He reached out and picked up the glass. Pa was sitting on a corner of the kitchen table, swinging a leg. The glass was near his knee. Hans reached by Pa and took it. Pa watched and swung his leg, laughing. The bottle was on the counter and Pa watched closely while Hans took it.

"Ah, you plan to drink some of my whisky, Hans?"

"Yeah."

"It'd be polite to ask."

"I ain't asking," Hans said, tilting the bottle.

"I suppose I'd better make some biscuits," Ma said.

Hans looked up at her, keeping the bottle tilted. He didn't pour.

"Biscuits, Ma?" I said.

"I ought to have something for Mr. Pedersen and I haven't a thing."

Hans straightened the bottle.

"There's a thing to consider," he said, beginning to smile. "Why ain't Pedersen here looking for his kid?"

"Why should he be?"

Hans winked at me through his glass.

"Why not? We're nearest. If the kid ain't here he can ask us to help him hunt."

"Fat chance."

"He ain't come though. How do you consider that?"

"I ain't considering it," Pa said.

"Why ain't you? Seems to me like something worth real fancy considering."

"No it ain't."

"Ain't it?"

"Pedersen's a fool."

"So you like to say. I've heard you often enough. All right, maybe he is. How long do you expect he'll wander around looking before he comes over this way?"

"A long time. A long time maybe."

"The kid's been gone a long time."

Pa arranged his nightshirt over his knee. He had on the striped one.

"Oh Pedersen'll be here before too long now," he said.

"And if he don't?"

"What do you mean, if he don't? Then he don't. It ain't no skin off my ass. I don't care what he does."

"Yeah," Big Hans said. "Yeah."

Pa folded his arms, looking like a judge. He swung his leg.

"Where'd you find the bottle?"

Hans jiggled it.

"You're pretty good at hiding, ain't you?"

"I'm asking the questions. Where'd you find it?"

Hans was enjoying himself too much.

"I didn't."

"Jorge, hey." Pa chewed his lip. "So you're the nosy bastard."

He didn't look at me and it didn't seem like he was talking to me at all. He said it like I wasn't there and he was thinking out loud.

"It wasn't me, Pa," I said.

I didn't want him to think I'd found it — not then anyway — but I didn't want him to know Ma had either. I tried to get Hans's attention so he'd shut up but he was enjoying himself.

"Little Hans ain't no fool," Big Hans said.

"No." Pa wasn't paying attention. "He ain't no kin to you."

"Why ain't he here then? He'd be looking too. Why ain't he here?"

"Gracious, I'd forgot all about Little Hans," Ma said, quickly taking a bowl from the cupboard.

"Hed, what are you up to?" Pa said.

"Oh, biscuits."

"Biscuits? What in hell for? Biscuits. I don't want any biscuits. Make some coffee. All this time you been just standing around."

"For Pedersen and Little Hans. They'll be coming and they'll want some bisuits and coffee, and I'll put out some elderberry jelly. The coffee needed reminding, Magnus, thank you."

"Who found the bottle?"

She scooped some flour from the bin.

Pa'd been sitting, swinging. Now he stopped and stood up.

"Who found it? Who found it? God dammit, who found it? Which one of them was it?"

Ma was trying to measure the flour but her hands shook. The flour ran off the scoop and fell across the rim of the cup, and I thought, Yeah, you'd have run, yeah, your hands shake.

"Why don't you ask Jorge?" Big Hans said.

How I hated him, putting it on me, the coward. And he had thick arms.

"That snivel," Pa said.

Hans laughed heartily.

"He couldn't find nothing I hid."

"You're right there," Hans said.

"I could," I said. "I have."

"A liar, Hans, hey? You found it."

Pa was somehow pleased and sat on the corner of the table again. Was it Hans he hated most, or me?

"I never said Jorge found it."

"I've got a liar working for me. A thief and a liar. Why should I keep a liar? I'm just soft on him, I guess, and he's got such a sweet face. But why should I keep a thief . . . little movey eyes like traveling specks . . . why?"

"I ain't like you. I don't spend every day drinking just to sleep the night and then sleeping half the day too, fouling your bed and your room and half the house."

"You been doing your share of lying down. Little Hans is half your size and worth twice."

Pa's words didn't come out clear.

"How about Little Hans? Little Hans ain't showed up. Folks must be getting pretty worried at the Pedersens'. They'd like some news maybe. But Pedersen don't come. Little Hans don't come. There's a thousand drifts out there. The kid might be under any one. If anybody's seen him, we have, and if we haven't, nobody's going to till spring, or maybe if the wind shifts, which ain't likely. But nobody comes to ask. That's pretty funny, I'd say."

"You're an awful full-up bastard," Pa said.

"I'm just considering, that's all."

"Where'd you find it?"

"I forgot. I was going to have a drink."

"Where?"

"You're pretty good at hiding," Hans said.

"I'm asking. Where?"

"I didn't, I told you, I didn't find it. Jorge didn't find it neither."

"You bastard, Hans," I said.

"It hatched," Hans said. "Like the fellow, you know, who blew in. He hatched. Or maybe the kid found it — had it hid under his coat."

"Who?" Pa roared, standing up quick.

"Oh Hed found it. You don't hide worth a damn and Hed found it easy. She knew right away where to look."

"Shut up, Hans," I said.

Hans tilted the bottle.

"She must have known where it was a long time now. Maybe she knows where they're all hid. You ain't very smart. Or maybe she's took it up herself, eh? And it ain't yours at all, maybe that."

Big Hans poured himself a drink. Then Pa kicked the glass out of Hans's hand. Pa's slipper flew off and sailed by Hans's head and bounced off the wall. The glass didn't break. It fell by the sink and rolled slow by Ma's feet, leaving a thin line. The scoop flew a light white cloud. There was whisky on Hans's shirt and on the wall and cupboards, and a splash on the floor where the glass had hit.

Ma had her arms wrapped around her chest. She looked faint and she was whewing and moaning.

"OK," Pa said, "we'll go. We'll go right now, Hans. I hope to God you get a bullet in your belly. Jorge, go upstairs and see if the little sonofabitch is still alive."

Hans was rubbing the spots on his shirt and licking his lips when I hunched past Pa and went out.


## PART TWO

There wasn't any wind. The harness creaked, the wood creaked, the runners made a sound like a saw working easy, and everything was white about Horse Simon's feet. Pa had the reins between his knees and he and Hans and I kept ourselves close together. We bent our heads and clenched our feet and wished we could huddle both hands in one pocket. Only Hans was breathing through his nose. We didn't speak. I wished my lips could warm my teeth. The blanket we had wasn't worth a damn. It was just as cold underneath and Pa drank from a bottle by him on the seat.

I tried to keep the feeling I'd had starting out, when we'd hitched up Horse Simon when I was warm and decided to risk the north corn road to the Pedersen place. It cut across and came up near the grove behind his barn. We figured we could look at things from there. I tried to keep the feeling but it was a warm feeling, like I was setting out to do something special and big, worth remembering. I thought about coming in from the barn and finding his back to me in the kitchen and wrestling with him and pulling him down and beating the stocking cap off his head with the barrel of the gun. I though about coming in from the barn still blinking with the light and seeing him there and picking the shovel up and taking him on. That had been at the beginning, when I was warm and felt like doing something big, something special and heroic even. I couldn't put the feeling down in Pedersen's back yard or Pedersen's porch or barn. I couldn't see myself, or him, there. I could only see him back where I wasn't any more — standing quiet in our kitchen with his gun going slowly up and down in Ma's face and Ma shooing it away and at the same time trying not to move an inch for getting shot.

When I got good and cold the feeling slipped away. I couldn't imagine him with his gun or yellow gloves. I couldn't imagine me coming on to him. We weren't anyplace and I didn't care. Pa drove by staring down the sloping white road and drank from his bottle. Hans rattled his heels on the back of the seat. I just tried to keep my mouth shut and breathe and not think why in the name of the good Jesus Christ I had to.

It wasn't like a sleigh ride on an early winter evening when the air is still, the earth is warm, and the stars are flakes being born that will

not fall. The air was still all right, the sun straight up and cold.
Behind us on the trough that marked the road I saw our runners and
the holes that Simon tore. Ahead of us it melted into drifts. Pa
squinted like he saw where he knew it really went. Horse Simon steamed.
Ice hung from his harness. Snow caked his belly. I was afraid the
crust might cut his knees. I wanted a drink out of Pa's bottle. Big
Hans seemed asleep and shivered in his dreams. My rear was God
almighty sore.

We reached a drift across the road and Pa eased Simon round
her where he knew there wasn't any fence. Pa figured to go back
to the road but after we got round the bank I could see there wasn't
any point in that. There were rows of high drifts across it.

"They ain't got no reason to do that," Pa said.

It was the first thing Pa'd said since he told me to go upstairs
and see if the Pedersen kid was still alive. He hadn't looked alive
to me but I'd said I guessed he was. Pa'd gone and got his gun first,
without dressing, one foot still bare so he favored it, and took the gun
upstairs cradled in his arm, broke, and pointing down. He had a
dark speckled spot on the rump of his nightshirt where he'd sat on
the table. Hans had his shotgun and the forty-five he'd stolen from the
Navy. He made me load it and when I'd stuck it in my belt he'd said
it'd likely go off and keep me from ever getting out to stud. The gun
felt like a chunk of ice against my belly and the barrel dug.

Ma'd put some sandwiches and a thermos of coffee in a sack. The
coffee'd be cold. My hands would be cold when I ate mine even if I kept
my gloves on. Chewing would be painful. The lip of the thermos would
be cold if I drank out of that, and I'd spill some on my chin to dry to ice;
or if I used the cup, the tin would stick to my lip like rotten liquor you
didn't want to taste by licking off, and it would burn and then tear my
skin coming away.

Simon went into a hole. He couldn't pull out so he panicked and
the sleigh skidded. We'd had crust but now the front right runner
broke through and we braked in the soft snow underneath. Pa made
quiet impatient noises and calmed Simon down.

"That was damn fool," Hans said.

"He lost his footing. Jesus, I ain't the horse."

"I don't know. Simon's a turd binder," Hans said.

Pa took a careful drink.

"Go round and lead him out," he said.

"Jorge is on the outside."

"Go round and lead him out."

"You. You go round. You led him in."

"Go round and lead him out."

Sometimes the snow seemed as blue as the sky. I don't know which seemed colder.

"Oh God, I'll go," I said. "I'm on the outside."

"You practicing to be a bird?" Hans said.

"Your old man's on the outside," Hans said.

"I guess I know where I am," Pa said. "I guess I know where I'm staying."

"Can't you let up, for Christ's sake? I'm going," I said.

I threw off the blanket and stood up but I was awful stiff. The snow dazzle struck me and the pain of the space around us. Getting out I rammed my ankle against the sideboard's iron brace. The pain shot up my leg and shook me like an axe handle will when you strike wrong. I cursed, taking my time jumping off. The snow looked as stiff and hard as cement and I could only think of the jar.

"You've known where that brace was for ten years," Pa said.

The snow went to my crotch. The gun bit. I waded round the hole trying to keep on tiptoe and the snow away from my crotch but it wasn't any use.

I got hold of Horse Simon and tried to coax him out. Pa swore at me from his seat. Simon kicked and thrashed and lunged ahead. The front right runner dug in. The sleigh swung around on it and the left side hit Simon's back legs hard behind the knees. Simon reared and kicked a piece out of the side of the sleigh and then pulled straight ahead tangling the reins. The sleigh swung back again and the right runner pulled loose with a jerk. Pa's bottle rolled. From where I sat in the snow I saw him grab for it. Simon went on ahead. The sleigh slid sideways into Simon's hole and the left runner went clear of the snow. Simon pulled up short though Pa had lost the reins and was holding on and yelling about his bottle. I had snow in my eyes and down my neck.

"Simon didn't have no call to do that," Hans said, mimicking Pa.

"Where's my bottle?" Pa said, looking over the side of the sleigh at the torn snow. "Jorge, go find my bottle. It fell in the snow here somewheres."

I tried to brush the snow off without getting more in my pockets and up my sleeves and down my neck.

"You get out and find it. It's your bottle."

Pa leaned way over.

"If you hadn't been so god damn dumb it wouldn't have fell out. Where'd you learn to lead a horse? You never learned that dumb trick from me. Of all the god damn dumb tricks I never seen any dumber."

Pa waved his arm in a circle.

"That bottle fell out about here. It couldn't have got far. It was corked, thank God. I won't lose none."

Snow was slipping down the hollow of my back. The forty-five had slipped through my belt. I was afraid it would go off like Big Hans said. I kept my right forearm pressed against it. I didn't want it slipping off down my pants. Pa shouted directions.

"You hid it," I said. "You're such a hand at hiding. You find it then. I ain't good at finding. You said so yourself."

"Jorge, you know I got to have that bottle."

"Then get off your ass and find it."

"You know I got to have it."

"Then get off."

"If I get down off here, it ain't the bottle I'm coming after. I'll hold you under till you drown, you little smart-talking snot."

I started kicking around in the snow.

Hans giggled.

"There's a trace broke," he said.

"What's so damn funny?"

"I told you that trace was worn."

I kicked about. Pa followed my feet.

"Hell. Not that way." He pointed. "You know about everything there is, Hans, I guess," he said, still watching me. "First little thing you figure out you tell somebody about. Then somebody else knows. So then they can do what needs to be done and you don't have to . . . Jesus, not there, there . . . don't it, Hans? Don't it always let you out? You ain't going deep enough. I never figured that out. How come somebody else's knowing always lets you out? You're just a pimp for jobs, I guess. You ain't going deep enough, I said."

"It ain't my job to fix traces."

"Hey, get your hands in it. It's clean. You always was that way about manure. Why ain't it your job? Too busy screwing sheep? Try over there. You ought to have hit it. No, there, not there."

"I never fixed traces."

"Christ, they never needed fixing while you been here hardly. Jorge, will you stop nursing that fool gun with your cock and use both hands."

"I'm cold Pa."

"So'm I. That's why you got to find that bottle."

"If I find it do I get a drink?"

"Ain't you growed up . . . a man . . . since yesterday."

"I've had a few, Pa."

"Ha. Of what, hey? Hear that Hans? He's had a few. For medicine maybe, like your ma says. The spirits, the spirits, Jorgen Segren, ha."

"I'm cold."

"Maybe. Only look, for God's sake, don't just thrash about like a fool chicken."

"Well, we're finished anyway," Hans said.

"We're finished if we don't find that bottle."

"You're finished, maybe. You're the only one who needs that bottle. Jorge and I don't need it, but there you are, old man, eh? Lost in the snow."

My gloves were wet. Snow had jammed under my sleeves. It was working down into my boots. I stopped to pick some out with a finger if I could.

"Maybe some of Ma's coffee is still hot," I said.

"Say. Yeah. Maybe. But that's my coffee, boy. I never got none. I ain't even had breakfast. What are you stopping for? Come on. Hell Jorge, it's cold."

"I know that better than you. You're sitting there all nice and dry, bossing; but I'm doing all the work and getting the snow inside me."

Pa leaned back and grinned. He clutched the blanket to him and Hans pulled it back.

"It's easier to keep warm moving around, anybody knows that. Ain't that right, Hans? It's easier to keep warm moving, ain't it?"

"Yeah," Hans said. "If you ain't got a blanket."

"See there, Jorge, hey? You just keep good and warm . . . stirring. It'd be a pity if your pee should freeze. And moving around good prevents calluses on the bottom. Don't it Hans?"

"Yeah."

"Hans here knows. He's nothing but calluses."

"You'll wear out your mouth."

"I can't find it, Pa. Maybe some of Ma's coffee is still warm."

"You damn snivel — you ain't looking. Get tramping proper like I told you, and find it. Find it fast, you hear. You ain't getting back up on this sleigh until you do."

I started jumping up and down, not too fast, and Pa blew his nose with his fingers.

"Cold makes the snot run," he says, real wise.

If I found the bottle I'd kick it deep under the snow. I'd kick it and keep kicking it until it sank under a drift. Pa wouldn't know where it was. I wouldn't come back to the sleigh either. They weren't going anywhere anyway. I'd go home though it was a long walk. Looking back I could see our tracks in the trough of the road. They came together before I lost them. It would be warm at home and worth the walk. It was frightening — the great bright space. I'd never wanted to go to Pedersen's. That was Hans's fight, and Pa's. I was just cold . . . cold . . . and burned by the light and sick of snow. That's what I'd do if I found it — kick it under a drift. Then later, a lot later in the spring one day I'd come out here and find the old bottle sticking out of the rotting snow and the mud and hide it back of the barn and have a drink whenever I wanted. I'd get some real cigarettes, maybe a carton, and hide them too. Then someday I'd come in and Pa'd smell whisky on me and think I'd found one of his hiding places. He'd be mad as hell and not know what to say. It'd be spring and he'd think he'd taken them all in like he always did, harvesting the crop like he said.

I looked to see if there was something to mark the place by but it was all gone under snow. There was only the drifts and the deep holes of snow and the long runnered trough of the road. It might be a mudhole we was stuck in. In the spring cattails might grow up in it and the blackbirds come. Or it might be low and slimy at first and then caked dry and cracked. Pa'd never find out how I came by the bottle. Someday he'd act too big and I'd stick his head under the pump or slap his skinny rump with the backside of a fork full of manure. Hans would act smart and then someday . . .

"Jee-suss, will you move?"

"I'm cold, Pa."

"You're going to be a pig's size colder."

"Well, we're finished anyway," Hans said. "We ain't going nowhere. The trace is broke."

Pa stopped watching me thrash the snow. He frowned at Horse Simon. Simon was standing quiet with his head down.

"Simon's shivering," he said. "I should have remembered he'd be heated up. It's so cold I forgot."

Pa yanked the blanket off of Hans like Hans was a bed he was stripping and jumped down. Hans yelled but Pa didn't pay attention. He threw the blanket over Simon.

"We got to get Simon moving. He'll stiffen up."

Pa ran his hand tenderly down Simon's legs.

"The sleigh don't seem to have hurt him none."

"The trace is broke."

Then Hans stood up. He beat his arms against his body and jigged.

"We'll have to walk him home," he said.

"Home, hey," Pa said, giving Hans a funny sidewise look. "It's a long walk."

"You can ride him then," Hans said.

Pa looked real surprised and even funnier. It wasn't like Hans to say that. It was too cold. It made Hans generous. There was some good in cold.

"Why?"

Pa waded, patting Simon, but he kept his eye on Hans like it was Hans might kick.

Hans let out a long impatient streamer.

"Jesus — the trace."

Hans was being real cautious. Hans was awful cold. His nose was red. Pa's was white but it didn't look froze. It just looked white like it usually did — like it was part of him had died long ago. I wondered what color my nose was. Mine was bigger and sharper at the end. It was Ma's nose, Ma said. I was bigger all over than Pa. I was taller than Hans too. I pinched my nose but my gloves were wet so I couldn't feel anything except how my nose hurt when I pinched it. It couldn't be too cold. Hans was pointing at the ends of the trace which were trailing in the snow.

"Tie a knot in it," Pa was saying.

"It won't hold," Hans said, shaking his head.

"Tie a good one, it will."

"It's too cold to get a good knot. Leather's too stiff."

"Hell no, it ain't too stiff."

"Well, it's too thick. Can't knot something like that."

"You can do it."

"She'll pull crooked."

"Let her pull crooked."

"Simon won't work well pulling her crooked."

"He'll have to do the best he can. I ain't going to leave this sleigh out here. Hell, it might snow again before I got back with a new trace. When I get home I'm going to stay there and eat my breakfast if it's suppertime. I ain't coming back out here trying to beat another blizzard and wind up like the Pedersen kid."

"Yeah," Hans said, nodding. "Let's get this damn thing out of here and get Simon home before he stiffens. I'll tie the trace."

Hans got down and I stopped kicking. Pa watched Hans real careful from his side of Horse Simon and I could see him smiling like he'd thought of something dirty. I started to get on the sleigh but Pa shouted and made me hunt some more.

"Maybe we'll find it when we move the sleigh," I said.

Pa laughed but not at what I said. He opened his mouth wide, looking at Hans, and laughed hard, though his laugh was quiet.

"Yeah, maybe we will," he said, and gave Simon an extra hard pat. "Maybe we will, hey, at that."

I didn't find the bottle and Big Hans tied the trace. He had to take his gloves off to do it but he did it quick and I had to admire him for it. Pa coaxed Simon while Hans boosted. She got clear and then was going and skidded out. I heard a noise like a light bulb busting. A brown stain spread over the sleigh track. Pa peered over his shoulder at the stain, his hands on the halter, his legs wide in the snow.

"Oh no," was all he said, "oh no."

But Big Hans broke up. He lifted a leg clear of the snow. He hit himself. He shook. He hugged his belly. He rocked back and forth. "Oh . . . oh . . . oh," he screamed, and he held his sides. Tears streamed down his cheeks. "You . . . you . . . you," he howled. Hans's cheeks, his nose, his head was red. "Found . . . found . . . found," he choked.

Everything about Pa was frozen. The white hair that stuck out from his hat looked hard and sharp and seemed to shine like snow. Big Hans went on laughing. I never saw him so humored. He staggered, weakening — Pa as still as a stake. Hans began to heave and gasp, running down. In a minute he'd be cold again, worn out, and then he'd wish he could drink out of that bottle. The stain had stopped spreading and was fading, the snow bubbling and sagging. All that whisky was gone. We could melt and drink the snow, I thought. I wanted that bottle back bad. I hated Hans. I'd hate Hans forever, as long as there was snow.

Hans was puffing quietly when Pa told me to get in the sleigh. Then Hans climbed awkwardly on. Pa took the blanket off Horse Simon and threw it in the sleigh. Then he got Simon started. I pulled the blanket over me and tried to stop shivering. Our stove, I thought, was black . . . God . . . lovely black . . . and glowed rich cherry through its holes. I thought of the kettle steaming on it, the steam alive, hissing white and warm, not like my breath coming slow and cloudy and hanging heavy and dead in the still air.

Hans jumped.

"Where we going?" he said. "Where we going?"

Pa didn't say nothing.

"This ain't the way," Hans said. "Where we going?"

The gun was an ache in my stomach. Pa squinted at the snow.

"For Christ's sake," Hans said. "I'm sorry about the bottle."

But Pa drove.

## II

Barberry had got in the grove and lay about the bottom of the trees and hid in snow. The mossycups went high, their branches put straight out, the trunk-bark black and wrinkled. There were spots where I could see the frosted curls of dead grass frozen to the ground and high hard-driven piles of snow the barberry stuck its black barbs from. The wind had thrown some branches in the drifts. The sun made shadows of more branches on their sides and bent them over ridges. The ground rose up behind the grove. The snow rose. Pa and Hans had their shotguns. We followed along the drifts and kept down low. I could hear us breathing and the snow, earth, and our boots squeaking. We went slow and all of us was cold.

Above the snow, through the branches, I could see the peak of Pedersen's house, and nearer by, the roof of Pedersen's barn. We were making for the barn. Once in a while Pa would stop and watch for smoke but there was nothing in the sky. Big Hans bumped into a bush and got his hand barbed through his woolen glove. Pa gestured for Hans to shut up. I could feel my gun through my glove — heavy and cold. Where we went the ground was driven nearly bare. Mostly I kept my eyes on Big Hans's heels because it hurt my neck so to look up. When I did, for smoke, the faint breeze caught my cheek and drew the skin across the bone. I didn't think of much except how to follow Hans's heels and how, even underneath my cap, my ears burned, and how my lips hurt and how just moving made me ache. Pa followed where a crazy wind had got in among the oaks and blown the snow bare from the ground in flat patches against their trunks. Sometimes we had to break through a small drift or we'd gone in circles. The roof of Pedersen's house grew above the banks as we went until finally we passed across one corner of it and I saw the chimney very black in the sun stick up from the steep bright pitch like a dead cigar rough-ashed with snow.

I thought: The fire's dead, they must be froze.

Pa stopped and nodded at the chimney.

"You see," Hans said unhappily.

Just then I saw a cloud of snow float from the crest of a drift and felt my eyes smart. Pa looked quick at the sky but it was clear. Hans stomped his feet, hung his head, swore in a whisper.

"Well," Pa said, "it looks like we made this trip for nothing. No-body's to home."

"The Pedersens are all dead," Hans said, still looking down.

"Shut up." I saw Pa's lips were chapped . . . a dry hole now.

A muscle jumped along his jaw. "Shut up," he said again after a pause.

A faint ribbon of snow suddenly shot from the top of the chimney and disappeared. I stood as still as I could in the tubes of my clothes, the snow shifting strangely in my eyes, alone, frightened by the space that was bowling up inside me, a blank white glittering waste like the waste outside, coldly burning, roughed with waves, and I wanted to curl up, face to my thighs, but I knew my tears would freeze my lashes together. My stomach began to growl.

"What's the matter with you, Jorge?" Pa said.

"Nothing." I giggled. "I'm cold, Pa, I guess," I said. Then I belched.

"Jesus," Hans said loudly.

"Shut up."

I poked at the snow with the toe of my boot. I wanted to sit down and if there'd been anything to sit on I would have. All I wanted was to go home or sit down. Hans had stopped stomping and was staring back through the trees toward the way we'd come.

"Anybody in that house," Pa said, "would have a fire."

He sniffed and rubbed his sleeve across his nose.

"Anybody — see?" He began raising his voice. "Anybody who was in that house now would have a fire. The Pedersens is all most likely out hunting that fool kid. They probably tore ass off without minding the furnace. Now it's out." His voice got braver. "Anybody who might have come along while they was gone, and gone in, would have started a fire someplace first thing, and we'd see the smoke. It's too damn cold not to."

Pa took the shotgun he'd carried broken over his left arm and turned the barrel over, slow and deliberate. Two shells fell out and he stuffed them in his coat pocket.

"That means there ain't anybody to home. There ain't no smoke," he said with emphasis, "and that means there ain't *nobody*."

Big Hans sighed. "O.K.," he muttered remotely. "Let's go home."

I wanted to sit down. Here was the sofa, here the bed, mine, white and billowy. And the stairs, cold and snapping. And I had the dry cold toothaching mouth I always had at home, and the cold storm in my belly, and my pinched eyes. There was the print of the kid's rear in the dough. I wanted to sit down. I wanted to go back where we'd tied up Horse Simon and sit numb in the sleigh.

"Yes yes yes, let's," I said.

Pa smiled, oh the bastard, and he didn't know half what I knew now, numb in the heart the way I felt, and with my burned-off ears.

"We could at least leave a note saying Big Hans saved their kid. Seems to me like the only neighborly thing to do. And after all the way we come. Don't it you?"

"What the hell do you know about what's neighborly?" Hans shouted.

With a jerk he dumped his shotgun shells into the snow and kicked at them hard until one skidded into a drift and only the brass showed. The other sank in the snow before it broke. Black powder spilled out under his feet.

Pa laughed.

"Come on, Pa, I'm cold," I said. "Look, I ain't brave. I ain't. I don't care. All I am is cold."

"Quit whimpering, we're all cold. Big Hans here is awful cold."

"Sure, ain't you?"

Hans was grinding the black stain under.

"Yeah," Pa said, grinning. "Some. I'm some." He turned around. "Think you can find your way back, Jorge?"

I got going and he laughed again, loud and ugly, damn his soul. I hated him. Jesus, how I did. But no more like a father. Like the burning space.

"I never did like that bastard Pedersen anyway," he said as we started. "Pedersen's one of them that's always asking for trouble. On his knees for it all the time. Let him find out about his kid himself. He knows where we live. It ain't neighborly but I never said I wanted him for a neighbor."

"Yeah," Hans said. "Let the old bastard find out himself."

"He should have kept his kid behind them fences. What business did he have, sending his kid to us to take care of? He went and asked for snow. He went on his knees for snow. Was he ready? Hey? Was he? For real snow? Nobody's ever ready for real snow."

"The old bastard wouldn't have come to tell you if it'd been me who'd been lost," I said, but I wasn't minding my words at all, I was just talking. I was thinking of the feel of the sleigh moving under me.

"Can't tell holy Pete," Hans said.

I was going fast. I didn't care about keeping low. I had my eyes on the spaces between trees. I was looking for the place where we'd left Simon and the sleigh. I thought I'd see Simon first, maybe his breath above a bank or beside the trunk of a tree. I slipped on a little snow the wind hadn't blown from the path we'd took. I still had the gun in my right hand and I lost my balance. When I put out my left hand for support, it went into a drift to my elbow and into the barberry thorns. I jerked back and fell hard. Hans and Pa found it funny. But the legs that lay in front of me weren't mine. I'd gone out in the blazing air. It was queer. Out of the snow I'd kicked away with my foot stuck a horse's hoof and I didn't feel the least terror or surprise.

"Looks like a hoof," I said.

Hans and Pa were silent. I looked up at them. Nothing. Three men in the snow. A red scarf and some mittens . . . somebody's ice and coal . . . the picture for January. But behind them on the blank hills? Then it rushed over me and I thought: This is as far as he rid him. I looked at the hoof and the shoe which didn't belong in the picture. No dead horses for January. And on the snowhills there would be wild sled tracks and green trees and falling toboggans. This is as far. Or a glazed lake and rowdy skaters. Three men. On his ass: one. Dead horse and gun. And the question came to me very clearly, as if out of the calendar a girl had shouted: Are you going to get up and walk on? Maybe it was the Christmas picture. The big log and the warm orange wood I was sprawled on in my flannel pajamas. I'd just been given a pistol that shot BB's. And the question was: Was I going to get up and walk on? Hans's shoes, and Pa's, were as steady as the horse's. Were they hammered on? Their bodies stolen? Who'd left them standing here? And Christmas cookies cut in the shape of the kid's dead wet behind . . . with maybe a cherry to liven the pale dough . . . a coal from the stove. But I couldn't just say that looks like a hoof or that looks like a shoe and go right on because Hans and Pa were waiting behind me in their wool hats and pounding mittens . . . like a picture for January. Smiling. I was learning to skate.

"Looks like this is as far as he rid him."

Finally Pa said in a flat voice: "What are you talking about?"

"You said he had a horse, Pa."

"What are you talking about?"

"This here horse."

"Ain't you never seen a shoe before?"

"It's just a horse's hoof," Hans said. "Let's get on."

"What are you talking about?" Pa said again.

"The man who scared the Pedersen kid. The man he saw."

"Manure," Pa said. "It's one of Pedersen's horses. I recognize the shoe."

"That's right," Big Hans said.

"Pedersen only has one horse."

"This here's it," Big Hans said.

"This horse's brown, ain't it?"

"Pedersen's horse has got two brown hind feet. I remember," Big Hans said.

"His is black."

"It's got two brown hind feet."

I started to brush away some snow. I knew Pedersen's horse was black.

"What the hell," Hans said. "Come on. It's too cold to stand here and argue about the color of Pedersen's god damn horse."

"Pedersen's horse is black," Pa said. "He don't have any brown on him at all."

Big Hans turned angrily on Pa. "You said you recognized his shoe."

"I thought I did. It ain't."

I kept scraping snow away. Hans leaned down and pushed me. The horse was white where frozen snow clung to his hide.

"He's brown, Hans. Pedersen's horse is black. This one's brown."

Hans kept pushing at me. "God damn you," he was saying over and over in a funny high voice.

"You knew all along it wasn't Pedersen's horse."

It was like singing the way it went on. I got up carefully, taking the safety off. Later in the winter maybe somebody would stumble on his shoes sticking out of the snow. Shooting Hans seemed like something I'd done already. I knew where he kept his gun — under those magazines in his drawer — and while I'd really never thought of it before, the whole thing moved before me now so naturally it must have happened that way. Of course I shot them all — Pa in his bed, Ma in her kitchen, Hans when he came in from his rounds. They wouldn't look much different dead than alive only they wouldn't be so loud.

"Jorge, now . . . look out with that thing Jorge. Jorge . . ."

His shotgun had fallen in the snow. He was holding both hands in front of him. Afterwards I stood alone in every room.

"You're yellow, Hans."

He was backing slowly, fending me off . . . fending . . . fending . . .

"Jorge . . . Jorge . . . hey now . . . Jorge . . ." like singing.

Afterwards I looked through his magazines, my hand on my pecker, hot from head to foot.

"I've shot you, yellow Hans. You can't shout or push no more or goose me in the barn."

"Hey now wait, Jorge . . . listen . . . what? Jorge . . . wait . . ." like singing.

Afterwards only the wind and the warm stove. Shivering I rose on my toes. Pa came up and I moved the gun to take him in. I kept it moving back and forth . . . Hans and Pa . . . Pa and Hans. Gone. Snow piling in the window corners. In the spring I'd shit with the door open, watching the blackbirds.

"Don't be a damn fool, Jorge," Pa said. "I know you're cold. We'll be going home."

". . . yellow yellow yellow yellow . . ."

"Now Jorge, I ain't yellow," Pa said, smiling pleasantly.

"I've shot you both with bullets."

"Don't be a fool."

"The whole house with bullets. You too."

"Funny I don't feel it."

"They never does, do they? Do rabbits?"

"He's crazy, Jesus, Mag, he's crazy . . ."

"I never did want to. I never hid it like you did. I never believed him. I ain't the yellow one but you made me come but you're the yellow ones, you were all along the yellow ones."

That's what the kid had done, I thought. Of course he'd seen his chance and shot them all — his Ma, his Pa, and little Hans. Of course that's what he'd done.

Then Pa took the gun away, putting it in his pocket. He had his shotgun hanging easy over his left arm but he slapped me and I bit my tongue. Pa was spitting. I turned and ran down the path we'd come, putting one arm over my face to ease the stinging.

"You little shit," Big Hans called after me.

### III

Pa came back to the sleigh where I was sitting hunched up under the blanket and got a shovel out of the back.

"Feeling better?"

"Some."

"Why don't you drink some of that coffee?"

"It's cold by now. I don't want to anyhow."

"How about them sandwiches?"

"I ain't hungry. I don't want anything."

Pa started back with the shovel.

"What are you going to do with that?" I said.

"Dig a tunnel," he said, and he went around a drift out of sight, the sun flashing from the blade.

I almost called him back but I rmembered the grin in his face so I didn't. Simon stamped. I pulled the blanket closer. I didn't believe him. Just for a second, when he said it, I had. It was a joke. Well, I was too cold for jokes. What did he want a shovel for? There'd be no point in digging for the horse. They could see it wasn't Pedersen's.

Poor Simon. He was better than they were. They'd left us in the cold.

Pa'd forgot about the shovel in the sleigh. I could have used it hunting for his bottle. That had been a joke too. Pa'd sat there thinking how funny Jorge is out there beating away at the snow, I'll just wait and see if he remembers about that shovel. It'd be funny if Jorge forgot, he'd thought, sitting there in the blanket and bobbing his head here and there like a chicken. I'd hear about it when we got home till I was sick. I put my head down and closed my eyes. All right. I didn't care. I'd put up with it to be warm. But that couldn't be right. Pa must have forgot the same as me. He wanted that bottle too bad. Now it was all gone. It was colder with my eyes closed. I tried to think about all that underwear and the girls in the pictures. I had a crick in my neck.

Whose horse was it, then?

I decided to keep my eyes closed a while longer, to see if I could do it. Then I decided not to. There was a stream of light in my eyes. It was brighter than snow, and as white. I opened them and straightened up. Keeping my head down made me dizzy. Everything was blurry. There were a lot of blue lines that moved.

Did they know the horse even so? Maybe it was Carlson's horse, or even Schmidt's. Maybe he was Carlson in yellow gloves, or Schmidt, and the kid, because he came in sudden from the barn and didn't know Carlson had come, saw him in the kitchen holding a gun like he might of if it'd been Schmidt, and the kid got scared and run, because he didn't understand and it'd been snowing lots, and how did Schmidt get there, or Carlson get there, if it was one of them, so the kid got scared and run and came to our crib when the snow grew around him and then in the morning Hans found him.

And we'd been god damn fools. Especially Hans. I shivered. The cold had settled in my belly. The sun had bent around to the west. Near it the sky was hazy. The troughs of some of the drifts were turning blue.

He wouldn't have been that scared. Why'd Carlson or Schmidt be out in a storm like that? If somebody was sick, they were closer to town than either the Pedersens or us. It was a long way for them in this weather. They wouldn't get caught out. But if the horse was stole, who was there but Carlson and Schmidt or maybe Hansen to steal it from?

He goes to the barn before the snow, most likely in the night, and knows horses. Oats or hay lead it out. He's running away. The blizzard sets down. He drives himself and the horse hard, bending in the wind, leaning over far to see fences, any marks, road. He makes the grove. He might not know it. The horse runs into the barberry, rears, goes to its knees; or a low branch of mossycup he doesn't see knocks him into a drift; or he slides off when the horse rears as the barbs go in. The horse wanders a little way, not far. Then it stops —

finished. And he — he's stunned. He's frozen and tired. The wind's howling. He's blind. He's hungry and scared. The snow is stinging his face. Standing still alone. Then the snow hides him. The wind blows a crust over him. Only a shovel poking in the drifts or a warm rain will find him lying by the horse.

I threw off the blanket and jumped down and ran up the path we'd made between the drifts and trees, slipping, cutting sharply back and forth, working against my stiffness, but all the time keeping my head up, looking out carefully ahead.

They weren't by the horse. A hoof and part of the leg I'd uncovered lay by the path like nothing more went with them. Seeing them like that, like they might have blown down from one of the trees in a good wind, gave me a fright. Now there was a slight breeze and I discovered my tongue was sore. Hans's and Pa's tracks went farther on — toward Pedersen's barn. I wasn't excited any more. I remembered I'd left the blanket on the seat instead of putting it on Simon. I thought about going back. Pa'd said a tunnel. That had to be a joke. But what were they doing with the shovel? Maybe they'd found him by the barn. What if it really was Schmidt or Carlson? I thought about which I wanted it to be. I went more slowly in Pa's tracks. Now I kept down. The roof of Pedersen's barn got bigger; the sky was hazier; here and there little clouds of snow leapt up from the top of a drift like they'd been pinched off, and sailed swiftly away.

They *were* digging a tunnel. They didn't hear me come up. They were really digging a tunnel.

Hans was digging in the great drift. It ran from the grove in a high curve against the barn. It met the roof where it went lowest and flowed onto it like there wasn't a barn underneath. It seemed like the whole snow of winter was gathered there. If the drift hadn't ended in the grove it would have been swell for sledding. You could put a ladder on the edge of the roof and go off from there. The crust looked hard enough.

Hans and Pa had put about a ten-foot hole in the bank. Hans dug and Pa put what Hans dug in small piles behind him. I figured it was near a hundred feet to the barn. If we'd been home and not so cold, it would have been fun. But it would take all day. They were great damn fools.

"I been thinking," I started out, and Hans stopped in the tunnel with a shovel of snow in the air.

Pa didn't turn around or stop.

"You can help dig," he said.

"I been thinking," I said, and Hans dropped the shovel, spilling the snow, and came out, "that you're digging in the wrong place."

Hans pointed to the shovel. "Get digging."

"We need something to carry snow with," Pa said. "It's getting too damn far."

Pa kicked at the snow and flailed with his arms. He was sweating and so was Hans. It was terrible foolish.

"I said you was digging in the wrong place."

"Tell Hans. It's his idea. He's the hot digger."

"You thought it was a good idea," Hans said.

"I never did."

"Well," I said, "it ain't likely you'll find him clear in there."

Pa chuckled. "He ain't going to find us neither."

"He ain't going to find anybody if he's where I think."

"Oh yeah, think." Hans moved nearer. "Where?"

"As far as he got." It really didn't make much difference to me what Hans did. He could come as close as he liked. "In the snow near that horse."

Hans started but Pa chewed on his lip and shook his head.

"Probably Schmidt or Carlson," I said.

"Probably Schmidt or Carlson, shit," Pa said.

"Of course," Hans shouted.

Hans scooped up the shovel, furious, and carried it by me like an axe.

"Hans has been working like a thrasher," Pa said.

"You'll never finish it."

"No."

"It's higher than it needs to be."

"Sure."

"Why are you digging it then?"

"Hans. Hans wants to."

"Why, for Christ's sake?"

"So we can get to the barn without being seen."

"Why not cross behind the drift?"

"Hans. Hans says no. Hans says that from an upstairs window he could see over the bank."

"What the hell."

"He's got a rifle."

"But who knows he's upstairs?"

"Nobody. We don't know he's even there. But that horse is."

"He's back where I said."

"No he ain't. You only wish he was. So does Hans, hey? But he ain't. What did the kid see if he is — his ghost?"

I walked into the tunnel to the end. Everything seemed blue.

The air was dead and wet. It could have been fun, snow over me, hard and grainy, the excitement of a tunnel, the games. The face of a mine, everything muffled, the marks of the blade in the snow. Well I knew how Hans felt. It would have been wonderful to burrow down, disappear under the snow, sleep out of the wind in soft sheets, safe. I backed out. We went to get Hans and go home. Pa gave me the gun with a smile.

We heard the shovel cutting the crust and Hans puffing. He was using the shovel like a fork. He'd cut up the snow in clods around the horse. He grunted when he drove the shovel in. Next he began to beat the shovel against the snow, packing it down, then ripping the crust with the side of the blade.

"Hans. It ain't no use," Pa said.

But Hans went right on pounding with the shovel, spearing and pounding, striking out here and there like he was trying to kill a snake.

"You're just wasting your time. It ain't no use, Hans. Jorge was wrong. He ain't by the horse."

But Hans went right on, faster and faster.

"Hans." Pa had made his voice hard and loud.

The shovel speared through the snow. It struck a stone and rang. Hans went to his knees and pawed at the snow with his hands. When he saw the stone he stopped. On his knees in the snow he simply stared at it.

"Hans."

"The bastard. I'd have killed him."

"He ain't here, Hans. How could he be here? The kid didn't see him here, he saw him in the kitchen."

Hans didn't seem to be listening.

"Jorge was wrong. He ain't here at all. He sure ain't here."

Hans grabbed up the shovel like he was going to swing it and jumped up. He looked at me so awful I forgot how indifferent I was.

"We got to think of what to do," Pa said. "The tunnel won't work."

Hans didn't look at Pa. He would only look at me.

"We can go home," Pa said. "We can go home or we can chance crossing behind the bank."

Hans slowly put the shovel down. He started dragging up the narrow track to the barn.

"Let's go home, Hans," I said. "Come on, let's go home."

"I can't go home," he said in a low flat voice as he passed us.

Pa sighed and I felt like I was dead.

## PART THREE

Pedersen's horse was in the barn. Pa kept her quiet. He rubbed his hand along her flank. He laid his head upon her neck and whispered in her ear. She shook herself and nickered. Big Hans opened the door a crack and peeked out. He motioned to Pa to hush the horse but Pa was in the stall. I asked Hans if he saw anything and Hans shook his head. I warned Pa about the bucket. He had the horse settled down. There was something that looked like sponges in the bucket. If they were sponges, they were hard. Hans turned from the door to rub his eyes. He leaned back against the wall.

Then Pa came and looked out the crack.

"Don't look like anybody's to home."

Big Hans had the hiccups. Under his breath he swore and hiccuped. Pa grunted.

Now the horse was quiet and we were breathing careful and if the wind had picked up we couldn't hear it or any snow it drove. It was warmer in the barn and the little light there was was soft on hay and wood. We were safe from the sun and it felt good to use the eyes on quiet tools and leather. I leaned like Hans against the wall and put my gun in my belt. It felt good to have that hand empty. My face burned and I was drowsy. I could dig a hole in the hay. Even if there were rats, I would burrow with them in it. I could curl up tight and warm my ears in my arms. Even if there were rats, I would sleep with them in it. Everything was still in the barn. Tools and harness hung from the walls, and pails and bags and burlap rested on the floor. Nothing shifted in the straw or moved in hay. The horse stood easy. And Hans and I rested up against the wall, Hans sucking in his breath and holding it, and we waited for Pa, who didn't make a sound. Only the line of sun that snuck under him and lay along the floor and came up white and dangerous to the pail seemed a living thing.

"Don't look like it," Pa said finally. "Never can tell."

Now who will go, I thought. It isn't far. Then it'll be over. It's just across the yard. It isn't any farther than the walk behind the drift. There's only windows watching. If he's been, he's gone, and nothing's there to hurt.

"He's gone."

"Maybe, Jorge. But if he came on that brown horse you stumbled on, why didn't he take this mare of Pedersen's when he left?"

"Jesus," Hans whispered. "He's here."

"Could be in the barn, we'd never see him."

Hans hiccuped. Pa laughed softly.

"Damn you," said Big Hans.

"Thought I'd rid you of them hics."

"Let me look," I said.

He must be gone, I thought. It's such a little way. He must be gone. He never came. It isn't far but who will go across? I saw the house by squinting hard. The nearer part, the dining room, came toward us. The porch was on the left and farther off. You could cross to the nearer wall and under the windows edge around. He might see you from the porch window. But he'd gone. Yet I didn't want to go across that little winded space of snow to find it out.

I wished Big Hans would stop. I was counting the spaces. It was comfortable behind my back except for that. There was a long silence while he held his breath and afterwards we waited.

The wind was rising by the snowman. There were long blue shadows by the snowman now. The eastern sky was clear. Snow sifted slowly to the porch past the snowman. An icicle hung from the nose of the pump. There were no tracks anywhere. I asked did they see the snowman and I heard Pa grunt. Snow went waist-high to the snowman. The wind had blown from his face his eyes. A silent chimney was an empty house.

"There ain't nobody there," I said.

Hans had hiccups again so I ran out.

I ran to the dining room wall and put my back flat against it, pushing hard. Now I saw clouds in the western sky. The wind was rising. It was O.K. for Hans and Pa to come. I would walk around the corner. I would walk around the wall. The porch was there. The snowman was alone beside it.

"All clear," I shouted, walking easily away.

Pa came carefully from the barn with his arms around his gun. He walked slow to be brave but I was standing in the open and I smiled.

Pa sat hugging his knees as I heard the gun, and Hans screamed. Pa's gun stood up. I backed against the house. My God, I thought, he's real.

"I want a drink."

I held the house. The snow'd been driven up against it.

"I want a drink." He motioned with his hand to me.

"Shut up. Shut up." I shook my head. "Shut up." Shut up and die, I thought.

"I want a drink, I'm dry," Pa said.

Pa bumped when I heard the gun again. He seemed to point

his hand at me. My fingers slipped along the boards. I tried to dig
them in but my back slipped down. Hopelessly I closed my eyes. I
knew I'd hear the gun again though rabbits don't. Silently he'd
come. My back slipped. Rabbits, though, are hard to hit the way
they jump around. But prairie dogs, like Pa, they sit. I felt snowflakes against my face, crumbling as they struck. He'd shoot me,
by God. Was Pa's head tipped? Don't look. I felt snowflakes
falling softly against my face, breaking. The glare was painful,
closing the slit in my eyes. That crack in Pa's face must be awful
dry. Don't look. Yes . . . the wind was rising . . . faster flakes.

## II

When I was so cold I didn't care I crawled to the south side of
the house and broke a casement window with the gun I had forgot
I had and climbed down into the basement ripping my jacket on the
glass. My ankles hurt so I huddled there in the dark corner places and
in the cold moldy places by boxes. Immediately I went to sleep.

I thought it was right away I woke though the light through the
window was red. He put them down the cellar, I remembered. But
I stayed where I was, so cold I seemed apart from myself, and wondered
if everything had been working to get me in this cellar as a trade for
the kid he'd missed. Well, he was sudden. The Pedersen kid — maybe
he'd been a message of some sort. No, I liked better the idea that we'd
been prisoners exchanged. I was back in my own country. No, it
was more like I'd been given a country. A new blank land. More
and more, while we'd been coming, I'd been slipping out of myself,
pushed out by the cold maybe. Anyway I had a queer head, sear-eyed
and bleary, everywhere ribboned. Well, he was quick and quiet. The
rabbit simply stumbled. Tomatoes were unfeeling when they froze.
I thought of the softness of the tunnel, the mark of the blade in the
snow. Suppose the snow was a hundred feet deep. Down and down.
A blue-white cave, the blue darkening. Then tunnels off of it like the
branches of trees. And fine rooms. Was it February by now? I
remembered a movie where the months had blown from the calendar
like leaves. Girls in red peek-a-boo BVD's were skiing out of sight.
Silence of the tunnel. In and in. Stairs. Wide tall stairs. And
balconies. Windows of ice and sweet green light. Ah. There would
still be snow in February. Here I go off of the barn, the runners hissing.
I am tilting dangerously but I coast on anyway. Now to the trough,
the swift snow-trough, and the Pedersen kid floating chest down. They
were all drowned in the snow now, weren't they? Well more or less,
weren't they? The kid for killing his family. But what about me?

Must freeze. But I would leave ahead of that, that was the nice thing, I was already going. Yes. Funny. I was something to run my hands over, feeling for its hurts, like there were worn places in leather, rust and rot in screws and boards I had to find, and the places were hard to reach and the fingers in my gloves were stiff and their ends were sore. My nose was running. Mostly interesting. There was a cramp in my leg that must have made me wake. Distantly I felt the soft points of my shoulders in my jacket, the heavy line of my cap around my forehead, and on the hard floor my harder feet, and to my chest my hugged tight knees. I felt them but I felt them differently . . . like the pressure of a bolt through steel or the cinch of leather harness or the squeeze of wood by wood in floors . . . like the twist and pinch, the painful yield of tender tight together wheels, and swollen bars, and in deep winter springs.

I couldn't see the furnace but it was dead. Its coals were cold, I knew. The broken window held a rainbow and put a colored pattern on the floor. Once the wind ran through it and a snowflake turned. The stairs went into darkness. If a crack of light came down the steps, I guessed I had to shoot. I fumbled for my gun. Then I noticed the fruit cellar and the closed door where the Pedersens were.

Would they be dead already? Sure they'd be. Everybody was but me. More or less. Big Hans, of course, wasn't really, unless the fellow had caught up with him, howling and running. But Big Hans had gone away a coward. I knew that. It was almost better he was alive and the snow had him. I didn't have his magazines but I remembered how they looked, puffed in their brassieres.

The door was wood with a wooden bar. I slipped the bar off easily but the door itself was stuck. It shouldn't have stuck but it was stuck at the top. I tried to see the top by standing on tiptoe, but I couldn't bend my toes well and kept toppling to the side. Got no business sticking, I thought. There's no reason for that. I pulled again, very hard, and a chip fell as it shuddered open. Wedged some way. Why? It had a bar. It was even darker in the fruit cellar and the air had a musty earthen smell.

Maybe they were curled up like the kid was when he dropped. Maybe they had frost on their clothes, and stiff hair. What color would their noses be? Would I dare to tweak them? Say. If the old lady was dead I'd peek at her crotch. I wasn't any Hans to rub them. Big Hans had run. The snow had him. There wasn't any kettle, any stove, down here. Before you did a thing like that, you'd want to be sure. I thought of how the sponges in the bucket had got hard.

I went back behind the boxes and hid and watched the stairs.

The chip was orange in the pattern of light. He'd heard me when I broke the glass or when the door shook free or when the wedge fell down. He was waiting behind the door at the top of the stairs. All I had to do was come up. He was waiting. All this time. He waited while we stood in the barn. He waited for Pa with his arms full of gun to come out. He took no chances and he waited.

I knew I couldn't wait. I knew I'd have to try to get back out. There he'd be waiting too. I'd sit slowly in the snow like Pa. That'd be a shame, a special shame after all I'd gone through, because I was on the edge of something wonderful, I felt it trembling in me strangely, in the part of me that flew high and calmly looked down on my stiff heap of clothing. Oh Pa'd forgot. We could have used the shovel. I'd have found the bottle with it. With it we'd gone on home. By the stove I'd come to myself again. By it I'd be warm again. But as I thought about it, it didn't appeal to me any more. I didn't want to come to myself that way again. No. I was glad he'd forgot the shovel. But he was . . . he was waiting. Pa always said that he could wait; that Pedersen never could. But Pa and me, we couldn't — only Hans stayed back while we came out, while all the time the real waiter waited. He knew I couldn't wait. He knew I'd freeze.

Maybe the Pedersens were just asleep. Have to be sure the old man wasn't watching. What a thing. She wasn't much. Fat. Gray. But a crotch is a crotch. The light in the window paled. The sky I could see was smoky. The bits of broken glass had glimmered out. I heard the wind. Snow by the window rose. From a beam a cobweb swung stiffly like a net of wire. Flakes followed one another in and disappeared. I counted desperately three, eleven, twenty. One lit beside me. Maybe the Pedersens *were* just asleep. I went to the door again and looked in. New little rows of lights lay on the glasses and the jars. I felt the floor with my foot. I thought suddenly of snakes. I pushed my feet along. I got to every corner but the floor was empty. Really it was a relief. I went back and hid behind the boxes. The wind was coming now, with snow, the glass glinting in unexpected places. The dead tops of roofing nails in an open keg glowed white. Oh for the love of God. Above me in the house I heard a door slam sharply. He was finished with waiting.

The kid for killing his family must freeze.

The stair was railless and steep. It seemed to stagger in the air. Thank God the treads were tight and didn't creak. Darkness swept under me. Terror of height. But I was only climbing with my sled under my arm. In a minute I'd shoot from the roof edge and rush down the steep drift, snow-smoke behind me. I clung to the stair, stretched out. Fallen into space I'd float around a dark star. Not the calendar for March. Maybe they would find me in the spring, hanging from this stairway like a wintering cocoon.

I crawled up slowly and pushed the door open. The kitchen wallpaper had flower pots on it, green and very big. Out of every one a great red flower grew. I began laughing. I liked the wallpaper. I loved it; it was mine; I felt the green pots and traced the huge flower that stuck out of it, laughing. To the left of the door at the head of the stair was a window that looked out on the back porch. I saw the wind hurrying snow off toward the snowman. Down the length of it the sky and all its light was lead and all the snow was ashy. Across the porch were footprints, deep and precise.

I was on the edge of celebration but I remembered in time and scooted in a closet, hunkering down between brooms, throwing my arms across my eyes. Down a long green hill there was a line of sheep. It had been my favorite picture in a book I'd had when I was eight. There were no people in it.

I'd been mad and Pa had laughed. I'd had it since my birthday in the spring. Then he'd hid it. It was when we had the privy in the back. God, it was cold in there, dark beneath. I found it in the privy torn apart and on the freezing soggy floor in leaves. And down the hole I'd seen the curly sheep floating. There was even ice. I'd been mad, rolling and kicking. Pa had struck himself and laughed. I only saved a red-cheeked fat-faced boy in blue I didn't like. The cow was torn. Ma'd said I'd get another one someday. For a while, every day, even though the snow was piled and the sky dead and the winter wind was blowing, I watched for my aunt to come again and bring me a book like my Ma'd said she would. She never came.

And I almost had Han's magazines.

But he might come again. Yet he'd not chase me home, not now, no. By God, the calendar was clean, the lines sharp and clear, the colors bright and gay, and there were eights on the ice and red mouths singing and the snow belonged to me and the high sky too, burningly handsome, fiercely blue. But he might. He was quick.

If it was warmer I couldn't tell but it wasn't as damp as by the boxes and I could smell soap. There was light in the kitchen. It came through the crack I'd left in the closet door to comfort me. But the light was fading. Through the crack I could see the sink, now milky. Flakes began to slide out of the sky and rub their corners off on the pane before they were caught by the wind again and blown away. In the gray I couldn't see them. Then they would come, suddenly, from it, like chaff from grain, and brush the window while the wind eddied. Something black was bobbing. It was deep in the gray where the snow was. It bounced queerly and then it went. The black stocking cap, I thought.

I kicked a pail coming out and when I ran to the window my left leg gave way, banging me against the sink. The light was going. The snow was coming. It was coming almost even with the ground, my snow. Puffs were rising. Then, in a lull when the snow sank and it was light enough to see the snowbank shadows growing, I saw his back upon a horse. I saw the tail flick. And the snow came back. Great sheets flapped. He was gone.

## III

Once, when dust rolled up from the road and the fields were high with heavy-handled wheat and the leaves of every tree were gray and curled up and hung head down, I went in the meadow with an old broom like a gun, where the dandelions had begun to seed and the low ground was cracked, and I flushed grasshoppers from the goldenrod in whirring clouds like quail and shot them down. I smelled wheat in the warm wind and every weed. I tasted dust in my mouth, and the house and barn and all the pails burned my eyes to look at. I rode the broom over the brown rocks. I hunted Horse Simon in the shade of a tree. I rode the broom over the brown meadow grass and with a fist like pistol butt and trigger shot the Indian on Horse Simon down. I rode across the dry plain. I rode into the dry creek. Dust rose up behind me. I went fast and shouted. The tractor was bright orange. It shimmered. Dust rolled behind it. I hid in the creek and followed as it came. I waited as its path curved toward me. I watched and waited. My eyes were tiny. I sprang out with a whoop and rode across the dry plain. My horse had a golden tail. Dust rolled up behind me. Pa was on the tractor in a broad-brimmed hat. With a fist like pistol butt and trigger, going fast, I shot him down.

Pa would stop the tractor and get off and we'd walk across the creek to the little tree Simon stood his bowed head under. We'd sit by the tree and Pa would pull a water bottle out from between its roots and drink. He'd swish it around in his mouth good before he swallowed. He'd wipe off the top and offer it to me. I'd take a pull like it was fiery and hand it back. Pa'd take another drink and sigh and get on up. Then he'd say, "You feed the chickens like I told you?" and I'd say I had, and then he'd say, "How's the hunting?" and I'd say pretty good. He'd nod like he agreed and clap Simon on the behind and go on off, but he'd always say I'd best not stay in the sun too long. I'd watch him go over the creek, waving his hat before his face before he put it on. Then I'd take a secret drink out of the bottle and wipe my lips and the top. After that I'd go and let the ragweed brush against my knees and then, sometimes, go home.

The fire had begun to feel warm. I rubbed my hands. Then I ate a stale biscuit.

Pa had taken the wagon to town. The sun was shining. Pa had gone to meet Big Hans at the station. There was snow around but mud was flowing and the fields had green in them again. Mud rode up on the wagon wheels. There was sweet air sometimes and the creek had water with the winter going. Through a crack in the privy door I saw him take the wagon to the train. I'd a habit, when I was twelve, of looking down. Something sparkled on the water. It was then I found the first one. The sun was shining. Mud was climbing the wagon wheels and Pa was going to the train and down the tight creek snow was flowing. He had a ledge beneath the seat. You could reach right down. Already he had a knack for hiding. So I found it and poured it out in the hole. That was the last year we had the privy because when Big Hans came we tore it down.

I ate an apple I'd found. The skin was shriveled but the meat was sweet.

Big Hans was stronger than Simon, I thought. He let me help him with his chores, and we talked, and later he showed me some of the pictures in his magazines. "See anything like that around here?" he'd say, shaking his head. "Only teats like that round here is on a cow." And he would tease, laughing while he spun the pages, giving me only a glimpse. Or he would come up and spank me on the rump. We tore the privy down together. Big Hans hated it. He said it was a dirty job fit only for soldiers. But I helped him a lot, he said. He told me that Jap girls had their slice on sideways and no hair. He promised to show me a picture of one of them and though I badgered him, he never did. We burned the boards in a big pile back of the barn and the flames were a deep orange like the sun going down and the smoke rolled. "It's piss wet," Hans said. We stood by the fire and talked until it sank down and the stars were out and the coals glowed and he told me about the war in whispers and the firing of big guns.

Pa liked the summer. He wished it was summer all year long. He said once whisky made it summer for him. But Hans liked the spring like me, though I liked summer too. Hans talked and showed me this and that. He measured his pecker once when he had a hard on. We watched how the larks ran across the weeds and winked with their tails taking off. We watched the brown spring water foam by the rocks in the creek, and heard Horse Simon blow and the pump squeak.

Then Pa took a dislike to Hans and said I shouldn't go with Hans so much. And then in the winter Hans took a dislike to Pa as he almost had to, and Hans said fierce things to Ma about Pa's drinking, and one day Pa heard him. Pa was furious and terrible to Ma all day. It was a night like this one. The wind was blowing hard and the snow was coming hard and I'd built a fire and was sitting by it, dreaming. Ma came and sat near me, and then Pa came, burning inside himself, while Hans stayed in the kitchen. All I heard was the fire, and in the fire I saw Ma's sad quiet face the whole evening without turning, and I heard Pa drinking, and nobody not even me said anything the whole long long evening. The next morning Hans went to wake Pa and Pa threw the pot and Hans got the axe and Pa laughed fit to shake the house. It wasn't long before Hans and I took to hating one another and hunting Pa's bottles alone.

The fire was burning down. There was some blue but mostly it was orange. For all Pedersen's preparing like Pa said he always did, he hadn't got much wood in the house. It was good to be warm but I didn't feel so set against the weather as I had been. I thought I'd like winter pretty well from now on. I sat as close as I could and stretched and yawned. Even if his cock was thicker than mine . . . I was here and he was in the snow. I was satisfied.

He was in the wind now and in the cold now and sleepy now like me. His head was bent down low like the horse's head must be and he was rocking in the saddle very tired of holding on and only rocking sleepy with his eyes shut and with snow on his heavy lids and on his lashes and snow in his hair and up his sleeves and down inside his collar and his boots. It was good I was glad he was there it wasn't me was there sticking up bare in the wind on a horse like a stick with the horse most likely stopped by this time with his bowed head bent into the storm, and I wouldn't like lying all by myself out there in the cold white dark, dying all alone out there, being buried out there while I was still trying to breathe, knowing I'd only come slowly to the surface in the spring and would soon be soft in the new sun and worried by curious dogs.

The horse must have stopped though he made the other one go on. Maybe he'd manage to drive this one too until it dropped, or he fell off, or something broke. He might make the next place. He just might. Carlson's or Schmidt's. He had once before though he never had a right or any chance to. Still he had. He was in the thick snow now. More was coming. More was blowing down.

He was in it now and he could go on and he could come through it because he had before. Maybe he belonged in the snow. Maybe he lived there, like a fish does in a lake. Spring didn't have anything like him. I surprised myself when I laughed the house was so empty and the wind so steady it didn't count for noise.

I saw him coming up beside our crib, the horse going down to its knees in the drift there. I saw him going to the kitchen and coming in unheard because of all the wind. I saw Hans sitting in the kitchen. He was drinking like Pa drank — lifting the bottle. Ma was there, her hands like a trap on the table. The Pedersen kid was there too, naked in the flour, towels lapping his middle, whisky and water steadily dripping. Hans was watching, watching the kid's dirty toes, watching him like he watched me with his pin black eyes and his tongue sliding in his mouth. Then he'd see the cap, the mackinaw, the gloves wrapped thick around the gun, and it would be the same as when Pa kicked the glass from Big Hans's hand, only the bottle this time would roll on the floor, squirting. Ma would worry about her kitchen getting tracked and get up and mix biscuits with a shaky spoon and put the coffee on.

They'd disappear like the Pedersens had. He'd put them away somewhere out of sight for at least as long as the winter. But he'd leave the kid, for we'd been exchanged, and we were both in our own new lands. Then why did he stand there so pale I could see through? "Shoot. Go on. Hurry up. Shoot."

The horse had circled round in it. He hadn't known the way. He hadn't known the horse had circled round. His hands were loose upon the reins and so the horse had circled round. Everything was black and white and everything the same. There wasn't any road to go. There wasn't any track. The horse had circled round in it. He hadn't known the way. There was only snow to the horse's thighs. There was only cold to the bone and driving snow in his eyes. He hadn't known. How could he know the horse had circled round in it? How could he really ride and urge the horse with his heels when there wasn't any place to go and everything was black and white and all the same? Of course the horse had circled round, of course he'd come around in it. Horses have a sense. That's all manure about horses. No it ain't, Pa, no it ain't. They do. Hans said. They do. Hans knows. He's right. He was right about the wheat that time. He said the rust was in it and it was. He was right about the rats, they do eat shoes, they eat anything, so the horse has circled round in it. That was a long time ago. Yes, Pa, but Hans was right even though that was a long time ago, and how would you know anyway, you was always drinking . . . not in summer . . . no,

Pa . . . not in spring or fall either . . . no, Pa, but in the winter, and it's winter now and you're in bed where you belong, don't speak to me, be quiet. The bottle made it spring for me just like that fellow's made it warm for you. Shut up. Shut up. I wanted a cat or a dog awful bad since I was a little kid. You know those pictures of Hans's, the girls with big brown nipples like bottle ends . . . shut up, shut up. I'm not going to grieve. You're no man now. Your bottle's broken in the snow. The sled rode over it, remember? I'm not going to grieve. You were always after killing me, yourself, Pa, oh yes you were. I was cold in your house always, Pa. Jorge, so was I. No. I was. I was the one wrapped in the snow. Even in the summer I'd shiver sometimes in the shade of a tree. And Pa — I didn't touch you, remember — there's no point in haunting me. He did. He's come round maybe. Oh no Jesus please. Round. Wakes. Sees the horse has stopped. He sits and rocks and thinks the horse is going on and then he sees it's not. He tries his heels but the horse has finally stopped. He gets off and leads him on smack into the barn, and there it is, the barn, the barn he took the horse from. Then in the barn he begins to see better and he makes out something solid in the yard where he knows the house is and there are certain to be little letups in the storm and through one of them he sees a flicker of something almost orange, a flicker of the fire and a sign of me by it all stretched out my head on my arm and near asleep. If they'd given me a dog, I'd have called him Shep.

I jumped up and ran to the kitchen but then I stopped and ran back for the gun and then ran back to the closet for the pail which I dropped with a terrible clatter. The tap gasped. The dipper in the pail beneath the sink rattled. So I ran to the fire and began to poke at it, the logs tumbling, and then I beat the logs with the poker so that sparks flew in my hair.

I crouched down behind a big chair in a corner away from the fire. Then I remembered I'd left my gun in the kitchen. My feet were bare and sore. The room was full of orange light and blackened shadows, moving. The wind whooped and the house creaked like steps do. I began to wonder if the Pedersens had a dog, if the Pedersen kid had a dog or cat maybe and where it was if they did, and if I'd known its name, whether it'd come if I called. I tried to think of its name as if it was something I'd forgot. I knew I was all muddled up and scared and crazy and I tried to think god damn over and over or what the hell or Jesus Christ, instead, but it didn't work.

The wagon had a great big wheel. Papa had a paper sack. Mama held my hand. High horse waved his tail. Papa had a paper sack. We both ran to hide. Mama held my hand. The wagon had a great big wheel. High horse waved his tail. We both ran to hide. Papa had a paper sack. The wagon had a great big wheel. Mama held my hand. Papa had a paper sack. High horse waved his tail. The wagon had a great big wheel. We both ran to hide. High horse waved his tail. Mama held my hand. We both ran to hide. The wagon had a great big wheel. Papa had a paper sack. Mama held my hand. High horse waved his tail. Papa had a paper sack. We both ran to hide. Papa had a paper sack. We both ran to hide.

The wind was still. The snow was still. The sun burned on the snow. The fireplace was cold and all the logs were ashy. I lay stiffly on the floor, my legs drawn up, my arms around me. The fire had gone steadily into gray while I slept, and the night away, and I saw the dust float and glitter and settle down. The walls, the rug, the furniture, all that I could see from my elbow looked pale and tired and drawn up tight and cramped with cold. I felt I'd never seen these things before. I'd never seen a wasted morning, the sick drawn look of a winter dawn, or how things were in a room where things were stored away and no one ever came, and how the dust came gently down.

I put my socks on. I didn't remember at all coming from behind the chair, but I must have. I got some matches from the kitchen and some paper twists out of a box beside the fireplace and I put them down, raking the ashes aside. Then I put some light kindling on top. Pieces of orange crate I think they were. And then a log. I lit the paper and it flared up and flakes of the kindling curled and got red and black and dropped off and finally the kindling caught when I blew on it. It didn't warm my hands any though I kept them close, so I rubbed my arms and legs and jigged, but my feet hurt. Then the fire growled. Another log. I found I couldn't whistle. I warmed my back some. Outside snow. Steep. There were long hard shadows in the hollows of the drifts but the eastern crests were bright. After I'd warmed up a little I walked about the house in my stocking feet, and snagged my socks on the stairs. I looked under all the beds and in all the closets and behind most of the furniture. I remembered the pipes were froze. I got the pail from under the sink and opened the door to the back porch against a drift and scooped snow in the pail with a dipper. Snow had risen to the shoulders of the snowman. The pump was banked. There were no tracks anywhere.

I started the stove and put snow in a kettle. The stove was beautifully black. I went back to the fireplace and put more logs on. It was beginning to roar and the room was turning cheerful. I wriggled into my boots. Somehow I had a hunch I'd see a horse.

The front door was unlocked. All the doors were, likely. He

could have walked right in. I'd forgot about that. But now I knew
he wasn't meant to. I laughed to see how a laugh would sound.
Again. Good.

The road was gone. Fences, bushes, old machinery: what there
might be in any yard was all gone under snow. All I could see was
the steep snow and the long shadow lines and the hard bright crest
about to break but not quite breaking and the hazy sun rising,
throwing down slats of orange like a snow fence had fallen down.
He'd gone off this way yet there was nothing now to show he'd
gone; nothing like a bump of black in a trough or an arm or leg
sticking out of the side of a bank like a branch had blown down
or a horse's head uncovered like a rock; nowhere Pedersen's fences
had kept bare he might be lying huddled with the horse on its haunches
by him; nothing even in the shadows shrinking while I watched to
take for something hard and not of snow and once alive.

I saw the window I'd broke. The door of the barn hung open,
banked with snow. The house threw a narrow shadow clear to one
end of the barn where it ran into the high drift that Hans had tunneled
in. Later I'd cut a path to it. Make the tunnel bigger maybe. Like
a hollow tree. There was time. I saw the oaks too, blown clean,
their twigs about their branches stiff as quills. The path I'd taken
from the barn to the house was filled and the sun was burning
brightly on it. The wind had curled in and driven a bank of snow
against the house where I'd stood. As I turned my head the sun
flashed from the barrel of Pa's gun. The snow had risen around
him. Only the top of the barrel was clear to take the sun and it
flashed squarely in my eye when I turned my head just right. There
was nothing to do about that till spring. Another snowman, he'd
melt. I picked my way back to the front of the house, a dark spot
dancing in the snow ahead of me. Today there was a fine large sky.

It was pleasant not to have to stamp the snow off my boots, and
the fire was speaking pleasantly and the kettle was sounding softly.
There was no need for me to grieve. I had been the brave one and
now I was free. The snow would keep me. I would bury Pa and
the Pedersens and Hans and even Ma. I hadn't wanted to come but
now I didn't mind. The kid and me, we'd done brave things well
worth remembering. The way that fellow had come so mysteriously
through the snow and done us such a glorious turn — well it made me
think of church. The winter time had finally got them all, and I really
did hope that the kid was as warm as I was now, warm inside and out,
burning up, inside and out, with joy.

# Kay Boyle (1903–    )

FIRST PROMINENT as one of the expatriate writers centering around *transition* magazine in the Paris of the twenties, Kay Boyle has long been one of the most esteemed American short-story writers. She is also well known as a novelist and poet. Boyle was born in St. Paul, Minnesota, but her writing is cosmopolitan in character. Her short-story collections include *Wedding Day* (1930), *First Lover* (1933), *The White Horses of Vienna* (1936) and *The Smoking Mountain* (1951). A few of her novels are *Plagued by the Nightingale* (1931), *Gentlemen, I Address You Privately* (1933), *Avalanche* (1943) and *Generation Without Farewell* (1960).

If there were no other scene in "Seven Say You Can Hear Corn Grow" than that in which derelicts in a line waiting for a night's free shelter break ranks and stumble through the dark toward a girl's voice crying, "Daddy! Daddy!" this story would demonstrate Kay Boyle's prowess as a writer. There are as well the finely drawn characters, the boy who collects "all kinds of odd information," descriptions of which are almost stories in themselves as are descriptions of the boy's crying mother picketing their street when he is late getting home and the mad girl pretending a weird municipal authority. It is such poignancy in writing that attracts so many readers to her short stories.

# Seven Say You Can Hear Corn Grow

DAN MINOS was a boy who collected all kinds of odd information from the newspapers he read, bits and pieces of things that had already taken place, or were still taking place, here and there in the world; such as the report that an octopus in the zoo in Berlin, Germany, was devouring itself at the rate of a half inch of tentacle per day. One of the aquarium officials had stated that the octopus was suffering from some emotional upset, and that by the end of the month, if the situation continued, it would certainly be dead. The boy read this and looked at his own gnawed fingernails, and then looked quickly at something else.

Once he read about how scientists are trying to dilute the venom in the stings of jellyfish that drift along the eastern seaboard like fringed umbrellas (as the paper put it), pulsing in and out among the bathers with limp curved handles hanging under them, while the tide, or some unseen hand, opens and closes them continuously. This poison, went the story, is stored in cups along the umbrella handles, and it acts in the same way as the stuff South American Indians tip their arrowheads with, causing paralysis, failure of the respiratory organs, and death in the case of small sea animals. Another time there was a half-page report on the remarkable navigating abilities of the green turtle, saying that the U.S. Navy was financing a study of how this large seafarer finds the pinpoint island of his birth.

When Dan's mother came back to their Brooklyn apartment at night, she would bring some newspaper or other with her that a customer had left behind on a table in the restaurant where she worked. One night it might be the *Herald Tribune* or maybe the *New York Times* that she carried with her handbag into the kitchen, and other nights it might be the *Journal-American* or the *Daily News*. But whatever paper it was, Dan would go through the pages of it in his room before he went to sleep, not noticing the name of the paper or the date, but reading the columns eagerly, as if in search of some final communiqué that would tell him how either beast or man had coped with the predicament of circumstances; as if seeking, in the silent doom of animals without precisely knowing what he sought, some indication of what his own vocabulary might one day be.

If you came to the conclusion that Dan Minos speculated on these things he read because the world of newsprint was the only world he functioned in, you would be wrong; for he had as well the daily world of high school, and he had major league baseball to follow, and television to present to him as reality the myths of power by which America lives. It was more that he carried the news items he read like a kind of shield between himself and others, a shield that was never emblazoned with any likeness of himself, but with that of aquarium official, or of scientist isolating the sting of jellyfish, or naval experimenter tagging green turtles at Ascension Island. Once it was the likeness of a German priest he carried, a priest who had been sitting in the front row of the circus when the lion tamer in the enclosed arena clutched at his heart and fell to the floor. The wild beasts had slunk down from their perches, the newspaper item said, and moved stealthily toward the fallen lion tamer while the spectators watched with bated breath for what was absolutely certain to take place. And then the priest had jumped up, pulled open the door of the caged arena, warded off the lions with a chair, and dragged the stricken man to safety. (Whether or not the lion tamer died of his heart attack in the end, the newspaper did not say.)

It was only the story of the harness racing horse that went berserk in an airfreighter eight thousand feet above the ocean that Dan couldn't put to any immediate use.

"Sometimes I've thought of being a pilot, a commercial pilot," Dan said to his mother that evening when she came home, "but then

I read this thing about the horse in the airplane, and maybe I don't feel the same about pilots any more."

"If my opinion was to be asked," his mother said, "I'd say go ahead and be a commercial pilot and forget about the horse." She worked as a waitress, and she never gave him any real trouble except when he came in so late at night that for hours she'd have been walking her high heels sideways up and down outside on the street. Sometimes it was three o'clock when he'd come home, and she'd be walking back and forth on the Brooklyn street without so much as a Kleenex to stop her crying, complaining about him to anyone passing by. "He doesn't know five o'clock in the afternoon from midnight," she'd say to anyone at all. "I don't know how he gets along. He can't tell good from bad." Or she'd give a description of him in case someone had seen him, saying: "He's nearly six foot tall, and his shoulders are broad, and he's nicely built, the way his father was. He'd be good-looking if he went and got his hair cut every now and then." She got up now from the kitchen table, and crossed the room, and took a can of beer out of the refrigerator, and she swore under her breath as the new-type, built-in-the-can opener tore a piece out of her nail. "But my opinion isn't worth anything to anybody, living or dead," she said.

Dan looked at her dark orange hair, and her face bleached smooth as a china cup, with the various features painted carefully on it.

"There were six horses in the plane," he said, thinking of this thing that had taken place maybe yesterday or the day before, "and this one, this champion, he panicked. He'd been winning harness races everywhere, Australia, New Zealand, all over, the paper said. He was worth seventy-five thousand dollars, and he was kicking and rearing like at a rodeo."

"All they had to do was turn around," the mother said, drinking exquisitely from the can. "Planes can always turn around and go back the way cars can't. You get yourself on a throughway in a car and if you're heading west you have to go to Chicago whether you want to go there or not."

"This plane was going to Montreal," Dan said. "They couldn't go back."

"What's so special about Montreal?" the mother asked, her small, cherry lip mustached with foam.

"The freight engineer, he said they'd tried cutting the sling around his ribs so they could get him to lie down," the boy said. "There were three of them trying to quiet him, but he threw them off, and his front legs were hanging out over the side of the stall. He was smashing against the cockpit, like trying to get to the controls. The other five horses had started acting up, so that's when the pilot told them what to do."

"I don't want to hear what they did," the mother said, taking another swig of beer.

"You can't change it by not listening," Dan said. "It happened. You can't make things different by just looking the other way."

"If you drank a can of beer every now and then, things would look different to you whether they were or not," his mother said. "It would relax you. It would do you good."

"The pilot of the airfreighter said the horse had to be destroyed," Dan said, perhaps not even having heard her speak. "That's the word they use," he explained. "But they didn't have a gun."

"They could have pushed the horse out the hatch," the mother said. She got up from her chair and carried the empty beer can across the kitchen to where it had to go. "For a horse worth seventy-five thousand dollars, they could have afforded a parachute," she said, daintily pressing her foot in a bedroom slipper trimmed with gilded ostrich feathers on the pedal of the garbage pail. When the white lid gaped open, she dropped the beer can inside. "Can't you see that horse parachuting out of the plane, pulling the rip cord and everything?" she said, and she gave a little scream of laughter. Then she took another can of beer from the refrigerator, and walked carefully on her wedge-soled slippers back to the table, and sat down. "So this time maybe you'll open it for me," she said, as she had said it on so many other evenings; and Dan took the can in his narrow fingers and twisted the flat metal tongue from its misted top. "I bought another pair of eyelashes today. Better quality," she went on saying. "Real dark long ones, with a new kind of stickum on them. If I go to the show tomorrow night, maybe you'll help me put them on."

"So when the freight engineer got the word from the pilot about what to do, he grabbed a fire ax," Dan said, and she still might not have spoken. He was seeing it exactly as it must have been.

"Stop it!" his mother cried out in sudden ferocity. "I don't have to hear it! I have a hard enough time working myself to death on my feet all day!"

"You have to hear it," Dan said. He looked at her small bright trembling mouth and her quivering chin, but he did not seem to see her. "If you don't know whether you're on the side of the horse they killed or on the side of the pilot, there's no sense trying to work out your life. You have to decide that first," he said.

"On the side of the horse or the side of the pilot? You're crazy!" she cried out in fury, her hand too agitated now to lift the can of beer.

And then, two nights later, on Christopher Street, in the city itself, Dan made the acquaintance of the girl. It could have been any month and any Saturday, with no extremes of any kind, and only the first beginning of chill in the bluish New York air. It had not yet begun to go dark when Dan saw the old man lying across the curb near the corner of Seventh Avenue, lying flat on his thin back with his legs sticking out into the street so that the passing traffic had to swing around them. His ancient trousers were slashed across as if by a knife, and his shoes were split by the bunions and corns he had carried around with him for half a century or more. His small head lay in a semblance of ease and comfort on the sidewalk paving, economically crowned with a crew cut of the purest white. The same white bristled without hostility along his jaws, and his cheekbones were bright as apples on either side of his short, scarlet nose. Beside him, in a turtle-neck sweater and slacks, the girl squatted, her face masked by a swinging curtain of long, straight, almost tinsel-colored hair. She was trying to raise the old man by his shoulders, and she was trying to push her bracelets and the black sweater sleeves back on her forearms, to get these encumbrances out of the way. "Repeatedly striking with force between the horse's eyes," the newspaper line kept going, for no good reason, through Dan's mind as he stooped down, "the flight engineer brought the frenzied pacer to its knees, and the ordeal of terror for man and beast was over."

"He looks as though he'd been here a week," the girl was saying.

"I'll get his shoulders," Dan said, and the girl shifted on the heels of her loafers out of his way.

The mottled-tweed jacket the man wore was soft and expensive to the touch; but however good it had once been, and whatever tall and elegant stranger had worn it once with grace, frayed wool now hung like feathers from the cuffs and from the jaunty lapels. As Dan drew him up onto the sidewalk, the girl moved on her heels beside them, her knees in the tight black slacks almost touching her chin, her bracelets ringing musically when she laid her palms beneath the old man's head. The three of them might have been quite alone in the crowded street. No one slackened his pace, no one turned to look in their direction, perhaps because of the sad sharp odor of grieving dreams and rotted teeth that lay in an aura around the sleeping man. Dan knew it well. It was there winter and summer, in snow or in rain, in the gutters and alleyways of the downtown streets he wandered. It lay in stupor under the park benches in the early mornings when drunks sobbed aloud to stone and grass the furious accusations of their pain.

"You'd better get that pint out of his hip pocket," Dan said to the silky lengths of the girl's hair, knowing, too, the exact size and shape the flask would be. "Sometimes when they fall, it cuts them up right through their clothes."

"You're sharp, aren't you, kid?" the girl said. For the first time now she looked up at him, and he saw that her eyes were wide and dark and stormy, and her brows and lashes were smudged like charcoal across her face. "I happen to live in this city," she said. "I happen to live right on this street." Dan held the little man under the armpits still, and as he looked down at the girl he thought of the things that might be of interest to say. He might tell her that in Japan a drunk is called *o-tora-san,* which means "Honorable Mr. Tiger," and that there are over a hundred and fifty sobering-up stations over there called "Tiger Boxes." He could give her the statistics even, saying that just last year one hundred and twenty-eight thousand and ninety-seven drunks had been taken to "Tiger Boxes" by the police to sleep it off. But he had got the little old man in a sitting position, with his neat skull fallen forward on his breast, and it did not seem the moment to speak. The girl reached into the little man's back pocket and took out the gold-and-red lettered bottle that had clung so perilously to his hip. "Two houses up there's an alley where he can lie down, where the fuzz won't see him," she said. She slipped the half-empty flask into the depths of her black shoulder bag, her bracelets ringing like sleigh bells as she moved.

They were walking now, the little old man held upright between them, and Dan thought of the Potawatomi Indians on Michigan's Upper Peninsula drinking for solace, as one newspaper had said. The professor who made the report had been drinking two years with them, and he said that alcohol now substituted for the tribal customs and rituals that had disappeared from their lives. Alcohol, the professor stated to the press, had given them the illusion that their ancestral rights had restored to them the high status that Potawatomi men had held until the white man had come upon the scene. "This professor said drinking was a way for them of asking for pity," Dan wanted to say to the girl, but he didn't say it. Nor did he tell her that in Brazil the police let sleeping drunks lie as long as they didn't block the sidewalk. With the little man propelled between them, they had come to the alleyway now, and there seemed no reason to speak of things that were taking place so far away.

"Get him to the end, back there behind the garbage cans," the girl said, and the pigeons who had been pecking at the paving stones hurried aside to let them pass.

The girl lowered her half of the little man to the ground, and Dan could not see the back of her neck because of the window shade of her hair drawn down across her shoulders. But he saw her slender, tightly belted waist, and her narrow hips, and the long, slim tapering legs in the black slacks, and he could not look away.

"I'll put my jacket under his head," he said, once the little man lay flat on his back in comfort.

The girl waited until he had folded it under the neat, impervious head, and then she drew the old man's right hand free of the elegant frayed sleeve and laid it, palm down, on his breast.

"Give me the other one," she said to Dan. It lay as if cast off, as if forgotten, on the alley stone, and Dan lifted it while she took the whiskey flask out of her bag. Then she bent the old man's will-less arm so that his two hands lay upon his heart, and she closed his fingers around the flask so that he, this ancient, malodorous infant in his asphalt crib, would find it there in solace when he awoke. "Regulations," the girl said. "Orders from the top." She stood up now, and Dan saw she was not tall, and that her hair was parted in the middle, and that she had no lipstick on her mouth. "This is my job. I get paid for it," she was saying, and a look of singular shrewdness was in her stormy eyes. "I've got quite an important position. I get paid by the city," she said.

"If they're hiring people, I'd be free to work every night," Dan said. They walked down the alley together, past the last of the pigeons hastening back and forth in the beginning of dusk, their eyes cocked sharply in their smooth, gray-feathered skulls. And every word that he and the girl exchanged seemed as reasonable to him as the story of that other, foreign pigeon who had hopped a hundred and sixty miles across Denmark with its wings bound. The newspaper had said that it crossed two rivers, nobody knew how, to get back to where it came from in the end. "I'd like a job like that," he said.

"You have to be twenty to work for the city," the girl said. "You look too young." As they entered Christopher Street again, the street lights came on in the early evening, and she shifted her black bag higher on her shoulder, walking now with that sort of frenzied dedication that takes people across deserts, across prairies, not caring about food, or drink, or sleep, driven toward some final destination that has no geography or name. "You have to know Spanish and French and Puerto Rican, and a lot about history," she said.

"I know about things like that," Dan said, keeping step beside her. "I read a lot." He thought of the green turtles' knowledge of the currents of the sea, and the Caribbean beaches they came back to, not every year, but whenever they could make it, navigating sometimes more than a thousand miles to reach the hot white sands where they were born. "The green turtles' lives are something like history," he said. "Anyway, Columbus left written records about them. I read about how they come swimming in to these beaches, and dig their holes, and lay their eggs. Columbus and the other explorers, like Leif Ericson and everyone, they used to eat their eggs."

"Did they eat them fried or boiled?" the girl asked sternly. "These are the things you have to know."

"That wasn't in the paper," Dan said, and his voice was troubled.

They had come to the corner of Seventh Avenue, and the girl turned left without any hesitation, and Dan followed where she led. "They have something like a compass inside them, the turtles," he went on saying. He and the girl were moving through the electric blue and yellow and red of the café lights, and through the spaces of city dark, and his head was turned to watch the side of her face changing as the lights and the diluted darkness changed. "I think I have something like that, too," Dan said. "I bet I could find New York wherever I was. I could come straight back across the country without needing maps or roads or anything like that."

"What country?" the girl asked, with the sharp edge of something different in her voice. "What country are you talking about?"

"Well, this country. The United States. I mean, America," Dan said, as if not quite certain of the name.

"You're pretty weak on geography," the girl said. She was stepping down from the curb, over rotting orange peels, over onion tails that had once been green, and flattened grapefruit rinds. "We haven't got a country. Wise up, kid. We've got New York," she said.

They crossed this side street as they had crossed the others, moving through the altering sections of dark and light. Wherever the girl was taking him was of no importance, and the impatience of the words she spoke was transformed to gentleness by the curve of her cheekbone below his shoulder, and the delicacy of her temple and brow when she swung back her hair. They were entering warehouse territory now, and high above the traffic hung the perpendicular letters of a sign not written in neon, but only faintly alight with the dying glow of bulbs set in its frame. "Volunteers of America," the sign read, and Dan knew that a queue of men would be standing beneath it, standing night or day, crippled or upright, sober or drunk, and no matter what time of year it was, waiting to pass through the double doors.

"They're waiting for something to eat," Dan said, and the girl did not take the trouble to turn her head and look at him. But she said:

"They're waiting for me. I make a report on them every night. I'm the only one in the field the city trusts." And even this Dan did not question, believing as he did that everything she said was true. Just this side of the slowly moving queue of men, she slipped without warning into the shadows of a warehouse doorway, and flattened her shoulders and her narrow hips against the wall. "Don't let them see you," she whispered, and Dan stepped in beside her. "If they start running after me, don't move. Stay out of sight. Some of them are still very strong even though they're old. If they once get hold of you, they squeeze you terribly in their arms," she said, her voice still hushed, "and they push their chins into your face."

"About us not having a country," Dan said. He was standing

so close to her in the darkness that he could hear the breath running in and out of her mouth. "Did you read that in the paper, that we only have New York?"

"Oh, the paper!" she said in irritation.

"Sometimes there're interesting things in the paper," he said. "Last night I read about the artichoke war they're having in France."

"Do you speak French?" the girl asked quickly. "Sometimes I need it. Some nights there're Frenchmen standing in line, sailors who jumped their ships, and haven't any place to go. I have to get their names. I have to make an official report on them."

Dan waited a moment, thinking of this, and then he said:

"Do you report back on these men? Is that the kind of work you do?"

"You're very handsome," the girl said softly, her breath running gently in the darkness, her voice turned tender and low. "I like your hair, and the way you talk, and everything, but you don't seem to understand things very well. I'm paid by the city to call them back from where they are. I'm the only one that can do it." And this might have been the whispered password, the valid signal given, that would cause the sentries to lower their guns and let the trusted through; for now the girl stepped out of the doorway, and her bracelets rang as she made a megaphone of her hands through which to call the words to the waiting men. "Oh, Daddy, Daddy, Daddy!" she cried out in almost unbearable and strident despair, and some in the slowly advancing queue turned their heads, as if aroused from sleep, and some did not. "Oh, Pa*pa*, Pa*pa*, Pa*pa!*" she cried as a daughter from a foreign country might have cried from the sucking undertow before the final music for the drowning played. "Oh, Daddy, Daddy, Daddy, help me!" she cried. "Oh, Popio, Popio, here I am! I'm here!" And now that she had summoned them four times, a wail of anguish rose from the throats of those who had broken from the line, and stumbled back through the darkness to where she was.

Brenda, or Shirley, or Mary, or Barbara, were the names they called out as they tried to run in other men's castoff shoes, in the outsized bags of other men's trousers, and could not. Jean, or Amy, or Pat, or Ann, the muffled voices sobbed like foghorns, and the men in whose throats the hoarse names rose fumbled their way past utility poles and fire hydrants, felt their way like blind men along the warehouse walls toward the sound and the flesh of all they had mislaid in the desert of their lives.

"We'd better get going," the girl said to Dan. She was standing beside him again in the shelter of the doorway, her breath coming fast. "Just run, just run," she whispered, and she pulled him out onto the sidewalk, her fingers closed tightly around his hand.

They did not stop until they had reached the flight of subway steps, and there she let Dan's hand drop. As she threw back her head to look up at him in the wash of the street light, she shook her bracelets savagely.

"You were faster than any of them," Dan said; and, without warning, the vision of the racing horse gone berserk plunged through his thoughts again. As it reared in terror, hammering the cockpit of the airfreighter with its frantic hoofs, Dan touched the girl's silver hair with uncertain fingers, saying: "But you'll have to stop running soon, before you get too tired."

"No, no!" the girl said, whispering it quickly. She stood close to him, looking up at him with her wild, stormy eyes. "You have to get somewhere, don't you?" she said; and then she did not say anything, but she put her arms in the black sweater sleeves tightly, tightly, around Dan's hips, tightly, as if forever, with her head pressed fiercely against the beating of his heart.

It was only for a minute, and then she was gone, running like crazy across Seventh Avenue. The green light turned to red as Dan got to the curb, and the beams of headlights poured between them, and he waited, understanding now with singular clarity the urgency of the choice to be made between horse and pilot, man and man. He could see the white of the harness pacer's eye, and the features of the airfreighter pilot's face, and he knew what should have been done in that interval when the election of either life or death hung in the balance eight thousand feet above the sea. He could not hear the pilot's voice saying *quiet, quiet,* to the stampeding terror. He could not hear it naming the destination to which they were, man and horse, committed, as the course of turtle and pigeon with its wings bound named it louder and clearer than catastrophe. Instead, the pilot's voice, not only heard but visible as are the words contained in comic-strip balloons, pronounced *destroy,* thus summoning death as witness to his fear. *We are not turning back. We shall complete this flight as scheduled,* he might have said, but he did not say it; and, standing waiting at the curb, Dan felt the failure of all men in the pilot's failure, and he whispered "Quiet, now, quiet," to the horse or the girl or the traffic passing by. When the light changed again and the cars halted, he crossed, running, in the direction the girl had fled.

But she was not in the alley off Christopher Street. The little old man was gone, and only his empty flask and the garbage pails were there. At the "Volunteers of America" the sign had gone dark and for once the street was empty. There was no queue of derelict men waiting at the door. It was growing cold, but Dan did not think of this as he walked up one street and down another, searching among the faces that passed in twos or threes through the lights from the cafés, and searching among the solitary others that lingered in the intervals of dark. If he did not find her tonight, still it would not be the end, he kept saying to himself, for he could come back to the city every night, whatever the weather, and on one of the streets, around one of the corners, he would hear her bracelets ringing or see her tinsel hair. If it was not tonight, it would be the night after, or maybe three nights later, or else at the end of the week; and after they had put the drunks to sleep, they would sit down on a curbstone together, and he would say, or try to say, "Don't call the lost men back from where they are. Don't make them remember. Just let them go." He would tell her about things that were taking place in other parts of America, beyond New York; about the Middle West, for instance, where seven university professors had made a tape-recording proving that you can hear corn grow.

It was three o'clock in the morning when he got back to Brooklyn, and his mother was walking up and down outside, complaining loudly enough about him for any neighbors who were awake to hear.

"Your jacket!" she cried out when she saw him coming up the street. "You had your good jacket on when you left the house! Oh, God, oh, God!" she wept.

Above them, as they went into the apartment house together, the one big planet was fading from the sky.

# Joyce Carol Oates (1938–    )

THERE MAY have been more prolific American writers than Joyce Carol Oates but none has surpassed her in the varied forms her multitudinous writings have taken. Short stories, novels, poems, articles, essays, plays, translations, book reviews, letters to the editor — you name it — Joyce Carol Oates is sure to have written it — and all in the space of a few years. Also, this literary cyclone is a professor of English at the University of Windsor in Ontario, Canada. She was born in Lockport, New York, graduated from Syracuse University in 1960 and received a master's degree from the University of Wisconsin. Among her many literary honors is the National Book Award for Fiction in 1970.

The title vividly describes the schizophrenic barrier that suddenly divides reality for the terror-stricken young girl of "Where Are You Going, Where Have You Been?" into what has been her normal life and what now awaits her. Joyce Carol Oates is noted for skill in developing tension in her characters with violence often implicit in the background. Even if the humiliated victim escapes alive, her future is forever scarred. Rape is the most devastating of crimes but unlike murder and other offenses practically never figures in the modern short story, although for literary purposes it presents great dramatic and characterization opportunities.

# *Where Are You Going, Where Have You Been?*

TO BOB DYLAN

HER NAME was Connie. She was fifteen and she had a quick nervous giggling habit of craning her neck to glance into mirrors, or checking other people's faces to make sure her own was all right. Her mother, who noticed everything and knew everything and who hadn't much reason any longer to look at her own face, always scolded Connie about it. "Stop gawking at yourself, who are you? You think you're so pretty?" she would say. Connie would raise her eyebrows at these familiar complaints and look right through her mother, into a shadowy vision of herself as she was right at that moment: she knew she was pretty and that was everything. Her mother had been pretty once too, if you could believe those old snapshots in the album, but now her looks were gone and that was why she was always after Connie.

"Why don't you keep your room clean like your sister? How've you got your hair fixed — what the hell stinks? Hair spray? You don't see your sister using that junk."

Her sister June was twenty-four and still lived at home. She was a secretary in the high school Connie attended, and if that wasn't bad enough — with her in the same building — she was so plain and chunky and steady that Connie had to hear her praised all the time by her mother and her mother's sisters. June did this, June did that, she saved money and helped clean the house and cooked and Connie couldn't do a thing, her mind was all filled with trashy daydreams. Their father was away at work most of the time and when he came home he wanted supper and he read the newspaper at supper and after supper he went to bed. He didn't bother talking much to them, but around his bent head Connie's mother kept picking at her until Connie wished her mother were dead and she herself were dead and it were all over. "She makes me want to throw up sometimes," she complained to her friends. She had a high, breathless, amused voice which made everything she said sound a little forced, whether it was sincere or not.

There was one good thing: June went places with girlfriends of hers, girls who were just as plain and steady as she, and so when Connie wanted to do that her mother had no objections. The father of Connie's best girlfriend drove the girls the three miles to town and left them off at a shopping plaza, so that they could talk through the stores or go to a movie, and when he came to pick them up again at eleven he never bothered to ask what they had done.

They must have been familiar sights, walking around that shopping plaza in their shorts and flat ballerina slippers that always scuffed the sidewalk, with charm bracelets jingling on their thin wrists; they would lean together to whisper and laugh secretly if someone passed by who amused or interested them. Connie had long dark blond hair that drew anyone's eye to it, and she wore part of it pulled up on her head and puffed out and the rest of it she let fall down her back. She wore a pullover jersey blouse that looked one way when she was at home and another way when she was away from home. Everything about her had two sides to it, one for home and one for anywhere that was not home: her walk that could be childlike and bobbing, or languid enough to make anyone think she was hearing music in her head, her mouth which was pale and smirking most of the time, but bright and pink on these evenings out, her laugh which was cynical and drawling at home — "Ha, ha, very funny" — but high-pitched and nervous anywhere else, like the jingling of the charms on her bracelet.

Sometimes they did go shopping or to a movie, but sometimes they went across the highway, ducking fast across the busy road, to a drive-in restaurant where older kids hung out. The restaurant was shaped like a big bottle, though squatter than a real bottle, and on its cap was a revolving figure of a grinning boy who held a hamburger aloft. One night in midsummer they ran across, breathless with daring, and right away someone leaned out a car window and invited them over, but it was just a boy from high school they didn't like. It made them feel good to be able to ignore him. They went up through the maze of parked and cruising cars to the bright-lit, fly-infested restaurant, their faces pleased and expectant as if they were entering a sacred building that loomed out of the night to give them what haven and what blessing they yearned for. They sat at the counter and crossed their legs at the ankles, their thin shoulders rigid with excitement, and listened to the music that made everything so good: the music was always in the background like music at a church service, it was something to depend upon.

A boy named Eddie came in to talk with them. He sat backward on his stool, turning himself jerkily around in semicircles and then stopping and turning again, and after awhile he asked Connie if she would like something to eat. She said she did and so she tapped her friend's arm on her way out — her friend pulled her face up into a brave droll look — and Connie said she would meet her at eleven, across the way. "I just hate to leave her like that," Connie said earnestly, but the boy said that she wouldn't be alone for long. So they went out to his car and on the way Connie couldn't help but let her eyes wander over the windshields and faces all around her, her face gleaming with a joy that had nothing to do with Eddie or even this place; it might have been the music. She drew her shoulders up and sucked in her breath with the pure pleasure of being alive, and just at that moment she happened to glance at a face just a few feet from hers. It was a boy with shaggy black hair, in a convertible jalopy painted gold. He stared at her and then his lips widened into a grin. Connie slit her eyes at him and turned away, but she couldn't help glancing back and there he was still watching her. He wagged a finger and laughed and said, "Gonna get you, baby," and Connie turned away again without Eddie noticing anything.

She spent three hours with him, at the restaurant where they ate hamburgers and drank Cokes in wax cups that were always sweating, and then down an alley a mile or so away, and when he left her off at five to eleven only the movie house was still open at the plaza. Her girlfriend was there, talking with a boy. When Connie came up the two girls smiled at each other and Connie said, "How was the movie?" and the girl said, *"You* should know." They rode off with the girl's father, sleepy and pleased, and Connie couldn't help but look at the darkened shopping plaza with its big empty parking lot and its signs that were faded and ghostly now, and over at the drive-in restaurant where cars were still circling tirelessly. She couldn't hear the music at this distance.

Next morning June asked her how the movie was and Connie said, "So-so."

She and that girl and occasionally another girl went out several times a week that way, and the rest of the time Connie spent around the house — it was summer vacation — getting in her mother's way and thinking, dreaming, about the boys she met. But all the boys fell back and dissolved into a single face that was not even a face, but an idea, a feeling, mixed up with the urgent insistent pounding of the music and the humid night air of July. Connie's mother kept dragging her back to the daylight by finding things for her to do or saying, suddenly, "What's this about the Pettinger girl?"

And Connie would say nervously, "Oh, her. That dope." She always drew thick clear lines between herself and such girls, and her mother was simple and kindly enough to believe her. Her mother was so simple, Connie thought, that it was maybe cruel to fool her so much. Her mother went scuffling around the house in old bedroom slippers and complained over the telephone to one sister about the other, then the other called up and the two of them complained about the third one. If June's name was mentioned her mother's tone was approving, and if Connie's name was mentioned it was disapproving. This did not really mean she disliked Connie and actually Connie thought that her mother preferred her to June because she was prettier, but the two of them kept up a pretense of exasperation, a sense that they were tugging and struggling over something of little value to either of them. Sometimes, over coffee, they were almost friends, but something would come up — some vexation that was like a fly buzzing suddenly around their heads — and their faces went hard with contempt.

One Sunday Connie got up at eleven — none of them bothered with church — and washed her hair so that it could dry all day long, in the sun. Her parents and sisters were going to a barbecue at an aunt's house and Connie said no, she wasn't interested, rolling her eyes to let mother know just what she thought of it. "Stay home alone then," her mother said sharply. Connie sat out back in a lawn chair and watched them drive away, her father quiet and bald, hunched around so that he could back the car out, her mother with a look that was still angry and not at all softened through the windshield, and in the back seat poor old June all dressed up as if she didn't know what a barbecue was, with all the running yelling kids and the flies. Connie sat with her eyes closed in the sun, dreaming and dazed with the warmth about her as if this were a kind of love, the caresses of love, and her mind slipped over onto thoughts of the boy she had been with the night before and how nice he had been, how sweet it always was, not the way someone like June would suppose but sweet, gentle, the way it was in movies and promised in songs; and when she opened her eyes she hardly knew where she was, the back yard ran off into weeds and a fence-line of trees and behind it the sky was perfectly blue and still. The asbestos "ranch house" that was now three years old startled her — it looked small. She shook her head as if to get awake.

It was too hot. She went inside the house and turned on the radio to drown out the quiet. She sat on the edge of her bed, barefoot, and listened for an hour and a half to a program called XYZ Sunday Jamboree, record after record of hard, fast, shrieking songs she sang along with, interspersed by exclamations from "Bobby King": "An' look here you girls at Napoleon's — Son and Charley want you to pay real close attention to this song coming up!"

And Connie paid close attention herself, bathed in a glow of slow-pulsed joy that seemed to rise mysteriously out of the music itself and lay languidly about the airless little room, breathed in and breathed out with each gentle rise and fall of her chest.

After a while she heard a car coming up the drive. She sat up at once, startled, because it couldn't be her father so soon. The gravel kept crunching all the way in from the road — the driveway was long — and Connie ran to the window. It was a car she didn't know. It was an open jalopy, painted a bright gold that caught the sunlight opaquely. Her heart began to pound and her fingers snatched at her hair, checking it, and she whispered "Christ. Christ," wondering how bad she looked. The car came to a stop at the side door and the horn sounded four short taps as if this were a signal Connie knew.

She went into the kitchen and approached the door slowly, then hung out the screen door, her bare toes curling down off the step. There were two boys in the car and now she recognized the driver: he had shaggy, shabby black hair that looked crazy as a wig and he was grinning at her.

"I ain't late, am I?" he said.

"Who the hell do you think you are?" Connie said.

"Toldja I'd be out, didn't I?"

"I don't even know who you are."

She spoke sullenly, careful to show no interest or pleasure, and he spoke in a fast bright monotone. Connie looked past him to the other boy, taking her time. He had fair brown hair, with a lock that fell onto his forehead. His sideburns gave him a fierce, embarrassed look, but so far he hadn't even bothered to glance at her. Both boys wore sunglasses. The driver's glasses were metallic and mirrored everything in miniature.

"You wanta come for a ride?" he said.

Connie smirked and let her hair fall loose over one shoulder.

"Don'tcha like my car? New paint job," he said. "Hey."

"What?"

"You're cute."

She pretended to fidget, chasing flies away from the door.

"Don'tcha believe me, or what?" he said.

"Look, I don't even know who you are," Connie said in disgust.

"Hey, Ellie's got a radio, see. Mine's broke down." He lifted his friend's arm and showed her the little transistor the boy was holding, and now Connie began to hear the music. It was the same program that was playing inside the house.

"Bobby King?" she said.

"I listen to him all the time. I think he's great."

"He's kind of great," Connie said reluctantly.

"Listen, that guy's *great*. He knows where the action is."

Connie blushed a little, because the glasses made it impossible for her to see just what this boy was looking at. She couldn't decide if she liked him or if he was just a jerk, and so she dawdled in the doorway and wouldn't come down or go back inside. She said, "What's all that stuff painted on your car?"

"Can'tcha read it?" He opened the door very carefully, as if he was afraid it might fall off. He slid out just as carefully, planting his feet firmly on the ground, the tiny metallic world in his glasses slowing down like gelatine hardening and in the midst of it Connie's bright green blouse. "This here is my name, to begin with," he said. ARNOLD FRIEND was written in tarlike black letters on the side, with a drawing of a round grinning face that reminded Connie of a pumpkin, except it wore sunglasses. "I wanta introduce myself, I'm Arnold Friend and that's my real name and I'm gonna be your friend, honey, and inside the car's Ellie Oscar, he's kinda shy." Ellie brought his transistor radio up to his shoulder and balanced it there. "Now these numbers are a secret code, honey," Arnold Friend explained. He read off the numbers 33, 19, 17 and raised his eyebrows at her to see what she thought of that, but she didn't think much of it. The left rear fender had been smashed and around it was written, on the gleaming gold background: DONE BY CRAZY WOMAN DRIVER. Connie had to laugh at that. Arnold Friend was pleased at her laughter and looked up at her. "Around the other side's a lot more — you wanta come and see them?"

"No."

"Why not?"

"Why should I?"

"Don'tcha wanta see what's on the car? Don'tcha wanta go for a ride?"

"I don't know."

"Why not?"

"I got things to do."

"Like what?"

"Things."

He laughed as if she had said something funny. He slapped his thighs. He was standing in a strange way, leaning back against the cars as if he were balancing himself. He wasn't tall, only an inch or so taller than she would be if she came down to him. Connie liked the way he was dressed, which was the way all of them dressed: tight faded jeans stuffed into black, scuffed boots, a belt that pulled his waist in and showed how lean he was, and a white pullover shirt that was a little soiled and showed the hard small muscles of his arms and shoulders. He looked as if he probably did hard work, lifting and carrying things. Even his neck looked muscular. And his face was a familiar face, somehow: the jaw and chin and cheeks slightly darkened, because he hadn't shaved for a day or two, and the nose long and hawklike, sniffing as if she were a treat he was going to gobble up and it was all a joke.

"Connie, you ain't telling the truth. This is your day set aside for a ride with me and you know it," he said, still laughing. The way he straightened and recovered from his fit of laughing showed that it had been all fake.

"How do you know what my name is?" she said suspiciously.

"It's Connie."

"Maybe and maybe not."

"I know my Connie," he said, wagging his finger. Now she remembered him even better, back at the restaurant, and her cheeks warmed at the thought of how she sucked in her breath just at the moment she passed him — how she must have looked to him. And he had remembered her. "Ellie and I come out here especially for you," he said. "Ellie can sit in back. How about it?"

"Where?"

"Where what?"

"Where're we going?"

He looked at her. He took off the sunglasses and she saw how pale the skin around his eyes was, like holes that were not in shadow but instead in light. His eyes were like chips of broken glass that catch the light in an amiable way. He smiled. It was as if the idea of going for a ride somewhere, to some place, was a new idea to him.

"Just for a ride, Connie sweetheart."

"I never said my name was Connie," she said.

"But I know what it is. I know your name and all about you, lots of things," Arnold Friend said. He had not moved yet but stood still leaning back against the side of his jalopy. "I took a special interest in you, such a pretty girl, and found out all about you like I know your parents and sister are gone somewheres and I know where and how long they're going to be gone, and I know who you were with last night, and your best girlfriend's name is Betty. Right?"

He spoke in a simple lilting voice, exactly as if he were reciting the words to a song. His smile assured her that everything was fine. In the car Ellie turned up the volume on his radio and did not bother to look around at them.

"Ellie can sit in the back seat," Arnold Friend said. He indicated his friend with a casual jerk of his chin, as if Ellie did not count and she should not bother with him.

"How'd you find out all that stuff?" Connie said.

"Listen: Betty Schultz and Tony Fitch and Jimmy Pettinger and Nancy Pettinger," he said, in a chant. "Raymond Stanley and Bob Hutter — "

"Do you know all those kids?"

"I know everybody."

"Look, you're kidding. You're not from around here."

"Sure."

"But — how come we never saw you before?"

"Sure you saw me before," he said. He looked down at his boots, as if he were a little offended. "You just don't remember."

"I guess I'd remember you," Connie said.

"Yeah?" He looked up at this, beaming. He was pleased. He began to mark time with the music from Ellie's radio, tapping his fists lightly together. Connie looked away from his smile to the car, which was painted so bright it almost hurt her eyes to look at it. She looked at that name, ARNOLD FRIEND. And up at the front fender was an expression that was familiar — MAN THE FLYING SAUCERS. It was an expression kids had used the year before, but didn't use this year. She looked at it for a while as if the words meant something to her that she did not yet know.

"What're you thinking about? Huh?" Arnold Friend demanded. "Not worried about your hair blowing around in the car, are you?"

"No."

"Think I maybe can't drive good?"

"How do I know?"

"You're a hard girl to handle. How come?" he said. "Don't you know I'm your friend? Didn't you see me put my sign in the air when you walked by?''

"What sign?"

"My sign." And he drew an X in the air, leaning out toward her. They were maybe ten feet apart. After his hand fell back to his side the X was still in the air, almost visible. Connie let the screen door close and stood perfectly still inside it, listening to the music from her radio and the boy's blend together. She stared at Arnold Friend. He stood there so stiffly relaxed, pretending to be relaxed, with one hand idly on the door handle as if he were keeping himself up that way and had no intention of ever moving again. She recognized most things about him, the tight jeans that showed his thighs and buttocks and the greasy leather boots and the tight shirt, and even that slippery friendly smile of his, that sleepy dreamy smile that all the boys used to get across ideas they didn't want to put into words. She recognized all this and also the singsong way he talked, slightly mocking, kidding, but serious and a little melancholy, and she recognized the way he tapped one fist against the other in homage to the perpetual music behind him. But all these things did not come together.

She said suddenly, "Hey, how old are you?"

His smile faded. She could see then that he wasn't a kid, he was much older — thirty, maybe more. At this knowledge her heart began to pound faster.

"That's a crazy thing to ask. Can'tcha see I'm your own age?"

"Like hell you are."

"Or maybe a coupla years older, I'm eighteen."

"Eighteen?" she said doubtfully.

He grinned to reassure her and lines appeared at the corners of his mouth. His teeth were big and white. He grinned so broadly his eyes became slits and she saw how thick the lashes were, thick and black as if painted with a black tarlike material. Then he seemed to become embarrassed, abruptly, and looked over his shoulder at Ellie. "*Him*, he's crazy," he said. "Ain't he a riot, he's a nut, a real character." Ellie was still listening to the music. His sunglasses told nothing about what he was thinking. He wore a bright orange shirt unbuttoned halfway to show his chest, which was a pale, bluish chest and not muscular like Arnold Friend's. His shirt collar was turned up all around and the very tips of the collar pointed out past his chin as if they were protecting him. He was pressing the transistor radio up against his ear and sat there in a kind of daze, right in the sun.

"He's kinda strange," Connie said.

"Hey, she says you're kinda strange! Kinda strange!" Arnold

Friend cried. He pounded on the car to get Ellie's attention. Ellie turned for the first time and Connie saw with shock that he wasn't a kid either — he had a fair, hairless face, cheeks reddened slightly as if the veins grew too close to the surface of his skin, the face of a forty-year-old baby. Connie felt a wave of dizziness rise in her at this sight and she stared at him as if waiting for something to change the shock of the moment, make it all right again. Ellie's lips kept shaping words, mumbling along with the words blasting in his ear.

"Maybe you two better go away," Connie said faintly.

"What? How come?" Arnold Friend cried. "We come out here to take you for a ride. It's Sunday." He had the voice of the man on the radio now. It was the same voice, Connie thought. "Don'tcha know it's Sunday all day and honey, no matter who you were with last night today you're with Arnold Friend and don't you forget it! — Maybe you better step out here," he said, and this last was in a different voice. It was a little flatter, as if the heat was finally getting to him.

"No. I got things to do."

"Hey."

"You two better leave."

"We ain't leaving until you come with us."

"Like hell I am —"

"Connie, don't fool around with me. I mean, I mean, don't fool *around*," he said, shaking his head. He laughed incredulously. He placed his sunglasses on top of his head, carefully, as if he were indeed wearing a wig, and brought the stems down behind his ears. Connie stared at him, another wave of dizziness and fear rising in her so that for a moment he wasn't even in focus but was just a blur, standing there against his gold car, and she had the idea that he had driven up the driveway all right but had come from nowhere before that and belonged nowhere and that everything about him and even about the music that was so familiar to her was only half real.

"If my father comes and sees you —"

"He ain't coming. He's at a barbecue."

"How do you know that?"

"Aunt Tillie's. Right now they're — uh — they're drinking. Sitting around," he said vaguely, squinting as if he were staring all the way to town and over to Aunt Tillie's back yard. Then the vision seemed to get clear and he nodded energetically. "Yeah. Sitting around. There's your sister in a blue dress, huh? And high heels, the poor sad bitch — nothing like you, sweetheart! And your mother's helping some fat woman with the corn, they're cleaning the corn — husking the corn —"

"What fat woman?" Connie cried.

"How do I know what fat woman, I don't know every goddam fat woman in the world!" Arnold laughed.

"Oh, that's Mrs. Hornby . . . Who invited her?" Connie said. She felt a little light-headed. Her breath was coming quickly.

"She's too fat. I don't like them fat. I like them the way you are, honey," he said, smiling sleepily at her. They stared at each other for a while, through the screen door. He said softly, "Now what you're going to do is this: you're going to come out that door. You're going to sit up front with me and Ellie's going to sit in the back, the hell with Ellie, right? This isn't Ellie's date. You're my date. I'm your lover, honey."

"What? You're crazy —"

"Yes, I'm your lover. You don't know what that is but you will," he said. "I know that too. I know all about you. But look: it's real nice and you couldn't ask for nobody better than me, or more polite. I always keep my word. I'll tell you how it is, I'm always nice at first, the first time. I'll hold you so tight you won't think you have to try to get away or pretend anything because you'll know you can't. And I'll come inside you where it's all secret and you'll give in to me and you'll love me —"

"Shut up! You're crazy!" Connie said. She backed away from the door. She put her hands against her ears as if she'd heard something terrible, something not meant for her. "People don't talk like that, you're crazy," she muttered. Her heart was almost too big now for her chest and its pumping made sweat break out all over her. She looked out to see Arnold Friend pause and then take a step toward the porch lurching. He almost fell. But, like a clever drunken man, he managed to catch his balance. He wobbled in his high boots and grabbed hold of one of the porch posts.

"Honey?" he said. "You still listening?"

"Get the hell out of here!"

"Be nice, honey. Listen."

"I'm going to call the police —"

He wobbled again and out of the side of his mouth came a fast spat curse, an aside not meant for her to hear. But even this "Christ!" sounded forced. Then he began to smile again. She watched this smile come, awkward as if he were smiling from inside a mask. His whole face was a mask, she thought wildly, tanned down onto his throat but then running out as if he had plastered makeup on his face but had forgotten about his throat.

"Honey —? Listen, here's how it is. I always tell the truth and I promise you this: I ain't coming in that house after you."

"You better not! I'm going to call the police if you — if you don't —"

"Honey," he said, talking right through her voice, "honey, I'm not coming in there but you are coming out here. You know why?"

She was panting. The kitchen looked like a place she had never seen before, some room she had run inside but which wasn't good enough, wasn't going to help her. The kitchen window had never had a curtain, after three years, and there were dishes in the sink for her to do — probably — and if you ran your hand across the table you'd probably feel something sticky there.

"You listening, honey? Hey?"

"— going to call the police —"

"Soon as you touch the phone I don't need to keep my promise and can come inside. You won't want that."

She rushed forward and tried to lock the door. Her fingers were shaking. "But why lock it," Arnold Friend said gently, talking right into her face. "It's just a screen door. It's just nothing." One of his boots was at a strange angle, as if his foot wasn't in it. It pointed out to the left, bent at the ankle. "I mean, anybody can break through a screen door and glass and wood and iron or anything else if he needs to, anybody at all and specially Arnold Friend. If the place got lit up with a fire honey you'd come runnin' out into my arms, right into my arms an' safe at home — like you knew I was your lover and'd stopped fooling around. I don't mind a nice shy girl but I don't like no fooling around." Part of those words were spoken with a slight rhythmic lilt, and Connie somehow recognized them — the echo of a song from last year, about a girl rushing into her boyfriend's arms and coming home again —

Connie stood barefoot on the linoleum floor, staring at him. "What do you want?" she whispered.

"I want you," he said.

"What?"

"Seen you that night and thought, that's the one, yes sir. I never needed to look any more."

"But my father's coming back. He's coming to get me. I had to wash my hair first —" She spoke in a dry, rapid voice, hardly raising it for him to hear.

"No, your Daddy is not coming and yes, you had to wash your hair and you washed it for me. It's nice and shining and all for me, I thank you, sweetheart," he said, with a mock bow, but again he almost lost his balance. He had to bend and adjust his boots. Evidently his feet did not go all the way down; the boots must have been stuffed with something so that he would seem taller. Connie stared out at him and behind him Ellie in the car, who seemed to be looking off toward Connie's right, into nothing. This Ellie said, pulling the words out of the air one after another as if he were just discovering them, "You want me to pull out the phone?"

"Shut your mouth and keep it shut," Arnold Friend said, his face red from bending over or maybe from embarrassment because Connie had seen his boots. "This ain't none of your business."

"What — what are you doing? What do you want?" Connie said. "If I call the police they'll get you, they'll arrest you —"

"Promise was not to come in unless you touch that phone, and I'll keep that promise," he said. He resumed his erect position and tried to force his shoulders back. He sounded like a hero in a movie, declaring something important. He spoke too loudly and it was as if he were speaking to someone behind Connie. "I ain't made plans for coming in that house where I don't belong but just for you to come out to me, the way you should. Don't you know who I am?"

"You're crazy," she whispered. She backed away from the door but did not want to go into another part of the house, as if this would give him permission to come through the door. "What do you . . . You're crazy, you . . ."

"Huh? What're you saying, honey?"

Her eyes darted everywhere in the kitchen. She could not remember what it was, this room.

"This is how it is, honey: you come out and we'll drive away, have a nice ride. But if you don't come out we're gonna wait till your people come home and then they're all going to get it."

"You want that telephone pulled out?" Ellie said. He held the radio away from his ear and grimaced, as if without the radio the air was too much for him.

"I toldja shut up, Ellie," Arnold Friend said, "you're deaf, get a hearing aid, right? Fix yourself up. This little girl's no trouble and's gonna be nice to me, so Ellie keep to yourself, this ain't your date — right? Don't hem in on me. Don't hog. Don't crush. Don't bird dog. Don't trail me," he said in a rapid meaningless voice, as if he were running through all the expressions he'd learned but was no longer sure which one of them was in style, then rushing on to new ones, making them up with his eyes closed, "Don't crawl under my fence, don't squeeze in my chipmunk hole, don't sniff my glue, suck my popsicle, keep your own greasy fingers on yourself!" He shaded his eyes and peered in at Connie, who was backed against the kitchen table. "Don't mind him honey he's just a creep. He's a dope. Right? I'm the boy for you and like I said you come out here nice like a lady and give me your hand, and nobody else gets hurt, I mean, your nice old bald-headed daddy and your mummy and your sister in her high heels. Because listen: why bring them in this?"

"Leave me alone," Connie whispered.

"Hey, you know that old woman down the road, the one with the chickens and stuff — you know her?"

"She's dead!"

"Dead? What? You know her?" Arnold Friend said.

"She's dead —"

"Don't you like her?"

"She's dead — she's — she isn't here any more —"

"But don't you like her, I mean, you got something against her? Some grudge or something?" Then his voice dipped as if he were conscious of a rudeness. He touched the sunglasses perched on top of his head as if to make sure they were still there. "Now you be a good girl."

"What are you going to do?"

"Just two things, or maybe three," Arnold Friend said. "But I promise it won't last long and you'll like me the way you get to like people you're close to. You will. It's all over for you here, so come on out. You don't want your people in any trouble, do you?"

She turned and bumped against a chair or something, hurting her leg, but she ran into the back room and picked up the telephone. Something roared in her ear, a tiny roaring, and she was so sick with fear that she could do nothing but listen to it — the telephone was clammy and very heavy and her fingers groped down to the dial but were too weak to touch it. She began to scream into the phone, into the roaring. She cried out, she cried for her mother, she felt her breath start jerking back and forth in her lungs as if it were something Arnold Friend were stabbing her with again and again with no tenderness. A noisy sorrowful wailing rose all about her and she was locked inside it the way she was locked inside this house.

After a while she could hear again. She was sitting on the floor with her wet back against the wall.

Arnold Friend was saying from the door, "That's a good girl. Put the phone back."

She kicked the phone away from her.

"No, honey. Pick it up. Put it back right."

She picked it up and put it back. The dial tone stopped.

"That's a good girl. Now you come outside."

She was hollow with what had been fear, but what was now just an emptiness. All that screaming had blasted it out of her. She sat, one leg cramped under her, and deep inside her brain was something like a pinpoint of light that kept going and would not let her relax.

She thought, I'm not going to see my mother again. She thought, I'm not going to sleep in my bed again. Her bright green blouse was all wet.

Arnold Friend said, in a gentle-loud voice that was like a stage voice, "The place where you came from ain't there any more, and where you had in mind to go is canceled out. This place you are now — inside your daddy's house — is nothing but a cardboard box I can knock down any time. You know that and always did know it. You hear me?"

She thought, I have got to think. I have to know what to do.

"We'll go out to a nice field, out in the country here where it smells so nice and it's sunny," Arnold Friend said. "I'll have my arms tight around you so you won't need to try to get away and I'll show you what love is like, what it does. The hell with this house! It looks solid all right," he said. He ran a fingernail down the screen and the noise did not make Connie shiver, as it would have the day before. "Now put your hand on your heart, honey. Feel that? That feels solid too but we know better, be nice to me, be sweet like you can because what else is there for a girl like you but to be sweet and pretty and give in? — and get away before her people come back?"

She felt her pounding heart. Her hand seemed to enclose it. She thought for the first time in her life that it was nothing that was hers, that belonged to her, but just a pounding, living thing inside this body that wasn't really hers either.

"You don't want them to get hurt," Arnold Friend went on. "Now get up, honey. Get up all by yourself."

She stood.

"Now turn this way. That's right. Come over here to me — Ellie, put that away, didn't I tell you? You dope. You miserable creepy dope," Arnold Friend said. His words were not angry but only part of an incantation. The incantation was kindly. "Now come out through the kitchen to me honey and let's see a smile, try it, you're a brave sweet little girl and now they're eating corn and hot dogs cooked to bursting over an outdoor fire, and they don't know one thing about you and never did and honey you're better than them because not a one of them would have done this for you."

Connie felt the linoleum under her feet; it was cool. She brushed her hair back out of her eyes. Arnold Friend let go of the post tentatively and opened his arms for her, his elbows pointing in toward each other and his wrists limp, to show that this was an embarrassed embrace and a little mocking, he didn't want to make her self-conscious.

She put out her hand against the screen. She watched herself push the door slowly open as if she were safe back somewhere in the other doorway, watching this body and this head of long hair moving out into the sunlight where Arnold Friend waited.

"My sweet little blue-eyed girl," he said, in a half-sung sigh that had nothing to do with her brown eyes but was taken up just the same by the vast sunlit reaches of the land behind him and on all sides of him, so much land that Connie had never seen before and did not recognize except to know that she was going to it.

# James Baldwin (1924–    )

THE SON of the pastor of a Harlem church, James Baldwin was born in New York and briefly planned to be a minister as his father had been but left home at seventeen and became an expatriate in Paris. His writing first attracted attention by the short stories he wrote while in France. A novel, *Go Tell It on the Mountain* (1953), about the members of a Harlem church, caused him to be hailed as the most important American black writer since Richard Wright. His *New Yorker* article, "The Fire Next Time" (1963), with its vivid account of the horrifying explosive situation in which black people find themselves, was a nationwide sensation. Baldwin's writing includes four novels, a book of essays, and two plays. His short stories have been published in the volume, *Going to Meet the Man* (1965). His most recent book is the novel *If Beale Street Could Talk* (1974).

When a reader finishes "Tell Me How Long the Train's Been Gone" he will know he has been to Harlem. He will have been in the Proudhammers' tenement home, got to know the whole family well; the father, a West Indian black who prides himself on his ancestors never having been slaves like American blacks, his gentle New Orleans wife, and their two sons. He will have faced an angry landlord, gone marketing with the family, learned some of the homely details of their domestic life, such as their Saturday night baths, and been terrified by the kind of reality they must daily face. He will know, with little Leo, what it means to be a small black boy lost in a big white city.

# *Tell Me How Long the Train's Been Gone*

MY BROTHER, CALEB, was seventeen when I was ten. We were very good friends. In fact, he was my best friend and, for a very long time, my only friend.

I do not mean to say that he was always nice to me. I got on his nerves a lot, and he resented having to take me around with him and be responsible for me when there were so many other things he wanted to be doing. Therefore, his hand was often up against the side of my head, and my tears caused him to be punished many times. But I knew, somehow, anyway, that when he was being punished for my tears, he was not being punished for anything he had done to me; he was being punished because that was the way we lived; and his punishment, oddly, helped unite us. More oddly still, even as his great hand caused my head to stammer and dropped a flame-colored curtain before my eyes, I understood that he was not striking *me*. His hand leaped out because he could not help it, and I received the blow because I was there. And it happened, sometimes, before I could even catch my breath to howl, that the hand that had struck me grabbed me and held me, and it was difficult indeed to know which of us was weeping. He was striking, striking out, striking out; the hand asked me to forgive him. I felt his bewilderment through the membrane of my own. I also felt that he was trying to teach me something. And I had, God knows, no other teachers.

For our father — how shall I describe our father? — was a ruined Barbados peasant, exiled in a Harlem which he loathed, where he never saw the sun or sky he remembered, where life took place neither indoors nor without, and where there was no joy. By which I mean no joy that he remembered. Had he been able to bring with him any of the joy he had felt on that far-off island, then the air of the sea and the impulse to dancing would sometimes have transfigured our dreadful rooms. Our lives might have been very different.

But no, he brought with him from Barbados only black rum and blacker pride and magic incantations, which neither healed nor saved.

He did not understand the people among whom he found himself; they had no coherence, no stature and no pride. He came from a race which had been flourishing at the very dawn of the world — a race greater and nobler than Rome or Judea, mightier than Egypt — he came from a race of kings, kings who had never been taken in battle, kings who had never been slaves. He spoke to us of tribes and empires, battles, victories and monarchs of whom we had never heard — they were not mentioned in our textbooks — and invested us with glories in which we felt more awkward than in the secondhand shoes we wore. In the stifling room of his pretensions and expectations, we stumbled wretchedly about, stubbing our toes, as it were, on rubies, scraping our shins on golden caskets, bringing down, with a childish cry, the splendid purple tapestry on which, in pounding gold and scarlet, our destinies and our inheritance were figured. It could scarcely have been otherwise, since a child's major attention has to be concentrated on how to fit into a world which, with every passing hour, reveals itself as merciless.

If our father was of royal blood and we were royal children, our father was certainly the only person in the world who knew it. The landlord did not know it; our father never mentioned royal blood to *him*. When we were late with our rent, which was often, the landlord threatened, in terms no commoner had ever used before a king, to put us in the streets. He complained that our shiftlessness, which he did not hesitate to consider an attribute of the race, had forced him, an old man with a weak heart, to climb all these stairs to plead with us to give him the money we owed him. And this was the last time; he wanted to make sure we understood that this was the last time.

Our father was younger than the landlord, leaner, stronger and bigger. With one blow, he could have brought the landlord to his knees. And we knew how much he hated the man. For days on end, in the wintertime, we huddled around the gas stove in the kitchen, because the landlord gave us no heat. When windows were broken, the landlord took his time about fixing them; the wind made the cardboard we stuffed in the windows rattle all night long; and when snow came, the weight of the snow forced the cardboard inward and onto the floor. Whenever the apartment received a fresh coat of paint, we bought the paint and did the painting ourselves; we killed the rats. A great chunk of the kitchen ceiling fell one winter, narrowly missing our mother.

We all hated the landlord with a perfectly exquisite hatred, and we would have been happy to see our proud father kill him. We would have been glad to help. But our father did nothing of the sort. He stood before the landlord, looking unutterably weary. He made excuses. He apologized. He swore that it would never happen again. (We knew that it *would* happen again.) He begged for time. The landlord would finally go down the stairs, letting us and all the neighbors know how good-hearted he was, and our father would walk into the kitchen and pour himself a glass of rum.

But we knew that our father would never have allowed any black man to speak to him as the landlord did, as policemen did, as storekeepers and welfare workers and pawnbrokers did. No, not for a moment. He would have thrown him out of the house. He would certainly have made a black man know that he was not the descendant of slaves! He had made them know it so often that he had almost no friends among them, and if we had followed his impossible lead, we would have had no friends, either. It was scarcely worthwhile being the descendant of kings if the kings were black and no one had ever heard of them.

And it was because of our father, perhaps, that Caleb and I clung to each other, in spite of the great difference in our ages; or, in another way, it may have been precisely the difference in our ages that made the clinging possible. I don't know. It is really not the kind of thing any-one can ever know. I think it may be easier to love the really helpless younger brother, because he cannot enter into competition with one on one's own ground, or on any ground at all, and can never question one's role or jeopardize one's authority. In my own case, certainly, it did not occur to me to compete with Caleb, and I could not have questioned his role or his authority, because I needed both. He was my touchstone, my model and my only guide.

Anyway, our father, dreaming bitterly of Barbados, despised and mocked by his neighbors and all but ignored by his sons, held down his unspeakable factory job, spread his black gospel in bars on the weekends, and drank his rum. I do not know if he loved our mother. I think he did.

They had had five children — only Caleb and I, the first and the last, were left. We were both dark, like our father; but two of the three dead girls had been fair, like our mother.

She came from New Orleans. Her hair was not like ours. It was black, but softer and finer. The color of her skin reminded me of the color of bananas. Her skin was as bright as that, and contained that kind of promise, and she had tiny freckles around her nose and a small black mole just above her upper lip. It was the mole, I don't know why, which made her beautiful. Without it, her face might have been merely sweet, merely pretty. But the mole was funny. It had the effect of making one realize that our mother liked funny things, liked to laugh. The mole made one look at her eyes — large, extraordinary dark eyes, eyes which seemed always to be amused by something, eyes which looked straight out, seeming to see everything, seeming to be afraid of nothing. She was a soft, round, plump woman. She liked nice clothes and dangling jewelry, which she mostly didn't have, and she liked to cook for large numbers of people, and she loved our father.

She knew him — knew him through and through. I am not being coy or colloquial but bluntly and sadly matter-of-fact when I say that I will now never know what she saw in him. What she saw was certainly not for many eyes; what she saw got him through his working week and his Sunday rest; what she saw saved him. She saw that he was a man. For her, perhaps, he was a great man. I think, though, that, for our mother, any man was great who aspired to become a man: this meant that our father was very rare and precious. I used to wonder how she took it, how she bore it — his rages, his tears, his cowardice.

On Saturday nights, he was almost always evil, drunk and maudlin. He came home from work in the early afternoon and gave our mother some money. It was never enough, of course, but he always kept enough to go out and get drunk. She never protested, at least not as far as I know. Then she would go out shopping. I would usually go with her, for Caleb would almost always be out somewhere, and our mother didn't like the idea of leaving me alone in the house. And this was probably, after all, the best possible arrangement. People who disliked our father were sure (for that very reason) to like our mother; and people who felt that Caleb was growing to be too much like his father could feel that I, after all, might turn out like my mother. Besides, it is not, as a general rule, easy to hate a small child. One runs the risk of looking ridiculous, especially if the child is with his mother.

And especially if that mother is Mrs. Proudhammer. Mrs. Proudhammer knew very well what people thought of Mr. Proudhammer. She knew, too, exactly how much she owed in each store she entered, how much she was going to be able to pay, and what she had to buy. She entered with a smile, ready.

"Evening. Let me have some of them red beans there."

"Evening. You know, you folks been running up quite a little bill here."

"I'm going to give you something on it right now. I need some cornmeal and flour and some rice."

"You know, I got my bills to meet, too, Mrs. Proudhammer."

"Didn't I just tell you I was going to pay? I want some cornflakes too, and some milk." Such merchandise as she could reach, she had already placed on the counter.

"When do you think you're going to be able to pay this bill? All of it, I mean."

"You know I'm going to pay it just as soon as I can. How much does it all come to? Give me that end you got there of that chocolate cake." The chocolate cake was for Caleb and me. "Well, now you put this against the bill." Imperiously, as though it were the most natural thing in the world, she put two or three dollars on the counter.

"You lucky I'm softhearted, Mrs. Proudhammer."

"Things sure don't cost this much downtown — you think I don't know it? Here." And she paid him for what she had bought. "Thank you. You been mighty kind."

And we left the store. I often felt that in order to help her, I should have filled my pockets with merchandise while she was talking. But I never did, not only because the store was often crowded or because I was afraid of being caught by the storekeeper, but because I was afraid of humiliating her. When I began to steal, not very much later, I stole in stores that were not in our neighborhood, where we were not known.

When we had to do "heavy" shopping, we went marketing under the bridge at Park Avenue — Caleb, our mother and I; and sometimes, but rarely, our father came with us. The most usual reason for heavy shopping was that some relatives of our mother's, or old friends of both our mother's and our father's, were coming to visit. We were certainly not going to let them go away hungry — not even if it meant, as it often did, spending more than we had. In spite of what I have been suggesting about our father's temperament, and no matter how difficult he may sometimes have been with us, he was much too proud to offend any guest of his; on the contrary, his impulse was to make them feel that his home was theirs; and besides, he was lonely, lonely for his past, lonely for those faces which had borne witness to that past. Therefore, he would sometimes pretend that our mother did not know how to shop, and our father would come with us, under the bridge, in order to teach her.

There he would be, then, uncharacteristically, in shirt-sleeves, which made him look rather boyish; and as our mother showed no desire to take shopping lessons from him, he turned his attention to Caleb and me. He would pick up a fish, opening the gills and holding it close to his nose. "You see that? That fish looks fresh, don't it? Well, that fish ain't as fresh as I am, and I *been* out of the water. They done doctored that fish. Come on." And we would walk away, a little embarrassed but, on the whole, rather pleased that our father was so smart.

Meantime, our mother was getting the marketing done. She was very happy on days like this, because our father was happy. He was happy, odd as his expression of it may sound, to be out with his wife and his two sons. If we had been on the island that had been witness to his birth, instead of the unspeakable island of Manhattan, he felt that it would not have been so hard for us all to trust and love each other. He sensed, and I think he was right, that on that other, never to be recovered island, his sons would have looked on him very differently, and he would have looked very differently on his sons. Life would have been hard there, too; we would have fought there, too, and more or less blindly suffered and more or less blindly died. But we would not have been (or so it was to seem to all of us forever) so wickedly menaced by the mere fact of our relationship, would not have been so frightened of entering into the central, most beautiful and valuable facts of our lives. We would have been laughing and cursing and tussling in the water, instead of stammering under the bridge; we would have known less about vanished African kingdoms and more about each other. Or, not at all impossibly, more about both.

If it was summer, we bought a watermelon, which either Caleb or our father carried home, fighting with each other for this privilege. They looked very like each other on those days — both big, both black, both laughing.

Caleb always looked absolutely helpless when he laughed. He laughed with all his body, perhaps touching his shoulder against yours, or putting his head on your chest for a moment, and then careening off you, halfway across the room or down the block. I will always hear his laughter. He was always happy on such days, too. If our father needed his son, Caleb certainly needed his father. Such days, however, were rare — one of the reasons, probably, that I remember them now.

Eventually, we all climbed the stairs into that hovel which, at such moments, was our castle. One very nearly felt the drawbridge rising behind us as our father locked the door.

The bathtub could not yet be filled with cold water and the melon placed in the tub, because this was Saturday, and, come evening, we all had to bathe. The melon was covered with a blanket and placed on the fire escape. Then we unloaded what we had bought, rather impressed by our opulence, though our father was always, by this time, appalled by the money we had spent. I was always sadly aware that there would be nothing left of all this once tomorrow had come and gone and that most of it, after all, was not for us, but for others.

Our mother was calculating the pennies she would need all week — carfare for our father and for Caleb, who went to a high school out of our neighborhood; money for the life insurance; money for milk for me at school; money for light and gas; money put away, if possible, toward the rent. She knew just about what our father had left in *his* pockets and was counting on him to give me the money I would shortly be demanding to go to the movies. Caleb had a part-time job after school and already had his movie money. Anyway, unless he was in a very good mood or needed me for something, he would not be anxious to go to the movies with me.

Our mother never insisted that Caleb tell her where he was going, nor did she question him as to how he spent the money he made. She was afraid of hearing him lie, and she did not want to risk forcing him to lie. She was operating on the assumption that he was sensible and had been raised to be honorable and that he, now more than ever, needed his privacy.

But she was very firm with him, nevertheless. "I do not want to see you rolling in here at three in the morning, Caleb. I want you here in time to eat, and you know you got to take your bath."

"Yes, indeed, ma'am. Why can't I take my bath in the morning?"

"Don't you start being funny. You know you ain't going to get up in time to take no bath in the morning."

"Don't nobody want you messing around in that bathroom all morning long, man," said our father. "You just git back in the house like your ma's telling you."

"Besides," I said, "you never wash out the tub."

Caleb looked at me in mock surprise and from a great height, allowing his chin and his lids simultaneously to drop and swiveling his head away from me.

"I see," he said, "that everyone in this family is ganging up on me. All right, Leo. I was planning to take you to the show with me, but now I've changed my mind."

"I'm sorry," I said quickly. "I take it back."

"You take *what* back?"

"What I said — about you not washing out the tub."

"Ain't no need to take it back," our father said stubbornly. "It's true. A man don't take back nothing that's true."

"So *you* say," Caleb said, with a hint of a sneer. But before anyone could possibly react to this, he picked me up, scowling into my face, which he held just above his own. "You take it back?"

"Leo ain't going to take it back," our father said.

Now I was in trouble. Caleb watched me, a small grin on his face. "You take it back?"

"Stop teasing that child, and put him down," our mother said. "The trouble ain't that Caleb don't wash out the tub — he just don't wash it out very clean."

"I never knew him to wash it out," our father said, "unless I was standing behind him."

"Well, ain't neither one of you much good around the house," our mother said.

Caleb laughed and set me down. "You didn't take it back," he said.

I said nothing.

"I guess I'm just going to have to go on without you."

Still, I said nothing.

"You going to have that child to crying in a minute," our mother said. "If you going to take him go on and take him. Don't do him like that."

Caleb laughed again. "I'm going to take him. The way he got them eyes all ready to water, I'd better take him somewhere." We walked toward the door. "But you got to make up *your* mind," he said to me, "to say what *you* think is right."

I grabbed Caleb's hand, the signal for the descent of the drawbridge. Our mother watched us cheerfully as we walked out; our father watched us balefully. Yet there was a certain humor in his face, too, and a kind of pride.

"Dig you later," Caleb said, and the door closed behind us.

The hall was dark, smelling of cooking, of stale wine, of rotting garbage. We dropped down the stairs, Caleb going two at a time, pausing at each landing, briefly, to glance back up at me. I dropped down behind him as fast as I could. When I reached the street level, Caleb was already on the stoop, joking with some of his friends, who were standing in the doorway — who seemed always to be in the doorway.

I didn't like Caleb's friends, because I was afraid of them. I knew the only reason they didn't try to make life hell for me, the way they made life hell for a lot of the other kids, was because they were afraid of Caleb. I went through the door, passing between my brother and his friends, down to the sidewalk, feeling, as they looked briefly at me and then continued joking with Caleb, what they felt — that here was Caleb's round-eyed, frail and useless sissy of a little brother. They pitied Caleb for having to take me out. On the other hand, they also wanted to go to the show, but didn't have the money. Therefore, in silence, I could crow over them even as they despised me. But this was always a terribly risky, touch-and-go business, for Caleb might, at any moment, change his mind and drive me away.

I always stood, those Saturday afternoons, in fear and trembling, holding on to the small shield of my bravado, while waiting for Caleb to come down the steps of the stoop, away from his friends, to me. I braced myself, always, for the moment when he would turn to me, saying, "Okay, kid. You run along. I'll see you later."

This meant that I would have to go the movies by myself and hang around in front of the box office, waiting for some grown-up to take me in. I could not go back upstairs, for this would be informing my mother and father that Caleb had gone off somewhere after promising to take me to the movies.

Neither could I simply hang around, playing with the kids on the block. For one thing, my demeanor, as I came out of the house, very clearly indicated that I had better things to do than play with *them*; for another, they were not terribly anxious to play with *me*; and, finally, my remaining on the block would have had exactly the same effect as my going upstairs. To remain on the block after Caleb's dismissal was to put myself at the mercy of the block and to put Caleb at the mercy of our parents.

So I prepared myself, those Saturdays, to respond with a cool "Okay. See you later," and then to turn indifferently away, and walk. This was surely the most terrible moment. The moment I turned away, I was committed, I was trapped, and I then had miles to walk, so it seemed to me, before I would be out of sight, before the block ended and I could turn onto the avenue. I wanted to run out of that block, but I never did. I never looked back. I forced myself to walk very slowly, looking neither right nor left, striving to seem at once distracted and offhand; concentrating on the cracks in the sidewalk and stumbling over them; trying to whistle, feeling every muscle in my body, feeling that all the block was watching me, and feeling, which was odd, that I deserved it.

And then I reached the avenue, and turned, still not looking back, and was released from those eyes at least; but now I faced other eyes, eyes coming toward me. These eyes were the eyes of children stronger than me, who would steal my movie money; these eyes were the eyes of white cops, whom I feared, whom I hated with a literally murderous hatred; these eyes were the eyes of old folks, who might wonder what I was doing on this avenue by myself.

And then I got to the show. Sometimes someone would take me in right away, and sometimes I would have to stand there and wait, watching the faces coming to the box office. And this was not easy, since I didn't, after all, want everyone in the neighborhood to know I was loitering outside the movie house waiting for someone to take me in. If it came to our father's attention, he would kill both Caleb and me.

Eventually, I would see a face which looked susceptible. I would rush up to him — it was usually a man, for men were less likely to be disapproving — and whisper, "Take me in," and give him my dime. Sometimes the man simply took the dime and disappeared inside; sometimes he gave my dime back to me and took me in anyway. Sometimes I ended up wandering around the streets — but I couldn't wander into a strange neighborhood, because I would be beaten up if I did — until I figured the show was out. It was dangerous to get home too early, and, of course, it was practically lethal to arrive too late. If all went well, I could cover for Caleb, saying that I had left him with some boys on the stoop. Then, if *he* came in too late, it could not be considered my fault.

But if wandering around this way was not without its dangers, neither was it without its discoveries and delights. I discovered subways. I discovered, that is, that I could ride on subways by myself and, furthermore, that I could usually ride for nothing. Sometimes, when I ducked under the turnstile, I was caught, and sometimes great black ladies seized on me as a pretext for long, very loud, ineffably moral lectures about wayward children breaking their parents' hearts. Sometimes, doing everything in my power not to attract their attention, I endeavored to look as though I were in the charge of a respectable-looking man or woman, entering the subway in their shadow and sitting very still beside them. It was best to try to sit *between* two such people, for each would automatically assume that I was with the other. There I would sit, then, in a precarious anonymity, watching the people, listening to the roar, watching the lights of stations flash by. It seemed to me that nothing was faster than a subway train, and I loved the speed, because the speed was dangerous.

For a time, during these expeditions, I simply sat and watched the people. Lots of people would be dressed up, for this was Saturday night. The women's hair would be all curled and straightened, and the lipstick on their full lips looked purple and make-believe against the dark skins of their faces. They wore very fancy capes or coats, in wonderful colors, and long dresses, and sometimes they had jewels in their hair, and sometimes they wore flowers on their dresses. They were almost as beautiful as movie stars. And so the men with them seemed to think.

The hair of the men was slick and wavy, brushed up into pompadours; or they wore very sharp hats, brim flicked down dangerously over one eye, with perhaps one flower in the lapel of their many-colored suits. They laughed and talked with their girls, but quietly, for there were white people in the car. The white people would scarcely ever be dressed up and did not speak to each other at all — only read their papers and stared at the advertisements. But they fascinated me more than the colored people did, because I knew nothing at all about them and could not imagine what they were like.

Underground, I received my first apprehension of New.York neighborhoods and, underground, first felt what may be called a civic terror. I very soon realized that after the train had passed a certain point, going uptown or downtown, all the colored people disappeared. The first time I realized this, I panicked and got lost. I rushed off the train, terrified of what these white people might do to me, with no colored person around to protect me — even to scold me, even to beat me; at least, their touch was familiar, and I knew that they did not, after all, intend to kill me — and got on another train only because I saw a black man on it. But almost everyone else was white.

The train did not stop at any of the stops I remembered. I became more and more frightened, frightened of getting off the train and frightened of staying on it, frightened of saying anything to the man and frightened that he would get off the train before I could say anthing to him. He was my salvation, and he stood there in the unapproachable and frightening form that salvation so often takes. At each stop, I watched him with despair.

To make matters worse, I suddenly realized that I had to pee. Once I realized it, this need became a torment; the horror of wetting my pants in front of all these people made the torment greater. Finally, I tugged at the man's sleeve. He looked down at me with a gruff, amused concern; then, reacting, no doubt to the desperation in my face, he bent closer.

I asked him if there was a bathroom on the train.

He laughed. "No," he said, "but there's a bathroom in the station." He looked at me again. "Where're you going?"

I told him that I was going home.

"And where's home?"

I told him.

This time he did not laugh. "Do you know where you are?" he said.

I shook my head. At that moment, the train came into a station, and after several hours, it rolled to a stop. The doors opened, and the man led me to the bathroom. I ran in, and I hurried, because I was afraid he would disappear. But I was glad he had not come in with me.

When I came out, he stood waiting for me. "Now," he said, "you in Brooklyn. You ever hear of Brooklyn? What you doing out here by yourself?"

"I got lost," I said.

"I *know* you got lost. What I want to know is how *come* you got lost? Where's your mama? Where's your daddy?"

I almost said that I didn't have any, because I liked his face and his voice and was half hoping to hear him say that *he* didn't have any little boy and would just as soon take a chance on me. But I told him that my mama and daddy were at home.

"And do they know where *you* are?"

I said, "No." There was a pause.

"Well, I know they going to make your tail hot when they see you." He took my hand. "Come on."

And he led me along the platform and then down some steps and along a narrow passage and then up some steps onto the opposite platform. I was very impressed by this maneuver; in order to accomplish the same purpose, I had always left the subway station and gone up into the street. Now that the emergency was over, I was in no great hurry to leave my savior. I asked him if he had a little boy.

"Yes," he said, "and if *you* was my little boy, I'd paddle your behind so you couldn't sit down for a week."

I asked him how old was his little boy, what was his name and if his little boy was at home.

"He *better* be at home!" He looked at me and laughed. "His name is Jonathan. He ain't but five years old." His gaze refocused, sharpened. "How old are you?"

I told him that I was ten, going on eleven.

"You a pretty bad little fellow," he said then.

I tried to look repentant, but I would not have dreamed of denying it.

"Now, look here," he said, "this here's the uptown side. Can you read, or don't you never go to school?" I assured him that I could read. "Now, to get where you going, you got to change trains." He told me where. "Here, I'll write it down for you." He found some paper in his pockets but no pencil. We heard the train coming. He looked about him in helpless annoyance, looked at his watch, looked at me. "It's all right. I'll tell the conductor."

But the conductor, standing between two cars, had rather a mean pink face.

My savior looked at him dubiously. "He *might* be all right. But we better not take no chances." He pushed me ahead of him into the train. "You know you right lucky that I got a little boy? If I didn't, I swear I'd just let you go on and *be* lost. You don't know the kind of trouble you going to get me in at home. My wife ain't *never* going to believe *this* story."

I told him to give me his name and address and I would write a letter to his wife and to his little boy, too.

This caused him to laugh harder than ever. "You only say that because you know I ain't got no pencil. You are one *hell* of a shrewd little boy."

I told him that then maybe we should get off the train and that I would go back home with him.

This made him grave. "What does your father do?"

This question made me uneasy. I stared at him for a long time before I answered. "He works in a —" I could not pronounce the word — "he has a job."

He nodded. "I see. Is he home now?"

I really did not know, and I said I did not know.

"And what does your mother do?"

"She stays home."

Again he nodded. "You got any brothers or sisters?"

I told him no.

"I see. What's your name?"

"Leo."

"Leo what?"

"Leo Proudhammer."

He saw something in my face. "What do you want to be when you grow up, Leo?"

"I want to be —" and I had never said this before — "I want to be a — a movie actor. I want to be a — actor."

"You pretty skinny for that," he said.

"That's all right," I told him. "Caleb's going to teach me to swim. That's how you get big."

"Who's Caleb?"

I opened my mouth, I started to speak. I checked myself as the train roared into a station. He glanced out the window, but did not move. "He swims," I said.

"Oh," he said after a very long pause, during which the doors slammed and the train began to move. "Is he a good swimmer?"

I said that Caleb was the best swimmer in the world.

"Okay," my savior said, "okay," and put his hand on my head again and smiled at me.

I asked him what his name was.

"Charles," he said, "Charles Williams. But you better call me *Uncle* Charles, you little devil, because you have certainly ruined my Saturday night." The train came into a station. "Here's where we change," he said.

We got out of the train and crossed the platform and waited.

"Now," he said, "this train stops exactly where you going. Tell me where you going."

I stared at him.

"I want you," he said, "to tell me exactly where you *going*. I can't be fooling with you all night."

I told him.

"You sure that's right?"

I told him I was sure.

"I got a very good memory," he said. "Give me your address. Just say it, I'll remember it."

So I said it, staring into his face as the train came roaring in.

"If you don't go straight home," he said, "I'm going to come see your daddy, and when we find you, you'll be mighty sorry." He pushed me into the train and put one shoulder against the door. "Go on, now," he said, loud enough for all the car to hear. "Your mama'll meet you at the station where I told you to get off." He repeated my subway stop, pushed the angry door with his shoulder, and then said gently, "Sit down, Leo." He remained in the door until I sat down. "So long, Leo," he said then, and stepped backward out. The doors closed. He grinned at me and waved, and the train began to move.

I waved back. Then he was gone, the station was gone, and I was on my way back home.

I never saw that man again, but I made up stories about him, I dreamed about him, I even wrote a letter to him and his wife and his little boy, but I never mailed it.

I never told Caleb anything about my solitary expeditions. I don't know why. I think that he might have liked to know about them. I suppose, finally, at bottom, I said nothing because my expeditions belonged to me.

Another time, it was raining, and it was still too early for me to go home. I felt very, very low that day. It was one of the times that my tongue and my body refused to obey me, and I had not been able to work up the courage to ask anyone to take me in to the show. The ticket taker was watching me, or so I thought, with a hostile suspicion. Actually, it's very unlikely he was thinking at all, and certainly not of me. But I walked away from the show, because I could no longer bear his eyes, or anybody's eyes.

I walked the long block east from the movie house. The street was empty, black and glittering. The water soaked through my coat at the shoulders, and water dripped down my neck from my cap. I began to be afraid. I could not stay out in the rain, because then my father and mother would know I had been wandering the streets. I would get a beating, and, though Caleb was too old to get a beating, he and my father would have a terrible fight, and Caleb would blame it all on me and would not speak to me for days.

I began to hate Caleb. I wondered where he was. I started in the direction of our house, only because I did not know what else to do. Perhaps Caleb would be waiting for me on the stoop.

The avenue, too, was very long and silent. Somehow, it seemed old, like a picture in a book. It stretched straight before me, endless, and the streetlights did not so much illuminate it as prove how dark it was. The rain was falling harder. Cars sloshed by, sending up she 's of water. From the bars, I heard music, faintly, and many voices. Straight ahead of me a woman walked, very fast, head down, carrying a shopping bag. I reached my corner and crossed the wide avenue. There was no one on my stoop.

Now I was not even certain what time it was; but I knew it wasn't time yet for the show to be over. I walked into my hallway and wrung out my cap. I was sorry that I had not made someone take me in to the show, because now I did not know what to do. I *could* go upstairs and say that we had not liked the movie and had left early and that Caleb was with some boys on the stoop. But this would sound strange, and Caleb, who would not know what story I had told, would, therefore, be greatly handicapped when he came home.

I could not stay in my hallway, because my father might not be at home and might come in. I could not go into the hallway of another building, because if any of the kids who lived in the building found me, they would have the right to beat me up. I could not go back out into the rain. I stood next to the big, cold radiator, and I began to cry. But crying wasn't going to do me any good, either, especially as there was no one to hear me.

So I stepped out on my stoop again and stood there for a long time, wondering what to do. Then I thought of a condemned house, around the corner from us. We played there sometimes, though it was very dangerous and we were not supposed to. What possessed me to go there now, I don't know, except that I could not think of another dry place in the whole world. I started running east, down our block. I turned two corners and came to the house, with its black window sockets. The house was completely dark. I had forgotten how afraid I was of the dark, but the rain was drenching me. I ran down the cellar steps and clambered into the house through one of the broken windows. I squatted there in a still, dry dread, not daring to look into the house but staring outward. I was holding my breath. I heard an endless scurrying in the darkness, a perpetual busyness, and I thought of rats, of their teeth and ferocity and fearful size, and I began to cry again.

I don't know how long I squatted there this way or what was in my mind. I listened to the rain and the rats. Then I was aware of another sound — I had been hearing it for a while without realizing it. This was a moaning sound, a sighing sound, a sound of strangling, which mingled with the sound of the rain and with a muttering, cursing human voice. The sounds came from the door that led to the backyard.

I wanted to stand, but I crouched lower; wanted to run, but could not move. Sometimes the sounds seemed to come closer, and I knew '' it this meant my death; sometimes they diminished or ceased altogether, and then I knew that my assailant was looking for me. I looked toward the backyard door, and I seemed to see, silhouetted against the driving rain, a figure, half bent, moaning, leaning against the wall, in indescribable torment; then there seemed to be two figures, sighing and grappling, moving so quickly that it was impossible to tell which was which, two creatures, each in a dreadful, absolute, silent single-mindedness attempting to strangle the other!

I watched, crouching low. A very powerful and curious excitement mingled itself with my terror and made the terror greater. I could not move. I did not dare move. The figures were quieter now. It seemed to me that one of them was a woman, and she seemed to be crying, pleading for her life. But her sobbing was answered only by a growling sound. The muttered, joyous curses began again; the murderous ferocity began again, more bitterly than ever. The sobbing began to rise in pitch, like a song.

Then everything was still, all movement ceased. Then I heard only the rain and the scurrying of the rats. It was over; one of them, or both of them, lay stretched out, dead or dying in this filthy place. It happened in Harlem every Saturday night. I could not catch my breath to scream. Then I heard a laugh, a low, happy, wicked laugh, and the figure turned in my direction and seemed to start toward me.

Then I screamed and stood up straight, bumping my head on the window frame and losing my cap, and scrambled up the cellar steps. I ran head down, like a bull, away from that house and out of that block. I ran up the steps of my stoop and bumped into Caleb.

"Where the hell have you been? Hey! What's the matter with you?"

I had jumped up on him, almost knocking him down, trembling and sobbing.

"You're *soaked*. Leo, what's the matter? Where's your cap?"

But I could not say anything. I held him around the neck with all my might, and I could not stop shaking.

"Come on, Leo," Caleb said, in a different tone, "tell me what's the matter." He pried my arms loose and held me away from him, so that he could look into my face. "Oh, little Leo. Little Leo. What's the matter, baby?" He looked at though he were about to cry himself, and this made me cry harder than ever. He took out his handkerchief and wiped my face and made me blow my nose. My sobs began to lessen, but I could not stop trembling. He thought that I was trembling from cold, and he rubbed his hands roughly up and down my back and rubbed my hands between his. "What's the matter?"

I did not know how to tell him.

"Somebody try to beat you up?"

I shook my head. "No."

"What movie did you see?"

"I didn't go. I couldn't find nobody to take me in."

"And you just been wandering around in the rain all night?"

"Yes."

He sat down on the hallway steps. "Oh, Leo." Then, "You mad at me?"

I said, "No. I was scared."

He nodded. "I reckon you were, man." He wiped my face again. "You ready to go upstairs? It's getting late."

"Okay."

"How'd you lose your cap?"

"I went in a hallway to wring it out — and — I put it on the radiator, and I heard some people coming — and — I ran away, and I forgot it."

"We'll say you forgot it in the movies."

"Okay."

We started up the stairs.

"Leo," he said, "I'm sorry about tonight. I'm really sorry. I won't let it happen again. You believe me?"

"Sure. I believe you." I smiled up at him.

He squatted down. "Give us a kiss."

I kissed him.

"Okay. Climb up. I'll give you a ride. Hold on, now."

He carried me piggyback up the stairs.

Thereafter, we evolved a system, which did not, in fact, work too badly. When things went wrong and he could not be found, I was to leave a message for him at a certain store on the avenue. This store had a bad reputation — more than candy and hot dogs and soda pop were sold there; Caleb himself had told me this and told me not to hang out there. But he said he would see to it that they treated me all right.

I went in the store one Saturday night, and one of the boys who was always there, a boy about Caleb's age, looked up and smiled and said, "You looking for your brother? Come on, I'll take you to him."

This was not the agreed-on formula. I was to be *taken* to Caleb only in cases of real emergency, which wasn't the case this time. I was there because the show was over a little earlier than usual, and since it was only about a quarter past eleven, I figured I had about half an hour to wait for Caleb.

When the boy made his invitation, I assumed it was because of some prearrangement with the owner of the store, a very dour, silent black man, who looked at me from behind his counter and said nothing.

I said, "Okay," and the boy, whose name was Arthur, said, "Come on, Sonny. I'm going to take you to a party." He took my hand and led me across the avenue and into a long, dark block.

We walked the length of the block in silence, crossed another avenue and went into a big house in the middle of the block. We were in a big vestibule, with four locked apartment doors staring away from each other. It was not really clean, but it was fairly clean. We climbed three flights of stairs. Arthur knocked on the door, a very funny knock, not loud. After a moment, I heard a scraping sound, then the sound of a chain rattling and a bolt being pulled back. The door opened.

A lady, very black and rather fat, wearing a blue dress, held the door for us. She said, "Come on in. Now, what you doing here with this child?"

"Had to do it. It's all right. It's Caleb's brother."

We started down a long, dark hall, with closed rooms on either side of it, toward the living room. One of the rooms was the kitchen. A smell of barbecue made me realize that I was hungry. The living room was really two living rooms. The far one looked out on the street. There were six or seven people in the room, women and men. They looked exactly like the men and women who frightened me when I saw them standing on the corners, laughing and joking in front of the bars. But they did not seem frightening here. A record player was going, not very loud. They had drinks in their hands, and there were half-empty plates of food around the room. Caleb was sitting on the sofa, with his arm around a girl in a yellow dress.

"Here's your little brother," said the fat black lady in blue.

Arthur said to Caleb, "It was just better for him not to have to wait there tonight."

Caleb smiled at me. I was tremendously relieved that he was not angry. I was delighted by this party, even though it made me shy. "Come on over here," Caleb said. I went to the sofa. "This is my kid brother. His name is Leo. Leo, this is Dolores. Say hello to Dolores."

Dolores smiled at me — I thought she was very pretty — and said, "I'm very happy to meet you, Leo. How've you been?"

"Just fine," I said.

"Don't you want to know how *she's* been?" Caleb grinned.

"No," said the fat black lady, and laughed. "I'm sure he don't want to know that. I bet he's hungry. You been stuffing yourself all night, Caleb. Let me give him a little bit of my barbecue and a glass of ginger ale." She already was beginning to propel me out of the room.

I looked at Caleb. Caleb said, "Just remember we ain't got all night. Leo, this is Miss Mildred. She cooked everything, and she's a might good friend of mine. What do you say to Miss Mildred, Leo?"

"Dig Caleb being the big brother," Arthur muttered, and laughed.

"Thank you, Miss Mildred," I said.

"Come on in the kitchen," she said, "and let me try to put some flesh on them bones." She walked me into the kitchen. "Now, you sit right over there," she said. "Won't take me but a minute to warm this up." She sat me at the kitchen table and gave me a napkin and poured the ginger ale. "What grade you in at school, Leo?" I told her. "You must be a right smart boy, then," she said, with a pleased smile. "Do you like school, Leo?"

I told her what I liked best was Spanish and history and English composition.

This caused her to look more pleased than ever. "What do you want to be when you grow up?"

Somehow, I could not tell her what I had told the man, my friend, on the train. I said I wasn't sure, that maybe I would be a schoolteacher.

"That's just what I wanted to be," she said proudly, "and I studied right hard for it, too, and I believe I would have made it, but then I had to go and get myself mixed up with some no-count nigger. I didn't have no sense. I didn't have no better sense but to marry him. Can you beat that?" And she laughed and set my plate in front of me. "Go on, now, eat. Foolish me. Now, your brother," she said suddenly, "he's a right fine boy. He wants to make something of himself. He's got ambition. That's what I like — *ambition*. Don't you let him be foolish. Like me. You like my barbecue?"

"Yes, ma'am," I said. "It's good."

"Let me give you some more ginger ale," she said, and poured it.

I was beginning to be full. But I didn't want to go, although I knew that, now, it was really beginning to be late. While Miss Mildred talked and moved about the kitchen, I listened to the voices coming from the other room, the voices and the music. They were playing a kind of purple, lazy dance music, a music that was already in my bones, along with the wilder music from which the purple music sprang. The voices were not like the music, though they corroborated it. I listened to a girl's voice, gravelly and low, indignant and full of laughter. The room was full of laughter. It exploded, at intervals, and rolled through the living room and hammered at the walls of the kitchen.

Every once in a while, I heard Caleb, booming like a trumpet, drowning out the music. I wondered how often Caleb came here and how he had met these people, who were so different, at least as it seemed to me, from any of the people who ever came to our house.

Then Caleb's hand was on my neck. Dolores stood in the doorway, smiling. "You stuffed yourself enough, little brother?" Caleb said. "Because we got to get out of here now."

We walked slowly down the hall, Miss Mildred, Dolores and Caleb and me. We reached the door, which had a metal pole built into it in such a way as to prevent its being opened from the ouside, and a heavy piece of chain around the top of the three locks.

Miss Mildred began, patiently, to open the door. "Leo," she said, "don't you be no stranger. You make your brother bring you back to see me, you hear?" She got the pole out of the way and then undid the chain. To Caleb, she said, "Bring him by some afternoon. I ain't got nothing to do. I'll be glad to look after him." The last lock yielded, and Miss Mildred opened the door. We were facing the bright hall lights: no, the building was not very clean. "Good night, Leo," Miss Mildred said, and then she said good night to Dolores and Caleb. She closed the door.

I heard the scraping sound again, and we walked down the stairs.

"She's nice," I said.

Caleb said, yawning, "Yeah, she's a very nice lady." Then he said, "Now, I don't want you telling nobody at home about this, you hear?" I swore I wouldn't tell. "It's our secret," Caleb said.

It was colder in the streets that it had been before.

Caleb took Dolores' arm. "Let's get you to your subway," he said.

We started walking up the wide, dark avenue. We reached the brightly lit kiosk, which came up out of the sidewalk like some unbelievably malevolent awning or the suction apparatus of a monstrous vacuum cleaner.

"Bye-bye," Caleb said, and kissed Dolores on the nose. "I got to run. See you Monday after school."

"Bye-bye," Dolores said. She bent down and kissed me quickly on the cheek. "Bye-bye, Leo. Be good." She hurried down the steps.

Caleb and I began walking very fast, down the avenue, toward our block. The subway station was near the movie house, and the movie house was dark. We knew we were late; we did not think we were *that* late.

"It was a *very* long show, wasn't it?" Caleb said.

"Yes," I said.

"What did we see? Better tell me about *both* pictures. Just in case."

I told him as well as I could as we hurried down the avenue. Caleb had great powers of concentration and could figure out enough from what I said to know what to say if the necessity arose.

But our troubles, that night, came from a very different source than our parents. I had just reached the point in my breathless narration where the good girl is murdered by the Indians and the hero vows revenge. We were hurrying down the long block that led east to our house when we heard a car braking and were blinded by bright lights and were pushed up against a wall.

"Turn around," a voice said. "And keep your hands in the air."

It may seem funny, but I felt as though Caleb and I had conjured up a movie — that if I had not been describing a movie to him, we would not have suddenly found ourselves in the middle of one. Or was it the end? I had never been so frightened in my life.

We did as we were told. I felt the grainy brick beneath my fingers. A hand patted me all over my body, every touch humiliating. Beside me, I heard Caleb catch his breath.

"Turn around," the voice said.

The great lights of the police car had gone out; I could see the car at the curb, the doors open. I did not dare look at Caleb, for I felt that this would, somehow, be used against us. I stared at the two policemen, young, white, tight-lipped and self-important.

They turned a flashlight first on Caleb, then on me. "Where you boys going?"

"Home," Caleb said. I could hear his breathing. "We live in the next block." And he gave the address.

"Where've you been?"

Now I heard the effort Caleb was making not to surrender either to rage or panic. "We just took my girl to the subway station. We were at the movies." And then, forced out of him, weary, dry and bitter, "This here's my brother. I got to get him home. He ain't but ten years old."

"What movie did you see?"

And Caleb told them. I marveled at his memory. But I also knew that the show had let out about an hour or so before. I feared that the policemen might also know this. But they didn't.

"You got any identification?"

"My brother doesn't. I do."

"Let's see it."

Caleb took out his wallet and handed it over.

They looked at his wallet, looked at us, handed it back. "Get on home," one of them said. They got into their car and drove off.

"Thanks," Caleb said. "Thanks, all you scum-bag Christians."

His accent was now as irredeemably of the islands as was the accent of our father. I had never heard this sound in his voice before. And then, suddenly, he looked down at me and laughed and hugged me. "Come on, let's get home. Little Leo. Were you scared?"

"Yes," I said. "Were you?"

"Damn right, I was scared. But — damn! — they must have seen that you weren't but ten years old."

"You didn't *act* scared," I said.

We were in our own block, approaching our stoop. "Well. We certainly have a good excuse for being late," he said. He grinned. Then he said, "Leo, I'll tell you something. I'm glad this happened. It had to happen one day, and I'm glad it happened while I was with you — of course, I'm glad you were with *me*, too, because if it hadn't been for you, they'd have pulled me."

"What for?"

"Because I'm black," Caleb said. "That's what for."

I said nothing. I said nothing, because what he said was true, and I knew it. It seemed, now, that I had always known it, though I had never been able to say it. But I did not understand it. I was filled with an awful wonder; it hurt my chest and paralyzed my tongue. *Because you're black*. I tried to think, but I couldn't. I only saw the policemen, those murderous eyes again, those hands. Were they people?

"Caleb," I asked, "are white people people?"

"What are you talking about, Leo?"

"I mean, are white people — *people*? People like us?"

He looked down at me. His face was very strange and sad. It was a face I had never seen before. We were in the house now, and we climbed a few more stairs, very slowly. Then, "All I can tell you, Leo, is — well, *they* don't think they are."

I thought of the landlord. Then I thought of my schoolteacher, a lady named Mrs. Nelson. I liked her very much. I thought she was very pretty. She had long yellow hair, like someone I had seen in the movies, and a nice laugh, and we all liked her, all the kids I knew. The kids who were not in her class wished they were. I liked to write compositions for her, because she seemed really interested. But she was white. Would she hate me all my life because I was black? It didn't seem possible. She didn't hate me now; I was pretty sure of that. And yet, what Caleb had said was true.

"Caleb," I asked, "are all white people the same?"

"I never met a good one."

I asked, "Not even when you were little? In school?"

Caleb said, "Maybe. I don't remember." He smiled at me. "I never met a good one, Leo. But that's not saying that *you* won't. Don't look so frightened."

We were in front of our door. Caleb raised his hand to knock.

I held his hand. "Caleb," I whispered, "what about Mama?"

"What do you mean, what about Mama?"

"Well, Mama." I stared at him; he watched me very gravely. "Mama — Mama's almost white."

"But that don't make her white. You got to be *all* white to be white." He laughed. "Poor Leo. Don't feel bad. I know you don't understand it now. I'll try to explain it to you, little by little." He paused. "But our mama is a colored woman. You can tell she's a colored woman because she's married to a colored *man*, and she's got two colored *children*. Now, you know ain't no white lady going to do a thing like that." He watched me, smiling. "You understand that?" I nodded. "Well, you going to keep me here all night with your questions, or can we go on in now?"

He knocked, and our mother opened the door. "About time," she said drily. She had her hair piled in a knot on the top of her head. I liked her hair that way. "You must have sat through that movie four or five times. You're going to ruin your eyes, and that'll just be too bad for you, because you know we ain't got no money to be buying you no glasses. Leo, you go on inside and get ready to take your bath."

"Let him come over here a minute," our father said. He was sitting in the one easy chair, near the window. He was drunk, but not as drunk as I had seen him, and this was a good-mood drunk. In this mood, he talked about the islands, his mother and father and kinfolk and friends, the feast days, the singing, the dancing and the sea.

I approached him, and he pulled me to him, smiling, and held me between his thighs. "How's my big man?" he asked, smiling and rubbing his hand, gently, over my hair. "Did you have a good time tonight?"

Caleb sat on a straight chair near him, leaning forward. "Let Leo tell you why we so late. Tell them what happened, Leo."

"We were coming down the block," I began — and I watched my father's face. Suddenly, I did not want to tell him. Something in Caleb's tone had alerted him, and he watched me with a stern and frightened apprehension. My mother came and stood beside him, one hand on his shoulder. I looked at Caleb. "Maybe you could tell it better," I said.

"Go on, start. I'll fill in."

"We were coming down the block," I said, "coming from the movies." I looked at Caleb.

"It's not the way we usually come," Caleb said.

My father and I stared at each other. There was, suddenly, between us, an overwhelming sorrow. It had come from nowhere. "We got stopped by the cops," I said. Then I could not continue. I looked help-lessly at Caleb, and Caleb told the story.

As Caleb spoke, I watched my father's face. I don't know how to describe what I saw. I felt his arm tighten, tighten; his lips became bitter, and his eyes grew dull. It was as though — after indescribable, nearly mortal effort, after grim years of fasting and prayer, after the loss of all he had, and after having been promised by the Almighty that he had paid the price and no more would be demanded of his soul, which was harbored now — it was as though in the midst of his joyful feasting and dancing, crowned and robed, a messenger arrived to tell him that a great error had been made, and that it was all to be done again. Before his eyes, then, the banquet and the banquet wines and the banquet guests departed, the robe and crown were lifted, and he was alone, frozen out of his dream, with all that before him which he had thought was behind him.

My father looked as stunned and still and as close to madness as that, and his encircling arm began to hurt me, but I did not complain. I put my hand on his face, and he turned to me; he smiled — he was very beau-tiful then! — and he put his great hand on top of mine. He turned to Caleb. "That's all that happened? You didn't say nothing?"

"What could I say? It might have been different if I'd been by myself. But I had Leo with me, and I was afraid of what they might do to Leo."

"No, you did right, man. I got no fault to find. You didn't take their badge number?"

Caleb snickered. "What for? You know a friendly judge? We got money for a lawyer? Somebody they going to *listen* to? They get us in that precinct house and make us confess to all kinds of things and sometimes even kill us, and don't nobody give a damn. Don't nobody care what happens to a black man. If they didn't need us for work, they'd have killed us all off a long time ago. They did it to the Indians."

"That's the truth," our mother said. "I wish I could say different, but it's the truth." She stroked our father's shoulder. "We just thank the Lord is wasn't no worse. We just got to say: Well, the boys got home safe tonight."

I asked, "Daddy, how come they do us like they do?"

My father looked at us for a long time. Finally, he said, "Leo, if I could tell you that, maybe I'd be able to make them stop. But don't let them make you afraid. You hear?"

I said, "Yes, sir." But I knew that I was already afraid.

"Let's not talk about it no more," our mother said. "If you two is hungry, I got some pork chops back there."

Caleb grinned at me. "Little Leo might be hungry. He stuffs himself like a pig. But I ain't hungry. Hey, old man —" he nudged my father's shoulder; nothing would be refused us tonight — "why don't we have a taste of your rum? All right?"

Our mother laughed. "I'll go get it," she said. She started out of the room.

"Reckon we can give Leo a little bit, too?" our father asked. He pulled me onto his lap.

"In a big glass of water," our mother said, laughing. She took one last look at us before she went into the kitchen. "My," she said, "I sure am surrounded by some pretty men! My, my, my!"

# John Updike (1932–    )

JOHN UPDIKE was born in Shillington, Pennsylvania, a state that has provided the background for much of his writing. He attended Harvard University and the Ruskin School of Drawing and Fine Art in Oxford, England. He worked in the editorial department of *The New Yorker* from 1955 to 1957 and it is in that magazine that most of his many short stories have appeared. His first published book was a collection of light verse, *The Carpentered Hen* (1958), which was to be followed by a number of short-story collections and novels. *The Same Door* (1959) and *Pigeon Feathers* (1962) demonstrate Updike's consummate artistry in the short-story form. Among his novels the best known are *Rabbit, Run* (1960), *The Centaur* (1963), and *Couples* (1968). In 1964 he received the National Book Award for Fiction.

His literary style is what has won the most praise for John Updike's writing and "Son" is a good example of why. Changing point of view and time sequences are problems that bedevil most writers. It is a marvel how skillfully in "Son" the author switches point of view back and forth from objective to subjective to objective again in the attitudes of father, son, and grandfather and how he moves from the present to the past to the present again without once disturbing the smooth surface of his writing. Small town life especially engages Updike in most of his writing and father-son-relationships. The latter he portrays with great emotional warmth.

# *Son*

HE IS OFTEN UPSTAIRS, when he has to be home. He prefers to be elsewhere. He is almost sixteen, though beardless still, a man's mind indignantly captive in the frame of a child. I love touching him, but don't often dare. The other day, he had the flu, and a fever, and I gave him a back rub, marveling at the symmetrical knit of muscle, the organic tension. He is high-strung. Yet his sleep is so solid he sweats like a stone in the wall of a well. He wishes for perfection. He would like to destroy us, for we are, variously, too fat, too jocular, too sloppy, too affectionate, too grotesque and heedless in our ways. His mother smokes too much. His younger brother chews with his mouth open. His older sister leaves unbuttoned the top button of her blouses. His younger sister tussles with the dogs, getting them overexcited, avoiding doing her homework. Everyone in the house talks nonsense. He would be a better father than his father. But time has tricked him, has made him a son. After a quarrel, if he cannot go outside and kick a ball, he retreats to a corner of the house and reclines on the beanbag chair in an attitude of strange, infantile or leonine, torpor. We exhaust him, without meaning to. He takes an interest in the newspaper now, the front page as well as the sports, in this tiring year of 1973.

He is upstairs, writing a musical comedy. It is a Sunday in 1949. Somehow, he has volunteered to prepare a high-school assembly program; people will sing. Songs of the time go through his head, as he scribbles new words. *Up in de mornin', down at de school, work like a debil for my grades.* Below him, irksome voices grind on, like machines working their way through tunnels. His parents each want something from the other. "Marion, you don't understand that man like I do; he has a heart of gold." This father's charade is very complex: the world, which he fears, is used as a flail on his wife. But from his cringing attitude he would seem to an outsider the one being flailed. With burning red face, the woman accepts the role of aggressor as penance for the fact, the incessant shameful fact, that *he* has to wrestle with the world while she hides here, in solitude, on this farm. This is normal, but does not seem to them to be so. Only by convolution have they arrived at the dominant submissive relationship society has assigned them. For the man is maternally kind and with a smile hugs to himself his jewel, his certainty of being victimized; it is the mother whose tongue is sharp, who sometimes strikes. "Well, he gets you out of the house, and I guess that's gold to you." His answer is "Duty calls," pronounced mincingly. "The social contract is a balance of compromises." This will infuriate her, the son knows; as his heart thickens, the downstairs overflows with her hot voice. *"Don't* wear that smile at me! And *take* your hands off your hips; you look like a sissy!" Their son tries not to listen. When he does, visual details of the downstairs flood his mind: the two antagonists, circling with their coffee cups; the shabby mismatched furniture; the hopeful books; the docile framed photographs of the dead, docile and still as cowed students. This matrix of pain that bore him — he feels he is floating above it, sprawled on the bed as on a cloud, stealing songs as they come into his head (*Across the hallway from the guidance room/Lives a French instructor called Mrs. Blum*), contemplating the brown meadow from the upstairs window (last summer's burdock stalks like the beginnings of an alphabet, an apple tree holding three rotten apples as if pondering why they failed to fall) yearning for Monday, for the ride to school with his father, for the bell that calls him to homeroom, for the excitements of class, for Broadway, for fame, for the cloud that will carry him away, out of this, out.

He returns from his paper-delivery route and finds a few Christmas presents for him on the kitchen table. I must guess at the year. 1913?

Without opening them, he knocks them to the floor, puts his head on the table, and falls asleep. He must have been consciously dramatizing his plight: his father was sick, money was scarce, he had to work, to win food for the family when he was still a child. In his dismissal of Christmas, he touched a nerve: his love of anarchy, his distrust of the social contract. He treasured this moment of proclamation; else why remember it, hoard a memory so bitter, and confide it to his son many Christmases later? He had a teaching instinct, though he claimed that life miscast him as a schoolteacher. I suffered in his classes, feeling the confusion as a persecution of him, but now wonder if his rebellious heart did not court confusion, not as Communists do, to intrude their own order, but, more radical still, as an end pleasurable in itself, as truth's very body. Yet his handwriting (an old pink permission slip recently fluttered from a book where it had been marking a page for twenty years) was always considerably legible, and he was sitting up doing arithmetic the morning of the day he died.

And letters survive from that yet prior son, written in brown ink, in a tidy tame hand, home to his mother from the Missouri seminary where he was preparing for his vocation. The dates are 1887, 1888, 1889. Nothing much happened: he missed New Jersey, and was teased at a church social for escorting a widow. He wanted to do the right thing, but the little sheets of faded penscript exhale a dispirited calm, as if his heart already knew he would not make a successful minister, or live to be old. His son, my father, when old, drove hundreds of miles out of his way to visit the Missouri town from which those letters had been sent. Strangely, the town had not changed; it looked just as he had imagined, from his father's descriptions: tall wooden houses, rain-soaked, stacked on a bluff. The town was a sepia post-card mailed homesick home and preserved in an attic. My father cursed: his father's old sorrow bore him down into depression, into hatred of life. My mother claims his decline in health began at that moment.

He is wonderful to watch, playing soccer. Smaller than the others, my son leaps, heads, dribbles, feints, passes. When a big boy knocks him down, he tumbles on the mud, in his green and black school uniform, in an ecstasy of falling. I am envious. Never for me the jaunty pride of the school uniform, the solemn ritual of the coach's pep talk, the camaraderie of shook hands and slapped backsides, the shadow-striped hush of late afternoon and last quarter, the solemn vaulted universe of official combat, with its cheering mothers and referees exotic as zebras and the bespectacled timekeeper alert with his claxon. When the boy scores a goal, he runs into the arms of his teammates with upraised

arms and his face alight as if blinded by triumph. They lift him from
the earth in a union of muddy hugs. What spirit! What valor! What
skill! His father, watching from the sidelines, inwardly registers only
one complaint: he feels the boy, with his talent, should be more aggressive.

They drove across the state of Pennsylvania to hear their son read
in Pittsburgh. But when their presence was announced to the audience,
they did not stand; the applause groped for them and died. My mother
said afterward she was afraid she might fall into the next row if she tried
to stand in the dark. Next morning was sunny, and the three of us
searched for the house where once they had lived. They had been happy
there; I imagined, indeed, that I had been conceived there, just before
the slope of the Depression steepened and fear gripped my family. We
found the library where she used to read Turgenev, and the little park
where the bums slept close as paving stones in the summer night; but
their street kept eluding us, though we circled in the car. On foot, my
mother found the tree. She claimed she recognized it, the sooty linden
she would gaze into from their apartment windows. The branches,
though thicker, had held their pattern. But the house itself, and the
entire block, were gone. Stray bricks and rods of iron in the grass
suggested that the demolition had been recent. We stood on the empty
spot and laughed. They knew it was right, because the railroad tracks
were the right distance away. In confirmation, a long freight train
pulled itself east around the curve, its great weight gliding as if on a
river current; then a silver passsenger train came gliding as effortlessly
in the other direction. The curve of the tracks tipped the cars slightly
toward us. The Golden Triangle, gray and hazed, was off to our left,
beyond a forest of bridges. We stood on the grassy rubble that morning,
where something once had been, beside the tree still there, and were
intensely happy. Why? We knew.

" 'No,' Dad said to me, 'the Christian ministry isn't a job you
choose, it's a vocation for which you got to receive a call.' I could
tell he wanted me to ask him. We never talked much, but we understood each other, we were both scared devils, not like you and the
kid. I asked him, Had he ever received the call? He said No. He
said No, he never had. Received the call. That was a terrible thing,
for him to admit. And I was the one he told. As far as I knew he
never admitted it to anybody, but he admitted it to me. He felt
like hell about it, I could tell. That was all we ever said about it.
That was enough."

He has made his younger brother cry, and justice must be done.
A father enforces justice. I corner the rat in our bedroom; he is holding

a cardboard mailing tube like a sword. The challenge flares white-hot; I roll my weight toward him like a rock down a mountain, and knock the weapon from his hand. He smiles. Smiles! Because my facial expression is silly? Because he is glad that he can still be over-powered, and hence is still protected? Why? I do not hit him. We stand a second, father and son, and then as nimbly as on the soccer field he steps around me and out the door. He slams the door. He shouts obscenities in the hall, slams all the doors he can find on the way to his room. Our moment of smilingly shared silence was the moment of compression; now the explosion. The whole house rocks with it. Downstairs, his siblings and mother come to me and offer advice and psychological analysis. I was too aggressive. He is spoiled. What they can never know, my grief alone to treasure, was that lucid many-sided second of his smiling and my relenting, before the world's wrathful pantomime of power resumed.

As we huddle whispering about him, my son takes his revenge. In his room, he plays his guitar. He has greatly improved this winter; his hands getting bigger is the least of it. He has found in the guitar an escape. He plays the Romanza wherein repeated notes, with a sliding like the heart's valves, let themselves fall along the scale:

The notes fall, so gently he bombs us, drops feathery notes down upon us, our visitor, our prisoner.

# Leslie Silko (1948–    )

BOTH A POET and a writer of fiction, Leslie Silko is a young American Indian
woman who was born in Albuquerque, New Mexico. She is a cross-breed,
being descended from two tribes, the Laguna and Pueblo, but says she
considers herself more Laguna since that is the culture in which she was
reared. The writing she has contributed to magazines has already attracted
attention to her as a writer of remarkable promise. She is currently a teacher
at the Navajo Community College at Many Farms, Arizona. Her home is in
Ketchikan, Alaska.

In his introduction to *The Man to Send Rain Clouds* (1974), an impressive collection of contemporary American Indian short stories, Kenneth
Rosen, the editor, rightly says Leslie Silko's stories are "so spare, so rich, so
finely honed has to stand as genuine literary works of unquestioned value."
Describing Yellow Woman's meeting with a cattle rustler and their love-
making, the author has interwoven subtly and poignantly the modern, everyday life of the Indians with the tradition of their grandfathers. This is no
secondhand Indian "folk tale" with pedantically edited overtones, which
white Americans have too long been accustomed to regard as an Indian story,
but the real living thing.

# *Yellow Woman*

MY THIGH clung to his with dampness, and I watched the sun rising
up through the tamaracks and willows. The small brown water birds
came to the river and hopped across the mud, leaving brown scratches
in the alkali-white crust. They bathed in the river silently. I could
hear the water, almost at our feet where the narrow fast channel bubbled
and washed green ragged moss and fern leaves. I looked at him beside
me, rolled in the red blanket on the white river sand. I cleaned the sand
out of the cracks between my toes, squinting because the sun was above
the willow trees. I looked at him for the last time, sleeping on the white
river sand.

I felt hungry and followed the river south the way we had come
the afternoon before, following our footprints that were already blurred
by lizard tracks and bug trails. The horses were still lying down,
and the black one whinnied when he saw me but he did not get up —
maybe it was because the corral was made out of thick cedar branches
and the horses had not yet felt the sun like I had. I tried to look beyond
the pale red mesas to the pueblo. I knew it was there, even if I could
not see it, on the sandrock hill above the river, the same river that
moved past me now and had reflected the moon last night.

The horse felt warm underneath me. He shook his head and

pawed the sand. The bay whinnied and leaned against the gate trying to follow, and I remembered him asleep in the red blanket beside the river. I slid off the horse and tied him close to the other horse. I walked north with the river again, and the white sand broke loose in footprints over footprints.

"Wake up."

He moved in the blanket and turned his face to me with his eyes still closed. I knelt down to touch him.

"I'm leaving."

He smiled now, eyes still closed. "You are coming with me, remember?" He sat up now with his bare dark chest and belly in the sun.

"Where?"

"To my place."

"And will I come back?"

He pulled his pants on. I walked away from him, feeling him behind me and smelling the willows.

"Yellow Woman," he said.

I turned to face him. "Who are you?" I asked.

He laughed and knelt on the low, sandy bank, washing his face in the river. "Last night you guessed my name, and you knew why I had come."

I stared past him at the shallow moving water and tried to remember the night, but I could only see the moon in the water and remember his warmth around me.

"But I only said that you were him and that I was Yellow Woman — I'm not really her — I have my own name and I come from the pueblo on the other side of the mesa. Your name is Silva and you are a stranger I met by the river yesterday afternoon."

He laughed softly. "What happened yesterday has nothing to do with what you will do today, Yellow Woman."

"I know — that's what I'm saying — the old stories about the ka'tsina spirit and Yellow Woman can't mean us."

My old grandpa liked to tell those stories best. There is one about Badger and Coyote who went hunting and were gone all day, and when the sun was going down they found a house. There was a girl living there alone, and she had light hair and eyes and she told them that they could sleep with her. Coyote wanted to be with her all night so he sent Badger into a prairie-dog hole, telling him he thought he saw something in it. As soon as Badger crawled in, Coyote blocked up the entrance with rocks and hurried back to Yellow Woman.

"Come here," he said gently.

He touched my neck and I moved close to him to feel his breathing and to hear his heart. I was wondering if Yellow Woman had known who she was — if she knew that she would become part of the stories. Maybe she'd had another name that her husband and relatives called her so that only the ka'tsina from the north and the storytellers would know her as Yellow Woman. But I didn't go on; I felt him all around me, pushing me down into the white river sand.

Yellow Woman went away with the spirit from the north and lived with him and his relatives. She was gone for a long time, but then one day she came back and she brought twin boys.

"Do you know the story?"

"What story?" He smiled and pulled me close to him as he said this. I was afraid lying there on the red blanket. All I could know was the way he felt, warm, damp, his body beside me. This is the way it happens in the stories, I was thinking, with no thought beyond the moment she meets the ka'tsina spirit and they go.

"I don't have to go. What they tell in stories was real only then, back in time immemorial, like they say."

He stood up and pointed at my clothes tangled in the blanket. "Let's go," he said.

I walked beside him, breathing hard because he walked fast, his hand around my wrist. I had stopped trying to pull away from him, because his hand felt cool and the sun was high, drying the river bed into alkali. I will see someone, eventually I will see someone, and then I will be certain that he is only a man — some man from nearby — and I will be sure that I am not Yellow Woman. Because she is from out of time past and I live now and I've been to school and there are highways and pickup trucks that Yellow Woman never saw.

It was an easy ride north on horseback. I watched the change from the cottonwood trees along the river to the junipers that brushed past us in the foothills, and finally there were only piñons, and when I looked up at the rim of the mountain plateau I could see pine trees growing on the edge. Once I stopped to look down, but the pale sandstone had disappeared and the river was gone and the dark lava hills were all around. He touched my hand, not speaking, but always singing softly a mountain song and looking into my eyes.

I felt hungry and wondered what they were doing at home now — my mother, my grandmother, my husband, and the baby. Cooking breakfast, saying, "Where did she go? — maybe kidnaped," and Al going to the tribal police with the details: "She went walking along the river."

The house was made with black lava rock and red mud. It was high above the spreading miles of arroyos and long mesas. I smelled a mountain smell of pitch and buck brush. I stood there beside the black horse, looking down on the small, dim country we had passed, and I shivered.

"Yellow Woman, come inside where it's warm."

## II

He lit a fire in the stove. It was an old stove with a round belly and an enamel coffeepot on top. There was only the stove, some faded Navajo blankets, and a bedroll and cardboard box. The floor was made of smooth adobe plaster, and there was one small window facing east. He pointed at the box.

"There's some potatoes and the frying pan." He sat on the floor with his arms around his knees pulling them close to his chest and he watched me fry the potatoes, I didn't mind him watching me because he was always watching me — he had been watching me since I came upon him sitting on the river bank trimming leaves from a willow twig with his knife. We ate from the pan and he wiped the grease from his fingers on his Levis.

"Have you brought women here before?" He smiled and kept chewing, so I said, "Do you always use the same tricks?"

"What tricks?" He looked at me like he didn't understand.

"The story about being a ka'tsina from the mountains. The story about Yellow Woman."

Silva was silent; his face was calm.

"I don't believe it. Those stories couldn't happen now," I said.

He shook his head and said softly, "But someday they will talk about us, and they will say, 'Those two lived long ago when things like that happened.' "

He stood up and went out. I ate the rest of the potatoes and thought about things — about the noise the stove was making and the sound of the mountain wind outside. I remembered yesterday and the day before, and then I went outside.

I walked past the corral to the edge where the narrow trail cut through the black rim rock. I was standing in the sky with nothing around me but the wind that came down from the blue mountain peak behind me. I could see faint mountain images in the distance miles across the vast spread of mesas and valleys and plains. I wondered who was over there to feel the mountain wind on those sheer blue edges — who walks on the pine needles in those blue mountains.

"Can you see the pueblo?" Silva was standing behind me.

I shook my head. "We're too far away."

"From here I can see the world." He stepped out on the edge.

"The Navajo reservation begins over there." He pointed to the east. "The Pueblo boundaries are over here." He looked below us to the south, where the narrow trail seemed to come from. "The Texans have their ranches over there, starting with that valley, the Concho Valley. The Mexicans run some cattle over there too."

"Do you ever work for them?"

"I steal from them," Silva answered. The sun was dropping behind us and shadows were filling the land below. I turned away from the edge that dropped forever into the valleys below.

"I'm cold," I said; "I'm going inside." I started wondering about this man who could speak the Pueblo language so well but who lived on a mountain and rustled cattle. I decided that this man Silva must be Navajo, because Pueblo men didn't do things like that.

"You must be a Navajo."

Silva shook his head gently. "Little Yellow Woman," he said, "you never give up, do you? I have told you who I am. The Navajo people know me, too." He knelt down and unrolled the bedroll and spread the extra blankets out on a piece of canvas. The sun was down, and the only light in the house came from outside — the dim orange light from sundown.

I stood there and waited for him to crawl under the blankets.

"What are you waiting for?" he said, and I lay down beside him. He undressed me slowly like the night before beside the river — kissing my face gently and running his hands up and down my belly and legs. He took off my pants and then he laughed.

"Why are you laughing?"

"You are breathing so hard."

I pulled away from him and turned my back to him.

He pulled me around and pinned me down with his arms and chest. "You don't understand, do you, little Yellow Woman? You will do what I want."

And again he was all around me with his skin slippery against mine, and I was afraid because I understood that his strength could hurt me. I lay underneath him and I knew that he could destroy me. But later, while he slept beside me, I touched his face and I had a feeling — the kind of feeling for him that overcame me that morning along the river. I kissed him on the forehead and he reached out for me.

When I woke up in the morning he was gone. It gave me a strange feeling because for a long time I sat there on the blankets and looked around the little house for some object of his— some proof that he had been there or maybe that he was coming back. Only the blankets and the cardboard box remained. The .30-30 that had been leaning in the corner was gone, and so was the knife I had used the night before. He was gone, and I had my chance to go now. But first I had to eat, because I knew it would be a long walk home.

I found some dried apricots in the cardboard box, and I sat down on a rock at the edge of the plateau rim. There was no wind and the sun warmed me. I was surrounded by silence. I drowsed with apricots in my mouth, and I didn't believe that there were highways or railroads or cattle to steal.

When I woke up, I stared down at my feet in the black mountain dirt. Little black ants were swarming over the pine needles around my foot. They must have smelled the apricots. I thought about my family far below me. The would be wondering about me, because this had never happened to me before. The tribal police would file a report. But if old Grandpa weren't dead he would tell them what happened — he would laugh and say, "Stolen by a ka'tsina, a mountain spirit. She'll come home — they usually do." There are enough of them to handle things. My mother and grandmother will raise the baby like they raised me. Al will find someone else, and they will go on like before, except that there will be a story about the day I disappeared while I was walking along the river. Silva had come for me; he said he had. I did not decide to go. I just went. Moonflowers blossom in the sand hills before dawn, just as I followed him. That's what I was thinking as I wandered along the trail through the pine trees.

It was noon when I got back. When I saw the stone house I remembered that I had meant to go home. But that didn't seem important any more, maybe because there were little blue flowers growing in the meadow behind the stone house and the gray squirrels were playing in the pines next to the house. The horses were standing in the corral, and there was a beef carcass hanging on the shady side of a big pine in front of the house. Flies buzzed around the clotted blood that hung from the carcass. Silva was washing his hands in a bucket full of water. He must have heard me coming because he spoke to me without turning to face me.

"I've been waiting for you."

"I went walking in the big pine trees."

I looked into the bucket full of bloody water with brown-and-white animal hairs floating in it. Silva stood there letting his hands drip, examining me intently.

"Are you coming with me?"

"Where?" I asked him.

"To sell the meat in Marquez."

"If you're sure it's O.K."

"I wouldn't ask you if it wasn't," he answered.

He sloshed the water around in the bucket before he dumped it out and set the bucket upside down near the door. I followed him to the corral and watched him saddle the horses. Even beside the horses he looked tall, and I asked him again if he wasn't Navajo. He didn't say anything; he just shook his head and kept cinching up the saddle.

"But Navajos are tall."

"Get on the horse," he said, "and let's go."

The last thing he did before we started down the steep trail was to grab the .30-30 from the corner. He slid the rifle into the scabbard that hung from his saddle.

"Do they ever try to catch you?" I asked.

"They don't know who I am."

"Then why did you bring the rifle?"

"Because we are going to Marquez where the Mexicans live."

## III

The trail leveled out on a narrow ridge that was steep on both sides like an animal spine. On one side I could see where the trail went around the rocky gray hills and disappeared into the southeast where the pale sandrock mesas stood in the distance near my home. On the other side was a trail that went west, and as I looked far into the distance I thought I saw the little town. But Silva said no, that I was looking in the wrong place, that I just thought I saw houses. After that I quit looking off into the distance; it was hot and the wildflowers were closing up their deep-yellow petals. Only the waxy cactus flowers bloomed in the bright sun, and I saw every color that a cactus blossom can be; the white ones and the red ones were still buds, but the purple and the yellow were blossoms, open full and the most beautiful of all.

Silva saw him before I did. The white man was riding a big gray horse, coming up the trail toward us. He was traveling fast and the gray horse's feet sent rocks rolling off the trail into the dry tumbleweeds. Silva motioned for me to stop and we watched the white man. He didn't see us right away, but finally his horse whinnied at our horses and he stopped. He looked at us briefly before he loped the gray horse across the three hundred yards that separated us. He stopped his horse in front of Silva, and his young fat face was shadowed by the brim of his hat. He didn't look mad, but his small, pale eyes moved from the blood-soaked gunny sacks hanging from my saddle to Silva's face and then back to my face.

"Where did you get the fresh meat?" the white man asked.

"I've been hunting," Silva said, and when he shifted his weight in the saddle the leather creaked.

"The hell you have, Indian. You've been rustling cattle. We've been looking for the thief for a long time."

The rancher was fat, and sweat began to soak through his white cowboy shirt and the wet cloth stuck to the thick rolls of belly fat. He almost seemed to be panting from the exertion of talking, and he smelled rancid, maybe because Silva scared him.

Silva turned to me and smiled. "Go back up the mountain, Yellow Woman."

The white man got angry when he heard Silva speak in a language he couldn't understand. "Don't try anything, Indian. Just keep riding to Marquez. We'll call the state police from there."

The rancher must have been unarmed because he was very frightened and if he had a gun he would have pulled it out then. I turned my horse around and the rancher yelled, "Stop!" I looked at Silva for an instant and there was something ancient and dark — something I could feel in my stomach — in his eyes, and when I glanced at his hand I saw his finger on the trigger of the .30-30 that was still in the saddle scabbard. I slapped my horse across the flank and the sacks of raw meat swung against my knees as the horse leaped up the trail. It was hard to keep my balance, and once I thought I felt the saddle slipping backward; it was because of this that I could not look back.

I didn't stop until I reached the ridge where the trail forked. The horse was breathing deep gasps and there was a dark film of sweat on its neck. I looked down in the direction I had come from, but I couldn't see the place. I waited. The wind came up and pushed warm air past me. I looked up at the sky, pale blue and full of thin clouds and fading vapor trails left by jets.

I think four shots were fired — I remembered hearing four hollow explosions that reminded me of deer hunting. There could have been more shots after that, but I couldn't have heard them because my horse was running again and the loose rocks were making too much noise as they scattered around his feet.

Horses have a hard time running downhill, but I went that way instead of uphill to the mountain because I thought it was safer. I felt better with the horse running southeast past the round gray hills that were covered with cedar trees and black lava rock. When I got to the plain in the distance I could see the dark green patches of tamaracks that grew along the river; and beyond the river I could see the beginning of the pale sandrock mesas. I stopped the horse and looked back to see if anyone was coming; then I got off the horse and turned the horse around, wondering if it would go back to its corral under the pines on the mountain. It looked back at me for a moment and then plucked a mouthful of green tumbleweeds before it trotted back up the trail with its ears pointed forward, carrying its head daintily to one side to avoid stepping on the dragging reins. When the horse disappeared over the last hill, the gunny sacks full of meat were still swinging and bouncing.

## IV

I walked toward the river on a wood-hauler's road that I knew would eventually lead to the paved road. I was thinking about waiting beside the road for someone to drive by, but by the time I got to the pavement I had decided it wasn't very far to walk if I followed the river back the way Silva and I had come.

The river water tasted good, and I sat in the shade under a cluster of silvery willows. I thought about Silva, and I felt sad at leaving him; still, there was something strange about him, and I tried to figure it out all the way back home.

I came back to the place on the river bank where he had been sitting the first time I saw him. The green willow leaves that he had trimmed from the branch were still lying there, wilted in the sand. I saw the leaves and I wanted to go back to him — to kiss him and to touch him — but the mountains were too far away now. And I told myself, because I believe it, he will come back sometime and be waiting again by the river.

I followed the path up from the river into the village. The sun was getting low, and I could smell supper cooking when I got to the screen door of my house. I could hear their voices inside — my mother was telling my grandmother how to fix the Jell-O and my husband, Al, was playing with the baby. I decided to tell them that some Navajo had kidnaped me, but I was sorry that old Grandpa wasn't alive to hear my story because it was the Yellow Woman stories he liked to tell best.